SARI AND CASS

A NOVEL

JAN SCHNEIDER LUND

This book is dedicated to my ain true love Blake Welles Lund
…and to the memories of

Jean-Pierre Farjon, DDS, PhD
and
Richard Baer

The real people, living or dead, who appear in this novel are set in completely fictional situations. Every other character in this work is fictitious. Any resemblance to actual persons, living or dead, is purely coincidental. Places, locales, events and incidents are used in a fictitious manner.

This book is not a memoir. Really. It's not.

1

"Bliss was it in that dawn to be alive
But to be young was very heaven."

— **William Wordsworth**, "The Prelude"

*"Il faut mieux rêver sa vie que
la vivre, encore que la vivre soit
encore la rêver."*

--**Marcel Proust, "*Les Plaisirs et les Jours*"**

"There'll be icicles, and birthday clothes,
and sometimes, there'll be sorrow. "

--**Joni Mitchell, "Blue"**

PART ONE:

IOWA CITY

Chapter One

"Little Green"...Joni Mitchell

WHEN PROLOGUE IS EPILOGUE

When they buried my best friend, it was horrid. It was the worst thing I had ever experienced in my short twenty-four years on the earth. I could barely stand to be there. I felt physically ill to the point of teetering on my ankles trying to navigate my way over the cemetery's only slightly rolling grounds. My husband usually uses **me** for support--he wears a brace on one leg, hasn't the use of one arm, and his whole one side is weak; but this time I was leaning into him like I'd keel over any minute. I felt queasy and dizzy, and on top of all that, I was pregnant. I'm sure he was concerned about it; I know I was acting weird.

I think I was nauseated because the ceremony had been so sickeningly cold, and that's ironic because I usually love the Anglican services; I take comfort in them even though I'm Jewish and don't believe in much of any of what Anglicanism is really about. It's the ritual I like, the music, the serenity.

The priest-- the Hydes' young priest who presided when they were at their Springfield church, as opposed to their Kenilworth church--hadn't known their daughter Cass from the proverbial Adam. He'd only been at the church in recent years, not when Cass would have been there visiting her grandmother at the summer house. He was just a hired actor for the ceremony, playing the role prescribed by Julia Bronwyn Hyde.

"*Cassandra Hyde, though grown to a woman, nevertheless was still her mother's child.*" He had looked straight through Mr. Hyde to Mrs. Hyde, who nodded her approval ever so slightly, almost cueing him to read. "*Almighty and merciful Father, who dost grant to children an abundant entrance into thy kingdom, grant us grace so to conform our lives to their innocence and perfect faith, that, at length, united with them, we may stand in thy presence in fullness of joy; through Jesus Christ our Lord. Amen.*"

I became ill feeling so much anger. It was anger at their abandonment of Cass, and, it must be said, at Cass' abandonment of me.

Cass had gone ahead and died against my vehement objections. It was really a suicide, even though she did die **of** something. She died of complications arising out of anorexia nervosa. When I first met her, I, and I dare say most people, didn't even know what that was. She was trendy.

Obviously the thing I got so worked up about at the ceremony was that her mother took control of it. Here was Cass, the mother of two children herself, **dead**. But her own mother was treating this death, the funeral, the whole thing like a society event she'd planned herself and put on-- just another like any one of such things she did weekly. She took full charge, made all the arrangements, set it up like some sort of macabre gala, and held it according to form. True to herself to the end and betraying Cass. It made me want to puke.

Julia just stood rigid, exhibiting little emotion, very little emotion for someone whose only child had died ridiculously young and whose grandchildren were now motherless. Looking the part, as always elegant, she was dressed in black with one of those veiled hats you see in the movies but usually not actually worn, except by Jackie Kennedy. John-Wilfred Hyde at least had his handkerchief out and was dabbing with it, but he too just stood there staring at the grave, as if waiting for a cue to leave.

I began to sob rather uncontrollably when it was over, and this, again, alarmed my husband, Polo, so much that he steadied himself on his cane and drew one arm solidly across my shoulders, as if I'd flutter away or vaporize on the spot.

I talked into his chest. "She deserves so m-uch-uch m-more," I sobbed. "What ab-b-bout the twin-in-ins for christsake?" I took deep, heaving breaths, and Polo just buried my head deeper in his shoulder probably to muffle my voice as much as my tears. He noticed, but I didn't, that Julia Hyde was coming right towards me.

She was in perfect control: "You were her best friend in the world, Sari, and I was her mother. There was nothing either of us could do."

4

I straightened up to meet her gaze but I found myself cowed by it. Was I her best friend? Why didn't she ask me for help? Why did she slowly starve herself to death?

"I--guess so, " I whimpered. "Even though--I knew she might --die--, I really didn't believe it." I wanted to present this dignified front, but it wasn't coming off at all.

She pursed her lips, bitter and rationalizing, "I believe my daughter was faced with a hard choice in the last year or so, and she just had to come to a decision: to get well and live, or to die. Cass had her mind made up to die."

Just as matter-of-factly as she pronounced these heartless words that didn't mean a thing to me, she added, "You and Jean-Paul will come back to the house won't you?"

John-Wilfred Hyde joined his wife to greet us. He had met my husband at the hospital where Cass died, and like most people who first met us, had been taken aback by the differences in our ages; Polo was closer to his age than mine. He treated him now deferentially.

"So good of you to come with Sari. Means a lot. Of course, please do come over to The Homestead."

Polo spoke up for us at that point. "Yes, thank you very much----we shall be there presently. Sarah is--you can understand--rather not herself. "

Polo's voice could always soothe my raging soul. He was calm but not indifferent and very compellingly wise. I could tell even in that fleeting moment when they'd first met, that Cass' father was impressed and her mother even somewhat fascinated by him. His English was technically perfect, though he was French, and his accent not very pronounced-- he'd already been in the States for over thirty years. The main thing people noticed about the way he spoke English was that he seemed truly bilingual, yet it did not sound exactly native. I don't know whether it was some formality of his speech or something else, but he could always give comfort when he spoke. And he rarely felt the need to shout. I often came off like a banshee in comparison.

It was depressing me at that moment to think of going back to "The Homestead." It wasn't just any house. It wasn't the house Cass had grown up in. But it was the loveliest, most magnificent house I had ever seen when I first went there in 1967. Cass, as it turned out, had professed indifference to it. She had only vague memories of childhood there. But I had been mesmerized. My childhood home was a suburban boxcar compared to this Victorian spun-sugar fairyland place she treated with nonchalance back then.

Back in 1967, which seemed like four lifetimes ago.

I sure didn't want to go there and be with them; but I wanted Polo to see it. I didn't want the pain of having to be there and not have her there; yet I wanted already, even so short a time after her death, to retrace her footsteps for him. I was already fantasizing about finding bits and pieces of her there, something, anything at all upon which to cling. I began to sob all over again.

We walked slowly down a hilly path to the makeshift parking area. By the time we got to our car, the assembly of mourners having dissipated, it would be easy for us to wend our way out. I always drove.

But in my sobbing fits as I stumbled down towards the road, I hadn't noticed that Polo reached for the driver's side door first.

" I shall drive the small distance to their house. You need to rest."

"Why? I'm fine, " I snapped, groping for Kleenex, trying to clean myself up. I wasn't mad at him and I realized the moment I said that that it wasn't fair to him for me to be crabby. However, he, too was unusually insistent.

"I believe Julia has veritably upset you."

"Well, I am fine, but if you want to drive---it's okay," I acquiesced. "But wait, though! I've got the seat up too close. You won't be able to get in." I leaned in and moved the seat back. He needed the room to get in, to position his leg and unlock the brace to bend his knee under the steering wheel. His left leg was in the brace, but he wouldn't need to use it; this particular car was an automatic. Actually, what we had there was the limo in which he was usually driven around. We'd given the chauffeur the day off; I didn't like being chauffeured. Anytime we were slated to go somewhere by ourselves, somewhere non-official, I always wanted to drive us. But Polo had decided I shouldn't drive to the funeral in Springfield--it was about a four-hundred-mile round trip--and he thought I would get tired. So he had called for the car, but then under my protests, had relented and given Jean-Luc the free time off. The limo was very comfortable, I had to admit, and I liked driving it. Otherwise we would have had the car I usually drove when we weren't on Foundation business--a *Citroën 1964 DS 23 Pallas.* That car had been his mother's, and she was the only person who drove it when she was alive. He wasn't ever able to drive it anyhow, with the brace leg having to work the clutch. His right leg was okay, though the weakness he experienced on his left side made it a bit hard to maintain driving. For all intents and purposes, Polo had simply given up driving. He didn't need to drive in Chicago; the Foundation provided a car and chauffeur for him. And I adored driving the *Cit,* so I drove it all the rest of the time.

Luckily, it was only a short trip in to Springfield proper from the cemetery out on Old Highway 54.

The "Springfield Homestead" was one of five residences Cass' family had, and Cass had professed to hate them all. The suburban Kenilworth house where she was mostly raised was more of a mansion; her parents had a massive penthouse apartment in Chicago proper, and they had a vacation house on Mackinac Island, which was the only one of these residences Cass said she could stand, since she was often sent up there alone in the summers of her childhood, with her parents only flying up on weekends. They also had an apartment in New York and a condo in Gstaad, Switzerland.

In the time I knew Cass, I visited her at both the Kenilworth and Springfield homes, and I have to say that even though the Kenilworth house was bigger and had impressive grounds, the Springfield Homestead was historically more accurate, architecturally more valid, a veritable little jewel box. It had been Cass' maternal grandmother's home, so it was also the place where Julia had grown up. It was a Queen Anne prairie style house with just enough gingerbread and gables and porch to make it ooze charm. They had always kept it painted cream colored with salmon trim matching the roof tiles and the two awnings on the attic level.

Upon arrival, one circled up to it from a long driveway. The American flag was flown on a pole near the sidewalk. Julia flew the Illinois flag on the same pole below the national one. She always insisted the flags fly when the family was there. Like the Queen of England in residence at Windsor.

When we pulled up, the first thing I noticed was that the flags were flying at full mast.

The house looked small from the drive, but that was a true illusion. It wound around a lovely lot with old growth maple trees which had surely seen pioneers' prairie schooners go by. The more you circled the house, the more wings of it came into view, flanked by bay windows and a long sleeping porch on the back. And all the yard was landscaped into beds of flowers with varying blooming times. That day in March of Cass' funeral, lilacs in every possible shade of purple, lavender, blue and violet were in full array.

"Oh, they are so beautiful!" Lilacs were my absolute favorite bushes.

"Et ça sent! It smells like heaven."

Every visible window on the facade of the house was beveled glass, even the front door. When we walked up to the entry we could see through the windows that Julia had things laid out on tables in the dining room.

"Only three steps," I announced to Polo over my shoulder. I took the cane so he could use his right arm to grab the bannister. If he held onto that he could boost himself up on the right leg, which would bend, and then bring up the left one. Stairs were always a consideration in places we went and often not as easy to maneuver as this porch, which had low banisters on either side of the shallow steps. We entered under a lovely arch.

Any other time under other circumstances, I would have been so happy to be there.

We let ourselves in but Julia and John-Wilfred Hyde were right in the foyer greeting people and directing them to the dining room, where the grand table was covered with an antique lace cloth and set with dishes of Fostoria and depression glass.

John-Wilfred Hyde approached me and made a bit of small talk—references to having known my husband's late mother. I guess he felt like they were already friends, since we'd all sat vigil in that hospital together.

"Very nice of you to bring Sari, Jean-Paul," he reiterated. "And, I'm glad you got to know our Cassandra, too, if only for a short while."

"I am so sorry *Monsieur.* Sarah is devastated by this loss. We are both very sad for you."

6

John-Wilfred Hyde looked squarely at us. "Really dreadful circumstances weren't they?"

"Indeed."

For a tiny second I'd let myself fall back into some sort of reverie, almost as though I were just seeing the place with Cass for the first time. I found my memory tricked into expecting her to come rushing down the stairs to greet us. I had forgotten then as I would for months and months to come, that she was gone. Gone forever. Never coming back.

"Sari, go on into the parlor, won't you?"

I nodded and leading Polo, turned out of the foyer and into the beautiful octagonal living room painted in the palest yellow and decorated with old furnishings clumped into conversation areas. Sofas and loveseats were covered in silk organza and thick damask fabrics in varying hues of blue and creamy yellow, some flowered and some striped, but all very muted. The drapes were drawn across the small-paned windows in there, but we could still tell the sun was beginning to set; and across the hall as we looked into the dining room where most of other people were still gathered, light from the sun low and weakening--was still streaming in through the leaded- glass windows above the buffet. All the antique furnishings in the downstairs took on a burnished look in the strange light. Three of the windows across the foyer from the formal parlor had long, narrow stained-glass scenes in them which twinkled in that waning sunlight.

We sat down on a small settee, the only two people in the room. Bookcases overflowed with leather-bound tomes flanked by china and crystal bookends. John- Wilfred entered.

"We are hoping you will stay longer--until the others have gone. We have some of Cass' things for you Sari. She wanted you to have them. You know, of course."

"Yes, we'll stay."

"Well, good! Please, help yourselves to food," he said, motioning to the tables across the hallway. "And feel free to look around the house, Sari. I know you used to like it."

John-Wilfred Hyde was a nice person, all things considered.

The house had been built in 1874 and still had every original thing in it that it had when Julia's mother lived there. Inside the dimensions were as deceiving as they were from the exterior. From the dining room you could exit into the kitchen through a pantry with cupboards almost twelve feet high; or across the hallway beside the gigantic curving staircase you could by-pass the kitchen and go straight on to the back of the house to a large circular veranda that wound around to the family room ("keeping room" in the lexicon of that house's era). Once one was all the way into the room, a squared-off bay window came into view flanked by a window seat (my dream!) and mounds of lace curtains.

That back room was done primarily in cream and rose with light blue accents. There was a grand piano, a blue satin canape and five tufted Queen Anne style chairs all with needlepoint seats in different floral patterns which picked up the cream, rose and blue color scheme. They were arranged around some casual cherry wood tables. Curio cases held Dresden and Staffordshire figurines of every sort. It was Victorian but not heavy or dark at all.

"The first time I stayed here," I whispered to Polo in the parlor, "I sneaked down the back staircase late at night and just sat in the window seat back in the other room, pretending I lived here and that all this was mine. I sure wish you could see the upstairs. It's just as magnificent as this--just a different place in time."

"It always amazes me about you," he said. "I cannot get over how a young American woman is so enamored with the culture of another century."

I did feel like I was born in the wrong era—he knew that.

And then he added, whispering in French, lest we be heard, " *Et tu n'as pas menti, chérie. Cette maison est un vrai bijou.*"

No, I had not lied, and yes, that house was truly a little jewel.

Julia startled me. "Come into the pantry, Sari, won't you?"

"Sure!" I followed her, carrying my glass of lemonade.

"She wanted you to have everything. She had it all written down here." Julia fumbled in her blazer pocket for a piece of notebook paper.

She thrust it at me and shook her head as we entered the pantry off the dining room. I looked back over my shoulder to see if Polo had any intention of coming, too. I gestured to him to come on.

The staff on kitchen duty for the after-funeral reception was busy cleaning up in there when we entered the kitchen. They scattered to the pantry and sink area. Julia Hyde waved me in with her usual perfunctory air.

"You knew we sent our people down to St. Anthony, New Mexico to empty out her house?"

"Yes."

"Well, this is it."

She had the kitchen table and all the chairs around it piled high with Cass' things: bundles of letters tied with ribbons, photos in open boxes, books, her paintings, lots of dusty old sketchbooks full of ideas for the doll designs she never finished. Boxes of clothes--all neatly piled or stacked or leaning against the table legs on the floor.

"Gosh. She told me, but..." I couldn't think straight seeing all this stuff. "I'll be happy to see that the children are sent--you know--the things she wanted them to have. It's just that it was all so, well, hypothetical when we talked about," I swallowed hard, "the possibility of..." Polo entered the room and Julia cut me off.

"Yes, I know." She went on, almost spitting out the words, "Naturally there isn't any estate to speak of. Just junk. But I'm sure the twins would like some of these things --photos--you know, mementos of their mother. For when they grow up and want to remember her. You may decide what they should have."

It wasn't worth arguing with her mother what with Cass in the ground less than a day, but the idea that she could say this stuff to me was just making me crazy.

"They remember her now." I felt tears well up in my voice.

But Polo interceded, "I can assure you, *Madame*, that Sarah feels a great sense of responsibility towards the children of Cass. She is their godmother, is she not?"

It probably made her seethe thinking of a Jewish college friend being her grandchildren's godmother, and truth to tell, that was nebulous, I had to admit. Of course, I could understand my French husband putting a lot of stock in it because in French culture the *marraine* is not only highly honorary but also quite serious. Children remain very close to godparents there. He was wistful about his even at his age. Maybe I couldn't be that, but I would always be "Auntie Sari" to those kids and nothing could change it. Not their grandmother, not their father, no one, not now, not later. I was making myself quite upset.

"Oh, I'm not worried, darling," she hastened to add, trying in her own way to soothe me--or probably Polo! "You just go ahead and browse through everything. Take your time. And if there's something you don't think will fit into your car, let me know and I'll make all the necessary arrangements to have it shipped." She turned to leave us but then, as if struck by something important she had forgotten, added, "Do you want her furniture? I've got it stored in the garage out back. I was going to give it to the Goodwill..." she smiled a terse smile and added, under her breath, "I'm sure that's where it came from."

"No, I doubt that I have a place for it." And I don't think I'll be taking any of the clothes." I had drifted over to where the clothes were draped over the kitchen chairs.

"Goodness, I don't blame you! Did you ever see anything so strange? Ten and twelve of the same blouse, the exact skirt!! It's crazy."

"Can you give them away? They look nice enough."

"The Junior League Thrift shop will welcome them with open arms."

I packed up the stuff I wanted -- almost everything else-- and drove the car around to the back so that the housekeeper and other staff could put boxes in the trunk for me. The back stairs were steeper and more numerous than the front. I had to help my husband down them rather carefully.

John-Wilfred Hyde came out back. He waved a piece of paper in my face.

"The children's current address, Sari! They're with their father in El Paso now. No one is going back to that hovel in St. Anthony."

I was truly grateful to him for that. I had, of course, seen them with their dad at the hospital the last time I saw Cass, but Alan, their dad, had shuttled them away so fast, I didn't even get a chance to say good-bye to them. And in the next minute almost, their mother died.

8

"Thank you. I--I feel so—I don't know—efficient-- with the remnants of Cass' life here. But, Mr. Hyde, I feel like I failed her when it counted."

"Well, you didn't. She loved you. Right at the end she spoke of you all the time. When you get home and go through all this stuff, maybe you can find some clue to her behavior that we all missed."

No lie. John-Wilfred was the better of the two parents, but he wasn't part of the solution when she needed one. Oh hell, I should talk.

"Well," I said, looking up and managing to eke out a smile, "we had better get on the road. Thank you again. We'll keep in touch."

"Yes, I'd like that. You know, Sari, I will always have an office in the City just like I did when you first moved to Chicago. I want you to call me if you ever need anything. Anything at all." He gave me a light little kiss on the cheek in passing and extended his hand to Polo. "It was a pleasure seeing you again. I'd heard so much about you from the girls."

"*Monsieur*, I wish it could have been under much different circumstances. I hope to see you and *Madame* again--perhaps in Chicago."

Julia had arrived on the scene by then and ignoring that last remark, chimed in "Have a safe trip, Sari dear."

"Thank you. And--if you call the children, will you please tell them that I love them. They'll be hearing from me."

"I will."

"Good-bye, Mrs. Hyde," said Polo, getting into the passenger side.

He settled into the seat, fastened the seat belt and turned to me.

"At least it is all over. Now you can relax a bit. When we get home you will have months to sort through the things of Cass. *D'accord? T'es pas trop déprimée après tout?*" He reached over and stroked my cheek. "You will be able to drive okay?"

"I'm all right." I had both hands on the wheel ready to pull out, when I hesitated and looked over at him. "It's just that, I know what's in all those boxes. You remember that I was always planning to go down there by myself---before we had to go rescue her? I just couldn't do it because of various circumstances getting in the way?"

"Yes, I remember. You were very disappointed."

"Yeah, well, the plan was for her to give me free rein to case the joint... go through her diaries, read through our letters to each other...from France and all; look through all her art, read her poetry. I wanted to do it, too, only I never got the chance."

"Ah, yes. Sarah? You are crying? You cannot drive with tears. Let me drive."

"No, no, I'm not going to cry on the road. I'm fine now. Really. I'm ready, let's get out of here. I'm not ever going to see this place again and I don't want to."

We slowly drove around the rest of the circular drive and out onto the country road that led to highway 97 where I could get the Interstate. We didn't talk about what had just gone on for most of the trip back to Chicago.

Polo put music on the tape player--Telemann. He took his cigarette case out, the one I'd given him for our first Christmas after we were married, and busied himself taking out and lighting a *Gaulois Blond*, with tobacco that smelled wonderful and reminded me of France. I settled back to drive and think about the minutiae of my life to date. It was good, it was bad. I felt lucky and grateful; I felt sorry for myself and bitter. And guilty for feeling that way when I knew better.

I was pregnant with our first child.

One minute I knew without a doubt that my life had never been better. The next I was almost screaming inside with anguish over why I had to suffer the loss of Cass. And when I should have been thinking only of her, I was shamefully thinking of myself in the same breath. Cass' death left two children dreadfully alone for all intents and purposes, and yet I felt like the orphan. She had in many ways given birth to me, at least as my cultural mother. She had truly "raised me" almost at Iowa U., sharing my first independent living spaces, which, if not homes, were nonetheless abodes I loved; romping through Paris with me, teaching me to really love art. That's not nothing! We had business schemes based on her amazing talent. We saw each other through many trials and tribulations of boyfriends, teachers, family--oh God, hers and mine; and she always said we were closer than any sister she could have imagined having.

How could she have left me? Now I felt scared that life could be so precarious. We were young! We had gone through a lot already, but not enough to die for! How would I ever remember her well enough to last me, to comfort me, the rest of my life?

I was surely a sinner to be so selfish at a time like this, I knew, yet the agony persisted. The feeling that I really needed to take stock of my life came upon me in a too familiar wave of nausea. It persisted even in the presence of this dear man, this husband and lover sitting next to me. At the end of that day I knew that I had a right to feel sad, but I didn't have a right to be angry with my lot.

I adjusted the automatic lumbar setting on the seat and felt my back melt into the leather. The drive home to Chicago wasn't too long and I did feel relieved to be going back there. As I drove out onto the highway, my thoughts raced backward, and I began to rehash a ride I had taken years earlier.

Chapter Two

"You've Got to Be Carefully Taught"...Rogers & Hammerstein

We were loading the brand new 1966 white Ford Country Sedan station wagon with my clothes, my typewriter, some books, my records and miscellaneous dorm necessities, like a hot plate and one of those cute little coils that could boil water right in the cup--the newest thing! My father had bought a rod which hooked onto the handles above the back-seat window and my clothes were actually going to hang there for the trip across Iowa to the university at Iowa City. He was proud of his handiwork.

"See that! Isn't that great? It sure beats packing everything in suitcases and boxes, I can tell you that." The king of hardware.

I was pretty happy with the clothes, because for the first time I actually had some. My mother's younger sister "Auntie G" must have felt sorry for me because one night she arrived at our house and brought me a whole armful of her clothes for me to take to college. She was ten years younger than my mother, thus fifteen years older than me. She could almost have been my big sister, and indeed, she acted a lot younger than her generation. She was a dancer, hip and cool, and lived in an apartment in Omaha decorated in Danish Modern. She was pushy and loud, a complete antithesis to my mother; but I liked her. And she seemed to understand that someone going off to a major university should have some clothes that didn't scream poverty-stricken small town. But unfortunately, neither did they exude '60's "mod". But I was happy to take them--they were free. One dress was a hot pink silk shirt-waist with a matching belt. That could look sophisticated with black heels and black purse, I decided. Another thing I really did love was a drop-waist orange and grey plaid jumper. I could see myself wearing it to class in the dead of winter with a thick turtleneck sweater underneath and tights and boots, looking quite the academic.

But besides the great hand-me-downs, something wonderful had happened before I was packed off to college. We'd gone to Brandeis in Omaha and I had got to pick out complete outfits for the first time in my life.

My mother hadn't gone to college, and I think she really was trying to send me off in some style she imagined one should be sent off in--within reason. I was, however, only vaguely concerned with the cost at that moment, I have to admit, and thinking back on it, I'm sure it was over her budget. I do remember her telling me once that she'd just paid Brandeis fifty dollars a month no matter what, like a utility bill. That was a lot for our family. I should have been more grateful. Instead, I was always terribly unhappy that I never had any clothes.

The freshman-going-off-to-college- shopping trip was the best one I'd ever experienced.

I got the outfit that appeared on the cover of *Mademoiselle* magazine, my absolute favorite thing in print. Later on in my life when I read *The Bell Jar*, I was completely floored that Sylvia Plath had been a *Mademoiselle* Guest Editor. I had wanted to be that! I tried out for it. How incredible. *Sylvia Plath--my idol. She was from the East Coast; I wanted to be from there. She went to a Seven Sisters College; I desperately wanted to go to Mt. Holyoke (I was living inside Emily Dickinson poetry at that time); she went to Oxford--well, at least I went to the Sorbonne. She became a great poet, she married a greater poet; she killed herself. The Bell Jar was seminal in my life, but there was always this one thing that nagged at me: I hadn't written it.*

The outfit was neat. I was convinced I was cool in it: black and white herring-bone tweed wool mini skirt; matching jacket with orange paisley-patterned lining and an orange pocket hankie; a paisley tie (so super-fab- Carnaby-Street!) and--could there be more? --a beret! Hmmm, I projected literary persona onto the purchase, and immediately deemed it a foreshadowing of things to come. My sister Roslyn, ten years old that summer, didn't see the sublime symbolism in any of this.

"That is the stupidest tie I've ever seen. You're not going to wear it are you? Gawwwwd, girls wearing ties. Barf me out!"

"It's the outfit. It goes together. People know that. You, of course, wouldn't. And nobody wants or cares about your opinion, so stay out of it. You're not a person. You are a pinhead. You shouldn't say 'God'."

To me at that time, and really, at all times, Roslyn was a complete pain in the ass. We were never friends--too many years between us for that. We didn't look anything alike. "One of you is an adopted princess," my mother would joke. I resolutely hoped it was me; but I always had the sinking conviction that even though I was the elder, she was the princess.

I was named for some long-dead relative, as is Jewish tradition, someone named Sarah that the family called Meema Sarah, and that certainly dated her. But Roslyn came along late enough to be named for someone even I had known. I had vague recollections of my second cousin Roslyn, known as Rozzy. Rozzy's parents were my father's cousins and he was very close to this particular cousin, Rozzy's mother. Rozzy got cancer when I was seven or eight years old and I certainly didn't know what that was, but even then I knew it had an aura about it that was deadly serious. First of all, she was in this wedding I got to go to, and she wore a neck brace coming down the aisle under her mint green taffeta organza bridesmaid's dress! How mysterious, I had thought! And she was smiling.

That's exactly how I remember her because I never saw her again. That was the last time she walked, too. (The adults always told this story years later.) After the wedding, she went into the hospital, and not too much longer after that, her parents were called to the bedside late one night by a nurse.

"She's going," the nurse had told them over the phone.

"Gosh," I remember telling my sister years later when recounting this story of her heritage to her, "they could tell when someone was going to die!" Right then I had decided that I didn't ever want to get a call in the night and be told my child was "going."

So my little sister born shortly after this death got named for someone who had got cancer as a teenager and had died far too young. The lucky baby. I did get a doll for the occasion of becoming a big sister, though. I liked that. I named her Little Roslyn Ann, and she became my favorite doll for many years (until the Gerber baby). I found out later that my mother had given me that doll so I wouldn't feel left out when the new baby came, and I marveled that she had known enough about child psychology to think that up on her own; she confessed later that she'd read it in a book.

I still have Little Roslyn Ann. She's a wreck--her rubber legs are shredded, but her head is fine. She's still dressed in a pink "house dress." Not very fancy. It was the 1956 model, but she looked like she was dressed for The Depression.

Roslyn was my father's favorite.

She was driving me nuts all the way to Iowa City. They all were. I didn't see why she had to come on the trip. They couldn't even give me their undivided attention on the way to my freshman year at college. She was taunting me the whole time from the "way far" as she called the back of the station wagon.

I sat on the seat wedged in between all the hanging clothes, pouting because I so wished I were on my way to Amherst, Mass. and not Iowa City, not comforted by the fact that I hadn't been accepted at Holyoke, and rationalizing that it was because of the small-town high school I went to in little Podunk, Iowa. I became more and more depressed as the miles melted down the new Interstate Highway 80. And it took all the energy I was willing to muster to ignore the inane conversation my father endeavored to start every ten minutes.

"And I'm telling you another thing, Sarah," he kept pitching his voice back over his shoulder, "you'd be better off joining a Jewish sorority. Stay with your own kind if you have the chance. You'll see I'm right if you do." It was the fiftieth time I'd heard *that* "suggestion."

I responded only enough to aggravate him, "I'm still not sure I'm even going to pledge. But if I do, remember I told you, I'd kind of like to be a Pi Phi. They're supposed to be the best. But if it's going to end up costing more, I'd rather save for Paris." I was living in pachuko dreamland if I really ever thought I'd end up in Pi Beta Phi, but he didn't know that. I just said it to assert myself over him; after all, I was going to college and he never had. It really galled him because he did feel some pride at being able to send the first grandchild in the family to college, let alone have to worry about affording a "junior year abroad." But Paris, France was all I ever thought about, all I ever talked about, all I ever dreamed about. Iowa City was a certain waste of my would-be French time.

"*Oy*, I wish you'd quit talking about Paris! Paris-schmaris. I'd rather see you have a good time in a Jewish house. Date Jewish boys. Go out. Go to parties."

Right, going out and to parties was okay in his eyes now. Now that I had Paris on my mind, dating was on his mind.

12

Roslyn had to join in on this one. "Who, **Sari**? Go out? That'll be the day!"

"Shut up."

"Do they have a wall-flower sorority at Iowa, Daddy?" Roslyn dissolved in giggles at herself.

"Roslyn," said my mom, making her presence felt like a diplomat at the U.N., "we'll thank you to keep out of this conversation." And then she added to my father, "Sol, can we just drop this subject for the time being? It's her decision."

"It's her decision and I'm her father. Doesn't that count for something? You're damn right it does. I'm voicing my opinion on this. It's my daughter and my daughter's future. Who's paying for this college anyway?" He projected his voice through the rear-view mirror this time. "I don't OWE you a college education, you know. Remember that."

And he carried on for another fifteen miles or so, as I closed my eyes tight and tried hard to imagine that the signposts we were passing said things like "Cape Cod National Seashore."

But the arguing in the front seat continued without letup until my mother intervened one last time.

"All right! Just calm down and drive. She'll get there, she'll go through Rush Week and she'll see if she likes it. If she likes it, she'll pledge. Probably Jewish."

"Probably Jewish! There you go." He was incredulous, or if not, feigned incredulity. "You mean you'd let her join a non-Jewish sorority, don't you!?! I'm telling you, that's how it starts. They go into the *goyishe* house and then pretty soon they're dating those boys and bingo!"

I could not stay silent at that point, sneering: "I LOVE the way we're not even there yet and you've got me married off to a Catholic."

"Watch that tone of voice! This is your father you're talking to."

And then from way far in the "way far," "I doubt that there are any Catholic boys who'd want to marry her anyway, Daddy."

I turned around to her this time. "Oh, cram it, will you? Just because you watch the Mickey Mouse Club's "Annette" series, all of a sudden you're God's gift to dating." Then I lowered my voice and got to the crux of the matter. "You just wait. Without me there, you're the only one, remember? I'm at least getting out."

"I always get my way, " she sneered.

On that point at least, we could agree.

The car rolled on over a seemingly endless ribbon of new highway meandering up and down small ripples in the prairie every five or ten miles with hardly a curve until it reached its destination. I didn't appreciate the land in those days. I had lived in the mid-west my entire life and had hardly set foot on a farm. Depression-era architecture depressed me though later I would come to love the idea of big wrap-around porches whitewashed or glossy painted, over which ceiling fans purred; later I would revere the prairie colonial architecture for its halcyon symbol of calm and simple elegance as much as I loathed it that day it whooshed by the windows of our car taking me to college.

My father thought the new interstate was pretty damn slick. "This is easy!" he fairly sang. "You'll be able to get back and forth in no time flat on this road. Not like the olden days."

Just what I feared. I had no intentions of ever coming home, let alone in jig time. I dreaded the thought of four hours in the car with them back and forth home for holidays and such-- to and fro. God help me I would figure out a way to avoid that. Maybe they'd be far too busy in the bar and grill they owned to ever come and visit me. One could always hope. Their weekends would not be free. Things were looking up already.

The moving-in scene in front of Kate Daum House was chaos personified with every man to himself grabbing for the few and far -between rolling carts, but we managed to get one and I didn't have much to put on it: no mini-refrigerators or television sets. But for our family on either side at that time, it was the first college dormitory experience in America. We didn't know what to expect.

The room was sparse but had its own bathroom. It was on the seventh floor of the recently added high rise dorm, which meant a cool view out the window, and, even better, it was at the very end of the corridor. Freshmen usually were not even housed in Kate Daum, but for some reason, maybe because I didn't have a roommate preference already, I was assigned in there and my parents were actually willing to pay more for the "private bath" the room came with. Daum was connected via a tunnel to Burge, which

13

was the freshman dorm, and our meals were taken in their dining hall. In the basement of Burge was a soda fountain, and the Burge lobby was a psychedelic nightmare of pastel-colored kidney-shaped vinyl couches and chairs, with a hotel-like front desk, a store for sundries, and a bank of mailboxes. The Kate Daum lobby was tiny in comparison and had nothing but a table with a non-descript lamp on it flanked by two armchairs and very small front desk.

In retrospect, I probably should have had some sort of idea who my roommate might turn out to be from her name: Cassandra Bronwyn Hyde. But we had not corresponded during that summer before I came, and had not done some of the things roomies might do, like coordinate who was bringing what. For one thing, at Iowa U. in the 60's you didn't need to bring furnishings like curtains or rugs as some of my friends going to other schools did; and anyway, my idea of decor was having a bookcase.

For another thing, Cassandra was a sophomore.

My parents and Roslyn stayed a mercifully short period of time. I think my parents imagined I might be upset to be left there if they prolonged the good-byes, and hadn't wanted to deal with those emotions. But it could also have been because my mother, especially, didn't have any emotions. At any rate, it was drop off the suitcases and boxes, a quick kiss, admonitions to write at least once a week, and bye-bye daughter.

I was just getting the first load of hanging clothes into the closet when there was a knock at the door.

"Hi!"

"Hi!"

"Hello."

"We're Dot..."

"And Mallory!"

There stood two thin girls about the same height, nearly the same color of reddish-brown hair cut short, in cute outfits wearing nearly identical Mogen David necklaces--all smiles and bubbly at my door.

"Sari."

"We know!" said Dot.

"How?"

"We've got the Rush list! So, can we come in?"

"Sure."

"Gee, why did they put you way over in this dorm anyway?" wondered Mallory as she looked around my room shaking her head. "Oh my gosh, you have a bathroom!"

"Then, I take it you are associated somehow with Rush?"

"Oh, we're just going through it, like you," Dot explained. "And we're Jewish, too!"

"Okay, so you know I'm Jewish?"

"Yeah," said Mallory, "but most of the Jewish freshmen are all in Burge--mostly even on the same floor, so..."

"Why, mostly on the same floor? Isn't that like being segregated or something?" I was pretty incredulous.

"Like colored people, you mean?" said Mallory.

"Mallory," Dot interjected at once, "don't use the term colored. It's Black now."

"Sorry."

"No, Sari, but, well, we like it that we're all together and I guess the university thought it would be to our advantage."

"Why?"

"Well, I don't know," Dot said, acting like she felt obliged to explain the rules somehow to me, "to not feel alone? We're all pledging SDT anyhow, right?"

" Well.....maybe." They had caught me off guard, it was true, but I also hadn't made any decisions at all at that point. I'd only been on campus three hours.

"You don't seem too enthused, Sari," Dot noticed.

"Look," said Mallory reassuringly, "don't worry that you won't get in! You will! " She turned to my closet project. "You're darling and you have all these cute clothes!"

"It's not that. I'm just not sure I want to be in a sorority. I kind of got talked into this Rush stuff by my parents. "

"Oh."

"But I take it you are not in that boat?" I added, trying not to come off immediately as so different from them.

"Oh, me?" said Mallory, "I'm an SDT legacy. Every girl in my family's been in it practically since its inception."

"I think it will be fun to see the other houses, " Dot added, "but I don't think I could ever pledge one."

"Not that they'd probably have us anyway," added Mallory. But then she chirped, "But who cares, right!"

"Why not? "I asked, obviously in the dark about the system and a true ignoramus in these girls' eyes.

"Well, I mean, it's not the '30's or anything anymore, but things haven't changed that much!"

"What do you mean, *things*?"

"Well, you know!" Mallory said in a tone that softened up her bubbles, "We're not exactly welcomed with open arms into non-Jewish sororities. I mean, if you're a potential Phi Beta Kappa or your father owns Neiman Marcus or something, maybe you could wheedle your way into Kappa or Pi Phi."

"Not those two--or Theta either." Dot shot Mallory a look of exasperation at her naïveté. "Maybe one that was hard up." Dot was speculating, but she actually found the thought repugnant. "Anyway, you had better not look Jewish."

And we all did.

"Okay, I don't get any of this. "

"That's all right. Come on over to our dorm and we'll explain it to you over dinner. Plus, you know, this year, SDT isn't the only Jewish house!"

"Oh my God, Dot--you're right. We almost forgot to tell her about AEPhi!"

"See, they're new! And they intend to give SDT a run for their money at Rush this fall."

"But they don't have a house, so good luck!"

And that's how I met Dorothy Sachstein--known as Dot, and Mallory Knoblauch. They weren't from the same Iowa town but had known each other all through high school due to regional synagogue youth group conclaves, conventions and exchanges. We all seemed to hit it off right away, and their rather instant acceptance of me intrigued me; but the more they got to know me, the more of an anomaly they thought I was. I had not grown up with many Jewish friends even being situated near a much larger Jewish population than either of them. I hadn't liked Omaha's Jewish culture, I tried to explain to them. It was insular and yes, very clique-y, even if that was a cliché. When I did go to their functions under duress and objections, I didn't have a good time and invariably came home with reinforced feelings of inferiority and low self-esteem. In those days, however, parents were not categorizing their children as such. Every time I came home miserable from one of these forced outings, as I explained to Dot and Mallory, my parents had told me to just get over it and try harder next time to make friends.

"The more they made me go to that stuff the more I hated it and developed unpleasant associations in my mind with Judaism period."

"That's just crazy!" Now Dot was incredulous.

"I know! You'd have thought they would have got the message or seen how unhappy I was and left me alone, wouldn't you?"

"No! I mean, that you were turned off to Judaism. That is so sad!"

"Yeah," Mallory chimed in, "but when you went out you didn't interfaith-date, did you?"

"No."

"At least!"

"I never went out."

Rush Week started the next day. The campus was warm with the temperatures of Indian summer and already awash in eastern Iowa's autumnal palette as groups of us huddled together in front of Burge Hall all that first day, somewhat fidgety and talking in excitedly hushed tones about what houses had been

15

the prettiest, who were the nicest housemothers, what would happen to legacies, and who would be blackballed. No one was really cut, of course, the first day. We all visited every house on campus and, at the end of that first round, *we* chose 6 houses to which to return the next day. They did not choose us yet.

I wore my Brandeis outfit and had to admit it might have been too hot out for it, but that it looked pretty great. We were jam-packed into cabs and driven from party to party, house to house. We spent the day drinking punch and making small talk about our hopes for life at university. I was actually fairly relaxed about it because unlike most of my new-found, if temporary peer group, I wasn't on pins and needles about whether the one I liked would take me, or the most prestigious one would cut me because I didn't care if I got into any of them or not.

We would be ushered into sunny living rooms, some decorated elegantly and others more cozy, as though alums had emptied out their attics for the good of the cause. But mostly the public rooms were meant to give the impression that we girls would be part of a lovely family and live in a place where we could feel proud if a date picked us up there.

The actual bedrooms upstairs looked more like camp.

"Oh my God, " moaned one rushee visitor after another, "three bunkbeds in a room the size of half a dorm room!" Not to mention one bathroom per floor shared by dozens. They all had something else in common: the most cramped closet space I'd ever seen. And in some of the houses the wallpaper was peeling.

The actives who were running Rush for each house would greet us at the door, take our wraps if we had any, and usher us into a seat. Sometimes on the first day they would start out with a little speech about their history on campus or about Panhellenic organizations, but mostly, the atmosphere was a cross between afternoon tea as it must have been for women four or five generations behind us, and some cocktail party as yet in our future. They had displays all over the houses with their chapter activities and photos with captions like "Tri-Delts Pepper and Muzzy helping with fun finger-painting project at Fairmont park summer day camp."

I began to gauge which answer to give when asked my major. There was the truth, of course, but that was too long a story to go into with girls who seemed under some pressure to only talk a few seconds to any one rushee. Explaining that *"I'd intended to major in music--voice performance-- until I found out from the orientation academic advisor that I'd have to also be able to play an instrument"* was akin to going into detail when someone asks "How are you?" expecting you to answer, "Fine thanks, and you?" and move on in the conversation. *"Undecided"* was a boring answer and a dead end, so I avoided that one. *"Maybe journalism, I'm not sure"* could lead somewhere, but for the most haughty of hostesses, and when I was "on my game", I would coo: *"I'm planning to study in Paris, so my major will be French."*

The second night over in the dorm, the little letters arrived inviting us back for another round. Some girls to my amazement had actually only put down one house rather than the six we were allowed. Of course that was their prerogative but it struck me as risky and stupid. The second night then, after most of us had seen six houses and narrowed them down to three, the letters came back--only this time there may have been all three, or two or one or...none.

There was more than a little crying in the bathrooms. Girls who had singleton desires of prestige only, such as Pi Phi or Theta, were the worst off. Having eschewed the "normal"-- or in their eyes, "unfit" --sororities to put all their eggs in one basket, if the one house they so desperately wanted cut them, their entire freshman year loomed ruined in front of them.

I saw a one of those up close, because Dorothy's roommate Penny McCallister was cut on the first round from Kappa Kappa Gamma. She was in their dorm room on the second night, packing to go home, when the three of us burst in to go over our little letters.

"Penny, you aren't serious!" exclaimed Dot when she saw her room in chaos, her sobbing roommate of less than a week throwing clothes in suitcases that had only just been unpacked. Dot put her arm around Penny and tried to be soothing, "You'll get into another one."

"You don't get it! " Penny sneered, jerking away.

"Well, but ...heavens, you can't up and leave the university!"

I asked, "Do your parents know you're coming home?"

"My mother's livid at her sorority! And my father says I don't have to stay here if I don't want to, and I DON'T!"

I had never seen anyone heave such anguished sobs. This just couldn't be that important, I thought to myself, and yet, here this girl was-- carrying on as though she seriously had no future life. I tried to empathize, to put myself in her place, relate to her sorrow, or at least understand it; but I honestly couldn't. I mean, I didn't like seeing her so hurt and I could tell she wasn't being fake, and I felt for her, but in truth I couldn't fathom it. And the more ironic thing was that seeing this display of emotions over not having received "the letter" didn't make me feel relieved or safe that I'd gotten three letters; it made me feel like I really didn't belong in a crowd of girls who put such urgency into whether or not they were accepted by some particular group.

I actually started feeling queasy watching Penny pack her bags. It did not seem right to me to see one's identity already start being wrapped up around outside factors. Was I a bigger snob than they were because I didn't even care about being one of them? Was I really just too insecure to even hope to belong, so I set up pre-emptive rejection defense mechanisms for myself? Was I just plain egotistical and only cared about myself first?

We left Penny to her packing and went down the hall to the lounge for some privacy as we opened the envelopes. But on the way to the lounge I pumped Dot for more information on Penny.

"Why is she THAT upset, that she would leave school before it even started? " I insisted.

"Well, " Dot started the explanation, "it's like this, Sarah, and I'm not sure you'll believe me."

"Try me."

"She's so unhappy that she didn't get into her sorority choice because what she's really unhappy about is having to room with me."

"Come on."

"No, I'm serious. She was flabbergasted that they put her in with a Jew in the first place. But I think she would have been able to stand it if she knew she was out of the room most of the time over at *the house*."

"Oh, get real, why do you think that? Did she actually say anything to that effect...seriously?"

"She didn't have to. She was surprised to see me when we were moving in and she asked me what *church* I'd be going to on campus almost before she asked my name. Then Mallory came in and we started talking. She knew. Plus, I'm not ashamed to be Jewish! I flaunt it right out there."

"I'm not insinuating that you should be ashamed. She should be ashamed of being so prejudiced. But God, I thought that stuff went out with Prohibition. All my father ever harps about was how people hated us during his high school days, and he still thinks that. I wouldn't like to see him proven right."

"Don't be so naive, Sarah. There are probably plenty of girls on this campus who will at least ask for a different room if they find out they have a Jew for a roommate. Yours might be one of them---she's not even here yet and hasn't met you!"

Mallory thought that was rather harsh. "Oh, Dottie, leave it alone. Don't scare her before she's even met her roommate."

But then she added her two cents on the Penny situation: "I was there, Sarah, and I saw Penny's reaction. I think it's sad that she obviously learned to hate before she learned to get along. Kids get that stuff at home, you know."

Dot rolled her eyes, "Yeah, Lieutenant Cable told us so."

"Okay, but look, you guys told me you were all in Burge together. But what you're saying is that there aren't that many Jewish kids that you all have Jewish roommates---you're just on the same floor?"

"Right, "said Mallory, "my roommate is Lutheran."

"So what's Penny's problem? There would be plenty of other gentiles for her to pal around with."

"Well, that's not a solution! "Dot interjected. "I don't want someone who hates me living with me for the next nine months! I say good riddance if she wants to leave."

"You know, this is a messed up situation," I concluded.

It might as well have been the Crusades revisited: religion was still causing the same damn wars it had for centuries.

We got to the lounge, flung ourselves on the couches and started to open the all-anticipated mail.

17

"Ooooh, " squealed Mallory, " just the two I wanted!" Then she got quiet--"But how will I choose?"

"Me, tooooo," sympathized Dot. " This is going to be haard! I guess we'll just have to judge between them."

They were referring to the two Jewish sororities on campus: one the venerated original one that had been on campus since the 1930's; and a new chapter just starting up where "we" would be not the charter members, but we would be the first pledge class at Iowa. They were just negotiating a fabulous house right across from the dorms.

"Well, Sarah?! " Dot turned to me in rapt anticipation and Mallory effervesced. "Oooh, yeah, tell us, come on! Did you get SDT or AEPhi?"

"Yes, both" I said incredulously, as I read them but didn't believe it, "and Kappa Kappa Gamma." I looked up at them more stunned than elated. I thought it must be a mistake; I thought someone would come in and grab the letter and apologize and renege on the offer.

"Kappa? Let me see that!" giggled Mallory uncomfortably as she grabbed it from my hand.

"You aren't going to join **Kappa**, are you?" asked Dot almost imploring me to assure her I wouldn't.

"Well, I don't know! I don't know how I got asked back to that house in the first place. "

"Yeah, but you have to have some idea, "said Mallory. "Did they...seem to...like you?"

I knew what she was getting at, especially after the impromptu little tutorial they'd been giving me since they first met me on the topic of **Latent Anti-Semitism among the Tribes of Iowa City**.

I looked Jewish and I wasn't cute. I had not had my nose done and only my straight hair was atypical. I was short and, while quite thin, rather too top-heavy. My eyes were my best feature, everyone could agree, but I hated my teeth. And even though liquor salesmen came into my family's bar and called out to me "Hi Gorgeous!" with phony Brooklyn accents, I was anything but.

The pre-teen fantasies about going steady by the time I was sixteen and doing homework with my boy-next-door boyfriend or long walks through Memorial Park on a Saturday before the high school football games, gave way to a reality of never being asked to prom or Military Ball, of sitting on the sides of the gym in pretty clothes waiting to be asked to dance at "regular" school dances, but only dancing once or twice with boys who were pals from biology class; of eating lunch with the wall-flower set.

What I had done to provide myself ultimately with protection from the effects of rejection, however, was to bury myself in academics; take on clubs and chores and the grunt work of back-stage scenery painting; throwing myself into feature writing for the newspaper, amusing my classmates with poetry and wit not generally associated with high school journalism; I had a column and saw myself as a younger, female version of Art Buchwald or Herb Caen in a godforsaken Baghdad-by-the-River. More importantly, I embarked on a great mission to please those teachers whom I respected and whose praise I craved-- and received-- far more than my parents', and to weave a dream for myself around a future life far away from all of it.

"I don't know why they would ask me back and not ask Penny," I shrugged.

"Oh, God, don't tell her!" Dot snapped.

Mallory continued her quest for answers, "You must be really smart!"

"I have grades, but..."

"Kappa's interested in that!"

"But I'm nobody from nowhere. I'm not cute. My family's not rich and I'm not a legacy. So, there you have it--it's just a mystery or a fluke."

"Well," said Dot finally, with an aura of conclusion, "You would be their token Jew then."

"You are, too! Cute, I mean." admonished Mallory.

"Oh, yeah, right."

"Anyway, " Dot went on, "This is the sixties! Like you said, 'The times they are a-changin' and all the rest of that. Maybe Kappa Kappa Gamma is making an effort at assimilation for all we know."

" Come on, " I said. "Assimilation? Non-Jews don't make that effort. Jews might, but I didn't set out to break any color-cum-religion barriers. Come to think of it, they didn't even talk religion to me. "

"Well, they KNOWWWW!" Dot was completely exasperated by what she obviously took to be my selective amnesia about the telling looks I carried around! "Maybe it's your name. Shrier isn't the dead-giveaway Sachstein is.

18

"Okay, okay. I am now at a loss. Don't ask me anything--I can't tell you. I'm just going back to my room and think about it."

"Oh my God!" Mallory was stunned again.

"What?"

"You're not considering actually pledging them, are you?!"

"Well, I don't know! Sheesh!"

I did go back to my own room and I did think about it. The way you think about something that *could* happen which would be so totally extraordinary that you can't let yourself think it really *will* happen; but still, you're in the grace period in which it hasn't *not* happened yet!

"The grace period, " I thought to myself, "is heaven. " And I fantasized about being a Kappa. That would be stunningly shocking to my parents.

What, me? Do the dishes? When I'm a Kappa? Iron shirts in the basement as a... Kappa? I don't think so.

Besides the fantasy, I actually thought about really being one. All of a sudden was I not being forced into Rush but actually liking it? What could have changed in forty-eight hours? Was the prospect of being in the in-crowd for the first time in my entire life really so overpowering as to make me forgive the certain potentially reprehensible aspects of this? What about being a part of a group who "really wouldn't have me" as the old joke went, but took me as a token and wouldn't take my equally deserving friends? Could I live with and later be an active and willing participant in any organization whose members were expected to blackball others for whatever reason? Well, so what; maybe Jewish sororities blackballed girls, too! I said to myself, and I was sure they did. What hypocrisy! And why weren't we all sitting around in the lounge having this discussion? Was I the only one agonizing over this aspect of Greek life, when all the others were ready to rend their garments over merely not being chosen for the one they wanted? Above all, what if the whole business were moot anyway because I couldn't stand any part of sorority life? Living in such close quarters with fifty other girls, most of whom wouldn't have spoken to me in high school; being supervised for study hours, doing busy-work as a pledge, feigning interest in rituals I would otherwise ignore and likely abhor?

Finally, as I contemplated all this, the thoughts came bubbling up to the surface about what if I were willing to join even after my misgivings, and then all that got in the way of what I really wanted to do: go to Paris?

I sat in my room alone that night and decided not to pledge a sorority, even Kappa if they asked me; and I fell asleep calm and convinced that I had made the right decision. I had also decided then and there to keep this information to myself until the end of the next day when the final invitations were delivered to Burge Hall.

The last day of the party rounds dawned cooler than the previous ones had been, so we were dressed in coats when the taxis pulled up to the sidewalk at Burge. But the crowd was considerably thinned as the soon-to-be-sorority girls were winnowed out with the remaining prospects only going to a few houses, and then not all at the same times.

Dot, Mallory and I were slated to be at the venerable of the two Jewish sororities first for a mid-morning affair labeled a "brunch" but without the requisite food — or so I thought. As we entered, friendly SDT's were ready to take our coats and, I observed, try to sneak clandestine little peeks at any labels in them. I did have some clothes with "Made Expressly for J.L. Brandeis & Son" labels in them, but no one would have cared about that. I guessed that what they were looking for were labels like Saks and Bergdorf's, but there wasn't a Saks Fifth Avenue within six hundred miles of my house, nor Lord & Taylor, Bloomingdale's, or even Macy's. So they were wasting their time looking at my coat, and that amused me.

Dot, Mallory and I were still together as we were ushered into the dining room to a table laden with lox, cream cheese, bagels, and fruit trays with crackers. Large antique-looking silver coffee and tea services were at one end of the table to be self-served, but the person I took to be the housemother hovered near them as if watching for drips. The chairs had all been removed to the living-room/parlor for us to sit around in groupings, but the dining room still had other furniture in it-- a side board, for instance, which displayed a very cumbersome soup tureen on a glass tray flanked by candlesticks which resembled the type of *Shabbos* candle holders *de rigueur* in every Jewish home; and a break-front china cabinet which held many sets of dishes including what was obviously a *seder* plate, trays with the special coverings for *challah*

19

at the sabbath dinners, and a set of silver *kiddush* cups, some of which rested on ornate bone china saucers. I immediately presumed they were for show, but then felt a pause. No, they were probably for the house's use, and on top of everything else I hadn't thought of, it all of a sudden occurred to me that the food was probably all going to have to be kosher and the rituals many more than just Greek.

Another round of small talk resumed and we passed an hour believing we'd all be sisters at the end of the day.   The same thing happened all over again at the Alpha Epsilon Phi gathering held not in a house because theirs wasn't finished yet, but in the basement soda fountain of Burge Hall. These girls were very enthusiastic in their quest for us, which I hadn't really noticed before. They were intent on forming a big chapter and luring Jews away from the other one. There were even some girls there I didn't think were Jewish, which intrigued me. Dot noticed it, too.

"Do you think they are trying to be open-minded, " she asked me in hush tones, "or are they just snobby?"

"Why snobby?"

"Because. They're trying to show us that they're more modern and with-it than SDT."

"They're prettier, I'll give you that," I whispered. They have different --well, a variety, let's say, of looks about them."

Dot shot me an exasperated look. So I continued, "Well, when you think about it, why are we presuming right off the bat that just because people don't look Jewish, they aren't? Maybe they are!"

"Doubt it!"

Dot and Mallory were done for the day and were planning to reconnoiter in Dot's room to decide what to do about the two invitations they were about to receive. I on the other hand, had the Kappa Kappa Gamma party left to go to mid-afternoon.

I didn't want to take a cab by myself, so I walked over there from Burge through a twisting path of quaint, small-town, tree-lined Iowa City neighborhoods. Iowa City did have some wonderful residential architecture; after all, it had been the capital of Iowa at one time. There were some vestiges of the late Victorian era which must have seemed quite genteel in its day there on the prairie: three-story tall turreted houses and stately, inviting homes which had yet to be made into apartments. I found myself trying to imagine what it would have been like to grow up on one of those sweet avenues, to play in those yards as a child, walk up to one of those doors with a date, and get married walking down the tall, curving staircases I presumed were beckoning right inside the doors.

The weather had turned crisper, but still sunny, and it felt great to be out walking around in it. I had almost forgotten for a moment that day how I hadn't wanted to be there at all, and how I should have been walking around South Hadley or Bryn Mawr instead.

I saw another couple of girls being welcomed in the door of the Kappa house as I approached it. I gave a last glance up from the sidewalk and for the first time at Rush, felt a small tingle at my life changing more than I ever imagined it would the first week of college.

They welcomed me in like the others and we sat around in the living room that had a more burnished patina about it than the SDT house had had or than the new AEPhi one ever could have. As I looked around the room, I tried to place myself among these other freshmen as a sorority sister with them. We would be the pledge class. We would share it all, and, I assumed, become great friends--maybe for the whole four years.

I didn't know any of them. I hadn't paid any attention at the dorm as to who was getting which invitations back, other than the two girls I already knew, and the drama over Dorothy's roommate.

Screwing up my enthusiasm, energy level and courage, I joined in the conversation with verve. We earnestly discussed study hours at the house, the duties of pledges, social functions and grades. One active gave a lovely testimony about getting pinned and what that ceremony had meant to her. Another told of the night she received a lavalier from her Sig Ep boyfriend and how having her sisters around her had made all the difference. I had questions at the back of my mind about hazing and any induction period rituals but repressed all of those. I was determined to bubble along and test out the waters of group identity as a Kappa.

When it was over, I joined three other girls in a cab back to Burge where the final invitations, the ones to join, would be delivered. Since I didn't have a room there, I just sat in the goofy pink and purple lobby on one of those kidney bean-shaped couches and read a magazine until the place began to fill up with anticipation-charged whispering, buzzing and squealing.

Dot and Mallory found me.

"WELL?" Dot said, smiling (at least). "Did you like it?"

"I did." I was surprised even to hear myself admit it.

"So, will you pledge Kappa?" Mallory asked with a lilt in her voice, too.

"I think I might!" And I finally laughed about Rush, feeling happy rather than cynical.

The cards arrived and were distributed. I had two and so did Mallory and Dot. I opened mine with greater anticipation that I ever thought I would. They were Sigma Delta Tau and Alpha Epsilon Phi.

My heart was pounding, which I decided was silly, but couldn't seem to stop. The two of them were staring at me with anticipation and expecting me to say something first.

"Kappa cut me. Oh well. That's the way the cookie crumbles, eh?"

"So, which one will you pledge now? You're in the same boat as us!" Mallory gushed. Dot didn't say a word.

"Well, I'm not joining any. I mean, let's face it, I wasn't going to, so I'm not going to." I tried to change the subject, hoping my voice didn't betray my brave front. "I've got to get back to Kate Daum. You know, my roommate will probably be here tomorrow-- or maybe now even! I'll see you guys. Have a good time pledging! It's not like we won't still see each other!"

I ducked out towards the tunnel that connected my dorm to Burge, hoping they would just let it drop. I didn't want to sit around helping them choose between the two Jewish sororities. But I saw them later at dinner that evening. They both pledged SDT.

I knew they were happy and I thought that was great.

21

Chapter Three

"Georgy Girl"...The Seekers

If I thought the frenzy of moving into the dorm was bad when I had arrived for Rush, it was nothing compared to the chaotic din that ensued when the rest of the freshmen and the returning students of the university moved in. Cars were double-parked in front of all the dorms and houses on Clinton street, with parents vying for a sidewalk spot and girls jockeying for those rolling hotel luggage carts in the midst of dorm officials trying to direct foot traffic. I watched out the window for a little while and then busied myself on the bed sorting through book lists and supplies until the noise and commotion seemed to die down, at which point Dottie, who had come over from Burge, burst excitedly into my room. She motioned for me to come back to the window, saying, "You won't believe this! We were coming back to our dorm when we saw this car pull up in front of yours, and I had to come over here. Look."

I again looked out. The car lane had advanced and taking up what seemed like more than one space was something no one could possibly be expecting to see in Iowa City: a grey-blue Bentley driven by a man in what could not be misconstrued: a chauffeur's uniform. He had emerged and come around to the passenger side, which we could see perfectly from our high perched window. Another person came into view from the car, also in a uniform-type dress, very plain with a prim jacket over it. She looked like a domestic servant from another era. Dottie and I looked at each other in amused disbelief.

"What the hell...?" I ventured. "Did they take a wrong turn on the way to Vassar or something?"

The two were followed by a willowy, waif-like, dark-haired girl with eyes so huge, that even from the seventh floor I could tell her facial features were uniquely striking. She wore black capri pants and a tight black tee shirt, with a pink sweater tied over her shoulders European-style. On her feet were ballet flats –no socks.

We just stood at my window and watched as they unloaded a real steamer trunk and about five other matching suitcases, plus an easel, paint boxes with little handles on them, an art portfolio-carrier and some crates, all neatly tied with rope.

"Wow, that was something, " said Dot. "I wonder what room SHE'S in?" But it was just a rhetorical question. She couldn't stay long enough for us to find out. "I've got to get back. Mallory and I have to be at the House in forty minutes for a pledge test on the Greek alphabet. We've been memorizing!" And she left my room with the door ajar, and me puzzling about why anyone that rich would come to a state school. Didn't make any sense.

With my door still open, I could hear a lot of commotion outside in the halls as people moved in; but I had decided to wait until parents left and things calmed down before presenting myself to meet neighbors. There would be plenty of time for that, and besides some girls, unlike me, would be sad to leave their families and would be, I surmised, going through touching good-byes. I went back to what I had turned to after going through all the bookstore information, namely reading *Mademoiselle's* college issue on the bed.

A man's voice interrupted my reverie and reading.

"Hello, Miss. Miss Cassandra's things, Miss."

HUH?

I looked up startled to see the chauffeur from a few minutes ago out the window standing at my dorm room's threshold!

I jumped off the bed. "Uh... come on in."

"Thank you, Miss." He wheeled in the trunk on what must have been his own dolly, as the dorms weren't giving those out.

He was followed by the woman maneuvering a cart with the aforementioned and stared at-- matching luggage, the easel and the boxes all piled up. The wispy girl came in last, carrying the art portfolio.

"Hi!" she effervesced. "I'm Cass! You must be Sarah?" She held out her hand.

"Hi! "I shook her hand. "How did you know my name? I ...didn't get anything in the mail giving me roommate information."

" Oh, you know, my mother's secretary must have called the school or something, " she laughed. And then she turned to her chaperones.

"Just put those anywhere."

"Very good Miss Cass."

"Oh, Miss Cass," said the woman mournfully, "we're all going to miss you!" She reached out to hug her. "Don't you want me to stay and unpack for you? Here, let me just get it started, " and she began opening the large steamer trunk and taking out tissue that was practically standing on its own. "At least I'll hang these up."

The trunk was overflowing with dresses, robes, pajamas, and skirts on skirt hangers. We each had the same amount of closet space allocated, so I really wondered where they were going to put all her things. One of the cases, however, was full of closet accessories: skirt hangers, hooks, storage bags that hung from hooks, folding lingerie cases, shoe bags. Things that I had never seen. The maid took all that out first and arranged the system into the tiny closet; it gave her twice the space. Sweaters were folded separately into tissue and could be arranged on the hanging shelf contraption. Good thing, I thought, watching that, because we certainly didn't have the drawer space in the dressers provided by the university for all the sweaters she'd brought: cashmere twin sets, wool cardigans, ski sweaters, Shetland sweaters in colors of heather, most of which matched specific skirts. But it was the dresses that most awed me. They were what my grandmother would have called "frocks". They seemed for the most part suited for a teenager, yet still had a certain sophistication about them. But they certainly didn't look as though you'd be playing dress-up in Mommy's clothes. These had a more innocent look about them: lots of navy blue and Kelly green together--mod-looking, mini-skirted. Or full skirts, one with a black background sprinkled with bright flowers across the layered fabric. And the *piéce de resistance* of all this: a midnight blue drop waist mini-skirted cocktail dress with a shocking pink sash, hip-level, tied low with a pink bow. Too luscious for words. No sorority chick would have had to look at its label.

I was utterly mesmerized. *What was this, Pollyanna or something? Who were these people? Did kids really have such servants who were sweet, kind, in-loco-parentis figures who actually loved them? Was I hallucinating? And if such a person could move into my room at Iowa like this, what must moving-in day be like at Radcliffe?! This was all just anathema to me.*

I caught myself staring again at them as they efficiently went about stacking *Miss Cass'* other things around the room. But then the girl was standing in front of me and I was staring at **her**. I snapped to and mumbled, "Sorry."

"No, it's we who are sorry we barged in here like this. And I promise I won't take up the whole room with this stuff. You must think I'm mad!" Did she mean crazy or angry? No one I knew used that term.

"No big deal," I said, and added, pointing, "I've put a bookcase there and sort of staked out my corner claim."

"Good!" Cass laughed, then turned to the maid and chauffeur who were still busying themselves with her things.

"No, really, enough! " laughed Cass. "I can unpack! You two had better get back on the road. It's still a three hour drive back!"

"She is correct, Miss Cooper," said the chauffeur, looking uncomfortable in being in the girls' dorm in the first place. Carrying things up was one thing; staying quite another.

"Well, I suppose he's right--as usual." She gave Cass another longing sorrowful look. "That's it then, Miss Cassandra. I must say, the Hyde household is just not going to seem the same without you there. You have a wonderful year, now, okay!"

"Well, I'll be back for holidays! We'll see each other sooner than you think."

The chauffeur shook her hand and sort of doffed his cap to her, and said, "Now if you've found that you've forgotten anything, just give a holler, Miss Cass, and I'll send it out."

"Thanks, Martin! That's really sweet."

The maid hugged her again and admonished her to write.

"Oh, yes, with all my mad, gay, exciting details of sophomore year no less, " she giggled. She walked with them to the door, and I think I just continued to stand there like this couldn't possibly be happening in my room.

Cass came back into the main part of the room and shrugged at me like, "what can I do?"

"I really really am sorry for all this commotion and mess. Honestly, I'll have these emptied in a minute and out of your way."

"It doesn't bother me." Brilliant conversation. I was still stupefied.

"So, anyway, shall we have formal introductions? Cass Hyde," she smiled and held out her hand.

"Right. And actually, I'm *Sari* Shrier. Only my father calls me Sarah."

"Got it. And you're a freshman, I take it?"

"Yes and you're a sophomore? Who was your roommate last year?"

"I had a single."

"Oh. Why?"

"Because that's the way my mother set things up when I registered. But I didn't like it! So I put in for a double at the end of last year and got it." She was all of a sudden fumbling with tissue paper and not looking at me. "Mummy wasn't too happy about that, but she let it go in the end. And that's how I got you!"

Mummy??!

"Well, I love this room. A bathroom to ourselves and all---God, what's not to like?" I ventured.

"You're going to love it here! Let me see your schedule. You did already register didn't you?"

I fished around on my desk for it. "Yes we came in mid-June for freshman orientation."

Cass read over my card and immediately asked, "How did you know to take Art History?"

"Well, because they said it could substitute for Western Civ and I thought it sounded better for my major. I want to study in Paris later and it would be to my best interest to know something about art and museums before I get there."

Cass just looked at me. "Boy, smart thinking. Especially for a freshman!" Then she added, "Just wait 'til you lay your eyes on Dr. Klampert! You'll freak out--he's so gorgeous."

"He teaches it?"

"Yes, but there are different sections. If you don't get him, we'll change you. I'm his T.A. for the core courses."

"You are?! Gee, what do you do?"

"Oh, set up slide trays for the lectures, correct homework--not tests. I sort slides for every lecture. I type his papers sometimes. Whatever he wants. I'm an art major and working for Klampert means everything. He's a god."

I was unabashedly incredulous. "**You** work. For a professor. And you are driven to school by ..." I was getting into territory that was none of my business here, and at least I realized it soon enough to shut up. But things were not coming together for me at that moment. I mean, I had heard of work-study but not for people driven to college in limos with a retinue of servants. Cass sensed my confusion at once.

"Oh, I know. Isn't that the queerest car?! My parents won't let me get a driver's license! At my age-- I'm nineteen! Anyway, I'm not on work-study. But I am an art major and I applied to be Klampert's T.A. because I just feel that anything I can do around the department is great for the experience. And Dr. K. needed some help. I really just volunteered."

Freshmen, it seemed to me at that instant, just didn't have a clue. I had no idea one could even get to know a professor or that you could work for one. Cass was already looming larger than life to me and I had only just met her.

It didn't take long for the aura of Cass to permeate my surroundings, however.

Dorothy, Mallory and a couple of their friends were dubious when they stopped me at the Burge mailboxes a day or two later to confirm what Dot had told them, namely that her little friend Sarah was the one who got the roommate brought to college in a goddam limo. We went into the tunnel between the two dorms and talked in hushed tones.

"I swear!" Dot reported again, "it was something like out of the movies to see a chauffeur for godsake and all that luggage!"

24

Mallory continued, "When we all heard that she was YOUR roommate, we just about died!"

"Well, heck-- you should see what she brought! I swear-- all the clothes she's got! I mean, you just wouldn't believe it. And she's an art major---tons of art supplies all over the place!"

They gave out a sort of collective "Wow."

It suddenly struck me to verbalize my innermost thoughts that I'd had since the day Cass moved in.

"Shit, I wonder why anyone so rich would come to this school?" I looked up at Dorothy who took offense at that remark and was giving me the dirtiest look.

"Look, Sarah! This is one of the best schools in the country--especially for writing AND ART! You ought to at least appreciate your own school!"

" I'm just saying that if someone's super super rich and half-way smart, they could've gone **anywhere**, that's all. Big schools let rich peoples' kids in for endowments of everything from libraries to soccer fields. You know what I mean."

"Well, you may be right about rich people but I don't get **your** attitude. I waded through four years of high school just so I could come here. I love this school! It really is an intellectual, literary, artistic oasis even if it is in the middle of nowhere! The faculty is fabulous, and I'm surprised you seem to have no idea of who they might be! You signed up for art history, didn't you? So you'll find out. We've got this great print-maker over here from the HOLOCAUST for godsake. I can't remember his name, but he's damn famous."

"Really?" Was that Klampert, I wondered? But no, he couldn't be. He was an art historian.

"And," she continued practically without coming up for air, "when you go to your rhetoric class in EPB just take a look at the roster in the lobby and see who all famous is here in the writing program! Not to mention the science department which is great, and the school of medicine and the law school and all the rest of that. *Gevalt*, Sari, you're here for the next four years. You'd better learn to like it!"

"I'm only here for three years." Lest there be any doubt--I had to keep myself convinced, at least. But I decided to appease her; after all, she was my very first friend on campus.

"But, you're right. I do like being here."

Hell, I'd have liked being anywhere out of my house.

"Okay, so what's she like already?" Dot asked in an appeasing sort of tone.

"Nice."

"Just nice?"

"Real nice. Yes. I mean, she's a sophomore. You'd think she'd be exasperated at having a freshman roommate; but so far she doesn't act that way at all. "

"Well, why didn't she have some friend from last year to ask to share a room this year, I wonder?"

"Don't know." I was beginning to feel defensive and didn't want to. I just wanted to be happy that I had a nice roommate-- one who didn't start packing back up to go home the moment she met me.

"Hey! Remember, tonight's *erev Rosh Hashana*. Maybe Mallory and I can come over to your room, you know, on the pretense of picking you up to go to services, and meet her!"

"You can come up to my room with the **real** reason of picking me up and meet her. Or you can come up **now** and just meet her!"

"Uh, no. We'll come by later. Say 6:45? It'll be crowded so we have to get there early."

"Fine. I--uh--don't even know where the synagogues are in this town."

Dot gave me another one of her starting- to -become- repetitive looks.   "There's only one-- conservative, but we all go to it. "

"Oh, right. Okay, see you at my room."

When I got back up there, Cass was waiting for me.

"Let me see your schedule again!" she bubbled. "I can't remember what P.E. you have."

"Oh, God, who knows. In high school my mother got me out of it. I had a heart murmur when I was little and that was a great excuse."

"Ooh, do you still have it?"

"I don't know. I think you grow out of them."

25

I found my schedule and it said Movement Principles, bowling, tennis, and golf. I looked up from the paper nauseated.

"Well, this looks a bit problematic. It can be changed, don't worry."

"Changed to what?"

"Get rid of the team sports, for a start. Bowling's ok and unfortunately Movement Principles is a required course for graduation..."

"Blech, I thought I'd be done with that crap after high school."

"But tennis and golf are populated by country club kids who already know those sports and are just taking them to get A's. You'll be at the bottom of your class the first day unless you played team sports for your high school."

"If you only knew..." I giggled at the thought, which produced in me a little reflex gag. *I was the proverbial last person chosen for any team on any playground, playing field or gym from the second grade on.*

"See, in college you can take dance for PE credit and you can take esoteric sports like fencing where the written tests will have a lot of French words on them and if you're in French, you'll be at the advantage! I'm taking it."

"Hey! I never thought of that! But I can't dance."

"It's not dancing, like fox trot. It's ballet, jazz, and like that."

"Oh I took ballet as a little kid! Maybe I'll remember some of it! That will mean more French vocabulary!"

"We can try to get into the same section. I'm taking it. And I already have the clothes--you can borrow some until you get yours--just leotards, a ballet skirt and soft shoes. No one in these classes gets to point. I've got mine here...somewhere," her voice trailed off as she rummaged through some suitcases looking for the dance class clothing.

"Okay, hold this up to you, " she said handing me off a black leotard.

"Looks fine." She was taller than me but we seemed to be about the same size –five or seven.

"Great! Now, tomorrow, we have to go over to the registrar's office and change your schedule."

"Ooh, tomorrow, I'm supposed to be in synagogue all day. In fact, I'm going tonight and I haven't even done my hair yet, yikes."

"A holiday?"

"Rosh Hashana."

"Do you have to go all day?"

" Well, come to think of it...noooo."

Some would, I presumed, but I just wouldn't. The wheels of rationalization began to turn: One set of services was plenty. At least I was going to something.

At home I had hated missing school twice--ten days apart at the beginning of fall semester, but my father was insistent and Betty, as usual, always just caved. It was never any use pleading our case to go back to class at least in the afternoon, get in half a day's work, take tests, ("They shouldn't give tests on a Jewish high holiday.") get caught up. Nothing would sway them and neither would it when grades were in jeopardy. You had to stay out of school and pull high grades, too, in my family.

One year my father was mad for some reason --at the world most likely, but it manifested in anger at the synagogue mucky-mucks-- and to our stupefaction, he announced that we would NOT be going to services. I was elated and dressed for school, whereupon he announced that neither were we going to school. No, a Jewish high holy day meant no school, and even though staying in my room listening to Ricky Nelson records was okay, school was not.

I went apoplectic at him and got in trouble for disrespect.

"Here I am, lucky to be in college, " I was explaining to Cassandra, "where the academic calendar starts so much later, so this year's first high *holy* day falls during the registration period and real classes didn't begin until the following Monday. But for Yom Kippur a week and a half from now, the dilemma will rear up again, and this time I'll be in class."

" Shit, " she sympathized.

"Holy shit."

The knock on the door a few hours later was tentative but the murmuring outside was an easy giveaway that Dorothy and Mallory were picking me up for services and dying to meet Cassandra. I had a funny feeling inviting them in, like I was the old-timer at the U and I was doing the introductions all around. Cass shook their hands and we all just stood there for a minute while they contemplated if they could have anything at all to say to her.

But Dot, looking around, chimed right in, "So, I hear you're an art major? Ooh, cute clothes!"

"Yes. I've got a lot of stuff in here now but in a few days I'll move it over to the studio."

"That's kind of neat that everyone gets some space over there," said Mallory.

"Yeah."

I suddenly noticed that what they were wearing, summery mini cotton sheath dresses and flats with flowers on the toes, was a lot less dressed up than me in my hot pink silk dress.

"Hey," I started, "you aren't even wearing heels!"

"Well, don't worry. It doesn't matter if you do. There aren't any rules."

"I know, but I guess I thought it was dressy."

"It's just synagogue."

"But it's Rosh Hashana."

Dot looked at Cass, as if to have to explain things.

"We don't have holidays like Easter where everyone gets dressed up."

"The hell we don't," I promptly refuted.

Who was she kidding! I may have been from a hamlet myself, but I knew that every Jewish woman from L.A. to Bangor dressed to outdo every other one on Rosh Hashana and Yom Kippur. I wasn't personally trying to outdo anyone that night in Iowa City, but I was certainly under the impression that you tried to show up looking like it was not just an ordinary service.

"Come on," said Mallory, checking the time. "We've got to get going or we'll be late."

I clomped out behind them giving a little wave to Cass.

Chapter Four

"Devil with a Blue Dress On"...Mitch Ryder and the Detroit Wheels

Without belaboring the point too much, it became clear to me in those first days, as we were getting to know one another, that Cassandra Hyde had led the poor little rich girl life even more stereotypically than I had ever imagined, read about or watched on the screen. She spent a large part of her childhood being sent away from the family's myriad of homes: to schools and camps and tours; to study art, horseback riding, marine biology, needlepoint, The Great Books; to New York, London, Wisconsin, Minnesota, Florida, Ireland, Norway, Switzerland and elsewhere.

"Why Norway?" I asked when she was listing the places.

"It's so beautiful and remote. It was a program like Outward Bound. But it wasn't the real Outward Bound - ha! I wouldn't have lasted on that."

"Which is what?"

"Oh, sort of where you learn to fend for yourself in the wilderness and get yourself into and out of situations."

"Like what?"

"Oh, like sailing in the fjords, hiking, tying knots."

"Come on, you can't be serious. Why would they want to send you to that?"

"They heard it was great, I guess. And it was! Norway is arguably the most pristine, beautiful place on the planet. Well, plus," she added, hesitating a bit, "it was long. Three months. We got to tour the country, too. I loved Bergen."

It started to hit me that while these parents, whom I could only guess at that time, cared about quality experiences for their daughter, they certainly seemed to have wanted her out of their lives for extended periods of time. I couldn't quite put my finger on why, but I already envisioned her having empowerment issues at home.

"The point is," I pressed on, "did **you** want to be so far away from home like all that--all summer?"

"But...I spent **every** summer away from home. If it hadn't been Norway it would have been somewhere else. Several summers in a row when I was little, I went to Porterstone Equestrian Camp. That's in Fairfax County, Virginia. Do you know it?"

"Nope."

"One summer I went to camp at an art colony in Door County."

"Door County?" *She might as well have said the Land of Oz.*

"Yes, it's really famous - you know the part of Wisconsin that juts out like a thumb into Lake Michigan? It's called the Cape Cod of the Midwest."

Now that I could relate to. I had never heard of Door County, but I was immediately jealous. "That sounds like heaven, all right."

"And all through my whole childhood I was sent to camps for the summer--it was just normal."

"Ritzy camps?"

"Well, nice ones."

I'll bet. Like in "The Parent Trap"??--girls brought to summer camp by chauffeurs. Boarding school would have been fine with me, but not summer camp. Every time I thought of camp, Auschwitz came to mind first.

"I guess you can get used to anything, and once you do, it would seem normal," I ventured, hoping I hadn't put her on the defensive.

"It wasn't a question of getting used to it. It was merely summer. I was never at home."

"Well, that's what I mean...did you want to be?"

"Not really. I mean, there was no one there but me. My parents weren't home a lot. Papa (*she pronounced it Pa PAH*) has businesses all over the world and Mummy travels with him. She always has. If I went off to camp or travelled, I was with a lot of other people---kids. You know."

"Right." At that point, I was already having to quell the strong urge to covet her life, and I only knew the half of it. I had to make a concerted effort not to be awed by her. All I could think was that it

28

certainly wasn't fair: I had schemed and plotted every summer of my life to get out of the house, and the farthest I ever got was to Brandeis on the bus.

"Now, " she added, "there was my grandmother's house. I did like to go there. Usually for the last two or three weeks before school started, after I was home from camp or wherever, I would be sent down to Gran's. It's a house in Springfield, Illinois that her family had built in the early 1860's when they homesteaded the land."

"Wow. Homesteading." *Did it ever end with this girl?* "What was that house like?"

"Neat! Very old. But they'd redone it a few times. Same house, really, though. Just with modern bathrooms and kitchen appliances. And small--it only had five real bedrooms, plus the attic."

"Oh, yeah, I can picture it... *small.*"

"Well," she laughed, "yes I can see what you think. It sounds big but the rooms upstairs were all sort of rabbit warren-like. The second floor was actually not even level, and rooms were tucked into corners up there. But, I mean, well, small compared to my parents' house in Kenilworth."

"Why do you call it your parents' house?"

"Oh, no reason." She laughed a little. "Okay. *My* house in Kenilworth. Maybe you can come home with me sometime and see the place... if you want to," she had ventured, that first time she told me about it.

"That'd be neat, " I replied, trying to sound nonchalant. I guess neat! I had begun at that moment to already fantasize about telling my parents I wouldn't be coming home for such and such holiday.

The part she left out that first time I heard about her family was that her mother's great- great-grandfather's side, a formerly Scottish banking family, settled nearly a huge swath of the territory that would eventually become the state of Illinois when Virginia ceded the area to the new United States in 1783; and that later, her father's family, early steel magnates in the state, had built an architectural empire on so much of the prime real estate in Chicago, that there was hardly a neighborhood on the North Shore they hadn't built on or sold.

Her paternal grandfather, Edward Custis Hyde didn't go into the family business, however, opting for a career in academia. He was a University of Chicago classical antiquities scholar, whose middle name came from the branch of the family he was descended from that included Martha *Custis* Washington. He had graduated from Yale where a fraternity brother (younger) was the man who would become Cass' maternal grandfather, Roger Bronwyn Scott. Roger's daughter Julia and Edward's son John-Wilfred married one another. John-Wilfred had gone to Yale also, in architecture and had become one of Chicago's preeminent and most successful architects with clients all over the country and the world. Julia sat on many boards and did the requisite volunteer work that matrons of her station are expected to do.

She was a great asset to John-Wilfred, who was ten years her senior. They entertained lavishly and often. The only job they didn't really take to was parenting.

Cass hadn't brought a lot of pictures with her to our dorm room, but she did have a little double framed portrait of her parents and one of her house, which looked like something on a movie set lot to me.

By the time Cass and I had roomed together all of my Freshman year, I would get to see her home in Kenilworth. Not exactly an estate, it did have the aura of a manor house in a bucolic setting not unlike something created on a Hollywood backlot. Situated on Abbotsford Road, the seven-thousand square foot Italianate villa was exactly what one would expect at that echelon but not at all ostentatious.

Cass had a bedroom that blew my mind when I saw it, however, complete with fireplace and old lace-fringed canopy bed. Her closet opened with French doors and the room had an en suite bathroom with a claw-footed bathtub, and a separate walk-in shower that was installed, of course, during one of the up-dating renovations the home had gone through over the course of twenty years. One whole wall of this bedroom was composed of windows with views to the grounds, which were more like a park than a backyard. Suffice it to say, I had never seen anything remotely like this house until I actually went there with her.

Their "pied-à-terre" in Chicago, where we also spent a few days once, was a three-story penthouse mansion in the sky. If the house in Kenilworth was actually a family home, this place was an art gallery that people sometimes lived in! White walls at various slants and angles had the express purpose of displaying art, paintings, fiber art and statues. The décor was modern and all glass and steel. The furnishings were stark. The parents had an actual bedroom of their own in this place, obviously; they spent a lot of time there. But Cass had one of the spare rooms when she spent the night there. She didn't have a say in how it was decorated.

Aside from these homes, her parents kept a studio in the Hyde Building in New York City, fully staffed and ready for their arrival at any unannounced time; and, as Hyde Architectural Industries had a branch in London, there was also a completely furnished flat in Mayfair at their ready disposal, and a chalet in Gstaad, Switzerland, where they spent New Year's. They would go to these places in the Hyde planes – a jet, a prop plane or a helicopter, depending on the distance, reason for the trip, number of people travelling. Cass Hyde had only rarely ever flown commercial in her life. (I had only been on a plane once.)

Cass intrigued me with the childlike innocence of an overprotected china doll on the one hand, and the worldly-wise nonchalance of a sophisticated maven on the other. It was still amazing to me that they sent her to such a mundane place as the dorm of a state university without anyone to oversee her daily needs. Doing laundry, for instance, had been new to her.

I finally screwed up the courage to ask her what I wanted to know from the minute the chauffeur had knocked on my door: why in God's name did she come to the University of IOWA?

"So all your family went to boarding schools and colleges in the East—grandfather and father at Yale, mother at Vassar, etc. Your grandfather was a professor at Chicago and you're a legacy there, too. Why are you here? If you don't mind me asking?"

"I'm interested in print-making."

"And? "

"Oh, yes, you're right---we've got the school of the Art Institute of Chicago, I know. *(I didn't know from the Art Institute of Chicago at that point but I played along.)* But Lasansky is **here**."

"Who? I thought you were all hep over Klampert."

"Mauricio Lasansky!!" *(My God, that must be who Dottie was trying to remember the name of that one day when she had admonished me to appreciate Iowa U more.)* Do you know that *Time* magazine called him the most influential print-maker in the nation? They said his U of I studio was the print-making capital of the world! I dream of working with him. But, ha! I've got a ways to go, don't you know!"

"Okay, can't say as I've ever heard of him, but I believe you. But here you are---living in a more or less slum of a dorm room –you know—for **you**, and having to do stuff on your own...like laundry? "

"Yeah, no problem… I've been in spartan rooms like this before. I wouldn't call it slumming. Rosemary Hall was very nice, frankly, and we didn't have to do our own laundry, but the camps I've been to are just like this. I mean, you're right and all, but I wanted to come here. I had made up my mind in high school to study with him."

"Well, shit, what did your parents SAY?" Weren't they upset?"

"Not really. They don't particularly care where I am, I guess. Plus it's pretty close to Chicago. They could send me here in a car."

"I'm afraid I **am** lousy with ironing," she told me one evening seeing me folding mine spread out all over the bed with the ironing board set up in the middle of the room and my little dorm-size black iron heating up. "I can't iron anything right."

"But you never had to so…?"

"No, not really. But I do think it's something one should know anyway. Who taught you?"

"I had to do all the ironing in the family, " I stated, "and my mother had a certain way she wanted it done, so she taught me. But it got to the point where it was one chore I liked doing. Helps if you have the greatest equipment and can set it all up watching soap operas. Once we got a portable t.v., I could put it wherever I wanted. That was heaven. Not that we had the greatest gadgets and appliances, but the iron at home was better than this thing."

"I brought an iron – it's a beauty--Rowenta, the Cadillac of irons. You can use it any time."

"Wow! thanks—could I even try it now?" She went to look for it and found it encased in tissue paper in one of her plastic shoe boxes that had been piled in the closet. She handed it over and I saw that this iron was glistening with brand-newness.

"Have you ever used this thing?"

She shrugged indeterminately.

I filled it with water through the top and let it heat up, which happened almost instantaneously. I took a blouse from the pile and began to iron it. I literally couldn't believe how different it was from mine. Cass just stood there and watched me like I was painting a masterpiece instead of ironing clothes. I showed her how I had learned to first do the collar and cuffs; then I went to the sleeves, each in turn; finally I'd start on the body, which was the fun part. I turned it out onto a hanger and buttoned the top button. It was now ready to put into the closet. Her iron glided along spouting steam all through my pile of oxford cloth shirts, making short work of this task. Pressing, flipping and finishing the material with the steam in my face felt good-- natural---like I had made a home out of our dorm room.

Classes were about to start. The schedules were fixed; I had Rhetoric, French 102, Spanish 202, Art History, Biology, Fencing and the dreaded Movement Principles. The clothes were readied in our respective closets. We had gone to the bookstore for supplies, and the sorority pledges were nowhere in sight in the dorms most nights now as they began their duties, their training and their parties. Cass noticed that she hadn't seen my Jewish friends around the room again.

"Are you kind of upset that you didn't join that sorority you were telling me about? " she asked out of the blue one night. "I mean, are you being shunned?"

"Oh, huh-uh. They're still friendly to me. My **parents** aren't too thrilled, though. My father acts like I did it deliberately to let them down. They love to wield that old perform-for-praise club. Do yours?"

"Well, when that you put it that way, no, not exactly. My parents don't pay too much attention to what I do as long as wherever I am and whatever I'm doing is within their stated parameters."

"So you can just do whatever you want and they don't have to know?"

"They can't be bothered with what I do, as long as I'm not in any trouble they might have to deal with."

"Come on! They're not putting any pressure on you to get grades or to date certain people...or not date certain people?"

"No, seriously, they don't ever mention dating because they already think they will choose the person I end up marrying--or at least there will be a sort of gene pool of eligible blue-bloods I will be expected to pick from."

"That's not possible!" I was flabbergasted as always. "You're certainly not going along with it are you? Aren't you dating people here?"

" Last year I met a grad student from the East - Joel-- doing his M.A. in Art Therapy and Child Psychology. I was helping out in an after-school art program at the lab school and met him there. He was so darling, so devoted to children----jolly, you know. I think I fell for him the first afternoon I saw him."

"And?"

"We went out. He was Jewish, it turns out."

"Oh, no."

"It didn't bother me but it did him."

"And your parents." I just assumed. But she didn't answer, as though it hadn't ever got that far.

"Does it hassle you at all to think of marrying someone who isn't Jewish, though?" she asked me instead of answering.

"I don't know-- frankly--what's the point? I hardly dated during high school. No Jewish boys asked me out---there weren't that many, of course, in our town."

She just picked up where she left off almost in a reverie, " 'Cause it always bothered Joel that I wasn't someone he could even get serious about. Made me feel so low...'til I finally just drifted out of his life."

"Is he still on campus? "

"Nope. Gone."

I could have bored her for hours with the way I'd been lectured to, up one side and down the other, about intermarriage. Every time there was a chance for me to be a captive audience in a moving car, or out to dinner or in some other enclosed space I would get to hear all about how I would be "disinherited" (now that was an oxymoronic thought) if I ever married out of the religion, or for that matter, got pregnant by any boy out of wedlock. Disinherited from what? Get pregnant by whom? It would have all been just a scream if we hadn't spent our lives actually screaming.

When classes began, most of mine were on the Pentacrest either in Schaffer or MacBride Halls, with the exception of Rhetoric, which was in the English/Philosophy Building that Dot had referred to as EPB; and Art History which was across the river from the Union.

Except for Biology in a lecture hall with three hundred students that I found too boring for words and very difficult to keep awake for, all my classes were intriguing and filled with so many smart and interesting people that I had to wonder what I was doing amidst some of them. I feared for my high school preparation; the subject matters seemed difficult indeed. I had courses scattered from the Pentacrest to the art building on the other side of the Iowa River, to the English-Philosophy Building and the old gym. Biology was in a modern lecture hall but the labs looked like Darwin could have used them. I liked the antique look of the rooms, though.

Spanish and French were in Schaefer Hall in an old, high-ceilinged room lined with a wall full of gigantic windows whose yellowing shades wafted in the light, early autumn breezes. Huge cream-colored globes hung from the ceiling, dangling above our heads on cables. The desks were vintage and there was a faculty desk in the front of the room which held a lectern.

Classes settled into a routine just as they always did no matter what level of education one happened to be at. Pretty soon I couldn't believe I hadn't always gone to that school, lived in Iowa City, and studied in little carrels in a big library.

I had confidently announced to the sorority girls during rush that I had come to Iowa a declared Voice major. I'd always loved to sing, had taken private voice and piano lessons at financial sacrifice to my parents, and had always sung in choirs all throughout school. I was not good enough on the piano to justify the expense of studying it, however, and had quit.

During the summer pre-registration my music career was nipped in the bud by the ridiculous requirement that one had to play an instrument to be a Voice major. WHY?

I also had thought about journalism. I'd been feature editor of my high school newspaper; I could write. I even had a column. I loved the idea of moving to New York and working on a great paper.

Truth be told, we didn't have to declare majors anywhere near freshman year, but halfway through the first month at school, I actually did decide to major in French.

Our instructor had come in the first day wearing black cigarette-leg pants and a silk blouse. Around her neck and over her shoulders was a brilliant purple, pink and green silk scarf tied to the side. She wore glasses that were not sunglasses per se, but whose lenses were darker than normal ones. She kept them on throughout the class. She tended to sit on top of the desk, her sleek pointy-toed flats hung over the side. She was the essence of chic.

Mademoiselle Genet conducted the class in French from day one.

"*Nous allons faire une révision pendant quelques jours des formes du passé en français. Tournez dans vos textes à la page trente.*"

A cute guy sitting next to me leaned over and asked, "What's she talking about?"

"Page thirty--the past tense--review." I answered trying to seem helpful.

"God," he muttered, "don't tell me she's going to teach this whole damn class in **French**."

It was daunting to me, too, though I loved it. I had "CLEPed" into a second semester French class at Iowa even though I hadn't had very much in high school. I had taken a lot of Spanish first, and wanted to continue with it because I did like it, but eventually the culture held little thrill for me, whereas France's had captured my imagination just from hearing my father's war stories. I had registered for them both at Iowa that first semester, but after Genet's class, I found myself drifting away from the Spanish sphere of influence and into the French and Italian department. And I began to look seriously at year abroad programs. Iowa had one---in Rouen, France, not Paris. I was disheartened, and determined to find another junior year abroad. And I vowed to catch up. I had one advantage, as I saw it: I was obsessing over Paris and nothing would stop me from going there.

In the lobby of EPB, on my way to the first Rhetoric class, I did pause to look at the building directory as I had been admonished to do by Dot. Sure enough, there under the listings for the Iowa

Writers' Workshop, though all unknown to me that day, were names like Kurt Vonnegut, Jr., Paul Engle, Donald Justice, Marvin Bell, Robert Coover.

*The Iowa Writer's Workshop was as famous as Dotty had said and more so. Of course, I had to admit that was pretty neat. Resentful as I was **still** to be at Iowa that fall, even I had to admit that this was awe-inspiring. Names that were not yet household words, John Irving and Robert Morrell appeared also on the roster. Philip Roth had just done a stint as a guest lecturer. Frederick Exley's A Fan's Notes would soon hit the presses. I would have classes with Stephen Grey and Greg Heyman before my years at Iowa were over, and there would be many references to the time Tennessee Williams and Flannery O'Connor spent there and how they had left their marks.*

I walked down the hall under an aura of exaltation at the proximity of so much literary greatness. As I later learned, almost every writer of stature in the country either went to or taught at or guest lectured in the classrooms of the Iowa Writer's Workshop. I grudgingly concluded that maybe it wouldn't be so bad to be on that campus for four--no three! --years. One year I would be in France come hell or high water, I reassured myself, as I made my way to a room filled with about 30 freshmen, spied a seat in the back, and took it.

Our teaching assistant instructor for Rhetoric sauntered in, tossed down a motorcycle helmet on the chair, and promptly jumped up on the desk and sat legs crossed in meditation style. He was not much older than we were, cute in a haughty but scruffy sort of way, flinging back his long blond hair and touching his straggly blond goatee as he looked over a sheaf of greenish data paper with lots of margin holes, paper that hung out over the desk two feet in length. The earliest years of technology had hit the U. of I., and our names were on those papers. He called attendance from this scroll, acting bored with such a teacher task.

"I'm Alan Jones. I prefer you to call me Alan. You'll find my office hours on the top of the course outline I'm about to hand out. This is the honor's section of Rhetoric, which means that anyone in here should have taken the placement test and been **put** in this section. If you just chose this section and wandered in, wander out now."

He paused a moment, expecting to see people leave, but no one did. He continued by hopping down off the desk, and passing out the syllabus, speaking to us as he went.

"You will see by the syllabus that the first reading is Barth. You might be wondering why I chose a **story** for a class that is essentially composition and not literature. Any opinions on that?"

One guy called out, venturing, " Because this is the honors class and we already know how to write or we wouldn't be here?"

Jones didn't dignify that with a response.

"When you're reading this, I want you to be thinking of Barth writing it---his purpose. This story, you will see, revolves around the grammatical commentary on an initial sentence, and the subsequent commentary on that commentary. A sort of James Joyce lost in the alphabet."

As college freshmen, we had heard of James Joyce, but most of us looked at each other in total confusion; a few students nodded as if to show the professor that they agreed perfectly with everything he had just said, which was, of course, complete bullshit. I had to admit, however, after only a few minutes in his class, that I was intrigued with Alan Jones. He appeared so young. He couldn't possibly really be a college professor, I thought. Tall, gangly even, blond, Norse-god-like....light blue eyes - so beautiful. So unkempt though. He wore jeans! To class! Still, he couldn't have seemed more the epitome of a writer.

Back on the corner of his desk, legs re-crossed, he took up again with his original line of thinking.

"One of your goals in this class will be to develop your writing skills. You have to write with a purpose. I put *Lost in the Funhouse* on the reading list as an example of a <u>feeble</u> attempt at purpose. Barth can do better. What do *you* think of Barth?" he asked after a pause to let what he had just told us sink in.

How should we know what we think of him if we've only just got the syllabus and haven't read a word? I was wondering to myself when I realized he was calling on me. Me? I gestured. He nodded. *Shit.*

I tried to conjure up the most sincere tone of voice I could when I answered, "Sorry! I've never heard of him."

"*Giles Goat Boy? The Sot-Weed Factor?* You've never heard these titles?"

"No."

Not missing a beat, he just continued, "Back to *Lost in the Fun House*. Personally my respect for Barth was considerably diminished when I read that book. He's saying, 'You must understand why I write. You see, my problem is that I'm quite neurotic.' I actually have no need for neurosis in **my** life, " Jones stated, adding, "See that you don't all make me crazy."

Students in the room laughed nervously. I didn't think any of it was amusing. I just thought he was ranting. I hadn't taken a single note, didn't have any sort of frame of reference for Barth, and wondered how I'd ever pass the class.

"You are dismissed," Jones said, looking up from his perch. "Go straight to the bookstore and buy everything on my list. Get it used if you can--save you some money. (Everyone called the bookstore "Iowa Book and Crook.")

Back at the dorm, I tried to explain the experience of my first Rhetoric class at the famed writing school of Iowa to my roommate.

"I mean, you should have **heard** this guy! I just can't get over it! He says this author Barth..."

"Oh, John Barth? --great writer!" Cass offered.

I just glared at her. "You know him. " I didn't pose this as a question. It simply figured that I was ignorant compared to her.

"Sure."

"Okay, anyway, our teacher--- his name's Alan Jones, have you heard of him?"

"No."

"Okay, so anyway, he said this guy Barth isn't good enough--or something-- to deserve self-pity. He goes, ' We must reserve suffering only for the man-god.' Whatever that means!" I shook my head perplexed. "He really blew my mind. I didn't understand half of what went on in there today."

"My God, he sounds fantastic," Cass cooed, almost in the same reverent tones that Dorothy always used to underline her point about what an inspiring place this university must be. Still, I was unconvinced. Cass continued, slowly forming her analysis of Alan Jones' thesis on Barth.

"And I think I know what he means: It's like reading Nixon's *Six Crises*. Nixon doesn't deserve **one** crisis. It's not fair that fools and lackeys should think they suffer." Her voice rose with enthusiasm for this train of thought. "Despair should be reserved for the very highest expression of mankind." She looked up at me anticipating a big reaction to this seeming enlightenment.

"Rigggghhhht." Then I caught the drift: "Like me living with my father!"

"Yours is probably a piker compared to mine, honey." But she chose not to elaborate.

34

Chapter Five

"Time of the Season"...The Zombies

Trying to live the University of Iowa life entailed trying to have a social life but priming yourself not to care if one didn't happen. I passed through the Goldfeather Room of the Iowa Memorial Union at least once or twice a day where students spent time studying or, more likely, not. People ran up huge amounts on their U-bill for food and recreation in the Union. I was not allowed to charge anything, so it didn't entice me; but I saw students while away whole months of academic terms playing bridge, watching soap operas and skipping as many classes as humanly possible. The imaginary malady Goldfeather Fever had a basis in reality.

Another favorite activity in the Goldfeather Room was fomenting political unrest. The place was a hotbed of radical thought expressed at poetry readings, jam sessions and verbal protests about the escalating and on-going war in Vietnam.

The room was always packed and it didn't much matter what "group" or crowd one associated oneself with there; the grad students and writers hung out somewhere else, like the River Room upstairs, and the frat jocks went to the Airliner. But sooner or later everyone wafted through the Goldfeather Room. I felt like a square peg in there, but found solace in the back of the room at any free table, where I would do homework, write in my diary, or read---or feign serious study. (For actual serious studying, I usually staked out a carrel in the library, normally after dinner.) I loved the idea that someone always had money to play the Goldfeather's jukebox and invariably it was a song I loved. We were living inside "Strawberry Fields" that first autumn. I had spent the summer ironing in my basement at home to "Eleanor Rigby." That one was played a lot, too.

Cass would come across the footbridge from the art building to the Union after late classes, and we would meet in the Goldfeather Room.

"How's it going at the studio?" I asked. It was one of those warm fall days when we met around four o'clock. She didn't look very happy.

"Lousy. Maybe I can't paint after all."

"Sure you can." I was about to expound on the subject because I had seen her latest sketches and they were outstanding. She was getting ready, she had explained, for a series of stylized flowers in abstract. But all of a sudden I saw my Rhetoric teacher Alan Jones come into the room and sort of gravitate towards us!

"Oh, God! Cass, that guy over there in the plaid shirt and jeans is Alan Jones! "

"So that's him, huh? He's cute. Whoa, he seems to be heading over this way," she noticed.

"God! I hope he doesn't ask me anything about Barth or anyone else."

But Alan Jones walked past our table without so much as a glance and joined a group of equally scruffy-looking guys who greeted him eagerly but seemed to be in deep discussion at the same time.

"Oh well, " I said, relieved that I hadn't had to be confronted, and interested in getting back to the problems Cass was having with her work. The art, drama, and English department regulars laden with drinks and snacks, were filing back and forth under the glare of the industrial lights, and in the fog of rock music pulsating through the room. I leaned on my elbows towards Cass on the other side of the table to hear her story better over the din around us. "So what's doing with your project?"

"If I knew that, I wouldn't be in this mess. I can't seem to get it to come together."

"It happens, I mean, with art, don't you think?" I ventured, not knowing what I was talking about, really, but thinking back to dinky little projects I'd worked on in high school, like set decorating for road shows and scenery painting. "It doesn't seem like much at first, and then---kind of evolves into what you want, right?"

She shot me a look that meant it was all she could do not to roll her eyes at me.

"I wish it were something like that. But this time..." her voice trailed off and I was amazed to see why when I looked up. There was a very cool-looking, clean-cut, wind-blown blond Adonis standing at our table. It figures, I thought, turning around

*Right, I haven't mentioned this yet: Cassandra Hyde was possibly the most beautiful girl on campus. Just her presence in that room must have sent waves through the crowd like Morse code signals. "Calling all guys-- abject beauty at ten o'clock." This is not an exaggeration. She could send that message with deep violet eyes that radiated out of her face like beacons from a lighthouse. When people saw her, they couldn't take **their** eyes off of her. It had happened when my other friends stopped by the room that first day. At first we were all just mesmerized by her **stuff**, but not long after, I, at least, realized that I was in the presence of true beauty, and not the common sort. This was no blond ponytail or flip-coiffed athlete, but a tiny hummingbird of a girl, wisps of dark pixie hair clinging to her forehead like Audrey Hepburn's Funny Face, only wispier. Like Audrey, she, too had a dancer's lithe body, and a smile of beautiful aligned teeth that could glow across her entire face when she was happy.*

But the kid tapped **me** on the shoulder. I jumped.

"Excuse me," he said haltingly. "But I think you're in my French class? *Mademoiselle* Shrier isn't it?"

"Yes, but how did you know my name?" I was stupefied.

" 'Cause she calls on you a lot, man!" He suddenly remembered we didn't know him. "Oh, uh, sorry. I'm Mick Delaney."

" I'm Sari. And this is my roommate, Cassandra Hyde," I stated.

They exchanged nods, while Mick pulled up a chair. Then Cass got up to leave.

"Wait a minute, " I said, catching her sleeve, still hoping to continue where we'd left off, but feeling rather incredibly occupied with Mick.

"No, listen, I've got to get back to it. I'll see you by dinnertime, okay?" She was already around to the other side of the table heading towards the door.

"Bye!" I let my voice trail off as I turned back to the matter at hand. "She's an artist, " I offered, shrugging.

"Umm, "he uttered, with not the least real interest. And then he took up with why he had come over to my table in the first place.

"The - uh -- guys I'm with over there, "he began, gesturing behind him, "are in the class, too, see, and well, when I caught sight of you sitting over here, we thought maybe we could ask you some questions. You know--that stuff she was talking about in class? *Imparfait* or something? I actually think I'm in the wrong section, because really, in high school, I don't think we got this far. Do you understand this business of what past tense to use and all?" He stared into my face like a lovelorn puppy.

"Well, sure, " I nodded confidently. This was not Barth, after all; French grammar I understood. "I know how to do it; it's not that hard."

"Well, **Mademoiselle** Shrier, then could you come over and explain it to us, 'cause I got to tell you, we're lost." He pointed over his shoulder and I looked around him to the table of well-dressed, frat-jock types huddled around some books.

"Sure. And, by the way, can you call me Sari."

"Well, alright!"

As we approached the table the conversation was building in intensity.

"Any takers here on my bet?" I heard a voice call out.

"This year they ain't gonna beat us. I'll take your bet, jerk. Betting against the Hawks! Christ. No way."

"You watch. The Hawks'll go down to Ohio State as usual. Homecoming won't make any difference, although we might be able to beat Northwestern in that game." In the middle of this debate, the speaker looked up and changed course, "Hey! The French whiz-kid. Way to be in there **Mickey**!" They started moving chairs around and clearing off a part of the table.

"Okay, okay, give us a break here, " said Mick, obviously expecting ribbing of some sort. "This is Sari and she's agreed to lend a hand to the ol' French homework. So listen up."

"Hi," I offered. I was puzzled because none of these boys looked the slightest bit familiar to me. Even though we'd only been in session a week, I couldn't remember them being in our class; and it turned out they weren't. They were all Sig Ep pledges in various sections of French 102 whose material was similar but who had different instructors. Pledges had to make grades, however, and Mick had taken it upon himself to scrounge up a little tutorial in the Goldfeather Room.

I had no trouble explaining the uses of the *passé composé* versus the *imparfait* to them, and I wasn't watching the time as we went through the various exercises in the workbook, each one of the "students" taking turns while I gave the yay or nay to their answers. They seemed genuinely grateful, not snotty or cavalier about getting help. Gee, I thought, getting into a frat must really mean something to guys. *That's kind of stupid, but oh well.* I was feeling great being of academic service to a table full of cute boys in the middle of the hippest place on campus. My pulse rate was rising right along with the music.

"Guys! " Mick suddenly announced. "Time! Look at the time!"

"Jesus!" one of them said. "We're going to be late!"

Mick looked at me apologetically. "Sorry to run off, Sari, but we're due at the house. Thanks a lot for all the help!"

"Yeah, man," they chorused.

"Any time!" I said, waving them off, and then looking around a bit bewildered at the abrupt clearing out of the place. It was late for me, too, but at Burge you could eat in shifts. I wondered if Cass had gone ahead to dinner without me, but I decided since I was so close to the art department, to run over there and just see if she had figured out what was going wrong with her painting.

It was still Indian Summer and that late afternoon sun was setting in a pool of pinks and purples and still strong enough to hurt my eyes as I watched it disappear behind the red-brick art building across the footbridge. The air still smelled like an evening summer in the Midwest and not like fall yet; up on that bridge I could hear the river gurgling through the concrete railing spaces. It wasn't the Pont Neuf, but at least it was a bridge crossing a river that divided a city in half.

I lingered on the bridge a few moments, admonishing myself to make an effort to like the place.

Once on the other side, I made my way to the only entrance to the building I ever used when going to art history lectures. I had no idea if that door would be open, and if it were, once inside, where I'd find Cass. I knew there were various departments in there---sculpture, painting, the famous print-making; but I had never been in the studio arts part of the building and figured I'd just have to explore around until I found her. I started in the hall where I knew my way around, and headed towards the office area. It occurred to me that this wasn't scary because the university had many evening classes which would be starting around the dinner hour, and besides, artists worked all the time at their craft. There was bound to be somebody in there.

As I came down one of the corridors I even heard conversation, so I gravitated towards it. Rounding the corner however, I came to an abrupt halt because right there in the middle of the hall stood Dr. Klampert with his hands gingerly cupped around Cass' face! I flipped back around out of their sight and waited just a bit because I could hear what seemed like Cass faintly sobbing.

"It can't be all that bad," he was saying to her in a soothing tone, "I hate to look into your beautiful blue eyes and see so much sadness."

Oh, brother! I peeked around the corner ever so slightly. But Cass wasn't reacting to this "line" like someone about to puke. She seemed hypnotized by him. He was stroking bits of her hair off the side of her face. His head bent towards her caused his own masses of straight hair to fall over his brow like a curtain. He had long hair to his collar, but not unkempt like Alan Jones' . He was far more professorial-looking than Jones, too; older of course, at least in his forties, I surmised, by the distinguished hints of grey around the temples of his sandy brown hair. He was dressed more professor-like, too, in light tan linen slacks with a pale blue cotton shirt --three shades lighter than his eyes-- tucked in, but pulled out a bit to fold over a black snake-skin belt. The shirtsleeves were rolled up to the forearm revealing a sleek gold watch on a thin black band. He wore black loafers barefooted, a look that affirmed chic yet casual, still summery, very cool, sophisticated and perfectly dreamy.

"I tell you what, " he continued, as I listened harder. "Come back over to the studio tonight and I'll give you whatever art historian critique I can muster. " He gave off a little laugh.

"Really!?" gasped Cass. "Oh that would be so super! Thank **you**! " she sort of drawled at him but with an intensity and a genuine earnestness in her voice.

37

Anticipating their imminent departure, I suddenly did not want to be found there, and darted back around towards the way I had come, leaped down the hallway towards the door, sprinted out over the footbridge and back to the dorm.

Cass found me in the dining hall of Burge and brought her tray over to my table.

"Did you get it worked out?" I asked.

"Not quite. I'm going back over there tonight and try again."

"Hmm."

"Hey! How about that guy Mick! He was cute. Did you help him?"

"I guess so. They had to leave before we were done, but I think it went pretty well."

"Cool. You'll be seeing him in class every day. Very good."

"Yeah, right. He's not interested in me. He's interested in making grades to become an active in Sig Ep. He is cute, though, and has some very cute friends, I will say that."

"So? Do you think he'll ask you out?"

"No," I snorted.

We sat there eating in silence for a while, me waiting for her to tell me all about her afternoon, which she did not. Dot and Mallory caught sight of us when they came off the line, as the place was clearing out, and they came over to join our table.

"How come you two are eating so late?" I asked them.

"Same reason you are?" Mallory ventured.

"Doubtful," I said. "I was tutoring some Sig Eps in French at the Union."

"Way to be in there!" Dot exclaimed approvingly, as if to suggest that I was making headway into the University Life I had so blatantly eschewed by not pledging a sorority.

"We had to do a service project after classes today for the house," explained Mallory," and that got us back here late. We just should have stayed for dinner over there, but I've got too much homework tonight to fritter away the evening at the house."

"You know," Dot said, looking around, "If you two eat alone like this over here, people will think you're *living on the bottom floor*."

"What's that?" I asked, bracing myself for more bullshit from Dot.

"Don't you know?!"

I looked at Cass and rolled my eyes. "Know what?"

"Well," Dot began, authoritatively, "the - uh - grad students live together in these double rooms on the ground floor back here by the dining hall."

"So?"

Cass interjected, as if to put an end to this becoming a saga: "Women grad students who live together in the dorm but aren't RA's, well, they kind of get the reputation for being lesbians."

"Well, have you seen them?" Dot haughtily asked Cass. "They parade around together in front of us. No wonder people think that. Plus, you've got to admit it's really **queer** --pun intended--that grown women would want to live in a dorm, besides."

"Oh come on!" Cass said. "You can't mean you judge them all on that?"

Now, it was the late sixties, and I wasn't from another planet, although, when I thought of my hometown, that wasn't so far-fetched. But I didn't really know what they were talking about here. And if, in the back of my mind, I sort of did know, because sometimes my father had complained about these two women who rode motorcycles, wore leathers, and came regularly into the restaurant part of our bar, as being "Butch" and "Fem", I had no idea that we were talking "lifestyle" here. My mother hadn't really wanted to explain it to me, either, when I asked her, and I knew she knew. She just said what she always said, "Let it go. People should just be left alone to live their lives."

"Yeah, but what's so special about these two?"

" They live as a couple, honey." And I had let it go.

Cass got up to leave and said she'd see me back at the room, but of course, I knew she wasn't going back to the room. Dot and Mallory stayed around to grill me.

"It's true, Sari, "said Mallory. "You and your roommate can't just always be by yourselves, or people will talk."

"For Christ's sake, " I said.

"Look, Sari, we **were** only kidding you when we came over here. Nobody's going to think you and Cass are... you know, " Dot said in a consoling tone. "But you've got to be aware of your surroundings. Just look over there" And she nodded her head in the direction behind me. I turned around slowly and saw a table with some older girls sort of huddled in deep conversation.

"I don't see anything." I said. "People can talk to each other without it starting a big *mishagoss*, can't they?"

"Well, you know what they do!"

"They? Who? Those two girls?"

"Lesbians, " Dot spat out, exasperated with me. "Come up to my room."

We left the dining hall and went up the elevator to the fifth floor of Burge, where Dot and Mallory were each in a triple. I felt rekindled with status as I noticed again how they only had a sink in their crowded Burge room and the bathroom was down the hall. Poor kids. I was livin' large over in Kate Daum.

"Are you really just stupid or have you learned to cultivate *naiveté*?" Dot asked me pointedly when we were settled on the three beds.

"Meaning what?" I asked.

"Okay, you're what--eighteen? Didn't you have high school friends who --who explained anything to you?" Dot asked.

Mallory chimed in, "Yeah, didn't you go to slumber parties in junior high or grade school and talk about all this?"

I shrugged, "Not really."

"Teeny boppers know more than you. This isn't real!"

"I did have friends in high school, but I told you, we were the wallflower crowd."

We did get together for sleep-overs, but we discussed stuff like whether the Virgin Mary should be actually worshipped and what the Virgin Birth really meant---that Jesus was born of a mother without sin, or that the mother was? It was a big debate among the Lutherans in my group of friends. They were very dismissive of Catholics, too. In my hometown a "mixed marriage" meant Lutheran-Catholic.

"Oh, you've got to be kidding." Dot was incredulous. Her eyes could not have rolled farther.

"Didn't any of you guys **date**?"

"Not really. "

"Ever?!"

"Hardly. There were rare occasions like being fixed up for a party or two."

And there it was. The ugly reality. Not a rumor at all but the naked truth. We were among the great minions of misfit girls Janis Ian sang of, whose phone didn't ring; who only dreamt of doing math homework with a boy who could explain it; who didn't get to shop for a fabulous prom dress, and never saw the view of glittery Omaha lights from the back seat of a car parked along the promontory of the Lewis and Clark Monument. Instead we would discuss calculus problems with the future valedictorian of the class who was so egg-heady she couldn't explain the stuff in terms we could grasp; make Nestlé Toll House cookies at three in the morning, and consult the Ouija board for all insights into our elusive love life. My love life consisted of pictures on the bulletin board over my bed of Steve Canyon, Illya Kuryakin and Young Doctor Kildare. There was nothing you could do if you were among the walking wounded in the halls of the American high school except pretend it didn't matter. You had to conjure up the façade that you had a fuller imaginary life than any of the rest of them, and constantly remind yourself that you were just there on the road to somewhere better. And you could feel smug in a way, that at the reunions to follow many years later, high school will not have been the highlight of your life, the seminal time period that defined who you were and would be, forever frozen in time. You'd have a real life by then.

"So, you're a virgin?"

Dot and Mallory tried hard to get over their incredulity enough to start an impromptu tutorial for me. It did not occur to me to ask the same question of them.

"Okay, look. You're going to be in some sorry state <u>here</u> if you don't know what's what, " Dot began.

"You DO know the facts of life?" Mallory asked hopefully.

Not that we had studied it too much in science classes at my school, but intellectually and academically, yes, I knew them. My father, however, had been the one to explain it to me right before I turned eleven. Mallory's jaw dropped.

"We had this playroom thing set up in our basement--where we kids played school mostly. And my father took me down there and drew diagrams on the blackboard. Told me what to expect when I got my period."

"You're making that up."

""He didn't want me to hear it on the street or from kids in just any venue. He said I had a lot of time before it would really happen and that I could talk it over with my mother, but he wanted to be the one to explain it to me. And then when I did get *it* the first time, I was only eleven and absolutely incensed, " I laughed. "I remember telling my mother I **refused** to go to school with *it*. But she called my grandmother and announced it all over the place."

"Well, at least you have a Jewish mother."

At that juncture, Mallory's other two roomies came looking for her and found out the purpose of the gathering. Patricia O'Bryan had gone to Marymount Convent School in Colorado before coming to Iowa and Mellanie Glazer ("Mellie", so as to avoid confusing her name with Mallory) came from Roosevelt High in Des Moines. I had already met them, and had felt kind of sorry for Pat being the only Catholic girl in the room with two Jews, and a transfer student to boot. But she could hold her own. She was very friendly and not around too much. Mellie had not pledged the Jewish sorority that Mallory and Dot had because she was holding out for the new one's more serious rush second semester.

Mallory didn't want to completely embarrass me with tales of my ignorance in front of these other girls, for which I was grateful, so she guided the conversation towards the general knowledge of sex and the virgin's need to know. Pat was happy to enlighten us on what pleased men, and I got the immediate impression she was speaking from experience. Her boyfriend was purported to be a complete hunk pre-med god.

Pat explained very efficiently how to massage the shaft. "Guys really like that."

I made a face. "You mean you put your hand on it?...I mean...."

"Well, to start with, yeah...." Pat replied. "But then you use your mouth."

"What!?"

"Absolutely, that's what they love best," Pat concluded.

"Nice Jewish girls don't give blow jobs," Mallory stated.

"Oh and nice Catholic ones do?" scoffed Pat.

"Well, I don't know. Do you? You seem to know all about it."

"No. I'm just telling you what I learned from my cousin. "

"Let's discuss multiple orgasm, " Dot interrupted, changing the subject.

I just leaned back against the wall and listened to this conversation unfold much like the one on Barth in rhetoric class. I didn't have much understanding for what anyone was saying, but kept quiet about it. They did get around to comparing homo- and heterosexual techniques, but by then I was thinking about real homework I hadn't done yet.

"Lesbians can't do much, of course, " Mellie was finishing with.

"Well, it must be enough, because they do DO it," surmised Dot.

"It's all relative, isn't it? Doing it to yourself can feel good," said Mellie.

"Eewoo, please," said Mallory. "I've got to get to studying."

And she pulled herself off the bed.

"Me, too," I said, relieved to be breaking off from this surreal study group. But I had decided then and there that I was ignorant, and that there must be books galore in the Iowa U. library just waiting for me to educate myself. After all, hadn't I looked up *impotence* when I first read *The Sun Also Rises*? I could do research.

I was, however, curious to know Cass' reaction to all that dinner talk, and almost forgot what she may have been up to with Klampert when she got back.

"Did you go to slumber parties when you were a kid?" I asked her.

"No. I was in boarding school, remember? Every night was a sleep-over, "she laughed.

"Okay, so then, during the summer? Did you go over to anyone's house to play?"

"I was never home in the summer."

"Even in grade school?"

"I started going to camp when I was seven."

"Holy shit, " I murmured, "that must have been awful." I didn't forget to ask about her painting or if she saw Klampert. But I let it go.

"Camp was okay."

Camp to me was synonymous only with Bergen-Belsen.

Chapter Six

Romanian Dances...Bela Bartók

I decided to let Cass reveal the Klampert relationship to me rather than asking her about him. I figured it would come out that I had seen them that night, and I didn't want her to think I was spying on her, because I wasn't! But she never spoke about him except in the most perfunctory ways, such as how great his lecture to my class on Picasso's blue period had been.

Fall of freshman year was growing cooler and people were appearing on campus in those wool skirts and Shetland sweaters and tights we all carefully shopped for and packed for college. I did wear my beret to class with the whole Brandeis suit...I didn't need a coat yet if I wore a sweater under it. But I have to say, a lot of students were wearing jeans, which had never occurred to me. I didn't even take jeans to Iowa that fall. I wore skirts or dresses to class.

My roommate and I were settling into a routine. The first of the four dreaded quarters of gym found us in the same class: fencing. Much to my amazement, I liked it and felt I would at least pass. This was a revelation to me: that I could actually do a sport. Cass, of course, was far more athletic than I was; plus she was completely at ease in group activities and had done many many years of sports and dance prior to coming to college.

In the hall on our floor, we practiced all our salute flourishes, our thrust and parry, our in-line moves, mostly after "hours".

"You've got to bend both knees," Cass gently coached me, "And remember, keep your body straight and distribute the weight to both legs evenly."

"God, " I sighed, "how many times has a gym teacher told me to do that? Is every damn sport the same?"

"Well, some, I suppose. It's the same with tennis sometimes."

I couldn't play tennis because I could never get to the ball. Having decided to take up golf, because that was my father's game, it turned out that I couldn't get the ball off the ground, and since one couldn't just play for the putting, which I actually could do, I never pursued that sport either. Whenever concepts like "follow-through " and "rhythmic swing" came into play, the coach/teacher/parent never got very far with me.

Cass and I especially liked to be deeply enthralled in fencing if someone else were coming down the hall and had to wait for us to subside before they could get to their room.

"Hey, let's try the feint!" she would call out with a glint of glee in her voice.

"Oh, yes! The feint!" I would chirp.

"No--not like that. You need to extend your arm without trying to touch!"

We chased each other up and down the corridor. Nobody cared if we were noisy, as most girls were up doing laundry, watching t.v. in the lounge, talking in each other's rooms, and listening to music. If people were trying to study or sleep, they weren't having much luck.

We tried not to bother our immediate neighbors across the hall in Kate Daum, because we actually *liked* them. JoAnne Williams and Sandra Delehante were both from northern Iowa near the lakes. They shared with us the obvious good luck to have a double end room. JoAnne was a musician and played the violin better than any kid I'd ever heard. She was sophisticated and worldly, knew she'd leave Iowa as soon as she graduated, head to a great music school and then to a city where a symphony orchestra consisted of more than volunteers who had day jobs like bookkeeping. Sandra was pre-med, a serious student, the daughter and granddaughter of doctors. She wanted to stay in Iowa City for her entire education, then settle in a small rural town and practice medicine there, "because the country needs that". She felt she would probably join her father's practice in Spirit Lake, but travel to the smaller communities all around.

But the girls right next door and down most of our hall were a mix of small-time Sorority Sallies and church-goers. Invariably, the religious ones were the most judgmental, intolerant and self-righteous.

42

Some didn't wear makeup and scorned anyone who did. Some had pitiful hair, always devoid of styling and sometimes even in need of a good shampooing. I just could not fathom women born and raised in an industrial country coming to college and not taking care of personal hygiene. On the other hand, some girls couldn't fathom coming to college a virgin either, so I kept fairly mum with my negative opinions of the squares like Kristiane Kitchener and Margaret Northrup; and on the other side of the coin, the sorority queen ilk like Candice Swensen and her Pi Phi sorority sisters down the hall.

Kristiane would always have something to say at my door when I came in. "Your roommate forgot her key <u>again</u>." She was the hall watch dog or something, butting into everyone's life because she didn't have one.

All Candy ever talked about were frat parties and which were the best to be seen at. She already had her sights set on being in the Dolphin Queen court and we weren't even close to winter sports season. But since she was so sure she was going to be in the running, Cass and I started calling her "The D. Q." right off the bat. She paraded around on the hall like her underwear was suitable for the runway, and she wrapped her fabulously long, thick, blond hair in towels that conjured up images of Grace Kelly. She had the right look for the genus *beauty queen*, it had to be said: turned up nose, large round blue eyes, perfect teeth. And she was thin but muscular, someone who preferred doing sports to studying, so even though the sixties were not yet known to be a decade of personal training and working out, hers was a precursor to the type of sculpted body people forty years later would be breaking their backs to have. She **knew** she was the prettiest girl in Kate Daum, but she also recognized that there was another, less run-of-the-mill beauty on the hall: my roommate.

Cass Hyde was exquisitely striking, which made her stand out on this small-town campus. Her dark auburn hair flicked against her face in little peaks that framed her eyes like a painting, her face awash in alabaster tinged with pink -- something Renoir would have conjured up. Her eyes were so blue-violet that they appeared fabricated, as if by colored contact lenses; but they weren't, of course, since if that idea had surfaced by the sixties, it was still only experimental or used on movie sets; and these limpid dark blue eyes were veiled by rows of lashes so long and thick that they also looked completely fake, but again, were not. Her hair was impeccably cut from salons whose caliber could not be duplicated in Iowa City, so as the college months drifted farther away from her Chicago hairdresser visits, she let her style become feathery long in the back like a bird's tail pressed against her slender neck. It started a trend that I began to notice on campus that first Fall: girls were purposefully having their hair cut like hers.

Cass would enter a room and women would look up startled, to see who she was, while men would just stare at her, mouths gaping. Her figure was proportioned for her height, taller than me but not tall per se. We were both rather top-heavy, to tell the truth, but she had much better lingerie and foundation underwear, so her indented waist and rounded hips presented the perfect wasp shape; and her bones were bigger than mine, so while I looked short, thin, and busty, she was voluptuously proportioned. I could pull off wearing her clothes, and she frequently allowed me to borrow them. She never asked to wear any of mine, it goes without saying.

The best thing about fencing class was that it was the last thing on the agenda Tuesday and Thursday afternoons, and we were together, so a sort of routine ensued where we went straight from the gym to the Goldfeather Room and rewarded ourselves with treats after the heavy workout of jousting.

Often we would use that time to go over the fencing quiz vocabulary while it was still fresh. Most of what we had to learn in the way of technical vocabulary was in French. Cass hadn't taken French, (but admitted she'd wanted to) but she knew Latin having done that in boarding school, which, I assured her, would help. We were swimming in handouts: the art of fencing, the history of fencing, invention of the fencing mask, development of fencing as a sport and the weapons. We would order coffee or hot chocolate and get to work.

What I really liked in fencing was way one had to position the feet, because it reminded me of some kind of violent ballet.

"The *en garde* position with its exact feet and arm poses is very ballet-esque," I would announce with an air of snobbish authority on the subject.

Cass and I had both taken ballet lessons as children, and neither of us had mastered it; but we had the basics, and were ahead of this game, planning to take dance for PE credit, too. *Point your fingers forward, towards your opponent's head*, we'd been instructed. *Let the wrist go limp.*

Life was good--as good as Phys Ed could be, at least.

43

If we thought it looked pretty neat in the hallway to be practicing fencing, we thought we were ultra-cool sitting at the table in the Union studying drawings of the 16th century Spanish fencing masters. Cass had it over me in class with the fencing coach because he loved the "Spanish school" and she could at least show a cursory acquaintance with Spain having been there with one of her summer tours. The guy had handed us out some photocopies of Spanish soldiers who all looked like Don Quixote or Carlos V. He showed us old movies in class, too, of matches where one guy used a two-handed sword against another with a rapier, or fencers using the Italian foils strapped to the wrist. None of that was in use in the modern day, but we still had to learn about it.

"They used to teach it this way," she said holding up a photo of the diagram from some ancient Spanish fencing school class. "A circle was drawn in the middle of a square divided by chords, and pupils were taught with this diagram."

"You mean they had to aim at it and practice like target shooting?"

"Exactly."

We also saw footage from old Olympic Games and tournaments of the *Federation Internationale d'Escrime* which ran international competitions during the off-years of the Olympics, and which formulated all the rules we had to memorize. We liked to pronounce our knowledge at the dorm dinner table to all and sundry. I felt it my calling to be the arbiter of all things French in life *anyway*.

"The great international meets were staged in Paris, " I intoned authoritatively to the bored throng eating with us. "America, however, did have the Intercollegiate Fencing Association which was started in 1894 and, later the NCAA held its first championship in 1945." They would roll their eyes. And when dessert came around, Cass and I would recite *ad nauseum*: "I scream, you scream, we all scream for *escrime*!"

During all meals that semester, we *had* to trot out our catechism --- memorized litany of the best performances of U.S. fencers in the Olympics; or our myriad of facts, like "in 1951 the United States team entered the first Pan American games in Argentina and won the foil and sabre team and individual championships." *Don't you know.*

If it had been only me and anyone normal doing this at the table people would have undoubtedly hissed or something and gotten up. But the girls of Burge and Kate Daum were fascinated by Cass Hyde and tended to study her as one would a zoo specimen.

A nightly routine was to test each other with the lists of vocabulary words. What was a *riposte* and why were there counter ones and parry ones? We had *remise, redoublement, corps-à-corps, coupé, engage and désengage*. One could fence with sabers, *épées*, or what we used in class, foils. "Curses, foiled again!" was another of our wink-wink secret messages to each other as we practiced in the corridors of Daum late at night.

"Why don't you two just give it a rest?" sneered the D.Q. whenever she had to pass us on the way to the showers. "Put a *chaussette* in it."

Hey! Go kiss Flipper's ass.

I aced all the written tests, the vocabulary quizzes with all that French content, the history and the rules. It was in winning matches where I came up short. Cass won more of her matches than I, and got only negligibly lower test scores, putting her in the grade area of A-.

The B that I received in fencing class for the quarter of college in the fall of 1966 was the first mark higher than a pity C ever in my entire life of physical education classes.

A pity we had to then go on to "Movement Principles," which I failed.

Chapter Seven

"For What It's Worth"...Buffalo Springfield

The word had come down from the University of Wisconsin that students rioted when Dow Chemical began to recruit on campus. In truth the students hadn't rioted; the police rioted against them. The students were peacefully sitting-in when they were violently attacked. The salient point here was that it made activists out of normally non-political students, a fact that was not lost on the campus in Iowa City. Our anti-war movement was nascent before I arrived at the university, and it was possible to go about your merry way to classes, to the library, to the union and back to the dorms without ever noticing it. But the U Wisconsin debacle was the galvanizing turning point for Iowa.

That and the fact that Dow Chemical also came to recruit on our campus.

Crowds started forming daily in front of the union to hear speakers set up on makeshift daises exhorting us to boycott baby-killing napalm-making war mongers like corporate Dow.

"Napalm," the voices warned us, "will torture its victims like Zyklon B tortured people in Auschwitz! And this company makes it! Profits from it! War-profiteers are recruiting Iowa students to work in their war machine!" I stood and listening to the talk but to me this seemed aimed at future graduates of the business school. They were the ones I'd imagined going to work for corporations like Dow Chemical. But it was not lost on me that the protests were taking place in earshot of the Chemistry building, too.

The administration of our university was infinitely more humane than that of Sewell in Madison. No riot police were deployed against our gatherings (of course, we weren't trying to occupy the buildings, either) and our campus still seemed the bastion of free speech and the protected environment we imagined all universities to be.

I was rather torn at this moment in time about the war in Vietnam because I was loath to disagree with anything President Kennedy had done in his thousand days. If he thought we needed to be there preventing the domino effect from toppling all over Southeast Asia, far be it for me to argue. Indeed, during my junior year in high school a bunch of us girls had rallied for the poor, lonely troops who had no sweethearts waiting for them at home, and we started writing to total strangers to bring them comfort and fun care packages. I was writing to a Stephen Mahoney stationed near Da Nang. I wasn't sure it resonated with him about how old we were, but he was only nineteen, so I couldn't see that it made any difference. To be nineteen and drafted as a grunt soldier in a war half-way around the world only struck me as bad luck, not heroism. He had been surprised to get my first letter, he told me, and didn't know that groups of girls were forming back stateside to write to soldiers they didn't even know. I told him we got the names from the USO but that was just malarkey; I had no idea where our junior class advisor at high school had come up with the names and addresses. She just called a meeting one afternoon as the school year was winding down in a sultry spring and organized us into a little club of volunteer cheer-bringers. It made us feel like we were thrown back in time to WWII and "doing our part for the war effort".

My boy's letters were typical and fairly plaintive; he seemed really bored and terrified at the same time. He had already seen some terrible things go down and some of his outfit were already dead, but he always assured me he wasn't scared to be there. I asked him that in every letter, especially as I began to pay more attention to the nightly news. Stephen wasn't in danger, he explained in his sloppy half-printing half-cursive writing, because he was in transport support, which meant that he worked as a truck mechanic or something fairly safe. I was glad of that so I could concentrate on the kind of newsy letters that would help him feel less lonely and didn't have to think about the issues such as if this war were morally reprehensible and how many innocents had been killed since my last letter.

The more he wrote the more I realized how different he was from anyone I would have ever been remotely interested in. He was just a high school graduate. His grammar and vocabulary were shockingly inadequate and incorrect, and he had been born and raised in a speck on the map town in Montana. He had no inkling of who I was

45

either. He knew I was from a small Iowa town and a high school junior, which meant that he was older and considered himself more sophisticated and worldly wise than me. He told me his faith in Jesus Christ kept him going and said that it was real great to write me because he didn't have a girlfriend back home.

Not that I tried to keep my identify under wraps; I just didn't know who I really was myself. That year, junior year, when I was obsessing over Emily Dickinson and the fact that I just had to go to Mt. Holyoke to college (and then everything would be okay), I spent a lot of time on the couch reading her poems over and over, hoping for some divine spark of recognition to hit me and give me a clue. My father had come home one night and noticed that I was sulky and moody (more than usual?).

*"You're **ungeblusen**."*

"It's just that I don't know who I am," I was stupid enough to respond.

"What kind of a thing is THAT to say? I'll tell you who you are! You're a young, middle-class Jewish woman. There. That's who you are."

And there it was. And that lovely encounter was my own damn fault. But I didn't tell Private Whosis who I was either. To him I might have been sweet, milk-drinking wholesome, dimpled. Or maybe sultry and mysterious. I had no idea what his fantasies were when he got the mail. All I knew was that they were fantasies, because I never got into the reality in my letters. I never met or tried to find that guy after the war was over. I don't know if he came back alive, and, if so, if he experienced the angst of coming home NOT a hero, like so many other Vietnam vets did. Did he turn against the war? Become bitter in the process?

When high school was over my own classmates started going off to that war, and all of a sudden I had real people to write to. Johnny North from our class was the first to die...in a helicopter crash. He was some hot shot pilot already in high school. His dad had a private plane and he had flown with him for years. It's all he ever wanted to do and he was pretty cocky about joining up. Most of the rest were drafted. Their numbers came up. Twice.

We sat around the pool at the Elks Club in the summer of '66, like we had done every summer; but now we spoke in hushed tones of people we actually knew who were dying in Vietnam. You heard of certain communities that had unusually high ratios of death from the war, and we wondered if we were one. I couldn't fathom how one minute, high schools all over America were brimming with kids all happy in school together, being in the musical, working on the newspaper, playing on the basketball team; and the next year or month, our government is shipping home body bags full of fallen youths. What was the cause? Who was the enemy? What was at stake? What was the suffering really for and who was winning?

When I went to the funeral of the guy who had played the lead in our senior musical production of The Music Man *(where I had played a mere townsperson but had been thrilled to be on the same stage with him) that was really the day I began to question my support of the war. I became consumed with the need to bring home every single boy I knew over there, and the rest of them, too. I suddenly felt that the Vietnamese people didn't even really want us there and that their government was corrupt. I began to read more and to realize the French had already suffered this defeat. Why should we go ahead and let history repeat itself so soon? I decided it was reprehensible to be over there giving up our country's treasure for nothing.*

My father, a WWII veteran, could not have disagreed with me more.

By the time my first year at college had passed, I was vehemently against the war, not that I really blamed the soldiers who were already there---it was so much more righteous to blame the government that sent them. I was rationalizing to myself that it was okay to be against the war by then as it was panning out; had JFK lived, the outcome would have been different anyway, I assured myself.

Cass on the other hand was already becoming politicized and active in the movement. She pressed me into service over at the union to make protest signs for rallies, carefully lettering "DOW BURNS BABIES" and "U.S. OUT OF VIETNAM".

It was at one of these poster-making sessions that Alan Jones came up and startled me.

"Miss Shrier! Are you a war-protestor?"

" Uh, oh, hi."

He leaned in over my shoulder and lowered his tone.

"Say, I know this is awkward and all, but you know that girl over there, don't you?" *Oh my gosh. He was referring to Cass.*

"She's my roommate."

"Ah! Do you think you could introduce her to me?" he nudged his elbow into my ribs a little and looked at me with a sweet, thin smile crossing his lips and his Delft blue eyes twinkling. All the while I was thinking *"she's involved with a tenured professor, pal; you don't stand a chance,"* but I just stuttered, "Um, yeah, uh---sure. Just a minute."

I went over to Cass. "My English teacher wants to meet you."

"Huh? Who? That cute Jones guy?"

"That's him over there---see?"

"Well, fine, then." She shot me a quizzical look and walked over to him. I watched him tentatively smile at her and gingerly shake what he recognized was her beautifully thin hand. He chatted with her for only a minute or two, then he took out a little scrap of paper and handed her a pen. She wrote something on it, gave it back to him, and he left. I stood there watching them and thought that even more than her physical presence, people could feel her spirit around them. She did have what I would call a haunting delicacy in that she seemed to float through space. I was already transfixed by this and decided it must be the artist in her. To boys she must have seemed unreachable in some way, I surmised. To men she must have been some sort of prize, something precious to win and then protect.

At that time, however, I just hoped she wouldn't date Jones until I wasn't his student anymore.

The anti-Dow Chemical demonstrations were big news on campus, and very exciting. Hundreds of students in the street by the Union, chanting, waiving the posters we'd created. We signed petitions against the military-industrial complex. The Goldfeather room actually became a hotbed of radical poetry readings, music jam sessions and ultimately the seat of the ferment of anti-Vietnam war protest on campus. The place was packed with the intelligentsia and artsy crowd; Greeks now tended to congregate elsewhere, so Mick and his gang, and for that matter, Dottie and Mallory, were never there. Students would give impromptu speeches about "the movement" and how soon, very soon, a wave of it would overtake us all.

Actually, marches did start shortly thereafter. One particular night, people showed up with candles for us to light and go out into the dark streets and up to the Pentacrest. All those flames illuminating our earnest, somewhat naïve faces made it seem very dreamy to me, not quite real. Yet I also felt a part of something important. People amassed from everywhere; I'd actually never seen so many crammed into a dedicated space. We were spilling out onto North Clinton Street.

Then out of nowhere police showed up in riot gear! Riot gear!

Watching American police in helmets and shields, wielding Billy clubs and maybe guns, charging into a crowd of young people essentially causing no problems, completely freaked me out. Someone bolted from the crowd and poured a pint of blood from a Red Cross container onto the street in front of on-coming traffic. Someone else was doing the same thing on the steps of the Union. That was enough for all hell to break loose.

"They're clubbing people!" I heard someone shriek. Police were grabbing for ones they thought were the instigators and leaders, and really, anyone who looked scruffier than normal students. Cass and I were in the back of the crowd on the sloping lawn up to the Pentacrest, and we saw it all pretty well. People started to sit down so that they'd have to be dragged off by police and hopefully get on t.v. because by now lots of press had turned away from the Dow recruiters on the hotel side of the Union and were talking to students. Cass looked panicked, which scared me.

"I need a loo!," she sort of whimpered.

"Come on!" I said, dragging her up the hill, around the periphery of the protesters and over to Schaeffer Hall, where a lot of my classes were. Amazingly enough, the doors were unlocked and not blocked either. We slipped inside. Cass ran to the bathroom and I climbed the stairs and went into a classroom with a view to the Pentacrest below. It had turned to pandemonium.

Once back outside, we threaded our way through what seemed like hundreds of people. It was never planned to be anything but a peaceful demonstration but by the time the crowd was dispersed, we were worried about making it to the dorm by "hours", which were 10:00 p.m. on weeknights.

"I may be naïve, " I said to her, "but with all the crime in our society these days and even on campus, you'd think they'd have better agenda for law enforcement than mustering a hundred cops to attack peaceful students. Sheesh."

"They think outside agitators came into town and did this, "she answered, sort of to herself.

47

"What? Why? Who told you that?"

"I don't know---some reporter."

We made it back to the dorm and I sort of expected to see heightened animation or at least excited girls coming back from the Pentacrest as late as we were. But there were just the usual routines at the door when it was nearing curfew: kissing, necking, sorrowful good-nights, exchanges of notebooks that had been carried, etc. Couples left a path open to the door and singles darted around and through them. Once inside a few people were talking about the demonstration but most were either uninterested or thought it was completely stupid.

"I hope I get a job with Dow Chemical," someone intoned.

"Why would they start something like that on THIS campus?"

"I bet it was SDS from Madison."

I chimed in with a group of girls I didn't even know. "Yeah, it was pretty awful."

"You were there?" asked someone I recognized from our floor but whose name I couldn't remember –or more likely never knew.

"Uh-huh."

"So idiotic," she sighed, shaking her head.

The next morning we were in Burge Hall's dining room for breakfast, at our usual table, when Dottie came bounding in waving a newspaper in my face. "Look! You made the paper!"

She thrust it in front of Cass.

"Who did?" I asked.

"US!" Cass said excitedly. You, me and my sign! She paused and put her hand on her heart. "My first hint of immortality." She was teasing but I wasn't laughing.

"Oh, God, what paper is that? *The Iowa City Press Citizen,* I hope?"

"No. *Register.*"

"SHIT!" I screamed and pulled it out of her hands. Yes, there we were. The picture was fuzzy but people could obviously tell who it was.

"What's wrong?" Cass wanted to know, incredulous at my reaction.

"My parents will see that and have a cow." *To put it mildly.* "Maybe it won't be in the state-wide editions, just the Eastern Iowa ones. Yeah, that's a possibility." I tried to calm myself down. But my father had already admonished me in various letters to "stay away from those crazy demonstrators" that he thought were infiltrating every college campus in America.

"When I go home for Thanksgiving there will be hell to pay. I can already hear him ranting and raving. He might even threaten to pull me out of school!"

"He wouldn't do that. Come on." Cass wanted to reassure me, but she had no experience with our kind of family. "Maybe I should go with you."

I shot her a look that said, "Yeah, like that's going to happen." It was touching, though, to think that this little sprite of a girl was ready to stand up and protect me from my father's wrath. So later on back in our room when I had thought about it and the future confrontation was looming more comical than serious, I brought up her idea again.

"So did you actually mean what you said? You'd like to come home with me for Thanksgiving?"

"Sure. Why not?"

"What would your parents say?"

"They are hardly ever home for holidays. They won't care; especially if I'm being invited by a friend. They'll think that's good for me! It's a terrific idea! And we'll have a jolly time in spite of them!"

I was amused at this thought. But then it hit me:

"But Cass...you've never experienced a house like mine---you know—normal... ugly. No one works for us. I do chores... the dishes...and at holidays I do them by hand even! We don't really even have a guest room. Maybe they'll let us sleep in the basement---we've got day beds down there." I was thinking out loud.

She'd be a real fish out of water there, that was certain. Not to mention at the time I didn't even know what kind of life she did lead in Chicago/Kenilworth. Had I actually seen her homes (plural), I probably wouldn't have invited her out of sheer mortification and embarrassment.

48

She reacted quizzically. "I'm up for it!"

When I phoned home to say I was bringing a guest for Thanksgiving, they didn't say a word to me about the newspaper article. "Whew, "I thought. "Dodged that bullet."

No such luck.

Chapter Eight

"Homeward Bound"...Simon & Garfunkel

We left on the Tuesday of Thanksgiving week and took the train to my hometown. To my surprise, the university, unlike high schools, actually closed for Thanksgiving on the Tuesday prior, after 4:00 p.m. classes. Neither of us had afternoon classes that day, so we could take the train that left around noon and wouldn't get into The Bluffs until the dinner hour. Iowa City was still served by the Rock Island Line and so was my town. The train was slow, but fun. I loved trains, even though this was a pretty sorry excuse for one by the late 1960's. The interiors had seen much better days. If there was still a dining car, we didn't avail ourselves of it, but brought snacks and pop on board instead. We didn't sit in compartments but the seats were like small sofas facing each other---two people on each side at every window. We left large suitcases on racks near the door, but put small bags above us at the seat. Neither of us had a real "train case" –those square little things that I would have killed to have; I loved them and thought them the height of chic. Even in her myriad of matched luggage, Cass didn't have a train case either. One of her paint boxes sort of looked like that, but she didn't bring any art supplies with her.

A cute boy entered the car and caught sight of Cass. I could see the wheels turning in his head – and, of course, I wasn't surprised. She just captivated people with that look of hers – that ephemeral beauty, like a breeze had just blown her in from some other world. He fairly lunged into the seat across from us. No one else sat in the other part so he had the banquette to himself.

He extended his hand to Cass. "Robert Brooks."

"Cass Hyde, "she responded, shaking his hand. "This is Sari Shrier."

He was, it turned out, also a U of I student, going to Denver.

"Golly, that's far," I ventured. "When we get off, you'll still have eight hours left to ride. Good thing you can spread out on the seat or something." I realized as soon as I said it that he was far too tall and gangly to be able to even rest part-way reclined on that little bench. "Well, at least partly."

"Yeah," he said, pointing to a duffle bag he had with him, "I've got a pillow in there."

When the introductions and train itineraries were finished, he settled back on his seat and took out some sort of small cassette player with earphones. I hadn't seen anything like that before. He let us each listen. He said he had personally made the tape (how? - I wondered) and he had made up a playlist of what was on it – a lot of Beachboys and some Seekers. Fascinating.

What he didn't have was any food, so after about the first hour, he got up and went in search of the Club Car.

"He's darling," I said.

"You got that right." She smiled. "I wonder what his major might be?"

"Oh, pre-med, don't you suppose? He's got that 'Young Doctor Kildare' look about him."

"Ho! I doubt that. More like poet. He definitely has a poet's eyes. Maybe he's set his sights on getting into the Workshop."

We did strike up some more conversation when he got back. He was a music performance major...piano. It then occurred to me to be surprised he didn't have Mozart or Chopin on his little player. He unzipped the duffle bag and showed me that he had half a dozen tapes in there, many classical.

Cass was interested and she knew a lot more about classical music than I did, even though I had taken voice and she hadn't done any music lessons, only ballet. She inquired, "Who's your favorite composer then?"

The guy thought a minute. "That's an impossible question to answer, isn't it? He looked up at her. "Well, I'm a piano major so speaking of that music, I suppose Franz Liszt," he said. "In his day he was considered the greatest piano virtuoso living."

"Wow," said Cass. "I never realized that."

I, in the meantime, couldn't think of one Liszt work I even knew.

It was dark when we pulled into the little Rock Island depot that The Bluffs still had in the late 1960's. My entire family was standing on the platform.

"Here goes nothing," I muttered.

What could she have been thinking about them and the greeting we were about to get?

Cass and I took our small bags down, lifted our bigger ones off the racks in between train cars, and headed off the steps of the train, which were awkwardly narrow to wrangle a suitcase down. My father stepped forward and took mine, then pivoted around and took Cassandra's.

"This is Cass Hyde, of course," I said, introducing everyone. "My mom Betty and dad Sol Shrier. This is Roslyn."

"Hi," she waved at Cass and clung to Betty.

"Very nice to meet you, Cassandra," said Mom, who naturally knew her full name. They all shook hands.

"Thank you so much for inviting me," said Cass.

"We're parked over there," said Sol, leading off to the station wagon where he flung open the tailgate and placed the bigger suitcases inside.

The three of us girls went to the back doors.

"You sit in the middle," I said to Roslyn, pushing her slightly onto the back seat.

It's a small town but the train station was in a part of it I never went to. The route home took us down the main street and past The Spot Bar and Grill.

"There's our business," my dad announced. "You'll see it later. Have you ever spent time in small-town America, Cassandra?"

"Cass." I corrected him.

"No, not really," she answered. "If Iowa City doesn't count."

"Well, then, you're in for a real treat."

I had to roll my eyes at her at that remark, and I think he caught me doing it through the rear-view mirror. Oops. But oh, well, I thought, I was in trouble already, so…

We all rode the next half mile or so without much conversation. Mom wanted to know how the train was.

"Fine. Seen better days, of course—the upholstery is kind of yucky."

"Have you ever taken the train anywhere, Cass?" she continued, trying to make small talk.

"Yes," Cass answered. "I've taken it from Washington, D.C. to New York from time to time. Oh, and Europe, too. Their trains are wonderful."

"She went to boarding school in Switzerland," I explained, lording HER life over my parents.

"Where's that?" piped up Roslyn.

"Don't they teach you anything in school?" I said in a sort of hiss.

"Sarah –knock it off!" Sol interjected.

"It's in Europe, honey," said Betty.

Roslyn had found her voice. "You guys are sleeping in MY room and I'm going to be in the den."

"Really." I said, more as a statement than a question.

*Her bedroom was, as it happened, **my** bedroom that she had usurped after I left for college. It was actually their idea to move her in there, and I knew it was going to take place before I was out of the house. Even as I was packing to leave, they were already installing toy shelving where I had had a study area. Along another wall they put up a long new desk made out of a recycled door, of all things. It was bolstered by little file cabinets on either end so that the "desk" height would be a bit shorter than a regular desk.*

Our house was a 1954 ranch of the most undistinguished style imaginable. It was in a very nice area, but to my way of thinking, was just about the ugliest one there, even though it had been custom built with many design elements from none other than Betty. Who knows what magazines she must have been reading at the time. In 1954, I was the only child, but I knew they were hoping for more. This house had three bedrooms, but one of them, a tiny square room, was used as a "den" – even though it was too stupidly small to be a real den OR a bedroom. It had a tiny closet and a wall of glass shelving, which was neither practical nor positioned properly to be a real bookcase. It was just a free-floating bibelot display area, too high for anyone to dust or really even look at what was there. Just a dumb idea. The room had two love seats and a t.v./record player combination. A coffee table held some books. It was a useless space.

*Nevertheless, I started campaigning for that stupid den for my bedroom when, in the fall of 1956, I found myself sharing my large back bedroom with a newborn. That previous summer they had already changed **my** bedroom into a partial nursery! Were they kidding? Where I had had twin beds separated by one of those magnificent round-mirrored vanities with a little stool in front of it like a Hollywood movie star might have, they took one bed out and put the dressing table on the opposite wall! Under the windows on the far side of the room suddenly appeared my old crib, its (wonderful) matching baby closet with drawers on one side and a door on the other that held hanging space; a bathinette, which in itself took up an inordinate amount of space, and a rocking chair! They placed a "baby" themed throw rug down on top of my carpet to sort of delineate the two parts of the room. The only thing they didn't put in there right away was the baby; she slept in a rolling basket in their room at the other end of the hall for the first four months or so.*

This entire setup incensed me, and I vowed then and there to not put up with it. It was beyond unfair! However, no one listened to me. To make it seem like I would be getting some magnificent new space elsewhere, they turned a quarter of the basement into a play room; workers laid down a huge square of linoleum with various classic nursery rhymes imprinted on it, put down some rugs, a large school-like blackboard, and some cutesy curtains on the basement window wells to lessen the undercroft effect. My mother conspiratorially began an all-out endeavor of military proportions to muster my most precious belongings, namely dolls, my doll bed, doll-clothes trunks, the metal doll house on its table, and all other playhouse accoutrements, and move the lot to the basement. And then workers came in and even finished off a powder room that had already been roughed in down there next to the laundry facilities. The parents managed to convince me that I didn't need to be in my bedroom very much other than for sleeping; and for good measure they put two small day-beds downstairs in case I invited a little friend for a sleep over. Once I even had a slumber party.

*It soon became apparent, (even after my parents had taken away the baby equipment and put the two beds back the way they had been and added a huge bulletin board behind the beds that took up the whole wall and was mostly used by me) that as a ninth grader, I'd still be sharing a room with a six-year-old! I redoubled my efforts on them to take the smaller room. I became very sullen and irritable and uncooperative. Ninth grade was looming large and Virginia Woolf notwithstanding, I wanted a **room of my own.***

"You want a room of your own so you can slam the door and lock it!" Sol had yelled at me.

*However, this time they relented. **But** rather than move me, they moved her! Right into the little den, now minus all its old furniture and sporting a small twin bed, a dresser, the rocking chair and toys. So once again, I had the big room with my own ample closet, my own study space, my own music (but no t.v.) and the privacy so essential to comforting one's teenage angst.*

The summer before I would be leaving for college, when Roslyn was turning ten, she reclaimed the room for herself, and for the second time, all manner of transformation of that bedroom went into effect. She was so completely and irrevocably already spoiled, that it was like they had two "only children", the trouble-making older one soon to fly the nest, and the resident princess.

So Cass and I settled in and because Sol had actually been rather deferential to us on the way home, I began to think maybe the *Des Moines Register* picture and any ensuing incidental fallout from it would just pass. It was after dinner when we got in, but Betty had food for us set up at the breakfast bar that separated the kitchen from the dining room, and she called us to come have some.

But Sol interrupted her by calling me out first to come have a little talk with him down the hall in their bedroom.

Cass went around the corner and into the kitchen with my mother, but she didn't sit down at the breakfast bar yet, waiting to see if I'd be back. Sol cuffed me lightly on the shoulder as he pushed me down the hall to their room. He shut the door behind himself.

"Your friend is a beautiful girl," he began. "I recognized her from her picture in the newspaper." He scowled at me.

I just stood there and said nothing.

"You're in big trouble, you know. I should pull you out of there. You have brought disrespect to your family. All our friends saw that picture. This is a little town, you know. People saw it and brought it into the bar."

"It was just a peaceful protest. At least it started out that way. We were just painting signs." I sort of chortled. "Much ado about nothing."

He began to raise his voice. "NOTHING? MY daughter protesting in public view against MY government!! You call that nothing? You know what will happen now? Do you?! You're going to have an FBI FILE on you, that's what."

"Oh, come ON, you can't be serious," I sneered at such a stupid idea.

"Don't use that tone with ME. I know what I'm talking about. I served with the armed forces of this country, and don't you forget it. (*How could I?*) I didn't send you to college to PROTEST against the United States of America."

"But I *am* against the war."

Both our tones escalated now and our heightened voices could be heard all over the house regardless of the door being closed.

"No, you're not. At least not while I'm paying for you to be there! You're just convincing me that you don't deserve to be there, that's what you're doing...right here and now!"

"Look," I shouted, "you've paid my board and room for the whole year and I have a full tuition scholarship! Are you just going to say goodbye to all that money? And I have decent grades. I can still go to classes and just live there on my own. And I WILL!" I was screaming now. I felt tears welling up and my throat contracting.

"You calm down!"

"Leave me alone! You want to threaten to take me out of school? Well, you CAN'T. I won't leave!" I pivoted and grabbed the doorknob.

It's not like I hadn't been expecting this and I'd actually been thinking of the ramifications. In that era, college semesters did not end at Christmas break. We had final exams in January when we got back. So I knew in my heart I would be going back to take finals and then my father really couldn't force me to come home.

"You stay in here!"

But I already had the door open and ran back down the hall to my old bedroom where Cass was standing in disbelief at what she had heard, closed doors notwithstanding. I slammed the other bedroom door behind me as I entered.

"He's just NUTS."

"Wow, kid...you really held your own in there."

I checked that the door had stayed shut, and we talked in softer tones so as not to be heard.

"Oh, this is just the normal way things go around here. He's only concerned with how anything I might do—ever—not just this time, will affect HIM. His friends saw the picture. Big deal. I'm so sick of it. Never mind trying to hear my reasons for doing what I do, or for that matter, being who I am. I mean, it's funny really. Do they ever ask me about how I like school? How my classes are? ANYTHING about Iowa? Hell no!"

"Well, you did say you thought they'd threaten to take you out of school. I have to hand it to you---you called that one."

"I just decided they can't do it, that's all. And I'm not coming home at Christmas either! Or next summer. I'll just stay in the dorm."

"Oh, ho ho ho! You can come to my house for Christmas!"

"But Cass, that's a two-week break. What would your parents say?"

"I'm thinking they'll say nothing. I've never asked them to have anyone stay at a holiday, and they'll be gone most of the time anyway. They go to Gstaad for New Year's every year. Don't worry."

Gasp.

"Uh, okkaaay. That would be great! And you know what we should do, too?" I didn't give her a chance to answer. "We should get an apartment this summer and stay in Iowa City!"

"Yes! I could work in the studio that whole time! Heaven!"

"And I'll have to get some kind of job. It shouldn't be that hard, though."

Cass added, thinking out loud, "My parents would probably foot the bill. I'd be working on my art."

"Wow. Far out! A plan!" We hugged each other.

53

"You know," Cass said, "you sort of blow my mind with the way you just plan things out. And how you're not intimidated by your dad."

"How come you find that strange?"

"Are you kidding? I don't really even talk to my parents, especially my mother. And they don't talk to me. If they need to tell me something, they have their staff do it."

"Really?"

"Mostly. My father is rarely home. My mother is very busy and she hardly takes time to expend any energy on me. I don't even know why they had a child. Seriously."

I thought about that. I couldn't put my finger on what was worse: neglecting your children or verbally abusing them.

I was certainly not ready, at that stage in my life, to give my own parents any credit for how they raised me.

I wasn't the first person in the entire extended family to go to college, but I was the first among the four of us; neither of my parents had gone past high school. My father enlisted in World War II and my mother went straight into her family business, a little restaurant called The Spot, which, after my father married her and came home from the war, they turned into the current establishment, twice the size it had been. Luckily for them, my grandfather had bought the building before the Depression, so no one could come along later and throw them out. Not only that, but he had turned an annex in the back of it into their home during the hard times. It wasn't typical to live "behind the store", but in that town, the main street backed onto a series of alleys that had fenced-in areas not all made into parking lots. So my grandfather put up a two-story addition to the building behind which was a sweet little garden. He added a garage and fenced it all in as though it were always meant to be a residence. There were mature cottonwood trees already there, and they put in a barbeque "stove" made of bricks. By the time Betty and her two sisters were in high school, however, they had all moved a few blocks away into a big old house. The annex apartment was always rented out until my grandmother, Nana, couldn't really take care of the big place anymore, and she moved back into the annex, quite comfortable there on the ground floor. She mostly always loved that little place because Grampy had built it. He died in 1952; she had been alone a long time.

We managed to get through Thanksgiving without any more histrionics, Sol and I, Betty, Roslyn and Cass. Neither one of my parents talked any more about taking me out of school. And we saw my grandmother a few times while we were home, too. I confided in her that I had gotten into trouble with Sol and she sympathized with me. One good thing about having parents who owned their own bar and grill: they were at work morning, noon and night. Sol left by 9:00 a.m. and sometimes didn't even come home until the wee hours of the morning. So that was great.

On Thanksgiving Day itself, The Spot was closed, but Sol used most of that day to go in anyway and work in his back room "office." The rest of us and Nana were home getting ready to have the traditional dinner with my father's side of the family from Omaha. Betty had wanted the same "restaurant quality" appliances in her house that she had in the business so her dream kitchen had it all: a six-burner industrial stove with two ovens; an oversized refrigerator with slide-out freezer on the bottom and a large dishwasher. This entire kitchen was copper and brown, accented in yellow. I couldn't fathom anything uglier but it was everything my mother wished for. They may have cut corners elsewhere in building that house, but not in the kitchen.

For someone used to cooking and serving multitudes, Thanksgiving was easy, even with all the other relatives who traditionally came to our house. Betty cooked and Nana baked. By the time she was through, three fantastic pies were cooling by the window and Cass couldn't believe the smells that wafted through the room.

"Look at THAT cherry pie!" Cass swooned, "I adore lattice crust! Ummm, the aroma seeping out of those squares---it's heaven!"

"Her apple one is also great," I added. "That sugar crust on top is my fave rave."

"I just can't believe all this food came out of this little room!" Cass said, mesmerized at first and then a little sheepish. "I didn't mean that your house is small," she added.

"No no, I get it. It IS small!"

I didn't get it until I actually saw her house a few weeks later. Then it was I who was mortified that I'd even had her at my house.

By the time the meal actually got going, around 4:00 p.m., the table was a proverbial groaning board of all the traditional Thanksgiving foods everyone in the entire country made on this one day. Whether you were seated in a mid-century modern, a Georgian colonial or a mansion, everyone imagined herself on the cover of the Saturday Evening Post inhabiting a Norman Rockwellian image of a happy family enjoying the fruits of a country awash in Thanksgiving plenty.

It was my job to set the tables and to do this I had to enlarge the dining room table with the extension leaves in it to seat twelve people. Usually there were enough cousins and children for us to need a card table which I also arranged in the living room, and which, this time, I happily laid claim to for Cass and me. I intercepted two of the older Omaha cousins as they came in, and told them they would be sitting with me and my guest at the card table! They were happy to oblige and were quite intrigued with her and the fact that I brought some stranger to Thanksgiving. Roslyn had to sit with the adults.

I set the tables with the "good china and silver" that I hand-washed and dried before and afterwards. The china service was grey-blue with grey roses on it and rimmed in gold. I didn't love the china—a rather strange pattern that echoed a frugal war-time marriage; but it intrigued me to think of Betty picking it out and going through the motions of a wedding that was held not in a synagogue, but in a hotel in Omaha. She hadn't worn a white dress either, but a navy-blue suit and a hat with a black veil. He had worn his uniform. It certainly wasn't a shotgun wedding; I wasn't born until three years after the end of the war. But he was about to be shipped overseas and they decided to marry before that happened.

There weren't many pictures of this occasion and if you did see some, you'd never think they were the wedding photos. She could have worn that same outfit to a funeral.

"That was really good food, "Cass said, helping me dry the blue-stemmed Fostoria crystal and line it up carefully on the breakfast bar.

"Yes, Betty can cook."

"Did she teach you as you were growing up?"

"Hell, no, not really. She just expected me to help so I did a lot of prep work as a kid. My job when I got home from grade school was to peel potatoes."

"Wow! You're joking."

"No. And I have to say, I did learn to cook somewhat working in the grill kitchen."

"I'll bet your mom was proud of you for that. Maybe that was her way of teaching you."

What an absurd idea. She was never home, and when she was, she was sleeping. But Nana had probably taught her to cook and to run the business, too, for that matter, because Betty was smart. Coming out of high school, Betty actually could probably have been a fine college student if it hadn't been at the end of the Depression when she graduated. Her younger sisters were able to go, and that no doubt galled her. She was already long married and settled into a life stuck working in the family business by the time those other two were packed off to college.

"I can't cook, " Cass said. "But once in a while if I did go into the kitchen, our cook would teach me how to do some of the things I loved that she made."

"Like what?"

"Bananas Foster."

"You're kidding. What does that entail?"

"Lighting it on fire, that's what! Ho! She wouldn't let me do that part."

"I'd say not! Geez. How old were you?"

"I don't know. I've loved it since I was a little kid."

"It's got rum in it!"

"I know."

On the Friday after Thanksgiving, I whisked Cass off on a bus to downtown Omaha and we retraced my pre-teen and high school habit of spending every Saturday of my life at Brandeis, Omaha's most wonderful (really, only) big department store. I took her to lunch in the Tea Room and we visited all my favorite hangouts: the book department, the third-floor Junior department and Chandler Shoes on the mezzanine, where, after ogling gold lamé flats, you could lean over the balcony and watch all the animated bustle on the Main Floor. I took her to the French Room; she could have shopped there; I couldn't. I just wanted her to see it because I had spent many a happy moment on the round tufted sofa in the middle of the room while Nana had shopped in there. If I were well-behaved, a root beer float could have been in my future.

I still didn't quite get it at that time, only having known her for a few short months, that Cass rarely shopped for herself, and when she did, it was shopping trips with her mother or grandmother to New York mostly; sometimes Paris. Or home, naturally, in Chicago where Marshall Field's and Carson Pirie Scott dwarfed Brandeis.

If Cass were bored out of her mind with my little life that day, she never let on.

Getting off the bus near 6th and Broadway after our Omaha jaunt, I did have a chance to show her our bar. Sometimes when Betty worked the same hours as Sol, and especially by the time I was of an age where I could drive and babysit, the grill cook would make up some dinners for us to have at home and I would bring Roslyn with me to go get them. We would sit at the bar drinking cherry cokes until the cook would show up at the window far down at the very end of the bar, and pass the food through onto a ledge.

I took Cass in for the same thing and we, too, sat at the bar.

It was a pretty bar, I couldn't deny that. Old fashioned, wooden with leather trim to rest one's arms. Sol kept it polished. There was the usual mirror on the other side, as well as a large, darkly dramatic painting that hung ominously from wires above the back counter, of some sort of Western mountain scene with a ram looking out over a cliff. Niches and shelving held the various assortment of liquor bottles. Beer taps were right in front of the actual bar and it was equipped with every other sort of glass-washing apparatus, refrigeration and various foods and garnishes for making cocktails.

Sol had kept the ancient silver cash register on the counter under the mirror, but by the 1960's it was only for decoration, as he really used a new electronic one that even calculated the change for you. No one had credit cards yet in the 1960's except for department stores. I got to use the Brandeis card once in a blue moon. But none of the bar patrons paid with credit cards. Sometimes Sol ran them a tab, but that was also rare. He'd been burned too many times to do much of that. He also only took checks from people who were his actual friends; The Spot was a cash-only establishment for the most part.

If you were sitting at the bar itself, looking into the mirror, the reflection was of the rest of the dining room behind you. Little four-top café tables and wooden chairs were the décor. If a larger party came in, Betty would put two tables together. Sometimes they would make three or four into a long table right across the far back wall if, say, the Chamber of Commerce were to have a lunch meeting there or something. But generally, the tables were at angles seating up to four people all around the room. The light fixtures were big cream-colored globes and though they gave off a soft light, were not very stylish. There was a chair rail running all around the room's walls, with light brown paint below and wallpaper showing a drab country snow scene above. Betty always had plans to have that removed.

I did like the floors: the original wood was very creaky and rather uneven. After closing Sol and the wait staff would place all the chairs upside down on the tables and then do the floors. Every night— actually wee hours of the morning, they first swept, and then he'd take out this polishing machine with a round buffing head about a foot in diameter, and wind around and through each table, the bar area and down the hallway. Once per week or more often in winter when the floor would have been tracked up, they would deep clean and polish it.

There was a narrow hallway leading to restrooms and then turning sharply into the kitchen or out a back door. They kept a cigarette vending machine back there and stored some wooden high chairs and booster chairs. The Spot Bar and Grill was not necessarily a family restaurant *per se;* it had evolved from a tiny restaurant into a large bar. But inevitably, they had expanded the restaurant, too, and someone would turn up with a baby or toddler who needed to be seated.

Cass seemed intrigued with the whole operation.

"This is pretty cool," she pronounced.

"Come on." I snorted.

"No, really---it's nice. Homey, like."

"I guess."

Sol came out of his back office, interrupting my little tour with his abrupt: "Well, Cass, how do you like it?"

"Very nice, Mr. Shrier!"

"Yeah, thanks for the coke," I added, as he handed me food to take home. "We're going to stop by and see Nana."

"You do that," he said, and since he was turning back towards the bar, I took Cass out down the hall and through the rear where we could slip across to the garden gate and be at the annex.

Nana was always happy to see me and she was quite taken with Cass already, having spent Thanksgiving with her. But she wondered why I hadn't brought along "the little doll. "

"She means Roslyn," I explained over my shoulder to Cass; and turning back to Nana, I said, "You mean the brat."

"Now now. She's the cutest little fireball in the family."

"Well, I was showing Cass the bar and besides, I don't take her with me places anymore."

I had done my share of that, though. I dragged her to school with me when I had musical rehearsals. I took her to Peony Park to ride the boats and play on the man-made beach. I took her on the bus to see Santa Claus at Brandeis. I schlepped her around plenty when she was little.

"Well, she's smart as a whip! The other day she tap danced for my mahjong group over at your dad's place. Sang to herself as she did it!"

"God. How embarrassing. Where did she dance?"

"On top of the table!!"

"Oh, please."

Nana had baked her huge, square, frosted cinnamon rolls and they were still warm and filling the little house with their unmistakable aroma.

She made coffee, too, so we all sat down at her small dining room table. I didn't really drink coffee but Cass did, so I had a cup---nearly half milk and a lot of added sugar. But I liked it well enough.

"These are the best cinnamon rolls I've ever tasted!" Cass effervesced.

"Thank you dear," Nana beamed. And then she got down to brass tacks. "So you protested the Vietnam War, did you?"

"Well," I started, "sort of. I mean, we made some signs and went on a march around the Union, but it really ballooned into something bigger."

"And how about you, Cass? Are you against the war?"

"I am, yes."

"She designed the posters!"

"It's not like World War II," Nana said, "No one was against that war."

"No." We knew *that*.

"But, "she continued, "I agree with you young people: I don't much like this war, and I don't like a war on the other side of the world taking away all our young men. I believe in the draft, though, so not just the poor, uneducated boys are made to serve. But still, it doesn't seem to be a righteous war."

"It's a mess!"

"Yes, well, I just hope we win and get out of there. I never saw such a thing—all these body bags being shipped back Stateside. Such a tragedy."

She changed the subject and asked us all about Iowa U and what classes we had. I explained to her that Cass was a budding artist and that she had steered me towards art history, too; and wouldn't that fit perfectly into my course of study when I went to France!

"Oh, I hope you go!" Nana exclaimed.

"I AM going."

"Oh, yes, and then you can write us letters every week, and I'll put them in a folder. When you get back, you'll have an entire chronicle of your time there."

"That's a GREAT idea, Nan!" I hugged her, burying my face into her plumpness. She wasn't really fat at all, but had a few layers a kid could get lost in. And she always smelled so wonderful...Chanel No. 5 mostly. Betty wore it, too.

Before we left, I pointed out to Cass some of my childhood-preferred oddities of Nana's that were around her house: her tin powder box that was actually a music box; her china slipper bedecked in porcelain roses that she kept strings of pearls in on the dressing table; and my all-time favorite—her set of three-- identical except for their sizes-- candy dishes.

57

"Those are called King's-Crown–Ruby- red- and- clear- thumb-print pedestal-compote-candy-dish bowls," she stated with an exact air of authority. "Aren't they grand? My husband gave them to me for our 15th wedding anniversary. In those days that was the 'crystal' one. These aren't crystal but I love them as if they were," she sighed. And then she reached over and tweaked my cheek teasingly, "Maybe I'll give them to you for your wedding Sarah."

"Oh, yes, please! That would be so fab."

She smiled at the word "fab" and shook her head a little. I, in the meantime, thought it was a long shot that I'd ever be getting married.

Cass chimed in, "They are just beautiful. I can see why you love them."

We left her promising to keep her up to date on all our—as Cass put it---mad, gay, exciting life at the university.

It was perfectly planned and lucky for us that we were taking the train back to Iowa City on Saturday and could get out of there early enough to get back into the swing of things at school. There wasn't any more talk of my being taken out.

The only other time Cass Hyde would see my parents was four years later on graduation day in Iowa City.

Chapter Nine

"I Should Have Known Better"...Lennon & McCartney

Cass was serious about inviting me for Christmas in Kenilworth and I was determined to accept. My parents would be expecting me to work in the Spot any free time I had when I got home for vacation, but I was **obliged** to work in the restaurant on Christmas Eve day, as was our tradition—to let the "help" have that day at home. Nana cooked, Sol tended bar and cashiered; Betty was the waitress, and I was either the greeter (we didn't really have a hostess) showing customers to a table and handing out menus. Or I helped wait tables. Mostly I cleaned up. Luckily Christmas Eve Day was never very busy. The Bluffs was a small town where the "regulars" in our bar were family folks and had things to do that day. We closed early and didn't open on Christmas.

"I'm probably not going to be able to come before Christmas day," I told Cass.

"Darn," she said. "We open presents on Christmas Eve."

"Well, " I said, thinking about that, "then it's better if I'm not there, right? You need to be together without interlopers for that." *What would I ever be able to bring to that table, anyway, I wondered. There wouldn't even be a hostess gift that I could possibly show up with that would be adequate for the Hyde family. Luckily I had some ideas of presents for Cass, though, and I'd earn some extra money in tips if I worked the few days before Christmas.*

So it was arranged by Cass that I would take the train to Chicago on December 25th and she would meet me at Union Station and bring me to Kenilworth. But Cass didn't make these plans with her parents. She made them with the woman who had brought her to Iowa that first day: housekeeper Evie Cooper. And Cass asked that Evie arrange to provide me with the ticket!

"You can't do that!" I protested.

"Sure I can. And that way, your parents can't refuse to let you come!"

"Gee. You're right. I don't know what to say. Thank you!"

I spent those weeks between Thanksgiving and Christmas of 1966 in a day-dream laden state of suspended animation. Class work came first, but every free minute I found myself imagining spending time with Cass in her house that, before I'd even seen it, I knew was a world away from mine. We could take the local train into Chicago every day and run around and shop; we could hang out in the art museums; we could go to parks and walk near the lake. And we could stay at her house and study for finals. And best of all we could plan our Iowa City summer.

Cass, in the meantime, was working hard on a Christmas gift for her parents: a miniature self-portrait. She'd been researching the whole genre of miniatures because Klampert was preparing to deliver a paper on them, and she had learned a lot. Plus she'd seen many of them already in person visiting European museums.

"I'm doing mine in oil, "she explained to me one night when she was trying to get the canvas the right size—tiny! "Usually...in the past that is, they were gouache, watercolor or enamel."

"God, I can't even imagine how someone dreamed up such an idea. Although, of course, they had to have some way to see what people looked like. Portable, I mean."

"Right. But Klampert's paper explains how this all developed out of techniques they used in illuminated manuscripts. Manuscript illustration advanced into woodcuts and such, and miniatures became popular for other reasons, like when they wanted to introduce people to each other over distances. Some nobleman who wanted to marry off his daughter might send his courier with her portrait to the courts of potential suitors. Soldiers carried a miniature of their sweetheart or wife off to battle, or the family might keep a miniature of their loved one off to serve."

"So what do you plan to have your parents do with yours? They have photos of you now."

"I know, but I just thought this would be really different and unique. My family has big portraits in oil all over the walls at my house, but no one has thought of a miniature before."

*No kidding. What **would** a kid do to come up with presents for these parents year after year? I had a hard enough time of it and mine weren't wealthy industrialists who "had everything."*

The thing was, I hated buying presents for my parents, Sol especially, and some of my worst memories were tied up in gift-giving. One Chanukah Sol gave Betty a diamond necklace. We were all at Nana's opening presents after the bar was closed. Betty took one look at it, became furious and threw it back at him. Nana had given her an exasperated tongue clucking across the table. At age twelve or so, I remember being flabbergasted at this drama. There must have been some backstory I didn't know about because I had never seen her blow like that, not like a smoldering volcano, but rather like a volcano hit by a thunderbolt. It wasn't pretty. Then Sol got mad at her for getting mad at him. Another holiday ruined.

I told Cass that story.

"But he was worse! Nothing I ever gave him was good enough, what he wanted, or nice. And he didn't have the couth to pretend that it was. One time after I was old enough to take the bus to Brandeis by myself (sixth grade) I went over to the big Father's Day sale. I picked out a pocket handkerchief and tie set for him for Father's Day. It was silk, in shades of beige and tones of brown with pale pink stripes on the tie. I thought it was so beautiful!! And I could afford it!"

"How could he not like that?" she wondered.

"Upon unwrapping it, he looked up and said, 'Is that it?'"

Yeah, that was it, you fucking prick. I wouldn't even waste my tears or my efforts on him again. Ever after that, it was golf balls and no thought put to them.

I continued, "So you can only imagine the next time an occasion arose with a birthday dinner I happened to be invited to. I was at a friend's house planning stage decorations for the high school road show. We were working with yards of muslin at her dining room table, when her mom asked us to clear out so she could set the table for the dad's birthday dinner that was going to happen that night. They invited me to stay for it, which I did, since we weren't nearly done with our project. We all had a wonderful dinner. Then the mother brought out the birthday cake, set it in front of her husband and my friend and her little brother came in with presents they'd had ready for their dad. He took the brother's small oblong one first, and tore off the paper. It was a candy bar! Oh shit! I remember thinking to myself. Here it comes. I actually braced myself for the barrage of chastisement that I assumed would be forthcoming from the disappointed dad."

"Oh, no, "Cass said, commiserating.

"Hell NO! He acted like it was the greatest gift anyone could have chosen! He thanked his son and told him it was his favorite!"

"How about that!" she exclaimed.

"And I just sat there staring at him and at the candy with my mouth agape and the wheels in my brain revving into gear. That was all it took for me to get it. I never forgot that lesson. You always just appreciate any nice efforts with gifts, even if it's not what you wanted, expected or needed."

"But I wonder how many people do that?" Cass said.

I told her I was sorry to have drifted into bad memories of gift-giving and urged her to keep telling me about miniatures, because it was fascinating, and she especially wanted to talk up Klampert's research.

"Klampert's paper is on Simon Bening and his daughter Levina Teerlinc. "

"Never heard of them."

"No. That wouldn't be in your class material. But Jean Fouquet might be and he was the earliest portrait miniaturist. Because he was actually a very famous manuscript painter and it was natural for him to turn to miniatures. You'll study him. Anyway, Levina painted portraits and she had moved to England to become a court painter. Her predecessor was the court artist Hans Holbein the Younger in the court of Henry VIII."

"So you got this idea after typing up Klampert's notes or something?"

"Sort of. I decided I wanted to do one after reading about her, it's true. But I wasn't sure I could do it. I made some sketches." She pulled out some papers from a pouch and sure enough, they were very true to life –the features and hair and her long neck.

"Wow. Neat. So you'll paint this in oils on a piece of canvas and find some little frame for it?"

"Exactly. I want an oval matt inside a square frame, with a piece of velvet ribbon for a hanger.

"Well, yes, that will look old."

"I picture something somewhat Victorian."

"Just perfect," I sighed, and then I added, "You can really draw. That does look just like you."

"Thus, the art major, you think? " She laughed. "Too bad we have to pass the rest of the classes."

"Tell me about it."

I was doing fine in French, and we had Fencing down; I was actually passing a Phys Ed class! But I was completely bogged down with the Biology course I had to take to satisfy a science requirement. The professor who lectured was actually pretty famous, it turned out, and his talks were probably interesting — if only I could have understood one word.

He would project a slide on the huge screen in the lecture hall: Cross Section of a Leaf, for example. And then he would expound. "The Stomatae. These porelike openings in the epidermis are connected with the air spaces within the leaf. These openings are regulated by two guard cells, one of each side of the stomata. Now, on which surface are the stomates most abundant? The bottom." Ad nauseum.

And take notes in a lecture hall seating 400 people? I would start out with good intentions, but as the writing dribbled down the page, it became apparent that these notes would serve no purpose. The notoriety in the field of Life Science of my esteemed teacher was soon lost on me.

The labs for this class were gruesome and difficult. The only thing I liked was the drawing. My amoebas, hydras, starfish and frog parts were little masterpieces. I worked them on heavy cardstock that I three-hole punched so I could keep them organized and illustrated them meticulously in colored pencil. I didn't, however, want Cass to see them because even though they were just drawings of blobs or insets of the vein system of a tadpole or some such, I didn't want her to really see at what a kindergarten level I drew.

Alan Jones' Rhetoric class turned out to be challenging. We were writing a lot— analyzing everything from Plato to Hemingway, lit crit to poetry. Jones would give notes but he seemed more disconnected from the subject matter of his course than I would have expected. I decided since he was merely a T.A., perhaps the syllabus had been thrust upon him and he would be better when he was teaching using his own. Being in the graduate writing program at Iowa at all was a major accomplishment, and he was under some pressures to perform with his own writing, which he never discussed with us.

He spent some weeks right before Christmas break preparing us for the study of *Moby Dick or The Whale*, which was actually the purview of Dr. Harry Oster, his English department mentor. He assumed we'd already have had to have read it in high school, but if we went on in American Literature or World Literature, we'd be studying it in a lot more depth.

Alan asked us, "What is *Moby Dick* in literature? Is it a novel? "He wrote novel on the board. "Is it a drama?" He put "drama" under "novel". "What else could it be?"

"An allegory, "someone answered, and he added that to the list.

"Autobiography," another student called out. Jones was skeptical of that, and didn't write it up there. He looked out at the person who had suggested that. "Is that what your high school teacher taught you? Because Melville was a whaler once?"

"I guess so." The guy was cowed.

"That's harsh, "whispered someone else in the row.

"And, " the first student continued, "the book has some elements of Melville's experience in it. We know that. They think Ahab is based on a real person. Plus there was a whale that they called the devil. I think it was Mocha Dick or something."

"You're right. And there were authenticated retellings of encounters with it. But Ahab based on a real person or not, that doesn't make Moby Dick an autobiography."

Alan cut off this line of discussion and instead we were admonished to find what was Shakespearean in the work, as well as what was biblical, factual, fantasy, comical, dramatic, erotic and banal.

Alan Jones was less than impressed with my finished product. He wrote on it, "Your initial ideas are good but you don't develop them and your paper loses focus. Miss Shrier, you could improve your skills."

"He sounds like a jerk, " Cass consoled me upon reading those remarks on my paper.

But then another paper I wrote for him drew enthusiastic praise, to my astonishment: "Guinevere: Too Good to be True or Too True to be Good?" was my homage to *The Once and Future King*, a book I had loved as a young high school student.

Of course that book wasn't part of our high school curriculum; I was just living inside the musical Camelot, so had the good sense to get the book it was based on and live in awe of T. H. White. I tucked that book into my bucket bag, and dragged it around with me for weeks reading it in study hall, backstage during down times of road show prep, and in between customers at the Spot. If you wanted to give in to living a fantasy life, the Arthurian myth one was as good as any.

Alan Jones liked the premise of my paper this time and wrote that my analysis led him to believe that I understood how White "harkens accurately to Mallory's *Le Morte d'Arthur* in its illumination of humankind's struggles and failures."

And Cass pronounced: "Okay, so he redeemed himself. Ha!"

Jones was not particularly friendly towards me in class, even after asking my roommate for her contact information. He was hard on all of us, and didn't brook foolish answers to his "penetrating" rhetorical quasi-Socratic teaching method. And even though he seemed to accept my answers more often than he derided me, he certainly didn't show me any favoritism, which would have been very detrimental to his T.A. "career" if other students had gotten wind of such a thing. Not that such things didn't happen all the time in college. One of Cass' English teachers cornered her after a lecture in EPB and pretty much propositioned her, saying that he and his wife had an "open marriage" and therefore she, the wife, wouldn't mind if he took Cass out.

"He sort of looks like Tom Jones," Cass told me, as I stared aghast, hearing this story. "He's cute - --short, though. Pretty smarmy, really. How come they think they're so desirable? Why did he presume I'd want to get involved with him? I just don't get it. He also intimated that my grade would not suffer if I agreed to see him."

"I guess smarmy! So that sounds, you know, like against the law---or at least against the college's ethics. What did you do?"

"Well, he is the professor, after all, and I didn't have much time to come up with an excuse; so I just said I was in a serious relationship already and faithful to my boyfriend."

"That was good thinking," I nodded approvingly. "You're lucky you only have this guy in a huge lecture class. You can disappear into the crowd. I'm amazed he knew your name. There must be a hundred kids in there."

But I wasn't really amazed that he had made it his business to find out who she was. I became, however, enlightened after that, as to the lengths some people would go to dangle your grade over you if you didn't do their bidding.

"You should report him," I added. "Women students shouldn't have to go around living in fear that if they don't succumb to advances, or even if they inadvertently bruise someone's precious ego, their grade would be at stake."

Cass sighed. "You're probably right, but I don't want to go up in front of any intercollegiate boards and all that rigmarole since he really didn't *threaten* me."

Cass did not go out with my rhetoric teacher as far as I knew that semester. Maybe they both thought it prudent to wait until he wasn't my teacher anymore, although no one said anything of the sort. And she didn't need my permission. Besides, Klampert was my teacher, too. But then, I wasn't supposed to know about her and Klampert. There was no grade involved there; Cass was not his student---merely his "work study" aide. And, of course, she never talked about their relationship other than that. I decided that if she were sleeping with him, she must have had her own reasons to do so and that it wasn't because he coerced her. But I admit I was curious to know if I was right.

In the end, it was I who was the naïf. Here was one young woman, my roommate, being pursued by three professors on this one campus; and it could have been happening to half the women students in school for all I knew. I heard later that "hardly any marriage can survive The Iowa Writers Workshop."

Chapter Ten

"Crystal Blue Persuasion"...Tommy James and the Shondells

In the '60's, with the exception of schools with things like special inter-sessions or the trimester system, no one had a month off between final exams and second semester. So part of the scheme, (which it was by then—a scheme for me to spend the majority of Christmas vacation in Kenilworth) was that we were studying for finals. Which we fully intended to do. I'm not sure exactly what Cass told her parents about my coming to stay, but as she had explained, it was probably done with the staff mostly. At any rate, they did agree to have me.

When I went home to do my usual drill, working over the holiday and especially in the bar on Christmas Eve day, it was still four days before Christmas and I had to plan out what to take to wear in Chicago. I wasn't trying to impress anyone; that would have been a fool's errand, but I did want to look presentable. I read a lot of magazines, like everyone else, so I knew at what level of taste to aim, whether or not I could actually attain it. For that matter, in my mind, if one merely copied Jackie Kennedy, one couldn't go wrong. She was still on the covers of ten or fifteen magazines at any given moment. One, where she was walking Caroline to school in New York showed her in a beautiful classic camel-hair long coat.

I went to see Nana.

"I'm desperate for a coat like this, " I said, thrusting the magazine in front of her. "I'm going to visit Cass and, well, my winter coat is from hunger. Do you think it would be possible for you to come with me to Brandeis and help me find one? It doesn't have to be expensive; it has to look like it is, though, " I laughed.

"Did you ask your mother?"

"No. I came to you first. I knew you'd understand my dilemma."

"Well, I do. You're a good girl, Sari. You work hard. I think you could do with a new coat."

"Oh Nan, you are so wonderful! I really appreciate this! When can you go? "

"Oh dear, you know...it's awfully cold out for a bus trip. I tell you what...I'll give you my Brandeis charge card and you can just put it on my account. "

"Really?! Gee, thanks!!"

"Be reasonable. Don't shop in the French Room."

"I won't. I'm hoping to find one for under $50. Is that okay?" It sounded like a fortune to me.

"Yes, honey, that's okay."

Nana had always thought Sol was hard on me, and I also believe in my heart that she knew her daughter was lethargic and not an enthusiastic parent at all. Betty did work every day and many evenings in the bar, but at home, she didn't do much. And she didn't show much interest in mothering. Looking back on her life, I can say now that it was probably part depression, part exhaustion. But to me at the time, it merely came off as indifference. I am lucky she didn't drink and pass out all over the place, but in a way, she gave off the same effect – she was often asleep on the couch stone cold sober. Other moms joined service organizations, baked for school activities, came to plays and shows and concerts. Betty came once in a while to some program I was in, and she showed up more to Roslyn's elementary school than she ever did to my high school, but she was never a Brownie leader or room mother or anything that required a certain leadership personality. Sol "could never get away" for my school events, but he was a community participant in business groups and the synagogue, and Nana had done a lot of work in those areas in her younger days as well.

I found a nice coat, and had to say so myself: I could shop on a budget. I didn't find one like Jackie's, long and drapey, but the one I did end up with--- thanks to Nana-- was camel-colored wool---what we called a "boy coat" with a belt in back and square pockets in front. It was double-breasted with no ornamentation except light beige buttons. I dearly loved that coat and was happy I could present myself to the Hyde household in a decent outfit. I had chosen my aunt's orange and grey wool jumper—the best thing I owned, in my opinion, at the time. I put on a grey wool turtleneck sweater with it, grey tights and

63

black boots. I wore a "pearl" choker over the turtleneck and it looked as classic as I could possibly muster. I longed to pass as Cass' equal when I met her parents, but there wasn't much hope of that.

The train ride was pretty grueling this time---long and not comfortable for someone dressed up. I didn't want to arrive all wrinkled and mussed, so I just sat pretty still for the eight hours it took to get there. Of course, I had plenty of material to study on the way; and at least I knew to bring food—cheese sandwiches and carrot sticks… nothing that could drip or flake all over me. The car was practically empty! Good job, traveling on a major holiday. At one point, completely bored rereading lab notes about the vascular cambium, I succumbed to the immense desire to sleep, spread out my new coat and curled up carefully on the seat lengthwise. I slept through the train's stop in Iowa City.

I walked off the platform in Chicago into the immense station hall, bedecked for Christmas with a very large tree in one corner and wreaths on the walls as well as bunting and banners hanging down from the beautiful coffered ceiling.

Cass was right there waiting and she hugged me. "Welcome to Chicago, kid!" Martin, the chauffeur, took my bags and we followed him to a different car than she came to Iowa in. This one was a 1965 Lincoln Continental Lehmann-Peterson limousine. It was sleek and quite long, whereas the other one had been very rounded and had seemed huge. I pressed Cass for some info.

"You know, I can't even tell you what all cars we have. That idiotic one they drove me to school in has a very large trunk; that's why we took it. This is my mother's town car."

Yes, the "idiotic one" was a Bentley S3. We were slumming it in the Lincoln.

Cass was still dressed up in her Christmas outfit that she'd worn to church that morning and then to holiday brunch at the Westmoreland Country Club, the family tradition. She looked very sophisticated standing there in the great hall waiting for me in a chic navy wool sheath dress with a thin red leather belt and a navy coat to match, the lapels and pockets piped in red. She had on knee high red boots and wore white leather gloves. She was not wearing a hat of any sort and it was really cold out; but then, she didn't have to be outside for very long.

Chicago, as we drove through it towards the north shore suburbs, was beautiful in the twinkling lights of decorations not only in the trees and on the street lamps, but also the city lights reflected on the lake itself all along Lake Shore Drive. I turned towards the window to take it all in as we floated out towards Kenilworth on the cloud that was that limo's suspension. I thought I was in a dream. I'd been sitting stiffly for hours, but now my whole body seemed to melt into those soft, squeaky leather seats as my boot toes disappeared into the thick backseat floor carpet.

"Oh, God, Cass," I said turning to her. "I brought your parents something stupid. I hope they don't think I'm a complete jerk. It's Glenlivet. Sol let me bring it. I mean, I couldn't think of anything."

"No, no! That's a great present. Can't have too much Scotch in the house, can you?" she sort of snickered.

"Well, I mean—my parents own a bar, so …it makes a certain amount of sense …."

"I'm sure they'll think it is very thoughtful. They weren't even expecting you to bring them anything."

"It's Christmas. I'm a houseguest for ten days!"

"Don't worry. Besides, you won't see them after tomorrow night. They won't be back before we head out to school.

Martin's route took us past Evanston and Wilmette on the way to Kenilworth.

"I would have gone to New Trier if I'd stayed home for high school," Cass said as we drove into Wilmette. "It's considered the number one high school in the United States."

"Well, if it's that good, why didn't you go there?"

"Because my entire family going back four generations has gone to Choate-Rosemary Hall."

"Did you like boarding school?" I ventured. I didn't know what she'd say, but to me, boarding school had always been my ideal.

Naturally I only imagined the wonderful campus in fall colors, the cozy dorms, terrific teachers (Mr. Chips), and the secret lives of great and good friends who would remain friends forever. I never let any alternate realities enter into it of mean girls or roommates who read your mail, diaries, grade reports, etc., or who stole things or used your homework as their own; freezing winter rooms, mediocre food and strict uncaring teachers.

"I really did, "Cass answered. "I had the most amazing art teacher in the whole world there. And I loved my English classes, too—all four years."

"What about your roomies?"

"Oh, it was pretty cramped in our room...three beds and a bit of personal space for each of us, and all...a nice room but you know, not very private. Sometimes girls did their space up really neat, though. I didn't add things to mine like a canopy but one of my friends made hers look like a Carl Larsson painting. It was darling."

"Who's Carl Larsson?"

"Swedish artist. Studied in France, though. I'll show you when we get to my place. Anyway, to answer your question, yes, I liked my roomies and made some good friends there—obviously since I attended all four years. But we had the same sort of problems anyone would have in a dorm: people stayed up all night typing which made noise, and if one of us were sick, coughing at night or whatever, no one could get to sleep. Luckily if you were really sick with flu or anything contagious, they had an infirmary you had to go to."

"So do you write to these girls or keep in touch at all?"

"Oh, sure. Sometimes. I've gotten letters from one especially, Terrie Simpkins. She's in school now in Williamsburg, Virginia at William and Mary. I've seen her once--- last year when I went back to visit D.C. and went to see some of my cousins near Richmond. All my grandmother's ancestors came first to Virginia. I still have a lot of relatives there, but they're very distant, of course. Mummy took me on one of her trips and she looked some of them up. Terrie was in final exam week because they get out a lot later than Iowa. So I didn't get to spend a lot of time with her. It was fun, though. She's from the Boston area, so when we were in high school, Wallingford, Connecticut was quite close for her. She went home on the weekends more than I ever did."

"But did she invite you to come sometimes?"

"No. She went home often to see her mother who was an invalid. She had polio. Actually Mrs. Simpkins died—of pneumonia."

"That's awful."

"Yes, and Terrie and her parents always were close. She and her dad grieved a lot---I'm sure they still are, even though they knew this could happen. I did meet her mother a few times. When we were newbies, they came together to bring her to school. Her mom couldn't get up to our room, but I went out to dinner with them several times. We had a third roommate, too—Brenda from upstate New York. She gave off all the vibes of a very snooty, spoiled brat and was standoffish as all get out. But she was a math genius and she really excelled at our school. She didn't bother us much, but she didn't join in either. She did stay in our room all four years, though. I always thought that was kind of strange considering her best friends were in a different dorm. She ended up applying to schools like Cal Tech and MIT. She got in to every one and ended up choosing Stanford. "

Hearing all this, I felt validated in wondering yet again just how, having come from a great private school like Choate-Rosemary Hall, Cass Hyde could have washed up on the shores of Iowa U; but since we'd already been down that road, I kept my feelings to myself.

Martin turned off Sheridan Road and onto Melrose and came to a long driveway where we went about halfway up and were stopped by an automated security gate that he could open from the car; others would have had to press a button and wait to be buzzed in for the gates to open. We were still far from the actual house, but rounding a shallow bend, it came into view: a manor house, more ersatz château than anything else, but with an aura of Italianate villa to it, as well. It was only two storeys but very long and symmetrical with a huge red-tiled roof and six floor-to-ceiling Palladian windows flanking the grand entrance. On the other side of the circular drive, the yard was actually a *jardin à la française* replete with stone "love seats" around a fountain. Everything was covered with snow that trip, but I could tell that flower beds were planted in quarter- circular patterns around the fountain and that the seating areas were positioned to give a secluded area in which to enjoy both. Eight windows on the home's second floor all looked out onto the fountain and flower beds and all the French doors on the first floor opened onto the

65

brick porch that ran the length of the entire house. Two huge urns stood on either side of the stairway leading up to the door. That night they were decorated with Christmas topiary, but most of the time they were planted with identical flowers and greenery.

A detached garage peeked out from one side of the house in back where the circular drive veered off, and that was confirmed when I saw it in the daylight. A six-car garage with a three-bedroom apartment above it bigger than my whole house in The Bluffs. In fact, as I entered the foyer, I realized our entire 1,700 square feet of living space could have also fit inside that one hall, too. My mind was reeling.

I began to furiously wipe my boots on the entry rug near the door, thinking at any minute I'd be instructed to remove them. So I just asked her, "Should I take off my boots?"

"No, don't worry. We only walked from the car to the door."

I stood on the white travertine floor and just took a look down the immense corridor to a beautiful, regal staircase leading up to a landing with those beveled glass French door-windows that house window seats filled with pillows for whiling away hours reading---the kind of windows I would have imagined Peter Pan flying into and out of! The entire staircase and stairwell were lit above the two-story opening at the top by a shimmering crystal and silver chandelier hung on thick velvet cords from a chain at the exact midpoint of the ceiling.

Martin took my luggage and instead of heading up that flight of stairs, turned down the hall and into the kitchen and up a back staircase to Cass' room.

"I'll show you the whole house later," she said, seeing I was completely mesmerized and must have been wondering what the rest was like. She took an audible breath. "First let's go meet the parents."

Luckily I had their gift and Cass' in my tote bag still on my shoulder, which I put down on a silk tufted love seat against one of the hall walls and took out the wrapped gifts and carried them with me, as Cass led the way through another set of doors into the living room. The color scheme was very light coral on the walls, cream ceiling divided into squares by plaster molding with medallions in every fourth square; and an enormous thick oriental rug of beige, coral and taupe tones on the parquet floor. Two identical sofas in coral silk faced each other forming a conversation area along with two wing chairs in front of a massive fireplace, above which was a painting of a pastoral scene flanked by decorative sconces on each side. Windows on either end of the mantel gave off into the back garden, and French doors on the wall behind one of the sofas led out into it.

The Hyde's enormous Fraser fir Christmas tree stood regally in the back of the room opposite the fireplace in a separate conversation area. A round antique game table with four chairs had been moved off to the side to make room for it. I had never in my whole life seen a tree like that in a private home; it looked more like the decorations Brandeis put up in the middle of the cosmetics department high on a pedestal, festooned in enormous bows and baubles. This was a Christmas tree done by an interior decorator, not a family. I was intrigued.

As we approached the fireplace area, Cass' parents both stood up to greet me. They were very formal but not unfriendly.

"How do you do, Sarah," said Julia Hyde, extending her hand.

"Welcome, Sarah, "echoed John-Wilfred Hyde.

"I'm very happy to meet you," I answered, shaking both their hands. "I've brought you this." I awkwardly handed the heavy package to Julia.

"Thank you, dear," she intoned.

Julia Bronwyn Scott Hyde was practically a specimen from Central Casting and, really, exactly what I thought she'd look like: perfectly put together, perfectly coiffed. At forty-four, she was taller than Cass, (who was slightly taller than me), at about five foot seven inches, with hair the color of burnished copper (but who knew if that was really her hair color; I doubted it), short in length but "done" swept up and around her head, dipping slightly into side bangs. She was wearing camel-colored wool pants which came to a tight halt at her ankles where they met creamy leather ballet flats; and she had on a lush tan cashmere sweater with a cowl collar and a pearl Christmas tree brooch pinned at the shoulder.

Her eyes were dark brown and rather small. She had a thin mouth that only slightly turned upward from pursed lips when she smiled, making it seem like she was smirking rather than happy. I noticed her slim hands right away because they were the same as Cass' only highly manicured. Her engagement ring was enormous, a square cut single diamond and her wedding band was all diamonds around the entire band, which I had never seen before then. It was absolutely beautiful, and seemed understatedly magnificent. She wore a gold link "identity" bracelet—the kind with a bar-- on one arm, and that was all the jewelry she had on that night at home. I imagined coffers of jewels somewhere in that house which would give the lie to understatement. In fact, Cass told me later, the ring she wore was paste!

"You're kidding! WHY?"

"Well, you get it—that ring is worth a fortune and could get stolen. She travels a lot."

"Okay, but why have wonderful things if you can't enjoy them?"

"It's an EXACT replica of the real ring, Sari, "Cass tried to explain to a dense me. "She had a private jeweler make it. The real one is in the bank. This is not uncommon, you know."

Well, I didn't know, but was schooled that night.

John-Wilfred Custis Hyde was tall and not really slim but in the kind of shape one would imagine of someone in middle age who still worked out at a gym. He had dark hair going ever so slightly grey, and he still seemed to have all of it...combed straight back and shiny clean but not glossy with products. His eyes were very blue and covered in masses of eye lashes, which obviously Cass had inherited. He wore thick horn-rimmed glasses and all he needed was a smoking jacket and a pipe to look like something out of Sherlock Holmes. But instead he was wearing beautiful muted dress Campbell Clan tartan wool pants and a fisherman-knit crewneck sweater. He also wore soft black leather "driving moccasins."

Cass wheeled around and went back towards the tree. "I've got one for you!" She came back with a beautiful box from Saks Fifth Avenue, not wrapped per se but their signature black and white box tied with an enormous red ribbon. I had hers in my hands still—wrapped in Christmas paper by myself and looking not so grand, especially after a nine-hour ride in a tote bag.

"Sit there, Sarah, " said Julia motioning me to the sofa. Cass sat beside me. "We'll have some champagne now John?" He nodded, stepping back towards the French doors where I hadn't even noticed a glass cart with a bottle of Veuve Clicquot brut champagne cooling in a silver ice bucket and four Waterford flutes on a silver tray. He poured two glasses and offered them to his wife and me first. Then he went back and brought two more for Cass and himself.

"This is for you, " I said, thrusting my gift at Cass. It was a sketch book that I had got at Things and Things in Iowa City and kept secreted away so she wouldn't see it in our room.

"Things" as we called it, was my first real introduction to a dark, squeaky-floored, hippie- boho boutique that smelled of scented candles and incense. They carried all sorts of wonderful stuff—like tie-dye curtains, bedspreads and long dresses; placemats and ironstone dishes; planters made of macramé hung from the ceiling; and all sorts of wooden toys and games, ash trays, beaded jewelry, woven baskets, bibelots and even some furniture. But mainly I loved the stationery corner where they offered artsy notebooks (as opposed to the University bookstore's up the street), journals, sketch books, cards, paper by the pound (I loved that!) and hand-made wrapping paper. I had found Cass a small, thick but pliable sketch book she could carry around all the time in a large purse or in her art bag -- at the ready for inspiration to strike. But what I loved was the cover: mauve suede with a suede hand-made flower on it in dusty muted violet and pink. The "stem" of the flower was stitched in green crewel embroidery thread going all the way down the front of the book. It had a leather page marker and even a back-page pocket to stick in little bits of paper or the occasional pressed flower or souvenir. This item, like all things in Things was too expensive for my budget, but I saved up and splurged on it, forking over $12.00 (outrageous!) and rationalizing that it was so beautiful, it was totally worth it.

Cass opened it up as her parents watched and drank their champagne.

"OH! I love this, " Cass cooed, flicking the pages as she cradled the suede cover in her hand. "Thank you, kid!!"

"You're welcome! Can't have too many, right?" *Same as with Scotch?*

"Open yours now."

And so I did, taking a swig of champagne as I untied the fat red ribbon on the box. As I opened the lid, tissue paper billowed up and when I reached down into it, I felt fur. I pulled out a hat...not a hat actually---a hood. With a long black gross-grain ribbon tie.

"Oh, golly. It's gorgeous!!" I exclaimed, lifting it out of the box altogether and holding it up. It was fox, lined in soft black fabric; and the ribbon stitched into the inside was to tie under the chin. "Thank you so much!!"

I really didn't know what to say.

That it was going to save me from ever being cold again trekking across the tundra that could be the U of I campus in the early winter morning? That it was going to look more chic than I ever could have imagined myself looking two years later as I made my way through the Luxembourg Gardens to the Sorbonne? That it would stand the test of time in both fashion and utility as I walked to work in cold and windy Chicago for years after that? I think I wore it until the gross-grain had literally wasted away. But that first night that I opened it in the Hyde's living room, I just held it across my lap and ran my hand through its softness, caressing it. Over and over.

Julia interrupted my reverie and I took another drink from my flute.

"I've had my secretary get you girls theater and symphony tickets, Cass, for next week and I think you two would do better to stay in the apartment rather than come back here. So we've notified the staff and they'll be ready for you."

"Oh…okay, thanks Mummy."

I'd heard Cass refer to her parents by what she called them: Mummy and Papa, (which she pronounced "puh-PAH"), but she never proffered any explanation for why, when she was nineteen years old, she still referred to them that way. I just had to take F. Scott Fitzgerald at his word: "…the rich are different from you and me."

Cass looked up at her father. "When do you leave for Gstaad?"

"Tomorrow morning, "said John-Wilfred, "very early. I doubt you'll be awake when we go."

"Yes, Sarah, " Julia added, "I'm afraid we won't be seeing you again after tonight. We won't be back here before Martin drives you and Cass to Iowa City. And, Cass, "she said rather pointedly, "don't forget you are invited down to the Springfield Homestead to spend time with Granny next weekend. The staff has all the details. My secretary Denise can take care of anything you need while I'm gone. As well as everyone else—you know."

Everyone else consisted, as I was to learn, of not only Martin and Evie Cooper, the maid I met the first day Cass moved into the dorm, but also housekeeper Lottie, to whom Cass was also very close it turned out; Maria Olivetti, the cook and Darius, the groundskeeper. Darius lived with his family in one of the large apartments over the garages, which allowed his children to attend the best schools in Illinois.

Evie Cooper came to work every day from somewhere else, but Lottie and Maria each had rooms the size of studio apartments in the house's basement. Basement was a misnomer in this case; there was nothing undercrofty about it. The ceilings were high and there were ample windows around the entire perimeter. Also down there were a huge "gathering" room with a t.v., a fully stocked bar with regular-sized refrigerator, and comfortable furniture, which served as a sort of family room for the staff; a wine cellar, the laundry room, which was bigger than my living room at home, and various organized storage spaces. Doors led out from that central room to a lovely sunken patio, and a garden lower than the one in front that I had seen as I arrived. The property behind the house sloped down for what seemed like acres until it ended in woods.

"Have a lovely time, Papa," Cass said, kissing John-Wilfred on the cheek. "What will you be doing…besides skiing of course?"

"A series of meetings with a French hotel group called Sofitel," he answered. "They've got about 40 luxury hotels world-wide and have asked me to consult on the refurbishing of the ones in Europe."

"Gee, you might be there a long time if you take that job, " Cass said wistfully.

"We'll be able to work out of the London office," he said casually. "It won't be much different than being here."

"So we'll say goodnight and also good-bye, Cass," Julie said, standing up. She gave Cass a little hug and then John-Wilfred did the same.

They both approached me and said their good-byes. I thanked them again for letting me come, for the gift and the theater tickets, and Cass and I headed out into the vast hallway.

"Maria's not here as you know," Cass said, "being Christmas day and all. But if you're hungry, we can find you something to eat in the kitchen."

68

"I'm fine," I said, "really. I ate snacks on the train." I was really tired, though, and drinking champagne on an essentially empty stomach didn't help matters.

"If you're sure?" Cass insisted. "Oh, wait, I know—there's Christmas candy and cookies in the library. Let's get those and take them up to my room."

So I followed her down the hall and through a different entrance that led past an enormous dining room and into a dark paneled room with floor-to-ceiling bookshelves, plus sofas, a mahogany desk flanked with leather Empire style chairs and elegant table lamps. Cass grabbed a tin container and a glass candy dish and we headed out. I realized then and there that I had no idea how to get back to the hallway that housed the magnificent staircase, but instead we went upstairs another way. Turns out there were three different stairways up to the second floor. Once up there, we were in another big corridor only this time we were walking on carpet so plush my feet once again seemed to sink into the depths. Cass led me past double doors that were the only entries on that side of the hall.

"Those doors lead into my parents' quarters. I'd show it to you, but actually, they keep it locked. And since they'll be gone, it will be locked the whole time. Now, mind you, I can get in there if I really want to because I know where Lottie keeps all the keys, so before you go, we'll see it. But not tonight."

We turned a corner and went into her room, which had an open door. It was also a space I could only have imagined a large hotel room would be like. She had pink and white Laura Ashley wallpaper on the top half of the walls, with white beadboard on the bottom. Her big double bed was very high off the ground, a canopy bed with a beautiful pink and white eyelet bedspread and six pillows of various sizes. And the room had a fireplace! And a mantle where she could display anything she liked. On the walls were HER own works of art: mostly prints but also watercolors and photographs she'd taken in remote parts of Scandinavia on that outward-bound type trip she had told me about. Double doors opened up her gigantic closet and she had an adjoining bathroom that had an aura of being very old-fashioned looking, until you realized the shower stall was the most up-to-date with five levels of sprayers and a steam feature! Her bathtub was a claw-foot free-standing tub and there were two small tables with shelving below them to hold towels of various sizes. The sink was a large pedestal one underneath a medicine cabinet. Normally pedestal sinks were a pain since they had no space to put things such as makeup cases or Kleenex boxes, but this one had unusually wide rims around the sink affording ample room for accessories. The whole room was predominately white with white subway tiling and a pink fuzzy accent rug. There was also a linen cupboard brimming with not only sheets and pillowcases, extra towels, washcloths and robes, but also an array of soaps and shampoos, hair supplies and sanitary products. That was handy.

"Wow." Just about all the eloquent vocabulary I could muster at that point. Her room had a bay window with a window seat, a chintz-covered tufted love seat, a coffee table, her stereo system, bookshelves built into niches, and something I had only seen in magazines: a portable television that sat on the corner of her sweet little painted writing desk and faced the seating area far from the bed.

The salient point of this room, to me, would have been that had I had such a room, I would never have left it, never left home. And here was Cass, who was hardly ever IN the room. Boarding schools all her life, summers in Springfield, or at camps or on bus trips around Europe. My God, she hardly had a chance to revel in this dreamy fantasy bedroom. And it really struck me by this time: what MUST she have thought staying at my house? I shuddered to think.

My suitcase had been brought up and I unpacked just enough to get into night clothes, wash my face and brush my teeth, and fall into that luxurious bed. The sheets smelled of lavender and I soaked that soothing scent in as my head sank down into the pillows and I was asleep before Cass had even turned off the lights. If she was talking to me, I wasn't answering. The next thing I knew, winter sunlight was flooding in the windows.

Chapter Eleven

"So Long, Frank Lloyd Wright"...Simon & Garfunkel

The Hyde house was bustling when we went downstairs for breakfast on December 26, 1966. Everyone there was back to work and the parents had been taken to O'Hare hours earlier. Maria had oatmeal for us and English muffins with Wilkin and Sons strawberry jam. She offered me orange juice and hot tea, also from England.

"Milk in your tea, Sarah?"

"Um...noooo. Do you put milk in it Cass?"

"Try it! Put the milk in first. It's really good."

I did and had that eureka moment when I realized I'd been missing out on something fantastic all my life.

Cass had been doing some thinking about showing me Chicago, and she had a plan all mapped out for our first day. We would begin, of course, with the Art Institute, where we would still be when lunch time rolled around, so we'd eat there.

"And then in mid-afternoon we'll work our way back down North Michigan Avenue and hit some or all of the great stores. After-Christmas sales will be on and it will be mass chaos, but I'm game if you are."

"You don't have to ask me twice." Too bad I didn't have any real money, but oh well, just looking at those chic stores...so much better than anything Omaha ever had...would make me ecstatic.

We'd go over to the Drake Hotel where we would take a cab to have dinner at a dive she loved – Lou Mitchell's, which was by the Union Station, and thus too far to walk in the twilight cold. Martin would pick us up there and drive us back to Kenilworth.

"Sounds like a plan to me," I said, happily.

Back upstairs, she made some space in her closet for me to hang up my few things and showed me what her mother had given her for Christmas.

"Here's my big present," she said, taking down a garment bag from the higher rod in the closet and unzipping it. Out came an absolutely beautiful charcoal grey velveteen empire-waisted Chanel jumper with ties at the sides and a jewel collar. It wasn't a mini but not long either.

She said, "You know I could wear it with a black or grey turtleneck sweater and black tights and ballet flats, and look artsy don't cha know—Audrey Hepburn in *Funny Face*. Or I could dress it up with a white silk shirt and pearls and shoes with squash heels and look like Jackie." She knew I would approve of that; I was obsessed.

It was so gorgeous I couldn't take my eyes off it. But I had no idea in those days of what a Chanel anything could cost. This piece was probably in the $3,000 range when dresses I bought were like $10.99.

"Are you going to bring that back to school?"

"Maybe. Don't know where I'd wear it there, though. But I'll wear it to the theater this week."

"Yes. Far out."

And so we began our fun-filled, --- "mad, gay, exciting" as Cass called it ---running around in Chicago. Luckily I had worn boots to her house, not knowing if it would snow more, and they were comfortable, because we walked miles—inside the museum and outside on the Avenue. I loved the art museum and had no idea at the time that this trip to it would mark the first of hundreds I would later make over the course of a life in Chicago. We ate Chicago pizza and Chicago hotdogs and had chocolate malts and more tea.

And later that week, we packed up overnight bags and headed into the city once more to stay at the penthouse apartment of Hyde Enterprises. Martin dropped us off and we were ushered in by the doorman to the lobby of the Hyde Building nestled in the Loop by the river but soaring high above most of its neighbors. Architecturally, the Hyde building did not stand out like the Wrigley Building or the brand-new Marina City that we could see really well glittering in the night sky right out the windows from

Cass' place. Of course Mr. Hyde and Bertrand Goldberg knew each other and John-Wilfred was one of the first architects in the field to praise the Marina City concept.

"Does he wish he'd thought of it? "I asked Cass, mesmerized by how people were actually living in there like the Jetsons.

"I don't think so, "Cass pondered. "It's not exactly his thing."

The apartment on the 35th floor was as mind-blowing-- in a completely different way-- as the house was to me. We entered into a long dark entryway only lit by spot track lighting shining specifically on modern sculptures placed at intervals on high glass shelves; a few larger pieces were installed along the walls on tables and pedestals. This hall gave into a great room of wall-to-wall, floor-to-ceiling windows. Draperies worked on an automatic system of degrees of open and close. They folded into the corners, but mostly they were kept open, except in the heat of summer days. The view was unobstructed that high and no one could see in, so we really weren't concerned about privacy and modesty.

The main living space was mostly non-defined except by conversation areas. One part of the space was sunken and I would have described that as the living room if there had been one. It had an artistic area rug of white and brown soft shaggy squares around which were placed modern sectional sofas done in brown leather with long pieces and square corner extensions. In front of those was a square glass box of a table with one large book of the art of Willem De Kooning resting on top of it. Back up in the space that was even with the entry hall, they had a black lacquer dining room table with seating for 15 people. A modern crystal chandelier hung above that but there wasn't much other lighting. At one end of the expanse, Japanese pocket doors separated a "den" type dedicated space that was a bit more normal looking with wainscoting and décor that gave off "office" more than living. They had a telescope set up at the window. The seating was utilitarian but comfortable.

An enormous wrap-around terrace was accessible at various points in the space, and there were different furnishings on that terrace, depending on which exit you took. One had a fire pit and deep couch seating around it. Another had a barbeque and outdoor kitchen with a long rustic table around which ten could sit easily.

At the other end of the apartment was the kitchen area, which was all open and consisted of a wide oblong island with a marble counter top and three burnished chrome lights hanging above it; and all the appliances and cabinets rather camouflaged themselves and hid in pale grey paint. The Sub-Zero fridge and freezer disappeared into the cabinetry and the only thing you could actually make out at first glance was the Viking cook top with its six gleaming gas burners.

Off the kitchen there was an actual wing of rooms that had doors: three bedrooms and a library. But what a library! Absolutely stark white with one wall of windows looking onto the river, which all the rooms on that side did, and three other walls of shelving completely full almost to the ceiling with books. There must have been a thousand of them! In the middle of the room was another two-piece cornered sectional, only this time grey-blue fabric and very comfortable. Two Louis XV armchairs covered in grey silk stood opposite the couches, and in the middle of that vignette was a big coffee table made of black engineered wood and steel. Right outside sliding doors of this room was yet another part of the terrace where the Hydes had put a smaller glass table and chairs with outdoor cushions on them. It was enclosed like a lanai and had a pergola over it with hanging plants. Container gardens and flower boxes flanked one entire end of this terrace.

In this glass-enclosed sky perch of a house, Cass' bedroom was the antithesis of her Kenilworth one: bare, modern, minimalist, yet whimsical with a big white bed, an architect's drawing table for a desk, plus bookshelves, and a white leather love seat. She had a white George Nelson bubble saucer light that came down on a retractable cord from the ceiling, and several smaller lamps around the room, too. Her room had the best natural light any artist could want for painting, but she didn't have any easels set up or any visible art supplies on hand that I could see.

When I asked her about that she reminded me, "I don't get to stay here all that often. This isn't really my room, ya know. But I use it when I'm here."

The apartment had staff, but except for the actual housekeeper of the penthouse itself, Mrs. Kritchfield, who was there waiting for us, they all actually worked for the company, showing up when the

Hydes were there and especially when they entertained. Mrs. Kritchfield asked what we wanted for dinner that night before we took off for the day. Cass was to choose from a list of menu items.

"What would you like to dine on tonight?" she chirped at me, as if this were living high on the hog for her as well as for me, when it turns out it wasn't.

"Make an executive decision," I giggled, still giddy from being in an actual palace in the sky. "I'll eat anything."

And when it was dinner time, a chef from Hyde Enterprises, whom Cass didn't really know, appeared in the kitchen, ready to make us whatever Cass wanted. She had chosen manicotti. What we got was an appetizer of antipasti meats and cheeses, olives, artichoke hearts and cucumbers, plus *insalata caprese*; followed by the main course: spinach chicken stuffed manicotti with green beans and bacon bits, and for dessert ricotta cheesecake with dark chocolate espresso sauce.

"You're going to have to roll me down the 35 floors to the car," I said, trying hard to finish what was served to me. The antipasti would have been a fine meal in itself for me. But the food was so amazingly delicious, I had a hard time declining anything that was offered.

Julia Hyde had gotten us tickets to *Barefoot in the Park,* a play that had done fabulously well on Broadway, and would be made into a movie before I got out of college. Their national touring company was in Chicago at the Oriental Theater, and we had great seats on the main floor. The Oriental had seen better days when we were there in 1966 but you could still see that the interior was more splendid than anything I had ever laid eyes on. Since the theater was so close to the apartment, Martin had gone back to Kenilworth, and the doorman sent us off in a cab. But afterwards Cass decided we'd just walk back.

"My parents wouldn't approve of this, but I promise you, it's less than a ten-minute walk."

"Well, I have my new hood ---I'll be fine."

Downtown Chicago wasn't safe at night by any means for young women, but there were two of us and enough people out and about--- coming from the theater, coming home late from work and dining out--- that we weren't afraid at all, and indeed we made it back to the building safe and sound.

When we returned to the apartment, Mrs. Kritchfield was up and waiting for us, but she wasn't about to be a babysitter, and said her goodnights. She was the housekeeper but she had her own apartment a couple of floors below and we didn't see her again until the next day. We weren't in the mood to watch t.v. but we tuned **WLS** on the radio in Cass' room and talked for a good two hours, just like we did in the dorm.

"So where do you want to live when you graduate?" I asked her. It would happen a year before me. I was curious as to her choices of lifestyle. "Would they ever give you this apartment?"

"NO! Are you joking?"

"Well, just a thought."

"I don't really know where I want to live. But I know I want to do art, so maybe grad school at the Art Institute? It's where they suggested I go in the first place, but luckily my high school teacher convinced them that I had to study with Mauricio."

"Which you'll get to do eventually?"

"Have to! I just hope I'm good enough."

"You are! So! You could be here, after all. I think that's cool. I like Chicago."

Yes, I liked Chicago--- what wasn't to like with what I had just seen? Nothing but luxurious digs and wonderful food, art, shopping and theater. Nothing like the real world I would probably have to be prepared to live in if I moved there after college: rents in the stratosphere, free time in the laundromat, eking out a meal or two---and that's IF I could find a job. I didn't want to become a teacher like my parents were already starting to insist that I do; but I wanted to use French in my work. That's exactly why I had to study in France.

"I want to show you something else, "Cass said rather hesitantly.

She went over to a wall of drawers and pulled out sheets of drawing paper.
They were children's portraits of some kind, done in pencil, not colored. I leaned over the drafting table where she spread them out.

"These are my ideas for... are you ready...dolls."

"Dolls?"

"Yes. I think I could design dolls to look like children themselves. When I was little my parents were in Germany somewhere, I can't remember, and they saw a doll in a little shop window. Germany has fabulous toys, you know? So does France, and all those countries. But Germany has these really famous dolls made by Kestner among others, and my parents thought one of them looked like me, and they bought it.

"So do you still have it?"

"Yes, but I didn't actually play with it. It's a porcelain doll. But MY idea is to design dolls that look like a certain kid, and have it manufactured like a regular toy that kids could play with—only it looks like them, so it could be a substitute friend, etc. And there's this other German company called Götz. A couple of years ago, the Götz company made the first reproductions of original artist dolls by Sasha Morgenthaler, the daughter of the Bauhaus artist Morgenthaler, and friend of Paul Klee. Do any of these names ring a bell with you?

"Nope. Well, yes, Paul Klee –we saw some of his works in the museum, right?"

"Yes—he's famous. This Götz company is the founder of the artist doll reproduction! I would like to sell them on my idea."

"That's a brilliant idea, Cass. But have you thought up a way to do that?"

"My fantasy is to take my idea to Germany and talk to them about it."

"YES! Even if they didn't grab onto the idea of you sketching actual children and making dolls to match their features, they should like your doll drawings anyway."

"Well, I don't want to be a commercial artist, and I really don't even want to work in the manufacturing end of anything. But last year we had to do a project where we developed an artistic product, and that was mine. I thought of it because of my old doll. And then one of the other students in the class, a guy named Evan, designed clothes for my doll idea for his project, and we worked together on it."

"Gee, did you get an A on that assignment?"

"Yes. The U of I isn't known for clothing courses, though, in our art school. Iowa State is. I'm not sure why Evan wasn't in Ames, actually now that I think about it; he really should have gone to the Fashion Institute or Parsons or somewhere. "

"Half my high school class went to ISU. Not an artist among them."

I was joking around but actually Cass had once again amazed me with her talent. What couldn't she do?!

"I think this summer I am going to get this back out and work on it," she announced, putting the papers into a plastic folder and returning them to the drawer. "I could get some sort of permission to hang around the University Day Care service and sketch the children. Maybe they could put the sketches up for parents to see or something."

"That's a neat idea." I said, pondering a room lined with the children's portraits done by Cass.

"Of course, my real goal is printmaking this summer. Oh, kid, it's going to be so cool with us living in Iowa City the whole summer, and working in the studio, isn't it?"

"Absolutely. I just hope I can find a job. "

She looked up and gave me a little smile. "It will work out, I just know it. When we get back there in two weeks, we should start lining up a place. I'm sure in the summer, apartments get snapped up."

"And I haven't sprung this plan on my parents yet, of course," I said. "But even if they don't like it, I'm still going to do it," I added, trying to convince myself.

We were back in Kenilworth for a few days before we had to start packing to go to Cass' grandmother's house in Springfield. I just loved hanging out in Cass' beautiful bedroom, and even though we had the run of the place, we decided to get some actual final exam prep in; and we settled in back up in her room. I loved snuggling into her chintz love seat and reading by the fireplace. The maid had stocked the log holder and kindling bucket, so we could have a fire going all day, while snow fell outside and temperatures plunged below zero.

I was re-reading *Gulliver's Travels* for my final paper for Alan Jones' class, comparing Swift to Rabelais; I had not yet read *Gargantua and Pantagruel* in French--- but soon would. I also had pages and pages of biology notes on our final experiment which was using the spectroscope containing a prism at the one end which we operated to see the spectrum of the visible light.

In the biology core course at Iowa, it seemed like I was always two weeks behind with one foot poised on the rocky precipice of failure. But the light chapter was different. My notes were pretty thorough, and didn't slide off the page for once, since I hadn't fallen asleep in lab like I tended to do in the lectures. I didn't like Life Science one bit, but I did pay decent attention on the components of the light in this section. I had actually liked doing these experiments.

We were working with the light spectrum, and this perfectly tied into my art history course when we got to Impressionism. In Claude Monet's time, the spectrum and light and wave theories were in their naissance, and being put into practice by Monet and his followers

Our experiments were probably NOT akin to what Monet was trying, but the role of light was foremost on our minds in Iowa City for this lab just the same. I imagined Monet making use of the same information in my notes: that when visible light is passed through a prism, it is separated into its different components according to their respective wave lengths. Red light has the longest wave length followed by orange, yellow, green, blue and violet in that sequence.

In our lab, we had had to obtain a spectroscope which contained a prism on one end. When the spectrum was clearly visible, we held a vial of chlorophyll solution in front of the spectroscope and we observed which portions of the spectrum were changed. Those parts of the spectrum which decreased or disappeared were being absorbed by the leaf chlorophyll solution. I made two rough sketches of the spectra before and after the solution test, and I designated on my pictures the portions important in photosynthesis because of absorption by chlorophyll.

This wouldn't have been so bad, but the light and chlorophyll work was just a tiny fraction of the material I had to master for this course's final exam, and I was pretty pessimistic of my ability to learn even half of it. Just for the second quarter of the course besides Photosynthesis and Leaves, we had digestion and respiration, angiosperm structure and function; a thorough study of the eye, and circulatory structures and processes. It was all too much!

"How's French going?" Cass asked me.

"French I don't have a problem with! I love French tests; they're too easy! What about you? Are you ever going to start a modern language? You should take French! I'll help you. "

Cass had passed out of a language requirement for her BA because she'd had so much Latin in secondary schools. But being able to speak another language was always something desirable for a liberal arts student of any major.

"You know I want to. I guess I'll start it in the fall."

"Well, I mean—you know, French…art…they go together like the proverbial horse and carriage."

"Yep. And so do Italian and German," she chided me.

"I suppose. But take French!"

"How about your Art History?"

"I've got that. Not going to be a problem. I'm just scared of flunking Biology and Movement Principles. Those two damn classes are on a trajectory to ruin my grade point average."

Physical education classes, a requirement for the degree at Iowa, were divided into quarters. We both did great in fencing, but after that I had to take Movement Principles, which was, in essence, an exercise class. Cass had already taken it the previous year, so she was in Modern Dance second quarter. I had to face Movement alone. They measured weight and body mass before the class began and again after it finished. If you didn't lose weight, you didn't pass. I had no weight to lose, frankly. I weighed ninety-seven pounds going into college; I had weighed the same the last three years of high school. My weight didn't fluctuate and I could eat anything.

Cass would laugh at me having chocolate malts in the soda shop under Burge Hall while she had phosphate, which they made the old-fashioned way with two ounces of some flavoring syrup (Cass preferred strawberry), plus ten ounces of carbonated "soda" water and a half teaspoon or so of acid phosphate. She said she liked it; I didn't care at all for the taste. Cass was not overweight by any stretch of the imagination, but she was bigger than me—bigger bone mass and taller. I could still wear her clothes, but she really didn't fit in mine, nor would she have wanted or needed to borrow them, which I knew and accepted as completely normal. She was slightly mystified by the idea that I had malts and cheeseburgers and pizza once a week and didn't gain a lot of weight. She always felt she would balloon up if she ate like that. Truth be told, I didn't pay much attention to weight.

We had a meal plan that I adhered to in the dorm, and on the weekends when they didn't serve us meals, everyone ate out. Cass and I usually had breakfast (when we made it up on time) and dinner together but I didn't normally see her for lunch. Neither of us liked the dorm food, but going down the line, if you really hated the main

74

course, you could usually find enough salads, breads and side dishes to make it seem like a meal. During freshman year, I was on a five dollars per week budget from my parents for spending money, which didn't go very far in the way of anything "extra" for eating out. I tried hard to save. And in those rare instances where I found a quarter in the bottom of a purse, for example, I'd think I could have a treat of some sort! Much to my absolute delight, once in a while Nana sent me extra money, and that was the source of relief and celebration with a malt.

Cass had tried to reassure me about grades, saying, "If you ace the three other academic courses, even if you fail life science and gym, you'll still come out okay."

She was right. I did get three A's, a C and an A in fencing with an F in Movement Principles that semester, and my grade-point did not dip below 3.0 like I feared. In fact, I got a 3.2 that first semester of university. Luckily those Phys Ed classes were weighted differently than the other ones. Whatever way it worked out, I was happy.

At the end of the second week in Kenilworth, as planned, we were packed up and driven in the Bentley to Springfield, Illinois, and the "Springfield Homestead." Her great-grandparents had named their place that ironically, since they had settled there from Springfield, Virginia., and it just happened that the place they settled already had the same name.

As we approached the house about half a mile from Old Route 54, and turned onto a long gravel road that led to a winding driveway which encircled the entire home, I could already see that this place was going to be magnificent. The house itself was very very old, a specimen of gingerbread-accented Queen Anne architecture, with a huge turret and windows divided into small diamond-shaped beveled glass panes. I had not gasped out loud when we pulled up to the Kenilworth house that night (though I might have had I been able to see its size in the daylight) but I did when we drove onto the striated dark and light gray paving stone drive of her grandmother's place. It was a yellowish cream and coral storybook structure like something off the set of Mary Poppins. Martin parked in front of a lovely wrought-iron gate with a fleur-de-lys motif and the top spear tips spaced every two feet apart.

The entrance wasn't that imposing, really, with only a few steps up to the narrow double front doors and a wrap-around porch defined by a white wrought-iron railing. But the house fanned out on either side towards the turret on one side, which rose three floors upwards - even higher than TWO chimneys on the roof of the main house, and had a widow's walk around it on the second level. Even in the turret there were little dormer windows which made the house some four or five floors high. On the opposite side it seemed to me that the home had been added onto during some previous generations, but the overall paint scheme tied it all in together. It had peachy pink trim everywhere with very extensive, elaborately detailed embellishments of hand carved wooded latticework.

"Oh Cass, " I gasped, leaning towards the car window. "This is just GORGEOUS. Oh, my God, if I had a house like that, I would never leave it."

"I do love this place, " she admitted in a soft voice.

The house was surrounded by lavish gardens—wildly "jardin à l'anglaise" and some old-fashioned benches, all completely covered in snow when we got there. The white drifts just added to the gingerbread design of the other white trimmings and made the whole picture look like a sugary pièce montée wedding cake.

Cass and I walked up the shoveled walkway and the few steps to the doors being opened in front of us by her grandmother. Cass flew into her arms, exclaiming, "GRANNY! How are you?"

"Oh, Cassandra, how wonderful to see you!"

• "And Gran, this is Sari Shrier, my houseguest for the winter break."

"How do you do?" I said, offering my hand to her.

"Welcome, dear!" she said to me, shaking my hand, but putting her other arm around my shoulders. "I'm so happy to meet you."

Anne-Louise Armistead Scott was Julia's mother, and the widow of Hamish Bronwyn Scott of the Scott publishing dynasty. Born in Philadelphia in 1883, he had moved with his family to Chicago to open the branch of HH Scott and Co. that would become even larger and more of a flagship of the family business than the Philadelphia office. Hamish went to Yale and knew Edward Hyde from the crew team, even though he was three years younger than Edward. This would become germane once their children were introduced to one another: Julia to John-Wilfred. It was a serendipitous coincidence that the two fathers had been pretty close friends, at least during the rowing seasons.

Anne-Louise's own family had been the ones to homestead the land, moving from Virginia in the early 1860's. Her great grandfather and grandfather increased the 160 acres the government gave everyone to more than ten-thousand acres at one time. A lot of it had been sold off over the decades, but the Armisteads still held many millions of dollars' worth of land holdings. Anne-Louise's father, Beauregard "Beau" Armistead was no farmer, however; he became a lawyer and then distinguished himself as an Illinois Supreme Court justice. His brothers and sisters all played a role in running the agricultural aspects of their family, and Anne-Louise, the eldest of all the children of any of these people, and thus, the matriarch, was given the rights to the original home and the land of the original Homestead farm. Her father had had many tenants farming this land, while his siblings formed an agricultural corporation with the rights and privileges to buy more land or sell it off; rent it, farm on it, have corporate farms on it or develop it for any housing or commerce they chose, as long as they didn't touch the original 160 acres, terms that were agreeable to all.

Anne-Louise was a homebody and didn't elect to go to the East Coast for college, but had stayed in the Chicago area and had gone to Lake Forest. She and Hamish had met at a Christmas dance at the Union League Club. Of course, the Scotts had a Chicago residence as well, a big brownstone in the city's Gold Coast neighborhood, but that home was sold when Hamish died; and Anne-Louise now had an apartment in the Hyde Enterprises building that she kept fully staffed and ready for any of her potential stays, but which she inhabited less and less in her dotage, preferring to stay down at the Homestead. Julia would, in time of course, inherit the Springfield place, as would Cass, eventually, I presumed.

Once again Martin carried our suitcases upstairs while Anne-Louise ushered us into the dark paneled foyer, past a grand staircase that we veered away from and into an elegant "salon" living room, decorated in Victorian tufted furniture that was more comfortable than it looked. Cass sat next to her grandmother on a royal blue velvet settee. Anne-Louise's maid brought in two trays of sandwiches, salad, fruit, tea cakes and hot tea. I luckily had taken a chair near a little round side table, because balancing a china cup and saucer on my lap while trying to eat sandwiches was not my forte; I was a klutz even when I tried to be really careful, as I had discovered only too well during Rush Week.

The food was divine. We were ravenous and ate it with gratitude and gusto. I put milk in my tea. It was my new fave rave.

Cass' grandmother was interested in our schoolwork and in our social lives. She wasn't prying but instead seemed genuinely involved in what we had to say. She knew all about Mauricio Lasansky and was keeping track of Cass' efforts to become his student while at Iowa U. And she was energetically affirmative of my dreams to study in Paris at a later date. In the meantime, she thought, we'd have a good time sharing an apartment near campus in the summer.

"College days are the best of your lives," she said wistfully. "Cherish them."

"Oh, we do!" Cass assured her. "And we brought a lot of materials to study while here, Gran. Finals are right when we get back."

"I remember," Anne-Louise said, "from last year when you came by yourself, Cass. I'm so glad you brought Sarah this time. I want you two girls to make yourselves right at home, all right?"

"Thank you, Mrs. Scott," I said, realizing that I hadn't brought her a single thing as a hostess gift. *Shit.*

"You know," Cass said to her grandmother, "Sari and I each have a maternal widowed grandmother. I met hers at Thanksgiving, and now she's met you! And she's close to her grandmother and I'm close to you! I think that's pretty cool." She sat back against the wooden framed sofa's tufted back, contentedly.

I smiled, a bit embarrassed at this mention of my family, but also happy to see the favorable comparison. *My grandmother was more of a bubushka when compared to this stately, elegant, svelte, society matron. That wasn't really fair to Nana Clara. In her own right, my Nana was a pillar of her community, too…a volunteer, a Jewish community leader and a business owner's real partner in every way. She could stand proudly at my grandfather's side at a Chamber of Commerce cocktail party in The Bluffs and she could stand behind an eight-burner stove in the kitchen of his bar and turn out vast amounts of wonderful food. She could balance the books as well as a tray of plates. Over the years she had managed to travel and having learned English right away in school, she began a lifelong habit of reading voraciously in order to educate herself in the subjects of literature, theater and interior design. But she was a first generation American, having come to New York from Russia at three years old, a member of a large immigrant family who wound up on the Great Plains as a matter of happenstance.*

We finished the delicious tea and conversation, and then repaired up to Cass' room, the THIRD absolutely stunning bedroom of hers that I would see on this trip. This time the dimensions were more "normal" but the jewel box of a room was still like something out of the movies to me, with its the semi-circular window seat below eight-foot high beveled glass windows swagged with cream silk valences. On the sides, matching silk draperies hung straight down and were never pulled closed. There was an antique writing desk, another Victorian tufted love seat, this time in the faintest blush pink; a beautiful fireplace with a gold screen in front of its marble mantel; and her bed: canopied once again, this time with fringe on the sides, indicating it came from at least three generations earlier than her one in Kenilworth. The bedspread, which covered a thick duvet, was the same faint pink as the sofa and the bed was smaller—a double one nonetheless. It was tall but when we laid on it, we sank deep into its featherbed of a mattress.

We turned on "the fire" and it seemed so perfect burning away in that old-fashioned room, lending its glow to the flocked wallpaper and shiny parquet flooring. A huge, thick pink and cream carpet with a small flower motif was laid under the bed and went far enough out to be able to also define the sitting room portion of the whole room. But there was still enough space for the hardwood flooring to make its statement and reflect the firelight.

"We have one problem, "Cass said to me as we unpacked.

What could that be? I wondered. Bathroom down the hall? Not enough blankets? No closet space? Hah! Wrong on all accounts.

"What?"

"I want to show you around Springfield, of course, and all the important Lincoln stuff."

"Yes, and I want to see it all. I love Abraham Lincoln."

"Well, I don't drive and neither does Gran. When I'm here by myself and want to go into town, Gran's chauffeur does take me, but I don't think it would be much fun to be chauffeured around this little town, do you? I think we should be free to go where we please without making him wait for us everywhere."

"Oh, well, I drive. I'm a good driver. "

"Yeah, I was hoping you'd say that. But you don't want to drive a limo, and I'm not sure what other cars are around here. There used to be some of my cousins'. And then here's the deal: will they let you take one of those cars if they are here? I think there's a Mustang! "

"Well, I can't drive a stick shift very well, so that could be a problem, you're right." *Not to mention the insurance situation, which we didn't.*

"I'll find out. "

And she left me to laze around the room. I had to peek into the bathroom and put some things in there. OLD! My goodness, I was surprised to see its octagonal floor tiles and a claw foot tub right in the middle, which had a hand shower but no other shower was present. White beadboard came up three-fourths of the walls, and the top fourth was the same wallpaper as in the bedroom. Pink towels hung from thick silver rods. There was a tall white radiator on one wall and above it, an old portrait of a distinguished man and woman hung down from wire. The sink was very old and supported on two sides by ironwork. It wasn't a pedestal sink but also not a built-in so the idea of space to put anything was not to be solved. Above that was a round mirror encased in a silver frame. The toilet was off to one side but not hidden away; all the faucets, knobs, and drawer pulls were silver with ivory. The hot and cold were marked in old type. In the middle of the ceiling, centered over the bathtub was a huge crystal chandelier, but over the sink someone had added track lighting, which looked very out of place, but which gave off needed light for doing one's makeup. Another door led out into the hallway, which was lighted by another lovely chandelier and some small sconces all down the corridor. We had come up the grand paneled staircase and the perfectly polished banisters of it turned a corner at one end and went up another two floors. If I leaned over the banister, I could see all the way down into the foyer and the marble entryway down there. When I made my way back to the bedroom, the floor, uneven in places, creaked under my shoes. But nothing gave the idea of "run down" or decaying. The place was as solid and as well-kept as a prized antique.

Cass came back and took a deep breath. "Well, you've got their permission to drive, but you'd better come out and see these cars! Hah! And grab your coat," she added, taking hers, too.

She led me down out the bedroom and instead of taking the big staircase, she directed me down the hall to an opening with a back staircase that led straight into the kitchen. Mrs. Scott's chauffeur, Eddie, was waiting for us. I was already wearing boots, but Cass slipped out of her ballet flats and into a pair of Wellington boots at the back door. Those were boots made for gardening or tramping across the moors or something, but I was amused that they were kept at the ready for her.

We went out to a garage that was more of a grange---not too far from the back door but out into a graveled part of the circular drive and across from a big cement bird-bath fountain flanked by those same little semi-circular cement benches her Kenilworth house had, positioned by a flowerbed lying dormant during the winter.

The big barn doors were open wide and several cars were parked inside, the main one being a black 1965 Cadillac limousine that was Granny Scott's regular car. But right away, I caught sight of the *pièce de résistance* in my mind: a turquoise 1955 Ford Thunderbird with wire rims and a white top that had that iconic little round window on the side; and on the trunk was a turquoise spare tire holder. It was so beautiful it took my breath away.

"Oh my God, Cass, THAT is my mother's favorite car!"

Indeed that was Betty's favorite car, so I knew it well. She would have died to have one, but it was waaaay out of our budget, and besides, Sol would only buy practical cars. At home I drove a 1959 Rambler station wagon with vinyl seats so worn out that they had to have towels stuck in them.

I couldn't drive the Thunderbird though, because it was a manual transmission.

"Any of these automatics?" I inquired of Eddie, as I turned my gaze round about to reveal a Chevrolet "Deluxe Four-Door Sedan" in yellow with a brown roof with gleaming wide white-wall tires, and a cream-colored steering wheel that seemed huge; plus another limousine-length navy blue Mercury Montclair, which was beautiful but also just enormous. I had a moment of panic wondering if I drove it anywhere, would I be able to park it?

"The Chevy here is, Miss. "

The old Chevy was about the most "regular" car of the entire lot, and reminded me of an old car my grandparents had back in the day.

"Well, then, the Chevy it is," I chirped. "Let's hope I can see out the windshield."

When we were ready to go out and about the next day, it had stopped snowing and the roads were more or less plowed. Eddie assured me that I wouldn't have any trouble with the car, but if we did get into any jams, we should find a phone and call home; he would come and get us.

I didn't have to back it out because he had it waiting for us and I just put it in drive and went forward around to the front of the house and down the straight part of the drive to the road, and then to the highway. It drove like a dream and really even though it looked fat and all, I didn't even need the extra little pillow he had put in there in case I actually couldn't see out.

"I love this car, " I said. "I like cars anyway."

"I love something, too, "Cass said, hinting at mirth.

"What?"

"Sitting in the front seat!"

"Come on. You mean to say that you never sit up front? Don't you and your dad or mom, sometimes, you know, just go off anywhere alone… no chauffeur?"

"NO! Are you mad?"

"Well, I guess I am. *Boy, I couldn't decide if that was sad or if she was just lucky!* You know, though, you ought to get a driver's license. Just to have. Pretty soon you're going to be living on your own, aren't you? I mean, let's say you go to the art institute and have an apartment. Won't you go grocery-shopping or take stuff to the dry-cleaners?"

"Sari. Think about it. I live in cities. You don't NEED a car in Chicago. You don't WANT a car in Chicago. I can get groceries delivered! I can send out dry cleaning with the doorman in the building--- well, if I live in my father's building. Even if not—most stuff is within walking distance; or you'd choose a place to live that was near shops."

78

"Geeze, when you were at my house, did you notice that we didn't walk ANYWHERE?"

"Yes, but we weren't there very long and had specific places to go."

"Yes, and we didn't walk to any of them, except to get the bus. And don't tell me you'd never take public transportation in Chicago."

"Taxis, yes. Not the 'El', but I took the metro in Paris and the tube in London," she hastened to add. "Now those are places you really do not want a car!"

So right then and there, I was once again confronted by the fact that Cassandra Hyde was oblivious to the life her peer group was living. She was nineteen years old and had never driven a car, shopped for food, done her own laundry (and when she did try it at Iowa U she was bad at it), shopped for her own clothing –only briefly and then not seriously to clothe herself; she had never earned any money, but I sensed that was about to change. Because she had designed and executed some of the most beautiful art I'd ever seen, not to mention from a teenager, and she was knowledgeable and serious about art far beyond her years. We just came from the proverbial two different worlds, is all. I had to laugh at the way I could easily glide right into her world, and she would probably rather die than have to inhabit mine.

She guided me through the streets of Springfield and the first important tourist "monument" we passed was the State Capital in downtown. We decided not to park and tour it, but I thought it looked impressive. There were other places she wanted me to see, more having to do with Abe Lincoln. So since we were in the town, first we went to the law offices where he had practiced law.

The Lincoln-Herndon Law offices were made into a state history museum by then and were very interesting. We parked as close as possible and went inside. There were also historic houses as part of the installation of the museum, which I loved. I liked the red brick colonial buildings on that block and the bronze statues of the President, Mary Todd Lincoln and Tad waving to passersby. Inside his office was restored and rather stark! But the big desk, with cubby holes like you'd have seen in an old post office, was imposing; and there were also glass-doored bookshelves holding law books. In the same building was a court room with candles on the green-covered tables and big iron chandeliers with tiers of candles above. Both rooms had huge black stoves, reminding us that these places must have been really cold in the winter.

We drove past what she called the Lincoln Library but it was in the process of being dismantled.

"They're going to rebuild it keeping the outside exactly as it was, but tearing the rest down to the studs. It will become the Lincoln Presidential Library as well as the Springfield public library, but who knows when that will all be done."

"Looks like it was quite nice. At least they're keeping the outward appearance."

We then proceeded to Eighth Street and Lincoln's Home. It was in the city proper and not on an estate of any kind, but it was run by the National Park Service and they had restored the whole neighborhood, not just his house, to look the way it had when Lincoln lived there.

The big tan clapboard house with green shutters was surrounded by a painted wrought iron fence draped with red, white and blue bunting every few feet. The house sat right at the sidewalk with hardly any lawn or garden at all in front of it. We had passes which Granny Scott had arranged, and when we entered, we first saw a film depicting life in Springfield in the seventeen years Abraham Lincoln had lived there. It was very cool to also meander around the streets and see the other old places which had been restored and were made examples of specific aspects of historic preservation. We went through all the twelve rooms; it wasn't crowded at that time since regular school was already back in session after the Christmas holidays, and besides, it was the dead of winter.

After about a two hour walk through the house with a guide, and then the rest of the area on our own, we were ready for lunch. I didn't have to move the car from where I parked it for the Lincoln House because Cass was taking me to one of Springfield's most well-known and oldest restaurants, Maldaner's, "started by Dutch settlers in 1884, " she explained tour-guide-like. We walked the snowy sidewalks towards a large maroon and red awning. And then I saw signage about Route 66 all over the windows.

"Noooo! Springfield was on the original Route 66?" I asked incredulously.

"Yep. Quite the notoriety this town has, eh?"

"I LOVE that show."

"What show?"

What? No. She could not be asking me that.

"Oh, GOD! You don't know Martin Milner and George Maharis and Glenn Corbet?! What planet have you been stranded on all these years?"

I didn't tease her too badly—I had barely heard of Paul Klee after all, when we were on "her turf." It's just that *Route 66* was seminal in my life: the Corvette, the THEME of the show, which was after all Kerouac-esque in its road-tripping.

"I don't want to belabor this point too much, Cass," I laughed, "but you're kind of out of it. *Route 66* was a really popular show! It portrayed the adventures of a very wealthy guy just out of Yale named Tod Stiles, who meets a working-class orphan named Buzz something or other, I forget, who had worked for Tod's dad on one of his ships. The dad was a shipping magnate."

She looked at me with the expression of someone who was waiting for a point to be made in there somewhere, so I continued.

"Buzz was a more 'beat generation' type. It's a long story but essentially the rich guy's father had gone bankrupt and the family didn't really know it until he died. The only thing he left his son was a new Corvette. So the son invites the working guy to join him on a trip straight across Route 66, looking for work, having whatever adventures that might befall them, and eventually finding out who they really were."

"Hmmm. Maybe I'll get to see it in reruns sometime."

"I hope so because besides how good the stories are, the music is primo. The theme song is one of my fave raves!" I started singing it for her: "*If you ever plan to motor west/ travel my way, take the highway that is best/ get your kicks on Route 66,*" I trailed off, rather embarrassed to have gotten carried away. "Did you know Nat King Cole wrote that?" I offered.

"Anyway, " I said, "here we are…getting our kicks on Route 66! Too cool."

Maldaner's was trippy in its own right. It had a large traditional old-time dining room, where we were seated in a green leather booth, flanked by glass partitions. Before we left, Cass showed me some of the private rooms, too, especially the Map Room, which had all brick walls with huge maps in frames on them. That room was set up for some sort of meeting with a podium and some hot tables. We didn't linger there. There was a public as well as a private bar, plus a dance floor. The place had everything and I loved it there.

"They're pretty famous for the home-made soups, " Cass said to me as we perused the lunch menu. Soup sounded good on a cold day like that was, so I ordered vegetable with beef and barley, and Cass chose their Tuscan wedding soup, which was a fancy minestrone, I found out. After that we split a BLT sandwich and I drank Coke. Cass had hot tea.

"Hot tea is great, "I ventured. (I especially loved it now, drinking it "white.") "But it doesn't quench thirst for me. I need ice."

"Coke eats the lining of your stomach," she chided me.

"I know."

When we were finished, we headed back out to the car for a ride a bit further to see Lincoln's tomb in the Oak Ridge Cemetery and the State Park housing some war memorials. The grounds were so vast that we made every effort to park as close as we could to the building that housed his tomb, which was in the center of a twelve-acre plot. His actual tomb was inside, down a corridor from the large rotunda of the memorial, in a "burial room" --very beautiful--, a large reddish granite tomb, behind which was inscribed on the wall, "Now He Belongs to the Ages." There was also a small reproduction of the great Lincoln Memorial in there, also done by Daniel Chester French, which I found delightful, only having seen pictures of the real one in books and magazines.

We didn't walk around outside for very long because we were cold, but I would have liked to have been able to see the historic memorials.

"There's a super huge bust of Lincoln down those steps, " Cass pointed out. "Everyone rubs his nose for good luck. That is so stupid, " she added, "treating Lincoln's nose as a rabbit's foot. It's all shiny now and the rest of the sculpture is tarnished with a brown patina. It looks ridiculous."

We skipped it. Back in the car, Cass announced that we were not done.

"You must see the Dana House. Can't be here and not see it."

"Okaaay. Just tell me how to get there." I had no idea what it was---another Victorian Civil War mansion?

"Three words. Frank. Lloyd. Wright."

"Oh wow."

"Oh, yes, wow. This is one of, if not **the** most magnificent of his houses. You haven't gotten to modern art yet in your class with Klampert, but you did do Impressionism and you studied how the Japanese print inspired Monet and his group, right?"

"Right."

"Well, they also had a big influence on Frank Lloyd Wright, and he interpreted it in architecture rather than another medium. This place is going to blow your mind."

And it did. The neighborhood was Springfield's ritzy district, formerly dubbed "Aristocracy Hill" and the Dana house was actually a REMODEL of a Victorian house, so I wasn't so far off after all. But remodel was not the word: tear down and rebuild, more like.

Growing up the daughter of a world-famous architect, Cass really knew her stuff, and she could demonstrate her command of architecture, art and art history without lording it over me or insulting my obviously inferior education.

"Susan Lawrence Dana commissioned Wright to redo her house," Cass explained, "and the two of them hit it off perfectly. He wanted to flesh out his ideas of his 'Prairie Style' and organic architecture."

"Organic architecture? What's that?"

"Well, you'll see…it's architecture he based on the flat Illinois landscape **and** Japanese prints' flat esthetic, too."

Among other aspects of this house, which was designed for showing off art and for entertaining as much as for residency of the owners, were four hundred fifty art glass windows, sky lights, door panels, sconces and light fixtures that he designed specifically for this house.

"Susan had a vast collection of Japanese prints, and Frank Lloyd Wright designed special easels for their exhibition. You won't see any inside, though—all the contents of this place were sold in the 1940's."

But we did get to see everything that had been built in, a hallmark of any Frank Lloyd Wright home, and all the modern stained-glass windows were intact. I may have been fairly ignorant of the great architecture of my country at eighteen years old, but at least I had the modicum of intelligence necessary to realize I was in the presence of greatness in that house; and I was very grateful to have been brought to it by Cassandra Hyde.

By the time we got out of there, we were exhausted, but also exuberant at all we'd seen and done. I drove the Chevy through the dusky streets west into the pallid winter sunset, retracing the path Cass had directed me on that morning. We pulled onto the long drive and made our way around the house and into the gravel courtyard between the garage and the back door. I lifted the gear shift arm into park, and turned off the engine. Eddie came right out to open the passenger door for Cass, while I opened my own door, and walked around to meet him with the keys.

"How'd she do?" he asked eagerly, meaning the car (!).

"Fantastic," I announced. "Love this car."

And so I got to drive it quite a bit while we were there. We went downtown another time to pick up some gloves for Granny at S.A. Barker's and I got to see Springfield's one and only chic shop; it still had a vacuum tube system for payments. We went through the store, (which was too big to be a boutique but not grand enough to be a department store), fingering all sorts of beautiful sweaters and trying on gold lamé flats.

And just before we were ready to leave, I spotted something that I "had" to have: a charm bracelet of the U.S. states. It didn't have all fifty—the point was you were to collect the charms as you visited/lived in the states. I hadn't been very many places, but I had faves that I HOPED to visit, so I bought the sterling silver bracelet, which set me back $10! And then I picked out Iowa, Illinois, New York because it was my dream to live there, and California—same thing; Nebraska where I spent quite a lot of time; Missouri—I'd been to Kansas City with the parents once, plus St. Louis was on Route 66. Each charm was three dollars.

81

I spent most of my Christmas money that day – a whopping $28, but I immediately rationalized that it was worth it. I had the best souvenir of my first sojourn with the Hydes, plus it really meant something to me. I still have it.

Chapter Twelve

"Tuesday Afternoon"...Moody Blues

Cass and I still had a lot of studying to do for finals, so we stayed in most of the three other days we were at the Springfield Homestead. In any event, it wasn't nice enough weather to take long walks in the country and see more of the actual farm, and hanging around the house gave me a chance to get to know Cass' grandmother. We spent long hours talking to Granny Scott about her life there, in Chicago as an arts maven, and as a very committed and successful "professional volunteer." She had seen a lot of changes in the Chicago culture scene in her day, but found herself weary of the politics of it all, and happy to be retired back to her home. She did, however, acknowledge what an exciting and vibrant city Chicago was. I began to hope I'd end up living there somehow some day.

This entire vacation flew by far too fast for me. Soon Cass and I were being driven back to Iowa City by Martin in the Bentley. This time, as that magnificent car pulled up to the curb in front of Kate Daum, I felt like I was having an out-of-body experience climbing from it. Who might be looking at that very minute down on the sidewalk from their dorm room? Ha! And see me getting out of a Bentley!

Final exams were always in January and afterwards we went through the process of registration for second semester at the Field House. During the '60's, there were only hints of any sort of data processing methods being used. Mostly then, it was all by hand as we stood in long lines and watched as people wrote on large white boards which classes were closed. As the sections were filled, little bits of paper, too small to see from where I was standing, were posted to the boards as groans would rise up from the crowd. Being a second semester Freshman, I was in line dead last, and worried I wouldn't get into any of the classes or sections I wanted. You had to be prepared to change your schedule on the spot and hope to hell there would be something else you could take!

Cass had convinced me to keep taking art classes, reminding me that I had told her repeatedly that art and French always went well together. So I took my first studio class, which was in linoleum block printing. I had often watched her carve small blocks in our room and I knew she had all the tools I would need and could borrow if I had to work outside the classroom. Might as well learn from the master.

I took another English class that was required: Masterpieces of Literature, which wouldn't be full, since it was a designated freshman/sophomore class. Miraculously, I got in the French class I needed; and I reluctantly signed up for the dreaded next two quarters of P.E., which, for me were bowling and archery. I had to take the second semester of Biology, too, which absolutely depressed me just thinking about it. I liked school and this course was ruining it. But on the very bright side, I didn't have to take a single math class to graduate.

As I already knew, Cass, coming out of Rosemary Hall, had been far better prepared for college than I had been. She had tested out of several required classes upon arrival in Iowa City the year before me, and was already headed into her major course work earlier even than most sophomores. But she still had to take some non-art studies, and so she signed up for a class of modern poetry and, at my fervent suggestion, French 101, which I assured her should be a breeze after all the Latin she had already studied. She had two studio art classes, including Print-Making... though still not with Lasansky; and she had to also take Anthropology.

Right down the street from our dorm was an old, white clapboard house with a big covered porch that had been taken over by the university for programming. This is where the International House was, and since I intended to study abroad come hell or high water, and since I passed by it every day, I just decided to go in and see what it was all about. I had been active in high school in all activities pertaining to foreign exchange students; and since I was planning to be one shortly, it couldn't hurt to get to know them, I reasoned.

I was surprised to find many older, graduate students, and not very many from any country with which I was even remotely familiar. But they were nice people, and soon I found myself participating in their activities, from talks on Burma, to a film on New Zealand, to singing with their amateur choir. There was be a big performance around Valentine's Day in the Iowa Memorial Union, and they needed all the voices they could get to sing in many languages. That was right up my alley and soon I was happily ensconced in the second soprano section.

Our choir director was a music major from India named Shook Patel. I had always assumed students came from places like that to America to study agri-business or social work or something, but not music. Plus in a school in the heart of America's agricultural belt, one would have thought Indians from the Punjab would be more inclined to want to learn our farming ways to take back rather than our music. Shook was minoring in math, so that made more sense to me, although I still for the life of me, didn't get what he was doing there.

"You know, " he said to me in his cute British-Indian accent, "this university is recognized as one of the most excellent university-based schools of music in your country."

"Come on."

"It is true. And people come from all over to study music here."

Well, I wasn't going to dip my toe back in that debating morass, so I just accepted what he told me.

Iowa had several music groups and choirs for non-majors, but I didn't think I had time to get involved with the most famous one, The Highlanders, for which, under other circumstances, I would have gladly auditioned.

Cass knew all about the roadblock I'd encountered that first day of being a music major, and when she found out I'd been so active in choir in high school, she, too, thought The Highlanders would be perfect for me. So I did look into it, but even before auditions were happening, I realized I couldn't do it.

"They have to travel so much, it turns out, " I lamented. "There's also a pretty hefty cost for the outfits they wear."

From the get-go I had my sights set on studying in France, and I always felt I had to put blinders on to keep me focused in the direction of Paris. Nevertheless, The Highlanders were prestigious and wonderful, and I thought it would have been be great to continue with music on that level. Oh well, The International Singers would just have to do.

Cass was all for the idea and came with me to several of our practices, just to hear us and gauge the level of our musical output.

"You guys aren't half bad!" she pronounced one night after our big concert rehearsal, which she watched, and even photographed with this fantastic Leica camera she'd brought to school with her. "And, it's not nothing to be putting on a show in the Iowa Memorial Union."

"Do you think I could borrow one of your dresses? "I asked her that night in February, walking back to the dorm from rehearsal. "They want us in our own clothes, 'something dressy'."

"Sure. How about the blue one you like with the drop waist and low pink sash?"

I was hoping she'd say that!

"Thank you soooo much. I love that dress."

The night of the performance we singers didn't really have to be backstage or in any sort of make-shift green room because we didn't have to change into costumes or get make-up on; so we congregated near the big double doors that led to the ballroom, set up theater style with chairs in front of a portable stage. We got to watch the whole show until it was near our time to go on. One of the ushers was a student I recognized from my lit class. He recognized me, too, and came over.

"It's a pretty great show," he whispered to me.

"Yes, there's a lot of talent here."

"I'm Soren Carlysle, "he said very softly, shaking my hand. He pronounced his name "Sair-en" – like mine but with an "en" instead of an "ee" sound at the end.

"Sari Shrier," I said in a stage whisper, amused that our two names were so similar.

"I know your name. He calls on you a lot! Will you return here after you sing?"

"I think so. Isn't there some reception or other downstairs afterwards?"

"Okay, yeah, that's right. So...look for me out here, okay?"

I nodded and left with the other singers to make my way around and through the side doors where we would end up behind the stage.

We did our numbers and I saw Cass in the audience with Professor Klampert! Cass took some pictures of us up on stage with her Leica camera and I was rather touched that she thought this was a big enough deal to schlep that heavy thing in its leather case again into the concert. The photos she took that night showed me in her dress and came out lovely.

We singers had to stay behind, it turned out, in order to take the final curtain call with the entire ensemble, and so the ballroom had pretty much emptied out when I finally got back out front. Cass was nowhere to be seen so I looked around for Soren. He saw me from a spot near some couches they had moved to a distant corner of the room to set up the concert. He motioned to me.

"Hey, Sari!"

I waved and started walking his way. No one had begun to take the chairs down yet, so we sat in the back row and talked for a while.

"So, your name? "I ventured. "Like Soren Kierkegaard?

"I'm afraid so. My parents had an existential sense of humor."

"I'll bet that was fun in elementary school...probably not. How much were you teased? A lot I'll wager."

"Oh, you know... you get used to it. "he laughed. "Someday I'll visit Denmark and they'll all think it's as common as Bob."

"Well, I like different names. It's interesting. Anyway, tell me about your ushering job here. Do you get paid to do it?"

"Yes, but not very much. It's a small stipend under the auspices of the Student Programming Organization."

"Oh yeah, SPO---I see all kinds of flyers and posters promoting their activities. The Valentine's Dance, Mardi Gras festival...that stuff?"

"Yes, but there is also an entire season of music and lectures. If you usher, well, naturally, you get to attend free. It's worth it."

That did sound like a good deal.

"So should you be downstairs at the wing-ding? "he asked me, smiling.

"Yeah. You want to be my 'date'?" I joked.

"You bet."

And that was my first encounter with the boy who would become my soul mate and great friend, first serious relationship, first love, first lover and first guy to break my heart.

In the meantime, Shook Patel also asked me out, and I began to see him rather regularly. He was absolutely fascinating, sweet, very polite, a lot older than me, and a person of very dark skin tone.

This did not go unnoticed by some girls working in the cafeteria behind the serving area, who, when I came down the line with my tray, felt it was necessary to ask me about him.

"Are you dating an Indian guy?" one of them snickered.

"He's a friend of mine, yes, " I replied, a little surprised they gave a damn about what I did.

"He's very dark."

"Is he?"

However, that wasn't all of it. Some boys from my hometown had also seen me out with him, and one of them, while home on a weekend trip to attend an anniversary party for his parents that **my** parents also attended, told Sol I must be dating a "colored person."

Betty called me at school, and Cass answered the phone on the wall of our room.

"It's your mom!"

"Oh God, I wonder what happened!" I stretched the phone's long curly cord to my bed. "Mom?"

"Sari, "she began slowly. "If you date colored boys, white boys won't ask you out."

"WHAT?!" I was incredulous. "You called here long distance to tell me THAT? Who has been talking to you about who I date?!"

"Never mind about that," she sneered. "You know I'm not prejudiced." *(Like your father is, she should have added.)* "But you're just new to Iowa; you don't want to be stigmatized right off the bat there, do you?"

"Mother. First of all, he's Indian. Secondly, if people won't date me because I've gone out with someone of another race, culture, --whatever, then I wouldn't want to date them anyway, now would I? Do you see what I'm saying?"

"You're wrong about this, Sari. Now do me a favor and break if off with this boy before you regret it."

"He's not a boy, Mom, he's a graduate student. I met him singing in the choir at International House. He's really nice! You'd like him."

"Oy, he's that old? And no, you're mistaken. I wouldn't like him, so please, just be a good girl, and do what I ask. I'm trying to be calm here; you notice I didn't let Daddy call you. He's furious. Just end this, Sari. Good bye." And she hung up.

Of course I continued to see Shook, kept singing in the choir, and found myself still going out with him, mainly to the one Chinese restaurant in Iowa City. Our cultures **were** different. He liked having hot green tea in American Chinese restaurants, but what he really loved was his favorite drink of *lassi*, which, as explained to me was curd, plus milk, plus powdered sugar. It sounded ghastly.

"Oh, how I miss it, "he would sigh. "That and *sarson da saag* and *makki di roti*. I shall some day make that dish for you. "

"What is it?"

"It is very good! You need spinach and mustard leaves. And for the bread, maize flour. "

"You mean corn flour?"

"I am not sure it is the same."

"Hmmm. Well, spinach you can find here but good luck with mustard leaves. My family owns a restaurant and I've never seen a mustard plant in my life."

"Yes, I know. It is very sad in America for an Indian. Perhaps in New York one could find the ingredients, but certainly not here in Iowa."

If we didn't go out for Chinese food, we went to the Ramskeller and I had cheeseburgers while he ordered only salad every time.

If my parents thought I had failed to take their warnings to heart, they didn't say anything or call me again. Luckily, I hadn't told my mom about a conversation Shook and I had had over green tea one night in late February. We were sitting at the little table lit by a pretty red candle in a brass lantern, when all of a sudden he told me that he thought we should be together.

"We will go to India, to my home, and my grandparents will bless the union."

"That is absurd, and you know it. First of all, I'm JEWISH. I doubt your grandparents would bless THAT. Secondly, I'm only eighteen. I have years of schooling left. I have plans to study in France. I'm not ready to "be together" with anyone!"

"Very well. We will not talk of this now."

Yeah, I thought. Not now or later. Jesus.

Spring break was in early March that year and just as we were studying for mid-terms and preparing to leave campus for a week afterwards, I came down with some sort of flu. I was practically delirious in the room, feverish, coughing and sniffling. Cass was worried.

"I think you need to call a cab and go to Student Health," she admonished me.

"Oh no, I'm okay. It's clear across the river."

"So what? They can give you something!"

But I didn't follow her advice and just toughed it out taking aspirins and rubbing my chest with Vicks Vapo-Rub that I'd picked up from Whetstone Drugs. I stayed in bed for a day, studying. Luckily it was Dead Week and no classes.

Shook telephoned our room late on the Friday afternoon before mid-terms were to begin the next week. In my stupor of illness, I had forgotten about the International House's Spring Fling dance. He had asked me to go weeks before and now all of a sudden, here it was!

"Oh, Shook," I pined. "I'm so sorry. I'm sick! I don't think I should go."

"I do not believe you, Sarah. I just saw you two days ago."

"Well, believe me. Can't you tell by my voice? It just came on fast!"

"But I am counting on you to attend. Please do not disappoint me on this. I do not want to attend without you."

"But Shook, for heavensake, you'll know everyone there. It's no big deal!" I wheezed.

"Please. You must come."

"OKAY. Sheeeeesh! I'll come. Pick me up at the dorm. We can walk since it's so close."

This dance party was being held in the lovely Congregational Church right on Clinton Street. They had a big social hall with a kitchen, of course, and a stage and band stand. The place was crowded. I had managed to drag myself out of bed, shower, and put on my aunt's pink silk sheath and black patent leather squash heels. I wore a heavy coat because I still had chills. We had gone down a flight of stairs to find some coat racks set up outside the social hall, and as he helped me out of my coat, I began to feel myself falling forward into the rack. I grabbed onto other peoples' coats and steadied myself.

"Are you fine?" he asked somewhat taken aback.

"I don't feel so well, " I answered.

"Well, come in and we shall dance slowly."

I was feeling hot and sweaty but shivery also. I knew I needed to get back in bed.

"Maybe some punch?" I asked him. He walked me to a table and I took a seat.

"I shall fetch it."

We stayed there for a little while and I began to feel slightly better, so I didn't make a big fuss of wanting to leave. But after a couple of other slow dances, I had just about had it.

"I need to get back," I announced. "You can stay, seriously. I can walk to the dorm---it's right here."

"Okay. If you say you must leave, you must."

"Shook, I'm SICK!! I'm sorry you can't see that. Here, feel my forehead!" I expected him to repel in horror at how hot I must be.

"It is all right. Just go. I am leaving for Chicago next week for the Spring Break. I shall not see you before then because you have examinations."

"Well, have a nice time. Listen, if you want, you can call me at home." I reached into my evening bag and pulled out a pen. Taking one of the cocktail napkins from the table in front of me, I wrote my Bluffs home phone number on it and gave it to him.

I didn't have any tests the first day of mid-term exam week, and by Tuesday I was feeling better. I took my tests, thought I did pretty well, and went home on the train. Cass, in the meantime was being picked up by Martin and driven to Des Moines this time, where she was to catch a plane to New York and then to Switzerland.

I teased her. "You mean, your dad isn't sending the Hyde jet to take you straight to Zurich?"

She looked at me with a puzzled look on her face. "The Iowa City airport isn't big enough for that plane to land here."

"I was JOKING."

John-Wilfred Hyde couldn't land his jet in Iowa City, but he had landed the contracts with the Swiss hotel chain and had been in Europe ever since Christmas practically, working out of the London office when not in Geneva. They wanted Cass to join them for Easter, so the staff packed for her, sent her passport, and arranged for her to fly out to New York and then on to Switzerland. After a week she would accompany her mother back to Chicago (yes, ON the Hyde plane) so she could attend an important Lyric Opera Board meeting; and then Martin would bring Cass back to school.

I got home and went straight to bed again. I was over whatever it was that I had, but I was still weak and sort of listless.

"I hope to God you didn't catch mono," Betty said tersely to me. I understood she was wondering whom I had possibly been kissing.

I took the opportunity, while home, to break the news to the parents that I would be staying in Iowa City over the summer, and I didn't couch it in terms of asking their permission, but of telling them Cass and I were doing it. I got surprisingly little resistance from Sol, except that he was adamant that I be back in the dorm for sophomore year, and not even consider living off campus. That was forbidden. I didn't mind; we hadn't planned on anything other than Kate Daum again for fall. Of course, they said they would not be paying my rent and that they'd probably have to hire someone else to work in my place at The Spot. I felt mildly guilty about that, but they took on part-time help all the time; I couldn't think about it. I told them I intended to get a job in Iowa City and I did plan to. I just hadn't found one yet. And truth be told, the Hydes would probably pick up the tab for the apartment. We weren't looking for Shangri-La.

87

On the Friday while packing to go back to Iowa City the next day, I got a phone call at home…long distance from Chicago. Luckily it was I who answered. The voice on the other end sounded very strange.

"Shook? How are you? How's Chicago?"

"Sarah, I am very ill. I now believe you. "

"Oh, no!" I couldn't help but giggle. I mean, it wasn't funny and I wasn't laughing at him, but of course, I had probably given him the flu *à la* Typhoid Mary.

"I'm really sorry, gosh."

"It ruined my trip. I have been in bed in the hotel."

"Wellllll, "I said, "See? I knew I shouldn't have gone to that dance."

"I am now very sorry that you did go. "

"Oh, well, great. That doesn't do you a lot of good, does it? You should have believed me." I was in no mood to take the blame for his wrecked Spring Break.

I didn't see Shook too much when I got back to school. I did, however, run into him one day at the Iowa Book Store. He saw me from the stacks on the other side of the room and came over. I greeted him as I always had, but he seemed unhappy.

"You have turned mean," he announced to me.

"What?!"

"I do not see you any more at the International House."

"Well, there haven't been very many events. I don't know what you're talking about."

The International House choir had no more rehearsals or performances, and once things speeded up towards end of semester, Cass and I were busy finding our apartment and some sort of job for me.

*It was unspoken but inevitable that Shook and I would no longer be dating. I didn't stop dating him owing to any admonitions by my family, but rather owing to my desire to not be blessed by anyone's grandparents at 18 years old and promised as a bride. If he were serious about what he had told me of my future with him, he was just being foolish; that was never going to happen. And he knew it! For one thing, when he told me about the blessings part, he didn't tell me the whole story. It was true that the groom's family met the bride first and actually showered her with gifts, as he did explain, but why? Because it was usually an arranged marriage and the groom could even be meeting her for the first time – or not seeing her yet at all! This was called **rokka** and the ceremony indicated that the search for the bride was over.*

After that they were engaged and it was the bride's family's turn to bring gifts to the groom's and make the match official. In every conceivable way, a marriage between Shook and me would have found neither family ever in agreement with it.

Even more importantly, to my way of thinking, where was my say in any of this? What had I ever done or how had I ever acted to make him believe I was in love with him? Did love matter at all? Where were my feelings being taken into serious consideration here? Nowhere. And speaking of me, not only was I ignorant of these marriage rituals, I was completely untutored in the rest of his culture, too! It was not prejudice. It was West not meeting East by any stretch of the imagination.

I went to the Union to look on various boards for summer job opportunities, when lo and behold there was one notice that seemed perfect: front desk receptionist in the hotel of the Union itself, Iowa House. I went over to ask for an interview in person and they gave me an appointment and said to come back with my resumé, which, of course, I didn't have, nor did I know how to write one.

Cass came to the rescue. "I'll have my mom's secretary mail me a sample one. She can post it overnight. You can copy it."

"Well, maybe. I don't have much to put on it. What have I done?"

"Are you serious? They'll love the experience you've had being the greeter at a restaurant. That's meeting the public."

"Yes! You know," I laughed, "I didn't even think about going around to Iowa City bars or restaurants and looking for work. God, it's like I'm repressing my entire past existence. "

"Ha! You just don't want to DO that work. This other job sounds perfect!"

And that's how it happened that I became one of the summer replacement desk clerks at the Iowa House. Nothing was computerized yet, and there was no internet with trip websites. People or their travel agent called in for reservations, checked in and checked out in person and needed to be handed an actual key. My bosses told me at the onset that I would have to learn how to use a telephone switchboard with those cords that plugged into holes in order to transfer calls to rooms, but that didn't sound too insurmountable. The best part was that I would make five dollars a day and not have to work on any weekends, which seemed unbelievable to me since it would doubtless be kind of dead during the week there in the summer. Things would get hopping in August, of course, with the moving back into dorms and parents staying overnight. But by August 20th my job would end, and full-time staff would be hired for the school year – probably someone on a work-study program.

When I told my parents that I got this job, they seemed more relieved than happy for me. Sol still had to come move me out of Daum because not only could we not keep our things in our room when school was out, we couldn't store them anywhere either! So Cass and I loaded what things she also wanted back in the dorm with her in the fall and kept them at my house over the summer. Sol and I drove back to The Bluffs and Cass proceeded to move into our apartment. It was a cute, if tiny, furnished place on Linn Street, part of an old house but with a rickety staircase in the back that was our private entrance.

My parents did surprise me, however, with the news that I would drive back to Iowa City in our old Rambler station wagon, bringing things like linens, a few pots and pans, and some dishes with me; and then I could have a car there over the summer. They made it clear that this was mainly so my father would not have to drive back and forth on so many four-hour trips with me, not because they wanted me to have it a bit easier in Iowa City. And I could drive it back and keep it in the fall if I could find somewhere to park it that didn't cost them extra money.

I was dumbfounded at the idea of having a car at school; but the parking idea didn't seem too feasible anyplace around the dorms. I would have to hope to hell I could find someplace in the neighborhoods to the north of campus and park it on the street. I had time to figure that out. In the summer, our little apartment house did have a side parking lot and having the car, crappy as it actually was, saved us! We could go get groceries and do laundry; and we could drive out Highway 6 to Coralville and get the best pizza burgers I've ever had at Tommy's Drive-In.

Meanwhile, Cass had made enormous progress on her art projects, and she was beginning to be recognized for it! She had done a series of wood cuts of a scene of mountain meadowlands above Lake Geneva that had got picked for an elite exhibit at the end of the semester which would showcase students' works. Students, yes, but not sophomores! Her prints were large – about 15 by 18 inches, and she did them on hand-made paper she had bought in Europe. Cass had a prominent place in the show and her works were rewarded with designation from the judges.

I, in the meantime, had handed in my *magnum opus* linoleum block print of a very yellow vase with unidentifiable flowers in it against a green background. Linocuts were much easier to do than woodblock prints. I only had three tools, and my cutting didn't have to be exact, since they didn't give the angular, grainy effects of wood. I thought I was really getting it when I figured out how to use the "reductive" print method Picasso invented wherein, instead of using a different block for each color, the artist used the same one, and, after each successive color was imprinted onto the paper, you would clean the lino plate and cut away more of what will be not imprinted for the subsequently applied color. So I had to plan what colors I wanted for which parts of the picture, and do the background first, and so on. Given that my forte was more in appreciating art than creating it, I thought I did well to master this technique and actually "get it." Because linoleum block printing was essentially done mirror-image reversed and I was something like dyslexic anyway when it came to putting things together, it was a miracle I'd even mastered it.

"Linoleum block printing, we learned was first used by the artists of Di Brücke in Germany between the years of 1905 and 1913," Cass had told me, "mainly for wallpaper printing."

"Why wallpaper?" I wondered.

"Due to how easy it was to manipulate," she explained, adding, "It was often done in children's art classes as an introduction to printmaking."

"Oh, like potato printing. Well," I sniffed, "linoleum's a lot harder to do than potatoes! I thought our instructor told us potato printing was often used right on the wall for a wallpaper-like design."

"Well yes, it was. But linoleum printing supersedes that for real art classes."

But I was proud of my accomplishments, nonetheless, and had really liked the class. It was part studio, part lecture. And the lecture on linocut printmaking also included notes on the contemporary art world and how the method was an established professional print medium used by Henri Matisse as well as Pablo Picasso! The first exhibition of it in America had been in 1949 at the Brooklyn Museum—large scale color linocuts made by Walter Inglis Anderson.

"So don't laugh!" I smugly told Cass as I unveiled my "Flowers in a Yellow Vase."

Cass didn't laugh when she saw it—she was too polite for that--- and instead I think she was pleasantly surprised if mildly shocked!

She encouraged me to try more, so I decided to make a series of cards for my final project. I went out into the neighborhoods at the end of the street the dorms were on, and tried to sketch the University President's house – a large red-brick Georgian Colonial mansion with a lovely little garden in the front. But my sketches were ridiculously awful and my senses of proportion and perspective were nil. So I bailed on that idea and went back to my room to come up with a different one.

Luckily, my own house in The Bluffs was just a rectangle with a triangular roof, so that was easy for me to sketch and carve out. I would forget about proportion, make it flat, and hope it would look like I'd planned to do that all along. I added some half-circles to represent stylized bushes in the front, and carved some curving lines to indicate a yard going down a tiered hill. Off to the side I put a stark, leafless tree. I printed it out on card stock in only two colors—light blue and white, so it looked almost like a winter scene Christmas card only in Chanukah colors. I finished it up with ink on the bottom of each picture where I hand-wrote in tiny cursive, "The Keeline Homestead" and signed my initials inside a circle. I made six of these prints and glued them to bigger folded cardstock cards that I creased with a bone creasing tool. I tied the cards in a bundle with ribbon and presented my project to the professor.

I got an A on the cards and in that class!

Cass suggested I go down to Things in the paper-by-the-pound section and find some envelopes of the right size for the card. That way I could actually use them. I sent one to Nana for Mother's Day. She loved it.

Second semester of freshman year had seemed exponentially harder to me than had First. I found myself studying all the time to keep up with all the reading, and the worst class was, again, Biology, but that was offset by how wonderful the class Masterpieces of Literature turned out to be. Professor Grenier was brilliant and his lectures and assignments insightful and inspiring. Since the class was in EPB, with the building directory in the lobby that read like a Who's Who in American Letters in those years, I could also read the notices on the bulletin boards there and keep on top of visiting guest lecturers and poetry readings.

W.S. Merwin was to be on campus that spring and though I had never heard of him, there was buzz around the various classes and in the Union about him, so Cass and I decided to attend.

Merwin, in 1967, was famous enough that, had I not been a small-town know-nothing with an inferior college preparatory education, I might have known him, at least his name if not his *oeuvre*. He did the reading that night from his early works, especially *The Drunk in the Furnace*, but he also gave us a preview of a work about to come out, entitled *The Lice*, which my professor, discussing the event afterwards in the River Room, pointed out to us that it was a manifesto of some consequence against the Vietnam War, "condemning modern man in apocalyptic and visionary terms." Cass and I were pretty enthralled that we had seen someone that illustrious who was on his way to becoming one of the most critically acclaimed men of letters in the country.

I started to believe that night, I think, that Iowa U was indeed a wonderful place for me to have washed up on its shores. There we were, in the company of thoughtful, articulate scholars in discussion of brilliance…right there on the plains of the Midwest, in a little oasis after all. A kind of euphoria swept over me.

The trouble was, when this enclave broke up, it was 12:30 a.m. and Cass and I had missed "hours" by half an hour. The doors of Kate Daum would be locked. We would have to go to Burge, ring to be let in, file a report and confess our sin.

The next day we got a notice that we were to be hauled before the Inter-Residence Hall Board to be punished for missing the curfew.

"Shit," Cass said, reading the paper. "I wonder if we'll need representation or something."

"What, like a lawyer?! Surely not."

"Yeah, I guess not. They just think they're the Supreme Court."

And so it came to pass. We had to appear and state our case. We didn't feel we had a lot to defend: it was a University sanctioned function followed by a discussion group consisting mostly of MY CLASS with MY PROFESSOR.

"And when you saw it going late, you could have gotten up and excused yourselves to come back on time, isn't that right?"

"Frankly," Cass started to explain, "we weren't paying attention to the time as much as to what was being said."

"Really, we were so enthralled with his works!" I echoed.

"We just made a miscalculation, " Cass stated. "We'll be more careful in the future."

That was good; I nodded.

But instead of letting us off with some kind of warning, our punishment was that we had to sign out and back in every day for two weeks.

"Fucking stupid!" Cass shouted in the tunnel as we went back to Daum.

I had never heard her use that word, and it had also never come out of **my** mouth.

"Fucking assholes! "I screamed back.

Chapter Thirteen

"If You're Goin' To San Francisco"...Scott McKenzie

In May of 1967 we had a visit by an even more famous poet than W.S. Merwin and this time, there was no danger of not getting back to the dorm by "hours". My poetry education was burgeoning and when flyers went up all over the campus, I was not so ignorant as to not recognize Allen Ginsberg's name and iconic photo plastered all over the place. He was coming to Iowa City for the first ever Gentle Thursday, a "happening." And that day was a poem itself, breezy and warm, so the Pentacrest was packed with students all day long.

You couldn't miss him: he was right in the thick of it, mingling with everyone, dancing around on the lawns with a flower crown in his wild, curly hair, performing a Buddhist chant intertwined with "Flower Power." Students were handing out candy and tabs of mescaline and other hallucinogens, amidst face painters, balloon distributors, and anti-war buskers. I stood on the sidewalk for more than an hour taking it all in, and then hurried back to tell Cass we had to go to his reading.

For this occasion, 1,500 people turned up in the ballroom. It was the poetry extravaganza of all time. I was sentient enough once again to realize that I was privileged to be in the presence of such greatness, and had the good sense to appreciate it. He read poems and he also gave an interview to student reporters saying that he believed drugs would soon be legal in the U.S. and that by the time children of today were adults, attitudes towards pot and acid would have changed accordingly.

"We may have an acid head on the Supreme Court one day," he told the throng.

"I think he means it," a voice called out from right behind Cass and me. I turned around and it was Alan Jones, smiling his broad grin and shaking his mass of blond curls.

"I know," said Cass, "but do you think it will really come to pass? "

"Oh, those cats in Washington are pretty buttoned up," he said, "I kind of doubt it." He laughed and touched Cass' shoulder, saying, "Would you like to go have coffee?"

Cass shot me a look of mild amusement and then went off with him. I was getting ready to press through the crowd and head back when I ran right into Soren Carlysle.

"Hey!" he said. "I thought you'd be here."

"Couldn't miss this," I said.

"Come on," he said, taking my hand and guiding me out of the Union. "Let's go someplace quieter."

So we headed out and uphill towards the dorms, walking slowly in the blossom-scented Spring night air. It was still early, and the soda fountain in Burge Hall was fairly empty, so we sat down in there and had cokes.

Soren was from an even smaller town in Iowa than I was. His family were practicing lawyers there since right after World War I, and they expected him to join that profession.

"But if I am going to do it," he said, "it won't be in Iowa. I want to do entertainment law." Then he corrected himself, "I don't really even want to do entertainment law as much as I want to write music reviews and criticism, but if I have to go to law school, it's going to be something to do with the arts."

"Wow," I said, "that is very cool. Is that why you took that ushering job? So you could see all the performances that come here?"

"Like I said...for free," he laughed. "Say, you should come next Friday. This incredible pianist is going to be playing a recital in the Union, but he's also giving master classes. His name is André Watts. Heard of him?"

"Nope." Ignorant again.

"Young, Black, talent up the ass."

"Oh wait a minute!" I exclaimed, coming to my senses and remembering I did know who that was. "I have heard of him! He's like **really** young, right? Wasn't he on t.v. in one of those Young People's Concerts with Leonard Bernstein?!" I was suddenly excited that I knew something for a change.

"Yes, that was him. On the show he performed a Liszt concerto. His mother used to hold Liszt up to him as a sort of bait to inspire him to play piano. Liszt was his idol."

Liszt again!

"You know what else happened?"

"What?"

"Well, Glenn Gould-- the most famous pianist of our time-- was scheduled to play with the New York Phil right after that same t.v. concert that Watts had appeared on. But Gould got sick and Bernstein called Watts at the last minute to be a replacement for him! It was on New Year's Day in 1963 and immediately afterwards, André Watts' career was set. He recorded his first solo album, won a Grammy ---the whole nine yards."

"And he's coming here. Wow."

"So is it a date? You can't miss this one!"

"Heck, yeah."

Soren and I began seeing each other regularly after that night. He was so darling I almost couldn't believe he was interested in *me*. He was not real tall but certainly towered over me. He had long dark straight hair that fell to his shoulders and shone clean as it blew softly around his face when we walked outdoors. Sometimes he would have to sweep it back out of his eyes. He had a goatee, too and it made him look hippie-cute. His eyes were blue-grey, and his nose was patrician. He had a lovely smile that was very sweet.

Soren's name was Danish but his actual ethnicity was Scottish and he was Catholic. He had gone to parochial school in his hometown of Imogene, Iowa, known for its Catholic church that dated from 1840, as he proudly stated, "It is so beautiful that it appears in many tourist pamphlets and guidebooks."

"Even if we all have a hard time believing any tourists come to this state, " I said.

"Kidding aside, you really should see St. Pat's some time," he said, "it's something else. There's a vaulted ceiling right over the altar that is painted to look like heaven. The high altar is white Carrara marble. The whole thing is Gothic Revival architecture. Imogene is not at all far from The Bluffs y' know!"

"Really! I'm sure I've never been there. The church sounds pretty damn fancy for a little town like that. So do you go to church here?"

"No. Don't tell my parents."

"Ha ha. I don't go to synagogue here very often either."

"Oh, so you're Jewish."

Remembering back to Rush Week when I thought I looked enough like every other girl in those Jewish sororities for us all to be cousins, I was taken aback by the idea that he was really asking me that.

"Mmm," I nodded.

Soren was a serious student so we had that in common, and many of our "dates" were just study sessions. We had the same English class and often worked on that together. We both liked what would now be called junk food but back then was just normal food, so we'd go to Pagliai's for pizza and Hamburg Inn for burgers. As we became "a couple", starting the summer before my sophomore year, when I stayed in Iowa City, we went out more and more to the iconic U of I hangouts: the Ramskeller, Joe's Place, The Airliner, where we always felt like we crashed a frat party to which we weren't invited; and even once in a while later when I had a car on campus, we would drive to the Amana Colonies and eat the fabulous food of the Ox Yoke Inn. And most of the time, even after some of these other places, we would end up at The Mill to listen to folk music.

When my father came to get me and collect my stuff for the trek home and back again to Iowa City with the car, he did not meet Soren. That would have just launched a four-hour barrage of admonitions and threats I would have had to put up with the whole way. I got enough of that as it was, and keeping a low profile of my doings in Iowa City was the new normal.

The junky turquoise and black box of a car that was the 1959 Rambler station wagon had oodles of space for all our stuff, and I was grateful for that. However, I had to hope the tires would last and the transmission wouldn't conk out on it. Nevertheless it was all mine for the next year and I was elated. Cass was a good sport about it, acting like it was just another car for transportation so why not be happy about it? But it was not an exaggeration to note that she had never ridden in anything that ugly or pedestrian in her life.

The summer of 1967 was one of several "firsts" for Cassandra Hyde. As previously noted, she had never really cooked for herself, except to make snacks once in a blue moon in one of her family's many glorious "chef's kitchens". She had never gone grocery shopping, had never stocked a pantry, had never washed dishes. She had done laundry in the dorm basement but had never gone to a laundromat. And Cass had never cleaned anything ever. At Iowa U when we were students, we actually had housekeeping: workers who would come in and change the sheets, mop the floors and even clean the bathroom if we had it neat enough for them to see the surfaces. Now we would be doing that ourselves in our own place. I had brilliantly thought to bring cleaning supplies with me when I drove the car back: a broom, of course, and also a cotton dust mop with one of those fitted mop heads you could take off the metal frame and wash; an old Eureka canister vacuum Betty said she could spare, along with two bags for it---if we used more than that, we'd have to find them to buy somewhere like a hardware store; a bucket, some sponges and dust clothes.

Cass had found the apartment all by herself when she arrived back in Iowa City after her Swiss sojourn and before I had even gotten back to town. And the Hydes agreed to pay the $85/month rent on it for June, July and August. Our apartment was furnished, and it wasn't just an efficiency one but had a separate bedroom, kitchen, bathroom and living room space. The bedroom was tiny, but still had enough room for a double bed, which, though nothing like the lush and self-indulgent canopy beds of Cass', was adequate for us and had a nice wrought-iron frame that would do for a headboard if we propped enough pillows on it. There were two little bedside tables that didn't match and had been painted over, each with a small lamp on it on either side. The room also had one comfy chintz armchair and a little round table near the window, and a fairly big walk-in closet, that doubled as a storage closet for our supplies as well as for clothes.

The kitchen was adequate with flower-print curtains on the high narrow windows over the sink. It didn't have many accoutrements, but came with all the appliances we'd need except a dishwasher, and cupboards full of pots and pans and oddly non-matching dishes. I packed those away in boxes and set them off in a small space that led to the back door and stairs down to the parking space, and I put my own dishes on the shelves instead. Mine weren't anything to write home about either—just some cast-offs of Betty and Sol's early marriage years that she had kept in our basement. But I felt better using stuff I knew had been properly and hygienically washed.

Off the kitchen in a small hallway, was the bathroom---right out of the 50's with coral pink and brown subway tiles on the walls and around the tub, a dusty coral pink toilet and sink, and brown cabinets. I really didn't mind it—to me it was kind of cute. Cass was horrified.

"If I'm ever sick in there, we won't know if it was something I ate or something I saw, " she proclaimed.

The main space of the whole apartment, of course, was a living/dining room that was more than adequate. There was a tiny dining room table because the kitchen was too small to afford any eating area; and the space fanned out to include a couch, a coffee table, some built-in bookshelves which were put into a narrow corner niche; an old console television (so I could put my little portable one either in the kitchen or the bedroom—such luxury!) and the best thing about the living room---a bay window that overlooked Linn Street where there were matching, if ugly, wing-back arm chairs and a round tier table with a pretty porcelain lamp on it in between them. The place looked like someone's maiden aunt had lived and died there, but we didn't care. It was ours.

The day I drove back with my laden car, Cass had been shopping already at Things and had bought us some really pretty screen-print batik Indian spreads to use on the bed and on the couch. They were those multi-colored cotton ones in hues of yellow, green, red and blue mandala-like designs. She also brought us some baskets from India—a big square one with a lid to use as a catchall for clothes and some round bowl-shaped woven ones just for decoration. One of them was gigantic in red and yellow stripes with a small flower motif woven all around every few inches. I really liked that. But the *pièce de résistance* of her shopping spree was a lamp shaped like a Chinese lantern that hung on a chain cord but just plugged into the wall.

"You hang it from one hook," she explained, holding her hand out to reveal two hooks she'd procured, "and you loop the cord up to a second hook and then down to the outlet. I thought we'd put it in the bedroom over that little table. That way, at least one of us could read under it."

There was still one very important thing which would make our little *sanctum sanctorum* perfect.

In our dorm we had been spoiled with a most miraculous source of music, thanks to Cass: an actual stereo system. It was a fabulous Philips system which consisted of a small turntable that sat on a receiver, plus two small speakers (small for the 60's that is; this was not a boom box, but components!) In Kate Daum we'd kept it on her desk, and even though it took away a lot of her surface space for studying, she made do. But it was going to be a real problem to move all that into the apartment without the help of Martin or my father, and besides that, we were in trouble finding somewhere to keep it until we did move. The dorm wouldn't let us store anything for fall, even though we had the same room reserved.

"It is just so stupid to have to move all this stereo stuff back to The Bluffs," I moaned, only to have to load it into the other car and drive all the way back here! That just doesn't make sense."

Cass agreed. "I'm going to talk to the landlord and beg him to allow us to stash the stereo over there---it's only a matter of a few days."

So she pleaded with the landlord of the summer apartment to allow us to just keep the stereo in a box right inside the back door. And he had agreed! We moved it over there ourselves in a taxi. *Voilà*.

So we would have music all summer! Now we just needed to find a place in the living room to set it back up. The bookshelf nook wouldn't work—too narrow. The coffee table wouldn't work—too far out in the middle of the room and away from any electrical outlets. So we went to a second-hand furniture store out at the end of Market Street and found a little table of nondescript style but that was low and rectangular. We had no problems getting it back in the station wagon and with both of us lifting, it went up the stairs easily enough. It fit on the wall by the t.v. and luckily there were two plugs on that same wall. We set up the system on it and declared total victory. At one end, Cass set the square Indian basket with the lid to hold records.

What with my salary about to start, the money I still had left over in my account from the academic year, which, albeit, was minimal, and Cass' comparative fortune, we were going to be fine for living expenses. Nevertheless, I felt bad that her parents were picking up the entire rent tab, so I offered to pay for groceries and do the shopping once a week when I got paid. I figured since I was making $30, give or take -- minus whatever they took out of my check -- I could probably afford $10 of it for food and other things one could buy in a supermarket like paper products.

"Look Sari, you know you don't have to do that. I can easily chip in."

"I know. But I want to; and if we run into trouble, don't worry—I'll hit you up."

So we agreed.

We were all moved in. My job was starting the next week. Cass was happily ensconced in her studio space in the art school across the river and we lived close enough to campus for both of us to walk to our various points each day—me in the Union and her across the bridge from there. I worked from 8:30 until 5:00 with an hour for lunch (a whole hour!) and she worked often into the late evening. We didn't care about having a schedule for dinner, although sometimes it did work out that we ate together and mostly I cooked. But more often than not, I made something for dinner and kept half of it for her when she got there.

Soren Carlysle had gone back to Imogene for part of the summer, but he returned to Iowa City earlier than he needed to for classes because he was actually going to be an RA that fall and could move into his room in the Quad at any time over the summer. Alan Jones lived in Iowa City off campus anyway, so he was around and had begun to see Cass on a regular basis. Professor Klampert was her summer faculty advisor, as before, and he lived in a beautiful little house on Willow Creek Drive just across Highway 1 from the art museum. As much as I traipsed around campus that summer, and hung out a lot in the Union, I didn't see anybody from the dorm. It was like a different population there in the off-season. Except for mid-summer freshman orientation when the Iowa House filled up and bustled with excited parents and their soon-to-be Hawkeyes, my job was mostly taking phone reservations for football weekends, and doing check-ins for people who came to the University in the summer to visit for other reasons. It was easy and it was fun. And I loved it.

Chapter Fourteen

"Let's Live for Today"…The Grass Roots

Piggy-backing on her enormous studio success of the semester we'd just finished, Cass was very productive with her print-making that summer we lived together in Iowa City. She worked on large scale self-portraits based somewhat on the miniature she had made for her parents at Christmas. Portraits of any kind in wood-cut or linocuts were stylized at best, and Cass' had a radiance about them that I thought was remarkable given the medium. She could illustrate emotions on her face that were mysterious in their moods; not really happy but certainly not sorrowful. I would say her self-portrait expressions were somewhat hopeful---perhaps foretelling her becoming an artist. She would print the first drafts out on normal paper first and work on the details on the block before finally printing the final version out on rag paper.

Some afternoons when I got off work, since I was close to the art school, I would cross the bridge and try to find her in the studio. Watching her work only emphasized how little I had really known of this process when I took that elective linoleum block printing course. She was dexterous as she wielded the chisels, choosing different sized ones for different carving effects. Even her trial sketches struck me as masterpieces.

Besides portraits, she began another series of Swiss village scenes that got more and more elaborate as she worked. She could actually turn a photo that she had taken herself into the scene on wood; I could hardly believe what I saw, sitting there mesmerized by her agility and savoir-faire. With each carving she would reveal more of the angular roofs and walls of the buildings, down to tiny cuts denoting crumbling stone. She printed them in black and white only on thin handmade ecru-colored paper. They had the patina of old-world etchings as soon as they were done. I thought she was quite pleased with the results; she seemed happy about her output. But it turned out that deep down she wasn't confident that the art faculty would feel anything but disdain.

"Why would you think that?" I asked incredulously one evening when she expressed real doubt as we were discussing her progress.

"Oh, you know…nothing's ever good enough for them."

I hadn't noticed that in my little class, but I didn't have any experience on the levels she had attained to argue with her. I thought her work was beautiful, frame-worthy and even saleable.

I didn't pick up the cues I should have as to Cass' insecurities that summer at all, because I was living in a state of bliss. For the first time in my life, I had total freedom, tied only to the schedule of my job, which felt like a privilege I got paid to do rather than any sort of requirement or chore. We came and went as we pleased, ate what we felt like having, spent free time exploring Iowa City, lazed around the apartment in the heat watching t.v. without guilt that there was some homework waiting or that parents would yell at us. There was no such thing as boredom either. Even hanging out at the laundromat over on East Bloomington I was enchanted to have time to just read for pleasure without any looming examinations or papers. I had always been a reader. I carried books around in my bucket bag purse all through high school and read them in study halls and sometimes even behind boring textbooks in one class or another. Reading was normal and hardly anathema to me, but it took on a new joy that summer, as I delved back into some old favorites like *Nine Stories* and most of Jane Austen.

I was reading Churchill's prolific volumes on his ancestor, the Duke of Marlborough, whose life and times would later become famous to all as *The First Churchills* on PBS, which was a network not yet on the horizon of our lives. I was curious enough intellectually, at least, to want to read about these people and go deeper into the stories. It was easy to go to the library and check out the biography of John Churchill to delve further into his life with Sarah Jennings, and to study the court of Queen Anne. A great side discovery of all this reading about the Marlboroughs and life at Blenheim palace led to my becoming cognizant for the first time of---and falling in love with--- Cavalier King Charles spaniels. Even if we had been allowed to have pets, it wasn't as if I could have gone out and found one of those dogs that summer;

I had never seen one anywhere in person, not at a pet shop or being walked on the sidewalks or in any parks in Iowa or Omaha, for that matter.

"They probably have some in Chicago," Cass had assured me when I pined for one. "Manet painted them, too, so at least you can find them in museums."

Cass had gone out several times with Alan Jones before inviting him up to the apartment. She wanted to have him over to dinner and suggested I invite Soren Carlysle, who was also around and often met me in the Union after I got off work.

"A dinner party?" I asked incredulously.

"Well, not a party. Just dinner. We could order it in from Pagliai's."

"Yes, let's do that."

"What about alcohol?"

"Well, we can't buy it."

I didn't drink. For the daughter of a bar owner, that was a contradictory situation. My parents had never forbidden me to drink at home; in fact, they even sort of taught me a few things I might need to know, like the names of certain cocktails and what they tasted like. This only happened in the house, of course, because had my father ever been caught serving a minor, he would swiftly and irrevocably lose his liquor license. And they never intended me to be a sophisticated drinker as a college freshman. But they thought if I knew a little bit about what was going on with drinks, I could navigate the social drinking scene better if that had ever arisen. It hadn't. Shook didn't drink in bars, and at the parties we went to, if the drinks or punch were spiked, I never liked it because I didn't really like the taste of alcohol in the first place. Soren wasn't of drinking age either and neither of us bothered to get fake id's of any kind.

"Alan can buy it for us. "

"Cass, do you drink with him?"

"Sure."

"In Iowa City bars? How do you not get carded?"

"We drink at his place mostly, "she laughed.

"Well, he can bring it, then, but I think I'll just stick with Coke. I don't know what Soren will want." And then changing the subject so I didn't have to really ponder what else Cass and Alan did at his place, I asked her what else we should serve.

"What about dessert? Can you make something?"

"I'll try. Maybe I'll have to find a cookbook at the library." It was actually my opinion that if one could read, one could cook. But then I realized that I had spent my entire childhood baking brownies. I'd just go buy a cheap baking pan, grab a mix, some ice cream and chocolate sauce at the supermarket, and declare victory.

We set up this "dinner party" and invited the guys over for a Saturday. Cass made a "table" out of the square basket that held records in our living room and we sat around it, Cass and I on the couch and the other two on the floor. I baked the brownies in the late afternoon and as they were cooling, left to pick up the pizza.

Soren and Alan hit it off fine, and Alan was quite deferential to me, I assumed due to the fact that I had been his student. He called me Miss Shrier.

"You can call me Sari now, you realize, " I said to him.

"Sure, Miss Shrier. I know." His eyes twinkled under that veil of curly blond hair falling down his forehead.

Alan wasn't a generation older than we were, but he was enough older that we tended to probe his taste and knowledge about topics that came up. Music was dominant, of course, not only because Soren had his sights set to a career in arts and entertainment law, but also because we all knew in those days that we were in the midst of some amazing musical renaissance, something that hadn't happened before, unless you counted the REAL Renaissance; but we meant popular culture.

We were the first generation to have music at our fingertips. We listened to the radio playing only our music, whereas, even though our parents grew up with radios, they had to remain huddled in their living rooms to hear it. It was never as ubiquitous in their lives as it was for us. They had to have a Victrola to play their big records on. I hadn't gone to soda shops and danced with boys from high school, like we saw on t.v. and in the movies, but some kids had. The juke box morphed into the portable record player – those little suit-case things people could move from place to place. By the time I was out of high school, we could carry around little radios; we had the ability to listen to tapes of music and people even knew how to make what we would now call mix tapes. Cars were beginning to feature the 8-track systems in them, although mine didn't. Soon we would all have AM/FM radios, and Chicago would to get its first Progressive Rock FM station WXRT; and on a clear night we would be able to pick it up in Iowa. So we knew. Even if we could never have predicted the miniaturization of it all, we knew we were livin' large.

"Rock and roll, "Alan said, "was dance music mostly, you realize. *Band Stand* for instance, introduced acts, but the criterion was 'can you dance to it', whereas rock music now is art."

"Yeah, "Soren agreed. "You know, there's this magazine, *Crawdaddy!* Man, I would love to work for them."

"In San Francisco? "Alan asked.

"YES!" Soren was amazed someone else knew what he was talking about. "Their reviews treat the music as an aesthetic medium, and the message as worthy of…well… art."

"Poetry in lyrics and the rest of that."

"Damn right. The Walt Whitmans of **our** time."

"Well, I think The Beatles' lyrics are the coolest, and I love Herman's Hermits" I stated.

"Huh? You mean, 'Mrs. Brown you've got a lovely *dawtah*'," mimicked Alan.

"Yes, I do mean them. I love them. I love the whole Mersey beat thing."

"So do I," said Cass, to help me out. "But you don't have that record do you?" She asked. "I haven't heard you play it."

"No, but I still love it. "

Soren chimed in, "Hey, I also really like that sound. 'Ferry Cross the Mersey' is outta sight."

"Yes. Jerry and the Pacemakers…can do."

And so it went, our first entertaining in our very own place. I served up the brownies à la mode and they were a big hit.

"Not bad, you little homemaker, "Alan chided me.

"Seriously, really good, " said Soren.

It was getting pretty late and no one had to be up in the morning, so Cass left with Alan for a while and Soren and I were alone in the apartment. He sat me down on the couch, pushing away the basket with the empty boxes piled on it. He put his arm around me and we just sat there for a while and didn't talk. Then he cupped my face in his hand and turned it towards him. We kissed a few times. It felt natural and like we'd been together for a lot longer than we had been.

"What time do you think they'll be back? " he asked me.

I think I knew what he was going to suggest before he'd even said another word. But I wasn't on the pill, though I knew I could get it from a doctor in town, of course. The thing was---me. I wasn't a prude, but I had always been a wall flower type. Sex when I wasn't in love didn't interest me, and getting pregnant would have been the end of my life. I wasn't brave enough to even remotely consider sleeping with Soren.

"No idea. But I'm not going to risk that. Anyway, I'm not on the pill."

"That's cool, "he said to me sweetly. "We can wait. "

"Thanks; I mean that."

And with that I curled up in his lap on the couch, and we spent the next few hours making out and listening to music before he told me he needed to be going. We kissed goodbye and he left down the stairs. I cleaned up the place and went to bed.

But Cass didn't even come back that night.

The next afternoon as I got back to the apartment from my job, I was surprised to find her home before me. She turned around when she heard me coming in our front door which opened right into the living room, and she had a broad smile on her face as she stood at our make-shift stereo table.

"I've got something fabulous here," she chirped. And she held up a record album. "Alan bought it for me…us."

It was Laura Nyro's *More Than a New Discovery*, and if I had to pinpoint a moment of life-changing proportions for me, that would be one. How Cass and Alan knew about Laura Nyro before me was a mystery; I'm the one who had the radio on night and day---in our dorm room, too. But I had never heard of her. I should have picked up on the phenomenon, because my faves Peter, Paul and Mary had already covered one of Nyro's early, wonderful songs, "And When I Die." Of course, by the time we were out of college, she was a household name, having become super famous for performing her own work and for other bands and groups covering her and turning her songs into pop hits. But it was her own versions and her own music that enthralled us both that summer. We lived inside these songs in the summer of '67 and the next year *Song to a Seagull* would start the great debate among us as to the superiority of Joni over Laura. In my mind, apples and oranges; I loved them both fervently. We had seen them both, and a host of others, in concert by the time 1970 had rolled around. Soren and I had actually camped out in a line to get Simon and Garfunkel tickets in Iowa City, too.

Our musical hearts were full with these as well as The Beatles, of course, and all the decade's renaissance rock/folk acts. I have to say, folk rock was my very favorite and soon there would be *The City* with Carol King and *Fotheringay* with Sandy Denny. The Ricky Nelson and Paul Anka and even the beloved Beach Boys I had listened to on the radio and on 45's in high school seemed like kindergarten fare compared to the music we listened to in the late 60's. Between Motown, bossa nova, folk rock, and all the "hard rock" anthems swirling around in our heads, we were swimming in the glorious ocean of musical Nirvana. When *New York Tendaberry* came out a few years later, some friends sent Laura Nyro a telegram congratulating her on her birth. And when I heard it, my friends might just as well have sent me the same one.

It was also thanks to Alan Jones that Cass and I were "educated" and turned on to such West Coast groups as The Byrds, The Doors and Buffalo Springfield, and albums like the Jimi Hendricks Experience's *Are You Experienced*, Cream's *Fresh Cream* and a lot of the Rolling Stones.

Soren's taste and mine were similar. He loved Jefferson Airplane so we listened to *Surrealistic Pillow* over and over. He also loved Otis Redding, Aretha Franklin and lots of Funk and Soul. We danced all night in the Union one unforgettable time that summer to Mitch Ryder and the Detroit Wheels in person.

Cass had a much larger record collection than I did, so almost immediately when we became fast friends, I availed myself of all her Beach Boys, and Mamas and Papas stuff. I had brought my own albums to school, too, of course, but mine included old favorites like Broadway cast recordings of *West Side Story* and *The Fantasticks*, movie scores like *The Pink Panther*, and all my Beatles records, especially *A Hard Day's Night* and the early ones. I was also deep into a lot of folk music like my beloved Simon and Garfunkel and Leonard Cohen, as well as Joan Baez, and Janis Ian.

Alan's most fervent accolades were always reserved for Bob Dylan and Soren agreed with him on that. They considered *Highway 61 Revisited* to be his masterpiece at the time. "Like a Rolling Stone" became an anthem around our apartment.

"*How does it feel?*" I would be singing as I did the dishes, and if Cass heard me she'd always answer, "Pretty damn fine."

Chapter Fifteen

"59th St. Bridge Song"...Simon & Garfunkel

Our summer in the apartment drew to a close, and we had to move back into the dorm. I wasn't completely oblivious to what was happening in San Francisco the summer of 1967, billed as "The Summer of Love" in the press, and even though it was far removed from my life in Iowa City, I felt a kinship. That one was my own summer of, if not love, then at least contentment. There would never be another one like it. This was the moment I would admit that Iowa City was more like home to me than I ever thought it could have been all those months during freshman year when I agonized over why I was there instead of Amherst, Mass. I began to love and appreciate the town for what it represented to me: freedom, self-actualization and a sense of belonging. I realized that I was grateful to Iowa City –and fate—for bringing me together with Cass first and foremost, and for opening up my world of intellectual pursuits, especially in the arts. I knew even then that it would stand me in good stead, and that, much as I wanted to deny it, I was truly becoming bathed in cultural enlightenment on that campus.

Cass and I discussed this as we drove to the Bluffs to reload the car with our stored belongings.

"So you admit it then?? She asked in mock seriousness. "Iowa is a fine university?"

"I admit it. Dottie will crow at me more than you are, " I laughed. "I may not let on to her that I've come around."

This trip, Roslyn didn't have to give up her room to us; we were only home for one night and slept in the basement. Sol, for his part, had been, if not pleasant towards me, at least non-menacing. Of course, Sol being Sol, nothing was perfect. He inappropriately told Cass what a beauty she was, but she just laughed that off as him being "quirky." Thankfully no one mentioned the war protest incident, and my parents and I did not argue, quibble or discuss anything except where I might park the car at school.

"Just make sure it doesn't get towed, and you don't have to pay anything extra to park it," Sol had warned me.

"It really is a problem to park cars anywhere on campus," Cass had commiserated with me. "The dorms have no parking lots, even if you wanted or could pay for parking."

"I know. Parking in any city lot is prohibitively expensive and I have no idea how that could ever work anyway; you can't leave a car overnight."

The only solution for us would be to stake out a space in the neighborhoods bordering campus and hope to hell it was safe enough, inconspicuous enough, and close enough that I could go and check on it all the time. Jesus.

After we unloaded our stuff at the curb in front of Daum House, I drove around until I found a spot for the Rambler on Linn Street...the nearest I could get to Clinton. Every day after classes I would go move the car...even just a few feet up or down the block. And I constantly worried about it.

"It almost makes it more of a hassle having it here than not," I had to admit one afternoon to Cass, who didn't like seeing me so unnerved, but couldn't come up with any helpful ideas.

Until she did.

About a month after classes were underway, Cas fairly burst into the room and crowed, "I have found a solution for the car! Oh kid! You're going to love it!"

"You did? WHAT?"

"Klampert's driveway! He said it would be okay to keep it parked there!"

"Oh my GOD, Cass! You have saved me!" I was completely shocked, relieved and grateful!

"He did."

"I will THANK him the next time I see him, but you do it for me, too, because I'm not over there for class anymore."

"I did. But I will again. I just asked because, well, you've been so worried! Mind you, it's not real handy, but hell, we can walk there from the art school and we can walk to the art school from here, so...problem solved. And we don't use it much except on the weekends anyway. By the way, Klampert agrees with you that I should learn to drive, so can he teach me with the Rambler?"

"Of course!"

Of course, that is, without thinking about things like liability insurance and who was allowed to drive the car on my parents' policy, or what it might cost to add a person, or what it might cost if she got in an accident. I didn't know a thing about any of that; Sol had never taken it up with me, so I was completely ignorant of what would happen if I ever wrecked it as well! Ignorance was, if not bliss, at least a comfort blanket.

I went to the hardware store up on South Gilbert Street and had another set of keys made for the car. Klampert would need one anyway in case for some reason he had to move it in his driveway, and frankly, once Cass got her license, we would be sharing it.

The offer of a parking spot for the station wagon had taken a most heavy load off my shoulders, and the semester got underway on a really high note. For one thing, I was no longer a freshman, so I got bumped up in the registration ordeal; none of my classes were closed. I was also ecstatic because I had satisfied the P.E. requirement even though an F in Movement Principles and a D in archery hadn't done anything to help my GPA. Archery looked easy but turned out to be ridiculously difficult for me. Every time I pulled back on the bow, the arrow fell at my toes. When it was nice out we'd had to shoot at hay bale targets set up in a little green area across from the Union. And if it rained, we had to shoot at things in a gym. Even though I wore a glove, my fingers were cut up and bleeding. I only passed because of the written exams, which, like with fencing, were easy compared to actually doing the sport. I got an A in bowling though! B, F, D, A added up to *pass*, and I hoped a few decades would *pass* before I ever had to set foot in a gym again.

My French classes were getting more and more advanced, now, and I was absolutely enthralled by all things French.

I had to give Sol some credit for this. My father had, without the remotest idea that this would happen when he enlisted to "fight Hitler," been assigned to an outfit that was liaisoned with the Free French. They started in Camp Crowder, Missouri and ended up in North Africa, and all over Europe. Early in their assignment, they had played a role in the invasion of southern France; and near the end of the war they had crossed the Rhine with the intent of demolishing the last Nazi strongholds, and chasing die-hard German soldiers from hide-outs in the Austrian Alps. He didn't talk about the war much, but if pressed, he would recount tidbits from his time as the Signal Corps radio operator. It turned out he did see concentration camps and dazed Jews and other prisoners on the roads; and he absolutely knew about the fear and degradation "his people" had suffered. But he mostly avoided telling me all that, and stuck to stories of taking cover in a French school house while shells were blowing up all around outside; or how he and his best buddy, another Jew, on his "team" (as they called themselves instead of platoon or unit or something with more military gravitas), had gone to visit Sidi-bel-Abbes where La Legion Étrangère, the French Foreign Legion, had its headquarters. He had indeed fought all the way from Oran, Algeria, through Italy, into France to Germany and Austria, and back to Paris. Since he wouldn't recount the war stories like we saw in the kinds of old newsreels that we would watch in history class, or describe to me the real horrors and the danger, the main impressions I got as a young kid were ones of nice French people who traded bottles of perfume for cigarettes and chocolate, and especially, Paris' glory after the liberation, which is when he was there. Unknowingly he ended up instilling in me a very great desire to go to France. I knew I could die happy if I saw Paris.

It was a revelation to me that, as long as I kept on track to finish required subjects for the B.A., I could take really whatever I wanted to, and since the U of Iowa had a large French and Italian department, there were many offerings. Thus, I took two French classes at the same time: one lit course on French poetry of the 19th century, and the other, a comp and con class required for the major. Satisfying requirements to major would become a moot point in one year, I reasoned, when I would be studying over there and racking up credits like so many seashells scooped up at low tide. Eyes on the prize. Always.

I had to take a social science course, so I chose Anthropology. Stroke of genius, I praised myself. Cass had taken it; she hadn't said anything about it being really hard, and she hadn't sold the textbook. I wouldn't have to shell out another exorbitant amount for at least one book!

I took Brit Lit and also a poetry writing class in the undergraduate Writer's Workshop, to which I actually had to submit some of my own writing to be accepted; and I was. That afforded me the chance to wander around in the offices where we picked up each week's reading assignment of other class members' poems, and read drafts on worksheets and galley proofs of real writers' works. Kurt Vonnegut was working on *Slaughterhouse Five* at that time, which would mean he was to become a household name by the time I graduated. And another grad student was writing his master's thesis, which would be titled *Setting Free the Bears*. I had seen this guy---John Irving, near the entrance to the football field at a game Soren and I attended. He sold souvenirs or some such. I recognized him there as a member of the Workshop. Those poor grad students must have always been starving, I surmised.

Cass was intrigued by my wanting to take a poetry writing class.

"Won't you be intimidated to take it there? I would be," she worried.

But I had decided that since Iowa was known for writing and since I was there, I might as well take advantage of it and see what all the hype was really about. I didn't know anything about the workshop methods. In the class I took sophomore year, there was part instruction, part peer review, and I just made my mind up to do whatever was required to get a decent grade. Grades were serious stuff to me and I didn't appreciate requirements like physical education screwing them up. But of course, math and science were also detriments to my ever achieving a superior GPA.

As for the peer "grading", I wasn't too scared about that. I didn't care what anyone said, would probably never see most of them again, and besides, I had come from a high school where I was at the top of the class in writing, not the bottom.

Little did I know none of that would mean a thing. It was brutal.

"So, how did you do?" Cass asked, meeting me in the Union right after I had the first poetry writing class.

"What could I do? I didn't cry, if that's what you mean. I didn't cry because this doesn't mean anything to me. It's just a class. I think I can take criticism, especially if it's actually helpful."

"Ha! If you can take criticism <u>there</u>, nothing else will ever stymie you." She seemed actually impressed, if a little surprised at my attitude.

"Well, I guess so." I handed her the poem I had turned in. "Here's my poem."

> **He repaired to an atelier in the**
> **Charming property, the blue and white tiles of an antique stove**
> **Glistening in the last afternoon sun.**
> **He reached for a glass on the table**
> **But instead of drinking**
> **Flung the contents onto a painting.**
> **A fine grey mist now covered the part**
> **Where his fingers could have traced the Dauphin's facial features.**
> **He had studied this painting for a long time**
> **Thinking he admired it.**

"How long did you work on this?" she asked looking up at me rather startled.

"For a while."

"What did they say about it?"

"Okay, so they mostly hated it. And several people wanted to know who HE was. Someone said, 'A monk?' I just said he was a lonely guy who wasn't satisfied with the work. That sounded plausible, don't you think?"

Cass laughed. "They can all relate to that." Then she thought about it. "But if he studied it and thought he admired it, why wasn't he satisfied? "

"Look, the *he* who threw the glass might not be the *he* who painted it. Did you think about that?"

"Not really, no."

"So yeah, I didn't give them too much of an explanation. One of the girls in the class said I should be writing about myself and not dreaming up silly scenarios. Someone else thought it was a cry for help from a muse. I mean, get real. I just tossed this first one out there. I didn't analyze it too much."

"Well, I mean, your imagery must have come out of somewhere," Cass said in a thoughtful tone.

"Truth be told, I was looking at some pictures of French chateaux and sort of imagined a court artist holed up in a little studio somewhere on the property."

"Well, Versailles, since you said the painting was of the Dauphin."

"Okay, I guess so. The point was, actually, it was about the act of creating something. Is anyone ever really satisfied with the creative process? Are you?"

"I get it." she said, softly. "Well! Pretty good for a first go-round, kid!"

"Oh, don't get excited. The professor didn't seem at all impressed, although he acted like he was merely a collector of the work, not an *adjudicator*, as he put it. I don't even know if we get grades on the output or merely on attendance. What do you think?"

"To tell you the truth, I have no idea how the Workshop grades. Alan would know, though. "

"Yeah, well this isn't the real workshop either, so…"

The first poem was just that — a trial balloon and yes, it did suck. But I got better. Intertwined with our own creative writing, there would be assigned forms to work out, sonnets, villanelles, haiku and cinquains, even limericks. We would study stanzas, free verse, rhyme schemes, versification, syllabication, the tercet, the quatrain among many other topics, trying each out and taking home the worksheets every week to dissect and report out on our progress. It wasn't what I would call fun.

I had more success in British Lit class where a paper I wrote entitled "*An Analytical Explication of Wuthering Heights*" earned an **A** when I wrote about its transcendental setting and dimension, an "extra-strange dimension compared to the ordinary world of the novel. "

I was wildly excited to have received that grade.

"Look what he wrote, "I said, showing Cass and sweeping it around in the air. 'Very good study… thoughtful analysis of structure and emotional content.' Yay me!"

"So, "said Cass thoughtfully, as though she'd just had a brainstorm, "do you think you might want to teach this stuff some day?"

"Oh hell, no."

Cass and I settled back into a routine of dorm life rather than apartment life, and, while more restricted in the area of where we could go and when we had to be back at night, things hummed along in the fall term of '67. She was still Klampert's TA, and he did indeed teach her to drive the car. She thought she got the hang of it pretty well; it was an automatic, and like me, she didn't know how to drive with a stick shift, which he thought we should both know, but said he didn't have time to teach us. Soon she was ready to try out for the license.

One night in early October she told me she was staying out all night, sleeping at his house because the next day he was going to take her to the Johnson County Courthouse DMV and she would take the written test and, if she passed it, the driving one the same morning. It goes without saying that it was against the rules to stay out, but bed checks were rare, and as long as I wasn't confronted by some roaming RA and questioned about her whereabouts, no one would be any the wiser.

Cass had, to this end, been studying the Iowa Driver's Manual learning all the rules and regulations most of us had done at 16 years old, and she was sure she had that stuff down; but she seemed unduly worried about parallel parking. Klampert also hadn't had time to teach her to do it well enough to give her confidence, so one late afternoon in the week before she was planning to take the test, she and I walked over to his house and I took her out to practice it.

Before we tried the street parking in downtown Iowa City where there were regular curbed metered parking spaces, I drove to the parking lot of the law school still on Klampert's side of the river, and had her pretend to be parallel parking where there weren't any cars around for her to hit. We found some space that would stand in for a real parking space, and I stood in it, acting as another car. She had to pull up parallel to me and then back in behind me, straighten out the wheels and "be in the parking space."

"You're not exactly a car, "she protested.

"Same difference. Just don't hit me."

The law school parking lot wasn't crowded since day classes were pretty much over and the night ones hadn't started yet. But there were still a few cars, and even though the lot wasn't set up like street parking, we were able to have her practice parking in line with cars that were in the lot. We found one sort of isolated by itself in a space and pretended that the area behind it instead of beside it was the parking space.

"Get ready because you're going to do this now. Pull up parallel to this car and then assume the space behind it is a real parking space. Back into it."

"Right."

And she did it.

"I get it!" she said triumphantly.

"To the streets! " I pronounced.

And so we started out in Klampert's neighborhood where the street was straight, and she managed to park it just fine. But the situation there was still not like downtown; the examiner would certainly make her park in a metered space. So finally, after about two hours of trying everything else out, we headed to South Linn Street and found parking meters.

"Go for it, "I said.

She nodded and drove right up to a car, lined up, backed up and straightened it out. Perfectly.

"You've got this, " I declared.

"I do! Don't I?"

We celebrated by driving back across the river and getting pizza burgers at the drive-in in Coralville before taking the car back to its safe little haven in Klampert's driveway.

The designated day came and no one bothered to wonder where she was when she didn't come to dinner. Why should they, I rationalized; we didn't always eat together. I retired to our room and it was totally normal for me to have it to myself to study anyway, just like it had been totally normal for her to stay out sometimes when we lived in the summer apartment.

The next day, Cass passed with the proverbial flying colors and proudly displayed her new driver's license to me back in the dorm. I swear she was the only person I've ever met whose driver's license picture was gorgeous.

Soren Carlysle was beginning to be "my boyfriend" that fall, and one thing I loved about him was his interest in sharing with me both what I liked to do and what he liked to do. What he was most passionate about was this idea of his that he would be a music critic, so he was taking a music survey course for non-majors, to hone his skills on identification of important works and composers. He suggested I audit it with him.

I was unfamiliar with the idea of auditing classes, and he convinced me that I could do it, especially when he also wanted me to get the same little job he had in the Union as an usher.

"You won't believe the terrific concerts and recitals you'll get to hear," he said to tempt me. "If you audit my music appreciation class, you'll like it even more."

The music appreciation class was an elective I never thought to take, but of course, it was an obvious choice. Registration was closed except that you could petition to audit, and since it fit into my schedule and only met twice a week, I went ahead and signed on. The class was lecture only; I didn't have to discuss and I didn't have to take tests. I just had to sit back and listen—to the talk and then to the examples of styles or periods or excerpts of composers' works.

I had taken choir my whole school life, and I had taken private voice lessons during high school, as well as some piano lessons—until it became evident that I had neither the talent nor the staying power to make Betty want to continue paying for those. But nothing could have prepared me for the realization I had, once I started in this class, that I was completely "nulle" in classical music, and knew absolutely nothing.

I complained to Soren, embarrassed more than anything else, that I had so far to go before I could even identify any major works or be able to tell Mozart from Benny Goodman.

"Don't beat yourself up," he said sweetly. "That's why we come to university---to learn, and master that which will prepare us for 'the examined life'."

"The examined life?"

" 'The unexamined life is not worth living,' "he quoted. "Know who said that?"

Oh God, I was also worthless in philosophy.

"Nope."

"Socrates."

At least I'd heard of **him**.

Luckily for me, the U of Iowa course I was auditing that semester, while not a fifth-grade music appreciation class, was still just a survey, and Professor Clyde Brandon was not expecting his students to be in there if they actually knew much about music. He peppered his lectures with anecdotes and stories from the various composers' lives and gave us background information about how the works were produced. Later in my life I would be strongly admonished to pay no attention whatsoever to the artists' lives, but to appreciate the works of art on their own. One should not have given one whit about whether or not Edward Elgar, for instance, had taken on a music student who was "to have a guiding influence in his life." Her name was Caroline Alice Roberts and he married her on May 8, 1889. Brandon told us that *"just when doubts – not of his own ability – but of the possibilities of being heard were tormenting him, his wife entered the scene to strengthen, sustain and direct his path."* None of that was relevant? I found it fascinating! Edward Elgar became my very first beloved composer and I could listen to his works day and night for the rest of my life.

It was a most amazing semester for me taking so much French and Brit Lit, auditing this survey of music, plus ushering at the Union all at the same time, and all at the moment when a young unknown English composer and choir director was coming to do a master class with the University choir. Soren left me a message at the dorm one afternoon to come to the Union the moment I read it because, as he put it, "...this guy John Rutter is putting the U of I Concert Choir through its paces. What I'm hearing is blowing my mind!"

I got there in time to see this rather wiry young blond man – only a few years older than me! -- in jeans and a white tee shirt with the sleeves rolled up around his shoulders, pointing out to the students that they were about to sing one of his own compositions, and that it "had influences of French and English choral traditions in it" and to be on the lookout for these. I, too, was enthralled with the sounds he got from this group and wondered a lot after that just what those French influences could have been.

Note to self, etc. etc.

Soren and I ushered at guest appearances by many musicians and visiting literary figures that scholastic year, and I was eternally grateful he had convinced me to work that job with him and take the class. The University's own symphony orchestra was a high enough caliber to impress even true music connoisseurs, and the astounding guests we had that year in Iowa City were a sprinkling of present and future Who's Who–level stars. The U of Iowa was indeed the cultural oasis everyone called it. Cass liked to rub my nose in this every time I came back to the room enthused about having seen the Guarneri String Quartet or when she accompanied me to a reading by William S. Burroughs.

Alan Jones and Cass Hyde were "an item" much as I suspected she was really Klampert's lover all along. She never once talked to me about being in love with or even about sleeping with Professor Klampert, and I didn't ask. But I knew Alan had his own place, too, although he had hangers-on and other quasi-roommates in his apartment from time to time. I thought, naively, that Klampert was more her mentor and link to desired future studies with Mauricio Lasansky; and Alan Jones was more her date-night-USA ticket.

"Alan is taking me to a party at Vance Bourjaily's farm!" she announced one afternoon excitedly.

Vance Bourjaily was already famous when we were at Iowa, and so were his parties, as it turns out; but they had come to a sharp drop off after a car accident a few years prior, which had killed his daughter and her little fifth-grade friend, and he had been the driver. The party to which Alan Jones was taking Cass turned out to be more of a small dinner party rather than the sorts of blowouts that had led to a famous Bourjaily quote, "The mark of a good party is that you wake up the next morning wanting to change your name and start a new life in a different city."

When she got back she had met various workshop members. Bourjaily was faculty advisor to John Irving, so he was there. A poet named Marvin Bell was there and Cass was brimming with enthusiasm over having met someone even more famous: Donald Justice. I had seen all these names on the directory in EPB, but rubbing elbows with these literary luminaries was another dimension.

"Do all these people know Alan?" I wondered.

"I would imagine. If they don't now, they probably will. I mean, it's not that huge of a program. You know because you see the mailboxes when you take your class."

"Right. Well, that's cool. Were their wives there, too?"

"Yes, almost everyone had a partner for dinner. I guess come to think of it, most were introduced as wives. Not sure."

"Were they nice to you?"

"Yes, but I have to admit, I didn't add much to the 'scintillating' conversation—ha!"

"Did Alan introduce you as an art student---or more accurately an artist!?"

"No. He introduced me as his friend."

Conquest more like, I thought, smirking. Alan Jones might be in the Iowa Writers' Workshop, getting an MFA, working on a chapbook and possibly headed for a literary career, but Cass Hyde was already showing signs of becoming a print making *wunderkind*. He would one day be eating her dust, I predicted.

Cass' reputation in the U of I art school really came into its own that semester.

She had decided to do a series of linoleum prints that would resemble stain-glassed windows. Instead of Bible stories, she would tell a tale of culture, and portray iconic scenes and architecture from everywhere---the US, Europe, Asia—any continent. They could be buildings or they could be mountains; they could be man-made monuments or nature. It was a brilliant concept and I wondered just how she would pull it off color-wise. She did massive amounts of sketching before starting to work any of this onto the blocks. I marveled at her work ethic and at her creative flow. It seemed to overtake and consume her. Over the three months of autumn and leading up to winter holiday break, she worked feverishly, and I watched the project take form. Klampert was beyond pleased with her growth and development as a student and as an artist. Cass was on her way to glory, I could feel it.

I, in the meantime, was on my way to Paris, at least in my mind.

I spent many hours in Schafer Hall perusing catalogues of programs abroad. Iowa U had one of its own –in Rouen, of all places. So I met with my advisor to talk about it.

"I'm sorry *Mademoiselle* Shrier, "she started, "you don't qualify for our program. (… WHAT?!!) You have to reach the 300 level in French to apply, and you're not at that level, as you know."

Really? Well, tough shit for Iowa; I didn't want to go to Rouen anyway!

I fumed to Cass, "Come ON. *Rouen*? It'd be like someone coming to the States to study choosing Omaha when they could go to New York?! Putting their program in the hinterlands of France is insane. I will find a different one."

"Normandy is just beautiful, though," Cass mused. "But you're right! PARIS or bust!!"

"I 'd rather take weekend trips to Normandy once or twice than have to take EVERY weekend trip to Paris. What is their logic?!!"

"Probably cost. I know you'll find a program. Keep looking."

And so I did. I poured through the catalogues with renewed vigor. And then, tacked right up on the bulletin board, a thin flyer from a place called Pella College, that I had completely overlooked, finally caught my eye. I couldn't believe it! This little college in an even tinier town in Iowa than where I grew up, had an amazing array of study abroad programs all over Europe; and their one in Paris put the students in the actual Sorbonne! I could be going to the Sorbonne!!

"My God," I told Cass, "That's even better than say, going to some colleges' study abroad programs, because they spend their class time with each other and not in the French university. I'll bet a lot of the other programs are like that. I mean, they are in Paris, for sure, but in class with Americans and American professors. This program I've found is better!"

"Absolutely! YOU will be in the French system. Hot damn!" she enthused.

"Now I have to get accepted. Then I have to convince my parents. But, let me just say: I'm not going to ask them. I'm going to tell them. I'm going."

And since Thanksgiving vacation was upon us, armed with brochures, application papers and dreams, I got in the Rambler and headed west on Interstate 80.

106

Chapter Sixteen

"Incense and Peppermints"...Strawberry Alarm Clock

The potential drama swirling around in my mind over this determination that I had to go to school in Paris didn't really materialize that Thanksgiving of 1967. I had all the application papers at home and filled them out. The parents had to sign. Betty was for it and Nana was delighted at the prospect. Sol didn't put up much opposition because, it turned out, he didn't think I'd get accepted!

"You're not there yet, " he said as he signed his name on the line.

"I'll get accepted, "I said haughtily. "My grades are good enough and I have a lot of extra-curricular activity, including International House. Maybe that will count for something."

Knowing what I do now about study abroad programs, what mostly counted to be accepted was the ability to pay the tuition. We didn't really have that, but I hoped against hope that my grandmother would pitch in if it turned out that was the only thing standing between me and the Hexagon.

The weekend of Thanksgiving I was working a few shifts in The Spot to earn some more spending money when one of Sol's best friends came in for lunch and a glass of Schlitz.

"How's school going, Sarah?" he asked me perfunctorily. He knew how it was going because his kid was there, too, and was one of the boys who had "tattled" on me for dating an Indian freshman year.

"Great, Arnie, " I answered. "I'm going to the Sorbonne next year, though."

Sol shot me a look from behind the bar that would have killed the Thanksgiving turkey.

"You ARE, eh? How about that!"

"Yes, sir! It's going to be epic."

"You're not there yet," Sol had to correct me.

This time, the Hydes invited me to spend Christmas vacation in Kenilworth by way of a written invitation to me and asking also for my parents' permission. They intended to delay their annual trip to Gstaad and take Cass and me to New York City for the week between Christmas and New Year's before heading across to Switzerland. They wanted to be sure I had the go-ahead from my parents to make both trips, and they indicated they would fly me to Chicago on Christmas day this time, instead of me taking the train. I was flabbergasted.

Of course, Betty and Sol said yes; I would have just gone anyway even if they hadn't. My parents couldn't even fathom who these people were, I could tell.

"Why are they being so nice to YOU?" Sol wanted to know, reading over their letter.

"Maybe they like the idea of their daughter having a good roommate and friend," I ventured, trying not to sneer at him too much with my tone of voice.

"And we're happy you have a friend like Cass," Betty added. "She's a sweet girl."

I looked up from the letter in horror, however. "What am I ever going to take them as a hostess-thank-you gift THIS year?!"

Betty looked at me with a blank face. Sol grimaced.

I had, however already found something I thought would be wonderful for Cass!

I had gotten lucky shopping at Brandeis the Friday after Thanksgiving: they were having a French trade fair--- special event--- and the main floor of the store was redesigned to be a marketplace filled with French products, displayed under the French tricolor and the fleur de lys. Besides serious export products like cheeses and wine, which were towards the back of the ground floor near the Tea Room, there were all kinds of different areas set up like boutiques and souvenir stands with everything from little affordable things to the most famous luxury items France was known for.

I went wild in the cheap sections displaying barrettes, journals, pens, soaps, coasters, trays, key chains, and all sorts of scarves with the major monuments of Paris on them. Everywhere I turned snaking around the entire main floor was everything my heart desired! And I even bought some of it, especially a gorgeous cloisonné key chain of -- what else – the Eiffel Tower. Ubiquitous Eiffel Towers, ranging from two inches to two feet high decorated the aisles.

They had one whole section of pricey leather goods, handbags, and luggage made in France. And then things got really expensive as you turned a corner to the perfume section. Brandeis didn't have any French designer clothing for sale that year, but they did have all the famous designers' perfumes, and I tried them all: Joy, Chanel No.5, Miss Dior, Calèche, and my personal favorite Je Reviens by Worth. I could not afford any of these. Even in 1967 a small bottle of Joy was $100!

Next to the perfume, as prices continued to climb, there were silk scarves, cashmere shawls, leather gloves; and off in one corner, a mini-department of interior décor items including fireplace irons, silver candelabra, Baccarat, Limoges, Lyonnais silk fabrics, and tapestry pillows depicting La Dame à la Licorne and various other scenes from French country life.

And that's what I got for Cass for Christmas! A brilliant and inspired find: a pillow! I reveled in it!

Because the pillows had a range of sizes, I could actually afford a small one. It had a beautiful petit-point front, backed in navy blue velvet and trimmed in braid. The picture was just a fragment of La Dame…the one where there's a toy Spanish spaniel at her feet. My love of dogs determined that Cass should have this particular small pillow to prop up to read in bed with or put behind her neck as she watched t.v. I knew she didn't have anything like it and I knew she'd like the idea that it came from France.

There wasn't, however, even one thing there that I could have bought for the Hydes. Even if I could have afforded Baccarat or Limoges, Julia not only probably didn't need any more of that, but of course, could have bought it for herself, which, I rationalized, was not the point of a GIFT, after all. It's a gift. But it was a moot point considering the prices of absolutely everything in that category.

"Maybe you could find them some monogrammed guest towels. They have many houses with many bathrooms based on your accounts of staying with them. Everyone can use those, " Betty had told me. "Come home a couple of days earlier this year and I'll help you shop."

"No, "said Sol.

"NO?! Are you kidding me?!"

"Just hold your horses and get that snotty attitude out of your voice, " he barked. "Come with me."

And he led me back behind the kitchen to his office.

"Salesmen bring things here all the time, " he told me. "The other day I got a couple of these…they want me to sell them in the bar over Christmas, but the pricing is too high for us. Twenty-five dollars! Who ever heard of spending that on a box of food?!" He snorted at the very thought.

And he pulled down a wooden divided tray filled with an array of beautifully displayed dried fruits, nuts and candies covered in glazed cellophane paper and tied around the corners in a huge bow. It was absolutely gorgeous and, I thought, quite unique. I had certainly never seen one like it in any store I shopped in. There were two and a half pounds of dried apricots, apples, figs and dates and even dried Bing cherries. Then in little square boxes tucked into the tray were cinnamon toffee almonds, roasted salted pistachios in the shell, and chocolate-covered giant cashews.

"You can take this with you and give it to them." He looked at me and handed me the tray.

"Gee…really??!"

"Well, it can be from all of us. After all, they're taking you to New York as well as putting you up for two weeks. Put all our names on the card."

"I will! And thanks, Daddy!" I wanted to hug him, but he'd already turned away.

We had a month still in school before leaving for Christmas break, and I spent a lot of it in the French and Italian department getting my Pella College application in order. My advisor was well aware of the program sponsored by the little school an hour and a half from the "big U", and she only half-heartedly helped me with letters of recommendation and other information. I sensed her attitude and reminded her that I didn't qualify for my own school's program.

"Well, Sarah, you must understand that most students who major do not start at the 102 level like you did. "

"My high school only had French by the hair of its chinny chin chin, " I said with resignation in my voice.

*And it was true. The only languages we had were Spanish and Latin. And we wanted French! Well, I wanted it. And my closest friends wanted it. These girls were in the class behind me when I was a junior at Bluff High. I had gotten friendly with them in American Field Service Club, and we all opined about how the Omaha schools all had French and we didn't! But there happened to be an English teacher that **they** had and loved, whom we knew to have gone to Catholic boarding school in Kansas City where she had had to speak French to the nuns. She was a young, beautiful charismatic teacher – only six years older than I was, to be precise, married to a med student at Creighton University, and teaching to support them and put him through.*

My sophomore friends had taken me with them into her room often after school just to shoot the breeze with her...we became her acolytes. We all called her Madame, even though she wasn't a French teacher. We talked to her at great length about some way to do French. Towards the end of that school year, we were in her room helping her pack up for the summer, when we petitioned once again:

"Can't you pleeeeease teach us French?" we begged. "We could come in after school next year like maybe three times a week or something?"

"I'm going to do better than that, " she told us, probably dreading adding an extra-curricular prep to her already busy schedule. "I'm going to try to get it in the curriculum. You girls have been asking for this the whole year; let's see what we can do."

And she did it!! That next year, we had an experimental no-text audio-visual course, French I, and we all joyfully signed up for it! We watched movies starring the revered Margot et son oncle. The first lesson was "Où est la bibliothèque?" and when I was taking notes from it, I wrote in my little spiral tablet, "WE" for yes. I loved French class so much and sang Madame's praises to all my other teachers. When my hitherto favorite venerated but much feared (not by me) American Lit teacher, Mr. Moreno, would pass by the open French classroom door on his free period, he would wave very discretely to me as he saw me in class seated in the front row. I had loved his class and he knew I loved this new one.

Midway through that first French course, Madame came to class in a beautiful grey wool peplum jacketed suit and when she removed the jacket and draped it behind her chair, we all of a sudden saw a noticeable bump on her otherwise slender form. A baby!!!

May would roll around and there would be a newly minted doctor father, a sainted beauty mother, and this heaven-sent bundle welcomed into their awaiting arms. We were all overcome with rapture over this, our holy family. I would be home the whole summer before going away to college, and I promised to baby-sit at the drop of a hat for them, which I did do. But by the time July came, they moved away for his residency match, and I never saw her again.

I managed to put together my *curriculum vitae scholasticae* replete with letters of recommendation and my official transcripts to date, along with the filled out and signed application, health record and $15 and mailed it off to Pella College. It was a waiting game now. I tried to remain calm, but truth be told, every night my head hit the pillow, I imagined life in Paris until I fell into sleep where I could continue to dream about it.

Soren and I spent the fall semester going to Iowa football games that we could all attend on our activity cards. His dorm sort of expected him to partake in university events of varying stripes because of his RA job, and, much as I hated football, I never minded the spectacle of school sports. During high school years, especially for wall-flowers of my persuasion, it was all there was to do on a weekend, and during college, well, Iowa was a Big Ten school and that meant something even though we only won a couple of games my entire college career.

Iowa U had the usual striation of status groups, and a subculture the whole country would later call *hippie* was beginning to emerge. Soren and I were not even on the fringes of that; we weren't townies, and, of course, we were not Greeks. So that left residence hall dwellers and that didn't appeal to my sense of style. So I decided we would be eclectic, quasi-iconoclasts.

We wore "mod" clothes. My favorite outfit for football games was plaid mini-skirt, black tights, black turtleneck sweater, thick oxford tie shoes, and my long camel coat. If it was cold out, my present from Cass, the fox fur hood, came out and wearing it I would saunter into Kinnick stadium on Soren's arm, like I owned the place. The games themselves bored me to death; I didn't drink beer, so there was nothing to do but try, without much success, to figure out why people were screaming at a bunch of guys running up and down the field. I took to bringing reading material and that made my football weekends more palatable.

Cass was dating Alan Jones almost exclusively, although many other BOYS more her age wanted to date her. She began to get a lot of calls and notes left for her. But Alan was the most successful suitor. He turned out to not have a car, and they rode around on his 1960 Norton 600 "Dominator" motorcycle. He wore a helmet but only had one, so more often than not, she was on the back with just the wind in her hair. Luckily they only drove around town and not on any highway trips. But you almost had to wear protective eyewear on any ride because dust and particles blew up in your eyes and really caused a sting; so she bought herself a pair of dynamite aviator-style cruiser goggles in a light shade of copper.

One afternoon in mid-December, she came into the room with red, puffy eyes.

"Oh no, did you forget your goggles and ride the bike with no protection? " I asked when I saw her face.

"No." And then she broke down sobbing. "We...g-g-ot into a f-f-fight."

"What happened!" I was incredulous.

"He h-h-ates my work."

"Your art!? Come on."

"Yeah...he...he said it was stupid. My stained-glass series. Kid, it's almost the end of the grading period. I can't start over now."

I looked at her, so dejected and defeated, standing there sobbing. I lost it and just went off.

"Start OVER?! Because of what Alan said? CASS! Get a grip! Who's fucking Alan Jones to criticize YOUR art anyway?! You don't critique his poetry for godsake! And Klampert and the others LOVE your project! They would have told you waaay before now if anything had been so wrong with it that you had to start over. It's BRILLIANT, and..and beautiful...and meaningful. You tell Alan to go take a flying leap!!"

She seemed to calm down in a short amount of time and we went back over to the studio together. Her finished sheets were hanging on the wall and her linoleum blocks were laid out waiting for the next colorations to take place. She had about five to go. I reiterated how great they all were. She had my beloved Eiffel Tower rendered rather cubism-like, standing amidst a swirl of shades in psychedelic oranges and yellows, with the sun setting behind it and the Seine at its feet swirling in blues and teals. She had *Mont Blanc* in its majestic splendor surrounded by clouds of varying shades of white, grey and beige on a blue background sky with snow coming down in the Japanese print style of Hokusai around it. That's what Alan had vehemently objected to, I was told.

"He said he'd fail a student who wrote a Japanese haiku instead of his own poem; that I was derivative and showed hardly any imagination."

"Oh, please. You're using their method; you're not plagiarizing Hokusai. I'm amazed you could do it and make it look like he did. It's so beautiful. "

She showed me the rest of the finished product: a Frank Lloyd Wright house — not the one we saw, but the more famous Falling Water; the Brooklyn Bridge, Versailles, and a pastoral rendering of London's Hyde Park.

"**Hyde** Park. How ironic -- I suppose he'll accuse you of stealing its name," I sneered. She managed to laugh.

Cass signed all her works in a way that I hadn't realized then was so cool. A year later when touring the *château de Chenonceau*: I saw what she must have already seen because she entwined her initials together CBH sort of on top of each other, the way Henri II had incorporated a D for Diane (de Poitiers) — his lover- - into his H for Henri and C for Catherine (de Medici) — his wife-- above all the doorways and fireplaces in the castle. (Catherine had not been pleased.)

I was a little surprised but not altogether unhappy that Alan had stopped calling her, but she was miserable about it, and seemed to sink into a gloomy place from which she could not emerge.

"Hell, I thought he was crazy about you, "I told her, "so where all this criticism of your work came from is a mystery to me."

I pondered the disconnect. Was he so insecure that he would resent her inevitable ascent to artistic heights he couldn't even fathom at that point? But if he really liked her, wouldn't he be happy for her success, as she was for his?

But I was also very -- that is to say **completely** -- preoccupied with my own schooling that semester. Every grade seemed to count for me to be able to go to France next year. Every paper I wrote or paragraph

I translated was like a tally sheet for the coming grade. I would not have a sullied transcript spoil my chances at such a life-changing all-consuming dream.

Right on cue, Anthropology threatened to be the next downfall of my GPA and I was determined not to let that happen. Luckily, Cass did snap out of her funk, and thus was available to talk **me** down from the ledge a few times. Doing research never interested me and the papers I wrote were, of consequence, more deductive than observational. I was not drawn to the field because of the excitement of research in a natural setting or even because of curiosity about how cultures originated …in a social science way. It did interest me, however, to discover customs of various peoples, and I was fascinated by the archeology side of things. That they could piece together a long-lost thread of civilization based on the ceramic shards it left behind piqued my curiosity. But I wasn't going to be staying with this field long enough to actually get into archeology, and in the meantime I had to muddle through an ocean of survey material exhaustively comparing many civilizations, many peoples, many species. I seriously had to work to stay afloat in that morass, but I came out of it in the end with a "B."

Cass was floundering a bit in French, but only for lack of effort, not because it was hard or because she wasn't bright. You actually had to hand in work and go to the lab to get the credit, and Cass had let both of those things slide.

"Could you just do these homework exercises for me?" she asked me one day when we met in the Goldfeather Room of the Union, which we weren't doing too often any more due to her lack of free time from the studio.

"Of course I could. What good would THAT do you? You have to take the quizzes and tests, and if you don't practice this yourself, you won't be able to."

She looked up at me all of a sudden as though she were going to burst into tears, but instead stunned me with a proposition: "You could take the final for me!"

"No, Cass."

"Wait, listen: they give them in this big exam hall or something, right? And you have to have your number out on the corner of the desk. I could give you my number; no one will know you're not me."

"Maybe not, but they'll know I'm ME. I've taken four classes in that department so far. They know I'm a declared major."

"So what---you're just a person in a room of 300 other ones taking a French I exam. No one who knows you will be proctoring that test."

I doubted that there were 300 French I students at Iowa in a given semester. French was still an elective; Cass was confused, thinking of classes like Rhetoric or Life Science where the scenario she described was accurate.

"I would do just about anything for you, you know that, " I stated. "But I can't cheat like that for you. We'd both get kicked out of this place if we got caught, Cass. We can't risk our collegiate careers on a stupid elementary French exam. Besides, this isn't hard stuff. I'll tutor you. You just got behind."

I motioned for her to sit down.

"Here, let's just do this together. We can knock it off in fifteen minutes."

"I CAN'T! "she practically screamed at me. She took my arm and led me over to a more secluded table.

"I can't stay here right now! I've got to get back to the studio!" She began to weep now as she had seemed about to before.

"What is wrong?!" I was actually becoming alarmed now. She didn't act like this!

"I was just doing my usual printing, "she muttered, between sobs, "when Alan came into the studio and I didn't see him. He came up behind me and said 'Boo!' and I jumped and the lino cutter slipped, so I made a long mark I didn't want! " She was heaving now and she lowered her voice to a whisper. "He—he—s-c-c- scared me and I... I wet my pants!!"

"Oh no."

She was crying now, but continued. "I couldn't sit there like that so I just told Alan to get out, and I ran into the bathroom. "

"And...?"

"Well, of course, I had to get some other clothes, so I ended up having to go back to the dorm."

111

"Oh, Jesus. Did a bunch of people see you?"

"I suppose.   "

"Well, just try to forget about it. Give me that assignment. I'll do it, and you go back to the art building."

She took my arm and pulled me towards her. We hugged; she sobbed, and I patted her back. She eased away from me and took a Kleenex out of her pocket to wipe her eyes, still sniffling.

"Thank you, kid. I owe you one."

"You don't owe me anything. Tonight after you get back, we'll go over the French so that godforbid someone calls on you tomorrow, you'll know the answer and how **you** got it, " I laughed.

"I'm a mess, Sari. I'm a complete mess."

"You're not. You're just upset. You'll figure it all out, fix your print, everything will be fine. Anyway, come on now — no one who's not the artist can tell if a line on a block print was a mistake or if you meant it to be there. Am I right?"

"Yeah, you're right. Hey...Sari. I love you."

"Love you, too. See ya later."

Chapter Seventeen

"Society's Child"...Janis Ian

Just as I predicted, Cass made the mark on her block print look like it belonged there. She got such a high grade on the whole ensemble project that the print professors showed it to Lasansky and her future as his protégé was all but sealed. They also exhibited her work with the senior art show, even though she was a junior; and we relished her fifteen minutes of fame on the University of Iowa campus, which, as a matter of course, did not escape the attention of Alan Jones.

"Alan saw my works displayed, " she announced to me during the last weeks before we were to leave on break. "He apologized to me. He wants us to go back to where we were."

"And how do you feel about that?" I asked trying to suppress any smirk.

"I really like him, Sari. Something about the poetic soul, you know?"

Not really.

"Oh, and you'll never guess what else...he applied to be a C.O.!"

Ah, the draft. Hanging worse than the sword of Damocles over every boy and unmarried man at the U.

"Well, I hope he gets it, but what will that mean?"

"He thinks he'll be able to do volunteer work for some agency like the Literary Council or something, and stay in Iowa City. He thinks he can keep his T.A. job and still do the volunteer work."

Cass was a lot less agitated now that her artwork was a huge success and her grades secured. She managed to do enough French to catch up, and write papers in her English classes. We were both studying very hard and were rather focused, at that.

Alan and Soren liked each other, so we made a few double dates, including a movie night out to see *Morgan!* We went to the Ramskeller afterwards for a happy analysis of the film.

"I thought the character was pathetic," Soren stated right off.

"Why?" we all wondered!

"Because he's so naïve and weird that he couldn't keep his relationship together even though the ex-wife is actually his art dealer and therefore can make or break his career."

"But didn't you love the whimsy? The character is obviously a Peter Pan type---he can't face the adult world. And he fought valiantly to keep her!" Cass chided him.

"Why would she come back to an idiot who crashed her wedding to the guy she really loved?" Soren continued.

"Who's to say she really loved him?" Cass answered.

I added my two cents' worth. "I just love Vanessa Redgrave. Thought she was magnificent in the film."

"I agree. And I thought the screenplay was terrific," said Alan.

Cass turned back to Soren. "So did you hate it?" Cass asked.

"I didn't hate it."

"I thought it was really funny!" I said.

"It was more than funny," Alan said, "it was actual farce. That is a higher art. And Soren's right about him being pathetic but that's what is so beguiling about the way Warner plays him. He's a child –a guy with arrested development emotionally and probably intellectually as well, but not sexually. It's funny but also scary, didn't you think?"

"Well, yes, *professor*, now that you put it that way," I said.

Alan and Cass left on the motorcycle and Soren and I walked back to Burge Hall and sat in the lobby on one of the hot pink vinyl couches. We weren't going to be seeing each other after that night until second semester started.

"You'll have a great time with them in New York," he said.

"What will you do? Home to Imogene?"

"Yep. Midnight mass on Christmas Eve with the 'rents and grands."

"But you like it, right?"

"I like it." He reached over and took my face in his hand. "I wish you were going to be with me." We kissed, and I turned and buried my head in his shoulder. We just sat there, entwined in each other's arms.

"Maybe someday I'll show up in Imogene, you know? And you can try to explain me away to your parents. That ought to be good. Your nice Jewish girlfriend from The Bluffs. They'll love that."

"They would adore you," he tried to convince me...or maybe himself.

Well, mine wouldn't adore you, I thought. But they'd be relieved you were white.

Cass stayed with Alan that night after the movie and for several other nights in that last week before we left school. She didn't make a big deal about it and waited until mid-morning to go back to the room so as not to cause any suspicion. She was back in the room the night we were packing to leave.

"I don't have many different clothes to bring to New York," I told her, realizing as I put the same old things in the suitcase that this could present a problem.

"Well," she said, standing at her side of the closet. "I'll bring this one." She held up the navy blue with the pink sash that I'd borrowed before and still loved. "And really, Sari, you can share my clothes there, too. My stuff fits you."

I was sorry I must have seemed like such a charity case, but relieved, too, that she was so generous of spirit and such a great friend.

I drove home to The Bluffs, radio blaring, happy as a lark. I worked my shifts at the bar, and because it was Christmas, tips were bigger than usual. I got some extra "Chanukah gelt" from Nana, who was delighted I had been invited by Cass' family to go to New York. She had several brothers and cousins I had never even heard of still living there. One day she came into the bar while I was working and pressed a little folded up paper into my hand.

"These are the names and addresses and phone numbers of my brother Ernest and my brother Leo," she said. "If you have a chance, will you call them up? I've already dropped them both a note to let them know you might be getting in touch."

"Of course! Do you think we can meet?"

"I don't know, honey. I have no idea what you will be doing there with Cass' family."

"Well, I'll really try to do it. "

Just before I was to leave, a large special delivery envelope showed up for me at the house. That had never happened before! In it was my plane ticket from the Hydes. My itinerary was Omaha/Chicago/New York/Omaha. I would not be flying back to Chicago with Cass nor returning straight to school with her either, because I had to drive my own car back. The logistics of all this were rather convoluted due to my obligation to work the few days before and including Christmas Eve.

I pored over the contents of the special delivery envelope and all my flight itineraries, which Julia's secretary had typed out for me. There seemed to be a gap: I saw all right that I was to fly the one flight from Omaha to Chicago and another from New York to Omaha. But Chicago to New York wasn't in there. And then it hit me: we must be taking the private plane to New York. *Ho-ly- shit.*

My head was actually spinning over all these various airplane reservations because I had only ever flown one time (round trip) prior to this: when I was fourteen and we went to Phoenix to see my mother's cousins.

It was just Betty, Nana, the six-year old Roslyn and me; Sol stayed back because when you owned a bar, you couldn't really ever close---not in America, at least. Flying United Airlines had been a real adventure. We got these cute square flight bags with the company logo, and we were all dressed up. We didn't fly first class, of course, but the plane wasn't very full and we could all spread out. The flight was non-stop, as were all my flights on the Hyde trip. Flying didn't scare me; I had total faith in the pilots, who were mostly the age of my dad – maybe a little younger, and most were WWII vets. I had never heard of very many plane crashes then. I had complete confidence in all crews and their ability to deliver me to my destination safe, comfortable and well taken-care of. Roslyn got a pin of little wings and was enthralled to sit by the window.

114

The Hydes had put me in first class for all the legs of the trip I'd take alone: from Omaha to Chicago and from New York to Omaha. A one-hour trip isn't really even long enough to get the benefits of flying first class, and in the 60's air travel wasn't the cattle call it is today, so being able to board first didn't mean much, if anything. But I did enjoy the extra attention; the hot towel dipped in lemon water for my hands, and the pampering with trays of hot food on china and silver ware.

However, let's be clear: nothing, no amount of reading up on it or watching tv or movies could have prepared me for travel in the private Hyde Industries jet.

So I packed up my best outfits --- I wouldn't have to be a complete free-loader on Cass--- of course, the same boots I wore all winter, my great camel coat, my fur hood (!), Cass' pillow and the fine dried fruit and nuts gift, and boarded the plane for Midway.

Cass met me at the gate just like she'd met me before on the train platform, and Martin was down at the luggage carrousel waiting for us. I had to show him my claim ticket and it had to match my suitcase, which of course, it did since I had the only light blue, round suitcase that came out. We drove back to the house in the Bentley and were greeted by her parents, who met us this time in the vestibule leading into the grand hallway. I offered Mrs. Hyde my present and she accepted it graciously.

"Welcome back, Sarah!" she intoned.

"How are you my dear?" Mr. Hyde said warmly, shaking my hand.

"Thank you so much for inviting me again," I said, "and for the trip to New York! I'm just so excited!"

They were indicating that Cass and I must follow them into the living room, which, to my amazement, was full of other people! What's more, there was a buffet table set up with staff carrying around trays of hors d'oeuvres and drinks, too. They were not the Hyde family staff, of course, since it was Christmas night and they still had the time off. These were catering company people. I guess a lot of people really do work on Christmas. It struck me as rather sad.

But I perked up as Cass ushered me through the buffet line and we took our plates off to the uncrowded corner of the room where the Christmas tree stood glimmering and laden as ever.

"Is your grandmother here? "I asked looking over my shoulder into the crowd to try to see her.

"No, no. She spends Christmas with the Springfield cousins. She hates to travel in snow anymore."

"So none of these people are your relatives? "

"No," Cass said, wondering why I thought that. "Just friends. Some are neighbors. Some are friends from the club. You know."

Okaaay. I guess people don't always hold holidays as sacred family time.

"Here, " Cass said offering me a long, narrow orange box unwrapped, like last year, tied with a brown woven ribbon with the iconic horse and carriage on it, the *calèche*. Now I had seen Hermès bottles of perfume before, and I knew that Princess Grace of Monaco had a bag named for her, "The Kelly." But I had never beheld anything Hermès as it came packaged, and was just floored when I realized where this gift must have come from.

I slowly untied it and lifted the lid, parting the tissue that covered a pair of dark brown glossed lambskin gloves with gold tone cuff ornaments, what, I learned were called "Medor" gloves.

"Oh, Cass, they're the most beautiful gloves I've ever laid eyes on. Thank you SO MUCH. "

"They should go great with your coat."

"But, really, Cass!! Too expensive."

And I had no idea!

I brought out mine to offer her, but I was beginning to hate the idea of giving her anything! No matter what I found, bought, wrapped up and presented to her, nothing could ever come close to these gifts I'd received twice now in Kenilworth. But hand it over to her I did anyway!

"Oh, wow! "she exclaimed. "From France?!"

I nodded.

"I LOVE this!! How did you ever manage it?"

I told her all about the French trade fair event at Brandeis.

"Ha! I can just see you in there. You must have been in your element!"

"I had fun, I'll say that."

"I can't believe you kept quiet about this between Thanksgiving and now!!"

Christmas Day fell on a Monday that year, and we weren't slated to fly out to New York until that Wednesday because John-Wilfred had meetings to attend to, and other business, which was another reason their Gstaad trip was put back. The Swiss hotel deals had gone so well that whole year, that representatives from Hong Kong were coming into Chicago to talk to him about replicating them in their city.

On Tuesday night the four of us were gathered for dinner and even though we practically had to shout to be heard up and down the huge table where Cass and I were seated across from each other and the parents at either end, literally yards apart, it was a jolly evening. I made it a point to praise Cass' art project to the hilt and make sure they knew how monumental it was for her work to be shown in the final seniors' exhibit. They seemed a bit surprised, and, finally, pleased.

"And what about you, Sarah? Do you do art, also?"

"Ha! No."

"She took a linoleum block printing class, though! And it came out all right, too," Cass added.

"Yes, but my final print was just a vase with some non-descript flowers in it. Although I did like learning the process and doing the colors. It looked like a kindergartener's picture being brought home compared to Cass' masterpieces."

We moved into the library this time and John-Wilfred walked over to a huge oak bar that occupied one entire corner of the room, and poured brandy into snifters.

"Sari and Cass? Would you like a drink also? "

"None for me, thank you," I said, gesturing with a little wave. Brandy, cognac, Armagnac and all those sorts of liquors burned my throat and made me gag.

Sol had, as I mentioned, tried to introduce me to alcoholic drinks one year. Not that I could ever serve them, but just as a sort of "education", and we had quite the assortment in our home liquor cabinet. Nothing like the Hydes' bar!

Cass took a small amount, and she and I sat on a deep leather Normanson sofa with brown braided tassels going all the way around the bottom. The parents took large leather wing chairs across from us.

Julia explained to us that we two would be staying at the Plaza Hotel rather than with them in the Hyde apartment, which was quite near there, on 76th and 5th Avenue.

Cass shot me a look of delight.

"Our *pied-à-terre*, as Cass can tell you, is quite compact," Julia said, "and I just thought you girls would have more fun at the Plaza. We'll come over there and have meals with you, too."

"So cool," I said, thinking of *Eloise at the Plaza.*

"It's a good location for sight-seeing," John-Wilfred added. "What did you have in mind to see while we're there, Cass?"

"Oh, gee — the usual stuff. Sari?"

"Anything! Statue of Liberty? The Met?"

"MOMA for sure," Cass said. "Oh , and you know what else we could do? We could go to some of the literary places, too."

"Oh!" I suddenly exclaimed, "Like the carrousel in the Central Park Zoo where Holden Caufield watched Phoebe and felt happy?!"

"Uh, okaaaay, sure," Cass said, "I was thinking more of the Algonquin Hotel Blue Bar---ha!"

"Can we even walk into a hotel bar, though?" I wondered. "And be served, I mean."

"Well, you've got a point. Maybe not."

She was probably thinking I was the one who'd give it away that we were not sophisticated enough to be there.

"But we must also go into the Village and for sure hit Washington Square."

Just then I remembered to ask them about calling my great uncles.

"Would you mind at all if I got in touch with two of my grandmother's brothers while I'm there?

"

"Not at all," Julia said looking a bit quizzical. "Do you know where they live?"

"Yes! I just found out---on 10th Avenue in Brooklyn."

116

"Oh. Goodness," she said.

Oh, no! I thought. The slums? I didn't know New York then, and of course, only had a cursory knowledge via books and magazines of "the Upper East Side" or for that matter any of the other neighborhoods of Manhattan. But I did register that a different borough would be a lesser one, a worse place, possibly somewhere the Hydes wouldn't be caught dead.

"I'm sure if you call them and if you want to go see them, we'll figure it out," she added, reassuring me.

Suddenly there was a commotion out in the hallway when the doorbell rang its Westminster chimes.

"Oh dear," Julia said with a nervous little laugh, "I hope no one thinks our party was tonight instead of last night!"

Mrs. Lotie Brandon was hurrying across the travertine tiles to answer it. And then, in a few minutes, who should appear in the doorway of the library, but Alan Jones!!!

Alan just stood there in motorcycle leathers with his helmet under one arm, his face flushed with cold, his blond curls tamped down on his head, very disheveled and tracking in wet snow with his "stompin' boots" as we teasingly called his dirty black Chippewa engineer's boots.

Suddenly he looked up and saw ME.

"Miss Shrier! What are *you* doing here?"

"I was invited for Christmas."

Cass jumped up, horrified, but trying to remember her manners.

"Mummy, Papa, this is Alan Jones." The Hydes rose.

Alan pulled off the glove of his right hand which he extended to John-Wilfred, who ignored the gesture.

"Excuse me," huffed Julia, "who are you again?"

"My- uh—friend from school, Mummy. He was Sari's freshman English teacher. We met that way."

Oh, great! Pawn it off on me would you!

"Cassandra," her father started, "did you invite this young man here?"

"No, but..."

"Then I think he should leave. Now." And he began to escort Alan back to the front hall.

"I'll show him out," Cass reached in front of her father, grabbed Alan's sleeve and walked towards the door with him. I followed them.

"What are you doing here?" she hissed at him in a whisper.

"I just wanted to see you so much! Had some free time...thought you'd be pleased."

"Well, you can't *do* it this way. Just show up. Jesus!"

"Alan, seriously," I said, "are you insane?!!"

"Well, Sari," he laughed, "I did not expect to see you here either!"

"Where will you GO? You can't just sleep outdoors...it's below zero out!" Cass worried.

"I'll find a motel. Can I see you tomorrow? Are they keeping you two locked up in here?"

"We're leaving for New York tomorrow. So no, you can't see us."

"Bad timing on my part, eh? Okay, we'll see each other as soon as school starts again, then."

"Just go! Hurry." She didn't want her parents to see them together so she pushed him out onto the porch and kissed him good-bye.

We closed the door and waited until we heard the motor of his Norton rev up.

We then went all the way back down the hall to face her parents waiting outside the library.

"What is the meaning of THAT?" Julia snapped.

"I'm sorry Mummy, I really am. I didn't know anything about it."

Her father spoke up rather more loudly than I'd heard his voice before. "Is he your boyfriend, Cassandra?"

"Wellllll, kind of. He's very smart, and he's in the famous Writer's Workshop—and a teacher in the English department. He's doing his MFA."

117

"I don't care if he's working on another rocket with Wernher Von Braun! I do NOT want you involved with anyone like that."

"Like what?" Cass was afraid to confront him, but she was also miffed.

"You come with us," Julia beckoned Cass. And then addressing me, she added, "Will you excuse us, Sarah?" And this time they all went into the library and he shut the door.

I sat on one of the needlepointed benches in the foyer waiting, while Cass' parents grilled her for what seemed an eternity. Julia was especially livid and was giving Cass all kinds of grief about how inappropriate it was for someone who looked like a vagabond to "**just arrive at the door uninvited!**" And how what he wore and how his hair looked were an abomination. John-Wilfred was very angry at the thought that Cass had never mentioned him to her parents, and had thus lied by omission that she was dating this guy.

I heard Julia practically screaming at Cass about how it was beyond her that someone would even deign to believe he could just show up out of the blue like that unannounced. "He can't have had a decent upbringing to do something like that, and therefore he is unsuitable to date **our** daughter!"

John-Wilfred also laid into Cass about riding on motorcycles and forbade her right then and there to ever do it again. And that was an ORDER.

And then the real clincher: Julia piped up with the "absolute humiliation if people found out her daughter was involved with a no-body motorcycle-riding grad student. It's unheard of in our circles!"

Both of them managed to express in no uncertain terms their anguish about how he wasn't her *caliber* of boyfriend, and how beneath her it was to even be seen with such a person. How could she be so disrespectful **to them**, dating someone so unworthy of her and her name. "He's just not our *kind*."

At first I could hear Cass whimpering a little and trying to get a word in, but after a while she just gave up.

I, in the meantime, was nervous that they'd cancel our trip to New York, out of sheer fury with her; but that didn't happen. I guess they thought it would be safer having their daughter under their thumb in New York, than sneaking around seeing Alan in Chicago.

Cass eventually was set free to find me and go upstairs to organize and pack. We were absolutely still going on our wonderful jaunt to New York on the private plane; staying in the Plaza Hotel and romping around at will.

"They'll get over it, "she assured me, more or less to try to convince herself maybe more than me.

"I mean, wow. Alan's got some chutzpah. How did he even know where you live?"

"Well, he said he was writing me a poem and he'd mail it to me during vacation, so I gave him my address and phone and all that."

"But Cass, it didn't seem like he was fully prepared to see you in your native habitat-- if I may use an anthropology term, ha ha—particularly since he just up and appeared on your doorstep. Didn't you ever clue him in on how –you know—-upper crust you are?"

"Maybe not, " she admitted, trying to sound nonchalant. But she was absolutely under duress.

"So all right then. 'I see said the blind man.' He's probably freaking out right now."

"Look, you should get this: there's a whole stereotype of *poor little rich girl* that was perpetrated plenty on us at Rosemary-Choate. I wanted to leave that behind the minute I got out of there. I mean, I liked that school—I really did. But I just want to be accepted at Iowa for who I am, not WHO I am. If you follow."

"Yeah, I do. But who you are IS being Cass Hyde of Hyde Architecture and Industries, too. *Noblesse oblige* …you're stuck with it."

"*Noblesse oblige*..and all that *rawt*, "she teased with her best fake British accent.

"You'll have to square the whole mess with Alan when you see him in a few weeks. But do you think your parents will be mad the entire rest of our vacation?"

"I don't think so."

But she certainly wasn't sure.

Chapter Eighteen

"Leavin' on a Jet Plane"...Peter, Paul & Mary (John Denver)

If Cass had a complex about being a poor little rich girl in anyone's eyes then I must have had one about being a poor little poor one. Stepping out of a limo and onto the tarmac at Midway Airfield, walking across to a parked jet and climbing the stairway were alien to me. Not only had I hardly ever flown, I had no way to even fathom how a private plane could be so different from a commercial one. Even in the 60's, the reconfigured interior of this de Havilland DH-125 was futuristic: all black leather and chrome seats, some in a "normal" position near the windows, and many others in conversation groupings with tables, and swivel chairs. Even the window seating had tables in between, and off towards the back was a larger seating and table arrangement. There were the usual loos but there was also a big bathroom in the back with a shower, a vanity, mirrors---everything you'd find at home. The farthest "stern" cabin made into a stateroom, and had a sleeper sofa the crew could make up for an overnight trip anywhere in the world. In the front, a wall separating the galley and cockpit from the rest of the plane had a large movie screen that would appear at the flick of a switch. We had several films on board in their metal containers, but no time really to watch one. The plane was equipped with telephones, dictating machines and a wire service, as well as an audio system where we could listen to five different channels of music at any seat or conversation area. The galley was not unlike a commercial plane's.

When we boarded, the Hydes settled into the sofa section while Cass and I took a window table. No one had said anything more about the Chicago Christmas drama, and we were driven to the airport with everyone talking about New York and acting like nothing had happened to change any of it. I was relieved. If something like that had happened at my house, I'd have never heard the end of it. My father would have made it a point to keep nagging and needling me until my mother would have had to tell him to drop the subject. Julia and John-Wilfred were cordial to me and perhaps just a bit cooler towards Cass, but then, I'd never seen them act any differently, so to me it seemed like either everything was back to normal or they had decided to stage a scenario of good-will...for now. Either way was fine with me.

The plane ride was fantastic and I was mesmerized. The crew literally waited on us hand and foot, from the first drinks—mimosas for all—I sipped it but would have rather had plain orange juice, which of course, I could have requested but decided not to be different right off the bat--- to the hot verbena washcloths, the delicious brunch food they served us—all on fine china with linen napkins and silverware that was the same pattern Cass' family used at home, "King Richard" by Towle.

At some point in the flight somewhere over Pennsylvania, Julia came up to us from her seat and told us that she had arranged some outings for us and the first one was that afternoon.

"Cassandra, it's been horribly hard for you to get a decent hair cut in Iowa City, hasn't it?" she asked but didn't give Cass enough time to react. "So I've booked both of you into Elizabeth Arden's this afternoon. It's an hour later there, of course, so you'll just have time to drop your things off at the Plaza and be taken over there. I've scheduled you both for manicures, a facial and a massage, and Cassandra you can do the haircut first and then at least have a mani-pedi and a facial. If there's not time for a massage for you, I'm sure you could get one at the Plaza. That okay, girls?"

"Thanks, Mummy," Cass said looking up at her with her huge eyes reflecting a hitherto unseen-by-me gratitude.

"Yes, thank you so much!" I echoed.

What was a facial anyway?

The flight was smooth thanks to the Hyde's pilot, Capt. Harrison B. Jenkins who flew the plane like a dream. Cass had known Jenkins all her life and called him "Captain J" when she took me forward at one point, to peek into the cockpit of the plane and meet him. There was space for a co-pilot and on longer flights they had one, but this time Captain J was flying solo. He was tall with a rugged build and a square jaw that really did remind me of Steve Canyon, from my favorite t.v. show as a kid.

In the fourth grade I was in love with and a devoted fan girl of Dean Fredericks, the actor who played Steve Canyon. Of course, I read the comic strip in our paltry little hometown newspaper, and the books Milton Caniff put out about the pilot dreamboat, **Steve Canyon: Operation Snowflower** *and* **Operation Convoy,** *which I carried with me to school every day and read over and over. But it was the television actor who prompted my heart's wings to take flight. Dean Fredericks was on my mind day and night. It lasted almost until Illya Kuryakin took his place.*

We landed and a limo took us first to the Plaza Hotel where the parents got out with Cass and me to register us and see that we were settled okay. Our room turned out to be a "junior suite" on the 21st floor with park views!

"Without belaboring the point," I whispered to Cass aghast, "once again practically my whole house could fit in here!"

The sitting room part had a full bar, a gorgeous white marble fireplace and beautiful Kelly-green silk draperies swagged and pulled back over enormous French-door windows. There was a cream-colored tufted sofa, the kind Cass must have thought was just a normal couch, so many of her houses had that same style. There were two large armchairs with bolster pillows on them, a coffee table, several end tables with beautiful lamps on them, and several other pretty chairs against one wall for extra seating if more people dropped in or something!

The bedroom part was also huge and so was the bed. I didn't know from sizes of beds in those days; my parents' bed was a double and my sister and I had twins. Period. Once or twice I'd heard the term "California King" ---mostly in conjunction with Jack Lemmon movies or on *The Price is Right,* but I had never bothered to determine just what that meant. This bedroom at the Plaza was more elegant and inviting than anything I could have ever dreamed up or imagined from reading *Eloise* stories, either!

I was still gawking around at everything when Julia's voice interrupted my reverie and brought me back to the present:

"Hurry up, now girls, we're going to drop you at the spa and head over to the apartment. Just grab your coats...maids can unpack for you."

So we followed them back to the elevator, back down to the splendid lobby and out down the steps to the waiting limo.

"Your mother and I will come back here at 8:00 o'clock," said John-Wilfred. "I've made reservations right here in the hotel... in The Palm Court for dinner."

"Groovy! "Cass called out to her father, and then turned to me. "You know there's another famous Palm Court in the Drake Hotel in Chicago, too, don't you? I guess it must be a common posh name for a hotel restaurant, huh?"

I had never heard of it so this was news to me.

Elizabeth Arden's Red Door spa-salons were too plebian for Julia Hyde, but because she was familiar with the services offered at the Chicago one, and since it was a chain and had that convenience element, she chose it for us as a place she could trust for her daughter to have good, safe treatments with decent products.

Suffice it to say the only type of **spa** I'd ever heard of was like Warm Springs, Georgia or some other thermal spa where people with health problems went to "take the waters." I knew Europe had places people called spas. One of my French professors had brought up the film *Last Year at Marienbad* and had told us that that place was a spa. And I knew people went to locations that were called spas but were like clinics built on natural springs or near the mountains. That they could be right in a building in the middle of a city astounded and, I must say, delighted me.

We were ushered in and shown where to change into the softest, thickest, terry cloth robes I'd ever had on *my* body, that was for sure. We were given pillowy little slippers for our soon-to-be pampered little feet. Cass and I met at the locker area to put away our coats and handbags. She said to me, "I'll take care of the tipping, so don't worry about that."

Huh? Tips? I had no idea what any of this even cost, so calculating a tip would have been impossible for me to pull off. Thank God she was in control of all that.

She went off to the hair salon part, and I was led through, yes a red door, into a hallway with a series of other doors, each marked with a red letter of the alphabet. My "aesthetician" as they were called, took me into one of these little rooms ("C") and told me to disrobe, put on the gown she provided, and climb up on the table sitting on a slant in the middle of the dimly lit room. Non-descript classical music — not Muzak but not the New York Phil either, was piped into the room. It was all to be soothing and calming. I got up on the table bed under the sheet and lay back wondering if I were going to fall asleep.

A knock at the door and the lady entered again. She adjusted the head of the table, pulling out a sort of pillow with a hole in the middle my head would rest in, took out a strip of linen ribbon and tied my hair back with it, turned off the lights except for one, and then pulled over a machine that blew hot air onto my face. She started with cold cream to remove all makeup, wiping my face over and over with a little cloth. She slathered something else cold all over my face, circled around my eyes, and laid a slice of cucumber on each eyelid. In the meantime, Pachelbel's *Canon in D,* which I recognized from music appreciation class, played on.

With my face covered in what I now know was a mask of wonderful goop containing things like clay, black moor mud, aloe vera, seaweed or algae, the facialist moved to the end of the bed, rolled back the sheet and spread, and began rubbing lotion onto my *feet.*

And therein lay the epiphany of my young life: foot massages were the *non plus ultra.* What they had to do with getting a facial was beyond me, but I was not going to argue.

"Please don't let this ever stop," I murmured to myself, entering into a complete state of bliss.

When it did, she walked over to the side and started massaging my hands laying limp at my sides. After that was done, the mask was also finished, so she took it off and began the second phase of the treatment with applications of toner, serum, moisturizer, eye cream, lip balm and, even though it was winter, a little bit of sunscreen. She then handed me a goblet of water and said, "Take your time, Miss."

I got back into the robe and took my water out to the hall with me, where I was led through more doors into a nail salon. Cass was there, with freshly cropped hair in her "signature" wispy, feathery back and sides, and shorter pixie bangs. She looked fabulous.

"How was it?" she sang out.

"The BEST," I answered trying to sound a little less like a kid-in-a-candy-store-for-the-first-time.

We both chose shades of red for Christmas nail polish and as it was drying, we were led away to yet another part of the hall for the massages.

So, right: if I thought the foot massage part of the facial was heaven, how would I ever survive the whole body massage without swooning?

The masseuse was gentle but when she began to knead my shoulder blades and up to my neck, she announced, "You have many knots."

I didn't doubt it; probably nineteen years' worth in there. Her hands and the sides of her palm worked alternatively like rapping drum sticks on my flesh causing a slight sort of burn I thought I was feeling way into my core; followed by her fingers caressing me like soft, swaying fronds making my skin tingle on top and giving me a little chill. Even though it would be years before I had another one, that day the happy phrase "professional massage" entered my lexicon.

By the time we were finished with all the services Julia Hyde had paid for us both to have, it was almost seven o'clock and I was starving. Dinner was still hours away, and there was nothing I could do about it.

I said to Cass, "Do you think we could stop at the lobby Coffee Shop and get some little snack to take up to our room? I'm a bit famished."

"Kid, there's a complete bar in our room. Didn't you notice it?"

I had not! And this wasn't some minibar that wouldn't even be introduced into hotels for almost another decade. This was a full-sized regular bar with many bottles of wine and spirits on glass shelving behind the polished wood console, a small ice machine underneath, glassware on side shelves and unopened packages of crackers, potato chips, peanuts, mints, chocolates, jellies and assorted other snacks. Well, that would do!

While we were in the room choosing what to wear to dinner with the parents, I decided I should call my great-uncles in Brooklyn, and asked Cass if that would be ok since the room would be charged, although I didn't know if Brooklyn was considered local or not. On the other hand, with the fortune they were paying for this room what difference did it really make?

"I don't know which one to call first... maybe Leo. I think she was closer to him in age." I was just thinking out loud.

"Listen, Sari," Cass said, "my parents have a dinner meeting tomorrow night so if they invite you over there, don't feel like you can't go. We're just on our own for dinner anyway."

"Well, that might be perfect. But you have to come with me!! If you want to, that is."

"Well, sure, but I don't know, kid. They might just want to see you."

"Nonsense!

So I called Leo first and his wife answered. I knew she was Celia and that Ernest's wife was Rose.

"Hello, Aunt Celia? This is Sarah Shrier from Iowa! I'm Clara Hershorn's granddaughter. I think she wrote you that I might be calling you?"

"Sarah! How wonderful! You're in New York! How are you dear?" said the friendly if elderly-sounding voice on the other end.

"Fine, thank you! And are you all well?"

"Yes, dear. We were so pleased to receive Clara's note! So! When can we see you?"

"Um, well, I am pretty much open to whatever will work for you."

"Well, Sarah, I can tell you, the family is so excited to meet you. Can you come over tomorrow afternoon and stay for dinner? Leo says we will come pick you up. Where are you staying?"

"Aunt Celia, I'm at the Plaza Hotel with..."

"Oh! My goodness! The Plaza! "and I heard her call out, 'She's at the Plaza Leo!'

"Aunt Celia, I'm here with a friend. May she come also?"

"Of course, honey! Tell her she'll be more than welcome."

I whispered the message over my shoulder to Cass that she was more than welcome.

"We will pick you up in front of the Plaza Hotel tomorrow afternoon at three o'clock, Sarah. Would that be good? I don't want you taking the subway."

"Yes! Thank you. Will you find us? I'll be wearing a camel hair boy coat and a fur hat that looks like a hood. My friend Cass is a little taller than me. She'll be in a navy-blue coat. Does that help? "

"We'll find you. Don't you worry."

After I hung up, I turned to Cass and said, "God, they sound a lot older than Nana! I wonder how it is that they want to face all that traffic and drive into the city to get us! Should we be scared"?

"Brooklyn's the city, too. I'm sure it will be fine."

Dinner in the Palm Court was far and away the most sophisticated thing I had ever taken part in to date. Cass wore her Chanel jumper from the previous Christmas and Julia was pleased. She put a white silk blouse with it, wore white tights and black patent leather Italian ballet flats by a shoemaker that I had never heard of until I met Cass because she had several pairs of them: Salvatore Ferragamo. She had not bought the shoes in the United States, but in Florence; and she had taken two pairs to Iowa but had many more at home.

I didn't want to confuse Julia right off the bat, by wearing Cass' clothes to dinner, so I dressed up my good old plaid wool jumper and made it as chic as I possibly could with a black wool sweater underneath, black tights, my boots and the double strand of "Jackie Kennedy" pearls for extra measure. I wore pearl earrings and tied a black gros-grain ribbon in my hair. We both dabbed on only very light makeup that night since our faces were still radiant (we surmised) from the spa experience. I wore lip gloss with a green apple flavor.

We met the Hydes in the lobby and went right into the Palm Court. I tried not to gape at the ceiling too much or give away that I was stupefied by the grandeur of the room in its entirety. But in truth I was in a soupy fog of "pinch me, is this real?"

Julia ordered a drink first—her usual when she dined there, a "Hemingway Daiquiri" that had lime, grapefruit and cherry juices "in a symphony with white rum" or so the drinks menu described it.

I made a mental note to tell Sol about this drink. Maybe The Spot could have a special Ernest Hemingway tribute night or something. On second thought...

John-Wilfred ordered a classic stirred dirty vodka Martini. Cass said she wanted a vodka gimlet but her parents thought she'd best not drink alcohol in public since bartenders could get into a lot of trouble for serving minors, as I well knew. I just wanted a coke.

We dined on the not very esoteric restaurant "winter food", but the presentation and the service were anything but usual. No one hovered over us, but they certainly managed to discern our every need and desire before we could even so much as blink at them. I had a wonderful dish of chicken cacciatore that came with rosemary potatoes, and onion straws. Cass ordered "Swedish baked young duck" filled with apples and prunes. The parents shared Chateaubriand and drank French red wine from the Pomerol vineyards. We all indulged in the most decadent desserts: *milles feuilles*, sticky toffee pudding and *crémeux*. I had never tasted anything so divine.

The dinner table talk between the Hydes and their daughter was all about our planned activities in New York. They didn't exactly ignore me, but they addressed their curiosity towards Cass. So I felt it was incumbent upon me at this table to bring up the fact that we were going to Brooklyn the next day, and staying for dinner with my relatives whom I had never actually met. Julia seemed pleased if a bit surprised.

"You have relatives here then?" John-Wilfred remarked. It obviously hadn't even registered with him when I'd mentioned it previously. "I think that's marvelous. And it's very nice of them to have invited Cassandra."

"So in the morning and for lunch we're going to be at the Met tomorrow," Cass added. "We can walk up there from here easily enough."

"Sounds like a full day," said John-Wilfred, and then glancing at his Patek-Philippe watch, noticing that it was almost eleven p.m., he turned to Julia, "Well, darling, maybe we should be getting on back and let these two have some sleep!"

"Thank you so much again for dinner and really, this whole wonderful trip," I said as we parted in the lobby.

And I really meant it, too. It was all I could do not to gush all over them in abject gratitude for everything I was about to experience in New York. It occurred to me to wonder if they had any sort of clue as to how normal people lived, or what kinds of vacations regular working stiffs took.

"Our pleasure," John-Wilfred said addressing us both. "So we won't be seeing you tomorrow night, but then later on this week we are all going to dinner at the Rainbow Room. That is really old New York, Sarah... you're going to like it!"

Cass gave a short "hee-hee" laugh. "That's my favorite restaurant since I was a little girl and Papa would let me dance standing on his shoes," she confided.

"What about Thursday in the day, Cassandra? Plans?" Julia wanted to know.

"Shopping!" she said, really to me. "AND the Empire State Building and probably we'll take the Staten Island Ferry ride to see the Statue of Liberty."

"Or you could take the ferry that actually goes to Ellis Island," her father suggested. His and his wife's ancestors came to America and landed at places like Jamestown, for all I knew, but he must have considered that mine all came through Immigration. Seeing it from afar might be better, I thought, because it would more closely replicate what my relatives must have witnessed as their ships pulled into New York harbor. I had only seen that in movies but it didn't take much imagination to feel the relief they must have felt, along with desperate homesickness, even if home were wretched.

Cass and I each took a bath and wrapped ourselves up on the couch in the Plaza's luxurious linens to watch some late night t.v. and...talk.

"Cass," I ventured. "What are you really thinking about with Alan and the debacle he caused. "

"That's a good question," she said. "I do like him, you know. I want to see him again, of course. But he was so incredibly stupid to barge in like he did."

"And of course, your parents have all but forbidden you to see him again."

"Well, there is that, " she laughed. "Come on. Don't tell me you'd *obey* if your parents forbade you to see Soren because he's Catholic."

"They don't even know about him but I'll bet at that point they would be glad he wasn't Indian!"

But I hadn't brought this all up to talk about myself and my situation. This whole time I'd known Cass, we had become very close. I loved her-- like a sister; nothing else. We often found ourselves sharing a bed, especially when I visited her, but there was absolutely nothing like sexual innuendo or tension between us. If that really was going on in the dorm like those kids had assured me it was, as a sophomore at Iowa I was still absurdly naïve. But I also thought enough time had gone by and we had had enough soul-letting between us, Cass and me, for me to broach the subject of her relationships with these guys she seemed to be entangled with. I finally decided to go for it.

"Cass, " I started out casually, "in terms of your future with Alan, what about Professor Klampert? You've actually never really talked to me about you and him. "

She looked at me like I had opened up her secret vault or something.

"Welll, "she dragged it out. "Klampert is my mentor. I sort of see him as a very good friend, but he's, you know, (she gestured) up here. I'm down there. I guess I hero worship him. "

"But, do you… sleep with him? "

"Let me put it to you this way: He has helped me so much, and guided my path to be able to work with Lasansky. I am so indebted to him and so grateful, that I let myself be…like…his, you know…playmate."

"His what?! Do you mean in the bedroom?"

"He's very sweet to me! And respectful! It's not like dirty or anything."

"Cass, you could get pregnant, though!"

"Oh, no, we take precautions."

"WHAT precautions? Are you on the pill? "

"No. We're careful."

"Oh. Oh, okay, you're careful," I chided her. *Puh-lease. Skepticism didn't begin to describe my reaction to that.*

"And he's not married, you know that already."

"Yeah, I hadn't even been thinking of that. But ---good to know. I think it would be awful to wreck someone's marriage. I couldn't live with myself knowing I was the *other woman.* Besides, that never works anyway."

"No."

"Why isn't he married!? "I said all of a sudden. "He so gorgeous. "

"I know! Well, he actually *was* married a while back. It didn't work out and I think he feels once burned, twice shy. He really loved her and she had an affair! It hurt him a lot."

"Jesus. So don't tell me Alan knows about you and Klampert."

"He doesn't."

"So…will you end it with Klampert if you and Alan become really serious?"

"I suppose I will."

She didn't seem so eager to discuss this in depth so I tried to let it go, reasoning with myself that she'd figure it out.

"And what about you and Soren? Do you love him?"

"I don't think so. Not yet anyway. And no, I haven't slept with him because believe it or not, I'm waiting until I turn twenty-one to have sex."

"What, you've got some sort of love calendar all set up?" she chortled. "It doesn't always work out that way."

"Look, I'm not saving myself for marriage or anything like that. This is the '60's after all. I'm not a prude…per se. Ha! But if I wait until I reach the age of majority, it's truly my life. I can't be accused of disrespecting my parents."

"Oh, you still can be, "she laughed. "But I get what you mean: emancipation and all. "

"Exactly. And besides, that's only a couple more years. And in case you haven't noticed, it's not like guys are lined up to sleep with me."

"Don't be ridiculous…they all would be." She paused and then looked up at me with a more serious look on her face. "You sure have your life under control and where you want it, don't you?"

"Why do you say that?" *Half the time I thought I was just hanging on by a thread.*

"Well, you came to the U and you went through Rush, didn't get the house you would have pledged, so you just gave the rest of them the ol' heave ho! You bucked the system by not caving to your father's wishes that you belong to a Jewish organization. Then you TELL your parents you're going to France and you compile all the stuff you need to do that all by yourself. You TELL your boyfriend what

124

the timeline is for intimacy. You never let anyone mess with you! You KNOW exactly what you want and you DO it."

"That's a stretch, " I said, taken aback at her candor.

"I just envy you, kid. You're going to set the damn world on its ear."

"Yeah, right. I have to pass Anthro next month first!"

But I seriously did not understand her envy of me. She was the one with the star power talent. She was the one with the art show! She was the one with the ideas and plans for manufacturing her own fabulous dolls. She was also the one with parents who could back her every dream and desire with enough financial wherewithal to pave her way fifty times over.

"I don't know about the truth of some of what you said about me, Cass," I said, finally, "but you should not shortchange yourself, either. You are the most stunning girl on our campus. I'm surprised there's not a line of guys waiting in our dorm lobby for you to say you'll go out with them. You're the most talented art student in the whole damn department. And you've been a great friend to me when a lot of girls wouldn't begin to give two shits about someone younger who washed up on the shore to be their roommate. Not to mention sharing your incredible wardrobe, inviting me to your **homes** *plural,* taking me on dream trips. This whole New York trip so far, I think I AM dreaming."

"Okay, okay, it's a mutual admiration society. I see that, "she laughed.

"I'm heading off to bed."

"Night. I'll stay out here for a while."

I got into the pajamas I had left in the bathroom, went over to the bar and poured myself a coke and took it to the armchair closest to the window. New York was lit up twenty floors below under my nose with the darkened part that was Central Park and the cars on Park Avenue leaving a trail of tail lights that looked like someone had spilled red paint and it was oozing between the buildings.

What a city! What must it be like to live here? Thinking back to a similar night when I viewed the magical lights of Chicago from the Hyde penthouse, I found it necessary to warn myself once again against falling in love with the lure of big city life. If I ever did actually move to either of these, I'd probably be living in a tenement. But it wasn't against the rules to self-indulge in a few moments of reverie. It never hurt anyone to dream.

Chapter Nineteen

"Bei Mir Bist Du Schon"...Cahn, Shad, Chaplin, Jacobs

There was, ironically, one thing I hadn't taken into consideration when contemplating meeting my extended family from New York: genetics.

Cass and I made our way out onto the red carpeted staircase of the Plaza Hotel's entrance, where cabs and limos came and went every thirty seconds or so. If I hadn't reckoned that the "normal" grey and white 1964 Oldsmobile that pulled into the line was theirs, just seeing my great-uncle Leo behind the wheel would have convinced me. He looked enough like a Dalkin to be Nana's twin instead of her older brother. I gave a little wave. Even as Cass and I were standing there in the outfits I said we would be and thus easily identifiable, I could see that, of course, it was them.

Leo actually got out of the car and came around to us, opening the back door.

"So nice to meet you!" I exclaimed holding my hand out for him to shake. He hugged me instead. "Thanks for coming to get us!"

"It's wonderful to have you here," he told me with a slight Russian accent. My Nana had lost her accent completely and it never occurred to me that anyone else in the family would still have one.

We climbed in and did more introductions all around. Aunt Celia talked the whole way as we headed over the Brooklyn bridge, which made me gasp, it was so beautiful and so famous from pictures. She was very animated, telling us about all the family that would be gathering tonight to meet us. She and Leo lived in the brownstone on 10th Avenue that they owned, and in that building, which was divided up into four large maisonettes, were many other family members: their daughter and son-in-law, Millie and Sammy Schwartz with their daughter Rochelle ("Shelley"); and their son Bernard, his wife Eve and their daughter Jenny, although Jenny had moved out. Shelley was older than me and still lived at home. I could not even fathom that.

"So," Celia explained, "we're not all living under one roof, but almost! Isn't it nice that the two little cousins grew up together? They're like sisters, really. Jenny lives in Manhattan now for her job. But she'll be here tonight and then she will take you girls back to the Plaza later tonight. You will go with her on the subway. It won't be dangerous!"

Cass and I exchanged glances: the subway!

Then Uncle Leo added that his brother Ernest and his wife Rose also lived in Brooklyn—on a different block. But they would be there for dinner, also with their daughter Penelope, called "Pinky", and her husband Ronald Cohen. They had two sons, Meyer and David who were both away at college.

"David is in Israel!" said Leo proudly.

"It's his spiritual side, "said Celia. "He's very religious. He writes us letters all about the yeshiva. *Oy*, what a year he's having! He started out in the summer staying on a kibbutz."

"Wow, "I said, "I can't even imagine that."

"Anyway," Aunt Celia continued, "we also have another tenant, Mrs. Berg who will be with us tonight. She's anxious to meet you, too! She has a very famous daughter, Beverly."

"Not Beverly," Uncle Leo corrected her, "not anymore." He glanced up to the rear mirror as if to address something to us in the back. "She changed her name when she wanted to dance! First she was Chan Richardson and now she's Chan Parker Woods."

I remember my surprise at that curious name change, but otherwise it didn't register with me in the slightest. Names of the family were being fired at us so fast I was just trying to keep everyone straight. But I had no inkling at all Chan Parker Woods would turn out to be the common-law widow of the jazz legend Charlie Parker, and was now married to another jazz great, Phil Woods. All I knew is that I was going to meet her mother Mrs. Berg.

"And Leo has to take the car to the garage where we park it, "Celia added, "so he'll drop us off at the butcher's and I'll pick up a few things for tonight right here on our block."

So that is what happened. Cass and I accompanied my great-aunt in and out of little shops that made 10th Avenue seem like a village. Everyone in them knew her and knew about US!

"Oh, the Iowans are here! "they would exclaim. One person asked if we had all the modern conveniences in Iowa.

"Like….?" I wondered.

"Electricity?!" one of them asked me.

I looked at her in disbelief and nodded "Yeeeessss." Someone else wanted to know if we had buffalo.

"Farther west, "Cass offered, trying not to burst out laughing at these moronic New Yorkers.

I whispered an aside to Cass: "We're the foreign exchange students from Iowa!"

We walked to the brownstone, Cass and I carrying the packages of food, and their building was indeed beautiful in the waning winter sun. It seemed huge to me. The stoop was large and there were more than a dozen steps leading to it. Aunt Celia and Uncle Leo must have been in great shape to do those every day even with the typical wrought-iron railings on which to help yourself up. Theirs was in a row of brownstone townhouses, but it stood out as being especially architecturally lovely with a big circular bay window off to one side and imposing doors. It was fitted with flower boxes at every main-floor window, but they were empty in December. It looked to me to be a three-story building but also had a basement entrance, so maybe that could have been another apartment, I wasn't sure.

Inside the big front foyer, we were in a dimly lit hallway with doors leading into the first apartments and a large staircase winding up to the rest.

The interior of their apartment, I was surprised to find, was decorated in blond teakwood, Danish modern. This entire decorating scheme was just the antithesis of what I'd expected walking in there, and when I saw it, nothing added up in my only slightly-educated brain that had understood this to be a late nineteenth-century building. The living space itself was distinctly *not* modern, with chopped up rooms and doors to close them off if desired. There were hard wood floors, high ceilings, and all-white walls everywhere I looked.

We were shown into the living room which had a very contemporary sectional that could seat a dozen people from end to end and sideways. There was an imposing white marble mantle with the fireplace blocked up with a black iron grate, so they didn't use it, but it was dramatic none the less. On either side of it were beautiful ornamental crystal sconces that may have been gas lamps back in the day.

The completely incongruous decor included, in the next room off the living room, a gigantic minimalist, again teak-wood, dining room table, long enough to be set for at least twenty people, but that night set for fourteen of us, with curvy wooden chairs and narrow black leather seats. There was a matching credenza against one unadorned white wall, with extra dessert plates and other platters set out on it. The chandelier above the table was long and pointy with little white bulbs on every tip, which gave off the appearance of many stars.

The table was set first and foremost with a white Scandinavian tablecloth embroidered at each corner and all down the middle with beautiful appliquéd blue and yellow flowers, green stems and leaves, and tiny brown dots. Matching napkins were put at every place, effectively setting off the dishes, which were stark white and shaped in squares and oblongs; the silverware was also very modern, the Cypress pattern by Georg Jensen. When I inquired about this---in a polite way, of course, Aunt Celia told me she had fallen in love with Scandinavian culture on a visit there with Leo in the late 1950's; and that, on a tour of the Georg Jensen factory in Copenhagen, she just made up her mind to have the Cypress patterned flatware and to create her own esthetic around it.

I sat there for a few quiet moments just looking at the dining room table, amused by how much more forward thinking she must have been than her Brooklyn Jewish peers in those days. But then I chided myself on stereotyping immigrant Jews like that. Besides, I didn't know a whit about her past. Not everyone who came through Ellis Island was fleeing pogroms and shtetls. Maybe she was educated and from wealth? And if not, people can always educate themselves, I admitted. I should take this as an example!

Celia continued with our tour. The kitchen was absolutely tiny compared to mine at my Bluffs home. I couldn't imagine how she cooked in there. And then I saw that actually she wasn't the one doing the cooking at all—they had a woman in there busy at the miniscule sink. Was she their maid? I had no idea. She wasn't in a uniform and didn't stay to serve the food, so maybe she just helped out. The part of the kitchen visible from the dining room wasn't the entire space, it turned out. There was an enviable butler's pantry behind it, with floor to ceiling cupboards, some with glass shelves, packed with dishes and cookbooks towards the bottom. Beneath its counter were dozens of other storage drawers and shelves housing pots and pans of every variety. And a large refrigerator was actually in a recessed niche around the corner. Whew, I thought, otherwise there would be no possible way.

Leo was anxious for Celia to put a cup of tea in our hands and sit us down on the sectional in the living room to talk about the family back home.

"My sister was so pleased to hear that you were going to be able to be with us today," he told me right off. "I telephoned her with the news. She seems to be in fine fettle. How would you say she is doing?
"

"Absolutely great!" I said. "Cass has met her, too---last Thanksgiving. We had a really nice visit with her."

"So, you are very close with her? " he surmised.

"Oh, God, yes. She's far and away my favorite relative."

"Well, I thought maybe you'd like to see some of the old pictures I have of her when we were young, " he said, and pulled out a dog-eared leather scrapbook from underneath a little square side table. Then he came and sat between Cass and me on the couch, so he could narrate. The pages were black construction paper, and the pictures were held in place by those gummed corners. Many of them had captions written on the tiny white borders of the photos, too small really to read. I was fascinated by these seemingly ancient photographs, some about one-third the size of a photo in the 60's; some the square shape of the early Brownie cameras.

"Look at this one—that is the three of us as children with our parents."

Sure enough! My great-grandparents! I had never heard much about them at all!

"My papa," he started (not pronouncing it like Cass called her father!), "had several brothers already in America in 1905 or so and they sent for—sponsored, really, the rest of the family. We all sailed from Odessa in Russia on a boat that first docked in Liverpool, England."

"Oh, gee! The Beatles are from Liverpool. You could have all stayed there and become English!"

"Well, we wanted to see our family in America, so we took another ship across the Atlantic, and settled first on the lower East side, Manhattan, and then eventually came to Brooklyn. Ernest and I started our business here. Your grandmother also lived in New York for quite a while—until she was a teenager, I'm sure she's told you?"

"Not really. I'm not even sure how she got to the Midwest, to tell you the truth."

"Yah, sure, I know. She met her husband at a dance! Yes, a dance. It was a young Jewish peoples' organization and they had dances."

"So…then they got married?"

"Not quite yet. He had family with a business---I think it was a restaurant---in Nebraska. They needed some more help, and asked him to come there. But the war was going on already in Europe and Hal Hershorn wanted to go back there and fight against the Kaiser. So he enlisted. Clara stayed in New York with our parents. When he returned home, then he and Clara got married, took a train to Lincoln, Nebraska and never looked back."

"So, I wonder how they ended up in Iowa." I said, sort of to myself. I was surprised I had never asked about any of this!

"The Depression. It is what hurt everybody. Your grandfather had heard of many bars and restaurants in trouble, some about to close, others barely making it. He had some friends in The Bluffs and it had a burgeoning Jewish community with a synagogue that many of the little Nebraska towns did not. So he decided to take over that bar, and he moved his family to The Bluffs, to make a fresh start, you might say. He named it The Spot. It was the spot they would plant roots and make a new way in life. He had the idea to enlarge it into a bar and restaurant—a grill, as I recall. But times were too hard to talk about expansion, so they didn't do that at first. He always had it in his head to go bigger, though, if they could just make a go of it. I remember worrying about them in those days. My little sister on her feet ten to twelve hours a day, cooking, waiting on tables, planning all the menus; Hal handled all the procurement of liquor stock and food, but I think Clara learned that, too! And on top of all that she was raising three children of their own! *Oy, vey ist mir.*"

"Yeah, that was a lot of work," I said, finally, having sat there, taking it all in.

"So now your father and mother have taken over the whole operation, and Clara is a lady of leisure?"

"That's about right. She still helps out now and then, though. "

"It's good, "he said, leaning back on the sofa. "Me, too. My boys handle it all here."

Before long the winter darkness had fallen definitively, and family members started to appear and file though the big entry doors. Everyone greeted us with kindness and also curiosity, as though our spaceship were parked just outside.

Shelley and Jenny could not have looked more different. Shelley was thin and lithe, with short dark hair and a rather flushed complexion. Her eyes were brown and pretty, but rather squinty, and she seemed to blink a lot like she was having a hard time focusing them on me. She struck me as the quintessential New Yorker, with a broad Brooklyn accent and an effervescent bounce about her. She was working in a borough office as a city clerk and wore a rather conservative outfit, a straight, dark green wool skirt that came below the knees, and a beige turtle-neck sweater with a long-tasseled necklace.

"Sooo, "she sang out at me, "you're my little cousin from IOWA? Pleased to meet you! "

"Likewise, " I called out rather loudly to meet her decibel range, as I introduced her to Cass.

She came at me rather abruptly, hugged me very quickly, and immediately lunged over to an anteroom right off the living room and threw her coat on a chair in there. She was obviously just as at home at her grandparents' house as at her own, and seemed totally used to making herself comfortable in this other charming space, which had the wide bay window overlooking the sidewalk below and the stoop to the side. The room functioned as a small den-cum-library, with built-in bookcases, a deep sofa and two armchairs with a television console in front of them.

When she came back into the living room, we all sat down on the sectional together, and I tried to make some conversation to show her I wasn't an alien. I knew, for instance, that Shelley had not gone to college.

"You work for the city, I understand. How do you like it?"

"It's just an entry position, but so far I really like it. "

She sat down on the end of the seat and smoothed her straight skirt. Then she reached for the album Leo had put back down on the coffee table.

"I've never met your grandmother, " said Shelley. "I'd like to, though! "

"You'll just have to come to Iowa one of these days, eh? "

She looked at me like I had just suggested something like "Let's go make reservations on the next rocket ship to Mars."

"I doubt that will ever happen!" she laughed. "But I wouldn't mind movin' t' Florida though! God, this weather!"

Jenny arrived at the house next, and I must have actually gaped at her because **she** looked more like an alien than I ever could have: she had that 60's folk-singer-esque long, blond hair, parted in the middle and worn completely straight down so that she had to sweep it back with a turning gesture anytime she wanted to talk. How stunned was I to see hair like that in our family, and how envious I felt! She must have been growing it out for 10 years. Jenny was a beauty, too, in a much more conventional sense than any of us except Cass. She had large, green eyes and a peachy complexion. She had also come from work, but was wearing a long denim skirt and a pink blouse tucked in and cinched with a wide black mesh belt. She wore boots and big hoop earrings.

Jenny turned out to be an assistant art director in a pretty well-known New York advertising agency. Not much older than I was, she had gone to college at CUNY and majored in graphic design, which in those days really was graphic design...with pencils and ink and not computers. When I told her Cass was an artist, she perked right up and they moved off to a corner to talk design. I overheard her tell Cass, "Our agency is handling an account that's going to have a Peter Max vibe for its commercial."

"Oh my! Cass exclaimed, "he's one of my idols."

129

Shelley's and Jenny's parents all arrived at different times from their jobs. The son and son-in-law were both in the family business with the great-uncles: a concession for supplying seltzer water all over the city! The son-in-law Sammy came in looking positively teamster-like, all bulked up in dungarees and a parka, underneath which he wore a long-sleeved tee shirt. His arms were huge and his build stocky. He oversaw and sometimes even drove in the fleet of trucks carrying canisters of seltzer water to bars and restaurants in three of the five boroughs.

Leo's son, my mother's cousin Bernard, was slight and more dapper. He wore a suit with a sweater vest and a beautiful silk paisley tie; he worked with his dad out of the offices of the company. As to their wives, each of whom entered the house and warmly embraced me, cousin Millie was a housewife, whereas Jenny's mom Ellie was a legal secretary.

When my great-uncle Ernest walked in with his wife Rose, daughter Pinkie and son-in-law Ronald, I was once again struck by the family resemblance. And there was even more cooing and fawning over Cass and me. Pinkie was not shy about telling Cass that she was the most strikingly beautiful girl she'd ever seen.

"Oh, my, what my sons wouldn't give to date someone who looks like you!" she exclaimed. Jenny shot me a look that said, 'Sorry—she has no filter.'

"I'm used to it, " I whispered. "Cass is the true campus beauty."

Towards the actual dinner hour of seven p.m., the doorbell chimed and Mrs. Berg let herself in without waiting for someone to answer it. She was slim and rather elegant looking, with a short dark brown bob, round black glasses, long slender hands and many rings on her fingers. She was very amiable, and began a conversation with Cass and me right away about university life and what great things we were doing in New York. She told us all about being a Ziegfeld girl and after that the Cotton Club where she used to run the hat-check section. And then she said,

"I have a granddaughter about your age— maybe a little older, in college here in the States, but her mother, my daughter, she's living right now outside Paris with her husband and younger kids."

"Oh, "I cooed, "Paris. It's my goal to be there for school next year!"

"Well, my goodness, if you go, you'll have to meet Chan and the children."

Cass and Jenny had really hit it off, and at dinner they sat together, talking about various art movements and their particular fields of endeavor. Cass was quite taken with the amount of art Jenny herself produced and they vowed to keep in touch since Cass did get back to New York from time to time.

I had a great time talking to everyone—they were so interested in my life, which was a very unfamiliar sensation to me. Cass and I were fawned over and treated like visiting royalty. The feeling I had of being the center of attention was not one I often experienced, and at first I was rather shy about it; but they were so warm and genuine that it broke through my defenses and I just started to enjoy it. Everyone seemed to genuinely love my grandmother, going back decades. She had visited Brooklyn in the 50's and some of the New Yorkers had even made it to Iowa to see her but that was before I was born. They remembered my mother Betty as a teenager!

Before we could say "boo," it was already past nine o'clock, and desserts were still being served and savored. The copious meal was delicious and courses never stopped coming. Millie, Pinkie and Eve bustled up and down serving and clearing dishes. I offered to help but they wouldn't hear of it, and the rest of us sat at the table and talked on and on.

Then suddenly Jenny was making overtures about getting us into the subway before it got late. We had passed the subway stop on our walk that afternoon; it was literally steps from the house.

"We need to get to a subway station at about 59th and Broadway," Cass told her (as if she didn't know where the Plaza was?).

"Piece of cake, "said Jenny, "and I'm going to take you all the way there and then head back to my apartment."

It was hard to say good-bye to everyone, and it took a while for all of them to hug us and wish us well. I told my great-aunts and uncles that I fervently hoped this was but the first and certainly not the only time we'd be seeing one another; however, as fate would have it, that's exactly what it was.

Chapter Twenty

"L'Amour Est Bleu"...André Popp & Pierre Cour

New Year's Eve fell on a Sunday in 1967 and we were all scheduled to fly out of New York on Saturday the 30th. Since Mr. Hyde had said he wanted to take us to the Rainbow Room before we left New York, he picked the Friday night to do it. This time I did wear Cass' navy drop-waist dress with the pink sash; and she wore her Chanel. Mrs. Hyde was pretty dolled up herself in a gorgeous (she didn't have any clothes that weren't) cocktail dress with a light grey silk *moiré* mini-skirt and a mauve sequined bodice. She wore her long black mink coat over it, fairly high heeled black pumps and a long pearl necklace clasped with a dark amethyst and diamond brooch at the side.

The Hydes' car dropped us in front of Rockefeller Plaza at the skating rink at Cass' insistence, so I could see it and the famous tree. I was beside myself to get to actually be there; the scene was so iconic in both the New York and American psyches.

The Rainbow Room atop Rockefeller Center took my breath away, as had so many other quintessential sights of New York on that trip. The ornate ceiling coving with its famed rainbow of colors fascinated me, as did the way they set the tables in a circle around the band and dance floor. The enormous chandelier dripping its crystals high above the room gave off shimmering reflections of the color-changing light display in the tray ceiling. Couples swirled around underneath it and the floor filled up with gowns sweeping past one another as they dipped and swayed to the music. They weren't playing rock and roll or folk music, but if I had heard of Astor Piazzolla or Noel Rosa in those days, I might have recognized at least some of what people were dancing to.

All the tables were round and fitted with long, flowing tablecloths. The seating was two-tiered and circular with some tables in front of floor-to-ceiling windows affording the unique view of Manhattan below; and other dining places on the dance-floor level circling off from the band box. We were seated at one of the window tables on the "upper deck," back from the dance floor but still within full view of the sophisticated scene unfolding under the lights. Bowls of flowers adorned all the tables and at various spots on the floor were three-foot tall crystal vases with cascading blooms spreading out of them. It was a magnificent setting and my great good fortune to be there with my friend and her parents was not lost on me.

The Hydes had been to this restaurant many times in their marriage, and even though they weren't actual New York regulars, we didn't get any less special treatment. The service was very deferential to every customer, and we were all the happy recipients of attention from an entire brigade of waiters. John-Wilfred ordered himself a Negroni, and for Julia, a gin and tonic before having the waiter bring a shared "appetizer" for the whole table, which turned out to be a huge silver lazy-susan platter of seafood of all kinds placed over a thick bed of ice. There were jumbo shrimps, oysters on the half shell, rock lobster tails, stone crab claws, and whelks. In the center was a large oval bowl of cocktail sauce, and in between the seafood offerings were small square dishes holding truffles and poached eggs. That could have been the whole meal for me and, except for the oysters, I loved every single thing I tasted. San Francisco sourdough French bread and pots of creamy, unsalted European-style butter accompanied this entrée. I was completely full by the time we were supposed to be ordering the main course. I had to beg off.

"Well, I hope you've saved room for dessert in that case, "said John-Wilfred not forcing me to order anything more, for which I was grateful. Julia glanced at me a little quizzically, but also didn't make an issue of my appetite being sated with the first course.

Cass ordered lobster pot pie with truffles (more truffles! I had never tasted a truffle in my life before that night) and the Hydes decided to share Beef Wellington. Mr. Hyde had a short talk with the sommelier about something on the wine list after which a bottle of 1959 Chateau Lafite-Rothschild Pauillac appeared on the table. I declined the offer to taste it; I wasn't 21 yet, but Cass took her father up on a glass of this ruby plum colored wine, which I only learned years later, was probably among the most sought-after in the world.

We all spent our last day together, this time at MOMA, after which we wandered through the Gagosian, and a few other of the Hydes' favorite galleries in Midtown.

I found that extremely educational, and, while I didn't love modern art, at least I knew enough to respect it. The art history survey I'd taken at Iowa didn't get far into the 20th century, but in speaking of the works of Impressionist painters being brought to American shores, professor Klampert had pointed out that it foreshadowed New York taking over from Paris as the center of the art world as both World Wars would change the European art scene completely. It goes without saying that I knew of Jackson Pollack, since our art museum at Iowa had a famous work of his, "Mural."

As we were packing to leave and go our various ways, me to Omaha, Cass to Chicago and her parents to Switzerland, Cass did confide in me that even though things seemed pleasant enough on the surface, her mother was still unhappy about Alan and somehow sensed that it might not be that great of an idea for Cass to return to Chicago without them.

"I was afraid she was going to cancel on Papa and come back with me," she said ominously, "but no. I'm returning on my own, thank God, and then Martin will drive me to school in another week or so. We can get into the dorm early, can't we? "

"Of course. Some people even stay, and others return to have plenty of time to start studying for finals, don't you think?"

"When are you going to be back?" she asked.

"Well, I have to stay until the 7th at least and work in the bar. He's actually happy I'll be home to do a shift on New Year's Eve! Let's just say I'll get out of there the second I can."

The Hyde Industries limousine came for Cass and me with Julia and John-Wilfred already in it, and whisked us all to the La Guardia departure terminal where Cass and I got out to go through the regular procedures, checking bags and getting first class seat assignments, and the parents stayed in to go to their private hanger and meet up with Captain J. The leave-taking wasn't particularly warm, except for mine: I bubbled over with thanks and gratitude for everything they had done for me taking me on this magnificent trip. Getting to meet my own family for the first time in that city afforded me about as priceless of memories as one could hope for in life. Not to mention how my every expense was taken care of! Whoever heard of such a thing?! I had to pinch myself time and again with Cass' family.

I flew non-stop to Omaha, and was met coming down the stairs of the plane at the gate by Betty and Roslyn.

"What did you bring me?" Roslyn asked, hardly greeting me.

"Something really neat. You'll dig it."

"Did you have a nice time?" Betty said, giving me a little hug.

"Oh, I can't even begin to tell you. The whole thing was fantastic…really it was like being in my own movie."

"What? That's stupid," said my sister.

"She just means it was unbelievably wonderful," Betty told her.

"Okay, so what present did you get me?"

"Well, just wait a minute, can you? I have to get my suitcase. It's packed in there."

I had gotten her something sublime; it's what I would have wanted at her age: New York Barbie. A Barbie doll whose box had a picture of the Statue of Liberty on the back and the writing said "Winter in New York". Barbie was wearing black pants, a black coat with red lining, buckled at the waist with a fur collar and cuffs, red gloves and a black hat with a red ribbon around it. She carried a big square purse. When Roslyn finally got her hands on it she squealed with delight and ran to her room to play with it.

"Well, you're back in the real world, now," my father harrumphed, when I was done recounting all the incredible things I'd seen and done.

"I'm sure my mother will want to hear every detail of meeting Uncle Leo and Uncle Ernest," Betty assured me. "You'll see her Monday on New Year's Day---we're having dinner at her place."

"I'll see her in half an hour!" I said pointedly. "I'm going right over there. By the way, Daddy, do you know the drink called Negroni?"

132

"Yeah, I know it. What's the big deal about that?"

"Oh, not a big deal; I just wondered. I'd never heard of it and Mr. Hyde had one, that's all."

"It's just sweet vermouth, Campari and gin. I don't know why that would cause anyone to get excited about it. "

"I'm just asking! Sheesh! Can't a person have a conversation with you*?!!" ASSHOLE. This man and I had so NOTHING in common we couldn't even be civil to one another anymore.*

Nana and I, on the other hand, had a great confab about her family and how much it meant to me to get to know them. She was delighted and I was thrilled to be sharing it with her. I only wished in the end that she had been there, too.

The week dragged on as I spent my time either working in the bar or studying for final exams. It had started snowing on New Year's Day and didn't let up. Betty was beginning to worry about me driving the Rambler back to campus without snow tires. I agreed with her, but I was holding my breath about Sol. The last thing I wanted was to be spending another long trip with him on the road if he decided to drive me back in his car. He finally consented to have snow tires put on the back two wheels of the station wagon, intending to switch them back again when I came home for Spring Break. So the car went into the Firestone store's garage across the street from The Spot, and the next day I was equipped to drive back safer than I would have been.

Then right in the midst of my work stint, still over a week from leaving to return to Iowa City, the mail brought the letter I had been anticipating with all my heart and dreading at the same time: Pella College's acceptance or rejection of me into their Sorbonne program. My mouth got all dry as I gazed at the envelope feeling to see if it felt a certain acceptance or rejection way.

Upon opening, my eyes fell on the first words after Dear Sarah, "Congratulations!"

"OOOOOh my GAWWWWWD!!!"

First I called Cass. She was still home in Kenilworth and as delighted as I was!

"KID!! That is so great!!! I knew you'd get it."

"You did not!" I laughed. "But isn't it TOO COOL???!"

I then grabbed the letter, pulled on my ski jacket, jumped into the car and drove over to the bar. Beyond excited and brimming with joy, I flung open the door and waved the envelope high in the air. Betty saw me first.

"Oh my!" she said, knowing right away what it was.

"Oh YEAH!" I screamed.

"Pipe down! "said Sol, "you'll scare the customers."

"I got IN!!!"

"So how much money do they want right now? I can just imagine."

"I haven't read that far."

It was determined that there would indeed have to be some money sent in right away to hold my place, and also there was a list of heath requirements I would have to attend to: a physical and a series of shots. I was up to date on boosters and such for college, but would now have to comply with obligatory World Health Organization specifications on immunizations for those traveling abroad. I could get some done at our pediatrician's office in The Bluffs, as well as be issued a little WHO book to keep safe with my passport, but the rest of the shots would have to be done at student health.

The day after the letter came, while I was still floating on air, Sol summoned me to get into "decent clothing" and meet him at the bank.

"I'm taking out a loan for your studies in Paris---$1,500. I want you to be there and see it. See what this is costing us."

"I can pay you back."

"That's not the point. The name on the loan will only be mine. But you should know that sacrifices are being made here. If you ever protest the United States government again, I will see to it that this is cancelled. Do I make myself clear?"

"Yes, Daddy."

I drove back to Iowa on roads that had, luckily, been cleared, though deep snow was piled up on the sides. I could have run the whole way, so pumped up on adrenaline and pipe dreams was I in that moment. I would be leaving FOR PARIS, FRANCE in mere months because the classes started in June; and I would not be back until the following July. Could it really be true? Could this actually be happening for real? Was I the absolute luckiest girl on God's green earth?! Yes, yes and YES.

Chapter Twenty-One

"Go Where You Wanna Go"… The Mamas & the Papas (John Phillips)

When I finally got back to Iowa City after the New York trip, the family mini-reunion, the Sorbonne program acceptance and working at The Spot, I felt my luck was continuing because I found a parking space close enough to Kate Daum that I could unload my stuff and raced up in the elevator to see Cass. She wasn't in the room and it looked like she also had just come back from Chicago and dumped her stuff down and left.

"It must be Alan Jones time," I thought to myself.

So I called Soren with my big news, and we got together and took my car back to its real parking space at Klampert's house, after which we went to the Union.

"So," he said grinning at me as we sat down with cokes, "Paris for a whole year!"

"I can't believe it!" I chirped.

"Maybe I can come over there next June and we can travel together before you have to go home. "

"Oh, my God! Do you think you could really do that?!! How neat!"

"Well, I'm not sure, of course, but I think we could make it happen."

That was the stuff of daydreams, too, and every waking minute that semester I spent pondering and envisioning my new life in Paris.

Soren also had news. Over the vacation he was also at home in Imogene and his parents had sat him down to talk about *his* future.

"They're pretty adamant that I get in to law school and then stay at Iowa for it. I'm a "legacy" so they're certain I'll be accepted if my grades are fine, which they are."

"And the rub?" I asked.

"Well, I told them I'd for sure be moving to one of the coasts and not joining the family firm."

"And what did they say to that?"

"Not very happy with it, but they admitted as to how they couldn't force me to stay in Imogene, Iowa."

"Yeah, 'the times they are a-changin' and all that," I offered, trying to remain optimistic for his plans. "You'll figure it out. Our parents can't dictate our lives. Nobody stays home like their generation did during Depression and World Wars and all. Except, of course, the boys who went off to fight with armies and what not. We're more adventuresome."

"Yes, I guess you're right," he said.

He walked me back to my dorm and right at the door we saw Alan and Cass. She saw me first from afar and began calling out my name. I leaped ahead to meet up with her and we hugged and bounced up and down like five-year-olds screaming to the world,

"PARIS!!"

"FRANCE!"

Alan and Soren laughed at us. They shook hands and Alan and I actually hugged each other. It was really cold out so we went inside and then, instead of leaving us to go up to our room, Alan suggested we all go out for something to eat. Since it was a Sunday, dorm dining halls were not reopened yet for us girls, so we all just decided to head back out. We walked downtown together, Cass and I bubbling over with tales of New York and plans for my own future triumphant landing on the beaches of Normandy. Alan talked about his applying for Conscientious Objector status and Soren talked about an interview with Pete Townshend in January's Rolling Stone Magazine that he had in his book bag. He actually read from the article, *"Nowhere in the world compares with San Francisco in what's in the air,"* Peter Townshend said during *his few free hours between the group's afternoon and evening spots at the Cow Palace. "The vibes that this place gives off are fantastic."*

"I think I may have to move there," Soren sighed.

"After law school?" I asked.

"I'm not sure that music scene will still be there in another four years. I may want to go sooner."

Second semester of my sophomore and Cass' junior year started to hum right along. We were now — at least I was now — old hands at Registration and we knew we'd get the classes we wanted. Rather unfortunately I was stuck with the second half of Anthropology, which I liked less and less; but happily I was taking a lot of French, English and Art. My French instructor was a FRENCH guy, another Writer's Workshop grad student who was doing comparative literature work translating Vance Bourjaily's poems into French for future publication over there. He was very French looking: dark hair to his collar; brown eyes and a rather long but very nice nose; thin lips. He wore dark glasses all the time — indoors, too, same as Mademoiselle had. He was very thin and rather on the short side---stereotypical, really. He wore something completely foreign to Iowa City in 1967: a cardigan sweater around his shoulders. He wore it every day to teach in; I supposed when he actually had to put on a coat, he put his arms though the sleeves, but inside, never. His name was Guy LeNotre, he lived in the 6th *arrondissement* in Paris, had gone to the *Sorbonne,* and was quite sweet in class, which was French 202 Comp and Con. It goes without saying that he had a devoted and serious student in me.

Monsieur LeNotre---just "*Monsieur*" in class--- was interested and supportive of my plans to study in Paris. I had to impose on him to proctor an oral placement test that was sent to me from France on cassette tapes. He actually had me come to his apartment in a house on Johnson Street after dinner one evening to administer it. I walked because Johnson wasn't all that far from the dorms and going to get the car on the other side of the river would be even farther. My boots crunched on the snow-covered sidewalks and I had to strain to see the house numbers in the darkened streets.

I found the address -- a big, rambling, green Victorian house -- which was all chopped up into apartments; luckily everyone had a bell, and the foyer was light enough for me to see his name and ring it. He came down the interior stairs to lead me back up to his door, and once inside, I saw that it was pretty nice, not like a lot of student apartments in old houses that always looked like they hadn't been really cleaned in decades. His apartment had a comfortable enough living room with an old, but substantial couch, an armchair and a nice desk laden with all his work over in one corner. We, however, went into the little kitchen and set up the tape recorder on his tiny kitchen table.

He started the tapes, which had instructions in French spoken way too fast for me to really understand, and then he took a seat and just sat there while I spoke into the built-in microphone. Saying I spoke French into the machine is a big leap: I tried to speak it and didn't do such a great job of it either.

"Oh, geez, "I said when we were finished, "they're going to put me in the lowest level ever!"

"Do not worry. You can only speak at the level where you are. You shall return much better!"

And in his accent, it came out like this: *"Due naht wohrry. You cahn ohnleee speak at th' layvelle whairh you ahrr. You shawl retourne much behttair!"* He could have read the grocery ads from the Press Citizen with that accent; I would have melted just the same.

Valentine's Day at the University of Iowa---dorms or sorority houses--- looked like a funeral where the only flowers allowed were red roses. Long boxes, every sized glass or ceramic vases, and bouquets in cellophane tied with ribbons were piled high on the front desks of Burge and Daum, although, really Burge had the vast majority. Everyone would be in there, either going to eat or getting mail or buying sundries in the little shop, and would pass the flowers and hope some were for her.

I passed this massive display and headed back to my room only to find three vases on the slim ledge in front of our mirror...all for Cass, and not from Alan!

"Good Christ! "I said as I caught glimpse of her reading a card. "Who sent you all these?! Really gorgeous and the smell is heaven!"

"I just can't figure it out, "she said, "because I don't really know these guys that well. This one, "she said showing me a large glass vase of long-stem red roses, "is from a guy in the art department — not actually a classmate but another art student, Sheridan Hayward. Do you know who he is? "

"Well, no, but I saw his name on some of those works that were on display where yours were. Wow, does he like you, too?"

"Not in any romantic way. At least I didn't think so," she laughed.

She picked up another, smaller glass vase of red roses mixed with sweet baby's breath and explained that it was from a guy in her lit class.

"He must want to go out with you?" *Who didn't?*

"I don't know…I doubt it."

And the third one was from Klampert. It had red and white roses with greenery and a lovely festooning ribbon winding its way through the flowers.

"That one," I ventured, "is really beautiful. I wonder if he told the florist how to do that ribbon thing."

I knew I wasn't getting anything of the sort from Soren; that would have cost far too much, though we did exchange cards. I made his out of a heart-shaped doily and traced around the cut outs in red and pink, à la Peter Max. I then mounted it on yellow construction paper and wrote on it in French "*Joyeuse St Valentin*" and signed it "Love, Sari." I thought it was quite the little psychedelic-cum-French work of creative genius. He gave me a "funny" Hallmark valentine showing a cartoon King Kong on the Empire State Building — to commemorate my New York trip — sweet! --- waving at planes with a giant heart in his hand and the dialogue bubble saying, "I'd scale the tallest building for you, Valentine!"

Notwithstanding three beautiful flower displays for the holiday from three different guys, Cass left for Valentine's night with Alan. She had also made his card: a drawing of the two of them on his Norton as they rode off into the sunset, which was a big heart setting into the horizon. It was very clever and even looked like them---from behind!

Soren and I did go out that night and it turned out to be the perfect Valentine's outing: to the film *A Man and A Woman* starring Anouk Aimee and Jean-Louis Trintignant. The Iowa Theatre was packed; obviously other romantic souls saw the symbolic gesture. Nothing could have prepared me for the *coup de foudre* to my heart that this film turned out to **be.**

The sound track alone changed my life forever. It was not my entrée to Brazilian music since I'd already been listening to Sérgio Mendes and Brazil '66, and loved them. I certainly could not dance the samba, but I loved the music others did dance to. But the true New Wave, Bossa Nova, would forever after permeate my soul in a way no other music of the '60's would. Yes, I loved the Beatles, Cream, Jefferson Airplane; and I was more than devoted to Simon and Garfunkel and Joni and Laura. But Antonio Carlos Jobim, Gilberto Gil and Vinicius de Moraes became the soundtrack to the rest of my life. Just from seeing that movie that night with Soren.

On Valentine's night, Cass didn't come "home" to our room, which didn't actually surprise me because she was staying over at Alan's more and more. We had the morning routine down pretty pat; either she'd "sneak" into breakfast stealthily in line with me, as though we'd come in together; or more often than not, just not come to breakfast---no reason — and be back in the dorm after 10:00 or so, as though she'd gone to a singleton class and was back. She could easily carry overnight things in her book bag; no one gave that a thought.

She also kept a few things at his place, and one day had asked me over to see where he lived. I had to bite my tongue to keep from criticizing his messy housekeeping. What a shambles! His digs were a studio in a big house like my French prof lived in, but way on the other side of town, out at the end of Market Street. It was run-down and housed at least eight small efficiency-type apartments. His was one big room with a bed off to one side, a big square oak table in the middle of the room serving as desk for his typewriter, dining table, and general dumping off place for clothes, books and everything else. There were four wooden chairs around that and only one comfortable chair in the room. A bathroom was separated with a pocket door and the kitchen, if you could call it that, was in the corner of the room opposite the bed. Nothing seemed clean. Bedclothes were wrinkled, curtains over the two windows the place did have were lopsided. The kitchen sink was rusting and the bathroom sink needed a good scouring, as did the rest of the place.

I was stupefied that Cass Hyde could even stand to set foot in the place.

In fact, that first time I saw it, she was as embarrassed as he should have been. The next time I was there, the clutter was picked up a bit more and Cass had done a few little things to the place to make it seem nice. For one thing she let him have our lovely Indian bedspread from our summer apartment, as well as the large woven basket we had used for records. Alan was able to use it as a hamper and that freed up space on the table. Still not ideal, but better.

I had a hard time trying to figure out Alan Jones, once I was no longer his student. I wanted very badly to like him; if Cass was in love with him ---a big IF---I wanted him to be great. He was certainly darling to look at, a square-jawed Norse god with a mop of curly blond hair and ice blue eyes. He had a mischievous grin and a hearty laugh.

"I just figured out who Alan reminds me of, " I announced to her one day after joking about his rugged good looks. "Dudley Do-Right."

"Ho! Does that make me Little Nell?" she laughed.

It certainly did, but I wondered: if she were ever tied to the railroad tracks, would he rescue her?

As for my actual relationship with Alan Jones, not as his student but just as a civilian, it hadn't been hard for him to figure out that I was Cass' best friend, and sometimes he could be so sweet to me. Other times he could be moody, aloof and judgmental, look right through me and pay no attention to anyone else in his presence either. He was generally deferential to Cass when I was there, and only that one time did Cass ever come back from any date or outing with Alan complaining about him. But there were other instances when, just based on his air of superiority, I thought he could have been nicer to her, too. Cass mostly ignored that and said she chalked it up to his being under work stress---he was still teaching Rhetoric to freshmen and doing his own graduate work at the same time. It took a toll.

Alan had pursued Cass quite ardently in the beginning, and he did seem genuinely scared of losing her with the whole art school drama he caused. However, after the horror story that was his unannounced Christmas Day appearance in Kenilworth, he refused afterwards to allow her to buy or pay for anything they needed: movie tickets, meals, books, supplies, etc. He had told her in no uncertain terms that her "Daddy's money" wasn't going to pay his way. When she told him she really had her own money, he refused to believe it.

"It's just his pride," she sighed.

"He's stupid, then," I said.

"Guy are like that, though, you know, kid?"

On February 14, near eleven o'clock that night, our dorm phone rang. Hours had NOT been extended for Valentine's night which fell on a Wednesday, and so I'd been back in the room for an hour already.

It was Julia Hyde on the phone.

"Hello, Sarah. I'm sorry to call so late, dear. May I please speak to Cassandra?"

"Oh, Mrs. Hyde," I said with worry in my voice. "Is something wrong?"

"Everything is fine, Sarah. I just need to speak to my daughter."

At 11:00 pm.?! No way.

"She's actually not in the room at the moment. I think maybe she went down to the study lounge. Or maybe the t.v. room? I just got back myself a short time ago."

Well, that last part was true!

"Study lounge!? At this hour?"

"Or t.v.?"

"All right, Sarah, I'll hang on---will you please go find her and bring her to the phone?"

"Uh...sure, if you want to hold. Do you? Or should I find her and have her call you?"

"I'll wait," she almost snarled.

I panicked. But truth be told, I didn't even know if Alan had a phone! I had no way to contact Cass. The apartment was way too far for me to run over to it. If I ran to my car it would still take me twenty minutes to get to it and then another 10 minutes to get to his place. How in God's name was I going to get back on the phone and LIE to these people who had been so kind to me, so accepting of me, so liberal with their hospitality to me? I had none of the righteous indignation against them that I had against Sol and Betty, to whom I really didn't lie much, but to whom I could have, with little remorse.

I went back to the room, picked up the phone, sounded breathless and announced to her that I just couldn't find Cass at the moment.

"She might be in someone's room having a chat about Valentine's Day, Mrs. Hyde. She got roses from three guys!"

"Sarah, I don't believe you, but..."

"NO! It's true. I looked for her! But the minute she comes back, I'll have her call you, I promise! "

"Well, don't bother if it's midnight or something. That is too late. I'll speak to her in the morning. Good night."

THANK GOD!!! I would get up really early Thursday, go over to Alan's and bring her back for the call!

But I didn't wake up early. And around 10:00 a.m. I was awakened by our room door opening up with a bang.

In swept Julia Hyde in her long Blackgama what-becomes-a-legend-most mink coat and matching hat covering her swept-up hair with tendrils hanging messily around her face. She had Martin with her and was flinging Cass into the room.

"Get packing, Martin."

I was startled, aghast. Cass ran into the bathroom crying.

Julia looked at me sitting up in bed, and over at Cass' empty bed. "I found her," she snapped.

Julia had ordered up the Bentley at the crack of dawn and been driven straight to Iowa City and first to the Registrar's office, which opened at 8:30, where she ascertained Alan Jones' residential address. Then she went over there, caught Cass with him and dragged her out to the car in the biting morning air.

"Cassandra!" she yelled towards our bathroom door, "get out here!"

In the meantime, I got up and put on a robe. Cass came out of the bathroom in her robe, too, having had to change out of her clothes. Again.

Julia was barking at her, "I'm going back over to the Registrar's office and terminate your enrollment at this school. While I'm gone, you and Martin will get all your things sorted and into the boxes and luggage.
"

"No, Mummy!! Please no!!" Cass sobbed. "I've …I've still got all my art supplies and projects across the river!!"

"I don't give a damn about your art projects. Just get your belongings that are here packed UP."

"Please please don't do this."

"It's done." She pulled Cass' pieces of matching luggage out of the closet, flung them in the tiny space near the door, and slammed out.

Cass sat down on her bed and heaved great sobs and floods of tears. Martin stood at the closet and picked out what he presumed to be hers. He wasn't happy about it, but he didn't try to comfort her either. I glared at him.

"This can't be happening," I said.

"She came OVER there, kid! She banged on his door and screamed at us," she sobbed. "She was so furious. I've never seen her like that!"

"Yeah, she must be really mad to come here herself. What did Alan say?"

"He couldn't say much. She called his place a pig sty and him a scum bag; and she threatened to have him fired from the University payroll and to ruin his chances of his ever getting his degree!! Can you imagine!! She was horrible!"

Jesus. I was betting she could do all that, too.

I went over to the bed and sat down next to Cass and hugged her tightly while she wept. She seemed so broken that I was afraid she would flutter away to the floor and disappear.

"Don't cry, Cass. We will still keep in touch. We'll find a way to see each other again. I'll come to Chicago and you can sneak into the city and meet me or something."

"I'd better get dressed."

I helped them load things into boxes willy nilly. No one was paying attention to details or being careful. When Julia returned, this time she knocked on the door and I answered it. She went right past me and surveyed the progress.

"You are officially withdrawn. Your grades will come back marked as such and maybe someday at some other institution of higher learning, you can recoup the credits, I'm not at all sure. "

She turned to me. "Sarah, I have paid in full for this room for the entire year, as your parents did, and I've told the University housing office that you may stay in the room as you wish, with or without a new roommate. I doubt there is anyone who is in need of a space at this late date in the year, but I leave that to them and you."

I'd been keeping it together up to that point, but I, too, broke down and began to cry. It was hitting me hard that Cass was leaving and I couldn't do anything to help her. I couldn't do anything to persuade her mother that she was making the **most** obscene mistake! I seemingly couldn't do anything to save my second semester sophomore year from turning into a nightmare when it had been so promising and happy. I would have to ready myself for Paris all alone; who would be there to share with me the trials and triumphs of my Junior Year Abroad preparations?

The packing done, desk drawers and closet shelves emptied, bathroom cleared, Martin went down to fetch the rolling cart and started loading up the car. Cass and I clung to each other sobbing until Julia had to intervene.

"All right, that's enough. Come on Cassandra. Let's go. Good-bye Sarah. "

"Wait one more minute, "I said, "Cass — I'll go to the art school and collect all your stuff. I'll take it home with me and ship it to you or something. Don't worry, okay?"

"'K. Thanks."

I grabbed her hand. "Bye, Cass. 'Keep the faith, baby'!"

Cass pulled me over to her once more and we kissed on the cheek and said goodbye. Julia took her by the coat sleeve down the hall to the elevator, her mink billowing behind her. A few other girls on the floor saw them. My nosey neighbor from across the hall had been in her room and had heard muffled arguing even over there, so she peeked out into the corridor, saw me and said,

"Your roommate was so weird! Is she GONE? Like for good?"

"Shut the hell up, " I said slamming my door from the inside.

The truth of the matter, still not sunk in on me, was that she *was* gone, like for good.

Chapter Twenty-Two

"Ohio"...Crosby, Stills, Nash and Young (Neil Young)

Sometimes we get a false spring in Iowa where you can be lulled into thinking warm weather had arrived and you were safe to go out in light clothes again and sleep with fresh air wafting into propped-opened windows. But that doesn't last and you find yourself hit by March's return of winter; newly blooming flowers tricked into thinking it was safe to show their beauty, are suddenly guillotined by a heavy snow.

Cass hadn't been gone a week when the phone rang in my room and it was Alan Jones.

"Miss Shrier! How are you?"

"How do you think I am?" *I still felt shell shocked, is how I was.*

"Can I talk to you? I'm down in Burge's lobby."

What?! Why didn't he just call me from his office or his apartment, if he even had a phone there---I had never ascertained that.

"Yes, okay. I'll be over."

So I went through the tunnel and met him on one of the purple couches. He was wearing a green heavy canvas army surplus jacket and carrying a walking stick of some sort.

"Are you taking a hike?" I asked, rather proud of my double entendre, which didn't seem to register at all with him.

"I really miss her, you know," he pronounced.

"I know."

I didn't have much to say to him. I blamed him for me losing my best friend and saw him as the person who controlled her. But she must have had something to do with the decision to start staying at his place all the time, too.

"So I was wondering if you would send this letter to her," he said reaching into his pocket. "They would never let anything I sent be given to her, I'm sure. "

"Well, I don't know how it works at her house; the staff do all that. "

"Yes, but you can bet they have orders to not let any communication from me get to her—letters, phone calls, packages, you name it."

"You might be right, Alan," I said. "But for all I know, I can't communicate with her either. We haven't so far. They may very well see me as complicit in all the drama. I was there, you know, and so they probably assume that I knew she was forbidden to see you and didn't tell them when she did!"

"Why would they expect you to rat on her?" he asked incredulously.

"I don't know. I guess I'm being hypersensitive."

"Paranoid."

"All right! So what?"

"It's okay, I can see your point," he said toning it down. "Will you do it? If they see a letter is from you, I'm sure they won't care and she'll get it."

"Give it to me."

And so it began, letters from me hiding letters from him. He didn't seem to care if I read them, since he just folded them small and flat—notes really, so that nothing nefarious could be discerned at the Kenilworth end. Cass wrote back to me but never sent any sort of replies to Alan via my letters, although she did express gratitude that I sent his. It dawned on me that she could write to him herself, and no one would be the wiser. She wasn't a prisoner in her house, after all, and not only did the staff love her, the parents were hardly there. She did also go down to Springfield and stay with her grandmother for part of the time. I didn't worry too much about her, even though in the back of my mind it still seemed incongruous that the Hydes' desire to end their daughter's relationship with Alan Jones could be accomplished just by pulling her out of school and physically separating her from him. However, it seemed to satisfy them, and they resumed their usual neglect of her.

Cass was very dejected about her art studies, her future career plans, and the lost momentum for her work. She didn't have to ask me; I had already decided to go over to talk to Klampert and get her things. He was happy to see me and wanted to help.

"I'm sorry my car is still in your driveway, also, " I told him as we gathered Cass' tools, sketches, prints and canvases.

"Sarah, that is just fine. You can keep it there. It doesn't cause any trouble to have it. We can even load all Cassandra's things in it if you like. I'll help you."

"That would be great," I sighed with relief.

"She was my muse, you know," he said to me with a fervent if far-away tone to his voice and a glint of sadness in his eyes.

More like you were her Svengali, I wanted to say, and then chastised myself for having such a snarky thought.

"Have you heard from her?" I asked casually. I presumed any letter from him was not kept from her.

"Yes. She and I have corresponded. She'll be relieved that you rescued all her things."

"Yeah---that was always the plan. I'm happy to do it."

"So, will you be taking more studio art classes or art history?"

"I am planning to take a lot of art history next year, Professor. I'll be at the Sorbonne."

"Will you! I think that's wonderful! And you should take some more studio art, too. You showed some promise with your linoleum block printing."

"Oh, you must be joking, Dr. Klampert."

I went over to his house and drove my car back as close to the art school building as I could park so we could load up all Cass' materials. I would have to get some boxes, I decided, and mail them off; and I changed my mind about driving with them all the way back to The Bluffs for Spring Break. I would send them from Iowa City if I could manage to pay for that. So I phoned Cass from our room and told her my plan. Phoning her was a splurge in itself because the long-distance call would show up on my "U Bill" and the parents would scream; but it was a risk I had to take, really, and given the circumstances, I figured they'd cut me some slack. I kept it short though I was dying to talk to her for hours.

"I'll send you the money for that," she said right off the bat.

"Thanks! I wasn't sure how I was going to swing it on my stupid allowance. I picked up boxes from the Safeway store in Coralville! Wasn't that smart of me?" I laughed, trying to seem clever and efficient.

"You're the best friend," she said solemnly. "I'm so grateful, kid."

"Hey, come on now---perk up. I'm happy to do it and soon you'll have all your stuff back."

"You'll need to go to the bookstore and get some of that heavy brown tape to wrap it with," she instructed me. "You know it comes on a roll and you have to moisten it-- like with a sponge."

"Oh, okay. I'll find it. I'll take care of everything. Don't worry!"

That semester I could have gone around campus like a zombie, missing Cass, but because I was in constant Paris planning mode, I couldn't neglect my studies. I couldn't let myself sink into some blue funk when my life's dream was about to materialize. I was buoyed by the prospects looming ahead of me in just a few months, and I was also heavily supported by Soren who had been my rock through the whole aftermath of Cass' leaving.

One of his intentions with me was to see that I wasn't moping around in my room, and to that end, he signed us up together for a lot of ushering at gigs that played the Iowa Memorial Union.

"You have to admit that Iowa U really is the oasis in this cultural desert," he admonished me as he showed me a list of the acts still to come to campus that spring: all kinds of touring music, speakers, play readings and recitals.

"Yeah, yeah---I'll give it that."

To wit, Mitch Ryder and the Detroit Wheels were slated to make a repeat performance in the Union ballroom but no ushering would be required; this was to be another fabulous concert-cum-dance. Soren asked me as soon as he heard about it, remembering how much I'd loved them before, as well as his professed admiration for these songs and what he called the "Detroit funk" sound.

"We all know Motown music is from Detroit, " Soren explained to me, "but Mitch Ryder is really the hero of Michigan rock and roll. "

"Why's that? " I had asked.

"Are you joking? Don't you love 'Sock it to Me, Baby' and 'Devil with the Blue Dress On'?!!"

"Yes, I LOVE them, " I insisted. *I watched Hullabaloo for godsake!* "And I also love 'C. C. Rider' and 'Come See about Me' and 'Little Latin Lupe Lu'. But how is he the hero of ..."

"Just because!"

If Soren was going to write music criticism, he'd have to be more articulate than "just because." Mitch Ryder was even more famous when he returned to Iowa City that year. He'd been on *The Ed Sullivan Show* and all over t.v. His songs were hits in the American tradition of feel good rock and roll.

We were, as we put it, "diggin' it," as we rocked out that night; it was the best time I'd ever had at a dance. I'd gone to many high school dances in the gym (never to Prom or a Military Ball), but had hardly ever danced. Always went with a group of girls who didn't have actual dates, and never thought I could dance anyway. But once I got to college, it seemed like dancing was easy; and if I did look ridiculous, no one seemed to care. I never cared about whether I was actually doing a real dance: the boogaloo or the frug or whatever. The music just swept me away on a voyage to a better place.

Soren and I were more or less going steady. We might argue good naturedly with each other, but we never fought. We didn't make love either. We were great friends, and that seemed to work out.

But I had had crushes on other guys at college, especially the kid from that first French class, Mick, who had also been in my Freshman Biology lab and whom I still saw on campus all the time. He was a Sig Ep so he wasn't even allowed to date me, a non-sorority person. But we had sort of bonded over dissecting things: a crayfish, which we had named "Rock On" and an earthworm we called "Henri the Earthworm". His favorite flower turned out to be my favorite, the daisy of all things, and I found that out when one time I was wearing daisy earrings and a matching pin on my sweater. He came up to me before class to tell me how fab they were.

"Thanks," I had cooed. "Daisies are my happy flowers."

"I love them, too," he replied. "At home we plant some, but most grow wild all over the place."

So I would make it a point to wear mine with as many outfits as I could possibly put together, even though my fashion sense led me to feel that they were out of place in seasons that weren't spring or summer.

Mick was so cute, I couldn't take my eyes off him, and any time he sat by me, I got all into a "pinch me" mode. He reminded me of a blond JFK. He was from Sturgeon Bay, Wisconsin and always talked about their Door County lake house and the sailboat he loved. I heard Sturgeon Bay but imagined Hyannis Port.

Mick and his frat brother Dick were always hanging around together and once in a while after lab or our French class, they would invite me for a beer. We would go to The Airliner, where "they" hung out, as opposed to "us". I didn't drink beer so I would have coffee and Dick always got a kick out of how square I was.

"Why didn't you pledge?" *Dick would ask – again and again.*

I would shrug and launch into my mantra. "No time. I've always planned to go to Paris, and by God, I'm going," *I told him.*

"That's really cool," *Mick said, grinning his perfect smile at me.*

I was what we would call "snowed" over him. I would hope and pray that he'd call and ask me out, even if they weren't supposed to date anyone but Greeks. I found myself hoping against hope that I would run into him at various places on campus; and then when I did see him, usually in EPB, it would seem to me that fate had brought us together. When he didn't call, I would tell myself that he had to be at frat functions, or that he went home to Door County on the weekends to sail. And when we did get together, even if it was very informally, I would write in my diary, "Reinstated!" *But then, inevitably, I would see him with some other girls – some I knew and some I didn't, and that would crush me, and I would record,* "Life is a piece of shit."

My University of Iowa dating life with Mick was mostly pure fantasy. But one time he really did ask me out: to go to the movie, Alfie, playing downtown at the Varsity. We had a great time, and he walked me back to the dorms, but we were early so we sat in Burge instead of saying our good nights in Daum. On a sudden whim out of nowhere, I invited him to the Spring Fling put on by the Residence Halls.

"You know what it is, don't you? Sort of the dormies' version of what sororities do. It's formal."

He knew all right, and no doubt couldn't be caught dead at it. But he was a gentleman, and declined the invitation graciously, explaining that he would be going home that weekend, "unfortunately" *but thanking me anyway. I have no idea if he really did go home that weekend; I was pretty heartbroken, but also upset with myself that I had asked him off the cuff like that.*

I didn't see Mick much at all after that first year, but in 1970 as we were picking up our caps and gowns, we did run into each other in the crowd. "Have a nice life," I called out to him, as we parted.

Another reason I kept busy that spring was that I had such great classes and teachers that were at the top of their game. Guy LeNotre made the French Comp and Con class amazingly interesting. It started off with the phrase "please forward" that we were to use on a letter we had to write someone. Since I was doing nothing BUT writing Cass, I just used one of my letters to her as the assignment, putting on it *"Prière de faire suivre"*. I got A's on every French assignment. I was confident that I had done good work for him, but it also occurred to me that, since he knew I was going to the Sorbonne after that, he'd taken it upon himself to boost my self-esteem.

My English class was called Masterpieces of Literature and was taught by Stephen Gray, a South African member of the Workshop who was possibly the best teacher I ever had at Iowa. He was becoming known for plays, novels, poetry, and even wrote journalistic articles. He was interviewed on the campus radio station all the time and gave literary reviews on air. While Alan Jones had treated us with more contempt than respect as his students, Stephen Gray seemed to love teaching. He was very secure in his knowledge and presence in the classroom. When we were studying Dante's *Inferno,* Gray brought in a fellow workshop participant, Sergio Rossi to read the part about Paolo and Francesca in Italian to us! I about swooned over both of them—Sergio and Stephen, that is. My grades in Masterpieces of Literature were hardly ever below A.

"The teacher really does make all the difference," I pontificated to Soren one night. "I mean, I am literally inspired to study anything Gray gives us. His enthusiasm is contagious and his intellectual prowess is prodigious."

"Sounds like you're infatuated," Soren observed, half-teasing.

"No! But I'm serious about this teacher-outcome correlation thing. I had an experience in high school with geometry where the teacher was a real asshole and I was getting D's! Me! I asked to change classes because this guy was sending me vibes that he didn't like me, that it was a personality conflict between us. But the principal was reluctant to put me in another section, since we were already into the term. I insisted, though, and in my new class, taught by a wonderful teacher, I suddenly began to get A's---because I understood it! "

"I guess that does happen," he admitted.

"Yeah," I added, "and Alan Jones could take a few pointers."

Half-way through March I was driving home once again. I would have made some excuse and stayed in the dorm in my solitary room over Spring Break, but since I was told to bring the car back for the snow tires to be taken off, I was obliged to obey. I also still had some more vaccinations to get of the diphtheria series, this time administered by my childhood pediatrician. It was sort of lucky that I was home, because I actually became very sick from it. I was in bed feverish and delirious, sweating when it broke, and shaking with chills.

Betty came to the conclusion that, "You must not weigh enough to be able to stand this shot in its whole form. They should have given you half."

"I weigh the same as I always did---ninety-seven pounds."

"Yes, well, you could stand to gain some."

This was crazy talk coming from her; my weight had scarcely ever fluctuated all through high school and so far in college. I hadn't put on the "freshman fifteen" and I hadn't lost any either. My mother simply could not have a conversation with me without finding something to criticize. She was so passive with her husband, so aggressive with me and so nurturing to my sister. It was the stuff of doctoral dissertations on the dysfunctional family.

We were actually starting preliminary plans for my exodus to France during the time I was home in March of '68. I would be leaving in just three short months and had to really decide what to take. Betty came up with two ideas: one, that I should have a set of very light-weight luggage, since I had to carry it; and two, that we should buy a footlocker and she would send that with more clothes for winter.

"In Paris you will have to figure out how to send it back," she said, "but I'm sure there will be a way to do that."

I didn't own any nice luggage and certainly nothing that matched. I had received a suitcase once for my birthday about ten years prior. It was the light blue hatbox I had taken to New York with Cass and her family. It ended up almost being destroyed, however, on its maiden voyage. This was during one of our very rare family vacations. Sol had tied luggage to the top of the Rambler station wagon. We were on our way heading north on U.S. Highway 59, and I was riding in the "way far" as Roslyn and I called the back of the wagon. I happened to see out the back window of the tail gate that all of a sudden, my suitcase had come loose from the roof of the car, had bounced off the edge, and was rolling down the road behind us! I screamed for Sol to stop the car and he did, pulling over perilously close to the ditch. The suitcase was probably almost a mile away by then, but luckily we found it, miraculously only slightly dented, but other than that not too damaged!

I would, however, not be taking an ancient round hatbox to Paris.

My grandmother, though, had a matching set of American Tourister luggage, fairly new, and with the modern rounded corner shape of the 60's. But even considering she was willing to let me take it away for a whole year, it was heavy. No suitcases had wheels in those days, and my mother said she couldn't see me trying to carry three pieces of it— train case, Pullman case and an even larger one-- plus a purse— the distance from the airport to a waiting coach or cab.

So it was decided I should have new luggage, and the way to get it would be with S & H Green stamps.

Betty had about five or six books filled with the little stamps pasted in. She got them certain places--at the grocery store and filling up with gas mostly, but sometimes at other stores. We had enough for me to get two pieces of plaid luggage. The frames were black vinyl but the red plaid part was stiff cloth that zipped closed. I couldn't believe how little they weighed empty, and mother assured me I would be easily able to lift them packed. She said we would put sponges on the insides of the handles, so my palms wouldn't hurt carrying them. *How'd she think that up?*

The program had already been sending out information packets about what to wear and what not to wear in Europe. One thing they made clear was that jeans were not allowed in classes, and that they really were not worn by women on the streets of Paris, either. Women did not wear *trousers* often at all in Paris, it said. It was too early when I was home on break that spring to actually gather clothes ready to take, but it wasn't too soon to do an inventory of what I would need; so we did that. I would pack summer and fall clothes, and she would send winter ones in the trunk.

I spent the rest of the break working in the bar and preparing for the mid-term exams I would have immediately upon return. Anthro lectures often were, in the vernacular of our day, "*v*-(for very) worthless", and I was thus always in danger of "flaggin' "it.

I also took the opportunity one evening at dinner to break the news to my parents and grandmother of Cass' abrupt departure from college and the ramifications of her boyfriend showing up unannounced at their place on Christmas when I was there.

"What do you mean, they took her out?!" bellowed Sol. "That guy must have been a real hippie *momzer*. Good for them!"

"He's an instructor in the English department! He'd been my teacher. He is a member of the exalted Iowa Writer's Workshop, for godsake." I suddenly felt defensive on behalf of Alan!

"Oh, great, so you were responsible for introducing them, I suppose?" snorted my father.

"Not exactly."

"But what will she do now?" asked my grandmother, still reeling from this report.

"I don't know. She signs her letters, *Cassandra Bronwyn Hyde, College Dropout.*" I laughed nervously; but no one else was laughing.

Roslyn suddenly got it: "So you've got that room all to yourself?! Lucky dog."

"Yes, and you've got mine all to yourself here. What's your point?"

"Will you get another roommate?" Betty asked.

"I don't think so. It hasn't happened so far. I can't see them putting someone in with me for only one quarter."

"Well, if that don't just beat all, " Sol said, still digesting both his meal and the news as I was clearing the table. "I would have done the same damn thing. Should have when you protested the war! But I have to say, what your friend did was even worse. I would have yanked you out of there if I thought you were skipping out of the dorm, too, believe me. To say nothing of shacking up with some *chazzer*." He just shook his head and walked past me to the t.v. "From that swanky WASP family, too. Just goes to show."

Show what?

Chapter Twenty-three

"Save the Country"...Laura Nyro

If someone hadn't already invented the phrase "That Was The Week That Was," I would have had to change "week" to "year" and coin it for 1968. Innocently at dinner in the dining hall on April 4, we were interrupted by an announcement on a p.a. system I didn't even realize they had. "Dr. Martin Luther King, Jr. has been shot in Memphis, Tennessee," a voice boomed over the loudspeaker. News was not instantaneous in those days, but the assassination attempt happened during the evening news broadcast period, and the t.v. and radio programs on at that hour were interrupted by a bulletin. Someone in the kitchen or down the hall had heard it and made the announcement to us.

Muffled gasping and shocked expressions resonated through the room. *I don't recall there being any Negro residents of our dorm that year, and if there were, for all I knew, they were segregated into their own hall or at least with their own roommates, as disgusting as that seems to me now.* We were all very saddened. I was relieved that no one in my presence that night took this news as anything but tragedy.

Students all across the campus repaired to various halls and lounges with televisions in them. I had a t.v. in my room and I watched it all night as reports of the shooting and then his death had come in at around 7:00 p.m. Five years earlier when John F. Kennedy had been assassinated was the first time I'd ever spent days in front of a t.v. screen wondering what would happen to the country in the aftermath of such a heinous act; and this was the second time.

We had already seen the nascent anti-war movement take hold on the campus of the U of Iowa, but as for a black student impetus to organize, that was a year or two off. No one on campus was yet using the term "black power" though we—and I mean white students---had been tapped to help register black voters in Des Moines the previous fall, and Cass and I had gone there and helped. But I didn't think too much of that as anything out of the ordinary. I wasn't happy when I found out that people didn't register, weren't told how to do it, weren't encouraged to do it already, or didn't think they had the same right to do it as I did. But had I made myself more aware of what was really going on in this country, I surely would not have been so naïve.

In the days that followed, the campus was solemn and several services were held at various churches in Dr. King's memory. It was a coincidence that during the one at the only synagogue in Iowa City, I had the opportunity to reconnect with Dottie from freshman year. When we left the service, she and I went to Hamburg Inn in downtown and talked over coffee. She was as surprised to hear about my various sojourns over the past year and a half with the Hyde family as about Cass' departure.

"Wow, " she said, after I'd regaled her with private planes and Homestead mansions and Chicago penthouses and New York. "They took her out of school. I'm not even sure my parents would take me out if they found out I was dating a *goy.*"

"Are you?" I asked.

"NO!"

In fact, she was lavaliered to a boy she'd met practically the first week of school when I knew her. He was in the Jewish frat and they'd met at the first mixer in the fall of '66.

"I'm engaged!" she announced.

"Well, that's so neat!" I said, thinking I had heard somewhere that one didn't congratulate the woman, only the man. "When's the wedding?"

"Next Thanksgiving! Can you come? "

"Actually, I can't!! I'm leaving in June for Paris! I won't be back until the summer of 1969."

"Oh my goodness! Well, when you get back, you'll have to come over and see us. We're going to be living in married student housing!"

"Incredible! What's that like?"

"Quonset huts!"

"Jesus."

147

"Yeah, Donald's a junior now. We'll live there for his senior year and then he wants to do grad school somewhere else."

"WHAT? You won't graduate from your beloved University of Iowa?! I don't believe it."

"Well, we'll see… maybe he'll want to be here after all. But I think he really wants to go someplace with mountains…like Vermont."

"Holy buckets. And what do your parents say about all this?"

"What can they say? They love him. I'm the youngest and only girl. Everything that's been done has already been done by my brothers, and my parents are thrilled that I found a nice Jewish boy and will give them grandchildren. "

"Even at our age? "

We were nineteen years old! I thought twenty was still far too young to get married. We weren't living in pioneer days for God's sake. The women's movement was about to be launched and how about a little self-actualization before you put on the ol' apron and started changing diapers?

"Well, we should get together before I leave for Paris," I said cheerily as we got up to go.

"Definitely! We'll do it. I'll call you."

But she never did.

It wasn't too long after the shock of MLK, that I got another big jolt with the initials CBH! A typed letter came to me postmarked Miami! Cass! Was in Florida? How could that be? And it was on stationery marked "Trans-World Airlines, " an even deeper mystery. I tore it open.

Dear Sari,

I know you are sitting there shocked to have received this letter postmarked Miami. I am indeed an employee of TWA, thanks to my father and his prevailing over my mother who probably would have locked me away for the rest of my life. My dad knows the president of the airline, and he got me into this program (although I probably would have been accepted without his pulling strings). They shipped me off for flight school, ya know, and here I am. Actually it has been much more exhausting than I ever dreamed. Classes are from 8:00- 4:30 every day and we work from eight texts, which we will have covered by the end of the five weeks. Reading assignment take approx. six hours (at minimum!) every night. The girls in my "class" are from everywhere—there are twenty-two of us—three Americans and the rest from Europe, Africa, Australia and Asia. Most—all but myself and one English girl---have college degrees (can you imagine?) and speak a minimum of four languages! HA! In language proficiency exams, I achieved the fabulous rating of "minimum" trying to use my French!

We "live" – ha! exist is a more appropriate word—at the Miami Airways Motel across from the TWA Buildings—we are quite close to Miami Internat'l Airport and so you would expect we would be miles and miles from beaches and peaceful parks, etc., but we are only a few blocks from them. The only problem is that the only times you can sunbathe are on the weekends. Seems like somehow we should be let out of our cage a couple times a day so we can develop the type of suntan you're supposed to get in Florida! Can you imagine my returning after five weeks and being as albino as before---I mean like "what'll my friends think?" Ha ha!

Let's see: what else to tell you. Oh yeah! The first week was "grooming" which was such a delightful experience ---mainly they decided my hair needed "body" you know, some ol' Gerald-Mc Boing- Boing- bounce, so off to the Beauty Shop and, oh, Sari, it's just awful. I could cry. I did cry, even. But I keep thinking it'll gradually grow out or something. I feel like wearing a paper bag over my head. I know you know about straightening hair and all. I'm sort of afraid to do that myself 'cause I worry about damaging my hair. It's still in good shape physically—I mean it's just giving me these God-awful emotional hang-ups!

I've actually been here two weeks already! Sorry to have not prepared you better for this news! Or at all---ha. The first week was general information about TWA—this second week has been Emergency Procedures class—whereby we learn about evacuation in case of ditching or land emergency landings—opening exits—doors, inflating emergency air slides, keeping a life raft group alive—how to escape burning wreckage, etc. Real fun stuff. Plus oxygen and fire extinguishing and a million other details. Yesterday was the final exam for that—we also had to memorize the location of all emergency equipment in the three main aircraft types TWA flies. It's amazing all we must learn, Sari, it's so crazy – I mean, it's harder than college. I look at the kind of job this is and it's just insane. We've been getting these shots like you had to get---every day though! The worst one was for cholera—it induced vomiting and chills and we got it the night right before the exam! UGH.

Next week is "Cordon Bleu" (oh right!) for learning to mix drinks (move over Sol!), work in the galley and prepare all kinds of food from steaks to some exotic stuff like squab ---I kid you not! Also, we've had uniform fittings. I look like I'm in a potato sack! TWA has about the oldest-fashioned ones still around. You watch at the airport when you go to Europe and laugh! Still, there are supposed to be uniform changes next spring, hopefully! But since I only plan on doing this just one year, well, the change won't do me much good.

WHEN exactly do you leave for Paris? Perhaps I would be stationed somewhere where I'd have your flight!! Oh you would be so impressed to see me stumbling down the aisle in my TWA turquoise potato bag, ha ha! Looking ahead, though, I plan on working for this next year and then spending next summer in Europe on my own---just traveling around. With TWA you get one month's paid vacation after a year, plus a 90% discount on flights, so I plan to take advantage of the money and discount. I would love to have you come with me if you are planning on just traveling next summer, too!

Now, to Alan. Sari, he has been so thoughtful, so wonderful about writing—he called the first weekend I was here, too, and ok, I just love him. I hope you and Soren have this kind of love some day. I mean, we've got things that have to be straightened out—the CO thing, college, etc., but still, somehow when you love someone, all is possible. As things are now, he plans to at least come visit wherever I get based for work. I don't know how all this will turn out. I fear he will become as exhausted as I am...but I guess only time will tell. Plus there's another problem...he never told me his old girlfriend had come in from Cedar Rapids last February to see him. It made me a little sick. You know, that's the thing that would've been nice if he'd told me. It leaves kind of an uneasy feeling. It's not that I doubt his motives or actions or anything like that. It's just how nice it would be to have him feel he could just mention other girls, etc. without feeling he was bearing his soul and "destroying" himself. Anyway, enough said.

Be sure and keep me posted on all the happenings about Soren, your blond elusive "other " *(she meant Mick)* classes, etc. You know there's nothing I like better than knowing happiness and sadness of yours because, well, I think you're my great and dearest friend. So keep all them letters rollin' in—now that you have my address. (Good old dear sweet Lottie forwarded your last letters to me, not to worry!) Did the U ever give you another roomie? My roommates are from Austria, Sweden and Germany and they're nice, but the one from Austria is really a lovely girl—so likeable. Still, you know there is no one here I can imagine living in an apt. with. If Alan were more certain of how long he could be with me, I'd do everything I could to get a single apt. But everything is so vague and changeable. Even if he were to put his degree on hold for a little while and if they'd save his place, there's still the CO job he'd be obliged to start in Iowa City. The older I get---ol' Granny Hyde talkin' now--- the more aware of life's utter chaos I become. All you can ever do is just keep the faith, I guess, huh? So we will and especially with those predictable (Soren) and unpredictable (Alan) guys we love. What was that quote you sent me a while ago about living in harmony with others as much as possible? Would you please resend it? I loved it and as usual when I love a quote and don't recognize it, I neglected to save it, leaving it henceforth lost to the "Hyde archives." So second chance, please?

How goes the planning for a European Year Abroad?!!! Gee, what fun you will have!!! And we can get together!! Often, too if I can just get a good base assignment. It's just luck about bases, so all I can do is HOPE.

Au revoir and smile and WRITE SOOOON.

Love always,
Cass (Alias the potato sack stewardess!)

To say I couldn't even catch my breath after reading that letter, much as I had flopped right down on the bed to do so, would be an understatement. Cassandra Hyde as an airline stewardess was about the last possible image my head could take in and not explode. Curly hair? Potato sack figure? I don't think so! But also work like that? What were her parents thinking that would do for her? Maybe they also would pull strings so she'd be based in Chicago and they could keep an eye on her. That was a harrowing thought.

I was, however, ecstatic at the very idea that we might somehow see each other in Paris!! If only it were true, I thought. We could have some gay, mad, exciting times! More to daydream over, more to plan. I wrote her back a huge long letter full of fab ideas, not the least of which was that she and I would plan an actual weekend and go to Germany to the doll factory and make that happen! Details to be worked on later!!

And then there came May, 1968. As if I didn't think anything else could disturb my equilibrium that spring, who could have predicted *"Les Événements de Mai,"* where once again, our television news was rocked by scenes of violence, this time in Paris!

"Paris '68" would long after have the same connotation in France as "D-Day" or "9/11" have for us. It had started out as early as February, with student unrest and striking against a satellite campus of the University of Paris (la Sorbonne) in the suburb of Nanterre. The unrest was triggered by, among other things, the political bureaucracy that controlled everything from the funding of the system to what students could study and who could attend. They protested against class discrimination, too, and published a sort of edict on their desires for change. The university administration had called the police in, but those protests ended peacefully with a few students being disciplined and the whole thing over with. However, by May, after there had been more altercations between the administration at Nanterre and students, the administration this time shut down the entire university. Students at the Sorbonne, which was summarily closed, got wind of a threat to expel those Nanterre students who were implicated, and they met to protest both that and the closure of all the schools.

French professors, teachers, and students were very unionized in those times, as they still are, and on Monday, May 6, they called a march to protest against the police having entered the Sorbonne.

Our news organizations all had the video of twenty thousand French students, teachers and others who supported them in the streets marching towards the Sorbonne. The pictures showed the police charging at the crowd and wielding their batons at the marchers. Then, in typical French fashion, people who had dispersed began making barricades out of cars, benches, tires --- anything they could find, and some threw paving stones at the police, who retreated, only to come back with reinforcements and this time tear gas. American news programs called it a riot and hundreds of students were arrested.

After that, something unheard of in the United States made our news: the high school students joined with the university students in solidarity, which prompted their teachers, and then increasing numbers of young union members from non-academic areas, to join in. They gathered at the Arc de Triomphe this time, demanding that the police back off, that the universities be reopened and that criminal charges against students be dropped.

I got a call from my parents that very week.

"Have you been watching the news?" Sol began, somewhat smugly. "We can't let you go to any city experiencing riots like that!"

"It's not a riot. It's a demonstration." I said firmly, but in truth I knew a riot when I saw one. Then a thought struck me! "Did you notice how they're dressed, Daddy?" I fired back. "Blazers and ties!! Rioters wouldn't dress like that!"

"She's got a point, Sol, " I heard Betty say.

"Okay, I'm putting you on notice, " Sol continued. "If this doesn't die down in a few days, your entire trip is OFF. Besides, there's no university for you to study AT, if the government has it closed down. That's my final word on it. Good–bye."

God DAMN him, I said to myself---or maybe out loud, about a hundred times. I wanted to cry but I was too mad.

At Iowa, our classes went along as usual….nothing happening here! American students couldn't have pulled together a massive demonstration like that at the drop of a hat if their lives depended on it, I reckoned. We discussed the whole thing in French class, though, and within two weeks' time after the initial *manifestation*, or *manif* as we learned to call it, Guy LeNotre's friends had expedited packets of French newspapers to him like *Le Canard Enchaînée* with their headlines, *"La Lutte Continue"* and *"Début d'une Lutte Prolongée."* The finer points had not made our news, he explained, which only reported that French students were rioting in the streets behind the barricades. He presented the facts to us that the students had returned to their classrooms on the announcement, which turned out to be just a rumor, that the police were gone and the buildings reopened. None of that was true, so they did get riled up exponentially into a near revolutionary fervor.

"Always negotiations broke down, " he told us. "So what could they do? And the student leader is Daniel Cohn-Bendit, who is a French-German, but whose name made the far-right assume he was a trouble-making leftist Jew; so then the student slogan became, '*Nous sommes tous les Juifs Allemands.*' I was very proud of my country that day!"

Something else that was not reported in the American press was that allegations were presented to the government that the police had been infiltrated by agents provocateurs *in the riots, and that they were burning the cars and throwing the Molotov cocktails.*

Our professor had explained to us that the government's reaction was very heavy-handed, and that this was what brought on a wave of sympathy for the students and other strikers. After the police brutality came to light, many famous singers and poets along with the bourgeoisie *joined in the protest. But the main thing that changed was that the major left-wing union federations, the* Confédération Générale du Travail, *or CGT, and the* Force Ouvrière (CGT_FO) *joined in with the students and teachers' unions, and they called a one-day general strike and* manif *for May 13.*

By mid-May our nightly news was having a heyday showing the million people marching through Paris, and I got another call from Sol.

"Now are you going to tell me this is just a student demonstration?

"Look, it was totally peaceful. Did you see the same film I saw? There weren't even any police menacing the crowds!"

"We shall see. You leave in one month? If things are not back to normal there, you don't go."

I was panicking now. Things certainly might not be back to normal. I wondered what was happening to the American kids who were there on study abroad programs now! The banks were closed; all the other workers were staging strikes all over the place. Those Americans over there might be in big trouble.

I went to Guy LeNotre.

"My parents are threatening to not let me go," I told him, practically sobbing.

"I shall telephone them, *Mademoiselle* Shrier, and I shall reassure them that you will be fine. Besides, you have had no word from your organization that they are cancelling, *non?*"

"No; that's a good point."

"And the State Department has not issued any travel bans for tourists going to France?"

"I don't know---do they do that?"

"Yes, indeed. One can ascertain this. I shall look into it."

"Thank you! And one other thing: you know this Cohn-Bendit guy—he's a Jew?"

"*Oui. Et alors?*"

"Well, I'm Jewish. Is he good news for us or bad? Will I be in more danger because I'm Jewish over there?"

"Of course NOT. Do not worry about that."

It was Wednesday, May 15, and I went back to Monsieur LeNotre's office and we called Sol and Betty at The Spot. There was an extension phone there and they could both get on the line. My teacher assured them that, as a Frenchman himself, he would not hesitate to go back home to visit that very week and that the demonstrators were not dangerous. Even if they got in some melee with the police, the American students would surely be kept very far away from the trouble, and their classes would go on as normal. He explained to them that the French semester started in mid- September and that any summer courses I would have would not be at the Sorbonne right away anyhow, (which was true! My program schedule made it clear that we had summer classes right in the girls' dorm, with the boys coming over there for class).

"And do you know, by the way," he finished, "that the student leader is himself a Jew? He is a hero now to the other students." *(That might have been laying it on somewhat thick.)*

After the phone call, things calmed down with my parents, and plans proceeded as if everything really was okay. I don't think Sol wanted to forfeit all the money he'd borrowed from the bank to pay Pella College; he probably wouldn't have gotten that back unless the trip had been cancelled on their end.

151

My parents really didn't know it, but things didn't get back to normal at all that summer, and the semester at the Sorbonne didn't start until October. But enough work got done away from the Sorbonne's actual building and no credits were lost. The banks were eventually reopened, but I didn't even have a French bank account, so I wasn't affected; Sol preferred to do business through American Express on the Rue Scribe. I never wrote to them that when I got to Paris, paddy wagons were parked on almost every corner of the Latin Quarter and a lot of other places, full of national police ready to spring into the streets; or about having to show papers at the merest request by any person in uniform. It was scary. They had the same riot gear and the same shields the Iowa City police had put on during the Dow Chemical protest in Iowa City. Well, what Sol and Betty didn't know...etc.

Chapter Twenty-Four

"For Emily Wherever I May Find Her"...Simon & Garfunkel

I was so caught up in the fear of not being able to go to Paris that I didn't have time to be rocked by Cass' new existence, but once the home front calmed down, I found that I was actually stunned to reread her letter and the words, "Alan called me..." and "Alan wrote me..." I wasted no time going to see him in his office.

"You KNEW about these plans to send her to TWA?!!!" I fairly screamed at him.

"Well, hey—take it easy, now. Yes, I knew, but it all happened really fast."

"Well, why didn't you TELL me?"

"She wanted to tell you. "

"I'll bet. You should have at least warned me that I'd be hearing something major from her or something!"

"I probably should have, " he laughed.

"This isn't funny. I almost had a heart attack reading that."

"I'm just so happy that she's free from her parents' clutches now, get it? " he said. "I mean, I'd much rather she were back here; but this way I can go be with her out of their reach!"

"I wouldn't be so sure about that. For all we know, Julia's having her spied on!"

It wasn't an empty or random paranoid thought; Julia was totally capable of doing something just like that.

"I don't think she'll go to all that trouble at this stage," he said after thinking for a minute, then rejecting my theory. "They know she's with a bunch of other stewardesses–in–training and that they have to maintain a rather rigorous schedule. That's why I'm not going down there right yet, or even after school's over in June. I'll wait to see what city she gets based out of, and then I'll go wherever that might be... to see her."

"That's probably when they'll put a tail on her, " I said, not able to drop the idea of Cass as some sort of prisoner of her parents.

"Naw, come on. She'll be working! They know that." He stood up and came around his desk to stand near me. "You know, we should get together every once and awhile---for coffee of something, and commiserate our loss of Miss Hyde!"

"Yeah, Alan, sure. Let's do that."

Soren was as shocked as I was at the idea of Cass newly washed up on the shores of Miami and in the skies of TWA. But he saw the glass as more than half full if she and I were going to be able to get together in Paris.

"What kind of stroke of luck would that be!" he exclaimed. "Think of the great times you'll have!"

"Well, yes. If she gets some real time off and I have some free time from my classes. I mean, she probably won't just fly in on the weekend, you know."

"It's PARIS," he yelled, " you'll FIND the time!"

And so I began to daydream for two. I had little inkling of exactly how many flights Cass might have to Paris in any given month's time, but it was fun to imagine us there together.

I did see Alan a couple of times before the end of term; once we met by chance in the field near the archery area across from the Union. He was coming from EPB and I was headed there. He was walking with his walking stick across the grass like he was in the Serengeti. He saw me from afar and immediately waved and grinned. I had to admit, he was looking pretty gorgeous just there. I couldn't go for coffee with him that day because I was on my way to class, but just as he was taking his leave from me, another girl called out his name and he waved at her. I looked at him like, "Wellllll? Who's that?" but I didn't ask. I was completely sure that Alan Jones was mad for Cass Hyde and not interested in other girls. Plus, as a teacher, he knew hundreds of students, half of them co-eds. He did, however, beg off talking to me in order to catch up with her. I never gave it another thought.

Then I got a second letter from Cass and these lines were in it:

"Sari, I have an enormous best-friend time question to ask you—that you must please never say to Alan or even Soren that I've asked: Did Alan ever to your knowledge date or see another girl since you've known we've been together? Perhaps this seems a little ridiculous to ask someone else about the person you may one day marry, but my trust and love for him could be mistaken. So I ask you as my dearest, most counted-on friend to tell me any and all things you may know but maybe have not wanted to say. And thank you-- I'm very grateful."

I wrote her right back that I didn't know of any such thing about Alan but that she should remember he's on the faculty so of course, he's going to "know" a lot of girls. But I believed him to be faithful to her, and frankly, I was fearful of upsetting her long distance like that, anyway, even if I had known anything. Luckily I didn't have to lie to protect her… I assumed Alan was not seeing anyone else certainly not seriously or even on a whim. But it did make me curious as to what plans they might be making when they were together!

In the midst of one drama after another, the campus was buzzing about something else, and Soren and I were in the thick of it. A much-anticipated concert by Simon and Garfunkel was to be held in the Field House, and a huge crowd was expected. Our little ushering gig did not extend to that, but because Soren knew they were my absolute favorites on God's green earth, he told me to be prepared to meet him outside my dorm very early one morning.

"Why so early? I groaned, upon hearing 6:30 a.m.

"Just because, " he laughed.

It turned out he was taking me over at the crack of dawn to *camp out* for tickets to the concert! The box office opened at eleven.

Cass and I had been living inside of *Parsley, Sage, Rosemary and Thyme* for a whole year by then, obsessing over both the lyrics and the harmonies. I loved both singers, but felt Simon to be the genius of the duo. Soren was tapped to write the review for the *Daily Iowan* and he'd got us both press passes to go backstage after the show; but we still had to buy our own tickets.

"You'd think the editor could at least get you free tickets?" I whined, dejected that we had to wait in line.

"I don't know about that," Soren responded with a tone that said in essence, *calm down; we'll get in.*

By the time we got there with an old blanket of his to sit on and wait, the line had indeed already formed and was wrapped half-way around the building. But when we got out around two that afternoon, the line was enormous and must have encircled the box office three or four times.

Going to that concert was a highlight of my life and accompanying Soren on his interview with Paul Simon behind the stage in the concrete hallway (Art Garfunkel drifted in and out during this q. and a. session that lasted almost an hour!) was the biggest brush-with-fame thrill I'd had to date.

Paul Simon was patient and funny; if he minded being interviewed by the not-so-professional press, he didn't show it. Soren had tried out several of his questions on me while prepping for the interview. He would ask him about our very favorite current songs: "Faking' It,'" "America" and "A Hazy Shade of Winter," and also the ones I loved like "59th St. Bridge Song, " and "Homeward Bound." Soren brought up what just about every review of their records considered to be the alienation theme running through these songs, which Paul Simon acknowledged was the popular press's mantra, not his.

Soren said, "Some critics have compared your lyrics to poetry by T. S. Eliot. Do you think you were consciously aware of writing lyrics as poetry?"

"Maybe a bit," came the thoughtful reply. "but I didn't set out to write poetry, just music and lyrics that fit it."

Paul Simon also freely spoke of doing marijuana and hashish and about the mental lethargy he attributed to drugs before he quit doing them.

Paul Simon had an animated demeanor that night backstage, especially compared to Art Garfunkel, but he was still pensive and reflective. He gave off nothing of folk-rock star or diva, even though they were bone fide famous people by the time we saw them, and had been selling out arena and stadiums at colleges all over the country.

Soren's review did not make the front page of the *Daily Iowan* due to the uproar going on in the country and all over college campuses over the death of Martin Luther King, Jr. But it had prominent column inches inside, where, in his opening paragraph, he took the university to task for the horrible venue in which they had held this concert, which, to me at least, still managed to come off intimate in front of thousands anyway. After complaining about the faulty audio system, to wit, *"no excuse for the failures that occurred during this concert in a building that is an acoustical atrocity,"* Soren praised the duo for *"their musical prowess and the truth and beauty of the poetry that is a Paul Simon lyric."* He talked about the enthusiastic standing ovations the appreciative crowd gave them and their willingness to play everything the students wanted to hear and more, followed by an hour-long back stage discussion of pot, the police and fans.

"Soren! "I called out breathless, waiving the paper in front of his face when we met, "it's wonderful!!" And it was. Soren was on his way to landing a spot on the paper for next year that would hold an entrée to the journalism career he hoped for. I was exceedingly proud of him and not a little snowed.

I wrote to Cass that the concert and the interview and the review in the DI had all gone swimmingly and that Soren was the man of the hour in my eyes. I told her I was inviting him to The Bluffs before I left for the year, parents be damned.

"I will be leaving for Paris so that could just be a mini-celebration before I depart," I wrote her, rationalizing the idea to myself. And just to hedge my bets, I also wrote to my grandmother and asked her permission for him to stay in her guest room rather than at my house. That would just avoid all acrimony on the part of Sol and Betty. She happily agreed and added, "You know, a little loving never hurt anybody." It made me wonder if she thought I'd be coming over, too, that we were sleeping together, but of course, we were not.

When I wrote Cass with that quote she replied, delighted with this turn of events, "Your grandmother is truly amazing. A little loving never did hurt anyone! Ha! As if we need to be told!"

I was very busy finishing the semester and packing up to leave the dorm for good. I had made up my mind to live off campus when I got back as a senior in the Fall of 1969, and, as previously, I had to clear completely out of Kate Daum… and also gather up anything remaining of Cass'. So, I told my parents that I wouldn't be home until June 7; that way I'd have time to sort through stuff and pack boxes with some logic. I had a lot of books and would need to segregate some of the French ones to take to Paris. I reasoned that if I at least had my own grammar book over there, which I understood and liked, maybe it would come in handy to look things up when I was lost in the Sorbonne books.

And then it happened: June 5, 1968. I wanted to think of 1968 as my dream year, my emancipation year, my rebirth year. Instead, news of another tragedy concerning another American icon and hero of mine spread through the campus. I was in my room taking a break from cleaning, lying on Cass' empty bed when I heard a really big commotion in the hallway and opened my door. There weren't that many girls left on the floor but the ones who were seemed taken in by hysteria.

"Someone shot BOBBY!!!!" one girl shouted at me.

WHAT?! Oh my GOD! Not again. That wave of nausea that had swept over me as a tenth grader in geometry class when a teacher had come in crying (!!)to tell us that JFK had been shot, came over me again as I stood in the hall too shocked to cry and in complete disbelief at what I was hearing.

My t.v. was packed already so I hurried to the 5th floor lounge and gathered with the others around the sofa in there, and we watched the events unfold in the kitchen of the Ambassador Hotel. How could this be happening just a couple of months after the last one? What was this country coming to? My head was spinning, my throat was closing up, and my mouth was dry. I was afraid I wouldn't be able to breathe in a minute so I ran back to my room and called Soren.

We met in the lobby of Burge and just clung to each other. I cried great heaving sobs, my head buried in his shoulder. We didn't want to be alone with our grief so first we went to the Union to see what was going on there, and then we went up to the newsroom at the school paper. One of Soren's buddies was already at work planning an interview with Vance Bourjaily whose book *The Man Who Knew Kennedy* was a critically acclaimed series of interviews with people about the first assassination. RFK's death actually occurred on June 6, which was a Friday, and I was slated to leave Iowa City the next day. But Soren suggested I stay until Sunday and attend the memorial for Bobby that the First Unitarian Church on Gilbert Street quickly put together.

"Bourjaily will give the eulogy," Soren told me. "I think we should go together."

I agreed.

The service was lovely and there were three speakers, not one. The minister of the church, Rev. William Weir, led the service. Another professor from the Political Science Department, John Schmidhauser who had been a classmate of RFK at Virginia and who was working on his campaign in Iowa, also spoke movingly of his friend.

Many of the students that spring had been swept up in "Come Clean for Gene" efforts, and had turned to the McCarthy campaign, but not me.

I made no secret of loving the Kennedys, flaws and all – not that we knew any of that stuff in the 60's when the press kept it all more quiet than they ever would later. Whether merited or not, in light of later revelations, I adored the whole Kennedy clan, and the "mystique" as they called it, of them really was larger than life, especially to me. As young as I was then, JFK's short time in the White House was a beacon of culture beaming the USA to the world. It wasn't just a presidency to us, but a phenomenon. With Bobby's death now, another violent and horrifying assassination, I was afraid the Europeans I would soon be meeting would have concluded that America was nothing if not filled with hate, and that we would all, by association, be painted with the same brush by the French.

"I wouldn't angst over that, " Soren had counseled me when I revealed my secret fears to him. "They will get to know you for you."

Soren was so sweet and also calm and wise. He helped me load everything in my car, and we made arrangements for him to be in The Bluffs that next week. I drove the four hours home on the one hand dejected over the state of affairs in a country that I saw as coming apart at the seams, and on the other hand elated over the prospect of flying into the arms of a country that, itself rocked by "events," would welcome me nevertheless with its culture that I was waiting on pins and needles to embrace with my entire being.

When I got home, I was happy to have parents who were also very sad and tried to comfort me, for a change. They were worried about their Democratic party and afraid the whole country was going to go up in smoke before it was over.

I couldn't expend too much energy on the fate of the Democrats right at that moment, however. My whole world was leaping and plummeting around me. So happy. So sorrowful. So much anticipation. So much abject fear. How different would school be there? Would I make any friends? Would I even pass; and what if I lost all those credits and came home still a sophomore? (Oh, who cared about that! It would still be worth it and if I had to redo the year, so be it.) What if Paris was so expensive (it was!) I wouldn't be able to actually partake in any of what it had to offer? What would happen if I got sick?

Soren did show up for the farewell celebrations that next week and stayed at Nana's, which was, after all, only a five-minute drive from our house. He met Sol and Betty first at the bar, where Sol was unusually non-confrontational, since he knew I'd be leaving, and figured that if this romance were even a little serious, which he was prepared to not let it be, it wouldn't survive the separation.

"So, you're… Catholic then?" Sol pretended to guess; (I had already told him he was). "I hear you've got a real beautiful church down there in Imogene."

"We do indeed, sir, "said Soren. We exchanged knowing smiles.

"And your family has the Carlysle law office down there? "

"They do, " Soren responded. It didn't surprise him that in the region of Southwest Iowa, his grandfather and father were pretty well known.

"So will you go to law school and join the firm afterwards?" Sol asked. If he were feigning interest, he did a pretty convincing job of it.

"That is the plan, yes, sir, " said Soren, "but I don't intend to actually practice law in Iowa. I hope to move to L.A. or New York and do entertainment law."

"Sarah will probably stay here," Sol said, "And teach."

156

I just let his manipulating little control gestures waft over my head and out the door. For once I didn't scream at him something like, *"Oh you think that do you? Well, knock yourself out, old man. Nothing could be further from the truth! You'll be looking at my dust the second I get out of school."*

As it turned out, nothing *could* have been further from the truth.

PART TWO:

PARIS

Chapter Twenty-five

"I Love Paris"...Cole Porter

In New York a day prior to flying out on Icelandic Airlines, I found myself in a hotel room with a sophisticated girl on my same program from Gross Pointe Farms, Michigan. She was friendly and told me much later that she had thought I was very wealthy because of my traveling outfit. Betty had gone all out to send me to school in Paris with a wonderful ensemble-- worthy of, well, Cass, actually. It was an absolutely unadorned beige knit sheath dress with a matching beige bouclé coat with a little round collar and three large off-white Bakelite buttons going down the front. I wore bright yellow leather flats with leather flowers on the toes, and I carried a small yellow leather cross-body purse on a gold link chain. My hair, as I left for Paris, was in a mid-short phase, sort of growing out from being very short. I usually wanted long hair, but I had kept cutting it off sophomore year, hoping it would resemble either Cass' or Audrey Hepburn's. It was a vain hope. By the time I left, it was long enough to be pulled back with a headband, and that's what I did. It was anything but chic.

Our hotel was in midtown and the room was tiny. I took the opportunity to call Uncle Leo and announce that I was indeed on my way to France! I longed to see them, but there wasn't time. Mrs. Berg was over when I phoned, and she took the receiver to wish me well and remind me that she was telling her daughter Chan of my imminent arrival. I gave them all my address at the *Maison des Étudiantes* in the 14th *arrondissement*, and we rang off promising lots of Paris-New York-Paris letters.

My grandmother had requested the same thing: a letter per week with a blow-by-blow report of what I did, saw, fell in love with, studied, ate—not necessarily in that order. She would gather them all in a file folder in chronological order, and in the end, I would have more than fifty of these making up a complete record of the year. I also kept a diary, but the letter file idea was really a better one; I did too much grousing and bitching in my journals. This way, I'd still have the record of my life in Paris without the dramatic overlay of angst, long-distance boyfriend woes, insecurity and the collection of emotions that would no doubt be plastered all over the journal pages. In the letters I would be truthful, of course, but bear in mind who was to be the audience.

Our flight over to Europe, via Icelandic, was in a turbo-prop jet; it started out as a prop plane and flew by jet engines later. The layover in Iceland was strange, too, with us getting out and going into the tiny airport outside of Reykjavik. This plane was a charter of all Pella College students going to France, Spain, Germany, Italy, Holland and Denmark. We did not land in Paris, but in Luxembourg, and from there, boarded buses to our various destinations. We had touched down in the wee hours of the morning; the bus pulled into Paris at the end of the day. What looked to be a distance like from Iowa City to Des Moines on the map, actually took the better part of ten hours!

We arrived grubby and fatigued, the girls dropped off first. The boys were staying farther away at the *Cité Universitaire* where they would be in the United States Pavilion, with more Americans; whereas we would start off being paired with an American, but that would change once the French girls got there. The boys, however, would be back to our dorm every day in the summer because our first term (trimester, really) courses were taught there.

The rooms in *La Maison des Étudiantes* were stark, but big. They all had large French windows that opened in and didn't have screens of any kind, of course. There were two twin beds, two armoires for clothes, no chests of drawers, (but some storage drawers built in with a ledge above them for some display area) and two desks with uncomfortable straight wooden chairs. The beds had the bolster pillow that all French beds had folded into the sheets and placed long across the head of the bed. We could have a normal *"oreiller"* pillow, too, if we wanted one, and I did. There was a bathroom *en suite* but it only had a sink, a bidet, which I had never seen before, and a mirror. A little shelf on the wall in there housed, of all things, a hot plate! Nothing else. The WC's or *cabinets de toilette* as well as the showers were down the hall, and that hall was always dark, by the way, and only lighted if you pushed a button that activated a timer. You had to keep pushing it on down the hall to have your way lit. I was on the actual third floor in *Chambre 24* because the first floor or *rez de chaussee* didn't count. Numbering started above that. Later I would change to *Chambre 45* on the fifth floor.

My first friend from the New York City hotel did not end up being my roommate for the summer; I had a Jewish roommate from Vero Beach, Florida. It struck me right away that Pella College, which was a Dutch Reformed Church school, had put us together based on our religion. We were the only two Jews on the program that year. It didn't make me very happy to be segregated and it didn't seem to make Johanna ("Jo Jo") Brechwald very happy to be in a room with me; she was snobby towards me. *I could just about not abide snobs, as had been shown in the Iowa dorm when we wouldn't tolerate the DQ's haughty ways.* Jo Jo deigned at first to go down to meals with me in the cavernous *Maison* refectory, but later, we went our separate ways. The most surprising thing about this seemingly worldly girl from Emory University was that her mother showed up at the dorm at least three times during that summer to check on her daughter. She would be in Paris to shop and buy things for antique businesses in several Florida resort towns that she owned. She would pick up JoJo and then they would go off and dine in fabulous places like the Ritz Hotel and Maxime's. They never asked me along, which was fine; I didn't resent her; it just would have been cool to have seen some of those places.

But the tables sort of turned between us when it was revealed that she called her mother "Mama" and was insecure and afraid to be in France without her family! I couldn't believe it! It was a bit of an eye-opener that all kids didn't actually long to leave their homes and be on their own. I began to see Jo Jo as my inferior, for whatever reason. Even though she tested in at a much higher language level than I did, she seemed to lack intellectual curiosity or any desire to experience Paris on her own. At the various holidays we had, Mama would be back to whisk her away each time. JoJo's father never traveled to Paris. She told me he was obligated to stay in Florida and oversee the shops in Vero, Boca and Palm Beach.

By autumn, after we had changed rooms and the real semester had begun, I rarely saw Jo Jo again. We were tracked into levels right off the bat based on those oral exams we had sent in on cassette. I was at the very beginning level of the language courses, and that was fine with me. It went so fast that in just the first few weeks of the summer session we had gone past all the grammar I'd had in French at Iowa for four semesters! The *Maison* had enough spaces in it to house our "*cours pratiques*" classes from elementary to very advanced in many rooms on the ground floor. There were actually three buildings hooked together by a courtyard. One, directly behind the entry gate, held the offices—Sorbonne *Cours de Civilisation* and Pella College Paris administration, along with the dining hall, and a laundry room with some washers and dryers—quite the luxury and really expensive to use; the second building was all dormitory. The third building, where my room was, held the concierge's cubicle, our mailboxes, and a Lilliputian black cage elevator to take up to the sleeping halls. In back of the concierge office and downstairs were classrooms. There were even vending machines in the courtyard! Boy, was I surprised to see those! France was keeping pace with America!

I had a few dubious adventures in my new city before the first week was even up. They began with the meal served on the night right after we'd arrived, a hearty meat stew that tasted a little too sweet, but pretty good nevertheless; and we all ate it. Then they announced to us that we'd eaten our inaugural Parisian dinner of HORSE.

I'm afraid I burst into tears. I wasn't one of those little girls who grew up horse crazy; how could I have been in the life I led in The Bluffs? But I had NO INTENTION of eating National Velvet, Black Beauty or Fury either! Most of the Americans were horrified; a few laughed. I sobbed into my dessert that night that "I didn't wait my whole life to come to Paris only to have to eat HORSE." The cooks had gotten a big kick out of that---they must have done it at least once to every new arriving group. I never ever ate horse again; I didn't care how healthy it was or how much the iron in it would stave off anemia.

The next adventure that befell me was a foray out of *La Maison* that I took one of the first weekends I was in Paris. Thinking what a stupid waste of a day in Paris it would be to stay in the room, I ventured out onto *Boulevard Raspail* and turned at the first corner and headed for the cemetery of Montparnasse that was right up the block. It purportedly was full of famous people, as were the other two big cemeteries in the city: *Père Lachaise* and *Montmartre*. *Père Lachaise* had hands down the most literati and glitterati, but the one near me had Samuel Beckett, Frédéric Bartholdi, the sculptor of the Statue of Liberty; Alfred Dreyfus

(!!—sooo, Jews were allowed to be buried there!); Henri Fantin-Latour (I'd already studied his works in my Iowa art history class!), Pierre Larousse of dictionary fame, and many more.

So I set out to find some of them and entered the grounds, only to be accosted by a group of people—women and some children-- gathering around me and trying to get my blue silk paisley headband off my head!! And they did! Then they waved it in front of my face and cried out, "Dollar! Dollar!" HUH? I didn't have any American and very little French money with me, and besides, I couldn't understand a word they were saying to me except "dollar." I said in English, "I don't have any money." The woman who seemed like the leader shook her head at me and looked at the head band and then back at me. I shrugged and thought, "Keep it! Who ARE they?"

I turned to leave and she followed me and gave it back. It and I were each worthless to her after all.

I ran back to the dorm and bumped into the Concierge inside the gate. I told her in French, "*J'ai rencontré des personnes!! Une femme, des enfants. Elle a demandé l'argent de moi! Elle a..a* ("**took**", what in hell was that verb? I changed it to "wanted") *voulu avoir ma bande de cheveux*! (I didn't actually think that was a real word, and it wasn't. I should have said "*bandeau*.") Our Concièrge with whom we would eventually become a tiny bit friendly as the year wore on, but who intimidated the hell out of us at first, began to laugh at me.

"*Les Gitanes!*" she bellowed at me. "*Attention!!!*"

"Gypsies!?" Oh for God's sake. So that was true.

So, my first week in Paris I had eaten horse and been attacked by gypsies. Things were not looking good. I needed something to comfort me and buoy my spirits. I was not going to admit any sort of defeat. I gathered up my courage plus a little bit of French money, kept in a tiny coin purse in my hand at all times, and set out to find a Coca Cola.

I couldn't have a soft drink in the cafés that surrounded the *Place Picasso* less than a hundred paces right up the street from me, because those cafés were among the most famous ones in Paris and outrageously expensive on my budget: *La Rotonde, Le Dome, Le Select.* And even the non-famous ones, *Le Gymnase* and *Le Raspail* were too expensive for me to sit in and drink a coke. No, I would buy a liter bottle of soda and keep it in the room.

Luckily, *La Maison des Étudiantes* was in the most wonderfully, typically normal residential section of Paris we could ever desire. An entire street, *Rue Delambre*, was right there, lined with every possible boutique full of one's heart's desire: bakeries, both *boulangeries* and *pâtisseries*; *crémeries, boucheries, charcuteries* and other food shops advertising themselves as *traiteurs* with gourmet delicacies already made and on display in big glass and oak cases; and besides those, there was everything else—two pharmacies, a dry cleaners, a laundromat, cinemas, restaurants and shops with a few toys and bibelots since there was an elementary school on the block. But up at the top of the street and across a space reserved for the outdoor market that would appear on a given weekday, was *Inno*.

Inno was a store like I'd never seen in the States: a store that was a combination of Woolworth's and Sears in a way, on the first floor, with small but numerous departments of clothes, luggage, cosmetics, cameras and film, school supplies, books and magazines, toys, and a few household items (no furniture). And then downstairs via escalator was a complete gourmet supermarket with a huge wine selection, all kinds of famous chocolates, every sort of vegetable and fruit, and all the other foods, dry, canned and fresh that any big market would have. In the States we had, by the 60's, big supermarket chains putting the smaller neighborhood grocery stores out of business one by one. But we didn't have any "discount" stores yet; Woolworth became Woolco and then Shopko, but that wasn't until later; Kresge's became K-Mart, etc. But we had no hypermarkets, no superstores; France was 20 years ahead of us in that respect.

Inno became my salvation that whole year. How I loved it! I was on the tightest budget ever: one hundred dollars per month, and at five francs to the dollar, that didn't leave me much wiggle room with Paris prices. Just eating out would have used up the majority of my funds. We got breakfast and one other meal at the *Maison*, except on Sunday when we just got breakfast.

I usually chose dinner for my one meal since having that in a café or restaurant would be more expensive than lunch, I theorized; once in a while I reversed that. Classes were from 9:00 to noon and 1:30- 3:30, so every so often coming out of class starving, I would opt for lunch as the main meal. That was

161

actually more French, it turned out; and for dinner I would go get bread and cheese with fruit and eat it all at my little desk.

Inno came to the rescue with stuff I could buy and keep in the room. Actually, having bought a filet for shopping, I could hang that outside the window and keep items cool in it. That worked well in winter, obviously; it wasn't ideal for summer. But that particular summer, the temps didn't get too hot. We had none of the canicule Paris would later suffer through.

Ice cubes were the rarest commodity in Paris, and I learned to like le Coca hot, as I coined it. There were no MacDo's yet in Paris; just Wimpy's, where you could get a facsimile of the fast food we had in the States, and the drinks came with ice. But Wimpy's seemed to be poison to me; I got sick every single time I ate there. You could, of course, ask for a drink avec des glaçons in a café, and much as I did frequent cafés often, mostly all I could afford to drink was coffee or hot chocolate. American soft drinks were laughably over-priced. However, I did learn that if one ordered a citron pressé in a French café, you got a glass with one-fourth lemon juice and the rest ice cubes, plus a little pitcher of water and a long spoon. You made the dilution of water and lemon to your taste, and then you added sugar, if desired, and stirred. One could nurse this drink for hours, pouring in a little more water each time until finally the ice melted. It became my go-to choice in a café.

The Sorbonne was still on strike when I got to Paris in June of '68, but it didn't really affect our routine. It did, however, elongate that summer since the lecture courses scheduled for September were pushed back and instead real school started in October. Meanwhile, I got the jolt of my academic life thus far when our *Cours Pratiques* began. We had been, as noted, tracked with that placement test almost before we could unpack our suitcases. Some of the other kids in our program placed very high; like Cass they had gone to highly academic private schools for secondary and were from colleges like Penn State, U Chicago, Oberlin and Vassar. Only a couple of students were actually from Pella College.

I had lucked into finding this program on the bulletin board in Schafer Hall, but actually it had a nationwide reputation.

Surprisingly to me, about a third of our group were grad students not going for the same certificate as the rest of us, the *Degré Supérieur de Langue et de Civilisation Française,* **but for the** *Licence.* **They took the same lecture classes as we did but they had to write a** *memoire,* **and their** *cours pratiques* **were exponentially more difficult than ours.**

As for me, I felt like I was preparing for a PhD, so overwhelmingly hard was the work. We were inundated with grammar exercises in the mornings, including dictations, or *dictées* that basically served to show me what I didn't know; and information and notes in the afternoon about every possible topic. My very first exam was on the history, art, religion and culture of the *Gaulois*!!

We had grammar textbooks with workbooks designed especially for the *Cours de Civ Française/Sorbonne.* But for the rest of our coursework, each professor designed and had printed these formulaic booklets comprising the readings upon which they were to base their lectures. The rest of our studies were from notes.

Part of what the French students were rebelling against in the "Evenements de Mai" had been the antiquated teaching methods of the French system, which dated back to Napoleon, the idea that they could not discuss anything with their professors and then just had to regurgitate what they had learned for the exams. No reforms were forthcoming by the time we were there, and so we had to memorize also and learn to be able to conjure it up at the moment's notice.

I was in deeply over my head.

Iowa U was not easy, as universities go, of course, compared to high school. But nothing in my Stateside studies could have prepared me for how much academic European universities were, with so much more of the responsibility for learning resting on the shoulders of the individual student. Even though I had placed in the lowest level of the summer grammar sections, we lowly beginners were doing the exact same work everyone else was as far as the civilization material was concerned. And it goes without saying: it was all in French. Every exercise, every paper, every lecture and all interaction in class was in French only. I considered myself just lucky that I was pretty good in grammar in the first place (thanks to my ninth grade English teacher), and that I loved French and had a strong will to learn it.

162

Because other than that, my self-confidence was at a low ebb and my nerves were shot after about the second week of being screamed at by the Concièrge whenever I had to interact with her.

"*Mademoiselle SHREEEE-AIRRRRE! Je ne vous comprends pas!!*"

Chapter Twenty-six

"Les Copains d'Abord"...Georges Brassens

I promised myself I wouldn't be homesick even for one instant, and if I felt twinges, I would just snap out of it. I urged myself in my head and in my diary to remember how I LONGED to be in Paris and how I counted the minutes to get out of my house, my town and my life back there.

I had a sort of malaise, however, walking around Paris, beautiful as it was ---(and it was in every season-- I was never disappointed); seeing so much public display of affection going on that it made me really wish Soren were there with me to share it all.

But what I really missed was being with Cass.

Much as I tried to make friends with Jo Jo, she was having none of it, preferring to study alone (well, we were not doing the same work, so I rationalized that), eat alone, and generally BE alone. I had to find other girls in the dorm to pal around with, so that is what happened. I got close with Antonia Rossi, (called Nonnie because her four little brothers could never pronounce her name); and I managed to relocate the sophisticated girl I had roomed with that first night in New York, Brenda Rutledge. She and I caught back up with each other during meals. Super nice, she had placed in the most advanced class and had a single room until her French roommate came, which we all considered the luckiest of happenstances.

But my second-best friend for the year would turn out to be another of the far-advanced speakers, Charlotte Carson, who went by "CC". She was from a family like Cass' and had even also gone to boarding school in Switzerland, before returning to the States and enrolling in the College of William and Mary. Her and Brenda's French were far and away the best in our group. Nonnie's was way better than mine, also. I didn't have grammar classes with any of these girls, but, at least for the summer, we all were on the same floor in the dorm.

Nonnie smoked, and she was happy to be in a country where almost everyone else did, too. She was extraordinarily nice and had an outgoing leader-like presence among us. She had a completely Italian name and *was* Italian on her father's side; but her mother was one hundred percent Irish and Nonnie looked just like her, she told me, with curly dark hair and gorgeous hazel eyes flanked by mounds of black eyelashes. If she wore something green, her eyes looked green, but mostly they looked blue. She exuded a happy personality, even though, it turned out, she was repressing a lot of sadness about things going on at home with her brother's health. When Nonnie spoke English, she had her own little slang vocabulary that we all more or less adopted simply from being with her, and we peppered our own conversations with things like "Oh, that *bateau mouche* ride was *great stuff*!" and "Let's go to my room and *rap*."

Nonnie became my closest Paris study-abroad-year friend. It began that way and it ended that way, because she had to leave the program early, before our graduation ceremony. I picked up her diploma for her and mailed it to her when I got back to the States. Nonnie's brother was ill the whole time she was in Europe, and she was secretly worried about it every day she was away.

" I'm the oldest child, " she'd told me, "and the only girl. I've got four little brothers!"

"Wow, " I'd chuckled, " what must that be like!" I couldn't even imagine.

"Well, sometimes they're a real pain. Actually, I'm closest to Adrian – he's three years younger than me and the nearest to my age. The problem is, he's really sick right now. He's got acute myeloid leukemia. You know what that is, right?"

"Um, cancer? " I was shocked. Cancer was a death sentence in those days.

"Yes. My parents even got him into some trials at Johns Hopkins, but things don't look too good. He doesn't seem to be responding." Her eyes filled with tears. "I almost didn't come on the program, but my parents and Adrian all insisted I not change my plans. And he was stable when I left."

It turned out that things held up okay with Adrian until the last month of our stay when she rushed back to Alexandria, Virginia on an emergency plane ticket sent by her father, to be with her family for the remaining weeks of her brother's life. Luckily she had taken the final exams and did not have to forfeit her year abroad credits; she got excellent results.

Nonnie and I made a pact early on to see as much as we possibly could, do all the touristy stuff as well as "go native," try not to speak English, try to meet French people (read: boys) and travel outside France together any time we could. She, like the rest of my Pella friends was not on as strict a budget as I was. One thing I couldn't do there was shop. Paris' expensiveness in all things continued to stymie me; except for essentials, it was all *lèche-vitrine* and no real purchasing. I just had to get used to this reality. I was poor in one of the richest cities in the world. But at least I was there.

However, I had made up my mind to ask the parents (and Nana!) for extra money from time to time whenever something arose that I really felt I should participate in. I vowed to pay them back working in the bar **one last summer** when I got home. Growing up, I wasn't entirely aware of my parents' financial situation, but I knew it to be moderate, at best, especially when I was introduced to the kind of lifestyle Cass Hyde led. Nevertheless, we belonged to a golf and swim club, lived in a mid-century modern ranch house they had built custom (on land paid for by my grandmother) and had two cars. We weren't poverty-stricken by any means. I figured they might see their way clear to coughing up a little bit of extra money given this was my first and maybe only chance to see Europe.

C.C. was very wealthy but not a snob at all...same as Cass. We might have been able to tell her status by her clothes, but she just dressed conservatively "preppy" and that was normal for us. What gave her away was that she had let it slip—in a non-haughty way, that her parents had given her a "baby Mercedes" for a high school graduation present and she drove it to Williamsburg. She was very sweet, friendly and curious about others. She and I were about the same size—she was a little taller and weighed more. C.C. wore her straight, dark hair in a shoulder-length flip, with bangs combed over to the side and sometimes she put on a headband ("*J'adore ton bandeau*" I complimented her, never forgetting that vocab word the rest of my life.)

Both C.C. and Nonnie got along famously with their parents, so my family situation was anathema to them. One would have thought with such diverse and polar opposite backgrounds, we never would have become chummy, but just the reverse happened. We all bonded, and that was really why, even with the tumultuous ups and downs I experienced that year, my Sorbonne sojourn stayed with me in mostly happy memory forever.

Not having Nonnie or C.C. in class with me meant that I spent a good part of each day without even seeing them. Girls in my level in the morning class, with whom I hung around, were Lizabeth Reynolds in particular, a very bubbly, friendly girl who loved to drink white wine in her room more than study; and Gloria Sullivan, one of the other Iowans, a homely string-bean of a girl with sort of dirty blond hair and demeanor to match, who came on the program hoping to become a bi-lingual secretary for some Iowa agri-business or other. I felt for Gloria, not only because she looked like some throwback to the Great Depression, but also because her French was much worse than mine!

For classes, we were separated by language ability, but for meals we were all thrown in together, and only Pella College had students in the dorm that summer; so I got to interact -- if not actually become friends—with just about all the other women, including the grad students, some of whom were surprisingly quite old, but most of whom were in their mid-to-late twenties, so not much older than us college juniors.

There were quite a few girls from the South on the program but there were no Negroes in our group. With the burgeoning civil rights movement going on in the States, that actually surprised me. One girl in particular, from Alabama, (a state about which I could never think of even one positive thing) was a real "sorority Sally" who only wore Lily Pulitzer pink and green sheath mini dresses, with a matching *bandeau* pulling back her curly short hair. She sat down across from me one night for dinner and, in true Southern Belle style, made small talk to me all smiles as she criticized how I was eating grapes. Her drooling southern drawl made her into a caricature of herself when she spoke.

"If mah daddy saw yew pulling those grapes off by the clump lahk that, Ah jes' don' know what he'd deeeew, "she clucked at me.

"Well, "I said, smiling back, "good thing he's not here, then, isn't it?"

I didn't give her time to snap back at me because I saw she was wearing a lavalier pinned to her Lily Pulitzer. "So, what sorority are you in?" I asked cheerily.

"Trah-Delt," she responded, "and Ah'm pinned," she added, patting herself on the lavalier, "to mah boyfriend. He's a Pahk." She meant Pike.

"Do you have any Negroes in your sorority?" I asked nonchalantly.

"NO! And yew up narhth don't either, don't kid me. Yew all are jes' as segregated as the south. Worse! We have colahed folk livin' *with* us! Ah greeew up with 'em."

"I'm sure you did, "I cooed back at her, *and thought*, *"Right. Black people are just fine and everyone should own one."*

She went on, "Ah have black folk livin' right in close proximity, lahke yew nahthenahs dew not."

"Oh, you mean, like your maid? Nanny? What? Sharecropper?"

"No mattah what, " she sniffed. At least they're not relegated to the kinds of ghettos y'all have. Y'all got a lap full o'woe up theah, an' that's a fact."

I let it go, but she didn't have anything more to do with me, and as a matter of fact, she quit the program, and went home at the end of the summer. Probably couldn't stand the thought of being in Paris during Rush Week.

It is not an exaggeration to say that I studied day and night. Homework mounted into an exorbitantly huge collection of readings and *devoirs* often due the next day. I had to get many supplies ("*fourniture*"), and much as I knew *Inno* had some, it was too wonderful to browse *Gibert Jeune* and the other *papéteries* in the Latin Quarter and buy far-out pink graph paper, (which was the normal loose-leaf paper in French schools); lovely pens, and fabulous tabbed *cahiers de textes*, or notebooks, some divided into days of the week, which I loved to use as regular notebooks and ignore the "weekifications".

My favorite *marque* was *Chipie*, whose front covers were often plaid and sported dogs. *Chipie* made all kinds of other products: kids' clothes and shoes and the school bags they wore on their backs called "*cartables;*" and it turned out, I learned later, that *Chipie* was slang for "bitch," but in a cute way. I also liked *cahiers* with covers that showed Paris monuments. But the brands that were the everyday garden variety like *Claire Fontaine* were also fabulous; and *Gibert Jeune* even had a house brand that I bought many of and saved for use my senior year at Iowa because they printed the address "*Gibert Jeune, 5 Place Saint Michel, Paris*" on the cover.

I also had to buy books, some to read for class and some for reference. Still happy that I'd brought my trusty American college French grammar text with me from home, it couldn't compare with the reference I came to consider my bible, upon which I relied, yes, religiously, namely Bescherelle's *L'Art de Conjuguer Dictionnaire des 8,000 Verbes*. Whenever we had a new verb presented to us in class, it was with all 8 tenses of the indicative, four tenses of the subjunctive, three tenses of conditional and two forms of imperative…all at once. We had to know this for every single verb. I considered myself so fortunate to have actually learned the conjugations of an English verb back in ninth grade, and by grammar name, so I knew the *plus-que-parfait* was the pluperfect and I actually also knew how to identify any given English form. That was a big boost and also a minor miracle. But I had never learned subjunctive anything in English, and it wasn't until I took high school Spanish that the word even entered my lexicon.

In grammar classes we did exercises from the book and we recited things and took *dictée*, but we didn't really speak to each other as in a "conversational French" class at home. Conversational French was a given; the teachers assumed we would be speaking it all the rest of the time, which was only true if we made a concerted effort to do so.

We also had separate classes of phonetics, taught in a different building by the venerable and oft-feared *Professeur* Filiolet. He was an imposing figure, who never seemed to change his clothing---ever; he chose to wear the very same brown suit to every class. Monsieur Filiolet had a distinct boom to his voice in class, and was a field linguist, who could pinpoint where all his students had been born anywhere in the world by how they spoke. One of the girls in our class was told, after she said a line of English for him, that she was from Champaign, Illinois. She was triumphant as she corrected him, thinking she had GOT him: "No! I'm from URBANA." And she over emphasized "ur-baaaaana" in that nasal twang they have. The two towns border each other and are not even divided by a river. The whole class laughed **at her**, because for all intents and purposes, of course, he was right.

For all my relentless studying and careful preparation, angst and fear, I managed to hold my own until the first big test, which I bombed. The *dictée* did me in. It was a one-hundred-fourteen word excerpt from Camus' *La Chute* that began "*C'était un beau soir d'automne, encore tiède sur la ville, déjà humide sur la Seine. La nuit venait, le ciel encore clair à l'ouest, mais s'assombrissait...*" *Dictées* were given on tape, which went too fast for me to be able to ascertain much meaning; I just had to strain to listen to the actual words, and make sure I wasn't leaving anything out. But I did leave things out and my paragraphs rarely made any sense. I had done rather well, I thought, on many of the other parts of the test, filling in missing words in context and changing tenses, etc. But it didn't matter, because, unlike what I was used to, if you blew one part, you blew it all.

I was devastated, and on top of that, my situation in the room didn't make things any better. Jo Jo had no sympathy for me and was even smug about her own results. Feeling sorry for myself about all this, I made a fatal error: I wrote the truth to Sol and Betty, complaining while I was at it about having such a bitch (and not a *Chipie*) for a roommate!

Ten days later a letter came from my father and he was furious-- first and foremost at my negative attitude towards rooming with a "nice Jewish girl," and secondly immensely unhappy that I should get such a bad mark on something so important. He admonished me that I had better work on "becoming fluent" (like he had any idea what that was), and "bring those grades way up!!"

Nonnie and C.C. were not having these problems, but they commiserated with me, and also couldn't believe I had a parent who would undermine my already low self-confidence like that.

"What I can't fathom is why he'd write you that after ONE test!" C.C. snorted.

Right. Someone who didn't have Sol for a father could not understand what that was like.

C.C. had a lot in common with Cass, one glaring exception notwithstanding: her parents were very attentive and approving of her. If they were as wealthy as the Hydes, I had no way of knowing it, but if so, that's where the similarities ended. C.C. was very close to her parents but not in the clingy joined-at-the-hip way Jo Jo was to hers. And C.C. adored them. Like Cass, too, C.C. never flaunted how rich she was. In fact, none of us really ever talked about money, and if the others just assumed that I, too, was wealthy because I was Jewish, they never mentioned it. Little did they know nothing could have been farther from the truth. I was pinching *centimes*, all right, but not out of some stereotypical avarice; it was purely out of necessity.

C.C. was an only child who, even though she had gone to boarding school in Switzerland, was not "shipped off" there, but rather lovingly sent because she wanted to go, and they could afford it. Her parents' business, like Cass', took them to Europe frequently so they found a school where she would be happy and where they could easily visit. Back in the states for college, she found herself accepted into every college she'd applied to, including the Ivy League, but had decided on William and Mary because she loved Williamsburg and the school had a superior academic reputation, was not huge, and had a campus that looked like a picture postcard.

Nonnie's family was typically by-the-book Catholic. Five children, mother didn't work outside the home; father owned an insurance agency in the network of a big national firm catering to patrician families like his. She grew up in a big, century-old house, went to parochial schools K-12 and was a student at Trinity Washington College in D.C., an all-girls school founded in 1897 by the Religious of Notre Dame de Namur. She went to Mass every weekend of her life, including in Paris, and she was going steady still with her "good Catholic boy" sweetheart, a pre-med student at Georgetown whom she'd met at a rowing meet, and whom her parents welcomed wholeheartedly into their midst.

C.C. had plans to move to New York after graduation and work for the UN. Nonnie wanted to teach. All I knew was that I didn't want to live anywhere even remotely close to my parents and I wanted to use French; but as for where that might be and what job I might have, I was *nulle*.

The guys on the program came to *La Maison* every day for classes, and one of them liked C.C. already, a fellow named Marty Olson, who went to Bethany College in Minnesota, a strict Lutheran school known for teaching foreign languages. I saw C.C. and Marty leave together often after lunch. They liked to walk over to the Luxembourg Gardens to hang out until the afternoon classes started. They ended up sitting together on bus trips and going out to concerts, movies and theater in Paris. Later on, in November at our end-of-term break, she took him to Lucerne to see her old school. They were an item by Christmastime.

Nonnie had her serious beau at home so she was completely uninterested in getting close to any guy on the program. I was open to making friends with the boys, but also thought of myself as "taken," which really wasn't the truth…more of a wishful thinking situation. But for reasons I wasn't exactly sure of, two of the guys showed interest in me and vice-versa. One was Eric Jensen who also went to school in Minnesota, at McCallister College; and the other was his roommate at the *Cité Universitaire*, an interesting guy named Taylor Hastings.

Taylor was an only child of "older" parents from Santa Cruz, California and a townie at UCSC. He was stereotypically surfer-tanned with washed-out blond hair and a little blond goatee. He also spoke in what I thought of as slang or "jive" and called people "cats," peppered his sentences with "man" or "hey, man," and, like Nonnie, used the word "rap" as a synonym for "talk." He was into jazz music big time, and, thus, couldn't have found himself in a better city for that passion than Paris, France in the 60's, and he knew it. It made him ecstatic. He invited me to his and Eric's room one weekend after our Saturday morning class to listen to his favorite album called "A Love Supreme" by, as I wrote Cass, "someone named John Coltrane."

Eric couldn't have been more different from Taylor, but they got along in the room just fine. Eric was quiet, studious and already spoke superior French. He had tested into the top tier and he was still an undergraduate. Tall, but slight of build, short blond hair and clear blue eyes, he exuded northern European heritage, and already had vacation plans to visit distant cousins in Denmark. He was from upstate Vermont and had easy access to sojourns into Québec. I liked Eric more than Taylor at first meeting, but it turned out they were each intriguing in his own way, and I befriended them both. Eric was more charming in a shy way; Taylor was physically more imposing, enthusiastic and self-confident. He was in Paris because, "it's like the coolest, man" and his parents had thought a year abroad would be beneficial to his studies. He wanted to continue on to grad school in psychology. Eric wanted to teach or maybe even go to seminary and head up a Protestant church somewhere, probably back home or maybe in Colorado because skiing was his favorite thing to do from November until May. When not visiting Denmark, he intended to be skiing in the Alps any chance he could while in Europe.

Taylor and Eric were, like the rest of our little "*bande*", in a more advanced class than I; but we all had a twenty-minute class break at the same time, and Nonnie, C.C. and I often found ourselves sitting in the courtyard of the *Maison* with Taylor, Eric and Marty, often listening to Taylor expound on some aspect of other of jazz. I think he felt a responsibility to educate us and have us experience the Latin Quarter *boites* with him. I arrived in Paris already steeped in a lot of music, and made no secret of my adoration of all things Beatles, along with my other faves. I was deeply immersed in "The Mersey Beat" by then, couldn't wait to spend my first holiday in England, and haunt Carnaby Street. The closest I got to any music respect from Taylor was my love of Bossa Nova.

"Yeah," he said, his face brightening, finally, "that Antonio Carlos Jobim cat can swing." But mostly he thought my musical preferences were lame. I should have defended myself more energetically; Eric Clapton was considered to be the finest guitar player on the planet and I had nothing to be ashamed of in loving him.

"And Laura Nyro is a fucking genius, " I insisted, brooking no arguments of his.

So it was a most unbelievably –but unintended—one-up-manship of Taylor that happened early in our stay, when I came out to the courtyard with a letter addressed to me in Paris from **Chan Parker Woods, 16 Quai Boissy d'Anglas, Bougival 78, France.**

Reading it as I approached the group, I looked up and asked Taylor if he'd ever heard of Phil Woods.

"Are you kidding!? Of course! He plays sax."

"Oh?! So, he plays the same instrument as John Coltrane? " I retorted coyly.

"Well, no. Not exactly. Coltrane plays tenor sax, but the guy can wail on just about any saxophone. Phil Woods is good though –on alto." He looked at me perplexed that I would be asking this. "Why?"

"'Cause I've been invited to dinner at Phil Woods' house in *Bougival*, wherever that is."

"Wait a minute! YOU?" he bellowed and stared at me incredulously.

"Here's what this letter says," and I read to them:

'Dear Sarah, my mother wrote to me all about you and what a nice girl you are. And I've been expecting to hear from you. I'd like to invite you to dinner. Phil has a gig in Copenhagen in a couple of weeks and we'll accompany him there. So, if it's convenient for you to come to dinner before we all leave, say, next week, give me a call. Otherwise you can come when we get back. Do you have a phone? Ours is 969-52-78. I'm home most of the time. Sincerely, Chan Woods.'"

"YOU know them?"

"Does it sound like I know them?" I teased. "I happened to meet her mother on a visit to New York."

"Yeah, but you don't GET it, do you? SHE is Charlie Parker's WIDOW, never mind she's now married to Phil Woods. CHARLIE PARKER! Shit, man, it doesn't get more far out than that! BIRD. Charlie **Bird** Parker."

The other friends didn't have much of an idea of who any of these people were, but C.C. had heard of Parker.

"You mean, as in Birdland in New York? West Fifty-Second St? It closed last year."

"Yeah, man, that's the one. **Everyone** played Birdland. Art Blakey, John Coltrane, Miles Davis, even your Bossa Nova guy Stan Getz, " he added, nodding to me. So are you going---out to their place I mean?"

"Oh, of course I want to. I'll have to call her and get the details."

"Wow." He said looking at me with some kind of deferential awe. "Just wow."

I did call Chan Woods and got the instructions for going out there, and it wasn't going to be easy, especially for little me who could only speak minimal French and had never negotiated the public transportation of a metropolis before. I was to take *métro* Line 1, *direction Étoile* (okay, so that was going to be easy enough) all the way to *Porte de Neuilly*. That was the end of the line in those days, so I was to exit up some stairs and look for the bus stops outside. The bus I needed was #258 and I was to take it into the town of Bougival and at two stops in, there would be the *église* and some stone lions. I was to GET OFF. That was their street, *Boissy d'Anglais*, and I would find the house number.

I had no idea what time to leave the *Maison* to go from *Vavin* to *Porte de Neuilly* on the métro, so I gave myself an hour and a half. Paris is on a very northern latitude and longitude; the summer sun doesn't even set until around 10:00 p.m. I had to be out there by 7:00, so I knew, even if I did get lost, at least it would still be light out. But luckily I found it and was even a bit early! I even knew I shouldn't arrive at this dinner empty-handed, so I brought flowers with me done up in clear thick cellophane with a beautiful ribbon, stapled with the florist's card.

I had crossed the Place Picasso from Boulevard Raspail and had gone to my local flower shop – they were literally on every corner, down every side street and on every rond-point -- round-about-- in Paris. My neighborhood was no exception.

I had, however, chosen a pot of chrysanthemums in a pretty decorative paper. The lady came out of the opened shop doors to help me.

"Bonjour, Mademoiselle. C'est pour offrir?" she asked me this question a little dejectedly.

"Oui, "I answered, (when I should have said, "Oui, Madame.")   "C'est pour un dîner."

"Ah non, alors."

She gently took the pot from my hands and placed it back in its spot. And then she explained something I didn't quite really understand except that I did get the "obsèques" part. In France the chrysanthemum is reserved for funerals only. One would never "offrir" this flower for anything else. She led me to the bouquet displays at the farther end of the sidewalk. They were all so beautiful---and cheap---; it didn't matter which one I picked. By the time she took it apart, rearranged the stems, added some greenery and a little baby's breath, and rewrapped the whole thing, it was an absolutely beautiful gift. She tied on the ribbon, secured it with a sticker, and stapled her card to it, and I walked away looking like I'd just danced the role of the Sugar Plum Fairy and been handed the congratulatory bouquet by some adoring fan.

I walked up and down the Quai a few times, not wanting to be too early, (happy I had got there any time but late), and then I went through an unlocked gate into a rather disheveled garden, and up the steps of a very large, very old house. I rang the bell and a woman of about the same age as my mother answered.

169

That was Chan Parker Woods. She stood there, taller than me, grinning. She had curly brown hair, eyes that smiled amidst a lot of lines, and a weathered complexion that hinted she may have spent a lot of time in the sun in her earlier days. She looked Jewish to me... well, as in Berg. She greeted me warmly and motioned me inside. I offered her the bouquet, and thanked her enthusiastically for having invited me.

There were young children running around in the hallway behind her, but she started out by telling me what Mrs. Berg had explained, that she had a daughter named Kim a little older than I was, who was in college back in the States; and then she had these younger kids. There were three of them at the table that evening but it seemed like there had been more children in the house when I got there---possibly friends over since it was summertime.

Chan showed me around the house. The rooms were vast but rather dark, with those ancient-looking iron chandeliers that don't really light up a room, but keep the light a faded yellow. Sunlight was, however, still reaching in through huge windows. The furniture was dark and the wood heavy. We passed by the dining room and went into a music room. On one whole wall, which was stone, there were niches and bookshelves full of albums, instruments and photos. And they had a rather large upright tape recorder also on that wall. I presumed some of that was memorabilia of Charlie Parker, but I didn't ask after him.

"This is Phil's studio, " she announced, making a sweeping motion with her arm, "where it all happens. The acoustics in this house are spectacular."

"I can imagine! " I answered, trying to.

"Maybe Phil can demonstrate it for you."

All at once there was a commotion of kids thundering down the hallway.

"Yeah, unfortunately music isn't the only thing that echoes in this place. Excuse me a moment, would you?"

When she came back, she took me into the *salon* for *apéro*.

By the time we sat down to dinner, Phil Woods had come home. He was rather handsome, striking really, with a widow's peak right in front of his head. He had also brought along another man, possibly another musician; I didn't even catch the guy's name. We all gathered around a very long table: three children—one was a French neighbor's kid, one was a little girl, and the third a bi-racial boy-- two women and two men. An older lady brought food in from the kitchen, and the meal was wonderful, especially for me who, had been acclimated only to the *Maison's* dorm food, which, if better than Iowa City's, was still pedestrian, for a country whose culinary reputation spread across the seven seas.

We had a starter course of *oeufs durs mayonnaise*, which was to become my very favorite hors d'oeuvre of any in France. The homemade mayo was divine and I just let it rest on the roof of my mouth as I savored it with the hard-boiled egg. I glanced over to see if the children were turning up their noses at this food, not having any of it! But no! They were gobbling it down. So, the American kids had become "Frenchified." Interesting.

The main course was roast chicken in a creamy sauce the French were known for (and not at all like pedestrian gravy), with crispy, golden new potatoes that tasted so heavenly in the same sauce. I got the impression the lady serving had also done the cooking, and that she was French. She brought out *légumes à la vapeur* to go with the main course, after which she cleared those plates and brought out smaller ones for cheese.

"Can I help her?" I asked, trying to somehow be polite and do some of the work. Chan shook her head and pursed her lips into a whispered "no." Then she asked me, "So how do you get on with my mother?"

"You know," I answered, "I only met your mother one time!"

"Well! You made quite an impression on her, in that case!"

"Well, she's good friends with my great-aunt and uncle—she lives in their building! That must be why she wanted me to meet you."

And Phil Woods said, "Tell us about your studies."

So I told them a little about the *Cours de Civ* at the *Sorbonne*, and how I got there---my dreams of Paris, and the route from Iowa. By the time the kids had left the table and the adults were drinking really strong coffee and eating *gâteau St. Honoré* from the local *pâtisserie*, I sort of blurted out to Phil Woods that my American friend and classmate was a big fan of jazz.

170

"Maybe if I could have your autograph for him...?" I asked shyly.

I wanted one, too, truth be told, but I didn't feel I could ask for another one without sounding like I had some ulterior motive for coming to dinner or seem like just another groupie.

"Sure thing!" he answered, and got up from the table and beckoned, "Come with me."

I followed him back to the music room. He pulled out two albums and reached onto a desk over by a bank of windows for what looked like a laundry marking pen.

"How about an album for each of you?" he smiled at me.

"Oh my GOSH, so great!" I was breathless.

He signed a **Pairing Off - Phil Woods Septet** album: "Hey, Taylor—Bon séjour à Paris.—Phil Woods" and said to me, "He might know these other cats on the recording, especially Gene Quill."

And mine was **Greek Cooking - Phil Woods.**

"My latest. "

"Thank you so much! I'm just thrilled to have these. This is going to blow Taylor's mind!"

He smiled at me and led me back out into the hall towards the dining room to rejoin the others. It was past eleven o'clock and I still had a bus and a *métro* to take. Chan spoke right up without my having to start making excuses why I had to leave an evening I really didn't want to see come to an end.

"I'm going to drive you to the Porte de Neuilly station, " she said. "The *métro* runs until 12: 30. You'll be okay."

I thanked her profusely and we said our good-byes, she and I, at the station. There wasn't any traffic to speak of, though Paris, like New York, "doesn't sleep". I expressed my profound gratitude for the dinner, for the records, for getting to spend time with her, for having met her mom.

"Oh, sure... you are entirely welcome. You know...we Americans who love France gotta stick together, eh?" she laughed.

I realized then that I had been in the presence of greatness in Phil Woods, but it turned out that Chan Parker Woods was also amazing, even though to me, she was just a wife and mother. Little did I even dream that I would one day see her memoirs on the bookshelves: **My Life in E-Flat** *mostly about her life with Charlie Parker. She would, in the end, divorce Phil Woods, but he remained her ardent supporter ever after. She gave interviews to Ken Burns and to Clint Eastwood for films. She was a dancer, a singer and a composer. And she was brilliant.*

The wonder of coincidence danced wildly around my mind as I rode the train back to *Étoile* and transferred to line 6 *Nation par Denfert* in order to avoid having to walk through *Chatelet* that late at night. I got off at *Edgar Quinet*, walked down *Rue Delambre*, turned the corner and was home. I had to ring the bell but I didn't get into trouble because I had told the night porter that I had been "*invitée à un dîner chez des amis à Bougival,*" and he had nodded approvingly at me and wished me "*Bonne soirée Mademoiselle Shreeee-air.*"

The next day I coyly approached Taylor Hastings in the regular court-yard place, only I slyly half-hid the album behind a notebook and sort of sauntered up to him , trying to hide a sheepish look.

He saw me coming and nearly flew at me. "HOW WAS IT?!!"

"Very nice, "I said matter-of-factly.

"Were they far out?"

"Very nice." I offered again, trying to keep a straight face.

"AND? Did he play something for you?"

"Well, no!" I said, giving up the act. "But he signed something for YOU." And I pulled away my notebook to reveal the record.

"Holy fucking shit!" Taylor blurted out, taking **Pairing Off** out of my hands and staring at it.

"He said you might possibly know Gene Quill on there? "I pointed to his name.

"Hell YEAH, I know who he is. This is far out, Sari!"

"You're welcome."

Taylor reached over and picked me up and twirled me around! "MERCI BEAUCOUP!"

That album solidified my friendship with Taylor, not that that was my intention. He knew I had a boyfriend back home, so it was not romantic in the least, but we liked each other. We were happy when we'd meet up. We went to cafés, and he invariably wanted to talk mostly about-- what else?-- jazz. Sometimes he would take me to a *jazz boite,* but if I found these boring in some way, it only served to amplify my ignorance. He invited me back often to his dorm at the *Cité Universitaire* to hear more music and hopefully convert me to *le jazz hot*. I wasn't too convertible! Jazz did not inspire me, and I just had to come to the conclusion---and so did he---that I wasn't intellectual enough to appreciate it. It got to the point where I was begging off these get-togethers with the excuse that I had to study and... that was always the truth.

Another simply amazing part of the program that summer were the excursions offered almost every weekend and at the end of term, which was to be a long three-week swing around the entire country of France. There would also be weekend field trips to the Loire Valley and Mont Saint Michel, the Normandy landing beaches and the Champagne region. All of this was *à la carte*, and we had to sign up and pay each time. But given that it was France, the government subsidized these trips because they wanted foreign students to get to know their country! The fees were dirt cheap; so much as I thought I would only be able to participate in maybe one or two excursions, I ended up going on them all.

Taylor and I sat together on some of these bus rides ---I really preferred sitting with Eric, though. Taylor mostly liked to talk about Taylor, but Eric was more interested in discussing politics, art, **other** music besides jazz, and important subject matter like which town had the best *crêpes*.

I got to the point where I was always nervous about grades and dissatisfied with the slow pace of my progress in spoken French, but I took pleasure in the circle of friends I had from the program, and the ways I was getting to know Paris. If I had insecurities about my ability to actually get the academic year's worth of credits I had signed up for from this experience, I gave myself full marks for acculturating myself with the wonderful city I would hereafter "own."

Chapter Twenty-seven

"Splitzing" (from The World of Henry Orient)…Elmer Bernstein

It was mid-July 1968 and the most amazing synchronicity floated into my life via the U.S. mail: **Cass had moved to Boston. and was indeed slated to start flying on a route from there to Europe every week!** Of course, it wouldn't always be to Paris, but right away she wrote me the news.

Dear Sari,
This is but a quick letter written to officially welcome you to Europe! And to tell you that I am stationed in Boston now –also official! —and that I already have two Paris flights in July!!! The name of the hotel at which we stay is Terrass Hotel (12 Rue Joseph De Maistre, Paris 18e) in the Montmartre neighborhood. If you can write me a letter there and mark it "TWA Stewardess: Please Hold" I will be sure to contact you when I arrive. I think my first flight is going to be next week!!!! Anyway, put your phone number in the letter so I'll be sure to call as soon as I'm in! And we'll be able to see each other soon!!
Don't you LOVE Paris? Ah, how I envy you! It and Florence are my two favorite places in Europe and to live there would be so wonderful. Now when I see you, I expect a full report on all your mad, gay and exciting Parisian adventures.
How did your goodbyes with Soren go? What are your plans as far as "you and he" are concerned? I would imagine true plans depend on how things develop and change, but still, what do you count on at the moment?
I can't wait to see you!! I want to know you are happy and wonderful as always—it will make me feel happy!
Love, Cass

I was in a daze after I got that letter, and my mind was reeling about the soon-to-be-fulfilled reunion. In Paris, of all things! How did this really even actually happen?!!

I told Nonnie, "It's so amazing we will get together here!" And she agreed with her usual comment, "Great stuff!" and said she also missed her best friend from home. They were planning a reunion in Europe, too---at Christmas time.

I wrote an elation-filled letter to Cass explaining to her that we went on break at 10: 15 every morning, and that if her plane got in early, like most of the Paris flights from the East Coast did, since they left the night before, if she timed her call right, I could maybe take it. I doubted they would call me out of class for it, though.

And sure enough, the following week, just as we were taking our break, the Concierge screamed *"Mademoiselle Shrrreeee-aaaaiiir! Un coup de téléphone pour vous!"* I went into the mail cubicle where the phone was and excitedly picked it up.

"CASS!!!???"

"Hi kid!"

"Where are you?"

"At the hotel. But you don't have to come up here. I'll meet you somewhere closer after your class."

"It doesn't get over until 3: 15, you know."

"That's fine! I am going to explore a little, even in the rain! It's been raining since we got in!"

"Tell me about it. Paris has more rain than I ever would have guessed."

So we made a *rendez-vous* spot just outside the *Charles de Gaulle –Étoile métro* station, on a bench I knew was just past the "up" escalator. Whoever got there first would wait. I had midnight hours but didn't ask to extend them, and decided to try to get back in time. I wasn't sure she'd still be there the next day, but knew we'd make as much of the first visit as we could.

After I ate lunch, I changed into a nicer outfit and grabbed my umbrella to take to class so the very second it was over, I could stow my notebooks and school stuff in my mailbox on the *rez de chaussée* without having to go back up to the room, dash up to *Edgar Quinet*, and take the direct *métro* to our meeting spot.

And there she was. I saw her immediately as the escalator stairs brought the *Arc de Triomphe* into direct view. We fairly flew into each other's arms.

"I'm so happy to see you," I panted, hugging her.

"Me, too, " she answered.

"*La bise!*" I shouted, kissing her on each cheek and then one more, like great French friends do. "I'm taking you across the street to *Le Drugstore!* The French named it that because they think it is American to have a pharmacy with also magazines, jewelry, a few food items, a restaurant --ha ha! like a soda shop only …not-- and all sorts of other items. I actually love it. It's not American at all! We're not talking Walgreens!"

We walked around the whole place weaving in and out of the "*rayons*" or departments of beautiful and expensive things for sale. In the *papéterie* part, we bought postcards.

"Here's one of Montmartre!" she exclaimed showing me *Sacré Coeur* overlooking *Place du Tertre* on it.

Then we went over to their café part and ordered something American! I had a Coke float since they didn't offer root beer, and Cass had a chocolate shake, which was too milky and not enough shake-y, but she drank it anyway.

We started right in with my tales of woe about my roommate and the Southern belle, and my happier outcomes with the other friends.

"Maybe the next time, I can come straight to the *Maison* and meet Nonnie and C.C.!"

NEXT time! I was so thrilled there was going to be one and then more! I felt like I was in a dream.

I told her about the Phil Woods visit, the jazz indoctrination I was reluctantly undergoing, and how great Chan Parker Woods had been.

"Who would have ever thought a chance meeting like that one afternoon in New York would lead to such a wonderful invitation, " Cass mused. "It's too cool."

"It was really thanks to your parents! If they hadn't taken me along with you to New York and then not cared that we went to see my relatives, none of this would have happened! *Tu te rends compte?!*" *(I excitedly threw in some French---it seemed normal to do so. Maybe I was making a modicum of language progress!)*

I wanted to hear all about how she got to live in Boston. I'd never been there, but the city always intrigued me whenever we studied American history in school, or when the Kennedys came onto the scene while I was young.

I wondered if her father had pulled some strings to get her the city of her choice.

"No, he didn't have to. It's funny," she said, her voice trailing wistfully off into some distant thoughts, "I just really wanted to fly a route that came here and told them I knew some French. They said if I learned the cabin speech we have to give in French, they would put me on that route." She snapped back into the present. "So I have it with me. If you could help me with it, I think I get tested next week!"

"Of course!!"

We just sat there in *Le Drugstore* and talked for the next two hours.

"I think a little information on you and Alan is due me, " I said.

"Well, "she started in, "we will be seeing each other next week---he's going to come to Boston!"

"That's great, but what will your parents say?"

"They won't know a thing. I have a stewardess roommate, and they are aware of that, naturally, and they don't think they have any cause for concern that Alan would be going to see me, since I'm technically never there, which is true. But neither is my roomie—she's got a boyfriend in town, and we rarely see each other. Don't get me wrong—she's nice enough. All the girls I've met in stew school have been pretty nice. They're all more talented than I am, prettier than I am, taller than I am! Ha! And they all love the job. I loathe it."

I smirked at her remarks about other girls being prettier, but I believed her about hating the job.

"I just so want to be back in Iowa City!" she lamented. "I want to finish my degree, of course, and I want us to have another apartment together for senior year---now we'll both be seniors together---isn't that a riot?"

"I hadn't even thought of that, " I said, amused at the idea. Cass had lost a semester, and we'd both end up graduating together.

"So anyway, before I left Miami, Alan came there, too! He rode 'the beast' all that way to see me!"

"Holy shit! He must be serious, then?"

"Well, it's not as simple as that. First of all, we can't be together for a long while—I have to stick with this faky job for at least a year. And of course, he only came to Miami for a short visit since he knew I wouldn't be staying there. We did talk about the future, though, and there's a problem. He thinks my living away from Iowa City and working for TWA indicates an unwillingness and an inability to 'make things work' with him."

"What!? That's the stupidest thing I've ever heard. Like you had a choice!"

"He thinks I'm under the thumb of my parents, which, " she hastened to add, "is true."

"Aren't we all."

"So I sent him away—rather dramatically. And also, I'm not at all convinced he's been so faithful to me back at school, either. Those little co-eds in his classes are very tempting, I'm sure."

"Oh, Cass, seriously, I don't think you have anything to worry about there."

"Plus, he's still waiting for his C.O. status and it's vague and uncertain, so even **he** doesn't know where he'll be. He hopes he can do it in Iowa, but who knows? He was even talking about joining Vista, Job Corps or something, but he doesn't want to screw up his T.A. job that pays tuition."

"Yeah, that's worth having. I thought you said he could fulfill the C.O. requirements in some programs in Iowa City, though."

"I hope so! But nothing is certain."

"Bummer."

"So not wishing to destroy what he really hopes for, he is just going to visit me off and on, and not leave his life in Iowa. Quite honestly, the qualms about our relationship and being together in the same city stem from our relationships with others. He's had girlfriends before me; my parents hate him, etc. I have fears of the inevitable alienation."

"From what?"

"From each other."

"Why?"

"Well, for instance, he told me he doesn't want to get married, especially not in a church like the Episcopalian one that I would want to marry in."

"You would?" I was surprised.

"Yes. But he just wants to live together eventually. He's trying to become a C.O., and he professes to be a Christian, too, like me, so why wouldn't he want to do the socially acceptable thing and wed me in a church union? That would establish us as bona fide members of society while still allowing him to be a C.O.!"

"Well, Cass, that's a stretch. I mean, he's not going to do religious work is he?"

"We don't know!"

"Gosh. Okay, so go on."

"Well, we can't really discuss this stuff too rationally. Maybe it will come up again when I see him, but after he came to Miami, I got mad and pretty much wrote him a good-bye letter."

"But he's coming to see you."

"Yeah, because he called me a few days after our big fight scene, and said he had definite plans for his life and wanted me in them! He said we are going to lay ourselves open and really figure out a future so that I can finish this job, get back to school and get my degree. And he promised me he'll have his plans solidified one way or the other with the C.O., and we'll go from there. One thing I can bring to the table is this TWA salary. It isn't half bad, and I'm not spending much of it."

"But Cass, you don't actually think you have money—uh—concerns-- do you?" I didn't say "money problems" because it was too out of the question to phrase it like that!

175

"I will if my parents find out I'm with him. They already said they'd cut me off completely."

"Yeah, but they won't. Come on."

"Oh, I think they would!"

"Jesus."

"Well, they've paid for all this TWA stuff so far, of course, since it was their decision. We have to buy uniforms, make-up, everything…and they give me money for it all, including rent. I don't have a car, but …"

"Even so, you still have so much money in your name in those trust funds and all that stuff! You never have to think about money."

"Well, speaking of that, look!" She reached into her bag, and pulled out a wad of francs. "This whole night is my treat and I'm also going to send you home in a taxi, so maybe we should blow this pop stand and see some more of the *Champs-Elysées*!!"

"Whoa, what's all that?" I squealed, staring at her fist full of bills.

"We actually get this *per diem*!! Can you dig it?!"

"God almightly. *Tu parles!*"

So we set out down the avenue and looked in all the windows—just *leche vitrine*; we didn't go in to any boutiques, although we did enter what would be sort of like a shopping center…an old building right in the middle of a block that was once probably an apartment building but now was divided into shops. We looked at the most beautiful lingerie I had ever laid eyes on. But the prices!

"My LORD, "I said stupefied, "five hundred francs for a bra?!"

"Yes," she agreed, "this stuff is really expensive. The matching panties are that much, too!"

"Two hundred dollars!??" I was incredulous. But people must have bought them; the place was an established business, and nothing in the windows had any lesser prices. Plus, as I would find out later, French women always liked to match that part of their wardrobe, and I don't mean the white Bally granny panties like I wore. I filed that information away for future reference, but I never intended to actually buy anything like that.

"Are you thinking of buying some?" I asked Cass, who, it had long ago been determined, didn't have any of the restraints on her that I lived under.

"No," she laughed, "even if Alan would appreciate it!"

We kept walking and happened upon a restaurant that had the menu outside. I was shocked with delight to see that they had a *prix fixe* on their "*étage*," i.e., upstairs, that was totally affordable at twenty francs including wine!

"Let's eat here, " I suggested, and we went in.

We had *hors d'oeuvre* of melon, accompanied by bread and white wine. That was followed by ham with a glaze over it, smothered in mushrooms with a light sauce over all that and the potatoes. Next the waiter brought a small board of *camembert* and *chevre* with more bread; and this feast ended with coffee ice cream covered in a mound of *crème Chantilly!* All for twenty francs per person! Four dollars! It was insanely cheap, even for the 60's. And on the *Champs-Elysées* no less! I could hardly believe our luck.

Afterwards the waiter, (who had flirted with Cass, remarking on her beauty) even gave us another half bottle of wine to take with us, plus two little plastic cups! So we strolled some more on the avenue and drank the lovely wine sitting on benches up by the *Rond-Point.* It was 10:30 at night and still light as day out. Cass suggested we jump in a cab and go back to her hotel so I could see it.

"Heaven!" I said, not having ridden in a car in weeks.

The *Hôtel Terrass* was a dream. The lobby was like an old gentlemen's club or something, with dark wood everywhere, flanked by mirrors, a grand piano and elegant seating. But her room!

"Holy magnificence, Batman!"

I hadn't seen the interiors of any *châteaux* yet, but when I did, I would harken back to Cass' room at the *Terrass.* The room's foyer was hotel-ish, with a modern bathroom, and a closet with the usual things, including laundry service, which Cass had already taken advantage of to have her uniform completely cleaned and pressed. But once in the actual room, it was a huge square with glorious French windows on two walls, a window seat under some of them, a very large bed, probably close in size to an American king, with curtains all around a square canopy in gorgeous brocade fabric. The floors were parquet stained very dark, and the oriental carpets on top were thick and lush. There was a desk full of *Hôtel Terrass* paper and envelopes, which Cass let me have some of, and a beautiful Louis XV chair with a silk-covered cushion seat. The room was divided into bed chamber and sitting room — where the desk was and a love seat; but then the windows opened out onto a balcony, with a view high above the most beautiful city in the world. You had a clear line to the Eiffel Tower from that window as it faced southwest. I was in awe and expressed my feelings with an eloquent, "Holy fucking shit."

Cass had another treat in store for me, that she would continue on all the subsequent visits.

"I have brought you goodies from the flight, " she announced, handing me a make-shift box that had stored napkins in the galley of the plane. She had filled it with all sorts of *petit-fours*, cakes, pastries, tiny cans of juice, little cans of Coke, and small tea sandwiches of water cress and egg, and cheese.

"And look, I raided the bar, too, "she said, pulling out miniature bottles of Grand Marnier, shaped exactly like the real bottle! — plus those very small bottles of wine. I wasn't much of a wine drinker, but heaven knows someone would be in my group. She also gave me a bunch of olives and cherries. They obviously had to mix some drinks on board.

"Cass!" I gasped. "This is a treasure trove!!!!" I could live off that for three days, I surmised!

"I thought you'd like it. They just throw the stuff out, by the way; I didn't technically steal it."

"Good Christian that you are, after all, eh?"

We turned on her t.v. — something else I hadn't seen in over a month, and watched a few minutes of a show I grew to love, which was *"Les chiffres et les lettres."* And then I started to get antsy that I would miss curfew. Montmartre was a long series of *métro* rides away from Montparnasse, and I'd forgotten already about her offer of a taxi.

"I'm sending you back in a taxi, Sari, remember? No arguments."

"Oh, my God, THANK you!"

She thrust a bunch of francs in my hand and we hugged again, tears streaming down my face. The joy of that evening stayed with me, buoyed me up when I felt "down", made me feel Parisian for the first time, and gave me a contentment that was palpable.

I took a dream ride across town under the lights that Paris is named for: City of Light. The streets were deserted more or less, compared to the daytime at least; the cobblestones glistened under the street lamps. I made it back before the gate closed, and I floated up to my room. Jo Jo barely turned from her desk as I entered and flung my purse and umbrella on the bed. I gingerly opened the box and walked over and offered her something out of it. She was stunned, to say the least, possibly at the contents but more likely at my gesture. She managed a semi-friendly *"Merci bien"* as she lifted a tiny *chou à la crème* from its resting place and set it on the corner of her desk.

"I take it you had a good time, " she said, not really looking up.

"Ah, *ouais, c'était vachement chouette,* "I responded. She wasn't the only one in the room who could speak French.

Chapter Twenty-eight

"Love is All Around"...The Troggs

The idea that I was going to be in Paris for a whole year was already thrilling enough, but the new fact that Cass would be coming every few weeks, sometimes even more frequently, filled me with overwhelming joy!

July was the most amazing of all the months. Cass was right back the next week as she had said she would be and this time, she got in really early in the morning, had time to change at her wonderful hotel, and then she took a cab and came to *La Maison* in time to go to class with me! She had a big tote bag full of goodies from the plane, and we tossed that in my room and ran downstairs. I asked permission for her to sit in on the morning classes, and when we were on break, I could introduce her to my friends Nonnie, C.C., Marty, Eric and Taylor. Cass looked a little disheveled having come right off the flight and not gone to sleep, but I could tell by the way the guys checked her out, that her beauty was still striking to people seeing her for the first time.

Cass took a folded-up piece of used-looking paper from her pocket and undid it, saying, "These are lines of dialogue I have to learn to say in French for my job. Sari's going to help me with it."

"Yes, and I'm also going to write you a little speech to tell the proctors or whoever administers the exam. You'll wow them."

"Gee, really?" Cass said, lifting her violet lash-rimmed eyes to me, all smiles. "Thanks, kid!"

"You guys should see what she brings me from the plane. We'll have to have a party!"

"Can do," said Taylor, gazing at Cass as though she were in a museum---the Venus de Milo.

I didn't waste any time cluing in the boys on just who Cass was, her art and our Iowa life in a nutshell. The girls had heard about her from the get-go. The whole group was very welcoming towards her, and break was over too soon. They went to their advanced classes and she and I returned to my beginning *cours pratiques*.

After the eternity it took for 10:30 to turn into noon, she and I retreated back up to my room. Jo Jo came in and I introduced them. Cass had already had an earful about Jo Jo, but she was as friendly as if nothing were wrong. Jo Jo wasn't rude, per se, but didn't give us anything but the usual short shrift. When she was gone to lunch Cass turned to me and said, "I see what you mean."

"Well, in a few months we won't be roomies anymore, thank God, so I guess I can put up with it. I mean, she probably thinks I'm some sort of geek. Or else she's pissed she got a Jewish roommate from a nowhere school or something."

"Oh no! Iowa is not a nowhere school."

"Oh, don't you start in on me, too!" I laughed. "You know what I mean."

"Well, where's she at? Harvard?"

"Emory."

"So what."

I had decided that I was going to skip the afternoon session that day. That way, Cass and I would have all afternoon and evening together. So we didn't hurry to lunch in the dorm. We decided to eat at a café. Even though Cass had her usual TWA per diem, I thought the famous cafés right down the street on *Boulevard Montparnasse* were still too expensive for us to patronize. But she felt differently, and we decided to go to *La Coupole* for lunch. Cass had a guidebook with her she'd picked up, and wanted to go there because her book reported that the theater-of-the-absurd playwright Eugène Ionesco lived above it.

"I can't believe your luck to live in such a famous neighborhood," she marveled as we turned up *Boulevard Montparnasse*.

"Well, I know Hemingway hung out at *Le Dome* right here," I pronounced as we passed the famous seafood display cases on the corner of *Delambre* and *Montparnasse*.

"You may be rubbing shoulders with the *literati* and not even know it," she admonished me.

"Well, yes, lah-dee-dah, won't the Iowa Writer's Workshop be impressed with that!"

Some of the other students had spoken about *La Maison des Étudiantes* being in a most opportune locale for the really famous cafés, *La Rotonde, Le Dome*, which was the closest to us and the one I passed every single day, *Le Select*, and *La Coupole*. But *La Coupole* was probably the most renowned of them all. Even during the events of May in that year, the leader of the student revolt, Daniel Cohn-Bendit, had stood on one of its tables to expound to the crowds.

Cass and I were eating outside, but she wanted to see the interior due to her guidebook's description of the walls and pilasters being "adorned with paintings by the minor masters of the 20th century, a temple of Art Deco."

"Did you know," Cass asked, already suspecting I did not, "that at the grand opening of this place in 1927, all the famous artists and their models, as well as socialites, writers and other 'stars' came and lent their panache to the place?"

"I believe you," I said. "And if I didn't, just look at the photos on that wall behind us inside." You could see it clearly from the terrace—behind the bar on the wall were images of everyone from Picasso to Sartre, Man Ray, Léger, Soutine.

She went on quoting from her book, "It seems that 'an unknown writer with little round glasses, Henry Miller'—HA!" she interjected, "unknown!---'took breakfast at the bar. Matisse sipped beer while Joyce lined up his whiskeys.' Wow," she said.

"I thought Sartre hung out at some other famous cafés in *St. Germain des Prés*," I told her, "but there he is in that picture."

"His regular table was number 149," she said, still reading. "It says he was a hefty tipper!"

"Is that a guidebook or a movie magazine?" I asked.

La Coupole was really more of a seafood restaurant at night, but for lunch their menu on the *terrasse* seemed pretty normal in food and abnormal in price.

"Jesus, this is expensive!" I reacted, typically.

"Don't worry," she replied.

So we had *entrecôte* (steak) *frites sauce béarnaise, avec salade* for lunch, which was more like dinner for me—so much the better---and for dessert, these amazing pastries called *millefeuilles* with *crème anglaise* and strawberries in them. I swooned over those. Cass giggled as she stuck her fork in one.

"So I want to hear your routine in that place. What do you do all day?" she inquired.

"Well," I began, "you know me---I love to sleep, right? No more! We have to get UP and get going by 7:45... and start right in by making the bed and cleaning up the room!! I take a shower at night because there's less chaos, but if we want to wash up in the room, we have to take a pitcher---it's in our bathroom— I don't think you saw that---and go down the hall to fetch hot water! It's medieval! Right now there are GUYS on the halls because in the summertime the place turns into a youth hostel so we have to be careful to wear robes! I hate that. Anyway, by 8:30 we have to be at breakfast, which is in a dining hall on the other side of the courtyard, sort of by where we met the guys for break."

"So that's pretty convenient?"

"Yes, and there's even a mini-laundromat in there, can you believe that?"

"Nice."

"It's expensive. Everything 'normal' is expensive here, I can't get over it. Anyway, breakfast is my favorite meal. We get these bowls of hot chocolate and two croissants plus any bread left over from dinner the night before."

"I had that in school in Switzerland, too! Loved drinking it from bowls!"

"Yes, so great for dunking! I never thought I would love anything so much as this French breakfast. I mean the **butter** in this country! How can something so mundane give me such a thrill?!"

She laughed, "So when does class start?"

"At nine. We do phonetics first, as you saw, and that lasted until break, which is typical."

"I'm impressed with that," she said softly.

"After break, like today, we take notes until noon. The lesson you sat in on was grammar, but it just as easily could have been some civ topic. We also have phonetics lab in the afternoon, and then more note-taking on lit or art or something. I don't usually go to lunch at *La Maison* because I save my meal ticket for dinner, but there are *boulangeries* and all the shops just around the corner and I'll get bread and cheese

179

for lunch and eat it in the room. And study, too." I paused and then told her, "Cass, I study all the time, you just wouldn't believe how much. This is really **hard**. So much worse than Iowa."

"And so when classes get over at 3:15 what then? More studying?"

"Yes, unless I take a break and go wandering around either in my neighborhood like up to *Inno* or to the pharmacy. OR, I get on the *métro* and go explore some other area. Dinner is at 6:30 and I'm always starving by then. Afterwards, a bunch of us might go up to the *pâtisserie* again, and buy a *pain au chocolat* or a *chausson aux pommes* or something. So gooood. Even worth blowing my budget. Really, the food in the dorm is probably horrible by French standards, but we're too hungry not to eat it. It's NOTHING like this meal was!! This was a real treat, so thank you so much for it...again!"

"I loved it, too. It's not like we can eat this way at home either! "

"Well, you can---haha."

Then she got a serious expression on her face and said, "I'm sorry your study time is so filled with my visit."

"Are you joking?! Shut up! If you weren't here, would I be cavorting all over, eating at a place like this, and spending a gorgeous summer afternoon and evening with my best friend in all the world?"

She looked up at me from her *demi-tasse* espresso cup and said, "I'm SO glad we have this time to get together. You are my soul sister, Sari---, and our friendship is one of the things that keeps me going in my dreadful job."

"It's what is keeping me together, too."

"I sense you're having some trouble staying afloat here, with all the course work you have, but I don't think you quite understand the difference between what you are doing and what I am doing. You are coming into your own! You will leave here a sophisticated intellectual! Me, on the other hand, well, ever since I started working at TWA, I often have sinister thoughts that the world isn't a place that's even worth the effort and loneliness it takes to get by."

"Oh, Cass! Don't say that! TWA won't last forever."

"Well, maybe not, but if it wasn't for getting to see you and spending time like this, I don't know what I'd do." Her voice trailed off.

I picked up the train of thought, telling her "Friendships like ours are pretty cool-- uncommon, really, aren't they?" I looked deep into her eyes and smiled. She still seemed forlorn, so I added, "But are you terribly lonely? For Alan?"

"Yes, I miss him. And how about you? Do you miss Soren, too?"

"I do. But I'm almost too bogged down with studying to have **time** to miss him!" I gave a little laugh. "But it's true—when you walk around Paris and see so many couples and so much 'PDA,' it's hard not to pine away for your one true love to share the city with."

"You know," she said, with somewhat more resolve in her voice, "no matter what happens with Alan and me, I feel stronger for having a dear friend like you in whom I can confide and listen to in return. I hope you feel the same way."

"You know I do."

"And you know what else? I think our experiences will somehow make each of us more aware and alive. I think, though my airline gig is somehow far less of a 'growth agent' than a wonderful year at the Sorbonne will be for you, I can't help but believe that what Tennyson wrote is true."

"What was that?" I asked, not being able to come up with anything Tennyson might have written.

"He said, 'We can but trust that good shall fall, at last, far off, at last, to all—and every winter turn to spring.'"

I sat there in *La Coupole*, my chin cupped in my hands, marveling at Cass quoting Tennyson off the top of her head, and I had one of those odd sensations of being conscious of my own self, that awareness feeling of being there at that precise moment in Paris, France...being me.

"So when you have a lonely day or weeks filled with crazy gypsies, a ridiculous roommate, difficult tests and no Soren Carlysle beside you," she told me, "your friend Cass Hyde will always be there to console you. And when things go great and you go off and make terrific things happen here...which you will –you must!.. then just remember how happy I will be for and with you! How's that?" She looked up at me, triumphant.

180

"Cass! You're too much! I am aware all the time just how really lucky I am to have a friend like you!"

I vowed in return to be the best friend she could ever hope to have. I knew in my heart, and it didn't need repeating, that I valued my friendship with Cass above any other, and I had to believe that she knew I would do anything for her, anything I could to help her find happiness. I was sensitive to her and whatever trials and tribulations she was undergoing, as well as the glorious achievements she had already made and would make tenfold. I didn't bother to bring it up for the millionth time, but the fact was always with me that I owed her so much already… in purely material things and money! …far too much to ever be able to repay. I renewed my silent pledge to make up for the largess shown me by her and by her parents. I didn't know how; I just knew I would.

"*On change de l'air?*" I said, gathering up my stuff from the banquette. "Sure you don't want to split the check?"

"Hell no, kid! It's all on me. I'm the one who wanted to eat here. And it was worth every *centime*, wasn't it?"

"It sure was! Thank you so much again!"

We left the restaurant and walked into a beautiful July afternoon, crossed the boulevard and headed down *Rue Vavin*, the street that led into the huge black gates at the back of the Luxembourg Gardens.

"I want to tell you about Alan," she said in a somber tone, "so shall we find a good bench and stay in here for a while?"

"Great idea."

She then spent the better part of an hour relating the details of their tryst in Boston. Things had not gone well.

"We fought a lot. We argued and we bickered, then we made up but it would start all over again. He's really anti-marriage, for one thing, and, kid, I don't want to merely live together."

"Well, no," I said, "I hear ya on that one. But, Cass, usually in a marriage, the man has the most earning potential and future assets. With you, if you marry him, you're likely to be cut off from yours. So maybe it might make sense to just live together."

"Yeah, I see what you're getting at. But if we lived together and my parents got wind of it, which they certainly would, I'd suffer the same outcome."

"I suppose, "I sighed. "So what do **you** want to happen?"

"The more I've thought about it, the more I think we're just not very compatible, I guess. I think I want to call it off with him."

"Wow."

"But I just can't do it," she hastened to add. "I just can't cut myself completely off from him." She looked at me with a renewed pained expression. "Nor can I bear the thought of severing all ties with my parents, in case you were wondering."

"The thought did cross my mind," I answered. "Do you think there's a solution?"

"No. That's just it. Between the job that I hate and my parents who hate the guy I love, I may just snap."

I looked up at her and she nodded.

"Suicide has entered my mind. It seems like a viable way sometimes."

"Cass, come on! Get real."

"I mean it. Sometimes I just hate living. Being alive seems almost an assault upon my integrity."

"You can't let yourself feel that way!"

"But Sari, if I cannot *resolve* the emotional chaos caused by my love and affection for Alan, that love will end up causing more pain and fear than pleasure."

I pressed her for her true feelings towards him.

"It's such a roller coaster ride, " she said. "I just ruminate about him over and over until I'm spinning…maybe out of control."

I scooted over on the bench and put my arm around her. There was one element missing in this conversation and I wanted to broach the subject delicately. "Cass," I finally said, "what about your art? I mean, to me, art defines you more than Alan, or for that matter, your parents. What about just concentrating on that?"

"I think about it, but only in terms of relinquishing any future with Alan. My parents said I could go back to school if I stick it out with TWA for one year. They think Alan will be gone by then or something. I'm pretty sure he won't be, but I don't tell them that."

"Yeah, I wonder if he'll finish even by next fall," I said, thinking out loud. "He might not! Your parents will monitor that situation—count on it."

"But you know what else, Sari? I do have doubts about Alan and me, even as I profess to love him. I'm not sure he loves me in a way that our life together would grow. I wonder if he feels about me in a lesser way, a way where love could not thrive—-maybe exist but not fill our days together with music and beautiful mornings. You know, the way it should be."

I thought of *Le Petit Prince*. Cass and I both loved it and we read it over and over in our dorm room at Iowa, she in English and me in French.

"You do remember what the Fox said, Cass. "*'Rien n'est parfait,*' right? I'm not at all sure perfection is attainable in any relationship. Take Soren and me. Not perfect!"

"You're right, of course, " she said. "I don't desire perfection from anyone. I just hope for a little peace of mind—-just a quiet place where everyone and everything is not up for grabs."

I wasn't used to hearing Cass Hyde sound so vulnerable. In the past she hadn't opened up—-even to me— about her love life, or for that matter, her home life either. This was a telling moment for me.

"Oh, and by the way, in case you haven't already guessed, I HATE flying, dammit. I'm just sick of it already. Get this… my billfold with seventy dollars in it was **stolen** on a flight the other day."

"WHAT?! That's awful!"

"Yeah, I was merrily preparing meals for the hundred or so souls in the back of the plane, and some brazen so and so somehow found my purse and took my wallet!! "

"Jesus! Was it another flight crew member then? Don't you guys keep stuff away from the passengers?"

"Yes, I suppose it was," she sighed. "I've just had it!"

The melancholy was unmistakable as we sat there amidst the precisely planted beds of summer flowers and the low-hanging tree branches of the *jardin à la française* part of the vast park. I tried to think up something to cheer her up, and I guess she sensed that because she looked up and said, "Sorry I'm rambling! I don't want to waste any more of our precious time together in Paris **boring** you with my problems."

"You could never bore me. Far from it. But I don't want us to be sad today either."

Before I could finish my thought, she lunged at me, engulfing me in hugs. "I love you, Sari Shrier! I'm so grateful for your listening ear!"

We hugged each other right there in the garden and no Parisian even gave us a second glance.

"What we need is some *lèche-vitrine*!"I said emphatically.

"What does that mean?" she laughed. "I guess my French isn't as up to snuff as I'd hoped it'd be!"

"Window shopping!"

We got up and set out for retail therapy, as no one, of course, called it in the '60's. I suggested we go off to *Boulevard St. Germain* and check out some of what Paris is known for: *bijoux de fantaisie*, as they called costume jewelry, chic eyeglasses, or the darling "doctor's bag" satchel purses I saw at *La Bagagerie* on one of my little forays into shopping that I could ill afford.

Cass had shopped in all the major department stores of the western world, it was fair to assume, with her mother and grandmother. But she really loved our little outings. She loved boutiques —-in Chicago and Iowa City, and, especially in Paris, a city with thousands of them.

I explained to her what I had found out the hard way about boutique shopping: they expect if you walk in, you want to buy something, since much of what they have to offer is on display in the window. I, myself, felt rather intimidated by not being able to "just look" and that did change over the years in Paris; but during the halcyon days of my student sojourn there, "*Je peux regarder*?" was not a sentence any French shopkeeper cared to hear.

We walked all over the *quartier*, and when all at once something caught her eye in the *vitrine*, Cass marched right into a chic little spot on the *Rue de Rennes* off *Boulevard St. Germain*, and asked to try on a gorgeous turquoise sleeveless silk cocktail dress with a wide contrasting black silk sash around the waist. She came out of the dressing room and modeled it for me. She had that Jackie Kennedy aura I recognized so often in her.

The clerk spoke some English; Cass didn't even pretend to know any French. I tried to run interference.

Cass liked it and nodded to the clerk. But the clerk was having none of it. She said, "*Un moment, Mademoiselle*" and went to the back room, only to return with a tape measure and some pins. She lifted the shoulder up and pinned twice. Then she cinched in the waist a little bit.

"*Trois jours, Mademoiselle. Est-ce que ça vous va?*"

"She wants you to come pick it up in three days, Cass."

"Oh, could you do it for me. kid?"

"*Avec plaisir!*" I said, and explained to the sales clerk that I would be the one to come for it.

"*Très bien*," she replied, smiling, and took Cass back inside the curtains of the dressing room to remove the dress from her.

Cass paid TWELVE HUNDRED FRANCS for that dress with a credit card that said "Carte Blanche"and was in her father's name. The dress was beautiful, I had to admit, but holy shit. That was two hundred forty dollars, and dresses in Brandeis in 1968 cost only a fraction of that, even in the French Room!

Cass explained, "I have this feeling my parents could drop in on me in Boston at any time, you know? And this way, I can pull out this dress to wear if they take me out—charged to them, of course---and it will allay their fears that I'm brooding over Alan and Iowa City."

"Umm," I said, a bit taken aback, "smart thinking. But do you like the dress, too?"

"I love it. Do you?"

"Of course!"

We walked up and down *Boulevard. St. Germain* and found another restaurant for dinner. It was around 8:00 o'clock already, so we did what we'd done the first time on the *Champs-Elysées*---just read the menus posted outside until we found one with things we thought we'd like. We had had such a filling lunch that I wasn't really even too hungry, but I "managed" to scarf down six *escargots* and a large *salade niçoise* with a *un carafe (un quart) de vin rosé maison*. Cass ordered an appetizer of *crudités* followed by a little turbot fish in a light white sauce of some sort, small fingerling potatoes and asparagus spears decorating the plate. We both skipped having dessert but had *un café* instead. We lingered over this meal, watching the *beau monde* saunter down the chic boulevard in front of us.

"I love the Left Bank," she stated.

"Me, too. Let's go on up to the church and see if there are any music rehearsals or concerts going on."

We crossed the cobblestoned entrance in front of *St. Germain des Prés,* but couldn't hear any music emanating from the nave, so we decided I would jump in the *métro* right there, and she would go back to the hotel in a cab, a queue for which was in the stand across the street.

We did "*la bise*" as though we were French. Nothing more needed to be said. She waved and called out that she'd be back soon!

And in three days' time, I made a dramatic trek back up *Rue de Rennes* to pick up the cocktail dress for her, took it gingerly in its box on the *métro* back to *La Maison*, and kept it safe for her return.

Chapter Twenty-nine

"Mas Que Nada"...Sergio Mendez & Brazil '66 (Jorge Ben Jor)

The next time Cass came, still in July, I couldn't possibly cut a whole afternoon of classes again, so I asked her to come to the *Maison* and get me at 3:15. We decided to stay in my immediate neighborhood, because Cass hadn't seen the *Montparnasse* area yet. We headed up *Rue Delambre* to *Inno*. Even though I didn't expect the merchandise to impress Cass at all, the supermarket in the basement certainly was worth a perusal. She bought a lot of great *chocolat* to take back with her as well as *Rosé d'Anjou*, the price of which was really cheap compared to the States. *Inno* had great cosmetics; we were both in love with *Bourjois* and *Roger & Gallet* products, which she also bought. She even deigned to look at the lingerie, which was the "store brand," *Miss Helen*, and she liked it.

"But I wonder why they use an English brand name?" she asked.

"I couldn't tell you."

Every quotidian item from toothpaste to clothes detergent in French stores was three or four times more expensive than I was used to paying in the States. Coca Cola, while exponentially cheaper in the supermarket than in the cafés, was double what it was at home. Wine was about a fourth the price, though, and being the daughter of a bar-owner, I also checked out the prices of such spirits as *Cognac* and liqueurs. But I wouldn't be taking any of that home to Sol. A nice bottle of expensive champagne would have been a good gift for the family, but it was still way out of my range.

After we left *Inno* we went past the *Montparnasse Bienvenue* train station and cut over to the *Rue du Cherche-Midi* where we'd seen some other cute boutiques the last time she was there. We went into one displaying less expensive but still nice knit dresses in the window that looked like long polo shirts with belts.

"Let's each get one!" Cass exclaimed, opening the door as its bell signaled our presence.

"Well, maybe---that will depend on the price."

The dresses were preppy-looking, in solid colors with contrasting collars and knit belts. I loved the navy dress with red trim and she liked a green one with yellow. They had no logos on them; this was decades before Ralph Lauren would launch his presence in Paris; and we weren't in a Lacoste shop, although those did exist then; Lacoste clothing was elite and pricey and reserved mostly for wearing to play tennis.

The dresses fit us and looked good! The price was one hundred sixty francs, so thirty-five dollars. I decided I could probably swing that if Cass could buy it then and there, and I could pay her back. My plan that day was to treat Cass to dinner, and that was all the money I had on me.

"Of course I'll buy it for you," Cass said, "and, sure, you can pay me back." But she looked at me with a twinkle in her eye and her lips pursed into a little turned up smile, as if to say, "Nope. That's not going to happen."

"I mean it, Cass. The next time you come, I'll have the money."

Back out on the street, we wandered more until we found ourselves on *Rue du Four*, right smack dab in front of *La Bagagerie*. I don't know if Cass secretly knew that's where we were going, but she seemed to want to be there.

"I must buy some of those sweet little leather satchels we saw here that other time," she announced, marching in.

She went right over to the display of the small, rectangular purses with two short leather handles on top and two patch pockets in the front secured with brass tab toggles. She proceeded to take a black one and two red ones up to the counter. I figured she was taking them to other stewardesses or something, but after paying for them (sixty francs a piece for the small size), she handed me a red one.

"Won't this look great with your dress!" she exclaimed.

"But Cass, I can't ..."

"Shhh. I won't be taking no for an answer, don't ya know. The black one is for me and I'm going to give the other red one to my TWA roommate. She'll love it."

I was so thrilled to have the dress and purse, I could have smothered her in hugs. But I was sort of in shock and just stood there. Finally, I did manage to thank her profusely.

I had planned all along to be the one paying for our dinner that night, but now I realized I would have to announce it and be insistent. We walked around the sixth *arrondissement* for a while more and then found ourselves near the *métro Duroc*. This was my opportunity to reveal dinner plans.

"We're going to take this *métro* back to my neighborhood, " I said, handing her a ticket from my *carnet*. "I'm taking you to a restaurant near the *Maison* and it's MY treat."

I had already decided that this time I would take her to dinner at the place we all went that was so super cheap, even I could afford to pick up the tab: *Mille Colonnes*. Some of the guys in the group had found it on *Rue de la Gaîté*, and I would go there with Eric and Taylor once in a while. *Mille Colonnes* was very old and venerable. It had a theatrical past associated with *Bobino*, the musical theater and cinema venue, and was, in its heyday, a popular restaurant-café, dancing and banquet hall. By the time we students went there, it was long past its prime, but still had a huge dining room where dusky twilight sun filtered into high windows even as late as 9:00 p.m.

It was there I reaffirmed, after my dinner at Phil Woods' house, that my favorite hors d'oeuvre of all time would be something as potentially pedestrian as *oeufs dur mayonnaise*, and I subsequently ordered it every time I ate there.

"How can something so totally normal like hard boiled eggs in mayo be SO different here than at home?" I mused to Cass as we settled into our rustic chairs.

"It's the homemade mayonnaise, of course."

"I know, but we can make it from scratch, too, I would assume."

"But we don't!" she laughed.

We had roast chicken in heavenly *beurre blanc* that covered the meat and oozed over onto the *frites*. The *salade* that accompanied this as a garnish more than a salad, had its own flawless *sauce vinaigrette* on it, the mustard of which turned it slightly yellow. We both soaked all the sauces up with the wonderful pieces of *baguette* from the basket on the table that the waiter would keep refilling.

I splurged and even ordered the expensive Coca Cola which came in a small chilled bottle, but no ice in the glass.

"The French think drinking Coke with meals is an abomination," I pronounced to Cass, taking a swig.

"It probably is," she said, "given that it eats the stomach lining."

"Yeah, yeah." I'd been through all that before about Coca Cola. Didn't make me love it any the less.

After dinner, for which I paid thirty-seven francs for both, including tip! -- we went back to my room where Jo Jo was at her desk studying, her back to the door. Turning to see who came in with me, because we were making noise, she saw Cass and said, "Oh, you're back!"

"I am indeed," said Cass.

Jo Jo stared at me as I dumped out my afternoon's purchases on the bed, and got out Cass' cocktail dress from my armoire. She watched with some interest as we emptied the tote bag full of airplane goodies, and repacked it with both dresses and the two purses Cass had bought that afternoon, and then tried to fit in her *Inno* provisions. The wine was pretty heavy, so we left that in the *Inno* bag. Luckily *Boulevard Montparnasse* right at the *Dome Café* had a taxi stand, and it would be easy for us to walk over there and put her in one.

"Thank you so much for picking up the other dress for me," she said, "and for dinner! It was wonderful!"

"And thank YOU for buying my dress today. I will have your money."

"I know," she laughed. "Stop."

"When do you go on that long excursion all around France?" she asked, taking a little calendar from her purse to mark it down.

"I'm not sure," I said. "Towards the end of August, I think."

"Oh," Cass said, looking up. "We've got oodles of time! I'll be back often before that."

"Yay!" I blurted out. "Practice your French so they keep you on this route!"

And I had to study mine so they'd keep me in the program!

Cass and I had explored various areas of Paris three times so far, and we hadn't even begun to take in what the city had to offer in the way of museums and galleries, antique shops, fabric stores, book shops, monuments, except for the Eiffel Tower, and more food. My mind wandered all the time she wasn't there of what we'd do next. A *bateau mouche* ride was certainly in our future. If only she could come on a real weekend, I mused; we could really cover a lot of ground.

Two days after Cass had left, I got a postcard from her. She had bought some at *Inno* and this one was a scene of *Sacré Coeur* at night shining above a filled *Place du Tertre* café. That was her hotel's neighborhood and it was as if she were announcing that it was her neighborhood as well.

Sari---Another beautiful time- and I thank you! And one week from tomorrow I shall return—I cannot believe it! I will come laden with goodies and force you to escape the delights of study! Ha! Gee, I thank you for picking up the dress---and wasn't the restaurant delightful? Note the mad, gay and exciting picture on this great postcard---got a little carried away, *n'est-ce pas*? Ha! (Guess where I got this little beauty, too!) Let's go shopping again in the area we visited last tonight, okay? Can't wait 'til next Thursday! Love, me

The following Thursday came, however, with no sign of Cass. In the days before any sort of fast communication other than telegrams, we really couldn't get ahold of each other if things came up to put a wrench in the works. She didn't call or leave word at the *Maison* for me and it wasn't until a few days later that I had a letter, and it had been written on stationery from the Intercontinental hotel in Frankfurt, Germany. She told me she was indeed to have had the flight to Paris on Thursday but it was cancelled, so her next one would be in another week or so. She would for sure let me know. And the rest of the letter was a broken record of her hurt feelings and pessimism over seeing Alan in Boston. He seemed to be lurking around the city, hoping to spend as much time with her on her non-flight days as possible. He had taken a seedy room in a house far from her apartment in the Back Bay area, but he stayed with her whenever her roommate was on a flight that didn't coincide with hers.

Their main bone of contention was still marriage, followed by his C.O. status. She said the C.O. indecision haunted his every step and that there was even fear of imprisonment, so that he couldn't concentrate on his work either. He insisted her reluctance to live together in Iowa City was a "hang up" of hers, and that if she really loved him, she wouldn't care what her parents thought of him and she would exit their sphere of influence. When they fought, he accused her of being a rich bitch who was "so tied to Daddy's money" that she couldn't bring herself to leave home and strike out on her own or for her art. All of this, she wrote me, stung so bad that she couldn't breathe afterwards and just wanted him gone for good. But then they would make up and he'd be back.

I hadn't taken seriously Cass' not-so-veiled threat to end her life, but now, as I read her letter and visualized what a ninth ring of hell she was inhabiting emotionally, on top of hating her job and feeling exhausted from it mentally as well as physically, it occurred to me to worry about her well-being. But I had to hope and to **believe**, (perhaps I was naïve to do so), that our plans to room together as seniors and get back into art would sustain her and keep her from doing anything harmful to herself.

I wrote her back emphasizing that we would figure it all out in mere days when she was back and to KEEP THE FAITH, BABY!

The dejected stab to the heart I felt when she didn't show up that last time only served as a wakeup call that I needed to snap out of the indulgent reverie that was Sari and Cass in Paris. I had a lot of work to do and should jolly well hunker down to doing it! My first set of real exams was coming up pretty fast; they would mark the end of the summer session and we would go on a month's hiatus, which turned out to be even longer since the Sorbonne was not going to open officially until October that year. The French students hadn't really gotten what they wanted yet, but the government was growing uncomfortable under the pressure to not disrupt their entire academic year, which was centrally controlled and rigidly adhered to.

186

July 14, *La Fête Nationale Française* was upon me! We Pella College program participants were unexpectedly invited to a grand celebration at the home of the American Ambassador to France for Bastille Day! The invitations were formal, engraved, sealed with wax and hand-delivered to the program directors at *La Maison*. Nonnie, C.C., Eric, Marty, Taylor and I all planned to go together.

We set off very early in the morning to first watch the parade down the *Champs-Elysées* and the fly-over of the French Air Force jets trailing vapor of *bleu, blanc, rouge*. We even had tickets stamped with De Gaulle's imprimatur to get close to the reviewing stand. I wasn't used to such heavy crowds at all; the *métros* were blocked way before the *Concorde* stop, and we were forced to get out and walk. I was semi-dressed up in my new blue dress, the white bouclé coat, and heels, so maneuvering the sidewalks wasn't that easy. Eric offered me his arm and I gratefully took it. And then all of a sudden, the sky darkened, the clouds opened up and it started to pour rain. No one had brought an umbrella. We were at least fifteen or twenty people deep in back of the crowd by the time we reached the Avenue, but I did get a glimpse of Charles De Gaulle standing up, despite the rain, through the roof of his *Citroën D.S.* limousine.

There must have been thousands of police, the regular *gendarmes* and the CRS, the national semi-military police of France. Every branch of the French armed forces flew over us in something, especially helicopters. There were horsemen dressed in Greek warrior outfits, galloping fast down the street, followed by marching bands, troops, and more dignitaries.

After the parade, we regrouped in a café near the *Rond Point* to dry off before heading up through the leafy treed part of the avenue towards the American Embassy at *2, Avenue Gabriel*.

"Well, that was pretty impressive," Eric stated, as we ordered coffee, and struggled to get dry before presenting ourselves at our Embassy.

"Awfully militaristic, if you ask me," I opined.

"Too much military!" sneered Taylor. "I hate that."

"Well," C. C. said, "De Gaulle is a general, after all."

We had to show our invitations at the heavily guarded gates, and then crossed a graveled courtyard to the actual building entrance. Once inside even though it was our Embassy, it looked more like a French palace. We were ushered into a mammoth room, more like a hall, flanked by Ionic columns with scrolled capitals. The parquet floor was covered by a circular blue and cream Aubusson carpet. A mammoth crystal chandelier hung over the center of the carpet, upon which a round pedestal table stood, and all the rest of the furniture had been swept off to the walls---brown horsehair sofas, a grand piano, some glass and chrome tables...all pushed off so that the crowd of five hundred of us could mingle and also get to the buffet table, which was laden with pastries and fruit, French cheese, caviar canapés and huge baskets of cut-up crusty *baguettes*. The champagne flowed like water and the guests swarmed onto the food table like locusts. This crowd was fairly well-heeled, but still acted like barbarians. I was actually embarrassed for America.

"You'd think these people had never seen a sandwich," Nonnie sniffed.

We did not even get a glance at the Ambassador, Robert Sargent Shriver, Jr. whom I would have died to get to meet; this whole affair seemed to be for ex-pats and other Americans stationed in Paris with their jobs or living in Paris for some other reason, like us lowly students. No one was allowed in without that piece of paper, so there was no risk of tourists who may have heard about it just dropping by.

The six of us stayed together the whole rest of the day; we strolled in the *Jardin des Tuileries* and sat down for a drink in the garden's shaded café. The rain hadn't lasted long at all and didn't start up again, so we were safe to sit on the chairs. We talked about classes, the up-coming exams and the long trip around France we would soon be taking that would span all the major regions we'd just been studying.

"It's going to be a long, loooong bus ride," Marty said unenthusiastically.

"But I can't believe how affordable it is!" I said. "This country really knows how to welcome foreign students." And I was right: The entire cost for us was only sixty francs! All the rest was going to be subsidized by the French government.

C.C. added, "You know the French: learning their language and studying their culture is the highest form of education they can imagine! So they want to roll out the red carpet for anyone doing that."

"I'm all for it," Eric said.

That July 14 was a Sunday and the French population was taking the next day off, too—*faire le pont,* but we were back in class, albeit with a guest lecturer, so the *cours pratiques* were suspended, and all the levels met in the largest classroom to hear about: the contemporary *dictionaire Larousse.* The speaker, from the publishing house by the same name, droned on and on at us for two hours! If we were supposed to be taking notes on all that, it was lost on me; but I liked getting the free books he distributed to all of us.

After lunch we split up again and my section took notes on Clovis, Charles Martel and Charlemagne. My head was swimming and my concentration levels were dangerously low. I went back to the room and slumped down onto my bed. My notes were too rambling to study so I got out some books and redid the material into something intelligible enough to actually learn from. And then I renewed my vow to myself to turn over yet another new leaf and really put my shoulder to the wheel.

Chapter Thirty

"Douce France"...Charles Trenet

The inter-continental mail was as fast as the trans-Atlantic one was slow. Cass had written me from London and the letter only took two days to reach me. She would be in Paris soon, she had assured me in her cheery note, but she had two London circuits to do first; so I wrote her back in London and thought myself quite clever to have a letter waiting for her at the Royal Lancaster Hotel upon arrival.

"I'm struggling," I wrote her, pouring out all my failure fears and fantasies onto the page.

And I **was** struggling. The grammar level I'd been put into might have been the most elementary one, but we were still responsible for the same readings and exams as everyone else. I huddled at my desk with Chateaubriand's *René*, where I made notes in my graph-paper *cahier* on "*la solitude de la nature*" and "*Il pense à se suicider*." The character "René" felt himself to be alone on the planet without family or friends, and, having no one to love, he's overcome with sadness, anguish and troubles. He comes to the realization that man's natural song was melancholy, even when he's expressing happiness. I pondered that for a good long while, wondering if it were really true. Was the heart, as "René" stated, "an incomplete instrument, a lyre missing some strings," which forced even the happiness it felt to be rendered as a sigh?

The passage I was stuck on also evoked autumn, a season, according to the author, that symbolized life in decline. Every description of the countryside where he walked dredged up feelings of solitude and desolation. Even when he described a little country church spire, it wasn't quaint or sweet, it was "*solitaire*" and symbolized exactly that: his solitude and the mystique of his own melancholy. Not only that, it seemed to me that this "*clocher solitaire*" personified was giving him permission to shuffle off these mortal coils himself, and depart the visible domain of the earth! However, the passage ended not with his demise, but with his newly rethought-out *raison d'être*! The clouds into which he stared constantly suddenly seemed to be telling him, "Man, the season of your migration has not yet come. Wait until the winds of death rise up. Then you will lament these flights towards the unknown regions your heart demands."

I had made copious notes on this passage. Certain verbs like *trembler* and *secher* implied an idea of the fragility of nature; I began to understand that his use of adverbs was a testimony to the slowing rhythms which signified abstract ideas like abandonment. Sentences were always flowing eloquently and effortlessly to the movement of his thoughts. I ended up thinking I could actually appreciate this author and that French Lit was going to be pretty damn cool.

But there was so much of it!

Chateaubriand was the first of **twenty-nine** nineteenth-century authors we would be responsible for reading. Prose and poetry! I was sinking in my own despair of ever being able to master this stuff, on top of the "*cours pratiques*" grammar classes, *la phonetique*, plus ten centuries of art history; geography of every region of France, and the plethora of other centuries of literature for which I would also be held accountable! *Dictées* from Proust. *Analyze logique* of Jules Romains' *Knock*. Balzac and Baudelaire! Mauriac and Appolinaire!

It was overwhelming to contemplate all that, and more than once, my heart was in my throat and tears welled up in my eyes, as I pictured the firestorm that would result both at home and back at Iowa U, if I didn't pass this year and get the requisite credit.

This time I was the one dumping depression on Cass when, as promised, she returned to Paris, and we once again roamed around, like the fictional René, combing not the countryside this time, but the city. My exams were looming and afterwards, I was to embark on that month-long bus trip, leaving Cass to come to Paris without me.

"Your letter made me so sad," she said, "that I picked up the phone to call you, but decided it wouldn't do any good, and besides I'd be here soon. And now I am!"

"Well, sorry to have alarmed you," I said. "I got a little carried away over the ramifications of failure."

"But you aren't going to fail!"

"You don't get it; it's **so hard**."

"Sure it's hard! You're now at one of the most prestigious schools in the world, which is just what you wanted instead of little ol' Iowa, if I recall! "

"Okay, okay, I'm with you. I've made my bed and now must lie in it. *(One of Sol's favorite things to growl at me.)* Unless and until they boot me out!"

"Come on. So, all right, maybe at Iowa you didn't have to toe the line as much..."

"Ha!" I interrupted her.

"But you **can** do it! You know the Pella College crew must think you're pretty great or you never would have made the program. So you won't be kicked out; just forget that line of thinking. Your letter was so hyped up that I just thought your mind was going blank on you! You make yourself feel stuck! It's certainly no indication that you can't do the work."

"Thanks for the vote of confidence, Cass, but this isn't just in my head; I'm really scared that I **do** study so hard and yet never seem to get out from under the amount of work expected of us long enough to come up for air. My parents are also making me nuts. My father already thinks I'm on a fast track to failure."

"I understand that this is really really difficult, and I'm sure your parents do, too. Don't think about them now. Don't think about junior year credits or anything else. Just concentrate and focus on the work. You'll pass the first battery of exams. You will remain in the program. You will succeed. You will come back to SUI *(she still used the older term for Iowa before they dropped the "State")* and set it on its ear!"

Where did that pep talk come from? I had to laugh a bit at myself and chide her.

"What ... so now TWA also gives you guys Dale Carnegie courses as well as lessons on how to walk with a tray on a moving aircraft?"

"Ho ho, you wish." And she cuffed me on the shoulder. "Let's go now and resume our mad, gay and exciting times in Paris, and not think about your studies for a few hours. Can you spare it?"

"I've been dreaming of nothing but that for two weeks!"

"You know, I have to pass that little ol' French test of my own in the next few weeks, too."

"We'll rehearse again."

So I spent yet another glorious afternoon and evening walking with my best friend along my favorite city's lovely quays, looking at the *bouquinistes* and getting *glace café* at *Chez Bertillon,* before having another indescribably great dinner at a little place we saw on Ile St. Louis, called *"Le Duc de Richelieu."* We chose a prix-fixe menu consisting of steak-frites and all the usual accompaniments of *salade vinaigrette, camembert* and *tarte Tatin.* To cap it off, we were back on the TWA *per diem,* and Cass had also faithfully brought the usual provisions from the plane, so once again, I was set for days.

My contribution to the festivities this time was a fresh *carnet,* and we took the *métro* all over, including back up to Montmartre where we stopped in a café near her hotel for one last *crème* before she would send me home in yet another taxi, the height of luxury in my Paris student days.

We settled into an old wooden booth with worn leather seats and Cass looked up at me with a gleam of anticipation in her eyes.

"You know, I've had an idea, " she said.

"Yeah? And what might that be?" I asked, only half believing her.

"Okay, so you're about to go on this long trip, right?"

"Right."

"And when you get back, the actual Sorbonne classes start?"

"Yes, if the strike is finished. But I think it will be."

"And then when do you have another break? Christmas?"

"No. We actually get ten days off around November first through Armistice Day."

"Wow! Great! Let's meet in London, in that case. You've never been there, and I'm getting to know it pretty well."

"YES!" I exclaimed with true glee.

"Wait, I'm not done. I mentioned to my parents that I was thinking we could spend Christmas in Amsterdam at the hotel Papa designed – I've stayed there before, it's fab, and Amsterdam is just a heavenly city you'd adore. And then we'd be close enough to go into Germany and look up those doll manufacturers."

"YES!! Oh my god, Cass! Fantastic idea!! I know they will want your dolls. Gee, just think of it! How fun!!"

"Well, that was easy. So London first and then Holland and who knows what!"

"But Cass," I said, suddenly realizing the flaw in all of this, " I get two weeks off at Christmas and you fly back and forth after only a day or two layover."

"I know. First of all, we will settle in the hotel room – it won't be the TWA hotel. I'll ask for a furlough of some sort, like for the holiday or something. I'll work it out. If I do have to leave, you can stay there---I'll pay for it, and then I'll *arrange* to come back...maybe in one day even! It can be done."

"Gee, really?"

"Well, not so you'd know it in Paris, since I can't always get *these* flights, ha! Can I? But I'm getting a bit used to the routine now, and I think by the end of the year, I'll have a tiny bit of time accrued or some such, one way or another, I'll work it out. I can maybe trade with someone else, for that matter."

"If you say so."

"Anyway, you can explore Amsterdam without me if I have to leave. And as for the Germany part, I will try hard to make sure I have some actual days off so I don't get called back on duty at the last minute and have to fly out."

"It all sounds like a dream. London, too. Maybe I can talk Nonnie into coming to London with me. That would be fun, wouldn't it? You could show us both around!"

"You bet! Great idea!"

Cass had been in a really fine mood the whole evening so I assumed either things with Alan Jones were worked out, or maybe they really did break up.

"And we haven't talked about Alan," I ventured, stirring up the foam in my coffee, hoping it would last and last. "Is he still in on the East Coast? "

Her face clouded over. "He is."

"And?! Is it going to work out?"

"I just can't say."

"But, when all is said and done, you really love Alan though?"

"Yes, I do. I do love him. But I still can't seem to reconcile my love and affection for Alan with the horrible future that all that will lead to if I'm cut off from my parents."

"You mean, financially or every way?"

"Every way — but financially, too. I don't deny that I have some money-fueled angst; I don't see myself living like a pauper. But it's hard to argue that there wouldn't be some peace achieved if I just relinquished a future with Alan and concentrated on school and art."

"I think you might be right about that, but it is still hard to flat-out deny love." Even after those words came out of my mouth, I felt a bit embarrassed. "Yeah, but how would I know?"

"Sometimes I find myself just overcome with a longing to be with him, preferably to be married to him rather than not married, but just BE together, going places---in the sense of working towards a future. God, if we could just finish school---working our hearts out---even struggling to make ends meet, I would give the world. I can think of nothing better than being back in Iowa City, getting our degrees, and sharing all that that entails."

I had to admit to feeling a little hurt that she seemed to be painting a picture of Iowa City where she and Alan lived together rather than she and I sharing the planned apartment. But I didn't press her on that, instead saying, "And avoiding the draft, of course."

"The C.O. business is making us both crazy."

"Would marriage help that?"

"Oh that's another part of it! Of course!"

"So why doesn't he WANT to marry you?"

"You know, Sari, the real problem in living with someone like Alan is, that he thinks if you really believe in marriage, fidelity and its potential, so long as you're living with that person and loving her, you

ARE married in every important way but name. But I still think it's important to have the piece of paper too."

We sat there for a few minutes with little else to say on the subject, so I remembered that I had part of the money I owed Cass for my wonderful new dress from her last visit. I took out fifty-five francs from my purse and started to hand it to her, when she pushed my arm away.

"I don't want your money for that dress. Get real. Do I need it? No. Do you need it? Hell, yes. So please...keep it."

"Well, I... owe you so much."

"Not another word about owing me money. Look, Sari, I am sorry to have subjected you to all my ruminations about Alan. It's just that you are the only person in the world with whom I can talk this over. I just love you Sari Shrier, the dearest and best friend a girl could ever have. And I only hope that if you need me to talk to about Soren someday, or for that matter, any of those cute boys at the *Maison*, you'll let me return the favor of lending you a great listening ear, okay?"

"Soren, yeah, that's a laugh. We write letters back and forth like pen pals, not boyfriend/girlfriend."

"Well, maybe that's because you didn't let things really heat up back home, and rightly so. You knew you were leaving for a whole year. That's a long time to keep someone 'in the bank.'"

"You're right. I guess if we were meant to be, the separation will prove it, eh?"

"Exactly. And I'll tell Alan to look him up this fall and keep the ol' home fires of friendship burning!"

"Thanks!"

"You know, come hell or high water, in a year from now I swear, married or not, I will be back in school and if I'm not married, we will absolutely put 'plan A' back in play and share our dreamy little apartment again, just like we said."

Ah, gratitude for that! Followed by my nagging fears coming through again:

"And shit, I hope we're both seniors!"

    *   *   *

July was over and the trip around France looming. I wouldn't be seeing Cass again for a month, and she took advantage of my absence, too, to get herself sent more to London and less to Paris, in anticipation of showing Nonnie and me around there later.

We all took the exams and muttered about their absurdly hard content as we boarded the bus --or coach as they called it. For a month, at least, I would forget about tests and any and all studying, even though, ironically, the bus trip was as educational as any book, and I faithfully wrote letters home to my parents and especially my Nana, chronicling my every activity, every chateau, every cathedral, mountain range and walled village.

We headed south first to the Loire Valley and marveled at the Renaissance works of art that were Chambord, Chenonceau, Cheverny, Azay-le-Rideau, Amboise, Villandry with the amazing kitchen gardens; Saumur, Sully Sur Loire (with the sweetest outdoor market I had ever seen to date); and Blois--- the gorgeous jewel town of Blois. We spent the night there in an ancient hotel with feather bedding and antique furniture. That evening we were served a scrumptious meal of vegetable soup, goose in wine sauce with mushrooms and fries, cheese and ice cream with the *de rigeur crème Chantilly* on top, the origins of which we had learned AT the *Chateau de Chantilly* just the day before! And in the morning before we had to leave, the elderly lady in charge of the dining room served our group hot chocolate in individual porcelain *chocolatières* that was so homemade from scratch, it made what we had at the dorm seem ersatz (which is wasn't). I had never tasted such divine velvety chocolate sliding down my throat. The croissants were huge, flakey, brown and crisp on the outside and soft layers on the inside. There were also baskets of crunchy *baguettes, confiture de Chambord* and pots of Normandy butter. Eating that breakfast was as close to an orgasmic experience as I'd had in my life at that point.

Our Loire tour was richly dense with both Renaissance and feudal castles: Angers and Chinon with all their Joan of Arc history; Chateaudun, and even some private ones. We didn't have to take notes, but since touring the Loire Valley is like a short course in French history, I did write down a fair amount of information at each place.

192

We used Tours as our base camp and bunked at the *Insitut de Touraine*, which was a school under the auspices of the *Université François Rabelais*, for mostly foreign students who come from all over the world to learn French in the region that was said to have the purest language and accent. We didn't even sit in on classes, just stayed in their dorms; but the place **looked** impressive, and there must have been two dozen or so students milling about after breakfast waiting to go to class, speaking every language one could imagine. Tours had a nice pedestrian mall part of the town center where we went after dinner and listened to---what else---jazz. Taylor was in his element.

At the end of a nice afternoon that had culminated in free time in the beautiful flower-lined streets of Orléans, our coach left the *Centre* region and headed west towards La Rochelle, and thence on down to the Dordogne, where we saw the original caves of Lascaux, before they were closed to the public and replaced by replica caves built next to the real ones. We were astounded at the cave art, the dwellings themselves, and the story of how the whole thing was discovered in the first place in 1940 when some kid's dog purportedly fell into a hole and when its owner, Marcel Ravidat, went to find it, he saw he was in some sort of shaft leading into a cave.

As this boy wandered further into the tunnel, he found himself in a "room" with astonishing paintings on the walls of larger-than-life animals, which seemed to be moving. Marcel told three other friends about what he had discovered. The boys had all decided to keep their find a secret but the news spread, and they ended up consulting the school master of their little village of Montignac, Leon Laval, who was a member of the local prehistory society. Laval at first thought they were trying to play a trick on him. However, when he saw the walls, he immediately felt sure that they were prehistoric and insisted no one be allowed to touch them or vandalize them in any way. The youngest of the boys, 14-year-old Jacques Marsal, persuaded his parents to let him pitch a tent near the entrance to keep guard and show visitors round. It was the start of a commitment to the paintings which lasted to his death in 1989.

Word of the discovery reached an eminent pre-historian, Abbé Breuil, who vouched for the paintings' authenticity. The news spread through Europe and the rest of the world, and in 1948, the family that owned the land organized daily tours that eventually brought thousands of visitors every year to see for themselves.

From the Dordogne, we headed over to Arcachon with its cute town center, the huge sand dunes and lovely beach. For a land-locked Iowan like me, being at the ocean was like experiencing a re-birth in the presence of God Himself. During this trip, we got to lay on the beaches of the Atlantic in the resort towns of Biarritz and St. Jean-de-Luz before heading on. As I marveled more and more with every beach, an older woman in our group, one of the grad students, chided me with "Haven't you ever been to Jones Beach or Miami?"

"Nope."

The itinerary continued to Pau and over to the walled city of Carcassonne in the region of Languedoc-Roussillon where we had free time, and Eric and I explored the fortified town restored in the 1800's by the now familiar to us name of Viollet -Le -Duc. On the coach, one of the directors had given a little talk about how Carcassonne was the first fortress to use hoardings in times of siege. Temporary wooden ramparts would be fitted to the upper walls of the fortress to provide protection to defenders on the wall and to allow them to go out past the wall to drop projectiles on attackers of the wall beneath. It was famous in legend as well as history, and Eric and I set about to discover the *cité*, as well as look for a nice café to eat in and some good ice cream after that.

For the actual start to the visit to the south of France, with Provence, and the Côte d'Azur, we were housed for a week in the university town of Narbonne and put up in their dorms, which made our own dorm seem like the Ritz.

God, was it awful!! Just one big hall with beds lined up "Madeline-style" in two straight lines, but without a sweet Miss Clavel overseeing everything. The mattresses were hard as tack; towels were like sandpaper, and toilet paper was meted out in little squares of brown tissue that tore up before you could really use them to do the job. The showers were also communal but at least not co-ed, and the water was never hot. There were no armoires, no cubby holes for our clothes, so everyone just kept their suitcase on top of the bed and hoped nothing would be stolen while we were out, as we were not the only people using this place as a make-shift youth hostel.

Since we were going to be there for a period of time and because being on the beach was the highlight of that stay, I went to a sort of primitive supermarket and bought a beach towel that was so big and soft, compared to the towels we'd been given, I used it for everything. I was attracted to it because it was the color combination I dearly loved: blue and white. But by the time we got to Marseilles and points farther east on the actual Riviera, I realized that without even knowing it, I'd purchased a towel in the replica print of the *Maison Souleiado*, the iconic Provençal manufacturer of household fabrics, bed linens, clothing, cloth bags, table linens, and décor that is one of, if not **the**, symbol of the good life in the South of France.

Narbonne was the jumping-off place for us to take day trips around to places like the Camargue with France's version of cowboys, which was also a sanctioned gypsy encampment locale. We also toured the famous Provençal attractions of Nîmes, Arles, and Avignon between long stretches of free time at the water's edge on Narbonne's *Plage*.

Once we left Provence we headed to Marseille *en route* to the actual Côte d'Azur. Having been a big fan of the movie *Fanny* with Leslie Caron and Horst Buchholz, Charles Boyer and Maurice Chevalier, I was only too happy to be in its city. The theme music started playing in my head the moment the bus pulled us up to the Old Port. We didn't stay in the city but we had a day there---not long enough but a taste. Some kids already knew what *bouillabaisse* was and ordered it in some iconic port restaurants. I had no idea what that was, but there was enough shrimp to keep me happy. We walked up all the steps to the beautiful Byzantine looking basilica *Notre Dame de la Garde* towering over the Old Port, and we entered the grand portals to gawk at the mosaic splendor of the walls and ceiling. I marveled at what it must have been like to march down the aisle of that church in a wedding procession!

Our bus took a route right through massive fields of lavender and mustard seed, the views of which out our windows and the scents wafting into the bus made me think we'd been lifted up and transported to some other planet, or maybe Heaven. We took this scenic wonderland route to the next stop, which was Nice, and another dorm, much nicer than Narbonne, thank God.

There were lots of things to do and see in that town, among which were the fabulous Chagall and the newer Matisse museums and the chapel Matisse had designed for some nun friends, (one in particular). The town had been the favorite winter watering-hole of the Russian aristocracy, so a Russian Orthodox church rose high on a promontory overlooking the city. I found its onion domes odd for France, although truth be told, the Marseille basilica had something similar. Nice was so beautiful with pastel buildings of adobe and stucco, houses with flowering courtyards, and shops selling lavender tied up with string to take home and perfume one's entire existence. We were staying close to the Place Massena and the flower market, so Eric and I took a stroll through there. I was enthralled with bougainvillea, though I had no idea what it was called.

As usual, the thing everyone really wanted to do most was get to the Mediterranean. And there was something even more special—that *cachet*-- about being on the beach on the French Riviera that no one wanted to miss. However, some of our group had been there before and warned us that the beach in Nice was not sand, but rocks! People who could afford it paid to go into the fenced-off private beach "clubs," where one could sit on *chaises-longues* under umbrellas with tables in between the chairs, order food to be brought to them and not worry about leaving their belongings if they wanted to take a swim in the sea. "Joining" one of these was $10 for the whole day, and I thought that was high, but I did it anyway. I loved every second I spent there, listening to the most beautiful music provided free from Mother Nature: the lapping of waves as the tide rolled in and out. This was, again, a soothing sound never ever heard in Iowa.

But some of our group did not want to pay or lie on rocks. They wanted to hitch-hike over to Cannes and the white sand beaches reminiscent of Miami Beach. That was too daring for me, but Nonnie and C.C. hitched with Marty. Eric came with me to Blue Beach on the *Promenade des Anglais*, and Taylor who really thumbed his nose at paying for any beaches, spread his towel out on the rocks just on the other side of our fence. We could carry on a conversation with him if we screamed.

One thing I couldn't believe was how many women went topless on French beaches. You didn't have to be on a designated beach for topless either; any beach would do. And we were not talking all Brigitte Bardots either. Women my Nana's age were un-self-consciously parading around sagging all over the place as though that was the most normal thing in the world. *(It was also absolutely fine and normal for little girls to not wear any tops at all for swimming; just the bottoms of what would have been a two-piece suit. This was, I found out, the same all over Europe. At some point I was taking slides of the water, and some of those ladies got in my pictures. A year later showing them at home, my mother would call out, "Where WERE you?")*

Soon our bus was climbing out of the Alps foothills and on towards Grenoble. This time, heading through the *Gorges du Tarn*, I kept gasping at the dizzying heights, hairpin curves and steep drop-offs to the valleys below.

"Wait, don't tell me," snickered the same grad student who had accosted me over the Atlantic beaches, "you've never been to Colorado."

"Nope."

Grenoble was another university town with wonderful accommodations for us in their dorms. Every view of the town from the bus windows or the dorm windows or the street level was more picture-postcard looking than the next. The Alps formed the scenic backdrop, but actually the town itself was flat, so we could walk everywhere without effort; rent bicycles and ride around easily; and otherwise just be tourists and enjoy the charm and bustle of the place that was already in preparations that summer of 1968 to host the winter Olympic Games. Because of the university's dominance over the life of the city, there were plenty of bars and *boites* to keep us happy in the late evening, which, unlike Nice and certainly Cannes, were inexpensive and geared to students. Some of the bartenders spoke English to us when they heard we were Americans. That was a first!

We stayed two nights in Grenoble and during the daytime toured the ski resorts that would soon be overcome with throngs of athletes and spectators: Mégève, Chamonix, Courcheval. We drove into Annecy, also, which seemed to me to be the prettiest little town I had seen to date.

It was still high summer, but the trip's turn into the mountains and the alpine towns made for a cool, green change to the scenery. I also saw village names go by like Évian, Vittel and Volvic and I wrote my letters home exclaiming that suddenly I understood where the bottled water I bought at Inno really did come from: the natural springs in actual places! And not only that, lo and behold, they were also spas, which, for some reason, had never occurred to me! French people came from far and wide to "take the cure" at these towns and if a doctor prescribed it, they didn't have to pay; it was covered under their "*sécurité sociale*"!

Our tour took us by-- but not into-- Lyon, which I thought was kind of sad. I certainly wanted to see a city with not one but two rivers dividing it, and also even though Julia Child was not yet a household name in America, we certainly knew about the culinary prowess of Lyon. JFK's press secretary, Pierre Salinger, would go on to do a many-episode feature on French chefs called "Dining in France," which portrayed him eating and drinking his way from Paris to the Riviera, with a heavy emphasis on the Lyon area. There he interviewed well-known chefs and showed Americans how the brigaded kitchens of the famous French restaurants hummed with activity. Salinger's show was to be a few years off yet when I was in France; still we knew Lyon was home to many famous cooking schools. Nonnie had already signed up for cooking lessons back in Paris at none other than the famous Cordon Bleu school, and I intended to accompany her and watch---if they'd let me.

But rather than stop in Lyon, we made our way into the region of Burgundy to Beaune and the famous "*Hospices*" a medieval hospital or *Hôtel Dieu*, with the most famous glazed, multi-colored tiled roof maybe in the world, certainly in France. The flamboyant Gothic architecture and the amazing display of medical---or more like torture—instruments inside were fascinating, but lent themselves rather well to imagining horror stories. Curtained-off four-poster beds were aligned down each side of the Great Hall, with its wooden vaulted roof built to look like the hull of a ship. There was a chapel at the end of the room with a polyptych representing the Last Judgment. It was painted by a Flemish painter I'd never heard of, Roger Van de Weyden. Our guide told us that patients could not see it except on Sundays and feast days. We also visited the kitchen, the pharmacy and the dispensary where an assortment of terror-inducing implements was on display in glass cases.

We had been on the road for twenty-five days at that point and my wardrobe possibilities were running dangerously low. In Beaune the calendar said August but the temperature said mid-October to me; I pulled out some knee socks that I had thrown into my suitcase and I was glad I did. I put on an orange pleated mini skirt, with a white long, flowing-sleeved "peasant" blouse, the white knee socks, black flats and my trench coat! It was my "dressy" outfit, but it did the trick in the cool weather.

Our last four days were to be in Normandy, and the route there took us west again, though the region of Champagne and an overnight stop in Reims, which, if unknown to me for champagne, was certainly on my radar of French history and the crowning of all the kings. That is where Joan of Arc had insisted the *Dauphin* be crowned-- at Reims Cathedral-- to verify and authenticate his throne. Reims was yet another picturesque little *bijou* of a town, with many "*caves*" where one could taste the sparkling bubbles that had induced Dom Perignon, a blind monk, to exclaim that he had "tasted the stars."

We got our own private tours of several wineries specializing in champagne, along with stories about its discovery and the differentiation between true champagne and other sparkling wines. Everyone bought bottles to take back to Paris and maybe even home to family. I bought one at the Charles Heidsieck cellars right in Reims that was *brut rosé*: pink champagne. I decided to give it to Sol and Betty for letting me come on this most magnificent year-long adventure. And I hoped with all my might that when I got back, we'd be celebrating my diploma attainment.

Our route to Normandy went through the town of Beauvais and on to Rouen. More Joan of Arc history galore. And Flaubert. And the famous Monet-painted cathedral. And the *Gros Horloge*, clock tower bridge. I could now see why the University of Iowa chose this quaint and beautiful locale as their study abroad headquarters, but I was still happy I went on the program that headquartered in Paris.

Rouen held a sway over me that still remains. For one thing, the iconic half-timbered architecture of the Norman region was first introduced to me there; and I loved it. Normandy became my favorite French region of all, and it started in Rouen.

We spent the night there in an actual hotel--wonderfully ancient with 14th century timber framing (14th century!!!) and full of history and culture. The lobby was more like a parlor and the dining room like a real dining room in a Tudor manor house. Since Rouen surrendered to Henry V of England during the 100 Years War, its English "look" was not by happenstance: Rouen was the capital of English power in occupied France.

It was the Duke of Bedford, John of Lancaster, who despised Joan of Arc and planned to destroy her. He had bought her from the Duke of Burgundy, thus freeing her from the jail where she'd been kept since May of 1430, only to put her on trial in Normandy. Her trial, which took place in Rouen under the auspices of the Church, was all orchestrated and financed by Bedford, who was in control of the entire proceedings; and she was sentenced to be burned at the stake there, which happened on May 30, 1431.

Rouen stayed English until 1449, when the Valois King Charles VII recaptured it, eighteen years after the death of Joan, and after thirty years of English occupation. That was the same year the young Henry VI was crowned King of England and France in Paris before coming to Rouen, where he was acclaimed by the crowds.

Our group tours included Flaubert's birthplace, which was an apartment in a hospital where his father practiced medicine. The whole place was turned into a museum; and same thing for Pierre Corneille's house. There would be many nights when I was reading *Le Cid*, and thinking back on Corneille living in Rouen, going to law school but wanting to be a writer and eventually, but while still young, moving to Paris.

Rouen's fine arts museum was a must for our group, as many of us were about to embark on a study of French art history. This museum had been established in 1801 by Napoleon I, and rebuilt in 1880. It held a collection that took my breath away with my first steps inside. I wrote Cass all about it: and hoped she'd one day be able to go back there with me.

"We always knew that Rouen was put on the Impressionism map by Monet et al., and this museum has so many of their works!! I wonder why Klampert never actually mentioned this collection? It has the original "Inondation à Port-Marly" by Sisley, and I'm sure he showed that slide. It also has Monet's "Rue St.- Denis" and of course, we've seen that a million times in books! This little museum also has a good representation of non-Impressionists, like Gericault, Modigliani, whom I adore, and David, Ingrès and Delacroix, for heaven's sake! I hope you'll be able one day to come here with me."

When I was a student in France that year, and we went to Rouen, we could visit the Place du Vieux Marché *where Joan of Arc's funeral pyre had been set up, but that was all. There was no monument to St. Joan. So on subsequent trips back to Normandy years later, over the course of my visits to my grandchildren, it surprised me that in the center of the Place du Vieux Marché, they put up a very modern church of St. Joan of Arc as her memorial. Dedicated in 1979, the form of the building is supposed to represent an upturned Viking boat and a fish shape.*

We left Rouen and headed for Deauville and Trouville, Honfleur and Cabourg. We were tracing the path of the Impressionist artists and some of the scenes, such as the beach in Cabourg, were as familiar to me as if I'd lived there, thanks to all the paintings I had already studied at Iowa.

And Cabourg held an even more special treat, as the Grand Hotel there was the actual place where Marcel Proust wrote parts of *À la recherche du temps perdu*. Luckily for me, we only had to read parts of his magnum opus for our exams, although I would absolutely plow through all of it once back in Iowa City. But some of the most famous passages were composed in that hotel! Cabourg was Proust's favorite vacation spot and he is thought to have modeled the seaside resort of "Balbec" in his book after Cabourg. I really wanted to see room 414, which was his room, they told us; it had been restored and decorated in period furniture, but we were not allowed in there. Proust sojourned there from the year it opened, 1907, until 1914, when the whole place was converted into a World War I hospital. Our guide did give each of us a postcard with a nice picture of the room showing just a hint of the view out the window and a quote from *À l'ombre des jeunes filles en fleurs*-- In the Shadow of Young Girls in Flower-- from a passage where he describes coming back to the room and watching a ship out the window, and being surrounded on all sides by images of the sea.

Jo Jo, of all people, caught up with me as we were exiting to go out onto the beach promenade.

"That translation is just gobbledygook," she said, pouting. "Don't you think?"

"Like I would know," I answered. I hadn't read many excerpts from Proust yet.

"Well, look, 'young girls in flower' –singular in the translation; plural in the original French. I don't get whether we're supposed to believe he means girls on the verge of blossoming into women, or girls wearing flowers---like in their hair?"

"You know," I answered, "it beats me. But from what I've already heard in various classes and read in articles, Marcel Proust is considered to be the finest writer of the 20th century in any language of any country or culture. So speaking only for myself, I am absolutely awed to be 'in his presence' so to speak. What about you?"

"I guess."

Oh Jo Jo. If only I had studied Proust by the time we had this conversation. How I would have gone on! His description of a dinner party could take one hundred pages, but at the end you have a perfect microcosm of the demise of the upper classes. How I would have billed and cooed at his use of humor on page after page-- dark humor, hidden humor, biting humor. He wrote a million words triggered by the bite of a tiny cake "dipped into [a] cup of tea or tisane."

None other than a writer of almost equal fame, Vladimir Nabokov, considered Proust's work the best novel of its era, describing its major themes and " effervescent, Mozartean style:" He said, "The transmutation of sensation into sentiment, the ebb and tide of memory, waves of emotions such as desire, jealousy and artistic euphoria---this is the material of this enormous and yet singularly light and translucent work." Remembrance of Things Past is rarely taught in its entirety in any university classes; it has not been kept alive by the academy. It is the readers themselves, all over the world, who keep it in prominence, reading and rereading it.

We finished off our whirlwind tour of France with the American cemetery on Omaha Beach, near St. Laurent, the Bayeux Tapestry in a too- short stay at that wonderful town; and then a final stop at Mont St. Michel. And, finally, after dinner in a great little café bistro on the only street on "the rock", sometime after ten o'clock at night, on August 31, 1968, thirty American students climbed back aboard the coach that had taken us all over France, and that would now drive us back on the darkened *autoroute*, back to Paris, avoiding as many *embouteillages*---traffic jams-- as we could. Countless other Parisians were also heading home that night for *la rentrée*, the great migration back to schools taking place all over the country.

Most of us fell right to sleep on the bus, completely exhausted after all that sight-seeing, hurried as it was at the end. The next day upon arrival we would have to face our exam grades, me with trepidation and abject fear; and then gear up for the real start of classes at La Sorbonne.

IF we were staying.

Chapter Thirty-One

Prélude de l'Après-Midi d'un Faun...Claude Debussy

Cass was the first person I wrote when I got the news.

"I squeaked by on the exams! I guess I won't ever complain about the American system again, since here none of the grades I got during the first term of class counted for anything; just the tests. And if you flunk even one of the 6 parts, you fail it all! No pressure, huh?! Luckily I scored high enough to pass them all. Whew."

I also let my parents know that I passed the exams, without sharing with them the fears I had before I knew the results, remaining upbeat and optimistic and all with them. The less they knew, other than the desired result, the better. *Voilà*, the autumn term would soon be in full swing.

And I also wrote Soren. He and I had been faithful correspondents, all through the summer, but his return letters left a lot to be desired. For one thing, like I told Cass, he was quite perfunctory in his communications. *Hi, how are you* and not much else. He didn't talk about his summer jobs—he was home in the summer of '68 working in the law offices. He didn't talk about his summer activities outside work, even though I knew they had a house on Spirit Lake straight up Highway 71 from Imogene-- on the Iowa Great Lakes-- complete with boats for water skiing and cruising around. I imagined him there with some summer crowd of kids who all knew each other from childhood and who all spent lots of time up there together. But he didn't actually report any such thing. He asked me a lot of questions about France and what I was seeing when out on tour; he wanted to know about my classes, and he talked a little bit about the prospects for The Hawks in the fall for football and in the winter for basketball. Mostly he said he was busy sending around sample reviews on music groups that came through the area, and had even gone over to Omaha to see the band Steppenwolf, which he proclaimed had the potential for greatness and was "solid" and wonderful.

I duly wrote back and answered all his questions and more, hoping not to seem like a travelogue, and to whet his appetite for coming over there and traveling with me in June, which, by the way, he never mentioned again. I wondered what was up but decided to let it ride for a while. I'd only been in Europe two months; it was way too early to think about next summer.

Everything changed for French students at "*la rentrée*", and likewise for us. First off, we were assigned different rooms in the *maison* with our much-anticipated French roommates, and had to go through the huge production of packing all our stuff up and moving into the new digs. We were all anticipating really being able to improve our French by having roommates who ostensibly did not speak any English (but of course that was hard to come by since French kids start English in elementary school). Hard as we tried and vowed to not speak English with each other in our old rooms, it had just come out anyway most of the time. Now there would be no excuse and no enabling!

My French roommate was Agathe Picard from a town near Chartres, too far away to be considered a Paris suburb, but at least commuting distance at any rate. She admitted to me that she didn't really want to go home on Fridays, but told me she would often be obliged to pay weekly visits to an elderly aunt who lived in another part of Paris. She also said she had an older sister working in Paris and they both spent almost every weekend "*chez notre tante*." Agathe was a small girl, looked and acted young for her age. She had short auburn hair, freckles, and a tiny bow mouth. She was nice (yay!) and didn't seem too surprised that she got an American roommate, *(but nine months later I was to find out that she had written in her journal exasperated over having to room with an American who didn't speak French, and whatever was she going to do?! She had decided to show it to me at the end of our time together because she was rather astounded at the progress I had made by May of 1969)*. Agathe was majoring in Italian and she had had a fair amount of English in school, too. I dare say she improved in English that year; not as much as my French took hold, though.

The first thing she wanted me to do was to teach her all our swear words and anything dirty. She knew the word "fuck" and wanted to use it as a noun, verb, adjective and adverb. I assured her that polite people didn't even use that word, but then, of course, that was a lie.

What she really wanted to know, however were the lyrics to *The House of the Rising Sun,* which she claimed to be able to play on the guitar she'd brought to college with her.

"*Qu'est-ce que c'est ce* '**tailor**?'" she asked looking up perplexed from the paper where I'd written out the lyrics.

"*Tailleur.*"

"*Ah! Alors,* '**sew**' *c'est coudre?*"

"*Oui.*"

Our new room was nicer than my old one with Jo Jo, for some reason. In America, rooms of a residence dorm or even a hotel are generally uniform, with certain exceptions like "the corner office" status or our Kate Daum room with its own private bathroom. But in France, you never knew what was going to be the accommodation; and that could be kind of refreshing, really. Hotel rooms, for instance, were often different because the buildings were converted *"hôtels particuliers"* or mansions . Some bedrooms in the previous manor house might have had fireplaces; some might have been sitting rooms of an apartment in there; one never knew. In the *maison des étudiantes,* it wasn't until I saw some of the rooms of my friends that I realized their rooms could be three times bigger than mine, or have wallpaper or built-in shelving! My new room did have shelves tucked into niches, and we had really nice armoires this time. The best thing about it, though, was that it was on a higher floor so that now when I looked out the open window facing west, I could actually see a tiny part of the Eiffel Tower peeking out from among the roof tops and chimneys! Plus our room was "in the trees", too. I loved its cozy nesty feeling.

Though the French students could not yet enter the Sorbonne, even on the day of the official national *rentrée,* our foreign student classes continued not only at the *Maison* but also at various other "borrowed" lecture halls and in one particular other building over by the bookstore *Shakespeare and Company.* This time the hours were all different, and when the strikes were officially over and regular sessions finally began in October, we didn't have class at the *Maison* anymore. That was kind of sad, really, and the convenience was, of course, over with, too.

Every week I had four lecture courses at two Pella College credit hours per class, and one "*cours pratique*" worth eight credit hours. The lectures lasted one to two hours each, four days per week, and the *cours pratique* classes were given for two hours **every day except Sunday**! Were they insane??! On Mondays I had XVIIth century French Lit from 10:00a.m. until noon, and the grammar class from 3:00 -5:00 p.m., also on every other day including Saturday. If that didn't mess up a weekend, I didn't know what could! On Tuesday for some reason I only had one shorter lecture course: art history, which I had from noon until 1:00; Wednesday started with geography from 8:00 until 10:00, followed by XVIIIth century Lit from 10:00 until noon, and more art from noon until 1:00. Regular French schools in those days tended to have Wednesdays off, but for us it was Thursday, when we did not have anything except the *cours pratique.* I had all my lecture classes in the famous Richelieu hall of the Sorbonne, once it opened back up.

I wrote to Cass explaining my new routine.

"Note that my *derrière* is paralyzed from sitting five hours! We are captives in there; the professors change! Luckily we can bring bottled water to the lecture hall. But I'm always starving."

Cass wrote back that her flight schedules had been "pretty messed up" with her being routed to Frankfurt more than any place else. But then she announced that she had passed her little French test and that she was promised more and more flights to Paris. I cut out an ad from the *Herald- Tribune* (another little splurge I indulged in) showing a perky stewardess in a chic Pierre Cardin uniform beckoning the readers to "Come fly with me… to Paris!", blocked out the **Air France** and scrawled **TWA** across it, and sent it to her at the Intercontinental in Germany.

200

France is on a surprisingly northern latitude and longitude, so when September really hit, it felt like fall, and what was more wonderful, it looked like fall. Paris could put on a coat of autumnal coloration to rival any other place in the world. Trees in the Luxembourg Gardens, through which I walked every day to and from the Latin Quarter, were as "*vêtu de broderie*" as the Charles d'Orléans poem described (only he was talking about Spring, so one could surmise every season in France was beautiful); the plane trees, all sculpted into the same square form and height showed their yellow and orange leaves among the green in the dappled light. My garden walks were on carpets of velvety scarlet leaves that reflected the bright, early morning sunlight hitting them. The *maison* also had a crawling grape vine that turned bright red-orange in September, decorating our wall as it creeped past the window of Room 48, putting me in a school mood for sure.

I settled into my study routine and, much as I couldn't really calm down because of the looming February battery of exams I would soon have to pass again, at least I vowed and rededicated myself to doing a better job of keeping my head above water this term. It still wasn't going to be easy.

When we were reading *Le Cid*, I saw in my *Pariscope* that it was playing at the *Comédie Française* and asked Eric to go with me.

"That's actually a brilliant idea," he said. "Sometimes plays are easier to see and hear than merely read."

"That's what I was thinking!"

So we made a date of it and I wore one of the very few really dressy things I'd brought with me: a beige and gold empire waist "trapeze" float mini-dress, gold mesh stockings, and black heels. I tied my hair, which was really growing long by now, with a black velvet ribbon and wore some gold jewelry. The dress had sleeves and since it wasn't too late in the season yet, I didn't need a wrap.

I thought being dressed up in the *métro* was stupid, singled you out for pickpockets, and just made it look like you couldn't afford a car or to take a taxi, which was true! But there was nothing we could do about it; we had to go over to the *Palais Royal* stop and I wasn't about to walk in high heels.

We had dinner on *Rue de Rivoli* and even though we went Dutch, it still felt like a real date. The restaurant was on the "*étage*," or upstairs, of a café called *Le Bon Boucheron* and the *prix fixe* menu was just the perfect thing: for a starter I had something completely different and simply amazing: half an avocado filled with seafood salad. *Mon Dieu!* It even surpassed *oeufs durs mayonnaise* as my number one fave rave. The *plat principal* that night was *boeuf bourguignon*, so tender and delicious with mushrooms and pearl onions, I nearly swooned. And dessert that I could have easily skipped, but of course, did not: *tarte aux pommes avec de la crème Chantilly*, exactly as it always was over there: scrumptious. I left the restaurant hoping not to fall asleep in the show.

Eric and I really enjoyed being in that venerated theater, the floors of which could have also been trod upon by Molière! It gave me chills. We had the cheapest tickets because the student prices were very low, but the seats were not half bad, up high in the balcony; and I preferred that since I could see everything below.

"I think that really did help me understand the play," I told Eric as we exited towards the *métro* right across the square.

He smiled at me. His French was far superior to mine but he concurred, "That was just the ticket. It will be far easier to follow the action now."

To my surprise, Eric got off with me at the *Vavin* station and walked me back to *La Maison*, which he certainly did not have to do. He was polite and caring, I remember thinking, and an all-around good guy. Like Soren, for that matter.

"This was really fun tonight," Eric told me as we stopped in front of the gate to *La Maison des Étudiantes*. "I can't do it too often, of course, with the budget I'm on. But once in a while…"

"I know. Me, too."

We didn't kiss good night, but we did what all French people do and gave each other *la bise*.

"I'm sorry you got out of the train and now have to use another entry on your *carte orange* to go back."

"Who cares? It doesn't matter at all; you know that."

"Well, it was nice of you anyway. Thanks."

"I think I'm just going to walk back from here actually."

"All the way to the *Cité Universitaire*?!" I couldn't believe that.

"It's not that far."

"Yes it is! God, it's four long *métro* stops from here!"

He laughed, taking off, and called out back to me, "*Bonne nuit, dors bien.*"

Crazy, I thought.

Soon Cass wrote, saying she would be coming back to Paris, having straightened out the Frankfurt mess.

"Some other stew had insisted she needed to be on a route through Italy, so they bumped me to Germany! It was all goofy," she said in the note.

Now she was set to fly to London, Paris and only once in a while Frankfurt. Since my own schedule was as stupid as could be with that grammar class clogging up the whole afternoon until five p.m., the best days for her to show up were Thursday and Sunday, which rarely happened, until: one weekend in September, she arrived on a Friday night! We agreed to meet when I got out of class around 6:00 p.m., at that same bench outside the *Charles De Gaulle-Étoile métro* entry on the *Champs-Élysées*, where we had rendezvoused before.

When I came panting off the escalator, she announced that she miraculously had a lay-over until Monday morning!

"Are you joking?!! That's *wunderbar*!!"

"And *très bien*, too!" she affirmed. And then she made like she had a big announcement for me. "I've brought you a present! We'll call it a **token congrats on your exam!**"

"Oh, gee, like I deserve another one after dresses and purses and food!"

"Let's go to Pub Renault again. It's close to here. We're early for dinner in Paris but we can snack there."

It was a great idea. I'd taken her there previously and we just got a kick out of sitting on antique car seats made into booths. It was a perfect place to talk. At seven o'clock in low-season, even if it were touristy and even if this were the Champs-Élysées, we had no problem being ushered to a spot and having menus placed before us.

"I'm having onion soup," she announced.

There was no bad onion soup in Paris in those days. Nothing was prefabricated, pressed, reconstituted or fake. But I made a mental note to take her to the Au Pied de Cochon *in Les Halles one of the times she was there for the best and most famous* soupe à l'oignon gratinée *in Paris.*

"*Deux gratinées, s'il vous plaît,* " I responded to the waiter asking us "*Qu'est- ce que je vous sers Mesdemoiselles?*"

"*C'est tout?*" he asked rather dejectedly.

I looked at Cass. "It's a whole meal for me," I said, "but what else would you like?"

"Nothing!"

"*Oui, pour l'instant, merci, Monsieur. Oh- une carafe d'eau fraîche peut-être?*"

"*Tout de suite.*"

Cass pulled an oblong package out of her tote bag. It was smaller than a shoebox but bigger than a box something like jewelry would come in. I didn't have an idea in hell what it could be.

"For you," she said lifting it up and replacing it in front of me.

I opened it up and found to my astonishment that it was a radio! A portable radio in a red leather case with a handle on it.

"Oh, a transistor radio?! Thank you!! I love it!!!"

"Ho! Not only a radio. Look on top under the carrier."

I took off the leather protector and saw that at the top were buttons that indicated it also played a cassette! And sure enough, the front slowly opened when I pushed down on "open".

"Wow! Unbelievable, Cass!! This is soooo perfect. I just can't thank you enough."

"And, what's a cassette player if you don't have a cassette, soooo," she cooed, reaching down into her tote, " here is one!"

"Oh my GOD!" I took it from her and instantly recognized the pink cover that mimicked the L.p. of *Un Homme et Une Femme*. "NO! Wherever did you find THIS?"

"Oh, I have my ways. When we're in London, I'll take you to where I bought it."

Also inside the box was a pair of the ear buds of that era, the kind we all already knew about for use with little transistor radios.

"You can listen to Radio Luxembourg, Sari, and not bother your roomie."

"Yes, good to know. I don't think Agathe would care, though! Jo Jo would have had a snit fit."

"So how is Agathe?"

"Listen, you'll have to meet her! She's sort of a hoot."

"Do you think I can visit some classes with you---how about the Saturday one? You know, I got really sad and depressed this month when I realized that school was starting in Iowa City and I was in Boston being a fakey stewardess. "

"Just one more year and **we'll be back, baby!**"

"Yeah! And I want you to know that the little speech you taught me probably did the trick with *my* French test. I'm sure my vocabulary and accent are both horrendous, but that little intro sounded good! So thank you again." Her voice trailed off.

"I'm happy if I helped you get to stay on the Paris routes, I'll say that! And I did talk to Nonnie, by the way, about coming to London. She's up for it!"

"Okay, get this. You can fly over there for really cheap! Not on TWA, of course, but there are student travel agencies and they can get you on flights for like ten dollars! So try that!"

"Okay, we will. I know several store-front places in the Latin Quarter that seem to be student travel spots. And there are lots of agencies on the street by American Express, too. I go by them every month when I'm over there collecting my check from home and cashing it."

We finished up our soup and ordered an ice cream extravaganza, as I called them, to share for dessert. It was really the perfect meal. We walked all the way down the *Champs-Élysées* and were heading towards the *métro* at *Champs-Élysées Clemenceau* which was direct via *direction Chatillon-Montrouge* to *Edgar Quinet*. I loved taking direct routes that avoided *correspondence* at *Concorde*, *Chatelet* or *Montparnasse-Bienvenue*, which were all huge stations you had to walk miles in and be vulnerable to getting "bothered" by low-lifes who would reach out to touch women and girls with no shame or self-control at all! I had learned that the hard way.

Cass seemed impressed with my take-charge knowledge of the system and was happy to accompany me back to the *Maison*.

"Maybe some of the other kids are there," I said. "But my roommate won't be; she goes home most of the time...or to her Auntie's house on the other side of Paris."

"So, then, what would be the chance of your just signing out until Sunday night? What if your— uh—cousins were in town and wanted you to stay with them?"

"Hmmm, I see what you mean! YES! Cass you are brilliant!"

So that is what we pulled off. No one thought a thing about it. I carefully put the food provisions she'd brought me in my armoire for later; put the new radio on my desk in a place of honor. I changed into my orange mini skirt and the white blouse --without the knee socks this time-- packed up some more clothes and toiletries in the tote bag I used for laundry, grabbed my *cours pratiques* notebook, and we were off to spend two glorious nights in the sublime luxury of the *Terrass* Hotel. We also took a taxi up there and the ride through Paris again could easily have been on a magic carpet I loved it so much. How amazing, I thought, would it be to have a car in this city! I didn't know one student who had one; hell, none of us were allowed to drive, and the French students I'd met only rode *mobylettes*.

Once at the hotel, we dropped my stuff off in her room---not the same one she had before, but even bigger with a newer, brighter color scheme on the fabrics and wallpapers---more like a country house than a château this time.

"Oooh, I like this room! Love the window seat and the desk! Just dreamy."

The bed was huge, especially for France, and completely enclosed in draperies and the usual square canopy. I just wanted to plop down in it, but she wanted to go down to the lobby bar, which we did. She had seen some TWA folk hanging out in there when we arrived, so she thought it might be fun to have a drink with them.

"Those guys are pretty nice, "she said, knowing no doubt that I was really wondering how she might interact among the "fakey" crowd.

We went down and were immediately welcomed into the fold. Cass introduced me as her friend the Sorbonne student, and that seemed to be an *entré* with them. There were two pretty girls, very tall and both blonds with blue eyes. They were already giggling a little too much for me to think they were not "in their cups" a bit. The guys were very ruggedly handsome and looked like men who had careers that paid real money and allowed them to travel the world. None of them was a pilot; they were all stews.

One of the three guys, Robert, called the waiter over and offered Cass and me each a drink---his treat. Cass ordered a glass of Chenin Blanc, but I didn't want to drink wine. I was the daughter of a bartender, after all, and thought I should order an actual drink. But I didn't know about French bars. Unless they were called "American Bar" like the Ritz Bar was or Harry's New York Bar, they didn't really make American mixed cocktails. I ordered a martini. Cass glanced at me with a quizzical look. Of course she had never seen me drink a cocktail in Iowa City; we were underage. I knew enough about the ramifications of **that** law to never order a drink in a bar or restaurant at home. But there was no drinking age in France. I was perfectly legal.

The waiter brought my drink over to the table. I wanted to laugh when it turned out to be Martini & Rossi on the rocks, but instead I acted like I knew that's what I'd be served. Just as well for me! A real martini would have sent me *under* that table.

Cass' co-workers were having a drink before heading out together to the kinds of real nightclubs Paris was famous for. They were trying to decide whether to go to the *Crazy Horse* or *Matignon*, all the way to the *Étoile* area again; or stay up in Montmartre and go to the *Moulin Rouge*, which I thought was in a particularly seedy area. But knowing nothing about this type of entertainment, I could offer no help whatsoever.

"Soooo, "Cass asked, sipping her wine, "do you want to go to a gay club or to a famous Las Vegas type one?"

Gay? As in homosexual??! I looked up at the guys; they all looked absolutely normal, and handsome as all get out to me. I wondered why she asked that! I could have been wearing blinking neon signs that flashed "NAÏVE" that night, because I was a complete ignoramus. I knew nothing about homosexuality, who they were, what they did, where they hung out—in the U.S. or in France. I had no consciousness about it. I didn't know what it was in high school and had only really learned anything about it at the love-in for Gentle Thursday in Iowa City. But even at university, I had no awareness of anyone actually gay in my classes, the union or in the dorms until that first Pride parade, when I saw many strange characters and many disguises; nothing that looked like any of the men sitting with us in the *Terrass's* bar.

When they were getting ready to go off, they invited us along. Cass and I declined the invitation to join in, mostly because I had nothing like the money it took to go to those clubs, but also because we were tired. Clubs and discos didn't even get going until around eleven o'clock at night, and most a lot later than that.

"So," I said nursing my drink that didn't really taste too great, "are they---all---or some of them gay?"

"Not the women."

"But all those guys?"

"Uh huh."

"Geez."

"The girls will have safe escorts that way," Cass offered, in some way of explanation, "although, I'm guessing these guys don't want to go to a straight club. But *Crazy Horse*, you know, that's like so famous—it's a revue really, that I'm thinking everyone goes there…gay or straight."

"Straight. That's the opposite of gay? Heterosexual then?"

"Sari, what planet do you really live on?" she asked me laughing out loud.

"I know! I'm out of it."

"You really are, kid!"

Chapter Thirty-Two

"Suzanne"...Leonard Cohen

"*On a fait la grasse-matinée!*" I announced to Cass, glancing at the clock which said 9:30—blissfully late for me.

"Huh?" she asked sleepily.

"We slept in!"

"So much the better," she laughed, hauling herself up on an elbow and reaching for the phone.

She ordered in breakfast from Room Service, hung up, and rolled back over; whereas I jumped out of bed and into the bathroom, where I took a shower in the fanciest, most wonderful shower I'd had since last being in the Hydes' Kenilworth home. She had offered me all the little products in the bathroom, explaining that she had amassed quite a collection of those already. Every cosmetic product in France was heavenly, from soap and shampoo to loofah sponges and thick French terry cloth. This was a country that knew how to do luxury even if their toilet paper was meted out in scratchy brown paper squares.

When I got back out to the room, a cart with coffee, *chocolat*, orange juice, a basket of *croissants* and *demi-baguettes*, Normandy butter and an assortment of jams had been delivered.

"I have an idea, " I said, tucking into the goodies on the cart. "Let's do museums in the *Marais* today. I need to take some notes anyway, and there are lots of interesting places to see right in the *Place des Vosges*. Victor Hugo's house is a museum there, and *Madame de Sévigné's* actual house is the *Carnavalet* Museum just a little ways away. I'm reading the letters *Madame de Sévigné* wrote to her daughter from the court of Louis XIV; I might as well see her house. The *Carnavalet* Museum is the best one for the history of Paris. "

"Sounds like a plan," she responded. "We'll be culture vultures for sure."

"The *Marais* used to be the Jewish quarter of Paris," I explained. "There are still some vestiges of that. We could maybe have a late lunch at Jo Goldenberg's Jewish deli---I've heard that's what it is, anyway. And then do you want to come to my class? Or I can meet you back here."

"Oh, I wouldn't miss your class! Will they let me sit in again?"

"Well, you'll be there; what can they do? If they kick you out, I'll leave, too. Won't be the worst thing that could happen, for me to have another few hours free. Class on Saturday just sucks, anyway."

So we left the hotel in a taxi hailed for her by the doorman, and headed for the *Place des Vosges*. We meandered in the park for a while and then did a complete tour around the four sides under the arches, looking into gallery windows and reading menus of the cafés and restaurants that lined the walk. Every place having anything to do with food looked inviting, if expensive.

On *Place des Vosges*, we entered Number 6 first, the Victor Hugo museum. An antechamber where we bought tickets (as usual, way cheap for students), led to the living room, all done up in Chinese motif with a black lacquer built-in cabinet on one wall, and on the opposite one, huge shelves with Chinese porcelain plates in each cubbyhole. The carpet in that room was teal colored and covered with flowers.

The next room was the dining room and could not have been decorated more differently: a very heavy, dark room with mahogany furnishings, a gas-lamp chandelier over the large dark table, and floor to ceiling repeating-patterned wallpaper of stylized feathery flowers that clashed with the similarly busy carpet. There were four free-standing Welsh cupboards and other pieces of dark wood furniture besides the table and chairs.

From there we headed to the bedroom where he died in 1885, which was also elaborately decorated with red flocked wallpaper and red brocade chairs against the wall flanking a large chest of drawers with a huge samovar on top of it. The bed was of the same carved wood as the dresser, and was a four-poster with a canopy made out of the carved wood and no draperies around it. There was another dresser covered in a red cloth, and a red horse-hair *fauteuil*, or comfortable chair. The bed itself was only a single but it was fluffy and covered in red silk.

I still hadn't read a lot of French literature yet by then, but nonetheless, felt awed by the moment. Such a literary giant, and so revered by his compatriots. The sense of retracing honored history continued when we exited and walked over to Number 1 where *Madame de Sévigné* was born.

"The plaque indicates she was born here, but the *Carnavalet* Museum was her actual home," I added.

Cass also wanted to know why so many of the designated numbered buildings were called "*hôtel.*"

"Because that meant high society single-family dwelling—mansion, really. And then, since this was built as a series of royal residences, you had the *Pavillons de la Reine* and *du Roi.* "

As we walked, I pointed out further luminaries' residences: Sully, the great minister of Henri IV lived at No. 7, and two famous writers—not as famous as Hugo—Théophile Gautier and Alphonse Daudet lived at No. 8. Number 21 was said to have been the home of Cardinal Richelieu.

We continued out into the *place* and around the corner to the *Carnavalet*, where I had already been once with class, and would go again and again, such a treasure trove it was---and free to the public in those days. Cass was fascinated and had never heard of the place.

"I'm sure you can find it in your guidebook, however," I told her as she expressed some amazement that her parents had never mentioned going there either.

The collection was essentially "historical artifacts"-- like an actual archeological stone from *La Bastille*, housed beside a replica of that infamous building; thousands of paintings, drawings, engravings, commercial signs that would have hung over the entrance of a business; a mock-up life-size diorama with the original furnishings representing Marcel Proust's bedroom; an entire floor of French drawing rooms you could walk through, all decorated in Louis XIV, XV, and XVI styles, one more beautiful than the next with green painted *boiserie* door panels against pink walls, and green silk chairs and *canapés* and *chaises-longues*. Another room was painted in Wedgewood blue walls with white *boiserie* décor to look like bas-relief sculpture. There were lots of gaming tables and many other pieces of period furniture in every room.

Their facsimile of Marcel Proust's bedroom, which he was purported to have hardly left after 1914, was decorated almost entirely in shades of brown and beige, thus much more somber and stark than the rooms on the other floor. It had cork walls, which he was supposed to have needed to stifle noise; a bed with a screen behind it; an armchair done in a subtle brown print fabric with heavy fringe around the bottom; and a bigger "fainting couch" of brown velvet and brocade top. There was a black desk, two small tables and a green-shaded lamp. I could stare at that room for hours, and every time I was there, I just lingered, imagining him writing that monumental work, propped up in bed.

We spent almost two hours in the *Carnavalet* having seen but a fraction of what was there, but too tired to go on without some sort of sustenance and rest for our weary feet. So we ventured back out and over to *Rue des Rosiers* to eat at Goldenberg's, where Jo Jo's parents had taken her, and which I had never heard of until she raved about it.

Eighteen years after I was in Paris for the first time, Jo Goldenberg's would be the site of the first terrorist attack in Paris linked to the Palestinian-Israeli conflict. Gunmen would enter and shoot the place up, killing six people including two Americans, Ann Van Zanten, a curator at the Chicago Historical Society, and Grace Cutler; and injuring twenty-two others including Mrs. Van Zanten's husband, David, who was an art history professor at Northwestern.

We sat down at an interior table near the zinc bar that was flanked by pretty red stools. Walls were lined with shelves of bottles and there were cases of foods along the back.

"I wonder if you can do take-out here," Cass said.

"I doubt it!" *The French to my knowledge at that point, had never heard of take-out or take-away, as the Brits called it.*

I had beet borscht with *crème fraîche* instead of sour cream, which I felt was an improvement over all the borscht I'd previously eaten in my life. Cass had gravlax, blinis and capers which came also with a small bowl of *crème fraîche*.

"You need a bagel for that!" I said staring at the large dinner plate of salmon piled on top of thin blinis. "How in the world are you going to eat it?"

So we got her a Parisian bagel which came from the Jewish bakery just across the sidewalk.

"Imagine that!" she exclaimed. "Here, have some."

I didn't mind if I did.

We had to watch the time because we were in the Marais at roughly *métro St. Paul*, and we needed to get to my class on the *Rue du Fouarre* in the 6ième at *métro Maubert-Mutualité*.

"By the time we go through *correspondence des lignes* at the dreaded *Chatelet*," I told Cass, "we could walk there faster."

So that's what we did: walked. We walked at a brisk clip over to *Rue de Rivoli* and zig-zagged through little streets that led to the *Quai des Celestins*. We crossed the Seine over to the *Ile St. Louis* at *Rue des Deux Ponts*, over to the *Quai de la Tournelle* on the Left Bank. We took a left turn heading west towards *Rue du Fouarre*.

"Ground floor, to the right," I called out almost panting. *"On est juste, quoi."* We'd just made it in time.

Once inside, Professor Filiolet said it was okay for Cass to visit, and in fact, he looked at her with interest. Her beauty, again, I surmised. He asked her to say in English, "My father is a banker and my mother stays at home," which she did, and then he proclaimed that she was from Chicago, USA.

"Yes!" she said, startled.

"He's good," I said.

He spent a good part of the class explaining what our next oral exams would be graded upon: he would count mistakes in articulation, rhythm, and intonation. Everyone groaned. We had already been notified in writing that the written exams would include explanation of words or expressions underlined in certain texts; justification of the use of tenses and moods in pairs of sentences; replacement of underlined words in sentences with personal pronouns; putting a given text into indirect style; and changing a text from the present tense to the past. And at the end of all that, we would have to write a paragraph of our own on a subject they would provide.

Cass looked at me with an expression on her face that said, in essence, "Yikes!" and I responded with one that expressed doom.

Not quite two hours later, he ended class a few minutes early, and he let us leave. I thanked him for allowing my friend to observe, and he shook her hand.

"I thought he was going to kiss it!" she laughed as we hurried out into the autumnal dusk.

"God, Paris is gorgeous!" I said, happy to have a reprieve from studying for a while. "We're near *Notre Dame*, as you can see, and I'm dying for *le hot dog* so I'll take you to the best ones in Paris! My treat. Don't argue!"

We crossed over to *Ile de la Cité* where crowds were gathered as usual outside the front of Notre Dame on the *parvis*; this time not so much for tourism as for actual mass. The café right straight ahead on the corner across from the side of the cathedral had hot dogs in a glass case on the sidewalk. The hot dog was a foot-long smothered with *gruyère* and placed in a hollowed-out space of a *demi-baguette*. They heated it for you, then slipped it into a paper sleeve, and off you went.

I paid, and then we jumped into a taxi to have them back at the hotel, where we could have lots of other food Cass had in the room, including "*Chipsters*" (which the French pronounced "Cheeepstair"), and fruit, and anything our little hearts desired to drink.

We plopped down on the bed and ate like we hadn't had food all day, when in fact, we'd had a magnificent breakfast and a fantastic lunch.

"I think I want to go to church tomorrow morning," Cass said all of a sudden.

I couldn't have been more taken aback. "Really?!"

"Yes."

"Okaaay, like Notre Dame?"

"No," she said thoughtfully, "though I'll bet that organ is out of this world."

"It is! But Cass, I know there's an American church in Paris, and it's yours: Episcopalian. Do you want me to look it up? I'm sure the service would be in English."

"No, I think I want French. If you were going to another church, maybe not as famous as *Notre Dame*, where would that be?"

"Oh, God, there are so many! But hey, let's go to *St. Germain des Prés*. Every time I see a flyer for music concerts, that's the one where they have them. So they must have a pretty great organ, too. And maybe a choir! Love that!"

"Well, that works! "

So it was decided. I did not have a *Pariscope* with me so we went down to the lobby to see if they had some. The *concièrge* was happy to oblige me by telling me the times of the masses at *St. Germain des Prés* rather than have me go out and buy a *Pariscope* just for that. We repaired to the room once again, both happy to stay in and watch French television that night. Around midnight I was still wide awake, and so I wrapped up in the hotel's thick robe and my knee socks under pajamas, a wool scarf around my neck, and walked out onto her balcony. The view over Paris from Montmartre was as spectacular as it was from the Eiffel Tower itself, which I could see clearly all lit right in front of me, off in the distance. I leaned up against the tiny balcony railing and I just stared at Paris rooftops and chimneys, reminding myself that to be there was the dream of my life, and I mustn't ruin it by flunking the next battery of exams.

"What are you doing out there?" Cass came stumbling to the French window-door.

"Nothing. Go back to bed. Sorry if I woke you up."

"No, no...you didn't. But isn't it cold out there?"

I came back in. "Not too cold...yet. This is probably the last throe of summer, though." But actually it was too cold to be standing outside in pajamas.

There were several hours of Mass to choose from, so we picked eleven o'clock, thinking that might have wonderful music. I packed up all my stuff in the tote bag I'd brought over there, and took it with me. We had breakfast in the lobby, which is what the *Terrass* did on Sunday, and it was a bigger spread than on weekdays: the regular French breakfast items were augmented with many different fruits and also trays of meats and cheeses, lots of different breads, like *pain de campagne* from *Chez Poilâne,* and sliced *pain d'épices.* And besides *croissants* there were lovely fat, round *brioches.*

We took plates full of every possible goodie and sat down on the ample couches and chairs that had little tables set in front of them for this weekly event.

"I am one hundred percent spoiled now," I announced, "and can never relish the *Maison*'s breakfasts again, you realize that."

"Ha! Happy to oblige!"

We finished around ten, and then took a taxi cross town to *Boulevard St. Germain* and sat in the tiny garden to the side of the church until it was almost eleven, after which we went in and chose chairs in the back. French churches had individual straight-backed chairs rather than pews. Each one had a kneeling step on the back that served for the one behind it. I didn't know if Cass actually intended to worship and if so, how she thought she'd be able to follow the service in French, which had been instituted after Vatican II changed from Latin. I myself had no idea how to compare the Anglican Mass with the Roman one, but decided she probably knew what she was doing. As it turned out, she really only wanted to be present at a house of worship on the Sunday, to hear the music and contemplate things. She didn't really care if she couldn't understand it at all.

Afterwards, we were right near the really renowned famous cafés where the Existentialist writers had hung out before the War, *Aux Deux Magots* and *Cafe de Flore.*

"My roommate Agathe told me these cafés are really 'snob' ---much more so than even the famous ones where I live."

"Well," Cass said, "I'm not hungry at all!"

"Me neither. Let's walk to the Luxembourg Gardens and sit there for a while. I probably have to get back to the *Maison* at a pretty early hour and study the whole rest of the day and night. But we can have dinner in that area, if you want to hang around."

"What I think we should do is talk about London and then I'll leave you to get some real work done," she said.

So we strolled on into the gardens and sat near where the children's toy kiosk was displaying the pretty balls and pails, plastic hoops and puppets. We took a bench in the sunny part of the far back garden — towards where I would exit for *Rue Vavin.* It wasn't at all cold in the sun and the fall colors were starting to be magnificent.

"I traded Anita some flights in order to take this furlough, you know," Cass said, "so I won't be able to come back to Paris before the end of the month or the beginning of October. In the meantime, I intend to fly in and out of London a few times between now and then and really get acclimated. So I can be your tour guide for a change! Ho!"

"Fantastic!" I said. "I'll let you know our exact arrival, and everything. "

"You might not be able to stay with me there," she said. "I hope that doesn't bum you out too much. I can sneak one person into my room, but probably not two."

"Oh, it'll be okay. Nonnie and I will figure it out."

"November first is a Friday, " Cass said, peeling back the pages of her worn purse calendar that had her flight schedules in it, "so that is just perfect. You guys planning to stay longer than just the weekend? "

"Well, we have off longer, but this time, they're not closing the dorm down like they do at Christmas, so we can come back any time; and frankly having some good ol' time off IN Paris, is just as well for me. I can do laundry and just take it easy."

"Have hot dogs at *Notre Dame* whenever you want!"

"Exactly. And you know what? Agathe actually brought a real tea kettle with her. We set it up in the bathroom next to the hotplate. I bought a little saucepan at Inno and I can make soup. Their packaged soup is really good here, believe it or not!"

We sat there for a while but had to admit it was too cool out to sit for very much longer in the garden, so we retraced our way out the side and went over to the *Café Ronsard* for some hot chocolate. I hadn't brought up Alan the whole weekend, thinking I'd leave it to her, but she hadn't either, so I asked her. She looked at me and her face suddenly took on a shade of grey pallor.

"I think it's over," she said finally.

"Why do you think that? Other than – what-- you told him to leave? I mean, and he actually did it?"

"He left and didn't come back. He also hasn't written or called me."

"Oh, wow. So he got the message, in other words."

"Looks like it."

"Cass, are you sad? You aren't…you know…mad that I brought it up, are you?"

"No. Neither one." She perked up a bit. "I don't think we'd make a go of it anyway. The only thing that bothers me is that, you know, you and I will be back there next year if my parents allow it, and he'll still be there."

"Yeah, that's not optimal. You'll meet new people! What about Klampert? Do you hear from him?"

"Yes! And he said I could rejoin his team, so to speak, any time I came back and wanted my old job. He's a dear."

"Well, then, for art! Not immature boy-men!" I pronounced.

"And what about your guy? Anything new on that front?"

"I probably would have been bursting with it if there had been! He writes me these inane letters. Although he does get more animated when he talks about concerts he's reviewed. "

"But what about coming over here and traveling with you at the end?"

"Well, that's still up in the air, but it's eons away, so I'm not too concerned that it all has to be planned now."

"Yeah, that's probably smart. You'll have to break it to your parents though, that you're not coming home and all when they thought you were."

"Yep. Have to cross that bridge later, too."

It was getting dark earlier now that September was waning. I had to get going back, and it was striking me as sad that we weren't going to see each other again for quite a while.

"I'll grab some magazines from the plane next time, too," she said trying to be cheery as we parted.

"Great! Thanks!" I let myself splurge on the *Herald Trib*, but I couldn't rationalize spending what few francs I had on things like *Time* or *Vogue*.

There was a taxi stand right in front of the *Ronsard*, and I watched her climb in one and wave. I crossed the street back into the park to cut through to the back and exit towards *Montparnasse*.

I had about a fifteen-minute walk during which to ruminate over the weekend and how great it had been to spend two nights at *Le Terrass*; what luck that the furlough had worked out; how cool that she had come up with the idea to "kidnap" me and take me there. I sensed myself trying to fight off feelings of "unworthiness" of all this good fortune, not the least of which was seeing Cass in Paris so often, which still struck me as a major miracle. Paris had been my dream and my goal. Having my best friend there at the same time had never entered my mind. It was as surreal now as it would have been impossible to fathom back in Iowa City.

So I resolved to be more grateful, more cognizant of my great good fortune to be there. I needed to show my parents that I was getting everything I could out of the year and the experiences I was having. I did write them and Nana very often and regularly, but I also needed to be more expressive of the fact that I realized they had sacrificed for me to get here, and that I had no intention of letting them down.

As I walked uphill on *Vavin* towards the Rodin statue of Balzac "in a bathrobe" as we students called it, which marked the beginning of *Place Picasso*, and "home," I gave myself the now-frequent pep talk about getting coursework under control and really doubling down. It wasn't too late, I told myself, and every week I'm here, I improve. All at once I felt the breeze come up and the temperature begin to drop. I tightened my sweater around my shoulders and bent my head into the wind.

"A change in the weather is sufficient to recreate the world and ourselves." -- *Marcel Proust* **("The Guermantes' Way," pt. 2, ch. 2, Remembrance of Things Past, vol. 6 (1921))**

Chapter Thirty-Three

"Adagietto" -- *Symphony No.5*...Gustave Mahler

October! The Sorbonne was finally reopening and my routine was changing... again! I didn't have to go to lectures all over the Latin Quarter anymore; all classes that had been at places like the Oceanographic Institute and the lecture hall at *Lycée Louis-le-Grand* were now all in the *Richelieu* amphitheater of *La Sorbonne*. We also had library privileges at *Bibliothèque Ste. Génévieve* across from the *Pantheon*, up by the *Fac de Droit*, the law school. I could study there at a table lit by an elegant lamp, but I could not go find books in the stacks. They brought them to you. And Paris didn't have any lending libraries. You read at the table and you left the books there for someone else to take back. I didn't even know what books to ask for, so I just studied my own materials.

By this time in my travels, I had not yet seen the British Library or the Bodleian at Oxford, so the *Bibliothèque Ste. Geneviève* was the most imposing academic structure I had ever encountered. It was a nineteenth-century building, but it housed the entire collection of manuscripts and other artifacts from one of the oldest abbeys in Europe, the Abbey of Sainte-Geneviève.

I found it very convivial to be in its venerable reading room with five hundred or so other students, scholars and researchers. Even though there was a lamp for every four places, light came streaming in from huge arched windows all along the walls high above the stacks; unless it was a rainy or overcast day, you could see very well in there.

Unlike during the summer when I did most of my studying in my room or in the little "library" as they called it at *La Maison*, when the Sorbonne actually opened, I found the Latin Quarter more conducive to serious work. Many days I would exit the courtyard after class and walk down the *Boul' Mich'* to any café that looked inviting; you could stay for hours having ordered anything, even just a coffee, and no one would bug you to pay the bill or leave. The tiny tables were crammed together and just right for one person to read or write, if not so great for two people to actually order food and eat. Of course, everyone smoked, and the fumes from *Gauloises* filled my sinus cavities and wrapped around me like a scarf. What the *madeleine* had done for Proust, *Gauloises* smoke did for me: it made me remember Paris the rest of my life.

Another great discovery took place once we were in the actual university of Paris. There were "*foyers*" with *resto-U*, or highly subsidized student restaurants and cafeterias scattered all over the *quartier*. You could get an entire meal of hors-d'oeuvres, main course with accompaniments of vegetables, potatoes or rice, fruit, cheese, a dessert and a drink for TWO FRANCS! It might not have been gourmet, but it was plentiful. Some days I would meet up with Eric and Taylor and go with them to try out the various ones. Sometimes they liked to go to the "*Foyer Israëlien*" because they both loved couscous and falafel, neither of which I could stand. But there the trays were often brimming with beet salad and blintzes, hummus, cucumber and tomato salad, tabouli and other Mediterranean cuisine favorites. I didn't start out liking much of it, but it grew on me. Especially for two francs.

Even though it was still months away, my exams were weighing heavily over every single assignment, paper and reading I had. None of the *cours pratiques* grades counted, even though we Pella students were awarded credits for taking the classes. If you failed the exams, you failed it all. And if you even failed one exam, as I had explained to an incredulous Cass, you failed the whole program. If I failed the whole thing, I would be obliged to return home in February instead of the following July. Luckily, very luckily, Pella's resident director at the *Maison* gave us sample materials of what would be on these tests. I carried those papers around with me the entire year, taking them out at every opportunity-- once I'd finished any work that was due imminently-- to write and write in preparation.

"Briefly indicate the evolution of the French nobility from the Middle Ages to the Revolution."
"What are the principal characteristics of architecture of the Renaissance?"
"Define 'Courtly Literature'. What are its principle manifestations?"

There were going to be four questions such as those in each subject matter being tested, and we had to write on three of the four. I had the subjects of French history, literature and art history, plus geography. For the *cours pratiques* side of the test, it would be a pre-recorded dictation given over a loudspeaker with no time to pause, to do a rough draft, or any other "aid" we might think we needed, and that part would be at least an hour. I couldn't prepare for that; it could be taken from anything. But I was grateful to be able to at least study for the other subjects, and I was truly appreciative of the study guide.

Nonnie and I got together often to study and sometimes C.C. would come, too. Our favorite place was the last café at the end of *Boulevard St. Michel* across from the fountain and just near the *quai*. This one had the *de rigueur* terrace of small tables which were enclosed with glass windows during the winter, but inside it also had booths and bigger tables where it was really warm. That's where we sat.

Nonnie was gung-ho for London, so we made our way to a student travel agency as Cass had suggested, to see about those flights that were dirt cheap. And Cass was right; they were! But we didn't buy them the first time we talked to an agent because Nonnie didn't know what date she wanted to return. When I started talking about London, she had envisaged a perfect way to visit some of her good friends who were also studying abroad that year. I already knew about her best friend's plans to come for Christmas holidays to Paris and then travel with Nonnie to Italy. But this way, she could see that girl and another one before December. She had another close friend from high school studying at Oxford that year, and her best friend from forever was the one studying at Trinity in Dublin. So she had already decided she might want to extend her part of the trip and go on to Ireland, flying back to Paris from there. I was warmly invited to come along, but not only could my budget not withstand any elongations of any sort, I didn't want to horn in on her time with her friend. So I thanked her and declined.

When Cass came to Paris in late October, we all reconnoitered about the London trip in my dorm room eating some of the snacks she'd brought me, as usual, and oohing and aahing over the magazines she'd also brought, like *Mademoiselle's* thick August "back to school" issue and the September *Vogue*.

"I will find you guys a London hotel you can afford," Cass told us, "and I'll meet your plane so that I can take you there---provided there are no TWA "snafus" *(a term I'd heard often from Sol, talking about his army days)*, of course. But in some dire case where I'm called back to work, I'll find a way to let you know."

Yes, I didn't even consider that, and didn't want to think about it.

She continued, "You'll arrive into Gatwick Airport and we will take a bus into London. TWA stays at the Hotel Thistle Kensington Gardens, but the last time I was in London, I walked around the neighborhood and saw lots of little hotels in that area, so I'm sure we can find one for you. They're called "bed and breakfast" and English breakfast is a whole meal—you'll see!"

"Gee, that's really nice of you," said Nonnie, relieved that someone was in charge and it didn't have to be her. "It all sounds like great stuff."

Cass and I didn't have very much time together that particular lay-over in Paris, so I suggested we head over to *Au Pied de Cochon* in *Les Halles* for onion soup---the **real** real deal, because I'd heard from my roommate Agathe and her friends that the French government was about to start tearing down the central market in just a few months; thus the iconic landmarks of culinary wholesale as well as the restaurants would be in danger of disappearing forever.

The *Au Pied de Cochon brasserie* was not crowded per se at the dinner hour; it filled up around eleven at night when the theater crowds showed up for "*souper*", or supper, the late meal. We had a wide choice of tables that night and Cass slid onto the red leather banquette while I took the chair across from her. We both ordered *soupe à l'oignon gratinée*, of course. Neither of us had any intention of continuing with actual pigs' trotters, but we did the inexcusable and asked the waiter to let us share a *plat principal*, to which he agreed without so much as rolling his eyes once! So we ordered one *escalope de veau, à la crème aux champignons, purée maison* and two desserts.

"*Quand-même*," he said approvingly. Cass wanted *Baba au rhum, crème fouettée* and I ordered *crème brûlée à la vanille Bourbon*.

The bill came to one hundred and ten francs! Cass was still "on the town" on TWA's dime, and by then, I didn't even make gestures to help pay for meals in great restaurants like that in Paris.

"I was full after the soup," I announced, "I feel like a bowling ball that needs to be rolled back to the *Maison*."

"Let's try to at least walk some of it off," she said, without much enthusiasm. "Do you realize that TWA makes us weigh in periodically?"

"No. That's ridiculous. Anyway, you're fine."

"For now. French food doesn't help!"

"You look great, as always."

But in the spirit of serious exercise, we took a circuitous route from *Rue Coquillière* in the first *arrondissement* over to the *Rue de Rivoli* to *Boulevard Sebastopol,* and across the bridge on to the *Ile de la Cité.* We walked along the *quai* and came to a kiosk of newspapers and magazines where we saw the now-famous photo of Jackie Kennedy's marriage to Aristotle Onassis.

Cass snorted at it, asking me, "What do you think about Jackie marrying that old coot?"

"Well, I read she freaked out when Bobby was shot, and decided someone was 'out to kill the Kennedys and her children are Kennedys."

"Jackie Kennedy's marriage to Onassis has the whole U.S. in an uproar. The great American dream of marrying for love has crumbled. Our symbol of royalty has gone and married a dirty old man."

"Well," I reasoned, "maybe she really did do it for her kids. She doesn't need his money."

"Ho! THAT kind of money? Everyone needs it. Her kids are back in the good ol' U.S. of A. attending private schools like they always would have."

"Well, I hope they'll be safe , at least."

"Yeah," Cass added, in an uncharacteristically snide tone of voice, "safe to grow neurotic amid ivy-covered walls like I did. I think Jackie Kennedy is pathetic."

"Come on."

"I mean it. Pretty soon no one will marry for love. It will be *passé.* We will all **evolve** into automatons and robots marrying for just the human necessities and not for anything remotely emotional."

"That's a pretty bleak outlook. What's gotten into you all of a sudden?"

"Well, do you think you'll defy all the conventions and marry Soren when you get back?"

"Given the fact that he doesn't even seem to see me in any romantic light whatsoever, I seriously doubt it! "

"But you love him, right?"

"I thought I could at one time."

At that moment she stopped walking and turned to me, "Sari, stop selling yourself short all the time! Soren doesn't love you; you're going to fail the semester; you can't get it together. I call bullshit!"

"What?"

"I mean it. You're someone any guy would be proud to date—you are smart! You have a darling figure—so tiny. You are funny. You have a work ethic that doesn't quit. God, kid, you'd better start believing it!"

"Jesus. Where did all that come from?"

"I don't know." She looked up at me apologetically. "I guess I'm in a bad mood because I have to fly right out of here tomorrow or something."

"Or something."

"Sorry."

"That's okay. We'll see each other in another couple of weeks and the time 'til then will go fast. I'm super excited about London. Oh, and I didn't get a chance to tell you this at the dorm: the little radio you got me has changed my life! I just love it."

"You found out all about Radio Luxembourg, I take it? "

"Hell, YEAH. It's fab."

We saw a taxi stand once we crossed over into the Latin Quarter, and she said she'd drop me off and then take it back to her hotel.

In front of *La Maison* I gathered my things and got out of the taxi, giving Cass *la bise.* "I still love Jackie!" I called out as the cab pulled away.

I didn't know it then, but that was the last time I would see Cassandra Hyde in Paris.

Chapter Thirty-four

"Ferry 'Cross the Mersey"...Gerry and the Pacemakers

Nonnie and I trooped back to the student travel agency and got our very cheap flights to London on Caledonian Airways, an airline I'd never heard of, that flew into Gatwick, the London airport Cass had mentioned which I also didn't know existed. The only London airport I'd heard of was Heathrow. We only bought one-way tickets because she was going off to Ireland and would fly back from there; the travel agent told me I could get a return ticket from that same airline's kiosk in the airport, and maybe try to fly stand-by. That way, I could decide when to return when I found out Cass' schedule in London.

"Even if she has to fly out, I might just stay longer. You can never know—she might be able to come right back," I reasoned to Nonnie, "We won't be on a strict time bind to get back to Paris after all." Ten days off seemed like an eternity to me then.

And thus when the *Toussaint*-holiday came on November 1, we set off for England. Upon arrival, the British customs officer was actually surly with us, which I had to find amusing since everyone thought the French were so rude.

Cass was standing right there when we entered the hall!

"Welcome to Blighty!" she called out.

"What?"

"How was the flight?"

"Fine! But it ain't TWA! "

"Yeah," said Nonnie, "I think my brother has a remote-controlled plane he built from a kit that's about the same size ours was!"

Cass led us towards the train into London.

"This is just easier and faster than taking a cab or the bus, I found out," she said. She already had one-way tickets for us.

"We get into Victoria Station and inside there is a tourist bureau that finds hotels for travelers! I looked in my area, but this will be better---they can arrange it for you to fit your budgets. And the service is free!"

"Wow," I mused, "Can you imagine foreigners arriving in New York and managing to find their way to, say, Grand Central Station? Would there be any such services there for them? Free?! I doubt it."

At Victoria station the queue at the free tourist service was quite long but we got in it and just chatted away until it was our turn.

"I've got a sweet little itinerary of the major sights lined up for you," Cass announced with an only slightly mocking tone. "But feel free to suggest different things, too."

"We know nothing!" Nonnie said. "We trust you."

"Well, we know a little," I said. *Quand-même.* "I'd be up for walking around Carnaby Street! I'm not a die-hard Beatles fan for nothing."

"Got that," said Cass. "Chelsea, too."

The lady at the desk helped us find lodging in the Otter House, which she did indeed call a "bed and breakfast," a format not on my radar at all in the 1960's. It was listed as a "guesthouse", and resembled what we might have called a boarding house rather than a hotel. The exterior was all white, as was the entire street of houses. They had all been Victorian or Edwardian townhouses at one time, and in fact, our room looked like it might have actually been a bedroom. It had a fireplace that did not work, a bay window overlooking the sidewalk two floors down, yellow flowered wallpaper, and a yellow and white chintz bedspread. Our room also had an en suite bathroom, which, though tiny, meant we didn't have to go out into the hall or share it with other rooms. Pure luxury! London was cold that November and even though our room ostensibly had central heating, it wasn't turned up any too high, so I slept in my raincoat over my pajamas, my robe and socks!

215

But the woman who ran the place was friendly and the breakfasts were epic, so we had no complaints.

The price for our lodging was seven pounds fifty—each-- per night, and even though that was within my budget, London still gave me sticker shock; and when I heard how much rooms went for at Cass' hotel, I just couldn't believe the discrepancy between ours and hers.

"You'll be surprised at how expensive life is in London," she assured me. "You're used to dividing French prices by five to get the equivalent in dollars. Now you'll have to multiply by one and two-thirds to get the price from pounds to dollars. "

"Oh, God, too much math," I moaned.

"Then just multiply everything by two and know that it's a little cheaper than that!"

We set out sightseeing the next day after breakfast, knowing we would not be needing to stop for lunch! The breakfast we'd been served was a truly huge meal—the antithesis of French breakfast. It sort of reminded us of home and tasted heavenly. There were, however, a few surprises on the plate: mushrooms, for one thing, and baked beans as well as eggs, bacon, sausage, tomatoes, cereal if we wanted it, and racks of toast with slabs of butter and pots full of jam to put on it. There was orange juice and milk and of course, wonderful tea.

"Here's what I'm thinking," said Cass, as she met us in our lobby, which was more like a tiny parlor. "We skip lunch and have afternoon tea. When you finish that, you might also want to skip dinner. It will be great for the budget!"

What a perfect plan that was, too. My first real English afternoon tea had been in New York with Cass on the Christmas trip, and that had cemented my love for the tradition right then and there. But over in England, it was even more glorious. I could not fully understand how the same simple foods we had in the States could wind up tasting so much better over there. Just a sandwich with the crust taken off the bread. Big deal. But it **was** a big deal, and I went absolutely stark raving mad for cress and cucumber finger sandwiches, egg salad, salmon and tuna, also cheese and Branston pickle. Besides the savory, the sweets were just as wonderful: usually some kind of layer cake, plus cream puffs and other French pastries. All of this was washed down with lovely pots of tea, to which I added milk and sugar, like at breakfast.

The tables were really turned in London for Cass and me. She was the guide and I knew nothing. She arrived bright and early on Saturday at our hotel just as we were finishing the huge breakfast.

"Did I lie?" she mused, noticing that we were stuffed to the gills.

"No, you did not," Nonnie affirmed.

No one had the word "cholesterol" in their lexicons in those days, but somehow I still knew we had consumed the equivalent of a year's worth in that first "full English breakfast" our *pension* boasted.

I noticed that Cass was sort of more elegantly dressed than I would have thought she'd be for sightseeing all day. She was wearing a darling brown wool mini straight skirt with cream colored wool tights, a beige cashmere sweater twin set, and sort of low chunky-heeled pumps; and she was carrying her trench coat.

"Cass," I ventured, "you're so dressed up!"

"You know, I was wondering if you guys could also wear something a little bit dressy today. Would you mind? I sort of have a surprise in store."

"Sure," said Nonnie, "but we'll have to go up and change."

When my trunk had arrived in Paris, it had my winter clothes that Betty and I had packed before I left with the understanding that she would ship them to me, and I thus wouldn't have to carry a suitcase laden with all that. It had wool skirts and sweaters, some corduroy slacks, plus my camel coat and the same good ol' boots I wore at Iowa.

She also sent me an outfit that I really loved: a light blue wool herringbone tweed skirt, blazer and Bermuda shorts and a cap that all matched! But the first time I wore the shorts with a white sweater, the jacket, cap, and white knees socks out onto the streets of Paris-- thinking it was the chic-est outfit ever-- I got stared at by people and outright heckled and laughed at by all the little kids in the Luxembourg Gardens.

"Petit garçon! Petit garçon!!" they had yelled at me. *French women, I discovered, NEVER wore shorts in public. Maybe to play tennis, but never out on the street.*

I had brought the wool skirt and jacket set to London—of course not the shorts. I went up and changed into them, wore my boots instead of knee socks, and was happy I had brought my trench coat as well. Nonnie changed into a red wool dress with a white Peter Pan collar and a full skirt. She had on stockings and loafers. The only coat she'd brought was her navy pea-coat.

"I didn't bring any dress shoes with me," she said, as I remembered she never wore heels because she was already so tall.

"You're fine," I said. Loafers can be dressy enough without socks."

Cass did not hurry us, but I could tell she was anxious to get the show on the road. She presented us that first morning with one-day Travel Card passes for the London Underground, and told us after that we'd buy them every day ourselves. She told us that she already knew all about the London tube would show us the ropes. She had even brought along tube maps for each of us.

"Gosh," Nonnie said staring at the map, "it seems even more simple than Paris': the lines are color-coded and they have names."

"See, you don't have to know the terminus to decide what direction to take," Cass explained, "the directions are north-south, etc."

But it was not easier. For one thing, you had to be on the right platform or you wouldn't be going to the right stops, and the platforms were shared between lines in some instances.

"And sometimes you even have to read the destination on the train's engine as it comes into the station or you might get on the wrong train by mistake even if you know you're on the right platform!" Cass explained.

"What?! In Paris, if you're going the right direction, standing on the platform, the train WILL be your train," I said, not without a little worry. My small-town non-sophistication was rearing its ugly head. Cass probably thought she was both tour guide and nanny, I mused.

"Luckily for us, we are only running around Central London and don't have to worry too much about which trains we are getting on," Cass said, and then she announced, "The South Kensington station is about the most confusing. We'll try to avoid that one. Except that will be hard," she corrected herself. "I stay at that one!"

There was another difference. When you got out of London's tube, you might not actually be anywhere near your destination. The city was gigantic, enormous, humongous---it seemed to dwarf Paris. In Paris, if you knew the right *métro* stop, once you went out the "*sortie*" you were pretty much there. One would rarely have to walk more than five minutes---ten at the most---to get where you were going. Not in London. With a few exceptions, like at Harrod's where the station really was right at the store, when you exited the tube system, you still had blocks and blocks to walk to get to where you were actually going. It was fine by me; we were seeing sights and the everyday bustle of the place as we walked all over, but it was not as convenient taking the tube as Paris' *métro* was.

Cass had planned for three full days of sight-seeing and was eager to show us as much as possible. Nonnie and I were grateful for anything and everything she had up her sleeve. We both loved museums, so that was easy. Cass had lined up The British Museum, the National and Tate Galleries, and the Victoria and Albert Museum. That was by no means all of the city's fine museums, but it was a start. She also wanted to show us neighborhoods, parks, Buckingham Palace and Parliament. And she wanted to take us shopping and to the theater!

"London is expensive," she said, "but theater is not! You'll be amazed at the great seats we can get for practically nothing!"

Cass also had a boat ride on the Thames planned, too, and the cruise would take us to Greenwich.

Before we set out for that first whole day's worth of activities, Cass wanted to check with Nonnie about the itinerary, the days she had planned to be with us, her Oxford student friend Patty's arrival, and also when she had intended to leave for Ireland. Cass surprised me by announcing that she didn't have to fly out until the following Wednesday, which was so wonderfully lucky for me. Nonnie said her friend Patty was due to arrive on Sunday.

"I'll get her to go to church with me," Nonnie said. "She's due to arrive in the morning and she knows where we're staying. I saw a Catholic church right by our hotel as we came in."

"You did?" I asked incredulously.

"Yeah, I tend to look out for stuff like that. In Paris it's easy because they're all Catholic! Here they're all Church of England."

"Yes," Cass said, "they're all mine." The American Episcopal church at that time was still a full-fledged member of the Anglican Communion, and Cass could easily attend any Anglican Catholic Church of England and feel at home, even though, as she explained, "the book of Common Prayer is different. And we don't call our priests 'vicars', although I'll bet some Americans use that term, haha."

"So which of those churches do you want to go to tomorrow?" Nonnie asked.

"Probably Westminster Abbey or St. Paul's," she answered. "On second thought, I think we should all go see Westminster Abbey. So maybe I'll go to services at St. Paul's."

No one even brought up the subject of synagogues or if I had wanted to go to my services. It was too late by then anyway, since we were making our way out at the same hour as any Shabbat service would be going on of a Saturday morning. And to be fair, I hadn't ever mentioned going to worship anywhere; and besides, I loved the Episcopal-cum-Anglican services I'd been to already – as well as the Catholic one in Paris with Cass that one time, too. The music was so great.

In a smaller English town, the main shopping street, or "High Street" would be crammed to overflowing with weekend shoppers on Saturday. In London, all the shopping and tourism districts were always jam-packed, so it didn't really make a difference that we were starting out on a weekend. Our "B and B" was closest to the Gloucester Road tube station on the Piccadilly, District and Circle lines, so we got on there and took the Piccadilly to Leicester Square stop and then backtracked to Trafalgar Square to look around it and the Nelson statue, before starting our real sight-seeing at the National Gallery. But right across the street from the side of the Gallery was The Church of St. Martin in the Fields, whose "Academy" had come up so often in my music appreciation class at Iowa, that I just had to see it. So instead of heading right in to look at one of the world's greatest art collections, I begged my friends to indulge me in a detour over to one of the world's most famous churches.

"This is just as I imagined it!" I whispered excitedly. "It's gorgeous!"

Row after row of dark symmetrical pews flanked both sides the center aisle, and eight perfectly placed chandeliers hung down from thick cords above them. The altar area was set up for a concert, with musicians and singers in jeans and mini-skirts gathering and taking their places; and we actually heard music coming from some antechamber up towards the front of the nave. All at once a man came and leaned over the harpsichord to give a starting note, when I gasped!

"Oh, my GOD!!" I fairly shouted, still in a whisper. "I KNOW him!"

"You're joking!" Nonnie said.

"Who is it?" Cass looked at me, stunned.

"That guy! That guest choral conductor at Iowa last year!! That English guy!"

"What's his name?" Cass asked.

"I can't remember! "

"But you're sure it's the same one?" Cass asked.

"Pretty sure. Almost positive. Don't you remember me coming back from the Union and telling you about him?" I begged Cass.

"Sort of. I remember you being very impressed with someone, now that you mention it."

"JOHN RUTTER!" I blurted out -- too loud! – and immediately hushed my voice. "That's his name!" I had remembered it, recalling him in jeans with a tee shirt, the short sleeves rolled even farther up on his shoulders. This time he was in khaki pants, a plaid shirt and a sweater vest. His hair was quite thick in back curling around his collar, and he wore the same glasses. His face had a cleft chin that was very distinguishable. I was sure it was the same person I'd seen at Iowa.

"I wonder what he's doing here!? I thought he was from Cambridge," I told them. "Let's sit down and listen for a minute. Maybe they'll play – or sing! My God, this is probably the choir of the Academy of St. Martin-in-the Fields."

"Do you think he would remember you?" Cass asked picking up on my thrill.

"No."

"But it was only a year ago," she argued.

"Come on."

"But maybe!"

"He's young!" Nonnie added, rather amazed.

"Gosh, he must be famous over here," I realized. "We certainly had never heard of him."

John Rutter was not yet famous when we saw that rehearsal in London in 1968. But obviously by the next decade, when the first Clare College Choir album came out his status had changed, at least in England. In the States it would be another ten years or so before his Christmas music would change the genre forever; and much later Volvo would use one of the most beautiful songs in a snowy wonderland commercial for their reliable car. Once that happened, classical music stations played more and more Rutter, mainly at Christmas, but sometimes his other repertoire.

We stayed for almost half an hour listening to the glorious sounds float up and all around us in the church, before Cass started getting antsy that we were off schedule. Walking ever so quietly out of the rehearsal we were taken aback by the bright sunlight outside as we made our way over to the National Gallery.

Nonnie and I deferred to Cass' knowledge of art in all museum visits, but especially here. She had already decided that I would be seeing every possible French art there was during my year in Paris, so in London we should concentrate on British but also other European art, Dutch, Flemish, and Italian especially.

"I'm anxious to see English," I announced. Nonnie didn't really care one way or the other. She wasn't as interested in art as I was, and was doing more French literature than any other subject at *La Sorbonne*. But she was absolutely open to broadening her liberal education with whatever art Cass and I had in mind.

"Okay, then I say we start with Constable, Turner, Gainsborough and Reynolds," Cass pronounced.

They were certainly all there...and so much more. It became a daunting task to even scratch the surface of this vast collection, as it was with any other major museum in the world. We were just like all the other poor tourists; we had to pick and choose what to look at. I did love JMW Turner and could easily trace the roots of Monet's theories of light back to Turner's depictions of the sun as the source of pure light, painted as a ball of color. The famous *Rain, Steam and Speed* was as Impressionistic as anything Monet or Renoir painted at Argenteuil.

Turner, it turns out, had bequeathed many paintings to the National Gallery along with specifications of which ones should be hung with which other ones. *The Rise of the Carthaginian Empire* should be hung with *Seaport, The Embarkation of the Queen of Sheba* and *The Mill*. It was all fascinating.

We wandered around and into the part that held 18th century British Portraiture, to gawk at portrait after portrait of the extensive collection of British Royal Family paintings, military and naval officers and statesmen.

Cass was also interested especially in the Dutch school and led us off to see her favorite, which was Salomon van Ruysdael's *View of Deventer Seen from the Northwest.*

"I've been to Deventer," she said, surprising me once again with the breadth of her travels. "This is just so hauntingly beautiful, don't you think?" Nonnie and I both nodded.

I also loved one down a ways along the same wall that showed an ice-skating scene by some artist named Hendrick Avercamp of whom I'd never heard a whit. What amazed me was that in 1616 when this work was painted, the Dutch people portrayed were socializing and having fun under the ephemeral pastel winter sky. It was a time period I mostly associated with wars, pestilence, starvation and ruin. But here was Holland, depicted with leisure activities, the people wearing red, yellow and blue clothes, and buildings looking solid and well-constructed. The painting told me more about my inferior education than it did about the time period it depicted.

We had stayed in the National Gallery until almost three o'clock!

"My tummy is telling me it's time for that tea break you were talking about," Nonnie said to Cass, as we headed for the exits.

"Mine, too. Even though this morning I decided I never need to eat again," I remarked.

"Never fear," Cass said, "sustenance is on the way!"

"Now for this – your first official English **afternoon** tea, I would like to treat you to a wonderful one. And if we do it again, we'll go to more 'normal' places. But this time we're going to a really special place. My grandmother actually brought me to London for my 14th birthday, and we stayed where I'm taking you. I just fell in love," Cass said wistfully.

*Oh, God, I thought, not the Ritz Hotel. I hadn't brought any clothing with me that would do for tea-- or anything else-- at the Ritz. Everyone, even kids growing up in Iowa, had heard of **their** afternoon tea. The Paris Ritz had one, too, and Jo Jo's mother had taken her there. She said the cost was $26 per person!! I about died when I heard that. Twenty-six dollars for a cup of tea and some sweets?! Why, that was a fourth of my monthly stipend!*

"Cass," I said, "I hope you don't mean the Ritz."

"No! Better! The Savoy!!"

I gave a little sigh of relief. "Never heard of it."

"You've heard of Gilbert and Sullivan, right?"

"Of course. Most fun musical we ever did at school, " said Nonnie. "I played 'Daughter Number Four — lah-dee-dah — in *Pirates of Penzance*. Type-casting, right?"

"Our school did *The Mikado*," I laughed. "And I also loved it."

"Did you have a part?" Cass wanted to know.

"Yes, in the chorus. No lines."

Story of my life.

"Well, then, you might know that the hotel was built by the producer of all the Gilbert and Sullivan plays, Richard D'Oyly Carte. If you have any of the albums of the musicals, they're still put out by the D'Oyly Carte Company of actors and singers now."

That didn't ring a bell for me; I didn't have the album of *The Mikado*, but I believed Cass.

"The Savoy was built in 1889 or so," Cass continued, "and for its day, it was the most modern, most luxurious, most appointed hotel of its kind. It was really Britain's first luxury hotel. You can just imagine the fortune D'Oyly Carte made on Gilbert and Sullivan!! And the same family has owned it for all this time."

"Wow," I said, as we approached the building. "It's beautiful."

Cass was still in tour guide mode. "It had the first electric lights and elevators; every room had its own bathroom which was just unheard of in those days. AND, hot and cold running water! Imagine!" Cass laughed. "And get this, César Ritz came from Paris to manage the Savoy! And he brought his chef with him: Auguste Escoffier!"

"Wow," I said again. "I wonder how he managed that!"

"Well, they must have lured him away. But you can dig it. Today the Ritz Hotels in both London and Paris are still the most famous ones, you know."

"This is going to be wonderful!" Nonnie said excitedly. "Are we dressed okay, really? "

"You are," Cass assured her.

It had been a surprisingly short walk from Trafalgar Square to the Strand, as it turned out. Cass had obviously planned the day that way. We entered the hotel via the Riverside entrance beneath a protective overhang under the huge sign. Cass led us to the Thames Foyer and teatime, where she had clandestinely booked us in and had guessed at the correct hour.

The room was absolutely stunning, with its gorgeous column- studded white walls, and the fabulous "Tiffany" glass dome cupola with the art nouveau ironwork gazebo underneath it, where a grand piano stood in those years. The tables all around were set with the fine linens, china and silver one would expect to see in as seriously elegant a place as this was --and is. The afternoon lighting in the room was soft, with most of the remaining sunlight still coming into the dome from above; but the tables were also lit with candlestick lamps. In every wall niche was a lit portrait.

The waiter escorted us to our table, and settled us into the soft pillows of the Chiavari chairs, and spread the heavy linen napkins across our laps. Cass told him we would all have the traditional afternoon tea. We were asked to choose from among all the tea types, but the only tea I knew of by name was English Breakfast. Cass chose the Savoy Afternoon blend, which was a blend of Ceylon and Darjeeling, and Nonnie and I followed suit, not having much of a clue not only what that was, but how it might differ from any other black tea.

And when the feast arrived, it was by far the most sumptuous one I could ever imagine. The food came on a giant silver-tiered tray and the tea in china pots. The savory things were towards the top and the sweets below, but it was all there in front of us at the same time. And when the portions are so dainty and sweet, you don't realize you may be gorging yourself.

"I love tea sandwiches so much that I could just sit here and scarf them down one after the other," I announced, taking a Scottish smoked salmon with lemon infused crème fraiche from the silver tray.

"Hmmm, egg salad," said Nonnie, "soooo good. And this 'classic white' bread, (*stated on tiny placards near the tray*) is different from our white bread, I'll say that! It must be *pain de mie*, don't you think?"

Cass took a "Coronation chicken on olive bread" and pronounced it delicious.

We had both raisin and plain scones served with clotted cream and pots of strawberry jam and lemon curd. Also on the tray's wide lower tiers were assorted gateaux, Genoise sponge and Bavarois crumble. They gave us citrus tarts, along with something called the "Classic Opera," which was a coffee-flavored butter cream; chocolate cookies; a "Savoy *éclair*" filled with mango passion fruit custard they called "cremeux" and topped with milk chocolat whipped ganache; and a strawberry sable, which was shortbread with vanilla custard and fresh strawberries. There were also three kinds of cakes.

The waiter offered us champagne to wash this all down, but I declined, as did my two friends; the tea was quite enough. We stayed there for two hours, part of the time regaling Cass with stories of our classes and the other program participants, some of whom, of course, she had met. She, in turn, told us of flying, her most and least favorite destinations, how they had to "bid" for routes; the grooming and body scrutiny they were subject to, which Cass hated; and how all the pilots slept with whomever they liked.

"Including you?" I asked, shocked to hear this.

"Nope. I tell them I'm spoken for and that, besides, I'm a 'good girl'---ho!"

"God, where do they all get off? Men, I mean. Why do they all think they're so irresistible that when they tell us to jump we say 'how high?'" Nonnie pined.

"Are any of us on the pill?" I asked, adding, "I'm not."

They shook their heads no.

"But I know someone at *La Maison* who is!" Nonnie added conspiratorially, "and she's sleeping with Matoré!"

"What!?" I was astounded that one of our very own participants was the lover of none other than the head of the entire *Cours de Civilisation Française* at the Sorbonne. Nonnie said she thought that by the time June rolled around, they would be engaged.

"How can stuff like that be happening and I'm completely in the dark," I wondered out loud.

"It's her naïveté," Cass laughed. "Legendary."

"No, but seriously, come on! Do you advanced students just get in on the good stuff and we peons are left to our own devices or what?"

"I couldn't tell you," Nonnie chortled, adding, "*Mais c'est scandaleux, non*? But I think it's kind of cute, too. He must really be in love with her!"

When we left the Thames Foyer, it was dark as night outside and the Savoy sign was lit in dazzling neon. We all walked along the Embankment trying to decide what to do next. Shops were not open late as in America, and we obviously weren't going to dinner.

Nonnie had the best idea. "You know," she said, "I heard that there's a *Le Drugstore* over here, modeled after the one on Boulevard St. Germain. That might be open into the evening."

Cass had brought a "Time Out London" along with her, which was the London version of "*Pariscope*" and she pulled it out and consulted it.

"Chelsea Drugstore," she read, "in west London near King's Road."

"Oh, King's Road is near Carnaby Street, I think!" I said, not knowing a thing.

"No, it's not, Sari," Cass said. "Sorry to disappoint you, kid. Carnaby Street is in Soho, not Chelsea. But we'll try to get there, too." She began to read out of the booklet about the Chelsea Drugstore. "It says that the Chelsea Drugstore—just recently opened, by the way-- has bars, a chemist—that's the pharmacy part," Cass explained—(but we knew that—we'd passed a gazillion Boots Chemists shops walking around--), "a newsstand, record store, and other things like souvenirs and even toys."

"Sounds like it will be open late," said Nonnie. "Does it say?"

"Eleven!" Cass announced. "That's cool."

The closest tube stop to King's Road, in our estimation, was Sloane Square so we just got back in the Underground at Embankment and took the District and Circle line towards where both our hotels were.

"That's coincidental," I thought. So far, the tube was a snap.

The Chelsea Drugstore was on three floors and more modern than the Parisian ones, which made sense since in 1968, it was brand new. We got some souvenir post cards in the newsstand part and then made our way to the music department. People were milling around listening to records with headphones.

"Wow!" I said, "they don't let you do that in Paris!"

"Look, they have cassettes, too!"

"Oh, look," said Cass. "Here's the Beatles' *Sgt. Pepper*. It would be neat to get this here in London."

"Well, *She's Leaving Home* is what they've been playing a lot on Radio Luxembourg now, Cass, and of course, since I have a radio, I listen to it all the time! Ha! But I'd really like to get a cassette or two. What about you, Nonnie?"

"Oh, my brothers would be thrilled with some record from London, too. Maybe the Stones?"

"Don't tell me your little brothers are Rockers instead of Mods," I kidded.

"They're American junior high school kids! They could care less about British nomenclature. But they do like the music!"

I loved the "British Invasion." It had already been going on for years.

"Maybe I can find a cassette of Herman's Hermits," I said. "That would make me happy."

We spent a lot of time in there trying out various songs and album samples before moving on to look at the very expensive array of costume jewelry and books, after which we repaired to one of the three bars. No one was hungry but even though it had gone completely dark by the time we left the Savoy, it was still not exactly late, and we didn't want to go back to the hotels.

"So this so-called 'swinging London,' where is it?" Nonnie asked.

"Well, we're sort of in the thick of it, but London is a town with a lot of private clubs and stuff," Cass said. "I think if we walked up King's Road, we'd find restaurants busy, though."

"We're just so used to having cafés to sit in at all hours," I said.

"Yeah," said Nonnie, "London isn't like Paris. It's not like the States, either, mind you."

"I really like it, though. It doesn't feel dangerous to be out and about in London."

We discussed the plans for Sunday and decided to sleep in, have the grand breakfast again, and by the time we were ready to leave for the day, it would be about ten. Cass and Patty would both be at our hotel, and Nonnie would go off with her friend. Cass and I planned to go on the boat ride, and Nonnie said that if they decided to do that, too, they would try to meet up with us. Everyone agreed we wouldn't be at the boat dock until somewhere around one in the afternoon.

Nonnie and I figured out perfectly how to get back from Chelsea to Gloucester Road tube stop, so Cass went off to find a taxi to take her back to her hotel. We had grabbed some salt and vinegar chips---crisps---to take back with us, and some Schweppes and Tango soft drinks. I was exhausted by the time we actually plopped down on our beds. Our room had a tiny little t.v., and as far as I was concerned, that made it perfect. We watched a game show and fell asleep. I woke up around midnight to white noise, turned off the set, and promptly fell right back to sleep.

Chapter Thirty-five

"Those Were the Days My Friend"...Mary Hopkin (Fomin & Bruhn)

Nonnie's friend Patty was super cool, and studying at Oxford had a cachet to it that more than rivaled that of the Sorbonne. Her experience was completely different from ours, we found out, as she didn't go to class, but "read" a subject with a "don" and met for discussion once a week in very small groups in the professors' offices. Americans could not "go to Oxford" to any college they chose; only certain ones were offered to foreign undergrads then; Patty was in Magdalen (she pronounced it as "Maudlin") College. All the colleges that made up Oxford University were autonomous and had their own mini-campuses amidst the greater university setting.

"That sounds kind of confusing," I ventured. But I had seen enough pictures of it to know how beautiful the whole place was and I was certainly dying to go see it in person someday.

Cass came over to the hotel, also, in keeping with our little routine where she came to our hotel rather than us having to make our way to hers. Nonnie left with Patty after our usual English breakfast, saying that they'd try to make it to the boat ride but not to wait for them if they didn't show up; and Cass and I sat and talked in my room for a little while.

"You could go back to sleep and I could come get you after St. Paul's," she laughed.

"Do I look that tired?" I wondered aloud.

"No! But I just thought you might like a little "lie-in" as they say here."

"Oh, no...I'm up for your church."

So we left for St. Paul's cathedral and it was worth the trip for this Jewish girl to observe once again, the magnificence of a place of worship so worthy of world class designation. We walked up the stairs and right on in, like we knew what we were doing as worshippers and not tourists. We stepped across the magnificent black and white marble floor to seats that were chairs rather than pews, as in French churches I'd been in; but the size and scope of this nave left me breathless. Choir music was already ringing out and the sanctuary was maybe a third full. We had no idea how many services were held on any given Sunday but Cass thought if we got there mid-morning, "we'll be able to take part in one no matter what", and she was right. We were towards the back, so the beautiful dark oak choir stalls with their little lamps on each post were pretty far away from me to actually see the choir, but I discerned little boys in red robes with white collars, flanked by men. I couldn't see if any women were present in the choir, and it turned out there were not.

I also had no idea of what clergy led what services. We were in a cathedral, so the man giving the homily out in the center may have been the Bishop of London, for which St. Paul's is the seat; but I couldn't tell from his vestments or anything else about him whether or not he was that exalted in the hierarchy. I asked Cass.

"Well, we know he's not the head of the whole Anglican church, " she answered with some assuredness in hushed tones, "because that's the Archbishop of Canterbury and he's at Canterbury Cathedral, no doubt. But I really don't suppose he's the Bishop of London either. This is only a Sunday service, not a holiday or an occasion of any kind. They must have dozens of clergy."

We were sitting there ostensibly taking part in the service that I was merely watching, but lots of people were milling around, albeit trying to keep quiet about it. In those days anyone could come into the church without charge, and Sundays were not yet closed to worshippers only. No one wandered towards the altar, of course, but the peripheries of the space were filled with items of interest and people gravitated towards the north transept to look at Holman Hunt's huge religious painting that hung in there, "The Light of the World."

I was completely entranced by the music and the choir. I didn't know an oratorio from a motet in those days, but I knew I was in the presence of a sweeping all-encompassing beauty that soared through the splendid architecture and swooped back down around us again and again like an invisible veil carried upon some magical breeze. To think that this was a "normal Sunday" and everyone could hear this kind of music every week!

I whispered very softly to Cass, "Your service is so beautiful; no wonder people come to church."

"Well, mine isn't this grand at home," she assured me.

"Still," I said, "I bet all the choirs in all the Anglican and Episcopal churches sing about the same music, don't they?"

"I'm just guessing they might, but again, not like this."

Once the actual service was over, we also walked around and toured the building. We, like all the tourists, went up to the Whispering Gallery where you could look down on the striking view of the choir stalls, each one carved uniquely with varied expressions in the cherubs' faces and differing flowers, leaves and fruits that made up the wreaths and garlands; or from high up there, you could get a closer look at the dome frescoes painted by Thornhill. Under the dome was an inscription commemorating Winston Churchill's state funeral three years prior; and also Sir Christopher Wren's own epitaph written in Latin, which when translated says, "Reader, if you seek his monument, look around you."

"That was really great," I said, as we exited. "I'm glad we went."

"Do you feel—you know---religious at all?" she asked. "Do you want to go to synagogue and reconnect with your own religion?"

"Ha! If it had music like yours, I might. But in answer to your question: no."

We headed out for Westminster and the boat ride to Greenwich.

It was cool and overcast weather once we got on board, but wanting to see the sights of London go by as we sailed, we braved the elements and took seats on a bench on the upper deck. However, the wind was sharp and the damp penetrated our coats, so Cass suggested we retreat inside and have a cup of tea rather than ride on the deck. We sat down at one of the tables that were set up near the bar in the interior of the boat. I told her to sit there while I went to the counter and came back with two steaming mugs of tea with milk and sugar.

I cupped my hands around mine to warm them up, and she stirred hers slowly and took a first tentative sip to see if it was cool enough to drink.

"I'm actually kind of glad we got some time alone with you," she said to me. "There's something I want to tell you."

"What?!" I was rather surprised. She hadn't let on that she didn't want Nonnie in London with us up to now. "Did you not want Nonnie here?"

"Oh no, it's nothing like that. I just wanted to tell you that Alan is coming to Boston at the end of the month."

"Oh, really?"

"Yes. He's coming for some big conference---the MLA, whatever that is."

"You know what it is. Every time we write a paper, we have to use their style sheet."

"Oh, yeah… I forgot. Anyway, since he's in the workshop, and since they also do literature in translation, they want him to go and do some kind of short presentation on it."

"The MLA conference is where people who are looking for jobs in foreign languages and English go to meet reps from schools seeking to fill positions."

"Ah hah. Well, maybe he'll play some role in that. I don't know. The U is paying for the whole thing."

"Wow."

"And he wants to see me. He said he only put in for it because it was in my city."

"I bet giving a paper at a national conference would look sweet on his resumé, too," I added.

"Can't hurt! But anyway, I'm a little worried about seeing him. Before he went back to Iowa City to start the fall term, we had a really terrible scene. I guess I became a bit –ho! --no, more like a lot-- hysterical at the thought of him going back and me stuck on the East Coast in a hated job."

"What kind of 'hysterical'?"

"I told him if we didn't make plans, real plans, I'd quit the relationship for good." Cass' face darkened. "I told him maybe I'd end up killing myself because it was destroying me."

"Oh, Jesus." I looked at her with more intensity. "But Cass, I take it he did go back? I mean, I saw you in October in Paris and he wasn't in Boston then."

"Right. And really, I didn't want to see him again. As far as I was concerned we were finished. And of course, he's not worth killing myself over! No one person is. It's just that when he left, I felt so completely unloved by him."

"So you're afraid if he comes you'll end up fighting with him again?"

"Oh, I'm in no mood to dredge all that up again. It's just that I hadn't heard from him until he called about this convention thing and you know, I was glad I hadn't had any contact with him. I was getting used to not having him in my life, much as I miss him. I really do miss him, Sari."

"But in your heart you don't believe it can work, right?"

"Well, after the big blowup, we did make up and we also made love again. But when push comes to shove, he just doesn't want what I do. And frankly, I just sort of feel a freedom without him in my life. I am actually kind of grateful to him---he has, in effect, set me free."

"So then you *don't* regret breaking up with him?"

"If I let myself feel regret, it just makes me depressed."

"You know," I said, suddenly feeling perturbed, "he doesn't seem to want what you want at all! " I saw Alan as being nothing but dismissive of Cass and her talent.

"I thought what I wanted was to be married! He doesn't want **that** for sure."

"Well, it seems to me that he didn't take into consideration what you wanted at Iowa either! What you really wanted was to be a printmaker, wasn't it? You can't tell me that you aren't even a little ticked off that he doesn't appreciate the fact that you are a gifted individual with a serious art career in front of you! Doesn't that even figure into it?!! Isn't it ART you miss and not Alan?"

"I don't know. I'm so messed up. I mean, you asked me if I regretted breaking up with him, but what you really mean is do I regret ever getting involved with him in the first place, isn't it?"

"Well— gee, maybe. Hey, that's not for me to judge. I thought you guys were in love. Weren't you? Really in love, I mean?"

"Alan's love—if you can call it that, was of a non-supportive sort, not the kind that wants to take care of someone, provide for real-world needs, share a life together under one roof. He had sort of idealized aspirations of love, I think. Dances and poems and kisses are all fine and nice, of course. But they dissipate or are snuffed out if stronger stuff doesn't exist beneath."

"So, do you wish you'd never gotten involved with him? Do you, you know, feel used?"

"No. To me, that would be to deny I really loved him. I am just as responsible for getting involved with him as he is. I hate that he has so much power over me because I love him. The problem is, there's no way around that. When we fight, it just leaves me numb."

"So don't see him! Book yourself on some extra flights. Come to Paris for Thanksgiving. Tell him you got sent at the last minute." This didn't seem so hard to me.

"Well, what I need to make clear to him is that we are going our separate ways."

"If I hear you then, you are saying that you are strong enough in your convictions to see him again and let him know the lay of the land."

"I think I am. I mean, the hard part is that I really want to be back at school and I hope I can be on that campus and not want to see him."

"Cass, get real. He will just come to Boston and mess with your head again. It looks like a pattern to me."

"I know. I'm fucked."

"Look, bottom line is, I hope you can be back in Iowa City and he'll leave you alone! But really, you also have to assert yourself! It seems to me that you've got to tell him that it's art that's your passion...and your priority! I mean, for God's sake, I am astounded that you aren't longing to be back in the studio in Iowa City. You say you miss school so much; it's your art you miss! You can't tell me you see yourself as a wife and not as an artist."

"Okay, okay, I do see myself as an artist. I just wanted both when I fell in love with him. Ha! I will be more objective in my relationships from now on! I mean, I would never give up the emotional side of life. I will just have to be more 'objectively emotional' from now on! How's that for a made-up expression?"

She laughed and I tried to go along.

"Look, it doesn't matter what Alan says or does, really, in the grand scheme of things. Stick it out at TWA for just eight more months and you'll have proven to your parents that you are responsible. Finishing out this stewardess gig for the year will satisfy Julia, especially, and then you can get back to art. You might even be on a path to greatness already with your doll idea. Holland and Germany are only mere months away from now!"

"You're right; I'm excited for that! But you know, my parents might not let me go back to Iowa. It's going to take some big convincing."

"Well, it's not as if the Art Institute of Chicago won't do!" I laughed, until I saw that she wasn't finding that funny.

"I just dearly want to be back in Iowa City. I just hope Lasansky will still have me after all this time."

"I know."

I was relieved that she still had the artist soul if not burning, at least smoldering inside her.

"For another thing," she reminded me, " we've been planning our senior apartment! I mean, it's not **just** that I want to be back in the Iowa school of art. I want to be back there with **you**. I really wonder how I got so very fortunate to have a **friend** like you---I feel we are in communion. We 'groove' together."

I took ahold of her arm across the table.

"I feel the same way; you know I do."

"But the thing is, you are empathetic, Sari, and I really am not. I am self-absorbed most of the time, especially now. I feel duly sorry for myself in this TWA purgatory. I'm overly analytical about Alan, and I'm scared about not being a good enough artist to even really consider it a 'calling.' Whereas you are always thinking about me, about your other friends in Paris, Nonnie and C.C., and even ol' Jo Jo. I've seen you stand up to your parents, and I was awed by that, but in the end, you do what they expect you to do, because you are a 'good girl' (she made air quotes) and if you're worried—like about your grades and all that, it's because you are afraid of letting everyone else down."

"Well, gee, when did you come up with all that?"

"I've been observing you, kid! And I get so lonely for you when I'm back in the States."

"Well, me, too, but you have to admit, it's a minor miracle we see each other so often this year, don't you?! I mean, *who'd'a thunk it*, eh?!"

"Yeah," she laughed.

"I should be the one who's grateful," I emphasized. "That fact that we got thrown together in that dorm in what seems like a lifetime ago already, that you were willing to 'put up with' a Jewish freshman was nothing short of pure luck on my part, and that does not escape me."

"I didn't 'put up with' you. We hit it off! We are kindred spirits."

"We are that! And nothing will change. God forbid your parents don't let you return to Iowa and if you're at the Art Institute, for instance, we'll still see each other. Christ, a one-hour flight away or four hours train ride is nothing compared to two continents! And after I graduate (or we both do) I'll move to Chicago! How's that for a plan? I'll find some sort of job—bilingual something or other. Maybe you'll go on to grad school. Maybe if we can't get back to our dreamy Iowa City apartment, we can room together in Chicago."

"I like your thinking, kid!"

"You're always telling me to keep the faith, baby. You have to, also!"

The boat ride was coming to an end and we were docking. The weather was still dreary but at least our, or I should say, her mood was lifting. We got off the boat having been philosophers, and turned back into tourists.

226

Chapter Thirty-Six

"Águas de Março"...Tom Jobim & Elis Regina (Jobim)

To my relief, as the boat docked in Greenwich, Cass seemed to feel better and had snapped out of her pensive mood. We first made our way up the pier to see the Cutty Sark and all the charts, sailing mementos and other evidence on display illustrating the history of the clipper trade. We then walked through a lovely park, teeming with people out for a Sunday, even in dreary weather, that led up to the Royal Observatory and the famous clock that shows Greenwich Mean Time. I was thrilled to see the clock telling what the BBC announcers always gave as the hour "GMT."

It was fitting, if only coincidental, that we had decided to come to Greenwich the same day we'd been to St. Paul's because in order to see the clock, we took the rather long tour of the Observatory, which, it was explained to us, Charles II had directed Sir Christopher Wren to build!

Our guide said, "He wanted a small observatory within the park at Greenwich upon the highest ground near where the palace stood."

Wren was, it turned out, a former astronomer as well as an architect, and he designed a house of red brick with stone decoration, an upper balustrade and miniature cupolas for the Observatory's residence "for a little pomp." The residence, we learned, was named Flamsteed House for the first Royal Astronomer, John Flamsteed, who had been appointed in 1675.

The guide also mentioned, to my astonishment, that when we descended back through the park along the slope below the Observatory, we would be walking on traces of giant grass steps designed by Le Nôtre in 1662.

"Le Nôtre!" I whispered to Cass as we walked through to the next room, "designed the gardens of Versailles! Gosh, he really got around!"

We didn't think we had time to tour the Tudor Palace because its guided talk took more than an hour and a half. But we lingered around the courtyard of the palace where King Henry VIII was born, and where the Tudors, including the first Queen Elizabeth, amused themselves with jousting exhibitions. We saw where there was a royal armory that was known to have made the finest suits of mail "equal to those in France or Italy;" and we peered over a wall down to the river where the sumptuous royal barges would bring nobles to the royal docks to inspect the ever-growing British fleet or to welcome it back from its far flung battles.

Cass and I decided not to take the boat ride back to Central London and instead opted for the train out of Greenwich station to Victoria, and then we grabbed a cab, which was easier because it was the weekend, and headed over to her hotel.

"I think my hotel's teatime is over," Cass said noticing that it was almost six o'clock. "But we can just have dinner there."

These were the days before there were any sorts of ways to communicate with anyone out and about, so I used Cass' room phone to leave a message at my hotel for Nonnie, just in case she and Patty were there. They hadn't been at the boat ride, so I figured they had just found other things to do to amuse themselves after church in London; but I had no way of really knowing.

"What do you want to do tomorrow?" Cass asked.

"SHOP!" I said without a moment's hesitation. There would still be a lot of cultural attractions to take in, but I was longing to see Harrod's, Miss Selfridges, department stores on Oxford Street and as many other stores, shops or boutiques as we could manage.

"Okay, I think we'll go to Knightsbridge tomorrow then, and start with Harrod's. It will blow your mind, especially the loo!"

"Why the loo?"

"It's blue and white porcelain!"

"Noooo."

"And speaking of china," she went on, "there's what's called the Reject China shop on Brompton Road, which is up aways from Harrod's. And," she said with a gleam in her eye, "also up there is the V and A, which you absolutely must see."

"What's the V and A?" I asked innocently.

"The Victoria and Albert Museum. Simply the most divine collection of...everything Victorian and Edwardian *arts décoratifs*."

"Heaven!" I pronounced it, sight unseen.

Cass accompanied me back to my hotel after dinner where we did indeed find Nonnie but no Patty.

"She had to take the train back to Oxford," Nonnie explained, "and I saw her off and came back here. I've been watching this soap called 'Coronation Street' and it's great stuff!"

"So what did you two do today?" I wondered.

"Well, we did go to church—which was very cool, by the way. We found this nice church right up the street from our tube stop called the Brompton Road Oratory."

"Oh my God!" I exclaimed. "We were just talking about going to Brompton Road tomorrow!"

"Yes, the V and A was right near that church," said Nonnie. "Patty told me I'd go ape in there."

"We all will!" I laughed.

"And after that," she continued, "we just walked around that area until we decided walking was stupid, and we got on a regular London double decker bus that had Paddington Station as its terminus. We just decided to ride it wherever it went, and look at anything and everything it passed. And Paddington is the train station for trains going to Oxford, so that was fortuitous!"

"Wow. Pretty brave. Where did it take you?"

"Oh, on a really neat route. We saw some famous places like the Royal Albert Hall, Harrod's, and Buckingham Palace! By the time the bus pulled into Paddington Station, it was still too early for Patty's train, so we were just going to stay on the bus and have another round trip before she actually had to leave. We showed our day travel cards to the conductor and he was cool with it, so we were sitting up there just shooting the breeze because the bus was going to be parked for a while. And then we noticed that we were across from a large nondescript building that I couldn't tell what it was at first and then realized it was a hospital called St. Mary's. And we saw this very crippled man struggling to walk with a walker but he wasn't really walking---he was dragging himself on it."

"Oh, dear," Cass said. "There is a student in Iowa City who sounds like the very same thing; I've seen him on campus. He really has a hard time of it."

"Yes, I've seen him."

"So," Nonnie went on, "you wouldn't have believed it---he needed to get up those steep concrete steps! And it was impossible. We watched as he laid himself down on the steps and folded the walker, which wasn't easy because it also had a bag hanging on the bar. And then he put it under his arm and proceeded to try to pull himself up the stairs! And it wasn't working out too well. It looked excruciating."

"Didn't anyone try to help him?"

"That's just the thing," said Nonnie, "no! We couldn't believe it. For one thing there really weren't too many people around, but the ones who did walk by, just kept on walking! We didn't know what to do because sometimes it insults handicapped people's dignity to offer to help them."

"Well, how dignified is it to be crawling up a flight of stairs?!" Cass blurted out.

"Exactly. So we got off the bus and ran across this rather huge street---I don't know what it was—and we got to him and asked if we could help him."

"And? Was he insulted?" I asked in anticipation of the worst.

"No! He was grateful. But we didn't exactly know what to do, so I took the walker and we helped him to a sitting position. Then Patty ran inside to get help! I mean, it was a hospital for God's sake! And she brought out someone—probably an orderly, but maybe a doc---with a wheelchair. It took all three of us to get him in it and up the rest of the staircase, too. I still had the walker in my other hand!"

"Wow, girl," Cass said admiringly.

"Good for you guys!" I chimed in.

"Well, I mean, anyone would have done the same."

"But they obviously didn't!"

"What did the man end up saying about all this?" Cass wondered.

"He took my hand in both of his hands and said, 'Thank you, Miss.' And he thanked Patty, too, and then I handed him the walker which he propped up on his knees, and the hospital worker wheeled him down the corridor."

I could see that Nonnie was profoundly affected by this incident, and it made us all ponder how in the world people with such mobility problems can even function in a huge fast-paced city like London...or for that matter on a college campus like Iowa. Or anywhere.

Changing the subject, Cass excitedly told Nonnie about our plans for the next day. Nonnie indicated that she liked the idea of shopping, but she broke the news to me that she had decided to cut her London visit a little short, and head on over to Ireland earlier than planned.

"I hope you don't mind," Nonnie said to me. Cass looked at me quizzically.

"Oh, no — whatever you want to do."

"It's just that my other friend called here right when I got back, actually, and said he had an invitation to the country with his Irish friend and that I was invited to come along if I could get there earlier."

"Will you still get to visit Trinity and see Dublin though?" I wondered.

"Oh, sure. But it would be wild to see a real Irish farm, too, don't you think?"

"Yeah, neat-o," I said.

Monday morning, our routine started once again with breakfast and Cass' arrival. Nonnie reiterated at breakfast that she was still up for going around with us that day, but that towards the late afternoon she would go back to the room and pack.

"But I've really enjoyed this great weekend with you and Cass," she repeated, making sure I knew.

"Me, too! I'm glad we did it."

"And I'll leave you my share of the remaining room fees, too," she said, "so don't worry about that. You'll have it all to yourself!"

"Well, sure, but..."

"I just mean you can spread out!"

We took the tube to Knightsbridge, and it let out right at Harrod's. Harrod's was everything I knew it would be and more. Very expensive, I could hardly afford one thing in there, but still managed to make a dent in my spending money buying some Harrod's branded souvenir plasticized linen tote bags and a little bear for Roslyn.

"Pearls before swine," I announced, showing the bear to my friends.

"Now, now," Cass chided me, "you know she'll love it. You're a good big sister to Roz."

We went all over the entire store, and spent a good two hours doing it. I loved the china department in the basement, and could have spent the whole day in there, but Cass wanted to head directly to the shoes.

There was even a sale going on and we all three bought shoes! Mine were what I called "Pilgrim" but, after a few more months in art history class in France, I would have been more accurate to have called them "Louis XIV" shoes! They looked a lot like the ones the king had on in the famous Rigaud painting. Mine were chunky shaped with a little square heel, in black patent leather with a hot pink silk bow across the entire vamp. They were very comfortable, looked "mod" and could be dressy or worn with jeans. I fell madly in love and had to have them, so I started to pray the cost would be somewhere near to what I could possibly afford, since in Harrod's, of course, one could see price tags that were more like the cost of a hotel room — or a yacht, for that matter -- than an article of clothing.

"On sale fifty percent off (!) for thirty Pounds sterling," I gasped. That wasn't half bad, about $ 50 dollars or so. I could swing it. Not that I would ever, **ever** tell my parents that I bought a pair of shoes for only slightly less than what they paid on their monthly mortgage in those days.

Nonnie also bought shoes of a similar style as mine, albeit costing more; and Cass bought grey plaid flats with squared-off toes and a soft insole. Hers cost one hundred and seventy pounds!!

In today's money, that would be over a thousand dollars! I couldn't fathom such a sum spent on one pair of shoes, even in 1968 money.

"My God, Cass. That's more than your flight attendants' take-home pay!"

"Shh. Don't tell my fellow stews!"

Naturally, I was not a wild spendthrift at any time on my European year-long sojourn. I was very careful with the stipend I received each month of one hundred dollars. But when my parents and, especially Nana, knew that a particular occasion was coming up, be it field trips or the true vacations and holidays when the dorm was closed, they augmented my allowance to accommodate, within boundaries, my need for extra cash. I really squirreled away that money and didn't touch it until the designated trip or time period when I'd need it. It goes without saying, too, that the extra cash Cass would thrust into my hands at various moments did not hurt either. In fact, on more than one occasion it made all the difference! I had no way to earn money in Paris. Even if I had had time, which I did not, working in France was strictly forbidden under my student visa. Some of the other students I met at the Sorbonne were working, mostly as au pair girls, but if they were American, they were doing that on the sly. The vast majority of those girls came from Scandinavia or Germany.

When I plunked down the thirty quid for those glorious London shoes, that was just about it for my spending money; I still had a tiny bit left for a little bone china floral with a flaw in one of the petals at the Reject China shop; and I bought a little note pad from the museum shop in the V and A. Cass, on the other hand, bought a beautiful kilt in Dress Campbell and an Irish fisherman knit sweater to wear with it. Nonnie had to take a collection of souvenirs home to her two youngest siblings, so she picked up lots of London or British things like police "Bobby" hats and double decker buses from street vendors.

We all loved the Victoria and Albert museum, as predicted, and spent several hours in there, happy to be able to meander throughout the place without having to hurry. In fact, when we were pretty exhausted and had seen much, if not all of it, we reconnoitered and decided what to do next: go off to Hyde Park and then have tea. After that, even though it was still early, Nonnie reminded us she wanted to get back and start the packing process, so Cass accompanied us.

"I think I have an idea," she said to me as we lumbered up the steps with our shopping bags and sacks. "It occurs to me that with Nonnie leaving, you should come to my hotel with me. Let me do the talking to your desk clerk, okay?"

"Uh—sure." But I didn't exactly get what she had in mind.

Cass stopped at the desk. She explained to the desk clerk that plans had changed and her friends would need to be checking out of the room early, and was there any penalty for it? The clerk went into the back room and the owner came out to the front. There wouldn't be a problem, she told Cass, and wanted to know if anything was wrong with the room. Cass assured her there wasn't; it was just a matter of one of us deciding to go to Ireland early. Suddenly I realized that Cass was making it possible for me not to have to stay there alone and pay the bill myself; and Nonnie didn't have to leave me money after all for her share when she wouldn't be there. Cass had arranged it all, and we would not be charged for the two other days.

"So pack up your stuff, too, Sari," Cass told me as we stared in disbelief at what she had accomplished for us. "You might have to sleep on the couch, but it'll still be fun. This time my room has two twin beds, but Anita might not even be in the room."

Cass' Swedish roommate from Boston roomed with her on trips where they both flew the same flights, but more often than not, she wasn't in the room since her most recent boyfriend was one of the captains. But as Cass had stated more than once, "you never know." Sleeping on the couch in their room at the Thistle Kensington Gardens would be just fine. My mind was still whirring with the money she'd just saved us.

Nonnie was also grateful to Cass. She said, "I have to go to Euston Station this evening to get a train to Holyhead and then the ferry across to Dublin. So you and Sari can ride with me—I'll drop you both at your hotel on my way."

"Gee, thanks!" I said, really appreciative.

"That will work perfectly," said Cass. "I'll go downstairs and wander around your neighborhood while you two do what you have to do." And she left us to our own devices for packing.

I was having trouble with the new clunky shoes in my little plaid suitcase and Nonnie was not faring much better trying to stuff in the toys and other things she'd bought.

"I might have to get a rucksack or something in Ireland," she said, exasperated at all the different angles she placed the policemen hats without any real solution. And then she looked up and said to me, "What will you do here when Cass has to fly out? Will they let you stay in that room?"

"Oh, God no. I can't even imagine what the price on that would be. No, I'll just go back. A few days in Paris with no classes wouldn't be the worst thing that ever happened to me!"

"Yeah, you're right. That sounds heavenly. You can really study."

"Yep." I paused and then remembering my manners, I added, "And I hope you have a great time in Ireland! It must be so amazing to see your American friends over here. Will Patty go over there, too?"

"She wants to, but it will depend. In any event, we've sort of made arrangements for her to be there, too, if she can swing it."

"You'll have to be sure to find me the minute you get back, so I can hear all about it."

"Count on it."

Leave-taking was actually a little sad; we'd become quite the *Trois Mousquetaires* in the days we'd been together. It was so fortunate to my way of thinking that Cass and Nonnie had hit it off so well.

"'Bye Sari. This trip was great stuff, and thank you, Cass, again-- for everything!"

Cass hugged her as the taxi pulled up to the Thistle Kensington Gardens Hotel. "Nonnie, it's been real. Have a great time in Ireland and I hope to see you again in Paris."

Cass helped me up to her fifth-floor room with my suitcase and shopping bags, and I saw her newly cleaned and pressed uniform hanging on the door still in its plastic sleeve. We had two more days of sightseeing and fun before the reality of her having to fly away would sink in.

The next morning she announced that she had another surprise for me.

"I've arranged for you to come to the airport with us on our TWA crew bus Wednesday."

"Really? Gosh, how'd you do that?"

"Oh, it wasn't too hard. A little unorthodox and probably against a few rules, but my crew are cool with it."

"You just astound me."

"Well, wait, it gets better: I put you on the stand-by list to Paris on TWA. Whatever plane can take you, will. When we get to the airport, I'll show you where you have to go. It should not be a problem; this isn't peak flying season and you won't be going back to Paris at the end of the holiday period, so that direction shouldn't be crowded. I got you a stand-by voucher. It was just easier for me to do it than for you to actually arrange to fly stand-by yourself. And you don't care what time you get in, right?"

I was so stunned at all this that I didn't really know what to say to her. "Right. Wait a minute, I fly stand-by on TWA? What is that going to cost?"

"Nothing. I took care of it. Listen, we fly for a fraction of the ticket price. I just bought it for you."

"My God, Cass! That's incredible of you! Thank you!" I lunged at her and hugged her hard.

"You're welcome! So now we have today and tomorrow still free and all to ourselves," she continued, laughing. "What do you want to do?"

"I'm up for anything, Cass. I just can't get over how you managed to do all that."

"I owe you one, kid! You've been my Paris guide for four months!"

"Oh, right. NOT the same!"

We decided to get a *Time Out London* from the front desk and map out our last two days. We would go to the Tate Gallery, see some more of London's famous parks, like Green Park and Kensington Gardens, which, were, of course, right out our front door; and spend two nights going to the theater.

Even though things in London struck me as very expensive, especially with the exchange rate of the dollar to the Pound, theater tickets, as Cass had promised, were very cheap, provided you didn't care where you sat. We went to *The Prime of Miss Jean Brodie* directed by someone named Ian McKellan; and went to the Palace theater the next night and saw *Cabaret* starring a young actress named Judi Dench. Going to live theater of this caliber was not something I did much, if ever, in my youth, and just breathing the same air as these glorious actors, sitting surrounded by the indescribably beautiful lighting and scenery, amidst the architecture of the buildings and the velvety splendor of the seats, just made the experience magical for me. I went back to the hotel both nights in a state of enchantment, which amused Cass.

"Well, what did you expect?" I laughed at her, "I'm a bumpkin."

"You might have arrived in Europe one---and that doesn't mean I think you are---but you won't go back one!"

London was a pure dream for me that November '68 trip. True, I had no other visits to compare it to, and true, I didn't live there and have to work, or manage the transportation system on a daily basis, or pay the exorbitant rents it would take to actually inhabit such a city. I just had fun for five unforgettable days with my dearest friend in the world, free from parents, with a respite from studying, with no cares and no responsibilities. If it got better than that, I could not tell how.

Chapter Thirty-Seven

"Come Ye Thankful People Come"...Henry Alford

Being with Cass in Iowa City was wonderful, especially during our summer sojourn in the apartment. However, Paris cemented our relationship into something beyond friendship. It was platonic love, sisterhood. We were each other's soul mate, pure and simple, and we were so used to pouring ourselves into visits and letters, that I fell into a sort of happy complacency that we were equals. Then it would be brought home to me in the starkest of realizations that, indeed, we were not. From time to time, I would come up short remembering just how wealthy Cass Hyde really was.

London had been a reminder of that, as both Nonnie and I watched Cass blithely spend nearly a thousand dollars – a veritable fortune to us then-- on clothes, shoes and taking us to tea at the Savoy and elsewhere. Cass had never been one to flaunt her wealth to me, and at Iowa, hardly anyone even knew about it; she was just my roomie and a student like me. But, of course, the glaring difference between my home when she visited, and my being a guest at hers---plural – could not have been more evident. The notion of the gap in our socio-economic levels was made manifest to me more than once in 1968.

One Saturday morning after I was back from London, I was having a little *grasse matinée*, sleeping in well past the normal hour, and missing breakfast on purpose, when a sharp rap on the door jarred me right out of any extra reverie I could have hoped to indulge in. The concierge's shrill voice echoed from the hallway!

"*Mademoiselle Shrier ("Shreee-air!!") il y a un coup de téléphone pour vous!*"

I leapt to the door and opened it a crack, giving her a chance to peer in over my shoulder and scowl at me as though she thought she'd see some clutter or contraband -- maybe a boy --in there.

"*Pour moi?!*"

(My God, I thought, who would be calling me? Surely it was transatlantic! And if so, only a dire emergency would warrant that.)

"*Merci, Madame. J'arrive!*"

"*Vite, vite!*" she barked.

So I threw on a robe and my shower thongs, and we descended the five flights of stairs she had evidently decided would be faster than waiting for the tiny elevator to come up and fetch us down. I saw the house phone receiver resting on the ledge in the little mailroom next to the office.

"Hello?" I panted, breathless not only from having dashed precipitously to the *rez de chaussée*, but also out of some fear.

"Hi Sari!" came the voice on the other end of the line.

"Cass?! Where are you calling from? Are you **here** in Paris?"

"No, unfortunately. I'm ensconced back at the Intercontinental Hotel in Frankfurt."

"But...how...why are you calling me? It's long distance!"

"I have news that I wanted to tell you rather than write."

"Geez, Cass, what is it?"

"Well, just that I won't be flying into Paris either this month or in December at all."

"Oh, gosh," I said, with perceptible sadness.

"Yeah, they've changed my route. But the good news is that our Christmas plans are solid, so you can count on coming to Amsterdam. Come the day, even, that your classes end, all right? What did you tell me that day was?"

"I think they end on December 21ˢᵗ—I ran out of the room without my calendar, so I can't look it up."

"That's a Saturday," she said, obviously consulting hers on the other end of the line. "Don't worry, we still have oodles of time to figure it all out. In any event, I should be there by then, waiting for you. Think about this, kid, I've put in for a ten-day furlough!"

"Wow! Do you think you'll get that?"

"I do!"

We didn't talk for very much longer, but rang off with her promising to send me a long letter that she'd already started before she decided to phone me. When it came, the news in it was even more astonishing.

Cass had talked up the notion of Christmas in Holland to me when we were together in London, and I had jumped at the idea, loving a chance to see another country with her, and, of course, to be able to continue on to Germany and go to the doll factory. But it turned out that the original idea had been her mother's!

"Julia," she wrote, using her mother's given name for the first time, instead of calling her Mummy, **"was so delighted that you and I could spend the holidays together—far out of the reach of Alan, no doubt—that she and Papa offered to pick up the tab for us to stay at the Amstel Hotel! This place is really going to blow your mind. It makes the Terrass look like a roadside motel."**

I didn't exactly believe that bit of hyperbole, but knew that Hyde Industries had redesigned the entire chain of Bilderberg hotels within the past fifteen years, and that Cass had already visited Amsterdam with her parents and had stayed there several times. They knew just about everyone in management at that hotel.

Her letter continued, **"If by some bad luck I don't get the whole ten days and have to fly out, but you still have time left on your vacation, my parents said that you should stay in the suite. It won't be on TWA's dime this time, but theirs. We can also eat in the hotel as much as we want."**

Besides this astounding news, Cass' letter contained more of those same fears and trepidations she'd expressed in London about seeing Alan on his Boston trip, but she admitted to me that she had told him it would be okay to come to her apartment.

"I feel frightened." she wrote. **"but have no other solution that is better. I resent having to pay such a high price in emotional turmoil."**

I would have worried more about her after reading that, except that she'd spoken so confidently of our time to come in Amsterdam that I put any concerns out of my head. If I were disappointed that I wouldn't be seeing her in Paris for the rest of that month, or for that matter the next one, I had enough on my plate to keep me from brooding about it. Whatever else I was doing, planning to do, or dreaming of doing, the January exams were a constant reminder that no matter what, I had to stay on top of the coursework. A prodigious amount of reading had once again piled up on me.

However, something else completely unexpected and miraculous happened to me the latter half of that first real semester in Paris, and it hit me right between the eyes one night in mid-November, after we had been back in classes for a week or so. I had sat down at my desk and, as had become my habit, flipped on the radio, tuned it to *France Musique*, my "studying" channel, and WHAM: all at once I realized that I was understanding EVERYTHING they were saying, not just the time and weather!

"*Je commence à comprendre le français!*" I announced excitedly to Agathe when she came in from studying in the library of our dorm downstairs.

"*Eh, oui,* Sarah, "she responded. "*Ça se voit.*" She'd been noticing it already.

This was a total revelation and one that needed amplification, so I left to find Nonnie and C.C. and plan a little celebration, maybe a coke float at *Le Drugstore* or something on the weekend.

"Great news!" Nonnie exclaimed, extolling my achievement.

"Hey," said C.C., "we should make a pact to not speak English any more amongst ourselves."

"Sure!" said Nonnie.

"Wait a minute…" I started to say, but was cut off.

"No no! You've got to!"

"*Eh, bien, d'accord!*"

And C.C. tried it out, explaining in French to us that she'd just been to the American Center for Students and Artists, where she and Marty had gone to a folk music concert, ("*Boff, oui, en anglais!*" she shrugged) and they had seen signs for a Thanksgiving dinner for any American students in Paris. The American Center for Students and Artists was not run by or for only Americans per se; many French young people also went there for their various cultural programming offerings. It had been founded in 1931, we learned from C.C., and had been a frequent gathering spot for American expat artists and writers before the Second World War, even as its present popularity rose in the 50's. Like the *Alliance Française* had French classes for foreigners, the American Center organized English language ones. But the Center's real draw were classes in everything else American: modern rock and roll---what I would have called "bebop" dance, which was still very popular with French young people; poetry readings, lectures on films, and art exhibits by Americans.

C.C. suggested we all make plans to be at that dinner. Thanksgiving was just about the only holiday you couldn't authentically celebrate in Paris, no matter what. Turkeys were not even in the markets until December, which was the only time they ate it---for *Réveillon* dinner.

So it was settled. "*On n'y perd rien,*" Nonnie added. What did we have to lose?

I went back to my desk, as I was deep into Stendhal at that moment, reading *Racine et Shakespeare* and *Le Rouge et le Noir*. It amused me no end how he put down the English people of Shakespeare's day and by consequence their most sublime art form.

"*Les anglais de 1590, heureusement fort ignorants, aimèrent à contempler au théâtre l'image des malheurs que le caractère ferme de leur reine venait d'eloigner de la vie réelle. Ces mêmes détails naïfs que nos vers alexandrins repoussaient avec dédain, et que l'on prise tant aujourd'hui dans Ivanhoe et dans Rob-Roy, eussent paru manqué de dignité aux yeux des fiers marquis de Louis XIV.*"

I studied this paragraph wondering if Stendhal's opinion actually could have been that the English were completely stupid and only loved to contemplate in theater, the troubles that the "closed mind" of their queen had eliminated from real life? He made the case that the Alexandrine verse, beloved by the French, would trump the blank verse of Shakespeare, which would seem completely lacking in dignity to anyone in the court of Louis XIV; but noting that this same form would be taken up by the English whole-heartedly in works such as *Rob Roy* and *Ivanhoe*.

After Stendhal it would be Balzac and we would be reading *Eugénie Grandet* and *Le Père Goriot*, as well as an excerpt from *La Comédie Humaine*. I couldn't decide if prose was easier or harder than poetry. By then I had taken copious notes on the poetry of Alfred de Vigny and Alphonse de Lamartine, and I had written them all in French! It was a milestone achievement but the sheer quantity of what I had to read was more like a millstone. But when I got to Victor Hugo's poetry and had marked up my copy with all the arrows and accents of reading aloud for Filiolet's class, *Les Contemplations* were causing me to contemplate jumping off the Eiffel Tower.

Thanksgiving arrived, and our entire group of friends, including the guys, traipsed up *Boulevard Raspail* to the American Center and the much-touted holiday meal. It did not disappoint. The bird---*la dinde française*-- was similar in look but different in succulent taste than its American counterpart. They tried to emulate the traditional foods but the French flair is hard to mask, and so the dinner was even more delicious than it would have been at my grandmother's table, which, coming from me, was high praise. Thanksgiving, however, was the only night I spent that entire year in Paris that made me kind of homesick; it is so quintessentially American that it just can't be replicated elsewhere.

We sang "Michael Row the Boat Ashore" and that made me cry. We danced with each other, even as a gaggle of French boys wanted to dance "*le bop*" with any American girl they could lure onto the floor. I didn't dance *le bop* at all, so I was useless, but Nonnie was expert at it. The scene reminded me of The Mickey Mouse Club's *Annette* series when the teenagers in saddle shoes danced at the malt shop. I had no frame of reference to that in my actual life.

Paris, as Christmas time approached, was breathtakingly beautiful. The streets were beginning to be festooned in white lights, especially on the *Champs-Elysées* — and in the many plane trees that lined the *grands boulevards*. Swags draped across smaller streets and met in the middle with a star or some other center point. And over behind *l'Opéra*, in the department store district, the fabulous fantasy holiday vignettes of *Galeries Lafayette* and *Au Printemps* in *les vitrines* — the display windows — were front and center, brimming with animated figures, toys, and displays that were street theater all on their own.

We'd had that to a certain extent in Omaha, too, at Brandeis, and it was de rigueur *for my sister and me to go see their windows. But the ones in Paris seemed on a par with Disneyland. It couldn't have been more of a wonderland if Tinkerbell herself had dusted it with her wand.*

The alimentary shops were also filling their windows with displays of holiday food and décor. Now the turkeys came out hanging in the windows still with feathers on; fattened geese were displayed in rows behind hams and other meat. Oysters were the most wanted hors d'oeuvre for the *Noël Réveillon* meal that every French family served on December 24 starting traditionally after midnight mass and going into the wee hours of the morning.

The holiday season officially started in France on or just before December 6, Saint Nicholas Day, when little children would anticipate getting toys in their shoes placed by the fire. Their behavior was held in check lest they got lumps of coal instead from "*le Père Fouettard*" who, legend had it, travelled with the Saint.

French people typically didn't decorate the tree until just around Christmas Eve, but in the outdoor markets all over Paris and all over the country for that matter, (or in the actual Christmas markets in Alsace-Lorraine that mimicked what Germany did almost to the letter,) trees, wreaths, garlands, and red ribbon appeared almost overnight once December arrived. There were big red candied apples on long sticks and warm chestnuts for sale everywhere in the markets, along with little hand-made toys and ornaments, garlands and holly.

Our program directors from Pella College even organized a December weekend field trip to Strasbourg to see the most famous Christmas market in France. My entire group of friends took advantage of this, and we had the most wonderful time wandering up and down aisles of booths.

Nonnie's mother had actually shipped her a miniature fake Christmas tree and a string of little lights, which we could not plug in due to their having the wrong prongs, and the fact that none of us had the requisite converter. She had sent some tinsel, a red metallic garland, and a set of matching tiny ornaments for the tree, too---all for Nonnie to put up in her room! I could not believe it! We all gathered in there for a party before everyone would be scattering to the four winds for the holiday.

We went to *Inno* and came back with champagne and orange juice for me to make Mimosas for everyone. I knew how easy they were to make from Sol, and I had also learned from my father that this cocktail was probably invented at the Paris Ritz in the 1920's! I thought it would not only be festive, but appropriate for our group as well. We also picked up some wonderful *saucissons*, a half dozen *baguettes*, a small wheel of *camembert*, a large wedge of *brie*, and, on the way back to the *Maison* some *langues de chat* cookies from the *pâtisserie* on *Rue Delambre*.

We invited our little crowd and everyone's French roommate as well as some of our other Sorbonne classmates.

Agathe opened the door, saw the tree and exclaimed, "*Oh, mais dites donc! Un petit arbre de Noël! Chouette, alors!*"

The other French girls were just as impressed …and delighted. I brought my radio and we tuned it to Radio Luxembourg to hear the hits rather than the classical music I studied to.

I actually had some other French friends by that time. We were not in classes with French students at the Sorbonne, but they were all back by then, and often we found ourselves studying in the same cafés in the vicinity. I was practicing my Hugo poem one day at a table near the back of a nice café on the Place de la Sorbonne-- quietly I thought, but still out loud,--when a pretty French girl with a mass of blond hair and gorgeous brown eyes, was all at once standing over my table. I looked up from the paper and she said, "You are English, yes?"

"*I'm American,*" *I said, wondering if that would make a difference seeing as how I'd learned that the French high schools and colleges eschew the American accent as being inferior and substandard, and they never allow it to be used in their English classes.*

"*Yes? Wonderful! New York? Chicago (ShEE-cah-go)?*"

"*Uh, no.*"

"***Peu importe!*** *Can you please help me with some words? We are all very confused!*"

I looked over at her table and another three girls were staring at me. I should have been staring at them; they were at the Sorbonne but dressed as though they were attending some posh private high school with a designer uniform: wool plaid kilts of varying tartans, but still "uniform-y", black tights, white , very expensive-looking sweaters, which I later learned were cashmere and you wouldn't be caught dead wearing anything else. And a necklace of pearls. I didn't know it then, but the pearls would have been for their sixteenth birthday, so "sweet 16" actually had some cachet in the French middle class; and to top off this "costume" a silk Hermès "carrée" or scarf, worn mostly around the neck, but sometimes tied onto the handle of a bag. If it started to rain, that scarf would come off and suddenly be worn as an actual headscarf which turned them all into their grandmothers...or Queen Elizabeth.

"Show me your lesson then," I offered.

"Yes, we have the lists...see here... the vocabulary. It is all the same, but the prof say – er – says ("sayz") we must pronounce some of them different."

I read: bow/ bough/ cough/ ought/ thorough/ through/ threw/ ear/ wear/ where/ yes/ eyes/ town/ mown/ moan.

"It is quite difficult, you're right," I told her. "But I'll be happy to pronounce with you and tell you what they mean."

"We are obliged to use them in a sentence," she said hesitatingly.

"**Pas de problème. Allez, je vous en prie.**" And I motioned for them to sit at my table, which they did enthusiastically, and we all introduced ourselves. When they found out I was a student in the **Cours de Civilisation Française**, they cooed with approval. Again, to the French, studying French was a most admired occupation.

I had also made friends with some of the international students from the *Cours de Civilisation Française* in my various expanded classes, and I invited one of them our little impromptu Christmas party. Anja Vander Hough was a Dutch girl working as an *au pair* for a family not far from the *Maison* in the 6th *arrondissement*. One day after class, she had invited me over to her room high up in the eaves of a beautiful Haussmanian building on *Rue Dupin*. We had to climb up the entire seven floors using a rear staircase far plainer and much more utilitarian than the majestic oriental carpeted stairs off the marble floored lobby that the tenants used if they didn't take the little cage elevator. Her room was a typical former maid's room with a slanting roof, but I loved it. Her view stretched over the rooftops all the way west to the top of the Eiffel Tower and reminded me of what you would look out on if you were a writer in a little garret studio with your desk pushed up against the window. She had a tiny sink but no bathroom, and the water down the hall was only cold.

"Jesus, it's the 1960's for heavensake," I expounded. "You'd think it wouldn't be asking too much to have hot water."

"We can have some in one of the bathrooms," she explained. "You have to put in a coin and then it comes out hot into a bathtub. The showers are all cold, though."

"*Sacré bleu.*"

Anja came to our little impromptu Christmas party, and I announced to her with great excitement and anticipation that I would be going to Amsterdam for Christmas.

"Then you must come to my home for the first night at least!" she chirped. "I invite you."

"Really? Gee, I'd love that. Do you live in Amsterdam?"

"Oh, no! I live in Bergen-op-Zoom. And my brother is coming to Paris to drive me there! You can ride, too, with us. And I can see you off on the train to Amsterdam from there. That will save you much money."

"You're kidding! That would be wonderful!"

"Kidding?"

"Joking. *Tu plaisantes.*"

"Oh! *Non, non, je ne plaisante pas.*"

I smiled. "It's just an expression. *Ce n'est qu'...une expression en anglais.*"

I had told Cass, correctly, that classes were over on December 21st, and the dorm was closing on December 23rd, and everyone would have to be out then. Knowing that we didn't all have places to go in Europe, or the means to travel for weeks, they conceded to reopen it for us on the *Saint-Sylvestre*, December 31st, even though the new term did not begin again until after January 6, Epiphany, which marked the end to the holiday season in France.

237

Anja still had family duties with her little French charges until December 21st, thus it was arranged that on the following day, Saturday, she and her brother Espen would pick me up at *La Maison,* and we would drive to Holland in his sweet little Simca. That meant that I would take the train on Sunday to Amsterdam to meet Cass, so I wrote to her in care of the Amstel, and expressed my joy at saving all that money by not having to take the train all the way from Paris.

I loved the car ride. Espen took the A1 north out of Paris straight to Lille and then the Belgian frontier, where I had to show my passport and they their identity papers. Over the border we had changed to the E17, which took us directly from Rooseveltlaan to Bergen op Zoom. The route skirted Brussels, and kept us in more of the countryside and farmland until we hit Antwerp. We made the trip in less than five hours.

We pulled up in front of their narrow, three-story dark green house with large picture windows shaded by lace curtains on every floor, and a red tile roof. The house was darling, and their parents couldn't have been more welcoming, showing me to a dear little bedroom where I would sleep that night. There was a single brass bed and a curly-carved Queen Anne chair with a navy-blue velvet seat. Up close I could see that those same white lace curtains had gorgeous cut-outs of town scenes, and the windows themselves opened out like French ones, and had that same handle as my window in the dorm had. Since it was already winter, of course I kept them closed.

On the floor at the foot of the bed was a hook-latched throw rug, and the rest of the flooring was ancient, creaking wooden planks. There was a tiny chest of drawers and a little mirror on the wall above it. I placed my suitcase on the floor, and draped my coat on the back of the chair. I would not be unpacking anything for such a short stay. I was charmed by the décor of the room. It could not have been more quaint.

Anja's grandmother also lived with them, which probably meant, I marveled, that she, too, had to climb stairs. By the time I had set my suitcase down in "my" room, and had gone back down to join the others, *Oma* had prepared and set out coffee and little cakes for us all in the front sitting room by a tiled stove.

"It is not antique," Anja announced, sort of reading my mind. "We have an electric one."

"It's very beautiful, however," I said.

It didn't take long before I realized that even though the adults had greeted me with "Hello" and "How do you do?" they really did not have any knowledge of English to speak of. Anja and her brother, therefore, had the task of translating, and did a great job of it. I had never heard Dutch spoken before; it sounded a lot like German to me. Disturbingly a lot like German. But I snapped out of that, reminding myself that had I been sitting in a room full of *alter kockers* from my own family speaking Yiddish, it would have probably sounded a lot the same way.

Dinner was absolutely divine. Real home cooking that I hadn't tasted in nearly six months. Much as fine French dining was nothing to sneer at, this was so good it made me blush with happiness and gratitude. The first course was *erwtensoep,* a thick pea soup. Truth was, I had never even tasted pea soup before in the US. My mother never made pea soup and it wasn't on the menu at The Spot either. The one the Vander Houghs served that night could have and probably should have been the main course because it was more of a stew than a soup, made from peas and other vegetables like celery, onions, leeks, carrots and potatoes; but it also had different cuts of meat in it— little round slices of smoked pork sausage that Mrs. Vander Hough added in just before she served each of us. We ate it with *roggebrood,* a delicious rye bread, and she put out cheese and butter to have on the bread, too.

After the soup *Mam* and *Oma* served some slices of the same sausage around mashed vegetables. This side dish looked like mashed potatoes with other veggies in them, but when I tasted it, it really was more the other vegetables than the potatoes. The sauce over the whole thing had cashews and mushrooms on top. They called it *stamppot.* I had so filled up on the stew-like soup that I barely had enough room for this course; and I was also worried I would burst, because I figured there would be dessert, which there was. Anja, her mother and grandmother all cleared the table, not allowing me to help, and then brought out dessert plates with a little round indentation for coffee cups plus a stack of *poffertjes* on the side, which turned out to be tiny, fluffy, pillow-shaped pancakes made with yeast and buckwheat flour. Their spongy texture was masked a bit by icing, butter and *stroop* or syrup.

238

Anja explained, "During our cold season and at street festivals and fairs, you can buy them from food stalls and eat them with a little fork in the street."

"Do you have to have a special pan to make them in?" I asked.

"Oh, yes. They have lots of shallow wells in them. Or you can make them in a normal one—you say skillet?- yes?—and turn them over with a knife in the oil. My grandmamma uses a knitting needle!" she laughed, thinking I'd also find that amusing.

"Yumm. So good!" I pronounced, taking a bite. The entire meal had been "yum, so good." I was so stuffed; I hoped I wouldn't be sick.

At the end of the meal, like in France, it was time for coffee. At home I hardly drank coffee, though I did drink the occasional *café crème* in Paris. I could not consider myself a coffee aficionado by any stretch, but this Dutch coffee with the special creamer in it they called *koffiemelk*--- was so delicious, I had two cups every time they served it. (However the next morning for breakfast, I was offered hot chocolate, "*warme chocolade melk met slagroom*" or whipping cream, and that was absolute heaven.)

When the plates had been cleared and we were still at the table, lingering over seemingly bottomless cups of coffee, Mr. Vander Hough said something to Espen and indicated that he should translate. Espen in turn, inquired of me if I needed some *guilder* or Dutch money. I said that yes, I supposed I did and asked if I could get some in the train station? I was planning to pay for my ticket with traveler's checks.

"Your ticket is not going to be so much," said Anja. "My father can exchange you some Dutch *guilder*—our money-- if you like."

"Really? Goodness, that's nice of him."

"Yes, he travels and sometimes needs dollars."

"Well, that is all very well, but the trouble is, I don't have much cash in dollars; mostly francs."

Espen translated. The father nodded and said "That is okay too."

Espen said, "So for your ticket to Amsterdam you need twenty-four *guilder*, so perhaps something like 12 dollars."

"Is that all?!" I was more than a little surprised.

Mr. Vander Hough nodded, so I surmised he could understand English better than he could or would speak it, which gave us something in common because that was the same for me with French at that time. He then said something in Dutch to which Espen turned to me and asked, "And after that you need a bus ticket once you arrive? Do you know where you are going there?"

"One second," I said, and jumped up to dart upstairs and come back with Cass' letter explaining to me where I needed to go once I arrived in the city. I knew the name of the hotel, but had no idea what street it was on. Unfolding the paper, I read, "The Amstel Hotel...it's on a street called Professor Tulpplein, and I guess the street number is **one**!"

I looked up to see Mr. Vander Hough's shocked expression. Mrs. Vander Hough had heard me, and dropped a spoon right into the cup she was stirring. It landed with a clank.

"My God, "said Espen whose thick Dutch accent made it sound like "My gut." "This is a palace!"

"It is very *LUXE*," said Anja, laughing. "What are you, a princess?"

"No no no," I sputtered out. "Please explain to your parents that I am the **guest** of the architect of the hotel... and his daughter. **She** will be there with me. I could never afford anything like that. My parents are not rich, good heavens, no. Huh uh."

They told my story, and the father said in English, "**Lucky** girl!"

"So," continued Espen, bringing over a book whose frontispiece was a fold-out map of Amsterdam, "you will not take the bus there. You will go by taxi, yes?"

"Yes."

"Here it is," he showed me. "You see? This hotel is right on the water of the River Amstel. A very beautiful location I think. And see here is the *Centraal Station*. This is where your train arrive."

"Arrives," Anja corrected him. "So, this is easy for you. You could almost walk there if you did not have luggages."

239

No, no I could not, I thought. But I just smiled and said, "Thank you for all this help. I feel a lot better now. I will also have to save back enough *guilders* to buy a train ticket all the way back to Paris, so how much do you think that might be?"

Espen consulted his father in Dutch.

"Something like thirty dollars so fifty-nine *guilder*. Father wants to know if you have fifty dollars with you. He can exchange you that in *guilder*."

"I think so," and I took out what I had *liquide*, as the French would say. Sixty- three dollars. It was a deal!

I also had one hundred eighty *francs* plus my travelers cheques which were in denominations of twenty, and I had a little book of five. So all totaled, I had the equivalent of one hundred ninety-five dollars on me. I had to save back thirty of that, so I calculated that I should save the *guilders* Mr. Vander Hough was going to provide for me in exchange for my fifty dollars, and that would leave me with a net amount of around one hundred fifty dollars for two weeks. I started to panic a little bit and hoped I'd make it, and still be able to buy at least a couple of souvenirs.

I didn't know if Paris was more expensive than Amsterdam, but I surmised it was. It was more or less wishful thinking. The souvenir I wanted to buy was a fur coat. In Paris, as soon as the cold weather hit, I saw every French girl at the Sorbonne wearing a white rabbit fur coat over her kilt and cashmere sweater, pearls and Hermès scarf. Every single one. I had already begun to daydream about buying a coat like that in Holland. But doing the math, conversion rates notwithstanding even, I doubted I'd have the money.

I went happily up to "my room" and having been shown the nice bathroom in the hallway, I took a short bath, changed into the flannel pj's that had been sent in my trunk to Paris, and drifted off to sleep, my head buried in a soft down pillow.

The next morning after a breakfast that included that heavenly hot chocolate plus bread with butter and chocolate "jimmies" (chocolate!!), and slices of what we would call cold-cuts of meat and cheeses, I said my goodbyes to the adults and was whisked to the train station by the brother and sister.

"I just can't thank you enough for everything, Anja," I said to her in complete sincerity. "Espen, you're so cool! Have a wonderful Christmas!"

"*Bon voyage!*" Anja called out.

"Thanks again!!!" I waved and took off to the ticket window.

Chapter Thirty-eight

"In the Bleak Mid-winter"...Gustave Holst

The train ride to Amsterdam from Bergen-Op-Zoom was fast, and by mid-morning on December 23rd, I climbed out of the taxi and up the majestic red-carpet covered steps to the doorman-guarded entrance of the Amstel Hotel and was greeted by a look that said, "Did you just get off the orphan train?" but also a smile and cheerful "Welcome to the Amstel, Miss," that made up for it. A differently uniformed bellman came and took my embarrassing suitcase as I walked up another –longer-- flight of stairs and across a shiny marble floor to the front desk, and announced to the clerk that I was staying here with Cassandra Hyde.

"Yes, of course," was the answer and he added, "my I see your passport please?" He wrote something in a book – probably the number – and handed it back to me. He then picked up a phone and said into it that Miss Sarah Shrier was there. So Cass had either pre-registered me or told him to call her when I arrived. And in a moment there she was.

"You made it, kid!" she exclaimed when she saw me.

I hugged her. "Hi Cass! Swanky joint you've got here."

Cass turned to the front desk clerk and explained, "Miss Shrier is to have all the same access to the room and the account as I do, Frederik."

"Yes, Miss Hyde, of course. Welcome, Miss Shrier," he said warmly, handing me a big brass key fob with the room key.

"Thank you!" But I was still a little puzzled as to why she had to tell him that. I was really just staying in her room and had no intention of charging anything on my own to the Hyde account.

Cass led me away into the elevator, her arm crooked in mine. "My parents are thrilled that you are here, that we are here together. They're so happy I'm not spending Christmas any place that Alan could find me, I think they would have paid to send me to the moon and back! We have *carte blanche* in this place! There's a spa, a huge pool, beautiful restaurants and ...and..."

Her voice trailed off but we'd reached the floor and the doors opened. Suddenly she sort of doubled over in pain.

"I'm feeling kind of sick," she said. "Can you open the door?"

She ran into the bathroom and I could tell she was throwing up.

"Cass! Are you okay? You don't have the flu, do you?"

"No," she called out.

"No you're not okay or no you don't have the flu?"

"I don't have the flu," she said, walking out drying her face with a fluffy monogrammed towel. "It must have been something I ate on the plane. I flew TWA as a passenger! HA! They won't like it if the food was bad! "

"How come you flew as a passenger?" I asked, as I unpacked my suitcase that had mysteriously beat me to the room.

"Because I'm on vacation and we can fly anywhere for ten percent of the cost of the ticket or free if we go stand-by. But I didn't want to risk getting bumped so I bought a reserved seat."

"Wow, that's still a perk."

"Hey, it's the swingin' sixties, don'tcha know."

"But seriously, are you going to be up for sightseeing around Amsterdam?" I asked.

"Oh, yes, and besides, we don't have to go out now. We have oodles of time. I did make a list. I got a sweet little guidebook. I'll leave it with you."

I looked up at her from my unpacking and wondered what she meant! Did she think Soren and I would come back there if and when he came over in June?

"Well, thanks. You are the guidebook queen."

"Just in case I get called back before the ten days are up. Even if that happens, you are going to stay here. I explained that to you, remember?"

"Yes, I remember. But I hope that doesn't happen!"

Cass just shrugged. "Anyway, let's get **you** something to eat. This hotel has marvelous afternoon tea every day so we can go down for that. But what do you want now?" It was only eleven o'clock.

"Oh, I don't care."

"Let me see," she said, taking a thick book with the room service menu. Hmmm, cheese board? With breads and –like what to drink? Coke? It's still technically morning, but ...go wild."

"That sounds great. Dutch cheese is so good!" I intoned, remembering dinner the previous night.

"Better than French?" she laughed?

"Well... no. Different!"

I finished putting away my clothes and changed into one of the luxurious robes that hung in our beautiful bathroom, a room that had black and white marble floor and porcelain sink and commode, gilt mirror, and upholstered Louis XV armchair next to the huge soaking tub! The bedroom itself was gigantic, all done up in *toile de Jouy* wallpaper and matching bedding in soft, muted grey-blue tones. There was only one bed, but it was enormous. There was a sitting room part with a grey brocade sofa and an identically upholstered armchair. Over on the other side of the room there was a desk with orchids blooming in a Dutch blue china pot, and a leather-cushioned chair; there was a niche space next to the desk, with shelves for small plates and silverware, and at the wall across from the bed was a glass cart on wheels holding all the accoutrements of a bar. Someone had already also delivered a large fruit basket done up in ribbons holding an enormous assortment of fresh fruit, some crackers and packets of cheese.

Our huge windows looked out over the city, and Cass told me I'd be surprised at what we would see on the other side of the hotel.

"This room faces the street where you came in, " she explained, " but if and when we go to the spa, out **their** doors is a terrace that feels like you're on board a ship! It faces the river and has deck chairs and umbrella tables and all sorts of relaxing ambience."

"Wow. You said this place would blow me away and just from what I've seen so far, you didn't lie."

My food arrived but Cass had already laid down on her side of the bed and fallen asleep! I had the waiter put the cart at the sofa seating area and tipped him two guilders, not having any idea at all of the prices of any of it. I saw that in true Cass fashion, she had put tiny bookmarks in the guidebook and I began to read it. But then I started feeling sleepy, too, and just stretched out on the couch. Soon I was also fast asleep.

When I woke up to clanging sounds in the bathroom, Cass was feeling a lot better and eager to go out on a boat ride through the canals, and then have tea back in the hotel. Amsterdam was truly at our feet in that place. The dock for one of the tourist boat lines wasn't fifty feet from the back of the hotel where I could look up and see the exact scene she described out the French doors of the spa. It was winter so nobody was "relaxing" in the cold, but there were heating lamps and a partial glass enclosure just in case some brave souls wanted to.

When we got to the dock, Cass saw that it was a river cruise and said we didn't want that, we wanted a canal tour, so we walked away from the river and back towards the *Centraal Station* where the other boats were docked.

"Gosh, I forgot it was Christmas!" I exclaimed as we rounded a corner, and the *Rembrandtplein's* enormous Christmas market hit us smack in the face. It was magnificent. The white lights were already on, even as it wasn't dark yet; in fact, many of the canals were lighted in white lights, some twinkly tree lights and other large round bulbs hung on wire garlands between buildings on either side.

Cass just walked up to a boat ride that had people lined up.

"Might as well take this one."

"How much is it?" I asked, reaching into my purse.

"Three *guilder*, but nope nope nope...all this entire trip is on my parents. You are not paying for anything except what souvenirs you buy. The whole time. Got it? And don't argue because that would be futile!"

"Cass, I..."

"Huh? Didn't you just hear me?"

"But, really..."

She wheeled around in front of me and put both her hands on my arms. "Sari...shut...up."

"Okay! Geez."

We took the most enjoyable and relaxing tour around some of the canals as the young---probably a student---guide pointed out various old warehouses and churches in five languages and also explained how the tax laws changed the architectural reality in the city by taxing width and windows, so that most of the buildings were very tall and narrow.

Cass said, "They told us at TWA that any time you take these boat or bus tours with guided talks, you can't take it as gospel; they could easily be just making up stuff on the spot."

"Oh, my goodness, I hope they don't do that on the *bateaux mouches*!"

We went by the hiding place of Anne Frank and her family.

"We'll come back and actually tour that," Cass said. "I don't know if they book tickets in advance for it. The desk can arrange it for me."

Back at the Amstel, tea was held in a part of the lobby you had to access from a double horseshoe-shaped staircase that led below street level. Both sides came together down there and spilled onto a vast space with more black and white marble flooring, not checkered like the bathrooms, but with large white slabs rimmed in black. A gleaming ebony concert grand piano stood in the middle. All around the perimeter were serving tables groaning with tall tiered china plates of crust-less sandwiches and mini quiches; fruit and cheese trays, baskets of breads and rolls. There were silver trays heaped with slices of meats; smoked salmon and all the embellishments for it, such as capers, onions, sour cream and lemons; herring; chafing dishes filled with meatballs in sauce; French pastries, cakes on glass trays, and a chocolate fountain, which I had never seen before in my life. Three large silver samovars surrounded by bone china cups and sauces, silver sugar bowls and creamers provide coffee and various types of tea.

I got the idea that the room was usually set aside for balls, dances—maybe even what I had heard called "tea dances," but on that day the dance floor, as it were, was filled with little loveseats, each with a small table in front of it and one or two extra small gilt chairs, depending on the need. Cass and I were shown to a table and then admonished to help ourselves to anything we wanted.

"So," Cass stated, "it's self-serve casual!"

I burst out laughing, taking in the serenely elegant surroundings that were the antithesis of casual! We would gorge ourselves like stuffed Christmas geese and, similar to England, not have to eat dinner.

"I don't see how anyone *could* eat another dinner after this," I said, stating the obvious.

"Well, dinner over here means eight or even nine o'clock, just like in France, I am assuming."

"Even so...I doubt I'll be hungry yet at nine."

"Well, guess what? Tonight we're going to a special music extravaganza! I have tickets to the *Royal Concertgebouw*'s holiday concert."

"The Royal what-guh-what?"

"Amsterdam's famous symphony orchestra: the *Concertgebouw*! Their hall is one of the most renowned in the world with like the best acoustics you've ever heard anywhere!"

"So we dress up?"

"Yep."

Luckily for me I had packed both my boots and my new Harrod's shoes, which could look very dressy with tights. I didn't own anything that could be construed as a "little black dress" but I had a black wool straight skirt and a white orlon sweater that had little rhinestone bits at the neck line. That would have to do. Cass had brought her Chanel jumper, still as beautiful as it was when she took it out of the box the previous Christmas. She had a white blouse to put with it this time that looked like a Shakespearian costume, with an ascot bow at the top of a band of ruffles going all the way down the front, and on the billowy lace-cuffed sleeves. She wore white tights and boots with higher heels than mine had. She towered over me in them. I just hoped the sidewalks wouldn't be icy; she'd kill herself in those things.

My hair was getting really long, I noticed in the mirror that night as I tied it back with a black velvet ribbon. Fortunately I could make it look half-way chic, and what's more, Betty had remembered to send the fur hood in my trunk, an effect which allowed my outfit to take on a more elegant aura. I had been wearing it for a while in Paris, too, and felt pretty damn Parisienne when I did.

243

We took a taxi to the *Koninklijk Concertgebouw*, the Netherlands Royal Philharmonic Orchestra's building in *Concertgebouwplein* and disembarked at one of the legendary concert halls of the world, "comparable," Cass said, "to Boston's Symphony Hall or Vienna's *Musikverein* in acoustics. My father told me that, and as an architect and a music aficionado, he would know!"

It was stunningly gorgeous in the *Grote Zaal* or Main Hall, with its red velvet seats and crystal chandeliers hanging from the highly decorated coffered ceiling, its balcony with the names of composers carved into the sides; its distinctive grey-green plaster columns adorned with gilt scrolls; and way up in front, raised high upstage center, its magnificent organ, which we got to hear that night because the sole work being played was Bach's *Christmas Oratorio*, and even though it was not written with an organ part, the Sixties being the Sixties, Bernard Haitink chose to put it in!

"Now, that's a choir!" I fairly shouted afterwards. I could hardly contain my awe, and came to the realization that even though I was not very familiar with the work itself, there wasn't much Bach I didn't come to love.

"Yes," Cass chided me, "I do know how to choose 'em."

"Tomorrow's Christmas Eve," I said all of a sudden remembering the date. "Shall we go back to that Christmas Market? It must be the most splendid one I've ever imagined. It's twice as big as Strasbourg's! I have to buy something!"

"Sure. What do you want to buy?"

"No idea!"

"And tomorrow night we must go to some church. Even if we don't understand a word being said, okay?" Cass added.

"Fine. Do you have one in mind?"

"I looked in the guidebook," she said, "and so I think Nieuwe Kerk. It's where all the Dutch monarchs have been crowned since the eighteen hundreds."

"Hmm, so like Reims cathedral or Westminster Abbey."

I wasn't completely ignorant.

I was mesmerized yet again by the wonderful market.

"Christmas is such a big commercial deal in the U.S.," Cass said, "I wonder that we don't have anything even remotely like this!"

"Yeah, or any other outdoor markets. If we do set them up once in a blue moon, it's just for some fair or special event. It seems sad to me, now that I've spent so much time here in Europe, that we're not a "market " culture like they all are."

We went all around the large square looking at every stall. We tried something Cass told me was like wassail that they called *Glühwein*, and we nibbled on gingerbread men and chocolate *Sinterklaases*. I bought some small hand-carved wooden ornaments of reindeer and forest scenes. Not having a Christmas tree, I thought I could just hang them from my cabinet handles at *La Maison* when I got back. They would remind me of Holland and another glorious time with Cass. We also found hand-knitted mittens in wild mod colors we each bought. They were only 5 guilders.

"The prices are crazy cheap," she said. I had to agree even on my budget, which was, due to the circumstances of the trip, now majorly augmented. I had even begun to think about the fur coat again.

We could not resist repeating that amazing Amstel Hotel afternoon tea extravaganza, and since it was Christmas Eve, the room was even more festive than the previous day! Two huge lit trees were taking center stage as we came down the broad staircase, with one on each side as high as the stair wells---more than ten feet. The tables were also festooned with greenery and glass balls. At the end of the serving tables and on each individual table in the hall were brass hurricane lamps with boughs of greenery tied with ribbon around the base and thick red candles inside. They gave off an old-fashioned muted light that still stood out amidst the dark sky visible from the high windows that let in a view of the little twinkling white lights outside in the trees.

There were many more hotel guests and other people there than had been at tea the day before; the little side chairs were being snatched up and crowded around tables. But the ever-vigilant staff never let the food run out, and afterwards I said to Cass, "Please have me delivered to the room on a platter. All I need is an apple stuffed in my mouth."

For the church service, Cass and I dressed down a little bit from what we had worn to the *Concertgebouw*. I had brought to Amsterdam my same grey-blue tweed skirt that I wore again with the white sweater and, this time, boots. Cass wore a red corduroy full skirt with a darling black piping decoration around the hem, the same white blouse as before, but this time with a black bolero jacket. She looked like Christmas personified, I had to give it to her.

The *Nieuwe Kerk* still had services back then, which it no longer does, and it was pretty jam packed with worshippers—and doubtless more tourists than just us ---when we arrived. Very different in interior appearance from St. Martin in the Fields, St. Paul's Cathedral, Notre Dame or any other church I'd yet seen to date, its Gothic Revival style was nevertheless magnificent in its own right. A Dutch Protestant church did not lack for ornamentation, as one might expect: the carved wood pulpit, the alter and the brass choir screen were deliciously elaborate, and the space with its not-to-be-believed forty-foot high vaulted wood ceiling seemed vast even when filled up with people.

We didn't understand a word of the actual Christmas Eve service even though the pastor or perhaps someone in the altar entourage---I couldn't see very well—somehow sensing that not all the attendees were Dutch, made a few attempts at instructions in English, such as "please stand." We did what everyone else did and that seemed to work, although following in the prayer book was not happening. Cass probably felt even more at sea than I, which I pointed out to her afterwards, since I'd sat in several Orthodox and Conservative Jewish synagogues not following the Hebrew either.

We retreated in the brisk winter night afterwards to our own little paradise at the Amstel, and promptly ordered up *heetchocolademelk met slaagroom* that I promised Cass would be the best she'd ever had.

"And I'm right, aren't I?" I crowed when she'd tasted it.

"You are!"

I went over to the Palladian windows to look out on the balcony. "I wonder if Dutch people go caroling," I said.

In grade school we sang some Thanksgiving songs, including my personal favorite, "Come Ye Thankful People Come" and the Dutch hymn "We Gather Together." But even as I searched the inner vaults of my memory I couldn't think of even one Dutch Christmas carol from any of the choral repertories that I had sung in any choir, including at the International House in Iowa City.

I stood there contemplating the carols I did know and love, and asked Cass, "Do you know of any Dutch Christmas carols? "

But instead of answering me, she jumped up and ran into the bathroom to be sick again.

Chapter Thirty-nine

"Why Are You Leaving"...The City (Carole King)

Cass came out of the bathroom and flopped down on the bed. She looked pale and in not some small distress.

"Cass, " I said rather coolly, with a serious determination to get to the bottom of this, "what the hell is going on?" *I had been eating the same foods as she and I wasn't sick.*

"You'd better come over here, " she said motioning to the sofa, "and sit down. I'm about to ruin your Christmas vacation."

So I walked over there naively not in any way prepared for what she was about to tell me.

"So, it's like this. I'm preggers. I've been throwing up for a few weeks now. By the way, morning sickness isn't just in the morning. I was sure you'd have guessed!"

Truth be told, I should have figured it out, because I'd known from her letters that Alan had indeed come to Boston right before Thanksgiving. She said it had been a cordial visit, no angst to speak of, and I had assumed they had gone their separate ways. I tended to take her at her word when she had told me they parted friends.

"WHAT?! Cass, no." And then another thing hit me: "But you KNEW about it? Why did you still keep this...this Christmas charade going?"

"So we could be together! So you'd have a mad, gay, exciting time in Amsterdam! With or without me!"

"Oh for godsake! What are you going to DO?! Are you going to get an abortion HERE?"

"No, Sari. Listen, before I came I had to call my parents and tell them. They're livid furious, of course, but said I should spend the weekend with you and then fly home—to Chicago, home—as soon as I could after Christmas."

"Oh, God." I really **was** in shock. "Did they scream at you?"

"I was the one pretty upset and they could tell. At first my mother just went into overdrive damage control mode and said we would go to Puerto Rico even before they left for Switzerland, and she would arrange for an abortion down there."

"Holy shit."

"But I'm not going to Puerto Rico with Julia. My father won't hear of it. He said my health is too important to risk such a procedure in a third world back alley dump of some kind."

"I tend to agree with him on that."

"So here's the deal they offered me: I must agree not to have any further contact with Alan Jones, and to come back to Kenilworth. I can stay there under the care of the people who've always taken care of me—whom they trust of course, until they get back from Switzerland; and then, more or less when I start to show---HA! won't that be a scandal in their midst!-- they will take me to a home for unwed mothers Julia knows about. It's down near the Springfield Homestead, actually. For the rest of the time until I have the baby. I would live there and I would have to agree to put the baby up for adoption immediately after its birth."

"A home for unwed mothers? Jesus Christ. You'd have to stay there six months or so. And then what?"

"Well, no more TWA, that's for sure. I guess that's the silver lining, huh?"

I said nothing, so she went on.

"My father already informed them that I needed to fly home—for a 'family emergency' now, but also that I must resign my job ASAP. And he's sending some of his staff east to close up my place and bring my things back. I'm sure his lawyers will be able to get me out of my lease."

"I just still can't believe you kept all this under wraps this whole two days! My God! I also can't believe Julia and John-Wilfred are taking it so well."

"Don't get me wrong, they're both apoplectic. They are horrified of any impropriety that would put them in the spotlight. They probably won't even wait 'til I'm showing---they'll send me away after a week!" She was trying to make light but she broke down sobbing instead.

I jumped up and hugged her. "Oh, Cass, what can I do to help you?"

"They d-d-id s-s-ay," she continued, between sobs, "that if I agreed to give the b-b-aby up for adoption---like I have any other possible solutions-- that I could resume schooling later, probably at the Art Institute." She paused to sniff. "I could live at home."

"Well, that's something, at least. And, really, Cass, you know that you would be doing the noble thing to give it up, right? There are a lot of couples who can't get pregnant and are aching to adopt infants. We talked about that in Biology class."

"In class? Wow, how did that come up?"

"Out of the blue one time he just took off on a rant about the pregnancy rates among unmarried girls. It sure wasn't on the syllabus!"

"Oh, anyway, let's get real. It's not like my parents would ever even *hear* of letting me raise an out-of-wedlock grandchild in their home. And let's face it, I don't know the first thing about mothering---certainly not by example," she sneered.

"Well, your staff would help you," I ventured.

"They've got their own jobs now!" She was getting agitated, and all of a sudden I had to think of her *condition* and try to calm things down.

"Yes, you're right. You know, your parents aren't the only ones. I've even had The Big Lecture on this at my house. If I ever got pregnant, my parents would do the exact same thing as yours, only probably kill me first before I could even be sent away. They would for sure disown me! They practically do now if I get mediocre grades!" I gave off a little nervous giggle.

"I guess," she said almost wistfully, "I think when push comes to shove your parents are like mine: they believe in us even if it doesn't seem like it at all! Your parents have sent you to the Sorbonne to get the best education and the best job later, so that you'll be happy. They love you, kid, and they're sacrificing to help and reinforce what you want."

I thought that was a stretch, but for the sake of not wanting to upset her further, I went along.

"I guess I believe what you're saying. Still, they have an odd way of showing it. They make me feel so guilty, like I'm in Paris but don't deserve to be. Yours, on the other hand, whoa! I would have expected them to go full-on nuclear war about this. Wow."

"Oh, my father made it abundantly clear that I **had** to promise not to see Alan, and agree to give the baby up for adoption. Only then would they let me continue living at home and possibly start back to school at the Art Institute---ha! if they'll have me."

"Of course they'll have you! Get real! Your art is wonderful. But, Cass, when all is said and done, are you in agreement with all this? Does Alan know? And does he think he has some stake in it? The baby is his, after all."

"I have to be in agreement. There are no other possible solutions. Alan does not know and I'm not telling him. I realize that's probably wrong. Somewhere in all this, he may have a claim to the baby. But believe me, my parents will never-- and I do mean never-- let him anywhere near me, now or in the future. If he did by some chance find out and want to fight them, he would lose in a heartbeat. My father would drop his lawyers on Alan like an atomic bomb, to use **your** reference."

"Yeah, I can believe that. They really hate him, don't they?"

"Oh, you know---they didn't like him before I got pregnant; now it is a matter of unbridled loathing."

"But they **are** going to help you, at least."

"As long as I do what they want, yes. They are paying up all my expenses and will support me, just as before---without Iowa City in the picture at all, obviously, because that would mean risking close proximity to Alan. I know they are furious, but right now they're keeping things on an even keel with me. I think after that phone call, they might be afraid I could, you know, do something drastic. I was pretty frantic when I called them."

I was also afraid she might "do something drastic" and didn't want to even entertain the thought.

"Look," I said, "we'll get through this. I'll always be there for you, you know that. It's just…well… I'm feeling so helpless right now."

Sucker punched would have been a better description.

She put her hands on my shoulders.

"Just please don't hate me too much because our much-anticipated romp through the European capitals is coming to an abrupt halt!"

"Don't be silly. We have had an amazingly wonderful time this semester. I mean it. If anyone had told me that day in Kate Daum when your mother literally tore you out of college, that we would be getting together again—often even—in Paris, France, I'd have laughed them out of the room."

"I know. And when you get back in July, I'll be HUGE. Will you come visit me in that awful place?"

"Count on it."

There we were, in a posh hotel suite high above Amsterdam, Holland, on Christmas Eve—turned to Christmas Day by then, since by the time I heard the whole story, it was two o'clock in the morning. The next day, she would be gone. What in God's name was I going to do for another week in Amsterdam without her?

"Cass," I said, "I know you think I should just stay here in Amsterdam for the rest of my vacation, but I feel really unworthy of your parents' largess staying here without you. It's too much!"

"Okay, cut it out! You've known me for over two years now, right? So please don't forget that my parents are extremely wealthy! Filthy rich, if you must know," she snorted.

How could I not know?

"If I tell you that the entire bill for this trip with the fancy hotel, all the food we could ever eat, and anything else—cash—spending money, which I'm going to give you, by the way, because God knows I won't be needing it now---all this is truly chump change to my parents! Do you believe me?! Because it's true! I mean it. Do not give the financial aspects of this another thought!"

"But, Cass…"

"But nothing! Look, I don't talk about our wealth; you know that. But I will just say this: what you've seen of it—my house in Kenilworth and the Hyde building, our penthouse in downtown Chicago, the trips, our stupid cars---none of that even scratches the surface!"

"Come on," I protested.

"I know you don't exactly have a frame of reference for this, but I want to assure you that they can afford all of it without blinking an eye. I'm not going to sit here and bore you with their net worth and all, but just believe me. It's beyond anything you could imagine."

"Okay, I get where you're coming from, but spending money on you is quite different from spending it on me!"

"Listen," she said sternly, "we've been over all this before! Twice as I recall! I can't insist enough on how thrilled they were when they thought we were going to be together for the holiday! They were only too happy to pay for all of it." She looked up at me with pursed lips. "And don't forget-- there was always the possibility before the actual events unfolded, that I would have had to fly out. It's the same deal, only I have to fly out and not come back. But you'll do fine!"

"Yes, I can see museums and I can go shopping and I can visit churches. But I can't seem to reconcile the idea that once again, the Hyde family is taking care of my every need! Your parents are going to see me as the biggest moocher on the planet, not to mention weak and not able to even support myself on a holiday."

"Well, no student could expect to be able to stay **here**, I grant you that, but that's not YOUR doing. Please cease with the guilt feelings. There is nothing weak or whiney or moocher-y about you. Just have a great time! And take my word for that, not necessarily my example! Ha ha."

"I know, but staying here is SO expensive. How will I ever—what can I DO to repay this in any way shape or form?"

"FORGET it. I am serious. This conversation is over. We're going to bed! Tomorrow—or actually today!-- is Christmas and I want to have a last great day together as I pack!"

So we each took a side of the enormous bed and turned out the lights. Cass was wiped out and I was also exhausted more emotionally than physically. I fell asleep fitfully, hoping against hope that I'd wake up in the morning and this would all have been a very bad dream.

Chapter Forty

"Don't Let the Sun Catch you Crying"...Gerry and the Pacemakers

When I awoke on Christmas morning, Cass was already up and had ordered room service. I fled into the bathroom when it arrived, and came back out semi-presentable after the waiter had gone. We arranged the food and pots of hot chocolate on our table, and then I went to the closet to produce Cass' gift.

"*Joyeux Noël!*" I sang out, handing it to her.

In the last few days before I left Paris to head to Holland, I had gotten very lucky to have come up with the perfect Christmas present for Cass. Usually buying things for her was impossible. I could never afford anything of the caliber of her clothing. I could never buy her accessories like jewelry---even bijoux *de fantaisie which I loved. Her hair was short, so the great French barrettes and hairbands were useless. I had already given her that special sketchbook, although truth be told, Paris had even more magnificent ones. Still, that would be a repeat. It was a recurring dilemma to try to find something for her. This time, though, I had hit the jackpot.*

Practically every day on the way to classes at La Sorbonne, *I walked up* Rue Soufflot *and right past a shop with the sign shaped like an artist's palette hanging from chains that said* Dubois 1861. *It finally dawned on me that I could get Cass some art supplies there of the sort that she could not get back home. To the best of my knowledge, she had not thought to get them for herself on her various trips to Paris---we had shopped nearby in* St. Germain des Prés *mostly, but never exactly in that part of the Latin Quarter. It would be meaningful, unique and ...I would find something I could actually afford! I declared myself a genius over this.*

Paris has many many ancient and venerable artist supply shops. Dubois *wasn't even the most famous one. Once I started doing a little sleuthing on these shops, I found out that one called* Sennelier, *over by the Louvre, was the most renowned in Paris, and boasted having been the place frequented for supplies by Cezanne, and was where Picasso had pastels made especially for him. But* Dubois *was touted as the supplier for* La Sorbonne et L'Académie, *and that made it perfect for me.*

One enters the shop and suddenly there's a feeling of being catapulted back into another century. Everything in there except the electric lights was original to the building-- the thick but uneven wood floors and the ancient beveled-glass display cases. The back part was all canvases, easels, watercolor papers on tables and counters in front of floor-to-ceiling shelving that housed cubbyholes of paints and pastels looking like multicolored candies on display. The front had other supplies including poster board, carrying cases, and more oak and glass display shelves that housed all different kinds of watercolor paints and sets, handmade papers, and stamps and inks.

Taking up one entire corner of the store were the brushes, and that is exactly what I decided to get for Cass. I was interested in giving her some variety, but I had little idea what brushes were used for which type of painting; because even though I had taken studio art at Iowa, I had only done block printing and no painting. Which brushes were best for oil versus acrylic, gouache, or watercolor? I could take an educated guess; but of course the clerks in the shop would help me. At least I was able to tell them I knew the brushes for each paint were different. However, I soon realized that there was also a choice of shapes and materials, like hog bristle and sable. In the end, I found some that I liked, and surmised that Cass would know how she wanted to use them.

*I chose three Manet brand brushes, with different numbers and markings on them, and stamped, of course, "Made in France," which went without saying. I hoped she'd be as pleased as I was, and when I took them to the counter, I told the elderly woman clerk excitedly, "*C'est pour un gateau *(cake)!" when I meant to say, "*C'est pour un cadeau *(gift)!" I caught my error and corrected myself when I saw the alarmed look on her face, but in typical French fashion, albeit in a nice way, she corrected my French further by saying, "*Ah, c'est pour offrir.*" Oui! She stooped below the counter, opened up a sliding door and pulled up a small wooden box just long enough for the largest brush. It was even marked "*Dubois 1861.*"*

*"*Je les mets ensemble là-dedans.*" Oh, my, yes...so perfect to put the brushes inside that. An extra gift! And then she wrapped it all up for me in a lovely antique-looking paper, which was even better than some Christmas wrapping paper, which I didn't have anyway. She put ribbon around it and tamped that down with a* Dubois *seal.*

*"*Voilà, Mademoiselle.*"*

"Merci, Madame, c'est parfait." *Perfect indeed.*

Cass looked carefully at the name *Dubois* but it didn't seem to register. She shook it a little bit, playfully and pronounced it too pretty to open. But open it she did, and she gasped with joy.

"Oh, WOW! French paintbrushes. *Manet*, no less –ho! I hope I'm worthy!"

"Do you think they'll be useful? I didn't exactly know what I was buying."

"I think they're wonderful and I thank you so much!" She rose to give me a big hug and sat back down saying, "I've got something for you, too. It's not wrapped, though."

I gave a "that's okay" shrug and she went to the closet and brought out the kilt she had bought in London.

"Oh noooo. I can't accept that," I said right away hoping to not insult her but leave no doubt that I couldn't let her give that to me.

"Hell yes, you can. I can't even fit into it NOW; what will happen in another month – or three? Someone might as well get use out of it! It's yours now, kid. Happy Chanukah!"

"Oh, Cass," I swooned, "it's the most beautiful skirt I've ever seen. I thought so when you picked it out; I think so now. It is absolutely gorgeous! EEEeeek!!"

"I love it, too, which is why it must go to you. You know, I'm only a few weeks along and already I feel my clothes getting way too tight. God only knows what I'll soon look like. I don't even want to think about it."

"You'll glow, like they all say expectant mothers do. *Voilà.*"

We took a good long while over breakfast not talking about her leaving or the *sturm und drang* to which she was about to be subjected.

Being without family in a strange city on Christmas Day is not the optimal way to spend a holiday; everything is closed and anyone who is still working, like the staff at the hotel or in restaurants, probably resent that they had to be there.

We didn't feel obliged to leave the Amstel. I was glad she didn't suggest another church service because even though I did love the music and the spectacle, I was pretty churched-out.

She took her time packing up her suitcase and we just lazed around the room. I read the Amsterdam guidebook.

"You know," she explained, "this country is so small that you can find out how to take the trams or buses and go to other towns easily from here. Since you are the Queen and 'Grand High Poohbah' of the 'blue and white society,' she teased, fully aware how much I loved that color combination, "you should really go to Delft and see the *Porceleyne Fles*. It's the great factory where they make all the best and really famous blue and white stuff. You'll go nuts."

"Oooh, that does sound like me. Maybe I'll do it."

"And what else? I want to know you're not moping around this hotel."

"Who could mope around THIS hotel? Surely you jest."

"Well, I want you out and about: the *Rijksmuseum* is a must, and there's also a separate Van Gogh Museum, which I would also tour if I were you. They are even close to each other---both over near the *Concertgebouw*. And we talked about Anne Frank's house. The hotel concierge can get you a ticket. You could do another boat ride. They have different routes."

"I'll be fine," I assured her, "and I promise I will get out. All the places you've just mentioned are high on my list."

"Okay, I'm going to hold you to that. Send me postcards to the Kenilworth address and write me also when you get back to Paris. I'll write you, too, of course. Hell, I'll even call you. We can time it out so you're there."

"That will cost a fortune," I started to say, but she cut me off...

"Uh-uh. Never mind. And by the way," she continued as she packed her carry-on bag, "I want you to take this money." She took one hundred thirty-odd *guilder* in bills and coins, plus a messy pile of *francs* out of her bag. "I still have TWA allowance left over from various trips. You take it. I don't need it and you do."

I knew better than to argue with her and I couldn't deny that this surprise windfall would come in terribly handy running around Amsterdam by myself; but once again, I was helpless to overcome the mixed emotions of gratitude, guilt and unworthiness that came over me. I was truly grateful but it made me unspeakably sad.

"My God, Cass, thank you. I don't really know what to say."

"Just take it," she said, thrusting it at me. "Have adventures."

"I will, but they won't be mad, gay or exciting without you."

Cass and I didn't leave the hotel room the entire Christmas day. We let the maids come in and make the bed and change the towels, but not much else. We ordered room service and just watched television. Dutch stations were broadcasting Christmas concerts mostly, and the music was very beautiful, even though nothing could really cheer us at that point.

Cass wasn't being very meticulous in her packing, and just sort of heaved her clothes in a pile in the case. She didn't even show deference to her Chanel jumper; it had become just another article of clothing she didn't think she could wear again for quite some time.

The next morning, I accompanied her to the lobby as they brought down her luggage and arranged a taxi for her. I was hard-pressed to hold back tears and for some reason had a sinking feeling that I might not see her again ever. I didn't want to admit it, but I was afraid. I was horrified at the thought that she'd arrive home and they would tear her to shreds emotionally if not physically. Maybe Julia would prevail and haul her off to get an abortion after all. I feared something terrible might happen to her either by her own hand or by things going wrong somewhere along the way in the pregnancy, or when having the baby.

But I fought all that back and kept up a brave front as I waved her off.

I went back to the room, hung up the "do not disturb" sign, and climbed into the soft nest of lavender-scented sheets and feathery duvet. It was ten o'clock on December 26th, a Thursday, and I fell asleep and didn't wake up until three in the afternoon.

Chapter Forty-one

"Dans le Port d'Amsterdam"...Jacques Brel

Determined to fight off shock and sorrow and not succumb to just plain sadness-induced inertia, I got up, bathed and put on the kilt and my white sweater with the little rhinestones around the collar, and went down to tea at the hotel. They had rearranged the grand room once again, as many guests were gone on the 26th and Holland didn't commemorate Boxing Day or any other post-Christmas doings. There were still small tables and the little chairs at the ready, and but there were far fewer of them, which made the room seem crowded with the remaining guests. Luckily I found a settee with a table and even an extra chair, and I took it.

All of a sudden, there was a rather tall young man with long, dark blond hair with his sweater around his shoulders leaning over me. He took the gilt chair from my table and said in French:

"*Pardon, Mademoiselle, vous permettez?*" He was wanting my chair.

Almost automatically, I gestured and answered in French, "*Mais oui, je vous en prie.*" I watched him move it over to another sofa with two people already seated on it, and pull the chair up to them as he seated himself. He glanced back over to me, and I smiled back as I got up to get some tea and food. I thought to myself, "*Gosh, he just assumed I was French. Must be the kilt.*"

As I was eating and wishing I'd brought something down there to read, the same guy reappeared at my sofa.

"*Excusez-moi,* " he said returning the chair that went with my table to its original spot and extending his hand. *Permettez-moi de me présenter. Je m'appelle Clément de Seignard.*

"*Enchantée,* " I answered . "*Je suis* Sarah Shrier." I said my name in English, of course, and not "Shreee-air".

"Oh!" he said, also in English, "then you are not French? I am sorry! But...you spoke French to me. " He was a little bewildered.

"I'm a student at the Sorbonne," I answered.

"*Ah! Bravo! Moi aussi, je suis étudiant à Paris. HEC.*"

He was older than he looked in that case because HEC is the "*École des Hautes Études Commerciales* in Paris, one of the "*Grandes Écoles*" or the equivalent of the Ivy League MBA schools like Harvard.

"Are you in Holland for Christmas?" I asked sticking to English because he could speak it well.

"Not exactly. I am here with my parents because my father has meetings at the Rijksmuseum and we stay for the holidays. I shall be here one more week."

"Oh, me, too. I came for the holiday with a friend, but she – uh- became ill and had to fly home to Chicago."

"Please," he said, "may I introduce you to my parents? They are right over there."

"Oh...well, sure."

We walked over and made introductions, after which he explained to them the whole bit about my being an American at the hotel. His father Renaud was an associate curator at the *Musée Marmottan*.

"Have you seen the *Marmottan, Mademoiselle*? " asked Renaud de Seignard.

"I am so sorry! I haven't," I admitted. "I don't even know where it is."

He turned to his son and said, "*Alors, Clément...faut que tu amènes Mademoiselle Sarah au musée, voyons.*"

The *Marmottan* collection, they explained to me, was housed in a "rather large and magnificent" former private residence right on the edge of the *Bois de Boulogne* in western Paris. It had started out as a showcase for the Marmottan family holdings of Napoleonic art and furniture, as well as their painting collection. The family bequeathed the entire lot to the *Académie des Beaux Arts*, so it came under the administrative auspices of the French government. Then in 1957, a distant cousin of Clément's father named Victorine Donop de Monchy gave that museum her entire collection of important Impressionist works.

"I had seen them at her home when I was a boy," Renaud explained to me, "and it made me want to someday work in the art field."

Clément's mother Blandine became rather animated at this point, and joined in the conversation, telling me, "Victorine's collection was inherited from her father who was Edouard Manet's physician! He also cared as well for Monet, Sisley, Pissarro and Renoir! Can you imagine?"

"No! I can't," I was incredulous.

"*Oui, oui,*" continued Blandine, "*le Docteur* Georges de Bellio was an avid supporter of the Impressionist artists early on."

Renaud interrupted her, eager to tell me the rest himself. "Then just two years ago, Michel Monet, the son of Claude, left our museum his own complete inheritance of his father's work, thus creating the world's largest collection of Monet paintings in one place. I have come to Holland to meet with other museum directors on behalf of our 'chef' (*his boss*), to compare how they have maintained large donations from the same artist. Here it is Van Gogh, of course."

"Gosh," I said, still wondering how this entire family spoke such good English, "I can't wait to see it."

"So you shall," Blandine said, getting up to signal our leave-taking.

"It is so nice to meet you all," I said shaking their hands once again.

Clément walked me up the staircase to the main lobby and over to the elevators.

"So, how is it that you and your parents speak such great English?" I had the temerity to ask.

"We've lived in Oxford and Philadelphia," he answered matter-of-factly.

"My God," I said. "I guess that would explain it. So where do you live in Paris?"

"On *Rue Singer* in the *seizième,*" he answered. It was a chic address.

"I'm on *Boulevard Raspail,*" I said. "Maybe we can meet sometime for coffee. I don't know where the *HEC* is, actually."

"Yes, we must do that, and I certainly want to invite you to the *Marmottan.* But before that, would you like to visit the Amsterdam museums with me tomorrow? Papa is in meetings and Maman has friends here she's seeing. I have nothing to do."

"Well, that would be super! I'd been planning to go to both the Rijksmuseum and the Van Gogh!"

So we made a date to meet back in the lobby the next day at ten in the morning. I retreated to my *sanctum sanctorum* where I read the guidebook Cass had left me, watched some t.v., and tried not to wallow in misery over Cass' situation, my being left in Amsterdam, and the exams that were once again looming over me. I considered leaving Holland earlier than planned, so as not to run up the Hyde's bill and also to get back to study, but the dorm was shut and I would just have to check into a Paris hotel, which the week before New Year's would not be easy to find. So I decided then and there to stay until the 30th as planned.

Clément was super nice. We ended up going out not only to the museums, but also to Anne Frank's hiding place, to dinner in the hotel, and even back to the *Concertgebouw* one evening.

On the third night after Cass had left, I stopped at the concierge desk with Clément to find out about going to visit Delft. It was easy — just an hour by direct train-- and Clément had already been there, and said he'd be happy to go again.

Delft was, as Cass had joshed at me, my dream. Besides being the blue-and-white freak that I was, the town thrilled me with its quaint marketplace, canals, lovely houses, beautiful church, and of course, the porcelain factory and all those shops, some of which sold the real thing, but most of which did not.

Clément and I laughed and laughed as I went from souvenir shop to shop looking at blue and white china everything from lambs and puppies to little jars and covered china boxes. "I must buy a blue and white COW, " I giggled, fingering a little milk pitcher that was not out of the range of my budget.

The authentic Royal Dutch china from *De Porceleyne Fles* was indeed expensive, but their shop had some seconds and I managed to buy a few nice things that were the real deal, a round jar with a convex lid that I could keep on the bathroom shelf, and a cup and saucer that would forever mark this trip for me as I drank hot chocolate from it. I was happy with my finds.

It was serendipitous and wonderful to have an escort to all these Dutch cultural things, someone to talk to and laugh with. It kept me from brooding over Cass' plight. I even told Clément a little about Cass and how we would see each other in Paris and all. He was intrigued and very surprised at the story of her being snatched out of school in the middle of her studies and the strict attitude of her parents. His own parents raised him in the very "*haute bourgeoisie*" *(and were probably* richisme *like hers, I imagined— well, maybe not rich like hers, on second thought)*, and he couldn't fathom them doing anything like that.

"It was just fate and irony that Cass and I found ourselves able to see one another in Paris after all that, don't you think?" I mused.

"*Oui, vachement incroyable, au vrai dire,*" he agreed.

One afternoon towards the very end of my stay, I told my new friend that I just had to get out to do some real shopping, and Clément said he would like to accompany me. He knew Amsterdam really well and knew where the wonderful boutiques were. But he was also amenable to showing me an actual department store, because that is what I said I'd like to see.

"There is only really one big department store here, " he told me, "*de Bijenkorf* or 'the beehive'. It is right near Dam Square, so very easy for us to walk there."

I confessed to him that I really desperately wanted a white rabbit-fur coat like all the French girls wore to university.

"I'm sure they will have them," he answered right away, and of course, they did.

I tried one on and it fit perfectly, looked elegant, and felt amazingly warm and cozy. I knew if I bought it that I would never freeze again walking to the Sorbonne in the early winter morning through Luxembourg Gardens, or home to *La Maison* in the blue dusk, as the damp cold bore down upon me.

But the price: 265 *guilders*. Wow, how could I justify that? That was a lot for my poor little budget even with Cass' extra money and everything I had saved. In the end, even though Clément pronounced it "*très beau*" on me, I couldn't buy it and pay that much. It just seemed to me like a fortune. My old camel-hair coat and the fox hood would have to do.

Soon the Amsterdam "adventure" was finished. I said goodbye to Clément and we agreed to meet up once we were back in Paris. He gave me his card; I did not have any reception cards to hand out, and of course, Clément wasn't expecting me to have any. Since he had lived in the States, he already knew that only American business people had such cards, which he admitted finding strange, since everyone from age sixteen on up in France had them.

"Will you telephone me?" he asked pointing to his number on the card.

"Of course! Maybe I'll even get some cards made in the *Montparnasse-Bienvenue* station and send you one!" I laughed. We gave each other *la bise* and parted ways.

I helped myself to some cellophane-wrapped packets of sliced gouda cheese, several Dutch chocolate bars, some chips and three bottles of Evian water from a basket in the room for my train ride back to Paris, and carried my plaid cloth suitcase to the lobby. They were pretty horrified to see I'd brought it down myself and came right over to the front desk to whisk it away to the bell desk while I checked out. I did not see the total of the Hydes' bill, and wasn't given a copy of even the amount of room service and meals I had charged to them. My gut felt queasy nonetheless, just imagining what the total might have been.

They put me in a taxi to the *Centraal Station*. I emerged after the short ride and went straight to the ticket window. The fare was so cheap, I couldn't believe it. I had more than enough to travel first class back to France, but I only contemplated for a minute how great that would be, before I bought the second-class ticket. There were no high-speed trains in those days, but the trip still didn't take even five hours. I enjoyed the ride and drifted off from time to time, but awoke almost in a cold sweat remembering I still had problems.

When I got back to Paris and took my suitcase in the *métro* to return to the *Maison*, I found to my surprise, that I wasn't too sad. My room was all mine for another ten days, until Agathe returned at the last minute, like she always did. I turned on my radio to *France Musique*, and let Francis Poulenc's *Concert Champêtre for Harpsichord and Orchestra* envelop the room as I unpacked and rearranged my armoire to house the new kilt. I took some time and *futzed* around displaying my new Dutch treasures on the shelves before I got out my study materials and placed everything neatly on the desk.

But before settling down to really study, I realized I'd need some fortification and sustenance for the next few days, so I pulled on my boots and coat, grabbed my trusty *filet*, and went up to *Inno* to supply myself with soup mixes, fresh fruit and more cheese, plus a couple of *litres* of Coca Cola and some little pre-packaged supermarket *crème caramels* to tide me over. On the way back down *Rue Delambre*, I popped into my favorite *boulangerie* for a *baguette*, a *chausson aux pommes*, and a *croissant*. If the *Maison* were not serving breakfast, I decided, I would go to a French café in the area and have "*un petit- déjeuner complet*" which would be a lovely splurge.

Soon the dorm would fill back up with the Americans, if not the French girls yet, and in the moments I could muster not angsting over exams or Cass, I was *gaie comme un petit pinson*...happy as a little lark.

Chapter Forty-Two

"She Came in Through the Bathroom Window"...Lennon & McCartney

The *Maison des Étudiantes* was only firing on two cylinders so to speak, that first week I was back after Christmas. The little alcove housing the mailboxes next to the tiny cage elevator was locked tight and we could not receive any mail, which was undoubtedly piling up in one of the offices. I tried not to obsess over the mail, but I knew I was doing so. I hoped there would be quite a bit accumulated for me in there. I was faithfully writing copious letters home mainly because of Nana's and my agreement that I should chronicle the year. I tried to be true to all that I did and saw, but I edited out a lot of my anxiety about functioning in French society, the kids on the program who bugged me, and my struggles with schoolwork. All I needed, I surmised, would be more of Sol's ridicule and lack of approval. I wrote to Soren often, too, and had begun to probe a little deeper into his intention to come over and travel with me in June. The months were stretching out in front of me now that I was "on the other side" and they would melt away fast if we didn't have a plan.

I sent a huge thank you letter to Anja in Holland, who surprised me just before I left her house with the news that she would not be returning for the new term. She had been offered a job she felt she couldn't refuse as a researcher in a publishing house in The Hague. I was happy for her, but sad that I was going to miss having her in classes with me. I felt eternally grateful for the welcome I received in her home. Her brother and parents were so nice to me and helpful! Her grandmother's food was among the best I'd have all year in Europe. I told her, completely truthfully, how much I had loved Holland and hoped to return to the country again and again.

It was good, however, for me to revert to a more normal life in my little room, which was more like a monk's cell compared to the splendor I'd been living in at the Amstel. I took comfort in the idea that my own world on *Boulevard Raspail* was adequate for study, and study was what I had to do. I liked having my souvenirs spread about, and took pleasure in looking around the room as I had fixed it up.

Nonnie got back from Ireland, and we reveled in being reunited. She had news that more of her American friends would be coming to see her in Paris in the near future.

"Besides the one you met from Oxford and my friend in Dublin, I have a good friend who's studying in Heidelberg, and she's coming to Paris to see me," she explained excitedly.

"You're going to be quite the tour guide," I pronounced.

"Yes, but get this—my **best** friend from home, Mary Ann, told me she bought a ticket, too and would be in Paris to visit me as soon as our exams are finished in February!"

"Wow," I marveled, "so she'll be here when we have another two weeks off!"

"Yes! It'll be great stuff!"

C.C. had spent Christmas in Switzerland with her parents, who took the opportunity to have a holiday with her in Europe. Marty, Eric and Taylor, on the other hand, had all roamed around Scandinavia.

C.C. and Marty were still "an item" but she had decided to put a moratorium on their constant companionship while they began the new trimester at the Sorbonne. It was all any of us could do to be studying for the exams we were all dreading. My fears of being sent home if I failed the tests were assuaged, as it turned out, because the new term for us foreign students continued seamlessly even as we were about to sit exams over the first term's material. We wouldn't get the results until March. Failure might cost me credit hours, but it wouldn't be a basis for being packed off. I felt better.

C.C. and I spent a lot of time together that first week back, running errands and just talking. We did laundry up on *Rue Delambre* at the *laverie*, where we could leave the clothes in the machines and run over to *Inno* to stock up. Sometimes we even splurged and got on the *métro* at *Edgar Quinet* riding straight to the *Étoile* for a hamburger at *Le Drugstore*. Since I'd been frugal in Holland, and thanks mostly to Cass' largesse, it was the first time since I'd arrived in Paris six months earlier that I had some discretionary spending money.

Soon the entire dorm reopened, and the first thing I found in my mailbox was a postcard of the *Arc de Triomphe* from Cass, one that she must have bought a long time ago in Paris and mailed from Schiphol airport. She had written in dark ink across the top of the picture of the arch: "**Shrier and Hyde**" and the body said:

"Symbolic of our <u>triumph</u> over loneliness, immature boys, and insecurity!" I surely enjoyed the wonderful, if truncated, holiday with you in Amsterdam and will write IMMEDIATELY upon return home. BEST OF LUCK on your exams--- I know you can do it!! And gee, happiness must be having a friend named Sari to talk to and be with and ECSTATIC happiness must be knowing we'll be back at U of I together!"

I read it and wondered if that could be true. I'd be back in Iowa City by late August, and she would hopefully have had-- and nobly given up-- a healthy baby by then. But would the Hydes allow her to return to Iowa? She must have been having a moment of optimistic fantasy.

It had dawned on me that, in a Dickensian sort of way, my time now in Paris would be the best of times and the worst of times. I was happily looking forward to seeing Clément in Paris, maybe traveling with Soren later, and studying hard but also enjoying the beauty and wonder of the place I had always dreamed I would be in. And now I was! However, knowing Cass would not be back there to enjoy it with me brought me down. Her delicate condition both physically and mentally scared me and I would start thinking about her as I studied, and I would fall asleep at night fitfully worried about her.

I wrote her long emotional letters trying to buoy her spirits and mine at the same time. But I had, after three weeks, heard absolutely nothing from her other than the postcard, and it sent panic through me. Luckily, though, I had the fortitude to realize that I could not, under any circumstances, let myself succumb to depression of any stripe, because sleeping all day or moping around would inevitably lead to more fatigue, more stress, and ultimately failure at the sole reason I was there: to get the *"Degré Superieur de Langue et de Civilisation Française"* from one of the finest universities in the world.

<u>Finally</u> a letter, the likes of which I would not have expected in a million years, arrived in my mailbox from Cass. Nothing could have prepared me for the shock of its contents. She was in Iowa City! With Alan! She would not be going to a home for unwed mothers and not only that, she was expecting TWINS.

This was all too much for me to take in. I sat on the bed and read her letter over and over.

Will you ever forgive me for not writing sooner? I "neglected" to do so out of a mixture of embarrassment once the time lapse occurred, and because my own feelings and very existence were so confused—a type of self-absorption and over-analytical and self-centered thoughts that left me incapable of thinking of others. And yet, always, I thought of you and felt lonely for you. This is a long confused and confusing tale.

When I returned from Hollard to Chicago, my parents were so furious at me! Their most pressing concern was for the embarrassment I was about to cause the family, and not, as had been intimated before, about my health. I almost couldn't believe it. I guess that comes from never having had a real relationship with them. But I managed to convince them that I would comply with their demands and go off to the dreaded "home" as soon as I started to show, which seemed to placate them-- enough at least that they took off for Switzerland at the New Year, like always. And that's when I called Alan and told him that I was going to have his child and give it up for adoption. He insisted he was coming to see and talk to me, so I arranged to meet him in downtown Chicago. I couldn't risk our staff seeing his motorcycle again on our property. Julia would have turned that jet around and come swooping back down on me---ha!

Once we were together, however, he insisted that I pack up whatever I wanted to take, and he would move me out of there. He had driven up in a truck, of all things! I think he knew all along that's what he was going to do. So I did it. I packed some of the clothes I especially like, much as I can hardly fit into them even now, and I took as many art supplies as I could put in my luggage. As soon as our kitchen staff was gone, I sneaked it all down to the back door. Alan drove up around the circular drive near the garages, and he loaded my stuff up. I know you are shocked to read this. I was uneasy and also nauseated the whole time...couldn't tell if it was anxiety or pregnancy or both. I felt like I was in some sort of nasty trance. And yet I was so happy to be getting away from there and the inevitable transfer to the ninth ring of hell. Going to a home for

unwed mothers was the loneliest thing I could have imagined. I felt I would have shriveled up inside and died. And I did contemplate my own death, which would, naturally cause that of the fetus, too. But when death appears in my mind, it feels so selfish, you know?

I am still upset all the time and the least little thing sends me into depression. I really wonder what is wrong—my mind, the situation…what? Alan was worried so he made me go to one of the U docs. They did another blood test on me and something called my HCG levels are elevated and the doctor thought the fetus was increasing in weight more quickly than it should, so he deduced that I was carrying twins!! They will do some test called ultrasound to make sure that is what is going on. I'm lucky to be in Iowa City where the U hospital actually has the machine.

Once my parents found out what I had done (and I think they were as stupefied that I had the gumption to do it as much as they were livid that I did it), their lawyer contacted Alan through the University to tell us they were disowning me and cutting me off from every possible thing, especially money. Alan is glad and said he wouldn't "take their filthy money anyway!"

I really believe Alan loves me. We even went to talk to the Episcopal priest that is his C.O. "advisor" for some counseling. He keeps expounding on the idea that trust breeds trust and how Alan's uncertainties frightened me before, and how Alan was in turn frightened by me. But Sari now I've got a kid—maybe KIDS inside me, and I -we- owe it to them not to give them away or terminate them.

I am so tired. And sometimes I recall our plans for an apartment next fall and our decorating schemes, and I long for our days together. And yet, now, that must of necessity be behind me. I must marry Alan if I am to be completely free of my parents. I want to think they are sad, as well as angry. I want to believe that they could love me and love their grandchildren, but I am very afraid that I'm wrong. So Alan and I will eventually marry, and I will give up my old ideas of courtly love and idealized marriage. I know that my love for Alan (and his for me) is a lovely, eternal thing, but also a fragile and battered one now.

You know what I would wish for you, my dearest and farthest-flung friend, is true love with Soren-- or for that matter even NOT with Soren-- but with whomever the lucky person will be who shares your life. That you will feel always loved honestly and patiently for ever and ever. Perhaps it is an impossible impractical dream, but I do not believe so. There must be a way that people are able to communicate and share with one another and grow without stifling themselves.

I got your letters and I hope you will forgive my not answering them. Forgiveness, it recently occurred to me, is the most elusive and difficult of commodities to acquire. I ask it of you, yet I find it hard to dole out! There are so many hard little spokes in my heart concerning Alan---I find that I am not the good and forgiving person I would have myself be. Rather I am hardened and even bitter when kindness and exoneration are in order. How people overcome this I am not certain. It is not something you "figure out" or scheme to be able to attain. Rather I suppose it is a gentleness, a free-flowing something that only truly fine, loving, self-demanding people attain. I hope with all my heart I someday, somehow do find a way to summon my better angel. But I'm really afraid that I'm so far from who I wish to be, what I want to do, and where I want to go, that I really feel as though I look at a stranger in the mirror.

I have let you down horribly not writing because of my own fucked up problems even though I love you dearly as a sister. So all I can do is ask ---even that old word pray-- for your forgiveness and acceptance of my clunky ways.

Alan is looking around for a house for us, so use his office address that's on the envelope and please please write to me that you're not mad.

Love ya, kid,
Cass

To say that my mind was reeling from this letter is to overstate the obvious, and yet I was so stymied by the news, I almost dropped to the floor. It's not that I wasn't happy for her; the thought of twins shocked me, but it was also wonderous. And I wasn't feeling sorry for myself that we wouldn't be rooming together as planned; that was inconsequential now. I just worried that Cass Hyde couldn't begin to fathom or comprehend what was in store for her, and how obviously unprepared she was for this life change. But I tried to convince myself that she wouldn't be the first person ever confronted with complete ignorance on how to run a household or raise a family.

I just had to have faith that she — they---would rise to the occasion. She'd have to find an OB-GYN in I.C. and go to pre-natal classes. Alan would have to step up!

As far as becoming a wife and mother almost overnight was concerned, Cass had a huge learning curve in front of her; she had, for instance, never so much as prepared food of any sort for more than herself. And part of that was my fault! That summer two years prior when we had lived together, I did all the grocery shopping and meal preparation. She'd eaten institutional food at every level of her education from boarding school to university. She'd had cooks and chefs at her houses in Chicago and she had relied upon me in Iowa City. I doubted she'd ever opened a cookbook.

I wrote her back and said all the right things to ease her angst. I promised to be there for her no matter what, no matter where. I didn't preach at her and certainly didn't go into my fears of her soon having not one but TWO babies to take care of at the same time. I just reaffirmed my love for her and joy at the prospect of welcoming their children into the world as soon as I got back; and I told her with unabashed glee that I was going to bring the babies something very French and wonderful also when I returned. Even though I was terribly worried, I told her not to worry — that everything was going to be all right, and that it must have been meant to be or it wouldn't have happened this way. It's not that I outright lied to her; I wanted to believe that.

Trouble was, I didn't believe it for a second.

Chapter Forty-Three

"She's Not There"…The Zombies

Classes began again for us foreign students the second week in January, even as the French university second term, which was preceded by a sort of intersession in January, really didn't start until mid-February. Our *Cours de Civilisation* exams were set for the beginning of February, after which there would be the two-week vacation that French elementary and secondary students went on: *école de neige*, or ski school. Schools took kids to the various mountain ranges all over the country and taught skiing as well as academics. Even our Pella College program offered a ski trip to Chamonix, which I declined to go on, but for which most of my friends in the dorm signed up. It would have, of course, been exciting to be so near to Mont Blanc, but I thought I'd prefer to see it from the windows of a coach. Besides the cost of doing this trip--which was substantial-- the main reason I didn't want to go was simple: I'd never even set foot on a mountain, let alone skied down one. Unless there would be ski lessons, I would be frittering my time away in a chalet, stuck with no way down.

Clément sent me a note just like he said he would when he returned to Paris, and as it was shoulder to the grindstone for me preparing for the exams, he offered to meet and help me with the material. His classes didn't begin until after his family's annual ski holiday in Mégève. He didn't seem at all concerned about his own exams when he so generously offered to help me prepare for mine.

The fact was not lost on me that this family, if not aristocratic, was at the very least, très aisée *–very well-off; and they invited me into their sphere, which was not typically French. I really wondered about it. They had only met me a short time ago, and much as Clément and I went palling around in Amsterdam for a week, the parents didn't know me or my background (or religion!) except that I was a student at the Sorbonne. Ordinarily that wouldn't have been enough to be taken into the fold, so to speak. But this family had lived in America, I rationalized; perhaps their guard was down or something. I had really hit it off with both parents and was so grateful for the chance to get to know them. Monsieur de Seignard reminded me that I had a private tour of the Marmottan Museum in my future and Madame de Seignard welcomed me to their home any time I was available* "peut-être pour un petit diner intime familial," *to which I would not say no.*

Clément was also very generous in introducing me to his *"bande"* of friends who got together almost every Friday or Saturday night in one or the other's apartments (most were still living with their parents!) to listen to music and dance. The younger, *"collège"* or junior high kids called this cultural phenomenon *"la boum"* and the older ones called them *"soirées."* But the first one to which Clément invited me was to be a "surprise party" (pronounced by them as "sur-preeze pahrTEE") so when I met him at the *métro Wagram* and he led me around the corner to the very nice Hausmannian building, and we went up to the fifth floor *"à gauche"* or on the left, we knocked at the door and Clément embraced the guy whom I had understood to be the guest of honor. Once we entered, I could tell that the party was in full swing.

"Oh, darn," I whispered to Clément, "did we miss the surprise?"

"Surprise?"

"Well, you called this a surprise party. Where I come from, if it's called that, all the guests hide or something and when someone brings the honoree, they all jump out and yell, 'Surprise!' The person isn't supposed to know about it. That's the element of surprise.

"How extraordinary," he responded.

"Well, what do you think surprise means?"

"No, I understand what it is; we just use the term to mean any sort of party."

I chalked it up to "the French," but it still baffled me. However, I was in for another—shall we say, culture shock: It was 1969, but even this sophisticated crowd was still dancing be-bop to fifties-style rock and roll. All the fantastic rock music of the sixties—American, English, all of it -- the veritable music renaissance-- was lost on these people. I couldn't even dance that teeny bopper stuff, so it was a return to my wallflower ways, which was fine. The buffet food was wonderful and the décor of the gorgeous apartment, typically French antiques and *toile de Jouy*, was delightful to just sit back and take in.

Most of Clément's group of friends were there: his three best guy friends, Gilles, Jean-Joseph and the resident of the apartment, Jean-Louis-Michel (three names no less!) plus four or five girls in his immediate circle, among which Mathilde, Florence and Sylvie, all of whom I had never met, of course, but also two girls I recognized!

"Believe it or not, I think I might know those girls over there," I said to Clément. "I met them at the *Café de la Sorbonne* one afternoon last fall. They were studying English."

"*Alors, c'est parfait,*" he said grinning. "They are both my great friends. One of them, Christine, is my cousin, in fact."

We went over to the girls and Clément introduced us.

"We remember you!" Christine said.

"Oh, *ouais!*" chirped Lorraine.

"So how did the English class turn out?" I asked them.

"You helped us," said Christine, "*mais de toute façon, ce n'était pas terrible terrible.*" It must not have been all that great.

Nonnie and C.C. were thrilled for me that I had met a nice French boy, and they hoped I'd introduce them some day. And my roommate Agathe was also happy that I had another outlet to practice my French. But several other of the girls in my dorm--the ones that lived on Nonnie's and C.C.'s floor-- were downright nosey and nasty about it. They were, shall we say, quite sur-PREEZED when they saw us in the courtyard one afternoon when Clément came by to pick me up, which, in itself was rare for a French guy to do. I could just about see their jaws drop when they realized he was there to meet **me**. They interrogated Nonnie about it, and she told me.

"They're obviously jealous, " Nonnie laughed.

"You know, it would never occur to me to wonder about their social lives; why can't everyone just mind their own beeswax?"

After the courtyard sighting, though, I felt funny looks on me whenever I ran into some of these same girls in the dining hall or just around the dorm. I was not in their level of *cours pratiques*, so they never saw me in classes. But I got the distinct impression that I was being shunned.

I complained once again, this time to C.C.

"My God, what's-her-name is sleeping with the director of the whole civ program, and she doesn't get this treatment! What is wrong with dating a French boy? We're in France!"

"Believe it or not, it's really just one girl who seems to not like you," C.C. confided to me. "Lindy. But she is kind of the big wheel in that group."

"Shit, she hardly even knows me! She's a snob all right, and I think she was friends with our former Southern Belle classmate who's long gone. But I've never had a conversation with her!"

"I'm sure I don't know what her problem is, Sari. Just forget about her."

"Maybe she doesn't like Jews," I wondered aloud.

"I suppose that's possible," C.C. agreed, "but she's never said anything like that."

"Well, they wouldn't, would they?"

Just what I needed: anti-Semites in the program.

The fact that Nonnie and C.C. were both included in Lindy's social circle didn't really shock me--- they lived on that floor; but it occurred to me that **they** could have invited me in—to sort of smooth the way for the other girls to get to know me. However, I mentally shrugged it off. We three were still as close as we'd ever been, especially me and Nonnie. If anything, she was more than happy for me that I'd been able to see my best friend in Paris more than half a dozen times first semester; and now I was entering a burgeoning circle of French friends.

Nonnie was the one person in the entire group to whom I had divulged my gravest fears of failure back at exam time, and she was the most attentive to me of the group, relieved that I had passed those first tests and could stay.

Those tests we took at the end of summer session counted, but not much…more for credits back in America than for our "*Degré Sup*". These exams that we were about to sit would determine our destiny. They would consist of a paper or what they called "*dissertation,*" written "*épreuves,*" an obligatory oral exam, and the dreaded dictation followed by questions of grammar and vocabulary.

When we got our instructions for the exams, I showed the dissertation topics to Clément. The dissertation had to be done while sitting the exams and they would give us three hours to do it that day.

"There are three different lit areas," I groaned, "*Littérature française du Moyen Age et de la Renaissance, Littérature Française du XVIIème siècle et du XVIIIème siècle.*"

"You could write on Molière." He pointed to the sample question on my sheet. "For instance this: 'In what sense was it true that Molière took for the object of his comedic ridicule the mores of the society of his time', " Clément suggested, adding, "We were always discussing that in school at *lycée.*"

"That's a pretty good one," I said, marveling that as hard as I thought my studies were, he'd been doing the same in high school! "I think I could expound on that. But I was always thinking I'd do mine on art history." All of a sudden something hit me, "You know, I'll bet you anything our professor knows your dad! She's a curator at the Rodin Museum! I never even thought of that until right now."

"Madame Goldschneider?"

"YES! God, Paris is a village. She doesn't know me from Adam, of course," I added, lest he think I would even suggest a good word be put in from his father.

"She loves Gothic architecture. Do your paper on that. *J'en suis très sérieux.*"

I wrote what I considered my first *magnum opus* in the French language: "The Evolution of Gothic Sculpture from the End of the XIIth to the Beginning of the XVth Centuries." I consulted Clément and he made some grammatical corrections on it. This draft was just for me; I had to rewrite the whole thing without notes on the day of the exams. Clément was very gracious and didn't pronounce my prose abominable, or warn me that I might not pass with what I wrote. He helped me condense my ideas into coherent paragraphs that got to the point faster. All in all, he was fairly happy with it and I was eternally grateful for his help.

But there was more than the dissertation to prepare. We were given sample questions in ten segments of study, from which we had to choose three, and in each one of those there were four parts that had to be addressed. They told us that in no case could the question section be the same as the one we chose for the dissertation, so art history could actually not even be one of my choices, but the subject matter treated would still have to come from among the courses we were enrolled in. The question part of the test would also last three hours, one hour per subject, and it went without saying that a blank paper would result in the grade of zero.

In French history, for example, I would have to write on the significance of the Royal coronation on the nation and political power; define a commune charter and trace the development of the bourgeoisie; tell how and when the University of Paris was constituted; and address what we knew of the historical role of the *Châteaux* of the Loire. If I took French politics, the subjects that had to be covered were how the president of the Republic is elected, what powers did the *Assemblée Nationale* have; what was the *Conseil Constitutionnel*, and how was the Senate elected. I enjoyed my geography classes, also with a woman lecturer, and her questions would entail citing the three most important French agricultural products; the decentralization of French industry, the two biggest French ports, and France's principal economic partners.

On the day of the test, we were mandated to arrive exactly on time to a building called the "*Maison des Examens.*" In order to be admitted into the hall itself, we had to present our *Sorbonne* identification cards, upon which we had already written the numbers of each exam we would stand. These numbers had been posted on a bulletin board at the university in our regular lecture hall, the Salle Richelieu. It made it official: they had displayed lists of our names with our chosen exams on them.

I noticed several students brought in *madeleine* cakes to the exam and I laughed.

"I should have thought of that!" I said out loud, whereupon a girl I didn't even know handed me one.

"*Beh, merci, alors!*" I sang out, still amused.

I wondered if we would even be allowed to take them in, since we were admonished more than once to not bring materials of any type: books, notebooks, dictionaries, personal notes, not even blank paper, since the exam booklets and some scratch paper would be provided for us.

We were to write *Monsieur, Madame* or *Mademoiselle* before our names on the exam sheets, as well as our nationality and table number on every piece of paper we actually wrote on. We also had to put the type of diploma we were working toward. I was a candidate for the Diploma of French Language and Civilization, and I was inscribed for the "*Supérieur*" level. There were also "*normal*" and "*élémentaire*" levels, as well as the lesser-status participation certificates one could earn on those same levels.

Once seated in the exam room, we were forbidden from smoking, from changing places for any reason, and from leaving the room under any circumstances. Only after one hour could any student leave the building. And it went without saying that anyone caught cheating "*in flagrante delicto*" would be summarily kicked out on the spot.

The first hour and a half was taken up by us giving a written resumé of a literary passage read out loud by a professor, and then written questions over that same reading. We were forbidden to take notes in "*sténographie*" and they really didn't want anyone writing anything during the first read through!

Next was the *dictée*. We were warned not to write the whole thing out as a draft on scratch paper because we would lose too much time. Sure enough, much to my-- and I daresay everyone else's-- chagrin, it was Proust. Those madeleines had better have done their job! I was petrified. The *dictée* was given from a recording. You could not ask for repetition but each line was read once through, then repeated slower, then read once again, just like *dictées* in class had been.

They gave us a fifteen-minute break and then we were back at the dissertation for three hours. We had walked into the test building at 8:00 a.m. and by the time the lecture, *dictée* and dissertation were over, it was 2:00 p.m. We had an hour respite and then had to report back at 3:00 p.m. for three more hours, which would be the written questions, one hour per subject.

The oral exams would be taken the following day and we could bring with us our *textes d'études*, a copy of *Le Cid*, and a list of what we had studied in the *cours pratiques*. The practical course tests were the only parts of this whole examination that made any distinction of our language ability levels.

The French grading scale in classes had always been "over 20" as in 12/20 rather than a percentage out of 100. However, in order to pass these tests, which had their own unique grade values, one had to achieve an overall total of 90 points; and any outright failure in any of the areas would mean non-continuation for diploma candidates. Presumably if one failed, they could stay in Paris and still obtain a certificate, but not the diploma. I really was under pressure not to fail any one particular category. The dictation was my *bête noire* in all that for sure. I was nervous and scared before, during, and after.

By contrast, my oral exams went a lot better than I had expected! They asked me things I recognized, and I actually knew the answers. Whether or not I expressed them in adequate French was another story.

It haunted me the entire year that even after I attained a certain level of fluency, my thought processes in French could not catch up in erudition with my native language. I had to come to terms with the fact that I was not going to be bilingual, even if I was thrilled to finally see that I was becoming more fluent.

But all those dark thoughts about my French and about failing my year abroad came to a halt on March 3, 1969, when I got the ecstatic news that I had passed with a grade of 108 and that was eighteen points higher than the cutoff. Eighteen points that would ease the burden of what I had to attain at the next battery of tests in May, which meant that, as it stood then, for the *Diplôme* I would need 72 instead of 90. That was huge.

Taylor scored 111 and was furious at himself. He and the other of my closest American friends all had been given harder *cours pratiques* questions than I, and so his 111 was probably a lot better than my 108. But he didn't see it that way. Marty, C.C., Nonnie and Eric all did great, but no one was happier and more relieved than I was. Agathe was thrilled for me, and had been waiting for the results to surprise me with an invitation to her home for a weekend in March. And I ran into one of my *cours pratiques* profs and she actually hugged me!

I went to the post office and sent my parents a telegram that read: **"I passed. Full stop."**

263

Chapter Forty-Four

"April Come She Will"...Simon & Garfunkel

The great exam hurdle overcome, I felt a transition wash over me, something akin to that day back in October when, turning on my little radio perched on the corner of my desk, I had realized all of a sudden that I was understanding what was being said. Once the threshold was crossed into the last third of my year, I felt that I was at ease in the French language, happy with French friends, and living as a Parisian more than a visitor.

At the February hiatus, since the dorm once again pretty much emptied out but did not close, I found I had my room all to myself and time on my hands. So I devised a plan---not too ambitious, after all, it was break---to explore at least half of the twenty *arrondissements* that made up the great city. I lived in the 14th and knew fairly well the area that bordered it: the 6th, as well as the Latin Quarter, the 5th. My idea was simple: choose an area, take a *métro* that landed me someplace in the given district, walk around and explore-- being careful to keep my *Plan des Arrondissements* with me at all times-- and finally, find a café to sit in and read, write letters, journal and people-watch.

Clément lived in the posh 16th, so I thought that might be a good place to start. I had already been invited once to his house—just to study-- and so I knew how to get to *Rue Singer*—it was right near the *métro* stop of *La Muette*. I went there and walked around his neighborhood and because the weather was icy cold and the sun a *boule menteuse* (lying ball of gas), I dropped into a café on the *Rue Passy*, not having gotten very far on my trek. I had a wonderful hot chocolate and wrote a letter to Cass.

When an hour or so had passed and I was revived, I had a last-minute change of heart. I set out **not** in the direction I had planned, which was through the *Place Trocadero* to *Avenue Kléber* and into the *métro* at *Charles de Gaulle Étoile*, but rather straight to the neighborhood of *Passy* itself, which was a happy find for me. They had a really old-fashioned chic department store called *Franck et Fils*, which I loved, and found inside that the only thing I could afford was a black velvet headband. I adored it and bought it, and wore that thing the rest of my life.

Passy also had an *Inno* and that surprised me at first because I thought of *Inno* as too inexpensive for that posh area. *Inno* was, after all, more like a Woolworth's with a grocery store, and I didn't expect to see one in upscale neighborhoods. On the other hand, there were *Prisunics* all over Paris, I reminded myself, and they were the same thing as *Inno*, even a little cheaper. The *Passy Inno* was smaller than "mine" but I still liked it. I found even more of that brand "*Chipie*" which I loved, and I got several notebooks, not for Spring term, but to use as journals. *Chipie*'s mascot was a little Scottie dog and that was perfect; I felt like a fifth grader but I liked the feeling.

The next day of my outing I dressed warmer and set off for the *Parc Monceau* area of the 8th *Arrondissement*, which bordered the "*bon 17ème*" the good part of the 17th. The "bad" part of the 17th was *Clichy*, home of prostitutes, drug dealers and the *Moulin Rouge*. I was anxious to see the *Parc Monceau* because I already knew about it from reading Art Buchwald. My mother Betty and I had actually bonded, for wont of a better word, over Art Buchwald's columns in the newspaper; and she had also bought his books in paperback which I read over and over. Many of the columns compiled in these books were stories of his life in Paris. I knew he lived in a grand apartment overlooking that park formerly reserved only for children of the royal family. When I got to the huge gold-leaf gates and looked around at the imposing apartment buildings that formed the periphery of the entrance, I was stunned by the opulence and realized that the Buchwald family must have had it pretty damn good. I'd never stopped to consider, up to that point, how an American salary would compare to what the average French person made. But even there as a student, I knew that no one except the most wealthy could live in one of these homes on the *Parc Monceau*; and I reasoned that if Art Buchwald was living in this neighborhood, he must have been pulling down one fucking huge salary.

The *Parc Monceau* was different from the other really famous Parisian gardens in that it was essentially a "*jardin a l'Anglaise*" with lawns that you could walk on, and great clusters of flowers rather

264

than manicured beds. It was famous for its statues of well-known French literary and musical figures, for its Grecian temple, its rotunda, a Dutch windmill and Corinthian columns.

The interior of the *Parc Monceau* was a little paradise for children, especially, as evidenced by the legions of nannies and young mothers pushing the kind of baby carriages that were navy blue and white: "baby Rolls Royces" called prams in England. It struck me that Cass Hyde's family would have been able to afford one for her children, but of course, now that wouldn't be happening.

The *Parc Monceau* was also notable for its snack kiosk selling all sorts of candy and even grilled treats to hungry after-school crowds, but I also saw the *Bertillon* sign over the counter, meaning that the park had a concession for the most famous ice cream in Paris. I had already tried and fallen in love at first bite with *glace café*, coffee ice cream that I had never even tasted in Iowa. But the *parfum* on this menu was called "*Cappuccino*" instead, so I decided that would be fine…must have something to do with coffee, after all, and even though it was February, and even though a *cornet boule simple* (one scoop cone) was four times more expensive than I thought it should have been, I ordered it. It was coffee all right, but with chunks of the most heavenly chocolate I had ever tasted, sending my mouth into a veritable orgasm of delight. I took it over to the playground area where you had to pay to have your kid ride on little merry-go-rounds or in miniature boats or rocket ships; or even to use the swing for allotted times. I sat savoring my cone and watching the interaction between the adults in uniform, indicating that they were caretakers, and others in quasi-uniforms of cigarette-leg pants tucked into boots, Lacoste wool sweaters and cashmere coats with their "*carré Hermès*" scarves and Kelly purses. Those were the moms.

It was a veritable parade of Hermès in that park. Sometimes the scarves were tied around the handle of their Kelly bags, which hung open draped on the strollers.

Madame de Seignard had a Kelly bag and it intrigued me even though, when I first saw it, I had no idea it cost "*cent mille balles*" -- the price in old francs quoted by French people in the 1960's who still spoke in terms of the franc before it was devalued by ten. *Cent mille balles* was *dix mille francs*, ten thousand new francs. Ten thousand new francs translated to two thousand dollars. My mind was completely blown that a purse could have such a price tag. Obviously, I had no notion of what *Hermès* bags, scarves, gloves, saddles or anything else they made sold for. I got the idea, however, that ordinary Frenchmen could never ever afford that kind of product, and that the French society was even more striated than I imagined ours to have been.

As I sat there watching all sorts of people come and go, it was mind-boggling to think of the socio-economic gaps between the different discernable French citizens. The French were divided into four identifiable groups that I could tell: the very very rich, almost a "*noblesse*", the *haute bourgeoisie*, a still very wealthy upper middle class; *la bourgeoisie* or middle class still pretty well off compared to the working classes, which were—put in simple terms-- the equivalent of the former peasants. France had also "invited" thousands of guest workers from their former colonies into the country after the wars to help rebuild and maintain its ravaged infrastructure. These people, many from North Africa—the *Maghreb*-- were relegated to the near-suburbs of Paris, in government-subsidized, very ugly high-rise housing, which I only saw that year a few times from the window of a bus or a train. The industrial revolution that America and England experienced before the 1860's had only arrived in France a century later!

The streets leading into the park, like those near my dorm which led into the Luxembourg Gardens, were lined with lovely boutiques displaying the most beautiful, if conservative, children's clothing and traditional toys in the known universe, and seeing all of these gorgeous boutiques got me to thinking about presents for Cass' twins. It would be easy for me to find fabulous treasures for them; whether I'd be able to afford them was another story. Luckily even *Inno* had beautiful baby clothes made by *Petit Bateau*, a venerable brand that also had its own boutiques in every major neighborhood. And a foray into the really famous shopping district at *métro Chaussée d'Antin*, the *grands magasins* of *Galleries Lafayette* and *Au Printemps*, would afford me the opportunity to buy anything and everything. Marks and Spencer, which I knew from London, was also right across the street and millions of French children were also outfitted by them.

Compared to New York or any major American city, Paris did not have many big department stores at all. Besides the two close together in the Opera district, there was *La Samaritaine* practically on the banks of the Seine near the *Pont Neuf*; and the oldest department store in Paris, *Le Bon Marché*. That one was over on the Left Bank, much closer to me than the other three; but I tended to ignore it for most of my year in Paris-- a big mistake. It had a most magnificent food hall, which turned out to be my fave rave, once I finally went there.

There were not many other establishments that could actually be called department stores, but there were literally thousands of boutiques all over the city. And the city's most famous toy store, *Au Nain Bleu* was not too far, coincidentally, from the "*grands magasins*," over on the same street as the *Hermès* flagship store, *Rue du Faubourg St. Honoré.*

If you shopped in boutiques, as I had mentioned shopping with Cass, (which seemed like another lifetime ago instead of only four months,) you'd better know what you wanted when you entered, because, as I had explained to my friend, browsing was not really in the French lexicon of that day. But in the department stores, I could wander around from floor to floor fingering and drooling over anything out on display. I tried to be reasonable and not get all depressed over what I could never afford. Rather I just tried to find "a little something" that fit into my very meager budget, but would still be representative of France and my year there. I was impressed that, unlike in America, French products were not "made in Japan" ---unless you actually bought a Japanese product, such as tea services that were sold in some of the housewares boutiques.

I had, towards the end of my experiment in Paris exploration, walked the avenues and boulevards and passageways and squares, and had discovered wonderful cafés in the 16th, the 8th, the 9th , the 14th, the 5th, the 6th and the 7th *arrondissements*; but I still wanted to go back to some of the older parts, which in my student days were a bit grittier, more "*moche*." One of these was *Le Marais*, which housed the former Jewish ghetto. *Le Marais,* which was really parts of two *arrondissements*, the 3rd and the 4th, had been royal and the official home of the king's brother over the centuries, not to mention many literary figures.

One of our assignments in my 19th C. French Lit class was to tour the Victor Hugo museum on the *Place des Vosges* where I had taken Cass that time; and our history group also spent a lot of time at the *Carnavalet* Museum. We *Sorbonne* students were even invited—with our professors-- into the *Archives Nationales* nearby, and shown some very impressive papers. One example of the astonishing things they brought out for us to see was the first page of an actual letter written in the hand of Louis XIV himself, which had been sent to the *Comte de Pontchartain*, telling him that an English fleet was approaching *Brest* and might bombard the city. All the archives that were procured for us, like one of Charles d'Orléans' poems written from prison in England during the Hundred Years War, were presented to us by curators wearing white gloves. The document there which absolutely astounded me the most was the trial transcript of Joan of Arc, which the curator placed right in front of me. I couldn't really read the French, which was in a very ornate printing font, and I didn't touch the paper, but I felt a chill go through me nonetheless.

I wanted to explore a bit of the city farther from my dorm, and Montmartre was often mentioned in art history classes. So it was very serendipitous when Clément phoned me on the Saturday morning before classes were to start up again. He was back from *Mégève*, and called me to see if I wanted to go with him to a concert at the Basilica *Sacré Coeur*. I told him I would love that, whereupon he offered to take me there in his car.

"You have a car?!" I was astounded, but I shouldn't have been. He was older than me and anyway, eighteen was driving age in France. I just hadn't met any students up to that time who had a car, and Clément had never mentioned that he had one, nor had he ever met me with a car or picked me up for any of our outings.

"I just got it. It was my grandmother's car in *Lyon*, and on this ski trip, she said I could have it. It's a 1958 blue *Renault Dauphine*. I shall come by to fetch you at 2:00 p.m., *d'accord?*"

"Fine!"

Well, that changed things. I had never tooled around Paris in a private car. The times I was sent back to the dorm by Cass in a taxi were the only times I'd ever ridden in a car in the city. This time it was fun...scary fun. Clément was an excellent driver, though, and I could tell he'd been driving in Paris long before he had a car of his own. Even though finding parking on the street was already a nightmare back then, Clément always managed to know where to park near enough to wherever we needed to be, as if he were endowed with some magical parking karma.

The concert he took me to was one of medieval choir music, and the resonance of those chants and *cantigas d'amor* inside *Sacré Coeur* captivated the audience unlike any concert heard in a normal theater or modern church.

"There is just something about hearing ancient music in an ambiance like that which sets the heart pounding, *n'est-ce pas?*" he whispered to me.

After the concert, we walked all over the area around *Place du Tertre* and ate *crèpes*. It was touristy, but in February-- not as much. We went to an old café at the foot of the steps leading up to the basilica, and warmed up with a *café crème*. He told me all about his trip to the Alps, and I told him all about my intrepid exploration of his city.

We had gone to the concert on a Saturday, and Clément invited me to his house for dinner for the next day, when I could also have the promised tour of the *Marmottan* Museum led by his father. I was thrilled to accept the kind invitation and happy I had the kilt to wear to it! Kilt, white sweater (not cashmere but nice enough), pearl choker (not real pearls but believable enough), black tights, boots, camel hair coat and the fox hood. It was as dressed up as I could muster.

The *Marmottan* was heaven, and being taken around by the assistant director was an honor not lost on me. Clément accompanied his father as I was shown first through the main floor collections with all the Napoleonic artifacts: the furniture and the bibelots, the paintings that had been collected by the Jules and Paul Marmottan family. The lovely and impressive Empire collection was just spectacular. But! They then led me downstairs to see all those Monet paintings Renaud had promised I'd see, gathered in one space. That just took my breath away! Monsieur de Seignard reminded me that it had only been two years since Claude Monet's son Michel had left the museum this--his personal collection of his father's work, and at the time that I saw it, it was the largest such collection in the world.

"Our space is different from that of *l'Orangerie*," Monsieur de Seignard explained, "but it was inspired by that rounded wall design." I had to take his word for it, as I hadn't yet even seen the *Orangerie* museum. I had already gone to the *Jeu de Paume*, however, and marveled at **its** collection of Impressionist paintings. I vowed to go back to the *Tuileries* Gardens and spend much more time in both of those museums.

Dinner at their house-- my first of several, as it turned out-- was wonderful. The family employed a cook and a small staff, but Madame de Seignard had made and served this meal of *blanquette de veau* herself. It started with *apéro*, followed by hors d'oeuvres before we even got to the table, and we had a wonderful time savoring the meal...and the conversation... for three hours.

Before dinner was served, I got my second tour of the day: around their home! The Seignard apartment was huge, airy, had the requisite parquet, floor to ceiling windows, and was situated in the building high enough to look out over the *Bois de Boulogne*. It was furnished in family heirlooms and antiques, but I had been ushered first into a *salle de séjour* that was completely modern! There was a brown velveteen sectional that turned a square corner, and could comfortably seat eight people, right in the middle of the room, amidst bookshelves, a bar, a writing desk, and two leather Eames lounge chairs in a shade of chocolate that made you want to dive into them head first.

As they took me around their apartment, they were especially proud to point out something which they considered quite new-fangled. It was in their hallway!

"*Voilà!*" called out Blandine, as she stopped in front of sliding-door closet storage for linens and folded clothing. I was informed that these had been newly installed and were "*à l'Américain,*" and the only ones of the sort in the whole building. I took it in without laughing or teasing of any sort, as Madame was obviously very proud of her design prowess, along with the fact that it was her idea to have had them put in.

I also got to see the living room, which they called "*double reception,*" and the room where we were to have dinner, the grand dining room, with a Lalique chandelier hanging over this magnificent mahogany table that could seat at least a dozen people easily.

I even saw Clément's room which was smallish but nicely furnished with an *armoire* that had been in the family since the French Revolution, and a writing desk that looked a lot like what I had seen in the museum a few hours earlier. His bedroom also had a private bathroom, which, noting my surprise, he admitted was not typical of apartments of that era.

"You know," he told me, "the bones of a building are just that. You can tear a place down to the *charpente*—how to you say that in English? the frame? ---and remake it any way you wish."

"Interesting," I said, actually not knowing anything about building construction or even the real phrase "down to the studs." I did know the *façades* were protected in Paris and that they didn't tear many buildings down ever, except in rare instances like the demolition and rebuilding that was about to take place in the area around the old *Les Halles*.

"Well, you've got quite the nice set-up here," I told him, looking around at the marble tiles and counter tops. "Love your shower."

I wasn't kidding. I had never seen a shower like it! It had multiple nozzles and spraying heads at different levels, plus a fancy silver and ivory hand-held one. All the fixtures in that bathroom were *Porcher*, a brand I came to find out later, had probably cost them a small fortune.

When we were called to the table, I saw that Monsieur de Seignard had brought up five or six bottles of wine from the "*cave*" in the building's basement, where each tenant had their own wine cellar. We drank a light *St.-Veran* white wine from the *Maconnais* with the first course of *potage aux legumes*. They offered me a choice between *Rosé d'Anjou* or a red wine from the *Médoc* with the veal dish, and I chose the *rosé*. Salad was served next, and I got to take a respite from alcohol, and drink *Evian*. But wines came out once again when he offered a *Châteauneuf du Pape* with the cheese course, and champagne with a dessert of chocolate fondant cake; at which point I had begun to pray to God that the meal would be over.

Clément suggested that he and I be excused before it got too late, because Jean-Joseph and Gilles wanted to meet us downstairs at one of the cafés close by. He begged off having coffee with his parents so we could have it with his friends. As I said my grateful thanks and farewells to the parents, Blandine de Seignard offered me her most serious compliment:

"Your French is really improving, Sarah."

I couldn't have been more thrilled.

Once we met up with "*les gars*," I saw to my shock that Jean-Joseph was sitting there reading Mao Tse Tung's *Little Red Book*… in French, of course. After greetings and *la bise* all around, I pointed to it, laughed, and taunted him.

"*Tu parles!* You have to be joking."

He lived in the same comfortably privileged, bourgeois family atmosphere that Clément did, and yet he was espousing Maoist ideas? They'd have his head!

"*Eh, oui, je suis maoist, moi.*"

"I seriously doubt that," I said in French. "*Ça je m'en doute. Franchement.*"

Jean-Joseph got up and asked Clément to accompany him to the *tabac* next door for more *Gauloises*, and acted mysteriously like he had to talk to him in private about something.

Gilles looked at me, smiled and shrugged. And then he said, out of the blue, "You know, Sarah, Clément will never be able to marry a girl who is not Catholic… and French. And, in fact, he has already a serious girlfriend, did you know?"

What? Where did that come from? I did not know! Clément had never mentioned having a girlfriend to me. But I feigned complete nonchalance and, laughing it off, I looked straight back at Gilles and said forcefully "*Oh, mais nous… on n'est pas petits-amis, voyons. J'ai un petit-ami en Amérique, moi!*"

We weren't boyfriend-girlfriend. I had a guy back home.

He acted like a huge weight had been lifted from his shoulders.

"*Ah! Mais…beh… voilà! C'est bien alors! Tant mieux!*" Yes, indeed, so much the better. Sheeesh. But then he added, "*Sarah, nous serons toujours vos amis.*" They would always be my friends.

"That's nice!" I said, "And by the way, all my friends call me Sari, not Sarah. But I know it's hard for you to pronounce."

Since it always came out "Sorry."

Chapter Forty-five

"The Letter"...The Boxtops

It had been weeks since any word from Cass graced my mailbox. I didn't know how she was doing physically, if the babies were okay and thriving, or if her mental state was stable. I didn't even know if her name was still Cassandra Hyde or if she'd become Mrs. Alan Jones. I wrote her letter after letter and sent them c/o Alan to the Writers' Workshop office in EPB, hoping—assuming-- she'd get them. I also wrote to Soren telling him to "find out where they're living for chrissake, go over and see them, and tell me how they are!" But nothing seemed to work and no one obliged me with any answers.

Time had a way of slipping by quickly in Paris, where my experiment in learning the *arrondissements* had been very successful, because I now had my own favorite haunts everywhere. I managed to still see Nonnnie, C.C. and the Pella College guys quite a bit, but mostly I studied in cafés, and met Clément and his friends on the weekend. The girls in his "*bande*" were friendly to me, his guy friends really seemed taken with me, and my French conversational skills were seeing an exponential improvement, which was just about the best thing I could hope for.

Classes were a vast improvement also. My reading fluency in the French language was making even greater strides than my conversational one, and that was a good thing, because we still had an enormous amount of reading material to cover before May. I went to *Gibert Jeune* and found most of the works I needed in the cheap paperback bins outside. We were to read Zola's *Assommoir* and Mauriac's *Le Noeud de vipères,* Bernanos' *Journal d'un Curé de Campagne* and Sartre's *La Nausée.* And that was not all, but it was certainly enough to keep me busy for the first half of Spring term.

Happily, as *prévue,* Agathe invited me home to the farm with her for a weekend in March. The place was near the town of Luisant-- not far from Chartres—on lands that the paternal side of her family had inhabited since before the French Revolution. This was a working agricultural operation, and even though I came from smack dab in the middle of the most fertile crop land in the USA, I'd never even so much as spent the night on a farm.

The first thing we did upon arrival from the train station in Chartres, where we were picked up by Agathe's mother, was to drop our stuff in her room, and head into the pastureland in back of their house. She wanted me to meet her father, who was driving a huge combine in the field near enough for us to go greet him. He jumped down from it and shook my hand heartily. Agathe's father was a gregarious guy, rather burly for a Frenchman and a bit gritty from the field work; this was no gentleman farmer, but a real farmer. He was very proud to have an American see his farming operations, and he invited me to climb up into the cab of the machine and sit in it, which I did. Another first.

While we were outside, they were all anxious to show me the animals they kept, as well as the 18th century grange on the property, where soldiers had evidently bivouacked during World War II.

"You see here, they...what is the word in English for *griffoner*...?" Agathe asked me.

"Scratched? Oh! Scrawled!" I answered, seeing where she was pointing.

"Yes, scrawled....because they had scrawled their names and some little messages onto the walls and dated it August 23, 1944. Look at that!"

"Wow," I answered. "I see it!"

The stone and wood farmhouse had to have been more than one hundred years old with ancient beams crisscrossing the ceiling, and a kitchen sink that had once been a pump-style before it had been modernized. Almost everything else in the entire kitchen was original, including a rustic square table in the center of the room, flanked by chairs made with caning instead of upholstery or plain wood. There was only a tiny refrigerator but there was a large stove with four gas and two electric burners. I had never seen that before. They had no other appliances like dishwasher or even a toaster, but they did have a clothes washer—also in the kitchen---*sans* dryer. Over in one corner were some drying racks folded against the wall for when inclement weather precluded drying the wash on the outdoor line.

"*Maman est ravie d'en avoir une,*" Agathe explained, tapping on the lid of the washer in the kitchen. "Do you have it also at your house in America?"

"We sure do," I said, explaining in French that we had both a washer and a dryer and they were in the basement. Agathe looked at me not believing that a washing machine could share space with a wine cellar.

"Oh, we don't have a wine cellar at my house. But believe me, I've spent half my life in what you would call *la cave* doing laundry and ironing."

"What do you mean, you did it?"

"Well, laundry and ironing were my chores at home always. Chore is *corvée*, but in my house, it was more like *boulot*—job!"

"And what is ironing?" she asked puzzled.

"*Repassage.*"

"*Non! Tu l'as fait toi-même?!*"

"*Oui – pour toute la famille.*"

"*Pour la famille? Mais,non.*"

"*Si si.*"

She was fairly surprised at the revelation that I was expected to do domestic work around the house, but she was absolutely stupefied that I did all the family ironing.

This topic of domestic division of labor in the American home compared to France had come up before in conversation…at Clément's house, for instance, and with other French friends. I always had to explain to French people that "normal" American families didn't have staff to do household chores. Some of my parents' crowd had cleaning ladies, but no one I knew had a maid, a laundress or a cook. My own mother and grandmother shared some cleaning help because unlike most American housewives of the 1950's and '60's, they always worked outside the home. Agathe's mother did not work outside the home, and she still had two village women who came to the farm every day to help with household tasks. Agathe and I were equally surprised at the differences in our mothers' situations.

The living room or "*salon*" as they called it had furnishings of an older vintage, but not at all like the few homes I'd been invited to in Paris thus far. The antiques were more "lived in," still quite beautiful, while also being inviting, something a Louis XV armchair was not. They had many items handed down from generation to generation: armoires in the dining room housing table linens and silverware; Welsh dressers with dishes on display; a beautiful oak dining table visible from the living room through French doors, which had ten chairs around it upholstered in fabrics reminiscent of the Provençal style. There was a huge old grandfather clock in the hallway leading to the front door and the stairs up to the second floor. The hall floor was a burnished red tile that shoes of all sorts reverberated upon.

On the *étage*, I didn't see the parents' bedroom, but the room I'd been taken in to put my suitcase was Agathe's room, which, while growing up, she had always shared with her older sister, Mireille.

Mireille, who had actually moved out of the house already, had come home with us for the weekend to be with the family as they hosted me; she kindly agreed to sleep on a couch downstairs. She and I had already met in Paris once when she came to visit her "*frangine*"(as I had learned was the slang term for sister) and go over to their aunt's house, which Agathe did almost every Sunday. I had liked Mireille immediately. She was four years out of high school (*quatre ans après le bac*), but had gone on to train in the *hôtelerie* sector. To do that she had not gone to university for the next degree, but to a specialized post-secondary training school for the hospitality industries, which were important and had a high "standing" in France. She was hoping to work for a resort hotel or a restaurant in the Alps ski country.

They had a younger sibling, future lady-killer Pascal, who was strikingly handsome, with a mass of dark curls and blue eyes.

"This is **not** a nice boy," Agathe teased, as she introduced her brother to me. "He always plays the tricks on me and Mireille." She tousled his hair, and he grimaced at her.

"*Enchantée,*" I said, offering my hand.

"It is nice you come to us house…to our house," he said, correcting his own error, as he gave my hand one shake.

.

Pascal was a *lycéen* studying for the *Bac Français*, so that put him at around sixteen years old, the equivalent of a high school junior in the States.

"Next year when he takes the *Baccalauréat*, he will have to speak English on one of the tests," Agathe explained to me, "so could you offer to help him by giving him a few topics, and we could discuss these?"

"I'd be happy to help!" I enthused.

He was overjoyed. Pascal was a darling boy and extremely polite, at least to me if not to his sisters.

The parents struck me as rather a-typical: non-educated but literate and well-spoken. They let it be known that they were tied to the land and to its traditions in a way that gave me an up-close peek at some cultural French anthropology. In the sixties, France didn't really have an upwardly mobile society like our country, but I could see that these "peasant stock" French farmers desired a more cosmopolitan life for their children. The elderly aunt who was in Paris was Agathe's mother's older sister, so not everyone had stayed on the farm; and the weekend I was there, many other cousins and relatives came for dinner, ostensibly to meet the American guest.

The Friday evening was filled with eating and talking. I could not keep up with the banter around the table too well, due, for one thing, to the numerous people talking at once; but I liked being among them.

Everyone agreed that on Saturday afternoon "the kids must take you" to see Chartres Cathedral. The town of Chartres was known since the Middle Ages as a pilgrimage town, and was now world-renowned for the cathedral which brought them there. I would marvel at, among other thing, the "Chartres blue" stained glass windows and the two different bell towers. We did the complete tour of the interior, and went around the outside to see the gracious flying buttresses.

I'd already studied Gothic architecture both at Iowa and the Sorbonne, and written on it for my exam, so it wasn't as though I didn't know about it. I knew any place as famous as Chartres would live up to the reputation that preceded it.

Both the cathedral and the little jewel town filled me with joy. Across from the cathedral's *parvis* there were some elegant, inviting cafés; but Pascal and Mireille wanted to go around the side street and find their favorite one on the market square. In heading that way we passed a beautiful toy shop with many dolls in the window of just the kind I had come to imagine Cass would produce. These were German dolls, too! I begged off the café for the moment, saying I'd catch up with them, and I went inside *Tartine et Trottinette*. I couldn't afford to buy a doll, but I could get a closer look at them, and in so doing, peruse the shop, and maybe pick up something for the babies due to be born later back in Iowa City. Not knowing whether Cass was having girls, boys or one of each, I tried to be gender neutral, but what I really wanted to do was buy one of every toy I saw!

The shop was darling, smaller than *Au Nain Bleu* in Paris, obviously, but simply laden with glorious things. I went straight for the toddler section, skipping many games and motorized vehicles, to plant myself firmly in the realm of baby dolls with all the doll accoutrements. The whole floor was brimming with stuffed animals, too, some life-size with a price tag to match. There were wooden train sets, little tables set for the Teddy Bears' tea; bath toys in beautifully colored shapes of every ocean animal and every type of boat. I could have stayed in there for hours, but didn't want to keep my friends waiting too long. So I settled on two little crocheted rattles-- one grey and white bear, and one yellow and white lamb. I was especially happy when the clerk wrapped my tiny gifts as though they'd cost a fortune, in red logo paper and bright blue ribbon. I hoped I could keep them wrapped just like that for the next four months until I could present them to Cass.

The next day Agathe and I, along with Mireille, got a ride back to Paris with one of the cousins, as it happened, going to visit his mother; so we didn't have to take the train or *métro* back to *Boulevard Raspail* with our suitcases.

Spending that weekend at her house sort of cemented Agathe's and my relationship. When I was about to leave at the end of the term, she showed me her diary where she had written many misgivings about having a "coloc" who couldn't speak French, and to tell me that she was wrong. I felt humbled and somewhat embarrassed, but honored nonetheless. I told her I kept a journal, too, and she said to write in it, "Agathe is a pure girl and angelique." And I did.

When we got back from the farm, there was---finally hallelujah!-- a letter from Cass. I fairly tore it open and read--with some not so small relief-- that she felt fine and had been to see a doctor in the University system. They did indeed get married so she could have the benefits of being a "faculty wife," even though he was a junior faculty at best and still a student. But never mind because it got the job done! The Episcopalian priest working with Alan on his C.O. status was the person who married them.

"Also being married emancipates me from the control of my parents once and for all," she wrote.

The letter contained the further news that they had found a little house to rent just south of town on Highway 1 and that she now had an address to which I could write to my heart's content.

"I really miss you, and when you get back, which won't be long now, please come often and happily to our little house. The one thing I want to somehow share with you is this: for you to feel like you can be easily with both Alan and me (and not just me), and for you to see how much I love him and love our life together. Somehow this evolved because of and through all the questionable, questioning problems and doubts you observed and shared with me. Do you know, Sari, that he has come through for me in a million ways that only I can ever know? That he is the person I believe and trust and respect above all others (not counting you, but you know what I mean.) It took so long for me to realize this, to discover what words like 'future' and 'marriage' mean in my life. This makes me feel not regretful but warm and good, that somehow a beautiful and fulfilling life evolved from it all. It is gentle and exciting to go to bed and then awaken to his dear face every day---not tedious and ordinary, but vital and real—a point of departure and strength to know he is my husband and I his wife. And yet, still lovers and soon-to-be parents! There is such beauty and happiness generated by a happy marriage--- with both the sorrow and the laughter that it entails. I may experience an 'attack' of depression or he may feel saddened by something, but the world does not collapse. After all, we are not heading across open fields in opposite directions, but going in the same one, and just being truly together makes all the difference. With a hand on your arm or an arm around you at night, all sorrows are bearable and so much less final and destructive.

And you know you always have a place not only in my life, but our life, because Alan and I have a relationship we believe extends beyond the mere us to and through to those dear to us. It is a major source of 'we' and also of 'he' and 'she'. And I want you to feel and know the good that is us and to know whereof it comes. Alan and I have changed. You have changed. Soren may have changed. And it is all wonderful, for it means simply that we are all alive and vital, vibrant beings. That we 'feel good together' is indicative that our general direction is similar."

And she ended it with **"We loves ya, kid."**

My emotions ran the gamut after reading and especially re-reading that letter. I vacillated from being really happy and terribly relieved, to being completely cynical concerning Alan's intentions. I admit I was a little sad at the prospect of me back in Iowa City not sharing an apartment with Cass. But I didn't dwell on that. I was more worried about her. She struck me as naively ignorant of a future that was bound to be so different from anything she could imagine, starting with being poor and having **two** babies! One child was enough to exhaust the most loving and sharing of couples. I had my grave doubts that Alan would rise to the occasion; but of course, I hoped I was wrong.

One thing that did hit me after reading Cass' letter was that it was mid-March of my year abroad, and I had kept Soren "in the bank." It wasn't fair to him or to me, much as we never really had plans or commitments either stated or inferred. Yes, I really liked him, and hoped he would come to Europe and travel with me after my classes were over. But was that really likely to happen? He hadn't said anything definite about it the entire year. We should have been making plans already had either of us really thought it would come to fruition.

I wrote him and essentially said that I understood it was more or less a pipe dream for him to come over, and that, in all honesty, I knew it wasn't going to happen. I'd be back in late June, and aside from working at the bar, I'd be free all summer; if he were planning to be home in Imogene, it would be easy

272

for us to get together. I did say sweet things about how I valued his friendship and that I felt close to him, but I didn't tell him I loved him, and I didn't expect that back in return.

About ten days later I got a reply from him, that, much as I tried not to read between the lines, felt like he was relieved to hear what I had to say. However, what he wrote at the end left me completely baffled: he said, "... and the thing is, I didn't want to give up Catholicism when push came to shove."

Give up his religion? Did I ever ask him to do that? No. Did we ever talk about us in terms of marriage in a synagogue versus a church? No. Did we ever talk about religion in terms of having children? Fuck, no!

(I was already pretty sure I didn't want children. I hadn't been parented well and it was too risky! Like the genetic risk factors we'd studied about in Life Science; if you can protect against passing that onto the next generation, you should.)

When all was said and done, I couldn't tell where in hell he was coming from with all this religion talk, but I suspected it was his mother. He'd told me she had been only lukewarm to the idea of his going up to The Bluffs to see me, and that, truth be told, she was adamantly opposed to his getting into a serious relationship with a Jewish girl. She thought he still went to church in Iowa City, and she certainly expected him to be at their side at Mass in their town when he was home. I suspected he was having enough troubles with his parents trying to assert his own future career decisions and all without the added burden of a girlfriend they wouldn't have approved of in the first place.

I confided to Clément what I had written to Soren, without ever letting on what Gilles had told me that night at the café.

"Eh, oui," he sighed. "*Je comprends. Mais de toute façon, c'est un peu triste quand-même. La vie est courte et en plus, ça va vite. 'Faut vivre Sari! Vive la vie!*"

I nodded. Yep.

Chapter Forty-Six

"Yellow Submarine"...Lennon & McCartney

The joke among my friends that Spring was that Paris was not Gay Paree but Grey Paree. The preponderance of monochromatic limestone and granite Haussmannian buildings, under relentless rain, could easily bring on melancholy, especially since I was at sixes and sevens about so much in my life at that precise moment. I was very worried about Cass, and also terrified of my May exams. I didn't know what I was going to do when the dorm closed at the end of term and there would still be ten days before we could pick up our diplomas, "**provided of course, I achieve that goal—ha!**" I wrote to Cass.

Even before that, I was also faced with another two-week hiatus in classes at Easter, and had no funds to go anywhere-- and really no one to go with. Nonnie was meeting her American friend in Munich; C.C.'s parents were coming back to whisk her and, surprisingly, Marty, off to Spain. I admitted to her that I wondered how that invitation had come about.

"We're just friends now," C.C. had tried to convince me, although I wasn't buying it, "but we've been close all year and I wanted my parents to meet him."

It completely astounded me that parents and their children could have such a close happy relationship.

Under the cloudy skies, and bundled against the damp chill in the air, I walked the avenues and parks with a firm resolve to stay positive. I was still fulfilling my dream; and no matter how real the impending threat of failure was, I seemed to have crossed over some "Maginot Line, " and had become a lot more confident in French, and able to tackle the difficult curriculum. *La Sorbonne* and *Rue Fouarre* classes had become a comforting routine by then, and I felt that it was just my life now, and that I had adapted to it. This had happened without fanfare and without sharp awareness on my part. All of a sudden it just became apparent to me that I was "getting it."

And I also hit upon the idea to use all of Easter vacation to STUDY…day and night, night and day. But not in Paris. I would get on the train and go back to Nice.

I saw Taylor and Eric in the courtyard of the university one afternoon after classes, and announced my decision to head to the *Côte d'Azur* for *Pâques*.

"It's my plan to lay on the beach and read read read," I announced to them.

"And stay in a Youth Hostel or something?" asked Taylor.

"Oh, God, no. I couldn't take another accommodation like we had at Narbonne last summer. I'll find some cheap little hotel."

"Yeah, but it'll be Easter, one of the high tourist seasons down there; the prices will spike up."

I hadn't thought of that, but undeterred by a depressing wrench in my works, I headed off to the student travel agency on the *Boule' Mich*, and solicited their help.

"Yes, he's right," a young woman travel agent told me, "but if you want to stay farther from the Place Massena or the beach---say around the train station-- we can probably find you something. You would have a fifteen- or twenty-minute walk to the sea."

That was fine with me; exercise never hurt anybody and I walked all over Paris all the time, I rationalized. So she found me a small hotel run by a family on *Avenue Berlioz*, the *Auberge Hortensia*, and booked me a room for ten days, nine nights, at the great price of only fifty francs per night. I thought I had really lucked out and thanked her profusely.

"FIFTY francs a night?!!" screamed Taylor at me the next day. "A Youth Hostel is around TEN francs per night."

"Well, why don't you come down with me then. You stay in the hostel, and we can meet up."

"That's not a half bad idea," he mused. "Maybe Eric will come, too."

So it was a plan, and Eric was on board. We would take the night train together on Friday April 4, "*le vendredi Saint*" and return on April 12th, the Saturday before classes started up again.

I wasted no time in gathering up materials to take with me to Nice. In various classes I was reading *Candide, Le Neveu de Rameau, Les Lettres Persanes*, works by Beaumarchais, Balzac, the essays of Montaigne, and more Proust. I didn't only have literature classes, either, of course, and was up to my kneecaps in architectural styles from *Classique, rococo, Directoire, Empire* and all the way to modern buildings with materials like *la fonte* (cast iron) *le fer* (iron), and *le béton* (concrete). I had to be able to identify the edifices and monuments of Delorme, Mansard, Le Vau, Hardoin-Mansart, Jacques-Ange Gabriel and Le Corbusier.

Several of my *cours pratiques* teachers had somehow befriended me, showing their pride, if not also shock, at my perseverance and mastery of the material in the autumn term, the results of which allowed me to continue. One of these, Mlle. Gardine, had invited us to her Parisian apartment in the ninth *arrondissement* for *"un cocktail,"* which was like the *soirées* Clément's *bande* of friends had. It was the first time I'd ever gotten a glimpse of a teacher's life outside the classroom, and it was exciting to get to know her, and talk to her one-on-one.

When the professor heard my Easter plans, she bubbled at me, "Oh, you know Henri Matisse's foundation is nearby and you must see the chapel he decorated in Vence!" Her suggestions were serendipitous because we'd just been studying the *Fauves* and the origins of cubism, too. The works of Matisse just made me happy, and the prospect of seeing more of them, and not just in museums, thrilled me.

As Easter approached and *La Semaine Sainte* was upon us, Paris seemed to morph into another wonderland almost as dramatic as it had been at Christmas. The streets were not lined in white lights, but everywhere festivity was evident. The shop windows were full of pastel-colored sweaters and dresses all of a sudden; the gardens began to come into bloom, and the glass enclosures around café terraces opened back up and flooded out onto the sidewalks. But the main attractions of that season were the bakery display windows, *les vitrines des pâtisseries*! Brimming with every sort of chocolate bunny, chick or lamb, wrapped in bright cellophane packaging tied with festoons of pink, green and yellow ribbons, these delectable tidbits vied for attention with all the regular pastries and cakes, set amidst festive paper grass and confetti-colored boxes.

Nonnie, C.C. and I planned a little pre-travel splurge on the *Champs-Elysées* to have our usual indulgences at *Le Drugstore*. But instead of getting off at *Étoile* and being right there, we took the other route, changing at *Concorde* to Line 1 that went up through all the stops on the *Champs-Elysées*. Exiting at FDR, we walked up the rest of way, so we could peer at the Easter displays in the windows of the really posh purveyors of confectionary. In those windows, the *pièces montées* alone, slathered in white spun sugar were worth the price of admission! I had never seen anything even one iota like this in the States, and neither had my friends who came from far more sophisticated cities than I did. We all marveled at how the French had truly cornered the market on window display.

A few days later, the guys fetched me (and my too-heavy suitcase full of books and notebooks) at *La Maison,* and the three of us set out together on a very crowded night train from Paris's *Gare de Lyon* to the Riviera. Arriving the next morning, I took a short taxi ride with my stuff to my hotel, and they took off on foot for their digs.

L'Auberge Hortensia, named for the hydrangea bushes that flanked the door, looked like a typical *Provençale "mas"* –a light pink stucco one-story house built around a square courtyard with rooms on three sides. All the rooms had French window-doors that opened up onto the central patio, which had a table and a few unmatching chairs scattered around it. The windows also had real, as opposed to merely ornamental, shutters that you closed at night to keep out the light; they really made the room pitch black.

My room was very basic but sweet. It had a wrought iron bed, covered in a pink flowered duvet, and that long bolster pillow that was so typically French. I also found a regular square pillow in the *armoire*, so I had the best of both worlds. The *armoire* was not antique but vintage nonetheless, with shelves in it for clothing, but no rods to hang anything, so I just folded my clothes into it. I hadn't brought anything dressy that needed to be hung up, and if I were going out, I could wear the knit dress Cass had bought me.

There was a reading lamp mounted above the bed, and a chair next to it, but no night stand. However, there was a small table and two more straight-back wooden chairs. I set up the little table in the room as a desk, scattered my books and notebooks on it, and placed in the corner my trusty portable radio, which worked out so perfectly for both the room and the beach.

My room also had a tiny *en suite* bathroom, which was the height of luxury as far as I was concerned. There was a sink, a toilet, a minuscule shower and, of course, a bidet, which I enlisted to hold my cosmetics bag, since there wasn't any shelf space in there.

My room had no t.v. Only the reception area of the *Auberge* had a television set with comfortable sofas and chairs around it; but I didn't feel the urge to watch anything with the other guests of the place. And not having a t.v. in my room was a good reason to get out and go study elsewhere during the day, and get more sleep at night.

I had arranged to meet Taylor and Eric that first night for dinner at a spot near the *Vieux Port.* I wasn't afraid to walk around the town in the daylight by myself, just as I did in Paris, but I had to confess it was better having guys with me at night. Nice had a distinctly Italian ambience to it, from the pastel plaster of its buildings to the wonderful influences of Italy upon its cuisine; but along with that came the rather unwelcomed catcalls and pinching that men were wont to carry out on unsuspecting girls. I was not unsuspecting per se, but I was sick of it. I had been grabbed at and prodded a few times on the *métro* already in Paris, but not right out on the street like what was common in Nice.

Our first dinner together was in an outdoor restaurant with Christmas lights strung in a square around its terrace, and little tables arranged in close proximity. I told Taylor and Eric of my firm plans to study the whole time, but I was also not averse to going to Cannes or Monaco or Vence to do some other sightseeing. They said they were up for that, but not right away, as they were already set to go hiking in the Alps foothills for the next few days, hoping, probably in vain, they admitted, that trails would be empty, with many other hikers taking a respite for Easter with family. So we planned to meet up later, and I reminded them that I would be back on Blue Beach every day; they could find me there.

The weather certainly cooperated that Easter weekend, and in the days beyond. While not as hot as in August, when I'd last been at the Mediterranean, the waves were still inviting, my study plans were solid, and Blue Beach was perfection itself. If I wanted food brought to my chair, I could order it from their menu. If I wanted to go up to the *Promenade des Anglais* and off into town to a café or a bakery to get something else, I could leave my things safely at my chair, and they would be guarded from intruders.

Even on my budget, I would not starve on this trip. I realized that I could easily make do with the breakfast that came with my room: croissants, baguette, butter, jam, hot chocolate and sometimes even cheese and orange juice; and then have a sandwich or salad for lunch and seafood or pizza for dinner. I didn't especially like "*pissaladière*," the pizza-like onion pie specialty that Provence made famous, but all the pizza places in town were owned and run by Italians, same as in Paris, and if I ate nothing but pizza *la Reine* for the whole week and a half that I was there, I concluded, it wouldn't be too much. I found the *ratatouille,* which turned up on every menu, to be an acquired taste, so I declared that if I didn't acquire it there, I wouldn't anywhere. I had that at least twice. *Salade Niçoise* was sublime, and I ate it at least once a day that week.

Sometimes the guys met me for *apéro,* where we drank kirs and ate Niçoise olives by the dozens. After the elongated cocktail hours we'd spend together, I wasn't even that hungry for a meal, so on my way back to *l'Auberge* I would buy a big *sandwich de thon baguette* from some boulangerie's sidewalk display, take that to my room, along with some Orangina, and have dinner *al fesco* on "my" patio. And more than once I picked up things like half an avocado filled with *salade monégasque* — the best seafood salad on the planet-- plus a *chou à la crème* or an *éclaire* to eat for lunch at my Blue Beach encampment. I would order a bottle of Evian, a coke or some *vin rosé* from them, and they didn't seem to care that I took my own food out of its bag and ate it there.

Quite simply, I was in hog heaven.

I had awoken on Easter morning to the pealing and tolling of many different church bells all over the place. France nearly had a state religion, the separation of church and state having only really taken place after the Second World War, but no one tried to cram it down anyone else's throat. In fact, we had just been studying the historical and literary convergence of state-sponsored religion in Diderot's *Enclyclopédie,* and I gathered up all those notes to put them in some semblance of order as I sat in my little Blue Beach enclave, which was still open, thankfully, even though it was a holiday. I wrote profuse amounts of notes for hours on end, lulled by the most beautiful music of God's own creation, namely waves lapping up against the beach. I didn't dare close my eyes, because I'd be asleep in two seconds, carried off to dreamland by the intoxicating sound of the surf. So I tried to just concentrate on reading and writing, and not let even daydreams allow me to neglect the matter at hand.

The matter at hand was taking the sample exam question prompts we'd been provided with, and trying to write a semblance of coherent thoughts about them.

En quoi l'Encyclopédie fut-elle illumée dans "la lutte philosophique?"

La lutte philosophique était un mouvement général de critique. Tous les grands sujets étaient remis en question. C'était une lutte contre tous les plans et pour la tolerance sociale. Ils étaient contre l'autorité réligeuse. Certains penseurs sortiront même plus ou moins franchement du Chritiansime pour instituer un déisme ou une réligion nauturelle. En face de la monarchie traditionnelle et son droit divin, l'on commence à parler du droit naturel et du bonheur des peuples. Un esprit positif et scientifique se répand: lumières. Croyance au progrès et confiance en l'homme caractérisent le XVIIIème siècle. Les abus sont condamnés par les philosophes: torture judicale, l'esclavage, inégalité devant les imports, justice, etc. Un certain nombre d'articles de l'Encyclopédie contiennent une critique du système politique et social: ils dénoncent les abus et définissent un monde plus digné de l'homme. Cette critique est souvent indirecte mais c'est son contenu audacieux et général qui a fait les poids et le prix de l'Encyclopédie.

Ouffe!
After a few days, my *confrères universitaires* got tired of laying out on rocks, and came to join me in the luxury of *chaise longue* cushions and drinks brought to the iconic blue-umbrella-shaded tables between the chairs. Even though we were in different academic levels, they, too, were going to be tested on the same literary material as I was, so we sat there together and discussed *Le Neveu de Rameau* and *Candide,* in hopes of coming to some easy-to-remember main points of the enormous amount of material we would be expected to regurgitate in another month.

"I really like Diderot," said Eric. "The fundamental problem he reveals in this work, as I see it, is the contradiction between materialism on one part..."

"And cynicism," said Taylor, interrupting.

Eric shot him a look and went on, "And on the other hand, sentiment...generosity, virtue."

"I agree with that," I said. "He seems to give a lot of credence to the idea that pleasure is derived from doing charitable deeds."

"So," said Taylor, challenging me, "should we assume that '*Moi*' is Diderot? "

"No. I don't think we should necessarily assume that," I said, "it seems to me more likely that there's an important part of Diderot in '*Lui*'. What do you think, Eric?"

"I think '*le neveu*' is more like Diderot, yes, because he is cynical, like you said, Taylor, and immoral and logical. He's more of an original, a Bohemian."

"Well, okay then," I said, adding, as though I'd had a revelation, "then wouldn't it be groovy if the dissertation subject was on a comparison between the characters of *le Neveu* and *Candide*? That would be perfect."

"Yeah," said Taylor, "Candide never becomes cynical even though he travels through the man-made hell of society, and witnesses all the horrors and stupidity of war, murder, theft, religious intolerance, and every other sort of injustice."

"That's right," said Eric, "*Candide*-- the work I mean-- is a complete critique of society, politics and the status quo. There are a hundred images of the Human Condition in that work. That would be an easy essay for sure."

"I wonder if Nixon's ever read *Candide*, " I pondered.

"Doubtful," they both answered, almost simultaneously.

I decided, towards the end of our stay, that I had to get more culture under my belt on this trip, and do some things that weren't just pure study after all. The guys were not taking art history, but I managed to convince them that since we were there, we all had to go see the Matisse works in the museum in Nice and also that famous chapel of his in Vence. We all wanted to lay out on a sand beach, too, and agreed that Cannes was the place to do it.

"I looked up the bus schedules to Cannes," I told them. "It's the same one that continues to Monaco on the way back."

"So we may as well go to Monte Carlo while we're at it," suggested Eric. "I've got a burning desire to see the Oceanographic museum there. It's Jacques Cousteau's research institute you know. He's the director."

"Gee, I wonder if the Calypso is in port there," said Taylor.

"Don't know," I shrugged.

"Jacques Cousteau's brother was a raving anti-Semite; did you know **that**?" Taylor asked me.

"No. But it wouldn't be the first time someone's relative was a piece of shit, and they were just fine."

"Right," Taylor went on, "but his brother wrote a collaborationist tract during the war called '*Je suis partout*,' and was sentenced to death afterwards for it."

"Wow, so did he die then?"

"Nope. Sentence was commuted. And he was actually released from prison in the '50's even though it had been a life sentence. It's all who you know in life, I guess."

"Well, Taylor, cynicism aside, I still want to see the place," Eric said.

We did go to Monaco on one of the cheapest and most stunning bus rides I'd ever---or could ever— travel. The Oceanographic center was amazing with all the creatures and model ships inside, as well as Cousteau's little yellow submarine outside. I left the guys and opted for a tour of the Palace, surprised that the line was short to get in; I loved it, and couldn't believe how much seemingly personal Grimaldi family living space the public got to see.

We met up and walked all over the town. We saw the cathedral, stopped in a pastry shop, and got some of the last of the Easter treats to take on the bus back to Nice, where we arrived at the Port in late evening. Though it was out of their way, they walked me back to my hotel, so I invited them to sit in the lobby-salon awhile and have some Grand Marnier—on me-- before heading back to their youth hostel.

The vacation was almost over. I felt pretty good about the amount of work I had done, the cultural things I had seen, and the relaxing way I had spent the holiday.

The next day, which was the last one, I went to the beach without any books.

Chapter Forty-Seven

"Mrs. Brown You've Got a Lovely Daughter"...Herman's Hermits

Spring had turned Paris into every wonderful cliché I'd ever heard: the parks overflowed with blossoming trees, and the gardeners were hard at work planting and cultivating the beds that would soon burst into Cartesian-ordered colors (decided "on high" in some bureaucratic enclave, we were told, but gorgeous nonetheless.) The birds had been singing outside my dorm window since February, but by late April they were a choir. Café sidewalks were filled with people lightened by not having to wear heavy coats and boots, as "*le temps a laissé son mateau de vent, de froidure et de pluie…*" Well, we still had *la pluie*, but less often and less harsh, and certainly no more snow, unlike Iowa where an April day could easily be dumped on by a late blizzard.

I was all routine, all business, and as French as possible in the waning weeks of my three-semester sojourn. I rarely saw the Americans except at meals in the dining hall, in classes, or in passing. When I did talk to Nonnie about what she intended to do when the dorm closed, she shocked me with her answer: she was going home right after exams and not staying either for the results or to get her diploma, of which, there was no doubt, she would be the proud possessor.

"Why?!" I asked.

"My brother's not doing too well. I should have gone home at Easter rather than head over to Germany, and live it up with the girls."

"I'm so sorry to hear that," I said sincerely, although I was shocked, and I couldn't really imagine what must have been going on to elicit this decision.

"Yeah, I'm pretty bummed out by it all." And then she looked up at me and added, "Oh, he's not going to die or anything …before I get there."

"I… gosh, Nonnie, I'm sure you're right. They would have told you, wouldn't they?"

"Oh, sure. He's been sick for a long time, you know."

Clément was helping me with *dictée* whenever he had a free minute, and once in a while we would even study together, although I had no inkling as to what he was working on for his own classes. He would sometimes show up in the courtyard of the Sorbonne as I was exiting the building. The look on the faces of my Pella College companions was priceless when they would see me walk over to this obviously French guy, standing there with his long blond hair falling onto his forehead and his sweater tied around his shoulders. And then we'd give each other *la bise* and leave together! More than once I caught a glimpse of what could only be called stupefaction among them.

No one had to tell me how lucky I was, and I wrote to Cass that once again, thanks to her parents, and just by pure chance of being invited to remain at the Amstel Hotel after she had left, I had met a really nice French family, and formed a friendship that would last the entire time I was there and possibly beyond.

"*Mon Dieu, tu te rends compte!?*" I marveled to Clément one day as I was reliving my good fortune at having met him. He laughed and said that stuff like that happens all the time; we just don't hear about it.

"I suppose. And I'd love to return the favor, so if you ever want to come back to the States and see '*L'Amérique profonde*' you always have a place to stay with me."

He smiled and seemed truly moved by this offer, to which he responded with an even better one for me: his parents were inviting me to spend the last ten days at their home after the dorm closed before I went back to the States.

"Oh my God!" I gasped. "That truly solves my problem!" I was so grateful to accept this offer, I could barely get the words out. I'm sure he must have begun to worry about how I'd ever pass those exams, hearing me stutter and make mistakes trying to express in his language my immense gratitude.

"And I will drive you to the airport to ship your trunk back," he also offered. Perfect!!

Word from the home front was the bad news that Sol's new game plan was to control my immediate future comings and goings, now that I was completely beholden to him for having sent me to Paris. The good news was that Cass and Alan seemed settled, and the babies were doing fine in their sixth month of gestation. The due date was

279

sometime in August, and if I could break out of the work schedule Sol had set up for me in the bar, my intent would be to get to Iowa City for the actual birth. I planned to go there the minute I got back, anyway, no matter what my parents had in mind otherwise. After all, I also had to find a place to live, and I had to appear at the Registrar's office to go over what credits had transferred and what my standing was before I actually signed up for senior year classes.

But I also wanted to work; I decided I had to earn some extra spending money to help Cass out with baby supplies right from the get-go. She was still vague in her few and far-between letters about how they were coping with having to buy double of everything, and it made me seriously ponder just how much in the dark they really were about their pressing needs. In any event, I was planning to show up there with a carload of stuff for them.

When the long-anticipated and daunting exam day came, and we filed once more into the examination building, I was more or less resigned to the idea that I either knew my stuff or I didn't. There was no grey area. What I did tell myself, when all was said and done, was that I had never worked so hard in my life; had never faced such a formidable curriculum, had never written so many papers or taken such an abundance of notes. I had never experienced such a stringent examination requirement; and most of all, I had never studied ten subjects at one time! Ten subjects that I could and would be tested on, and with little real knowledge of the parameters of the exam materials. This was not the American university system at all, and if I could survive it, I could survive anything, probably even including graduate school, I reckoned, because when this was all over, no educational system could ever seem as difficult or challenging to me. And as a result, I made a solemn vow to myself that I would never **ever** study this hard again. "You deserve a break today" would become my motto.

After the first battery of written *épreuves*, we all spilled out into the courtyard, me included, completely devastated. I was especially deflated by the art history dissertation and almost broke into tears with Nonnie that instead of Rodin or Impressionism, I had to write on Cubism.

"What ROT," I hissed.

She commiserated, not because she also had that course-- she didn't--but because all the history she had prepared for hers was left out, too.

"I expected to have to write on something like the general characteristics of France in the 19th century with all that upheaval and the socialism that sprung out of it...stuff like that."

"And instead, what did you get?" I wondered.

"Well, if you want to know precisely," she answered, my topic was '*les causes et consequences de la politique de stabilization en 1963*'."

"Oh shit," I said, "if I had gotten that I wouldn't have been able to write one word!"

"No kidding," she sighed. "I've never done so poorly. I left out more than I put in."

When the written exams were done, we all felt the same way: *On est dans la merde.*

Even Taylor was apoplectic. Notwithstanding his self-inflicted anger at his low score after the February battery of tests, he was usually very confident, even cocky about coursework. This time he saw me and exclaimed angrily, "That was the hardest exam I've ever taken in my entire college career!"

Before returning to his room at the *Cité Universitaire*, he told me he intended to detour to the post office on *Boulevard St. Germain* and send his parents a telegram telling them that he was not going to stay for the diploma ceremony or fly back to the States with the group; but rather that he'd decided to stay on and start a European tour to take his mind off a perceived failed academic year.

"Don't you think that's jumping the gun somewhat?" I asked, feeling certain he wasn't going to fail the whole thing.

"Fuck it," he said, adding, "I'm still not going to the ceremony."

His attitude puzzled me; I'd never seen him so down. In the meantime, the person who really was in danger of failing, namely me, worked myself up into a high frenzy preparing for the oral exams. However, just like in February, compared to the written ones, they were not that bad.

I appeared before a committee of professors, ones whom I had seen around the halls, but who were not my actual teachers. I got *Dominique* as a topic, and it struck me as sadly ironic because out of all those authors whose works I'd prepared, and all those books I had read, Fromentin's work did not strike me as monumental enough for this, my culminating exam. But I had liked the story and the premise, and had not found it difficult to read, which boded well for my being able to talk about it. I was asked to give the synopsis, which was easy: characters making do with their lot in love and life, even as their aspirations were far beyond their fulfillment. My explanation wasn't perfect but I was hoping for a "*moyenne*"—just an average grade. Twenty or thirty points would have been great--if unattainable!

And then it was over. It was really over.

All that remained was waiting out the results and hoping for the best. I tried to channel my inner "Candide" but sadness lurked around every corner. Nonnie was packing to leave; Taylor had already gone, and saying good-bye to him had, surprisingly, really got to me. We had taken one last foray out together to the *Jeu de Paume*.

"You know, looking at Impressionist paintings can make anyone forget their troubles," I told him, "including grades and any impending doom they might foretell."

Afterwards, strolling in the *Tuileries,* Taylor told me he "hated with a purple passion" to say good-bye so; he just said, "We'll write, right?" And I had answered, "Right." And that was it. I had read once where friendships made in "year-abroad" experiences were deeper and more intense than others, and I believed it.

C.C. and Nonnie had conspired to give me a huge surprise for my twenty-first birthday, which would come after we had to leave *La Maison.* I was flabbergasted to find out that Betty had sent money to Nonnie for a celebration with cake, champagne and presents! Nonnie had even got Clément involved, and he had told her he would provide the champagne, so as not to spend any of the funds buying that.

They all surprised me (as in a **real** surprise party!) at *Le Gymnase,* the café right next to the *Maison* where we had all studied and hung out for so many hours that the staff there knew us. Not only did they let Nonnie push some tables together and set up a little buffet that the chef had prepared, but they also provided champagne flutes, even though the wine wasn't bought from them.

Nonnie and C.C. had shown up at my room and invited me to drop everything I was doing and come "*prendre un dernier petit pot*" with them (go for a little drink) for old time's sake -- a last hurrah.

I noticed C.C. trying to hide the fact that her eyes were all red and puffy. She and Marty had decided to break up after the entire year of dating, since they were going home to completely different schools in diametrically opposed ends of the country. It had been his doing, really, and she thought it was really because he had gotten cold feet of having a long-distance serious relationship once they returned to the States. I felt for her; I'd had a hard time saying good-bye to Taylor, and we weren't even dating. It would even be worse with Clément, and I didn't want to think about that.

When we walked in, there they all were: Marty had come, as well as Eric. It seemed strange to not have Taylor with them, but Clément had brought Jean-Joseph and Gilles. Jo Jo was there, which was an even bigger surprise. I shot C.C. a look of amused bewilderment, and she just shrugged. Agathe came, and it was revealed that she had helped set the whole affair in motion; and about a dozen other Americans from the program were invited, too (not Lindy!).

People gave me the *de rigueur* gag gifts: a replica Eiffel Tower and a plastic Arc de Triomphe; a bootlegged Sorbonne t-shirt like they sold from carts on the Boule' Mich; a fake water color "painting" of Le Pont Neuf—I really liked it anyway!—and some lovely blue rhinestone Eiffel Tower dangly earrings, "because we know you love blue!" One of the girls from the group handed me a small box and said she got it for me in the little merchandise corner inside Notre Dame.

She smiled as she told me, "So it's not a gag gift." When I opened it, I found it was a nice rosary. Trying not to react in a way that would hurt her feelings, I just looked up and thanked her, and glanced at Nonnie who was cringing as she tried not to giggle. C.C. rolled her eyes. I tucked it back into its box and put it in my jacket pocket. I would be handing it to Nonnie as she climbed into the taxi that would take her to Orly.

We had a cake that resembled a *Saint Honoré* one from the patisserie on *Rue Delambre* that we had all frequented since the first week we arrived in Paris; and they had put sparklers on it instead of candles. I had never been to a French birthday celebration, so I didn't even know that tradition. Nonnie and C.C. also gave me a real gift—a beautiful long Indian silk scarf. No one wore long scarves like the French, and I was thrilled to be able to wrap one three times around my neck and tie it high like they did. It was yellow with a faint print of blossoms on it.

`" I will wear it home," I announced to them, "and people in Omaha will have a cow when they see me!"

Another thing that happened was that Betty, Sol, and Nana sent me some "serious" money for my birthday.

"You'll have a blast with that!" said Nonnie when I opened the card and about fainted. Finally, a real shopping trip was in my future.

I was completely blown away by this party. Not only the thoughtfulness of my American best friends, but also by my parents' hand in the festivities. It was so unexpected.

Finally, it was time to pack up. I carefully filled my foot-locker trunk with as much as possible since I didn't care how heavy it was---Sol was paying for it on delivery. Of course I put in all the winter clothes I'd been grateful to have received from home, as well as many of my notebooks, and the souvenirs for the family and friends. I even packed a special bottle of champagne for my father, nestled in some styrofoam that the *Nicolas* shopkeeper on *Rue Delambre* had nicely gone to the back and retrieved for me. Not risking it even for a second, I buried it in every heavy wool thing I could find to cover it. I had to pray it arrived intact or else my entire contents would arrive soaked in *vin mousseux*.

The day Clément showed up to get me with his magnificent—in my eyes---car, I didn't say my final good-byes to the people who ran the *Maison* because I knew I would be coming back to do that in the next week or so, and maybe bring them some flowers or other small token of my appreciation. I still didn't much care for the *concierge,* who'd been a nosy banshee the whole year; but I really liked her young daughter, and had struck up a friendship with her and her big white cat, who strolled around the courtyard of *La Maison* like he owned it. It would also be rather hard to say good-bye to the various maids, cooks and maintenance staff. Much as some of the year had held trauma and setbacks, I still loved the place, and could tell I would be nostalgic for it. It would always symbolize, like Iowa City did, my emancipation and self-actualization.

Clément loaded the trunk of his *Dauphine* with my two suitcases, what would end up as my eventual flight bag, and a box of books to be taken to the post office and mailed home, (since France had really good rates for sending "used books" through the mail). Everything packed in, we headed for the *16ème* and *Rue Singer.* Once arrived at his building, since he couldn't park in front of it for very long, he ran in and summoned some of their housekeeping staff to come down and help carry everything inside. We left the trunk and the box, however, since we were taking those to other locales.

Both shipments turned out to be a piece of cake, maybe the smoothest of any "functionary" thing I'd done all year. It didn't hurt to have a sweet, preppy French guy helping me maneuver through the paperwork and provide transportation. Lucky. I kept reminding myself how lucky.

Clément was not done with his classes at HEC, as it turned out, so some of the days I was at home alone with his mother. We talked about a lot of topics: the differences between her life and my mother's; the school and university systems; the Vietnam war.

"We French cannot understand why the U.S. is waging it after having seen our "*échec*" –failure— in *Indochine. Cette guerre est tellement stupide*," she told me, and I did not disagree. "*Ça finera mal, je t'assure.*"

Blandine de Seignard had domestic staff that did the cleaning and the laundry. The sheets I slept on in that home smelled so strongly of heavenly lavender I thought I was dreaming in a *Provençale* field. She also had a skeleton kitchen staff but she did her own grocery shopping, and not with a car, but on foot every morning, and sometimes twice a day if she were free in the late afternoon.

I went with her several times, and one particular day, I could not help but comment to her how much I admired her lovely navy-blue *Hermès* Kelly bag. Even a country bumpkin like me-- in budget if not taste--couldn't live in Paris an entire year and not know about *Hermès.* (Of course, Cass had already given me those incredible gloves at Christmas in Kenilworth, and she and I had been to the venerable store over on *Rue St. Honoré* to drool at the windows.)

"It's just that a handbag of that price is so unheard of where I come from; I can't seem to get over it."

I didn't mean to embarrass her in any way, but you couldn't see one of those bags and not acknowledge "wink wink" that you knew what it cost to own one.

She smiled at me. "You have good taste," she said. "I will show you something. I think you will like it."

We turned down a small street that led towards the *Bois de Boulogne,* and right around a corner was a tiny shop displaying purses looking for all intents and purposes just like hers.

In France in the 1960's no one was selling fake designer purses spread out on blankets in the tourist districts, easy to wrap up and flee if police appeared. And there were no faux bags from China or Italy sold anywhere either. Rather, a small manufacturer could indeed replicate a style, of course without any of the logo branding that would mean one were offering a provocative fake.

The purse Blandine de Seignard pointed out to me in the window was a Kelly-looking bag, not of the same actual measurements, it turned out; and this one was two-toned in cream linen, "*toile*" and navy leather. It was beautiful and it was perfect. Perfect for me, the blue and white (okay, cream) queen of the world.

We went into the shop and Madame de Seignard spoke to the clerk who was also the owner, a thin, frail-looking elderly lady who exuded the panache -- "*bon chic*" of the French upper middle-class. She brought the bag out of the window for me to peruse up close. Its leather was not as soft as Blandine's purse, but I didn't mind that. It had the same closure, the padlock (no H on it) and the keys hidden in a tiny navy leather cover. The price was one hundred seventy-five francs, so thirty-five dollars. The most expensive purse I'd ever bought to date at that time was under ten dollars, so thirty-five was still a lot (not like ten thousand!) but it was my birthday, and I had that birthday "mad" money... and any other rationalization I could conjure up.

I happily — no, ecstatically-- bought it! I didn't give a second thought to whether or not, as I got off the plane in Omaha wearing it on my arm, even one person would recognize its iconic style, and wonder if (assume?) it were real. I didn't care about that at all. The purse was so beautiful and so well-made (in France!) that it would not only stand the test of time stylistically, but last my whole life, too.

When I went back to 214 Boulevard Raspail to bid a final farewell to people, it occurred to me to take pictures of all my favorite haunts following my route from there to the Sorbonne, through the Luxembourg Gardens, and all over the Latin Quarter. So I took my little camera and did just that; and when I told Clément about my day's efforts, he offered to take me in the car with his (great) camera and document the entire city. I could take stills and he'd take slides. He would give me all the film and I could have it processed at home, where it was about five times cheaper than in Europe. What a souvenir that would make! And we had a fabulously fun time doing it.

Inevitably it was time to return to the Sorbonne and see if, indeed, any diploma would be given out with my name on it. The list was posted in a locked case on the wall behind glass. And my name was there!! The relief, the ecstasy, and the reality of it all hit me at once. I went a little weak and couldn't catch my breath for a minute. The diploma ceremony would take place in the *Maison des Océans* , the *Océanographique Institute* of the Sorbonne, on *rue Saint-Jacques,* which had a big amphitheater. I'd seen the building before when we were taken as a group on a tour of the university, right at the beginning of our program ; but I never imagined I'd be participating in a prestigious ceremony in there myself.

I could invite someone, so I asked Clément, but was actually a bit reluctant to do so, first of all because he, too, was busy with end of term projects and exams ; and secondly because I didn't want him to think I was using him as my French boyfriend to trot out in front of my erstwhile American friends. (But of course, if they thought that, what could I do about it?) Naturally I wore Cass' gift dress and my London shoes. I pulled my hair back and secured it with the black velvet headband, and I wore the blue Eiffel Tower earrings, for just a bit of kitsch.

They called Nonnie's name at the beginning, because she had « *mention bien* » which was their version of *cum laude.* I went up and accepted for her, which our program director knew I was going to do, and had okayed it. My name was called among the students with no « *mention,* » but I was just so glad to have the paper in my hand, that honors were the last thing on my mind. The diplomas were elegant enough, much bigger than American ones. These were scrolls which we could and would later have framed. They would take about a twelve-by-fifteen inch size. On the diploma were listed the courses for which we got credit and earned the « *Degré supérieur de langue et de civilisation française,* » to wit on mine : *littérature française du XVII siècle, littérature française du XVIII siècle, littérature française du XIX siècle, littérature française du XX siècle, Histoire d'art français du Moyen Âge, Histoire d'art français modern, Géographie de la France, Les régions françaises,* and finally *Langue française pratique.*

When we got back to Clément's house that afternoon I was floored to have a telegram waiting for me! It read :

DIPLOMA RECEIPT FANTASTIC NEWS. SHRIERS PROUD TODAY.

Chapter Forty-Eight

"On The Road Again"...Canned Heat

The fanfare that awaited my return at the beginning of July wore off pretty quickly. I had a few days of "grace" free from criticism from the parents about anything that went wrong with me in Paris, and free from nagging me about what came next.

They seemed happy to greet me at the Omaha airport, and as I descended the stairs from the plane, Roslyn came running on to the tarmac to take my picture with a little camera she had. After a year, she seemed more grown up, which was entirely noticeable to me. Maybe it was the new hairstyle—a high ponytail that changed her look. She suddenly resembled a bona fide teenager more than a kid.

"Did you bring me something really neat?" she asked breathlessly.

"Yes."

"What? An Eiffel Tower?"

"Sure. And a notebook with dividers for the days of the week—written in French, of course. You can draw in it. They have paper with little squares on it, called graph paper. Or you can write in it. Do you keep a journal?"

"No, what's that?"

"Oh, you know... a diary....where you write down what you did today or your most private thoughts. Stuff like that. You could use this for one."

She acted uninterested in that idea, but thumbed through the graph paper pages anyway. "What else did you bring me?"

"Well, I brought you some fab French candy, some socks and a keychain."

"Oh, good."

I should have been tired and eager to sleep for a month when I got back, but the adrenalin kicked in and I had energy. Nana had not come to meet me at the plane, and I was really anxious to go over to her place and tell her all about my year. She had a surprise waiting for me when I walked in: the file of my letters.

"The whole story is in here," she laughed, waving it around. "Look what I've made." And I saw that she had taken a file folder and punched two holes in the top where she inserted a two-pronged clasp. "This is how we used to keep the 'tabs,' the house account files in the bar", she explained. You can see things in order that way. Same thing with your letters. I have them all chronological with the most recent on top. You see, I've punched the same holes in the tops of your letters. Then I can slip the fastener through the holes and fold the ends over. Doing it this way also means that whatever size paper you used fits in here. If I can punch it, it can be put in!"

"So...I can flip through these and relive the whole year, eh?"

"That's your chronicle of it all, right there."

"Super neat! It will be a gas for us to go through it together."

"Yes, fun!" she laughed, but then got serious and asked after Cass. "You didn't go into too many details in your letters and I'm sure there are some."

"It was a nightmare, Nan," I said. "She was so sick those days in Holland and I didn't even 'get' it. I thought she'd picked up the flu. So I'm going to Iowa City in a few days and will get the low-down and report back."

"Good. You tell her to take care of herself. *Oy*, two little ones at the same time. It takes super human strength to be a mother of twins."

I had brought the immediate presents with me in my flight bag, and I distributed all that first: the gifts I'd brought for Sol, an art print to hang in the bar and a silk pocket square; for Betty --Joy perfume and a Christian Dior coin purse; the champagne in my trunk would arrive later. For Nana, I brought Roget et Gallet soaps and a spoon of the city of Paris with the "navire" or sailing ship on it for her collection; plus a French style photo album with the tissue paper page separations. I figured she'd find more pictures to put in it, and of course, I would have dozens, too, that she could share. I got slides made of the photos that Clément took and we viewed them one night.

My trunk even arrived not too long after I did, and all the contents were unscathed, so I spent a few days unpacking and looking over my Paris life again, as I arranged my books and notebooks from the year abroad on my bookshelves and placed the bibelots that were my souvenir treasures among them.

I had to go to the Omaha National Bank to exchange the remaining francs I'd brought back, and the parents let me keep the money which came out to $87; much as Sol thought that might be a bit extravagant.

"I guess you earned it," he grunted.

"I've never worked so hard," I assured him.

I drove around Omaha and revisited some old haunts like Brandeis, which, after *Galleries Lafayette* and *Au Printemps*, seemed banal and lackluster to me. The money I had left over would have bought quite a few skirts and sweaters for the Fall semester, but I held onto it. The only thing I did buy myself in the book department of Brandeis' basement was Julia Child's *Mastering the Art of French Cooking*.

I had been so anxious to share my new culinary tastes with them that I tried in utter vain to find croissants and make hot chocolate with the cocoa I'd brought back from *Inno*, but there wasn't a croissant to be had in the land of Omaha in 1969. So I used Pillsbury crescent rolls and even after dipping them in the hot chocolate, they still tasted like sawdust rolled in glue. With Julia Child's help, I was determined to learn to make real ones.

My father had it all mapped out that I would work the entire summer on a certain schedule at The Spot, which included weekends. I was resigned to have to work in the bar even before I got back from France, and that was okay with me since I needed to earn quite a bit before returning to school. But I let him and Betty know right away that before I settled into the work routine, I had to get out to Iowa City and find an apartment for Fall and check on my credits with the registrar.

"Well, go ahead then," he said, "I don't want you in jeopardy of losing a year's worth of work and staying on another one!" Dollar signs in his eyes helped with any scheme I might have to get out of there.

Before heading east, I walked up the street from The Spot to our own downtown Montgomery Ward and perused the baby department. I chose that store because I reasoned that I could get more things for the money I would spend at a fancier store and baby accoutrements were all the same: white cotton. I went looking for diapers first. A sales clerk on the floor saw me looking at them and gave me the once over, noticing I had no wedding ring, and said with an air of exasperation, "Did you know you can buy these little gauze liners for the diaper now? They make clean-up a lot easier. You place one in the diaper and when it's time for a change, the liners have caught all the poopy stuff and you can just flush it."

"Genius," I mused.

"Not only that," she continued, "but we also have these disposable diapers. 'Course, they're real expensive. But you tape them! I never seen anything like it. Look!"

I looked at them and saw immediately what a time saver they would be. But oh, the cost! A box of ten cloth diapers (that you could wash probably fifty times and still be good) cost $2.99. The twelve-pack of disposables cost $4.50!

"Who has that kind of money?!" I asked her astonished.

"Nobody. We don't sell too many of 'em; you're right," she laughed.

So I picked up two boxes of the cloth ones with a package of liners, and went over to the layette display. Cass would need shirts and gowns for the babies. I got everything in white since I didn't know if she were having boys or girls and anyway, for a layette, what did it matter?

"What else would I need to buy?" I asked the clerk.

"Well, you're going to need to bathe the baby so you need baby towels, don't you?"

"Okay, yes, but you misunderstand. I'm not the one having the baby. These things are gifts."

"Oh! Well, I didn't mean to imply…"

"Yeah, that's okay. So towels?"

"Yes! Here are some cute ones. Yellow with little giraffes on them. See, they have a hood."

"Okay, I'll take two of those."

"And receiving blankets. The mommy will want some of those."

When all was said and done, I got Cass most of the layette items she would need right at the beginning: diapers, four white shirts, four drawstring gowns, the two baby bath towels with hoods, two bibs with Mother Goose themes, and two sets of booties. Plus I had the French rattles from Chartres. I would tie it up in a pretty box and put the rattles on top as decoration. I knew it wasn't nearly enough but it would get her started. The entirety of what I bought ended up costing me around $15.00. I had also gone around and fingered lots of pretty baby clothes: little sweater sets crocheted with caps to match; darling snowsuits. But that would have to wait. I did the best I could with the money I thought I could spare.

On the way to Iowa City, rather than listen to the car radio, which had nothing in the way of decent rock music in the depths of Iowa, I took my trusty transistor radio and played cassettes in it the whole way. *Un Homme et une Femme* was the perfect road music in any case, given that "*À 200 à l'heure*" was one of the tracks. I also found I could sing along with it in French and know perfectly what the lyrics were. That was progress right there.

I got into Iowa City around noon, and I knew I would be staying with Cass, because I would just ask her if I could crash on the couch, provided they had a couch. So I first went to the registrar's office and hoped to get an appointment for the following day, but luck was with me, and they could see me right then. I explained who I was and where I'd been for the year, and sure enough, Pella College had sent over my transcripts already. My GPA was going to drop, the registrar clerk told me, since some of the results from the French exams were not high enough to translate to A's or even B's. But when all the credits were tabulated by Pella College and converted into American grades, I had earned seventy-two credit hours in French! The number needed in the major for a B.A. at Iowa was twenty — four, and I'd already had half of that when I left!

"You actually earned enough credits for a master's degree," the secretary told me as she handed me all the paperwork to take. "But of course, you weren't taking graduate-level classes."

Truth is, my cours pratiques courses were not, but we had all taken the same Sorbonne course-work in literature, history, art, etc., and except for writing the "*memoire*" or thesis that the grad students in my program had to do, I obviously had done graduate-level work. No wonder it had been so hard!

But I was happy that I was a senior in good standing even if Iowa wasn't about to award me anything higher than a B.A. when I graduated in eleven months. I left the Registrar and headed straight for the French and Italian departments in Schafer Hall to get the lay of the land for Fall term. Dr. Marianne Ilke was chair and since she also happened to be in the office that day, I waylaid her and asked if we might have a little chat.

"Dr. Ilke!" I called out to her from behind. She turned rather startled and saw me approaching her with my hand thrust forward to shake hers. Ever since I'd come back, everywhere I went, I would automatically extend my arm and start to shake hands with whomever I met...it was the French custom that I had inculcated. Some people were taken aback. Dr. Ilke was French, so it didn't faze her.

She invited me into her office. She had been aware that I had turned up my nose at going to Rouen with Iowa's own year-abroad program, but then remembered that I hadn't by then taken the prerequisite classes to get on the Iowa program; so I was "excused" in her eyes for having gone with Pella College.

"I trust you had a marvelous experience at the Sorbonne then?" she said with her eyes twinkling a bit at me.

"Marvelous and harder than hell," I replied.

I showed her the transcript I was still carrying and looking it over, she saw that I had already taken much of what would be offered to me from her department next term.

"I'm afraid you will have to repeat French Pronunciation. It's a requirement for all our majors."

"But, I had FILIOLET (expecting her to know who he was!) for that in Paris!! How does that not transfer?"

"Oh, you earned the credit, but we need to see our exact course title on your exit transcript in order for you to get the major."

Ah, red tape. I reminded myself that I should be used to that after the amount of it in France that practically strangled us foreigners, so I didn't say another word.

"What else do I need to take?" I asked, wanting to be completely sure I didn't miss anything that would prohibit getting the degree.

"Well, there's no class in 18th Century French Novel on here."

"Yes,…see, Littérature du XVIIIème right there."

"I know, but we focus on the novel. So take ours, too. If it's a repeat for you, that will mean you'll earn an easy A."

"Gotcha."

I left the campus that day in July really happy: I'd be registering first and would easily get into the sections I wanted; I would be taking mostly electives since I'd done the vast majority of requirements even before I went abroad; and nothing academic would ever again be as hard as what I had just gone through, so I envisioned a lot of free time for the coming year. So much the better as I could offer babysitting services up the ying-yang to Cass, and thus begin to repay the myriad of life-saving kindnesses she and her parents had shown me in Europe, and really ever since I'd first become her roommate. And the best thing of all, I mused, as I drove out of town south on Highway One to Cass and Alan's farm house: I would work six more weeks in The Bluffs, then pack up my car and head out, and, if things went my way and luck prevailed, I would move to Chicago after graduation, find a job, and never look back.

I pulled off the highway into the gravel drive leading to a grassy parking area in front of a ramshackle farmhouse. There was even a little pond in front of it where an actual duck was swimming! Cass had heard the car and had come to the front porch, holding onto her back and protruding far out in front. She was enormous.

"Cass!" I cried, as I got out of the car and walked up to her arms outstretched, "You're HUGE!"

"Oh, God, don't remind me," she said, not really laughing. "How are you?! You look gorgeous, kid!! Very French!!"

"Hah. I wish. So how the hell ARE you? You have a duck!?" I said in wonderment.

"Yes, that is Maynard le Canard! Do you love the name? I'm about ready to give birth on this porch is how I am!"

She actually seemed to struggle a bit getting back into the house, and went straight over and sat down in the one comfy chair in the room.

"I'm spent," she said. "Just going to the door took all the energy I have! But I'm so glad to see you."

"Same here. And can I crash here tonight?"

"You MUST!"

"Will Alan care?"

"Hell no. He'll love it."

"So everything's fine with you guys?"

"Great." She tried to sound convincing, but I was not entirely buying it.

"I brought goodies!" I announced, and bopped back out the screen door to my car and got the package, plus my overnight case.

Cass was wide-eyed as she opened the gift I'd brought, and just as she did, Alan's motorcycle pulled up and he came in.

"Look what Sari's brought for us!" Cass cried, holding up the layette items for him to see.

"Well, hello Miss Shrier. That was certainly thoughtful of you!" He beamed at me with a glorious smile the likes of which I hadn't really ever seen on Alan. Perhaps things were going to be fine with this marriage after all.

"Least I can do. I'm also offering my babysitting services this whole year, too. Free! You can't pass that up!"

"Indeed!" he said.

"Sari, this is just the sweetest present," Cass said. "The rattles are so cute, too! The babies are groovin' to them!"

"They are from France. The other stuff is from good ol' Montgomery Ward."

"Nothing wrong with that," Alan chimed in.

"Hey Alan, I'm spending the night; that okay?"

"Sure," he said.

"Yeah, Sari," said Cass, "you don't have to ask permission."

"Well, okay then, thanks. Listen, while I was on campus, I picked up an Iowa City *Press Citizen* to look through the want ads for an apartment and I found one. I called on it from Schafer Hall, and I'm going to go look into it now, so on my way back, I'll pick up a pizza and we can have it for supper. Does that work for you guys?"

"Heck yeah," said Alan.

"Okay, so what kind would you like?"

"Anything's fine with me," Allan responded enthusiastically, as though pizza take-out were a real treat. "Where are you getting it?"

"Pagliai's of course."

"Groovy."

"Cass? What kind?"

"Well, you don't know this yet, but I've sort of become a vegetarian, so anything with veggies is great with me."

"You're pregnant with twins and now you decide to become a vegetarian?! Is this the time?"

"Just sort of I said, not entirely." Her tone was a bit menacing but I laughed it off.

"Okay, I'll get two mediums instead of one large, and one will be veg."

"Will you be wanting some money from me, Sari?" asked Alan.

"My treat. See you in a while."

I made my way back up the highway to the town. They really only lived 10 minutes by car from the English Philosophy Building on the edge of campus, so they were hardly out in the country. The actual farm that had been adjacent to where their house stood had been sold off to the Iowa City Airport Authority years prior when a new runway was added, so the house was merely a rental now and not a family home. Alan rented it for a song: $55 per month, unfurnished. I was hoping to find an apartment for that amount, and knew I probably wouldn't be able to, but I was on my way to see a tiny furnished apartment in the upstairs of a house on Brown Street that would rent for $60 per month including utilities, so that was about the same bargain.

That location was perfect: close enough to walk to campus and quiet enough to leave my car parked right out on the street in front. I spoke to the landlord, a Mr. Breck, who lived on the first floor. He was very nice but made it clear that he wanted a quiet, studious student above him. He wouldn't care if the tenant played music—he was rather deaf; but he could feel stomping around and didn't want that. I assured him I was quiet and, thinking ahead, I had also brought personal and financial references.

He accepted me and told me I was smart because I had hopped right on the ad that he'd only just put in the paper the day before. I said I felt lucky, and thanked him, and also said I wouldn't be moving in until the term actually started, which was fine with him since his summer session student had only recently moved out.

"Shall I show you the apartment now?" he asked. "I haven't had it cleaned yet, but I will."

"That would be great," I said eagerly.

So he got the key and we went out his apartment door inside the foyer of the house, and up an interior stairway to the door of the other apartment. The door opened right into the living room which was painted in a shade of light green. Down the hall was a bathroom first and then a bedroom next door. A tiny kitchen was at the very back of the place and there was no exit from it. So in theory if he were so inclined, he could watch or hear all my comings and goings out his front window. I wasn't planning to do anything untoward, but I hoped, nevertheless, that he made a habit of minding his own business.

The furnishings were like any college town digs: sparse and ugly, but adequate. I had all my own cooking paraphernalia, bedding and linen, so anything else that was included was icing on the cake. And I was happy contemplating having the place all to myself. Much as Cass and I had been perfect roommates, I knew what imperfect ones were like, and began to consider living alone as luxurious.

The deal done, I signed a preliminary letter of intent, left a $25.00 deposit and went on my way. I had gotten a lot accomplished in one day in Iowa City! Pizza was a just reward.

289

Back at the farmhouse, I took the meal to the kitchen table which wasn't really even in a separate room. It may have been at one time, but they told me that the original farm owners (who were their landlords) had knocked down a wall, and extended a bathroom that they enclosed on all sides, which left the otherwise designated kitchen area exposed to the living room. Cass' and Alan's bedroom was also just off the living room, and back down the hallway past the bathroom was a closet and tiny storage room that had previously been a back porch. There was no other bedroom and nothing for a nursery. Thus the Jones' two babies would be in cribs in the front room against the outer wall of the house right to the side of the front door. I didn't like the potential draftiness of that arrangement, but Cass was excited to show me how they'd found two separate old, used cribs, and she recounted her adventure in scouring them down with Lysol.

"These are new mattresses, though, right?" I asked, worried that they didn't look like they were.

"Well, no, but..."

"Wait," said Alan, "what's wrong with used ones?"

"Are you really asking me that?" I glowered at him.

"No, but we have new sheets on them—see? -- and these neat-o bumper pads and all," Cass tried to assure me.

"You really need to put new mattresses in those cribs," I maintained. "Baby ones can't be that expensive."

"It doesn't matter what they cost," said Alan. "We can't afford them."

"Anyway," Cass cooed, trying to lighten up the mood, "look over here Sari. We have a bassinette for them when they're newborn. Isn't it sweet?"

"It is. Will they share it?"

"Yeah. They won't be very big...too tiny to put in the cribs right away. We'll keep it in our room when the time comes," she added, which made me feel better at least about the drafts.

The rest of their living room consisted of the armchair which Cass had availed herself of when I first got there, and a couch situated in such a way as to block off the kitchen table from the rest of the room, creating the illusion of a little "salon" vignette in the space. There was a low table in front of the sofa, and another table to the side with a really ugly brown glass lamp on it.

"We got all the stuff at Goodwill," Cass said, anticipating my next question. "They changed stores since you've been gone and the prices have gone up some, but their merchandise is still not expensive. And see over here? I even got this bathinette-changing-table thingy. Like it?"

"Well, it looks like it came from the 1940's, but, yeah, I like it. It has some good storage underneath, too. You are going to need that."

We sat down to eat the pizza off a ragtag collection of dishes and mismatched glasses. Cass offered 7-Up in bottles, and I gladly took one. The two pizzas I had ordered at Pagliai's were fantastic. Even though I loved French pizza, it was so totally different from ours, and I had missed sharing slices with a group. We devoured a sausage and black olive one, and the vegetable one got eaten more slowly, mainly by Cass and me.

"You amaze me," Cass said to me at the table. "You blow into town in the morning, and you manage to see about your credits, talk to someone about the Fall schedule, and secure a place to live---all before dinnertime!"

"You're a little go-getter, aren't you Miss Shrier?" Alan was only teasing me calling me Miss Shrier like he had when I was his student.

"Gosh," Cass added, "that pizza is so good."

"Of course," I agreed. "Pagliai's is the best. Don't you guys go there all the time?"

"We actually don't go out much," said Cass.

"Not in the budget," added Alan.

"Was it heaven to see your Nana again?" Cass asked, changing the subject, and before letting me answer, added, "I got a horrid dressing down from my grandmother when she heard my news. She's really uptight about early babies and about all the pain I am 'deliberately' inflicting on her only daughter. That upset me."

"Well, that actually surprises me to hear! So are they still in contact with you even though they said they were disowning you?" I asked hopefully.

"Oh, no. That was when I first got home. It's pretty much over, I'm sure."

"And good riddance!" Alan added, raising his voice. "I don't want one cent of their dirty corporate money and if they can bear to never see their own grandchildren, then what kind of people are they anyway? Nobody I want in my life."

"It's not dirty money," said Cass softly. "They earned it. At least he did."

"You know what I mean…they're capitalists no matter what. It's all ill-gotten gains."

"Not necessarily, come on," I said, wanting to deflect the argument away from my eight-months-pregnant friend who probably didn't need the stress of fighting with her husband.

"I'm going back to my office," Alan announced getting up. "Summer session grades are due next week and I have a pile of themes to grade."

"And I'm going to the bathroom for the umpteenth time," Cass said, trying to get out of the chair gracefully, but not succeeding.

"You poor pregnant woman!" I laughed. "I'll bet those babies are pushing on your bladder!"

"Ugh, you wouldn't believe how much!"

After Alan had left, Cass and I had a good chance to talk. I told her about breaking up with Soren, "if we were even a couple, which of course, I thought we might be, but we never consummated anything, so an argument could be made that we were not." I related the trials and tribulations I went through taking my exams, but compared to her becoming pregnant, threatened with a home for un-wed mothers and then snatched from her parents and married in haste, my little problems paled… and had a happy ending. *I fervently hoped she would also have a happy life with him and their kids, and I did not bring up any of my anxiety about how ill-prepared she still was to be a wife and mother. After all, in some parallel universe like, say, the Dark Ages, girls used to be married off at thirteen for chrissakes. What could they have known?*

"Oh Sari, but you passed! You got seventy-two fucking credits! You are golden. Here you are--- back from a year abroad-- like in the movies or something. You glow, you are infinitely bright and intense and so loving-- to us and our babies with all the loot you brought today. You deserve --and will have-- a special happiness that few are capable of. You have much to do and many to meet. This will be a glorious year for you, I can feel it."

I was taken aback by the passion of that speech… out of the blue like it came. I giggled and said, "Maybe you're feeling contractions!" But she didn't laugh.

"And now that you know where we are, will you promise me to come back often to our little abode?"

"Of course, Cass. I wouldn't miss being with those babies for all the world. I'll be your babysitter-in-chief."

"And I'll frequent your Brown Street dwelling, too, because, you know, I have really missed you. I can't wait until you are here permanently. We'll have to plan something gay, mad and exciting that doesn't include changing diapers!"

One month later--earlier than expected, but really, with twins they should have suspected it could happen -- Cass gave birth to a baby boy and a little girl. Alan phoned me at home and Betty relayed the call to me at the bar where I was finishing up a shift.

"Slightly early but full-term, they were healthy and Cass is doing all right."

It was a Saturday night, and the instant the bar was closed, I raced home, packed a few things in an overnight bag, got in my car, and drove four hours out Interstate 80. I arrived in Iowa City at three-thirty in the morning exhausted from night driving but tense with anticipation. I went straight to University Hospital and walked right into the only part that was open, which was the ER. I told them I was Cass Jones' best friend from The Bluffs, and that I had driven all night to see her. They let me in and said I should just get some sleep on a sofa in the lounge and I could see her and the babies in a few hours. I grabbed my makeup case from my bag and threw it in my purse so I could at least have a toothbrush later.

Alan was there and he and Cass were very surprised to see me when I walked into her room.

"My GOD, Sari, how did you get here so fast?" he marveled at me.

"I drove all night. They let me sleep in there," I explained pointing out into the hall towards the lounge. "SO!!! How ARE they?"

"They're so beautiful, Sari. I'm just so thankful."

"And??? Names??"

"Oh! You're going to like it: Paul for Paul Simon and Laura for Laura Nyro!"

"I LOVE IT!" I said. "Paul Simon Jones... and Laura Nyro..."

"No," Cass interjected. "Paul Hyde Jones and Laura Bronwyn Jones."

"Oh, right," I sheepishly corrected myself, adding, " I think that's cool, though, you guys; keeping those family names in the mix. Way to stick it to Julia!"

"Exactly," Cass confirmed. "Teach her to abandon her own flesh and blood, the bitch."

"So do you want to see them?" Alan asked me.

"Of course!"

"I'll take you. Cass, you coming?"

"It will take me too long to get up," she said. "I hurt. You two go down there. They'll bring them to me soon anyway."

So Alan led me to the nursery window, where I peered in. And there they were: so tiny, but big enough to not be in an isolette, which was the very best news.

"Oh Alan, I've never seen anything so beautiful."

Chapter Forty-Nine

"Time Won't Let Me"...The Outsiders

On the trip to see the new twins, I was in a limbo of bad timing. It was mid-August, and I figured to work another two weeks at the bar before moving my things to Iowa City; but there I was in Iowa City with no apartment to stay at yet. After that first encounter with the infants, I had gone over to Alan and Cass' house to freshen up. I then headed right back to the hospital, figuring to leave in the early afternoon, but found Cass in a state of high anxiety, so I hung around longer.

"I can't think how I will breastfeed two babies on my own," she said breaking into tears. "A nurse had to keep propping them up on me the last time. How do I even know they're getting enough milk?" She was sobbing.

I went over to the bed and put my hand on her shoulder. "They'll help you. They might even have someone on staff whose job it is to help you," I offered, trying to sound like I knew what I was talking about, which I did not.

"Y—y-yes, they dooo," she tried to say, as Alan came in, fairly echoing her.

"There's a lactation specialist who will stop in today," he assured her. I felt relieved. "She's from the La Leche League."

"The la-what-league?" I laughed.

"La Leche. Deadly serious, Miss Shrier," Alan said with mock authority in his voice.

"Okaaay. If you say so."

And sure enough, a perky brunette, with a volunteer badge pinned to her knit top, came bounding into the room all animated, on a mission to see Cass.

"Good morning, Mommy!!" she called out. "I am Dede from La Leche and I am SO glad you decided to breastfeed!"

Oh brother, I thought, immediately wishing a) that I were not there and b) that all proselytizing be held in check, which of course, it would not be.

"We're Cass and Alan," Cass answered, motioning her husband to her side.

"Now, first things first, do you have a doctor who is on board and supportive with breastfeeding?"

" Well, I guess so," said Cass . "Aren't they all? I never asked him."

"No, my dear, they are not. They are men, after all, and the big formula companies get to them first! Did you know," she continued, turning her attention to Alan, "that we in the La Leche League have calculated that breastfeeding---especially twins!—can save you about $1,200 per year! Formula is expensive. And it's not good! Plus, all that bottle washing and sterilizing, prepping the formula and warming takes up about an extra three hundred hours!!"

"Whoa," said Alan.

" I'll say! I know, I know—you're thinking: but it seems like they want to eat every half hour or so right now, and my life will consist of nothing but feedings and exhaustion! Am I close?" she quipped, not coming up for air. "But it will get better, I promise."

Cass looked shell-shocked at this disclosure, and Alan gave off a sort of snort-laugh, which Dede caught.

"You'll have to make yourself available to help her, Daddy," she stated.

"Yeah, but the term will start here in a few weeks. I've got a lot of meetings and...and preparations of my own to do now."

I just glared at him in disbelief.

You've got TWO children you just brought into the world, you fucking blockhead.

"Then getting into a routine will help you," Dede said, without missing a beat or letting Alan's answer stand. "What we have to master here is how to support and balance the babies -- one on each breast--and to teach them to latch on. After that, it's a piece of cake!"

Dede's enthusiasm was clearly not contagious. I found her to be cloying and hard to stomach in doses longer than a minute. She went into the bathroom adjacent to the room and brought back two towels, which she rolled up and placed under each of Cass's arms.

"This is how we position the babies," she explained. "You can do it either in the cradle hold –see here---right at your chest," and she leaned over Cass and placed the towel. "Or, football hold! That's where you lay the babies along each side under your arm…like you were carrying a football! Touchdown!"

I gave Cass a **"spare me"** look from my perch on the window radiator across from her bed.

Dede turned back to Cass, "Are you planning to demand feed or be on a schedule?"

"I don't know."

"Demand feeding is being more flexible. Babies are individuals, you see, so one twin might decide he wants to nurse, and the other one may still be sleeping! One may want to feed every two hours and the other every three. But we suggest that you not feed separately. Let the hungrier one dictate the time of the feeding for both."

"The nurse just brings them both right now for me to feed in here," Cass said.

"I know. Hospitals tend to use a scheduled feeding approach. Not so easy to do at home. You won't want to hear them cry all the time."

"It's just so overwhelming," Cass whined, starting to sob again.

"I know, sweetie," cooed Dede. "Just remember that Mother Nature won't let you down. The laws of supply and demand will work in your favor. Trust your body to supply enough milk, and alternate breasts at every feeding so that if one twin is a stronger eater, the switch will help the breasts produce an equal amount of milk on both sides. That will lessen the chances of blocked milk ducts, too."

"Blocked milk ducts?!!" Cass cried.

"Now now," said Alan. "Don't jump to conclusions. It probably won't happen."

"And just remember that low milk supply can almost always be corrected by nursing more often."

"More often?! You just said I'd be nursing them maybe on the half hour! How much more often can I be expected to do it than that?"

"Just remain calm, Mommy! You can always pump if you need to."

This was all too overwhelming for Cass. She was finding it exceedingly hard to cope with the barrage of information, when the nurse wheeled two newborn bassinettes into the room. Tiny Laura was swaddled in a pink blanket and little cap, while red-faced Paul was screaming in his blue one. Dede scurried up to the bed with her rolled up towels to position them in the cradle way, and the nurse placed each baby up to Cass's exposed breasts. I watched as this ballet of getting the infants in a position to latch on played out; Alan just stood there acting like he thought he might be in the way. It occurred to me how little he could be called upon to help with feedings unless Cass did pump, and the babies learned to suckle at both the teat and the bottle's nipple.

Cass turned her attention to the floor nurse, whom she suspected of having more actual medical knowledge than Dede. "How can I tell if they're done and if they've gotten enough?" she asked almost desperately.

"Well, since you are the parents of multiples," she explained, "we're going to send a nurse practitioner who is a lactation specialist, to your home in a few days." She saw the need to reassure Cass. "And she will be able to tell whether the babies are getting enough milk by how much weight they gain. Newborns tend to lose nine percent of their birth weight before regaining it by the time they are two weeks old. They should be gaining an ounce a day by the fifth day after birth," she said.

Cass's huge violet eyes just grew wider as she looked up from her babies, who seemed to me to be eating-- but who could tell? –and she stared at Alan as if to say, "You got me into this; you'd better help me!" I could see that they were both anxious to be calm and reassured by everything Dede and the nurse had told them; but that they were also only too aware that once they left the front door of University Hospital, they were pretty much on their own to get the job done.

Dede announced that she had to take her leave, but called out that she would be stopping back with pamphlets galore for Cass; and the nurse took the babies back to the nursery. I told them that I thought I'd better be hitting the road again and explained that I had another few weeks to work to earn some more money for the upcoming semester.

"I wish you could stay," Cass moaned.

"Me, too! But I'll come back as soon as I can. My academic load will be light this year; I'll come over to your place early and often! And I'm going to call you once you're home, so keep the phone where you can reach it, okay?"

Alan walked me out and into the hall. I turned to him and tried to elicit his solemn word that he would do everything in his power to help his wife: cook for her; keep the place clean, help with the babies.

"I promise," he laughed. "Don't you worry about us, Miss Shrier!"

"Knock it off, Alan, I'm serious. And by the way, just because Vance Bourjaily lives on a farm, did that mean you had to move out to the hinterlands away from drugstores and laundromats? Wasn't that kind of **not** thinking!!?"

"Cass loved that place! It's what I could afford. She's the one who wants farm animals, too! She pined for the duck. She wants a goat, for chrissakes."

"Yeah, come on. You're going to be back in your cozy little routine of coffee with the grad students in the River Room, and she's going to be stranded and isolated 'out on the farm' with two screaming infants. Well played, you."

"Give us a break, Sari," he said suddenly more serious. "Anyway, you said you'd come out and help her."

"And I will, Alan, but I'll have classes, too, and I live on the other side of the campus."

"Yeah, I know. Maybe my mother can come and help Cass out."

Oh, that's all she'd need, I thought, but kept it to myself.

Nevertheless, when I got back in three weeks, they had become a little family unit, and had settled into some semblance of a routine. Cass was healing nicely from her episiotomy, and said she felt well, if sleep-deprived. The baby bassinette they kept in their room was working out for the time being because, as she predicted, the babies were still terribly small. Cass was grateful that Alan would help her at night, getting the towels situated and babies to her; but she confided in me her exasperation that he had a tendency to complain about all the sleep **he** was lacking, due to his class prep, teaching and grading chores. But Cass brushed that off, and didn't rub his nose in it that all this was as much his fault as hers.

In the meantime, I had settled comfortably into my own little place. Cass had given me several of the accessories we'd shared in our summer apartment, in what seemed to me another lifetime ago. One thing she insisted I take was the Chinese lantern lamp, and I strung it up beside my bed. It gave off a pinkish glow that made me feel happy. I also used the same Indian bedspread we'd had in the other place; and I bought some inexpensive slipcovers for the couch and chair in my living room…a sort of ocean blue that I thought would make for a calming effect in the place.

I had also brought and set up my own record player, a small Bang and Olufsen stereo system with a receiver, a turntable and speakers, which had been a present from all the Omaha relatives on the occasion of my Sorbonne degree. None of these people had an inkling of what the Sorbonne was or anything I'd gone through to matriculate from there; but they knew that in our family it was a first, whatever else it was. I was delighted to accept the gift with much gratitude.

Besides getting together with Cass and her children, one of the first things on my agenda once back in Iowa City, was to seek out Soren, and have a talk. I felt bad that things had sort of deteriorated with him, and I didn't want him to feel like his friendship hadn't meant the world to me, because it had. He was once again an RA; only this year he was head of them all in the Quad. Soren was an L1—a first year law student; but having the dorm job, which, barring any emergencies, he could do with his eyes shut, gave him free room and board, which saved hundreds off his U-bill.

Soren took the liberty of inviting himself over to my place for the big confab, saying he couldn't get any privacy at his digs, and maybe we'd rather not talk in public. I didn't see this as any big deal, but agreed, and invited him over. I went down to the front door and out onto our "communal" porch. Right away we both noticed my landlord peer out his curtained window, and watch me invite Soren in.

"Oh, don't tell me he's going to spy on you this whole year," Soren said laughing as he entered.

"Yeah," I moaned, rolling my eyes at the thought, "that will creep me out."

He came into my place, pronounced it "bitchin'," and then grabbed me and took me in his arms for a serious and seriously unexpected kiss.

"I missed you, Sari," he whispered, clutching me closely.

"I missed you, too," I said, when I could get enough air to talk.

We sat down on my slipcovered couch. It was awkward all of a sudden, when being with him used to feel so easy.

"I'm sorry my letters were boring," I started.

"No! They were not boring. I liked hearing about all the stuff you were seeing and what your classes were like. Why do you say they were boring?"

"Well, in all honesty, it sort of bothered me that you didn't ever have a lot to say back to me. I figured you were pretty uninterested."

"No. That's my fault. I'm sorry. I was having sort of an on-going battle with the parents last year over law school and all."

"Yes. Well, you're **in** law school so did they win?"

"You could say that. But I'm still intent on entertainment law and not ending up in Imogene, Iowa. I think they get that now."

"Good."

"What about yours?"

"Parents? Oh, the same. I'm finishing up and moving to Chicago after this. I think they get it, too. No discussion, anyway. I'm twenty-one now. Emancipation, baby."

"And financially you're still beholden to them?"

"Well, yes. Therein lies the rub, of course. But I don't think they'll cut me off until I have the parchment in my hands. Ha!"

And then he added, "By the way, my mother had a minor shit fit about me leaving the church and all… assuming you and I had stayed serious, that is."

"You know, what is she even getting worked up about? You and I never talked marriage. We were never even promised to each other when I left for Paris."

"I know, but you are the first girl outside my hometown that I ever dated exclusively."

"Is that what we did? Date exclusively? Go steady? Mostly we just studied, Soren. Yes, we went for pizza and to The Mill and whatnot, but it's not like we lived together, and we still aren't."

"Yes, about that…I don't think we should break up, though. Let's GO steady this year…see where it takes us."

"Yes, but you just said, in so many words, that your parents would go apeshit if you got involved with even a non-Catholic, to say nothing of a Jew."

"Well, we're not talking marriage per se; let's just take it slowly and see where it goes?"

"Sure," I said, "I'm all for that."

With that, Soren pulled me towards him and resumed kissing and caressing me, his hand exploring under my sweater and then gradually moving down my back. "So," he said after a while, very hesitatingly, "I've got condoms. Shall we take them into your bedroom?"

I just looked at him for a minute.

This was pretty far from the romantic first time I had always imagined my having sex to be. I liked Soren a lot. I might have even loved him. Yes, my body was my own to do with as I wished; I was of age. But I wasn't seeing stars or hearing bells. I almost felt squeamish knowing what was about to go on up there was what the landlord thought was going on up there.

"Okay, but we have to be quiet about it," I cautioned.

Jesus, at least one, possibly two virgins in for a little afternoon delight. Who'd a thunk that?

We undressed each other solemnly. That part went okay. He fumbled to put on the Trojan, and I sort of lay there waiting. Then he awkwardly positioned himself over me and cupped my breast in his hand, kissing my neck and chest. I kissed his forehead before we finally found each other's lips and locked into a loving and perfect embrace.

I felt the increasing pressure of his erection against me as he tried, as gently as possible, to enter me. I let out a small gasp of pain when my hymen gave way. As he moved within me, the discomfort continued for a while, but mixed with new sensations of arousal.

296

Soren could feel me tensing up beneath him and seemed to conclude that saying something would help overcome the awkwardness of the moment.

"Man, you're pretty tight."

What did you expect?

Then things happened faster than I had imagined they would, and soon it was over, and we were both panting, sweaty on my new sheets. We looked over at each other and smiled at first, and then laughed, as he rolled over towards me, and wrapped me in his arms again. We snuggled in bed for about half an hour, and then got up and took a shower together. He held me in his arms under the water, backing me up against him. We soaped each other off, and kissed as the warm water cascaded over us. We wrapped up in towels, and sat at my kitchen table while I grappled with my long hair in tangles.

"We should walk out together carrying some books or something," he laughed. "So your spy thinks we've been up here studying."

"Sure, we can try that," I said.

It was dusk when I dropped Soren off at his dorm for a dinner meeting, and I headed out to the farmhouse.

"Ça y est," I announced to Cass as I bounded of my own volition into her unlocked home. "Soren and I are a couple again."

"Oh kid! That's so great! We love him."

"I do, too, it turns out. We're an actual *couple*, if you get my drift."

Cass looked up, surprised and somewhat vindicated. "Well! Sari! How was it?"

"Heavenly," I said, wanting to believe it.

Cass flashed a smile at me. "Our little girl is growing up," she teased.

"Yeah, yeah, go ahead, razz away."

"No, I'm so happy for you. I'm really serious."

"So," I said, desperate to change the subject, "How are my two little lovies?"

"Well," Cass said, "signs are that all is well. We have been feeding every two to three hours eight times a day!"

"Wow."

"And they're wetting and pooping right on schedule. How much of the grueling details of stool colors would you like to be made privy to?"

"Ha! That's terrific! You're doin' it!"

"That's about all I'm doing, though, just like she said that day---you remember… that Dede chick."

"Of La Wretched League?"

"Ho ho, very funny."

"Has she been over here all the time?"

"Not all the time. Quite a few times. But I'm breast feeding; she's preaching to the choir. It's like even after you've sworn your allegiance to them, they have to keep on you to swear you mean it. I **mean** it already, lady! Sheesh!"

"Oh, please, why don't they just butt out?"

"Well, they're zealots."

"So are you a zealot now, too?"

"No. But I want to do it. Alan is thrilled at the idea that we don't have to buy formula, but, naturally, he's only thinking of the cost."

"How about pumping milk so he could at least feed one of them for you? Doesn't he want to bond with them, too?"

"I haven't had any luck pumping, Sari, but I want to do that, too. I hope the lactation person can get it going with me the next time she's here."

"I hope so, too. Pardon me for being frank, but from the look of things around here, it doesn't seem as though your husband is giving you a lot of other help. Is he at least cooking dinners?"

"Sometimes. For himself, mostly. I don't eat the stuff he brings home very often."

"So what do you eat? What's in this fridge right now?"

"Well, I have some herbs ---I'm going to start growing my own, too. And eggs. So I can make a mean omelet."

"Okay, what else?"

"Some fruit is in there. And we have tomato soup - Campbell's."

"Well all right! How about if I make dinner? Soup and *omelette aux fines herbes*, if that's what you have; or *fromage*---you got any cheese?"

"Yes. We—uh—went to the food pantry at our church and they gave us stuff free!"

"Wait a minute. He's salaried, Cass. He must make enough for food! What's going on here?"

"He just came up a little short, that's all," she said, her voice quivering.

"For heaven's sake. I have some money! You can have it all."

"NO! You need it, too, Sari. Let's not talk about this anymore. If you make dinner, when Alan gets home, maybe he'll watch the babies, and you can drive me to the laundromat."

"Yes, sure."

So that's what we did. I put the soup on very low, and let it heat over a long enough period of time for me to wash dishes and wipe down the kitchen/dining room table thoroughly. I busied myself picking up dirty clothes from the living room and their bedroom, and I grabbed the diaper pail, and put it in the back of my station wagon. Cass watched and didn't even try to stop me, but thanked me profusely.

"You're so take charge," she marveled. "As soon as we're done eating, everything will be ready to go!"

When Alan got home, he helped Cass situate the babies for feeding, and he even offered to put them back to sleep while we ate. I tried to take that as a positive sign that they were both into this formidable parenting job ahead of them. But I still felt uneasy. Mostly about my dearest friend.

When Cass and I were in the car, I ventured an opinion on her looks: "Cass, you're very thin. Are you positive eating vegetarian while nursing is a good idea? Are you taking iron tablets at least? Vitamins?"

"Yes and yes," she laughed. "Don't you fret about me."

Laundromats were not fast institutions in the 1960's, but the price was right. The wash was 35 cents and drying was ten cents. The machines were big, and we used two of them. The diapers had to be washed separately in very hot water with Dreft, which I bought her-- because I insisted on it. Since the cycles took over an hour, we had a nice long time to talk. She told me again about the details of her escape from Kenilworth and how she managed to get her art supplies gathered up, along with her clothes, in such a short time.

"It was just lucky that I knew where I'd put everything when I left Iowa, and that I could still get to it."

"So do you plan on doing some art? Have you contacted Klampert?"

"No. Not yet. But something interesting did happen. I gave a block print to our priest—you know the one who married us—and some people in his office saw it, and thought it would make a neat Christmas card. They might commission me to make them a set."

"Cass! That's fantastic. That would be pretty easy to do, right?"

"Yes. I have some left-over blocks about the size of a card, plus all the inks and the brayer and such. But I don't have any paper anymore. I'd need to get some paper by the pound at Things and make them on that. But we don't have any money for me to go out and buy paper."

"Well, that's simple, silly. I'll buy it and you can pay me back—or not---after the sale."

"Gee, kid, could you do that?"

"Consider it done. You shouldn't even hesitate to ask me stuff like that. You know how I feel: I **owe** you... gobs."

"Well, I don't have the job yet, so this is really not anything but conjecture. I'll keep you in the loop, though."

"Another thing, Cass---I think you should go apply for food stamps. I read a pamphlet about it in the hospital waiting room. It's great for low-income families. You'd probably be eligible for a lot of food and supplies. I think you can even get diapers on them.

"Gee, for free?"

"I think so! And you know what else? You can get infant formula with them, too, in case breastfeeding doesn't work out. I can take you tomorrow. We'll bring along the babies if Alan can't be home."

"He doesn't teach tomorrow until late afternoon."

"Perfecto. We'll go in the morning after you feed them. Just think—more money for food! And speaking of that, I'm also going to pick up some stuff tomorrow and make dinner for you guys. I've got my grandmother's recipes for meals like the bar serves, pot roast and Salisbury steak and stuff like that. Does that sound good? Those last for two days, too; the leftovers are better than the meal, even, " I laughed. "I know you're not too keen on eating meat, but if I make it, you'd try it, wouldn't you?"

"Well, you'd win Alan's heart, that's for sure! It's been lean pickin's for him ever since we moved in together."

I could see -- her eating habits notwithstanding-- that she didn't have the time, energy or inclination (or for that matter, housekeeping know-how), to do much of anything around there at all. The place needed a good scrubbing, and the fridge and pantry both needed to be stocked.

"I'll shop for all the food...you won't have to do anything."

"Well, say, you need to know, then, that there's a new food co-op in town, too, kid. You should go there instead of the supermarket. All the food is in bulk and you can even bargain."

"Umm. But I'll be willing to bet it's not like the Paris outdoor *marchés* is it?"

"Well, sort of. The foodstuffs are straight from the farms, but no, it isn't pretty like in France. Ho! What **could** be?"

I did end up going over to the co-op, but it didn't live up to my imagination at all. Vegetables and fruit on tables were fine, but grains in bulk, spilling out of bins, did not inspire me; and their meat selection was, well, from hunger. I didn't buy anything from the co-op, but instead headed straight to the local Piggly Wiggly, and stocked up to the tune of $20.00. I got a lot, and it included cleaning supplies like dish soap and Lava hand soap, Old Dutch Cleanser and Pinesol. I kept thinking about how their place needed a good cleanse, so I also bought a broom, a bucket and mop, paper towels—a real splurge to be used sparingly-- some O-Cel-O sponges, and a couple of cloth dishtowels. The idea hit me that that for Christmas I would save up and buy them an electric broom. It wouldn't work as well as a vacuum cleaner, but it would be something.

Like I told her I would, I took my own Dutch oven over to their place, and made Swiss Steak and potatoes in the same pot. With that I served corn-on-the-cob and a salad. I didn't have time to make a dessert, so I chopped up fruit and served it with cheddar, cut into squares. I also took over my tea kettle, so we could have tea and instant coffee, which I'd purchased at the store, but intended to up-grade when I could get to a coffee grinder shop in downtown Iowa City.

As Cass predicted, Alan was impressed with my culinary skill, and he expressed enthusiastic gratitude for what we would call today, the "comfort food" on his plate. He took a bite of the steak, looked up at me, and burst into a grin, his blue eyes twinkling under a messy array of blond curls.

"Miss Shrier! You've outdone yourself."

I was afraid Alan might nix the idea of government benefits like food stamps—on the grounds of pride or something else threatening to his manhood; but he didn't. He realized he'd bitched so much about money, and how Cass's family money was forbidden, that he couldn't really turn down help of a more public assistance nature.

"If we even qualify," he said, "I am faculty, after all."

"Yes, but really, you're just part-time when the salary part of it is separated out from the free tuition, isn't that right? I think you'll qualify."

And they did. In a few weeks Cass began to receive some supplements of income, free samples, vouchers and various other perks from Uncle Sam. Thanks to Hubert Humphry in particular, and the war on poverty in general, America had a *soupçon* of a safety net.

Luckily, Cass calmed down about her worries over breastfeeding and became quite adept at it. Alan did help her, especially at night and the babies gained the requisite weight. The lactation specialist pronounced them a success, which made Cass happy. I was afraid every day there for a while that she would plunge into post-partum depression, and for the babies' sake, I hoped fervently that that didn't happen. But Cass turned out to be more resilient and adaptable than I ever would have imagined a very privileged woman to be. Perhaps the TWA stint had made her grow up a bit faster, I reasoned.

Then one day when the children were about a month old, Cass surprised me by announcing that baby Paul and baby Laura were to be christened in the little Episcopal church on campus; and how thrilled she would be were I to agree to be the godmother!

If you look up the authentic duties of a godparent, like the French culture has, this was a very big responsibility…and honor, too. But as a Jew, I was fairly ignorant of godparents; there were none in my life, of course. Cass understood that I could play no key role in the preparation for the christening of the infants, or even as the children grew in their faith.

"But the role also extends beyond just christening," she told me, "to actually take charge of the children in case of our deaths. You would be the one to raise Paul and Laura into adulthood. But don't worry, kid, that's not going to happen."

"Well, I hope to hell not. Plus, Cass, you and Alan would have to have a will, wouldn't you? Like wherein you would name me as their guardian in the case of your deaths? Otherwise, his relatives would probably be the ones to come in and swoop them up. Which might not be all bad. What do I know about childrearing?"

"A heck of a lot more than I do!" she said. "Actually, getting back to being their godmother, in the olden days there would also be relatives to seek out to fulfill this role, but I don't have any relatives I would ask to do it, as you very well know. Shit. So anyway, Sari, it's just really more honorary these days."

"Well, in France, it's real. The *parrain* and *marraine* actually do play a part in the child's life: they give a second birthday party on their 'feast day,' and take the kids places, and do things with them."

"Okay, I give you permission to spoil mine all you want. You can be godmother and honorary auntie combined, how's that?"

"Deal. Ha ha! Luckily I have your kilt to wear to the ceremony."

"Oh, thank you!" she said with relief. "And you might have the kilt to wear, but my kids don't have anything resembling even in the slightest a christening dress. So those lovely white gowns you brought for them will do just fine. Symbolic even! And from you!"

"Okay, yes, I shall be their fairy godmother."

Now where did I put that damn wand?

Chapter Fifty

"Children's Corner"...Claude Debussy

Christening day, a Sunday in mid-September, arrived very warm out, so the little white cotton gowns I'd brought for the twins actually were good choices. But I thought they should look slightly fancier, so I went to Woolworth's and found two very light receiving blankets, each with a little row of cotton lace around the edges. One was a sweet print with tiny flowers, perfect for Laura, and the other one had a duck motif and yellow suns, which was fine for Paul. I also bought little crocheted white booties for both of them and called it "outfits." Cass was very pleased.

The ceremony was to take place in the early afternoon, once the Sunday service crowds had dissipated. Alan had intended to borrow a pickup truck, but I offered to drive us all in the Rambler; so Cass sat in back with the baby basket, which both babies were still sharing, and Alan sat up front with me.

"Awfully good of you to do this, Miss Shrier," he said, tapping me on the knee.

"Sure, Alan... since that truck really didn't have any seating, you mean?"

We got to the church on College Street and, as if ordained from on high, there was a parking space right there. We walked into the cool, semi-dark space, and sat down on a pew towards the back. The young priest, friend and mentor to Alan and his C.O. status, was preparing to perform the ceremony. There were a few people lingering in the sanctuary, which surprised me.

"So, did you invite some friends or fellow parishioners after all?" I asked Cass.

"No! I have no idea who those people are, but if they want to witness our happy occasion, that's fine by me."

We all gathered around a baptismal font in the middle of the back of the church, and the priest gave some blessings and priestly-sounding benedictions. He sprinkled drops of holy water on the babies' heads. I was glad he didn't pour it on from a vessel and really wet their hair. Much was made of their names: Laura Bronwyn Jones and Paul Hyde Jones. I, on the other hand, amused myself thinking "Laura Nyro Jones" and "Paul Simon Jones" instead.

I had thought to bring my old Polaroid camera that had been a gift for high school graduation. Luckily I'd taken it to Iowa City with me, along with the few boxes of film I could still find. I got a couple of cute pictures of them holding the babies, with the priest at the side.

We hung around a little while to wait for my photos to develop, and chatted with Father Steven. And just like that, it was over with. We had no reception planned, no party to get back to. So, we decided to head over to a coffee shop near campus called Victor's and have some refreshments by ourselves.

"Maybe they have tea and some kind of cake," I suggested, thinking it would give things a bit of flair.

The babies, at six weeks old, were far too small to sit in any high chair the place had, so Cass and I each propped one up in the crook of an arm, and drank our drinks with the other hand. Cass and I had tea; Alan had coffee. There wasn't any cake, but they did have banana bread and a sort of lemony bar; so I ordered us the last two slices of the bread and one bar. Cass ate her banana bread as though she were swallowing cyanide.

"What's wrong with it?" I asked, startled to see her have to force it down.

"Oh, nothing! It's good! Well," she laughed, "it ain't the Savoy."

"I think it's fine," I said, frowning at her. "Tastes pretty delish to me."

"My lemon bar is great," Alan said.

The twins were fussy, and Cass didn't want to start the production of breast-feeding both at once in public, so we gulped down the rest of the tea, and I paid the bill, so we could all pile back in the car and head home.

"I really want to thank you, Sari, for everything today. The blankets and the booties and our mad, gay outing and you driving us," Cass said, hugging me.

"You're welcome, Cass," I said, noting without the slightest doubt as she hugged me, that she was skin and bones.

I walked out of their house back to my car really starting to worry. How could those kids be getting any nourishment if their food source had none to give? Did the body of a lactating woman just make up for it? My knowledge of the science of any of this was as thin as her frame seemed to be. If I pushed my concerns on her, would I be a nagging fishwife? Maybe I should just show up more often with food and cook for them.

At the end of the day, I decided that the problem was time and energy on Cass's part. And to be fair, she was so busy caring for two babies at once, every minute of the day, that she just had no strength left to make wholesome meals and eat them! I had no idea what she was eating when I didn't cook it; Alan had alluded to them having nothing decent for dinner, and he sure wasn't pitching in.

So this time I went to the store and bought six Anchor-Hocking glass refrigerator containers, as well as lots of aluminum foil, and all the ingredients for five meals: macaroni and cheese, tuna casserole, another casserole consisting of penne pasta tomatoes, cheese and meat; a meatloaf and more Salisbury steak. I decided that I would show up there WITH the food already prepared, having cooked it in my own kitchen. That way they couldn't refuse my offer. I had a few pangs of guilt and worry that Cass would think I was ignoring her vegetarian status, so I also stocked in cans of tomato soup and blocks of cheddar so she could make grilled cheese sandwiches.

I spent one entire day midweek preparing these dishes and packing them into the containers I'd bought, which could be frozen and then go straight into the oven. Cass's and Alan's fridge had been a sorry mess, but once the babies were home, I had cleaned it all out, and had even taken a dishpan full of hot water to the freezer compartment to thaw all the frost. It had worked, and after that, there would be enough space in it to store several fully-prepared meals.

The farmhouse had a phone, and Alan, at least, had acknowledged the importance of having it hooked up. He hadn't argued with the idea that, with two children at home, there had to be a way for his wife to reach him in an emergency. So, I was just about to phone Cass and tell her that I was coming out, when I got a call instead, and it was she on the other end of the line. She sounded really upset.

"Sari, you've got to help me! I don't know what I'm going to do!"

"WHY? What's wrong?!" I yelled, panicked.

"Oh...don't scream at me!"

"Sorry, Cass. What is it? You scared me."

"That lactation nurse-person was just here. The babies are not thriving!"

"What?!! But they look fine! Are you sure that's what she said?"

"Yes. She wants them on formula now. She says my milk must have dried up or something. Alan will be furious with me!"

"Oh, no he won't. These are his children! He'll want to do whatever they need."

"No, he'll blame me and say we can't afford it."

"Cass, get a grip. You have food stamps now. You can get formula. I'm coming over...I was anyway. It's four-thirty. Alan will be in class. I will drive us to go get formula. You can pay with those coupons-- or I can give you the money."

"It's expensive, kid!"

"It can't be that bad. The only problem is we'll have to take the babies, because I can't buy it without you there; I wouldn't know what to get."

"Okay," she said. "The nurse left the name of the formula. It comes in a powder or in liquid. The liquid is more expensive, but it's accurate. The powder you have to measure."

"We'll figure it out. I'll be right there. And Cass, I've made you some meals to keep in the freezer. Don't be mad. Some of them have meat."

"You're a doll. Alan will love you."

So, the Jones children went on formula, and their weights did improve. We had to buy bottles and brushes, a large pot to sterilize them in, plus a rack. Luckily Woolworth's had it all. We got the formula from Drugtown in Coralville. Food stamps did cover the cost, and she started them out on the ready-to-feed canned milk rather than the powder, since she dreaded not knowing how much to give them. Alan wasn't angry, which was lucky for him, since I was prepared to tear him a new one if he made any to-do

302

about this. And having the babies on the bottle made life a lot different around their place. Cass could calm down and get herself organized around a feeding schedule. Hallelujah!

Alan was also thrilled at the meals I'd brought, and Cass was only too happy to set them before him. Whether or not she ate any of it, I didn't know, but I hoped so. The house, too, was looking better--- more kept up. She had made little nooks and crannies for play areas and napping areas, and had even set up a small table in that space in back of the house to use as a mini art studio.

A couple of weeks after the christening, Cass asked me to come so she could talk to me about enlisting babysitting help for the weekend.

"I love it!" I exclaimed walking in to the tidy and clean-smelling home. "You've been busy!"

"Ho! Not only this but look here---the kitchen is organized; bottles are sterilizing away as we speak! And go peek at the bathroom! I cleaned it all up and made it pretty. And then I took a bath while the babies slept!" She paused, and reflected, "It was a miracle, really."

"I'll bet. So how do you feel? Better?"

"Better. You know, I worried all along about breast feeding. I never was fully convinced I could do it."

"Well, you did it. You gave them some of the immunity that's supposed to be the main reason anyone does it. But it's not always the method that works best, that's all."

"I know you must be right. I still feel like a failure, but it's over now. I'm not going back to it. The formula is working fine."

"Right. So, what time do you want me here Saturday?"

"Well, it's another faculty thing at Red Bird Farm, so like around 6:00? I think it's a barbeque."

"No problem."

"You could even bring Soren! He could help you. They're still a handful."

"If I bring Soren out here, he'll think I'm laying a trap for him to play house with me and get him to ask me to marry him or something."

"That's ridiculous."

I can't say babysitting the twins came naturally to me or that I wasn't nervous being alone with them. We were woefully ignorant of crib death at that point; I'd never heard of it, but if I had, I would have been even more on edge. However, they were at a very cute age -- two and a half months old; they cooed and even smiled a tiny bit-- that didn't seem only like gas. I put them both on a big blanket on the floor to change them "assembly-line style," and then took turns giving them their bottles. At that age they were still little enough to share the bassinette, and I put them down in the gowns that tied at the feet, with their heads at opposite ends of the basket. Feeling full and dry, they went right to sleep. It wouldn't be too long now, I surmised, before they'd need to be inhabiting their own cribs.

I busied myself picking the place up, and checking on the food supply. Cass and Alan – or at least Alan-- had eaten most of what I'd brought that one time; of course, I had been expecting that, since it'd already been a few weeks. The glass containers were washed and stored. Maybe the next time, I thought, I could get Cass to cook with me in her kitchen and fill them up again.

I peeked into their bedroom; it had not been tidied at all. Clothes were spilling out of baskets, and I couldn't tell if they were clean or dirty. The bathroom didn't exactly sparkle anymore, and I realized another thing: they barely had a towel that wasn't in terrible condition, and of course, none of them matched. At least the two hooded baby towels were hanging up to dry, and seemed clean enough.

Back in the former sleeping porch area, Cass's work table was spread with designs which I took to be her commissioned Christmas cards. There were sketches of a Madonna-looking figure with undulating shallow peaks behind it, possibly sand dunes. In the fore ground was the vague outline of an animal's head. She had sketched gothic-looking lettering on top spelling out NOËL. Another sketch had a modern-looking Christmas tree with two cartoon teddy bear figures in stylized diapers with big diaper pins on each side, seated leaning up against each other under a tree, one holding a baby bottle and the other a rattle. Little old-fashioned toys were scattered around the floor. The designs were both nice, and the small array of supplies on the table told the tale: Cass was getting back into her art.

About a week later, she called me excited on the phone, once again asking if, after my last class the following day, I could come out.

"My curiosity is piqued," I understated.

"Oh, it's good news! Nothing bad."

When I got there, she was waving a check in my face for twenty dollars!

"Whoa...that's a lot! What is it?"

"I got an advance!! The people who want the cards! They want two orders of twenty-five cards each—all the same design—my Madonna. They told Father Steven that they knew I'd probably have to buy supplies and stuff, and since they want fifty cards, they paid me this."

" Still, though," I worried, "fifty cards!? Jesus."

"But twenty dollars is a fortune! Just think, kid! And it's not going to be hard, you know? It's a print ---they're all the same. I just have to get the paper and the inks. That's where you come in. If you'll drive me to the bank and then to Things, I can get the paper; you won't have to pay for it! I'll use that paper-by-the-pound this time because the envelopes match. I can make cards out of cardstock, but making envelopes is a pain, so this one time, I'll buy them. I figure it won't even be that much...maybe three to five dollars. The inks are cheap. Just imagine, I'll have a fifteen-dollar profit or more!"

"That will come in handy all right."

"So, here's what else we need to do," she went on, "I need to have a drying place and our back room will have to do. We'll need to get some twine and some thumbtacks, and make a sort of clothesline on the wall. I'll be hanging the cards there to dry. And the only other thing," she added sheepishly, "is if you could come out and babysit for a couple of hours, while I'm doing the actual printing?"

"Of course. So do we go into town and get the paper now?"

"And to the bank! And we can take the babies in their basket."

"You know, Cass, that basket isn't going to work for much longer. You need some little seats. Let's go into Cedar Rapids and see what Montgomery Ward's has."

So we did that, and found the 1969 version of car seats. They fit on the back of the back seat and hooked over the other side. They were $7.98 each and I bought them for her. They were bronze colored and had a polyurethane seat. There was a lift-up guard rail of padded foam and even a safety belt. This was the be-all, end-all of its time.

We thought at first that these car seats would really only work in my car; that panel truck they drove didn't have a back seat. But Cass figured that in their panel truck, they could hook them over the front seat-- facing backwards in the back-- so actually they would also work in the truck! Whatever the vehicle, these two seats would be a great boon to the transport of Paul and Laura.

Cass also needed some sort of little baby seats to feed the kids in when they could sit up. So since she didn't have a high chair yet, let alone two of them, we decided she might actually bring in these car seats, and use them that way, too! When we tried that out the first time, hooking them to the kitchen chairs, Cass pronounced it a stroke of genius.

Thinking back on it, I now realize it was unsafe as hell, and sheer luck the babies hadn't tumbled out of them right onto the floor.

The card-making plan took shape, and Cass did the Madonna card as originally designed, since that one was the version of the print she'd given Father Steven, that the clients had seen. In the original, there were four colors –gold for the sand dunes, green for the cloak and hood, brown for the donkey and red for Noël. But that would have meant having to ink these smaller cards four times, which Cass thought would be a royal pain. So she bought gold-colored cards and white envelopes. She did a reductive technique whereby the uncarved sand dunes would just appear in gold once all the other figures were carved out. She did the cloak in white, and the silhouette of the donkey, as well as Madonna's face, in black. That way she only had to ink it twice, and you could still tell exactly what it was. Cass carved a separate block that she inked in red, and stamped Noël onto the finished cards on the front. She left the inside blank. She carved out CBH backwards, and stamped that on the back of each card.

The process took a few days, so I went out to their place "on demand," and took care of Paul and Laura while their mommy worked. When Alan came home and saw the disarray of all the linoleum blocks, the inks, and the cards drying on the string, he became grouchy about it.

"I just don't think she has time to go into the card-printing business, that's all," he told me out on the front porch, where I had hustled him to tell him to get off her case.

"Yes, she does. And she'd have more time if you did a little something to help around here. I'm watching the kids when she prints. YOU could come home early once in a while and do the same."

"I bring home the bread, don't I?"

That was questionable.

"Being a father entails more than that."

Once the order was done, Cass phoned and asked me to bring her out one sheet of poster board from the bookstore. It only cost a dime, and from it she made two little boxes-- just the size for the cards-- and put twenty-five of them in each. She then made lids. Cass was a pro wielding the X-Acto knife, and she knew how objects fit together, a skill which I sorely lacked.

My complete ignorance of spatial relations caused me to fail miserably on all those standardized tests that we had to take in school, where they showed you a flat version of a three-dimensional object, and you had to tell what it would be when put together. I never had a clue.

She presented the finished cards in their boxes and called out, "**Voilà**!"

"*Voilà* indeed! You are a genius!! Cass, you should make up lots more boxes of fewer cards, say… ten…and take them to the bookstore!! They would sell!"

"Oh, no," Alan responded. "The card-making factory is out of business as of right now."

"But Alan, for chrissake, she already made $20.00! She could make more!" I turned to Cass. "Sell the other ones for $2.00 a box."

"It's okay, Sar…he's probably right. We only bought fifty of the cards anyhow. But you've got a point. It wouldn't be too hard to keep doing this."

"I know I'm right." I shot Alan a look, but let it drop.

Ironically, I was walking on campus near the EPB the next week and ran right into Alan. He approached me and began to talk in a distinctly contrite tone.

"I'm sorry I snapped at you the other night, Miss Shrier. I really do appreciate all you've done for us." He laughed, adding, "And if it weren't for your meals, we would have starved a while back!"

"Come on."

"No! I'm serious."

I was afraid he was.

He went on. "Those car seats you bought for the babies are really workin' out great doubling as places where we can 'park' them for a bit in the house, too. I just want you to know I **am** grateful."

I answered him coolly. "That's fine. I'm happy to help." And then I added, "It's not going to get easier, you know. Sooner than we think, they'll be up and about and into everything! This phase is fun; before long it will be non-stop hectic!"

"How do you know so much about babies anyway?"

"I'm a lot older than my sister. I remember."

Chapter Fifty-One

"We Gather Together"...Dutch Hymn attributed to Adrianus Valerius

Besides actual school, my Fall semester of senior year at Iowa was pretty loaded up with babies, meal preparation for the Jones family, and trips to the laundromat with Cass, which we did fairly often. Either she didn't have enough diapers and baby clothes, which was obviously true; or babies, especially two of them, went through clothes at a pace a sprinter would find hard to keep up with. I made a mental note to bring back things from The Bluffs when I went home for the holidays. I even began to wonder if our basement held treasures in the way of baby items left over from Roslyn. I seemed to have remembered a high chair being down there.

As far as actual academic pursuit was concerned, my classes were certainly not the challenge my coursework had been in France; so all in all, I was having a pretty dreamy Fall term. Soren and I were together, and we became involved in new ways with campus life. His first-year law student cohorts had projects going with Legal Aid; and Iowa City, itself, was pulsating with civil rights and anti-war activism. There was a different presence now than there had been when I left: the Black Panthers were in town organizing. I went into one of the meetings in the union, all fired up, and looking around, discovered that virtually no other white people were there. I was approached and promptly informed that I would not be welcome.

.   "But I worked on civil rights issues before this. I registered voters in Des Moines two years ago."

I thought my bona fides would impress the guy.

"Well, yeah, that's fine and everything," he told me. "This organization is for black folk."

"You know, since when do black or any other **folk** not need all the help they can get?"

He looked at me with pursed lips. "I know you mean well. It's just that... we're recruiting blacks. Thanks anyway."

I didn't sing any longer with the International House chorus, nor did I continue as an usher for events in the Union either; but I did join *Cercle Français,* run by the department under Ilke's auspices; and I continued to attend the readings and lectures by visiting Workshop writers and other distinguished faculty and guest scholars. There was a seemingly unending parade of famous people on campus, and one of our own, Kurt Vonnegut, Jr., had become a household name the year I was gone.

Soren was all abuzz one night when he came over. "Philip Roth, for God's sake! He's coming back to do a reading from *Portnoy's Complaint.* Have you heard of it? You've got to read it!"

My grades from the Sorbonne had not been the most stellar, and had even set my overall GPA back by a few points, to a 3.4. But the massive amount of credit hours I received for that year's work put me far ahead of any other French major on campus that year. There wasn't much left for me to take, so I did Advanced Comp and Con --a five credit-hour class--and found it to be a piece of cake. My French vocabulary was superior, my pronunciation as good or better than anyone else's in the class; and, unlike students who had not studied abroad, to me speaking French was not angst-producing at all; it was second nature.

I took another round of art history courses, and wrote what I considered to be very informative and revelatory papers on Matisse and the Fauves, French Academic Art and its Foibles, and Mary Cassatt's relationship to Degas.

I got few grades below A.

I was ecstatic at the thought of no further science or social science course requirements, and really patted myself on the back for slogging through them all before I left for the year abroad. Because almost everything I took that semester was elective, it worked out that I was left with a luxurious amount of time to read for pleasure; so I turned to Sylvia Plath, Leonard Cohen, and Proust for deep and welcomed forays into other lives.

By the time Thanksgiving vacation was upon me, with the annual family dinner looming, I made a momentous decision to skip it. I asked Soren what he thought about both of us staying in Iowa City and having Thanksgiving at Cass and Alan's. I would cook. He could help me.

306

"I think it's a great idea," he said, "but I'm not sure how good an idea my mother will think it is. She really looks forward to Thanksgiving with everyone being home."

"Yeah, mine, too. I used to, also! It's one of my fave holidays. But I'm not interested in going home this year. I think I'll just tell my family that Cass needs help, and I'm staying here for her."

On the phone when confronted with this news, Betty said, "You can invite all of them here. We can find room."

"Now, Mother," I protested, "we can't have infants staying with us. Get real. Plus I'm sure Cass and Alan wouldn't come. They'd think it was far too big an imposition."

I didn't talk to my father about this decision. I was sorry to miss seeing Nana, but I didn't want to hear about dating a Catholic boy or what I owed them now that I was back from France; or why my grade point average had suffered, even the minuscule amount it did. I didn't want to be held accountable for my plans after graduation at this early date, either. I had already made up my mind to move to Chicago, but they didn't know it yet.

It seems that all Sol wanted to know about me at Thanksgiving was whether or not I'd be home at Christmas to work in the bar. I said I would, and hoped to hell it would be the very last time.

I was slated to be home three weeks at Christmas. That was pretty long, but gave me more time to earn money. My last hurrah. I had already been thinking of what to bring back for Cass's present, and had made up my mind that, instead of the electric broom, it was going to be a twin stroller. I had seen one in a Sears catalogue that was just what they needed: two square seats side by side with a large square canopy lid over both, sitting on one frame with one wide handle to push. It had a basket underneath as well. And the amazing thing was that this all folded down together so that you could travel with it, albeit you'd need a station wagon or a truck! It was going to set me back something like $26.00, but I was determined to buy one for them. It would be great, and they really had to have some way to walk around outside with the kids. I also remembered how badly they needed towels, and I planned to get some of those, too – a nice matching set with large soft ones, plus hand towels and washcloths. I was leaning towards the color turquoise. Turquoise reminded me of the sea and any harkening back to Blue Beach in Nice was welcomed.

Soren had already asked me out for New Year's Eve in Omaha. He and I would drive home together in my car, and I would drop him in Imogene. For December 31, he would use his parents' car, come up and spend the night at my house, so that he didn't have to navigate dark, icy roads back to Imogene. A week after that, I would drive us both back to Iowa City. Soren didn't have a car in Iowa City; he never had wanted one there since he lived on campus, and the U, as we'd already established, made it very hard to have a car anywhere near the dorms.

I pitched the idea of my cooking Thanksgiving dinner to Cass one afternoon in late October as we sat on her porch with the babies, taking in the autumnal view across the highway of fallow fields off in the distance, and trees in wonderful hues of muted oranges and yellows.

"Turkey is cheap," I said, bobbing Laura on my knee, "and there will be lots of vegetarian side dishes you can eat to your heart's content. I'll make my Nana's rice pudding—it's the best thing ever. And of course, green bean casserole and candied yams with marshmallows, cranberry sauce...all the usual stuff."

"Pie?" she asked.

"Of course, pie! Pumpkin and one other. I'm not too great with pie crust, though. You?"

"Never made one."

"Well," I said, "they have frozen pie crust now, and also pie crust kits in a box. Either way, we'll have pie."

Later I told Soren, "I talked a good game to her, but the truth of the matter is I have never cooked Thanksgiving dinner by myself before."

"Your family's in the restaurant business. You probably got cooking know-how by osmosis," he offered.

"Ha, maybe...maybe not."

"Well, we'll tackle it together, then, because I've decided to stay and help you."

"Hot damn!"

Yes, I'd been around the kitchen when holiday meals were being made, but with my grandmother and mother cooking, I never had to do the heavy lifting. But, forging right ahead with my steadfast belief that if you could read, you could cook, I pushed any qualms to the back of my mind and made myself believe I could do this.

Alan only had had a smattering of cooking utensils when they moved in together; Cass had none. I'd brought a few things back from when we shared an apartment together, but really they didn't have enough "*batterie de cusine*" to make this meal. Luckily lightweight inexpensive roasting pans were already on the market in 1969, and I grabbed one of those at the grocery store. Soren and I packed all of my own pans and casserole dishes in a box, along with two bowls and all the miscellaneous gadgets we'd need, and moved them out to Cass' before the big day, so I'd have an arsenal ready to use.

Soren and I shopped for all the food, and he even shared the cost with me, which was so great of him. He had also picked up two bottles of wine at the state liquor store.

"Wow fancy," I said when I saw them.

"It's not French wine," he announced to me, even though I could see that. "But it will go with the dinner okay. I just think we should drink wine with a holiday meal."

"I think it's great! Thank you so much!"

I needn't have worried about pies. The Piggly Wiggly sold both Morton's and Mrs. Smith's frozen ones. I'd seen those before, but had never tasted them, since my mother and grandmother had always made their own pies from scratch. I didn't feel I could pass up the chance to not have to concoct real home-made desserts, however, so I sprang for one each of Mrs. Smith's pumpkin and apple, and I baked them in my own apartment the Wednesday night. I wrapped them in dishtowels and packed them into the car where it was cold enough out that they stayed nice and fresh.

Soren and I showed up out at the farmhouse around 10:00 o'clock Thursday morning, and began the prep. The bird came with directions, and except for not having a roasting rack inside the pan, we followed them just fine. Soon the house started smelling like Thanksgiving should! I methodically went from side dish to side dish and prepared them. The oven was a bit crowded; cooking Thanksgiving dinner needs two ovens, it turns out, but like the myriad of families around the country with only one oven, we made it work.

Cass and Alan only had one big table in their house. It had to serve as kitchen and dining table both, and was the only decent workspace they had. So I commandeered it that day. As I cooked, Soren washed pots and pans right when they were used, so as to avoid a big pile up at the sink. And as soon as the dinner was ready, we turned the table into a buffet where everyone could just walk around it, and take what they wanted.

Cass had decided we would all eat in the living room, and she cleared off the coffee table in front of the couch and pushed the chairs closer to it. We would still have to sort of eat on our laps, but it was cozy and festive. She surprised me by finding actual Thanksgiving-themed paper plates and napkins in Woolworth's and she had bought them! They were really kind of cute and, of course, alleviated our having to do mounds of dishes afterwards.

The turkey was beautifully browned; I had tested it often to see if juices were running clear, since this was in the days before the pop-up timers and we didn't have a meat thermometer. But I did not know how to carve. Soren didn't think he did either, and Alan was thus deputized to do the deed.

"Pretend you are the dad in that famous Norman Rockwell painting," I instructed him. "You know what it should look like." He didn't do too bad of a job, and, using the only sharp knife we had, which was much too small, he carved out enough slices for us to feast on.

Cass, as I predicted, did not eat turkey, but she did partake of the rest of the meal, and I actually stopped paying attention to what she put in her mouth. She and Alan both praised the food. Soren put his arm around me and gave me a little squeeze of recognition, adding, "Your talents in the kitchen know no bounds."

"You helped plenty," I praised him, and meant it sincerely. "This isn't gourmet cooking by any stretch, but thanks. I do love Thanksgiving."

"I hardly ever went home for Thanksgiving," Cass said. "I either ate the school dinner in the refectory, or my parents came East and took me out to a restaurant."

"I just can't believe you know how to cook so well! I sure haven't had a meal like this in a good long while," added Alan, who, whether for show in front of Soren and me or because he was actually a *mensch*, got up and took it upon himself to retrieve the babies' bottles from the fridge and warm them on the stove in a water bath. He took Laura, and Cass took Paul, and they sat on the couch feeding and rocking them back to sleep. Alan was being a help-mate to Cass, who exchanged a knowing glance with me and smiled contentedly.

Cass and Alan had a more extensive music collection than I realized, and, after the babies were down, Cass came back out to the stereo system, and put on a record she had brought home from London, *What We Did on Our Holiday* by Fairport Convention, which set a wonderful tone to the dessert part of the meal.

"'Meet on the Ledge' says it all," Alan proclaimed, flopping down on a pillow near the coffee table, and he was right about that. There we were, four far-flung friends together again, sitting around after a big meal, snuggling infants, talking, laughing, singing, drinking wine. Everything was "for the best in the best of all possible worlds"…in our little world, at least.

Chapter Fifty-Two

"Tell Her No"...The Zombies

Right after Thanksgiving break, I got a call from my academic advisor to meet in her office. I hadn't the foggiest idea why I was being summoned.

"Maybe she wants you to be a T.A.," Cass suggested, "If she doesn't, she should."

"I don't think so. I've never tried out to be one, and I've never spoken to her about that at all. I just hope there's nothing wrong with my credit transfer, though. It would really screw me up not to graduate on time."

"Well, don't worry about it. But let me know!"

I need not have worried about it.

"I have a friend in Chicago, " she said, motioning for me to sit in the chair in front of her desk, "who works for a private foundation there, which is French. I doubt you've ever heard of it, but just so you know, the governmental French consulate is also in Chicago, and this is not their organization; however, they work closely together---it's a bit too long a story to go into here. The point is, the foundation is organizing, or reorganizing, I should say, their library of French films, and they are looking to hire someone to be the librarian. Now the position won't officially open until June, so my friend contacted me, because she thought some graduating senior French major would be interested in the job. And I thought of you."

"My goodness!" I exclaimed. "Thank you! Yes, I'd be interested!"

"Well, I'm not offering you the job. I'm putting your name forth for an interview for the position."

"I understand."

"So you would get in touch with them and set it up---perhaps for over spring break? The organization is called French Cultural Foundation or *Fondation Culturelle Française*---F.C.F. either way. And the office manager to whom you would address your inquiry is Madame Marie-France de Piaget, who is an old friend of mine from school. Like I said, this is a private foundation, and the family who own it is called d'Arivèque. It was a mother and son, only the mother died two years ago, and her son Jean-Paul has taken it over." She looked up and smiled at me. "Marie-France is a wonderfully kind woman who was very devoted to Madame d'Arivèque, and is to her son, also. She's really like a *seconde maman* to him."

"How old is he?" I wondered ...aloud. She wrinkled her nose.

"Oh, I don't know. Maybe in his forties by now. His father was killed during the war, and the mother was part of the first French delegation at the United Nations-- before she founded the FCF and then moved it to Chicago. You will no doubt hear all about the history of the organization." She handed me a slip of paper with the address and phone number of the FCF. "You could probably just set this up by phone, I would imagine."

"Well, I can't thank you enough, Professor Ilke. I'll get right on this."

"And don't forget, Sarah, you must register for the last two required classes in the major in our department: 18th Century French Novel and French Phonetics. They're only offered second semester."

"Got it," I nodded to her, even though I was still flummoxed as to why Iowa would require me to take phonetics when I already had it at THE SORBONNE. Sheesh. "And thanks, again!" Then it occurred to me to ask her, "Are you also recommending any other of your Iowa students to Madame de Piaget?"

"Just you. *Au revoir!*"

I left her office still rather stunned, pondering what this could mean. An alignment of the stars?! The "Age of Aquarius" upon me? How incredible that the job would be located in the city I'd already made up my mind to move to!

I looked up the date for Spring break, and discovered that it was Easter Week, March 22nd to Monday the 30th. I would probably have to make the appointment for mid-week, I reasoned; their office would no doubt be closed on Good Friday and Easter Monday.

"I feel like I'm going to have to go up the day before" I said when I told Cass the news. "First of all, as you know, because the train is slow and undependable if you have to actually be somewhere on time..."

"Oh yeah, ha ha! That's the truth! This isn't Europe!" she laughed.

"And also because I'd need a good night's sleep, don't you think? Before the interview?"

"Oh KID!, " Cass gushed at me, "You will be sensational! You'll start a whole new life in Chicago, speaking French and working with French people, and well, being French!"

"Whoa. First of all, I'm far from getting it..."

"You'll get it!"

"And secondly, it's a library job. Whatever that is. My degree will have nothing to do with library science. I may not even qualify for the post."

"Anyone who's been to college can find their way around a library, you know that. Why did they ask the French department for referrals and not the library science department if they need a real librarian so bad?"

"Probably because the friend is the French department chair! But I take your point!" I laughed, happy at this "logic" of hers.

I packed my car to go home for Christmas break with all my superfluous summer-weight clothing, as well as books to study for finals back in the Bluffs, and drove over to pick up Soren for the ride home. I would be exiting off the Interstate an hour out of The Bluffs to drop him in Imogene before finishing the journey to my house.

"I got an invitation to be on Law Review next year!" Soren said waiving a paper in front of me at the steering wheel as he got in the Rambler.

"Wow! Congrats! That's truly fab! And so prestigious! Now we'll each have a big announcement to hit them with at home, won't we?"

"So you're intent on moving to Chicago, then?"

"Well, I set the interview up for March 27th. I'll go up the 26th. After that, I'll either announce that, yes, I'm moving to Chicago to take a job in a French office—hope, hope--or I'll announce that I'm moving to Chicago to look for a job. Ha ha, so either way..."

Soren laughed, and said, "You always know what you want."

"I do?"

"Yes! If I had half your resolve, I'd be on the short list for a Supreme Court clerk gig."

"Making Law Review, you might be anyway!"

I had brought along the ever-faithful portable radio-tape player Cass had given me in Paris, and popped in the cassette to *Un Homme et Une Femme* so I could convert my boyfriend to Bossa Nova as we sped across Iowa. But Soren had also brought a tape, and he surprised me by insisting that I would have never heard of it, but that I would love it.

"It's by 'The City', " he said, showing me the little box as he took the cassette out.

"Oh, God! You told me about this album. How did you find a cassette version already?"

"The album's a year old now. You lost a year."

We put it on. It was indeed wonderful, and I did love it. Carol King was already famous for writing a lot of top 100 hits for girl groups that I had grown up hearing on AM radio, but this was her own band, and the album was their only one. Soren and I played it at least twice through before we got to his hometown.

When I pulled into his driveway around four in the afternoon, I felt I had to do the polite thing and go in to at least greet his mother, who would be the only one home.

"Unless my grandparents are already at the house, that is," Soren offered, more precisely. "Dad will still be at the office, and the other kids are doing school activities or playing basketball at the church gym."

Mrs. Carlysle peeked out the living room drapes as she heard the car motor in her driveway, and then met us at the front door. Soren and I briefly discussed his staying over at my house for New Year's, and my driving us both back to Iowa City the next week. His mother smirked a little bit, but didn't say anything that would spoil our plans, which were actually completely innocent. What kind of hanky-panky did she think could take place under my parents' roof after all?

I only stayed for a few minutes, begging off having coffee so that I could get back on the road. It was all small highways up to The Bluffs from there, and I had another hour drive ahead of me in the pitch blackness of the shortest days of the year.

Upon arrival, I left my stuff in the car for the moment, and went in to find Roslyn looking at comic books and Mad magazines scattered all over the living room floor. Our house was festooned in Chanukah banners, and the blue lights Sol had strung around the high rectangular windows of our living-dining room twinkled on the outside too, when lit up.

"Hi Scary Sari," Roslyn greeted me.

"Hello pin-head. Where's Mom?"

"Doing laundry down the basement. How long are you here for?"

" Too long. You on Christmas vacation yet?"

"NO! But tomorrow's our program. Wanna come?"

"Maybe." I went over to the basement door and called downstairs to Betty. "Mom! I'm home!"

"Sari! How was the drive? Did you take Soren?"

"Yes, it was fine. I'm tired, though. I've got stuff still in the car."

Betty came upstairs with a basket of laundry in her arms, which she put down and hugged me.

"Sari, can you work lunch and dinner shifts for the few days before Christmas? Nana hasn't been feeling well, and I've got to take her in before this really turns into something like, I don't know, flu or godforbid, worse."

"Yes, that's fine, but between shifts I've got to get out and do some Christmas shopping."

"Yeah, what did you get me?" Roslyn chimed in.

"Roslyn, set the table please," said Betty.

" Mommm, Sari's home," she whined, "why can't she do it?"

" Oh, just put a sock in it, and do what you're told," I snapped at her. "You're fu…you're thirteen years old now. Take some responsibility around here."

"You shut up!"

"Girls, please," Betty sighed. "Roslyn, go on…get with it."

I went back out to the car and brought in my summer clothes, took them straight to the basement, and hung them up on the pipes that stretched across the length of the un-finished part where the washer and dryer were. They would just hang there until I needed them again. Then I went into my room, closed the door, and unpacked the clothes I'd actually be wearing while home. I flopped down on my bed and looked around. My high school room seemed about the same as when I left it. Glossy photos sent away for-- or torn out of movie magazines-- of Dean Fredericks as Steve Canyon, David McCallum as Illya Kuryakin and Jackie Cooper as Hennesey, were still pinned to the bulletin board next to a big poster of the Eiffel Tower. I had to laugh remembering how, since I never went on dates in high school, I just lived inside television shows, and, of course, dreamed of going to Paris. My room was a testament to that, as if preserved in amber.

I didn't want to stay on the bed, however, afraid I'd just fall asleep until morning, so I went back out into the kitchen to ask my mother what was really wrong with Nana.

"We don't know. She's just dragging a bit."

"So you don't think it's serious? You didn't call your sisters, did you?"

"Oh, no. It's flu season. She's probably just got it worse than a younger person."

"Yes, I hadn't thought of that. I'll go see her tonight."

"You might not want to do that, Sari. If you catch it, you won't be able to work, and you could be sick for the holidays."

"Well, gee, that seems harsh. I have to see her."

"Just wait 'til I take her to the doctor. Maybe they'll put her on some medicine or something."

"All right," I pouted, thinking of her being ill, and my not being able to do anything for her.

Even though The Spot was open for dinner, as well as evening and late-night drinks, my father came home to eat some supper with us, leaving the bar in the hands of "the help" as he called the cook, the other waitress Bonnie, and his second-in-command bartender Mo, short for Morris.

I didn't much like Mo, and when I was young, I would tease him and call him Mo the Shmo, which was nipped in the bud by both parents admonishing me to be polite to him. He was an obnoxious sports fanatic who lived and breathed Nebraska football, so by the time I was in junior high, I never gave him the time of day if I didn't have to.

My father deigned to acknowledge my presence as he came in the house, having, obviously seen the Rambler station wagon on the drive.

"So, you're here?" he kissed me on the cheek and expected me to do likewise. "Did you take the Catholic boyfriend home?"

"Yes."

"And?"

"And what?"

"Is he coming up here for New Year's after all?"

"I told you he was. I mean, I asked your permission," I hastily corrected myself.

"You know," Sol started in with me right away, "I'm not going to have the talk with this boy because you're not going to end up with him. There's no future there. Forget it."

"You astound me," I said, catching a glance from my mother that said, "let it go." "I'm not going to end up with him because I'm moving to Chicago next June. But I am going to go out with him until then."

"Oh, now you're moving to Chicago."

"Yes! I have big news! My academic advisor recommended me for a job! I even have an interview lined up! I'll be going up there in March during Easter break for it!"

"What kind of job?"

So I told them all about the referral, and how this sounded like my dream job.

"I figured you would teach," Sol said. "Didn't we say we wanted you to become a teacher? I thought I made it clear to you how I feel about this. During the Depression, the teachers always had a job."

"Daddy, at the risk of repeating myself, I need to remind you that I never said I wanted to teach. I haven't taken education courses. I won't be graduating with a teaching degree from Iowa."

That didn't set well.

"Oh, you don't want to teach? Well, isn't that great? What DO you want to do?"

"I want to use French! To speak it on the job, maybe every day — or at least most of the time. There must be some jobs that need French. I'm just not sure what they are; but if I have a lead on this one, I'm certainly going to follow up on it."

"Well, good luck with that. You'll come crawling back here when you can't get anything and can't live on the economy of a place like Chicago. The rents there must be five times what they are here or even Omaha."

He had me there about the rent, but I would never come crawling back. I'd be a nanny for some family before I came back home. I'd work in a hotel, wait tables, or answer phones in an office.

I didn't know what I'd do. I just knew what I wouldn't do.

313

Chapter Fifty-Three

"Deep River"...African American Spiritual

I spent the rest of the vacation trying to avoid my father, which wasn't that easy since I picked up a lot of hours working at the bar; but I still made myself busy and unavailable for any of his "heart to hearts," where he did all the blustering-- really just taking the occasion to hear himself talk. I was, however, willing and able to have meaningful conversations with my grandmother, who was interested in hearing about Soren and our up-coming plans for New Year's.

"I didn't save myself for marriage," I confessed to her a few days after my arrival, when it was determined that she didn't have the flu after all, and I was free to visit her. "But at least I waited until I was of the majority age before I had sex."

"So do you think he's the one?" she had asked me.

"Maybe," I 'd answered. "I don't know."

"Well, like I told you before, I've always believed a little loving never hurt anyone," she answered.

No wonder she'd been "the fun mom"-- so much more modern and open than her peers-- to hear Betty and my aunts tell it.

Soren did arrive, as arranged, in the middle of the day on December 31, and we had made plans to go to a "hip" new bar in Omaha called The St. Moritz.

"So I guess they want to invoke a ski resort?" Soren wondered.

"Like anyone here would even know that," I sneered.

Nevertheless, that's where we would go, and at least try to conjure up some feeling of being in Europe.

Soren had driven up to The Bluffs in his father's fancy Buick roadster, so we took that to Omaha. A snow squall had come up, and driving was getting treacherous as we made our way quite far west in Omaha for those days. But the car was heavy, and Soren was a good enough winter driver that it didn't turn into a white-knuckle ride.

When we got there, the parking lot was packed. As we left the car and ventured into the freezing night air, our faces were hit by tiny ice pellets that seemed to be falling as crystals before our eyes.

"Geez, I can't see shit!" Soren laughed.

But I could see. I caught a glimpse of a crowd of people going in ahead of us, and I recognized some of them as being from my high school.

"Oh, God," I sighed, "those people went to school with me," I announced, pointing them out to Soren.

Within a bigger group, there was a foursome of former football stars and their dates. I explained to Soren that I'd been in British Literature with one of the guys.

"He actually got me into trouble with the ol' battle-axe teacher of that class because he always made me laugh!"

It was true. All through high school he'd dated one of our classmates of whom he said, completely straight-faced, "If she had an IQ a few points higher, she'd be a plant." And there they were! Still together? It didn't look like they were a couple because he was paying a lot more attention to the other woman in the group, whom I did not recognize. I did, however, know the other guy, a friend of Mr. Football but less popular. I knew I'd have to introduce Soren to them if they noticed us, and I hoped if I didn't call attention to myself, they wouldn't.

The St. Moritz did indeed make an effort, however pathetic, to have a continental feel. There was even a small fireplace---like a firepit really---in the middle of the large room, with a white lacquered bench surrounding it, and leather pillows spaced around that. All along three sides of the room were intimate booths, with other tables of varying sizes, filling the rest of the space. Each little booth had leather banquette seats and its own lamp. On the fourth wall was a raised platform stage. There was room for a small dance floor in front of that, and the long bar was at the end of the room nearest the entrance. Just like in my parents' bar, a narrow corridor could be seen off to the side, with pay phones and cigarette machines, leading to the restrooms.

The rest of the décor was ski-lodge chic, and you could, if you stretched your imagination, pretend to be in a lovely alpine resort, except for the fact that when you left the place, you walked out into a barren West Omaha landscape without a mountain for five hundred miles.

As we entered, fervently looking around for any empty area, we both caught sight at the same time of a miraculously open booth, and headed for it. As we wound our way through the throng, we passed by a large round table with leather armchairs, which my former classmates had claimed, and were placing their coats on the backs of the chairs.

"Sarah Shrier!" I heard above the din, and turned around.

"Hello," I said giving them a little wave and trying to sound friendly-- in an aloof way.

"How ARE you?" exclaimed Mr. Football.

"I'm great, thanks. How about you?"

"Couldn't be better. Happy New Year!"

"Same to you!" There was a pregnant pause with the group just watching Mr. F and me awkwardly reconnecting; and then I snapped back to my senses and introduced my date. "This is Soren Carlylse. We're at Iowa together." I had no idea where these people were in school, if indeed they were.

"Nice to meet you," said Soren offering his hand, which they all shook in turn, and, in a gesture of hail-fellow-well-met, gave their names, which let me off the hook because I doubted I could actually even come up with them. They were, it turned out, Bob McVaney, Victoria Brand (she of the low IQ), the high school football star whose name was Steven Turkle, as well as a woman named Janice something, whom I did not recognize. Victoria looked at me, as though reading my mind-- even with her amoeba-like brain-- and said, "I'm with Bobby now," as though needing to set the record straight that she and Steve were no longer a couple.

Soren and I got out of more conversation with this group by making it clear that we had to "grab that booth!" and doing so required hurrying away.

"So who **did** you run around with in high school? I'm assuming it wasn't that group." Soren asked me once we'd settled in and were drinking White Russians.

"I didn't run around in high school," I laughed, knowing he didn't mean it literally. "I was part of the wall-flower crowd: no dates, but, you know, smart; like… active in lots of clubs. I lived in my own little world. What about you?"

"Well, in my town, you couldn't **not** go around with everyone, especially with my being in a parochial school. My best friend, as I've mentioned to you before, was Martin --the one at MIT—and we hung out and did everything together. He was my tennis partner on the school team, too, and my lab partner. "

"Yes, I remember. Is he home now? "

"No, he didn't come back for this holiday, but I've seen him whenever we've been in town at the same time."

"And your school was all-boys, so did Imogene have an all-girls Catholic high school and then a mixed public one, too? It doesn't seem big enough."

"Oh hell, yes. Far be it for the kids who were in the same-sex grade school their whole lives, to be tossed into one high school building with raging hormones. All the girls we palled around with were from the girls' Catholic high school. I really didn't go out with anyone from Imogene Senior High itself."

"Why, because your parents didn't allow it?"

"Well, not exactly. They couldn't have kept that kind of tabs on me. It's because for three years of high school, I was dating a certain girl. And, Sari, I haven't really ever talked to you about her."

Well, that was the truth. Soren had never mentioned any serious relationship that he'd had. I suddenly wondered if we had been as intimate as I assumed we had.

"No, you haven't said anything about any other girl. I guess I should have asked, huh?"

"Well, it's not a big secret. She died the summer before senior year."

"Oh, my God, Soren. How awful. What happened?"

"It was a freak boating accident, and we were all there. Her parents had a ski boat, and they let all the kids use it out on Spring Lake. Their son usually drove the boat, and that hot summer day, we were skiing, as usual. My girl, Melinda... er ... Mindy... had gone down, so her brother put the boat in reverse to go get her. But her tow ropes got tangled up and... strangled her."

"And you all saw that happen!? That must have been horrific."

"I still can't really even believe she's gone," Soren said, and even in the dim light, I could see real sadness overtake his expression.

"Yeah, I don't know how you ever get over something like that. Or her brother! Godalmighty." I paused and looked at him. "Well, I guess you never do."

"Right." He took my hand across the table, and said, "Let's not ruin New Year's Eve talking about sorrow."

"Okay," I agreed, "but I get it that you might want to talk about her some time with me. I'm fine with that."

"Thanks, Sari. I mean that."

The more I pondered Soren losing his girl in a tragic boating accident, the more I realized that maybe his parents "tolerated" me because they'd seen, and no doubt worried over, their son's deep grief. It probably occurred to them that he'd never get over that girl Mindy, and be scarred the rest of his life. Soren was older than me. He'd been at Iowa a year before I got there; yet I was the only girl he'd taken home to meet his parents since the accident. Maybe the Carlyles had just been thankful he'd started to date again, and had stifled, for the time being, their inevitable great disappointment at their son dating a Jewish girl.

The St. Moritz had a band that came on about an hour after we walked in there, and we got up to dance to their covers of "Give Me a Ticket for an Airplane" and many Beach Boys hits. It was fun, and at one point, as I was doing my version of something like the Frug, I noticed Steve Turkle staring at me out on the dance floor. He must have been in shock that I had the moves. I couldn't blame him; I shocked myself.

Soren and I hadn't made fancy dinner plans for the evening because we knew the restaurants would be booked and expensive to boot, so we had decided that after a few drinks at the bar (I changed to Coke after my one "gown-up" cocktail), we would find a coffee shop or diner somewhere and just get cheeseburgers before seeing in 1970. I knew a little restaurant that fit the bill, Petey's Place, and it was actually about twenty-five blocks or so east on the same street as the St. Moritz. We left the bar about 11:00 o'clock, and headed off for food. Petey's was not very crowded at that hour, and we were still there when the new year struck. We leaned over the table and kissed each other.

"I hope 1970 is a great year for us both," he said.

"I think it will be!"

Heading back to my house, we rounded the corner of my street where, at the top of the hill my house was visible...and all lit up!

"My God!" I said, absolutely shocked to see all the lights on. "They had a New Year's Eve party and I didn't even know it? How can that be?" I let out a little snickering giggle.

But when we got to the driveway, it wasn't full of cars.

"What the hell?" I wondered.

We walked into my kitchen, which was the door closest to the where Soren parked, and there were my parents... Betty pacing around with a horrified look on her face, and Sol on the phone.

"What's going on?" I asked.

"Nana."

"OH GOD! Is she sick again?"

"Sari, she...we found her...she... passed away tonight."

"WHAT!!?"

I felt my knees give out, and the blood drain to my toes. I flung myself on a kitchen chair and began to wail.

"This can't be happening!! I just saw her! She was fine!!"

"She wasn't really too well, you know. It turns out she had a burst blood vessel in her brain and it caused a cerebral hemorrhage---a stroke."

"You, you, should have caught it," I sobbed. "The doctors! We all should have."

"It's hard to do, honey; no one knew this could happen."

"They should have seen it coming!! GOD how can this be?!" I was inconsolable, but then I realized, too, that my boyfriend was just standing there, stunned.

"Sorry, Soren," I sobbed, "here, have a seat."

"Let's all go into the living room," Betty said. "Soren, would you like some coffee?" He shook his head. Poor guy, he was a deer in the headlights with all of us going nuts around him.

We moved through the dining room and into the living room. Sol got off the phone and came in, also.

"Okay, I've talked to Arlene, and she'll fly out here tomorrow. Now we've got to call your other sister." He looked up and acknowledged my friend in the house. "Hi, Soren."

"Hello, sir," Soren answered. "I'm so sorry for your loss."

"Thanks." He said nothing to me.

"I'll call her," said Betty, "if I can find her number."

And from that moment on, the weekend unfurled in suspended animation for me. Soren spent the night sleeping in our basement, and then he drove back the next day. My two aunts, one of my uncles, and their entire families all arrived on various airplanes, so we had to make several runs to the Omaha airport to get them and bring them to The Bluffs. Roslyn moved in to sleep in my room. Auntie Arlene and her brood stayed with us, doubling up on our roll-a-way bed in Roslyn's room. Her husband would follow in a day or so. My other aunt, Gloria, her husband and one son went to stay at Nana's house. Auntie Arlene had two boys, Jason and Jeremy, who were teenagers now, I noticed, rather surprised when I saw how big they'd grown; plus their youngest, a sweet little six-year-old girl called Rhonda. My other little cousin Lionel, Gloria's only child, was nine. I was the oldest of all these cousins, some of whom were, however, older than Roslyn. We rarely ever laid eyes on any of these kids; once their parents had moved away, they hardly ever came back to visit.

Jewish funerals happen fast, but this death occurred on a national holiday, after which was Friday, and Jewish funerals were never on the Sabbath, so Sunday, January 4th would have been the first day they could have even had it. However, things were set back a few days, what with all those relatives, as well as some other people, needing to come from far away. The service had to be postponed one more day, when Uncle Gregory couldn't get a flight out of Phoenix, where he'd been on a business trip. It was unpleasant to think about delaying the matter, though. I didn't know much, but I knew Jews were never embalmed. I reasoned that since we were living in the modern world, however, they could refrigerate the body after all, without breaking any Talmudic laws.

My mother busied herself planning the meal of bereavement which would take place after the burial. It intrigued me that she was acting very particular about what would and would not be served. Even more shocking to me was when I found my mother and her sisters huddled with their heads together, going over the potential execution of Nana's will--of which Betty was executrix-- and the distribution of her things. Gloria, staying over at her Nana's house, had already started putting what she liked in boxes, which didn't set well with Arlene. Betty said she didn't care what her sisters took, that she didn't really want "any of Mama's *tchotchkes*."

As far as I could tell, Arlene and Gloria had each "married very well" and had all the material trappings of their own—fur coats and jewelry--that anyone could wish for; far more than my mother. But I found it to be normal that everyone would be sentimental for something of Nana's; I was, too. It was Betty's attitude I could not fathom. She really did have ice water coursing through her veins.

"I only ever gave her the very best --whatever gift –whatever the occasion," sobbed Arlene, "for Mother's Day, her birthday, the holidays."

(What she really wanted was to be with you and your children. She often lamented not being able to see her far-flung younger grandchildren grow up.)

Sol overheard me telling the aunts that I hoped they would let me have something of Nana's, too.

"I don't really care what," I told them, "but secretly I 've always been dreaming of having a string of her pearls. That would be so meaningful…oldest grandchild and all."

317

Sol yanked me away from them and pulled me into another room. In a loud whisper, he admonished me to keep out of it.

"You just keep still about getting any of your grandmother's stuff! " he barked at me. "This isn't the time or place."

"But they're talking about it ...and already packing her house up!" I argued.

"Stay out of it! It's their inheritance, not yours."

"OKAY! I was just hoping for some little thing...that's all. Leave me alone!"

"Hey—another tone with me, if you know what's good for you."

"YOU SHUT THE FUCK UP—how's THAT for a tone!"

I actually couldn't even believe those words came out of my mouth to him, but then, all of a sudden, he swerved around and his arm came up, extended out! He cuffed me across the shoulder, just catching himself before he struck my face. I stood there for a second and gave him a look that conveyed, I hoped, what a pathetic old worm he was, and then I started to laugh, which made him really mad.

I turned abruptly and left the room before he could regain any sort of composure. From that moment on, I vowed to have nothing more to do with any of them. I would be leaving for Iowa City right after the funeral and not looking back.

I called Cass long distance on my home phone and told her the whole story.

Soren phoned me, too, wondering if I wanted him up there at the service. I thought that was so sweet, even as I said, no, but would he mind heading back to school a few days earlier than I had planned?

The little Bluffs synagogue was pretty crowded on January 6th, when we finally had the funeral. We, the family, all sat behind a screen that had been set up, and Betty kept pulling out Kleenex tissues from her pocketbook, and handing them down the row of seats to me, Roslyn and the cousins. There was no music whatsoever: no organ, no choir, nothing recorded. And no one went up to eulogize her except the rabbi, who did know my grandmother, but still seemed perfunctory. Our Rabbi then was just this little nebbish we had all detested in Hebrew school. If he was an actual scholar, he kept the fact nicely hidden. Instead of talking about my grandmother and all the wonderful things she was known for, like baking the best cinnamon rolls in the known world; or instead of paying tribute to her for things like having come to America after emigrating from Russia, like thousands of others without two nickels to rub together, and having eventually run a business; or for being a leader in her religious community where we were all gathered (!), or even for having raised her children alone after her husband had died young from a heart attack... instead of any of that, he gave a garbled treatise on the meaning of Kaddish.

"Kaddish, " he said, pronouncing it "Kah-DEEESH," was believed to have been brought down from heaven by angels (*oh, so Jews believe in angels and heaven after all?*) as a bond to chain together heaven and earth, keeping those left living tied to those in the other realm, the realm of the dead. "This prayer is the guardian, if you will, of the people by whom alone it is uttered."

I didn't even know, or couldn't remember if I had once known, what I was saying when I said the prayer. The translation was always on the page, but I was too busy paying attention to the Hebrew to read it. I did know that the word death was never mentioned in it, that the prayer didn't acknowledge death because you were supposed to believe that whoever had died was going to come to life again in your heart; that this was a sanctifying power that the prayer gave the mourner. But I felt I would have been more soothed in my grief to hear a little Bach or read a little Emily Dickinson for Godsake, than to try to gain solace in trying to decipher some Hebrew enigma.

Someone who worked in our bar when I was younger—a Christian-- had once told me she thought Jewish funerals were so very sad because there was no afterlife to look forward to; it was all so final, especially for babies and children who died. I just thought Jewish funerals were so sad because nothing beautiful was permitted.

After the synagogue service, the adults all piled into a limousine provided by the funeral home, with the rest of us ushered into various peoples' cars to follow the hearse up Pearce Street to the Jewish part of the Catholic cemetery. We all huddled in a biting wind under a little canopy set up next to the grave, sitting in chairs placed on uneven Astroturf which appeared to undulate in waves under the congregation. Everything was in Hebrew. Again there was chanting but no real music, no flowers, no eulogies. Just the ceremony of people putting dirt on an upside-down shovel and pouring it over the casket, followed by the lowering of the body into the grave. And that was that.

We returned to the social hall back at the synagogue for the luncheon Betty had so carefully planned. In this, at least, she had departed from the typical, and ordered excellent, delicious food, some of which was the traditional noodle kugel, lox on a long silver tray flanked with hard-boiled eggs and capers, cream cheese and bagels; but the rest she augmented with wonderful pasta and vegetable salads, oil and vinegar coleslaw, tuna and egg salads in cut-glass bowls; huge trays of beautiful fruits of every kind, all cut up and heaped high. She had no sandwiches, especially not the typical funeral ones that churches served, which my mother always said she abhorred. Since this was taking place in a synagogue, she had to observe the rules of *kashrut*, even though we didn't keep Kosher, so no cheese and meat together or casseroles like lasagna. But she managed to provide copious offerings of everything she did serve, because she also detested buffets that looked empty or that ran out. For dessert there was an entire separate table filled with cakes, pies, and another of Nana's specialties: *mandelbrot* — not as good as hers — and my favorite sweet thing of my entire childhood: thumbprint cookies.

My family could probably have used my help some more, either in the bar or at home, corralling the cousin kiddos, or cleaning Nana's house. But instead, after the luncheon I packed up my clothes and schoolwork, as well as the presents I was taking back to Cass, and packages of left-overs from the funeral luncheon, and hit the road.

I went to Imogene and spent the night at Soren's, having sort of invited myself to do so, and the next morning we would set off back to Iowa City. Soren's family was friendly enough to me, knowing the great loss I had just suffered. They treated me as though I were just a friend driving their kid back to campus, and not his girlfriend. There was no drama.

The Carlyle house couldn't have been more different from mine — a rambling Cape Cod split level indicative of being in the wealthier class of the small town, but by no means a stately mansion. It was the sort of architect-designed bespoke subdivision home that would be among the finest addresses in Imogene. It sat on a deep lot with a carpet of lawn spreading out in front and yew bushes flanking the limits of the property. While mostly covered by snow and barren in winter, the lawn and cluster of rose bushes by the doorway would be beautiful in spring and summer.

They had a comfortable den where I slept on a sofa-bed in one of the lower levels — not a basement, but far from the other bedrooms. There was a powder room down there, so I had my own little guest quarters.

I neither asked my father's permission to miss those last work shifts I was supposed to do, nor waited for my last paycheck. I forfeited the money to be able to clear out of his sphere of influence. Much as I figured I'd have to be back home at some point after graduation, before taking off for good to Chicago, the thought depressed me, and I wouldn't let myself dwell on it. The further along I drove with Interstate 80 spreading out in a trail behind me, the better I felt.

I dropped Soren off at his residence, and since it was on the same side of the river as Cass and Alan's house, I just headed on out to the farm before returning to my apartment.

Cass greeted me warmly, but with a subdued manner when I pulled up to her front door.

"I was worried about you, kid, " she said, hugging me tight. "Are you okay? What a terrible loss for you. I sure did love your Nana."

"I know," I started to cry. The floodgates just seemed to burst. "I don't know what I'm going to do without her. I feel like an orphan."

We just stood there clinging to each other for a minute; then I dried my eyes, and went around the back of my station wagon. My mood lifted as I lifted up the tailgate.

"Look what I've brought you! Merry Christmas! Sorry it's not wrapped," I said, pulling out the folded-up twin stroller. I undid some latches and the basket bottom fell down, followed by the two seats. I attached the yellow gingham canopy to it and *voilà*! An alluring sight to behold: two seats, one handle, one canopy lid, a big basket for storage. It was a thing of beauty! Cass couldn't help but gasp.

"Oh SARI, thank you SO MUCH!" she chirped, calling up to the house, "Alan! Come see this!"

Even though there wasn't snow on the ground in Eastern Iowa like The Bluffs had, it was still very cold out, and Cass had come out to greet me with just her sweater, no coat; so I suggested we take it inside to show Alan.

"It may be a little bulky to get in and out of the house," I warned.

"Well, we can just leave it on the porch then. No one will steal it out here!"

Alan came to the door and expressed his own surprised approval of the gift.

"That is so thoughtful of you, Miss Shrier!" he exclaimed. "Isn't that just something!"

"And how are my little snuggle bunnies?" I asked.

"Anxiously waiting for their Auntie Sari to be back!" Cass cried, telling a fib, of course, since they were too young to know me, really.

"I also have another present," I announced, and ran back out to the car to produce the towels wrapped as a bundle in left-over Christmas paper I'd found at The Spot, where Sol had obviously given gifts of some kind to his best customers. I had tied mine with string, because I didn't have any ribbon.

Cass opened it up: two of each: bath towels, hand towels and washcloths in that soft turquoise hue. All the linens were trimmed in monochromatic embroidery along the edges.

"Oh, gads," she said lifting them up. "If these aren't gorgeous! And so soft!! Ha! Whether we need them or not, eh?" she winked.

"Well, I did notice that you could use some," I said a bit sheepishly.

"We thank you!!! Over and over and for everything! We thank you! To the ends of the earth we thank you! " Cass sang.

*As if I could ever **ever** repay Cass (and her family, it must be said) for everything they'd already done for me---with more to come. I would have brought her and the kids the moon if I could have.*

Chapter Fifty-Four

"Put a Little Love in Your Heart"...Jackie DeShannon

The Sorbonne stint had done a number on my GPA and probably kept me from getting into Phi Beta Kappa or graduating with honors; but at least after that first semester back, and the ensuing final exams, my grades were high again. I finished the term with a 4.0.

However, my final semester at the U of Iowa was starting off with both a whimper and a bang.

At the end of the first week of classes, I had phoned Cass to tell her I was coming out there to take her to the laundromat, as was our routine, but I had to warn her that I was in a state of high dudgeon. For one thing, we'd had a major snow storm, which meant I had a long haul to dig my way out of drifts, both nature-made, and left by the snow plow. That took more time than I would have desired. But mainly, I had to unload on Cass about the two-- shall we say-- wrinkles in my otherwise smooth last semester of university. I drove out to the farmhouse, pulling up and around the gravel drive as close to the door as possible, and stomped up the stairs kicking as much snow off my boots as I could before going in.

"My French lit professor is certifiably insane," I announced to Cass, taking off my coat, and flinging it on the sofa. "I wonder if Alan knows this guy: a Brit named Hugues Berry? He pronounces his first name in French 'ugue' like 'fugue.' He told us that he's descended from the Dukes of Berry. But guess what? Anyone descended from the Dukes of Berry won't have the last name BERRY! That's such a crock."

"What would it be?" she laughed, slightly bemused by my mood.

"Well, if I remember correctly...we toured the chateaux of the Loire, as you know... I think they said the name was d'Alençon. Anyway, the Dukes of Berry were royal. He obviously doesn't know what he's talking about; but it's also evident that he thinks little students sitting in the middle of corn fields wouldn't realize that."

"Is that why you think he's crazy?" she asked looking at me askance.

"Not only that! He came in today and accused someone in the class of leaving a thumb tack on his chair! What is this, kindergarten? Of course no one copped to doing it. I don't believe college students would do that. They'd put LSD in his coffee or something more creative!"

"I'll ask Alan if he knows him. Most foreign instructors are here in some other capacity, too, like in the comparative lit department or the Workshop," Cass assured me.

"And besides that, he's only teaching one book this entire semester: *Candide*. Don't get me wrong, I love Voltaire; *Candide* is a great work of art. But really a whole eighteen weeks on a short book? I know...philosophy, yes, but come on! We did *Candide* in my 18th Century Lit course in Paris, because it was part of 18th Century LIT. Now I'm about to embark on a whole semester of this one book? He's nuts. I mean it."

"You've made a pretty good case. What does Ilke say?"

"Well, I haven't gone in to complain about him or anything. I'll bet she's heard from people in the department though. This kind of stuff gets around."

"What else are you taking this semester?" asked Cass, looking glum.

"Oh, funny you should ask. My other *bête noire*. I have to take French Phonetics! The University of Iowa requires it for every French major, which is fine, but they don't recognize the actual course I did at the Sorbonne in that! I have to take ours in order to graduate with Iowa's French major. And get this: FRENCH nationals are in the class!!"

"What?" Cass asked, amazed.

"Yes, indeed. Quite the shocker. Did I go to Paris and take English classes? NO! So why are they allowed in my class? And all of them are grad students to boot!!"

"I have no idea. You're right, that makes zero sense," Cass commiserated with me.

"And first thing, he put a word on the board, '*abbaye*' and asked for the pronunciation. So aside from the French students, I was the only one who knew it. He said, 'Oh, full marks, Mademoiselle Shrier,' and I said, 'Well, thank you, but I just got back from a year with Professeur Filiolet at the Sorbonne.' I fully expected him to know that name in his own field! But it didn't really register with him. This is going to be a long semester."

Cass and I gathered up the baskets of laundry, put the babies in as many layers of clothes as we could find, and took them and the little car seats to my car. We liked a particular laundry place next to our favorite pizza parlor, Pagliai's on Bloomington Street, where the wafting scents of baking crust never failed to entice us to take some home after the clothes were done. That was reward enough for the drudgery of schlepping kids and clothes out in the winter chill.

I was worried for Laura and Paul again; Cass and Alan didn't seem to dress them warmly enough for my quasi-Jewish-mother standards.

"The kids need snowsuits," I announced to Cass as we sat on the floor, and tried to entice the babies to engage with some toys the laundromat kept in a little play area by the window.

"I know, but they're expensive, and the thing is, kids grow out of them so fast!"

"So let's go look at Goodwill or the Salvation Army store or something then," I suggested, "because whatever we find will be cheaper than if you have to end up buying antibiotics!"

"You are, as usual, spot on. Maybe we could find two that could fit them through this Spring." She took her billfold, pulled out three dollars, and held them up.

"Well," I said, "that won't do it, but I've got some money. Part of which is going for a large mushroom pizza before we leave here. I'm dreaming of it already!"

Cass smiled at me her gratitude, both for the idea of buying the kids snowsuits, but also for a vegetarian pizza.

The Salvation Army store had one snowsuit that would fit Paul, so we bought that for $2.50, and then we headed off to another place in Coralville that Cass knew — a nondescript thrift store that had baby things. Right away we spotted one that would be great for Laura, but it was more expensive. Cass then did something I'd never seen her do: she bargained with the clerk for that baby snowsuit, making the case that they were poor grad students living on a T.A.'s paltry salary, with two children, and what did the lady think she might be able to do for them? Cass began bouncing Laura on her hip. The clerk looked at her and lowered the price by three dollars to six. Cass looked at me and I nodded "ok" and paid for it.

"So Miss Laura Bronwyn Jones, you have the fancy one!" sang Cass, as we left with the package, and tucked the kids back into the car. I felt a hundred times better seeing them both in those fat snowsuits. Paul's was yellow with an embroidered train on the front and a fluffy yellow hood. Laura's was all white, quilted, sporting a white ruffled hood, and little stitched pockets. It had the mark of a fancy brand name that Cass recognized: Canada Goose.

"This probably originally went for something like eighty dollars, " she told me, zipping Laura into it.

"You have to be joking," I snorted. "Who would pay that for a baby outfit the kid would only wear for a few months!?"

"Oh," Cass sighed, "you'd be surprised." And I realized Julia probably dressed her like that her whole life.

"Well, weren't we lucky to find it, then?" I declared, even though I phrased it as a question.

I should have realized that expensive clothing had its merit. Cass's own wardrobe was holding up beautifully, even as she went from privileged student to TWA stewardess to impoverished wife and hausfrau. Her navy-blue wool Saks Fifth Avenue winter coat was the same one she had brought to Iowa three years ago, and had worn in Chicago with me, and it still looked like a million bucks. Her shoes and boots were also beautiful, showing little sign of wear. The sweaters she wore with her jeans were mostly cashmere, and even the underwear we washed every week was of such fine quality that it never seemed to wear out. Everything Cass owned now was the same as it had always been; she'd bought nothing new since London.

Alan's clothes, on the other hand, were all pretty raggedy, but then Alan wore that as a badge of honor. He could dress in jeans for class, and did so with a tweed jacket that had the time-honored and de rigueur patches of brown suede on the elbows---his one nod to "professionalism." He rarely wore a tie, but if there was a meeting with the dean or a faculty function, he gussied the outfit up with a tie and maybe some khaki pants. His shirts were threadbare at the collars, and his shoes left a lot to be desired. He wore

Converse basketball shoes to class, and his dress-up shoes were loafers. He still had those motorcycle "stompin' boots" as we called them, but that was all. Once it turned cold out, Alan seemed to forgo dressing like a professor, even for class, and wore a ratty sweater under an old black leather jacket, and jeans.

I didn't worry so much about Cass, and I didn't care about Alan's lack of warm clothing or how he coped with the weather. But I confided my angst to Soren about the kids. They were turning six months old now, and growing like the proverbial weeds. I didn't see how Cass and Alan were going to keep up with the stuff they would soon need...times two! I didn't have the kind of money that could support myself in my apartment and their children, too.

"You know," I told Soren, "I can't really lend them any more money. I've got this trip to Chicago coming up in a few weeks for the interview, and I'm going to have to save up for the train, plus the night in a hotel. It's not going to be easy. It isn't as though I can ask my grandmother for money now." I started sobbing just thinking of her and wished I hadn't invoked her name.

"Sari, I'll give you the money for the hotel if you want."

I looked up in disbelief. "I couldn't do that," I told him flat out.

"Sure you could. You can pay me back...right out of your first paycheck."

"But Soren, that won't be until June! IF I get the job, that is."

"I think you're good for it!" he laughed.

I didn't know if I were going to take him up on that offer, but it made me feel so relieved and grateful that he'd made it to me. I hugged him and kissed his face all over. He kept laughing, delighted he'd cheered me up so.

"I do adore you, Sari," he said, in a rather subdued tone all of a sudden. "I just wish my parents could know the you I do; you're generous to a fault, you're sweet and kind and oh yes, outspoken."

"Well, what do you mean? You are all those things, too. They've met me; don't they recognize that we're alike?"

"They don't. All they can see is the big difference between us—religion."

"Well, Soren, we've been through all this. We're not going to go off and get married or anything, so what are they so worried about? Don't they like me—for a friend to you?"

"Not for a girlfriend."

"Because I'm not Catholic?"

"And my mother also said you weren't 'cute' enough, " he made air quotes.

I was taken aback by that remark, but didn't let it upset me. I sort of smiled at the cut, and said, "Well, sure---she's entitled to her opinion, I guess."

"I don't agree with her!! Don't get me wrong!"

It was anathema to me that people in "our day and age" were still judging others by their looks. It only occurred to me to like people for their personality, their character, and the way they treated me. IF they were handsome, cute, beautiful like Cass was, or good looking in any conventional sense, that was a perk. What really counted was if they were sweet, kind, not snobby, intellectually curious, thoughtful and loving.

I pondered all that for a few minutes before snapping back to what I really wanted to talk to Soren about-- besides my looks. I announced to him that I had an idea: "I'm going to write to Cass's parents and tell them they ought to at least meet their grandchildren. I think if they did, they'd lift the ban on helping Cass financially, and that would solve her problems."

"Oh, whoa, there, Nellie. Are you sure that's such a good idea? You'll risk driving a wedge between her and Alan. He hates them and they hate him."

"I'll cross that bridge when I come to it. Let's just see if they're amenable to the idea of visiting her first. Maybe they could send a car for her to go to them."

"Alan would be furious."

"Yeah, I guess so. Okay, I'll suggest they come into Iowa City-- for even just a day-- and see her. They can time the visit to coincide with Alan's classes so as to not run into him."

So that is what I did. On the coldest, bleakest night yet, in early February, 1970, I sat at my kitchen table and composed the following letter to Julia and John-Wilfred Hyde:

Dear Mr. and Mrs. Hyde,

323

I hope this letter finds you both well, and I'm sorry if writing to you out of the blue strikes you as very strange. I just want to assure you that I still have feelings of deep gratitude to you both, and I wanted to take the opportunity to tell you that you have twin grandchildren, Paul Hyde Jones and Laura Bronwyn Jones, who are absolutely adorable! I know you would fall in love with them at first sight. I fervently hope you will get in touch with Cass, and come to Iowa City to see her and the babies. I think I know how angry you were with her, but she's in rather dire straits now, and I'm hoping that if you saw her, you could forgive her and perhaps give her some financial help with the babies. I'm just asking you to consider this. I am at your service for any arrangements. Cass does not know that I'm writing you. Thank you both very much for reading this.

Sincerely,
Sarah Shrier

Before Soren could talk me out of sending it, and before I could change my own mind, I took it to the Iowa City post office and put it in the drive-up box. By the time I was leaving for Chicago in mid-March, I still had had no answer.

Chapter Fifty-Five

"Intermezzo Op. 118 No. 2"...Johannes Brahms

As I had noted on the calendar when planning my Chicago trip, the University timed its closing for Spring break that year to coincide with Easter week, which was convenient for me. Easter was relatively early, falling as it did on March 29, so we had the last classes on Friday, March 20, and didn't have to resume school until March 31. That was an Easter miracle right there.

I found that I was becoming exceedingly nervous before my scheduled departure on the Tuesday for my Wednesday interview at the F.C.F. Obviously, one of my main concerns was what to wear for it. I consulted with Cass.

"Of course, your kilt is my number one choice for all things dressy, " I told her, "but we aren't in the dead of winter anymore and it gives off 'Christmas' really. I could wear your blue dress with the pink sash, again, but it's sort of too dressy, don't you agree?" I was rambling, thinking out loud with her.

"I think you should wear navy blue," she said finally, giving the problem her full attention.

"Yes, the French do wear a lot of that color, " I agreed. "But what do I have that could even be construed as chic?"

"Well, you have white blouses, and you have the faux pearls. So all you really need is a skirt, and not a flouncy summer one. You need a straight skirt and wear it with nylons, not socks."

"And a cardigan?" I wondered. " It's hard to match blues, so maybe a grey sweater?"

"No cardigan."

"Okay, I have a navy-blue box pleated skirt. Will that do? What about a grey blazer with it?"

"Listen, wearing a box pleated skirt and a blazer, you're going to look like you just got off the bus of a private school. Why don't you skip the jacket? A skirt and blouse is professional looking enough."

"All right...if you say so."

She paused and then added, "Also—and this is just my opinion--don't carry your blue fake Hermès purse to the interview. You don't want them to think you're so wealthy you don't need the job. Once you get it, though, then by all means, carry that puppy all the time!"

"Good thing you told me that, " I confessed. "I wouldn't have thought about looking TOO good. Ha!"

A few days before I was to leave for Chicago, a package came for me with a letter from my Aunt Arlene in Phoenix. I hadn't even heard from my parents since I'd stormed out of the house after Nana's funeral, but I figured maybe Betty and the aunts had spoken a bit about the incident with Sol, and that's why she was writing me. I felt validated for my feelings about Nana, no matter the coldness of Betty and the outrageous antics of Sol.

But the letter wasn't about that. Auntie Arlene explained in it that she knew I was wanting a little memento of my grandmother's, and she had picked something out for me she hoped I would like. I read this letter enthralled, and was excited to see what was in the box. It turned out to contain two small items: a green leather passport case that Nana had carried on a European tour aboard the HMS Queen Elizabeth in the 1950's; and a miniature travel clock, which had a latched fold-down cover that acted as a base when you set it next to the bed. She must have taken that on trips as well. I didn't recognize it, but if Arlene said it was Nana's , I believed her. I would use the clock on the trip to Chicago, certain that it would bring me luck; and I would cherish both of these things for the rest of my life.

Cass called on the Monday night to wish me all good karma and the best of luck, and to cheer me on to victory and a most wonderful job. Soren showed up early Tuesday morning to drive my car and me to the station. He would keep the car and pick me up late Wednesday night. The train left Iowa City at 7:30 and would take four hours to get to Chicago; but it was cheap, and nicer than a Greyhound bus, which was my only other alternative.

I arrived at Chicago's Union Station and, for the first time, was not met by a limo! "Knowing Cass certainly had had its benefits those other times!" I laughed to myself. I lugged my stuff out to the curb, got in the queue, and took a taxi to the Allerton Hotel, where my parents always stayed when they went to Chicago.

The next day dawned bright and cold, even for March. I bathed, did my makeup—very sparse, as usual, dressed meticulously, and took my coat and gloves to the hotel lobby, along with my suitcase that they were letting me store, because I had to vacate the room by noon. I had decided to have at least a cup of tea in their coffee shop. Hotel food was really expensive, so I didn't have lunch; but I figured even if they charged me a dollar for tea, I had to drink something hot. However I found I was so hungry, that I felt I had to have something in my stomach or I'd faint; so I splurged on toast, too.

At noon, I was still early, so I went out onto Michigan Avenue to find the exact location of the building that housed the French Cultural Foundation offices. I didn't have anything but the address, and I didn't know the street well enough to gauge how many blocks it was from the hotel. In fact, it wasn't too far, and I still had almost an hour before my appointment. So I walked on much farther-- up to the Art Institute and sat in its garden. Luckily the sun had heated the benches up nicely, so I could sit there and not freeze.

I tried to go over what I thought the interview would be like, but the truth of the matter was, I had no idea. I'd never been on an interview before except at the Iowa Memorial Union, and that had been a mere formality. I had my resumé with me, but even that was slim and probably not in the correct form, either, since I'd just copied the old one from Julia that I'd used before…when it didn't really matter.

Finally, it was twelve-forty-five, and I made my way to the 800 block of North Michigan Avenue. I would be about ten minutes early but I didn't mind waiting. Maybe there would be forms to fill out anyway. I found *Fondation Culturel Française* in the building directory, and took the elevator to the twelfth floor. That had to be near the top; the building wasn't very tall and pretty much dwarfed by its neighbors. Stepping out of the elevator doors, I entered a foyer that was right in the offices, which surprised me. I went over to a high mahogany counter with a switchboard behind it and two receptionists, one wearing a headphone, answering calls, and the other facing the lobby. She spoke to me in French.

"*Bonjour, Mademoiselle. Puis-je vous aider?*"

And I answered, "*Bonjour, Madame* (even though I really didn't know her age or marital status), *je suis Sarah Shrier, et j'ai un intervue avec Madame Marie-France de Piaget.*"

She beckoned me to have a seat with "*Je vous en prie, Mademoiselle,*" and I waited to be summoned. At precisely the hour, a much older, very elegant-looking woman appeared. She was about my own height--so fairly short-- wearing a beautiful Chanel-style (real Chanel even?) black bouclé wool suit with a boxy jacket and a white blouse under it and an (obviously real) Hermès scarf draped around her thin shoulders. She extended a charm-braceleted wrist to me and I shook her hand as she introduced herself, and then invited me to follow her to her office. She led me down a beautifully decorated corridor painted the lightest of blue and trimmed in white crown molding . The walls were dripping with French art. Her office was in a corner and had two banks of windows looking out towards Lake Michigan and the Chicago shoreline. I sat on a Louis XV style chair in front of her glass-topped cherry wood writing table, a small desk with cabriole legs and little claw feet. She spoke to me in English -- sort of..

"May I have your *curriculum vitae studiorum?*" she smiled at me across the table.

I presumed she meant my resumé because that is all I had with me, but I had never heard it called anything in Latin. She took it from me and tucked it into a leather zipped pouch on her desk.

"I shall explain a bit about the *Fondation*. I know Dr. Ilke referred you, so I am going to assume she told you something already about our organization?"

"A few things, " I answered.

"We are a private foundation, fully privately funded, but we work in close association with the actual French consulate here. We are not, however, under the aegis of the French government." She went on to tell me that their relationship with the consulate was one of mutual cooperation, and that they collaborated on any variety of projects; but otherwise, The FCF was an entirely separate entity.

"Professor Ilke explained to you, did she? -- that the foundation's founder, Madame Marie-Aveline d'Arivèque, had had close ties to the French delegation of the nascent United Nations?"

I nodded. She continued explaining that it wasn't unheard of for the FCF and the UN to take part in joint ventures, and that the Foundation still had a presence in New York, even though the headquarters offices had been moved decades earlier, as I understood her to be saying, to Chicago.

"We also have a satellite office in Paris, and our Foundation has major family ties in Geneva."

She did all the talking, telling me that if I started to work there, the organization's mission would become clearer to me than it was during this interview. She said that before I left, she wanted to give me a tour of the offices-- to show me where the new lending library of "mostly films but also other materials" would be. That would also house the librarian's office.

"We are currently under major construction," she explained, "which is why the job really doesn't start until June."

"That is perfect for me, as it turns out, " I offered, "since I graduate in May."

"Precisely, " she answered, and then leaning ever so slightly forward towards me, asked me a question I found most strange: "Tell me, are you uncomfortable around a crippled person?"

Crippled? Do we even use that term anymore? Surely this was a poor translation of what she would have said in French?

"No!" I answered, "Of course not."

"Do you wonder why I ask it?"

"I— I guess— so," I answered, befuddled.

"Because many people are, and they do not admit it." And then she switched into French. *"Notre président est un handicappé."*

I didn't say anything, but I nodded to let her know I understood.

"You will, of course, meet him, though possibly not today."

And at that, we got up and headed back out to the hallway where she led me to a section of offices blocked off by a large wall of plastic to keep construction dust out of the rest of the space. However, she, to my surprise, lifted up a flap, and we went inside. I saw a fairly large theater-like room with a projection booth being built. The walls were lined with shelving and the half-dozen or so theater seats, as yet to be installed, were propped up against the raised portion of the booth's outside wall. The floor slanted, so the seating would go in like an actual movie house, I surmised. Down at the bottom was an office desk that already had a phone on it as well as an IBM Selectric typewriter, and a Rolodex. There were some file cabinets and a coat rack in the corner, but no outside windows in this place; it was a true soundproof room.

"We are in the process of reconfiguring this space to be an actual film library and mini *cinémathèque*, where films may also be previewed. Why? Because we shall be loaning them out to schools and universities or other organizations. The post we have created is, therefore, first off, one of curating and cataloguing the collection, which grows and changes all the time, by the way. And secondly, we anticipate that the librarian will advise the schools and interested parties as to what is available, and will coordinate the loans, and keep the records of them. We shall lend them out free of charge."

"Free?! Wow, that would be quite a boon to someone's class!" I said, immediately wondering if that sounded too enthusiastic.

"Yes. We are trying to implement our founder's vision to expand our offerings as an educational as well as cultural service."

Before I could ask what the cultural components were, other than films, she began to explain more about the library's construction, and how there would be a wall of windows to the corridor side of the room so it wouldn't be like working in a bunker.

"The room is to be designed to not let sound out, and also those curtains would probably need to be drawn if a film were being played. Light from the hallway would get in if they were left open."

"I see, " I said, wondering just how much of this job would entail watching films!

"Perhaps you are wondering why we would like to hire an American-English speaker first and foremost?"

"I... well, sure..."

"Because the librarian will be a liaison to schools in the entire region, and indeed, nationally, too, if it comes to that. The French consulate here in Chicago encompasses a twelve-state area; we are hoping to be wider than that even, in scope. We need someone who can talk to schools anywhere. We would also

327

like the librarian to preview all the films that come in, and write short synopses in both languages to be put in with the mailings. *Vous comprenez?"*

"*Oui, Madame. Parfaitement.*"

"And will you be earning by chance, a degree in education as well as French?"

"I'm afraid not, Madame, " I answered, thinking that might be the end of this interview.

We left the construction zone and walked back through an area of cubicles, past a lounge-type room and a copy center. People greeted Madame de Piaget with "*Bonjour, Madame*" every time we passed someone's desk. Some of them smiled at me.

When we got back to her office, she offered me a spot on a small sofa, and she sat in a wing chair next to it. She then took out my resumé and gave it a cursory read-through, as I sat there, more and more worried about my lack of education courses, but happy I had seventy-two credit hours of French from the Sorbonne. She looked up and handed me a brochure on the Foundation, and then she elaborated on some of the other aspects of the work the organization did: lecture series, concerts, scholarships for French study abroad programs, a local newsletter to the Chicago-area French community, and all sort of information dissemination.

"The post of librarian is new because we are expanding our offerings. We very much need someone to coordinate all of them."

Besides films to lend out, there would also be film strips, slide sets, recordings, travel information on France, its regions, and *La France d'Outre-Mer*; illustrated brochures on France and its culture like the one she gave me. They even provided a wealth of useful information about art exhibits coming to the U.S. from France. And to that end they had a strong working relationship with the Art Institute of Chicago. Another area of interest was the French culinary world, and the FCF was a great source of knowledge about it in the United States, with lists of French cooking schools, chefs, restaurants, places that sold French foodstuffs and cooking supplies. They put all this in their monthly newsletter, and had an entire publishing department within the offices.

"There is one other thing we — we members of the *équippe*, so to speak-- do that I should explain to you, " Marie-France de Piaget told me after about an hour of touring and interviewing. "Our president lives in a very large mansion on Lake Shore Drive, which also serves as a sort of welcome center for visiting French dignitaries. And as such, he entertains often in his home, sometimes several times per week. Part of all our jobs is to help where we can and be of service to Monsieur d'Arivèque, making ourselves available, for example, as dinner guests or perhaps being part of an audience of spectators for a lecture or discussion group, or even a musical recital he might hold. The home is so large that it has a staff resembling a hotel, and indeed, many of the rooms are guest suites where the various luminaries who come to Chicago can, and often do, stay. He offers that service to the French consulate because his mother did it previously, and also because he has the means to do it. He's a very generous man. We work in tandem with the Consulate on that part of it, of course. They are invited to house their guests at *la maison Arivèque* rather than using a hotel. It is a great boon to them. "

I had no idea what to say to that, since I couldn't even imagine the scope of what she was describing. I ventured the opinion that , "The house must be incredible" and smiled.

It sounded like this family had more money than the Hydes...and God.

"Would you be willing to participate in this aspect, as well as the library duties?"

"Yes, Madame."

What was I going to say... no?

"Even before I saw your c.v., I knew that you were a graduate of *La Sorbonne* because my friend Marianne Ilke mentioned that. My brother-in-law is Yves Brunsvick. Perhaps he was one of your *professeurs?*"

Ah hah. So maybe that was how my name came up when she and Dr. Ilke discussed this job opening. Dr. Ilke hadn't said a word to me about her knowing a Sorbonne professor's sister-in-law. Yves Brunsvick was not only a teacher in the *Cours de Civilisation Française* — that was his hobby! He was Secretary General of the French delegation to UNESCO in Paris! Everyone knew him.

328

"I did not have Monsieur Brunsvick for a teacher, Madame, but I was very fortunate to be able to go on a tour of the UNESCO building that he gave my group from Pella College; and so, yes, I did meet him. I was awed by him...and of course-- that building and all the art in it! I'm doing an art history minor."

"Good!" she said. And then she looked straight at me and said, "I would like to offer you the position."

I almost couldn't believe my ears. I hoped I hadn't gasped, but I'm afraid I might have. I just sat there for a second, as though in shock. She must have seen this reaction because, as if to reassure me that I had indeed heard correctly, she added, "You come highly recommended, Mademoiselle Shrier. Follow me to my administrative assistant's desk and she will finalize your employment."

She took me over to another part of the office to fill out some forms and at the end, we talked a few minutes about when the position would officially be open. I said I could be there almost immediately after my May 15th graduation, so she set a June 1 start date.

"Je vous souhaite un très bon après-midi, Mademoiselle."

We shook hands. I thanked her profusely, gathered up my things, and exited down to the lobby, ecstatic to be back out in a sunny Spring day on Michigan Avenue in my new town. I understood immediately why That Girl had twirled around with her parasol on the streets of New York.

Chapter Fifty-Six

"Sisters of Mercy"...Leonard Cohen

Soren picked me up and was thrilled with my news as I got off the train and cried out, "I got the job!!"

"This calls for celebration!" he said as we embraced on the platform. "But it's too late to get Cass and Alan in on it, isn't it?"

At almost midnight, it certainly was, and Iowa City was still practically deserted for Holy Week, with students not due back for another four days. Soren drove my car from Wright Street, where the station was, over to South Clinton, and then across the river into Coralville, where we pulled into a parking lot of a bar called The Birdy. I looked askance at Soren, whose face was lit up by moonlight flooding through the windshield. He turned to me and said,

"Yeah, it's a dive, but let's just go in and have a drink anyway."

We walked into the dark room with votives in glass pots on the tables and an aura of sleaze about it. There weren't very many women in the place; just middle-aged men on barstools, and a couple of grad student-looking guys sitting at another table.

" This is where we're going to toast my good luck? It makes my parents' bar look like the Paris Ritz."

" Let's just see if they have any champagne."

We sat down at a table and the bartender called out to Soren, "What'll it be for you two?"

"Do you have any champagne?" Soren asked, making the few heads that were sitting there turn.

"Sorry, kid, " came the answer. "How about white wine?"

"That will be okay, " Soren said, and looking at me, "right?"

"If you say so. It'll probably be Gallo or something from a jug," I laughed.

The bartender came from around the bar and brought us our wine in the correct narrower white-wine glass, of all things. I gave Soren a look of "well how about that."

"Here's to your new life in Chicago, " Soren said, "you knew what you wanted and you went right out and got it...as usual."

"Come on."

" I mean it. You are one of a kind, Sarah Shrier."

"Well, thanks, Soren Carlysle. You are, too. *Unique au monde.* I'm giving a nod to St. Exupéry if you must know."

"I got that!" he said, laughed and clinked glasses with me.

"I will be making four hundred twenty-five dollars a month," I said, rather proudly. "I can pay you back the hotel money you loaned me right away in June. I'm not sure where I'll be living, but for the first few months anyway, it can just be a room or something. I haven't figured any of that out yet."

The next day when I saw Cass and Alan, they, too were happy for me.

"Way to go Miss Shrier!" Alan clipped me on the shoulder in a teasing way.

"Of course they wanted you!" Cass cried, "Just look at you! You're so French! So tiny and perfect!" *I didn't know what my size had to do with it.*

"I really have Dr. Ilke to thank for all this, " I said, "so I guess I won't go in and bitch to her about ol' Hugues Berry after all."

"Oh," Alan said, "I meant to tell you about that: you're not the only one who thinks he's a nutcase. The U isn't renewing his contract because of all the complaints."

"Where did you hear that?!" I was startled. "Too bad he has to finish out the semester, though. Blech."

It was a lazy weekend over Easter Sunday, and instead of being depressed about the town feeling so deserted and closed up, I relished the chance to hang out in my own apartment, get caught up on some reading, work on yet another *Candide* assignment, and mostly day dream about my new life to come. I decided to phone my parents and tell them the news, wondering if they'd even take the call.

Betty answered, as I hoped. "Mom, I just want to tell you I got a job in Chicago and I start right after graduation on June first."

There was a moment of silence on the other end of the line and then she said, "That's real good news, Sari. I'm happy for you. It's what you wanted."

"Yes, so I guess I'll come home for a few days after graduation and pack some stuff up. Maybe you can send it to me if I box it?"

"We'll work something out. Daddy and I were just talking about graduation. We want to come to the ceremony. That okay with you?"

"Sure. I'll find out all the logistics closer to the date. Also, would you ask Daddy if we can leave my car here for Cass? I mean, I know it's not my car. But it's a beater; you guys won't need it. Roslyn still has three years before she's driving, and she won't drive the Rambler. Cass really needs a car."

"I'll talk to him about it."

"Thanks. Okay, so talk to you later?"

"Bye, honey."

Bye, honey was the closest she came to saying I love you, and that was okay by me.

Around the middle of the next month, I came back from class one afternoon to find a very unexpected letter addressed to me from Hyde Industries. I took it up to my place and actually experienced a sort of dread opening it up. Would they be livid with me? It had taken literally months for them to write back.

It wasn't from Julia and John-Wilfred, however, only John-Wilfred. He started out thanking me for writing and said that his wife was immoveable on the subject of their daughter, but that he would like to take me up on my suggestion to see Cass and meet the babies. He would fly in with his pilot in one of their smaller planes, and if I would pick him up at the Iowa City airport, he would spend the afternoon, timed for Alan to be in class; (he appreciated my suggestion, and, of course---he refused to see Alan in any case). Then I could take him back to his plane. The other part of the "deal" was that I tell Cass that I had written to them, and assure him by phone to his office that she was open to the meeting. If all was well, he would come in a week.

A week! Oh Lordy.

So I also waited for Alan to be in class before driving out to the farm the next day to confront Cass with what I had done.

"So, I wrote your parents a few months ago and …"

"You did WHAT?" Her eyes darted at me.

"Please don't be mad. I just told them that it would be great if they could see their grandchildren! I'm sorry I didn't ask your permission or tell you. Cass, you just seemed like you were in such a terrible situation out here with these kids and no money! I didn't know what else to do."

"I'm not mad—exactly-- kid," she harrumphed, "but I'm surprised that you did it! Did you think they'd come?"

"Well, yeah…"

"HA! That's a laugh."

"But your dad finally wrote back, Cass, and he is coming." I held up the letter.

"You must be joking. Let me see that."

I let her read it, ultimatum and all. "Are you up for it?" I finally asked her.

"Yes, I guess so. What can I say now for heaven sake anyway?"

"Maybe he'll help you out at least! And he should see Laura and Paul. He'll fall in love. Who wouldn't?"

"Oh, don't count on that," she said shaking her head.

"But we'll make an effort, okay? We'll clean the place all up, and put the kids in cute clothes for the visit."

At least clean ones, I should have said. It didn't matter how often I took her to do laundry, we never seemed to get caught up for more than a minute.

331

The day before her father was due to arrive, Cass and I did some major rearranging of the living room part of the house. The two cribs were still side-by-side against one wall, but we positioned the other furniture closer together to make the space seem bigger between the conversation area and the kitchen/baby area. We placed the two car seats inside on the kitchen chairs; they doubled for feeding chairs anyway for a little while. We took all the bedding along with the baby clothes to wash, just so the bedroom would look and smell fresh. Since it was spring, we could open up the windows and air the place out , too. We positioned the stroller on the front porch so that John-Wilfred could see that this was a real, functioning family. Taking her kids out for walks in the clear Iowa air was the highlight of Cass's day.

I brought over one of the baskets Cass had given me from our summer apartment two years prior, thinking they now needed it more than I did.

"This will make a cute toy box!" I announced placing it in a niche near the cribs.

The kids didn't have any big toys yet at eight months old, but Cass had picked them up a few playthings when she got paid for her Christmas card sales. She had gone to thrift stores and had found a Fisher Price gazing-ball toy with carousel-looking animals that went around and around inside of it and played music. I had also bought them a bath toy—a big boat with other little boats and men that floated on it. They had some soft plasticized stuffed animals Cass had found at a garage sale, and I brought over some baby books, one of which was cloth. I liked to hold them on my lap on the floor and pretend they understood what I read to them. They were sitting up now just fine, too, to play, and they were not crawling, so Cass didn't really need a playpen…yet. But I wished we could get them a bouncy seat or a swing that hung from the door jam, or a little seat with wheels—anything that they could "move around" in. Those things existed; I'd seen them in the Montgomery Ward catalogue. The expense, however, was beyond what we could justify. If John-Wilfred saw it, or if he recognized the lack thereof when he did see the place, maybe he would chip in. I was also not afraid to ask him nor adverse to doing so.

I drove past the farmhouse the afternoon I was picking him up, and verified that Alan was gone; the plan was working perfectly. Alan had office hours before his four o'clock writing seminar, and was long gone out of the house by two. I was to meet the private plane around two-thirty so I high-tailed it right out there. I was truly embarrassed to have to take him back and forth in my 1959 wreck of a car. It would certainly be the ugliest, most horrible car in which he had ever ridden in his entire life.

I pulled up to the airport departure/arrival hall but I realized all at once that he wouldn't be coming out of that building! So I drove over to a hanger farther afield, and I was right; the private planes came into "Sky Harbor" rather than the main terminal. I saw a Beechcraft King Air land and figured that was his. I parked and got out of my car, and was standing there as it taxied over and came to a stop. He and his pilot got out—I didn't think this was the same pilot I'd met that other time, but I couldn't tell. They exchanged a few words, and then John-Wilfred Hyde walked over to me.

"Thanks so much for picking me up, Sarah! How are you?"

"I'm fine, thank you, Mr. Hyde. I'm so glad you came!"

We shook hands and then the moment of dread when I led him over to my car.

" I apologize that you have to ride in this!" I said, trying to laugh it off. "So sad!"

"What year is it?" he asked rather stupefied.

"1959! Can you believe it? I'm actually rather amazed it's still intact."

"And is it road worthy?"

"No comment, sir!" I giggled.

It only took ten minutes to drive down the highway back to Cass's place. I wasn't sure how it was going to go, but I was more than happy to leave them, and come back for him at the end of the afternoon. He got out of the car and just stood there looking around the former farmstead. Cass didn't have any garden to speak of or really any yard in front, thanks to the gravel driveway. But there was a little cement birdbath off to the side at least, and Cass's duck was happily swimming in the pond. John-Wilfred didn't give away his feelings about what he saw and stoically walked up the steps. I followed, but only long enough to get my marching orders.

They greeted each other amicably and Cass had a baby in each arm so they didn't hug one another. John-Wilfred cooed a little bit at his granddaughter and ruffled the downy hair on his grandson. Cass put them in one of the cribs, and offered her father something to drink.

"Coffee? Tea?"

"Nothing for me, thanks. "

"Sari?"

"No, thank you, I'm not staying, Cass. I just need to know when you want me to come back."

"How about this Sarah," Mr. Hyde interjected, " if I could have some time alone with my daughter, maybe you could take the babies for a walk in that nice stroller that's on the porch? You don't have to go far."

"Oh, sure…that's a good idea."

Cass and I got them into socks and sweaters; it was fairly warm out…too hot for jackets. She took one and I took one and we put the stroller on the ground before we put them in. Cass went back in the house, and I left with the kids. There wasn't, of course, a decent place to walk a stroller on a highway. It was about half an hour from there to the campus, so I set out in that direction, hoping I could make it. But without a real sidewalk, wheeling babies on the shoulder of a small road was not ideal. I walked them on the left towards the traffic so I could see cars coming. Luckily it was flat and had no ditch, so I could move pretty far out of the way.

I took about an hour coming and going. The babies had fallen asleep and were slumping over in their seats, so I had lowered the seatbacks to let them nap. Paul woke up kind of fussy when I turned back onto the gravel leading up to the house. I took him out and rocked him a little bit, sitting on the steps.

Cass heard us through the open window and came out without her father.

"How was it?" I asked anxiously.

"Fine, " she said.

"Okaaaay, " I said when she wouldn't elaborate. We went back in.

"Do you want to hold one of them, Papa?" Cass asked, pronouncing it as she always had: "p'PAH".

"Sure! Hand me Paul." I sat down next to him and put his grandson in his arms. I picked up Laura, and Cass glowed at her sweet children in this domestic scene.

"They're both beautiful little tow-heads, aren't they?" he observed.

"That they are, " I said. "And they're so good!"

"I imagine you've got your hands full at all times even so, " he said, looking up at Cass.

"Yes, I sure do."

We traded babies after a few minutes, and John-Wilfred bounced Laura on his knee. He seemed to be really relishing and enjoying his granddad role. Cass excused herself to go to the bathroom, and John-Wilfred turned to me and asked if, instead of taking him straight back to the airport, could we stop somewhere---maybe on campus---and get coffee?

"Of course, " I answered, careful to not suggest the River Room where Alan could easily show up with his students, not that I knew he would, but it could happen. I wracked my brain about where to take him at four in the afternoon, and settled on The Airliner. Absolutely no one I knew would be there, and the mostly frat-boy crowd would ignore us.

Cass didn't seem to have fought at all with her father, but nor did they seem to have reconciled. It was more like a business meeting and not a truce, not a forgiveness fest, nor a battle royal. But at least, I thought, as I walked back to the driver's side of my car, they got together, he saw the kids, and he saw his daughter for the first time in over a year. Maybe some good would come of it. I watched Cass give a little wave as we drove away.

Inside the bar it wasn't even as noisy as usual given the hour, and we got a booth easily. We ordered coffee.

"I wanted to talk to you, Sarah, because of the long conversation I had with my daughter today. I understand you've done more for them than she could have ever imagined. I want you to know how grateful I am."

"She's my best friend, Mr. Hyde, from the first day, almost, that we met in the dorm. I'm sad that things went wrong for her with you and Mrs. Hyde, but I could never abandon her. She needs a lot of help!"

" I know she does. Unfortunately, things are not simple. Her mother refuses categorically to welcome her back into the fold if she remains married to Alan Jones. I am almost that adamant, too. I've changed the parameters of her trust funds and that is difficult to do, believe me. We do not want that disgusting fellow to be able to put one finger on Cass's money…or ours, for that matter, and because of that, we have taken all her inheritance and the money she came into at her majority, and put it somewhere where he will never be able to access it under any circumstances. "

I didn't say anything, but just listened. I was hoping he'd give me some indication that he had realized that something had to be done about his daughter's predicament.

"From what Cass told me, without being disloyal to her husband exactly, is that he is very tight with the little money they do have, and that you were the person who got her on those government food stamps! "

"Well, yes, she probably mentioned that I had seen some articles about it and thought she qualified. Alan's salary as a teaching assistant really isn't very large, and they both think they were pretty lucky to get that house for a tiny rent. The greatest thing is that she sold some of her art! That was exciting."

"I see. Well, Sarah, I gave her a hundred dollars just now, but that is not going to get her very far." He reached for his wallet. "And I'm giving you the same amount in cash. Here."

I was stunned as I took his money.

"Thank you so much! It's very nice of you. This will help getting the kids some new clothes! They really grow out of stuff fast."

"No, Sarah, this cash is not for the kids. It is to pay you back. Cassandra made no secret of how much you did for them out of your own pocket. You keep that for yourself. The fact is, I'm intending to give her more, but I'm not going to do it within the reach or purview of Alan Jones. When I give that money, I'll give it to you, to distribute to them as you see fit."

"But, Mr. Hyde, they'll know. I don't have any money! And if I all of a sudden start buying them things, or even if I slip money to Cass, Alan will wonder how in the world she afforded whatever it is she does with it."

"You and Cass will just have to figure something out. I understand you are moving to Chicago after school gets out. I intend to open an account in your name at my bank, and I will put five thousand dollars in it to start with."

"Wow, that's…that's so very generous!" I could hardly hide my shock at the sum of money he was talking about—*nearly thirty-thousand in today's dollars*. "I'm sure she's grateful. But again…I'm uncertain how this will ever work. It's so…so …clandestine." I stared into my coffee cup, as if the answer could be read in there like tea leaves.

"You two will have to devise some scheme. She knows about the money arrangement, so you don't have to be sneaky around her, just around him."

Before I could protest again, he began a new speech.

"There's something else. Cass tells me you have babysat for her, done endless errands for them, taken her to the laundromat, gone grocery shopping and cooked meals for them both. I think she looks terrible, by the way. Whatever is she eating?"

"Well, she's a vegetarian now and she walks the kids a lot, so she's keeping pretty trim."

"Nonsense. She's far too thin. Don't tell me you haven't noticed."

"I have."

"Anyway, she asked me to do something for you and I'm only too happy to see to it. She said you don't have any place to live yet in Chicago. I want to help you out with that. What I propose is to have you live in one of my buildings rent-free for a year. After that, you'll have saved up enough to be able to afford the rent on a small Chicago apartment. Coming from The Bluffs as you do, even Omaha, you don't have any idea of how expensive it is to live in Chicago."

"I know I don't; you're right. But really, Mr. Hyde, I can't take you up on that offer. I mean, I can use the help finding maybe a room to rent or something, and the truth of the matter is that I did think to ask you about the real estate scene, of course. But I can't live rent-free for a year. "

"Certainly you can. Hear me out—this isn't exactly what you think; we're not talking about the Hyde penthouse here, " he laughed. "I have a building, in a very nice and safe neighborhood, on which we are right now commencing a total refurbishment. We call it a brownstone…not the kind you saw in Brooklyn that time; the Chicago ones are often brick, as is this one. This place of mine has eight large apartments and two small one-bedrooms, plus a studio in it. We want to reconfigure them into four townhomes and two smaller one-bedroom apartments within the building. In the front now is a *concièrge's* efficiency apartment, *concièrge* in the French sense, the caretaker—that's the studio. It's right up the front steps and to one side of the hallway. The rest of the apartments are upstairs now, and there's no elevator, but we're putting one in. We are starting remodeling from the top down and from back to front. We are leaving the utilities turned on, and there is a security fence now up around the entire perimeter of the lot. It's not a row house—there are side yards, a parking area in a neighboring space we also own, and a tiny front garden with a large gate already there. My security fence goes around the ironwork gate and encompasses the entire property. It is locked by an electronic locking system that the foreman opens in the mornings and locks at night, but which you will have access to at any hour. I have a private security company, and they are patrolling the property from 6:00 p.m. until 8:00 a.m., even on weekends. We would be doing that even if you weren't going to live there, because I don't want any of our tools and equipment or building supplies stolen. So you see… you'd be helping me out by being a presence in the building. And except for a few overlapping hours, you won't be there during the noisy times. It's really a good deal for you. "

"I don't know what to say."

"I appreciate what you mean to my daughter, Sarah. You've been a true friend to her. It's why we invited you to New York and it's why we wanted you to have the Christmas holiday in Amsterdam. Those were dark days for Julia and me. But you've been steadfastly loyal to my Cassandra no matter what her hare-brained decisions have been. I feel we owe you quite a lot, really, and so does she."

"She has—all of you have-- done so much for me---far more than anything I've done for her. I feel I can't do enough to repay any of you."

"Well, I think it's mutual then. I am going to make these arrangements with my staff, and when you come to Chicago in a few weeks, you stop up to my office, and one of my secretaries will take you to the house. I understand your future office will be on North Michigan Avenue. The property is about six blocks north and three blocks west of where the Water Tower is. I know you stayed around there when you went in for your interview. You can walk to work--- or there must be a bus. You're young and healthy…walking will be right up your alley. As far as the amenities of the area, they are all there---small markets and laundromats. In the new units we'll be putting in laundry facilities and the best, most up-to-date equipment, but unfortunately it's not there now. You won't want a car in the city, either, Sarah. Too much bother. "

I dared not tell him I was leaving my car for Cass if my parents agreed to the plan.

"And one other thing, " he added, "I will make sure my staff leaves or puts some furniture in your studio. I'm actually not sure at all what is in there now, but the basics will be there for you. Cass says we need to find you a television, too, " he laughed. "So I will direct my staff to do so."

"I can't ever ever thank you enough for this, Mr. Hyde. I'm serious."

"I know you are." He smiled at me. "I'm glad we have a deal, then. He extended his hand for me to shake, and then added, " I'd better be getting back to the airport."

We stood up to leave and he put his hand on my shoulder. I looked at him and the bleak expression on his face. He said, "I am…well…her mother and I that is…are extremely unhappy about all this horrible situation, you know. I would like for her to leave that preposterous ass of a husband and come home to Kenilworth. We could help her with the kids in some way, maybe not at our home, but somewhere. She has ruined her entire life being with that man. All our hopes and aspirations for her have gone up in flames. Her grandmother is beside herself."

"I can't even imagine how hard it must be to know you have grandchildren and not be able to see them grow up, " I said, not wanting to get in the middle of the real fight.

"Yes, " he said, "that, too. So we are in agreement about the bank account also, then?"

"I'll do whatever you want me to. It's not that I'd ever stand in the way of benefits to Cass and the children--- you understand that, right? It's just the logistics."

"You two work it out."

Chapter Fifty-Seven

"Pomp and Circumstance March No. 1"...Sir Edward Elgar

I admit I was afraid Cass would be mad at me for having contacted her father, so I tried to ready some excuses that would appease her and not compromise my reasons for having done it. But it turned out that she was more relieved than anything else to have broken the barrier between them and to have had him see her children. The money didn't hurt either. She and I worked out a preliminary plan.

"For the time being, " she told me, "I want you to be the one buying the kids things and not me. I could buy some more art supplies and Alan wouldn't think anything of it because he doesn't really know what I took with me from home. But kids' gifts are a different story. He'd get suspicious."

"Yeah, accuse you of being an artist and selling your work is what he'd do. Idiot."

But I accepted her plan.

"When I go home after graduation and come back with the car, I can bring plenty of stuff with me; Alan will just think I was flush with graduation money."

" Once you get to Chicago, he'll believe you're spending your salary on us! I'm not sure that's such a good idea."

"We'll think of something to make it all work, " I said, hoping it was true.

The trouble was, Mr. Hyde hadn't told Cass the amount that I would have at my disposal for her: five thousand dollars. Alan's adjunct teaching assistant salary went mainly towards his tuition. The rest of the money netted out to less than two hundred dollars per month. Their rent was fifty-five dollars and they had to live on what was left over. I imagined that a teaching assistant salary was never meant to raise a family on. My new four-hundred-twenty-five-dollars-per-month salary wasn't any great shakes either, considering I had to live in a big city on it, but not paying rent would put me comparatively on easy street. Alan wouldn't know any of that nor what I made, so if we were lucky, and he didn't become too suspicious, sending things to Laura and Paul would just seem like I was spoiling them, like "aunties" do.

I was coasting towards graduation after easy mid-terms when, in late April, I received a written notice in the mail to see my academic advisor at my earliest convenience.

"What do you think it means? " I asked Cass over the phone when I opened it up. "It's sent on official University department stationery."

"Oh, gosh, probably nothing. They do a senior check of some sort to make sure you got all the credits. Stuff like that. I'm sure it's routine."

"I hope it's not something gone wrong with my new job, though," I said worried.

"She wouldn't send you an official university memo if that were it, would she?" Cass offered.

"No. You're right. Must be routine."

But it wasn't routine.

I showed up in Dr. Ilke's office and, right away, she told me to sit down. She, on the other hand, was pacing around in front of me with a paper in her hand.

"Dr. Berry has lodged a complaint of plagiarism against you, Sarah, " she finally said, looking up.

"WHAT?! PLAGIARISM? Against ME?" I was flabbergasted, unhappy, and not a little frightened.

"Yes, he's convinced the last paper you did on *Candide* was not your own French."

"But Dr. Ilke, I would never cheat!! I annotated that paper; the footnotes were all correct. He could check them all!"

"I pursued that avenue, and he said he did check them, but that it still didn't seem likely you wrote it."

"But that's absurd!" I protested.

It was as though Ionesco were sitting in the office, dictating the script.

"I know it seems incongruous. I am prepared to defend you, Sarah; I have the paper now. I will recheck your sources. But can you give me any additional verification of your work? Do you have any notes or drafts you could provide?"

" I do have my rough draft!" I remembered. "And I have my own handwritten notes from last year." I heaved a deep sigh. "I've already studied Voltaire, Dr. Ilke, in depth, as you may remember. I used those notes in the paper, but that's not against the rules, is it?" I suddenly became panicky and started to sob. "What will happen if he brings me up on charges of some sort in front of some university inquisition? I can't not graduate!!"

"Try to calm down," she said with some degree of soothing in her voice. "Let's not get that far ahead. You bring me all your notes and the draft, and let me re-verify the sources. I do believe you, Sarah. We here at Iowa have not had many student fabrications of research cases. I have a feeling Dr. Berry isn't being entirely rational about this. Would he have any reason to dislike you?"

"Well, none of us respect him much, if you want to know the truth. We all think he's off his rocker."

"Hmmm." She was careful with her response to my put-down of him. As chair, she probably couldn't comment on that, especially to a student.

"But I haven't ever been outwardly disrespectful to him. At least not to his face," I had to give a little laugh at that. "Truth be told everyone in the class considers him a ding-bat."

"He also said he checked with one of the other professors you've had for French comp and con, Dr. Hotka, and he told me she had the same, as he put it, 'trouble' with you."

The fuck she did.

"WHAT?!" That's not possible! He's lying to you. She never said a word to me. You can see on my transcripts-- I got A's in her class!"

" I did look that up, and I concur with you. What is bothering me about this whole thing is why, when you give accurate documentation, should he assume what he is assuming?"

"Yeah," I puzzled, "Is his primary complaint that the paper is too good?! Why should excellence arouse suspicion? Don't make me laugh."

But it wasn't a laughing matter to think I'd be called on the carpet, with the onus on me to prove my innocence, because some prick professor lodged a false plagiarism charge against me that could ruin my university career and the entire rest of my life! I was shaking by the time I left her office.

I sat on Cass's couch and cried and cried. She put her arm around me and tried to assure me that he didn't have a case to bring against me, that Alan, as a faculty member who had taught me, would vouch for me to the U, and so would all my other profs.

"Klampert has weight on this faculty, " she said, "and he would defend you! You're a good student ! You've done nothing wrong. The burden of proof will be on Berry."

I hoped she was right, but as it turned out, it never came to that.

On May 4, 1970, the shootings at Kent State University by the Ohio National Guard that left four students dead, rocked the campuses of colleges across the nation, and Iowa was no exception. Students marched on our National Guard Armory, and things became violent enough—with the breaking of windows not only at the Armory but of some of the downtown businesses-- that the Iowa City Council gave the mayor curfew powers. Two days later, the student leadership called for a complete boycott of all classes and staged a "sleep-in" on the Pentacrest in front of Old Capital. But it didn't end there.

I did not join the protest this time, figuring I couldn't risk being near any more trouble what with my pending woes with Berry. Instead I offered to be out at the farm babysitting so that Alan and Cass could go demonstrate. But Alan and Cass also came home earlier than expected, and Cass announced breathlessly, that someone had actually broken into the Old Capital building, and set off a smoke bomb.

"We got out of there," Alan said. "I couldn't run the chance of being arrested either, and we had to get Cass back here, too, just in case they did round everyone up and take them into custody or something."

Most protestors left voluntarily when told to do so, but some did not, and around 2 a.m. the next morning, President Boyd authorized the arrest of everyone still at the scene. The Iowa City paper reported later that he had regretted doing that, since he'd been given false information; but no one believed him. I felt sorry for him, truth be told, because I'd always liked him, as really, most students did. But this war, and the Nixon administration's escalation of it with the invasion of Cambodia, was just too much to keep things peaceful on campuses.

The next day, right after the mass arrests, was supposed to have been a Governor's Day ROTC observance. President Boyd called it off. ROTC was alive and well on the Iowa campus all through my years there, and, much as students and also faculty called into question the amount of credits that could be earned for being in it, for the most part no one had bothered them until now. After the anti-war demonstrations really escalated, we started to hear of movements to get rid of ROTC on our campus. But President Boyd said he would not abolish it, nor would he cancel classes, as many other schools did that week.

Nevertheless, most of the buildings where classes were held were relatively empty. Dr. Berry decided to hold our class—one of our last ones—at his own home in town. Everyone in class thought that was a disgusting idea, and a few were cutting it just to spite him. I decided to go, if for no other reason than to show him he hadn't intimidated me. I was innocent and I needed to act like it.

We were all milling around on his porch at the appointed time, mostly mocking the stupidity of his holding this session. When he came to the door, I distinctly felt he was sneering at me as he motioned us in. We sat around the dark little living room, some on the floor and others on the seating, which was minimal, and discussed, for the millionth time, the "*optimisme*" theme in the book.

"In light of what we are seeing in this country with the Vietnam war and the eruption of violent demonstrations" he began, "was the brutality displayed in Voltaire's tale conducive to the master Pangloss's persistent optimism? Or was the real theme of the work evil and the theoretical existence of evil in all entities, from government to theology, and every other thing of human design?"

Not many of us wanted to get into this with Dr. Lunatic Berry. Someone offered the obviously overly simplistic observation that whatever Candide's horrid fortunes, Pangloss, professor of "metaphysico-theologo-cosMORONology" always said it was "for the best in the best of all possible worlds." That brought groans. We had already discussed that line over and over in class, and Hugues Berry always dismissed it as mere satire on Voltaire's part. I had done the majority work in my own paper on Candide's ultimate repudiation of his master, but I felt too vulnerable to baiting by Berry to participate in this discussion; so I kept mum.

By the time he dismissed us and I was back home, I had a phone call from Dr. Ilke saying that President Boyd had decided-- and was about to announce-- that all students were free to leave the university, taking the grade they had at that moment.

"But…what about graduation?!" I asked, afraid I was about to burst into tears.

"Graduation will take place just as scheduled in another two weeks," she assured me. "It's just that, essentially, if not officially yet, the university is about to be closed."

Then came the next bombshell: Dr. Ilke said she had already consulted Dr. Berry on my behalf to determine what my grade would be, in the light of this turn of events.

"He told me that he would be giving you a C."

"It will ruin my grade point average, " I sighed.

"But not your life."

So I jumped on the offer. She also told me that she had reviewed all my documentation, saw that it was in order, and restated her belief in my honesty.

"If you did go ahead with the hearing and quasi-trial," she said, "I believe you most certainly would win. But it's a moot point. Dr. Berry has withdrawn the charges against you. The only question now is the grade. Can you live with a C?"

"I suppose I'll have to."

The path of least resistance was preferable to me at this point. I could, however, just hear my father bellowing at me about getting a C in a French class. It was almost funny.

"What a fucking nightmare!" I whined to Cass later at her house, where I had gone with a mushroom pizza to celebrate my liberation from Hugues Berry!

"It's a hard lesson to learn that some nut case in a position of power can wreak havoc in an innocent person's life. But you prevailed, kid!"

338

Two weeks later, I walked down the aisle and collected my diploma, the first grandchild on my mother's side to do so. I moved the tassel to the left-hand edge of my mortar board, along with the other thousand people in the field house, and walked off the campus a graduate — without honors.

Sol, Betty and Roslyn drove in for the ceremony, and seeing them all there just made me sad about my grandmother's absence, because I knew for sure that Nana would have come with them had she lived. Betty brought me cards from my two aunts, so it was evident that they had discussed the momentous day. Soren came over to my apartment to greet them all, but didn't go to the ceremony with us. His own family were all in town to attend the Law Review announcement dinner with him, and Soren and I had decided in advance that the two families would be kept separate from each other. I didn't really want to have to encounter his mother anyway.

Sol and Betty were anxious to go to Cass and the babies, so we all piled into their Ford, and I drove us out to the farm. Cass was looking rather frazzled, but she greeted us at the door and, once inside, offered everyone coffee. Unfortunately, one of the twins must have had a bout of diarrhea or something, because the place had a distinctly sickening smell to the interior. Sol and Betty were noticeably uncomfortable, and Roslyn just sat there not interacting with the babies. But I got down on the floor and scattered some toys around me, bouncing Paul on my knee as I played the "rings" game with Laura.

Alan was not home to help Cass "entertain" my family.

Once my father saw the house, he started acting almost put off by being there, much as he and my mother had always liked Cass, and going out to see her had been their idea. He gave the place the old once-over in a judgmental way that I noticed right off, if Cass didn't. His suspicions were aroused as to the cleanliness of the plates Cass served cookies on, and of the spoon he was given to stir his coffee. Betty was less obtuse, but I could tell she was also disappointed in such an environment for raising children.

"You're a little crowded in here, aren't you?" my father asked Cass, although it came out as more of a statement than a question.

"Yes, we are," Cass answered with a lilt in her voice instead of despair. "But we're contemplating making our bedroom into a nursery-slash-playroom, and putting our bed in the back of the house. It may just fit!" she laughed.

"That might be a good solution, " Betty said, "to get two cribs out of your living area."

Once we were back in the car, the barrage came, however.

"I do not understand for the life of me," Sol ranted, "how decent people can live like that! It is a shambles! It is dirty, it is depressing, and it is beyond the pale!"

"I can't imagine how she can keep her children clean if they crawl around on that floor, " said Betty. "They must be in the bath three times a day."

"You know they aren't, " I said, but vowed not to get into a big argument on the subject. "Cass has her hands full, and she doesn't have any help," I offered.

"Well, where are her parents, then?" Sol wanted to know. "Why don't they just take her home?"

"She's married! And they are not in the picture. End of discussion."

My family did not stay overnight in Iowa City, but headed straight back after dropping me off at my apartment. Soren came over the next day to help me pack up my car.

"Thank God I didn't have to drive across Iowa with them! I'd have probably jumped out of the car before Des Moines."

Soren and I parted sadly. We would not be seeing one another again, even though I'd be back in Iowa City in a week, leaving my car with Cass, and taking the train to Chicago. He planned be in Imogene over the entire summer before returning to law school in August.

"Chicago's not that far," he observed, as we held one another before I got in the driver's side. "Let's just not even say good-bye."

"Au revoir, alors, ".

Moving away with only two suitcases and a purse to start life over in a new place was not easy. I had to decide what was really important to take, what could be shipped later, and what had to be jettisoned. I was afraid the more I left behind of my "life", the more Betty would just throw out. So I got some boxes and went down into our basement to see if there was anything of utmost importance from my childhood that should be saved. Roslyn had commandeered all the toys, so she had mine and hers: my original Barbie doll and her new generation one; my metal doll house with the pink and blue plastic furniture (none of the dolls that "peopled" the home were still around, however); my roller skates with the key on a leather bracelet, my walking doll, and my white boot ice skates. I decided none of that was salvageable. But there were some high school mementos kept in a little box along with my childhood and teenage diaries; those shouldn't slip into the wrong hands! I stepped lightly around the playroom and then headed over to the storage closet where my winter clothes were. Even though I hated them all, I had no choice but to pack some if I wanted anything to wear in six months.

Up in my room, I carefully wrapped the souvenirs of my European sojourn that were displayed on glass shelves above my bed. They, at least, were small, and could fit in my suitcases. I put my Sorbonne books and notebooks in a bag to take with me, also, figuring I never knew when I might need some French grammar or literature references on my new job.

I packed some household items in the rest of the small boxes I would take in the car and leave with Cass to mail to me in Chicago. Even though I figured I would buy most of it there, if I didn't have to right away, that would be good. I was ever mindful that I owed Soren money immediately from my first paycheck. I had asked Betty if I could just have some old Melmac dishes from the bar because they were lightweight. They were so ugly that I figured she didn't care about them. She let me have four plates, four cups and saucers and four bowls. I took table settings of some old silverware, too, and four glasses. It occurred to me also that I would need the same towels I had in Iowa City, plus a bathmat. I also took a set of twin-sized bed linens, much as I had no idea what size bed would be in the apartment.

Before leaving Omaha, I headed to Brandeis to outfit Laura and Paul with Mr. Hyde's money. Not only would Alan have been suspicious; so would my parents. So I brought the packages back stealthily and put the items in my suitcase before they could even see them. I had a great time buying them sizes 12 and 18th month clothing: sleepers, rompers, sweaters, three sweet cotton dresses for Laura, which were more fun than the little pants and shirts I could find for Paul. I bought them both play clothes: little bib overalls in pastel mint green for Laura and light tan for Paul, with contrasting patterned shirts for underneath. For dressier occasions I chose for Paul a darling light blue sailor suit with red piping on the collar and a navy tie at the chest; and for Laura a pink ruffled dress with a white dotted Swiss pinafore over it. The apron part was embroidered with pink and green flowers, and tied at the sides with white bows. I got them socks and some soft shoes in varying sizes; and lots of white undershirts they could share.

On the way down from the store's Fourth floor where I'd been busy in the children's department, I took a detour to Three just for old time's sake and the vaunted Junior Department. I passed a brown and white checked mini skirt and a white short-sleeved camp blouse on display right near the escalator. It didn't take long to rationalize I needed just one new outfit to have as I began what could really become a career, even if that were unlikely just yet. I would use some of Mr. Hyde's money and absolutely pay it back the instant I got paid. The skit was $8.98 — ouch! — and the blouse was $3.98. It was really cute but still not quite "professional" looking, so I also bought a brown neck scarf in silky rayon ($1.98), and went down two more escalators to the I. Miller Shoe Department where I found a pair of mod brown Amalfi leather shoes with beige piping along all the edges and cool beige leather tassels on the front. They had a chunky two-inch heel, and were the perfect dressy-casual-office-dinner all around great shoes! Cost: $14.00, easily the most expensive ones I owned, not counting the Harrod's shoes, of course. The grand total of what I "purloined" from the Hyde funds would come out to around thirty dollars, and I rationalized that Mr. Hyde would not begrudge my feelings of needing to look put together my first day on the job.

As it happened, I needn't have worried about borrowing from the Hyde money. The night before I was to take off, Betty and Sol absolutely shocked me with a graduation present of a small t.v. and five hundred dollars!

"Nana would have wanted you to have this money, " my mother said softly, as my father acted uninterested in it. I thanked her profusely and my gratitude was genuine. I didn't have the heart to tell them that Mr. Hyde had already offered to have a television put in my place, because their present was so generous. It would be easier to just have the luxury of two of them… temporarily.

"I'm going to ship the t.v. and your stereo to you on the Greyhound bus," she announced. "That way you just have to make arrangements to pick it up. It's better to not have it be delivered to you when you're not home."

"Well, that's...smart...I guess, " I said, wondering how I'd ever get to the bus station to retrieve the package. Cass would be mailing me the other boxes from Iowa City to my office.

When I was set to depart from The Bluffs, I insisted that leave-taking would be brief and devoid of sentiment. This was, after all, my most adamant decision, and nothing was going to make me look back with any possible or visible regret. I could not expend any energy on arguing with them or getting into any sort of negative discussions, crying jags or screaming matches. I needed all my focus and attention to be on the road trip, the train trip, the logistics of getting to Mr. Hyde's office once I arrived, and the start of my job.

But when I got ready for Cass to drive me to the train in Iowa City, the floodgates of tears burst.

"You'll be back for Thanksgiving, " she sobbed. "It will go fast."

"You will write me all the time, okay?" I slobbered over her shoulder.

"All the time! You'll be having a mad, gay, exciting new life, and I'll be at the laundromat, as usual, " she laughed, trying to sound convincingly optimistic about us both.

The tears flowed again as we stood on the platform at the Iowa City train station, hugging and clinging to each other. I think Cass felt my leaving this time acutely. I believe she saw it as the end of her getting any more real help-- with cooking, laundry and the kids. She may have been experiencing a kind of abandonment. I, on the other hand, had a strange feeling of being kicked out of the nest and expected to fly on my own. Cass was my sounding board, my mentor on all things aesthetic, my confidant. Even as we knew intellectually that the bond of our great friendship, our love, really, could not be broken just by physical distance; still, facing the reality of not being able to be together at the drop of a hat was unsettling to us both.

I watched her get smaller and smaller as the train pulled out.

PART THREE:

CHICAGO

Chapter Fifty-Eight

"Summer in the City"...The Lovin' Spoonful

My new job was set to start on Monday, June first, so I arrived in Chicago several days ahead to have some time to get settled. I'll admit it was daunting to find myself alone in a huge city knowing I was going to make a new life there, not merely visit.

I'd made the requisite arrangements with the Hyde organization per John-Wilfred's instructions, and when I checked into the Allerton Hotel again, a message was waiting for me saying keys were ready. I had an appointment for Friday morning with a Miss Peggy Bergman who would be taking me to the apartment.

When I got to the twentieth floor of the Hyde Building, Peggy was summoned to the Reception and she greeted me warmly.

"Welcome to Chicago, Sarah!" she said, brushing her light chestnut brown hair back from her face.

"Very nice to meet you, " I said, offering her my hand.

"Come on back to my office for a minute. I'll order us up a car."

She led the way and I followed her down a thick-carpeted hallway into an executive suite of offices. I didn't see Mr. Hyde at all and wondered if he were indeed behind one of those closed doors.

Peggy was very pretty and seemed to me to be in her thirties. She wasn't wearing very much makeup, although I did notice that the red lipstick she had put on seemed to match the color of polish on her impeccable manicure. She looked very professional in a light blue suit skirt and a paisley blouse that tied in a bow at her chin. She grabbed a suit jacket from the back of her chair and pulled it on as she sat down at her desk. The lining matched the fabric of her blouse.

"Chic," I thought.

"We'll swing by the hotel and get your luggage, " she said to me, replacing the receiver after ordering the car. "I've got all the keys here with me, so shall we go on down? You're going to like your neighborhood."

"I'm sure I will. " I smiled, and followed her.

The black 1968 Lincoln town car was waiting for us, and we both slid in the back seat. First stop was my hotel. I hopped out and up the stairs to fetch my luggage, but the Hyde Industries chauffeur was close behind, to carry it all down for me.

"You're not very far from Oak Street Beach, " said Peggy, cheerily as we drove up North Michigan Avenue from the Allerton, and turned west away from the Lake. The streets were leafy and wide with older brownstone-looking houses and some modern high-rise buildings scattered in among them.

"Gee, I never think of Chicago as a beach locale, " I said truthfully.

"Oh, you'll be surprised at how hot it gets and how inviting the lakeshore can be."

I saw the house even before we got there because just like John-Wilfred had described, there was one property with a huge link fence thrown up around it. If there had been another house next door, it was torn down now, so the workers had a lot in which to park trucks and enter from the back. Nevertheless, we parked on the street, and Peggy and I got out. Inside the fence was the actual gated property, but it was the fencing that had the first lock; the wrought iron gate was open.

"You have three keys, " Peggy explained, handing me a packet. "One for the fencing. See there--- you have a lock to get in this first opening in the fence. The work crew have a different opening in the back that they will use. Once up the stairs, you have a key to the front door. And then once inside, your apartment is the one right there, " she said, pointing to a window to the left of the entry. "All the other apartments in the building are on the next floors up. You'll see—there's a staircase inside the hallway.

Eventually it will be closed off, though and they'll be installing an elevator. But that's not for some time yet. Let's go in."

As the driver put my suitcases on the sidewalk, he offered to carry them up the steps for me, which I really appreciated since there were so many steps up to the front entrance. I could tell that the house had once been quite pretty; it was reddish brick and limestone with gothic overtones to the design. The apartment above mine had had a magnificent bay window overlooking the street and the top ones had turrets. On the exterior, there was only the stone staircase and no railings. I could tell I was going to get a big workout every time I took groceries or laundry up those stairs.

Once inside, the place wasn't as much of a wrecking-ball work zone as I had pictured. Like Cass's father had told me, they were working from the top to the bottom, back to front, so where my apartment was hadn't been touched yet. Peggy opened the doors for me with her own keys, and she surveyed the main room.

"I want to make sure everything works, " she said, going around the place switching on lights, running the hot water and flushing the commode. "This part of the building was just an efficiency apartment, kind of like a studio, " Peggy explained, "for the caretaker, as Mr. Hyde no doubt explained to you. This room is a pretty good size, really, and some of the furniture was already here, like that dresser for clothes over against the wall, and the Welsh cupboard there. You can use that for linens, dishes or really anything you want. We didn't like the bed that was here, so we brought in that new day bed — you can use it as a couch, too. The comfy chair over by the window seemed in good enough condition to leave, so you have that, and the other little tables will come in handy. I could only find one floor lamp that was decent enough, but the small table lamps will work, too, for more lighting. The one over by the day bed can be used for reading in bed, if you like."

Furnishings were indeed very sparse and looked as though they had perhaps been culled from other apartments; but it was fine to me.

"Yes, this will be great, " I said, looking around the room and trying to take it all in.

Everything would be great since it was all FREE!

"And there's a tiny kitchen through this door, " she said leading me into it, "and a bathroom on the other side. Will it do?"

"Perfectly, " I said. "I love it."

"Since the front window gives onto the street, we left the old draperies on it for you, even though they are pretty awful in that heavy cotton velvet. The other windows in the house are high enough that no one can see in, and the bathroom window is frosted. The kitchen window looks onto a brick wall, so there's no view, but then again, no one can see in either."

There was actually a tiny old-fashioned chrome and Formica drop-leaf kitchen dinette table inside the small kitchen space, and it even had two chairs. The stove was very narrow, but adequate and the fridge was also smaller than a normal one, but still bigger than some I'd seen in Paris, for example. There was a large sink with a few cabinets below it, and a broom closet next to the fridge. The floor was faded yellow linoleum, but it was clean.

Back in the main room, the heat was from radiators which, Peggy advised me, would probably make some noise in the winter, but for the summer they wouldn't be on. The apartment was also not air-conditioned.

"That will take some getting used to, I'm guessing, " she told me, "because it can get really hot here. Maybe you'll have to buy a fan. At least you do have a nice window and if there is any breeze at all, you should feel it."

"I'll be fine, " I assured her.

"I took the liberty of supplying you with some bedding, " Peggy said walking over to the closet nearest the door and pulling down a set of sheets and a pillow from the top shelf, "and I put some towels in the bathroom."

"Gosh, that was nice of you!" I said. "I have some coming but my stuff is not here yet, of course. I did bring a towel in my suitcase."

"There's one other thing, " she said, turning to me, "the phone." She pointed towards the kitchen and we went over to it. I hadn't even noticed that a yellow wall phone was in there! "I had it installed for you and I put the number right on the dial on the front. See?"

"I… really… appreciate all of this, " I stammered.

"Mr Hyde wanted you to be comfortable. He really likes you. He told me you've done a lot for his daughter."

"Please, when you go back to the office, thank him again for me. I'm just so grateful. I start my job on Monday and this place is a dream."

"Can you walk to work from here? " she asked. "Where is the –uh– office is it? Business?"

"Office. It's on North Michigan. I'm guessing, given the car ride over here was about ten minutes, that I will have to give myself probably half an hour to walk there. Maybe a little longer. I'm not in such great shape."

"That's not bad, " she said. "There is also a Red Line bus that goes into the Loop from here. You'll soon get the hang of the CTA. The neighborhood is pretty great."

" I can see that! We passed a little grocery store and a laundromat, so right off the bat, that's about all I need. But CTA?"

"Chicago Transit Authority."

"Oh, of course. Duh."

"But Chicago is a pretty walkable city, " she remarked, and then caught herself. "But not at night---don't go out alone. Later on this Fall it will be getting dark when you get off work. That won't be so dangerous because it will still be early. But don't go venturing out alone after, say, eight or nine. Not that this is a bad area, don't get me wrong. But be cautious. Now, speaking of that, though, do not worry about this place. Mr. Hyde has Jake from Blue Light Security who will come on duty at six p.m. every night and patrol the block keeping watch on this house. You'll meet him right away, and he will be on call until at least eight in the morning, maybe a bit later. Blue Light is a subsidiary of Hyde Architecture Industries. Jake has been working for us for decades. He's wonderful --and don't let his age fool you---he's extremely capable. You will see his car and its – yes, blue light! He'll probably patrol a bit at first, and then park on the side lot over where the workers do, to keep watch on the property. Even though this is a work site, you have nothing to fear about being here alone at night. We do not want any of our tools or materials stolen, so he's there for that as well."

"I can't thank you enough for all your help, "I told her as she made her way to leave.

We shook hands and she said, "My pleasure, Sarah. If you need anything, you can always call me. Here, I have a card." She put it down on the Welsh cupboard and opened my apartment's door. We walked together to the front entrance.

"Thanks again!" I called out as she made her way down the steps and back into the town car.

So there I was: ensconced in my own little flat with my own phone, my own everything and no rent to pay. I just sat on the day bed in wonder at it all…and again, how lucky I was to have a best friend whose family owned a huge property business, who would let me live in the place rent-free, set it all up, and send a staff member to move me in! And provide a security cop to keep me safe! It was all surreal.

I unpacked everything I had brought, which, it turned out, wasn't much at all! Those boxes could not get there fast enough. But I arranged what I had, set my cosmetics bag in the bathroom, where Miss Bergman had conveniently also left a bar of soap; and filled the chest of drawers in the main room first with my folded clothes and underwear. I mentally praised myself for having had the foresight to have brought some clothes still on hangers; I would have to get more on Monday. I placed my shoes on the floor of the one and only closet, which was really just a coat closet but would be my everything closet. At least it had one shelf.

On the table next to the day bed, I put out my grandmother's travel clock and the little transistor radio tape player Cass had given me all those months ago in Paris. It was still working perfectly and I was in heaven when I found WLS-FM right off the bat. FM radio was the new wonder in our lives in those days, and I was spoiled right away with the Chicago stations.

And then I began to realize I was feeling hunger pangs. What to do?

I needed to explore the area more in order to get a feeling for where I really was in relation to that more commercial street we had passed. I gathered up all my keys, and went out with the intent of not bringing back too big a load of anything right away. I just needed some food to get me through the weekend. I was to find out that literally hundreds of little grocery markets dotted the Chicago landscape in those days, and the bigger chains there were A & P and Jewel; but I had no idea where they might be.

I went into the first food shop I saw, which was called Ernie's, and picked up a small basket—that way I wouldn't buy too much at one time. I went straight for the dairy case and got a quart of milk and some butter. I then put in a loaf of bread and a box of Rice Krispies. Next I went to the soda aisle and as I reached for the Coca Cola, suddenly realized that I would be repeating my Paris faux-pas! I immediately ascertained that Ernie's had a limited housewares section, and I could pick up a bottle opener. A flash of insight also had me buying one ice-cube tray as well.

Since my dishes and silverware wouldn't arrive for at least a week, I had to get paper plates, a small sleeve of paper cups, a plastic bowl, utensils, some napkins and, while in that section, I grabbed a roll of paper towels and a two-pack of toilet paper. Obviously I had no pots and pans yet, so buying anything like canned soup or frozen pizza would have been useless. I concluded that I would have to subsist, at least that first few days, on sandwiches and cereal. A package of ham and a pack of sliced cheese would make that happen.

The elderly man with white hair and mustache (Ernie?) rang up my items to the tune of $ 13.45 (pretty expensive!), and put it all in a couple of brown paper bags that did not have handles. Even though what I bought was not all that heavy, it was still bulkier and more awkward to carry than I had planned. I lugged the bags back to my house and up those stairs, making a mental note to not do this again. I wished America had net filets or least those little plaid carriers on wheels I had seen so many French women take to market-- and even onto the *métro*.

The fence locked automatically behind me once I was inside of it, and the front door lock was easy to operate once I had the right key in it. (Note to self: mark the three keys.)

All this moving in and figuring out sustenance took my mind off being nervous about starting the actual work on Monday. I settled into the chair by the window. My drapes were still open and dusk was descending upon the sky outside. I saw the Blue Light car pull up to the curb and contemplated going out to meet Jake, but decided it could wait. Instead I took out a brand-new blank journal I had brought with me for just this occasion, and made the first entry under the title: Congratulations! This is the first day of the rest of your life.

346

Chapter Fifty-Nine

"Upstairs by a Chinese Lamp"…Laura Nyro

I set the alarm on my grandmother's clock, but needn't have because I awoke godawful early for my first day on the job. I had no real idea how long it was going to take to walk to work or the route that would be the most advantageous, so since I was winging it, I gave myself plenty of time. I didn't want to hurry that morning and make some mistake; I wanted the luxury of time to get it all right.

Chicago seemed far more bustling than any place I'd lived in prior to it, but that was a false equivalency; I couldn't compare sleepy little Omaha to it. Even though I could certainly compare it to Paris, in that city I rarely had to insert myself into a rush-hour situation; I always had classes right down the stairs or else ones that started after 9:00 a.m.

I found my way easily enough, as it turned out; the main street nearest to me, Dearborn, was not that far from Michigan Avenue, and when I got to that street, of course I knew my way straight to the building that housed the *Fondation Culturelle Française*. I remembered there was a coffee shop in the lobby of the building, and people were milling around there outside its doors. Since I was, as luck would have it, too early after all, I ordered a small orange juice and sipped it sitting on the edge of a leather couch. Finally as the appointed starting hour of 8:30 a.m., approached, I went on up.

The elevator opened right into the office, as I knew from my interview, and I straightened my skirt before the doors parted. I had chosen the brown checked skirt and white blouse that I'd bought at Brandeis, and had carried the Bagagerie purse that Cass had bought me in Paris. I was especially happy with the new brown shoes, too: very comfortable for walking. Instead of wearing the little brown neck scarf, I tied my hair back with it. I wore the pearl choker necklace and pearl earrings, feeling great that no one could ever tell real pearls from fake. The color scheme of brown and white was thus accomplished. My skirt was short enough to be hip but the ensemble gave off conservative chic.

As I entered the space around the receptionist's desk, I was greeted warmly by Bernadette Cabriot, and told that Madame de Piaget had asked for me to be shown into her office upon arrival. So I followed her to the beautiful corner office I'd seen in March. I could not have found it myself, however, as the myriad of hallways and cubicles seemed even more confusing this time than when I was taken on that first brief tour at the interview.

Madame de Piaget also greeted me just as warmly in French, and she took care to pronounce my name Shrier rather than "Shree-air," unlike most of the personnel at the *Maison des Étudiantes* . She offered me a chair and said she'd like to take me to meet the President of the Foundation, Jean-Paul d'Arivèque, but first she wanted to reiterate that I shouldn't be shocked to see him because of his being *éstropié*. That was a word I did know, but still could not believe she used. She had said it before…in English. It meant "crippled." I cringed to hear that word again, but couldn't correct her.

Even in 1970, we were no longer calling people by that term. Not that there was anything like the Americans with Disabilities Act even on the national radar at that time; people said "handicapped" and thought they were being respectful.

She made it a point to say that she wouldn't be so concerned with my reaction if she hadn't seen worse before. She made no reference to his actual condition or what I should expect to see, but just about how she'd seen people recoil, either out of pity or derision. Throughout the whole time she was talking to me, I still felt it was ridiculous. How crass and rude did she think people were? Was it a French thing? Did she feel Americans were worse? I'd grown up during the polio epidemic, and more than one kid in every school I ever attended, including Iowa U , had students with the aftereffects of the disease. I didn't think I could be too shocked at any physical limitation anyone had.

But something had obviously triggered this line of questioning, and then she added, "You know, it's usually a fear element. People are afraid of crippled people. It is as though they think they can catch it."

She took me down a beautiful, paneled-wall corridor to intricately carved French doors, which opened into another wide reception area, where two more people had desks on either side of a large glass-enclosed corner office. Jean-Paul d'Arivèque was seated on an elaborately decorated chair behind what was at once recognizable as a very grand Louis XV-style Rococo writing desk. It looked like it came straight from a museum with its elaborate parquetry and elegant gilt edging. The chair neither swiveled nor rolled, so it took some effort for him to get out of it--which he did--to stand and meet me. He held out his right hand to me, and I could see that his other arm was hanging rather limp at his side, although his hand seemed to be able to move, and he could balance his weight on the desk with it. He wore a brace on the left leg, which he reached over and locked with his right hand as he stood up, but he was really only standing on his right leg behind the desk.

And that was all it was; nothing I would have had to be prepared to be shocked about. It puzzled me even more why this was made out to be such a big deal.

Madame de Piaget introduced me as *"la nouvelle cinématequaire, Mademoiselle Sarah Shrier."*

"Enchanté, Mademoiselle," he said giving me a nice smile.

" Je suis très heureuse de faire votre connaissance, Monsieur, " I answered shaking his hand –one pump-- and smiling back.

Madame de Piaget said, *"Je m'excuse, alors, et je vous laisse, "* and she quietly left the room and closed the glass doors behind her. Monsieur motioned for me to take a seat and then he rather laboriously sat back down, too. He switched to English.

"Perhaps you are wondering why the Foundation wanted especially an American for this position?"

"Um… yes… Madame explained to me about being a liaison of some kind to schools?"

"The Foundation was begun by my mother. You have not, I think, as yet had the opportunity to learn about us except most briefly. One of her dreams, yes, that is the word, was to enhance our engagement with the academic world. We have much to offer to schools and universities of all sorts, and the means to do so with no cost to them. But we must have more visibility. Do you see what I mean?"

"Yes, Monsieur, I understand. I'm not a teacher myself, but I can venture a guess that once they hear 'no cost' it will pique their interest and enthusiasm."

"Exactly. And I am hoping as you get the film library up and running, *au fur et à mesure*, you will liaison, as Marie-France explained, with schools, and provide them with films and information from us."

"Absolutely!"

"Everyone on our staff, from our publication people to the public relations department to the various departments of the arts—right down to the mailroom speaks some English. *Évidément, on habite à Chicago.* But few of them have English as their native tongue, and I wanted the film librarian to be American…with a strong understanding of French, it goes without saying."

"Oui, Monsieur."

He paused and looked up at me, not exactly smiling but with a rather kind expression, especially in his eyes.

"So," he said, extending his hand once again to me, "welcome, and I hope you will soon be comfortably settled into the library and your duties. I am afraid after the remodeling we just did, it is a bit of a *bazaar*---a mess in there? "

I couldn't answer him because I still hadn't seen it yet. So I said, "I'm sure it's fine."

"Good," he said. "If you would be so kind as to wait in the outer office, I shall send for Madame de Piaget once again to take you."

I thanked him and did as he instructed me. Soon Marie-France was by my side once more, and we headed out of the presidential suite of offices and back into the corridor. I had no idea where the library was from there. It was becoming more and more obvious to me that the first time I was there for the interview, I hadn't seen half of the place. We came to an intersection of two corridors, where off to one side I could see the main reception again with the elevator doors; and straight down yet another hall I saw the film library now visible without plastic barriers.

"Oh, wow, " I almost gasped. The library was accessible by glass French doors and you could see everything: the projection booth at the top of the room, the new theater seats in front of it on an incline, and my desk at the bottom of the room, which was lined in shelving. There were also file cabinets, a long table on one end of the room, and on the wall to the side of my desk was a little "conversation" corner of two rounded leather armchairs and a small table with a lamp on it. My desk had a phone on it, and there was an identical one in the booth, I noticed.

"You have a special phone, " she said pointing at it. "It has an '800' number, so people can call in and order films or ask questions and so on without paying a long-distance fee."

"Oh! My goodness! Really? It's a free call for them? "

"Yes. And if you need to call long distance for any reason to verify a mailing or return a call if you miss it, it is also free for you to do so. We ask that you log the outgoing calls. See, here is a logbook you will use. You can log the incoming ones, too, but we do not actually keep track of those."

I didn't have to think about this long: Cass and I would be able to talk on the phone to our heart's content! I'd also give the number to Soren in case the idea moved either of us to chat. What a windfall!

"Another thing I need to show you, " continued Madame, "is the screen. It can be automatically lowered from a panel in the ceiling by a control in the projection booth. Shall we start in there then?" And she led me up there asking, "And do you know how to run a projector?"

"I think so. We had one at home and showed movies when I was a kid."

"The professional ones are bigger, of course, " she said. "But there is a little illustration of the threading right on the machine. If you follow it, you should not have any problems."

"That's handy," I admitted, but had a twinge of panic when I saw the huge machine. I flashed on reels of celluloid flowing down from it and onto the floor. Yikes.

"Your first task would of course be to catalogue the film collection. After that, Monsieur Jean-Paul feels you might want to watch any films with which you are not now familiar, in order to be better able to advise potential clients as to the content and so on."

"Oh, that would be a great idea." I didn't tell her how woefully ignorant I really was of film. I'd never taken a film class, and although a fan and a steady movie-goer, even in Paris, I was nowhere near expert on any of it. But I vowed to myself that I would do my best to learn it. I was going to be paid to watch movies all day. There were worse jobs!

Madame de Piaget then talked to me about the supply room and the break room, where there was always coffee.

"We in the office even try to take breaks at certain times to stagger the people who help on the front switchboard, " she said, and then explained that I could take my own breaks when I wished, since I was not going to be called upon to join that switchboard relief team any time soon.

"But some day we will probably train you on it just in case."

The other place I needed to see-- and figure out how to get to-- was the copy room. Normally copy assistants ran things for the office on the large Xerox machine, she explained. They were in charge of the operation of it, changing paper and putting in toner. But we were allowed to make our own copies if they weren't there, or if we wanted to do it ourselves.

"When the library is functional," Madame spelled out to me, "you will be sending the films with a return label and a form cover letter which you will type. We do not use carbon paper anymore," she continued, "so each time you will make a Xerox copy and file it. That way we will build up a client base record automatically."

I felt like I should have followed her around with a steno pad in my hand and taken notes, but I didn't; so I hoped I could remember half of what she said, and find a path at least to the main reception area where the elevator was, not to mention the bathroom!

Even though I felt my first day on the job didn't really get going until it was almost time to leave, it didn't take long to settle into the office routine. By the end of the first week, I was already loving it. My desk area was stacked from day one with film canisters, and the task of getting them sorted, catalogued, and onto the empty shelving units was my first order of business. I was impressed with the titles we had, among which were the *crème de la crème* of French cinema: *La Belle Dame sans Merci; La Cousine Bette*, based on the Balzac novel I'd read in Paris; *La Glace à Trois Faces*; Godard's *A Married Woman*, and hundreds more. It seemed like it would take me forever to even make a dent in this undertaking; but no one seemed to have me on a deadline, and I wanted the results to be meticulous when I was done.

I hadn't been in Chicago very long when suddenly I had a message that my mother's boxes from home containing the stereo, new t.v. and all my goodies were waiting for me at the bus station; and almost simultaneously to that, the boxes Cass had mailed me to the office address also arrived, only instead of two there were three. She had taken it upon herself to send me the Indian bedspread and the Chinese lamp we'd had in our Iowa City summer apartment. I was thrilled but also in a quandary as to how to take them home, and pick up Betty's to boot. I decided that even though I was new to the job, I would have to ask to leave a little bit early one day soon, and take a taxi with my three boxes to the bus station in order to pick up the other ones. If I got home before five o'clock, one of the workers at the place could probably be cajoled into helping me schlep all that up the stairs. It was a plan.

But whom to approach? I was friendly with the front desk receptionist, but I didn't think she had any authority to grant me an early release. I didn't really know any of the staff of the Foundation at that point.

One of the secretaries had sort of accosted me in the break room the second day I was there, and even though I vowed to be friendly with absolutely everyone in the office, she had rubbed me the wrong way almost immediately.

Her name was Henrietta Vargane, Hennie for short. She was another American – of French descent-- and her personality had an intense edge to it. She was taller than me, slim and wore a sort of uniform every day of neatly put-together pencil skirts and sweaters. She had the leathery complexion of someone who'd spent her youth – maybe her entire life – in the sun. Her lips were pursed tight which gave her an angry air, and her light blue eyes had lines around the edges. She had freckles on her nose and longish, curly blond hair. She had explained to me right off that she worked in the legal department.

"Sooo, we have a legal department?" No one had pointed that out to me.

"Oh yeah, it's almost connected to the presidential offices. Daniel Rosier de Molet is the chief legal counsel. Have you met him yet?" she had asked, not coming up for air, and I had shaken my head. "I'm not his personal secretary, of course. Suzanne Lefevre is his actual secretary. I work for her, and another girl also works in our office for the other lawyer, whose name is Madeleine Guerin. Rosier and Guerin also serve on the board of the Foundation, so a lot of what we do is for the board."

"I'm the new film librarian, " I had offered as soon as I could jump into the conversation.

"Oh, I know!" she said, sitting down with her cup of coffee and smoothing her tight skirt. "I'm a very sociable person," she added …apropos of what, I had no idea. People who had to define themselves like that the first time they were introduced, raised a red flag to me. I had tried after that to tune her out if we met in the coffee room, and if I did run into her, I would usually try to make myself busy with coffee and something called Cremora, a product I had never seen before.

So not wanting to go to Hennie for advice, I decided the obvious path would be to seek out Madame de Piaget's secretary, Annie-Laure Lebeau, and ask her the protocol. I surmised she would know how I should go about it, and I knew she was friendly; she, too, was one of the staff members I'd met early on, and I really liked her. She was a little bit older than me and had been working at the Foundation for six years already, having come over from Lisieux, France on an exchange program during high school and met Marie-France de Piaget at the Chicago *Alliance Française*. Madame de Piaget, who knew the host family, had taken to Annie-Laure immediately, and had told her about the Foundation. When she turned eighteen, and passed the "Bac," Annie-Laure jumped at the opportunity to work in the U.S., and moved to Chicago. Once there, she applied to and started night classes at U Illinois Chicago Circle. It had taken her five years to get her BA, but she did it, as well as obtaining dual citizenship.

I decided to wait until almost quitting time to approach her in her office area, and ask if the next day I could possibly leave an hour early.

"Yes, of course, I shall ask Madame, but I am sure she will allow it, " she said, smiling at me. "Do you have problems?"

"Not really problems, " I said, "but I have a few moving issues. I had some things shipped to me here instead of to my apartment, where no one would be home. So I need to take a taxi with these boxes that I already have, and go pick up some other ones at the Greyhound Station on my way home. "

I also explained to her in the briefest of terms why I needed to get there before five and catch a worker to help me.

"Oh!" she suddenly exclaimed, "but I have a better solution for you!"

"You do?"

"*OUI!* My boyfriend is Jean-Luc!"

I just stood there, not registering why this would help me.

"He is the chauffeur to Monsieur d'Arivèque and he can drive you! You will not have to leave early because he doesn't drive Monsieur until at least 6:30, and you are not that far from the office, no?"

"I –I guess that's right. What about the bus depot detour though?"

"Yes, yes, it is close enough. I shall ask Luc. Maybe I will accompany you, also, and help you carry things, yes?"

"Really?! Thanks!"

"I will let you know what he says. You want to do this tomorrow, is that right?"

"That would be great."

It was great, except that when she came into my office later to tell me the good news, she said that "Luc" had asked permission from Jean-Paul d'Arivèque to take the Foundation car, the limo.

"Oh no, " I said, "I didn't want to bother him with all this! Let alone make him think I wanted to be driven in his limousine. "

"But that was his idea! " She pronounced it "i-deee" … French people could never seem to get that word right.

"You have to be joking."

"No, no. It was all his idea. Tomorrow Jean-Luc and me, we shall both help you get the boxes down to the car. Do not worry!"

I just sort of sat there, stunned again at my good fortune to have found this job. After the main office closed, I sat down at my typewriter, the fabulous IBM Selectric with the interchangeable balls—one with the English keyboard and one with the French!—to write Cass a letter. I had not yet told her about the free phoning we would be soon be taking advantage of, and I had to give her instructions on how to call me, because I didn't think I should call her on the toll-free line—at least not for a while. The library wasn't functioning, so there would have been no reason for me to be calling out. And I didn't want to NOT log an outbound call. So I wrote her a long letter (so much faster and easier on an electric typewriter, I couldn't believe it) with the amazing "magic" number. I was sure she would be very surprised.

Dear Cass,
The boxes arrived! Thank you so much! And thanks for the extra one, too---sneaky!! But I love our old stuff, especially the lamp. I will use them! I love my apartment. The chaos of builders and machines and all that doesn't bother me. And of course, Jake the security guard is my protector! I haven't talked to your father since arriving –just his secretary—but I do thank him for all this…again and again. And, by the way, I will also be reimbursing you for the postage, just like I said I would. I can tell what it cost you from the boxes.

Anyway, you are not going to believe what I'm going to write next: It's the most incredible news: after you get this letter you can call me any time and we can talk for free! So keep this number handy: 800-323-3324. It's called a toll-free number! You can use it to call in to me and never have it show up on your long-distance bill. Can you believe it?! And, though this sounds a little funny, I can't really use the phone to call you—you're not a school, etc. and I have to log the out-going calls. I think if you call when Alan goes to late afternoon classes, if that's convenient, that would be about perfect, because I can talk more towards the end of the workday, and it doesn't matter when I leave here. People work late all the time. There are not many people who work in my area of the offices, either. Hell, I could stay all night if I had to (but I'm only joking---some cleaning crew must come in---my wastebasket is always empty when I get here).

Work is going great. I'm deep in up to my knees with film canisters to catalogue, but I'm getting it. I can also take the movies out and watch them—they even want me to-- so if someone asks about the film I can speak with at least the authority of someone who has seen it. But I can't watch them all---we have hundreds! You know that film festival we went to last year in the Union? Well, they can borrow films from the Foundation in future and not have to pay royalties on them! The Foundation pays for everything! Just imagine!

Of course, I met the President and he seems really nice. He's probably twenty years older than us and he's French and looks it, except that he's kind of paunchy for a Frenchman. I don't know how long he's been in America but it's probably our food that did it. Anyway, as I had been informed, he's handicapped, but not much! I don't know what my immediate boss was so

concerned about my reaction for. So he can't walk very well---big deal. I think what gives him more trouble is that his arm is also sort of out of commission. His hand "works" okay but he really can't use the one arm. So one side doesn't function fully. I figure he must have had polio or something; I didn't ask. Anyway, he's even quite handsome –in a mature way. He's got dark hair--longish compared to American executives--- and he has brown eyes, a rather patrician nose and a lovely smile. My boss treats him with great reverence and I think other people around here really like him, too. It turns out I have to also attend "functions" like dinners at his home because that place operates like a Foundation hospitality center of some sort! Can you dig it? They host important guests to Chicago with ties to the French community. I guess the first one I will attend is coming up soon…and, as per usual, I have nothing to wear; it's summer, so your kilt won't do. By the way, in case you were wondering, we only have a loose dress code at the office: no jeans or shorts of course. Hardly anyone wears pants, but my job involves a lot of climbing on library step stools and ladders, so I've been wearing them. I also wear my denim skirt; so far no one has said anything to me. No one sees me anyway.

I like the people I work with, more or less (ha!) One secretary has sort of befriended me on the grounds that I'm one of the other few Americans on staff. We've gone to lunch a couple of times, but she never shuts up about herself and it's starting to bug me. She's from California originally, and got divorced---just walked out of her house with hardly anything---got on a plane and came here. She lives in a boarding house she says, and got this job right away because, in her own words, she's a hot-shot legal secretary. (We have an entire legal department, don't ya know. Hell, we have a bunch of departments: music events, literary events, education, film, visual arts, performing arts, kids and families, grants administration, public relations, marketing. We put out a slick little newsletter quarterly! I mean, I had no idea when I came here in March that the office was so big.)

I can't wait to hear all about what those ten-month- olds are doing. Can you believe how fast they're growing!? Now that they're on the move, are you going crazy? Don't answer that. I'll talk to you SOON!
    Love, Moi

    The next afternoon at regular quitting time, Annie-Laure and Jean-Luc Moreau--whom everyone called Luc, as she had the previous day--showed up in my office. We each carried a box to the lobby, where just outside at the curb, the limo was waiting. Jean-Luc and I were introduced to each other. He was cute! Pretty tall for a Frenchman, with dark curly hair and a broad, friendly smile. He wore a real chauffeur's uniform like in the movies. I couldn't believe it.

    Annie-Laure got in the back seat and beckoned for me to follow, while Luc loaded the boxes in the trunk. He drove us first to the bus station where I picked up my other boxes at the will-call window of the freight office, and then on to my house, where they were, not unexpectedly, a little more than mildly surprised to see the barrier of fence and gates I had to go through to get in.

    "What is…wait… this is it? Where you live?" Annie-Laure asked glancing incredulously at the mess off to the side of the building.

    "Is this place deserted except for you?" Luc wanted to know looking at me with an expression of non-belief.

    "It's all fine!" I said, "I am kind of a squatter, but with permission! It's completely safe---look how I'm behind the fence---two locks!"

    "But," protested Luc, " the back of the building is…almost…open!"

    "Yes, but notice, the property is surrounded by that high fence. And there's a security company that patrols all night starting when the workers leave. So…really, it's not dangerous."

    I thanked them profusely for all their help and apologized for not having anything to offer them other than water in the house! I felt very embarrassed at that and vowed to rectify the situation once I got paid, making a mental note to what extent my first paycheck was already going to be eaten up the minute I deposited it, but still happy I was actually going to get a paycheck!

    Once I was alone I got down to seriously setting up housekeeping with my motley collection of pots and pans and Melmac dishes, sheets and towels, Indian bedspread, the Chinese lantern lamp, and the second television set! I turned it on and tuned in WTTW, soon to become Chicago's nascent PBS station. It wouldn't be long before I'd be hooked on my very first British costume drama, The First Churchills. Life was especially good.

Chapter Sixty

"Along Comes Mary"…The Association

I had to face facts: I had never worked in an office before. I'd worked in my parents' bar and grill. I'd worked in the Iowa Memorial Union behind the desk. But I'd never been part of a large organization with any office hierarchies, office politics, cliques or the ensuing crap that came from all that. Hennie was only too willing to give me a full-blown orientation on office gossip, but I had to put the brakes on it; I just didn't want to know. I wanted to do my work and not take the office home with me at night. Luckily I was in the perfect position to do that, isolated as I was, far from the larger reception area, miles from the Presidential suite, and nowhere near any of the other departments. My space was, in fact, in a deserted wing.

As I began getting the films catalogued and more in order, I started to wonder who was ever going to find out about this library and our services. So I approached Annie-Laure with the intention of asking Marie-France de Piaget about an idea I had. I broached it with Annie-Laure first, and she was enthusiastic… and got me right in.

"Do you think the research department of our office could find me a list of all the French teachers in the Chicago metro area?" I asked Madame. "I could send out information on Foundation letter head, giving them a short introduction to the Foundation's ability to provide them with films for class."

"Why, I think that is a good suggestion! " she exclaimed, rather startled, it seemed to me, that I had come up with the idea. Since she knew that her secretary and I were becoming friendly, she had Annie-Laure take me to the marketing department and introduce me to someone who could look up the information for me. They said it wouldn't take too long to generate a list.

In the meantime, I still had a lot of work to do to get the lending part of this project up and running. There had to be a dating system, some way for me to know what films were out at any given time, and when they were expected to be returned. Everything was no cost to the borrowers, but on the other hand, we weren't giving the films away for them to keep either; they had to come back to us. I decided two weeks would be a long enough period to lend out films, and made up form letters with the lending time-frame information. I also stopped into our copy room and asked Pénélope, the clerk in there, if we could make some sort of return address label template.

"That way, I can just copy sets of them onto label paper that I can then peel off and affix to every return mailer, " I explained.

She was happy to oblige, and I felt I was making progress.

When I got the list of teachers a few weeks later, I noticed that one of the schools was right in my neighborhood, and indeed, had I taken a slightly different route to work in the mornings, I would have passed just in front of it. So, I purposely walked over there one morning in late June, expecting to see nothing, since schools were out for the summer; but instead the place seemed bustling! I saw on the marquee at the edge of the school property that summer school was in session June 15 through August 1. Stunned by this realization that Chicago schools must have offered nearly year-round classes, I decided to check out what was being taught during the summer: remediation, enrichment or possibly both.

I was new to Chicago, but I realized that you couldn't just walk into a big urban high school, even in those days, and expect to be able to see a teacher; and I didn't want to be misconstrued as a solicitor of any sort. So I continued on to my workplace, and phoned Lincoln Park High School, asking to speak to the first French teacher on the list from there, a Mr. Dominique Lambert. I didn't know if he were French or American or if his last name was pronounced "LAM-bert" or "Lahm-BAIR," so I asked for him by the English variation first, and they seemed to understand who I meant. In about five minutes, he was on the phone.

I introduced myself, with apologies for bothering him at work, explained what the *Fondation Culturelle Française* was, and briefly mentioned our film service. I wondered if I could stop by the school on the way to the office in the next few days and meet him, all of which was amenable to him. He said if I got there by 8:15, he would still be free to talk for a little while before his summer classes started.

It wasn't yet 8:00 o'clock when I walked into the huge high school on Orchard Street, and was escorted to the office by a student greeter in the lobby. Even though students were present, the atmosphere seemed decidedly more relaxed in June than it would have been in September. Classes didn't get underway for about an hour, so I did as Lambert had advised on the phone, and waited for him to come meet me in the office. There, I was given a visitor's badge, and invited to follow him to the teachers' lounge.

"Thank you for seeing me, Mr. Lambert, " I said sitting down with him at a long table.

"You can call me Dom, " he said, smiling at me.

"Okay, I will, thanks."

I explained what the Foundation was--in more depth this time--and what our film library services to teachers would be once we got it all functioning.

"I'm sorry I'm here without any formal brochures or written catalogue lists of our offerings, but those are coming," I explained. "I was just wondering, " I continued, a bit timidly, " if, when we get this all going, well, if I could prevail upon you to spread the word to the other French teachers…and any other faculty who might want to show a French film… and tell them about how they can borrow them for free and all."

"I'd be happy to spread the word," he said, "but better yet, you should be asked back here in the Fall — maybe during our back-to-school in-service week, to address the Foreign Language department and explain all that you offer yourself."

"Well, sure, " I said, "but do you think the other languages would be interested in receiving information about French culture?"

"Give them food for thought about how they could be better utilizing their own consulates. You did say that your organization was part of the French Consulate, didn't you?"

"No! Gee, I hope I didn't confuse you. Our organization is private. We do work with the Consulate and the Cultural Attachés here in Chicago, but we're not under their auspices."

"Got it. Well, we have three other French teachers, some of whom don't do French exclusively like I do; but I'm sure it would interest them. I think the others would find it helpful, too. Leave me your card and I'll get back in touch with you."

Card. It never occurred to me to have one, yet I remembered Clément in France, and how whenever I met French people, even students, they all had their cards. One of these days I'd get some made up, I swore to myself.

"I'm afraid I'm still so new that I don't have a card, yet, " I answered trying to think on my feet.

"It's all right. Just write down your information on this, " he laughed, handing me a piece of paper he'd grabbed from a mimeograph machine parked on a little rolling cart behind us.

Arriving at the Foundation, I stopped by Marie-France de Piaget's office to report on my morning's meeting. I didn't have an appointment, so I conveyed my news to Annie-Laure first, and, since it was fresh in my mind, I hesitatingly told her of my need for business cards eventually. She readily agreed to look into the matter for me.

I was pleased with having made a connection in the French education community with Dom, and I felt a bit of confidence well up in my abilities to promote our films. I saw Hennie in the break room that day, and regaled her with my encounter at the high school.

"You took it upon yourself , eh? To go there and all? Now you're thinking like me!" she exclaimed approvingly, placing her finger to her forehead, adding, apropos of nothing, "What a mind I have!"

I looked at her and thought "spare me" but didn't say anything. No amount of self-promotion was ever going to come from my lips if it sounded like that.

Even as Hennie was already getting on my nerves, she was also taking me under her wing. One Sunday she invited me over to her boarding house, the Ensonia, and I met several of the other people living there. We all went out for brunch. Hennie was involved with one of the fellow boarders, a man she introduced me to as her **French** boyfriend, Jacques Simonet, but whom everyone called "Mop," due to the obvious fact that his hair sat upon his head in curly clumps resembling an old-fashioned rag mop. Mop was a man of few words but, as Hennie had already made me feel uncomfortable when she divulged it, "the sex is outstanding!"

There weren't very many women in Hennie's circle, but one named Jeannie, also a resident of the rooming house, was a *danseuse manquée* with the Chicago ballet, which I came to learn meant that she had got one role a few years prior in the *corps de ballet* on a one-time contract, and ever since had been clamoring to get hired on as a member of the troupe. She took many dance classes, but also must have indulged once too frequently in Chicago's signature deep-dish pizza, because she did not have that ultra-slim profile of a ballerina by any stretch. What she did have was a heightened sense of attitude about herself and her ballerina persona. Nevertheless, Jeannie intrigued me, and she was friendly, so that was welcomed.

"I'm a White Russian, " she told me the first time we met. "My great-grand-parents immigrated in 1917."

I only knew the term "White Russian" as a cocktail. I just didn't know enough about Russian history to be more impressed with her.

"My family came here as émigrés from the Russian Revolution," she said with an aura of smugness.

"I guess I'm pretty nil on the Russian Revolution, " I admitted.

"So…there were the two armies, basically . The White Army fought against the Red Army who were staging the Revolution. The White movement," "she explained in a perturbed manner, "wanted nothing to do with so-called 'soviet' organizations. They rejected the creation of nation states and wanted to keep the Russian Empire intact." She paused and added, "We loved the Czar."

"My great-grandparents and their children immigrated from Russia, too…about ten years before yours! They were fleeing pogroms. Russia wasn't very friendly to Jews, you know. In fact, Czarist Russia was very anti-Semitic," I reiterated, looking straight at her with intensity.

"Hmmph, yes. I see."

So she knew I was Jewish. She didn't seem to mind. In fact, the funny thing was, she and I sort of looked alike, which I was also sure did not escape her.

Jeannie and I actually did become friends, and in spite of her living in the Ensonia, she was still very close to her mother, who lived on the West Side and whom she visited faithfully each week. One time she invited me back to her mother's tiny apartment over on Damen Avenue. This lady was a wonderful cook, and her home was filled with tantalizing aromas when we entered. The place was also a little shrine to Ukrainian artifacts and Russian Orthodox icons. Jeannie's mom was very nice to me, and asked after my Russian roots, much to my embarrassment and chagrin.

"I'm so sorry I'm ignorant, " I told her. "You know, I was a kid in elementary school during the '50s, when we were all hiding under our desks because of the Soviets and the H-Bomb, and the last thing we did was admit we were of Russian descent. I said I was German and left it at that."

Shrier didn't sound Russian, so I got by with the lie. And in fact, my not-so-distant family had already entered the realm of myth by the time I was growing up in the American Midwest. I didn't even know the circumstances of their Russian life or why they came to America in the first place. It was much later on that I found out that my other side, Betty's family, were called Dozlovsky before the name was changed to Dalkin at Ellis Island.

"I knew they were from a shtetl near Minsk and that was about all," I told Jeannie and her mother, between heaping helpings of the very un-Russian dinner of veal scaloppini in sweet red pepper sauce.

"What do you think about the Ensonia?" Jeannie asked me as she poured me a glass of chianti from one of those bottles that looked like it was seated in a basket. "Half the time I refer to it as 'The Insania,'"she quipped.

She wasn't half wrong; they were a motley crew, but I did begin, after meeting Jeannie through Hennie, to hang out a bit on weekends with that crowd. Some were students, others had what we'd call "entry-level" jobs. Still others worked "temp" or held odd jobs for short periods of time. Some were stoners, and the aroma of weed, punctuated by incense, wafted through the halls.

One particular guy, Ray, a licensed practical nurse who worked in individuals' homes, took a liking to me, and asked me out for dinner. I met him down in the Loop one night after I got off work. Summer time in Chicago was noted for long scorching days with heat and humidity lingering into the evening. So being outside, especially near the lake, where we ended up going for a walk, meant less time sweltering in my little studio.

"Well, " he said, as I was getting ready to catch a bus from where we'd walked to on Lake Shore Drive, "are you going to ask me over to your place?"

"Umm, no. I can't, sorry" I answered. "It's a long story, my house isn't any too conducive to late night visitors."

"Nosey landlords? What?"

" Something like that." I wasn't about to go into it; I didn't necessarily even want him to know where I lived, and my living circumstances were too convoluted to explain to most people. He wasn't too happy about this turn of events.

"Seems like after a nice dinner, we might want to get to know each other a little better, that's all," he said stroking wisps of my hair back behind my ear and making an awkward attempt to nibble at it.

Pulling his hand away from my face I said, "I'm not going to be living there after next year, so I'll have more say about who comes and goes then."

"Next year!? What makes you think I'll be hanging around that long?"

"Nothing makes me think that." And with that, I thanked my lucky stars the bus pulled up. If it had been France, we would have still parted ways with *la bise*, but since I got the distinct impression he wanted after-dinner sex rather than a good-night kiss, I just hopped on the bus with a little wave to him.

Of course, the next time I saw Hennie at work, she knew all about this brief encounter.

"Didn't you think he was a nice guy or what?" she asked me rather curtly.

"Not the point, " I said, trying to sound nonchalant. "I'm not interested in sleeping with men I don't know, and I don't consider one dinner a chance to get to know anyone on that level. And for that matter, I told him the truth. My apartment is like Fort Knox. It's a big hassle to take someone in there, and then have to go back down and unlock the fence for them to leave. What if I **were** to sleep with someone? Am I going to get all dressed again to go back outside? I don't think so."

"Well, why can't they stay?"

"Because a night watchman is watching the place! And, much as I'm an adult and can do what I want, I don't want !"

"In that case, " she concluded after a moment's reflection, " you've got a fucked living situation!"

"Yeah, well, it's a gift horse , so…I can't really look it in its mouth."

Chapter Sixty-One

"Victim of Circumstance"…The City (Carole King)

Mid-summer hit, and with that, the French national holiday loomed on our horizon. French organizations like the Chicago branch of the *Alliance Française* and the French Consulate were already advertising their big events for Bastille Day. The French Cultural Foundation was right in there with them, although our party was not for the general public; it was for the office, plus invited dignitaries, and it was to be held at Jean-Paul d'Arivèque's residence.

When we came in one morning in early July, we all found beautiful engraved invitations on our desks. They were printed in red ink on white cotton stock paper, and festooned with blue ribbon braid. Pinned to the back of the invitation was a pretty tri-color *cocarde* we could wear on our clothes or in our hair. It was to be an indoor "*pique-nique*" and the dress was marked "casual. "

I told Cass on the phone when she called, "Casual to me means jeans, but I've never once seen any of the people around here in denim. This event will be populated with people who don't know the meaning of the word casual—namely French people!"

"Well, you could wear white pants and some sort of nautical top, " she offered. "Something crisp."

"Crisp, hmmm, that's close, " I laughed. "I'll have to search around for something meeting that description."

"It sounds mad, gay and exciting, though, " she offered. "What is his house like?"

"No idea, " I said. "But I understand it functions like a hotel. Oodles of staff work for him, and lots of important guests are invited to stay there. I heard that one of them coming to this thing is the new conductor of the Chicago Symphony."

"Whom my mother probably knows, " Cass laughed. "She and my grandmother have both been on and off that board forever."

"Oh, Christ, it didn't even occur to me that your parents might be friends of his! But hell, yeah, they could be there!"

"I hope not, for your sake," she said.

I didn't even want to think about that, so I changed the subject

"Anyway, how's it going with my favorite twins?!"

"Well, not speaking of mad, gay or exciting… things are going okay. I can't wait for them to see their Auntie Sari! They're all rosy-cheeked and crawling everywhere! I can't corral them both at once, and they do not like staying in their cribs."

"You need a playpen."

"You know, the words 'I need' are always on my lips, but the thought of one more baby thing in this tiny little house makes my head spin."

"But you have to have a safe place for them to keep out of trouble, don't you?"

"I have made an area with pillows, bordered with my couch and some chairs. So far that keeps them in. Won't last for long, though, I know."

"Cass, I have an idea! Go down to one of the appliance stores in town and get some cast-off refrigerator boxes. Cut them down and make a pen out of them. And put duct tape on it so it will fold but also stand up. Then paint it to look like a picket fence or a castle or something! It will work!"

"Hey, kid! I like that! You're a genius! No wonder you're the Auntie with the mostest. That doesn't exactly rhyme like 'hostess' does it? Ha!"

"Yeah, that's why they pay me the big bucks. Seriously, though, I think it might even work so that you'd have a moment to yourself to do art!"

She didn't readily agree or say much of anything.

"Cass, what's wrong?"

"Oh, you know, art…I don't have a second to do art."

"But what about when you put them down at night? Surely they go to sleep early?"

"I wish. No, I'm too exhausted at night. Plus I have to make meals and clean up and clean the house. You know, all the usual stuff."

"I'm afraid to ask, but doesn't Alan help at all?"

" He doesn't do much. And he hates my cooking, as you saw when you were here. But I'm giving it a real effort. I'm trying to do healthy stuff now, too! You know this organic movement? Have you read about it? It's hit Iowa City! I'm diggin' it!"

"So what is that, exactly? I haven't heard a thing."

"Well, I go to this co-op now! All the time-- for organically grown food. I hardly ever even shop at the regular supermarket. And I add stuff to the meals to sort of sneak in the healthy part. And I never fry anything… just steam or broil and roast. I make my own baby food so I don't buy that stuff in jars in the stores. I got a blender at the Goodwill. It works great."

"Are you giving the kids meat?" I asked, afraid to hear the answer.

"YES, don't worry! I made them beef and noodles the other night---puréed my little heart out."

I was relieved. While I didn't especially believe that safety and good nutrition were the hallmarks of store-bought processed baby food, I was afraid her kids wouldn't thrive if they ate what she ate. I didn't want to nag Cass at this point, believing that she was emotionally, as well as physically frail to begin with, but I was concerned for Laura's and Paul's growth and development.

" Uh, well… all right! I think that sounds great. If you make your own, then you needn't worry about all the chemical colors and preservatives we hear so much about. "

"And get this: I got some ice cube trays, and I can label and date the contents and freeze what I make. It keeps for up to five months! "

"Brilliant," I admitted.

"You know what else I made?" she asked excitedly, and didn't wait for my response: "Yogurt! And I added dried apricots — those were expensive! — and they just love it."

"Wow, where did you find yogurt culture?"

"Oh, the co-op sells that. They also sell some ready-made organic yogurt. I use that, too, to blend in with fruits. But you know, Sari, my ultimate goal is to grow most of our food ourselves and not shop in stores at all. I want a big garden next year. I can't wait!"

"Lots of work."

"Labor of love! And NO work at all to grow sprouts! You don't need anything, no plot, not even a window box if you don't want one. And they grow free of pesticides, bugs, or poison fertilizers. Sprouts are a foodstuff we can grow humanely with its own vibrant life-force!"

"No kidding. So are you doing it?"

" You better believe I am! You should see my soybeans. Did you know that while sprouting, soybeans' vitamin C increases by 500% or something?! It's a miracle of life, Sari. I'll show you everything when you come. When can you, by the way?"

"Well, probably not 'til Thanksgiving at this rate. I have no vacation time yet, of course. I wish I could come for their first birthday though! Damn! I'll send you guys a huge box of goodies, to be sure. How are they doing on clothes?"

"Still good. Listen, you don't have to go all out or anything."

"The hell I don't!"

I couldn't talk much more that day, but rang off telling her we'd have to speak after the party. "Be sure to call me!"

The office phone thing was working out well, but she did say that she had the urge to talk to me later at night, and might start writing more letters, since calling me at my home phone would run up bills neither of us could afford. I told her letters were good, too, and the truth of the matter was, some days, I could carve out a bit of time to sit and type at my desk as well.

As the big day for the party at d'Arivèque's approached, I asked Hennie what she was wearing to the wing-ding, and she shocked me by saying she wasn't going.

"But won't he expect us all?"

"I'm really just in the legal department, " she said, "and I don't want to bring Mop to something like that; it would bore him to tears. We're going to celebrate Bastille Day down at the beach."

"And you won't just put in an appearance? Go by yourself for a little while? I am!"

"I don't want to, " she said.

"Gosh."

I was pretty taken aback by this, especially from "I'm Miss Social" and all. It never occurred to me that we had a choice. Of course, when I interviewed, I had been told I would be expected to attend functions. Maybe the secretaries weren't. I asked Annie-Laure if she were going, however, with Jean-Luc, and they were, so I thought Hennie might actually get in some trouble for not being there.

I did angst over what to wear but it wasn't like I had much of a choice, and decided on my brown and white checked skirt and white blouse. It looked summery, if not nautical. I had no white pants, or any cute middy shirts. I couldn't go out and buy clothes for this thing.

The party was called for 4:00 p.m. and the air temperature alone at that time was still 98 degrees. I decided not to even tie a sweater over my shoulders like Parisians wore, because it would be superfluous. I attached the little *cocarde* to my cute Bagagerie purse, though, and thought it looked perfect pinned to the red leather.

Not wanting to risk getting lost or going to the wrong place, and mostly not wanting to walk or take buses in my outfit and arrive rumpled and sweaty, I called a taxi to get to the d'Arivèque mansion on North Lake Shore Drive; and in the back of my mind, hoped Annie-Laure and Luc might somehow be able to give me a ride home.

I arrived a little past the appointed hour, hoping not to be the first one there. I needn't have worried. People were streaming in from limos and cars; some who knew what they were doing drove around the side of the house and actually down into underground parking! I couldn't believe that. The place really did seem more like a hotel than a residence.

Except that it **was** a residence. I followed people up the sidewalk through an ornate low black iron gate, past carefully carved box-wood hedges, *à la française*, and into a cool Carrara marble floored entry hall, which led to a strangely long corridor with a lot of closed doors, all of which were private-looking and had numbers on the them. I just followed the group into an elevator, which stopped one floor up and spilled out into a very huge and formal foyer.

I must have made an audible gasp because Marie-France de Piaget, who was standing in the hall-- called the "reception," I later learned-- turned towards the sound and greeted me.

"*Ah, Mademoiselle Shrier. Bienvenue! Entrez.*"

"*Bonjour, Madame.*" I dispensed with the usual niceties of asking how she was because I found myself nearly approaching a state of stupefaction at what I was seeing before me. When I managed to close my jaw and look around, I still couldn't help but stare, gaping at the vastness and opulence into which I had been ushered. This man lived like Louis XIV in Versailles! The square footage of the room we were standing in dwarfed anything I'd seen at Cass's houses. It really resembled the American Embassy in Paris where we students had gone that rainy Bastille Day in 1968, with reception rooms large enough for 500 people or more. *Who lives like this?*

"My God," I murmured, "the place is a museum!" I didn't see one comfortable chair or sofa on which to sit; all the furniture was tufted and claw-footed and covered in silk brocade. I knew I'd be afraid to drink water, let alone wine, sitting on those chairs. The enormous room held a nine-foot black Steinway concert grand piano off in one corner and it looked tiny. The wall panels and doors had very ornate patterns of intricately carved wood, and were painted boiserie style in shades of cream and light green… and then gilded! The furnishings were also the same color -- light green with accents of the barest blush pink. Actual tapestries hung on the one wall that was not paneled, and the entire length of the room gave out onto a terrace overlooking Lake Michigan.

I wandered over to look out the French door floor-to-ceiling windows, and saw benches arranged around many topiary trees and even some fruit trees in boxes, just like one would see at the *Orangeries* at Versailles and the other French *châteaux*. Also outdoors were smaller conversation groupings of furniture around glass-topped tables or square hassocks made to withstand the elements. I only had a glimpse out there, however, because I heard my name and turned back to the room. Our host was standing by me, leaning rather heavily on his cane, I noticed. I was a bit startled by his immediate presence, but managed to sputter out a greeting in French.

"Bonjour, Monsieur d'Arivèque! Your...your house...home...is dazzlingly beautiful!"

"Mademoiselle Shrier, bonjour, " he said, placing his cane in his left hand and offering me his right one. I took it, but instead of the typical French one pump, he just sort of held my hand for an instant and then shook it. I looked up at him and smiled. He was, as I predicted, decked out in a "kit" as the Brits would say, of nothing casual at all, except that his white cotton dress shirt was open at the neck with no tie. He wore beautifully pleated light grey "summer weight" slacks and a stunning double-breasted navy-blue linen blazer with six gold buttons and a red pocket square. All he needed was an ascot and a yacht.

"This place is so lovely, " I repeated, finding my voice. "I'm just ...well, *épatée*, blown away."

He smiled at me with a look that said "questionable English vocabulary" but let it go. "I would like to introduce you to one of my guests, " he said. "Would you? " He motioned me to go in front of him with *"Je vous en prie,"* to which I replied, *"Pardon"*, as I passed him but then stepped aside to let him lead me through a congestion of guests. People were mingling everywhere, taking Baccarat champagne flutes from trays held by very proper waiters. On the other side of the room was a tall figure, a distinguished middle-aged, balding man with a very square jaw and rather heavy-lidded soft brown eyes. When he saw d'Arivèque he let out a delighted "Polo! My dear chap!"

POLO? I sort of looked around for someone else to be standing there.

"Maestro, how are you? " They kissed on each cheek and the man held on to d'Arivèque affectionately for a few seconds.

"Thank you for having me here ...again! "

"It is always my pleasure to welcome you back. I have someone here to introduce to you. Maestro, this is Mademoiselle Sarah Shrier our new film librarian at the Foundation. Sarah, this is Maestro Georg Solti."

My boss called him **George** in English, not the French softer pronunciation, nor the German "Gay-org" .

"Enchanté, Mademoiselle," Solti said, taking my hand in his as if to kiss it rather than shake it.

"Je suis très heureuse de faire votre connaissance, Monsieur...er...le ... Maestro. " I didn't know what to say to him so I took cues from d'Arivèque calling him Maestro; but even that seemed too familiar for me to use.

"Please call me George, " he said squinting a little smile to me. "Polo," he said, turning back to our host, "you wouldn't believe what I heard myself being called on the radio the other day...not in Chicago, I'm thankful to report. This moronic announcer pronounced my name "GERG". He looked back at me and added, "I am Hungarian by birth, Mademoiselle, and my name was György and I changed the spelling to the German Georg—'Gay-org'-- when I moved to work in Germany and Austria. But I live in England now, and when I settled there, insisted upon calling myself just the English 'George.' Like Handel did before me!"

A tuxedoed waiter showed up just then with champagne, which the maestro and I each took. Monsieur d'Arivèque wasn't really able to hold onto a glass and a cane, so he excused himself at that point, and went off to talk to other guests. Georg Solti led me into a part of the room with some empty seating.

Even though I'd heard that the new conductor of the Chicago Symphony would be at this gathering, and had told Cass that very thing, it still didn't register with me to whom I was speaking! After all, I'd never heard of him by name.

"So you're just visiting Chicago then? " I asked, giving away my state of stupidity right there.

"No, no. I started with the orchestra here last year. I stay with Polo sometimes because my new bride and I do not yet have a place here. She's in London, by the way, expecting our first child!"

"Congratulations!" I said, sipping on the best champagne I'd ever tasted and being taken aback by how good it really was. *(It was so good in fact, that I was reminded of Dom Perignon's pronouncement of "tasting the stars" when he supposedly accidentally invented the drink.)*

"I know what you are thinking! I'm old! Yes, I am fifty-eight and this will be my first child...second wife, however."

"Well, it's wonderful. Will they be moving here, too?"

"Sadly, no, at least not for a long while. My wife is English and we love London. I work in both cities, so for the present time, I will *'faire le trajet'* so to speak, and commute."

"I'm new to Chicago, too, and think I was very lucky to get my job at the *Fondation Culturel Française.* "

"Your boss is a wonderful person, " Solti said. "I know his uncle, well…he befriended me in Geneva a long time ago when I knew hardly anyone there. It was during the War. I'm a Jew, you see, by birth, and I could no longer stay where I was in Karlsruhe, or Salzburg, and I couldn't go back to Budapest, even though many famous musicians and conductors thought they would be safe there. So I went to Switzerland. Unfortunately, in doing so, I never saw my father again. But I met *Le Duc de Beuvron*, Polo's uncle, and we became close friends, even though he is twenty-five years older than I am! We still see each other often when I'm in Europe. He's very fond of Polo, you know. He thinks of him as his son, especially since he and his dear wife Madeleine lost their only son in a tragic car accident in the Alps some twenty years ago."

I didn't stop his narrative but if I had, it would have been to express my complete shock at the word **Duke**, for starters.

"My God, " I managed to say, "how terrible."

"Very sad. They were both devastated and heartbroken. Madeleine died not long after her son. No doubt from that. The Duke lost his only child, and Polo became his heir."

A waiter came around again, and we both took another flute from a silver tray.

Maestro Solti paused and looked at me, no doubt by now noticing my blank stares of non-recognition of the implications of what he'd been telling me. My head was swimming and not only with champagne.

HEIR? Did that mean d'Arivèque was something titled, too – a **noble de race** *for chrissake? What were the nephews of Dukes anyway? Counts? Earls? Barons? I barely knew the British system, let alone the French one. I knew there still were quasi-royals in France, but whenever I had heard of "royalists"it was only in conjunction with right-wing politics and people who showed up at the Basilica of St. Denis on January 21 to mourn the death of Louis XVI.*

Georg Solti saw that I wasn't tracking, especially, so he explained that he'd been on the staff of the Hungarian State Opera, mostly working as a *répétiteur*, coaching singers in their roles and played at rehearsals. "It gave me a better education at becoming a conductor than my classes at the Academy had, " he laughed. He went to Germany to become assistant to Josef Krips, but it was 1932, and within a year, Krips was warning young Solti to get out of there and return to Hungary. Austria hadn't fallen to Hitler yet, so in 1937 Solti was offered another post, as assistant to Arturo Toscanini at the Salzburg Festival.

"Toscanini was the greatest musical inspiration of my life, " he told me. "Before I heard him live in 1936, I had never heard a great opera conductor. Not even in Budapest. It was like I'd been struck by lightning."

"That must have been unbelievable," I said, thinking how it must have been like me meeting Paul Simon or The Beatles.

" Yes, it certainly was. It was the first time I had heard an ensemble singing with absolute precision. It was his *Falstaff*. Do you know this opera, Mademoiselle?"

Oh no, not another conversation topic where my ignorance would be in the spotlight. I just shook my head no without offering anything in the way of explanation.

"Well," he continued, as if he were actually not speaking to an ignoramus, for which I was grateful, "the impact upon me at the time was life-changing. And I had never expected to meet Toscanini. It was a chance in a million. I had a letter of recommendation from the director of the Budapest Opera to the Salzburg Festival. Toscanini received me and said, 'Do you know *Magic Flute*? Because we have an influenza epidemic and two of our *répétiteurs* are ill.' So I played that afternoon for the stage rehearsals. Can you imagine it?"

Yet another waiter appeared at our sides offering more flutes, and I took a third glass, grateful to have something to do other than talk.

He continued, "But the war spread and I had to leave again. My family really insisted that I not even return to Hungary—they were instituting the same sorts of anti-Semitic laws as in Nuremburg—you know, restricting Jews from professions. So I left intending to go to London first, but then rethought that and sought out Toscanini in Lucerne in hopes that he could find me a position here, in the States."

"Oh, so is that how you came to be here?" I asked.

"No, it was not to be. I stayed in Switzerland and it was there that I met Polo's uncle Charles. He knew all the singers in Geneva who could use my services, and I was able to find security there during the war. Charles suggested I apply to be vocal coach to the tenor Max Hirzel who was learning the role of Tristan in Wagner's opera. I stayed through the war, but unfortunately my father had died – oh, not in a concentration camp; in a hospital from complications of diabetes, of all things. So that is how I never saw him again. But I was reunited with my mother and sister after the war."

"Wow!" I said. "That must have been like a miracle!"

Before I could hear more of his illustrious career, about which he hadn't even really gotten started, one of the staff who seemed to know Solti, came over and said, glancing at me rather perfunctorily in passing, "*Excusez-moi Maestro, mais on vous demande au téléphone.*"

"Thank you, Robineau. I am coming. Will you excuse me, Mademoiselle Sarah?" he said getting up. "I hope Polo will bring you to the Chicago symphony with him sometimes! I should be very happy to see you there." And as he was leaving, Jean-Paul d'Arivèque was making his way back over to where I was still seated. Solti called out to him, laughing, "Polo! I've just invited *la belle petite* Sarah to my concerts as your guest!"

Jean-Paul smiled and said to me, "It would be my pleasure to have you as my guest. *Maman* was on the board of the CSO and we have had seasons tickets for years."

"I'd really like that." I said, but as I stood up to give him more space on the settee, I felt that horrible rush of nausea and the saliva in the mouth that precedes thinking you're going to vomit. How many glasses had I drunk, anyhow? I became sweaty and panicky. By the time Monsieur had unlocked his brace and sat down, I knew I had to get out of there and find a bathroom. I begged his pardon, and slipped into a throng of people near the door — some door — I didn't know where it led, and I ran out into a long corridor. There had to be a bathroom in that hallway somewhere, but where?

I was reeling from dizziness and terrified I'd throw up, which I didn't do very often, frankly, and only when my mother was there to hold a wet rag over my forehead! I saw a door and tried to open it...locked. I looked down the hall and also down another side hall. I was getting farther and farther away from voices and the party, and feeling sicker and sicker. Finally up ahead I saw double doors and prayed to God that they would open into a bathroom. I ran towards them and they did open but not into a loo.

I was all of a sudden inside a boudoir the likes of which I had never seen in America. If the green silk canopied bed had been festooned in ostrich feathers, I'd have thought I'd been transported to the Marie Antoinette bedchamber I'd seen at Versailles. The huge bed was draped in gauzy curtains that gathered at the top into a crown-like ring. The spread was green quilted silk. I was walking on carpet so thick I thought it was sponge.

Please have an en suite, I begged in prayer.

This room was three or four times the size of my studio apartment! There was a large and very ornate gilded mahogany writing desk off to one side, a chaise longue with a pink tufted cushion, three or four armchairs around a low table, and what seemed like a wall of windows shaded in more gossamer green silk drapery. Then taking up one whole other wall, the largest, most elaborately carved armoire I had ever seen. It was at least four doors wide and was a veritable architectural wonder, with burnished wood grain and metal locks. I'd seen pretty armoires in my day, having been to dozens of museums, but I'd never ever even imagined anything like this. I couldn't take too much time out of my emergency, however, to admire it further, because at any moment I was about to be sick.

Suddenly I noticed a little light coming onto the floor from the other side of the room and ran over towards it. YES! A door opened onto a white marble floor and I flung myself over the toilet. Mostly I had dry heaves; I hadn't had a chance to eat anything while I drank champagne, which was probably my downfall. The lurching of my stomach stopped, but at the same time my head became heavy and I was listing to one side. Afraid I was going to pass out and possibly conk my head on something porcelain and hard, I just grabbed for a towel and laid down on it on the bathroom floor. It was not soft, but it was cool and, overcome with the urge to sleep, I closed my eyes. And that's all I remember.

Someone was jabbing at me as I awoke in a groggy state of abject panic.

"*Mais, qu'est-ce que tu fabriques ici?! Bon DIEU!*"

I looked up from the floor. It was that same Robineau guy who had summoned Solti. Being very rude, I might add. Calling me "*tu*" when he didn't even know me, but knew I was a guest there! And I wasn't "up to" anything!

"I… I just felt ill, " I managed to spit out. "I couldn't find a bathroom."

"Do you know where you ARE? You're in Madame d'Arivèque's bedroom!"

Oh, Christ. His mother's room. Well, how was I to know? And what difference did that make anyway? They should have had signs or something.

"I'm sorry. I'll be leaving now." But when I stood up, I couldn't. Oh fuck me! Was this being drunk or was something else wrong with me?

"You are DRUNK!" he shouted with a tone of abject disgust.

"I'm …just… sick. I'm sorry. Can I just sleep here for a little while?"

" NO! The party is over, Mademoiselle. It is past eight. No one could find you!"

"Oh, shit."

And then Jean-Paul d'Arivèque was standing there, too, and he instantly became alarmed at seeing me on the floor.

"*Mais, qu'est-ce qui se passe Robin?* "

"She is drunk. Got sick. Said she could not find a bathroom."

"Oh *mon Dieu*, " he said sorrowfully. "Please, help her to the chaise longue."

"Do you mean in THERE?" Robineau asked incredulously, pointing the bedroom.

"Where else? Can you stand up Mademoiselle Shrier?"

"Nooo, " I whined.

" *Allez*! Come on, " said Robineau, yanking me up.

"*Attention Robin! Doucement, doucement!*"

I struggled into a standing position and was led physically to the chaise longue that was thankfully not too far from the bathroom door. I collapsed into it, relieved at how deeply I sank into its lushness.

My head was still very foggy but I managed to thank Monsieur d'Arivèque. And I was seriously grateful…grateful that I didn't feel like puking any more, and grateful to sleep.

And sleep I did.

Chapter Sixty-Two

"You Were On My Mind"…We Five

Even though the drapes were drawn as I awoke still sprawled out on the chaise-longue in someone else's night clothes (!), light was filtering in through the slits of the curtains, and from under the bathroom door; and I was startled, remembering with horror what had happened the day before. I sat up and realized I had a burning, acidly dry taste in my mouth that was abominable. A maid was sitting on the settee about ten feet away from me, and she jumped up and rushed over to me with a robe when she saw me stir.

"Do not worry, Mademoiselle!" she said reassuringly once she saw that I was very confused about what I had on. "You are wearing a nightgown of Madame d'Arivèque. Your clothes are there."

"But…what happened?"

"Nothing. Monsieur thought you would not want to sleep all night in your clothing, and he asked Madame de Piaget and me to put that on you. Do you not recall?"

"I don't remember anything! I mean, I do…know.. that I got sick and lay down on the bathroom floor. Some man came in and was mad."

"Monsieur Robineau found you, yes. He is the *valet* of Monsieur."

"Valet?"

"*Oui, Mademoiselle.*"

Do people even still have those these days?

Almost as if someone had cued him that I was up, Jean-Paul d'Arivèque came to the door, knocking perfunctorily to come in—he didn't have to knock, it was his house. The maid slipped out and I slipped into the robe she had laid on the foot of the chaise.

"Are you feeling all right this morning?" he asked with a slight lilt in his voice that soothed my fears of seeing him there.

I was so appalled at myself after what I did that I couldn't even muster any French to speak to him. "I'm so so sorry. Please don't fire me!" I blurted out. His voice may have been soothing to me; mine was panicky.

"But, I am not firing you."

"Oh, thank you. I'm so dreadfully ashamed at…what I must have…I mean, how much I must have drunk here. I don't have any idea why it had that awful effect on me. I'll just get dressed and be going." But then I had the presence of mind to add, "I'm terribly grateful for your having let me stay. Thank you for the loan of your mother's nightgown! "

Ignoring my eagerness to get out of there, he went on, as though giving me a medical reason for my blunder: "You had too much champagne and, *évidemment*, nothing to eat. You are quite thin and perhaps the alcohol was more potent than you are used to? "

"You're being kind. I think the alcohol was fine. Very good, as a matter of fact. It was my judgement that was the flawed part. I'm sure I'll be the talk of the office tomorrow. I deserve it. "

"Do not be anxious about that. I have had my staff put some toiletries in the bathroom for you. You will find everything you need in there. Perhaps when you get dressed, you would like coffee…or orange juice? Can you find your way back to the salon? Ah, no…probably not. I shall have Béatrice show you."

"I …well, thank you, but you've done so much already. I **will** brush my teeth, though! My mouth feels like a …"

"Yes, I shall leave you to it. But I would like to accompany you home, and Jean-Luc will drive us."

"Oh, you don't have to do that. I'll be fine to walk. Maybe take the bus part way. I don't know what buses run on Sunday, but I'll find out."

"I insist." And he left the room, closing one of the double doors behind him.

I took my own clothes and went into the bathroom, which I could really get a look at this time around, and saw that it was a most splendidly beautiful space, equipped like a five-star hotel. The flooring was not just tile but little green and white octagonal glass bubbles. No wonder they'd seemed softer than I expected when I lay down on them. The subway tiles on the walls went up three-fourths of the way to the ceiling, and the white ones were interspersed every few feet with pastel- painted ones showing whimsical *toile-de-Jouy-* type pictures of the leisure life of 17th century courtiers. The walls above the tile were painted in that same pale green of the bedroom, and the coverings on the high windows were blush pink silk festoon shades. The bathtub was set back in a large niche at the rear of the room; I hadn't even noticed it the night before.

A very large pedestal sink with beautiful nickel fixtures took center stage in the room, and that's where I found a toothbrush in a little paper wrapping to show it was brand new. There was Roget & Gallet soap in a Sèvres dish --verbena, which smelled so wonderful when I lifted it to my face. A little Lucite box held toothpaste, shampoo, cotton balls, and even some fizzy bath salts.

Feeling human once again, I carefully hung the gown and robe on hooks in the bathroom, got dressed, and went back out into the bedroom. Then a sinking feeling came flooding over me: my purse! With my keys! Where in God's name had I left that the night before? But I looked up at the chair where my clothes had been and there was my little bag...as if I'd put it there myself, which I had not. So relieved! *But Christ, I needed a keeper!*

I walked out of the bedroom and sure enough, the maid was there to lead me to the room where Monsieur sat next to a small, round ebony lacquered table with a coffee service on a silver tray, and a glass of juice next to the cup and saucer that were obviously meant for me.

"*Je vous en prie,* " he beckoned, pointing me to the chair across from him.

I wanted to protest and argue and reject the offer, but I just sat down and reached for the glass. My hand was surprisingly shaky. I wasn't hung over and I wasn't scared. But I guess I was nervous. My comfortable office anonymity was shattered now. I felt utterly self-conscious and awkward. A stupid dolt who couldn't "hold her liquor." *Oh, God, what would Sol and Betty think if they ever found out?...which they would not!*

D'Arivèque had not missed my trembling hand. "Are you quite all right?" he asked, worried. "Would you care for something to calm you, such as *une tisane*? Perhaps you are hungry? Would you prefer a *croissant*? Some *baguette*?"

I shook my head no! *Absolutely no more fussing over me or tending to me. I couldn't take it.*

"No thank you. Really." I sipped the juice and didn't have coffee. Cold liquid felt great in my mouth and I couldn't risk spilling hot anything all over myself or his furniture.

"How did you find Maestro Solti? Interesting?"

"Lovely. He was very nice to talk to me as long as he did."

"I shall avail myself of his request to invite you to the next concert of the Chicago Symphony."

I didn't know what to say to that. I couldn't quite figure out why he wasn't angry that I had done such a ridiculously idiotic and juvenile thing at his party, and it seemed like there should be a catch somewhere in all this. He sensed my discomfort, too, because he reiterated to me,

"Mademoiselle Shrier, I feel that you do not believe me when I tell you your post at the Foundation is not in jeopardy. Am I correct?"

"I was petrified that you would send me packing, yes."

"*Pardon?*"

"*Je me suis trouveé paralysée de terreur que vous me renvoyerez.*"

"I am not going to sack you, " he said again, using the British expression. *Restez assurée.*"

"Well, I sure appreciate that. I mean it. *Monsieur.*"

When it was evident that I wasn't going to eat or drink anything else, he picked up a phone on the other side of his chair, and called for his car.

"Come, " he said, rising up with some difficulty, it seemed to me, locking his brace leg and steadying himself on his cane, "and we will go to the lower level. I can show you some of that part of the house. I have a swimming pool...did you know?"

Of course I didn't know...about that or anything else this place had, but I was soon realizing that nothing should come as a surprise. I was to find out much later that the lower level also housed a vault!

We had taken the elevator down one floor past where I'd come in previously. The lowest level led to the underground parking, and to get there you had to wind through carpeted hallways with more numbered rooms.

"This is living quarters for the staff, " he explained, as we slowly walked for what seemed like forever. "They do not all live here, of course, but they can if they like. I do not charge them rent. All these doors lead to small apartments. The big doors ahead go into to the gym and the pool." He tilted his head for me to look inside when we got to heavy double doors like you'd see in a school. I opened them, and peeked into what seemed to me like a strange gym. Oh, it had all the equipment... a few weights, those machines any gym would have for working upper and lower strength, and a small treadmill. But this room also had a set of free-standing stair steps, two leather-topped examination tables of the sort one would find in a doctor's office or massage room; and parallel bars-- like patients had to use to learn to walk again. But the biggest difference between this gym and others was that on the wall were hung various leg braces and canes, as well as some arm crutches. Three different wheelchairs were also parked against one wall.

"Physical therapy?" I asked looking back at him.

"Precisely," he said, pleased that I understood. "And the pool is through those doors at the far end, " he pointed out with his cane. "Water is very therapeutic, as I am sure you know. I have therapists who come regularly."

"Well, it must certainly be—uh-- convenient to have that all here, " I said, not knowing what if anything to comment on, and not wanting to pry any information out of him that he didn't want to freely give.

We walked through the final set of doors and found ourselves in the garage, where Jean-Luc was waiting with a Mercedes limousine. I was surprised he had a German car--- however, I didn't say anything. But then I noticed, parked a ways away, a stunningly beautiful , powder-blue and silver-trimmed Citroën DS. Its white roof with those distinctive bright yellow lights, gleamed in the sunlight pouring down on it from high, narrow windows in the garage. It was so absolutely magnificent that I gulped, and exclaimed, "Heavens! Would you look at that!"

Jean-Luc had come around to take d'Arivèque's weak arm and help him into the back seat, but Monsieur, turned to me, concerned. "What is it?" he asked touching my arm.

"That Citroën! It's the most gorgeous car I've ever seen!"

"Ah! La voiture de Maman! Elle est belle, n'est-ce pas? Une DS 23 Pallas"

"Ohhh, oui."

He laughed. "And can you drive a manual transmission, Mademoiselle Shrier?"

"Sort of," I said, and he looked surprised. "Well, not really. And certainly not one of those. I've never driven a car with a column gear shift."

"Especially not that one, " he said, "because it is the reverse of American cars. First gear is selected by moving the gear lever forwards, and second gear by pulling the lever backwards through the neutral position...and so forth. Third gear moves to the right and fourth to the right and down."

"Oh , boy, " I said. That sounds hard."

Sol had tried to teach me one time to drive a car with a four-on-the-floor manual transmission. He thought I should know how to drive a stick shift, and had borrowed my uncle's – his brother's-- Fiat. We went to a quiet street in Omaha to try it out. I wasn't very adept at it, and Sol wasn't patient. When I finally got the hang of it on a flat surface, he took over and drove me to a cemetery with gently rolling roads in it, and made me try to drive the car there. But I was bad at it, afraid of killing the engine on every hill. Sol kept yelling at me to stop riding the clutch. After about half an hour he gave up, and he drove it back to my uncle's.

"She's hopeless," he announced, tossing the keys back down on their kitchen table.

"Well, cars shift themselves just fine with automatic, so why should I have to do it anyway?" I pouted.

"You'll get the hang of it with more practice, " my uncle said.

"No," Sol sneered, "she's through. Waste of my time."

"Maman drove Citroëns very successfully her entire life, " Monsieur d'Arivèque continued, with a hint of pride in his voice. "She always said the engineer who designed this car was so very clever." He paused. "And, of course... I cannot drive it. Perhaps if you promise not to drink champagne, I could have Jean-Luc here teach you to drive it, " he laughed.

367

I gave out a little giggle, too...and didn't even dream that I could take him seriously.

"It really should not just sit there, " he said softly. "Maman died nearly three years ago, now. No one drives this car."

The garage doors automatically opened as we approached them, and so did a gate that enclosed the driveway once we got to the street. Jean-Luc knew where I lived, and when we arrived at my house, I could see Jake's car was parked right out in front. He would certainly be wondering where the hell I'd been. *Jake didn't judge me and he didn't care what I did or where I went or with whom. But it would have been common courtesy to inform him if I were not coming in, so he wouldn't worry and could get on with doing his job.*

We pulled up to the curb and I opened the car door before realizing that Jean-Luc would be expected to do so.

" But...what is this!" d'Arivèque said brusquely, seeing the big perimeter fencing and the heavy machinery off to the side of the house. "Are you living in a condemned property?"

"No no no...let me explain. It's kind of a long story."

"This is unacceptable!"

"No, really, it's fine. See that car...that's the night watchman who works on weekends. He patrols the entire property until the workers arrive. I am perfectly safe here. Really."

"You are a squatter here, *alors*?"

"Not exactly." I smiled a sort of grimace at him, hoping he'd drop it. I knew it would be too complicated to explain so I didn't want to go into it, and besides that, it had occurred to me even before this that he would likely know the Hydes and then explanations would really get arduous. "And there aren't any other...er...tenants...or... anyone living here. Just me."

"You live all by yourself in Chicago in a construction zone? I find this quite unbelievable Mademoiselle!"

"I know...it's a bit unconventional."

Not wanting this conversation to proceed further, I jumped out onto the sidewalk, and turned back into the car to thank him again for the ride and for everything else. I gave a little wave, and, as if Jean-Luc got the idea that it was a signal that no more confrontation should take place, he drove off rather precipitously. I then walked over to Jake's car to apologize to him, too.

I unlocked the fence, went through my gate and up the stairs, unlocked the front door, entered the hallway, unlocked my apartment door, tore off my clothes and threw them on a chair, and feeling even more exhausted, fell gratefully onto my daybed where I slept until four in the afternoon.

And when I woke up, showered and changed into pj's, I finally got myself some food after nearly twenty-four hours of not eating anything, and called Cass on my home phone.

"Sari!" she exclaimed worriedly when she answered, "why are you calling me instead of me calling you!?"

"Because I've made such a fucking mess out of things, " I said, and proceeded to tell her the whole sordid tale, ending with "I was so sure he was going to fire my ass."

"Well, come on kid, buck up. It looks like your job is safe!"

"Yeah, but his office chief of staff -- the woman who hired me --- was there, and I'm sure she was appalled. The entire legal department was there, and who knows, they might have something to say on the matter. My God, Cass, I've only been there for six weeks and I may have just kiboshed the whole damn thing! "

"But again, I don't think you'll get fired if the boss says he's not firing you."

"If I do get the boot, I'm just going to come back to Iowa City and take any old damn job and live there. Period. I don't give a shit. It'll have been my own fucking fault anyway."

"Okay, let's not cross that bridge yet!" And then she added cheerily, "But I'll love having you back here if it does come to that. "

Chapter Sixty-Three

"Tous les Garçons et les Filles"...Françoise Hardy

The Monday after the fateful Bastille Day party, Hennie stuck her head into my office with the greeting of, "So, you got shit-faced at the big bash, eh?"

"I have no defense. Your bosses were there; are they talking about it like I'm about to get the axe or anything?"

"Oh, hell no. The word in the office is that you drank on an empty stomach and since you weigh next to nothing, it had its effect on you rather immediately. No one acted like JPA was angry with you. I think it's a scream!"

"JPA? Is that what you guys call *Monsieur*?"

"It's how we refer to everyone in the office...well, not everyone, mainly the brass: MFP; our head attorney, DRM. He's Jewish, did you know?"

I shook my head no.

"Yep, a French Jew. Came to the States as a little kid after the Holocaust. I gotta run."

Hennie was never one to stick around and make small talk unless it was about her, and I didn't see her much after that for quite some time, because I made it a point to lay low. Nothing ever took me even close to the presidential suite of offices and hardly anyone came to mine.

Things were still pretty slow with the film library's lending part, so while I was busy cataloguing and viewing films, the "business" part of my job—sending and receiving—hadn't picked up at all by the end of the summer. After I had catalogued over three hundred films, however, and shelved them alphabetically, even I could see that this system was not going to work. So I tried out regrouping them by genre and theme: "education," for instance, and then maybe "geographical" under that. Or maybe culinary; there was a documentary about a cooking school called "Food, Glorious Food." I knew I would have a big section on Paris, but again there were so many sub-categories even to that. It made me realize that this, too, was an imperfect system.

I knew I would have to figure something else out.

I used the alphabetical list as a master, and with that, I began a system of cross-referencing by theme and subtheme. It was the best I could come up with to guarantee that when some organization or school called in and requested something, if they had the title, that would be easy to find; and if they had a genre, I could suggest a title from what we had. Since we had few clients at all that whole summer, I didn't have a good chance to try out this idea and see if it were actually the solution or not.

The other way I filled my time on the job was to write short synopses and even took it upon myself to prepare quasi lesson plans to go with each film. I intended to spring this idea on Marie-France de Piaget when I had completed enough so that I could show her samples. The first one I chose to tackle was *Le Ballon Rouge*, a film with almost no dialogue, that could be shown and discussed on every level of French studies. When Cass called me one afternoon in early August, I tried out my discussion questions on her.

"You remember seeing *Le Ballon Rouge* with me in the Union that first year we roomed together, don't you?"

"I loved that film, " she sighed.

"Well, do you get the idea that alienation is a theme of it?"

"What?"

"Alienation. Does the boy seem lonely before he meets up with the balloon?"

"Well, I guess so."

"So like on the most elementary level, the teacher could discuss the idea of *l'amitié* with the class—having a friend. Having unconditional love, really. And on the more advanced level, they could get into the flip side -- the loneliness, alienation and eventual redemption."

"Okaaaay, " Cass said, wondering where this line of reasoning was going, "but I don't follow."

"Yeah, so like Pascal, the little kid, is 'chosen' by the 'magic' balloon to be his friend and they're very happy together, right?"

369

"Yes."

"But later Pascal is also singled out for bullying, and tormented by the other kids because of the balloon. The balloon has put Pascal on the outs with everyone else. Even the priest kicks him and his grandmother out of church because of the balloon. And then, by the end, the balloon is the victim of a mob!"

"Oh, okay…I'm beginning to get the drift."

"So do you realize that some critics think this is Christian allegory? I wonder if Lamorisse set out to make the balloon a Christ figure? I mean, it was hunted down, tortured and pummeled on a bleak hill."

"Goodness! Who would have ever thought of that watching The Red Balloon?! I wouldn't have."

"Well, think about the ending…the balloon is essentially destroyed, but it comes back with many other balloons and takes Pascal off into the sky!"

"The Assumption?"

"Well, what else?"

"So, the same themes as Le Petit Prince, really, and also…a children's masterpiece that turns out to be anything but just for children."

"Exactly. Open to interpretation on levels peeled away like layers of onion skin."

"Well, brilliant! I'd say you've got yourself a lesson plan in spades!"

"Good. I hope so. And speaking of children: cough it up. How are they?"

"Great. Nearly one! It's crazy how fast time flies! They scoot around—almost walking. Can you dig it? As a matter of fact, my little son just flashed me a beaming face—lights up the entire room. Must be meant for his Auntie Sari. Can you come for their birthday, Auntie Sari?"

"Oh, crap, Cass, I don't think so. I have no days I can take off . I'll be lucky to get to Iowa City for Thanksgiving, and that will be really short."

"Then in November you take some of that money my father gave you, and fly out here. I mean it. You won't have to waste your whole day on a train. Just come the fastest way possible. And you don't have to spend time cooking, either, once you get here. You know what I saw in the grocery store the other day? A turkey breast. Just the breast. That might be perfect for us this year. I can even make the side dishes…I'm trying out all sorts of organic vegetable recipes."

"I must say, Cass, that is all, if you'll excuse the expression, food for thought. But don't tell me you were shopping in a normal store?" I teased her but was legitimately surprised.

"Yeah, well, there are still some things that are cheaper in the supermarket than the co-op. I don't need organic dish soap! Ha!"

I told her I would look into what planes flew out of Midway to Iowa City, if any, because under no circumstances would I schlep all the way out to O'Hare. That cab ride would cost as much as the plane ticket. But I had to ring off anyway because Marie-France de Piaget came into my office and startled me. Cass, per our sneaky plans, always called me late in the afternoon, and we'd been talking for half an hour already. It was almost quitting time.

"I'm sorry to bother you," MFP said, to which I protested that she wasn't. "I do not think you know this but Monsieur d'Arivèque is in the hospital. He was taken in last night as a precaution."

"Oh no! I didn't know. How is he? What was it?"

"Well, he has agonizing pain from time to time, and this particular bout was serious enough that his doctor was called in the night. They admitted him around five in the morning. He is doing better. He is in a private room, of course." She didn't give me time to comment, and continued, "Anyway, late this afternoon some papers came in from France that he must see, and I am awaiting a call from New York on another matter, so I cannot take these up to him. I was wondering if you could leave early today and do it on your way home? He is at the Chicago Medical Center hospital, and as you probably know, that is not far from here."

"No. Yes! I'd be happy to do it. Can he have visitors?"

"Yes, évidemment."

"Well, I only mean…strangers walking into the room? Maybe I should leave them at the nurses' station?"

"No, no. You must give this portfolio directly to him. I shall telephone his room and say you'll be there shortly.

And with that I gathered up my things, and headed out into the still hot summer afternoon, carrying a brown leather zippered pouch under my arm. Huron street was very close to our North Michigan Avenue location, just as she said. I'd passed that street many times, and turning towards the lake, could see the hospital campus.

I found out from the front desk that his room was on the fifteenth floor, so up I went. Once out of the elevator I proceeded to a nurse's station and was directed to go straight to the corner, turn right, and head down another corridor to the very end. His room was not a typical one, I found out. It certainly didn't look like any rooms portrayed in shows like *Dr. Kildare* or *Ben Casey*. It looked more like a hotel room. Of course there was a hospital bed of the normal type, a bedstead table and a tray table on wheels next to it with i.v. poles and blood pressure cups behind the bed. But the room was huge and had a regular table in it, plus comfortable chairs and a window seat sort of thing placed over the radiator. The open drapes revealed large windows with a panoramic view of Lake Michigan dotted with sail boats.

I stood at the door and knocked hesitantly. From where I was, I could see the bed and no one was in it!

"Come in," a woman's voice said. It was a nurse who came towards me from a corner of the room where she had a sort of high podium-like desk with a lot of papers on it.

Jean-Paul d'Arivèque was seated in an armchair near the window, dressed in a hospital gown and a long cream-colored silk robe over that. A doctor was kneeling in front of his brace-less left leg, which d'Arivèque hurriedly covered by pulling part of his robe with his right hand over it as I came in. But he wasn't fast enough, and I glimpsed his shriveled leg and misshaped foot and then averted my eyes to address him face to face.

"*Bonjour, Monsieur.* Or should I have said *bon après-midi?*" I gave out a nervous laugh. It wasn't even five o'clock yet, so too early for *bonsoir*. I was flustered and I realized that I was yammering, so I shut up, and, smiling hesitantly at him, I handed him the pouch. "I brought you these papers."

"*Merci bien, Mademoiselle* Sarah. Please take a seat."

"Oh," I motioned towards the door, "Shouldn't I wait outside? Am I taking those back to the office? I'm not sure anyone will still be there." Marie-France had said to leave early, as in go home for the day, but I was certainly willing to take them back and had plenty of time.

"*Je vous en prie, Mademoiselle,*" he said rather pointedly, gesturing in the vicinity of the window seat, where I sat down and waited as he perused the papers. "I would like to speak to you after I have read through these. Have you enough time to stay a little while longer?"

"Oh. Of course. I'm not in a hurry or anything."

The doctor was using one of those little rubber mallets to see if he could get a reflex action on the left knee, but nothing was happening, so he folded the robe back over it and stood up, saying he would return in a short while. The nurse had also left the room; it was just the two of us.

D'Arivèque grimaced and set the papers down on the window seat not far from me. He then turned to me and said, "I need to adjust my robe. Could you help me by chance?"

"Yes... sure, " I answered, having no idea what to do for him.

"Fine. I cannot grasp your arm with my left arm, so when I stand up from this chair, could you hold onto my left side? That way I can tie this robe!"

So I went over to the left side of the chair and he eased himself onto his good leg holding onto the chair with his right hand. He seemed wobbly and I silently prayed for nothing to happen that would send him reeling to the floor "on my watch." I took hold of his arm, which even though it couldn't be moved far, seemed healthy enough. He steadied himself on the good leg and let go of the chair in order to reach across his body for the tie which he endeavored to place in his left hand, leaving it there long enough so that he could maneuver the two ends together with his good arm.

But it wasn't working too well. I saw that it would be hard for him to get those ends together enough to tie them low like that.

In 1970, no one was too keenly aware of the rights and desires of "handicapped" people – as we said in those days--, and I wasn't any different. I didn't know what to do for him or what not to do. I hadn't had any sensitivity

371

training about what would or wouldn't insult someone I perceived as needing help. I did know then that some people couldn't bear to even look at a handicapped person on the street or in a shop; and some people jumped right in and assumed the person needed help and just took over, which wasn't a good idea either. So I hesitated to offer assistance until it just seemed ridiculously futile for me to be standing there watching him fumble with it. Hell, I thought, if I offered aid, all he could do was tell me to bug off.

"May... I...would it be okay if I... help you tie that?" I asked shyly.

"Yes, please, " he said, almost heaving a sigh of relief. He let go of the belt pieces and grabbed the chair arm again , leaning heavily against it on his right leg while the left leg hung limp. Once he was steady, I let go of his left arm and straightened up the sides of the robe, brought them together, and tied the tie around his middle. I then returned to holding his left side as he settled back down with some effort into the chair. I couldn't tell for sure, but had a feeling that pain was playing a bigger role in this mini-drama than anyone knew.

"*Voilà,* " I said. "Better?"

"*En effet.*" He took my hand in his, not to shake but to just hold for a moment, as he added, looking deep into my eyes, *"Merci beaucoup. C'est gentil."*

I just gestured that it was nothing and sat back down, turning to look once again at the lake view while he replaced the papers in his lap. After a couple of minutes, he looked back up at me and said he was glad I'd brought the documents over because he was wanting to talk to me. I panicked, thinking that I was back in hot water for the drinking incident of the preceding month, and that the consequences, like "the other shoe dropping" were going to fall after all. I took a breath and prepared myself for the worst.

"I am in negotiations with the *grand magasin*, Marshall Field's to provide some films to them during a certain French trade fair that they are planning for their flagship store in the Loop. This will take place at Christmastime. I shall have several meetings with one of the vice-presidents, a good friend of mine, and I would like you to perhaps attend some of these, and participate in finding him what they want. I have only sketchy details at this point in time, and of course, their goal will be sales of many French goods, not merely activities to put our culture into the spotlight."

So Marshall Fields was doing what Brandeis had already done? Fancy that, little Omaha!

"I'll be very happy to help however I can!" I said, so relieved, I wondered if it showed.

"*Très bien.* We shall discuss this further at the office, of course. The other thing I wanted to say to you is that soon the season of the Chicago Symphony will begin---I believe it is in mid-September. Georg has been at Ravinia, of course, for the summer concerts, but it will not be long before he will back rehearsing for the regular season. I have not forgotten to invite you. You would be amenable to attending with me?"

" Oh-- uh-sure! I'd like that. Just tell me the date."

"Dates. I have season tickets. *Maman* and I went together every year for decades. I'm going to be delighted to once again use her ticket."

The next time I spoke to Cass and recounted that entire afternoon, I confessed to her what I could never have asked him, namely that I was mystified as to why he hadn't been using his mother's ticket since she died almost three years prior.

"I mean," I said, "why would he hesitate to ask someone out to the symphony---or anywhere else for that matter? Who wouldn't want to date him? He's still fairly young...well, not really. *(Forty-something must have seemed old to me then.)* He's not half bad to look at, and he's richer than Croesus. I can't imagine women wouldn't be flinging themselves at him."

"Well, Sari, my naïve little friend, think about what you just said."

"What?"

"That he went with his mother for years to the symphony. His mother. With whom he lived until her death."

"So?"

"Have you seen him out with women? Did he have a date at any of those functions you have to attend?"

"Well, no, I guess not. I'm not privy to what he does in his off hours, though!"

"Sari! Think! Someone perceived as a confirmed bachelor is perfectly accepted in polite society. But a man of his stature could not be seen out with another man. Someone like that would need a foil—some woman with him—in public. That's probably why he asked you to the symphony."

"OOOOooooh. You mean…you're saying he's —like—queer or something?"

"Bingo."

"Holy shit, I should have guessed that, I suppose."

"Yes, and didn't you tell me he had that valet who was mean to you? Probably a gay who hates women. There are such types, you know."

"Well, but there are plenty of straight men who are misogynists, too, Cass. Come on."

"Just think about it, that's all."

"Okay, so he's gay. So what? Why hasn't he had anyone over to our office gatherings at his home? They're not really in public."

"Because he has a reputation to maintain, silly. Homosexuality isn't legal! In England it was only decriminalized like, a couple of years ago!"

"And what about here?"

"Laws against it are still on the books! It's called sodomy, in case you haven't heard."

"Jesus. You're right."

Well, what did I know? It wasn't as though television or mainstream films portrayed characters who were gay. It would be two years before "That Certain Summer" would be shown on ABC, where a gay man was raising his kids, and even that didn't contain any scenes of explicit relations between men. I was ignorant, but I assumed I wasn't alone. Like most people at the U of Iowa until the first Gay Pride parade was held, I thought I didn't know anyone who was gay.

Cass then brought up the other point. "And besides that, from what you've said, he can't walk well, he certainly can't drive. He has trouble dressing, obviously. He can't do a lot of stuff that takes two arms. That's probably off-putting to someone seeking intimacy."

"What do you mean? What's that got to do with someone liking him? He seems to be a true gentleman, if such a beast exists! He's genuinely nice. Everybody in the office loves him. I'm serious, Cass, they really are devoted to him. And as to the other stuff, he has a chauffeur to drive him and a valet to dress him. It seems to me that women…men…anyone would be anxious to go out with him."

"No. How can you be intimate with a man that has a couple of caregivers hovering in the same room with you all the time. What someone **would** be anxious to do, more likely, would be to get their hands on his money. What do you guess his net worth might be? "

"Cass, I have no idea."

"Well, one time I overheard my parents talking about their estate being worth in excess of a quarter of a billion dollars. Do you think his is more than that?"

"Billion??! With a B?"

"Yeah, two hundred and fifty million dollars."

"Well, much as I can't fathom that amount of money, I guess I think yes, he may be worth more than your parents. The mansion in Chicago is the size of a palace! It's more like a big apartment building, only it's all his…a single-family residence, even though it seems to function like a private hotel. He has many more staff than your parents do. He's got an apartment in New York and one in Paris, and from what I understand the actual family seat is a *château* somewhere in the French provinces. And another branch of the family is in Geneva. So yes, I know he must be very, very—ULTRA-- rich."

"Then I repeat my opinion that everyone will be after his money. Especially if they get the idea that he's frail or ill and not long for this world."

"Well, gosh, I wouldn't go that far."

"No, but I am just saying that some women would love to marry some old guy who might die pretty soon and leave them fortunes. Don't kid yourself, Sari, everyone is after the loot."

"How can you say that? You of all people! Is that why boys dated you at Iowa? That can't be why your parents married!"

"Sari, no one at school knew me or my net worth –then nor now-- ha! ----now it's more like zero! And as for my parents, they both came from wealthy families. Their union was like the merging of two dynasties. I'm only kind of joking, really. You know I'm right. Very wealthy people are often pursued for their money alone. You watch soap operas, you know the conniving money-grubbing that goes on."

"Since when did soap operas mimic real life?"

"In this case... they do!"

I was not about to stay on the line arguing with Cass, but the more I thought about it, the more I decided Jean-Paul d'Arivèque was gay, and I surmised that given the state of the legal and social ramifications of that, it was a bigger handicap than anything physical he was contending with.

Chapter Sixty-Four

"Sit Down, I Think I Love You"...Buffalo Springfield

As the summer of 1970 was drawing to a close, I couldn't help but feel some real satisfaction with the way things had gone after I'd left home. I was living by my own means (but of course, not paying rent was making it possible, so I couldn't gloat about that); and much as Cass admonished me from time to time to feel free to dip into her little windfall from John-Wilfred, I did not. I only used that money to buy things for the kids and send cash to Cass. Out of my very first paycheck, I had faithfully repaid Soren, and my conscience was clear. It was never far from my mind, though, that a year later, when I presumed I'd have to move, I'd need to have some savings built up; so I was trying to be frugal. I had done a lot of *lèche-vitrine*, literally drooling over the store display windows, but I hadn't actually bought much the whole time I'd been in the city.

However, finally, there came a time where I just had to have some different clothes. This culminated in a meeting with Marie-France de Piaget, wherein I was called on the carpet-- so to speak-- and hinted at that perhaps I needed to step it up a bit in the wardrobe department.

I had to call Cass.

"You won't believe what I'm going to tell you next, " I said to her as I began to regale her with the saga. "The other day the office manager---she's really like the chief of staff--called me into her office and asked me rather gingerly—you know, so as not to offend me, as she put it—ha!-- if I thought I had enough clothes for the position I had at the Foundation."

"Oh, my God, that sounds just like TWA! " she exclaimed, commiserating. "You can't imagine the uniform lectures I used to get." She paused and sighed audibly. "So does the FCF have a dress code or something? You said you wore pants to work... didn't they approve?"

"The first time I wore pants, I did get some funny looks, but really I needed to wear them to climb library ladders, so they cut me some slack..er..slacks! Ha ha." She laughed at my little attempt at humor, but then I got serious again. "No, to answer your question, we don't have a dress code; but you know the French: navy blue is all they wear."

"I remember!"

I wasn't done with my story, though.

"But anyway, you have to hear the rest of this. Marie-France de Piaget started sort of lecturing me---not in a mean way or anything, she was actually quite sweet--- about me having to be at various dinners, meetings and more of those *soirées* or *salons* or whatever they are at *Monsieur's* house. So, get this! She told me not to take it as an insult or charity or anything, but *Monsieur* had a lot of clothes of his mother's still at the house, and how his mother might have been about my size, and would I be interested in having some!"

"Oh my God, Sari, you **are** joking. Could you imagine what she must have had!? Probably nothing but Chanel, Hermès, Givenchy, and maybe the odd Yves St Laurent, Celine or Dior for slumming around! Ha! I can just see her...'Oh, yes, grocery shopping in this old Dior thing, don'tcha know.' I'll bet those *armoires* are groaning!"

"Oh, I seriously doubt she ever did anything as normal as shop for food, Cass," I remarked.

"Yeah! That's probably true."

"I mean, does your mother ever do the grocery shopping?"

"Oh, hell, no, " she admitted.

"I rest my case."

" So what did you say?"

"I was so taken aback I didn't say anything at first. But then, it started to sink in that JPA was like, paying attention to what the hell I wore! And then I **really** didn't know what to say. I didn't want to take him up on the offer to have his mother's clothes! I just stammered at her how generous an offer it was, but that I couldn't possibly...and when she realized I probably didn't want to do it, she said I should just consider the offer."

"But Sari, they probably **are** all designer. Maybe you should!"

"NO! Please. How old must she have been when she died? He's in his forties. She had to be at least pushing seventy. Come on."

"You're right. So what are you going to do? If I remember right, your boss is going to be inviting you to the CSO, too!"

"Well, that might not happen. He hasn't said anything about it since the hospital. I doubt if he remembers."

"But if he does, you will be dragging out the blue dress or the English kilt over and over again. You have to do something about this. You take some of that slush fund my dad gave you and go buy some clothes!"

"No, Cass. We've been through that. I'll not be using that money for me. He's already like **giving** me a couple of hundred dollars per month in rent I'd otherwise be paying. It's up to me to find money in my own budget for whatever my needs are."

" Ha! You sound very adult, kid!"

"But I do intend to go shopping, " I laughed. "The antidote for everything!"

End of summer was a perfect time to be able to shop in Chicago stores I couldn't afford normally because of the sales. These sales were very good. Even though stock was depleted, there were still bargains on last-season's fashions and especially in the junior departments, where back-to-school was the focus. I could find leftover items on sale, and be able to afford them. So I began to use my lunch hours to hit the fancy stores like Saks and Bloomingdale's on North Michigan Avenue, and go to Marshall Field's after work on Thursdays when the store was open late.

I first struck gold at Saks. There it was: a fabulous outfit marked down way more than fifty percent. It was a Georgio di Saint Angelo (*I'd never heard of that brand so I didn't even know if it were a real designer or just a made-up name*). The outfit was very unique: a wool knit sweater and skirt that looked like a dress when worn together. It had wide orange, black and green stripes, and in the middle of the sweater, knitted right into the design, was a picture of a biplane. A plane flying across the sweater! The skirt was pretty short and a little bit flared, which would look great with black tights. No one else would have this outfit in our office, I reasoned...correctly.

I described it to Cass on the phone later, and said, "It's actually not as loud and crazy as it sounds...more like designer-y. I didn't own anything chic of my own, as you know...only your stuff!"

"I think it sounds neat!" she said. "I'm sure they were getting a bit sick of seeing you in that blue dress of mine."

"If ever a dress got its use, though," I said, "that one sure did. Does. I still wear it."

"Well I can't wait to see the new one. Wear it here on Thanksgiving!"

"Okay, I will."

Actually, I got the chance to wear it sooner than that because two events happened almost back to back. First, Hennie showed up in my office one day and asked me if I knew when the Jewish High Holy Days fell that year, and I actually did since I carried around a little Hallmark calendar the shops gave away free.

"Why?" I wanted to know.

"Because, DRM wants you to have this." She held out a ticket for me to take.

"What's this for?"

"Well, what do you imagine it's for, silly? Beth Emet synagogue's high holiday entry. It's in Evanston where he lives, and you probably don't know this yet, but you take the subway from Chicago direct to Evanston Dempster station and the synagogue is right there within walking distance. You will not get lost trying to find it."

"Wait a minute! You have to have a ticket to attend services? I never heard of such a thing." It was true. The Bluffs wouldn't have had that, but even the Omaha synagogues didn't. "And also, Hennie, how did Daniel Rosier de Molet find out I was Jewish?"

"I told him, what'd you think? But guess what---he already knew it. I guess JPA had informed him of it."

"Jeez, I don't remember ever telling him. But Madame knows. I guess they discuss everything about the office, eh?"

"Believe it."

"Well, I'll come to your office and thank him."

"Do you think you'll go...to the services I mean?"

"I might." At least I really did have something to wear.

The next thing that gave me an opportunity to dress up was at Lincoln Park High School. I got a call at the office from their chair of the foreign language department. She invited me, no doubt at Dom Lambert's behest, to give a short presentation on the Foundation to the French teachers at their in-service before the start of the Fall semester.

Public schools in Chicago started way later than they did in my little Iowa town, and I liked that. It was beginning to feel like autumn by mid-September and I actually found myself a bit nostalgic for school. *Grade school and high school had been respites for me, little sanctuaries where I could fling off my family and just be whoever I wanted to be for those six or more hours per day. And who I wanted to be was a good and serious student, so teachers would like me. It wasn't rocket science; in those days I longed to have some adult acceptance in my life.*

I didn't figure I needed the office's permission to go to Lincoln Park High; after all, I had stopped in there months earlier of my own volition and planted the seed of promoting the Foundation's offerings. Still, I went to Madame de Piaget with the news that I'd been asked over there, and to clear it with her that I could have our marketing or PR departments do up some materials for me. While I didn't as yet have any sort of glossy brochures about the films, I could at least take some Xerox copies of my titles list. I also showed her a mock-up of my sample lesson plans for teaching and discussing *Le Ballon Rouge* on all levels.

"You also wrote this up as a lesson example? " she asked astonished as she looked it over. I was braced for her to tell me to can that part, or table it until later. "This is very good initiative, Sarah. Of course, you can have our office make copies."

I arrived at the high school in my sweet little airplane outfit, and Dom met me in the front office to escort me to the meeting.

"You are stylin'! That outfit is a gas!" he said looking me up and down.

We went to a lecture room and I gave an overview of the Foundation, and what we had to offer French teachers in general, before I got to the film part. As I had predicted to Dom, they were quite surprised all our services were free. I handed out copies of the titles we had, and then I took the liberty to spend a few minutes on my ideas for lessons built around one film. I went through it from elementary to advanced, and from what I could tell, it held their attention.

"This is just one idea, of course, " I said, wrapping up. "As you'll see if you peruse the list, we have many more films that you could easily build lessons around...Molière plays, the regions of France, the city of Paris, French cuisine and, of course, many classic titles from French cinema. Thanks very much for your time!"

And they all applauded, happily took my hand-outs and thanked me!

Dom and I walked out together.

"Say, would you like to meet up with me and my friend Peter at the Art Institute Saturday morning? There's a lecture at eleven on Gothic architecture."

"Really? I'd love to go to that."

I did take him up on the offer, and met them that weekend. That was how I started hanging around with them. Peter worked for an agency which brought music groups to Chicago; and part of his job was to work the shows as a lighting technician. He had also done lighting design for Chicago's burgeoning theater scene, and worked in many different venues. He was anxious to tell me about one with a French tie-in he was about to work on.

"If you like Edith Piaf music, you would really be blown away by it, " he said, and Dom nodded. "But there's a twist...have you ever been to a drag club before?"

"A what?" I answered.

"I'll take that as a no, " Dom laughed. "Not even in Paris?"

"Nope, 'fraid not. Can...I mean...do straight people go to them?"

"No place of business can discriminate about who can and can't enter their establishment, " Peter answered. "Straight people tend not to frequent gay bars and clubs more for the comfort-level reasons rather than because of any outright discrimination."

"But I take your point, " said Dom. "It would be easier for me to accompany you to a straight bar than for you to walk into a gay bar and order a drink. So that's why I'm inviting you to come with me to the most famous drag club in Chicago on Thursday night. It's called *La Ferronnerie*—on Rush Street."

His implication was not lost on me.

"So if I go with you guys to this place Thursday, it'll be okay?"

"Sure, and besides, Lou Limone is so well-known as Piaf, " Peter explained, "that there will be many people in the audience who are not gay. I think a lot of the French community knows her. They've had to add a show."

Since Peter would already be there, Dom and I made arrangements to meet after work, and go to Pizza Uno first for a couple of slices to tide us over before heading off to hear Lou Limone. Peter would have to work both shows, but I would not be staying for the second one, since I had to work the next day.

The club was a true ratskeller deep underneath street level right in the heart of Chicago's theater district. You went down one flight of stairs from the door and were in a sort of mezzanine where there was a coat room, restrooms and cigarette machines. The hallway was quite long but it wasn't very wide. To get to the bar, stage and dance floor, you had to descend a narrow and winding wrought iron staircase which opened onto a vast expanse of beautiful carved wooden tables and booths in dimly lit surroundings. The stage was barren---no curtain, but big enough for a band to set up behind the singer.

"She'll sing two sets per show, " Dom informed me. "It's a pretty long gig. Peter may even get to come sit with me out front to see her second set of the first show, but even if he doesn't, he'll hear everything fine, and be able to watch a monitor in the booth. And we've both seen Lou before, so ..."

"I'll bet doing these 'gigs' as you call them is pretty lucrative, huh?"

"Are you joking? Honey. Lou Limone has made more of a fortune being Edith Piaf than Piaf did!"

Even though we got there in plenty of time, the huge room was already filling up. Dom and I took a high-top table midway between the stage and the entryway, which was still pretty far from the dance floor.

Dom surveyed the scene. "I think they might have to add chairs on the dance floor, " he said, "because no one will dance to Piaf songs and they might have an overflow house from the looks of this."

We ordered drinks and were chatting away about the gothic architecture lecture we'd attended when I almost spit out my Tom Collins. Coming down those horribly winding stairs was Jean-Paul d'Arivèque helped by Robineau and another guy, who really had to practically carry him because there was simply no possible way for him to maneuver both down and around.

"Oh, holy shit! I can't believe it."

"What?" he asked, more than mildly surprised at my outburst.

"See that man being helped down the stairs? That's my boss!"

"Polo d'Arivèque is your boss?" Now he was flabbergasted.

And again: POLO?

"But, you knew I work for his cultural foundation."

"I know you work for **the** *Fondation Culturelle Française*; I never knew it was run by him."

"It's owned by him! His mother started it in the 50's. Why do you call him **Polo**?"

"Well, I don't. But see those guys with him?"

"Of course—the one is his rude creepy valet Robineau whom I've only met a couple of times and already despise."

"Yeah, I can believe that. Thing is, the other guy is Robin's boyfriend, and he's managing partner in this club! Peter often works with him to bring in acts and do lighting design. He and I have known Robin for years. Actually the boyfriend, whose name is Maxime, is a pretty nice guy."

" That's funny, I heard Monsieur d'Arivèque call his valet 'Robin' like you just did, one time. But I wonder how come this Maxime is with him if he's such a nice person, like you say?"

"They've been together for decades, so there must be chemistry there!"

378

"I just hope they don't see me!" I said, sort of turning my back towards them and talking to Dom more from the side.

"I can tell you, Robineau is very devoted to your boss."

"Oh, I know that. So then who is my boss' — er — lover or boyfriend or partner or whomever? I have been to his house a few times now and there's never anyone I can discern who is 'with' him."

"Well, Sari, what makes you think he bats for our side?"

" Huh?"

"What makes you think he's gay?"

"Come on. He's single in his forties and lived with his mother his entire life."

"Yeah, well, I think Peter would know if he were. He's never mentioned him to me in that context, and he knows Maxime pretty well."

"Are you sure?"

"I'm not positive. But I've never heard of or seen anyone who is his lover. Robineau never talks to me, but from what I understand there was a woman once whom everyone thought would marry Polo. It didn't happen."

"So what's your best guess?" I asked. "Is he maybe closeted and when he was about to marry her — you know, to keep the charade going, she just couldn't go through with it? Or maybe he couldn't because that sort of marriage would have just been a sham? What? "

"Well, your little imagination is working overtime tonight! I have no idea, but I don't think he's a closeted homosexual. I really don't."

"But listen, just consider…look how well known he is in this town! You know him. "

"Well, I know who he is. I've never met him."

"Obviously you-- and everyone-- know he's richer than God. He can't 'come out' — homosexuality is against the law. So naturally, a marriage would shield him from public scrutiny."

"You're right -- homosexual acts are illegal if the law gets involved. But in today's world, there are no *lettres de cachet*. People don't report you just for being gay. No one's going to show up at the door and arrest anyone. No one's going to be shunning anyone. I mean, some do… yes, there are some bad-ass fringe churches with pastors and congregants who think, for instance, that I'm a product of Satan living in abject sin, of course. Some of the faculty at my school are ignoramuses who believe stuff like that. But even they aren't going to turn me in to the police or anything for being gay. Mind you… as a teacher, I'm not giving anyone reason to single me out for it either! Nor would I."

"I hear that. And I'll admit I'm pretty naïve about homosexuality in general---I've been told that. I'm sure gay teachers would be singled out for scrutiny. But even **I** know that molestation of kids and young people is rampant among **straights**. Happens all the time! In families, in schools –probably even in churches ! *(Little did I know!)* I don't personally care what adults do behind closed doors, but if children are involved, it's disgusting, in my opinion, no matter who's doing it."

Just then the room got even more dark, the candles at each table took on an ethereal glow, and the stage lit up to reveal a backdrop of a Parisian street scene which was very convincing. Lou Limone, as Edith Piaf stepped out to raucous applause. "She" looked the spitting image of Piaf.

As Limone began to sing "Non, je ne regrette rien," I whispered, excitedly, "Wow, if you close your eyes you could swear you were hearing the real Piaf!"

I was stupefied at the level of talent I was witnessing. She sang five more songs, including all the greatest hits: "Padam, padam" and "La vie en rose", (my fave rave), "Hymne à l'amour", "l'Acordéoniste", and "Milord" before taking a break. The audience reaction was electric, as the lights went back up for a short intermission before the second set.

"My God, she'll be doing encores until two in the morning at this rate, " Dom laughed.

"She's so wonderful. Thanks for suggesting this! I wonder if the Foundation got word of it and more of my co-workers are here." I looked around but didn't see anyone else I knew.

Suddenly, almost as if on cue, Jean-Pierre d'Arivèque with Robineau in tow, appeared at our table. Since it was a high top and I was sitting on a high stool, we were about face to face, as he greeted me.

"*Mademoiselle* Shrier! I am pleased to see you here. Did you enjoy that first set?"

"*Bonsoir, Monsieur.* I did…very much. *Permettez-moi de vous présenter un prof de français du Lycée Lincoln Park: Dominique Lambert.*"

"*Enchanté, Monsieur,* " d'Arrivèque shook hands with Dom and Dom answered with the same formality and then turned to Robineau.

"Robin, how are you? " he asked, nodding at him.

"Hello, Dominique, " Robineau answered in English, coldly. But he was really glaring more at me than at Dom.

Jean-Pierre d'Arivèque seemed somewhat taken aback that they knew each other and wondered about that. Robineau explained that he knew Dom and Peter through Maxime.

"Ah, " he said, "it seems Chicago is a village." He then turned and addressed Dom, "Will you be accompanying Sarah home after the first show, or are you staying for both?"

"Well, I'm staying. My friend — my boyfriend-- Peter is doing the lights for these shows. But Sarah here thinks she has to get home after the first one."

"*Mademoiselle* Shrier, I would like to offer you a ride home in that case. Will you join me after the performance?"

"Oh, goodness, that's okay, *Monsieur.* I can catch a bus or something. But thank you!"

"*Il ne faut pas faire de bêtises,* " he said to me sharply. "You cannot go home late at night alone. Please accompany me upstairs after the show. I shall insist that Jean-Luc wait with the car."

It wasn't going to do me any good to argue and truth be told, a ride home was a godsend. "Thank you, *Monsieur.* I will find you afterwards, then."

"Edith Piaf" sang another whole slew of wonderful music for the second set, ending with the fantastic "Sous le ciel de Paris" and "Autumn Leaves." Encores were demanded and she did "Ne me quitte pas", the Jacques Brèl anthem that thrilled me to the marrow.

Dom, seeing me practically swoon over that song, said, "Brèl was quoted, you know, many times insisting that it's not a love song."

"So what is it then, a love plea?"

"Actually, no. He said it was a –and I'm quoting here, 'a hymn to the cowardice of men' and the degree to which they were willing to humiliate themselves."

"Well," I mused, "it strikes me, then, as rather brave for a man pretending to be a woman, to sing it."

When the second set ended, and the ovations died down, people began heading out, and I saw Robineau make his way again to the stairs with Jean-Paul d'Arivèque but without Maxime. It seemed to be easier to climb up than go down, but getting around the spiraling part on the narrow stairs was still an ordeal. I noticed that d'Arivèque didn't seem bothered by needing help, which spoke to his self-esteem. He obviously did not lack any, and I admired that trait. Or maybe, I thought, he was just a regular at this club.

I met them near the car, which I recognized even though the traffic was heavy, with double-parking going on. Jean-Luc greeted me cheerfully, which made Robineau roll his eyes and give off a distinct sigh of exasperation. D'Arivèque evidently didn't hear him, but instead beckoned me to enter the back seat before him, so I slid in, while Robineau helped him into the car from the sidewalk side, and then he himself got into the front passenger seat.

"Did you enjoy that?" d'Arivèque asked me smiling kindly in a street-lamp and moonlight-bathed aura.

"I just love 'Ne me quitte pas' so much!" I sighed. "I didn't realize Piaf covered it."

"*Ah non*? But you did realize, did you not, that when Brèl wrote the part that starts '*Moi, je l'offrirai des perles de pluie venues de pays où il ne pleut pas*' he set the lyric to a theme borrowed from one of Franz Liszt's *Hungarian Rhapsodies*?"

"Um, no, I certainly did not know that. Did he plagiarize it? How could that be?"

"Songwriters do it more than you know, " he laughed. "Liszt's andante section of *Hungarian Rhapsody No. 6* dates from 1847. By the time Jacques Brèl wrote his version, 1959 I think, Liszt's original tune had gone into the public domain."

" Really! Gosh how about that."

In 1970 I didn't have the slightest notion that pop singers were ripping off classical musicians right and left, but by the end of that decade, and the ensuing musical education under the tutelage of Jean-Paul d'Arivèque, I was going to recognize the egregious plagiarism by Barry Manilow of Chopin and even worse, the chutzpah with which Eric Carmen blatantly stole the theme for his song "All by Myself" from Rachmaninoff's Second Piano Concerto, for which he ended up subsequently settling with the Rachmaninoff estate.

Our friendly musical conversation was abruptly called to a halt as we drove up to the sidewalk outside my house and Jake the night watchman was out of his car, shining a very bright flashlight at a dark figure sitting on what looked to be a duffle bag on the ground near my front fence. They seemed to be arguing, and the figure whose face I could not make out was gesturing with one hand as if to say "stop".

Suddenly the flashlight hit where I could see him and I gasped! "Oh, my Lord! That's my college boyfriend!!" I leaped out of the car, yelling, "Jake! Jake! It's ok!! I know him!"

Soren jumped off the bag and picked me up and actually twirled me around. "Sari! It's so good to see you!"

"What are you **doing** here? " I said still incredulous. "Put me down a minute, I have to go explain this."

Jake had backed away, apologizing for the hassle, to which I said, "No, no—you were right to be suspicious. But everything is fine." And I walked over to the limo where d'Arivèque had his window rolled down and was looking perplexed, and a bit unhappy at me.

" You see, *Mademoiselle* Shrier," he said in a serious tone while extending his hand out the window to me, "why I think your living situation is so unsafe for you?"

I touched his arm through the window of the car, and assured him, "*Monsieur*, I do understand how you might be concerned, but this time, at least, you mustn't be. This is someone I know very well. I just...sort of...well, didn't know he was coming to visit me! That's all. I'm surprised, but not scared, and it's all fine. Thank you so much for the ride home. See you tomorrow!" I waved and turned back to Soren, who put his arm around my waist as I unlocked the fence. I glanced back to see that the limo was not pulling right away but had stopped for a moment longer and Monsieur was slowly raising his window as it drove away.

"Soren! What the hell? Couldn't you let me know you were coming? I would have stayed home!!! Plus, you can't get in here---there's no buzzer or anything."

"I got that! You live in a virtual chastity belt!"

"Ha ha. But seriously, what gives? Isn't law school in session? " I knew the rest of the university was coming back to life, even as I wasn't positive of the start date to classes. "What about your dorm resident job?"

"Sari, I quit."

"What?!"

"I quit the job and I quit law school. I risked incurring the wrath of my parents and letting down the entire family, but I quit."

"So...what are your plans? Are you going to stay in Chicago?!"

"No."

"Oh."

"I'm going to stay for the weekend though! Can we play tourist and guide?"

"Hell yes!"

"Good. On Monday I'm going to walk you to work and then I'm catching a train to New York. I wanted to come here and say good-bye to you in person. But I'm moving to where I can do what I longed to do in the first place. I don't want to be a talent attorney or a corporate agent or a manager. I want to write music criticism. It's all I ever wanted to do. I want to write for Rolling Stone or Variety or something."

"Variety? But don't both Variety and Rolling Stone publish out of L.A. or San Francisco or somewhere?"

"Oh, I'm sure they must each have a New York bureau. I mean, I'll write for any publication, as long as I can write about rock. What we're going through...what we've been going through, is nothing short of a Renaissance. I have to be a part of chronicling that."

"Well, I admire your ambition, Soren."

"You should! I took my cue from you. I mean that. I don't think I ever knew anyone who had as much conviction as you, Sari. Nobody — not your family or anyone was going to tell you what to do with your life."

"Oh, I don't know about that. If I'd gotten along with them, who knows what my decisions might have been. I wasn't in a very appeasing mood when I graduated Iowa, as you jolly well must recall."

"Yes, but you stood up to them. I watched you. I couldn't do it. My parents didn't approve of our current or future — uh — union, if I can use that word, and I acquiesced to them! I'm not happy about it."

"Look, we weren't ready to get married, either of us. I didn't want marriage, although, I admit I wanted you in my life."

"But you went off to Paris."

"Yes, and then I realized I couldn't just" I gestured -- making air quotes---"keep you 'on ice' all that time. "

"We had fun though, didn't we?"

"Yes we did. And we will this weekend, too. I can't wait for you to see the film library and all my progress in there!"

My little single day-bed was a challenge, but we were both exhausted after talking so late into the night, and we scrunched in together, and, after making love, spooned to keep warm. The alarm went off punishingly early and I ran into the shower first so I could get ready for work, leaving Soren to languish more comfortably, at least, without me in the bed. He was awake by the time I had to leave, however, and I explained to him that he really was a prisoner in my apartment for the day, but I would come straight home and even try to leave the office a little early.

"Eat anything I've got in the house, " I said. "Make tea! Plus, there's cereal and milk… and I think some ham. Maybe cheese. And soup! I've got soup."

"Don't worry about it. We'll go out for a great dinner, how's that?"

"Bitchin'! I'm not cooking."

"And I'm just going to crash all day. I didn't think you were ever coming back last night!! That sidewalk was hard."

"Poor baby! See you in a few."

"Bye, sweetheart."

Even though I'd gotten little sleep that night, there was still a discernable spring in my step on the way to the office. How I had longed for him to be in Paris with me, I remembered, and now here he was in Chicago and we would have two days to play. It was bliss.

Cass called me that afternoon and there was a distinct air of conspiracy in her voice.

"Did you get a little surprise last night?" she asked, not succeeding at feigning ignorance of my answer.

"You KNEW he was coming?"

"Uh -huh. But not until he was actually on his way. He stopped here to say good-bye. Wasn't that nice of him? I drove him to the station while Alan watched the kids. I'm going to miss him, kid."

"Well, Cass, it's just lucky I was out last night and came home to find him, because if he had just shown up at my fence, there would have been no way to signal me that he was here. He would have had to beg the security guard to let him in, and I'll bet that wouldn't have been easy."

I told her all about going to the drag club and seeing the Piaf impersonator and running into my boss.

"My God," she said, breathless, " things are never easy with you, are they? HA!"

Chapter Sixty-Five

"Ne Me Quitte Pas"...Jacques Brèl

I came back after work on Friday to find Soren up, all showered and refreshed, sitting at the kitchen table reading *The Strawberry Statement* by James Simon Kunen.

"Is it good?" I asked throwing my arms around his neck and kissing him on the forehead.

"Someday our kids are going to remember us as the generation of college radicals, " he answered, as he put it down and pulled me onto his lap.

"Hmmm, " I answered, tacitly in agreement but not with the "our kids" part of it. "Hey, I want to go out for a really nice dinner tomorrow night. My treat. I owe you anyway."

"No you don't –you paid that back."

"I know, but I owe you an emotional debt of gratitude, too. I want to go to this famous Chicago restaurant called *La Cheminée*. I already made reservations from my office this afternoon."

"Well, that's neat. I even have a tie with me someplace."

"Oh, I hadn't thought of that. Do you have something resembling a sports coat, too?"

"Yep, if I can wear it with jeans."

"Oh, I suppose so...you'll look pretty cool. It's not that fancy of a place, just really nice. French."

"Duh."

"Okay, smartass. So, I'll bet you've got cabin fever about now, eh? Let's get out of here, and I'll take you to this sweet diner Cass and I ate at one time. You'll like it. There's a bookstore on the block and after that we can walk to the Lake."

"Sounds like a plan."

So Soren and I retraced Cass's and my steps, and ate cheeseburgers and malts at Lou Mitchell's place, before heading over to a bookstore called The Dolphin. This venerable shop—another Chicago landmark-- had an interior more reminiscent of a general store from the turn of the century than a modern-day book seller. The main floor had comfy chairs and a table or two among the stacks; there was a counter with coffee always on. The hip, young proprietor's office was off to the side but open into the room, too, so he could observe what was happening from inside there. The stairs up to a loft area were rickety and they creaked. I went up them, and picked out Eric Seagal's best seller *Love Story* intending to merely leaf through it, sitting on the top step. An hour later, I had read the entire book, and liked it. Soren, who had immediately headed for the music section, came over and found me, and laughed when he saw what I had.

"I finished it already!" I said surprised even at myself. "It's pretty good!"

"Come on."

"Well, okay, it's not *Moby Dick*."

"I like this place, " he said. "No wonder you hang out here."

We left and walked, as I planned, all the way to Oak Street Beach and the shores of Lake Michigan. We found a bench and just sat there as darkness took hold of the city. The air turned noticeably colder, so Soren moved over closer to put his arm around me and snuggle. He had seemed like he wanted to have a serious talk with me almost from his arrival, but perhaps sensing I'd be unhappy after it, he'd put it off. Now we had nothing else to do but talk.

"I want you to know that I'm sad to be leaving you, " he said. "I was already sad when you moved here."

"But we talked about that in Iowa City, " I said, not wanting to rehash anything about how his parents didn't approve of me. "I'm not angry that we didn't end up getting married or anything."

"I know, but I just feel bad that if we were going to make future plans of some sort, my family's attitude ruined it."

"Look, it's not like my family was any better. Yours was just more up in our face about it. My father was completely against the idea, too, don't you worry."

"Well, the trouble is, Sari, the more I thought about all this, the more I think they're right. Religion is a tough nut to crack. I imagine I'll only marry someone Catholic…in the end, I mean. There's no one else now, in case you were wondering."

"I wasn't." *I have to confess I was a little shocked…and hurt…to hear those words "I think they're right" come out of his mouth.*

"Well, don't you agree?"

"I think religion is a royal pain in the patootie!" I snapped. "Instead of bringing people together in peace and love and all that, it drives the biggest wedge in the world between people."

"Like that hasn't been happening since the Inquisition."

"Doesn't make it right." I sat and pouted for a minute, but then came around to at least admit religion would probably make a difference in my future marriage. "Okay, I give, " I said. "I'll admit it would be really hard for me to watch my little girl go down the aisle in a white dress and receive her First Communion. So, your point is well-taken in the end."

"I get what you mean. You can see that it would be easier for me to marry a Jew simply because I believe in your religion's basic teachings because they're mine, too."

"Sort of. I've got bad news for you, though, if you think that all Judaism consists of is the Old Testament."

"Oh, okay, yeah, maybe. But in any case that's not true for you. I could sit there and be just fine watching my son have his Bar Mitzvah. But it would be tough for you to see him as an altar boy, am I right?"

"You are."

We sat there for a few more minutes in silence and then he said, "There's another thing, too."

"What?"

"When I move to New York, I'm not coming back. Not to Iowa City or Imogene. I intend for this move to be permanent."

"Well, so did I when I came here. I'm not planning to ever move back to The Bluffs, that's for sure. But, " I hastened to add, "if my Chicago dreams don't pan out, I could see myself back in Iowa City, though."

"Yeah, well, you don't have to contend with the draft."

I turned to look straight at him. "Oh shit! Did your number come up or something?"

"Not yet. But it's when, not if. And when it does, I'm going to saunter right across the Canadian border and not look back."

"Can you do that?"

"Canada lets people in who are 'evading induction' more readily than they do if you're a deserter. And Canadian immigration officers can't ask about immigration applicants' military status now when they show up at the border seeking permanent entry. Plus there are a lot of agencies in Canada that are being set up to help us."

"Wow. Would you really dodge the draft, though, Soren?"

"In a New York minute." He laughed at his pun, but then got serious again. "I'm not going to go through all that C.O. crap Alan did."

So this was it: possibly our last weekend together ever. Facing that made me want to cry, but I didn't want the next two days to be cloaked either in anger or despair. We'd already gone our separate ways once as friends; this was not a rupture of that, but a continuation.

"At the end of the day, Soren, I think we'll always love each other, " I said, "whatever we do otherwise."

"I agree, " he said and hugged me close.

We didn't "talk this into the ground", as my mother used to call endless discussion. In fact, we took our next day mood cues from the weather-- bright and sunny…even a little on the warm side for September, and we spent the day doing tourist activities all around the North Side. We went on the architecture tour on the Chicago River, and we strolled along Navy Pier before heading to the Art Institute where we spent most of the rest of the afternoon.

When it was getting time to start thinking about dinner, we went back to my place and cleaned up. I put on the kilt with a white blouse and pearls, white tights, and my London shoes. I carried the Hermès replica bag and draped my trench coat over my arm. Soren looked cute as hell in jeans, a light blue oxford cloth dress shirt—could have been more crisply ironed, but I didn't care-- and a cool navy-blue silk tie splashed with little sailboats all over it. He'd brought a beautiful navy-blue camel hair blazer with him, which he lifted out of his duffle, not even too wrinkled. I was shocked to see something that fine come out of his bag.

"Wow, that's pretty. *Chic, alors!*"

"Thanks. I got it for job interviews. It is New York, after all."

"I'd wear it on the train if I were you, " I said, offering unsolicited advice. "Take it off to sleep, though, " I laughed.

Our dinner was glorious. *La Cheminée* gave off vibes of a cozy little French country inn. The walls were exposed brick and the ceiling was heavily beamed. Tables for two, four or even six persons, all covered in red cloths, were close together but still seemed intimate. There was a huge fireplace in the main room that one could imagine held a heavy iron *marmite*, which, "in days of yore," would have needed to be stirred every hour. Behind latticed doors was an immense wine cellar.

We started with drinks in their upstairs cocktail lounge, *Le Grenier*. Because we were in a French restaurant, I decided to forego cocktails like Tom Collins, my usual "can't-taste-the-alcohol" choice, and opted for a Martini and Rossi on the rocks, which I didn't much care for and nursed the whole time. Soren had a kir.

The dinner menu prices were quite steep with most entrées in the $9.00 range, but I'd decided it didn't matter; this was a special dinner and cost be damned…to a point. I ordered *quiche Lorraine* as a starter and Soren went with lobster *mousse*, which, when I begged for a bite of his, was so delectable I couldn't believe my taste buds weren't dancing right out of my mouth.

"Umm, sooo good, " I managed to mutter.

"How's the *quiche*?"

" Good, too, but not as wonderful as yours."

Our very attentive but not pushy waiter may have guessed we had, as it were, "lesser means" than some of the other diners, so he suggested we might want to share a *plat principal*, and there were two marvelous ones: Beef Wellington which of course was called *filet de boeuf en croûte* on their menu, and *châteaubriand*. We opted for the first one; I'd actually never before had it. The filet of beef was smothered in *pâté de fois gras* and *duxelles*—mushrooms sautéed with onions, shallots, garlic and parsley-- before it was covered in puff pastry and baked until only rare. It was sublime. The meal also came with *petit pois* and *carrottes à la vapeur*--a much used method in France, which turned ordinary vegetables into a dish that tasted so much better than anything I could ever conjure up in my own kitchen. *(We had a pressure cooker at home, but Betty rarely made use of it, and I didn't blame her. The thing scared me to death.)*

Soren ordered a half bottle of *Château Neuf du Pape*, offering to pay for it himself if that would help me out, but I demurred. We finished up with *Grand Marnier crèpes flambée* at the table, which we also shared, and espresso. I thought, once again, I was going to have to be rolled back to my place, and thanked my lucky stars we could walk slowly, very slowly, right down Dearborn to get there.

"Oh, my God, "I said enraptured as we left the building, "I will never eat again."

"Sari, that meal was far out! I mean…wow… really choice."

"I loved it, too. I did good, huh?"

"You did great. It was memorable. And I may have to rely on the memories of it because I doubt I'll ever eat that well again."

"New York will have plenty of French restaurants."

"Yeah, but will I have the bread?"

"Well, you'll just have to go out and earn *beaucoup de baguette!*"

Sunday morning I got up early and ran out to get the *Chicago Tribune* so we could laze around and read it. I made tea and toast.

"Sorry I don't do coffee, " I told him, but of course, he already knew it. "You could take the keys and nip out to the little coffee shop two blocks from here and see if they'd let you take some in a to-go cup or something. I'm sure they have that, " I explained hopefully, since I didn't really know if they did or not!

"Tea's fine, " he laughed, taking the cup and kissing me on the forehead.

We spent a quiet day inside reading and repacking his bag, and, of course, I brought up the subject of Cass and Alan, whom he'd just seen on his way out of town.

"I didn't go over there as much as I should have, " he admitted. "I saw Alan alone more often than the both of them together. He was usually in the union with some students."

"Students or student?" I asked, only half kidding. "Cass mentioned more than once to me that he spent an inordinate amount of time 'in his office', " I said, making air quotes.

"Well, I only saw him with groups, but who knows. They don't seem all that happy out at the farm. Although they did do some work on the place. They sleep in that tiny little back room, now and the twins have the bedroom as a real nursery. It works out a lot better for the clutter."

"She told me they were going to do that, but I wondered if it would actually get done. She loses her make-shift art studio, but the kids needed a room, so…"

"So what do you think they'll eventually do…when he gets his degree and all?" Soren wondered.

"I don't know. I guess you go where the jobs are. But they've got another couple of years to figure that out, don't they? He's got to stay and finish that community service for his C.O. status, no matter if he graduates or not. He's also got to put together a chapbook for the MFA, so…that's probably not happening any time soon."

"No, but he is giving a reading one of these days."

"Well, that's something. I wish Cass could do her work. She's so damn good and has so much talent. It's such a waste."

"She's the mom of twins now. I can't think she has a spare minute to sleep, let alone paint or make prints. And from what I could tell, he's not exactly pitching in."

"I know he's not."

Monday morning we awoke before the alarm and just sort of held each other in bed for a while before getting going. We walked to Michigan Avenue, and he got a coffee in my building's lobby, before heading up to the Foundation offices so he could see the film library, and maybe meet a few of my co-workers. We came upon Hennie in the hallway first. She almost spit out her coffee when she heard me call him Soren.

"Oh! So, you're the famous Soren, " she greeted him, before I could make formal introductions.

"And I'm guessing you're Hennie?" he said teasing.

"How did you know?" she chortled, and passed us by without any real conversation, for which I was thankful.

Annie-Laure was also coming out of the break room with her coffee, and ran into us. I introduced them, and she smiled happily back at us. I had already told Soren a lot about her and Jean-Luc, and how great they'd been to help me move in.

"Are you bringing him up to meet everyone in the Presidential suite?" she asked me.

"Oh…no, I don't think so. We don't have an appointment. Besides, he's catching a train."

"Well, all right, then. It was so nice to meet you, " she said turning back to Soren and offering her hand. "I hope to see you again."

"Um, you, too!" he answered, somewhat awkwardly, since he and I knew he likely would never see her again.

We roamed about the office a few minutes more, stopping in at the publications department, which was doing my brochures. Back at my office I showed him my amazing projection booth, the progress I'd made with film cataloguing, and a sample of a lesson plan I was in the process of writing.

" You like it a lot here, don't you?"

" I love this place, " I admitted.

But by then it was time for him to be leaving for the train station and his journey to a new life. I was going to accompany him back down to the street lobby, but he picked up his duffle bag from one of the theater seats, and said he'd decided he should just go by himself. So we embraced and held each other for a little while and then, with really nothing left to say except the *de rigueur* stuff about keeping in touch, I led him down the long hall to our reception and the elevator. I wondered if I'd ever see him again.

I made it a point not to mope around the office, and busied myself with film summaries. Around mid-afternoon, however, I was summoned unexpectedly to the Presidential Suite. I had that same momentary feeling of panic, which was still all too frequent. I admonished myself to cut it out.

JPA was seated behind his enormous *escritoire ancienne* and did not get up, but motioned for me to take a chair in front of his desk.

"I had a phone call from the head of the foreign language department at Lincoln Park High School, " he said, not hinting at whether this were good news or bad. "She was quite taken with your presentation the other day." He looked up at me and smiled. "She went on to explain that she was program chair for something... I wrote it down..." He reached into his pocket, took out a small pad, placed it in his lap, and turned the page over.

"Yes, here it is, Mid- States Conference on the Teaching of Foreign Languages. Have you ever heard of it?"

"No, " I said, shaking my head.

"No...well... it is a fairly new organization, she told me. Formed last year. This next spring---in March, I believe-- they are having their annual meeting in Lake Delavan, Wisconsin, which is not too far from here. She has invited me to be keynote speaker at a luncheon. She would like me to explain all about the Foundation and how the education component of it would be of interest to French teachers. She said that even though other languages would be represented, of course, they could also learn about what, if any, similar services might be available in their own field, say from the Spanish or German consulates, et cetera. "

"Oh, my! Well, I must say, that is fantastic news. With all those French teachers from everywhere in the same venue, you could really disseminate a lot of information in one fell swoop. That's going to be really...just what we need."

"I would like you to attend, also, and of course, the Foundation will provide all your expenses."

"Oh. Gosh—me?" He nodded. " Well, okay...sure... I'd be happy to go. Maybe do you think I'll have brochures by then...hint... hint?" *I wasn't really sure if I could joke with him, but did it anyway.* "Do you have something in mind specifically for me to do?"

"*Bon, bref,* I do not know---help me hand out information or perhaps just talk to teachers about the films they can order." He smiled at me and winked. " As you say, you may have catalogues to offer by then."

"Thank you!" I said. "I think this will be just the shot in the arm our film program needs!" I was genuinely enthusiastic about the film part, but as I was saying that, I realized that these teachers were going to have their minds blown finding out about all the other aspects of the *Fondation Culturelle Française*, too, and I didn't want to downplay that. But I couldn't think fast enough to come out with anything actually articulate, and just added, "Your speech is going to bowl them over!" And with that eloquence, I started to get up to leave.

"Oh, one thing more, *Mademoiselle* Shrier. I'm having a dinner salon at my home next weekend with the curators of several Parisian museums, who will be in Chicago to meet at the Consulate with the executives of the Art Institute. This is an event to which the entire staff will be invited. And you are welcomed to bring your...euh...your friend... from college. The one who came to town. Would you both be available?"

"Umm... yes, I will be. Thank you, *Monsieur*. My college boyfriend, Soren, left town today for New York, where he will now live. We...aren't really...we aren't... together anymore. But thank you for thinking of him."

I looked up at him and saw that his expression was a mixture of feeling sorry for me, but also something like relief. He probably didn't really want some non-French speaking hanger-on at the party, I thought. To lighten the mood a little bit, as I was exiting his office, I called back to him, "And don't worry...I'll just drink club soda!"

Chapter Sixty-Six

"Desafinado"...Antonio Carlos Jobim

The height of the autumn colors in Chicago really reminded me of being in my Paris dorm, because just as I'd experienced there, the ivy climbing up the façade of my building burst into oranges and reds overnight. By next year, I thought wistfully as I climbed the stairs admiring it, they will surely be gone; the renovation would be complete, and the outside would have been refurbished, with the spiny spider-web-like vines all removed. But for this year, it was glorious.

My walk to work, as well, took on the feeling of a scenic tour. I made my way down sun-dappled sidewalks, brushed through un-raked leaves crunching under my feet, and lingered under block-long canopies of color just above my head. Red brick homes and big city apartment buildings with old growth trees lining the curbs, always conjured up images of quintessential Americana to me. I hadn't grown up in a place like that, but had admired vistas of it portrayed in paintings, photos, even greeting cards. Now I was trekking routes daily, where I could ponder the irony — or perhaps great good fortune — that I was living in those scenes.

The evening of Jean-Paul d'Arivèque's salon arrived, and I knew I would wear my little airplane outfit. I felt confident that it was right for the occasion, even though when I walked in and handed my coat to one of the maids — yet another one I didn't know-- heads turned towards me with expressions that were more quizzical than admiring. Oh well, I thought, too late now.

The outer reception foyer was crowded with about twenty or thirty people, but when we were led into the vast living room, we were so dwarfed by the dimensions that it seemed more like an intimate group of friends.

JPA had looked up to give me a little wave when I arrived, but hadn't really greeted me or taken me around to meet anyone; he was engaged in some deep conversation with two men who turned out to be the French *Consul Général* and one of the head curators of the French collection at the Art Institute. I was almost immediately stopped, however, and offered a flute of champagne by a waiter with a tray.

I motioned for him to lean in so I could whisper in his ear, "May I have some club soda or Seven-Up, please? "

"Certainly, *Mademoiselle*. Wait one moment."

But suddenly, someone called out my name in a tone of such utter surprise that I turned on my heels, and came face to face with, of all people, Renaud de Seignard! I was almost as stupefied to see him as he was to see me!

"*Mademoiselle* Shrier! Is it really you?" he asked delightedly, taking my hand and kissing it. He had called me by name so forcefully that everyone in our immediate vicinity stopped what they were doing and looked at us, including Jean-Paul d'Arivèque.

"Oh!, *Monsieur de Seignard, c'est vous?! Ça me fait grand plaisir de vous revoir!*" And without thinking, I gave him a hug *"à l'américain"*, at which he was a little taken aback, but recovered nicely. It could have been construed to be a big faux pas on my part, but at that moment I wasn't thinking about formality.

"Sarah, *moi aussi ça me fait un grand plaisir!*" We both just stood there smiling, not knowing what to say. " But... what are you doing **here**?" he asked at last, after we got over the incredulity.

"I work for the *Fondation Culturelle Française! Monsieur* d'Arivèque asked me to come tonight. I'm the film librarian, actually. "

And as the waiter appeared at my side again, this time with a fizzy drink that was obviously not champagne, it all of a sudden dawned on me that this was the gathering of museum curators. Of course! Stupid me, I might have guessed that de Seignard would be coming from the Marmottan!

Another waiter followed with a tray of *canapés*, from which I carefully took one toast point with chicken-liver *mousse* and raspberry jelly.

"And you must be here representing your museum? This really is so fantastic to see you!"

"And I am also very delighted to see you. How marvelous that you work for Polo!"

POLO? Again? My God, did the whole world of music and art know him by that name?"

" Um…yes, I've been working at *La Fondation* since June. I got the job right out of college. I'm so happy to be a part of the organization. I have nothing but admiration for it."

"*Et alors,*" he said shaking his head, " I had no idea you were even living in Chicago. Clément will be very happy to hear that I have seen you. I am truly *stupéfié.* I am only sorry Blandine was not able to make the trip with me. She had surgery for cataracts… removal of them."

"Oh, dear," I said.

"No, no. It was…do you say?… *routine.* She will be fully recovered soon. But, yes, she would indeed have wanted to see you."

"And Clément? How is he? You must tell me everything. He hardly ever writes."

It was true. I had tried to stay in contact with my Sorbonne friends throughout the ensuing months, now years, since Paris, and I heard fairly often from Nonnie; less from C.C. But I didn't hear much of anything from the boys; only a few letters from Clément were ever written to me in Iowa City.

"Oh, he is wonderful! He will be married at Christmastime!"

"Married? Already?" *I had to admit I wasn't expecting that!*

"You know," Renaud said, taking my arm and leading me over to sit down on a curved Louis XV settee, "he was nearly twenty-five years old when you met him. His girlfriend was rarely in Paris in those years. Did you ever meet her?"

"I can't quite remember, although I knew he did have a girlfriend. Is it the same one then?"

"Yes. He only ever had one serious girlfriend, Éléanor. She was not there too much---just at holidays, because she was doing her studies in Rome and Florence. She was a student of the classics. When she returned, well, the events just took their course, and they are engaged since a year."

(Mr. Seignard's English was good, but like many French speakers, he didn't quite grasp the usage of "since" with time and "for" used with the present perfect tense. It was an error d'Arivèque or de Piaget wouldn't have made because they'd been in the States so long that they'd become quite bilingual.)

"So you like her a lot then?" I asked awkwardly; it certainly was none of my business.

"Oh, yes. We do love her."

JPA came over to our couch and sat down on the other side of me. He seemed relieved to be seated, and a waiter came over directly with a champagne flute. Standing and talking to people made it impossible for him to hold a glass of anything, as I had observed in previous gatherings. It really brought home to me the problems one had without the full use of one arm. It seemed even worse than not having two good legs.

"Polo, *mon cher ami,* " Renaud de Seignard said to him sort of leaning around me, "I see how lucky you have been to have hired Sarah Shrier. *Tu as bien fait, mon vieux.*"

"I am aware of it!" he laughed and held his flute up to clink with Renaud, leaving me in the middle to wince a little bit. "We are very happy with her work."

"She is a dear friend of Clément."

I had to interject my voice in here somewhere because all this talking about me was making me uncomfortable.

"So you all know each other, then?" I said tentatively, even though it was totally obvious.

"Yes," said Renaud, "well, the *maman* of Polo was very well known to me, of course, and in the art circles of France… Paris, New York…everywhere, so I knew her first. But it was not long before we all became great friends."

"I have known Clément since he was—what?-- perhaps four or five years old?" JPA asked.

"Precisely, " affirmed Renaud, and continued… to me, "I was not yet with the Marmottan, but was working in a well-known art gallery in Paris where *Madame la maman de* Polo frequently came to make important purchases. I was always happy to advise her. You can see many of the works on the walls here."

My God, I thought, I hadn't even looked at or paid any attention to the art on the walls of this home. I guess I was too busy running around panicked the last time I was there.

Dinner was announced, and without even giving it a second thought, Renaud got up and went around me to help JPA to his feet and hand him the cane, which made me immediately cringe, "Oh no! Here it comes." That was one of those "too forward" actions that I just assumed you were supposed to avoid with handicapped persons. But d'Arivèque seemed fine with it, and didn't even flinch. They must really be close friends, I decided. Strange how small the world really was.

Then Renaud offered me his arm. "*Vous me permettez,* Sarah? " I took it happily, and let him escort me into the dining room.

Hooooly shit! What I had not had a chance to see in this house while being sick in a far-off bathroom in July, now gleamed in front of me, drenched in the autumnal moonlight pouring in from a wall of glass doors each leading out to the spacious terrace that circled this floor of the house. And the interior, with its enormously long dining table, sparkled under five huge crystal chandeliers. The room was the size of a football field!

"My goodness, I exclaimed to Renaud, "this table is set for thirty people! It's bigger than that famous one in the Napoleon III apartments in the Louvre!"

"Ah, yes," he laughed. "This home is without parallel."

Seating was preassigned and I found myself very separated from de Seignard, but thankfully close to Marie-France de Piaget, who was seated directly to the right of the head of the table where Jean-Paul d'Arivèque was standing to welcome everyone and give a toast for the evening. First course wine glasses had already been filled by a veritable retinue of waiters, staff that would have been called footmen in the great houses of times past. With Jean-Paul d'Arivèque addressing his remarks to the *Consul Général* first, then to the curators of the most prominent museums of France and their guests, we drank to one another's health and to a successful conference, which, I learned, was starting the next day at the French Consulate's suite of offices.

Dinner was divine. It began with a simple soup that harkened more to the American Midwest than to France, but done with French culinary flair: *potage parmentier,* a thick but not heavy cream-based soup with mainly leeks and potatoes, but also a few other harvest vegetables added. This was followed by *sole meunière* with rice pilaf, after which came a simple but elegant curly endive salad in raspberry vinaigrette.

Throughout the meal, which lasted a good two hours, I was served an assortment of wines (Château de Crezancy Sancerre with the main course; Dom Perignon throughout the meal if we wanted it). I didn't refuse alcohol, but just sipped mine, paying attention to eating without spilling anything, and to the fascinating conversation to which I was privy...all about the various collaborations upon which these museums and galleries were about to embark with the Chicago Consulate, the Art Institute, and, by extension, with our Foundation. Not eager to lend my own remarks to topics about which I knew very little, but always polite and eager to speak if spoken to, I answered a few questions about where I had studied art in France, and what my job with the *Fondation Culturelle Française* entailed. Luckily MFP included me in on some of her exchanges with the assistant curator of the Orangerie, which I had visited on several occasions in Paris in 1968-1969. It was soon due for a complete overhaul, she was explaining, and she was very excited about an eventual addition to the building and an augmentation of the permanent collection. I guess the expression on my face upon hearing this must have signaled that I was worried about changing such a venerable Paris landmark, because she quickly added, "Of course, the original rooms that Monet designed for his monumental works of *nymphéas* will not be altered."

Desserts were brought in on rolling carts so people could choose mini *amuse-bouches* from among every famous French dessert: *gâteaux,* fruit *tartes, choux à la crème,* three flavors of *mousse, millefeuilles, réligieuses, éclairs* -some with vanilla *crème anglaise* and some with caramel and chocolate; *crème brulée,* and *crème caramel,* which is what I chose. Even though it was small, it was heavenly...thick custard that jiggled in a dark caramel "bath." I just let it slide down my happy throat.

We were encouraged to take our pick from the cart more than once, and to then rejoin our host next door in a more intimate space, in what we would perhaps call a "drawing room," where the décor was less "museum" and more "home." Here there were lots of seating areas with tables so we could have coffee served and not have to balance everything on our laps. I wandered in there gazing around at beautiful blue and cream silk brocaded sofas, wing chairs—some with ottomans—and gorgeous table lamps, which were not overly frilly but still elegant enough! Everything in this room was certainly tasteful, while not giving the impression of being priceless antiques like in the other, more public rooms. Hallelujah, I thought, finally! A *petit coin* with some half-way comfortable furniture!

The party broke up rather early, for which I was grateful, and as the crowd dissipated, I held back a few minutes to look at the art hanging in that salon. I was amazed to see things I would have expected to see in the Art Institute or the Jeu de Paume, not in someone's living room. There were works by artists whose names I didn't readily recognize, like Aristide Juneau's painting of a pastural scene in a nondescript locale. But then there were a Boudin and a Pisarro that were museum-worthy. I was gob smacked.

When all of a sudden I realized I was quite alone in the room, I scurried out through the dining room, retracing my steps, so thankful I wasn't lost again. Once back in the great reception hall, as I was being handed my coat, Renaud de Seignard came up to me with his own coat over his arm.

"So, you're not staying here with Monsieur?" I surmised.

"*Si*, yes I am," he answered, "but Polo, Marie-France, and a few other of us are having a little pre-conference meeting at the bar of the Drake Hotel now. May we drop you at your place? Jean-Luc is driving us."

"Oh, no, " I insisted, "the Drake's just over a few streets from here and right up the block. It's too far out of your way to where I live."

"I'm so sorry to hear you say it, " he said--truly sad, but then his face lightened up. "Would you join us then for a while at the bar?"

"No, really, I couldn't. I'll tell you what, though. If it's okay with Monsieur, I'll ride up to the Drake with you and catch a cab from there, how's that?"

"*Parfait*, "he exclaimed. "*N'est-ce pas* Polo?" JPA and MFP, within earshot of our conversation, had joined the small contingency heading up to the hotel.

"*Avec plaisir*," he said, and motioned us all into the elevator.

Once in the underground garage, Jean-Luc pulled up in a stretch limo, since there were the four of us and five other museum officials. JPA was helped in last, and we all sat across from each other on white leather banquettes. A mini-bar was in the back, but we didn't partake of it; the trip over to Michigan Avenue and straight north up to the Drake lasted less than seven or eight minutes, with little traffic.

At the steps of the Drake, I said good-bye to Monsieur de Seignard. He was there, holding his arms out to me, as though to hug me like I had hugged him, which we did, as well as give one another *la bise*.

"It was such a joy to be with you again, Sarah, " he said taking both my hands in his. "Now that I know where you are, I am sure this must happen again. Blandine and I will most certainly return to Polo now and then."

"I am so happy I got to see you, too! " I said in earnest. "Do congratulate Clément from me on his upcoming marriage. I'm truly happy for him. And please give my very best to Madame de Seignard."

I thanked Monsieur for the ride, took my leave of Marie-France de Piaget also with *la bise*, and got into a waiting taxi. I thought, as I rode off into the gleaming city caverns, what an unexpected, incredible night that had been. I looked up from the cab window into the starry sky. One of those shining pinpoints was my lucky star. It had reunited me with someone who represented the happiest time in my year abroad.

And that lucky star had also kept me from repeating my *bétise* — although, ironically, I would still have been, in the words of the blind monk Perignon, "tasting the stars."

Chapter Sixty-Seven

Sarabande...**George Frideric Handel**

Having met the Chicago Art Institute's various mucky-mucks at that Foundation dinner, it occurred to me that I'd better get far more acquainted with the French art collection they oversaw, since it was the largest one in the world outside Paris. So sometimes together with Dom and Peter, sometimes alone, I began to spend Saturday mornings there, like I'd done every weekend in the Louvre when I was a student in Paris. At the Louvre, it goes without saying, even once a week for nearly a year, hadn't been enough time to see it all; but I did, at least, get fairly familiar with the various departments. I hoped to do far better in Chicago.

When these Art Institute Saturdays included Dominique Lambert, we would invariably walk through the breathtaking French Impressionist collections, discussing our faves and admiring the rest; and, usually thereafter we would go have coffee in their café. I liked to bounce ideas off Dom about what the FCF could offer teachers... sort of audition my lesson designs with him. I found I was always in the throes of some latest and greatest scheme to augment what we could do with our films in the field of education.

"I have in mind to provide the wherewithal for teachers to show films or film strips about the regions of France, and then, for instance, build classroom activities around that, " I announced enthusiastically to Dom. "You know...theme-like. Normandy, for instance, so perfectly dovetails with Impressionism. What do you think?"

"That sounds like something I'd be interested in, " he said, "especially with my sophomores. Sophomores are the 'middle child' of high school; they need something special in their lives."

"Yes! I think a cultural component, really in any level, would be a great incentive for your students. See, here's one idea I had: you could divide them into teams of some sort and assign a region to each--- there are at least a dozen---and they could research the history, geography, cuisine specialties, tourist attractions, and on and on. They could present this to the class, maybe even with food. Kids always love food. Sound like a possibility?"

"As a matter of fact, " he said, "you wouldn't believe the number of professional papers people have presented at conferences on the regional cooking of France! Not to mention the different wines and what other things they drink if the region isn't known for wine."

"Yeah, well, you couldn't do a wine tasting, " I said, a little bemused, " but it can't be against the rules to learn about it, can it?"

"Of course not. As for your cooking idea, if I butter up the home-ec department, maybe I could even use their kitchens some time, and the kids could prepare a classic dish."

"Yes, or have a chef demo. Maybe some famous Chicago restauranteur could come and give a lecture! "

"Or some culinary arts student or sous-chef, more likely."

"So I'm going to organize all our regional films and make up a unit on this, " I said, writing down notes on a paper napkin. "This could really end up being great stuff! I'll have to run it all by my bosses, of course."

"You heard, I'm guessing, about the touring exhibit coming here a year from now? It will be shown in the other wing of this place, and will focus on life at Versailles."

"Yes, there was mention made of that the other night."

"I told my advanced class about it, and they asked if it was going to be about all three Louis, and I said, '*OUI*, three kings!'"

"That's actually clever, " I said, looking up at him and chortling.

"Well, what does the Foundation have that would complement an exhibition like that? If you dream something up that teachers can do to prepare their classes before it gets here, wouldn't that be a coup?"

"Hmmm. I'll get on that. I can see a lot of elementary school interest in things having to do with life at Versailles---*Mousquetaire*-oriented and all, but is there any French taught in elementary schools in this city?"

"Maybe more in the private than public sector, but I'm sure if you invent it and get the word out, the interest will be there for kids even if they don't take French."

"Yes, getting the word out will be key."

"Well, hey, I heard my chair invited your boss to Mid-States next Spring. He can talk it up there, for sure."

"Well, that means I'd better get on it!"

And that is what I did. Our lending service was still in its infancy, but I decided that if I started with some lesson plan sheets to put into the big film bubble envelopes, I could expand that into ideas for teaching the content with other things the Foundation could provide: puppet theater instructions and scripts; costume ideas for dress-up role-play; coloring activities.

About mid-October when Yom Kippur was on the horizon, I took a detour into Hennie's part of the office to thank Monsieur Rosier de Molet for the synagogue tickets, which I did intend to use. Since I had to ask Marie-France de Piaget for the day off to go, I decided that when I was in her office, I would broach the subject of some of my teaching ideas with her and maybe get her to take them to JPA. My pitch was going to be that libraries lent all sorts of things nowadays, and since we wanted to keep an eye out for ways to further Madame d'Arivèque's stated wishes for the Foundation to be ever-expanding educationally, this could be a logical next step.

She held her cards pretty close to the vest when bombarded with my ideas, but she also had that gleam in her eye that led me to believe there was a kernel of possibility there.

"Why don't you write up for me a short treatise or abstract enumerating your ideas, and I shall present it to Monsieur. He will, of course, have the last word."

So I got right to work on three initial proposals. I had no mock-ups as yet, but I described in as much detail as possible what they might look like once the art department or marketing could make them for me:

Idea A: a box with costumes of a certain period, made out of inexpensive materials and only stylized—not perfectly authentic of, say, a Louis XIV or a Marie-Antoinette; some wigs; maybe some spats kids could put on over their shoes; plastic swords, stick horses. There could be instructions for the class to make other props like a big cone with some gauzy fabric coming out the top to represent a Medieval noble lady or an oversized man's hat with feathers in it.

Idea B: A Guignol theater that would fold up; hand puppets or puppets on sticks—could even be laminated thick paper; various themes from the original Punch and Judy-type characters, lending themselves to reenactment of Molière scenes or *La Révolution Française* . There could easily be one for *Le Petit Prince* with a pilot, a prince, a rose, a fox, a lamplighter, a businessman-- characters who influence the story most.

Idea C: The Regions of France, with a master calendar of a month laid out for daily activities from filmstrip viewing to research, to cooking and oral presentations. It would have sample quizzes and tests, pamphlets and posters depicting each region's costume. We could include a big map of the regions showing the various famous historical tourist attractions or culinary specialty for which each was known.

That got me started, and apart from worrying that I had too much of a "money is no object" air about all this, I was pretty pleased with my inventions so far. I took the document to Annie-Laure's desk and asked her to please give it to MFP, which she was happy to do. I asked her to read it first.

"If you think these are lousy ideas, would you tell me so I can fix them before the other two see it?" I pleaded with her.

"I've some news for you, too, Sari, " she said with a little lilt in her voice. "Jean-Luc would like to start teaching you to drive the Citroën...before the snow falls on Chicago, you know?"

"Wow, he does? I'd sort of forgotten about that. Well, tell him I'm game!"

"*D'accord.* Perhaps he can come see you in your office with all the details?"

"Sure!"

Later that afternoon I was on the phone with Cass up in the projection booth.

"So I'm going to get to learn to drive this groovy, gorgeous French car, " I was telling her.

"Oh, kid! Maybe he'd let you drive it here for Thanksgiving! You could make a lot better time than taking the train."

"Hold on a minute, there. THAT'S not happening. What if I got in a fiery crash on Interstate 80? I'm not on their insurance or anything. Besides, that's only a month and a half from now. I can't master this thing in that short of time."

"Oh, I bet you could. And if it's bad weather, well, I remember you telling me yourself, you're a great snow driver."

"Cass, get real. Please." But just as I was about to expound on my fears of driving his car to Iowa, Jean-Paul d'Arivèque appeared through the glass doors of the hallway and came into the lower part of my office.

"Oh, Jesus, Cass. I've got to go. JPA just came in. Call me tomorrow?" And I'm afraid I had to hang up the phone quickly on her.

He looked up to see me careen out of the booth and down the steps of the aisle toward him. He sat himself down in one of the theater seats behind my desk and motioned for me to sit in one, too. He was carrying my proposal.

"I am very pleased to tell you that these ideas of yours are wonderful," he said holding up the paper. "I had never imagined any of this... what you have thought up here... I must admit that I... and also Marie-France... we are very impressed! You have gone beyond the film aspects---although of course, all these ideas revolve around our films---and into the realm of educational enrichment." He softened his voice and added, "Le rêve veritable de Maman."

"Well, " I said, "that's good then?" I was also happy.

"So, " he continued, "how do you envision for example, the box? Tell me your ideas for its implémentation."

"Okay, so first of all, I think we'd have to have two—maybe even three, but perhaps they wouldn't all have to be the same—so that we could loan them out simultaneously. We would follow a theme, like I explained in the proposal. If it were the one on, say, Life at Versailles, we could put in some wardrobe items—doublets or princess-type dresses-- that we could easily get from the places theatrical organizations use. But if we didn't want that level of expense, we could find some kid dress-up costumes , like for Halloween. Or have them made for us. I'm sure there are lots of avenues we could explore. We would use a generic size—it wouldn't have to fit each kid—just enough to give the impression—a stylized costume. We would pack up the box with all the accoutrements, including an inventory of what all was expected to come back to us, and mail it off like we do films, with the expectation that the schools wouldn't steal the stuff, and the teachers would return the box... after a designated, agreed-upon time period."

"And if the children tear them or ruin them?"

"That's a risk alright. There may have to be some signed agreement that in the case of damage, the school is responsible. As for cleaning, we'd have to do that after every loan, either paying to have it done if our costumes were, shall we say, 'real;' or we'd just replace the cheaper ones." I stopped babbling and looked up for his reaction. "Are you worried I have just dreamed big with carte blanche?" I asked timidly.

"You are right to do so, " he said. "Ça se peut... tout."

"Wow, that's so cool!" I was not used to, in any part of my life, being given free rein to spend money.

"Of course, this will take some time before it comes to fruition, you know that, do you not?" he asked me.

" Oh, yes, sure. I understand."

"You will need to work closely with our other departments, especially at first, to create a model of what you actually would like to see. And it goes without saying that in due course, this would also be put before our Board of Directors. Not now--that is down the road a bit. They do not have to give me their permission for any expenditures, but I would like them to be kept well informed of it."

"Of course."

"And now I have a more pressing item to discuss with you."

Momentary panic, once again.

"More pressing?"

"Yes, " he said, smiling, "the Chicago symphony concert. It is this weekend. May I once again extend the invitation of Maestro Solti and invite you to accompany me?"

It occurred to me that he probably had a lot more people he could take using his mother's tickets, if that was indeed what he was using, so I tried to give him an out, saying with a nervous laugh, "You know, he was probably just kidding. You don't have to take me if you don't want to."

He looked at me for a moment with a furrowed brow and then said, "*Mademoiselle* Shrier, I would not be asking you if I did not want to take you. It would be my pleasure."

"In that case, I happily and gratefully accept, " I said, feeling silly that I had made this into a federal case.

"And something else, " he added, but before he could finish I interrupted.

"Yes? Oh, wait, I bet I know: you don't want me to wear my airplane sweater outfit."

"*Mais non!*" he stated emphatically, "I have no preference for what you wear. Wear what you like. No, I was going to speak about your driving lessons. I am pleased that Luc is taking the opportunity to start them."

"You know, I feel bad he's giving up his free time."

"He is very willing to teach you. And *de toute façon*, he is being paid to do it."

"Well, then, that's okay, " I laughed. "I hope I can master it and not waste his time. Thank you so much for this…this …incredible opportunity to drive such a magnificent car. I'm so excited!"

"*Je vous en prie.* Well, until Friday evening then?" He used his right arm to push up from the chair, and locked his brace with the left hand this time since he didn't have to lift his arm to do that. "I shall pick you up at seven. Curtain is eight o'clock but if we get there early, we can have a drink. Have you ever seen Orchestra Hall?"

"As a matter of fact, yes. It's beautiful. "

"Good! *Alors, tout est prévu.*" He took my hand to shake and seemed to hold onto it for a bit longer than I expected. I thought maybe he was getting his balance, but actually, it was a rather tender gesture. I felt myself blushing a tiny bit.

Yom Kippur was that same week, and MFP had, of course, granted me the day off with pay. I took the train to Evanston and had no trouble finding my way to the synagogue; at least a dozen other passengers got off and headed there as well. I did indeed have to show my ticket at the door, which still floored me. And if I thought I'd see Monsieur Rosier de Molet anywhere in the crowd, I had another think coming. There must have been eight hundred people in that place! There were four sweeping, curved sets of pews with three great aisles separating them, and the rows went forward from where I stood at least twenty-five deep. I could not believe I was in a Jewish place of worship and not a cathedral. One would seriously need opera glasses to see the *bima*.

A half dozen massive iron chandeliers with dangling lights hung from the domed ceiling and luckily, winding around the entire sanctuary was balcony seating, so even though the capacious main floor was too full for me to find a seat, what with open spaces in the pews marked off with the random purse or coat draped across the bench to indicate that they were being saved, I climbed up to the balcony with another throng, and found a spot.

To say that this was a much different Yom Kippur than I had ever experienced in my little hometown synagogue, would be to state the obvious. It was a Reformed temple with an organ and a choir. I had missed Kol Nidre the night before, but in the slot on the row ahead of me, I saw on a flyer that they'd had a cellist, so I knew immediately they must have heard Max Bruch's adagio.

My music appreciation professor at Iowa had called Bruch's Kol Nidre "probably the most beautiful Jewish music ever written by a Protestant." He'd gone on to explain to us how Bruch became acquainted with Jewish music when his teacher, Ferdinand Hiller, took him to meet the chief cantor of Berlin, who was on friendly terms with many Christian composers of the day, and who took an interest in Bruch's curiosity with Hebrew folk melodies. "Was Bruch's music Jewish then?" he had asked us. Answering his own question, he had told us, "No. Bruch never pretended he was writing Jewish music. He was taking inspiration from the traditional songs' melodic traits to incorporate some into his own compositions."

The service itself was dotted with some nice choral renditions of the prayers, but I didn't actually get any religious fervor out of it, even though much more of the entire service was in English than the Bluffs' ever had been. I sat there, but, rather than follow along, I leafed through the special *mahzor* looking at random prayers and readings, hoping something would lead me to a sense of awe, since the high holy days were often called the Days of Awe. I wasn't feeling it, although I certainly was aware of how much better I liked Reformed than what I had grown up with. Even the Iowa City congregation had been Conservative, and thus conducted mostly in a language I could neither read any more nor understand.

"If I ever do get into religion on my own accord, " I told Cass the next day, "I will absolutely go Reformed."

Cass was amazed that I brought up religion that particular day because she had major news to tell me. Her church, the campus Episcopal one, had a day care facility, and she had never even known that. She said she'd been approached one Sunday by some of the, "yes, church ladies," (of which she hastened to add, she was not one), and told that they wondered whether she might need but not be able to afford, some babysitting.

"So they said they would take Paul and Laura in the church's basement childcare rooms one or even two days a week! For free! They said it was as a favor because they liked me, and could tell I was a harried mom in need of respite and some help."

"Hey, how about that!" I was very happy for her.

"I was so stunned by the thought of this miraculous offer, " she enthused, "that I didn't quite know what to say, except thank God I did manage to choke out a heartfelt thank you! It was truly a Christian thing of them to do, don't you think?"

"Yeah, I do! I'll bet Alan is pleased he doesn't have to pay for anything!"

"Alan was only lukewarm to the idea, " she said with a tinge of sadness in her voice, "thinking it was not needed, number one and charity, number two, which irked him. But I reminded him that it was probably his own pastor—you know, the one helping with his C.O. status-- who had given them the heads up about us in the first place. "

"Well, what is religion anyway, if it's not good works?" I asked. "Isn't that especially prevalent in yours?"

"Exactly. So anyway, that's not the end of the story."

"Oh, dear," I worried, "there's more?"

"Oh, it isn't bad! I was in town with the kids in their groovy stroller and guess who I ran into?"

"Some idiots from our dorm days?"

"Oh, hell no... Klampert!"

"Far out! How is he?"

"Very surprised I had two one-year-olds, that's how he is! No, he's great. He wants me to come back! Says I should reapply for the program and really finish my damn degree in art, and get the B.F.A. He's certain I must have satisfied all the core requirements when I almost had the B.A., so this would mean just a lot of studio time. He would be my advisor, he said."

"CASS! That's wonderful!"

"And with two-- or maybe I could even eke out three-- days of babysitting with no charge, I could do it!"

"Hey, don't forget that you really don't even have to worry about it. I will send you some of that money! Remember, it's yours."

"No, Sari. Alan must never ever know of that money, and it must all seem like it's coming from just you. And you can't afford to send me to college."

"Oh, fuck yes I can! I can send you enough to cover all sorts of things-- the kids' food, for example, and Alan won't suspect anything. He accepts that I am their auntie Sari, merrily spoiling them with clothing and toys---lots of toys. You can surreptitiously spend it on art supplies and sneak in the tuition. No problem!"

"Well, we'll see. I don't really think Alan can object to any of this if I tell him that I have the chance to get an art department scholarship through Klampert's patronage."

"So would you go back next semester? Wowie zowie, that's so exciting!"

"I hope so!"

I hoped so, too. What with the news from Soren that they had fixed up the place they were renting so that it sounded a lot more livable, and with the prospect of free child care, and going back to finish her degree, I thought things would really be looking up for Cass-- that she was on her way to getting her creative groove back, and the old art juices would flow again. I had convinced myself that Cass doing art again for real would allay any of her fears of not being a success in life.

A blossoming art career and being a fine mom could go hand in hand, and she was the person who could prove that.

Chapter Sixty-Eight

"Moments Musicaux"...Franz Schubert

Orchestra Hall was brimming almost to its 2,500-person capacity the night I accompanied Jean-Paul d'Arivèque for the first time to hear the Chicago Symphony in concert. We were dropped off by Jean-Luc, who came around to help JPA out of the car. We entered directly off Michigan Avenue and it was easy...no stairs...for which I was relieved. It was late October but the weather was unusually balmy that night, and JPA didn't even wear a coat over his beautiful bespoke light brown three-piece Dormeuil Guanashina suit. It was far too warm for my winter coat, so I wore my trench coat, which, I realized as I handed it to the coat-check person, was looking pretty sad. I was sure my boss noticed it, too, and I felt justifiably mortified.

Dress for the event was not as fancy as for the opera, but this certainly wasn't the little Omaha symphony or a concert in the Union at the U of Iowa. I was wearing the kilt-white-sweater-London-shoes kit...my usual dressy choice from Labor Day to Easter...figuring that the airplane outfit had been hauled out enough for one month.

The d'Arivèque seats were, surprisingly, not in a box, which, in that hall were on the next floor up. Instead JPA led me to a row eight back from the stage, on the aisle to accommodate his brace leg. He explained to me that he didn't want to sit down too far ahead of time because that would mean he'd have to get up to let other people in, so he suggested I walk with him down to the high footlights of the actual stage, where I could turn around and get a sweeping view of the entire house, with its massive curved balconies. It was breathtaking. Everything was bathed in red with row after row of sparkling white lights and white plaster trim setting off the seating and stage. The loge area which was designated the "First Balcony and Boxes" was right over the main floor, but above it were not one but three huge balconies, the uppermost one of which was called the gallery.

I oohed and ahhed at the view, which prompted Monsieur to remember that I'd said I'd been there previously.

"Yes, it's true, " I affirmed. "I'd been visiting my college roommate in Kenilworth, and her parents gave us tickets. We sat in their box that night. But for some reason, I have to tell you, I did not appreciate the splendor of this auditorium when I was up there before."

"I can well imagine that. Do you believe this rivals the Paris Opera?" he asked me almost teasingly, with a little glimmer in his eyes.

"Well, if you mean the size of the house, maybe, " I answered. "But the entryway and the lobby sure don't rival the *Opéra Garnier* at all. And the Paris stage is probably twice as large as this even though this one is huge!"

"I agree with you, " he laughed. "The seating area in Paris is considerably smaller than this, which, by the way, is why they are contemplating building a new one."

I didn't remember ever seeing seating above and behind a stage before, so I asked him what those seats were for.

"They look like a choir loft, " I proposed.

"Yes," he said a bit surprised at my remark, " I've seen them used that way. Other times, it's just more seating. Like tonight—you will see. The seats will be all filled for Isaac Stern. You have heard of him, have you not?"

I had, but did not want to give the impression that my knowledge was anything but cursory, so I just nodded.

"He first played with this orchestra in 1940 when he was all of nineteen years old, " JPA stated with a little chuckle. "Imagine it. "

When d'Arivèque saw that the row had filled, we took our seats and I glanced at the program. What, if anything, would I recognize, I wondered, leafing through the book and noticing that Maestro Solti had a full-page bio in it. He would be leading the orchestra in Dvorák's *Carnival Overture* to open the evening. I was thrilled that I did know that one.

"Oh, *Monsieur*! The Dvorák work is a favorite of mine!"

"So you like Dvorák tone poems then?" he replied smiling at me. "The *Carnival Overture* is one of his set of three tone poems: life, nature, and love. The *Carnival* is the second one. Very famous."

I was at least a bit familiar with Dvorák, even though I didn't really know what a tone poem was. However, as it turned out, at least I did know and love his 9th Symphony. I explained to my host that "From the New World" had really been my introduction to classical music.

"My parents didn't have many classical records at home, but we had that. It was a gift from one of my uncles, and I used to listen to it a lot. But that's not the reason I know *Carnival Overture*."

"No?"

"No. That music was featured in one of my most favorite movies. It's called *Interlude*. Have you seen it?"

"No, I have not even heard of it, " d'Arivèque answered, puzzled.

"Well, it stars Oscar Werner as an orchestra conductor, and his musicians play the Dvorák---we see them rehearsing."

"Ah, Oscar Werner. I like him. Obviously *Jules et Jim* is a masterpiece. We have it in our collection at the Foundation, as I'm sure you already must know."

"Of course! I also love that one."

Indeed, and ironically I was working on curriculum to accompany that film right about then, but didn't want to get into that at the concert. I hoped he would be pleased with my ideas for Jules et Jim, *though, when I did present them.*

I returned to reading the program. Isaac Stern would be second on the roster, a featured slot, playing Brahms' *Violin Concerto in D*. Not good news for me; I couldn't place it at all. Maybe I'd recognize it, though, I ventured, from having taken that class at Iowa. However, sitting there waiting for the concert to begin, it wasn't ringing any bells. After intermission the program would have Beethoven's *Symphony No. 3 in E-Flat Major*.

As if reading my mind, JPA said to me, "I'm sure you will recognize the 'Eroica' symphony of Beethoven. It is one of the most often played ones in the repertoire. And Maestro Solti is a Beethoven specialist as well, so it should be quite impressive. I hope you will like it."

I turned to him and smiled. "I'm prepared to like anything Maestro Solti chooses."

That night I still didn't know much, if anything, about Georg Solti. I knew he was nearly sixty and had a new, young wife in London, Valerie; and that earlier in the year, right before I met him at the fateful Bastille Day party, they'd just had a baby girl and had named her Gabrielle. But that didn't tell me anything about him musically. I had grasped the idea that, at the time, he was new to the CSO, but could not have had any insight, of course, into the fact that one day he would be considered the force majeure *behind that body's becoming one of the three greatest orchestras in the world. I didn't know that in his early career he was sometimes considered an almost draconian taskmaster in rehearsals, but that he exhibited a captivatingly relaxed demeanor during performances, which the musicians appreciated. It seemed to me that first night I saw him conduct in person, and sitting rather close like we were, that all he had to do was glance at them or flick his hand and they responded perfectly. He had done away with the baton, I found out later.*

Carnival Overture was rousing and lilting at the same time, and Maestro Solti seemed full of its zeal up on the podium. It only lasted about ten minutes but it set a vivacious mood for the ensuing offerings.

Isaac Stern walked out on stage and was immediately greeted with a standing ovation, which surprised me, but should not have. JPA did not stand up for it but since everyone else around me did, I, too, stood. Isaac Stern had already been lauded not only as one of the great virtuoso musicians of his time, but also as having been instrumental in saving Carnegie Hall in the early 1960's. He was beloved around the world, and the Chicago audience showed its appreciation and esteem before he'd even played a note.

The Brahms was enchanting, and I was mesmerized by both conductor and guest artist. I could feel d'Arivèque's gaze upon me from time to time, and although we glanced at one another, we did not exchange any words. I thought to myself that he must have been wondering if he'd brought someone who could appreciate what she was seeing and hearing, and I hoped he didn't think he'd wasted his ticket on me.

After another protracted standing ovation for Isaac Stern, it was Intermission. Monsieur got up and beckoned me to follow him out. There were multiple lobbies and spaces with bars in Orchestra Hall, but of course, we stayed in the one associated with the main floor. He called my attention to the sign pointing towards restrooms, but I shook my head, so we proceeded to the bar.

"May I offer you something to drink? White wine perhaps?"

" Thank you. That would be nice."

Monsieur was anxious to know my reaction so far.

"So *Mademoiselle* Shrier, what are your thoughts?" he asked, not teasing me… but actually interested.

"I love it! It's so wonderful. Isaac Stern's playing just…blew me away."

He gave me a smile of slight amusement at my language. "I do admire the Brahms, " he said. "It has always been one of my favorites. The adagio movement strikes me every time I hear it as the soul of the entire concerto."

Much later on I would come to realize that in almost every work I would ever hear where there was an adagio movement, that one would be what I would love the most.

We were standing at the bar sipping glasses of Chenon Blanc when one of the bartenders handed a note to him. The idea that they knew him struck me as rather amazing, given there were literally hundreds of people in that space.

"Oh, dear!" I said, as he took it. "Is something wrong?"

"No, no. Maestro would like us to meet him afterwards at the stage door entrance."

"So, will you have to get word somehow to Jean-Luc? Do you want me to do it? Is he parked out there someplace?" I made the offer, but realized almost immediately that I didn't have the slightest clue how I'd ever find the car.

Monsieur looked at me with an expression of gratitude, and touched my shoulder. "He knows, but thank you for the offer."

"Oh? Goodness. That's rather remarkable, isn't it?"

"Well, no, it was all *prévu* with Georg *(he pronounced it "George" in English, just as the maestro had told us he himself said it)* that we would be going to the bar at the Palmer House afterwards. He had his assistant phone my house and confirm with Jean-Luc that the plans were on for him to fetch us at the side entrance. "You and I, we shall proceed to the Green Room after the Beethoven. Would you like to meet Isaac Stern if he is there? He will not, unfortunately, be coming with us afterwards."

He stopped talking when he noticed my perplexed look. "*Excusez-moi*, Sarah, that I did not inform you of these plans ahead of time. I needed to make sure that Maestro was not under an obligation to go out with the board or the money people and Stern."

"Um—it's fine."

What was I going to say? That I didn't want to come to the Palmer House and they should take me home first? Ha! And meeting the guest star backstage would be a blast, but I was pretty happy he wasn't coming out with us afterwards. Besides "How do you do, " I couldn't imagine even one thing I'd be able to do to hold up my end of a conversation with Isaac Stern. I had enough trouble talking intelligently to Georg Solti.

JPA finished his wine and I set my not-yet-empty glass on the bar, and we made our way back inside.

The Beethoven piece was long and majestic. I recognized bits of it which served to alleviate some of the anxiety I thought I would feel spending the next part of the evening in the company of the conductor! Even if he and JPA knew in their hearts that I was a know-nothing, I felt fairly certain they wouldn't show it.

Maestro Solti was in a jovial mood when we met him afterwards, and acted extremely happy to see me.

"So, how were we?!" he exclaimed as he saw me.

"Oh, I'd say you were pretty fair, " I teased.

"She's funny, Polo," he said as they clasped arms.

"No, I loved it all, " I said more seriously. "The music was all so wonderful. I can't thank you enough for---er---inviting *Monsieur*... to invite me!"

"Yes, well, Polo must bring you to the entire subscription series! You will do it, won't you? " he said turning to his friend.

"I would be most happy to," JPA assured him, and then addressed me, "Would you be amenable?"

"I—uh—I'm sure that would be-- great." But I still couldn't figure this all out, so I added, "That is, if maybe you wouldn't rather ask Marie-France or someone else also?"

"Oh, she goes already—to the matinée performances."

" Ah. Well, then, thank you so much. I'd be thrilled."

"I am pleased," he said, and then turned back to the maestro. "Is Mr. Stern still here, Georg?"

"He was kidnapped by the fundraising vultures, I'm afraid. There's a big *soirée* at the Board President's house, as you know! You were invited too."

"Yes, I sent my regrets."

"Of course, I am supposed to be there, but I begged off because I must fly out early tomorrow back to London and *ma petite Gabrielle*. I'm sorry. It is a pity you cannot meet him, Sarah."

"That's all right, " I said. *"Phew" would have been rude.*

"You know, Polo, it is the part of the job I hate most. I do it, but I cannot stand it."

"Heureusement, I am in the business of giving money away and not asking for it," JPA answered.

Just as *"prévu*," Jean-Luc was waiting for us, and we headed out into the much chillier night air, and over to the Palmer House Hotel's bar, which was in the gorgeous lobby. As we walked in, Maestro took my arm and motioned for me to look up. The ceiling was worth the price of admission! I let out an audible gasp.

"Oui, c'est un oeuvre d'art. Français, en plus!" said Solti, who spoke passable French. And then he switched back to English. "The story of Bertha Palmer is interesting, perhaps, to you, Sarah. She was married to Potter Palmer, and she was twenty-three years younger than him---so you see some similarities between Valerie and myself, " he laughed. " He gave her this hotel for a wedding present. And even though it burnt down mere days later in the Great Chicago Fire, they rebuilt it."

Monsieur added, "Bertha Honoré was her *nom de jeune fille*, so you see she had some French origins in her family tree. She had gone to France where she met and befriended some of the Impressionist painters, most notably Claude Monet."

"That is correct," said Solti. "She met the painter Mary Cassatt there, too, and she, too, figures into this story."

"You know already, I think, *Mademoiselle*, " said d'Arivèque, "that the Chicago Art Institute has the largest collection of Impressionist art outside Paris? *Alors, Madame* Palmer at one time had the largest collection of it outside France, and it was she who bequeathed it to the Art Institute. As for the hotel, much of her art work hung in there for decades. And she had also convinced her husband Potter to commission another French painter, Louis Pierre Rigal, to do this formidable ceiling fresco."

"And do not forget, " added Solti, "all over this place you see chandeliers dripping in garnets and lamps and stained-glass windows---all masterpieces-- by Tiffany."

"Wow, what an extraordinary story, " I murmured , settling into a big leather club chair, one of three arranged around a small table flanked by beautiful iron sconces on the walls and elaborate standing candelabra on the floor.

"Shall we have a bottle of Veuve Clicquot?" Maestro Solti asked d'Arivèque.

"Why not! We can toast your *triomphe* tonight."

"Oh, but perhaps not, " said JPA looking at me for approval of the idea.

"You know, do you think they'd bring me some tea?" I asked timidly.

I didn't mind drinking champagne, but truth be told, much as I thought I was fine, you never could know. I was certainly once-bitten-twice-shy about drinking bubbly since the July incident.

"I don't see why you cannot have anything you want, " Solti said.

"Tout à fait, " d'Arivèque agreed. "But, you are not feeling ill, no?"

"No no, I'm fine. "

Their champagne was brought to the table by a very nice waiter who greeted us warmly, poured their first flutes, and then and set the bottle up in an ice bucket beside the maestro, who could take care of the next round. A different waiter brought a tray with my pot of tea and my cup and saucer. I poured my own.

"So, Miss Sarah, " Maestro Solti addressed me, "how did you enjoy the Beethoven?"

"It was magnificent, " I answered. *As if I could have said otherwise.*

"Imagine if events had not changed the course of history and Beethoven had stuck to his original plan of dedicating it to Napoleon! Instead of 'Eroïca' it would have been called 'Bonaparte!'" the maestro chortled.

"But we do know, Georg," Monsieur said, "that during its composition and at its completion...and even when he was negotiating its publication... Beethoven surely intended it to be a piece for and about Napoleon."

"That is true, but the original dedication to Bonaparte was defaced by Beethoven himself."

"**That** is the stuff of legend, do you not agree?"

"We know from several accounts, my dear Polo, that when Napoleon grabbed the crown from the Pope and made himself Emperor, he became, for Beethoven, a tyrant. Beethoven could no longer live with his *chef d'oeuvre*, his *magnum opus* being associated with that sullied reputation. After all, he was inspired to write the largest-scale composition ever at that point in his career by the profound human, philosophical and political motivation he saw in Napoleon **before** he styled himself Emperor."

D'Arivèque nodded, " I shall give you that, but perhaps he was also willing to change the symphony's dedication in order not to jeopardize the fee due from a royal patron?"

"*Touché,* " Solti laughed, and then turned to me. "He's quite a cynic, this Polo d'Arivèque, eh Sarah?"

I could hardly comment on that. So I just smiled and drank tea.

"In a few weeks when Daniel and Jacqueline arrive, " Solti said, "you can reconnoiter with Barenboim and see what he thinks."

Monsieur laughed and turned again to me, "Do you know who Daniel Barenboim and Jacqueline du Pré are, Sarah?"

I was startled. It was the first time he'd ever called me Sarah without a preface of Mademoiselle or Miss, or without my last name in there somewhere.

"I'm sorry, I don't, " I answered.

"Oh!, "said Solti, "You are in for such a treat! Those two youngsters are like...pop stars!"

"Yes," Monsieur added, "I'm hosting them at the house, and we will give them a light supper when they get in, because they will be arriving from Lansing, Michigan that night. It will be November 5, I believe. Something like that."

"I will not, unfortunately, be here then, " said Solti, "and Daniel will conduct the orchestra."

"Wow," I said, "you're turning over your orchestra to a young person?"

"He is a prodigy. She even more of one!"

Monsieur turned to me and explained, "He's a pianist and conductor. She is a cellist who is world-renowned at a very young age. They will be giving a special series of concerts with the CSO at Michigan State for the Beethoven Bicentennial Festival and then recording later that next week for Angel Records in Chicago."

"Yes, Polo, you must invite Sarah."

"Would you like to come?" he asked me.

"I'd...certainly...I'd love that!" I replied. *More invitations, but what was I going to say, " NO"?*

On the day of the "casual dinner party," as our invitations stated, for the visiting super stars of classical music, I stayed at the office in order to accompany Marie-France, Annie-Laure, Daniel Rosier de Molet and d'Arivèque all in the car driven by Jean-Luc, who, it was arranged, would be taking me home later that evening. I had dressed up for work, which wasn't uncommon now that I was no longer clambering up ladders in the stacks. I dragged out my old orange and grey plaid jumper to wear this time; the office had seen my—or rather Cass'-- kilt and the airplane outfit more by then than they ever needed to.

We were offered *apéros* while awaiting their arrival with much anticipation. Robineau was, of course, hovering over the group but pretty much ignoring me. I made no attempt to get his attention or to even talk to him, but it didn't escape me that his blatant fawning over the others and snubbing me was on purpose. On the other hand, the rest of the staff were always friendly and accommodating to me above and beyond, so happily his mysterious bias had not spread.

Finally the elevator doors opened to reveal a tall young man carrying a leather satchel. He had a mass of dark curls on his head and long sideburns, and was dressed in a navy-blue overcoat and plaid scarf draped dramatically about his neck. Jacqueline du Pré was a very pretty, young blond woman, lugging her own cello in its oversized case, which Robineau offered to take for her (at least!) and put in her room; but she demurred and leaned it up against the wall in the foyer. Introductions were made and we were all ushered into the beautiful d'Arivèque library, where Daniel Barenboim and Jacqueline du Pré were each offered at drink before the meal. The young couple seemed quite at their ease and comfortable in the d'Arivèque home.

Daniel Barenboim was very animated as he pulled some newspapers out of his bag and read to us, " '*Miss du Pré, cello soloist with the symphony, must be heard and seen to be believed.*' Isn't that terrific?" he said, pausing for our reaction.

"Come on, Danny, " she interjected, "they don't want to hear all that."

"Yes, they do. Listen, it goes on, '*Her beautiful playing of the Dvořák Concerto for Violoncello enthralled the capacity audience. Barenboim, who conducted, gave the most sensitive support, perfectly controlling the ensemble.*' Well, this was nice of them to add that, " he said a little sheepishly, I thought. He didn't seem to mean to take anything away from his wife's acclaim, but they were both hailed as the brightest of bright young things. He continued quoting from the article, " '*The effect was that of a large orchestra listening to a solo instrument with the closest attention. Though loosely knit, the music was brilliant and dramatic and Miss du Pré played it gloriously with all her wonderful tone, technique and style.*' There you have it."

"Really, Danny. Enough. But I'll tell you what, we shall play for our supper...afterwards!" she laughed.

Dinner was served not in the ornate dining room where Monsieur had entertained the museum curators, but in a part of the reception salon where the grand piano was kept in a corner over by the sweeping windows and French doors leading out to the terrace. A considerably smaller dining table had been set up, and the regular collection of Louis XV furnishings had been rearranged in more intimate seating clusters for the after-dinner mini concert. I thought it couldn't have been more perfect.

Trays of hot covered plates were wheeled in on small cloth-adorned, rolling carts. The meal commenced with *hors d'oeuvres* of *crudités* and a *salade de crevettes et écrevisse*, those little crayfish that are more work to get out of the shell than actual food to eat once it's been accomplished. This was followed by a scrumptious *blanquette de veau* served with baskets of crusty *baguette*, *salade verte*, a selection of cheeses from the Jura area---*comté*, *bleu de Gex*, *Roblochon* and *vacherin*, and for dessert, *mousse au chocolat*, coffee and Chambord *liqueur*. One again I was afraid I would burst. Luckily we didn't have to go far to sit back down and hear the music.

Jacqueline du Pré fetched her own cello and set herself up with it on one of the dining chairs from our dinner, not too far from the piano. We all settled in to listen to this essentially private first-class cello concert. She and Daniel, who had seated himself at the piano, began the first strains of the work called *Après un Rêve* by Gabriel Fauré, a piece they would go on to make a signature work of their careers. Barenboim seemed detached, as though he could play his part in his sleep, but as she played, Jacqueline sort of drifted into some melodic trance, embracing the instrument as if it were her lover, her shoulder-length golden hair swaying from side to side as she and her instrument produced, as one, the most heavenly sounds imaginable. I was mesmerized by her playing and pretty much speechless when they were done. Luckily Jean-Paul d'Arivèque was anything but tongue-tied as he praised the beautiful playing, and we all clapped enthusiastically. Then Jacqueline came over and sat next to me on the settee, as Daniel Barenboim rose and stood in front of us, saying eagerly, "And now how about we partake of a little of the Divine Franz?" And he sat back down on the leather piano bench.

"Oh!" I just blurted out, "Liszt! How wonderful."

He pivoted around sharply and glared at me. " Not Liszt! SCHUBERT!"

Mortified, I let out a nervous little laugh, "Ooooh, ooops! Sorry."

I had never felt so humiliated. Why had I even done that? On top of it all, Robineau was overseeing the staff clearing away the dishes, and gave an ever-so-audible sneer when he heard the kerfuffle.

Jacqueline du Pré put her hand on my wrist and whispered, "It's okay. Danny's bark is far worse than his bite." I saw from the corner of my eye that Jean-Paul d'Ariveque was watching my sorry reaction with a look on his face that took pity on me.

Barenboim swiveled back to the piano, with a wave of his hand, seemingly making light of my *faux pas*, as he, in his own turn, set about completely enrapturing us, playing all from memory, the second of Schubert's six "Moments Musicaux", Andantino in A-flat Major, which, from that night on would become one of my very favorite pieces of music, for my entire life.

"Did you like it, Mademoiselle Shrier?" he teased me again when he had finished the last note with a little flourish.

"So much!" I said, adding, "I'm very impressed that you played it all so wonderfully from memory!"

"Camille Saint-Saens knew and could play all of Beethoven's thirty-two piano sonatas by heart!" he stated, as though what he had just done was nothing by comparison.

Before we parted ways, the other Daniel—Rosier de Molet-- approached me to ask if I had liked the Yom Kippur services at his synagogue, which conversation was overheard by Jacqueline du Pré, who came right back over to me and exclaimed, "Danny and I are Jews, too! I converted in Israel when we were married. We had wanted the ceremony to be get at the Western Wall, but we ended up being wed at a lovely home overlooking Jerusalem instead!"

"Wow" was about all I could come up with. I knew she was British, but not much more than that. But I figured she'd either been Church of England or Catholic, and wondered how her conversion must have gone down in the family. "How'd your parents take that?" I ventured.

"Not too well! " she laughed. "But what could they do? We were so desperately in love; we wanted to be married. Danny wasn't about to convert, so I did. I wanted to become Jewish."

In the middle of the workweek that followed, Jean-Paul d'Ariveque showed up in my office just after lunch one day, and announced that this was the afternoon for the recording session he'd mentioned to me previously, and that he was heading over to listen to Barenboim and du Pré record for Angel Records at the Medina Temple on Wabash Avenue.

"You would like to come along, yes?"

Of course, I jumped at the chance, and so Jean-Luc drove us to the very Byzantine-looking building, and accompanied us inside to help Monsieur with any unforeseen stairs.

"The architecture of this temple is Moorish Revival, " Monsieur said, as if reading my mind and instructing me. "This place is a former Shriner's Temple...where they had ceremonies and such. Do you know they once had the Shrine Circus in here?"

"My God, " I said. And it was huge all right. The interior was almost as amazing as Orchestra Hall and it seated almost twice as many people on twice as many levels!

JPA went on to tell me that the CSO had used the space to record many times previously, under the baton of John Martinon, the music director who had been there before Maestro Solti. It seems the Medinah Temple, with its gigantic perfect dome, had acoustics like no other auditorium in the city---maybe in the country.

There was no actual recording booth. The orchestra was set up on the stage as usual, but the stage floor protruded quite far out into the house, and the seating was arranged in a big U shape around it. A table full of equipment was set up sort of over some rows of seating and two engineers in headphones ran the board. We were ushered silently to seats behind and to the side of this make-shift control room, so we could see better.

Jacqueline was playing the Dvorák *Cello Concerto* and Daniel was conducting the CSO. The acoustics in that place were truly as marvelous as advertised. There were a few stops and starts, takes and retakes; and then when that part was over, no one applauded, and she went right into another of Dvorák's vast repertory and played *Silent Woods* and *Rondo in G minor*. Once again my mind was blown by her seemingly effortless articulation of this gorgeous music.

There was a short break, during which Jacqueline saw Monsieur, and came right over to greet him, and, by extension, me. They gave each other *la bise* and I think she was almost on the verge of doing the same with me, but I had held out my hand to greet her, and she shook it instead. She sat down with us and then almost on cue, Daniel Barenboim came back into the recording space and took a seat at the Steinway grand that had been pulled out from the back of the orchestra to the very front. The room got dead quiet again, and he proceeded to join Jacqueline in a performance of Brahms' *Sonata in E Minor* and Beethoven's *Sonata in G Minor* as well!

"Brilliant, Danny!" Jacqueline enthused when he had finished.

One of the engineers called it a wrap, and Monsieur and I, along with Jean-Luc made our way to the back of the Temple, while Daniel thanked the musicians, and Jacqueline disappeared to retrieve her cello. We sat down in the very back to wait for them, because this time Daniel Barenboim had invited Jean-Paul d'Arivèque for drinks and, even though they were still staying with him, they wanted to take us all out somewhere rather than go back to d'Arivèque's house, where they felt the staff was already waiting on them hand and foot. They had chosen the Coq d'Or bar at the Drake hotel. It was a godsend choice for me, since I could just take a cab straight home from there, like I'd done before.

Because I had gone to work not planning on an afternoon or evening out, I felt particularly under-dressed as we walked into the Drake. My winter coat was almost as pitiful as my raincoat had been at the concert the week before, and I was wearing a short black skirt, white blouse and black vest with black tights and black penny loafers. Already short to begin with, it didn't help now that I looked like a kindergartener. If only, I thought to myself miserably, I'd had on my London shoes, it would have helped the lack of height situation. I felt lowly walking in with these celebs and their wealthy host. None of them said anything, but I was pretty sure that my discomfort was evident. I really wanted to be there with them; I adored both Barenboim and du Pré, but I desperately wanted to bolt, also. I took heart in the fact that one drink would not take very long.

The Coq d'Or bar was actually rather crowded for a Wednesday evening, I thought, but Chicago was not Omaha after all, and this was a world-class hotel full of people on the move, literally and figuratively. I had followed the other three in and hadn't been paying too much attention to the surroundings when all at once I was hit by the breathtaking scene: red leather everywhere---even padding the edge of the bar itself. There was a long red leather banquette with seating for at least fifteen people along one side, and in the rest of the room were clusters of low, four-top tables surrounded by more red leather on captains' chairs with black lacquer frames. The entire room was made up of oak paneled walls with murals interspersed in them of stylized golden roosters, and every few feet, hung high up, were large glass lanterns like you might find lighting some *porte-cochère* of a colonial mansion. On the tables were small hurricane lamps, giving off soft, burnished light. The room was impressive and inviting, cozy and imperious at the same time.

We found an open table and all took a chair. Daniel Barenboim was looking at me and grinning, as if he expected me to start the conversation. I smiled back but didn't say anything.

"So, what did you think of that?" he finally asked.

"Well, there wasn't any Schubert, but…"

He burst out laughing. "Next time, eh?" he said mocking seriousness.

"Actually, you shall have some Schubert in a few months," JPA said looking up from the drinks menu he'd picked up from the table. "Margaret Price will be in town, singing his lieder."

"Oh, my God, " said Barenboim, "Solti cannot seem to abide that woman. He wasn't very kind to her in London awhile back."

"Oh dear, " I said, having not a clue who she was. "But maybe, was his bark worse than his bite?"

"No!" Jacqueline piped up. " He had a clause written into her opera contract at Covent Garden that she could never sing the lead roles, and should always be expected to sing the mezzo… minor ones. Too awful."

"He thinks she lacks a certain charm, " said Daniel. "But she has improved, after all. She took singing lessons! And besides that, Otto Klemperer has taken her under his wing."

We ordered drinks and, thankfully, they also offered food. Not only was I starving, but my boss was ever so sensitive to my previous embarrassment, which had been diagnosed (*ad nauseum*, by this time) as "drinking on an empty stomach." JPA ordered what would have been aptly deemed a plate of *charcuterie* in France; here they just called it antipasti. It came with a glorious array of lovely *paté* with *baguette*, a splendid *Terrine des Trois Rois*, layering chicken with creamy *fois gras* and boozy cognac-soaked prunes; *rillettes, boudin*, which I eschewed, together with *saucisson* and *jambon de Bayonne,* both of which I loved. There were also little ramekins of olives, *cornichons* and some kind of jam, as well as three cheeses: a triple *crème*, some *chevre* and a lovely Pont l'Évêque. With the addition of all that for the four of us to share, I did not worry at all about having a gimlet.

JPA ordered a scotch and water, which I'd not seen him order before, specifying Glenfiddich, that he must have known they had. Jacqueline du Pré asked for a drink called "French 75" which, when it came in its martini glass, looked yummy and consisted, she told me, of gin and champagne, plus some lemon zest and a little bit of sugar. Daniel Barenboim ruminated over the drinks menu, and went back and forth before deciding to order a brandy Alexander. We all settled in, and I sat back and mostly listened as JPA interrogated Daniel about some remarks he had made to the Chicago press earlier that week on Wagner.

"Yes, I was asked if I …being Israeli…would ever conduct an orchestra playing Wagner. Of course! That was a silly question. Perhaps not in Israel yet; it is still too soon. But one must separate the person from the art."

"Well, Wagner is certainly not my favorite, " Jacqueline observed.

"Nor mine, " stated d'Arivèque.

"Wagner the person is despicable and appalling…absolutely: Barenboim conceded, "But this is very difficult to put together with the magnificent music he wrote, which so often invokes the opposite kind of feelings…noble, generous."

"Yes," said Monsieur, "I do agree with you. But he was such an anti-Semite. You can understand the reluctance of orchestras to want to play his music with their patrons to consider, and the widely accepted fact that he was revered by Hitler."

"You are right, of course, " said Barenboim, taking a long sip of his drink, "his anti-Semitism is obviously monstrous. But we also must face the fact that Richard Wagner did not cause the Holocaust."

As the evening wore on and dinner plans began to be discussed, I begged off, arguing rightly so, that I was not dressed for dinner out with them. They all pooh-poohed that, and tried to get me to change my mind, but I held firm and told them, truthfully, that I was sad to not be staying, that it had been an incredible thrill for me to hear their music and get to watch a recording session, that I desperately hoped to see and hear them again and that I would most certainly be in the audience for any future Chicago appearances.

Jacqueline got up and accompanied me to the lobby, which was so sweet of her.

"Polo really likes you, you know?" she said to me almost in a whisper, her mouth curling up into an impish smile. "Maestro Solti told me so."

" Excuse me?" I said, astonished.

"Yes, he does. I can tell, too. He's a pretty wonderful man, isn't he?"

"He's a generous and gracious employer, " I answered, "and I hope he likes my work because I love my job at the Foundation."

"Well, I'm sure he likes your work, too, but I'm not talking about that. I can see you're a little embarrassed by my remarks, so I won't press you. But Solti just adores the guy and says that if anyone deserves to be happy, he does."

I didn't know what to say to that, even though I did agree with her. I didn't want to come off like I had set my sights in any way shape or form on having a relationship with my boss that was outside of work.

She gave me a little hug at the door. "See you next time," she said.

I never saw Jacqueline du Pré again. Three years after this phenomenal encounter with her in the autumn of 1970, it would shock us all to learn that she was struck down in the prime of her astonishing career by multiple sclerosis; and we would all anguish at one of the music world's greatest tragedies which would unfurl for the next two decades until her death in 1987 at only forty-two years old.

Chapter Sixty-Nine

"Drive My Car"...Lennon & McCartney

Even though it was November and thus becoming increasingly cold in Chicago, no snow meant I was afforded an elongated opportunity to learn to drive the Citroën, and Monsieur d'Arivèque had not reneged on his offer to have his chauffeur teach me how to do it. So one Saturday morning, Jean-Luc picked me up in the beautiful car. He brought Annie-Laure along ("to provide you with moral support"), and we drove all the way north on North Shore Drive to Winnetka, where he had decided my first lesson would be in the parking lot of New Trier High School. The ride was like nothing I'd ever experienced before in a car: soft, undulating, like riding on a water bed, which wasn't too far wrong, since the hydraulic suspension system that made the company famous, was so superior to shocks.

When we pulled into the empty parking lot, he shut off the car and it slowly began to sink down to a non-road-clearing resting position. I marveled at this, and Jean-Luc said, "You know, it is capable of raising one wheel up while the other three sit on the ground." It was like a circus act.

"So," he began my lesson, "do you know how to drive a manual transmission car?"

"Not really. My father tried to teach me one time. I bombed it. That means I failed, by the way."

"That's actually better, because if you had driven an American one or a VW Beetle or something, you'd have to unlearn what you had mastered in order to drive this car. This way, you can learn once."

"Okay. Why?"

"Because this car, she is a four-speed shift on the column, and the gears shift the opposite way that other cars do, namely, first gear is up and to the right slightly, second is down, third is up and farther to the right, and fourth is down from that. Reverse is out and down."

"Jesus."

"Do not worry, I will show you."

He took the keys out of the ignition, and we changed sides so I got in behind the wheel. He then handed me the keys. He wanted me to feel the key's positions.

"Turn the ignition only part way so you can adjust the seat height and posture."

The ignition was located strangely super low between my knees, but I found it, and then with the engine switched on, the driver's seat could be moved in several ways by a toggle on the side. I drew my seat closer and higher. When I turned the key all the way, the car rose up to driving height, adjusting for the weight of the three of us in the car. It felt like being in an elevator.

"So you know that a manual transmission shifts by engaging the clutch, do you not? "

I nodded.

"*Alors*, the clutch is to your left...the third pedal. The first one, which is long, is the accelerator, middle one is the brake. *Voilà.*"

Well at least that was the same.

"So I press all the way down on the clutch pedal and then I can put the gear shift in first?" I asked.

"Exactly. Do that now."

I did, and then the car responded by rolling forward an inch or so.

"Give it some gas. *Doucement.*"

I did, and just like that, we were going. He told me to stop. Of course, I killed it.

"*Bon*, I need to tell you this: the car does not have synchromesh. Do you know what that is?"

"Nope."

"*Alors*, in cars that have it, you can easily shift through the gears and you do not need to be very precise about the rpms because the gears will not strip. This car does not have that, so in order to shift from one to the next, you look at the tachometer. The needle should never be above the 2...or you are not in the right gear. Pretty soon when you get used to the car, you will feel the engine and hear the motor and you will know when to shift. But for now, look at the tach."

"Criminy."

"*Bon, alors*, try it again."

So I started over with first gear, and we got going in the school parking lot. I had to master putting in the clutch and shifting gears at the same time, then letting it out without killing the engine. It took many tries before I got it right.

"Gee," I said dejectedly, remembering how I struggled to learn to drive the Fiat, "automatic transmissions are so much easier. This is a pain."

"Yes, Sari, " said Jean-Luc in a soothing tone, "but the great drivers would never be caught dead in an automatic. The ones who race are constantly changing gears, feeling the road and their engines working as one."

"She doesn't want to be a great race driver, "Annie-Laure piped up from the back seat. "She just wants to get from here to there."

But I kept at it and suddenly, I was getting it. I made it to third gear, but there wasn't room enough in the lot for me to speed up to shift to fourth gear.

"That is fine, " Luc said. "I want to practice reverse *de toute façon*."

Reverse was down and to the right. I was afraid of getting it mixed up with fourth gear, which I hadn't actually driven in yet, but Jean-Luc assured me I'd find it okay, and I did. I practiced backing up, turning to see behind my shoulder with my right arm bracing against the top of the buttery soft leather of my seat. He made me practice parallel parking between two big light poles (just like I had done with Cass!) , and then when I'd done it about five times, and driven the entire perimeter of the lot, he announced that we were ready for the street.

My hands were suddenly clammy and again, I harkened back to my first solo driving from the Bluffs over the Aksarben Bridge to Omaha when I was sixteen years old. Before the sessions with the manual transmission, Sol had actually taken me to learn to drive our own car first, and notwithstanding his constant yelling at me, I learned well. But driving over the Missouri River made me squeamish. I overcame the problem by purchasing a fab pair of yellow leather driving gloves that snapped on and had perforations in them. It did the trick, and was the start of my love affair with driving.

Luc had me drive out to Winnetka Avenue and from there to Sheridan Road, which we took north. I had a chance to put the car through all four gears on that route.

I drove as far as Ravinia, where the CSO plays in the summers, and it was neat to see that. I switched places with Jean-Luc for the drive back into Chicago, because I didn't feel ready to tackle the big city streets.

I actually felt good for the first lesson. The Citroën was a dream to drive as well as look at.

As we turned back towards my place, I thanked Jean-Luc profusely for taking the time to teach me, and mustering up all my courage, knowing what I was about to ask for was against the odds, I addressed both of them, "Do you think if I really learn to drive this car well, by any chance Monsieur would possibly let me drive it to Iowa City over the Thanksgiving weekend?"

I didn't hold out much hope that they would think it would work, and Jean-Luc pretty much verified that by hesitatingly explaining that I wasn't on their insurance and the liability for this car would be too great, especially driving it out of state.

"I would have to check with Monsieur on that. He is letting you drive it with me, but you would probably have to be put on a special rider on his insurance or something."

"Yes," I replied, "I knew it was a long shot. It's okay."

However, I wasn't prepared at all when Annie-Laure said, "But Sari, our office is not closed for the day after Thanksgiving. You would only be able to drive there for the day."

"Really?! Are you joking? Bummer!" *My God, I'd spent my entire life to that point in school, and school was always out the Friday of Thanksgiving week. It never occurred to me that other places weren't. Yeah, my parents' bar was open on that Friday, but that was different, and, besides, I never worked that day. Still, I might have realized it; a French office was not interested in giving its employees off more than one day for an American holiday. Nevertheless, I was actually in shock.*

"Sari," said Annie-Laure softly, "if it is any consolation, the office will close for more than an entire week at Christmas. You will soon get a memo on that. We will be closed from Christmas Eve until after the Saint Sylvestre."

"Oh, sure. Right. That's nice. Of course. I can spend a longer time away then."

But I was still heartbroken that I would have to break this news to Cass.

As we pulled up to my curb, Jean-Luc offered me some city driving lessons after work the next week, and I gratefully took him up on it, as I slid out of the passenger side to let Annie-Laure come into the front seat. I thanked them again and waved as they drove off.

I decided not to wait for Cass to call me at work, and called her long-distance as soon as I got back up to my apartment.

"Sari! Why are you calling me?!" she said, surprised and worried to hear from me out of the blue like that on a Saturday.

"Well," I said, hesitating to get right to the point, "I've got a problem."

"Oh?"

"It's a big one: our office is open the Friday after Thanksgiving. I can't come to Iowa City."

"Oh, Sari. Well, damn."

"I know. I should have asked about this before making plans. I'm such an idiot."

"I'm really sad!" Cass said. "The kiddos would love to groove with their auntie."

"And she would love to see them. But, you know, I can't see coming for just one night."

"No." Cass sounded dejected.

"I'm so sorry Cass. But there is a silver lining."

"What's that?"

"The office is closed Christmas week! So I can come on Dec. 23 after work on that late train and stay until the 30th!"

"Yay! At least."

"And I'll bring bundles of goodies with me."

We talked for a little while longer about what had been going on in Iowa City and about my learning to drive the Citroën. I didn't want to spend too much time talking to her long-distance on my dime, so we rang off with the prospect of our regular calls resuming during the work week.

I did feel terrible about Thanksgiving, and realized I had probably ruined Alan's chances of having a decent dinner. Cass was turning more and more vegetarian and, besides worrying about the twins' growth, I wondered what in the hell Alan had to look forward to in the way of meals at home. I had decided to broach the subject with her when next we spoke, but she brought it up first.

"Well, I can tell you Alan will be sorely disappointed you're not coming and doing your cooking magic. He's still not at all fond of mine."

"How do the children take to it?"

"Oh, they don't care. I can sneak in every healthy thing in their diet."

"Well, if they're thriving, that's all that matters."

"Why wouldn't they be?" she asked suddenly on the defensive.

"Oh, I didn't mean to imply that they weren't! "

Wow, she must have been more mad I wasn't going to be there than I realized.

"So what are you going to do for the actual Thanksgiving holiday next Thursday?" she asked with lingering notes of regret in her voice.

"I hadn't really thought, " I answered. "Maybe PB&J?"

"Ha ha! I hope not!"

I decided to switch the attention to Christmas rather than give her an entrée into some debate with me on the new love affair she was having with the organic food movement, something I still knew nothing about.

"Cass, it's only another month until the big holidays when I can be there and cook up a storm for you guys and spend oodles of time with you…and help you! So…keep the faith baby!"

Chapter Seventy

"Passarim" (Little Bird)...Antonio Carlos Jobim

"It will be the first Thanksgiving I've ever spent alone," I said to Cass on the phone, as the holiday was coming up. "It's almost funny."

"But isn't it really also depressing?" she asked, adding, "I mean, wouldn't you be better off going out rather than being stuck at home all day?"

"You mean to a restaurant?"

"Or someone's house."

"Well, no one has invited me to it and that doesn't surprise me. People tend to celebrate this holiday with their own families. But the idea of going alone to a restaurant does depress me. I won't be doing that."

"You won't believe this, but we did get invited over to someone's house for it."

"Really! Who? Workshop people?"

"Church people."

"Well, I think it's pretty neat how the Iowa City Episcopal church is helping you guys out. First with the CO support and then the day care offers, and now this."

"Yeah, I'm happy about it. That day care thing has been my saving grace. When you come for Christmas we will actually be able to drop them off there and do something mad, gay and exciting."

"Well, I'll look forward to that! But I'm also dying to see the babies. Hell, they're not such babies anymore. You need to get out that camera of yours and make me some Auntie Sari photos to keep in my office. Have you been taking any pictures of them?"

"Not so's you'd notice. But you're right; I need to get on that. So, back to you---what will you do about this holiday dinner? Cook it for yourself?"

"Well, the meal is the same whether you're making it for two people or twenty, but no, I don't think I'll be doing up a turkey and the trimmings in my minuscule and ill-equipped kitchen. I'll go to the store, though, and see if some idea flies off the shelves at me."

I liked Thanksgiving as a holiday. It was one that every single American of every stripe, ethnicity and religion could embrace equally. There were no gift exchanges involved. At home since my immediate family had the professional-grade kitchen at its disposal, we were the ones who hosted all the relatives in the area. The Spot was always closed on that day, but my mother and Nana availed themselves of its ovens to roast at least two turkeys, and Sol would go fetch them and bring them back to the house, where I would have had the job – which my mother saw as more of a privilege –of setting the table with the good china and silver. After the meal I would also have the "pleasure" of washing and drying all that by hand. Even though they got married during the War, with my grandmother's taste guiding the way, Betty had picked out really beautiful Wedgewood china in a pattern of blue flowers on a white background with gold veins running through the leaves, and a gold rim. Her silver was Grande Baroque. It was all kept in those quilted, zippered protective bags and the felt-lined silver storage box in our living room cabinet. None of those pieces ever saw the inside of a dishwasher.

When I ended up at the supermarket on my way back from work on the Wednesday night before Thanksgiving, the place was bustling and the lines long. I thought about soup—perhaps some turkey soup--but there wasn't any, and the idea of chicken noodle or tomato didn't do it for me. Finally, I ended up in the frozen food section (a mere shadow in 1970 of what it would ultimately become,) and decided it might have to be a pizza for me the next day. Suddenly, however, there it was: a Swanson "TV Dinner" that was made for Thanksgiving. It had sliced turkey with dressing, "whipped potatoes and gravy," peas and carrots in a seasoned sauce, and some permutation of a cranberry-apple cobbler. The price was ninety-nine cents. I put it in my cart, knowing it would be terrible and taste at best like cardboard, or at worst would be completely inedible.

One thing I did relish on the actual day off was being able to sleep in. I had only started sleeping late as a teenager; in fact, sleeping parents on weekend mornings or my mother, especially, taking naps in the afternoon, made me gloomy as a kid. Now I understood it, as I myself was tired from sixteen years of having to wake up early to prepare for school and work. My morning routine usually left little room for error. The Foundation wasn't my first real job, since I'd been working in the bar or that one summer at the Iowa Memorial Union, but it was my first full-time one, and I was never late, nor did I ever slack off. But up to that point I hadn't "brought the job home at night" either. My nights were luxuriously free to do the three things that filled my free time: read, watch television, and listen to the radio.

Television with only four channels left a lot to be desired; one had to take what one got. Nevertheless, I found myself still mightily hooked on it. The trouble with Thanksgiving, however, was that if you were awake early enough, which I was not, the Macy's Thanksgiving Day Parade was about the last interesting thing on for the rest of the day. Football dominated the air waves all that afternoon and into the evening, which, to me, was unacceptable. So I turned to the radio, and was not disappointed to hear on Chicago's classical station, a program of Thanksgiving hymns and songs, many of which we'd sung in school.

I made a sandwich for lunch, and took it with a cup of tea to my window-facing wingback armchair. The weather that day was unforgiving, with snow flurries swirling around in a wind that also picked up the remaining dried leaves and deposited them elsewhere. I was happy to stay indoors and retreat into L. P. Hartley's Victorian world of *The Go-Between*, which I'd been reading, enthralled, each day at the office on my lunch break.

Midway through the afternoon, I decided to strip the daybed, put on newly washed sheets and pillowcases, and snuggle back down to nap. It felt so different to not have to do any of the chores or errands that tended to fill up the weekend. I could drift gloriously off to one of those deep, restful sleeps where you wake up not feeling like you'd been in a coma, but actually renewed.

When I awoke—again—it was almost dinner time. Surprisingly, I didn't feel depressed or sorrowful at all that I was alone for this auspicious occasion. It did feel strange, but then, that was probably due more to the absence of food than the lack of company. Of course the meal was bad, as predicted, but once in a while the smells emanating from the plate seemed almost authentic. Probably in 1970, even a frozen meal was composed of more real food than it is now.

Thus my first Thanksgiving alone passed without a bang, but also without a whimper. It did strike me as patently ridiculous that I faced the prospect of having to get up early the next day and go to work, only to come home and be tossed immediately into a weekend and two more days off. The ironic thing was that it was so not French. The French would *"faire le pont"* for any holiday that fell close to a weekend, and stretch it over the ensuing days.

Cass and Alan were weighing heavily on my mind as I wondered how their holiday went with church friends. Or maybe not even friends, which would be even more awkward. I wondered about their contribution to the meal, about which I would have to debrief Cass in great detail when I next spoke on the phone to her. I wondered if Alan had stepped up and helped her. Feelings of guilt welled up in me, and I vowed to redouble my efforts to bring them wonderful Christmas surprises. I would make a huge shopping list at work tomorrow and set out next week to try to fulfill it. There was still a small fortune in that Cass bank account her father had set up, and this was just the thing I needed to spend some of it on. Trains didn't restrict one's luggage allotment in those days, and I began to plot how much I could pack in two suitcases and some shopping bags.

The idea also came to me to bake for them. My baking equipment was nil but that wouldn't cost much to buy, and the ingredients for cookies would be easy. I had an empty freezer and could stock many goodies between now and the third week of December. That would also free up more time once in Iowa City for us to gallivant around and still have jolly holiday treats. Splendid idea if I did say so myself!

The other thing I decided to do besides bake over the weekend, was to forego my previous non-working-at-home status, and bring home more of my lesson plans and outlines for films, and really tackle them. If I did them over the weekend, I'd have a nice big stockpile to type up on Monday. I felt I was making real progress with this film-lesson idea and the boxes. Once we had a real clientele built up, which, albeit, was still going rather slowly, I had a feeling my ideas would take off. I made a mental note to go over to our marketing department and brainstorm with some of them about how to reach more schools.

However, when I got to the Foundation Friday morning, I was stunned to be greeted at my office door by Jean-Paul d'Arivèque!

"*Bonjour, Monsieur,* " I said, worried that I'd made some other faux-pas that had to be discussed, but not having a clue what that might actually be.

He motioned me to precede him into my office and he sat down on one of the theater seats. I just stood there until he said "Please." And I sat down next to him.

"I am afraid I owe you an apology, *Mademoiselle* Shrier, " he said, motioning to me to not talk, as he continued, "I understand that you wanted to be absent for the Thanksgiving weekend, but were told that the office was not closing."

"Well, yes, but…it's okay."

"No, you would have been most welcomed to miss a day. I wish you had come to me."

"*Monsieur,* I've been in school for the last umpteen years, and I made a stupid assumption, based on that, that everyone got off work on the Friday after Thanksgiving. I should have realized that was silly since my own parents' business and all the retail were always open. But I guess I just had a mind-set that offices and schools were closed."

"Yes, I understand, but of course, you could have taken time off. We do not adhere to the strict absentee policies of perhaps other businesses or offices. We are more of a family concern here at *La Fondation,* and I would have been more than willing to grant you an extra day. We are very happy with your work here, *Mademoiselle.*"

"Thank you, *Monsieur!*" I was so relieved, I was afraid I was completely red in the face.

"And in that vein, I have also come down here to advise you of the meeting to which I referred some time back, which will take place next week at Marshall Field's. I would like you to accompany me to it, as we will be discussing some films they would like to have playing in the store's auditorium during their French Market Days promotion. Will you avail yourself of the time to come with me?"

"Certainly. What should I prepare?"

"Oh, I believe this to be more of a fact-finding meeting, but perhaps a current list of films you think might be suitable to show in conjunction with the trade fair. It is to be a sort of holiday market, from what I understand, but as I say, I am not too certain of all the facts myself. We shall find out together."

"You know, we do have a documentary-type film about the region of Alsace-Lorraine and the real Christmas markets Strasbourg has. That might be an idea for them to show."

"Yes, of course, be sure to mention that one. "

"And also what about films set in or about Paris or France, but that aren't French?"

"I will leave it to your judgement what to suggest. I believe we can procure the rights to showing any film. I shall have the legal department look into it."

Since he was sitting there in my office, not angry with me, I found myself emboldened to take out my drafts of lesson plans written in long-hand on legal pads, and show them to him. I told him that I had been drawing them up all weekend, and would have these samples ready to go as soon as they were typed.

"So I see you worked this weekend rather than traveling back to your family?" He smiled at me with a look of regret on his face nonetheless.

"Oh! No! I wasn't going home, in any event."

Chapter Seventy-One

"I Shall Be Released"...The Band (Bob Dylan)

Around the first of December, I was thrilled to find a huge envelope in my mailbox from Nonnie! It was an invitation to her wedding, and I had never received...or even seen...such an elaborate one. It was a large ecru card wrapped and tied with a golden bow, which, when undone, opened like French "window panes" behind which were the details: her parents requested the honour of my presence at the marriage of their daughter Antonia Evangeline to Dr. Patrick Alcott O'Hara, son of...blah blah blah...on Thursday, December 23rd at the Cathedral of Saint Matthew the Apostle in Washington , D.C. at four-thirty in the afternoon. I gasped. Nonnie was getting married in a cathedral on the day before Christmas Eve?! How could they swing that? It would be epic!

And then a realization hit me. Of course I couldn't go.

I could not and would not back out on Cass again. Going to Nonnie's wedding would be out of the question. She'd understand. I wouldn't even tell Cass I'd received this invitation, or she would do something noble like insist that I go, while in reality doing so would wreck our plans to be reunited for the first time since June. I would write Nonnie a sincere letter of regret, explain it all to her, and tell her how sorry I would be for missing this momentous milestone in her life. Then, I would use all my shopping prowess to find her a "champagne" wedding gift on a "beer" budget and send it to her.

But as luck would have it, on the heels of the arrival of the invitation, another, actual letter came from Nonnie! Her news was that I would be seeing her right after the new year! They were driving across country for a honeymoon in San Francisco and the start of the next phase of their lives in that much venerated city. Patrick was to begin an interim special project before his residency in orthopedic surgery, hopefully at the same place--the University of California San Francisco hospitals. They would come through Chicago, stay two nights at the Drake Hotel---what could be more perfect--- and visit me! It was going to be GREAT STUFF.

Having not paid rent for five months, I took stock of my finances as the holidays approached and, having been frugal—up to a point—I found I had about $1,400 saved up from my salary, plus the money my parents had provided in the name of Nana for graduation. I earned $400 a month net, and tried, not always successfully, to live on only half of that in order to save for the day when I would be moving into a place I had to pay for. I thought I was safe for another six months in the Hyde property, so I hoped to have more than enough to face the shocking (to me) rents that were Chicago apartments in 1971.

Naturally I could spend Mr. Hyde's money on his grandchildren and on Cass, but I was also determined to bring them Christmas presents that I bought with my own money, too, and I set aside fifty dollars in cash for that purpose. I already knew I would be bringing Alan a box of the famous Chicago treat, Frango Mints, and since I was going to be at the meeting at Marshall Field's anyway, I decided that would be the perfect time to stay after and shop. They would be open late for the season, and it would be a piece of cake to get a cab home near the front entrance right under the clock on State Street.

On the afternoon of the slated Marshall Field's meeting, I gathered up my own draft catalogue of films, and went to meet JPA in our lobby. I admit I was a bit surprised to see that it would be just the two of us attending, and not MFP or any of the legal team. He motioned me to go ahead of him to the elevator with "*Je vous en prie,*" and we went down to the street where Jean-Luc was waiting with the limo. Monsieur seemed more subdued than normal, and he winced as he brought his brace leg into the car. It occurred to me to wonder if he weren't having another bout of the pain that had landed him in the hospital before; but I didn't say anything.

Nor did we talk in the car. I had no idea what to expect from this meeting, and I couldn't even think of any questions to ask. I wondered if I had dressed appropriately enough. I still didn't own a real business suit, but I tried to look professional in my chevron-striped light blue tweed skirt and jacket. I wore it with a white blouse, white tights, and my same old boots. I wore my only winter coat, the camel one, and my faithfully beautiful fur hood, and carried my little red Bagagerie purse. It was about the best I could do other than my regular uniform -- Cass' kilt.

When we arrived, Jean-Luc helped Monsieur out of the car and we headed in, where, all senses engulfed at once with the opulence of Christmas right in my face, I gulped to the point of almost choking.

If I had thought Brandeis at Christmastime was dazzling, or Galleries Lafayette was splendidly elegant, I had never seen anything so breathtakingly beautiful as Marshall Field's that year. The sheer dimensions of the holiday decorations were over the top. The main floor was draped and festooned in huge red clusters of enormous glass balls on thick red velvet ropes, all converging in a canopy-like structure above the gigantic, elegantly decorated and lit, three-story tall Christmas tree in the center of the store. Like Galleries Lafayette, the interior floors were open balconies onto the center space, but unlike the Paris store, which was round inside, this was rectangular. I used to marvel at the view from the various departments in Galleries Lafayette, but the one of the main floor from any one of those Marshall Field's balconies was even more striking.

"It is beautiful, is it not?" Monsieur said, rather amused at my initial reaction. "Do you like the ceiling? It, as well as the chandeliers, was designed by Louis Comfort Tiffany, whose work you know, of course?"

"I do, " I laughed. *Was he having me on or did he really think me an ignorant country bumkin, even with an art history minor?*

"It is, in case you were wondering, the largest Tiffany dome in the world of its kind. It contains one and a half million pieces of Favrile glass hand-blown in Tiffany's own workshop."

"Wow, " I murmured, as usual too gob smacked to be articulate.

He seemed to know just where he was going in the throng of holiday shoppers, so we made our way to a side elevator and took it to a suite of executive offices on the fourteenth floor. We were met by a Mr. Walter Pierce who was one of the operation's executives, and the man in charge of the French trade fair. We were ushered into a conference room with a stunning view of the Chicago Loop all the way to the lake. There were several people already there, including a cultural attaché I recognized from the Consulate. Marshall Field's was pulling out the big guns.

Once we all were seated, Mr. Pierce introduced everyone, including me (!), and announced that the great French trade fair idea was for NEXT Christmas, not this one. Goodness, that made more sense, as I couldn't fathom how it could have possibly been ready in three weeks, and fit into the locale we had just walked through, which was already packed.

"We will have it in a separate part of the building, " he announced, as if reading my mind, and, gesturing to a store map on an easel that was set up, he pinpointed the seventh floor, "near the Frango viewing kitchen."

Everyone nodded and expressed approval. I had never heard of the Frango viewing kitchen, but made a mental note to view it as soon as I could.

The meeting went on with Mr. Pierce soliciting from various people ideas for the products and trades that would likely be represented: all of France's world-famous luxury exports, plus regional specialties… in fashion, perfumes, food and drink, pottery, porcelain and leather. Five wine regions would be featured even though there were many more than that.

I had a film in mind to suggest, so I decided to ask a question about the content of the exhibits and what was going to be for sale.

"Excuse me sir, do you intend to import the actual crafts sold in the *Marchés de Noël*, say from Alsace?" I asked.

"I would hope to do just that, " Mr. Pierce answered. "Which do you like best, Miss Shrier?"

"Oh, I have only seen the ones in Strasbourg," I answered, "about three years ago. But as film librarian for the FCF, I have curated some films for you that show Strasbourg's, plus some smaller regional markets. The Strasbourg Christkindl market had things like mulled wine, fois-gras, chocolate of course, ginger bread, these huge red, hard-candied apples on long sticks, kuglehopfs—that sort of thing. And, oh my gosh, the decorations and handmade toys!"

"I can imagine it!" he said, and the cultural attaché nodded. JPA sat there smiling at me, seeming to be intrigued by my, shall we say, exuberance.

Buoyed by their reaction, I continued, "Not only that, but several of the markets also have choir concerts outdoors and, for instance, the one in the town of Obernai has a choir called Saint Odile. Maybe you could even bring them over… or something like that?"

"That is a splendid idea!" Pierce said, and the others agreed, including my boss who beamed at me.

The Consulate and the Foundation, it was determined, could work together on public relations for this endeavor, and, as usual, Monsieur d'Arivèque offered to house any visiting dignitaries who would attend. He suggested that they could invite mayors of little villages-- to see Chicago and promote their towns at the same time. Various wine merchants and *négociants* who worked with the store would be involved, and the Cultural Attaché would take the responsibility to gather promotional materials from the major French "*marques*" or brands, manufacturing houses, factories and small craft workshops all around the country.

When we adjourned, it was late afternoon. I turned to my boss and told him that instead of riding back to the office with him, I would be staying after in the store to Christmas shop.

"So, as Jews, does your family also celebrate Christmas?"

"We celebrate Chanukah, or should I say, they do. I'm shopping for the children of my very best friend. She has twins! They are eighteen months old. It's a really long story, *Monsieur*, but I'm their sort of 'Auntie Sari Santa Claus' and I'm taking things to them at Christmastime---when the office is closed, of course. They live in Iowa City, where I went to college. Their mom was my first college roommate. "

I finally came up for air and looked at him. He was sort of mesmerized by my saga.

"May I…would I be able to…ah… accompany you on your shopping?" he asked, **surprising the hell out of me.** "Do you mind?"

"Well, sure…of course you can. You don't think you'll be too bored?!"

"*Mais non!* I am very curious to see what *La Tantine Père Noël* would buy for these children. After the shopping, I should be pleased to invite you to dinner in the Walnut Room here in the store. Would you like that?"

"Yes…I…uh…well, sure, but… but that's not necessary. You certainly don't have to."

"But I would like it. Very much. You were wonderful in that meeting. You seemed to be simply brimming with good ideas. Your enthusiasm is appreciated also. A dinner would be the least I could do."

"Well, thank you very much. I'm happy to accept!"

I didn't know what the Walnut Room was, but Brandeis had a cafeteria, too, where we would go as kids after shopping, often at Christmas time, with Nana -- sometimes even with the parents. I figured it was the same idea…a dining room in a department store was not uncommon.

"I shall telephone Jean-Luc in the car, and have him fetch us at nine this evening. Will that give you enough time?"

"Oh, no doubt. That's when the store closes, right? But… you said call him in the car? Is there a phone in the car?"

"Yes, Sarah. I decided to have one installed in the larger limousine. It is up in the front, a Motorola Car Telephone, with a unit that is the receiver, and a part that looks more or less like a regular phone. It operates on Illinois Bell Telephone. I shall ring him from a telephone in one of these offices. Wait right here."

It continued to amuse me that French people are taught British English. They were always using locutions totally uncommon in America, like "ring" someone for "call." I noticed it most acutely when I was a student in Paris, and here it was again.

I watched as he made his way rather slowly to the inner offices, then I turned away to the wall of panoramic windows, and marveled at the view, while my mind wandered to worrying about whether shopping for toys may be strenuous for JPA, given little chance for him to sit down and rest if he needed to. "We'll just have to see how it plays out, " I thought to myself.

He came back and said, "Shall we?" and led me to the elevator where there was a store directory and we could see that toys were on Four. Stepping out onto the sales floor, I paused to look out over the array of decorations and animated displays in all their abundance-- shelves and rows of toys of every variety imaginable. Once again, comparisons to Brandeis were meaningless; Marshall Field's dwarfed what we had in Omaha. I turned to JPA who was as transfixed as I, it seemed, and said that since these kids were only 18 months old, I would head off toward the toddler section and also find the plush collection.

Cass was always talking about getting real farm animals---goats and lambs-- and although I thought this was crazy, it had given me the impetus to look for a stuffed lamb. She also mentioned that the kids loved a stray cat that had appeared on their porch one day and stayed. Paul and Laura called it "Booch" and that's the name that stuck. So I thought I could find a plush kitty, a lamb and some soft boyish toys, like a small truck or tractor for Paul. Laura was still too young for a really good doll, but I decided if I could find Raggedy Ann and Raggedy Andy, that would be a good first foray into dolls.

"Maybe I can score a book about those two dolls, too, " I told Monsieur. "I used to have one, so I know they exist."

"I am not familiar with these Raggedy *personages*, " he said.

"Oh, it's terrific: the books came first. The author had a daughter named Marcella and she's a character in the book, too. Raggedy Ann was her doll. And when the grownups weren't looking, the doll came to life...in the story. The brother doll was introduced some time later. Then someone got the brilliant idea to manufacture soft toys to go with the books. You'll see when and if I can find them up here. They are iconic in the States."

So we marched up and down, fingering toys and testing them for weight, packability and cuteness. I found the stuffed lamb I wanted...it was the perfect size for a toddler now and maybe even a sleep companion later.

" How do you like this lamb? "I asked holding it out to him.

"It is truly lovely, " he answered with a sort of amazement and reverence in his voice.

I also found a crocheted clown doll with the outfit in harlequin pattern knit right in, and a little bell atop his pointy hat. That would be cute for both of them. I easily located a stuffed kitten. I didn't know what color "Booch" was, but thought a plush calico cat toy covered a multitude of sins.

Then I made my way to the boys' area with JPA following behind. I couldn't find any small tractors or farm implements except the John Deere ones that were too advanced for a baby, but I did see a soft plastic train with big red wheels and a rubbery engineer sitting in the cab. I snatched that up!

Then I saw another toy I had to have.

"They don't live on a working farm, " I explained to JPA , "but since my friend is always talking about raising animals, the perfect toy is this one." I held up a round "See and Say: The Farmer Says" edition where the farmer arrow points to a picture of the animal, and the child hears what the animal sounds like.

"*Alors*, it is a game?" he wondered.

"You can do a lot with this toy, " I explained. "You can, of course, teach them the names of the animals and what sounds they make, but later on, you can count the animals, sing 'Old McDonald Had a Farm' and play little quiz games with it. "

"But...how do you know all these things?" he asked me, admiringly.

" Oh, this toy has been around for a few years now. I saw it a long time ago, so I have to hope they don't already have one." *But I doubted it since Cass and Alan rarely bought them anything new.*

I had thus amassed quite an assortment by the time I found Raggedy Ann and Andy, so I piled them on, and headed for the cashier desk. Marshall Field's was by no means a discounted store, so the tab was going to be pretty hefty, I knew. The lamb alone was a Steiff and quite pricey. I decided to buy it anyway, since I could spend the Hyde money, but it occurred to me that Monsieur, who knew full well what salary I made per month, would think this overly extravagant.

"I think you may be curious, " I said to him, "as to how I can afford all this?"

"Not at all, " he answered.

"Well, at dinner, I'll explain it anyway."

The clerk wanted to know if I intended to take the lot to gift wrap, and I declined, which I felt needed explanation.

"I'm not going to have any of it Christmas-wrapped, " I told JPA, as the young woman tucked them all into a big Christmas shopping bag in the store's iconic dark green color, decorated with a forest of

416

white fir trees and Victorian-looking people walking among them. "I like it when kids wake up and find toys left under the tree as if Santa had been there."

"I am really marveling over how you think of all this, " he said as we made our way to catch the escalator back up to the Walnut Room, "---what the toys are for, and how they work, and the way they are to be received. What a wonderful mother you shall make one day."

"Um, yeah...no. I'm not intending to have any children."

"I do not believe you!" he said, flabbergasted.

"No, it's true. I had a psych prof at Iowa who gave a lecture one time on parenting. He said that good parents are people who, they themselves, were parented well. And then he added that very few people were...parented well, that is. I know I was not one of them. I won't be inflicting that on more children. It's like spreading a disease when you could have avoided it."

Monsieur had that furrowed brow look on his face, but didn't have a response to my "mini rant." I couldn't tell if it was because it angered him, saddened him or shocked him. Or perhaps he thought what I said was merely bullshit, and he was too polite to answer back to me. It occurred to me that he might be upset because perhaps he wanted to be a father and maybe even loved children; and I briefly considered the possibility that being homosexual made him sad because it precluded any of that. There was, for sure, no such thing as gay adoption, I surmised, as I mulled it all over.

The Walnut room was under yet another atrium and there was yes, another magnificent forty-five-foot Christmas tree elevated onto a platform right in the middle of the room. We sat at a table not far from the tree, and it was hard for me not to stare at its enchanting decorations and the humongous array of fake presents laden under it.

"Gosh, " I purred, "I've never seen so many wonderful Christmas displays. I know I sound like a broken record. Maybe it's being Jewish that has me so enamored of something I couldn't ever have."

"Did you never have a tree?"

"Never. Our bar did---a little countertop one." I hastened to explain, "My parents own a little bar and grill."

"Your parents own a bar?"

"Yes. It was started by my grandparents, and my grandmother cooked there for a long time. It's a bar and -- little restaurant-- combined. It's in a small Iowa town. Have you been to Iowa?"

"I have not, no."

"Anyway, " I continued on, "about the tree-- I always wanted to be the one to trim it, but our decorations were stupidly mundane. Just blue and silver balls. I did manage to beg them for some tinsel, though, " I laughed. Suddenly I was self-conscious; this story must have been boring him to death.

But far from changing the subject, he encouraged me, "Tell me more."

"Well, we had a few metallic snowflakes we would hang from the rafters, so that when the furnace kicked in and the blower started, they would turn and sparkle in different colors. I really liked them. But as to real tree decorating, we had these nice neighbors on the street who let us help decorate their huge tree. If you ask me, every Jewish kid secretly wanted to decorate a Christmas tree."

" But, I believe some of the Jewish people I know in Chicago and New York do have them!"

"You don't say! I guess the times, they really are a-changin'.'"

He didn't get the Bob Dylan reference, and directed my attention to the menu.

The Walnut room had specialties, but since I'd never been there, I was surprised to see that they were some of the same things we served at The Spot. One was a pot pie, but not just any pot pie: Mrs. Hering's 1890 original chicken pot pie, the menu stated, based on her own recipe.

"Wow, it has leeks in it. I've only ever had them in France. I think I might have to try that."

The other Walnut Room traditions were things like oven-baked meatloaf, fish and chips, which was touted as "Alaskan Cod almond crusted and Chips," which were their seasoned fries. It came with lemon caper sauce, and house made coleslaw.

"It all sounds yummy, " I said, noting that those were just the specials. "I still think I must try that pot pie."

"I shall do the same, " he said.

417

I was relieved at his choice, and hoped I didn't show it. I found myself worried that eating out was problematic for him with an arm that could not be easily used to cut food. I was certainly in no position to offer to do anything for him, and the truth was, I couldn't recall ever having seen him struggle at his own home when I'd been there for dinners; so I imagined whatever he had in the way of meat must have always come to him pre-cut. But I wasn't at all sure about that-- all I knew was that I'd never seen him cut anything. His left hand actually was functional, but lifting the arm up to use it did not seem to be in the cards. It became obvious to me again that having no use of an arm was certainly worse than wearing a brace on one leg, that was for sure. Anyway, the pot pie would be edible with one hand.

"So, " he said, looking straight at me, "do tell me about these children for whom you are being such a *Père Noël*."

"I really need to warn you, like I said, it's a long story."

"Please," he gestured as if to say, 'go ahead.'

So I began at the beginning of Cass and me as college roommates, her mentoring of me, her art---I kept coming back to her art. I was sure he would know her family, and he did, showing some no small surprise that I was talking about Julia and John-Wilfred Hyde's daughter.

"*Mon Dieu*! " he said in that French way, "Her grandmother was a friend of my mother since we came to Chicago twenty years ago!"

"That makes sense since your mother was active with the symphony and the arts in general. I've met Cass' grandmother, and I like her. 'Course, I like her parents, also. Sort of. Well... especially her dad."

It suddenly struck me that I was sitting there, eating dinner and talking to my boss as if we'd been old friends. He was so easy to talk with that I almost forgot who he was! I amused him with the tale of my taking Cass home for Thanksgiving and meeting my family, and how she'd never stayed in a "normal" house or had chores to do growing up, or a part time job, like I did. I covered our various other antics, like fencing in the hallways of the dorm, and protesting the war. And I regaled him with my trips to Chicago and New York, staying in the Hyde penthouse, the Plaza Hotel, and Springfield. He alternated listening with great concentration and laughing at my account of all that.

Trying also to eat my dinner before it became cold, I continued on about how Cass had met my English instructor and had begun to date him, which precipitated her removal from school by a furious mom.

Which brought me to the most important part of the story yet, of how Cass began coming to Paris was I was studying there, and all the fun we had.

"It was really a miracle, our reuniting in Europe, " I said, wistfully. I didn't go into much detail of my time at the Sorbonne, except to remind him that it was during this year in Paris that I met his friends Renaud and Blandine de Seignard and their son, Clément. I also related the part about the Amsterdam shock of finding out Cass was pregnant, and her family's ensuing ultimatum about the home for unwed mothers, which had led Alan Jones to go to Chicago to, essentially, " liberate her".

Finally, I came to the part about the kids-- how I was present right after the birth of the twins, and what Cass' life was like now.

"After I was back from Paris, for my senior year, I tried to help Cass out as much as possible, " I told him. "She really can't cook, and that whole year I tried to make them as many meals as I could. I think Alan appreciated that, and Cass did, too, although I think she would have been more embarrassed than grateful, if she hadn't been so exhausted all the time."

I didn't mince words about how hard it was to have twins and how, with my car situation in Iowa City, I would drive her to the laundromat, to the babies' doctor's appointments, and shopping, among other places around town.

"She needed SO many supplies all the time; it's just crazy how much stuff two babies at the same time go through. You have to plan on double everything, really. "

I explained how her need for so many necessities, and my inability to provide her with any kind of real monetary help, played a part in my contacting her father, and his flying into Iowa City in his private plane. I spilled the beans to my boss about how the bank account came to be, as well as Mr. Hyde's offer to put me up somewhere without rent. I had previously made references to my apartment situation, but he understood that much better now.

"So John-Wilfred Hyde did not think I would pay you an adequate salary, is that it?"

"Oh, no no no. **No**." *Oh shit, Sari. Open mouth, insert foot.* "I think he was under the impression that any entry-level salary would still leave me shocked at Chicago housing rates. Anyway, the construction has been delayed quite a bit, and I'll bet I'm pretty securely ensconced there for at least another six months…maybe even more than that. "

To get off the sticky subject of my living conditions, I extolled the virtues of Cass' art to Monsieur.

"I can't overstate enough how wonderful her talent is. If she never gets to go back to art in a serious way, it will be a true tragedy."

"Yes, it seems as though she needs some help…some support from her husband?"

I really didn't want to cast Alan in a bad light, but his recalcitrance at Cass self-actualizing with art, and his insistence not to accept any financial help from her family-- should she ever reconcile with them--was not a pretty picture.

"I hate it that he more or less insists they live in poverty, " I said, taking the last bites of my dinner. "It—the poverty-- puts Cass in a terrible position, which I try to abate," I added, "albeit rather sneakily."

I reached for my water glass, and all at once, Jean-Paul d'Arivèque put his hand gently on mine and clasped it from across the table.

"Your story is quite astonishing, " he said gravely. "I did not expect such a portrayal when we sat down at this table tonight. She is very lucky to have you as a friend. Does she know it?"

"Oh, Lordy, I'm the lucky one." *And that was another story!*

The restaurant was pretty much cleared out as we got up, and I gathered my film catalogue, my purse and the big shopping bag of toys. More Christmas shopping was in my future, but I felt I'd made some real progress that afternoon. The store would be closing soon, and the chauffeur was picking Monsieur up. I thanked him profusely for dinner, and announced that I had planned all along to be taking a cab from State Street; but d'Arivèque wouldn't hear of that and insisted I accompany him to the other entrance. He had placed his coat over his good arm, preferring to not put it on himself, but I wore mine so I wouldn't have to carry even one more thing. When we got to street level, Jean-Luc was waiting and helped JPA on with his coat.

We rode in some silence except for Monsieur chiding me still about the empty apartment house situation, and how, when one pulls up to my place, it is so dark.

"Remember, there's Jake, " I said trying to sound reassuring.

"*Au moins,* " he replied without much conviction. "Jean-Luc will carry your purchases in for you."

I got out of the car first, and then, to my surprise, the chauffeur helped him out onto the sidewalk, too.

"You know, " I said, suddenly remembering my manners, " I would like to invite you in and offer you a drink. But as the daughter of a bar owner, I am even more ashamed to tell you that not only do I have no home bar set up-- and literally nothing to serve you-- I have nothing to serve it in! Isn't that pathetic?"

I knew in all honesty that he would never be able to climb my stairs in a million years unless the faithful Luc practically carried him up there. I felt sure he wouldn't want to do that in front of me, but even if he did, coming back down would also be a nightmare. So my little speech---all true, of course, saved him having to decline any invitation.

Still, he said to me, "*De toute façon,* I would not be able to go up with you…to the inside. *Vous comprenez?*"

I nodded, and thanked him again, and very sincerely, for the lovely dinner, and his infinite patience listening to me the whole time.

"I very much enjoyed watching you choosing all those wonderful presents!"

"It was fun to have someone to shop with, " I said, smiling at him.

It was the truth.

We stood there for a minute while Jean-Luc gathered my bag, and then JPA offered me *la bise*. I was a little startled but air-kissed him back. He watched me as I waved over my shoulder, unlocked the first fence gate, and followed Jean-Luc up those stairs to my front outer door. Jake had appeared out of nowhere, and shined his car lights on the path for us. I went inside. Jean-Luc could get back out and the

419

gate would lock behind him, or Jake would lock it. I looked out from the window as he once again helped his boss into the back of the car, got behind the wheel, and drove off.

Chapter Seventy-Two

"Holly Jolly Christmas"...Burl Ives(Johnny Marks)

So taken up with Christmas plans was I that first December in Chicago, that I hadn't even thought about Chanukah at all. So you can imagine my surprise when I stopped into Woolworth's on North Michigan to have lunch at the counter, which was easily becoming my routine, and saw a display of little metal menorahs! Woolworth's! I had to laugh as it hit me that I now lived in a city where being Jewish was far from the minority it was where I came from. The price was right: $1.99! They were long rather than candelabra shaped, and had a tiny lion on the end holding up the *shamas* "candle well." All the wells were so small, they would take birthday candles instead of the normal ones. So needless to say, I bought one to put in my front window. It would be dwarfed, and no one would even be able to see it, but I felt it was something. I would only be able to light it the first night, Tuesday the twenty-second, because I was leaving the next day. But I would be back in time to light all the candles on the eighth night.

Woolworth's also had another item I bought. I'd been doing more shopping for the kids, especially restocking their clothing sizes, but I longed to buy them some kind of little riding toy to share. However, in Chicago's department stores, I only could find heavy wooden ones or ones like miniature motorcycles and cars made of metal; I wanted something small and light. And then... there it was---right on the shelf in the dime store! A plastic bulbous green inchworm with bright yellow "feelers," googly eyes and a happy smile. It was about two feet long, had a yellow molded saddle, and sat up on wheels mere inches from the ground. I figured I could carry it with me if I could get someone to help me on board the train with all my stuff.

I also shopped for Cass and Alan with my own funds. I found Cass a beautiful red chenille bathrobe with a self-tie and high puffy shoulder pads that made it look Victorian. I figured not only would she need this, she'd love it. For Alan, the de rigueur Frango Mints were perfect; and I also got them both Joni Mitchell's brilliant album *Ladies of the Canyon*. It had come out in April of that year, so I had to hope they hadn't gone out and splurged on it for themselves like I had!

So the baking was done, and the presents organized. I had submitted my lesson ideas to Marie-France for her approval, and she would take it from there if she thought Monsieur would want to see them. Everything was ready for my departure, and the excitement of seeing Cass and the babies was mounting.

On Monday of Christmas week, which was December twenty-first, I arrived at the office to find a long envelope on my desk. I figured it was my paycheck, and thought that was nice that we were getting them a little early, probably because of the holidays. Opening it, I first read a hand-written note from Jean-Paul d'Arivèque inviting me for a *"petite soirée pour la Saint Sylvestre"* on New Year's Eve at his home, beginning at 4:00 p.m. and including light supper. I presumed people would be expected to stay until midnight to see in the New Year. That would be nice. I was planning being in Iowa City for at most a week anyway, so the dates would work.

I didn't consider myself a normal guest at Cass's and neither did they, but trying to be more considerate of Alan and their privacy, I planned it so as not to wear out my welcome either. Plus I'd be sleeping on the couch in the living room, and that could get old for all of us, let's face it.

But when I looked further into the envelope and took out the other item in there, I gave out a squeal! It was my paycheck, all right, but the amount! The check was for an entire month's salary ON TOP OF my regular salary, with the memo line marked "Christmas Bonus." A Christmas bonus the likes of which I'd never even dreamed of!

I called Cass this time, too excited to wait for her call.

"Can you imagine?!" I fairly screamed into the phone, "Do businesses DO that?"

"Yes, I've heard of it," she said laughing. "I hope my father does something similar for his employees."

"My God, Cass, it's a windfall!"

"So do I see a new winter coat in your future? Maybe a raincoat, too?" she chided me.

"Yeah, I hear ya!"

"And wait until you see **my** big surprise for you," she said mischievously.

"Can you give me a hint without ruining it?"

"I can tell you! I made papier-mâché ornaments with my own silk-screened designs for the paper and actually sold some at a Christmas street bazaar in Mount Vernon! I have many left over for our own tree. We can decorate it together if you want. Alan has even got lights for it!"

"Far out! I can't wait! That will be dreamy to sleep in the same room as the tree."

"Oh, lucky you, " she chided.

"And Cass, I had another idea. For Christmas Eve, I say I make chili, and we can open presents that night---and then when the kids are down for the count, we can set theirs under the tree to find the next morning. And then, let's not make a big dinner on Christmas day."

"Really?" She sounded intrigued.

"Yeah, let's just do Chinese like every other Jewish family in the world. What do you say? There are a lot of vegetarian offerings in that cuisine."

"Sounds great," she said, "although I'm a little surprised that you don't want to cook up some extravaganza. "

"I know, but with the time we save not slaving over a stove, we can play with the kiddos and go places."

"Wonderful, Sari, truly. I love it! And don't worry, we can have meat in the chili. I will supply it because I have to tell you, I do something ingenious with ground meat these days."

"Oh? What's that?" *I didn't suppose she was going to tell me she actually **ate** it.*

"I have the butcher grind up heart, lungs and kidney or other organs into the round or chuck, and I have him make me several one-pound packages of it to use in all meals. I make it over brown rice, in stuffed peppers, and all sorts of ways. See how healthy that is for the kids? And at half the price!"

"I can dig it, " I said enthusiastically, if surprised.

I told her I'd be getting into Iowa City, barring any unforeseen snow or conditions that would slow things down on the railway, at around 6:30 p.m. Wednesday night, and rang off.

I had Nana's recipe for chili and would take the requisite ingredients and spices with me on the train. Nana's called for both paprika and chili powder, each of which I could easily take. But she also used kidney beans that she soaked overnight, a method I rejected in favor of canned. And I could also buy stewed tomatoes in a can and save even having to do that step. This was going to be supremely easy.

What wasn't going to be so easy was getting to my workplace with all the luggage, grocery items, and gifts, and then to Union Station. The office was closing at noon on Wednesday, and my train was at two. I could take a cab in the morning, but I decided to throw myself on the mercy of Annie-Laure, and see if Luc could take me from the office to the station.

"It's just that I'll have all this stuff---you won't believe it, " I explained to her as I made my case for a ride, hoping, shamelessly to garner a little pity.

"I can go with you, " she said, "and help!"

"Oh, heavens, I'll owe you big time. "

I absolutely looked like a refugee getting out of the cab on North Michigan Avenue with my purse, a large plaid suitcase, a big green shopping bag, two smaller plastic bags, and the jolly inch worm riding toy. The driver helped me inside, and the lobby concierge looked at me and smiled, saying, "You need a Sherpa!"

"I do, " I confessed, laughing, "I really do."

So he carried the lot into the elevator for me and dropped everything in our office. I realized I should be tipping him, and pulled my purse around to the front to get into it, but he waved me off, and left in the same elevator we came up in.

"*Mon Dieu!*" blurted out our receptionist Bernadette, "Are you going to France?"

"Iowa."

Annie-Laure called me on my house phone to say that she and Luc would in fact be able to drive me and my stuff to the station, that the car would be free since Monsieur would be working until later, and at any rate, "none of it will be a problem."

"I can't thank you enough, " I crooned. "It's all who you know in life, eh?"

In the car on the way to the train, Annie-Laure seemed agitated and giggly. Finally she said, "Jean-Luc and I have a little secret. Do you promise not to tell if I reveal it to you?"

"I promise. Shoot."

And she showed me she was wearing an engagement ring.

"Oh, I'm so happy for you both! This ring---it's gorgeous!" I cried, taking her hand, and it was. It had a series of Ascher-cut diamonds in an antique setting of oxidized silver on a platinum shank. There was intricate hand-made *repoussé* metal work around the stones, and I could tell this ring was old, but had kept its beauty flawlessly.

"It was Jean-Luc's great-grandmother's ring. I am so proud to wear it."

"Well, I'm delighted for you two!! When will you announce it? At the Saint Sylvestre party maybe? " I said winking.

" The what? No, we shall still be in Aspen for the New Year."

"Aspen, eh? Pretty fancy!"

"The trip is an engagement gift from Monsieur."

"Ah ha! That is incredible!"

"Oh, and there's an even bigger surprise, but we will have to wait and tell you with the others--- after the first of the year."

"Wow, " I said, "you guys are pretty mysterious." And I made it a point to look right at her and not avert my eyes to her belly.

They both helped me get on board, and waved me out of the station. I made a mental note to find them something stellar for their wedding when I was out shopping for Nonnie and her Patrick.

I settled in for the ride with *The Go-Between's* last chapters and my transistor radio's cassette player with earpiece. The trip was uneventful, and the time passed quickly. I read or just closed my eyes, lost deep inside *New York Tendaberry* with *Sergeant Pepper's Lonely Hearts Club Band* in the queue. At one point about two hours out, I went and got a Coke from the bar car, but didn't bother with food since when I got in, either Cass would have cooked or I'd make a pizza run to Pagliai's. As we pulled into Iowa City, I saw Alan leaning against a pole on the lighted platform. Cass was, however, not with him.

"Alan! "I called out waving, and beckoning towards the train coach so he could help me. I handed him things down from the steps and then got off. We hugged, and he laughed at my "haul."

"I'm amazed you got here with all that!" he said, taking my luggage.

"I got by with a little help from my friends…obviously."

"So how are you Miss Shrier?" he asked kidding around and addressing me as though I were still in his class.

"Great, " I answered. "You?"

"Everything's copacetic here. Your car's still running, as you can see over there — look. I've brought the chariot for you."

"Good ol' car, " I mused.

"More old than good, " he answered.

"And how is everything with your job? Chapbook done?"

"Almost! I'm thinking it isn't going to be much longer. Maybe a real teaching position is in my future sooner rather than later."

"Oh, is it? Good! " That might have come off sounding like I didn't believe him, but I did. I wanted to. Cass hadn't complained to me or anything, but she never did sound all-together happy.

"I heard also that Cass sold some cool ornaments at a craft fair or something?"

"Yep. Been busy."

"No shit. I don't know how she does it, but I'm very glad to hear there's art in her life again. Having that church nursery a couple of times a week really must make a difference."

"Hmmm."

Iowa City was having a white Christmas, evidently, because the snow ruts in Alan's gravel driveway looked fresh, and it was cold enough out for the snow cover to stay around. The property didn't seem as run-down in the snow; it took on that Currier and Ives patina. We circled up in front of the steps, and Cass immediately appeared on the porch with a too-scantily-clad toddler on each hand.

423

"Here she is!!! Auntie Sari!!!" she called out.

The twins didn't exactly react to that, and I scurried them all inside before Cass and I exchanged *la bise* and held on to one another for a long drawn-out hug. It was as though we hadn't seen each other in fifteen years instead of six months. Cass seemed distinctly thinner to me, but I chalked that up to vegetarianism. She looked healthy enough, except for her previously beautiful hair, which now had lost its luster and was clinging in patchy clumps to her head instead of fanning out bird-tail-like around her neck.

I let Alan bring everything inside except the riding toy, dumped my coat on the chair, and gathered Paul and Laura up in my arms. They were absolutely beautiful children, both complete tow-heads with thick curls exactly like their father. But they had their mother's wide, deep-set eyes and a combination of their smiles. Laura was considerably smaller and more frail looking than Paul, who was a stocky little cherub of a boy, full of rambunctious energy and babble. Laura would point to things and say, "Bah!" but she didn't run around. I could just see Paul on my Inchworm toy, which I'd told Alan to leave in the car for now.

"My God, you two...what a work these gorgeous children are! They're miniature people already! You did yourselves proud."

"We're on the brink of destruction with them, " said Alan, "Paul's already trying to climb, and we've had to empty all surfaces. That's why we had to block off the tree here with that little table."

The tree was indeed up and balanced on two crossed boards. It wasn't the worst tree I'd ever seen, but it was pretty short, just a bit taller than Alan. The strings of lights were on but no ornaments; we would all decorate Christmas Eve, as planned.

I saw, too, that they had electrical sockets covered and kitchen cabinets secured with long locks.

"I like your safety precautions as well, " I commended Alan.

"Yeah, if one toddler could get into everything, with two you've got a real threat on your hands."

"The saving grace is, " Cass added, "that so far they still like their cribs, and go down willingly. That is a Godsend."

"Must be, " I said.

"We don't even give them bottles before bed now, " Cass explained. "We read a story, and let them play in their beds until they nod off."

"And they don't cry?" I marveled.

"Usually not. Schedules, kid, " she pronounced. "God Sari! I'm so happy you're here. We both are. Aren't we Alan?"

"Yes, ma'am we are, " he echoed, in mock Western lingo. "I'm diggin' the idea of some gooooood home cookin'. What 'cha fixin' t'whip up fer us, there, little lady?"

"Chili. Christmas Eve. And I promise to leave your larder full, how's that?"

"Good news, " he said, and then getting serious, lowering his voice, "because she still can't cook for shit."

"Hey!" Cass said, "I caught that. Tonight we're having something just divine," she said. "You'll see, Sari."

"Oh, yeah? What is it, I'm afraid to ask, " Alan taunted her.

" I tried a new casserole, " Cass announced proudly. "It's called 'Chicken in the Garden of Eden.'"

Oh, dear, I thought. I hoped she wasn't turning into a church lady herself, cooking more from the Bible than Betty Crocker.

She proceeded to call off the ingredients. "It's got chicken, of course, plus apples, honey, apple cider, and safflower oil."

"Where in hell do you find safflower oil, Cass?"

"At the co-op, of course."

Of course.

We went through the twins' bedtime rituals, just like she'd described, and they cooed away in the nursery for a little while; then we heard nothing. So Cass called us all to the table she had set with everything mismatched-- but pretty enough-- and dished out the Garden of Eden contents onto our plates.

I tasted it. Pretty damn good!

" Cass, this is really delish!" I exclaimed.

"You doubted me?" she laughed.

"Uh, yeah, sort of." And turning to Alan, "You've got nothing to complain about, Mister."

"It is pretty fine," he admitted, "but that's not the norm around here, what with all this organic, raw, unprocessed, healthy crap I have to put up with."

"Drop it, Alan, " Cass said. "Sari doesn't want to start her holiday listening to your blather."

"Anything for dessert, Mommy?" I wondered, trying to cue her to let it go.

"Carob brownies and sorbet. I went all out for you, Sari!"

"Well, thanks. What's carob?"

"A chocolate substitute, if you must know. Much healthier. You'll like it."

"You won't, " said Alan, " but the sorbet part sounds righteous. What kind is it?"

"Cherry, " she stated. "Store-bought."

"Praise the Lord! " he teased, winking at me.

I told Cass to stay seated at the table, that I'd clean up the kitchen. After I had cleared, washed and stacked the dishes to dry on their own, I boiled water in the tea kettle to rinse the silverware…and make us tea. As we drank it, she apprised me of our schedule for the next day, Christmas Eve Day.

"So the kids will go to the church day care, and we can roam around Iowa City all day if you want to."

"I'd love that."

"Plus," she said, "did you notice that Alan and I sleep in the back room now? I think I told you on the phone."

"Yes, and Soren also told me you'd fixed it up. Cool!"

"It's minuscule but really, it's so much better letting the twins have that bedroom space and keeping all their stuff in one place. I've even made them a toy box for Christmas. We'll pick it up tomorrow. It's at a woodworking shop of an artist friend of mine."

"What do you mean, you made it, though?" I was incredulous.

"Well, it was an unfinished box with a hinged lid. My friend let me use his space and I painted it, and stenciled a design all over the front. I found an old glass knob handle in a junk shop and am using that on the front. Their chubby little hands will be able to grasp onto it pretty soon, and eventually open and close it-- even maybe put toys away some day! I'm really happy with the way it turned out."

"Sounds like a true labor of love, " I told her.

"That's exactly what it was, " she agreed.

"HA! Good thing you did that because I've brought a shit-load of stuff to fill it with !"

Alan was watching a Perry Como Christmas Special in the living room, which wasn't really a separate room, so Cass and I hunkered down at the table and spoke softly.

"Alan mentioned when he brought in your bags and sacks that he thinks you must be making a tidy little fortune on your job."

"Well, let him think that. Anyway, in December, I did! Listen, Cass, I've brought you five hundred dollars this time."

"What?! That's risky, kid."

"But this is your money. I don't like controlling the purse strings of **your** money."

"Well, I'll squirrel it away somewhere, but you know, I really can't spend it on anything without rousing his suspicions."

"Yes, I know. Damn it, anyway. What about when you sell art of any kind? Do you have to turn over the money to him?"

"Well, actually no. In any event, not yet."

"So, if he questions you about anything—spending or whatever, just tell him one of your pieces sold. Does Klampert still have some of your work?"

"Believe it or not, he does. Oh, and guess what? As a matter of fact we're meeting him for lunch tomorrow in town after we drop off the kids!"

"Neato!"

"Also, while we're at the church, I'll take you upstairs to the sanctuary and you can see a banner I did for them. I mean, I had to—wanted to-- do something, since they took my kids in for free and all. It's a big blue dove in profile with an olive branch. It hangs from the rafters. "

"Sounds positively Woodstock-esque, " I said, recalling the logo of the bird on the guitar.

Alan came over and announced he was retiring to the back room to read and leave me a little privacy. But what he meant was that he wanted privacy, and I felt bad.

"I'm sorry to cramp your style for a week, Alan, " I said.

"Now, now, Miss Shrier, never! Don't give it another thought. Say, by the way, are we going to see Soren while you're here?"

"Don't you remember?" Cass prompted him, "Soren moved."

"He went to New York, Alan. I saw him though, on his way out there—he stopped in Chicago. I miss him."

"Yeah, I get that. Sorry I forgot."

Cass said she'd turn in, too, even though it was only around ten o'clock. But I had to admit I was tired, and kind of running on pure adrenalin.

"Thank you so much for coming, Sari, " Cass said as she handed me a thread-bare towel , a sheet, pillow and blanket to put on the sofa to at least simulate a bed.

"Don't thank me! I've been dying to come!! You know that; I'm just so sorry about Thanksgiving."

"Done and gone. Forget it. " She hugged me again. "Sleep tight. Oh, the bathroom's still in the same place, of course. "

"You guys go ahead, and I'll use it last."

"Okay, " she said, and added, " and, there's bubble bath."

"Gee! What is this, the Amstel?"

Chapter Seventy-Three

"Christmas in my Soul"...Laura Nyro

The Christmas Eve day sun streamed right into the living room window above my bed on the couch, and woke me up, so I arose early, put on my robe, and foraged in the kitchen cabinets for a stock pot in which to start my chili. I knew Cass and I had used a big pan to sterilize bottles two summers ago, so I figured she'd still have that. But to my surprise I found a few additions to her culinary supplies, indicating maybe she **was** getting into cooking. I got out a big pot and a frying pan, found the meat in the fridge to fry up with some diced onion, and within the half hour, I had it all going on the stove. I would let it simmer until mid-morning, and then turn it completely off, to reheat closer to dinner time.

I had placed my very full suitcase in the baby room when I went to bed the night before, so I just padded around in my pajamas and robe until everyone was up. Babies do not let their parents sleep in, of course, so it didn't take long before Cass was in their room changing and dressing them. I joined her in the nursery.

"How do you like what I brought them?" I asked, displaying things around as I unpacked them.

"You are the best shopper!" she said ogling the new supply of clothes and pajamas for Laura and Paul.

"Well, it's not so hard to spend other peoples' money, now is it? But really the only splurge are these little Italian outfits I got at Saks. Aren't they gorgeous?"

And with that, I held up a red knit pleated skirt and sweater set with Scottie dogs on it for Laura, and a powder blue and white knit slacks set for Paul. It had a darling train motif on the sweater.

"I'll bet that's not washable, " Cass laughed.

"Cass, I tried to be really careful and not buy anything you had to dry clean, but I couldn't resist those. So I'm sorry in advance."

"It's okay, " she said fingering all the other outfits, most of which were cute little corduroy or cotton ensembles with flared tops for girls and little shirts for boys. I'd brought them each three sets in sizes from eighteen months to toddler two. I included one of the outfits in identical colors, just in case Cass and Alan actually wanted to dress them as twins.

"I know you could care less, but I love the idea of people seeing they are more than just siblings," I said to Cass pointing out the twin pair.

"Well, I'm going to give you 'Auntie-Sari-Creative-License' on that one and indulge you."

"Yay. And did you see the toys!! I love them all."

"This is quite a haul, here, *Mademoiselle Shreee-air!*" she said pointedly, mimicking the way they she'd heard them call my name so many times at *La Maison*. "Did you get spoiling them rotten out of your system this time?"

"For a while, maybe. I didn't get them winter coats, though, and it dawned on me yesterday when they came outside, that those first snowsuits we bought way back when don't fit these kids anymore, huh? "

"No. But they're making do with some jackets I found."

"Well then, it looks like we may need to shop some more today."

"I suppose we could stop in at the rummage shops and see if anything else came in that would fit them."

"Or we could actually go to a normal store."

I knew, and could feel, that Cass was in a tough spot with the money situation of her marriage, so I didn't push my agenda too much. But the truth was, her children did not have to want for anything, and she would just have to figure out a way to reconcile that with her own and Alan's attitude towards her family money, plus their new-found commitment to living the simple life. I, on the other hand, had made no such deal, and thus felt free to indulge my two "God-children."

When the kids were ready for breakfast, Cass set up the high chairs near her kitchen table, and made oatmeal for them. I observed her. She seemed to really relish her role as mommy, and acted far more comfortable with it now. Cass had changed and evolved even since I was last there.

She smashed up some blueberries and put those on top of each bowl, and let the babies try to eat with little spoons, which was a chore for them. But they liked the food, and soon just stuck their hands in it. Some of it even made it into their mouths. It was cute to see them eat.

"I tell you what, " Cass finally said. "You feed Laura and I'll help Paul, and this show will get on the road faster."

She had read my mind.

Alan came out of the back bedroom dressed, pronouncing the smells on his stove very enticing. He told me that he had to meet with some of the faculty at the River Room for coffee, but he'd see me later. He gave Cass a peck on the cheek, and took off on foot.

"He walks to campus?" I asked, surprised.

"Well, usually he rides the bike, but not in the snow."

"The bike" was that same old, blue Norton 600 that he'd had already when I first met him as my teacher. I was rather shocked that it was still around, but then, they were also driving my 1959 Rambler, so it shouldn't have been that surprising.

"Alan rarely drives the station wagon," she said, "because he knows I need it."

"I'm sure he wouldn't want to be caught dead being seen in that."

"That's not true. We're grateful to have it! What would I do without it? Perish the thought! That boxy old thing gives me the perfect space for two car seats and the double stroller?! Who'd- a- thunk **that** when you drove it up here in the summer of '67, huh?"

"Happy to help in that case, " I laughed.

After I finished overseeing Laura's breakfast, I went in to get ready myself. The chili had been simmering for nearly three hours by the time we had everything and everyone cleaned up. I turned off the stove, and sneaked out to the car to retrieve the Inchworm toy, and hide it with the others to be set out that evening.

Cass and I packed the kids into the car and drove into town. When we parked at Trinity, I took her up on the suggestion to peek into the sanctuary and see her banner. It was even more beautiful than I pictured from her description. Her lovely dove was done in batik. It was a real masterpiece.

Cass was excited to be meeting up with Professor Klampert for lunch in downtown Iowa City, and we found him waiting in front of The Mill. He greeted us both—but not by name-- and even though I figured he knew me, I preempted the awkwardness with the first question.

"Do you remember that I was in your art history survey class, Professor? Sarah Shrier. " I offered my hand to shake his— a reflex more from French customs than anything else.

"Of course, " he said somewhat startled, leaving me to wonder whether that were true. It was. "You parked your car in my driveway, too, didn't you?"

"That's right! Cass and I were roommates all those years ago."

"And after my survey class, you took a studio one, if I remember. You worked on linoleum block printing?"

"Wow, that **is** a good memory, " I said, pretty astonished.

The Mill hadn't changed one iota since our student days, and we took a table inside the pine-paneled booth area for a little more privacy and quiet. The Mill could be jumping and very loud, but not at lunchtime, and not on Christmas Eve Day. We had a jolly time with him, as he was very enthusiastic over Cass' works—old and new.

"He's the reason I got that order for Christmas cards last year, " she said.

"Your terrific print was the real reason you got the commission, " he corrected. "Did you do more for them this year?"

"No," she said, regretfully. "But this year I made ornaments for the Mt. Vernon holiday arts fair, and I sold a lot of them! We're going to put up the rest of what I have left this afternoon, aren't we, Sari?"

"Yes!" I enthused. "Trimming the tree is always fun. And it's so European to do it this late! Well done, you!"

428

We laughed at my British English. Given that was mostly all I heard when anyone spoke English around my office, it wasn't hard to conjure some up.

Cass told Klampert all about my job in Chicago, and how this was the first time I'd been back since graduation week and all. I didn't think that would interest him, so I tried to steer it back to art, her art, the art department, and the collection at the Art Institute that I was beginning to know intimately.

"I guess you don't realize this, " I told him, " but I did enough art history in Paris to have a minor in it when I got back."

"I'm impressed!" he said, nodding in approval at me. And then he turned his attention back to Cass.

"Listen, I want you to prepare some works to submit to the actual Johnson or Linn County Fairs next spring, " he told her. "I'm not judging, but I am heading up the panel to place the judges all around the state, and if you win at these fairs— or the State Fair in Des Moines---it looks good on your resumé, not to mention you actually win monetary prizes as well as ribbons."

"I'm not sure I…"

He didn't let her finish. "You can always use studio space in the department, " he said. "In fact, I wish you would work on several pieces and then really finish your degree. Wouldn't you like to do that?"

"More than anything, " she said, and added with a nervous little laugh, "I just wish I could find a way."

"I know you have two little kids, " he said, not wanting to sound unsympathetic to her plight. "Just think about it."

He announced that he had an impromptu faculty holiday function to attend that sounded like Alan's, so he excused himself, telling me how nice it had been to see me, and giving Cass a friendly kiss on the forehead as he left.

"He's a pretty neat guy, " I said and repeated my oft-quoted truism: "It's all who you know in life, isn't it? I get free rent in Chicago because I knew your parents, and you get free childcare and studio space here."

"Most of the time I just feel so far from ART, " she sighed. "I feel like I could reconnect with it, but I just have no time to sit and think during the day without baby sounds in the background. They can't amuse themselves yet, of course, and I'm too scared to start working on some project, and then have to get up and go to them if I detect distress signals coming from elsewhere."

"I hear you, Cass, but you have to admit, they're little works of art in themselves! Laura is as beautiful as any child in a Mary Cassatt painting and Paul looks like a tiny Michelangelo's *David*. Curls all over their heads…really I could just sit and stare at them all day."

"Yes, well, last month you wouldn't have thought that. They were both sick, and I realized at one point that I was spending my sixth consecutive day stuck out on our little 'farm' together with them! I thought I would lose it. "

"Yeah, that doesn't sound fun."

"But today is fun!" she said, changing the subject. "Isn't Klampert fab? He's even cuter now with his hair in that short ponytail. That is different than when you had him for a teacher, isn't it? I'm so glad he took the time to meet up with us both. I know you find him beautiful on the inside, too… like I do."

"I'm really happy you're in contact with him, and I hope it will afford you the opportunity to keep one foot in the art world."

"Yes, I'm grateful to him, all right. God knows I don't have much other support system…except you of course. You are my constant."

"So, nothing from the parents at all, huh? Not even for the twins' first birthday? Christ you'd think they'd just get over it."

"Well, contrary to what I would have said before, I think my father might have actually come if I'd put out feelers. But Julia is such a hard nose when she wants to be. I fear reconciliation will never be possible with her, and consequently probably not with him either. They just cannot forgive me for being with Alan, and they refuse to see their own grand children because of it. Poor Paul and Laura don't have any luck with the other side either. Alan's parents are divorced, and his father is all wrapped up in his

429

own problems. His mom is on the East Coast--he never sees her. I wonder if she even realizes he's married with kids! 'Course, that's as much Alan's fault as hers. He doesn't make contact at all."

"Well, how **are** things with you and Alan? Sometimes on the phone, you have to admit, you give the impression you guys aren't doing so well."

"Life is good for the Joneses at the moment," she said sparkling it up a little. "Alan is doing a great job with the C.O. stuff—the literacy council and all, and his workshop classes are going well enough, I guess. He's still working on his own chapbook, of course. He's setting some of his poems to music on the guitar even."

"Whoa! When did that come about?"

"Oh, pretty recently. I think it's a great outlet for him."

" But, is changing diapers also a good outlet for him? "

"Ha ha. I get where you're going with that. He doesn't really help much with them, but..."

"But what!? There's no but about it. He has to chip in. He's their dad!"

"Now, wait. What I started to say is that you saw how different our little place is now. He took the initiative on that---fixing the place up, painting every room, making that back bedroom ours and moving the twins into the nursery—so called. And he's on board with my ideas of living as nearly self-sufficiently as possible—raising crops—I have a few in the works for planting in the spring, believe it or not. I even went to the county extension office to get information. I'm also learning more about sewing. Some day you won't have to buy the children's clothing. Their mommy will sew it! "

"But, do you two even go out anymore? What do you do as a family?"

"We do manage to have a date night once in a while. If there's something we really want to do, we do it. We go picnicking, hiking, driving, etc."

"Well, good. At least you've got that. How do the kids react to those activities?"

"Well, I'll be honest, it was easier that first Fall when they were little and the weather was better. But we really dig sharing everything with Paul and Laura. They're like our own little cohorts, and they keep us on our toes! We all experience collective exhaustion, I'll tell you!"

"I believe it."

"And, let me tell you something else, Sari. Love. Love is so fine. There's always the beauty of the person beside you in bed. And warm hands and hearts together. And when **you** marry, like, the heavens will open up and throw white gardenias and daisies and doves all down upon you."

" They will, huh?" I laughed. "Oh, goodie. I'll be sure to look forward to that."

"You know what I mean. And I hope it's sooner rather than later. Are you meeting people in Chicago?"

" Oh... you know a few, but not really. I work all the time and I come back to my little place and that's about it. "

"I know you like it there, " she said, "but is loneliness your enduring menace? Even in groovy apartments or big mansions, you turn around and there you are...just you and no one else. And you can become LONELY. Even if you live alone by choice."

"Well, sure, but Cass, I like living alone."

"Yes, but what about friends? I know you've got some jerks in your orbit. You've told me about the creepy valet and the crazy secretary—these are almost hyphenated words like fakey-stewardess." Her voice trailed off.

" I don't have a lot of friends yet...a couple. But I still love Chicago."

" But I'm wondering—don't you find it a hassle to live alone?"

"No, I honestly don't. I can see what you're getting at, though. I hope to connect soon to 'real' people...and I mean really connect. I do have two great friends in Dom and Peter. And I think Annie-Laure in my office is one of the good guys, too. She's dating the chauffeur and they seem genuinely happy together... two people who could become my friends."

"Maybe the chauffeur has got a buddy? Ha!" She laughed and then became serious again, adding, "It's hard to find close 'soul-mate' friends, I know. I wish I had that here, and I don't."

"Well, you're stuck out in the boonies."

"Yeah, I have to admit I feel like a little house-frau occasionally, as though I were married to the place. I caught myself a few weeks ago daydreaming about a new couch and chairs, and I didn't like that! I fear becoming attached to **things**."

"Cass," I said, trying to broach the subject delicately, "you can't be expected to give up every aspect of your previous life, can you? Is this self-imposed, or does Alan expect you to make do living at the poverty line?"

"Oh, probably a little of both. I want to rid myself of materialism. And he agrees with that."

"Well, he **would** since he makes zero money. But you've got these two children who need **stuff**!"

"And you are providing it, aren't you? " she laughed. "What they really need is you! They love it when you're around…can you tell? Because I can. And I love it, too. And Alan, too. You know you are always welcome here any time… on vacations and 'R and R' stints---anything. "

I could see that the conversation wasn't going further, so we got up and went to retrieve the wooden toy box (which impressed me no end); pick up the kids, and head on home for our Christmas eve.

Once back at the house Cass brought out a tote bag with her hand-made ornaments inside. Their beauty took me by surprise. They were real works of art---little jewels that sparkled and gave off an aura of expensive heirlooms.

"My God, I can't believe you made these!"

"I saved one out specially to give you. Take it home with you…I know you don't have a tree, but you can hang it from a hook somewhere in your place."

"I know just where, too. Thank you! I'll really cherish this." I hugged her.

"And here we have some little store-bought ones, just plain gold and silver glass balls, but I thought that would look good, and make mine sort of stick out. And I bought a Jiffy Pop! We will make popcorn and string it!"

"Brilliant idea."

My chili was ready to go, so I relit the burner under it, and then stepped aside again and watched anew as Cass took over the kitchen. She explained how she made the babies' dinner of brown rice with vegetables she had cooked right in it, plus always served them fruits and foods with lots of calcium like broccoli, cottage cheese and milk.

"I know what you are thinking, " she teased me, " that there's no protein here."

"Hey, I didn't say a word." And frankly that hadn't even occurred to me. I was certainly not on a healthy food kick of any sort!

"No, but I can tell you are a skeptic of a vegetarian diet. Anyway, look what I have. " And she went to the fridge and took out a small package wrapped in freezer paper. "It's a little bit of cooked salmon that I'm going to lay in pieces right over their rice. They love that."

I put my hand on her shoulder. "You're a great mom," I said, and meant it, "And not just because you know enough to give these kids some fish."

Alan came home, and we all played with Paul and Laura until it was time to put them in the tub, into pajamas and into their cribs. While they were still in the bath, I went into the nursery and took out all the toys I wanted to place around the tree for them to discover in the morning. I also brought out Cass' and Alan's gifts, as well, and did not forget to fetch the boxes of home-baked Christmas cookies from my suitcase, where they'd thawed out nicely and could now be displayed.

While Cass (with Alan pitching in--- I couldn't help but think, almost snarkily, for show and my benefit), dressed the kids for bed and then read to them, I set the table and grated some cheddar cheese for the top of my chili creation. Cass had bought saltines at my behest and everything was ready for our Christmas Eve dinner.

When they both came back out of the nursery and seated themselves at the table, I told them I marveled at how easily the babies seemed to get ready for sleeping through the night.

"Do you think they know they have each other in there?" I wondered. "They just gurgle away—as if they understand what the other one is saying."

"I think that's more than a theory, " said Alan. "Twins are a unique unit."

"It smells good in here!" Cass sang out as I approached with the pot containing our dinner.

431

Cass actually ate some of the chili, even though it had meat in it; and I, in turn, had to admit that all that healthy ground-up organ meat did taste great. Alan had two bowls full of it.

"You are a fine cook, Sari, " he said, "which we've known for a long time. Thank you for that meal!"

He got up and put on some music which we all loved, *Liege and Lief,* and we hunkered down on the couch to string the popcorn and decorate the tree. When we finished hanging the last ornament, we were ever so pleased with our artistic effort.

"I LOVE it, " I enthused. "You know my theory---Jews secretly want to decorate Christmas trees. Actually it's no secret with me. I adore doing it. This one looks especially fantastic."

"Not bad at all, " said Alan, and Cass nodded happily, almost in a trance.

"I wonder if the kids will even really notice it tomorrow, " she said.

"Well, they'll see all those toys, that's for sure!" Alan chimed in. "Miss Shrier's outdone herself! You must be doing pretty well on that job, eh?"

"Yep, I am, " I said. "I'll have to tell you guys all about it. I really love my job. Can you imagine getting a whole month's salary as a Christmas bonus? I thought I'd faint!"

So even though Cass pretty much knew everything from our phone calls, I proceeded to regale them with tales of meeting famous musicians and conductors, giving in-service talks about my ideas to high school teachers, creating the period-piece role-play boxes, and doing lesson plans for films. Of course I didn't gloss over my horrible moments, either, like getting *shickered* on champagne, embarrassing myself over The Divine Franz, and running into my boss at a drag club. Then there were the stories of what a dipstick Robineau always was to me.

"God, he sounds like a complete candyass, " said Alan when I stopped and came up for some air, "but your boss is a real sweetheart, right?"

"He's very nice, yes, " I answered.

"So...are you kind of crushing on him? Tell the truth," Alan teased.

"Uh, noooo!"

Cass hadn't said anything, but she then spoke up, "He's gay, Alan."

"Oh, okay. Never mind, then."

Feeling the need to change the subject, and also keep the spirit going of our holiday camaraderie, I suggested they open my presents. I handed Alan the Frango Mints and he tore it open. Cass was delighted to see that familiar green box, too. Alan waved it around.

"Not carob either!"

"Oh, neat-o! I've missed them!" she admitted, laughing.

"And here's one for you, " I said handing her the one containing the red robe, which she took smiling, and gingerly opened. She lifted it out and just fingered it for a moment, running her delicate hands through the deep chenille pile.

"I absolutely adore it!" she said holding it up to her and twirling around. "It's the color of Christmas to boot! Ha! And I love the sash."

"I think it will look very nice on you, " said Alan.

"I agree," I said.

"Kid, "she said, standing over me, "you really know how to pick 'em."

"Don't I just!"

"And I needed one, too!"

"Yeah, I thought maybe you might."

"Okay," said Cass, setting down her gift. "Yours isn't under the tree, so I'm going to go get it." And with that, she left the room. I turned to Alan who smiled and shrugged at me.

When Cass returned, she had a familiar looking box with her, unwrapped but tied with a black grosgrain ribbon.

"OH, NO, " I said. "If that's what I think it is, oh, hell no." I saw the two crisscrossed C's in all their embossed glory on the box, and I knew it was the same one she had opened from her parents four years earlier.

"Yes," she answered matter-of-factly, but also a little hurt.

432

"Cass, you know I can't accept this."

Alan didn't let her intercede. "You have to because otherwise..."

"What he means is this, " she said, looking squarely at me, "Sari, I will never wear this again. I have nowhere to wear it, nothing to wear with it, and besides all that, it doesn't even fit me anymore. It's too good to give away and too expensive to sell to second-hand shops. This isn't New York; there are no consignment boutiques where I could take it even if I wanted to sell it; and the little rummage shops we do have wouldn't know what they were getting if I did take it to them. You, on the other hand, are now mingling in the public eye at occasions where you must dress up. It would be tragic to let this piece of clothing to go to waste when you really need it!"

She set the box down in front of me and thrust it towards my hands.

"Go on, " said Alan, "no more protests---just open it."

"I-I-I don't know what to say, " I managed to stutter, taking off the lid, pulling back the tissue paper and lifting the beautiful charcoal velvet jumper out of its box. "When you got this and wore it for the first time, I remember thinking it was the single most stunning article of clothing I had ever laid eyes on."

"And you never even asked to borrow it!" she laughed.

"Well, I couldn't. And I wouldn't! Really, Cass, I just can't accept this."

"This is non-negotiable, Sari Shrier. It's yours now. Do with it what you will. You can take it back to Chicago and sell it for all I care. Chanel never loses its value. You'd be able to pay rent for the next ten years if you could sell it for what it probably cost my parents. The trouble is, you can't."

Ten years might have been an exaggeration, but I got the point. However, I would never sell it, and told them so.

"Then wear it. It will make me so happy to know you have it and are getting use out of it."

Part of me wanted to scream with joy and amazement; the materialistic part of me, the part of me that Cass had only hours before condemned in herself. And part of me wanted to refuse still, on the grounds that Cass might just be going through a phase with the lifestyle, if you could call it that, she was currently living; and that, contrary to her own protestations, she really would wear it again, that it would someday fit her again, and more importantly, she, herself, would need it.

So I tried one more tack: "Cass, you will be a professor's wife one of these days, and you will be invited to holiday parties at Deans' homes or fancy graduation events, and all that. You really might wish you had this again."

"Not happening, " said Alan. "We're just not the social types, and even if we were, nothing on a college campus is going to require the level of dressing up as what you go to in Chicago with that French business. You're already hobnobbing with the movers and shakers. We are the hoi-polloi. "

"I don't know about that, " I said, and then relented. "Okay, I'd like to stay nonchalant about this, but truth is, I am beside thrilled !! I will accept it, and I thank you so much. SO much!!"

Cass jumped up and put her arms around me. "Finally! Good deal."

And Alan pronounced to me with a twinkle in his bluer than blue eyes, "**You** will be the belle of the ball."

"Well," I replied, "if that isn't the damn truth!"

Chapter Seventy-Four

"Our House"...Crosby, Stills and Nash

"I have three days left in Iowa City, " I said as Cass and I fed the kids early on the Monday morning after the big Christmas celebration. We had spent the long holiday weekend playing with all the toys and eating Chinese takeout. The house was a complete wreck. Alan had taken refuge in the back bedroom and hadn't come out. "I propose we clean this place up and by 'we' I mean, Alan and me."

"Huh?" she said, looking up from the oatmeal. "And what will I be doing?"

"I have an idea, " I said. "You and I will drive the kids to the church, after which I will drop you off at your chosen hair salon for a long-overdue cut, style and relaxation. Are there any places in this town that have a real selection of services like in Chicago? You know, facials, massage and all that?"

"Yes, one. It's right downtown. But I don't have an appointment."

"I know, but it's the day after Christmas weekend and students are gone. They can't be that busy."

I was actually surprised she didn't argue with me; it just told me that she, too, thought she needed some pampering. I let her finish up with the twins, and I went back to talk to Alan. Knocking, even through the door was open, I saw that he was up and dressed, working at a make-shift table-cum-desk in the corner of the room. I walked in and laid out my idea to him.

"I'm treating Cass to a little spa day, " I said, giving him no time to respond, "and after I drop her off, I'm going to hit the grocery store and stock up on all sorts of stuff to make oodles of meals for you guys."

"Bless you my child, " he said, perking up and turning towards me.

"Yes, yes, you're a lucky guy. But wait, there's more. I'm also going to get a bunch of cleaning supplies, and while she's still out, you and I are going to deep clean this place."

"Are we now?" he laughed.

"Don't laugh. I mean it. It's the least you can do for all the yummy and delectable treats I'll be leaving here."

"Okay, it's a deal. What do you intend for us to do?"

"I wish we could steam clean the carpets, if you want to know the truth. Your kids crawl around all over the floors, and they are not clean enough, **Daddy**. But we can't; so I'm going to get that stuff you sprinkle on and vacuum up, and hope it works. As for all the other floors, they'll be easier. Pine Sol, baby. And same for the bathrooms. You and I will divide the labor. Are you diggin' it?"

He got up, stood at attention, pretended to click his heels---not possible in socks—and gave me a Nazi-like salute. "*Jawohl, mein general* Shrier!"

"Shut up. Not funny."

So the plan was the plan, and it was put into action. The beauty salon was open for business and they got her right in.

"When you get done, " I said, "go on over to the bookstore and get yourself a bunch of art supplies, okay?" She looked at me wide-eyed and smiled.

I had taken her in at nine-thirty and we weren't getting the kids until six. I felt I was going to need about forty-five minutes in the market, and then the drive back, so I was figuring Alan and I could clean from around ten-thirty until half-past noon, if we really worked at it. Then I would cook.

"I'm going to need until about five o'clock in the afternoon at your place, " I told her, "so you've got some time to kill."

"Oh," she said, almost wistfully, "don't you worry about me. I can plop down somewhere in that bookstore and just sit and read."

"Okay, so I will assume I can find you there at the end of the afternoon, and we'll have time to get a coffee or something before we have to pick up the kids. And on the way home, we'll stop and get a Pagliai's pizza."

"But—what about all the meals you're cooking all day? You still want to do take-out?" She was incredulous.

"Come on! Seeing your kids and having Pagliai's are the two reasons I came!! I can't wait to have thin-crust pizza again. I may be the only person in Chicago who doesn't like theirs!"

The supermarket was the same as ever, and I knew every nook and cranny of it. Working very fast and not missing any aisles, I stocked the cart full. I intended to do most of this cooking from scratch, which was cheaper and of course, healthier, so I bought many fresh vegetables and fruits. My *pièce de résistance* was going to be Nana's carrot cake, and I was damned if I was going to use any of Cass' buckwheat or soy flours in that, so I bought regular old bleached flour. She'd just have to live with it.

Thinking ahead, and giving myself full credit for it, I also bought a few freezer and fridge containers. In 1970, if you didn't go to a Tupperware party, there were few options for storage that weren't glass. And if the grocery stores even carried them, these were a luxury. But as luck would have it, the Iowa City one that was "my supermarket" had a line of Rubbermaid products, the poor woman's Tupperware. They were also made out of a heavy plastic with "locking lids," which would suit my needs to a T.

Once in the store, I couldn't help but also pick up a few convenience items like some jars of Gerber Junior foods. I was determined to try to convince Cass to get back to the art she could produce for those scholarships or prizes, and if she did that, she might need some emergency time-saving provisions on hand for the kids. It was just a thought, and I had no idea if she'd ever allow processed food to touch her children's lips, but I went ahead and bought it. She could accuse me later of being a little passive-aggressive, and I wouldn't argue with her.

When I returned from the store, Alan helped me carry everything in, no doubt wondering how much it all had cost, but not asking me. We unpacked and stored the food, and then turned our attention to cleaning. I "assigned" him the entire bathroom---every surface: tub, sink, windows, and floors. In the meantime, I gathered up all towels, bedding, crib sheets and blankets, and even the curtains, and drove them over to the laundromat next to Pagliai's. I splurged for them to do the wash-dry-fold thing, and made sure they knew to do the baby stuff in Dreft, which I also provided. I said I'd be back to pick it all up before six.

My first order of business when I got down to brass tacks, was to take over the living room carpet cleaning, hoping it would work with that powdery stuff I'd bought. The chemical needed time to set before I could vacuum it up, so I busied myself cleaning all the kitchen surfaces and floor with Pine Sol and Spic and Span. Luckily Cass still had all the mops and broom I'd taken her the summer the babies were born. I'd brought in two new large sponges and several packages of paper towels-- a luxury they didn't feel they could afford and never kept on hand. I had decided to buy some because she didn't have the kind of cleaning rags I needed for all these jobs.

Alan and I Windexed the entire array of the house's windows, (not that many, after all the house only had five rooms); and in the nursey, I wiped down the changing table/dresser and both cribs. Alan did the floor.

After a couple of hours of cleaning, and when I had finished the living room carpet, the place was looking and smelling a lot better.

Alan went back to his writing, and I began to lay out recipes. I might not get it all done in one afternoon, I told myself, but at least I could try and stock their place with as many meals as possible. I liked working alone, being able to organize and do things my way, even if I did have only that tiny space to work in.

I found myself caving a little bit to Cass' wishes for healthier foods. I would make my same recipes---Nana's--but substitute in a few more healthy bits. I had told Cass that I, myself, wasn't going to the co-op, but I would use whatever organic supplies she had on hand as I cooked, and thus, try to satisfy her need to eat "natural." I decided upon two meat loaves, and of course, had to take advantage of the ubiquitous mixed organ ground meat she'd left for me. I knew I could doctor it up and disguise it with enough spices and seasonings to make it taste just as great. My meatloaf recipe called for egg, breadcrumbs, onion, mushrooms, and garlic, plus I used Cass' sea salt in it. I laid slices of green pepper over the top, which was slathered in ketchup, as usual. I made my Nana's rice pudding, but used brown rice instead of the usual kind. It came out fine. I did tuna and noodle casserole with whole-wheat noodles. Who even knew those existed? I'd never seen that, but Cass had them.

I had bought the biggest piece of boneless chuck roast the grocery store had that day to make two pot roasts and still have some meat left to make vegetable beef soup the way my grandmother made it for the bar. I added barley to it, even separating out a portion of that minus the meat, so she could have her own veggie version. I only realized too late that the broth was beef broth, therefore, it didn't count for true vegetarian. So I did another soup, with corn and beans, onion, celery and even some soybeans Cass had been soaking. I felt like I had complied with all her wishes on that one.

The pot roasts took the longest time to make, but at least they could be done on top of the stove in a pot that was the closest she had to a Dutch oven. Of course, the soup cooked that way, too, which left the oven free. I was able to put together the casseroles assembly-line style, and bake them more or less together.

While things were simmering and baking, I cut up fruit for salads that would store well for a few days, and I also made a quite healthy carrot and apple salad with raisins and yogurt, which, I had to admit, was a huge nod to Cass.

My grandmother's carrot cake recipe had been the hit of The Spot for decades. I saved making that for last, since I had to have the oven ready to bake it at 350 degrees after everything else was done. The cake took all the usual ingredients: flour, baking powder and soda, salt, cinnamon and two cups of sugar, which I was sure would disgust Cass if she knew. I also used a cup and a half of vegetable oil, four eggs and a can of crushed pineapple, along with the raw carrots and chopped walnuts. No carrot cake is good plain, so the traditional cream-cheese frosting was called for. Nana's needed a stick of butter, an eight-ounce package of Philadelphia Cream Cheese, a whole pound of powdered sugar and a teaspoon of vanilla. It was the best frosting on God's green earth, probably because of all the sugar.

Alan came out from time to time to put on music and watch me work a bit. We really didn't talk much because I was so busy, but he did manage to thank me for all the food.

"It smells so good in here!" he enthused, extolling once again my virtues as a cook. "My wife still can't cook worth a damn, you know that."

"Your wife is an artist, Alan, and a great one. Why don't you give her a break and let her BE one?'

"I do. I mean, I do in a way."

"Oh, like volunteering to watch the kids a couple of nights a week so she can get some studio time in? The art department has offered her free space, did you realize that? She needs to take them up on it."

"Who gave her that?"

"You know who. He was her advisor forever, for chrissake. He knows her talent. You can't possibly begrudge her that. Get real. She's really going to be famous one day."

"Well, aren't we all!" he said, trying to lighten up the conversation and assuage his obvious guilt — or, quite possibly, inferiority complex. "And you, Miss Shrier? What fame is going to be coming your way? Will you open up a restaurant some day in Chicago?"

"What? NO! I love my job just the way it is. No fame involved."

The two pot roasts with their garnishes of potatoes, carrots and onions finished cooking around four o'clock, and the casseroles were already out of the oven and cooling. The soup was ready to be ladled into serving sized containers, and everything was wrapped up either for freezing or storing in the fridge. Only the carrot cake remained to be frosted before I could slip a cover of wax paper propped up with toothpicks over the top of it.

And then Alan came over, faced me, grinning, and put his hands on my shoulders. "I'm going to give you a little shock right now Miss Chef extraordinaire!" And he made a flourish with his hand right in front of my face. "I'm going to wash up all these pots and pans and dishes for you."

"You are?! Wow, Alan, I am shocked…and impressed. And grateful. Thanks!"

"Yep. You've worked your ass off today. You go on into Iowa City with my lady, and have some fun together."

I found Cass in the bookstore, and we repaired to Hamburg Inn for coffee. She looked fabulous — like her old self, with once-again chic hair and a glow in her cheeks. By the time we picked up Paul and Laura, the car was packed to the gills with the clean laundry, the pizzas, and all of Cass' purchases of art supplies and several books.

When she got home, Cass was quite literally astounded at the clean house, much of it done by Alan, and the array of food in her fridge and freezer. She stared, mouth agape, at the sheer quantity of what I had prepared in one day.

"You little firebrand, you! You astonish me!"

I was, I had to admit, exhausted, but very happy that I could fulfill my mission---a sort of extra Christmas present to them. Yes, I had used money from the Hyde account, as did Cass for the beauty treatments and the art furnishings; and Alan wasn't any the wiser.

As we sat around eating pizza and drinking chianti, listening to Joni Mitchell and talking about everything from their plans for self-sufficient future living, to my soon-to-be faced real apartment hunt in the big city, the twins' pre-school in another two years or so, and the ridiculous Viet-Nam war, I harkened back to Cass' and my Paris days, and how all three of us and our relationships were born out of the luck of the draw of roommates and section instructors. I was struck by the randomness of life. Had my department chair not known Marie-France de Piaget, would I have ever had the chance for my fabulous job? And what about my free apartment from Cass' arrangement with her father?

"It's all kinds of crazy, " I told them, marveling, "that I got to meet Chan Parker and Phil Woods because of a connection through my relatives in New York, whom I would not even have been able to see if Cass had not invited me to go with her family, and then their agreeing to let us trot off to Brooklyn! Or what about running into Clément de Seignard's father at my boss' house! I mean, really! Who could believe that! If your parents hadn't insisted I stay in that fabulous hotel in Amsterdam after you left, I would never have met that family either!"

Reminiscing was fine with Alan, until it involved giving Cass' parents credit for anything good, at which point he said he'd check on the kids, and got up and left.

"Sorry." I told her, shrugging. "I guess I shouldn't speak too highly of John-Wilfred and Julia around him."

"Oh, ignore him, " she said to me, pouting. " He's the third baby in this family."

The next day, far more leisurely, Cass and I took Laura and Paul shopping in Cedar Rapids where there was more choice of toddler clothing than in Iowa City. We found the cutest coats, and bought them big enough to maybe even last until the next Christmas! Laura's was red wool with black velvet collar and cuffs with the same fabric-covered buttons going down the front. I also insisted on the mittens that were on a string of yarn that went into one sleeve and came out the other, so that she would never lose them even if she pulled them off, as toddlers were wont to do. The coat even came with a plaid tam o'shanter, and the ensemble was super chic. Paul's coat was a navy-blue pea-coat with a little military-looking insignia on the breast pocket. It had leather toggle closings. The boys' mittens did not come tied with yarn, so we bought the little clips the store had, and a pair of navy-blue mittens for him. His coat came with a hood, so all we had to get him was a little stocking cap to keep his ears warmer.

Cass and I had the same taste. We both thought her kids were just darling in those coats, which we did buy even though they were expensive. But I knew she was worried that Alan would think they were too fancy to play in and not practical at all for their non-social lifestyle.

"Just blame it on me, " I told her. "Tell him their Auntie Sari once again spent all her hard-earned salary on your kids."

"All right," she agreed. But I could tell she thought there would be blowback from Alan.

"Okay, just to be on the safe side, and because I think those thrift store jackets you had them in are completely inadequate, I'm getting them new ski jackets, too."

All too soon, I was packed for the return trip much lighter than when I arrived, and was headed back to the station and the train for Chicago. Alan stayed home with the twins this time, and a teary-eyed Cass stood on the platform linking arms with me, not believing I really had to go.

"Please, just call and tell them you got way-laid and have to stay until Sunday, " she pleaded, sobbing.

"I don't want to leave either. You know, though, that the office is having a New Year's Eve party---French style—another *Réveillon*. I need to be there." I hugged her tight and also wept. "Thanks for **everything**. I had the **best** time."

"Why are you thanking me? You did all the work… cleaning, cooking, baking."

"You know why. NOT only for the Chanel *tour de force*, either. You save my spiritual being."
"You save my damn life, what are you talking about! I'm just going to miss you SO much."
"I thought Jesus saved your life, " I giggled, trying to joke through the tears.
"Yes, Him, too. But mostly you."

Chapter Seventy-Five

*Sicilienne Op. 78...*Gabriel Fauré

My bags were considerably lighter on the way back to Chicago, even though Cass had insisted I take home the remains of the five-pound bag of sugar I'd bought for 35 cents. The more precious cargo was, of course, the Chanel outfit, and I planned to wear it to the party at JPA's. My London shoes would still be fine with it and so would my white sweater. But the coat situation was dire.

When the taxi from Union Station dropped me at my apartment house, Jake was not on patrol, but I met Perry.

"Jake took some vacation time knowing you would be away, " he explained, as though he knew me and the job. He did know the job, and he also offered to carry my luggage up, for which I was truly grateful. He told me not to worry about staying out late on New Year's Eve, as though he'd read my mind.

"I really don't think it will go too late, " I said, purely guessing.

"That won't even matter. I'll be here in any event."

He was as laid-back ...as *décontracté* as Jake, and also just as nice. It had not escaped me that I'd been ever so fortunate with this housing situation, weird as it was to be living in a construction zone for six months. Jake and now Perry were my guardians. I wondered just how much their salaries were for being on duty almost around the clock, and really also at my beck and call. I mused that if my parents really knew the truth of how I lived in the big city, they'd probably drag me precipitously back to Iowa. I had only told them I was being "allowed by Mr. Hyde to live rent-free" in one of his many properties until I could get on my feet financially. It was true enough.

Up in my studio, it struck me that much as I had filled Cass and Alan's freezer and pantry, mine were pretty bare. It hadn't even occurred to me to lay in a few supplies before I left; I'd been so fraught over packing all their presents and the foodstuffs. Luckily I had cans of soup and some crackers. Those, along with a pot of tea, would do fine for supper, and then right to bed.

I had a day of shopping to look forward to.

On the train ride back, I had spent a goodly amount of time determining the lay of the land budget-wise. If I really splurged, it would set me back paying rent even as much as a few months; and I didn't know how many more free ones I had. On the other hand, I had gotten that nice bonus. Wasn't expecting it. Hadn't planned for it or computed it in my income. It was frosting. Why should I have to budget it? On the other hand, that would go a long way towards taking more than a little pressure off when paying rent time came. And finally, for all intents and purposes, I still had control over Cass' money to the tune of thousands of dollars, and if I did dip into that to cover the cost of this new coat, I definitely would pay it back.

On the other hand, that was a slippery slope, so... no. No borrowing from the Hyde account.

Cass would certainly have wanted me to buy a coat with her money, and had been the first person to caution me that I'd need a better one than I'd brought with me. She was right about that. No matter what anyone said about relative seasonal temperatures, winter in Chicago seemed colder than anywhere else I'd been. Factoring in wind-chill was necessary in order to undertake any outing. Wind blasts were unrelenting coming at my face on Michigan Avenue. So it wasn't like I had to rationalize buying one. I determined, without any guilt whatsoever, that I needed to come up with a better winter coat than the one I was still wearing from having been invited to her house nearly five years earlier.

I would need to find a really nice coat in some price range that was reasonable. It didn't have to be inexpensive; I had the funds. But I couldn't go completely bonkers either. I made up my mind to shop very adroitly at the wonderful post-Christmas sales. My goal was to find something utterly fabulous on a budget of two hundred dollars, which, after all, was four times what the original coat had cost.

I started with Saks. Saks Fifth Avenue was my favorite store of all American department stores. In the 1960's and 70's this store epitomized for me the pinnacle of having "made it" in life. It had the highest of the high end, and it had less expensive things, too, but still with great style and chic. It was rare in those days that I could ever really afford to shop there; but the few Saks items I did own lasted forever and were well loved. So I headed straight for the coat department and to the sales rack.

And there I saw it-- my dream coat: a Fleurette, camel colored seventy percent Italian wool and cashmere blend "boy" coat, with a wide-lapel collar and square pockets, belted. It was so beautiful I had to stifle a squeal. And it was in my size, which was even more surprising since this coat was generally seen on taller women, and indeed, trying it on, I worried that it would be way too long for me to look right in it. But by some miracle, the proportions were correct. I stared at myself in it. Already right in the store I could tell that the coat itself would be toasty warm, maybe even too warm! But the actual weight was not untoward. I could wear it without feeling as though it were wearing me.

So finally I mustered up the courage to look at the tag, which, perhaps someone else would have done before they tried it on and fell instantly in love with it. Shit. Two hundred eighty-nine dollars and ninety-five cents marked down from five hundred fifty. My God, five hundred dollars for a coat. That was two months' rent in a place I wouldn't have been able to afford anyhow, having been hoping to find a studio for around two hundred, when I did start looking in earnest. And that was also ninety dollars over my self-imposed limit, I reminded myself.

But I had to have it. I just blithely promised myself I would scrimp for the next however- long-it-took to make up the difference, and, I also realized, let's not kid ourselves here, that it wasn't out of the realm of possibility for me to have to get a second job. I could certainly wait tables or work behind the soda fountain at Woolworths if push came to shove. I could be an evening hostess at some restaurant like I'd done my whole life. I had skills, and for all intents and purposes, my evenings were free since I rarely took papers home from the office. Rationalizing complete, I decided I could buy the coat.

There was a Saks saleswoman on the floor, but she hadn't really been paying any attention to me. I took the lovely bounty up to the desk and then she snapped to attention.

"That is one gorgeous coat, " she said, taking it from me.

"You know, I think I'd like to wear it, " I suddenly heard myself announcing. "Do you suppose you could put this one in the bag for me instead?" And I handed her my old coat.

"Certainly, " she said, doing her very best to act like she could touch my old one and not get cooties.

"Oh my God," I thought, heading back down the escalator to the main floor, feeling that softness against my neck, and knowing it looked not like two hundred or five hundred but a million dollars. I was Princess Grace in my mind. Of course I needed better boots—maybe "riding ones"—black with brown tops. Whoa! Nothing doing on all counts! My same stupid boots would have to last awhile longer.

When it was time to get ready for the party, I carefully laid Cass' jumper out on the day bed while I bathed and did my makeup and hair. I had sent Cass to the hairdressers in Iowa City, but truth be told, I should have gone with her. My stick-straight hair needed trimming, too, and the idea of styling it was anathema to me. I either wore it "down" with the black velvet Paris head band; tied back into a low ponytail with a ribbon; or half up and half down, secured with a barrette or a bow. And always, bangs. I could cut my own bangs, but I didn't dare take the scissors to the rest of my hair myself. And even though curling irons had been invented almost a century earlier and perfected in 1959 by—who else— two Frenchmen, I didn't own a modern one, nor did I ever sleep in rollers. But it sure would have been nice, I thought that afternoon, if I'd made some effort to have a few tendrils, a little curly top knot, anything that made me look at least a bit worthier of wearing Chanel. I decided on half up and half down with a black velvet bow this time. I thought I came off Gigi-esque and that would suffice.

I took a taxi to d'Arivèque's house for the mere selfish reason that I didn't want to sit on the bus in my new coat and Cass' amazing outfit. Just my luck, I had worried, someone would sit down and spill coffee on me; or I'd be standing at the bus stop and get splashed. And even though snow threatened, I was wearing the Harrod's shoes rather than boots this time. I couldn't be expected to walk in those shoes through slush and snow from the bus stop all the way to Lake Shore. Excuses, excuses.

I hadn't wanted to be there first, so I made it a point to arrive—not late---not even fashionably late, but just a bit past four o'clock, so as to join others going in. As the cab pulled up, I really expected to see a line of cars heading to the underground garage, and certainly a few other stragglers gathered around the front door. But no one was there. I paid the driver and got out as panic swept over me. Did I have the wrong date, for chrissake? *Le Saint Sylvestre* is New Year's Eve, so that was right. Had I misread the time?

That was always possible. I began to doubt myself and doubting made me angry at myself. What if I really had fucked this up?

I rang the bell with trepidation. No one answered in person, but the intercom came on and it was Jean-Paul d'Arivèque's voice! What the hell??

"*Bonjour*, Sarah, I shall buzz you in. Please take the elevator to the *deuxième, d'accord?*"

"Yes, thank you, " I answered timidly, but did so.

The elevator door opened into the foyer with which I was familiar by then, and there he stood, waiting for me. No maids, no butlers, no Robineau (thank God), just him. He was dressed in an honest-to-goodness smoking jacket in dark maroon, piped in black satin. It did not look like a pajama top or a robe, but was, nonetheless, of that ilk. He wore the palest pink silk shirt opened at the collar, no tie of course, and soft navy pants that looked like the same wool and cashmere as my new prized possession.

I took off my coat and laid it gingerly over a settee in the hallway. He couldn't take it from me, and I didn't know where there was a closet to hang it in anyway. He smiled warmly at me and said I looked "lovely." I blushed a little, I suppose, half expecting him to say something like, "Where in the world did you get that dress" but he didn't say anything of the sort.

I then asked haltingly, " I'm not....like, you know...the first person to arrive, am I?" I sort of glanced fervently around him and down the hall into the reception room.

"As a matter of fact, *effectivement*, you are the only guest."

"Excuse me?!"

"Does this distress you, Sarah? I perhaps should have asked you in a different way? I hope you do not think I used false pretenses to get you here."

"I'm not distressed, *Monsieur*."

"Do you think you could call me Polo?"

"I...uh... well, but...surely not in the office!" I gave out a nervous little laugh. "Not Jean-Paul?"

"Well, yes, Jean-Paul if you prefer. However, all my friends call me Polo."

As if I hadn't noticed.

"But I'm your employee."

"And also my friend? "

I smiled up at him. "Yes, also your friend." And then I added, "Thank you." *That sounded awkward!*

"And how was your holiday with your friends? Did the children of Cass like all those things you brought them, *Tante Père Noël?*"

"Yes, they did. It was great. The lamb was a big hit. And you should have seen Paul with that train! He loved it. The dolls didn't go over real big, but later on when they read them the Raggedy Ann books, I think they'll dig it."

" Ah, very good," he said, " it sounds like it was a great success. "

" I think so. We all had a fun time being back together, too."

So," he continued, "shall we go into the library? I have something to show you."

"Sure."

"*Je vous en prie, "*he gestured to me to go ahead, but I really didn't know exactly where it was from our meeting point.

"Oh, " he said realizing my predicament. "*Par ici*. This way."

We by-passed the formal reception I'd been in so often before, with the Versailles-type antique furniture, and, as we walked together down the long corridor, I thought I again perceived him to be limping even more pronounced than usual; however, I couldn't see his face to tell if he were in pain. When we got to a junction in the hall, he stopped, touched my arm lightly and nodded that this was where we went inside.

I knew I'd been in the library once previously, at one of the dinner parties, and we had gone past it on several other occasions the way to other rooms, too, but I knew I could have never found it by myself. I did remember how much I loved the room. It was a very ornate and tastefully decorated room with, to my delight, real furniture and not museum pieces!

The focal point was an enormous Chesterfield sofa with deep leather tufts that were soft and comfortable. The room had two walls with floor to ceiling bookshelves, and a ladder on a track, like you

441

see in movies, to use in obtaining books from them. One wall was windows and French doors leading out onto the terrace, which encircled the entire back of the house that faced Lake Michigan. Heavy, white silk brocade draperies were pulled open and secured with thick braided tassel cords. The fourth wall was made up entirely of beautiful pickled wood cabinetry that housed professional audio-video equipment built into the storage units. Four of the pocket doors of that part were opened to reveal a screen that had to be forty feet wide. I didn't realize it, at first, but a projector unit was behind the sofa set up on a table.

I found myself gasping as I turned almost three hundred sixty degrees to look at the entire expanse of space.

There were also distinctly delineated conversation areas in this room due to its gigantic size. One cluster had leather club chairs around a round table with pretty brass lamps and a magazine rack. Another one had wing-back chairs in the same silk as the drapes, with a square glass and wood coffee table, similar to what was in front of the Chesterfield sofa. The corner of the room housed a completely stocked bar, and the end closest to the hallway had two narrow but ornate mahogany writing desks with identical leather desk pads and Tiffany style lamps on them.

"Gosh," I managed to get out, "this room is so pretty."

Oh! You couldn't come up with anything more eloquent than that?!

But the thing that really caught my eye in there was over at the window…a small table with a most beautifully decorated Christmas tree. It was typically French to have a table-top-sized tree, and this one was perfectly shaped and smelled as wonderful as any tree three times its size. The lights on the tree were only white ones, and the ornaments placed nearest to them caught their bright reflection. The sun was already setting at four-thirty in the afternoon, and the tree dazzled in the fading dusk at the window.

"That's one exquisite Christmas tree!" I exclaimed to my host. "Gads, those ornaments! They are spectacular! Are they your family collection?"

"That is exactly what they are, you are right. Maman had them sent over from France after the war, and she had the staff put them up every year. I keep her tradition."

When I got closer to them, I saw that these were not the normal ornaments most people had, but crystal, as in Crystal Saint Louis, Lalique and Baccarat. Some of the clear ones I found out later were Waterford. His mother evidently wasn't completely chauvinistic. A few of the ornaments were not crystal, but bone china figurines, like delicate ballerinas and a little white train trimmed in gold and decorated with red roses, which was tied onto the tree with a ribbon that said Royal Albert. Even the garlands were glass beads.

Jean-Paul placed his cane in his left hand so he could reach up with his good arm, take one down, and hold it up to me. It was a red Eiffel Tower made of sparkly filigree metal with encrusted crystals all over it. "I got her this one in 1938. Papa took me to *Boucheron* in Paris. Do you know it? On *Rue de la Paix*?"

"I've never been in there, but… um, yeah, I know where it is, " I laughed. I'd walked through *Place Vendôme* many times and had heard of all the jewelers that had their shops and *ateliers* there: *Cartier, Van Cleef et Arpels, Boucheron, Piaget, Chaumet*. Not places where I would have ever had a reason to cross the thresholds.

"Would you like to hang it back on the tree? Perhaps you can find a better spot for it."

"Oh! I'd better not." I gestured to him to not hand it to me. " Be just my luck to drop it or something. Your ornaments are certainly not the run of the mill kind. Every one of them looks like it could be a priceless, breakable heirloom."

He took my hand and placed the little Eiffel Tower into my palm. Then he said, "Here, I will hold onto you and you choose the spot. We shall both place it." So I found a branch where, if we hung the ornament near the tip it would look like it was suspended in mid-air and the crystals would catch the light even more.

"*Voilà*," he said.

"It's really the prettiest Christmas tree I've ever laid eyes on," I repeated, feeling a twinge of disloyalty to Cass.

I was still marveling at the tree when the other two doors of the library were opened and a man and woman rolled a long table inside. It was covered in a white cloth and had a pretty centerpiece that looked like a Victorian house decorated on the outside for Christmas.

442

"*Merci bien*, Martine, " Jean-Paul called out, and then turned back to me, "That is for our dinner later. I shall explain to you."

We walked over to the table as Martine, in a white chef outfit with the high shoulder buttons and her name embroidered on the breast pocket, and Léonard-- either her helper or an actual sous-chef, I couldn't tell--brought the table to a halt near the bar, and began uncovering and arranging the dishes and platters on it.

"I have given almost all the staff today off, " he said, "but Martine and Léonard, here, graciously agreed to stay on tonight. They have prepared us some nice, simple things to sort of…partake in as the evening goes on."

"Umm, nosh? That's actually my favorite."

He laughed again. "Yes, noshing … as you say…that is precisely what this is. I asked for only cold buffet, to cut down a bit on their work, you see."

I saw, but it didn't look like any effort had been spared.

Martine finished setting up the food and Léonard put serving tongs, fish forks, and various spoons and spatulas in their appointed places.

"*Bonne Année, Monsieur, Mademoiselle!*" Martine wished him and me.

"*À vous aussi, vous deux.*"

"*Bonne Année,* " I mimicked, adding, "It looks…wow… fantastic," realizing as soon as I'd said it that that was the understatement of the evening, since it really looked more like a magazine photo spread of some New Year's Eve party for fifty.

The feature of this evening of "snacking," and the item that took center stage nearest the Victorian house, would be the required French *Réveillon* staple: oysters on the half shell, which, even though I had tried to learn to like them in Paris, I just couldn't eat. Luckily there were so many other choices that I would have no trouble at all finding sustenance. Two big platters buried in ice contained peeled shrimp, whelks, crab legs, and lobster tails, all open and ready to eat, with small ramekins tilting on the edge filled with cocktail sauces, and a larger one over a flame of canned heat that contained melted butter. There were also lightly seared scallops with their beautiful orange coral, and steamed cockles and mussels. The buffet also held a plate of *paté de fois gras* and *baguette*, a whole smoked salmon with lemon and capers, cheese boards, and, at the far end with a coffee carafe, was a tray of mini French pastries of all sorts.

Sensing perhaps, my astonishment that so much food was put out for just the two of us, Jean-Paul explained that houseguests would be arriving the following week from France, and none of the food we didn't consume would be thrown out. There would be a cocktail reception for them, he explained, and that would take care of any excess. He didn't have to justify himself to me, but I was glad food wasn't going to be merely tossed out.

"I have something to show you, and then I thought we might watch a film together. I brought one in for the evening. Even though you have already seen it , I thought you would not mind."

I looked up, "Oh?"

"*Interlude.* It came highly recommended…by you, *n'est-ce pas?*"

"Yes!" *Far out. I wondered how he got ahold of a copy of that!*

He smiled. "Good! So first, would you help me take something from the shelves? *Venez*, Sarah. And he gestured for me to follow. He led me over to the wall behind the bar where the shelving was enclosed in glass-doored cabinets. "Do you see the box standing amidst the books…there? Could you bring it down and over to the sofa?"

I reached up to the ornate door knob, opened the door and took down the box. It was rather heavy. I carried it over to the couch and we both sat down. There was a coffee table in front of the Chesterfield and just enough space between them for Jean-Paul to be able to seat himself, unlock the brace, and pull his leg up. I sat on his right and laid the box on the table.

"Could you open it, please?"

Even though I didn't know what the box contained, I got the distinct impression that it might be fragile or very valuable. I lifted the lid off and there was a large book inside, looking somewhat like a strange photo album. But the pages were not filled with pictures; rather they were separated with vellum, like many French albums are, and in between those pages were sketches, some in watercolor and some in graphite.

"OH! My God!"

I stared at the album, astonished. What I was seeing were pages from *Le Petit Prince*. Not just any pages, but hand-drawn original illustrations for the book. Some looked familiar, and other seemed not to have been used in any edition I'd ever seen, at least.

When I glanced initially at the first one, I turned a bit on the couch in order to face him better, and blurted out, "Jeez, did you buy these at some art auction or something?"

"Look a little further."

I turned over another piece of vellum and the picture of the prince in his green outfit, on watercolor paper this time, was signed "*Pour Polo-- et à ton amical souvenir, St. Ex.*"

Simply flabbergasted, I looked back up at him and managed to mutter, "But... how can this be?"

"It is why I wanted to invite you tonight. I want to tell you my story."

Chapter Seventy-Six

*Gnossienne No. 1...*Erik Satie

Thus we sat in the library, and as it became dark outside, he asked me to go around the room and turn on the lamps. The light from them was subdued, not bright, but rather shimmering, and as they came on, the Christmas tree seemed to give off even more glow. I went back over to the sofa, and leafed anew through the drawings of *Le Petit Prince*, feeling guilty that I was touching them without wearing the white gloves an archivist would if handling precious pages. Sitting right beside him, though, was not optimal for listening to the story. I was in no position to kick off my shoes and curl up on the end of the couch and face him, so I got up and pulled one of the little desk chairs across to the sofa and sat facing him.

Jean-Paul d'Arivèque began at the beginning with his autobiographical rendering of how he came to be the owner of these works of art, and it entailed going back to his childhood in France.

By his own admission, Jean-Paul as a little boy, lived a very privileged and sweet life, typical of a "certain aristocratic stratum" of the French population, especially in pre-war France. He was an only child, which was not especially typical in a Catholic family, but wasn't due to any lack of desire for many children on the part of his parents. His mother "couldn't seem to carry a baby to term," before finally getting pregnant with him and somehow staying pregnant. It meant that even before he was born, he was a very special baby in the entire extended family. He would one day be the sole heir to a fortune so vast, he was unsure if I could even comprehend the amounts, which, he explained, he didn't really want to elucidate for fear of my thinking he was boastful. I assured him that I understood his wealth was significant just by working at the Foundation, and he took that as an acceptable rejoinder, even though he knew I didn't have a clue. Wealthy French people rarely spoke about money in any case.

His idyllic childhood included a very comfortable, yet not ostentatious apartment on the Rue Madame *in the* sixième *near enough to Luxembourg Gardens that he could play there any time his nanny or governess-- and often times, his mother-- took him. His paternal grandparents, on the other hand, had a magnificent home on the* Parc Monceau, *which was the ducal seat in Paris.*

"I spent many happy hours there, too, with *Mamie* and *Grand-Père*. Our own apartment in Paris belonged to my mother's side of the family. She was more at home there."

He went to l'école maternelle, primaire et élémentaire privée catholique *run by the Jesuits, and was on the preparatory road to the* Lycée St. Louis *which would, as I knew, send him directly on the path to the* Grandes Écoles *after that. There was no school on Wednesdays, and often he didn't go on Saturday mornings even if they did have class, because the family tended to leave Friday after school by train or car for their* résidence secondaire,*"a manor house, we would call it, not a* château," *(but as I would see later, of course it was a* château!*) near the town of Vierzon, with the Sologne forest bordering the property. The house had twelve bedrooms but he described it as intimate and welcoming, a perfect place for a little boy to grow up in the happy company of friends and extended family, his closest relatives being cousins on his mother's side, who lived in a* château *of their own less than an hour away in the other direction from the town.*

By the time he was ten years old, there were no other family left in France on his father's side, and yet the country house, which they had named La Pérégrine *when it was built in 1764, was the d'Arivèque family seat. In fact, it was the ancestral seat of the Dukes of* Beuvron, *but the current duke, his uncle Charles, made his actual home in Geneva, Switzerland, where, for all intents and purposes, he ran the family business, a conglomerate of shipping, banking, money management, real estate and art collecting. Because Uncle Charles and his wife Aunt Madeleine, themselves had had only one son, who had been killed in a tragic car crash in the Alps in 1948, Polo's father would have been the rightful heir to the title and the fortune had he, too, not died.*

(I had to admit I was rather stunned to listen to all this business about the *Duc de Beuvron* and all, and remembered that someone I met at one point had referred to Jean-Paul with a title. However, I think I sort of repressed that thought. I decided not to bring it up there.)

"The death of my cousin Thiéry precipitated that of his mother," Jean-Paul said softly. "She passed away in 1950, I think from the great grief and a broken heart. Uncle Charles never remarried."

"Do you ever see him?" I asked.

"Oh, yes. I would like to see him more than I do, it is true. He is in his eighties now, into *'la troisième âge'*, so I should make more of an effort because I dearly love him. He has been to Chicago quite often. Most of the time we meet in Paris."

"Uncle Charles, " he continued, "was the reason there was even a fortune left to the d'Arivèque family, because he was—and is-- the steward of the entire dynasty, the caretaker and, more importantly, savior of it during the war. I was still in elementary school of course, at nine years old, when things began to deteriorate for France."

The family were still going about their merry ways in Paris and at La Pérégrine *on the weekends and holidays, but even at such a young age, Jean-Paul could sense that his parents were over-wrought. There was a lot of hushed talking taking place among the household. For one thing, Uncle Charles, who had an earlier perception of what was happening in Germany and other parts of Europe than the French side of the family did, summoned his younger brother to Geneva to discuss the family holdings.*

"When Papa returned, he announced that we were to empty out the two Paris apartments as well as *La Pérégrine*, and ship everything to Geneva! This would be a massive endeavor because we had to pack up most of the furnishings---anything of value---and the art, all family jewelry and the antiquities. He told my father to have the family stay, however, but not live in Paris."

"So... your uncle was tuned in to more of the political stuff going on than your father was?" I wondered.

"Exactly. And it was he who suggested that my father would want to work for General De Gaulle. You see, my father's other brother, the one who was killed in World War I, knew De Gaulle when they were fighting in the Battle of Verdun. De Gaulle was older and a senior officer; my uncle Jean-François was a newly-commissioned officer, and much younger. He was, however, in command of a unit under De Gaulle, and it sustained quite a rout. De Gaulle was injured and subsequently taken prisoner of war. My uncle was killed outright. After the war, *"le Grand Charles"* as my family called him, paid a visit to my grandparents at *La Pérégrine* and spoke kindly of his young *protégé*, Jean-François. That had endeared him, of course, to my grandparents."

In fact, his Uncle Charles, who had contacts in cities all over the world, started hearing rumblings of German aggression far before the Nazis actually invaded Poland in September of 1939. He had many university contacts and friends in the arts world who were either being summarily kicked out of their positions or making plans to flee when they saw what was happening to their colleagues and friends. Charles feared early on that Germany would invade France, and brought his brother back to Geneva to discuss plans to evacuate the Jewish employees and their families to Switzerland from all the offices in harm's way: Paris, Lyon, Marseilles, Toulon, the Côte d'Azur.

"So, did your family business have a lot of Jews employed in it?"

"Not a large number, no, but my father felt, and he was right, that every worker we had was integral to the entire operation. We had also found some jobs, at that point, for several Jewish refugees from more recently menaced countries like Poland. It turned out that they would be the most in danger."

*Jean-Paul's father could travel fairly freely right up to and even during the occupation, it turned out. Besides knowing people in high places, which never hurt, he was a well-known intellectual and businessman who was the typical "citizen above suspicion," and, as such, the perfect kind of recruit for the Resistance. The **real** Resistance.*

"After the war, of course, everyone and his brother---and mother, father, sister, et al., were in the *Résistance*," he scoffed, making air quotes. "Or else collaborators. The truth lies somewhere in between. We French were neither all Resistance fighters nor all *collabos*. But there were, *évidemment*, some of each."

The parents took their young son out of school in Paris, as Charles had advised, and closed up their family apartment there in late 1939. The school would soon be shuttered anyway, and they were more than anxious to move out of the city and to the perceived safety of La Pérégrine. *Many of the household staff served them in both places, but some servants who only worked in the Paris apartment, had families they couldn't leave.*

"*Maman* was especially upset and fearful of an outright German invasion, as she saw horrible things happening, such as the formation of the Black Market, which she and my father found especially *honteux*—shameful."

Soon, as in Germany, Jewish professionals would be fired and stripped of their positions in France, and one of those people was a good friend of the d'Arivèques who taught philosophy at Lycée Henri IV, *a man named Gabriel*

Schwartz. His students would actually join a student league of the Résistance, les Volonaires de la Liberté, *but the Schwartz family would have fled before that happened.*

One day shortly before Jean-Paul and his parents were to leave Paris, Madame Schwartz appeared at the door of the apartment, nervous and upset. She and the professor were trying to get to Portugal, she said, and thence to America or even South America, but they didn't have enough funds.

"*Maman* was only too anxious to help this lady, " Jean-Paul said, "and right away offered her money. But *Madame* Schwartz demurred. What she had in mind instead was to sell my mother her jewelry."

"Oh dear, " I said.

"This was not uncommon. What was different, however, was that she came to us---a private family-- to sell it. She must not have trusted anyone at that point. *Alors*, of course my mother had a large and valuable collection of her own jewels handed down for five generations on both sides, but as a matter of principle, naturally, she offered *Madame* Schwartz as much as she could convince her to take, saying that after the war she would find her and give her jewelry back!"

"So you were there and witnessed all this?" I asked, imagining him as a schoolboy with no real comprehension of what was happening in the world.

"I was there when *Maman* greeted her at the door, but then they went into our study for privacy, and I did not accompany them. When she left, though, *Madame* Schwartz was weeping, I could see it."

"And after the war did your mother find her?"

"My mother, as it happens, looked diligently for them-- and several other families-- after the war. She had many resources at her disposal. It took quite a while but in the end she did find the records on the Schwartzes. They had, it seems, escaped before the roundup of *Vel d'hiv*—you know of it?"

"Yes."

I had indeed learned of the mass arrests in Paris and imprisonment of Jews in the *Vélodrome d'Hiver* on the *Rue Nélaton*, with subsequent deportation to the French concentration camp in a suburb called Drancy before being hauled off-- mostly to Auschwitz.

"Sarah, " he said solemnly, looking straight at me, "the round-up of Jews in Paris—all the women and children—was abominable, and when my parents found out about it, they were truly horrified. My mother was actually overcome, once the truth came out about it. Yes, it was under Nazi orders, but make no mistake, French officials carried them out. But it took place in June of 1942, and by that time *Maman* and I were in New York, and we had been there for six months already. I shall get to that shortly, here in my story."

"And did the Schwartzes make it out?"

"Well, it seems they got to near the Loire Valley, but must have been denounced or turned in somehow by *collabos*. They died in Auschwitz."

"But how did your mother know they were those Schwartzes? That's a pretty common Jewish-- and German-- name, for that matter."

"Yes, but the two given names matched—Gabriel and Sophie-- and the records showed deportation from Pithiviers on a certain date that seems to suggest they must have tried to stay and find refuge in France rather than going to Portugal. I am not exactly sure of the circumstances of their flight."

In 1940 fully one sixth of the French population took to the road in a futile attempt to flee invading German troops. In Paris, Jean-Paul's father suspected the Germans would shutter his business and take it over, as they were doing with the assets of many wealthy families, which was why he had taken the advice of his uncle, and shifted most of his operations to Geneva almost a year before the actual invasion. Jean-Paul's mother was afraid soldiers were going to expect to be billeted in their country house, which was located just to the south of the River Cher, the demarcation line between the Zone Occupé *and the* Zone Libre *at the start of the occupation. But they were spared that, although many families'* châteaux *and country houses were not.*

"My father, like my uncle, had studied law, and he was also greatly interested in history all his life. He had also amassed a coterie of important intellectuals and artists, as well as engineers and international business contacts---our family business started out as shipping before the French Revolution---- which was what helped make him a valuable asset himself to De Gaulle and the *Résistance*. Charles De Gaulle would not accept the German takeover of France and neither would my parents. *Maman*, especially, detested the Vichy government, and both, as I said, hated the black market. Some people said the black market was an act of resistance because it certainly went against Vichy policies. But my father dismissed that. The hypocritical Vichy government condemned it out of one side of their mouths, but recognized the necessity of its existence and even participated in it. German soldiers were also willing participants. *Papa* was completely disgusted."

"You know, I never learned anything about the real black market during my schooling. But I did watch one of the films in our collection, *La Grande Vadrouille*, and saw some of it depicted in that."

"Both of my parents, but most pointedly my mother, were terribly *déçus* –fed up with the French at that point---people denouncing each other---not just once in a while, but often. Women were also very culpable. Households hid their provisions and people became suspicious and stingy. *Maman* told me later that she could see how accusations became a tool, just as they had during the French Revolution. There was an incident in a *château* near us where women working in the kitchen were conducting affairs with German soldiers quartered there. *Papa* was just as outraged at this as *Maman*. He proclaimed these sordid events as anti-French and a betrayal of our entire nation."

It was true, however, that the countryside didn't suffer as much as the urban centers with their lack of food and other provisions. Yes, some farmers prospered on the black market, but it was dangerous and risky to be a supplier and there were severe penalties if you got caught doing it. Nevertheless, an intolerance grew among people living in cities against peasants and farmers. Urbanites imagined their rural counterparts to be in possession of an enormous wealth of supplies, which cultivated a simmering overlay of distrust and suspicion.

"Money was the best answer for survival under the Occupation, " Jean-Paul told me. "The right amount of money made anything possible, even when France was plagued with nationwide scarcity. The price was high, but those with money still had access to goods if they were willing to pay."

Jean-Paul's parents tried to maintain a semblance of normalcy at La Pérégrine, but for the most part, Marie-Aveline was running the place on her own. Georges-Henri, once in contact with General De Gaulle in London, had to absent himself often from the little family huddled in their now-stripped-down country manor house.

"*Maman* was glad to have me there, though, because she was deathly afraid I could have been exposed to diphtheria, which was rampant in Paris at that time, as were tuberculosis and influenza."

I asked more about his everyday life in the countryside during the Occupation. He told me he was taught at home rather than enrolled in the local school, with tutors arriving in the morning for two to three hours, and then again at two o'clock for three more in the afternoon. Sometimes the tutors were invited for lunch with him. Even though there was an acute shortage of many foodstuffs in the shops, it did work out that the farms near La Pérégrine could still be counted upon to provide some dairy products and vegetables. White flour was scarcest, and the French population did not like eating rye bread, or "dark bread" as they called it. But any bread was better than none at all, and Madame d'Arivèque insisted that dark bread would do just fine.

"All raw goods went to the German war effort, so paper mills, fabric manufacturers, furniture plants and other factories shut down for lack of materials. We had to register our cars and could barely drive anywhere since the petrol — *euh*-- gasoline rations were so strict. Making do, you know, was the order of the day. There were no cigarettes — no tobacco was left in many cities. I would see the adults making their own cigarettes from dried grasses and herbs. They called it '*système D*' for '*débrouiller*'. And no sugar! To replace sugar, our clever cook used liquorice and boiled pumpkins. She even made a sort of coffee from acorns, substituting for the coffee beans — that is until my father would show up with wonderful packages under his arm from England or Switzerland. I do not even know to this day where he got the marvelous things he managed to bring us."

"Did you have pets at the country house?" I asked him. "And what did you feed them?!"

"We did have a dog...she was a chocolate lab called Medea. But she was really *Papa's* dog and not my pet. I had horses. I am actually not sure what the dog ate...perhaps scraps from our kitchen, and the like. But my horses ate grass, mainly. Hay if our stable hands could procure it."

"You rode, then? Were you good at it?"

"I'd been riding since I was five years old! First ponies and then my horses. I really took to it, yes. My favorite horse was a blond palomino I called Corneille."

"Corneille? Like the author?"

448

"Precisely. We were studying his works when I got the horse, so I took that name, " he chuckled remembering his childhood logic. "It is amusing, no? A majestic name for a very tall horse."

"But my **God**, you were reading Corneille as a little kid? I struggled through it at the Sorbonne."

Unfortunately, his last memories of the equine Corneille were not happy ones.

"My father was due to come home in December for Christmas of 1941. I was very excited at this prospect, even as I had no idea if he could find anything in any shops to bring us as presents, or if we would have *Le Réveillon* as usual with any of the foods we loved. *Maman* did not have a precise time we would expect to see him. In fact, we did not even know how he was getting there... if by car or train or on foot. I decided to set out on Corneille to meet him in the road. But of course, I was not sure where he would be. Our property, as I mentioned, was on the edge of the Sologne forest, so I decided to cut through there a bit, and ride a shorter route to the train station. But it was late afternoon and the light was dimming. *Maman* did not really want me to go out, but she realized my excitement was brimming over, and since it was soon Christmas, she knew how much I anticipated seeing *Papa*. I rode off, and had not gone too far when a loud boom rang out."

"Oh no! What was it? The Resistance blowing up train lines or something?'

"*Mais, non,* " he chuckled at my naïveté. "Yes that happened...mostly in films...but this was more like a car backfiring. Corneille reared up and...I fell off. "

"Oh. God."

"His front hoofs also came down on me, first on my shoulder and then on my leg, crushing me. I was lucky he didn't land on my head, eh?"

Jean-Paul thought he must have passed out from the pain. His horse was unhurt and, like one would expect in this situation, easily found its way back to La Pérégrine. When the stable groom saw the rider-less horse return, he knew immediately something had gone terribly wrong. They got together a search party headed up by his mother, took lanterns and set out on foot. Eventually they heard an approaching motor, and flagged down the only car on the road, which, as hoped for, was Georges-Henri heading home. Both parents were sick with worry, and all thoughts of a happy holiday homecoming were set aside. The only thing that mattered was finding their little boy in a forest dark as pitch looming ominously before them.

Jean-Paul's mother had recounted the story to him many times. They stayed pretty close to the road in their search, and it wasn't too long past the entrance to the forest proper that they heard moaning, and followed the sounds. They found him still lying in a mass of bramble bushes and pine needles, and they saw at once that he was badly hurt.

"*Maman* said she was scared to death to lift me, but what could they do? They had to get me somewhere near to where a doctor could see me, so they decided to take me home and call the local doctor to come. Most of the younger physicians in France were called up, or else had left to join the Free French. Our village doctor was too old for any type of conscription. We were just lucky he was there."

The country doctor was not at all optimistic about what he saw; he was, however, a good doctor and examined the patient thoroughly. He told the parents he had some morphine he could give, but that Jean-Paul needed to have x-rays taken to determine the damage, and even after that, he himself would not be able to operate. They needed to see surgeons and specialists. At that point he was already suggesting Lyon or even Geneva. Georges-Henri decided to call his brother Charles and talk it over with him, but time was of the essence, so they packed Jean-Paul gently into the car and drove to Vierzon, the closest hospital. The doctor came along.

"X-rays showed multiple fractures and crushed bones, " said Jean-Paul. "My shoulder and arm were placed in a sling just to hold them stable. There wasn't anything they could do for that. They finished by putting my leg in a sort of temporary cast--just so I could be transported elsewhere."

But where? The next day the call came back from Uncle Charles in Geneva. He told them his inquiries disclosed the best doctors to operate on such an immensely complicated case were in New York at Mount Sinai hospital.

"Oh, my God, " I said, realizing this must have been how he came to America. But had he stayed all this time since he was twelve years old? "What about you at that point? Were you in agony?"

"*Remarque,* Sarah, I do not remember much of that—the injury. I do recall weeping constantly...probably from pain. I remember *Maman* burrowing her body over me to console me. She was always there beside me."

With that *dénouement* in his story he looked up at me, smiled, and wondered whether or not I was getting hungry.

449

"Come, " he said, "I shall show you where you can freshen up and we shall begin dinner. "Could you please lend me your hand for a moment to help me up?"

I offered my arm and he struggled a bit to right himself. "I can neither sit in one spot nor stand for a very long time, " he said with a little sigh of resignation in his voice.

As for me, I was only too eager to know where the bathroom might be in that part of the house, since I still had lingering nightmares of searching down endless corridors that fateful time back in July. The thought crossed my mind that he remembered it, too.

Chapter Seventy-Seven

"Man Without a Dream"...The City (Carole King)

When I thankfully found my way back to the library, I was a little bit surprised to see that Martine and Léonard had returned, ready to serve us. I should have figured it out: we couldn't eat buffet style unless I carried both plates over to the sofa to sit, and even then---very awkward. No, it made infinitely more sense for them to create a seating area at the end of the long table on wheels, and for us to use the library desk chairs to sit there. Actually, I did get to take my own plate and chose what I wanted from among, let's face it, every single thing I loved spread out right before me. While Martine served her boss, Léonard popped open the first of the champagne. I made sure to avail myself of a lot of Evian water on the table, too. The seafood was so delicious I nearly swooned. I hadn't gained the freshman fifteen in Iowa City, but I sure could see myself doing it in Chicago.

It was still early, even though darkness had long since spread out over the lake, and the terrace outside the library doors was twinkling with lights that decorated evergreen trees in low square crates. Jean-Paul wanted us to have dessert back on the sofa so Martine set up coffee and all the fixings plus the pastry tray and more champagne over on the table where I'd put the box of *Petit Prince* drawings.

"Shall I continue my story?" he asked rather rhetorically, since we hadn't even gotten to the part about the illustrations, that I realized had to be coming.

"Oh, yes," I said, getting comfortable beside him this time, so I could also drink coffee.

When x-rays had been taken in the small-town hospital, his parents took him back home, along with the films. Nothing more could be done for him there besides the cast for his leg and a sling for temporary stability of his left arm and shoulder.

Back at La Pérégrine, they waited frantically while his father and uncle in Switzerland devised a strategy for them to leave France. A plan developed that Uncle Charles would arrange all transportation and Georges-Henri would get the mass of necessary paperwork done, with a little help from every diplomat either of them knew in Switzerland, England and France, using even the aegis of De Gaulle if it came to that. They would go to New York via Lisbon. Owning a shipping dynasty came in handy when one needed a boat, and Uncle Charles procured a trawler out of Arcachon that would sail them to the Portuguese capital. From there they would take the Pan Am Clipper to New York.

"You needed exit visas from France, transit visas for Spain and the Portuguese entry visa, which sometimes depended on having already booked transportation out of the country. *Papa* also got several more sets of visas and papers, having decided that more of our household staff should accompany us and help *Maman*. You see, once in Lisbon, he could not go with us to New York."

"Why ever not?" I asked astounded that the mother would have been faced with making this daunting trip on her own, and arriving in New York with no one to greet her or see her through.

"He was being called back to London. When he came home that night of the accident, it was only to have been here for two or three days—just to have Christmas holidays with the family. He had to rejoin De Gaulle."

But it turned out that there was quite a French ex-pat contingent already in New York, and by the time they got there, Uncle Charles would have arranged letters of introduction for Marie-Aveline. Not only that, but she had some friends in New York who had been working there for years, and even though she hadn't seen them in a good long while, she still felt she could look them up.

"But in reality, we met someone in Lisbon who was a great help. I shall get to that part shortly, " he said.

Jean-Paul's mother knew she would need to travel light. Even with help, she would either be carrying her own suitcase or pushing her son in a make-shift wheelchair or both. Everyone had to be super careful when lifting him, not only because he screamed in pain, but also because of the numerous broken bones that still hadn't been set.

They found the fishing boat in the harbor easily enough, per Uncle Charles' instructions, and the fact that it carried the emblem of the family dynasty on it: the Peregrine Falcon. It flew the flag of France. The boat wasn't tiny but it wasn't a ship either. Jean-Paul could be propped up fairly comfortably below in the cabin, and his parents could administer morphine daily to keep the pain abated. The waters were thankfully calm for December, and the temperatures off the French and Spanish coasts were mild that year, 1941.

Arriving in Lisbon, they found that the city was already becoming a haven for refugees, especially the wealthier Jews who had managed to escape, carrying what, if anything, was left of their lives before things got so desperate in Germany and other places. Getting out of Lisbon wasn't easy, however; lines at all the consulates stretched around whole city blocks. Within two years, Lisbon would be experiencing shortages of every supply, living space, food and everything else, a situation that made for an ugly existence. When the d'Arivèque family arrived, however, because of their money, they could maneuver more easily than the refugees.

"Uncle Charles had booked us into the Aviz Hotel which was a luxurious extravagance at the equivalent of six dollars per week! It was there that we made a much serendipitous acquaintance. A Jewish couple who were both doctors, were in the same hotel as us. The husband was a clinician and the wife a researcher! They were Hermann and Bertha Lowenstein, and they had their little boy Harry with them."

Jean-Paul's father at once saw how he could help these people, and they could help his wife and son, so he quickly changed the visas for the household staff – (who didn't want to go to America anyway, but would have) – to accommodate these two doctors and their child, and also managed to book their passage on the plane to New York.

"They were so grateful, they practically flung themselves at my parents. But also they were doing a great service to us in that they would be able to care for me on the trip, and once in New York, Dr. Lowenstein knew people at Mount Sinai."

The arrangements were already being made from Switzerland by those medical specialists whom Uncle Charles had consulted, but it also meant a great deal to have personal contacts upon arrival.

The Pan Am Clipper was a Boeing 314 sea plane – a flying boat! It was divided into compartments with reclining seats and tables. There was a dining room, and at the very back of the plane was an area of deluxe accommodations called "honeymoon suites," which is where Jean-Paul and his mother rode, with the Lowensteins in compartment six. There were also berths, bathrooms, galleys and crew quarters. The bridge where the pilots' cockpit was could be reached by stairs leading to a level high above the nose of the aircraft. He described it in great detail and I couldn't help thinking what a cool time he would have had on that plane under normal circumstances.

During the plane ride, Dr. Lowenstein administered the pain meds, and checked the little boy's vital signs. He helped Marie-Aveline lift and reposition her son and keep him calm and stable. Bertha and little Harry also visited in the back suite from time to time. Marie-Aveline could not take her son to any dining area for meals, so food was brought to them.

"Harry shared with me some airplane pilot's wings the crew had given him," Jean-Paul mused, "however, I was too knocked out to enjoy anything about the plane ride."

"Did you ever see him again?" I asked.

"As a matter of fact, I saw him quite a lot in New York City through our teen-age years. We have kept in touch."

"That's so cool."

When the plane arrived in New York Harbor and the Lowenstein family helped Marie-Aveline get the boy onto the dock and through customs, an ambulance took all of them to the hospital. The doctors knew the patient would be arriving, and also the fellows Hermann knew were there to greet the party. It was determined when the first surgeries would take place, and then Madame d'Arivèque went to find a hotel near-by to stay until she could look for an apartment. The Lowensteins first went to be with their relatives on the lower East Side, and thus they ended up living far from Jean-Paul; so he and Harry didn't go to the same schools …in fact, Jean-Paul didn't go to any schools until he started high school – almost two years late – at the Lycée Français de New York.

Even though the surgeons who operated on Jean-Paul were those recommended to Uncle Charles, and even though they were among the best in the world, things did not go perfectly. His shoulder's deltoid muscle was pretty much beyond repair and the physical therapy that would ensue for that was tantamount to torture. Jean-Paul d'Arivèque would spend two years in the hospital and another year after that in and out. He had nineteen operations in all.

"I had surgery after surgery to set the bones in my leg, and there was the rather large chance that the two legs would never be the same length, which would cause the limp, of course, but also much pain."

Marie-Aveline stayed in the hotel Chastiagneray for the first two weeks in New York to be very near the hospital, but after that, with introductions and help from various groups of French ex-pats, she found a townhouse on the Upper East Side, and began to make friends. The French in exile in New York during the War were divided into

452

various factions: some were Vichyists, pro-Petain; others – the majority – were pro-De Gaulle. Jean-Paul's mother hated Petain and also Laval, and loathed the way their supporters in New York were so quick to denounce others, just as she had hated that while still in France.

"She felt some of them were even outright *collabos*, " Jean-Paul said. "When my father's friend Raoul Aglion came to New York to beat the drum for De Gaulle, he was stupefied to have to present his credentials and pitch his cause for the General at more than one address. Antoine de Saint- Exupéry was in New York then, and it was he who exasperated Raoul the most, according to my mother. He stubbornly refused to support De Gaulle even while he was staunchly anti-Vichy. *Maman* told me that this was what, *effectivement*, hurt the general's cause the most. Saint-Exupéry was famous already when he arrived in New York, and everyone who was hoping for the United States to enter the war wanted him to help rally the American government behind De Gaulle. But he would not do it."

Marie-Aveline met St. Exupéry several times, at parties, but also, surprisingly, in the hospital. Upon return from a sojourn in Québec, he had suffered from high fevers and had checked himself in to Mt. Sinai. One day he was taking a walk on the ward and in the far corridor near the windows, which had seating in front of them, he recognized Madame d'Arivèque and approached her, shocked to see someone he knew. She explained that her young son had been in the hospital for over a year and it was breaking her heart to see him in such agony. She told him the saga of leaving France through Lisbon, which astonished the famous writer, who explained that he had sailed from the same port on the last day of December, 1940. They were also surprised to learn that they were almost neighbors in an area around Beekman Place where he had moved.

"May I visit your son here?" he had asked her.

"He would like that, " she had responded, thinking of all the aircraft Saint-Exupéry had flown and how interested her boy would be in flight. "Please, do not discuss with him the fact that you do not support De Gaulle, however. His father is an enthusiastic aide-de camp *for the general."*

Thus, the visit took place in Jean-Paul's hospital room, and the famous author brought with him some sheets of onion skin with drawings of Le Petit Prince *lying on his stomach with his feet in the air, and of the birds carrying him off like a kite to explore other worlds.*

"But you didn't really know who he was at that point, " I verified.

"No, not yet. Shortly thereafter *Maman* recounted to me an evening where she was invited by the Swiss writer Denis de Rougemont, who was a great friend of my Uncle Charles, to accompany him to a dinner at the Saint-Exupéry's, at the behest of Saint-Ex, of course. It was winter and the city was having a blackout test. After the meal, Saint-Exupéry assembled all the guests in his study and read *Le Petit Prince* to them from beginning to end. Maman described it as almost magical, as snow fell outside the window, while inside the rooms were all lit by candlelight. It was only mid-way through the reading that his wife arrived for the dinner that had been over for quite some time."

"Did your mother end up ever liking him, though – when she got to know him?"

"Yes, and no. *Maman* characterized him, much later, to me as someone impossible to live with, and she concluded the same was true for Consuelo."

"Gee, I wonder that their marriage worked then, " I said.

"In fact, they did not live together, " Jean-Paul told me, "but had dual penthouse apartments in the same building. They tormented each other and often one or the other did not come home at night. Of course, none of that was of interest to me as a child."

"Well, no, obviously not as a kid. But you liked the book?"

"I, like most people, did not understand the layers of his book until much later, and then his life, with its mounds of personal problems served to provide some background to the meaning of it. We do know that the book was born out of his own despair brought on by, among other things, his conditions of ill health and not being able to fly. Writing this little book was proposed to him by the wife of one of his publishers, Elizabeth Reynal as a sort of therapy, did you know that?"

"No, " I said, pretty stunned at how often I'd studied St. Exupéry and still didn't have all the facts.

"Even when he was at my bedside, he let on that he was experiencing doubts and frustration. He showed me a picture of a baobab tree that he was then currently having problems drawing. He said he was going to have to turn the picture half-way around and start again."

"Incredible, " I said, marveling over a famous author taking an unknown kid into his confidences.

"He came back to my room two more times, and each time he brought me more drawings."

"Did he read you the story, too?"

"Parts of it. I especially wanted to hear about the pilot repairing his own airplane."

"And did he oblige you?"

"Oh, yes, " he laughed, "he loved talking about flight. He was tremendously friendly towards me. We could see that we had something in common, " Jean-Paul, added, finishing his story, "we were both in excruciating pain."

Chapter Seventy-Eight

"Things We Said Today"...Lennon & McCartney

I offered to put the drawings back in their box and return it to the shelf, hoping as I said it, that I could find the place again in the expanse of the books. I opened one of the glass doors and he called from across the room that it was the next one to the right.

"So now you know my story, " he said, as I returned to sit by him, "and how all... **this**... came about." And with that he swept his right arm down his torso.

I nodded, giving a little grimace of recognition and concern. "And since you one time showed me the physical therapy room downstairs, I guess it means that you never get a respite from rehabilitation, do you? Even after thirty years."

"You could say that, " he laughed. "I am not making any further headway, really, but I must continue to have therapy to ward off atrophy and to try to get even minuscule improvements in my arm-- its range of motion. Losing so much deltoid muscle inhibits the lifting of my arm. That as well as axillary nerve damage."

"What about pain?" I dared to ask.

"There is always some pain, *oui*."

"Must be awful, " I said in a hushed tone.

"Sarah, " he said looking at me with a different intensity, "you have never acted at all...well...that is...repulsed by my physical appearance. We have been together many times in public and you just take it in stride, yes?"

"I'm not repulsed. Why would I be? Neither are any of your other friends and people I've met here."

"My friends, no. But many people are afraid to even approach a man who looks like me."

Was that true? I grew up in the era of the polio epidemic in this country, and I didn't recall anyone being afraid of handicapped kids in school or on the streets of The Bluffs.

"Well, why in heaven's name are they afraid? That just seems rude."

"Oh, it is an entire substratum of fears, " he said, "and perhaps fits into the area of generalized anxiety disorder---probably fear of 'catching' it or having it happen to them."

"Hmmm, no, I never feel like that. Since you — uh — brought it up, though, I'll tell you what I think is awkward--out in public with people in general---who are handicapped."

"What is that?"

"It's that you...I mean I... never know when or if to offer help. I was asked to take notes for a blind girl at school---at Iowa---and I agreed to do it , writing my own notes with a special stylus on this lap board they gave me, and you know what? My notes got automatically transferred to Braille. It was really neat. But they cautioned me never to guide her or help her in any other way in class. After class we sometimes walked back to the dorm together, and she would take my arm... but I wouldn't offer it. She had a cane, too, but she was really terrible with it! I guess she was new to being blind, or uncomfortable in a different setting or something. Anyway, you just wouldn't believe it. There were loads of times when she almost killed herself tripping up curbs and stairs. One time she ran head-long into a railing for God's sake. And I didn't say anything. But I felt stupid! What would be wrong with guiding her, like away from a pole or something? Sheesh." I shook my head.

"*Non, je comprends.* The thing is that people are rarely like you, Sarah. In my case, they are often ill at ease with how I look, how I walk and move. They either feel so sorry for me and show such a great deal of pity that it becomes awkward. Or they feel duty-bound to grab ahold of me and give me what they consider to be aid. **Or**, they become fed up and impatient about it."

"What?! Why?"

"Oh, you see...it makes some people very uncomfortable to watch me struggle to make my way doing anything."

"Well, forgive me for being bold here, because first and foremost, you **are** my boss and I have precious little right to address your issues, but you aren't … well, actually, **very**…handicapped, are you? I mean, you're mobile, you are not affected intellectually, you're very…uh..nice looking…*(I realized with that comment I was in the danger area of overstepping my bounds of employee, but plunged in anyway)* you wear gorgeous clothing…and you have every possible advantage-- uh—living in this mansion and all. What's there to pity?"

He laughed out loud, "Oh, Sarah! You are too marvelous. And your *naïveté* is charming."

"Am I? Naïve?" I bristled a little bit at the label.

"Yes! But it is what I admire about you."

Sensing, however, that he may have made me feel uneasy, he suggested that we get on with our evening's entertainment. " Shall we watch our film?"

"Sure."

It was going on nine o'clock. Plenty of time remained until the holiday witching hour. I offered to go around and switch off the lights I had turned on, and he instructed me that there was a button to push that would release that enormous screen and cause it to advance from the wall toward us.

"Whoa! My goodness, that's huge," I said, never before having even seen any home theater set ups.

I left the little light on the table at the projector for last, thinking, correctly that it could even stay on---it was far enough behind us to not bother our film viewing. The movie was threaded through already; all I had to do was flip the "on" switch and adjust the sound. I circled around the back of that table and took my seat again next to Jean-Paul on the sofa. Luckily that Chesterfield not only had the beautiful patina of aged leather, it had the soft, sunken luxury of it as well.

"Ah, yes, you said that this film starred Oskar Werner, " Jean-Paul said, as the first scene came up and he, too, settled into the cushion, "the apotheosis of his career was most certainly *Jules et Jim.*"

"Hmm, " I said. I couldn't dispute that, but Werner was older and so gorgeous in this movie, it wasn't even worth arguing about.

Several times though the film, I felt him reacting. The love scenes were pretty steamy, but of course, not lewd. I wondered for a minute how a gay man would react to heterosexual love-making. At the time I really didn't even know what "they did. " I wondered, though, if the tables had been turned, and I was watching a movie with a homosexual love story (of which, it goes without saying, there were none in any movie theater I'd ever been to) would I have been shocked out of my gourd? But it also occurred to me that probably nothing could offend as worldly a man as JPA.

He seemed afterwards to have enjoyed the film. How did I really know, though? I did not have a clue to his taste in movies or anything else. I certainly loved seeing it again, and luckily, it was not a film that made me cry, even though Barbara Ferris' character Sally sniffles throughout. What I adored about this film, really, was the music. I loved the theme song, and the soundtrack was a lot of orchestral music he would recognize, as well as a gorgeous Georges Delerue score. Couldn't go wrong with that.

"I hope you enjoyed watching that again? I think so. *Merci de m'avoir prévenu de ce film.* I am so happy that you mentioned it at the concert. I did like it very much."

"I'm glad!"

"But what did you think seeing that plot unfold though, about their handling of the *–euh –* affair?" he asked me.

"Well, of course, they were both sympathetic characters to me, " I answered, honestly. "But then there's the wife—she's beautiful, intelligent and the mother of his children. She certainly doesn't deserve to be thrown over. I guess, even when I find the character so supremely attractive as I did Stefan, I don't really get why no one considers their marriage vows!"

"So you do not give credence to the possibility that love could have blindsided the two of them…that that can happen?"

"Well, yes, I guess so, " I conceded. "I'm sure it happens more than we know."

"And what if it had happened to you? Would you be like Sally?"

"No." I didn't even have to ponder that question.

"What if my friend George Solti had taken the kind of interest in you that Stefan took in her?"

456

"No! I would never have an affair with a married man. I adore George Solti. I would maybe have met him for drinks or dinner, and I would be thrilled—am thrilled---that he showed interest in my music edification. But sleep with him? Out of the question."

"Even if he considered it merely returning a favor?"

"Even then. I would hope to never have put myself in a position where that could have been misconstrued, either. Nothing would ever entice me to become the cause of someone's marriage breaking up."

"Well, I only presented it as a hypothetical case, " he said, laughing.

I couldn't tell whether he thought me a prude or a goody-goody, but I had to be honest with him, even though it struck me as rather unfair to bring up George Solti. That had never entered my mind.

As if he also felt like he might have gone too far, he abruptly changed the subject and asked me, "What other films do you consider your favorites?"

"Oh, geez…movies that were seminal in my life…gads there are so many. I guess the first one would be *The Parent Trap* with Hayley Mills. I'm guessing you don't know that one?" I looked up at him and grinned.

"*Buh*, non," he admitted with a look on his face of mock concern.

I went on, "Then there was *The World of Henry Orient*—one of my all-time faves. Every Audrey Hepburn film but especially *Two for the Road* and *How to Steal a Million*; and speaking of Peter O'Toole— which we were not, but I am now-- *Lawrence of Arabia*, of course. *The Graduate* was a big hit with me. Do you know this one?

"Yes, that one I have heard of."

"I saw it again in Paris with a friend who came into my dorm room and begged me to go since she was missing Berkeley."

I paused, remembering that incident and laughing about it. He, however, wanted to know more, so I kept on rattling off movies.

"I love Peter Sellers, so *Dr. Strangelove* and the first *Pink Panther* movie are two more in my personal pantheon. I adore Omar Sharif so *Dr. Zhivago* has to be on the list, and it has Julie Christie so that opens up the inventory to include *Far from the Madding Crowd*, *Darling* and *Billy Liar*. She's so wonderful."

"Yes, I agree. And what other genres of films do you like?"

" Well, naturally…I like musicals so *An American in Paris* was a big one for me, and of course, *Funny Face*---fits in both categories of Audrey and music. And since I LOVE the Beatles, I adored *A Hard Day's Night*. I wanted to see it so much that I actually agreed to let my father take me and a friend to the drive-in movie—I couldn't drive yet in 1964-- and put up with his snarky comments all through the film… just so I could see it."

"Snarky?"

"Negative, judgmental. You know, running commentary on their hair cuts. He was fit to be tied over how they looked. Could not shut up."

"I understand…I think. What else did you like?"

"Well, let's see. I loved *To Kill a Mockingbird*, and I admired the book, of course. And there is a wonderful quirky movie that my college roomie Cass and I adored: *A Thousand Clowns*. She had seen the play it's based on, and turned me on to the film." I looked over at him to see how bored he must have been listening to my litany. I felt like I had to come up for air!

"There are just so many!! But does that give you an idea?"

"Well, it would if I knew more of those, which I do not."

"So you didn't go to the movies much when you were a kid?"

"Sadly, no."

"Luckily you have a film library at your disposal and, need I add, at your service, Sir!"

"I must say, I believe I have chosen a very competent film librarian."

I noticed the chimes of a small clock on the other side of the room just then, that I realized we must have ignored all evening, because it surely had struck---I'd been there for hours. I glanced at my watch and saw that it was a quarter 'til midnight.

"Gasp! It's almost the new year. We have fifteen minutes."

"Ah, then I shall ask you to do two favors for me . First go get that other bottle of champagne cooling in the bucket. The ice is no doubt melted by now, but the bottle will still be cold enough. Bring it over here and I shall pour us a toast. Also, if you would, go to that cupboard in the bookcase just at the door. Inside you will find a shawl and a cape. If you bring them, and help me on with the cape, and you wear the shawl, we can go outside on the terrace and watch fireworks in the distance over the lake. They are the best kind---you can see the beautiful colors but the noise is very much muffled."

So I did just that, and while he poured us the two Baccarat flutes, I fetched the articles of clothing. The shawl was a large wrap—what we would now call a pashmina–of thick mohair; and the cape was a black wool man's opera cape lined in grey silk satin.

When the clock struck twelve, we clinked glasses and took a nice sip of the Moet et Chandon, and then it was time to go outdoors.

I helped put the cape over his good shoulder, then swaddled myself in the voluptuous mohair, thinking I must have died and gone to heaven. He took my arm instead of his cane as we made our way outside into the very cold air. He let go of my arm long enough to make sure the shawl covered my neck and even part of my hair, and then, as if afraid to lose his balance, grabbed ahold of me again. Snow was falling, as we stood out there down at the end of the terrace where we could have a view unobstructed by his container garden of trees and shrubs , and sure enough, as if out of nowhere in the void, the sky lit up with red, green, silver and gold hues. I didn't know how many miles away they were or under whose auspices this gorgeous fireworks display took place, but the city of Chicago did itself proud that night with a spectacular show, of which, due to the freezing temps, we only saw a few minutes' worth.

"That was very nice!" I said blowing on my hands as we came back in through the French doors.

"I agree with you. I enjoyed it."

"I must thank you for all of tonight. It was really fantastic. The dinner was terrific. Please convey my thanks to your chefs for all they did. Seeing your drawings and hearing the story just left me...well...wowed! I'm so honored you wanted to share it all ---your past, that is, with me. I really mean that."

"So you are all right with the party not being a party after all?"

"I'm **a-okay** with that."

At this point, under any other circumstances, were I standing with a lovely man who had just wined and dined me and told me the most particular details of a harrowing early life, and shared a movie that I loved, that he had picked out in order to experience it with me, I would have at the very least wanted to hug him. Gay, straight, whatever, who cared? And I desperately did want to hug Jean-Paul d'Arivèque and just hold him and be held by him. But this was a preposterous inclination on my part, not the least since he was my boss; and naturally, I didn't act upon it in any way. I hoped nevertheless, upon my leave-taking we would exchange *la bise*.

"I have pondered the situation of how you will return home tonight. The most logical thing would have been, I now believe, to have had you spend the night in one of our guest rooms. However, as we did not arrange that and you haven't any provisions, I would like you to drive *la* **Citroën** back to your apartment and keep it over the weekend."

"But...wait. What about a taxi?"

"I am told they are next to impossible to obtain on New Year's Eve."

"But...I... well, gosh, I don't know about that. You realize I don't have a garage or anything! Your car would have to be outside all weekend! I can't let you risk loaning it to me. My God, what if something should happen to it? "

"I believe your night watchman person would look after it, no?"

"Well, yes, but...no! I mean, he's there, but what if someone were to slide into it in the snow or something awful like that?"

"So, would you rather stay? I can have you wear some night clothes of my mother, and in the morning my staff will have resumed their posts. Jean-Luc is still away, but I can have Robineau drive you."

WHAT?!

"No. But thank you." I feared that may have come off slightly abrupt, but little did he know that what I meant, of course, was **no fucking way**.

458

"Alors, la bagnole de Maman?"

Bagnole *indeed! Calling that magnificent machine a jalopy?! Say rather the luxury wonder car of the world!* I nodded.

"You need only drive it back here Monday morning. The garage door will open as you approach because you will have the remote control on the driver's side visor. Do not worry about where you park it---place it in a spot that is easy for you."

"Yes, sir, I understand."

"And then come upstairs, and I shall accompany you to the office."

"Oh, gee, no...that's okay...I'll walk to work. I wouldn't want you to go in at any hour you don't normally. It's only a short ways, really." Our North Michigan Avenue office wasn't that close to the Lake Shore Drive mansion, except as the crow flew, but compared to my usual commute it was a piece of cake.

And luckily, I remembered that there was indeed a side pedestrian door out of the garage. That would have been awkward if I'd had had to go back up to the main floor of the mansion and out the front door! I felt a huge relief.

We made our way back to the elevator and down to the first floor, that he called the ground floor, or *rez de chaussée* in the French fashion. My coat was still on the bench. I put it on, and he and I descended to the lowest level, where we retraced those steps we'd taken many other times past the pool and the gym and the staff quarters, to the garage part.

"The keys are in the car, " he said, placing his cane in his left hand and taking my hand in his right. I had gloves on by this time so he just held my hand for a moment, very gently, and leaned down to give me the first kiss of *la bise*, as I reciprocated.

"Good night, Sarah."

"Good night, *Monsieur*, " I responded almost automatically, even though I'd been using his first name all evening. It was as though the clock had struck and I'd turned back into an employee.

My coach was certainly no pumpkin though. I got in behind the wheel and engaged the key in the ignition. The car's hydraulic system lifted it slowly up on its wheels and obtained the proper height for driving. I re-familiarized myself with the dashboard and the gauges, the lights and the turn signals. I let off the emergency brake, put it in gear and inched forward. I was aligned already with the garage door about a hundred feet away and I set off for it, waving goodbye to my host, and waited for the door to lift automatically.

"Holy buckets, "I said out loud to the car as much as to myself. "Please don't let some drunk hit me on the way back!"

Arriving with no problems, I parallel parked the fantastic beastie right smack dab in front of my gate and saw Perry's lights as he approached, not knowing it was me. I got out and carefully locked the car, and motioned to him.

"Gracious Sari!" he yelled out, "what is that!?"

"That, my friend, is a cherry Citroën DS Pallas. It's going to be parked here all weekend. Guard it with your very life, okay?"

"Shit house mouse!" he exclaimed as he walked over to it. "I have never seen one of these up close and personal before."

"It's a dream car, Perry. Say!" I added, noting the path that had been shoveled for me, "Thanks for clearing the walk and steps! What a guy! Happy New Year!"

Chapter Seventy-Nine

"Wave"...Tom Jobim

The office reopened on Monday, January 4, and I dutifully returned the Citroën to its stall and began the commute to work on foot. Due to the fact that the wind was howling even through my new coat and the faithful fur hood, and that the morning sun provided no warmth whatsoever, I got off Lake Shore, and made my way "inland" to North Michigan Avenue. That way I could trek straight down a more protected street. It afforded only slight respite but even a little helped.

People at work all seemed happy to be back and to see everyone after the long holiday break. The receptionist was greeting people with the news flash that there was to be a *vin d'honneur* that afternoon right there in the main lobby, and for all of us to stay around for it after closing. There was to be a special announcement.

If I'd been thinking, I would have guessed what the special occasion was, but instead was just as floored as everyone else when it turned out we were toasting the engagement of Annie-Laure and Jean-Luc, who had just returned from Aspen, and were as bubbly as the glasses of Dom Perignon being handed out to us by some of the staff from back at the house. Jean-Paul d'Arivèque asked for our attention, and then made two surprising announcements:

"We send all our most sincere good wishes to the happy couple, and I am pleased to offer them the wedding in France at my family home, *La Pérégrine,* next summer." Everyone oohed and aahed and raised their glasses to toast, whereupon Jean-Paul made another stunning statement. "Also I want to tell you today that Marie-France de Piaget will, at that point, go to *La Pérégrine* prior to the wedding to open up the house and ready it for guests, and then, she will retire there and stay. Annie-Laure will take her place here at the Foundation, and Jean-Luc will continue as head of my motor pool." More clapping and wild congratulations from the gathering of Foundation staff, as I just stood there stunned. Annie-Laure was talking now, about how generous the offer was, and how grateful they were to be able to be married in France with both their families present; all I heard was blah blah blah.

Marie-France retiring. Living in the country house, the ancient seat of the Ducs de Beuvron. Wow. He must love her like a second mother.

Well, I sighed to myself, at least this wasn't happening for another six months...I had time to get used to all of it. I snapped back out of my reverie and congratulated all concerned. I really was happy that once married, the couple would be back in Chicago, and I'd still get to see them both. It was a terrific promotion for Annie-Laure and I knew she'd do a great job. She loved the Foundation, just like all of us who worked there did.

Upon reflection, I didn't know how they managed to do it---hire people who all got along and who didn't partake in the office dramas we all read about and saw in movies. No one had ever, for instance, tried to sabotage any idea I'd come up with to date; no one treated me like an outcast, even though they hardly saw or knew me. Wacky Hennie drove me a little nuts but she was the exception to the rule around there and, much as I had no knowledge really of how she was accepted by the rest of the crowd, I believed no one judged her as having any malice aforethought; I certainly didn't.

When I got home that night there was a letter from Nonnie "on the road" in Pennsylvania saying they would arrive in Chicago by January 7. I wondered if they'd chosen the Drake Hotel on purpose to be close to my office, or if that was just a fluke. In any event, it was convenient!

In the envelope was also an article—almost a full page!-- from the local Arlington, VA newspaper telling of her wedding. The picture of her was astonishingly beautiful. She was in profile with a huge bouquet of flowers that the writer called a **"cascade arrangement of mauve Cymbidium orchids, Stephanotis, white roses and heather"** held right in front of her very tiny waist. Nonnie looked as though she had lost half her body weight from when I knew her.

The huge article told of the nuptial mass having been celebrated amidst an altar **"banked in Christmas greens and poinsettias with brass candelabra marking the pews entwined with smilax,**

" which I knew from the woods behind my grandmother's house to be a holly-like plant with little red berries.

Nonnie, or as they called her, **Antonia**, wore her mother's wedding dress! It was described as a **"gown of imported Swiss organdy with a three-tiered cascaded skirt edged with bands of lace and forming a circular train. She wore matching organdy gauntlets and a fuchsia velvet ribbon at her throat."** The article made a point to say that her headdress was **"a two-tiered veil of imported silk tulle that fell from a crescent demi-Camelot headpiece enhanced with Swiss embroidered floral motifs appliqued on fichu *point d'esprit* embroidered edged trim."** That was in English and French, and I still didn't understand it.

The four column-wide article went on to name the entire bridal wedding party and continued in great detail as to who the maid of honor was and what she wore; the names of the five bridesmaids and what they wore; junior bridesmaids and their outfits; and what her mother wore! Nonnie changed for the reception and they reported on that, too!

Then there was a paragraph about who the groom was, (Patrick O'Hara came from Binghamton, New York, I found out.) where they'd each gone to high school and college, and the Sorbonne, and medical school, and what Greek organizations and national honor societies they'd belonged to at college. It ended with **"Dr. and Mrs. O'Hara will be leaving on a cross-country motor trip to their new home in San Francisco, California, and for the departure Mrs. O'Hara has selected a pants outfit in navy blue with a white turtleneck sweater and a blue suede jerkin worn over the blue tweed pants."**

My God. I had never seen a wedding announcement like that published in either my local newspaper or even the Omaha one. I found myself taken aback by how prominent her family must have been for such a spread to appear about their daughter. Nonnie had given the impression to me in Paris of being a normal college coed. She had talked about her high school because I met those girlfriends of hers— all bridesmaids it turned out – and knew they had gone to a private Catholic girls' school together; it hadn't sounded high falutin at all. But I guess it was.

January 7th came very soon after her letter, and I admit I woke up that Thursday morning with great anticipation and joy at seeing Nonnie again. I decided to dress up a little more than usual---nothing too fancy-- the kilt and sweater. I figured we'd be seeing each other probably for dinner. When I had first found out she was coming, I'd given her instructions to phone me at work, and that's exactly what did happen, at about eleven o'clock in the morning. I got the call from the receptionist since Nonnie didn't know my direct line.

We greeted each other on the phone with much jubilant screaming. No one could hear me, of course, in my soundproof booth.

"Can you come to the hotel after work?" she asked breathlessly.

"I can come at lunchtime!!"

"Yay! We can't even get into our room yet---we'll meet you in the lobby!"

So that's what I did. I left early, even, and didn't, of course, have to worry about punching any time clock to be back; although I wouldn't take much more than an hour. It was a wonderful reunion and I immediately loved Patrick. We ducked into the coffee shop and they treated me to lunch. I told her I was delighted-- but also astounded-- by the wedding article, and she said even she thought it was over the top, and that she hadn't had much say in any of it.

"Virginia's really the South, you know?" she said. "They just do it everything the old-fashioned way there."

"Geez, I guess that explains it then, " I said. "I mean, it was *vachement chouette*, don't get me wrong." Of course I was envious. I'd never have an announcement like that in a million years if I ever got married.

"So tell us all about your JOB!" she enthused. "Do you still love it?"

"I still do. Do you guys want to come back with me and see the offices after lunch while you're still waiting for your room to be ready? It's really close to here."

They were enthused at my invitation. I didn't take them on a real tour all over the entire Foundation. We flashed by the art department on the way to my office, though, and I introduced them to the team making up the teaching boxes that were my idea, and showed them the *Trois Mousquetaires* one.

461

Predictably, Nonnie pronounced them "great stuff, " and we went on down to my theater projection room-cum-office. Patrick was impressed with the layout and equipment, as well as the sheer number of films I had catalogued on the shelves. I also showed them my collection of lesson plans and other things I'd been working on. Nonnie intended to teach French eventually, and I valued her opinion.

"My next idea is to provide little classroom activities or reading tidbits to accompany each film that we have on the various regions of France," I explained. "I've already written a couple of examples…in French and English. See?" I handed the papers to her and she glanced through them.

"Genius ideas!" she said.

"I thought I'd call them *Moments Culturels*, " I added, quite proud of the title I'd come up with. "I think if I were a teacher who ordered a film, say on Normandy, and it came with a little blurb to start conversation in the classroom with… well… I'd find it useful."

"I like that, " said Patrick.

"I love it!" Nonnie said.

I showed them out, and we made arrangements to meet back at their hotel for dinner. Patrick had also invited a friend of his, a resident at the hospital where Jean-Paul d'Arivèque had been a patient the time I delivered those papers to him.

"Well, that hospital is right in this neighborhood, too!" I told them. Funny how stuff worked out.

"Yes," said Patrick, "that's why we chose the Drake."

"Oh," I said, not really able to hide my dejection, "that makes sense."

"Close to you, too!" Nonnie was quick to add, when she caught a glimpse of my expression.

"Pax told us about it."

"Pax? That's your friend?"

"Yes," said Patrick. "Paxton, but he goes by Pax."

"It's Ambrose Paxton Hubley, if you want to know the whole truth, " laughed Nonnie.

"He was a year ahead of me in med school, but we became great friends and sailing buddies. He's already in the residency program here."

"You'll like him, Sari, " said Nonnie. "He's really nice. Sweet guy."

As I was getting ready to leave later on and go meet them, Jean-Paul came around to my office, which surprised me.

"I saw you showing a couple of people around the offices, " he said.

"You did? I'm sorry I didn't see you. I would have introduced them."

"Teachers?"

"Uh, no… they're friends… newlyweds---she and I went to the Sorbonne together. They're actually on their honeymoon and visiting Chicago from the East Coast on the way to San Francisco. They mainly wanted to see my office. I hope that's okay."

"But, of course! It is fine for you to invite them here. I would have been happy to have met them."

Oh, he would have been happy to have met them! And I had ignored him! Idiot! But how could I have just traipsed into the Presidential Suite uninvited with a couple of tourists in tow?

"Gosh, I'm so sorry. I didn't want to interrupt you…just show up in your offices unannounced and all. They're staying at the Drake so I'm headed up there now."

"*Alors*, do not let me keep you. *Bonne soirée*, Sarah." At least he smiled.

"*Merci, Monsieur…à vous aussi.*"

I fled up North Michigan Avenue in the ever-present bitter wind, and met the group---now three---in the lobby. Introductions ensued all around and I was face to face with Dr. Ambrose Paxton Hubley. I admit I did a double take. "Pax" was absolutely gorgeous in the most dream-boat way. He looked like a cross between the youthful John F. Kennedy — that same square jaw and chiseled features-- and some surfer dude with sun-bleached hair falling in disarray on his forehead. He was tall and buff—very athletic looking, except for his hands, which struck me as delicate and already fine-tuned for doing surgery. I tried not to stare at him. Patrick, after all, was very cute, too, with dark hair and blue eyes. But he looked like *vin ordinaire* next to this bottle of *Romanée Conti*.

Originally from New Orleans, Louisiana (yes, he pronounced it "Nawlins"), Pax explained that he was here in Chicago by way of American University in Washington, D.C. and Georgetown Medical School.

462

He verified that he was indeed a year ahead of Patrick in Med school but he seemed so much older than that. It was then explained to me that he had deferred entering Med School so he could "serve when 'Uncle Sugah' called me, " meaning he'd been drafted right out of undergrad.

"I fooled them though, " he said with a still- prominent, if gentrified Southern drawl, " and spent my wartime at Bethesda Naval Hospital."

"Whew, " I said, "that was a close call, then. But what did you do there? You weren't a doctor yet."

"You're right, darlin'. But I'd been pre-med and I got assigned to the hospital as an admitting clerk."

"Tell her the rest, " Patrick goaded him.

"Ah, right. My daddy knew the commandant. He may have pulled a few strings."

Oh, really, I sneered to myself. Christ.

"What? You thought maybe it isn't all who you know in life?" Patrick laughed.

"No, you're absolutely right." *(I should know.)*

"In any case, however, " Nonnie interjected, "you obviously got lucky."

"Yes, indeed. But what I saw was almost as bad as being in a M.A.S.H. unit in the Mekong Delta or somewhere. Weekend passes, however, were definitely better, " he laughed.

"So do you like Chicago? How did you end up here? Someone trying to make a Yankee out of you?" I asked, trying to show I also could lighten things up a little bit.

"I got my first choice in the match, " he said seriously, " working with the greatest surgeon in the U.S. of A. right here."

"Oh? Who's that?" Patrick was curious.

"Dr. Fabrizio Garabanti. He's one of those 'last of a generation' of real general surgeons. He has the most superb technical expertise in a wide variety of areas, and is an outstanding teacher."

"So you just heard about him and wanted to come here?" I wondered.

"That's about it. One of our profs back at Georgetown told me that any residents he trained would be the fortunate recipients of a short course in medical ethics and procedures, while learning their surgical skills from a master. And I can tell that's exactly what I will have once I'm done on his service. I've never seen anyone develop such a special relationship with his patients as Fabrizio does. He's very sensitive to their pain and suffering."

"Wow, " I said, " he sounds like a wonderful doctor. I'm wondering if my boss might know him." And I guessed he did.

Patrick, it turned out, was also taking a risk on residency. He had graduated mid-year, in December, and was headed for a much sought-after practicum at San Francisco General Hospital, they told me. The big match day, which was the third Friday in March, would happen while he was there, and he intended to put in just for that hospital.

"It'll be a gamble, just like yours was, Pax, " Nonnie said, " But it seems he is pretty sure to be guaranteed that hospital once he was already in their program. At least that's what they told us."

"You're betting the farm, though," Pax laughed.

"Yeah, " Nonnie said, "but we're prepared to reapply and move if we have to. I'm going to start grad school wherever we end up."

After a little deliberation, we decided to stay at their hotel for dinner in the Cape Cod Room, which I loved and so did they, as it turned out. Afterwards I said I had to get back since I had work the next day.

"But tomorrow I am inviting you to dinner at La Cheminée, and I say we meet there at seven o'clock. The hotel concierge can tell you how to walk to it, or if you take a cab it would be a short ride."

"That sounds great," Nonnie said, " and I hope we could do some serious sightseeing on Saturday. Are you free, too, Pax?"

Suddenly I realized I'd invited my friends to dinner but not Dr. Hubley, so I hastily addressed him with, "I'd love to have you come to La Cheminée tomorrow night, too, if you can! Do you know this restaurant? It's my favorite French one in the city. So far."

"Thank you, Sarah, but I'm afraid I'm on duty tomorrow night…into Saturday, too, I believe. I'll recheck about that, though, and get ahold of Patrick if it turns out I can make it."

463

And just as I was turning to leave them, Pax offered to drive me home.

"I'd be happy to give you a lift, Sarah, if you would be able to walk back to my apartment building near the hospital where I garage the car."

I knew the apartment high-rises near that hospital, and was mildly surprised a resident doc could afford to live in them. I said that would be great, and off we went at a fairly brisk pace I could barely keep up with.

We got to the building which was non-descript as urban residences go, but which had a lovely lobby. Instead of going into it, however, we went underground through a stairwell on the side and ended up in the garage where parking spots were numbered and in his was a 1965 Volvo P1800 roadster coupe. It was pale seafoam green, sleek and hip as all hell.

"Oh holy shit!" I exclaimed. "What a nice ride!"

"She's a beauty, isn't she?"

"You could say that."

He unlocked my side first and held the door as I lowered into the seat. The interior of sienna brown leather was like being in the cockpit of an airplane more than the front seat of a car. The dashboard gauges were three big round ones, the speedometer, odometer and tachometer, and three little round ones, the fuel, oil and clock. The shift was "four on the floor" but the car actually had five gears because the M41 gearbox had an electrically attached overdrive that served as fifth gear. The steering wheel, compared to the one on the Citroën Pallas, was very narrow but with a larger circumference.

"Boy, " I sighed admiringly, "I'll bet you can peel out in this baby."

"Yes, darlin', I can, " he laughed, "but we won't… in downtown Chicago."

It only took six minutes to get to my place, as traffic was light.

In true southern gentlemanly fashion, he parked and got out to open my car door again. I didn't ask him in---it was late and I hardly knew him—but he gave me a peck on the cheek, and said he was looking forward to seeing me on Saturday if he could get time off.

I was talking to Cass on the phone in my office the next day debriefing her on Nonnie, and still bubbling over about New Year's Eve with Jean-Paul.

"But don't you suppose Nonnie was trying to fix you up with Pax?" Cass asked gleefully.

"Oh, hell, no, " I said. " They wanted to see him and they wanted to see me."

"But do you think he'll ask you out?"

"I doubt it, " I answered. "Let's get real. For one thing, he's gorgeous. He's more than that…he's an Adonis. Every nurse in that hospital would be at his beck and call. Secondly, from what I could gather---I'll find out more tonight--- he's the scion of some rich, Catholic, Southern, Louisiana dynasty or other. Probably goes back to the Civil War there. I don't know how I manage to hook up with the landed gentry when I'm so hoi polloi, as Alan calls us. Ha! Just lucky I guess. Anyway, he wouldn't want to date the likes of me in a million years, so put that out of your mind."

"I can't get over how, after all this time, you still do that!" Cass said exasperated. "Stop putting yourself down."

"Yaaas'm, " I answered, "oh, and did I mention he talks in a peculiar Southern manner…not really a drawl, but of course, it is a drawl. Said he was raised by a Scottish governess and picked up her accent! Ha! But he calls women 'darlin' –no g sound—and pronounces I like ah. It's a scream. Next thing I'm expecting him to say is that he's got a 'lap full o'woe' or something."

"I'm the one with the lap full of woe, " Cass replied, catching me off guard all of a sudden, and causing me to come up short, worried.

" Why, what's wrong?"

"We're all sick---it's pestilence and locusts around here. Four days and no let up! Alan has the stomach virus with diarrhea…"

"Oh yuck, that's the worst."

"Yeah, and Paul has an ear infection. Laura has a cold and I have the same as Laura Bronwyn Jones."

"Poor **you** guys! Hang in there!" Brave words, but I was imagining the chaos that comes with not feeling well enough to take care of children and oneself. I was afraid to even think of the cleaning up that would be needed around their house, and how neither one of them would be up to it.

"It's times like these when we're really feeling isolated, too, you know?"

" I wish I could just get on the train and come there."

"Well you can't! You've got guests to show around and mad, gay, exciting adventures to take them on. Don't worry about us. I just brought it up because I'm feeling duly sorry for myself."

I told her I loved them all and would talk to her again on Monday, in the hopes that everything was sunnier by then. I left in haste to get home and change for my rendezvous dinner.

Pax did not come, and poor Patrick had to sit through hours of Nonnie and me reliving Paris and catching each other up on the two years since we'd seen one another. They said they were anxious to start a family, but would have to wait at least to see if Patrick got San Fran for residency and where they would be for the foreseeable future after that.

"So how many kids do you want? " I asked offhandedly.

"Four," she said.

"Five," he said with no visible hesitation.

"Jesus, " I said, "you'll be busy."

The next day I met them at their hotel and we cabbed it to the Art Institute, where we stayed all morning, long enough to also eat lunch there. After that we took a long taxi ride to Andersonville, the historic Swedish neighborhood of Chicago, because I thought they should see something ethnic, and I had discovered the area quite by accident when on my little exploring weekends in the warmer months. We walked down Clarke street and saw Scandinavian flags flying off a mast at Simon's Tavern.

"Let's just pick this bar, " I suggested, not even realizing I'd chosen a historic landmark, famous for Al Capone legends and bootlegged whiskey during Prohibition. " I'll bet they have *glögg*! That'll warm us up."

We drank for a while and then decided to stay around that area for dinner since the place seemed to be bustling with eating establishments, too. Afterwards they wanted to see where I lived, so the taxi we caught in Edgewater took Lake Shore all the way down to North Dearborn, which was right near me. With the meter ticking, we bid our fond farewells right there in front of my fencing. They would be taking off in the morning for Omaha and the next stop on their way west.

"Too bad I can't go with you and show you a boring town after this great one, " I sneered. "Don't blink or you'll miss it. Where are you staying?"

"Some place called the Town House, " said Patrick. "Do you know it?"

I nodded and shrugged it off. Didn't bear talking about. We hugged and promised to keep in touch like we had done, which, I told them, made me so happy, as did our reunion.

I sat up listening to *Liege and Lief* that night when I got in, and wrote in my diary about how I wasn't unhappy living alone or even, essentially, **being** alone, but that friends could certainly change the emotional topography, and add sustenance to one's meager diet. I suspected Cass would definitely agree with me on that one.

Chapter Eighty

"Blue Rondo à la Turk"...Dave Brubeck

The Foundation had a newsletter, which went out bi-monthly to the entire French population of Chicago, and when the features editor wanted to do a substantial article on the film library, she came to interview me about it. I took this as a chance to highlight my two ideas for classroom enhancement of the film experience, namely my lesson plans for discussion of the movies, and my recent addition of "*Moments Culturels*" to go with our collection of media about the regions of France. But since I hadn't exactly cleared that last idea with the powers that be, I begged off doing the interview for a couple of days until I could get the necessary permission I thought I needed.

I wrote up a proposal for MFP with some sample blurbs on Normandy and Brittany for starters. Those two areas of France were easy, and had more than enough interesting facts--foods, points of interest, history, etc.--to make for educational copy. I wrote them in English, then in elementary French, using as many cognates as possible, and then in more advanced French. That way I could show her how we might be able to appeal to varied levels of French students. However, before submitting anything to Marie-France, I ran the ideas past Dominique Lambert.

I asked him over to the office one afternoon in January, when his workday was finished, met him in the lobby of my building, and invited him for coffee so we could talk before we went up. Dom taught all levels, but I zeroed in on his advanced classes. I gave him a sample of my discussion questions over *Jules et Jim* and a *Moment Culturel* about following the Impressionist painters through Normandy. He was enthusiastic.

"I really have to hand it to you, Sari, " he said patting me on the shoulder, "these are very good."

"You aren't really my target teacher, " I explained to him, "because you already know all this stuff, but I wanted to get a classroom educator's opinion before I present it to my bosses."

"I'm just as grateful as the next guy to have lessons already made up, don't kid yourself," he laughed. "If all I had to do was create units and teach them, my job would be a lot more wonderful. But of course, you can guess, even though you've never taught, our workdays—and nights-- consist more of grading papers, meetings, keeping records, counseling, sometimes even policing, and a load of other crap besides what we were hired to do, which is teach. So... any port in a storm."

"Well, not having taught, but having **been** taught, I already know that there are many teachers who don't create the kinds of lessons that would turn kids on to different aspects of their material; and that's my 'targeted demographic' so to speak."

"Well, more power to you. Go get 'em."

After that, I took him up to my office to show him more *Moments Culturels* and a role-play box mock-up, just to get his take on them. He said he loved the idea of the box, and could even see his high schoolers getting use out of something similar for skits. I offered to have him pick out a film or two while he was there; and he in turn invited me to his place for dinner the following week, saying that his boyfriend's cooking was "outta sight."

"Cool, "I said, accepting the invitation, "and you won't even need mailers to send the films back. I'll just pick them up when I see you."

With my projects in full swing, I needed more organization in my office life, so when I went in to ask MFP's permission to give the interview, I also asked her if I could procure some extra filing cabinets from our supply room, to which she enthusiastically agreed. Then I invited her down to see the newly delineated areas of my space.

"The ones here, " I explained, showing her a bank of cabinets, "house lessons alphabetically by title of the film. Those others will contain all the *Moments Culturels*, and maybe some elements of the culture boxes, too."

"I see how your culture boxes might need their own area, " she remarked, "because they seem to grow exponentially with every new idea."

I laughed. "Yes, they are taking over my office!"

"I noticed you have placed the *Moments Culturels* nearest to the shelves that house our media on French regions and geography. I like that."

"Thanks," I said, pointing out that there were not just films but lots of filmstrips in little square boxes that were also kept in the library, along with posters and pamphlets that had to be organized.

"And where did you get all those?" she wondered incredulously.

So I explained, a bit sheepishly, that I had taken the liberty, using Foundation letterhead, of sending written requests to a long list of French departmental and regional *syndicats d'initiatives* and had been showered with positive responses in the form of print and audio-visual media. I knew from my own time in France that the role of these offices was to amass all the forces of tourism and organizations whose goal was to attract business and industry to the area, and then to disseminate this information to any interested parties. But I was still surprised at the amount of material I was offered from every corner of France.

I had taken it upon myself to start all this without consulting anyone else, and when it was time to gather up the evidence and get in front of the top administrators, I fervently hoped I hadn't overstepped my bounds. I anticipated that Marie-France and eventually JPA would be on board, but I didn't take it as a foregone conclusion by any means.

Every minute I wasn't viewing and cataloguing films, or physically filing and organizing material, I was writing. Marie-France had seen my office layout, but she hadn't actually yet read anything I'd written, so I made an appointment to see her again, and laid my ideas all out for her. She already knew about the lesson plan proposal, so she asked me to present her with two dozen of what I considered to be the most popular films for which I had written material. And she also asked for samples of my newest suggestion-- the culture lessons that could accompany anything we sent out on the regions of France and France d'Outre-Mer.

It was about a week later when I took her a packet of everything she wished to see.

"You did all this already?" she asked in a rather amazed tone.

"It's a start, " I answered. "I hope to — I mean, I **will** do all the regions and as many films as people borrow."

She just sat there wide-eyed, so I continued, "The thing is, we've got to get our information in front of more teachers. If you give the go-ahead for me to be interviewed for our newsletter, that's, obviously, a start. I think a nice article like that will enlighten **some** people as to what we offer. But what I'm really hoping for is that, when *Monsieur* gives his speech to the Mid-States Conference in the Spring to all those hundreds of teachers, then they will become our grateful and enthusiastic patrons. I mean, the word **free** should do the trick!"

She stood up and came out from behind her desk and sat down in a chair next to me on the other side.

"I am overwhelmed by your accomplishment, Sarah, " she said smiling at me. "You have taken our idea of a film library in new directions. I believe *Monsieur* will be very pleased, and I shall see him today about it."

"Oh, thank you. And, so I have the green light to present all these ideas in the article for the newsletter interview then?"

"Of course I give you permission to do the interview. Feel free to mention anything and everything you have done. However, I might also suggest that you yourself may want to write up some short synopsis for our editor explaining your projects, since you are the one who knows best the details. As for the pieces you are preparing for inclusion with the films, I believe anything you do write should also go through our editorial staff before dissemination. Would you also be amenable to submitting your copy?"

"Oh, by all means, " I answered, "That goes without saying. I'd want them to for sure correct *fautes de français* in any articles I might write!"

"Good. *Alors, très bien fait!*" She rose from the chair and I also gathered my files and stood up, at which point she walked me over to her office door and gave me *la bise* as Annie-Laure looked on.

When I stopped at Annie-Laure's desk she teased me, "Ah, so it's *la bise* now is it? You must have really impressed her."

I smiled and said, "Maybe. Hope so."

Back in my office, I got a call and, noticing the time-- just before noon-- I knew it was too early for it to be from Cass. But on the other hand, who else could be calling me? I immediately became concerned that something was wrong in Iowa City. I was both surprised and relieved to hear that the voice of our receptionist Bernadette, announcing in French that someone was in the office to see me---a Dr. Hubley. I was flabbergasted and headed up to the reception area, knowing he'd never be able to find his way to where I hung out.

There he was---standing in scrubs, a ski jacket and stocking cap, looking this time like Young Doctor Kildare meets Jean-Claude Killy.

"Pax! Hi!"

"Sorry to barge in on you, darlin'," he said in a quiet tone. "But I didn't have your number, so I thought I'd just bop on over here on my lunch break. Your office is really close to the hospital!"

"Yeah---I know!" I laughed. "I'm so surprised to see you here, though."

"Well, I don't have time to take you to lunch, but would you be free for dinner tonight? I'm off duty for twenty-four."

"Um...okay...sure!"

"Well, all right then! I'll pick you up at seven. I remember where you live."

"Okay, cool! I'll be outside by my fence."

A bit dazed, I went back to my office, and this time I called Cass. The illnesses that had plagued her house the previous ten days seemed to have abated, and she sounded more chipper.

"Soooo," she cooed, "you've got yourself –what is it, the third—Catholic boyfriend?"

"He's certainly not my boyfriend---yet, haha. Seriously you could have knocked me over with the proverbial feather when I heard he was here. He just came over on his lunch break!"

"Well, kid, he must like you. You surely made an impression on him that first time. "

"Well, it is, after all, every Jewish parents' wet dream for their daughter to be dating a doctor. Except of course, if he's Catholic."

"Oh, the irony!" she mocked. "But showing up like that. I still can't get over it."

"That makes two of us. So anyway, how are you guys? The kiddies better?"

"Thank the Lord, they are and we are. Toddlers are very active little people. I'm worn out."

"Gosh, you must be!"

"But they're really cute! You should see them—they love that inch worm toy you brought them. And they're babbling now. I even let them watch Sesame Street on t.v. Here I'm the one who said no television, and I'm so desperate for a couple of minutes down time that I plunk them right in front of it!"

"I've never seen that show but I hear good things about it. What about Alan...is he feeling okay now?"

"Yes, Alan's over his bug. I made him chicken soup—ha! Talk about stereotype. He'd be happier to know that one of these days you're coming back to cook, though! Do you think you can come soon and visit again? Your couch awaits you...always."

"I will really try to get there before too long. Maybe around your birthday, how's that? March isn't so far away."

"Oh, yes, please. That would be jolly!"

"So what about Alan's degree? Is he progressing? Does he have a TA gig lined up for Summer school?"

"I think so. Everything's going on about the same with him. He's back in class now, of course, and also doing his CO work at the Literacy Council, too. That's going well. They like him but...get this... they want him to cut his hair. Naturally, he won't. He's also got to finish his own chapbook and then with any luck he'll get the MFA degree... hopefully in August. That's when he'll begin the search for an eventual real job."

"Well, that all sounds promising, at least. What about you? Are you looking to go back to classes, too?"

"Missed it for this semester. No bread."

"Cass, come on. You know you can have all the money you want from that account."

468

"Let's not go through **that** again, okay? Anyway I am working on my own art, so that's all that matters. I'm going to get some things ready for the fairs this summer, like Klampert mentioned. "

"Well, hot damn! I'm really glad to hear that!"

We hung up, and I felt a little better knowing she had not abandoned art, which, if nothing else, I thought, had to be a catharsis for her.

As for me and my ramped up social life, dating Pax meant, for one thing, that I could wear all my old outfits and they would be all new to him; so that made me feel good. That first outing was dinner at a place near his apartment, a French restaurant I'd never been to called "*Jacques*", which had no normal sign, just a small placard on a chain and only tiny exterior lights. No one would ever suspect it was there since it blended in seamlessly with the lobby of an adjoining high-rise. The food was wonderful. The cuisine was tilted towards Alsatian, which could have been the chef's nod to the cold weather, but whatever the reason, sharing *choucroute garni* and drinking Riesling was perfect in the dead of the Chicago winter.

Out of the blue during dinner, Pax asked me if I liked jazz and blues, so I took the opportunity to regale him with tales of my jazz "education" in Paris and meeting Phil Woods, whom he professed to have heard of.

"Do you know The London House? " he asked me, and when I shook my head no, he said, "Well, then, that's what we'll do tonight. It used to be a restaurant, but lately it's an afterhours jazz club and it's not too far. Shall we go to it?"

"Near here?"

"Not **here**… in this neighborhood, no, but we're close to my car, if you recall."

I thought taking his car was a great idea. I really didn't yet know the neighborhoods of Chicago, but I knew that even in my own area, I could be walking somewhere that seemed chic enough, and then go around the block or across a street and all of a sudden see bars on the windows of seedy looking buildings. It made me realize that any place in the city could be dangerous and any place could be safe, and I decided that I couldn't go around living in fear or I wouldn't be able to live there.

Luckily for Pax, whose glorious car stood out in every neighborhood-- not just bad ones-- there was London House reserved parking.

Inside, the stage was cavernous, the sounds produced on it were superb, and the acoustics in the room were extraordinary. Square four-top tables filled up the space in front of the stage, and they were covered in thick linen tablecloths, each with a little hurricane lamp on top. The place was crowded with an eclectic mix of young and old, couples and singles, lots of women, and people of varying races. Even though it was super crowded, we could still get a table to ourselves.

The Teddy Wilson Trio, whom I did not know, was on the bill along with someone named Dan Kingsley.

"You know," Pax said, pulling a chair back for me and then taking his own next to mine, "Ramsey Lewis plays here, too. His band was the house band here. Do you remember the song 'Function at the Junction' from your college days?"

"No. Never heard of it. But I sort of recognize the name Ramsey Lewis."

"What about Dave Brubeck? He's something of a star who's played here."

"Oh, sure, I know that name. Can't say that I own any of his records, though. If I remember, my friend had one, come to think of it."

"*Time Out*? It had the song 'Take Five' on it."

"Oh, right. He's famous! Is he here tonight?"

"Unfortunately not," Pax laughed. "Trust me, if he were the place would be three times more crowded than it is now."

One other thing I did remember from college was how much I loathed beer, so when Pax ordered a Coors, even though I didn't want to look like a tee-totaling teeny bopper, I asked for a Coke. He gave me a side-eye glance so I explained, "I hate American beer, sorry."

Midway through the second set as someone was singing "Mas Que Nada," and I was digging it more than I ever thought I would, Pax got this funny look on his face and left the table. I didn't think he could possibly be sick on just the glass of wine he'd drunk at dinner and a couple of beers; but I couldn't think why else he would bolt from the table without me.

469

When he came back he leaned over and told me he was sorry but we had to leave, which we did. Once outside, he explained to me that he wore a paging device, and it had vibrated, which meant the hospital was summoning him back.

"Comes with the territory, darlin', " he told me as he put his arm around me and we walked back to his car.

"It's fine, " I said. "I understand."

It actually **was** fine with me. It got me off the hook of the awkward first date and who got invited in, and when they would leave, and the rest of that. I thanked him for a super evening, and said how much I enjoyed both the French restaurant and the blues club. I admitted to being a jazz and blues neophyte, but made the observation that with exposure comes appreciation and knowledge. *Hell, I should know. After all, I was at that very time in my life being given an education in classical music by the masters.*

"I do like your attitude, Sarah, " he said.

"You know, hardly anyone calls me Sarah…only my father and people who don't know me or, like in the office where we have to be formal. I'm Sari."

"So your father doesn't know you?"

I laughed. *A very astute comment and truer than he ever imagined.*

Soon after that, it hit me that my little dance card was starting to fill up. All of a sudden I had a social life, which was new territory. I went to dinner and hung out at Dom and Peter's place. I went to the Chicago Symphony with Jean-Paul d'Arivèque, and I went out on real dates with Dr. Pax Hubley, when he was free, which wasn't all that often, as it turned out.

And then there was Jerry Cohen. Jerry was a few years older than me, and a junior executive at a brokerage house, where his job was in research and development of the industry side of professional sports in America. Jerry was *mishpucha* – extended family. I'd met him visiting my cousin's house. He was her brother-in-law.

It turned out that one of my Nana's nieces, Rebecca, called "Becca, " lived in a Chicago suburb. She'd grown up in Fremont, Nebraska, and of course, I knew her parents, even if we rarely got together, because her dad was my grandmother's youngest and favorite brother. But because Becca was my second cousin and ten years older than me, we never really knew each other. That, and the fact that Becca was practically an alien in our family. She was tall, athletic, and a blue-eyed beauty. Her hair was a sleek blond shoulder-length pageboy, completely foreign to our clan.

I hadn't been in town too long before she'd gotten in touch with me, and asked me to her (predominately Jewish) club to play tennis. But I warned her that I couldn't play my way out of a paper bag; so I begged off, and just watched her and her real partner play. Afterwards, her husband Rod joined us for drinks by the pool. The weather that first September in Chicago was still warm and we spent a pleasant afternoon at the club, had dinner there, and then Rod drove me back into the city, which was above and beyond.

Becca had met Rodney Cohen at the University of Nebraska in Lincoln, and she had dropped out of college to marry him, and move with him as he accepted a promising position with Sears Roebuck and Co. She never had to work a day in her life after that, and spent her time being a trophy wife and raising their three sons. She was the consummate mom, lady who lunched, mahjong player, and sportswoman, who perfected her culinary skills as seriously as she did her swing.

I liked them both, and thought it would be great to have some relatives in the vicinity. I was a little surprised to hear they rarely came into Chicago from their home in Skokie, though. They didn't have symphony tickets, never went to jazz places, and rarely came in to go to the museums. If they went out to dinner, it was usually just to their club.

"I love to cook at home, " she told me, "and I hope you'll come to dinner one night."

"Oh, sure, I'd love to, " I answered, truthfully.

But it was a pretty long time before I heard from her again, and then out of the blue she called me up one weekend in February and said that they'd like to have me come out. She explained that I wouldn't have to take public transportation because Rodney's brother Jerry lived in the city, and would be happy to drive me.

"He's a babe, " she had said, in a conspiratorial tone.

More like a *shlub*, it turned out, an opinion which I kept to myself. He picked me up at the office, wearing, under his short tan topcoat, an outfit of dark brown polyester slacks and a beige knit shirt open in the front to reveal his hairy chest and a gold-chain "man necklace" with a *chai* hanging from it. Both he and his brother still wore crew cuts, the likes of which had all but disappeared from the U of Iowa campus while I was still a student there. Each of the brothers had dark hair and swarthy complexions, made darker by the amount of sun-bathing they all did in the Summer and travel to places like Florida or the Mexican Riviera in the Winter.

Becca's meal that particular night was fantastic, and I was happy to spend time with my extended family, even though their ulterior motive of fixing me up with Jerry was not appreciated. Throughout dinner he seemed to fidget, just a little too anxious to leave and take me with him. Becca made it a point to tell me how groovy his apartment was, in a doorman high-rise on the north side, and how I should see the view from his twenty-second-floor balcony. I agreed to let him show it to me on the way home, but regretted that decision immediately, even though I felt secure enough in the idea that this was family, and nothing to worry about. Jerry was a *putz*, but he wasn't mean.

The view of Chicago at night off his Juliette balcony was indeed beautiful, with the other apartments and office buildings lit up so close and personal, at varying heights, arrayed right before me. As we stood there admiring it, he put his arm around my shoulders, and offered me a drink back in his living room. We sat on his white leatherette couch, in front of which was a chrome coffee table where he had placed a tall pitcher filled with a magenta-colored liquid with orange slices floating in it. He made a production of stirring it with a long spoon.

"Sangria, baby!" he sang out. "Have one." He poured my drink into a wine glass (*at least!*) and we clinked glasses.

"*Skol!*" he pronounced.

"*Santé!*" I responded. But when I tasted it, it was all I could do not to gag.

"Like it?" he asked eagerly.

Like it? It was absolutely disgusting, a cross between sour wine and turpentine.

"Well, it's...uh...different! "

"Oh, sure. You can take the girl out of Iowa, but you can't take Iowa out of the girl, is that it?"

"No! Remember, I lived in France. I guess I—uh-- like French wine more than Spanish. I just got acclimated to theirs, is all."

"Yeah, sweetie. I remember you went to school in Paris. Pretty lah-dee-dah."

"Actually, it was hard. But it's the reason I got my cool job, so..."

"Want to listen to some trippy music?" he asked, cutting me off.

"Sure. Beatles?"

"Nope."

"Stones then?"

"Huh-uh."

He got up and went over to a large console record player and flashed a Montovani album at me. "This!"

He handed me the album, titled "*Songs to Remember*, "and I read through the list on the back to see if there was anything of interest on the record.

"I used to watch his t.v. show when I was a kid, " I offered.

"He's famous you know, for writing the main theme for the movie *Exodus*."

"I know, " I answered.

"Did you see it?" he wondered.

"What do you think?"

"Well, I didn't know if maybe you only liked French movies," he mocked me. "Montovani is just such a classic!"

Montovani was a classic bore, synonymous in my opinion, with elevator music. I sat there, taking tiny sips of the horrible drink, and thinking of ways to let him know it was time to drive me home. I knew what his plan was. I realized he was trying to get me "loose" by alcohol consumption and "relaxing" music. Not happening. But I didn't really know the guy, either, and it occurred to me that this little "*soirée*" could have ended with some sort of incident. However, when it was obvious to Jerry that I wouldn't be finishing my drink, let alone staying over, he seemed just as eager as I was to call it a night. I offered to have his doorman hail me a taxi and save him the trip back to Dearborn Street. He took me up on the suggestion.

We never dated again. I rarely saw Becca after that, and when I did, Jerry's name never came up.

By the time the Foundation Newsletter interview was done and the article printed, d'Arivèque summoned me to his office. For once I didn't go with trepidation. I saw my work was being recognized, and that made me happy. I hoped it pleased him and I was pretty sure it did. I wasn't, however, expecting the degree to which he went out of his way to heap laurels on me.

"You have done more to bring the vision of *Maman* to fruition than I could ever have imagined, " he told me. "I am so very impressed."

"Thank you, " I said. "And I really feel, like I told *Madame* de Piaget, that when we can get the word out in Spring with your speech to the teachers' group, the library will take off. "

"Precisely. That is why I asked you here now. I am calling a meeting of the board of the Foundation to acquaint them with the new offerings and plans, including the Mid-States appearance, and I'd like you to be there to assist me in presenting to them the ideas you have developed."

"I'd be honored to attend. Shall I make up some handouts for them? "

"Very good idea. And, thank you, Sarah. Truly. I find I am *bouleversé* by your talent and abilities. You are a great asset to the Foundation."

Oh my God. He was blown away by my talents? My abilities? Was I dreaming?

"I hope you know, *Monsieur*—er—Jean-Paul, I love this job, and I'd do, well, anything, for …the Foundation."

"That is very much appreciated. Would you also dine with me on Friday before our concert? I do have one or two things I should like to discuss with you. Would you be able to leave with me right after work?"

"Um…yes, sure. I can come…uh… dressed up that day?" My voice lilted up into a question but it was really to myself and not to him. I felt stupid.

"Good, " he said. "Come here to my office at closing and we shall leave together."

I didn't even really wonder what that was all about, figuring we had a lot of kinks to iron out before the board meeting and the convention. Months had a way of melting into no time at all when so many plans were in the works.

It would have been too ridiculous to wear the Chanel jumper to work, even though it was my go-to-symphony uniform by now, so I just hauled out the airplane skirt and sweater set, and brought pearls to put on as I was leaving my office. My London shoes were still fabulous, but my boots, sadly, had really bitten the dust, and I hadn't had a chance to get another pair yet. So even though I had worn the horrible boots in on my commute to work, I changed into the pumps and hoped against hope we'd be dropped at the door wherever he was taking me, and I wouldn't slip and slide around.

It turned out dinner was at the Palmer House, but this time in their Empire Room restaurant. He wanted me to have an aperitif and hors d'oeuvre, so I obliged by ordering a *kir royale* and shrimp cocktail. He had the same drink and a half-dozen blue point oysters. We both had salmon for a main course, and it was heavenly—super moist and awash in creamy sauce with a rice pilaf accompaniment. He did not need help cutting it, which was also brilliant.

We were done with the appetizers and waiting for the main course, and he still hadn't brought up the subjects he had said he wanted to talk to me about, so I was beginning to wonder. But then he leaned closer to me and asked about my living situation again.

"Have you heard when will you be asked to move? " he wanted to know. "The construction must be nearing completion, *non*?"

"Yes. Mr. Hyde assured me they were doing my little studio last, and so far, the workers are not there yet. But the apartment house has no more open spaces—all the work is being done now on the interior. And pretty soon that guard fence will come down, and when other people start moving in, I'll be able to just enter the front door without going through double locks! That will be different!"

He then leaned over even farther towards my ear as if what he had to say were very private.

"You will be obliged to move in any case, yes?"

"Yes, that is what I envision."

"I should like to offer you one of my staff apartments in which to live. You know where they are located, but you have not seen them yet, so I would be happy to show one to you. They are like a studio with a kitchen, perhaps a little bit larger than the one you have now. You would be on the lower level with access to the car of my mother in the garage. You would be closer to the office. It is a secure building, of course. And you would not have to pay rent."

He smiled at me and his eyes twinkled in anticipation of my loving the idea.

But I was completely taken aback, and entirely unprepared for such an offer.

"Oh, my goodness! That is too generous. But I couldn't possibly do that and… especially… I couldn't… not pay rent."

"But you accepted the offer of *Monsieur* Hyde and you do not pay rent to him."

"Only for a year. And his apartment building was empty. He did do me a huge favor, it's true, but I just can't let you give up staff quarters for me."

He again smiled at me, but through pursed lips. "Your arguments are weak, Sarah."

This time I took his hand…**in mine**. I didn't care who saw it or if it embarrassed him. I was so moved, so blown away by his offer, that I threw caution to the wind, held onto his hand, looked him in the eyes and said, "You are the kindest, most generous man I've ever met. I see it at the office and I see it at your home. I'm so grateful to be working for you. I thank you so much for thinking of me with this idea…offer. But I simply cannot accept it."

He gave my hand a little squeeze and then extracted his. "Very well. I shall respect your wishes. What I would ask is that you might think it over. I am afraid I have surprised you, perhaps even shocked you a little bit with my suggestion, *non?*" I nodded. "So just please say that you will give me your final answer later."

"Okay, I'll agree to that." Later was vague and far off, so that was okay with me.

"*Bon.* Now my next topic to discuss. Perhaps some dessert first? We still have time before the curtain goes up and, *de toute façon*, we are very close to the concert hall. What would you like?"

"I'm afraid I'm too full for dessert. But thank you anyway."

"Just perhaps a sorbet? Cleanse the palate?"

"Well, I…"

"Yes, I shall do that, too." And with that he motioned for the waiter, ordered us each a sorbet assortment, and turned back to me with a serious look on his face but still a twinkle in his eye.

"I shall be making a formal announcement in the office about this, but I wanted to tell you first. I am creating a new position at the Foundation, which we shall also take up at the board meeting. It shall be the Director of Education, and I am appointing you to the position."

"What?! Really?! Oh, gosh! I don't know what to say!"

"Say you will accept this one at least!" he laughed.

"How could I not? It's so…also…unexpected and …wonderful!"

"And it comes with an increased salary…two times what you make currently."

"Twice the salary?! But…"

"Yes, because the duties will also double. You shall need another librarian to help you with the day-to-day details like mailing out and checking in the films because, if, as you so fervently desire, we go before many hundreds of teachers in this area…perhaps even nationally, the amount of exchanging back and forth could be enormous. I propose an office for the new person in the area of the mailroom. We shall see to the details later."

"I just don't know how to thank you, not only for the salary increase but for your confidence in me. I promise not to let you down. I'm very serious about that."

"Of course you will not. And *effectivement*," he added with a hint of resignation in his voice, " with this salary increase, you would be able to afford to pay for a better apartment. *Il va sans dire.*"

We left the restaurant and were picked up by Jean-Luc who helped my amazing benefactor into the car and took us to Orchestra Hall. I know Maestro Solti was on the podium that night. I know the program consisted of many wonderful pieces of music: Ravel's *Pavane pour une Infante Défunte* and Bartok's

Concerto for Orchestra in the first half and Fauré's *Pelléas et Mélisande* in the second. But all I could do was daydream about what had just happened. Did it actually happen? What if I hadn't really heard him right? But then, eight hundred dollars a month?! Eight hundred in one month? My God, with the savings I had socked away over the rent-free period, I really could move into a nice place, even if it was at the exorbitant Chicago rates. The rule of thumb was to not spend more than twenty-five percent of gross income on housing, so my budget would be in the two hundred range, but maybe I could even go higher. My mind reeled at the possibilities; I pondered this whole thing all through the entire concert.

I wasn't a very practicing Jew at that point, and I wouldn't have been such a hypocrite as to have prayed for something like this to happen. But I knew enough to thank God Almighty for my great good fortune. What were the odds? How did I manage to have been a student of someone who knew Marie-France de Piaget? How did it happen that I was graduating right at that particular moment that she would be interviewing for an entry-level opening in a wonderful organization in the exciting, promise-filled city to which I'd planned to move anyway?

I thanked God that all the stars had converged to make it happen. And I thanked God that Iowa U had been my state school, and that even contrary to my wishes, I wound up going there and rooming with Cass Hyde, whose father, also against all odds, gave someone he hardly knew the wherewithal to take that opportunity of a lifetime.

I was thinking drippy thoughts all night. This was all a miracle. My having passed my Sorbonne exams and gotten that degree had been a miracle. Hadn't Oscar Hammerstein II written the lyrics "A hundred million miracles are happening every day?" And here some of them were, all right, happening to me.

Chapter Eighty-One

14ième ordre Pièces de Clavecin (Le Rossignol en amour)...François Couperin

As if on cue, shortly after I found out I was getting promoted at work, I came home to see that all the scaffolding was off my building and the perimeter fence had been removed also. Jake, who was back to patrolling, got out of his car and came up to me when we saw me standing there in disbelief.

"Wow, this is a change, " I said.

"I'll still be on the job while they're finishing the inside, " he told me. "As soon as people start moving in, though, I think my assignment will be changed, " he said.

"I've certainly felt safe with you here, " I said, knowing that I would really miss him. "You and Perry, both."

"Well, you've probably got us for another three months or so. How's that?"

"Great! And what about this key to the outer gate that I still have? Do I turn it back in to the Hyde company?"

I think you can just keep that key for a souvenir. They'll change the locks on that fencing."

Of course I had known the writing was on the wall and the time would come when I had to leave. I had just repressed the thoughts of having to start looking for an apartment.

I got to see Pax's amazing one not long after that and it made me daydream about what it would be like to live in his building. He had a small one-bedroom, corner apartment on the twenty-eighth floor, with these incredible sky-box-like lake views from both the living room and the bedroom. It was on Huron Place not two minutes from the Memorial Hospital complex. I couldn't imagine how a resident doc could afford such a home, and surmised that he must have had an independently wealthy back story, which turned out to be true. For one thing he had a maid, Mabel, whom he referred to as a cleaning lady, but who came every weekday. She cleaned, did his laundry, took out and picked up his dry-cleaning, and also cooked things he could heat up at all hours.

What the place lacked in square footage, it made up in exquisite finishes. Everything in it was top of the line. The first time I walked into the tiny vestibule I encountered art on the walls and a revelatory musical instrument in my line of vision.

"What is **that**?" I asked, looking at the light green and gold gilt, low wooden piano-like thing before me. "It looks like a harpsichord!"

"Well, that, darlin' **is** a harpsichord. I built it myself."

"**You** built it? Do you play it?"

"Yes and yes. I built it from a kit, and I play it every night. Almost every night, I guess I should say if I want to tell the whole truth."

"My God!" I got closer to it. I thought that the instrument was very beautiful even before I heard a sound come out of it. It had a single keyboard as opposed to double ones I had seen mostly in museums or at the U of Iowa in the music practice rooms. The soundboard was exposed, and the interior panels had a floral motif I thought was painted on but that Pax told me he had stenciled.

"It's cheating, " he laughed.

"No it's not. And you sure did a terrific job of that. That gold paint trim is a nice touch, too."

"I modeled it after one I saw in Paris, " he said, "at the Carnavalet Museum. Do you know that place?"

"I do."

He sat down at the keyboard and, without availing himself of any of the music that was neatly stacked on a small table behind the bench, played from memory a little Sarabande from Handel's *Suite No. 4 in D minor*. I was thoroughly enraptured. He was really good.

His living room also had a small terrace reachable by a sliding glass door, but other than that, it was the antithesis of the d'Arivèque one. The seating was all comfortable, one long couch and one elongated chair, both entirely of grey leather, modern in look and feel. The walls were painted a soft grey and accents were white. It certainly was not like the Hyde penthouse, either, in that it wasn't merely an art receptacle, but had a lived-in vibe. He had a pair of tall bookcases which held all books and no bibelots, with the exception of some fancy jade bookends shaped like the seated Buddha. There was no separate dining room, but one corner of the main room held a striking glass and chrome table and four grey chairs with crisp lines and comfortable seats.

His galley kitchen was also small, but had sleek white cabinetry and white appliances, light slate-colored Corian counter tops, and every possible amenity for the times: a microwave oven, a refrigerator with a slide-out freezer compartment below, a little "garage door" storage area on the counter that held a fancy Italian coffee maker, a toaster and a stand mixer inside. The sink was deep and square, if small, and it had one of those pot-filler high faucets, as well as a spray attachment. Everything was spotless.

"Oh! Do you cook?" I wondered upon seeing all his accoutrements.

"Not very much, I have to admit, " he laughed. "I leave that to Mabel."

"Well, yeah. It'd be a shame if a great kitchen like this went to waste," I muttered, completely envious.

There was a powder room next to the kitchen and attached to that a double-doored closet which opened to reveal a stacked washer and dryer on one side and floor-to-ceiling linen and storage shelves on the other.

Finally, the only room left to see was the bedroom with its attached bathroom. Another "study in grey," it had corner west-exposure windows that warmed the place up in the chill winter afternoons, and whose thick thermal shades kept out the summer's oppressive heat. His huge bed was another California King. The bed-frame was black and modern and the headboard was black tufted with inset flat button accents. Two tasteful black end tables with Chinese motifs flanked the sides of the bed, and a bench was at the foot. Directly in front of that was a dresser with a television set on it, and across from that, to the far side of the bed, was an Eames lounge chair, (with no clothes draped across it) and an ottoman to match. Above the dresser was a large mirror that mostly reflected the view out the window to anyone in bed. He also had another low bookcase on the other wall and this one did have some little personal things that may have been souvenirs from travels, it looked like to me, and one vase, devoid of flowers or plants, but decorative nonetheless.

A wide pocket door led to the bathroom, which was the main bath of the place. It was gigantic by apartment standards, with a beautiful black and white tiled shower, a separate soaking tub, and a vanity with one sink set into the same Corian counter as the kitchen. To the side of the shower was a walk-in closet where all his clothing was meticulously arranged, and which also had loads of storage for every sort of supply and for his luggage.

"This place is fantastic, " I swooned.

"Wait 'til you try out the bed, " he said as he drew me close to him and began to unbutton my oxford-cloth shirt.

We kissed, short at first then longer and more intensely. He moved on to removing the rest of my clothes, quite adeptly. I was more awkward undressing him, but we finally snuggled down naked in his bedclothes. He propped himself up on one arm and asked me, "Are you on the pill?"

"I'm not, " I answered.

He then reached over into the little drawer of the night stand and pulled out a package containing a condom.

"I think you're gonna like this, " he said, and put it on himself.

When I felt it inside me, it was soft and fuzzy! What was this? Shearling? That's what it felt like. *(Note to self: you're such a neophyte.)* "That's nice, " I whispered in his ear, but he was already not listening. Pretty soon I, too, was rising to a crescendo of pure joy.

Afterwards he asked me if I wanted to shower.

"What I'd really love to do is have a bath with those tub jets of yours," I answered.

"You got it, darlin', " he said laughing and jumped up to fill the tub and fulfill my wish.

When I ventured into the bathroom, the tub was also full of bubbles.

"Oh, you keep bubble bath here?" I laughed teasingly.

"As what man wouldn't?"

He lowered himself in one end motioned for me to get in the other. The tub was so big, we hardly touched. The jets felt like a heavenly massage. I leaned back against the sloping end and stared over at Pax, noticing again how beautiful a specimen he was. I had to marvel anew that I was the girl in bed with him and now in the tub with him, when, as I had protested to Cass, he could have anyone he wanted and they would all want to have him.

"You've got a bitchin' body, Sari. Your waist is tiny and you are very amply endowed on top--- for such a little girl, I mean. I'll bet you've also the best legs in the joint at work."

I just looked at him, expecting to see signs of sarcasm, but there weren't any.

He continued by asking me what I weighed.

"I am at my all-time high of one hundred seven, " I told him truthfully. "I've gained ten pounds since high school and college, because until I moved to Chicago, I always weighed the same, ninety-seven pounds. Probably cooking my way through Julia Child this past year did it." *That plus the fact that I kept eating out in fabulous Chicago restaurants or in the home of my boss, which obviously didn't help either.*

Pax's schedule didn't leave him any time off for the next ten days after our initial love-making, but he called me to say that later on in the month, he had a semi-free weekend scheduled, and he wanted me to block out the time and go with him on a short trip up to Algoma, Wisconsin.

"Algoma, Wisconsin? Where's that and what's there?"

" A few hours north of here. It's a really sweet little town...nicer in the summer, of course, than now, because it's a port city. But they're having a sugaring off festival and some tall ships will be in their harbor, provided it isn't iced over."

"Sugaring off? Like what they do in Québec?" I was astonished and had only seen that in the film library's Canada collection.

"Yes, exactly. More places in North America have sugar maples than just Canada, you know. Goofy girl. Do you want to go?"

"Okay, sure, I could dig seeing that."

"I have a half-day meeting at the medical center up there, " he said, "but you'll have plenty to do and see in the town. I'll find you as soon as I can get out, and we'll have a great dinner and stay the night Saturday. What do you say?"

"Sounds groovy."

He paused a minute and then said, "And since you'll be bringing an overnight case, pack in some work outfit or other because you should stay here with me Sunday night, and just go to your office from my place on Monday---it's a lot closer than yours anyway."

Boy, that was the truth; he lived just minutes from my office.

"Deal," I agreed.

So that's what we did. He arranged to pick me up very early on the Saturday morning for the three-plus hour drive up there along the highway that skirts Lake Michigan. In front of my house he took my bag and put it in the trunk of his car and then he suddenly looked over at me and asked,

"Can you drive a stick shift?"

"Yep." I answered, about to explain that I could even drive a French one. But instead of letting me continue, he popped the keys into the air and said, "Here, catch! You drive."

I caught them but was incredulous. "Me? Drive this...machine... of yours? You'd actually let me?"

"Sure. You know you want to."

I couldn't deny that, but it was the last thing I expected.

I got behind the wheel and adjusted the seat. He pointed out a few things, like the order of the gears in the gear box. Of course, there was a diagram on the knob, and, naturally I knew which pedals were which. However, I didn't know about the overdrive stuff, so once I got on Lake Shore, which turned into U.S. Highway 41 heading north, he told me to put in the clutch. I did it and then he shifted the car into fifth gear from the passenger seat.

"Clutch out now," he ordered, and I let it out.

He taught me how to downshift once I had to slow down and then how to get back into that overdrive gear again when I sped back up. I got the hang of it quick enough.

477

The trip took three and a half hours, but the route was fairly simple. At a point north of Milwaukee the road changed numbers, but it still pretty much went in a straight line to Algoma if we stayed on the highway that ran along the lake. He had to get to his meetings by eleven, and offered to drive the last third of the way. My back muscles felt pretty sore mostly because I probably hadn't adjusted the seat well enough, but also because I had tensed up driving that car for the first time. They don't call it horsepower for nothing. The Volvo roadster acted like a racehorse wanting to bolt, and I was timid about letting it do so. It made me nervous.

I was curious to know more about his job, but at the onset of the trip Pax had put a moratorium on "talking shop, "i.e. medicine, so he asked me — politely of course, if I could make a point not to bring it up.

"You've no idea what I have to listen to day in and day out, " he told me. "Yesterday one of my patients was sure his **blood** was hurting. He was showing me exactly which veins and which arteries felt the worst. Christ."

"Yes, but that's your chosen field, " I had remarked. "Who else are they going to tell their troubles to, if not you?"

"Yeah, well, please don't try to pinpoint which veins have what blood in them, okay?"

Upon arrival in the little town of Algoma, we parked his car near the hospital and he went in, leaving me to meander about the place for a few hours. He thought he'd be done by two at the latest and said for me to start making my way back towards the hospital, that he'd find me. He said if I got lost, which he doubted would happen, I should just ask someone to direct me towards the hospital; and he said if I kept track of where the lake was I couldn't get lost.

The town was indeed as cute as he'd described — a throwback to another era. Teenagers dressed as town criers were announcing festival activities. People had to go out into the woods around the outskirts to actually see the sap that flowed into the buckets attached to the tree trunks; but on their Main Street, they'd set up little sugar shacks for us to try out the syrupy substance on ice chips, or eat the candy they were making from it right there. I wandered in and out of little booths and shacks; when I got cold, I found the town coffee shop to sit in and have hot chocolate.

I was dressed pretty warmly in brown dungarees and Cass' fisherman-knit sweater, but it was still winter, and the wind coming off Lake Michigan was as biting there as it was in Chicago. I had put my hair in a low ponytail tied with a brown velvet ribbon and tucked it into my fur hood, and of course, my new camel coat kept me protected. But the best part of this outfit were my new boots: dark brown with a contrasting reddish-brown top and adjustable crisscrossed- buckled straps at the instep. I loved them. With the dusty brown jeans tucked in and my camel coat flapping around below the knee, I felt chic.

The sign coming into Algoma placed the population at around 2,300, and there was no college there, so the little commercial center of the town was a tad thin on boutiques or retail shops. I did, however, find a bookstore, went in and perused its aisles for an hour. When I was warm enough to brave the elements again, I went to the harbor and sat down on a bench there.

The tall ships were gorgeous and impressive. No one was allowed to board them unless they were crew. "Sailors" in old fashioned uniforms were scrambling up and down the ropes of the mainsail, no doubt for the amusement of the crowd. "Officers," in colonial-looking dress uniforms with shiny brass buttons and lots of braid, were prancing up and down on the deck, pretending to make preparations to depart. Many families with children made up the spectators, and the enthralled kids clamored to board the ships, but were dissuaded from doing so. I was also mesmerized by the sails and rigging and I, too would have liked to have climbed on board.

"Do you sail?" asked Pax when he found me sitting there. He'd gotten out of his meeting even earlier than planned.

"Who me? God, no."

"I'll teach you. We'll wait for warmer weather, though."

"You have a boat, too? Where do you keep it?"

"I don't have one in Chicago, but we can rent them, " he replied, giving me a little cuff on the shoulder and then putting his arm around me to walk along the dock.

478

Later we had dinner in a nice enough restaurant that was doing a bang-up festival business right near the little pier. It was in an old converted factory building and had an antique car parked in front with the sign "Hilltop Manor" propped up against it. The specialty was New England clam chowder, which amused me. The place was more like my parents' bar and grill than anything I could picture in New England.

Pax told me he'd made reservations at a "cute place" for us to spend that night. It turned out to be a quaint motel complex he seemed to know existed on Highway 42, called Blue Top Knolls. It consisted of a Scandinavian looking lodge, which was quite spacious with an A-frame design, where one checked in, got keys and could also get coffee; and then the sleeping quarters, which were ten small white cottages scattered around a circular drive, which all had blue roofs and blue shutters. The place looked like a holdout from the forties, which I loved. If snow hadn't been piled up where they'd cleared the drive, a fountain would have been visible, marking the center of a communal garden for all the cabins.

"This is a sweet little set up, " I said. "How do you know about it?"

"I've had meetings up here before, " he answered nonchalantly.

"Yeah, I bet you bring all the girls here." I said, meaning it.

He laughed. "No, just you."

The interior was arranged like a child's playhouse with a Lilliputian living room, minuscule bedroom and kitchenette, and a tiny bathroom. As hard as it was to believe, the furnishings were normal sized, with the noted exception of the stove and fridge which seemed to be on a scale of half the regular dimensions.

"I bet some people actually live in spaces like this for real, " I mused.

"Unfortunately, you're right. In Louisiana whole families do. It's one reason we needed Johnson's war on poverty."

"Are you a Democrat? I mean, one can imagine there are such animals as wealthy Democrats. Rare species that they may be."

" Darlin' my family's been Democrats since the Civil War. And yes that was the wrong side to be on then, but we feel vindicated now."

"You'll have to forgive what I'm about to say, but I'm going to say it anyway, " I chided him. "The South is a foreign country to me. I especially don't know how any Jews can live there, and yet, we do."

"Well, they certainly do. I'm guessing you don't even know this, but there are Jewish graves in the Confederate section of Hollywood Cemetery in Richmond, Virginia." He paused for a minute and then said, "And so you're Jewish?"

"You couldn't tell by looking at me? " I asked, knowing full well the answer.

"No!"

"Yes."

"I'm Catholic."

I looked up at him and took his chin in my hand, brought it to my lips and kissed him. "I knew that."

"How did you?"

"Never mind."

The next morning we went to the lodge hoping to find breakfast, but all they had was the same coffee laid out as the night before.

"It's okay by me, " I told Pax, "I don't really eat breakfast anyway."

He crinkled up his nose and shot me a look. "You should, though. Let's go get some."

One thing every small town in America usually had in common was some great local diner or coffee shop where you could gorge on eggs, pancakes, waffles, bacon and sausage. But this was Sunday morning and the thing Americans did on that day in places like Algoma, Wisconsin, was to show up in church. So we hit the road---he drove—and made our way to the bigger towns where businesses were likely to buck the Sabbath thing and be open.

Five hours later, we pulled back into Chicago, parked his fabulous car, got our stuff out, picked up the *Chicago Sun Times* from his front lobby, headed straight up to his apartment, and tumbled back into bed. We made love, read the paper, and fell asleep. When I awoke it was nearly seven p.m., and he was up watching t.v. in the living room with the newspaper spread all over the place. I hadn't even heard him leave the room.

"You were tired, " he said.

"I guess so! Wow."

"And hungry?"

"Sure. Do you want me to cook something? What have you got on hand here?" We had known each other for a few weeks, now, but we hadn't gotten around to where I came from and my background with the restaurant business.

"Oh, hell no. How about if I order in Chinese food? What do you like?"

"Well that's a fab idea. I like everything except… please nothing Szechuan. I ordered that once in Paris, took one bite, and spent the rest of the night in the bathroom of the restaurant with my head under the faucet. I thought I'd drown myself gulping water. Death would have been preferable to the burning in my throat."

He laughed, but then said, "I'm sorry. I can imagine that wasn't funny then."

"Well, it wasn't. My God, who can eat that stuff?"

"I won't order anything hot, " he said.

"Merci beaucoup.

"De rien."

"I keep forgetting you speak French."

Soon there arrived wonderful take-out that he buzzed in, and they brought right up to the apartment door. It was a different world, I thought. We looked like lovers in the movies, sitting around in our skivvies on his leather sofa eating out of those ubiquitous little boxes with chopsticks. He tossed me a fortune cookie and opened one for himself.

"What does it say?" I asked, having trouble tearing the wrapper off my cookie.

"Mine says, ' You will sing like a nightingale under the stars. Lucky numbers 2 4 5 7 and 20.' What about yours? If you can get it open."

"I know. I can never unwrap sealed cellophane. If I were stranded on a desert island with just crackers in those little packages, I'd starve to death."

"Here…give it to me."

"Oh—I got it, " I said giving it the final yank that tore it. "Okay, mine says, 'You are lucky to have an eager and enthusiastic audience.' Lucky numbers are…Oh, my God! …listen to this: 12 30 48. My birthday's the 30th, and I was born in '48! Not December, but still…"

"You must be lucky!" he laughed. "What's the audience?"

"Well, I couldn't tell you. I'm not destined for any stage that I can think of."

Pax had set the alarm for pretty early. I wanted to be at work by 8:00, but he had to be on duty even before that. I only had that short walk from his place, so he said I could linger over the Italian coffee he would make and just let myself out.

"That's a plan," I agreed.

We got in the steamy shower together. I turned to soap him down first, and he cupped his hands over my breasts, and stood behind me pressing against me as he reached around and lathered my front. When all at once he stopped.

"Here," he said solemnly, guiding me under the water, "rinse off."

"Uh, okay." I thought maybe he was later than he realized.

He got out first and snapped a towel around him, dried off with it, and then handed me one and said, "Towel down and then just put this around you and come back into the bedroom."

"Yes, sir, doctor!" I said sarcastically.

All dried off, I wandered into the bedroom and batted my eyelashes at him teasing, "Is this a clinic? The love rotation?"

"Lay down on the bed, Sari, and put your arms over your head. Do you give yourself monthly breast self-examinations?"

"Huh-uh, "I said, still not getting what he was up to.

"I felt a lump in your breast in the shower, " he told me. "I want to verify that."

480

"What?! Come on."

But he was serious, and as I lay there with my arms up, he used both hands to manipulate the tissue back and forth, pressing down and then scooting over a bit and repeating it. He did each breast.

"I'm feeling something at one o'clock on the right breast, " he said. "I'm going to mark it." And he reached over for a ballpoint pen and actually put an "x"on me! "Here, I want you to feel this. It shouldn't be in there." He put my fingers on the spot and I felt it.

"Thanks a lot. That ink will never come off! Anyway, I'm a little young to have breast cancer, don't you think?"

"Actually, I do think it's probably benign. I can move it around. It could be a fibroadenoma. But you have to have it checked out. Like today. You have an Ob/Gyn don't you? Make an appointment as soon as you think their office is open."

"I don't have any Chicago doctors yet."

"Okay, then show up at our clinic and they'll assign you someone. You have to get this started today."

"No! I can't just leave work."

"Today."

"Look, I'll talk to our office manager and ask her who her doctor is. Maybe she can make me an appointment. I'm sure she'll do it. Or one of the other women will."

"Promise me you'll do it though, darlin'."

"Yeah, okay, I promise."

"Try not to worry too much. Most of these lumps are cysts."

"You're more worried than I am."

I wasn't worried. I didn't know shit about breast cancer in 1971, and there was no internet to look anything up. I would have had to go to the Chicago public library because I doubted I could even get access to a medical library over at some university. But really, I wasn't concerned enough to even start the process of research.

First thing when I got to the office, I went to Annie-Laure and asked if Marie-France could see me that morning some time. She checked MFP's calendar and told me she was free all morning, and that sure, she'd see me. And she did.

"I felt a lump in my breast today, " I told Marie-France matter-of-factly, "and I was wondering if you could give me the name of your Ob/Gyn, and maybe I can make an appointment to see him."

She looked up from her desk right at me with a look of terror in her eyes.

"Oh, *mon Dieu*, yes, of course. Here, let me call her. Sit there." She motioned for me to take the chair in front of her desk.

She had a rolodex right by the phone and dialed a number. When the other party answered, she asked if a Doctor Bertrand could see a new patient at her earliest convenience, and gave them my name and a few details…that I worked with her and was new to the city so I didn't already have a doctor. Marie-France placed her hand over the mouthpiece and told me they said they could get me in at two o'clock that afternoon. I nodded.

"*Parfait. Je vous remercie, Mademoiselle*, er… thank you very much, " she said, a bit flustered, remembering there at the end that she wasn't necessarily talking to a francophone. She replaced the receiver, and turned her attention back to me. "I shall write down for you where the office is. She is associated with the hospital right near us…you know it… you took papers there to *Monsieur* that day. Her offices are in that complex. The grounds are rather large. You may have to ask someone."

"Yes, I'll find it. Thank you so much,"

How lucky was that? Pax's hospital, too.

"And, Sarah, you may possibly not be aware of this, or perhaps you forgot, but you have health insurance working here. So do not worry too much about the bills. They often let you pay monthly, too, if something is not covered. We shall work with you on that."

"Oh, gosh, thanks! I wasn't even thinking about that."

"I am writing down the name of the insurance company. We may have to have a card issued for you. I shall check with Personnel. Try not to worry."

Gads, people thought I should be worried about this. I decided to see what Dr. Bertrand had to say first. But it was only ten in the morning, and I had to stew about this whole turn of events for another four hours. It certainly killed my appetite, and I didn't go out for lunch; but at about a quarter to two, I headed over to find the office.

Dr. Bertrand was French. No big surprise there. She had done her initial medical training in Paris, but having come to Chicago on a research exchange in the early '60's, she had decided to stay. It was easier for doctors to get visas, green cards and resident alien papers, and after a few years, she became a U.S. citizen, she told me, not that I had asked. She was still pretty young looking to me...her light brown hair—not short but not as long as my hair-- fluffed in curls around her face. She had big brown eyes, a rather long nose, and a friendly smile. One thing I noticed was that she had very delicate long hands. Just like Pax.

Her nurse had asked me to change into a gown open in the front, and had directed me to get up on the examination table with the paper protector on it. When the doctor came back in, she had me lie down and covered me in another papery drape, which she pulled back, then spread open the sides of the gown, and did the breast exam. I had to explain the X.

"My boyfriend is Dr. Paxton Hubley, " I explained, sort of lying about the "boyfriend" bit. "He... uh... marked the lump location for me."

"I see," she said, smiling. She did not laugh, but I bet she wanted to. "He speaks excellent French."

Her breast exam was eerily like the one Pax did. "I would like to get a ' *radio*' of your breast, " she said using the French term. "So you will sit at this desk against the wall, please? And we shall bring in the machine. Just sit right there for a minute."

I got off the table and sat down, whereupon a cart was rolled in with a funny looking object -- shaped like a cone-- sitting on it. They put a lead apron on my stomach, which really wasn't in range of the cone anyway, since I was sidled up to the table, and moved the cone over to touch my bare breast. Dr. Bertram stepped out and a tech of some sort came over to me. There was a push button remote control gizmo on the cart, like a camera shutter activator, and after the young woman had set up a huge film frame, like any other x-ray film of that era, she picked up the remote, told me to take a breath and hold it and not move, and stepped away from the machine to take the picture. That's all there was to it. There was no compression of the breast. All that standing with one's breasts squeezed between plates of glass was still decades away.

They told me to get dressed and the doctor would be back to talk to me.

"I would like you to see a surgeon, " she told me.

"So...what do you think it is?" I asked tentatively.

"I honestly do not think it will be malignant, " she said, and I breathed easier. "But we cannot tell either by feeling it or by having this mammogram, which, as you can see, is like an x-ray. We need to have a biopsy. But I will say, it's rather large."

"Oh boy, " I sighed.

"I want you to see Dr. Fabrizio Garabanti here at our hospital."

"Oh! I know him! Well, no I don't know him; rather I know of him," I corrected myself.

"Good!" she exclaimed. *Tant mieux.* He's the best there is. My secretary will set it up. He probably cannot get you in for a few days---perhaps as long as a week. But that is still soon. Do not worry."

There was that caveat once more. However, I was elated that I was going to be set up to see that doctor Pax had raved about. I was lucky. Again.

Chapter Eighty-Two

"Monday, Monday" …The Mamas & the Papas

The surgeon's office was going to take another week to be able to get me in, so I called Sol and Betty. I didn't expect them to come hold my hand through it or anything; at that point I still didn't think I had anything to be overly concerned about. But they were my parents, and I certainly didn't want them hearing through some third party if anything bad had happened to their daughter.

"Oh, Sari, no!" Betty exclaimed with a tone of panic when I told her about the lump. "Sol! Get on the extension."

"They don't think it's cancer, but no one can be sure until they biopsy it. The OB also said she thought it was rather…er…large."

"So, why don't you just come home, then, " said Sol in an uncharacteristic quiet voice.

"Come home? For the surgery? Oh, no…that's not necessary. They've already begun the process here. I have a preliminary appointment with the surgeon next Friday."

"No, I mean, come home. MOVE back here. You don't have to live in Chicago. You gave it a try…got it out of your system. Now come back."

"Daddy, " I said, "I'm not moving back there. Whatever gave you that idea?"

"Well, you tell me…just what is keeping you in Chicago? Your job?"

"Yes, as a matter of fact. That's the other reason I was calling! I got a big promotion. What do you think about that?"

"A promotion from what to what? Sounded to me like you were a glorified mail room attendant."

"Why would you think that?"

"Well, you said you mailed films out and re-catalogued them when they came back in. What's the promotion? To a secretary now? Is that what I sent you to college for?"

"The promotion is to Director of Education for the Foundation, and all along I've done more than mailings. I write lesson plans that go with the films, I have created role-play units for elementary classes and put together all sorts of materials. I do lots of things."

Finally Betty joined in and added, "That all sounds real good, Sari. "

"No lie! They're doubling my salary!"

"Sari, I think I should come out there and go with you to the doctor's appointment, " Betty said. "I can take the train in on the Thursday night before and leave on Saturday morning."

"Well, fine…if you want to. " Right away I would have to figure out where I'd sleep if I gave her the day bed. Too bad I didn't have a sofa.

"Yeah, you should, " my father echoed.

"Yes, it's settled. That's what I'm going to do."

I had another call to make about this also. Cass had been very excited for me when she heard the news of my promotion, and started fantasizing with me on the phone about all the fab things we could do when I came for my next visit. She said she had some great ideas on art projects that would tie into French films and "You should take all the credit for coming up with them. We will work out the details when you get here."

I was slated to go to Cass' around her birthday at the beginning of March. This was now going to be impossible and I had to tell her.

"Oh, my GOD, Sari, you have a LUMP in your breast? How horrible! You must be scared to death."

"Well, I just don't think women my age are at so much of a risk. Besides, Pax and my new OB both think it's benign."

"But how can they know that?"

"They can't know it definitively. But I guess there are indications they look for between cancer and non-cancer. I'm afraid I can't tell you what those might be. Pax talked about it being movable, and I took that to be a good sign. But Dr. Bertram said it's big, and I take that to be a not-so-good sign. So who knows?"

"But how are you going to handle it?"

"That's why I'm calling, Cass. I'm having surgery in 10 days and then there's a week at least recuperation period, plus check-ups and post-op stuff. I'll also miss a week of work. So, the thing is, damn it, I can't come to Iowa City in March. I'm so sorry to have to miss your birthday, especially when I said I was coming."

"I'm sorry, too, of course, but you could maybe come in April!"

"In April I have to go to the Mid-States conference and hand out stuff. My boss is going to give a huge presentation---he's the key-note speaker and I'm the side-kick. The preparation for that will be big, too."

"Your health comes first and foremost, kid. Don't give it another thought. I just wish I could come there and be with you for the surgery!"

"Well, if you ever want to come to Chicago you always have a place with me, although there's no there there, to quote Gertrude Stein. Ha! Betty's coming next week to go to the surgeon consultation with me and I'll have to sleep on the floor or something."

"I'm worried about you Sari. You keep me in the loop, okay? Promise?"

"Sure. No sweat."

"What did your parents say? Did they flip out?"

"Oh, get this... my father says I should move home and doesn't give a shit that I got a huge promotion or anything. Betty's more sympathetic. I think she sort of assumes I have it...cancer. I didn't call them to get their sympathy. I called them because their daughter could --but probably doesn't—have a life-threatening disease. Wouldn't you want to know if you were a parent?"

"Hmmm." Cass probably wondered if her parents would.

I met my mother at the train and we took a cab to my house. The temporary fencing was down, which showed off the original black iron gate that was behind it; and the façade was devoid of vines, so the bricks looked pretty bare. Still, it was a handsome building and would only get better once they redid the windows. But climbing up the steps with me all Betty could manage to say was how lucky I was that my father didn't see where I was living because he'd "yank you right out of here."

"Yeah? What's wrong with it?"

"It looks like a tenement."

"Oh my God, are you joking? Do you know what a real tenement even looks like?"

Inside things went from bad to worse. She froze when she entered my place and looked around. Even though I had only minimal belongings in it, and no adornments of art or nice furniture, my tiny studio was clean and tidy, respectable and efficient.

"You live like a pauper, " she said, looking around.

"Yes, because I was one. But since I've saved on rent money and now just about to get a promotion, I'm doing all right!"

"So where will you move?"

"Don't know yet. I'm not even sure what I can afford or what's out there to rent. But all I know is I'm a hell of a lot better off now than I was a year ago, and I'm happy with that. I super love my job, as I'm sure you know. Sorry I'm taking tomorrow off or I'd show you the office."

So that was a fib. I did take the day off, but I could have easily taken her up to see the offices and meet everyone. The doctor's appointment wasn't ten minutes from my office. But she didn't know any of that.

She settled in on the day bed and I sat in the chair by the Chinese lamp.

"I do think, Sari, if it turns out to be cancer after all, that you should come home. I won't be able to come here and take care of you."

"I realize that."

"If you have breast cancer and they have to remove your breast, you'll have to start chemotherapy and probably radiation, *oy gevalt*. You'll get very sick. Living alone is out of the question. Especially here."

"Why especially here? " She was beginning to enter "getting on my nerves" territory.

"Well, all those stairs, for one thing. How will you ever drag yourself outside to go to appointments or buy groceries? I just told you. You're going to be very very sick."

"We don't even know that I have it! Don't expect the worst and don't project crap onto me. Please! Let's see what happens, first."

"Do you promise to just think about what I said?"

"I'll think about it."

People kept trying to elicit promises out of me!

We went to the doctor's appointment the next morning, and were both impressed with what a nice man Dr. Garabanti was. Just as Pax had described, his "bedside manner," even though not at my bedside, was caring and reassuring, and his expertise showed-- even to us ignorant lay people.

He had my mammogram up on the lighted board and reiterated that he did not think it was cancer. I glanced at my mother as if to throw a little smugness at her, but I could see the fear was almost melting away from her face, so I just smiled. I remained calm throughout the consultation, as he outlined specifically what the surgery would entail. It wouldn't be a needle biopsy, but a lumpectomy. I'd be put under general anesthesia.

"We will need to remove that tumor, " he explained, "but there won't be any side effects except for some residual pain. We'll give you something for that. You'll be pretty bandaged up for a while." He smiled at me. He was a sweetheart.

"So," Betty asked the doctor, "do you think I need to come back here when she has the surgery? We live pretty far away."

"I can't make that decision for you, Mrs. Shrier, but I can say that Sarah is an adult and I'm pretty sure she can manage this. If everything goes well, she shouldn't be too incapacitated."

For the remainder of her stay, Betty and I refrained from getting into any more arguments. We put a moratorium on nagging and judgmental accusations with each other until I put her back on the train the next morning. I had slept on the floor rug for two nights, folding my bedspread into a very thin sleeping bag, which was totally uncomfortable, but luckily, I had a second pillow to use. We had eaten out rather than cooking any meals in my apartment, but I did make her tea.

"I'll eat breakfast on the train, " she said.

"That will be best, " I concurred.

I agreed to call them as soon as the ordeal was over and to check in periodically as well.

She stopped before going up the little steps onto the train and ran her hands through my bangs. "Nobody ever thinks cancer can happen to them. It's always the other guy," she said, as we stood there awkwardly, not hugging or kissing.

"Well, it hasn't happened to us yet, has it? Let's just try to keep this all in perspective until we actually know something."

It occurred to me that I was the one sounding like the mother.

Chapter Eighty-Three

"If You Leave Me Now"…Chicago

The surgery was scheduled for late February and I had enough time to alert the office that I'd be taking a few days off, which I didn't expect to be paid for because I didn't realize we had sick leave as a benefit; but we did. As I came out of Marie-France's office, Annie-Laure beckoned me to her desk and said that she and Jean-Luc at least wanted to pick me up and take me to the hospital the morning of the surgery so I didn't have to take a cab. I knew by now that if anything was planned using any of Monsieur's cars, he knew about it, so I assumed he knew I was going in for the operation. I hadn't said anything to anyone else there, but all things had a way of finding their way back to him.

When the scheduled day arrived for surgery and I had to be there at six in the morning, they appeared out front at five-forty-five and I climbed into the limo with my little overnight bag. I figured I'd be spending one or possibly two nights, but no more than that.

"I really appreciate this, you two, " I said.

"We plan to come visit you, too, "said Annie-Laure.

"That's so sweet. But you don't have to. I'm not going to be there long, I'm sure."

"We hope not!"

They dropped me at the front entrance and I went in through the wide revolving door, to a desk, where I found out where to report on the surgical floor. Once up there, I was assigned a bed in a room with three other beds and given a gown to change into. There was also a locker for my personal things. I was to remove all jewelry, which, as it turned out, I hardly wore at all.

I got into "my" designated bed and then there was a series of doctors, technicians and nurses who came in to do different things to me: draw blood and blood gases; measure, re-mark the spot (another X!), take my pulse, hook on an I.V. and start a sedative through it. The anesthesiologist came in and introduced himself to me. His initial statement was off-putting, "I'll be putting you to sleep." And with that he taped a sign that said "Nothing by mouth" above my bed and left.

The there was a barrage of paperwork. They'd taken my insurance card at the first desk, and they returned it hooked under the top of a clipboard full of things I had to sign. One of the papers was permission to do a radical mastectomy if needed.

"Why do I have to sign that?" I asked, incredulous. "Dr. Garabanti didn't tell me anything about doing a mastectomy on the spot."

"We just have you sign it so that we don't have to wake you up and then put you back under in case it turns out that we must do further surgery."

"Well, I'm not sure I want to give permission for that."

"It would make things a lot easier if you sign it, " she said matter-of-factly, like it was a mortgage contract or a bill for car repairs or something.

I signed it and then when she left, I lay there saying to myself, "Shit shit shit."

Another young woman was in the same room but the other two beds were empty, so it was big and we had it all to ourselves. She came over to my bed.

" I'm Jenny. What are you here for?" she asked me.

"Sari. Breast biopsy."

"Me, too!"

"We're too young to have cancer, don't you suppose?" I asked her, laughing –a little too nervously, it turned out.

"You think so?" she replied.

"I do think so."

"Shall we play cards later this afternoon when we're back in here?" she asked me.

"Sure, you're on."

Pretty soon they came in and started me on a heavier sedative, so much so that I really didn't realize they had transferred me onto a gurney and put me in the hall. I came to just slightly – enough to see subway-tiled green walls -- and then drifted out again.

I woke up back in my room with Jean-Paul d'Arivèque sitting at my bedside, holding my hand! There was a beautiful pink rose in a tall thin vase on the table.

He leaned over and kidded me, "God has been playing marbles on your chest?"

I wanted to laugh but it hurt. I tried reaching up to feel if I had two breasts still there or not. The bandages were really tight, and I couldn't even tell.

I looked up at his soft features and kind expression. I tried to ascertain from his demeanor if I had cancer or not, which was, of course, futile. How long had he even been there? The room was already getting dark.

"Water?" I managed to articulate with a hoarse voice.

"No, Sarah. I am afraid you cannot have anything yet."

A nurse came in just then so he asked her, even though he knew the answer, if I could have something to drink.

"Nope! Nothing to drink or eat. How about ice chips?"

I nodded, hoping they'd dump them in my mouth. I felt like I had just dragged myself across a parched desert.

But then all at once I was overcome by a wave of nausea, one of my worst fears. I retched, and the nurse saw me.

"Oh no, honey, we don't want you throwing up." And she left the room in haste.

Right on the heels of her leaving appeared Paxton Hubley!

"PAX!" I exclaimed in a hoarse whisper, since I was still hardly able to talk.

He approached the bed and saw that I also had a visitor, which I realized he wouldn't be expecting. But he leaned right over anyway and kissed me on the forehead.

"Hi, darlin'. You're fine!" announced. "It was benign, just as we were hoping."

The nurse came back in with a shot for me and she handed the syringe to him. He administered it and then I turned my attention to introducing him to Jean-Paul as best I could with my croaky voice.

"Dr. Paxton Hubley, this is my boss, *Monsieur* Jean-Paul d'Arivèque."

Pax offered his hand and said, *"Enchanté, Monsieur."*

"Enchanté, Docteur. Vous parlez français?"

"Oui, monsieur. Je viens de la Nouvelle Orléans, d'une famille qui est moitié française."

"Bon, mais alors,tant mieux! Voulez-vous que je vous laisse avec votre patiente?"

"Merci. On n'en a que pour quelques instants."

And with that, JPA struggled to his feet and made his way outside the room to leave the doctor with his patient.

"So I have both boobs?" I asked more for reassuring myself.

"You most certainly do! Nothing else to worry about. Dr. Garabanti saw some moles on you and took off several of those, too. He may have saved you a lot of headache down the road doing that."

I nodded, still very groggy. At least the anti-nausea meds were kicking in. I felt better on all accounts.

Pax came around the other side of my bed and sat down in the chair where JPA had been. "Your boss must really like you!" he said. "I didn't expect to see anyone here. Does he maybe have a thing for you?" he asked laughingly but in hushed tones.

"He... well... bats for the other team, " I said.

"Ah! Got it. So, listen, Sari," he said, leaning right over me and brushing the side of my cheek gently with his elegant hand , "the thing is...you're on my service now, so...we can't... I mean, I can't go out with you."

"What?! Why ever not?"

"Because my boss is Dr. Garabanti and you're his patient. So you're my patient. And the ethics rules are clear. I can't risk anything to do with my career, now can I?"

"But I won't be a patient for long!"

"You will, 'Sugah'. I'm sorry that's just the way it is. Them's the breaks."

"For God's sake, Pax, " I said and felt my eyes well up.

"I know, darlin'. But don't fret…I'll come back later and see you in here, okay?"

"Ok−k−ay," I said beginning to sob.

Pax left and I could hear him tell JPA, "She's all yours, *Monsieur. Allez, je vous en prie.*"

When he came back in the room and saw me crying, Jean-Paul was very worried.

"*Mon Dieu*, what is wrong, Sarah? What did this doctor tell you? You seem to know him?"

"It's nothing," I sniffed, trying to regain composure, but failing, mostly due to still being out of it on residual anesthesia.

"Are you in pain?"

I nodded affirming that, and reiterated, "Thirsty."

"I am so sorry, Sarah. Soon she will bring the ice, I expect."

And shortly thereafter, not a nurse but an orderly came in with just that. It was in a bowl with a little plastic spoon. I was in no condition to sit up and eat it, though. Jean-Paul's weak arm was next to me on the side of the bed where the chair was, so he got up and moved over to the other side. He set his cane down and proceeded to lower the railing on the right side of my bed. Then he moved in close to me and, cradling me in his good arm, lift me up a bit so that I could maneuver the bowl of ice. Finally! Cool against my palate.

"*Merci bien*, " I ardently said to him and meant it. I wanted to kiss his cheek, but I had a mouth full of ice. "I'll bet I look like death warmed over," I added, embarrassed by the little display of emotion he'd witnessed earlier.

" I am happy you no longer feel like you wish to vomit, " he said. "And how do you know the doctor who speaks French so well?"

"Do you remember when I brought the visitors to our office? The newlyweds? He's a friend of theirs and I met him that weekend through them."

"Ah, " he said nodding, "*très bien.*" He didn't ask me any more questions and I didn't offer any further information.

Just then Annie-Laure and Jean-Luc came into the room. She was also carrying a bouquet of beautiful yellow Asiatic lilies and purple statice mixed in with pale green mini carnations, white baby roses and greens. It had a pretty green ribbon around it and she had also brought one of the crystal vases from the office cupboard, which she ducked into the bathroom and filled with water. They greeted their boss, and then turned to me.

"How are you doing?" she asked setting the bouquet next to the rose on the bedtable.

"*Salut, ma vieille*, " said Jean-Luc. "*Ça va mieux comme ça?*

"I'm great. Thanks."

"She is still very tired," said Jean-Paul, "and in some pain."

"*La pauvre*, " said Annie-Laure, touching my arm.

Jean-Paul laid me gently back down and moved again over to the chair as the other two stepped away to clear his path. He wanted to talk to me into my ear.

"Sarah, I have asked Annie-Laure and Luc to come here in order to pose a question to you and I hope you will agree to what I say."

I was loopy but I was cognizant enough to really wonder what the hell was coming next.

"I would like to have you recuperate from all this at my home, rather than go back to your apartment. Therefore, I would like Luc to take Annie-Laure over to your place to pick up some more clothes and bring them back. She will need your keys, will she not? Do you agree?"

"No! I can't let you do that. Seriously. Huh-uh. No."

"But I must insist. You cannot take care of yourself in that apartment. *C'est hors question.*"

"But, *Monsieur*, I can't stay at your house."

"And why is that?"

"Because it's too much trouble. Your staff have their real jobs to do. They don't need to be waiting on me hand and foot. It's a lovely offer, really, and I am very appreciative, don't get me wrong. But I can't let you do that."

"My plan is *impéccable,* you must agree. We are set up for exactly this! I really must implore you to do it."

"Honestly, I can just lay around my place and watch t.v. for a week. There won't be any need for anyone to take care of me."

"Sari, please, " Annie-Laure broke into the middle of the argument. "I can't even see you being able to go up your stairs! Luc would have to carry you, *voyons,*" she said with mock exasperation . " No, you have to do as *Monsieur* suggests. You know he is right."

I just lay there, too groggy to argue, too tired to think.

Finally I looked up at them all and said, "Okay. My purse with the keys is in this locker over here by the window. The larger gold key is to the front outside door and the smaller one to my apartment. Just bring my nightgown and robe and some underwear. And a change of clothes or two, I guess. There are some brown dungarees and some sweaters. Pick out whatever you want. "

When all my visitors had left, I tried to stay awake in case Pax came into my room again. It was a losing proposition, however, and I drifted in and out of sleep, sometimes fitful and sometimes the sleep of the dead. At least the anti-nausea meds were working great. It must have been around midnight when they woke me up to take vitals, and brought in this cylinder thing for me to blow into and make a little red ball rise because post-surgical tests showed my oxygen levels weren't up to snuff. When they finally let me have some water, I then wanted Seven Up.

I woke up again around four in the morning, but I thought it was still evening. I looked over at Jenny's bed, remembering we had said we would play cards. But no one was there. The next time the nurse came in, I asked after my roommate.

"She had to be moved to a different room, " she said.

"How come?"

"You get some rest, now, hon." And she left the room.

489

Chapter Eighty-Four

Après un Rêve...Gabriel Fauré

Two days later I was discharged and taken down to the lobby and out to the car in a required wheelchair, where Luc and Annie-Laure were waiting to take me to JPA's. I'd had enough time to regret agreeing to this. For one thing, I'd have to see that jerk Robineau up close and personal again. I tried to put him out of my mind. Hopefully, since I was an "invalid," and a girl, he'd keep his distance.

When we got to the house, Jean-Luc also had a wheelchair for me to ride up the elevator in! It must have been one I'd seen in the therapy room...Jean-Paul's wheelchair from the past. Robineau was in the foyer as Jean-Paul welcomed me and informed me that I would once again be in his mother's room.

"Really? Are you sure you don't want me in one of the guest rooms?" I asked.

"*Mais non*, Sarah! You are familiar with the room and the *en suite* is right there. It is very comfortable, non?"

"Oh, very! It's not that. It's just that...that room is so big and..."

I heard Robineau give the slightest "hrummph" noise, but Jean-Paul was already drowning him out, "It's exactly what you need. I am also having a television put in there. *Voilà.*"

What could I say? I gave up. Me thinks I doth protest too much and all that.

This time I wasn't on the chaise longue next to the bathroom door, but in his mother's grand sleigh bed with about half a dozen beautiful pillows fluffed up for me and her luxurious million-thread-count sheets and eiderdown comforter to snuggle into.

A maid was already in the room when I was wheeled in, but it was Annie-Laure who handed her my bag to unpack, and who helped me put on my nightgown and get into bed. Annie-Laure also had brought the flowers from the hospital, which still looked beautiful, and she had set them on a dresser near me.

Jean-Paul came in after ascertaining that I was not in some state of undress, and told me, as he pointed towards the distant wall, "You see, the *en suite* is far from this bed. I do not want you to risk a fall. Do you know it takes about two weeks for the anesthesia to wear off from your body?"

I actually did not know that. No wonder I still, even three days since the operation, felt like shit.

"Therefore, you must dial *numéro six* on this phone for the help to come for you. *Comprenez?*"

Oh, like that was going to happen. I would certainly not be dialing any such thing.

Then as they were all gathering around the bed, another staff member brought in a television on a mobile serving cart, for wont of a better display table. It had a large, square remote-control device. Talk about being smack dab in the middle of the lap of luxury.

Annie-Laure took her leave telling me she'd see me back at the office in about a week's time. Jean-Luc said good-bye, but left the wheelchair parked in another far corner of the room. The maid excused herself, and then Jean-Paul asked if I would like some company for dinner, and offered to have his brought in there, to which I agreed, grateful for his offer to stay with me.

I had no dietary restrictions to speak of, but that sweet man must have thought I needed a sick person's array of light food, so he had them bring me broth and cottage cheese, fruit and a fluffy rice pudding, Scandinavian-style, not like my Nana's. This was delivered to me on a tray, and he asked for the same food to be set up on a tray table next to my bed for himself. We drank *rosé d'Anjou* and Vittel water with it.

"You're going to have to go down to the kitchen and have them broil you a nice steak when you get done here, " I teased. "You shouldn't have to eat what I do!"

He laughed, protesting, "No, no...it is just what the doctor ordered." When we had both finished, he said, "I will leave you now to sleep. I hope you get some restorative rest."

"I don't know how I'll ever thank you for all this, " I said, wondering exactly that, "but I just want you to know how much I appreciate it. I really don't know what I can do to ever repay you."

"Sleep now. " And he lifted my hand to his lips and kissed it.

490

He wasn't out of the room two minutes when Robineau knocked once at the door, and proceeded to come in without waiting for me to say *Entrez*. I was hoping there'd be enough time that I could pretend I was already asleep, but he was too quick.

He put the dishes on the cart, rather noisily at that, and lifted the tablecloth up to cover it all before moving it out. He turned abruptly, and—this was not some paranoid imagination on my part---he glared at me.

"Well, well, here you are again? *Nom de Dieu*! You must think you can wheedle your way into his life, *n'est-ce pas*?"

"What?! NO!"

"Do you believe *Monsieur* welcomes you here as his equal? Well, I am telling you something now: he will never accept you as one of us because you did not know *Maman*. It is as simple as that. *Voilà. Jamais. C'est tout.*"

I was completely dumbfounded at his rudeness and the tirade, but I came to my senses immediately, and let him have it.

"Now you listen to me, " I fairly barked. "Didn't you mean to say, *Excusez-moi, Mademoiselle, de vous déranger, mais*… before you started your little speech? And for your trouble-making information, I'm not trying to wheedle my way into anywhere! You haven't liked me from the get-go. You are the one who's a manipulating little prick, *espèce de con*. YOUR BOSS invited me here, and I'm going to quote you VERBATIM to him. We'll just run **that** up the flagpole and see who salutes."

I was furious to the point of tears. He was stupefied at my anger, but it wasn't over yet. I was perfectly willing for this to escalate into some kind of battle royal, him and me, and I was livid that he assumed he could walk in there and make me feel so bad. And to accuse me like that!

He gave me a dirty look, but didn't say anything else, and turned to leave with the cart.

"One more thing, " I called out. "*Tu te prends pour qui*? Don't you **ever** walk into this room again while I'm in it. You are persona non grata inside those double doors, *comprends? Je te previens*!! I used the familiar form to warn him, as though I were his superior, which could not have been lost on him nor have been more clear. He got it. He turned on his heels and huffed out of the room.

The trouble is, I didn't quote him to Jean-Paul. What would have been the point? My boss obviously needed his valet and, while I suspected he would be very angry if I told him what had gone down between Robineau and me-- really since my arrival at the Foundation-- any complaining about him would just put Jean-Paul between a rock and a hard place. In the end, I felt it was a lose-lose situation for me, so I stuffed my feelings and kept quiet.

Robineau never returned to my room—*Maman's* room—but later in the week, two of the maids who'd been caring so nicely for me came to alert me that he was spreading vitriol about me to the rest of the staff, telling them I was trying to ingratiate myself with *Monsieur*.

"*C'est très méchant de sa part. Il vous accuse de vous insinuer dans les bonnes graces de Monsieur!* " they said. They told me they didn't believe that for a second, but that I should beware of him. "*Méfiez-vous, Mademoiselle* Sarah."

I thanked them and said I wasn't worried, that he couldn't do anything to me, but that I hoped they would set the record straight to the other maids and valets, cooks, etc. about me. It went without saying that I had no malicious intentions. Everyone knew that I'd been invited at the behest of Monsieur. They agreed.

Nearing the end of my stay, Jean-Paul was having breakfast in my room with me, as he had done all week, when he told me that he hadn't mentioned this before, but Fabrizio Garabanti was also his doctor.

"Oh! You've had more surgery? In Chicago, then?"

"Yes, that is right. A little bit more. Nothing too major. I was very pleased you were referred to him. He is still a bit young to receive a life-time achievement award, but one day he will, and he will truly deserve it."

"Yes, my doctor friend was delighted to have been matched to his residency here with him. "

"Well, I spoke to him about your case since you are staying here, and of course, he will want to see you to clear your way for coming back to work. So I have arranged for him to come here, rather than you having to go out."

"Oh, Jesus, what must that have cost? Doctors hardly ever do house-calls anymore."

"In Paris, it is very common. Well, perhaps not a surgeon, " he laughed. "So, I am wondering if you would like my staff to wash your nightgown and some other clothes? Yes?"

"Oh, yes, please. I guess I'll just get dressed for the visit, then."

"He will need to check your bandages and the stitches, " he said. "I would like to offer you something to wear other than your normal clothing." And with that, he made his way over to his mother's armoires against the wall, where, balancing with the cane in his left hand, he opened the first doors and then an interior drawer, and pulled out a silken peignoir. He tucked it under his weak arm and came back over to me, whereupon he motioned with his head for me to take it.

"It's lovely, "I said, feeling the luxurious silk satin. "I'm not elegant enough to put on such a thing."

"*Si, si.* I am glad you like it. She would have been most pleased to have you wear it."

"So, forgive me, again, for prying into your personal life, but, have you… you know…kept… her clothes and things all this time? Didn't she die in '68?"

He looked down at me with the most despondent look I'd ever seen on his face. "I confess I cannot bear to give them away," he replied.

Naturally, I realized right away that I should not have asked. "I'm so sorry if my remark brought back sad memories for you, " I said, angry at myself for opening my big mouth and reopening his gaping wounds.

"*Non, non, ce n'est pas grave,* " he replied.

492

Chapter Eighty-Five

"Polovtsian Dance No. 8" (from *Prince Igor*)...Alexander Borodin

By the first week in March, I was back to my old routines, living in my little studio again instead of d'Arivèque splendor, and playing catch up in the film library. I still had many follow-up doctors' appointments with both doctors, too, and it worried me to be constantly asking for time off or leaving early, but no one batted an eye.

I also had a pile of bills. I wasn't too panicky about that since the insurance had covered a lot of it, although not the actual doctor bills or the anesthesiologist. But the hospital business department said I could be put on a payment plan and so I embarked on the first debt settlement scheme of my young life. Sol had taken out loans to send me to Iowa and the Sorbonne, and had not expected me to repay him — (so far; frankly, I was always waiting for that other shoe to drop), and I had no car, credit cards, or school loans, nothing that would qualify as experience with debt.

My new salary at FCF would kick in after Board approval, but that meeting had been postponed when it turned out I couldn't be there. That is why, the first day I was back, JPA called me into his office right away to discuss its rescheduling.

"I am anxious for the Board to meet you and approve your new position, " he told me.

"Thank you. Like I said before, I'd be happy to present them with an overview of our projects so far and even have samples available and everything."

"That would be very good. I am convinced they will approve your work and your new title with full unanimity. In the meantime, I am aware that I outlined your new salary, but that it has not begun yet. Do you have many outstanding hospitalization bills?"

There wasn't much he didn't know about hospitals.

"Some."

"I should like to take them over and pay them off."

"Ooooh, no. But thank you."

"Hear me out. I am aware that we offer our employees medical insurance, but no plan is perfect. They rarely cover the physicians or some of the tests, either, I would imagine. Did you have bills for any of the tests you had?"

"Uh... gee, I'm not sure. I guess I'd have to take a closer look at the itemized statement."

"Yes, perhaps you do not have experience in the business of all this?"

"Maybe my father's accountant can help me, " I laughed nervously.

"Are your parents paying for any of it?"

"They've made no offers to do that, actually, no, but if I asked them for some help, they might."

"Then please allow me to intervene. I can assure you, Sarah, the amount of money we are talking about would be nothing for me, but quite substantial for you...even with your increase in salary." He sat there looking at me intently, hoping for an affirmative answer.

"I just can't let you pay for any of that. You've already done so much for me."

"No, I have done nothing out of the ordinary. It is you who are extraordinary. You have---I think still unbeknownst to you-- fulfilled my mother's greatest wishes for this Foundation, namely, as I have already mentioned, to enhance and greatly expand the educational mission she dreamed for it. "

"But, really, anyone you hired could have done the same."

"If you think so, you are, once again..."

I interrupted him to finish his sentence, "...being naïve?" I laughed.

"Precisely!"

He got up from behind the desk, and picking up his cane, came around to where I was sitting and, unlocking his brace, took the other chair beside mine.

"Sarah, at my house, you asked about my mother, and then you regretted that your question had conjured up my sadness. I apologize if I made you feel bad."

" No, please. I'm the one to blame."

" It has not escaped me that I have not finished the story I was telling you on New Year's Eve. Shall I continue with it?"

"Please do."

And he began the narrative where he had left off—with him in the hospital in New York.

What started out as a temporary detour for medical treatment elongated first into two years and then longer. The war was raging in Europe and the United States was still not in it. When Marie-Aveline was not at the hospital, she was, for all intents and purposes, acting as a lobbyist for the cause of De Gaulle and France. She had taken an apartment on the Upper East Side, as he had already told me, where she held many gatherings and "salons" to promote the idea of helping France's war effort.

"She was vehemently anti-Petain, " Jean-Paul reminded me, "almost as much as she was anti-German."

All that time, she was also waiting for her husband to join her in New York, at least to visit, if not to stay on, if for no other reason than to assess the medical situation of their son and what might be the next phase of his treatment…and where. But De Gaulle relied heavily upon Georges-Henri d'Arivèque's ability to weave in and out of both worlds, the Occupied one and the Free one, and he could not get away from the war.

By December of 1943, when the U.S. was now in the European Theater but before any Second Front, Jean-Paul was just getting out of the hospital, at age fourteen, and Marie-Aveline moved him into her townhouse on East 76th Street, and began making plans for him to start school the next Fall at the Lycée Français of New York, a venerable secondary school four blocks away that had already been established for nearly a decade before that. She knew many of the French families by now who sent their children there, and also a lot of the faculty, some of which she had already brought in to tutor her son while he languished in the hospital.

Jean-Paul was not mobile at all at this point. If he did attend the school, which he really wanted to, he would do so in a wheelchair accompanied by an adult aide. Even that idea did not deter him.

"I was so very weary of being confined to a bed, " he said.

The curriculum was as rigorous there as it would have been in France, and combined with the more pragmatic American tradition of promoting intellectual inquiry and creativity , that high school offered the best of both cultures. The results were that Jean-Paul became completely bi-lingual and academically prepared for either country's post-secondary system. He would be awarded the Bac three years later.

Then, as terrible fate would have it, the ultimate tragedy struck for both mother and son: Georges-Henri was killed aboard a commercial B.O.A.C. DC-3 flying from Portugal to Britain. It was attacked and shot down over the Bay of Biscay by a squad of German Junkers JU-88 planes. De Gaulle's office in London called Marie-Aveline personally to convey the general's deepest sympathies. They told her that her husband was a true hero of France, but also that no remains could be located at all. There would be nothing to bury.

"There was no body, " he said solemnly, "but there was also nothing clouded in ambiguity. *Papa* was gone. Lost forever. Our world was very nearly destroyed. *Maman* put up a brave front for me. I could tell she was inconsolable, and I could not be very much help to her. We were each floundering in our own way now."

"I'm so sorry about your father, *Monsieur*."

"Thank you, Sarah. You see, in the end, I really did not know him very well."

"So she decided to make a life for you in New York, then?" I asked.

"*Maman* was very angry…at France, more precisely at the French people for the capitulation to Hitler. She was very much like De Gaulle in that. She could never accept that surrender had happened. With the death of my father, she felt no compunction to return."

Uncle Charles in Switzerland was equally devastated by the death of his brother. He knew now that his nephew Jean-Paul would one day become Duc de Beuvron, and, more importantly, the head of d'Arivèque Industries, the banks and every other holding. He undertook to guarantee as much help financially and any other way to his sister-in-law for the care and upbringing of the boy, and also for her, informing her that as the widow of Georges-Henri d'Arivèque, she was now, if not the wealthiest woman in the world, certainly one of them.

Having decided to stay for the foreseeable future in New York with her son, she became active in various war works, hoping to somehow carry on the patriotism and memory of her husband. She worked on committees for displaced persons and refugees in the city, and became vitally interested in using any spheres of influence she could to try to find missing persons.

494

"She even made several trips to Paris in the late 1940's," he told me, "to be at the Lutetia Hotel and work with relocation groups to find missing persons, including the Schwartzes, who, as I explained before, were never among those returning from the German concentration camps. Do you know this hotel? It is on the same street as you lived, Boulevard Raspail."

"Yes, I do know it. It's a pretty posh place. I used to pass by it all the time, because it was right on the way to *Le Bon Marché*, you know? But I learned about its war-time history, too, yes."

"My mother's work came to the attention of De Gaulle, and after the war was over and he was back in France as President of the Fifth Republic, he tapped her to serve in a semi-official capacity with the French delegation to the newly formed nascent United Nations."

"Wow," I said, upon hearing this part. "That's quite something!"

"*Oui, c'est normal.* She was the perfect choice," he relied. "It buoyed her spirits somewhat, too."

"So what about you and school? Were you bullied? Did you have friends?"

"Ah. I was not bullied at all, and I had several good friends. I was older than the other classmates when I began, and also behind them in my studies; but I quickly caught up and joined the ranks of the class *en troisième*. When I was fifteen, things changed for me. I no longer used the wheelchair. After months and months of physical therapy, I was fitted with a different sort of brace on my left leg that provided more movement, and I walked, limping of course, with one arm crutch—the kind proposed by the nurse Sister Elizabeth Kenny. Do you know of her?"

"No," I admitted.

"Well, she had theories about treating polio, which of course, did not pertain to my situation, but one thing that she also advocated was a different kind of crutch -- one that hooked onto the forearm. I could not use a crutch of any sort on my left side, but on the right side, the Kenny 'stick' as they were called then, worked better."

"You know," I told him, " I think I may have mentioned to you already, when I grew up in the 50's, even in my small town, we had quite a few polio victims who went to our schools. But I have to say, with the use of both arms, they could really maneuver pretty well with crutches. Most of them had the underarm ones, but a few had the other kind, like you described."

"Yes, Sarah, I think you could see, even from when you initially met me, that the useless arm inhibits me even more than the leg."

"So you could go to school without an adult supervising you?"

"No, not really. I still had a companion---an aide-- with me. I was used to this. It was a good paying job for someone then, and they did not have to do any work!" he laughed. "As you would imagine, I had trouble with stairs and I had real problems carrying things at lunch. I could not participate in any sports or go to the homes of my friends after classes. Sometimes, however, my friends came to my home. I was extremely fortunate to have such good friends, including Harry Lowenstein, who came often but did not go to my school. He helped me...*beaucoup*. They were very dear that family. "

"And at school were kids helpful, too?"

"My friends did help me."

"But anyway, you and your mom stayed in America and you were able to go to high school...and college?"

"High school in New York and university at the Sorbonne. As you."

Well, not exactly "as me."

"So what year did you graduate from high school?"

"1949."

"The year after I was born!"

"*C'est vrai? Dis-donc.*"

"And then what did you do?"

"After that it was time to go back to France and continue my education. *Maman* and I sailed on the S.S. Normandie, and, at the strong behest of *Oncle* Charles, we moved back into the original family home in Paris, my d'Arivèque grandparents' apartment on the Parc Monceau. *Maman* still did not wish to live in France, but she felt I could not go there alone yet. Paris is very difficult for *les handicapés*."

"I know! You would almost need a tag team."

"C'est vrai."

"What did you study at university?"

"My father had studied history very seriously and I wanted to emulate him, so I began those studies at *La Sorbonne.* I liked it well enough, and obtained the *License.* But I soon realized that perhaps I should go in another direction. The great thing about being back in Paris was that *Oncle* Charles was closer there, and we saw him often. He was anxious for me to study *hautes études commerciales, H.E.C.,* because, after all, I needed to prepare to one day take over the reins of our –uh—businesses and organization. So I stayed on to do it—what you would call post-graduate work, yes? Charles was so happy that we had made the effort to have me do it there. The school was in the midst of post-war modernization and the curriculum was beginning to adopt the model of Harvard Business School just as I arrived there."

"Did you go to *La Pérégrine* on the weekends, too?"

"Non. That was still too painful for *Maman.* Except that we did go down there one time to symbolically bury *Papa. La Pérégrine* has a chapel, and it has a small burial area housing the graves of the previous family members and the *ducs de Beuvron.* But *Maman* decided, since we had no real ashes…or anything else…that she would make a different place, deep inside the gardens where she put up a folly— you know? It is a small temple of Venus—I think she got the idea from the Parc Monceau because we could see one from our windows in Paris. She placed a vase in there, as though it had his ashes in it. And she commissioned a plaque with the words by George Sand engraved on it: *'Il n'y a qu'un bonheur dans la vie, c'est d'aimer et d'être aimé.'"*

"That's lovely," I said.

"Maman wished to return to the States after I received my *diplôme.* She had discussed with *Oncle* Charles the idea… the dream… she had of starting a charitable organization…a trust or a foundation to provide funds to disseminate the truth about France, that we were not all *collaborateurs* and *Pétainistes,* nor all *Résistance* fighters either. She hated that after the war, so many…really everybody… claimed to have been part *of La Résistance.* She felt that watered down the real *Résistance* and the memory of *Papa."*

"I agree with her. So, what about your childhood home? Do you still own that?"

She had sold my family home in Paris, which was hers, after all, but kept the d'Arivèque house always at the ready for visits---I still have it; and she did not close *La Pérégrine.* Every so often—very rarely--we would go back in the late 1950's and '60's; but she wanted to live in America."

"But why not New York where she knew so many people?"

"For one thing, the French Embassy in Washington, D.C. was spreading out its consulates. Chicago's was not very well established as yet. She felt she could be a sort of adjunct to them. They would do all the official governmental jobs, of course, like issue visas. But she, with her private Foundation, could augment their offerings in other cultural and educational areas."

"So with her background at the U.N. why didn't she just join forces with them?"

"For one thing, she could not. She had no *diplôme* from the *Sciences Po.* For another, she wanted autonomy from the French government. She had the financial resources to make her own vision a reality and did not want to come under any restrictions."

"So you moved to Chicago and the rest is history, " I said, making a flourish.

"Au fur et à mesure, oui, " he laughed. Then getting serious again, he looked at me and said, "You see, I wanted to tell you all this so you have a clearer idea of why I'm so grateful to you for your work here. You have only been here a short period of time, and yet, you have accomplished a great deal. I'm so very pleased."

"Thank you."

"Alors, our Board meeting will take place here in our conference room. I shall call it for Friday of next week and I shall send you a memo later with verification after I hear back from the others as to their availability to come. *D'accord?"*

"Oui, Monsieur."

I rose to leave. We shook hands formally—as a matter of habit as much as anything else. He leaned forward slightly before letting go of my hand, and I wondered if he had an impulse to give me *la bise* as well, but perhaps thought better of it. His office was, after all, entirely made of glass.

Chapter Eighty-Six

"Insensatez"...Jobim and Moraes

Cass phoned just as soon as I was back on the job; she told me she wouldn't have dared call at d'Arivèque's house, but was anxious to hear the outcome of the surgery. I assured her all was well, but that I just felt so bad having to miss her birthday.

"Well, speaking of missing birthdays, Alan has now hit the trifecta: he missed Valentine's Day, our anniversary and my birthday."

"What the hell?"

"Yeah, see, he thinks these days are just ordinary ones...no big deal."

"So, he didn't really forget..."

"No! He was unconcerned about it. He couldn't even manage to wish me a 'Happy Birthday.'"

"I'd be pissed."

"I was hurt."

"Yeah, well, I'm disgusted to hear this. I don't think it's out of the realm of reason for you to feel the way you do. Anyone would."

"Frankly, Sari, you can't make other people feel things like that if they don't already. But when my husband does this kind of stuff, then hate seems to take hold of **my** feelings towards him! Guess I'm not really prepared to accept him as he is. I can't refrain from wishing to have a kind word, an event of some sort on special days."

"Did you get him something for your anniversary?"

"That's just it! I got him the Neil Young album we didn't have... you know it, I think...called *Everyone Knows this is Nowhere*. His great one from a couple of years ago. I mentioned this to Alan...that I had gotten it for him, but he just laughed! I swear I don't even know him anymore. And I'm so weary of it."

"Maybe you should leave for a while. Bring the kids here. I mean it. I don't have any place to sleep four people, but bring a sleeping bag; we'll make do."

"I wish I could take you up on that. I do think I need a respite! It's not just that I think I need to escape from something. I need to escape TO something."

"Hell, yes. You need some TLC for the soul."

"Right! It would be great to be in some situation where I can respect and value myself. He won't even talk to me about any of this. I bring stuff up and he just turns off. He'll snap at me, 'This conversation is over' and just walk away. It makes me so damn mad I could spit."

"Who would ever say that? For God's sake, Cass."

"I know. He always says I make such a big deal out of nothing. But it's not nothing to me. I've explained to him a million times that to me a kind word or smile---any damn crumb would mean a lot. He just shrugs and says, 'What's your problem?' I think he's said **that** a million times, too."

"If you keep hearing that, you're going to come to the conclusion that it is your problem, " I told her. " You need to seek some people---like me--- in a safe place where you can share your thoughts and feelings. I mean, I saw it, too, when I was at your place, Cass. I could see you were exhausted, and never had any real blocks of time to devote just to yourself, do your art or see friends."

"I don't really have any friends here. And when you come, hell, you do all the work—ha. But the real thing is that when you're here, I have an ally and someone I can talk to---I mean really rap. It's damn hard to be in a relationship with someone you feel you've lost touch with. I don't think Alan values me or our relationship anymore."

"Put the onus on him, then, Cass...don't doubt your own self-worth."

"You know, I'm ashamed to say this-- but I can tell you won't judge me: I felt so close to the edge one day a while back that I screamed at him. He sat there, all bored and uncaring and even yawned! I had tried to talk to him and had got nothing, so I screamed. It's so humiliating to just wait for him to say something—anything. All of a sudden, rage just overtook me. I flew at him and physically pushed against

497

him.

"Oh shit.... What did he say?"

That sounded like a plea for contact, all right... of any kind.

"Oh, he didn't say anything. He slammed me back against the kitchen cabinet...as hard as he could. I burst out crying and sobbed and sobbed on the floor."

"Oh my God, " I said, not believing what I was hearing. *They'd entered a new dimension now. Physical violence...the American way.*

"Oh, there's more. Laura began to scream. Nothing could console her. Alan took her outside to calm her down. Paul was crying, too, and scared...he just sort of toddled off into the living room and stood at the sofa sobbing. I went over to him and picked him up and cuddled him."

"Then what happened? I imagine Alan couldn't stay out in the cold for very long with Laura?"

"Yeah... no. Luckily we're having kind of an early spring. He came back in with her and he was a little shame-faced — or at least I imagined he was. Physical violence is the only thing he ever really regrets."

"Wait a minute, so you're saying there've been other incidents of it — violence, I mean?"

"Yes."

That was a revelation to me that gave me a terrible sick feeling-- a wave of pure nausea-- that came over me in the midst of the conversation. She was really in trouble and I was two hundred miles away.

Domestic violence wasn't anything new in the country back then, but there certainly weren't any services for women available. I doubt Iowa City even had so much as a hot line she could have called in 1971.

"Cass, I'm glad you told me. You have got to get out of there — as much for your kids as for you."

"Do I? Am I the one who has to bear the responsibility of staying or going? Is this whole marriage now on my shoulders?"

"It might just be."

I couldn't think of any other rejoinder to what she was saying. Was she reticent to leave someone who hit her? Would his temper fly at the kids next? This was not a hard decision in my eyes, but then, I wasn't the one in the marriage. I knew all about women who stayed in rotten relationships. They'd rather "face the hell they knew...."

"Cass, listen. In a few months, I'm going to have to move out of my place, and now with my salary increase, I can afford a bigger one. You and the kids can move in with me...I'll help you with them."

I knew she was too fragile for me to bring up what would really save her: to try to reconcile with her parents. But who was I to talk? I wasn't about to do what my father wanted me to do and move home, so I couldn't expect that of her. But moving away from Alan's violence was another story.

"You can't stay in a situation where at any moment you could be slammed up against a wall, a buffet, a cabinet or anything else!"

"Sari," she said in a low, exasperated voice, "I also freaked out on him and pushed him."

"Okay, so he was provoked! So were you! " I fairly shouted into the phone. "He's ten times stronger than you and obviously your pushing him didn't do anything to harm him physically, but he could have broken all your ribs — or worse."

"Maybe."

We sat on the phone without talking for what seemed like quite a few minutes. I was afraid she was going to cry at the slightest rebuke, so I backed down from anger at Alan.

Finally I said, "Cass, you know I'll always be there for you. I'll always help you and I'm always on your side."

"I know. And I'll think about coming to Chicago. I still have the money you gave me before."

"We'll talk about this seriously later, okay?" And we rang off.

Sure enough, a few days went by and, in fact, she did call again. This time, almost as I expected would happen, based on the little I'd studied about psychology in college, she was embarrassed about having laid that whole trip on me.

"The storm clouds have lifted, " she cooed into the phone. "Hearts are again sun-filled and warm."

"And you expect me to believe that?" I said.

"Alan finally consented to talk to me, and we somewhat repaired the damage."

"Somewhat?"

"He said he just wasn't ready back then to cope with my problems---what I mean is -- feelings."

"So he's prepared to cope with them now? Yeah, right."

"My plans for flight have ceased, at least. Flight from or flight to? I guess I won't have to decide just yet, eh?" she laughed.

I didn't laugh.

"Okay, Sari, " she said, sensing my unhappiness at this turn of events. "I can see up-raised eyebrows from your direction right through this phone line. Ha! But seriously, my confiding all this shit and hassle to you was probably unfair to you."

"It's not unfair. If not to me, then to whom?"

"You **are** right. You are the soul I am most in communion with and sometimes, well, when it's friends we're talking to about everything, the sorrow just spills out, doesn't it? But I hope happiness does, too. Love is both."

Yes, but just please don't tell me this was never going to happen again, because I wasn't buying it.

Cass' drama made my little woes of not being able to date Pax anymore seem piddling, but she asked me about him, and even though I was able to truthfully regale her with his seeing me in the hospital, and how nice he'd been when he told me we couldn't date each other anymore, I had a hard time hiding my disappointment from her, which elicited a flurry of sympathy from her.

"Now it's my turn to wish I could be there for you. I miss you more than I can say on the phone or that my pen could write, " she told me. "I so hoped you would find someone to fuel yourself with, to share your dreams...and nightmares. I thought Pax could have been the one. You are, to me, the epitome of a best friend, so keep the faith, baby. Someone will come."

"If you say so," I laughed. "Pax probably wasn't the one, anyway, " I said, seriously. "He was far too beautiful and far too Catholic to have ever wanted to marry me. But we did have fun together while it lasted. I mean, you haven't lived until someone's serenaded you on the fucking harpsichord that he built himself!"

"Oh, well, you'll be interested to hear, in that case, that Alan has taken up his guitar again---plays it almost every night. It's an outlet for all the poetry in him that doesn't get written. He sure loves that Goya."

What I really hoped was that Alan "sure loved" his wife.

Chapter Eighty-Seven

"Prélude Te Deum"…Marc-Antoine Charpentier

I was making a mock-up culture box on the French Revolution and doing the lesson ideas that would accompany it, when I got what could have been my greatest educational idea yet for the Foundation. I hated to inundate JPA with idea after idea, especially since he'd be footing the bill for all of them, but this was a good one, and I really thought we should discuss it before we went to the Mid-States Conference, because if it were a "go", it would be advantageous to present it to teachers there.

So I ran it past Dom first.

"What would you say to a two-day seminar, sort of thing-- a 'teaching institute'--where teachers would meet for lectures on a subject in depth, sort of intense-like, and then there would be break-out sessions with films, lesson planning and bulletin board ideas? I was thinking of one, say, on the Marquis de Lafayette for starters. What do you think?"

"Well," he said in a tentative voice, "that sounds like an intriguing idea. Tell me more."

"Okay," I began, taking out notes I'd made on a legal pad, "we convene say, at the Foundation, and have a *vin d'honneur* and introduce the speakers. Then the next day we have the lectures by experts in their field…it could be French history, American history, both revolutions, French culture of the 18th century, music and art of that century, the French in America at that time…all sorts of neat stuff."

"Yeah, I'd get behind that."

"And see, my idea is that we would limit it to a certain number of teachers, say ten, and put them up at d'Arivèque's home for free, and then take a jitney each day to the location of the classes. I was thinking the *Alliance* might let us rent out some space for that short period of time in their building. They have a school, as you know, and we could plan it for when they were between sessions or whatever. I mean, I even think they'd also profit from having their own teachers either take our institute or teach in it."

"So what about other costs to the teachers? I am assuming you think this won't be just local, so you're putting them up. What about feeding them?"

"I admit I'm going to ask if the Foundation can pick up all the costs, including supplies for anything they might make in the break-out sessions. But I can't guarantee he'll go for the idea. Maybe there could be some nominal charge."

"I think they'd pay something. "

"You know what might even be a better idea for starters, " I said, thinking out loud really, "is to limit it to in-town teachers…sort of do a trial run, before we start inviting out-of-towners. It could be a weekend deal—a Thursday night, Friday and Saturday all day. That would probably work to start with. If the first one's a success, we could expand it in future. Maybe have annual ones."

"Gads, Sari, looks like you're on your way to figuring this whole thing out."

"Not quite, but I'm getting there. He's made me Director of Education, did I tell you? So I've got to live up to that."

"Congrats! *Bien-meritée!"*

"*Beh — merci, alors!"*

"One thing if you do set this all up…"

"What's that? I'm all ears."

"Make a rubric for evaluation of it at the end. See what the teachers think, and get their input on how they would do anything differently."

"Great suggestion. You know, he and I are going to the Mid-States Conference. I hope we can present this idea."

"See if you can talk just to the Chicago French Teachers Association, rather than the entire group. The 'AAT's' — that's the American Association of Teachers of French-- each have their own local meetings that weekend."

500

"That's another good idea. Thanks! You know, my boss is the keynote speaker at the Saturday luncheon. And I'm going to be there to hand out all kinds of info on the Foundation. We're making up packets."

"You guys should have a booth at that."

"Yes, maybe next year. I think if we disseminate enough information about what we have to offer this time and people really know what we do, a booth would be great for next time."

"If your boss is giving the keynote, does he realize that he'll be talking to teachers of other languages, too?"

"I think so. I'll mention it to him. I guess when they asked him to do it, they figured the other languages could take note and see if their own Consulates or Embassies had something similar. There are certainly no other cultural foundations like ours!"

"You got that right. I think the Goethe Institute does some of the same kinds of things for the German teachers, but nothing on the scale of what yours does, and certainly not as free. D'Arivèque must be one of the richest men in the world."

"I guess so."

So ahead of the Foundation Board meeting, I mustered up my courage and once again, asked for a meeting with JPA.

"I'm sorry to bombard you with ideas, " I said searching his face for any signs of rejection, "but I came up with something I would like to propose for teachers."

"*Oui? Vas-y.*" He smiled at me as if to say, "You're at it again, eh?"

So I told him of my plan. He sat and listened intently, sometimes nodding.

"The whole point of this would be to bring the classroom to life with quality materials--some we would create and some they'd create themselves. But whichever, they would all be helpful to teachers because they would augment planning and instruction. Everyone would be for that. Our sessions would tie the material into thematic units and would work for team teaching… like, say…the American history teacher might want to collaborate with the French teachers. Very few of our American schools have elementary foreign language, but I've heard that is up and coming, and these materials would dove-tail right into our culture-box project. One idea, for instance, for a break-out session could be game-construction. Another could be making bulletin boards. I might need to get our art department in on that."

I stopped to come up for air and test his reaction.

"Sarah, you are a visionary!" he praised me. "Again, I am most impressed!"

"You are? Oh, good!"

"Truly, you have originated something very interesting here. I believe such a weekend of activity could elevate the enthusiasm for teaching French. I also believe we would be offering strategies for inspiring students to go further in their studies."

"And teachers, too, " I added. "Taking an institute-type intensive course could give them more confidence in the classroom, especially when they would leave with some ready-to-go lessons."

Of course, putting all this together would take a lot more time than I had before the conference, let alone the Board meeting, but I agreed to write up the proposal, and have the idea ready to present at each, maybe in more detail at the Mid-States. We would later determine dates, venues, logistics, and who would be our guest lecturers and session leaders. I told him I thought the teachers at Lincoln Park High could be a great resource for us, and he was pleased with that, and added we could perhaps earmark our first one for six to eight months from then…around the first of the year.

"It might be a great break for the January doldrums, " I suggested.

"Yes, you and I will be able to work out the details by then, I believe," he agreed.

The day of the Board meeting I knew I would be invited to not only the meeting itself, but also a cocktail party and dinner afterwards at JPA's home, so I dressed up for work, pulling out all the stops with Cass' Chanel jumper, my London shoes and pearls. I wore a pink velvet bow in my hair—half up and half down. Thank God, I thought, that outfit was almost all-season. I couldn't wear it in the dead of summer, but could make it work for a dressy occasion practically the entire rest of the year. But as I put it on, it made me realize that maybe, it was time, even though I had to budget now for real rent and medical bills, to actually spring for some new clothes. It was 1971 and I was still wearing what I took to college in 1966, fortified by Cassandra Hyde's hand-me-downs.

I approached our domed conservatory-like conference room up in the Presidential Suite at the appointed hour, was greeted by Marie-France, and beckoned to go in. The room was full of men, some of whom I knew, like our chief legal counsel Daniel Rosier de Molet, who approached me with his hand out and also gave me *la bise*; and our publications editor-in-chief Quentin Masson, who addressed me as Sarah, since we'd had so many dealings with each other already. There were six or seven other men I thought I might have seen some time or other at *soirées* at d'Arivèque's , but then there was a very elderly gentleman who stood up as I entered, whom I did not recognize at all. Jean-Paul came over to me and led me to meet him. I swear I detected a glimmer in his eyes.

"*Mademoiselle* Shrier, *permettez- moi de vous présenter mon oncle,*
Charles-Albert d'Arivèque, Duc de Beuvron."

I stared at him in awe and disbelief as I held out my hand. "*Je suis très heureuse de faire votre connaissance, Monsieur…er… Monsieur le Duc,* " I stammered.

He took my hand and kissed it---in front of all those people. I think I must have turned flame red.

"*Enchanté, Mademoiselle,* " he said, adding, "*C'est mon grand plaisir de vous connaître. Mon neveu parle souvent de vous.*"

Was he joking with me? How could that be? How often did people talk trans-Atlantic?

"*Vous êtes venu toute la longue distance de Genève jusqu'ici, Monsieur!*" I remarked with astonishment.

"*Eh oui, Mademoiselle,* " he chuckled. "My nephew Polo sent his airplane, so it made things easier."

I was pretty sure the head of the d'Arivèque dynasty had every possible means of transportation of his own at his fingertips, but the idea that Jean-Paul had put his plane at the disposal of his uncle seemed sweet to me.

Marie-France de Piaget, and another of our legal team, Hennie's boss, Madeleine Guerin, both came in and took seats at the long oval conference table before the meeting was called to order. Annie-Laure entered with a steno pad, as the meeting recorder. I felt relieved to have other females in the room with me.

JPA presided. They went through all the normal business meeting agenda approval and procedures. My head was still swimming with the idea that Uncle Charles had been summoned, but I had to focus and get my act together, because soon it was New Business, and my promotion was announced. They turned to me with many congratulatory salutations. Then it was my turn to speak.

I began by reiterating what an honor I felt being tapped for the position, and thanked JPA once again for having faith in my abilities to handle it. I passed around a one-page summary of what we had implemented to that point in the film library.

"Our Foundation library is, in all reality, becoming a teaching resource center. Soon we will have a large variety of educational components. You see on the handout that I've noted a few of them—lesson plans to accompany films, learning activities stemming from a culture box, vignettes on the regions of France to enhance those audio-visuals, and so on."

I noticed one of two of them refer to the paper I'd handed out. They seemed intrigued, but when I finished with my presentation no one said anything, and I thought for a moment that it had landed like a lead balloon on a disinterested crowd. Marie-France, at least, was smiling at me. However, the motion was made and carried for my new position to be adopted, along with its salary--which still blew my mind—a round of applause broke out. I was embarrassed all of a sudden, but elated, too.

Many people came up to me afterwards to say that the Director of Education was a much-desired new post, and what a splendid idea it had been to put me in it, with all due credit, of course, to Jean-Paul d'Arivèque for initiating everything.

The glass doors swung open and some of the staff from the house, as was often the drill, entered with bottles of Krug *Clos du Mesnil* in silver ice buckets, and the de rigueur Baccarat flutes for us to toast a successful meeting.

Jean-Paul instructed everyone who did not have a car there already to meet in front of the building and ride to his home in the stretch limo, so I made my way down with Annie-Laure and Marie-France.

Both of them told me how pleased and excited the staff were to hear about my ideas and that everything possible would be done to help me bring the Institute to a reality.

"I am certainly impressed with your schemes!" said Annie-Laure. "How do you come up with so many great ones?"

"I don't know," I answered, "I might be a teacher *manqué*! I mean, I wouldn't want to put up with all the administrative bullsh—uh stuff-- they have to do, but I find I really like to create things to do in a classroom!"

"It sounds like you could perhaps make quite a wonderful teacher, though, "said Marie-France.

I shook my head. "No, " I demurred. "I love what I do now."

If only she knew. I saw Dom in his classroom. I saw him dealing with bureaucratic crap and paperwork. I knew he took hours and hours of grading home every night. No, thanks. What I did was exponentially easier than teaching. Dreaming up lessons, especially built around films and culture and geography was the fun stuff. If I was good at it, then **tant mieux! Dieu Merci**!

Once arrived at d'Arivèque's, which, after my recuperation sojourn, seemed a little bit like home to me, I had to steel myself to have to be in the same room again with that asshole Robineau. Luckily, he had too much to do with all those dignitaries there to pay any negative attention to me. He didn't dare disparage me within earshot of his boss either. I did wonder if he thought I hadn't really ratted him out like I threatened to, since there obviously hadn't been any rebuke. But I liked the idea of keeping him guessing. I didn't show any reaction to him whatsoever. I didn't acknowledge his presence, nor did I do anything that could be construed as a snub of him. I simply shrouded him, like I swore to do forever after that. He didn't exist. But he was still *le roi des cons;* that was for sure.

The person who did show attention to me that evening was *Le Duc de Beuvron*. He also used a cane and seemed quite frail, though not handicapped at all, and actually surprisingly high spirited for an octagenarian. His face was still handsome, if wizened and marked with lines and folds. He was not very tall—maybe due to shrinkage, for all I knew, in his advanced years. He carried himself with some effort, more as though he were tired than in pain of any sort. His clothing was as impeccable as Jean-Paul's. He wore a wonderful blue wool and silk suit-- not navy blue, but lighter than that-- with a light blue pin-striped shirt and a red Hermès tie with little figures of sunbursts on it. He was dapper, there was no doubt about it.

He came over to me and, startling me, took my arm to lead me to a place on the settee.

"Polo is enthralled with your ideas, Sarah " he told me in perfect, if accented, English. "May I call you Sarah?"

"Of course, *Monsieur le Duc*, " I answered.

"Please call me Uncle Charles, would you?"

"Am I allowed to do that?" I asked incredulously.

"I am giving you permission, " he laughed. " I hear from my dear friend George Solti that Polo also has taken on somewhat your musical education. What works have you found to be your favorites so far?"

"Oh, gosh, there are so many. I have to say I'm very grateful to the maestro for being so welcoming to me at the Chicago Symphony, and to *Monsieur*—er—your nephew, for seeing to it that I get to go. In answer to your questions, I guess you could say that I'm currently hung up on Gabriel Fauré. I love his *Sicilienne*."

"Yes, it is very beautiful. And to think it was to be incidental music of his for a rendition of *Le Bourgeois Gentilhomme* that never got produced!"

"The Molière play?"

"Yes, of course. It was never used because the production fell on hard times. It was meant to be a revival of the play for Paul Porel's Eden-Theater. Do you know it?"

I shook my head. I didn't know the theater or the name Paul Porel for that matter! *Monsieur le duc* brushed off my ignorance.

"*Ne vous en faites pas.* The theater went bankrupt in the 1890's *de toute façon.* Fauré never got paid for his work. So he then rewrote the piece for cello and piano only, which was played from time to time. But, it gets interesting! He eventually passed the score along to a pupil of his to re-orchestrate it, and the piece was used again as incidental music, in Maurice Maeterlinck's play *Pelléas et Mélisande*. So you see, we almost did not have it!" He looked up at me with a kind, jolly expression.

"Well, that would have been a great loss."

"Indeed."

Trying to make conversation that wouldn't expose me as a know-nothing, I changed the subject and asked if Charles met the maestro's new little daughter Gabrielle.

"Oh, no no, I have not been able to travel to London. But I know he is ecstatic about her. I was very fond of Hedi, you know, his first wife, but I do admire Valerie, and I know he loves her very deeply."

The dinner part of the evening was not held in the big "state"-- as I called it--dining room, but instead tables were set up in the part of the reception main room by the piano, and we had an intimate repast listening to Cole Porter and Aaron Copeland, which struck me as odd, but I did enjoy it.

I always liked it when music evoked the era when my parents were, if not my age, at least young. It made me try to imagine what they would have been doing when they heard it. It was anathema to me not to be able to have music around anytime, anywhere I wanted it. But their Victrolas and radios were not portable, and they had to go to dance halls and places that had a band.

After dinner coffee was served over in the seating area of that same space, so we were once again on the silk Louis XV furniture that always made me so nervous that I would accidentally spill even one drop on it. I politely waved off the server, not wanting to risk anything.

Annie-Laure sat with me and said that, as usual, Jean-Luc was charged with taking Marie-France and me home in the limo, and she would come, too. She told me that the time she went to get my clothes when I was in the hospital, she hardly recognized my place without the perimeter fencing and the ivy-covered walls.

"I believe you! I had the same reaction the first time I saw it. They've sort of changed the character of the place, " I admitted.

"Where will you go when you must move?"

"Don't know."

Board members actually approached me that evening, too, and wondered about this or that program I'd mentioned. (*It was different for me to be at a Foundation event at d'Arivèque's where* **my** *opinion was sought after. I was so used to playing the fly on the wall there, barely chiming in.*) Our head of marketing said he liked the idea of the unit on Lafayette, but wondered what other things I thought would lend themselves to an Institute weekend. I said I had a notion to do a region of France in depth.

"Normandy comes to mind. It would tie in, for example, with the film of *Madame Bovary*, which would enhance the teaching of the novel. Not only that, but there is another obvious American connection there, what with the World War II invasion onto Omaha Beach and all."

"Of course! That is a perfect tie-in. We would certainly be able to market that idea, " he offered, beaming at me.

"That particular region is famous for so many things! Their cuisine, the history, the architecture, the art—with the Impressionists following the Seine to Honfleur and all the other villages… so much!" I could have just rattled on!

Finally, people started to leave and I looked to take my cue from Annie-Laure; but she didn't appear to be in any hurry. Jean-Paul came over and sat down by me.

"My uncle is very fond of you, " he said. "You **wowed** him."

"I did what!?" I laughed. *I'd never heard him utter one word of English slang.*

"I am very happy you and he had the opportunity to meet. "

"Well, after your story of coming to the U.S., he's practically legendary."

"Yes, and I am really all he has in the way of family, so it is so good to see him."

"It was very thoughtful of you to send your plane for him."

"Ah, he told you that, did he? Well, I wanted my own people to accompany him to the meeting if he could come. He's not so able to travel very easily these days."

"So will he be staying into next week?"

"No no, he flies back on Sunday. Tomorrow we shall go over Foundation business. It will be very helpful to have him here in Chicago where all the records are. And he keeps me apprised of the state of the family enterprise. You can imagine his staff is quite enormous, and one day I shall have to deal more directly with them, also."

"That must be daunting, " I said.

"It is a challenge, but I also have many people to help me."

"That's…uh…lucky."

"The sad thing is, of course, that I do not have children to carry on after me, to whom all of this may be left."

Well, he had me there. In the 1970's no gay people could adopt in the U.S. and, while things such as surrogacy must have existed, it would be the better part of the decade before in vitro fertilization was even on the horizon. I had no idea where anyone could have their sperm frozen, or how he might go about finding someone who could be an egg donor or womb-for-hire. Even if he could find someone, whether or not she would carry the child to term and then relinquish it to him loomed as a big question in my mind.

I didn't know how to respond. It was none of my business, and I had nothing to offer in the way of expertise or experience. I just kept quiet. He didn't elaborate about having children, much to my relief.

"You were very poised today at the meeting, " he said, smiling at me. "You will do our organization a great service putting the spotlight on us with teachers. Our board recognizes that and, speaking for myself, I cannot thank you enough."

"Thanks to you! " I replied, trying to take the compliment gracefully, when in reality the remark made me wonder if all along he had been secretly afraid I'd blow it.

Chapter Eighty-Eight

"Color My World"...Chicago

I knew it was only a matter of time until it would be lights out, literally, on my rent-free living situation. So when I got a call from Hyde Industries informing me that Peggy, John-Wilfred's same secretary whom I'd met when I moved in, needed to see me, I wasn't at all surprised. At least they were giving me fair warning that the studio must be vacated in three months, which would be June first. She asked if she could come over to my building and talk to me about it in person, and, while I thought it unconventional for someone in her lofty position, of course I agreed. She would come over on a Monday evening after work.

There was still no bell or buzzer system at my place, so I watched for her from my vantage point at the window. When I let her in, she told me that Mr. Hyde was aware of my situation, so she was there at his behest, which made me wonder if Cass had again had something to do with it. Mr. Hyde didn't know that I'd gotten a raise, but he did know that since I had lived almost a year rent-free, as was the plan, I must have saved up a good amount of future rent money. So he had sent her to offer me an amazing deal: rent one of the newly created smaller one-bedroom apartments in this same building! She said they would give me a break on the price, too, and charge me three hundred dollars for it, including all utilities.

Wow, if that's the discounted rate, what must the normal rent be?

I just sat there for a second trying to do math in my head, always a challenge.

"Is that too high for you?" she wondered, when I didn't act enthused right away.

"Oh...that seems very –uh—fair. I **think** I can swing it...hope so, because I would dearly LOVE to stay here."

"We could probably let you keep the furniture you now have in the studio if that would help."

"Yes, thanks! A lot! I'd just have to get a sofa or something."

"You know, I think I can be of some help to you there, too. Several of these apartments we just renovated had the odd piece of furniture. I'll look for you. Do you want to see the apartment? It's not quite done yet, but you'll get an idea."

Boy, did I! She had keys, and we set off just down the hall past a beautifully redone central stairway, behind which an elevator had been newly installed, too. The extensive millwork was just magnificent. All the while I had known workers were in and out, but I'd never explored to see what they were doing! I was astounded. No wonder the place would be expensive.

"You see, there is one apartment in the back on this floor, " she explained. "That's the door."

We went in to a little vestibule where there was a tiny coat closet, and then to the immediate right of that was the kitchen. It was splendid: a narrow galley kitchen but appointed in gorgeous, modern appliances...even a small dishwasher and stacked washer and dryer over in a corner...the height of luxury to me! The stove was electric, the top of the line Tappen, and above it was a new-fangled Amana microwave oven! Also there was an apartment-sized, but appealing, white fridge. The floor was black and white large square tiles. The cabinets were all white, the countertops were blue; and one had an integrated white farm sink. I could just see some blue and white gingham curtains on the window over it in my future!

"This is Corian, " Peggy told me brushing her hand over the counter, "the newest, most sought-after material in kitchens today. I think you're going to love it."

Of course I recognized it as the same material as in Pax's kitchen, and I was blown away that I might have it, too.

Continuing down the hall, we came to the living room, which wasn't all that small, really, and had a view out to the side parking lot.

"You'll lose your pretty front street view," said Peggy, "but you'll gain a bedroom."

At least I could still see some foliage, as no other building could block the view on that side. The living room was an el-shaped one with space for a small dining table if I could find one. My kitchen table from the studio was ugly, but there wasn't any room in the new kitchen for it, so I guessed it would go there. The living room had a brick fireplace with green and blue square tiles around it looking like holdovers from the art deco era, and it came with a beautiful mantel stained in dark reddish-brown tones. I admired the fireplace. *(Even Sol and Betty hadn't put one in our house when they had it custom-built. Talk about a stupid cost-cutting measure. They always regretted it.)*

Peggy told me, "If you put a mirror right above the mantle, the room will seem even larger."

Flanking one side of the entry was an original–to-the-house bookcase built into a large niche. I adored that and could think of many things with which to fill it.

"Notice we kept the crown moldings and the original baseboards," Peggy pointed out. "The room is certainly prettier that way and seems elegant-- from a by-gone era."

"I love it."

We went back down the hall, and she showed me the bedroom next. It was plainer than the other rooms without any decorative features like moldings or bay window or anything, but it did have a spectacular feature: a walk-in closet with more space than I'd ever had, even at home in The Bluffs.

"So will you use that day-bed from the studio?" Peggy asked.

"Well, it's the only bed I have, so I'd be grateful to keep it."

"Like I said, we'll try to get you a couch for the living room. I can't guarantee it will be pretty or even comfortable, or in any style you like, though," she laughed.

"Hey, I'll take it no matter what." I should have added, provided it's clean, but I trusted that she would be hep to that.

Finally, she showed me the last room: a sweet bathroom painted in light green with all the bells and whistles I could ask for: a nice-sized vanity, two cabinets, a large one, perfect for linens; and a small "medicine cabinet" with a mirror on it, built in above the sink. The tub had a normal, good-sized shower head, and the surround was tiled in a darker shade of green than the walls. This was the only bathroom, as the bedroom did not have an en suite, but I couldn't have been happier or more appreciative.

She informed me that I would get the new keys before the end of May, and would not even need to turn in my present one because the remodeled front entrance, and the new efficiency apartment there, would entail a completely new door.

"We are keeping the studio and completely redoing it for a concierge-slash-landlord or landlady to live in," Peggy told me, as if reading my mind. "It's not a doorman building, of course, but that way there can be someone to get packages or call repairmen or whatever tenants need."

"That's great, " I said. "Are the apartments being advertised yet to the public?"

"Not yet. But we think the building will fill right up. There are really big units upstairs, " she explained. "One has four bedrooms, which would make it ideal for a family with an *au pair* or a summer girl. There could be children in this house soon."

I'd heard that term 'summer girl' for full-time vacation babysitter or nanny. Is that specific to Chicago? I wondered, because at home we don't call them that.

I had Cass on the phone as soon as Peggy left.

"So I told her that I would be **thrilled** to take the one-bedroom for the rent stated, that, besides the couch she would hopefully find for me, I can move the furniture from the studio in there. The workmen might even be prevailed upon to help me move the stuff! I'm in clover once again, thanks to your father!" I told her breathlessly.

Cass was overjoyed for me and I broached my suspicions to her.

"You didn't have anything to do with this rent deal I got, did you?" I asked her point blank.

"Nope. Haven't spoken to my father since he came here to see us---on your invitation, if you recall."

"Well, once again, Cass, I'm in his debt."

"Oh, he'll get his money from you. He didn't give you that great a bargain."

"Ho! I think he must have. I would have probably had to spend at least two hundred dollars just renting a room somewhere. This city is unbelievably expensive!"

"Well, all's well that ends well, then, isn't it?" she laughed.

I was still very worried about Cass and Alan, but Cass did sound up-beat at this time, telling me that the *Iowa City Press Citizen* had written an article about her and her art.

"I'll send you a copy of it, " she sang.

507

"Oh, you have to!! That's is the greatest news! You're going to be famous; I've always said so. "

"Ha ha. "

"Are the twins in it, too?"

"Of course! They were very active when the reporter came out here."

"What did Alan say?"

"Not much. I mean, he was pretty happy about it, I guess."

That's what I thought she'd say.

She did send me the article. I thought the journalistic "style" was a little too cloying, but, as far as getting Cass some publicity for her art, an article of this magnitude was fabulous! It took up almost an entire page—spanning four column inches in size-- and had photos! There was a big picture of her holding up a large block print self-portrait, plus one of the Switzerland scenes, a smaller inset of the Christmas card design she'd done, and finally, a fourth picture of her with the twins. No Alan.

"Good," I thought, "serves him right."

The article recounted, among other things, that Cass lived in a sweet little farmhouse right outside Iowa City (I'm not sure sweet is the term I would have used for it). The reporter wrote:

"You are met by a welcoming committee of friendly animals and children when you approach it. You take a glance around the place, and you feel you are in an old childhood dream."

What the hell did that mean? I guess the next sentence told it.

"You see a little pond off in the distance with large fluffy white ducks floating slowly in it, while in an enclosed pen to the side of the house you find an indifferent goat munching on grass. Cass said she bought the goat ostensibly for the milk and cheese it could provide, but the truth is she will grab onto any excuse to give an animal a home."

Really?

It went on, **"Toddlers abound! Cass and her Writers' Workshop member hubby have adorable eighteen-month-old twins, a boy Paul and a girl Laura. They are sweet cherubs with tousle-headed blond curls and wide blue eyes. 'They take after their daddy,' Cass explains. Paul chases around the room on a riding toy that resembles a jolly inch worm, (yes!) and Laura clings to her mommy's long, paisley skirt. Your first thought is: lucky is the husband who comes home to this menagerie every night."**

We wish.

"We'll pretend that Cassandra, who was distinctly reticent to talk about herself, was in a particularly revelatory mood. I can tell you that she was born in a suburb of Chicago and went to boarding school on the East Coast. She came to Iowa U because of Mauricio Lasansky's position on the faculty and even though she'd chosen to take time off from finishing her degree to raise her children, she kept up with the art school and found time to work there. 'I find that even in the midst of this hectic home life I can escape into my own world of art,' she explained. As she holds up the linoleum block print self-portrait shown in inset photo, she admits that it makes her seem rather unhappy because it is very solemn, but the other one, a magnificent scene of Swiss alpine villages will be presented in a few months at the Johnson County Fair art show this summer. If it wins, it goes to the Iowa State Fair."

The reporter noted that although the care and feeding of babies and animals made demands on her time, Cass usually sat down every day—not from habit, but from a longing or need inside—to create. She wrote that Cass had largely abandoned oil and watercolor for block printing, partly because it was less expensive, and partly because it lent itself to the more angular lines of her recent drawings; and, more importantly, because she still wanted to show her work to Lasansky someday. Cass was also quoted in the story as having become **"intrigued with textures, and the carving of the linoleum block as well as the chance to use papers with interesting surfaces,"** all of which afforded her a satisfaction she couldn't get from painting. The article ended by Cass affirming that when she created a work of art she wasn't thinking, just feeling and the feelings had to do with her life and God, so many things that summed up her **"self"**.

I fervently hoped all that were true, but I had my grave misgivings. To me Cass didn't sound philosophical in the piece…more like desperate.

Chapter Eighty-Nine

"Pomp and Circumstance March No. 4"...Sir Edward Elgar

Jean-Paul d'Arivèque had called me in to go over what I would like for him to mention to the teachers in his keynote address to the Mid-States Conference, and also what role I would be playing on that occasion since I had agreed to accompany him.

"I am delighted to have you attend with me, " he said.

"If I can be of assistance to you, I'm happy to do so, " I replied. Not to mention, it couldn't hurt for me to see how language association conferences go, since I was going to be planning a mini-version of that in the coming months.

"Yes, it will be a big help. I liked so much your handouts to the Board, that I am anticipating your disseminating similar materials at the luncheon."

When it came to giving out materials, I felt like a cheerleader for the Foundation.

"I'd love to give them all sorts of goodies …like the film catalogue and maybe a sample lesson plan to go with a certain film, and perhaps also a "*Moment Culturel*" on a region. I think I'd also like to include a description of one of our culture boxes, and give them a preview of what they could do with that in their classroom. I love the idea that we'll be reaching a wide target audience of educators, don't you?" I fairly gasped for breath.

"Yes, Sarah!" he laughed. "We shall do all of it."

"I think this could do the trick, you know. We may become more popular than we can handle!"

"Well, since you mention that, I have not forgotten the idea of your having an assistant film librarian on the job, like I told you previously. Would you be able to start interviewing when we put the word out?"

"Of course."

Then he told me that we would be going up to Wisconsin in his car and that Jean-Luc would drive. We would be staying over one night in the Delevan Lodge, which was attached to this sort of convention center where the big events would take place. I would have my own room, of course, as he would, and there would be another one for Jean-Luc and Robineau.

"Robineau! **Fuck** it, " I told Cass on the phone. "I'm thinking I must have visibly bristled at the thought of having to see that shithead again, but I guess JPA didn't pick up on it. He didn't say anything."

"I wish you would tell him already. Why should that weasel s.o.b. get away with making you miserable?"

"I've made up my mind to completely ignore him, but if he ever even looks at me cross-eyed, I will go to **my** boss **and** his, and rat him out."

Further arrangements were that the packets, which I would be offering to the attendees after his speech, would be delivered up there by messenger so that we---meaning Jean-Luc and the valet—wouldn't have to carry in boxes. Also Jean-Luc would be taking Robineau back after he helped JPA get dressed on Saturday morning because he had work to oversee at the mansion. Then Luc would come back up there to get us that evening.

"So," I told Cass, "four two-hour trips for that poor guy!"

"Chicagoans don't think anything of a two-hour commute, though, " she said.

"You're joking."

When the limousine arrived to pick me up, I came down with my tote bag, and Jean-Luc who was already out of the car, took it from me, opened the door for me to get in the back, and then he put my bag in the trunk. Robineau was seated in the passenger's side of the front seat. Luckily for me, I only had to see the back of his ugly head, and even that was separated by the glass partition. He never acknowledged my presence, nor I his.

JPA greeted me with *la bise*, which, if Robineau had seen that, it might have given him a well-deserved comeuppance. I settled into the luxurious seat and looked over at my travel partner and smiled. Two hours in that car would probably put me right to sleep. I hoped I wouldn't accidently topple over onto his lap.

Once we were underway, JPA took out his speech and asked me to look at it. He was very used to giving speeches, and certainly did not need any editing from me. But he wanted me to check that he had included the points I felt were most salient to our cause, especially the parts that were "the fruits of your labors."

The talk began by giving the audience a brief history of the Foundation and how his mother had started it with private funds, which remain private to this day with no government oversight either from France or the U.S. It stated the Foundation's mission to promote the culture of France and the French-speaking parts of the globe, but especially those in North America. He went on to explain how the FCF differed from the Embassy and its consulates, but how we did programming in partnership with not only them, but also the Chamber of Commerce and arts organizations. He made it a point to talk about scholarship and grant opportunities that the Foundation offers to students in high school, college, grad school and also to professionals. He then described the newsletter we put out that would surely be of interest to teachers, and could be used to enhance their classrooms. Finally, the last third of the speech was devoted to my recent additions in the realm of film and education.

"Have I sufficiently covered your major topics?" he asked.

"Very nicely, " I reassured him, and then, trying to lighten up the conversation a bit, I added with a bit of tease, "Are they going to introduce you as *Monsieur le Comte de Beuvron?*"

"No, no, " he laughed.

"Well, you'd probably be mobbed for your autograph afterwards if they did."

We pulled onto the grounds of Delevan Lodge on a ring road in a bucolic setting of old growth forest that led to Lake Delevan off in the distance. It could not have been more quaint or more inviting. A second- floor terrace that wrapped around the building was in view from the road, with blue iron café tables and parasols standing empty and at the ready. Park-like manicured lawns spread out around the perimeters of the compound below.

The Lodge and its convention center were conveniently located right together. The hotel part was older, brown clapboard, green-shingled roofs and lots of rock on the façade. All the outside window casings were painted in blue and some had blue shutters with steep Scandinavian-looking gingerbread-trimmed eaves. A large blue canopy marked the main entrance.

Inside the furnishings were "lake lodge" rustic but very beautiful. The lobby reception area was called the Great Hall, and it had a massive stone fireplace as its focal point that reached from the floor right up to the beamed ceiling. On either side of it were gorgeous windows with squares framing the glass. The room was furnished in heavy wooden and leather sofas, and scattered throughout the space were lovely conversation pits with beautiful pine log benches, tables, and chairs. The entire color scheme was tan and green, with accent pieces of large azure urns holding tall pampas grasses.

Robineau and Jean-Luc came in with the bags, and handed them over to a bell-hop. Jean-Luc took his leave , giving me *la bise*, which annoyed Robineau, who glared at me as I stood at the desk next to JPA. I ignored him, and waited for the clerk to hand me my key.

" *Alors*, we shall repair to our rooms and unpack?" Jean-Paul said, turning to me, "and then may we meet back here to pick up our convention credentials? Would half an hour be sufficient for you?"

"That would be great, " I said, smiling at my boss and giving the valet a smirk, smug this time.

My room was huge for one person, and had two incredible features: a stone fireplace and old *armoire à la française*. I wondered how they came upon having that type of cabinet. I reveled in the flashback to Paris, but when I opened it up, the inside of this piece of furniture had been converted into housing for a television, thus removing any drawers or hanging spots for clothes. A large closet served that purpose. The room screamed another era, but the bathroom was modern. I could be very happy in there for weeks.

When the three of us (Robineau was back with him! What the hell? I wondered.) reconnoitered at the hotel front desk to pick up convention materials, there were thick envelopes with our meal tickets inside, along with schedules of presentations and their room assignments, and a list of the vendors. The

510

clerk also informed us that a message was left for JPA that he was invited to a presenters' reception later that afternoon and to that end, his also contained a badge with a ribbon on it which would admit him to the function. Only him.

"May I please have another of these for my colleague here?" he asked at the desk. But that person's only duties were hotel-oriented; he had nothing to do with the convention registration which was under other auspices.

"I'm sorry, sir, " he replied. "You'd have to talk to the Mid-States folks about that."

"Can you please call one of them here in that case?"

Soon a young woman appeared and asked what, if anything, she could do for us. JPA introduced himself, and she immediately recognized his name from the program with which she was obviously familiar. JPA told her he wanted me to have a badge for the private reception that afternoon.

"Oh, I'm so sorry! Registration closed weeks ago. I do apologize, but it's not possible to add anyone now."

"But that is preposterous, "he said unamused. "She is with me."

"I do apologize." She didn't know what else to say to ameliorate the situation we all found ourselves in. My boss was not pleased. I touched his arm and said,

"No, no, that's fine. You go. I'll see you in the morning."

Robineau looked down his nose at me, as if to say, "serves you right." He took Monsieur's manila envelope and left the lobby. He had presumably realized that our boss would not be able to carry that around with him all evening.

JPA looked forlornly at me, and said how unhappy he was at this turn of events.

"It seems neither of us has any experience at these things," I said, "so please don't give it another thought. You go… and enjoy it!"

"Sarah, I want you to order room service---anything you like. And just sign for it. Will you do that?"

"I'll do it!" I laughed. "And thank you!" I turned and went off to my sweet room.

In the morning when we met up again at the conference breakfast--for which I did have a ticket, of course! --we were greeted by the chairwoman of the entire convention, who made it a point to tell me she had been " mortified" by the slight to me the previous day. She wanted to be sure we saw the ball room where the luncheon would be held so that I could become familiar with the back, where I would be stationed with my materials.

As we walked in, I told JPA that I'd also brought along sign-up sheets for the teachers interested in getting on the Foundation's monthly newsletter mailing list.

"You have thought of everything, " Jean-Paul d'Arivèque warmly complimented me.

The convention center itself looked like any other large auditorium or arena. It had a skylight over the humungous exhibition hall, and another whole area with meeting rooms. The huge ballroom was set up with fifty round tables of ten places each.

Once in the ballroom, however, there was a major shock. JPA pulled me to the side and in a low voice, sounding very distressed, told me to look at the stage. Indeed, I saw that it was one of those portable ones that conventions often brought into rooms where there was a need for a raised area on which to do presentations, hand out awards and such. They had placed upon it a large podium with the microphone.

"But do you not see the problem?" he said to me with a note of apprehension I'd not heard before from him.

"Uh, wait a minute." And I took a better glance around the space. "Oh."

I saw it all right. The steps leading up to that stage were right in front…six steps, high risers, no railing. Nothing. Bare stairs.

"I cannot go up those steps, " he said.

"Um, let's tell her, and maybe for your speech, they can move the podium to the main floor. You'll be hard to see from the back, but the microphone should carry your message loud and clear."

So I approached our hostess, and asked whether the podium could stand on the main floor for his presentation.

"No, I'm afraid not, " came the reply. "The cords won't reach down there. They're connected to the back wall." I couldn't tell if she was "getting it" that we had a big problem here.

"I see, " I said, "so can the mic be taken out separately and just held?"

" Sorry, no. It's not portable. Why?" she seemed perplexed.

"We have an issue."

Jean-Paul couldn't have given his speech on the ballroom floor in any case, I realized after I asked. He had to hold his cane or lean against something, and hold his speech. It wouldn't be possible to also hold a microphone.

I went back to where he was standing, looking both forlorn and panicky. Jean-Luc and Robineau had left to go back to Chicago hours ago. There was nothing to do but offer to help him.

"I'll go with you up the stairs, " I said matter-of-factly.

"You cannot, Sarah. I am too heavy and if I start to teeter, we should both fall down all those steps."

"Well, then, I'll get some guys to do it, " I offered. "There will be plenty of waiters or teachers or... other... men... around. I'm sure someone will be happy to help out."

"No, " he said, and looked at me. "You see, at my home or the office, I am happy to let people assist me even when it makes me seem feeble or helpless, because I know they know otherwise. But I cannot be seen here being lifted upstairs like that in front of a banquet room full of strangers. I am sorry. I cannot."

"But, " I said, trying to think, "if you just give your speech on the floor without a mic, no one will be able to hear it. This room is cavernous as it is."

"I agree." He transferred his cane to his left hand and put his right hand on my shoulder. "Sarah, would you deliver the address for me?"

" I—uh—but...no! They invited you! They don't want to hear me."

Okay, so I'm sure the director of the conference was just as taken aback to see that her keynote speaker was disabled, as we were to see that stage. And I certainly wished we'd made the fact known ahead of time, but no one was thinking of special accommodations in those days. I pondered whether or not it had occurred to my boss, and he just hadn't voiced his concerns. I wondered what he did in other speaking circumstances. But there wasn't any time to research solutions to our immediate dilemma.

"Please, Sarah. Do this for me? I am convinced you could handle it beautifully."

What could I say?

"Well, they'll be sorely disappointed, but...of course, if you really think I can...if you want me to... I'll do it for you." *Jesus! What had I just agreed to?* "Only...holy buckets!..let me take it off somewhere and practice a little!"

"Je t'en remercie, Sarah!" he exclaimed, visibly relieved. *"Voilà."* And he handed me the folded papers from his interior suit coat pocket.

Jean-Paul informed the chair of the change in speakers, and gave her a brief bio of me in exchange for the long intro she had prepared on him.

We oversaw the unpacking of our boxes containing the packets to be distributed from the back of the room, as planned. Except that now I'd need to finish the speech and then get back there. Well, too bad, they'd just have to wait for me; what else could we do?

The luncheon menu of sliced chilled beef tenderloin with sandwich rolls, New Orleans shrimp salad, potato salad or garden salad vinaigrette plus honey vanilla cheesecake was not bad; but I just sat there too nervous to eat. My stomach was doing flip flops.

"You are not hungry? " Jean-Paul asked me, worried, when he saw I wasn't eating much. "This is better than most convention food, I should imagine."

"I'm sure you're right."

Finally, it was show time! Our introduction presenter explained without really giving an explanation, that the speaker would be the "film librarian from the *Fondation Culturelle Française,* Miss Sarah Shrier." Polite applause and tittering ensued.

I went up those steep steps --lucky that I didn't fall myself-- and looked out among the crowd of about five hundred people! I lowered the microphone in its adjustable cradle and began.

"It is my great pleasure to be with you here today, to represent the *Fondation Culturelle Française* and its president *Monsieur* Jean-Paul d'Arivèque, and to address you on his behalf. He's here, by the way,

" I added, not realizing until it was too late that I'd just put him on the spot, "seated over there, so be sure to meet him before you leave." I nodded in his direction, and he waved awkwardly to the crowd, having been brought into the limelight…by me.

"It is our goal to introduce you to the Foundation, and give you an idea of what our mission is-- what we have to offer educators. We realize not all of you are French teachers, and we want you to know that our services are open to anyone. Granted our content is geared to French, but it is our hope that the ideas transcend the languages. Many are also interdisciplinary."

That was an educationaleeze term he'd got from me! I got it from Dom. It was an up and coming trend in high schools.

I continued with the seed idea for the organization having been *Madame* Marie-Aveline d'Arivèque's dream child and all about the private funding.

I talked about our mission and how we were not diplomats but that we worked closely with the French Embassy's consulate in Chicago to collaborate on programming.

"We partner with museums, the symphony, the opera, and also with businesses, either via the Chamber of Commerce or with specific ones, for things like the French Christmas markets that Marshall Fields will be doing this December."

I spoke of all the scholarship and grant opportunities we fostered, and emphasized that we could put teachers in touch with programs where they could perfect their language skills in France or Québec with opportunities to live and work there. I managed to plow through his nicely written prose, and even to glance up once in a while, so as not to appear to be reading it robot-like.

Finally I got to the part I could do without his notes—the information on the educational component and the film library.

I offered what I saw as the *pièce de résistance* by saying, "We provide our services to the public, but our goal is educational, and we have specific areas geared to reaching students at all levels, elementary to university. Our Foundation produces a monthly newsletter of interest to you in your classrooms with French history stories, cultural trends, and language articles. There are frequent offerings on sports, or cuisine, and art. Each issue contains a wealth of informative content on wonderful French destinations, in-depth feature articles on such topics as the French educational system or French elections. This is sent absolutely free of charge and in the back I will have a sign-up sheet so that you may begin to receive it next month."

Gasps and more applause. I glanced over at JPA, and he was smiling broadly back at me. Buoyed by the response, I launched enthusiastically into the programs for which I was personally responsible.

"Next I want to tell you about another service we offer at the *Fondation Culturelle Française:* a newly restocked and redesigned French film lending library. In the packet we have provided, you will find our catalogue of films that you can borrow—again without any cost to you…we even pay the return shipping! Our library also contains film strips, and slide sets, documentaries, travelogues, posters, in addition to all the current and historic French movies. We have recently begun to add lesson plans to accompany some of the films with discussion questions and prompts for conversations in your classes. We have them in all levels of French.

"In the realm of non-fiction, our film library is replete with documentaries on every region in France, France d'Outre-Mer, and Canada's French-speaking areas. If you do a unit on those, you know you cover history, geography, cuisine, and tourism. To that end, we at the Foundation are prepared to provide you with little articles written on two different language levels called *Moments Culturels* that you can use to enhance the learning experience.

"In the areas of elementary and junior high-level language, we have created role-playing boxes--- we call them Culture Boxes--- that you may check out. They contain anything from simple costumes and wigs to play swords and even *Guignol*-style puppet theaters for your students to study, say, Life at Versailles with *Les Trois Mousquetaires* or Louis XIV. "

Now I was hearing "wows" and exclamations like "far out" from the crowd. So I deviated completely from the written speech and brought it all home.

"I am happy today to also announce an exciting new concept for the Foundation, as concerns educators. There is an introduction to this in the packet---we're calling it a **Mini-Institute**, and greater details of it will be forthcoming. Essentially, the idea is to hold a two-day workshop on a specific topic-- such as *Le Marquis de Lafayette*-- to have lectures about his role in French and American history, and then to provide you with breakout sessions, like you have here, to make lesson plans based on the theme that you will take right with you that day. You might also make a bulletin board or a game. Once again, this will be at very minimal cost to the teacher. We 're hoping to set this all in motion for next January, so stay tuned! "

The audience was agitated, and it seemed, in a good way.

"In all our educational arena, we want to offer you the highest quality engaging materials that have one primary objective in mind, and that is to elevate your enthusiasm for your job and to make you a more effective teacher. All of this, let me emphasize again, at no charge to you!"

I thanked them for their attention, apologized once again for being there instead of their original keynote speaker, and bade them see me in the back of the room for all the swag. There ensued wild applause and a bit of a stampede to the back table. When I saw it could get out of hand, I assured them we had plenty, and not to worry; and I exited the stage to really, thunderous applause.

It took a fair amount of time for me to hand out the *exemplaires* to all who wanted one, and, in the end, our stockpiles were depleted, and my newsletter sign-up sheet was completely filled up. After the last person left my table, I got up to head back out to the lobby.

To my relief and pleasure, people were flocking around d'Arivèque, congratulating him on providing such a windfall for teachers. I passed by him, deep in conversation with an adoring fan, and, exhausted, I made a beeline for a gigantic leather club chair in the Great Hall. It was happy exhaustion, but, thinking about it in retrospect, having been asked out of the blue like that to give his speech, and having had to get up in front of that crowd, the sheer numbers of which had been daunting, I found myself sort of surreptitiously done in! My relief that the whole thing was over was palpable.

Convention participants filed by me with their packets and waved or called out "Thank you!" but mercifully didn't stop to ask me anything else. And then Jean-Paul made his way into the area, looking around, presumably for me.

"Sarah! " he called out, struggling to control his gait and his enthusiasm at the same time, "*quel triomphe, mon cher collègue!* " He leaned over to give me *la bise* and sat down in the chair next to mine, taking my hand in his, and addressing me in the familiar (!). *Tu as fait merveille!* I am so proud of the way you represented *La Fondation. Brava!*"

"You're welcome! It did go well, I think. We gave away absolutely everything we brought. And look at all these teachers who want to receive our newsletter!" I waved my list in his direction. "Far out, eh?"

"Yes, Sarah. Thanks entirely to you!"

Just then, the chairwoman found Jean-Paul and me, and insisted on an impromptu meeting on how we could best promote our programs in the future. So we went off with her to the bar to discuss the possibility of sessions or a booth-- or both --at their next confab in a year. I excused myself after a bit, thinking she just wanted to talk to him, and did a quick tour through the vendor exhibits in the arena hall, and then went back to my room to pack. Monsieur called me on the house phone.

"I have asked Luc to pick us up around eight. I should like to invite you to dinner in the restaurant of this Lodge, before we have to leave."

Since I had barely touched the lunch, I was famished. The Lodge's main dining room was gorgeous, and I was only too eager to go there. I offered him the requisite enthusiastic thanks.

All through dinner he praised and lauded me. I told him I thought anyone would have done the same, but he wouldn't hear that.

"You are such a poised speaker for someone so young! If you were anxious at all, you certainly did not show it!"

"I can't say I wasn't nervous. But I had a professor once who said that if you couldn't express what you knew, then you didn't know it. I guess public speaking comes easy enough for me." I think I was blushing by that point, not anxious to talk about myself like that, but hoping to accept his acclamations gracefully.

514

I found myself perturbed at one thing, though, and brought up to him the fact that the convention seemed highly unprepared for last-minute glitches like that of the stairs.

"And why have that kind of set-up" I proffered, "with not even a railing! What if someone were in a wheelchair for heaven's sake?! No ramps! Nothing!"

"You sound like you could be an advocate for handicapped people, " he laughed.

"Oh, you know…it just irks me. *C'est normal.*"

In the limo on the way back home, I was drained. I closed my eyes and felt myself sinking deep into the leather seat and drifting off to the swaying of the car. When we stopped and I woke up, I was nestled in the good arm of Jean-Paul d'Arivèque, and there wasn't anything I could say about it. I didn't know if I'd fallen over or if he had voluntarily enveloped me. All I knew is that I slept the sleep of the dead, awoke and… almost died!

"*Tu es très fatiguée,*" he said tenderly, lifting his arm slowly from my shoulders.

I thought for a fleeting moment he was going to lean down and kiss me, but of course, that would have been ridiculous. And yet, I felt …something.

Chapter Ninety

"Plus Fort Que Nous"...Francis Lai

Word of my achievement in speech-making spread through the Foundation to the extent that I was met with thumbs up signs and pats on the back when the new work week started. People came down to my office to congratulate me and the receptionist fielded many phone requests for materials and films. The swell of activity in the film library kept me very busy for the next month, and I found that I was actually doing something new for my job: taking serious amounts of work home at night. I was writing "*Moments Culturels*" to go with the regions films because that was what was being requested most. My Regions of France sample units had evidently been big hits.

Our outings to the CSO continued, although Maestro Solti was not in town for all of the concerts that spring, since he had previous commitments to Covent Garden in London. He was sharing the job with Carlo Maria Giulini, whom Jean-Paul had also met numerous times. Due to the fact that Marie-Aveline had contributed so generously over the previous decade to the symphony's endowment, her son was still invited-- in her memory, really--to every meet-and-greet, fundraiser and gala they put on.

When I did see Georg Solti, he seemed genuinely pleased that Jean-Paul had brought me to the entire season of concerts, which, as he reminded us, had been at his behest.

"Next you must take her to the Lyric Opera, Polo," he chided one day. "Would you like that, Sarah?"

"I would...certainly. My musical education continues! Ha!" I made light of it but I worried my boss would feel put-upon or obliged, and I did not want that.

We, in turn, asked after baby Gabrielle constantly, and scolded the maestro for having hardly any recent pictures of her to show and brag about. He promised us he would see to it that Valerie put some in his suitcases the next time. Even without them we knew he was besotted with his new daughter, and missed both "his girls" when he came to Chicago and they stayed in England.

For the last concert of the season, which Solti would be conducting, Jean-Paul told me he was still in a celebratory mood from the Mid-States conference and its aftermath of interest in the Foundation, "thanks to you," (as he always put it and I always denied) and let me know in advance that he would like to invite me to a special pre-concert dinner at the Palm Court. I found myself again on the horns of a dilemma. My wardrobe was not working, even with the infusion of the Sant'Angelo outfit and Cass' clothes.

It was not a secret that I loved clothes, although, truth be told, the styles of the '70's didn't do much for me, as I was still happily ensconced in the 60's---not the hippie stuff either— the Carnaby Street vibe of Twiggy and The Shrimp. My heart's desire ran towards Pappagallo, Daniel Hechter, Mary Quant, Lacoste, and Yves St. Laurent. But I couldn't afford any of that. Nana had always said that if you have taste, you can shop almost anywhere. So I tried to augment my ridiculous closet by shopping very astutely and finding things on sale. But the fact was, when dressing up to go out, it came down to Cass' blue dress with the pink sash, which was losing its panache. I had worn it so often that I almost couldn't bear to throw it on.

Note to self: you must get some new clothes.

I wasn't the only one who thought so, it turned out. Jean-Paul and I were seated across from each other at a rather small, intimate table, especially for that room where large round ones were the norm, and he seemed a bit agitated as he looked at me, and took a breath as if to start an important announcement.

"Sarah, please do not take this the wrong way..."

Always an inauspicious way to begin a conversation, I thought to myself and immediately looked up with a sense of dread.

"...but I am wondering if perhaps you need some new —uh— dresses, blouses...skirts? Do you feel as though you cannot afford to shop even with your augmented salary?"

"You're sick of seeing me in these same old outfits aren't you? " I laughed... nervously.

"No, not at all. But I am concerned that you are denying yourself and I am wondering why."

I looked at him directly in the eye and said, "*Monsieur*, you know how ever so grateful I am for the raise. I'll admit I've been a little under the gun with my money situation since coming to Chicago, but I fully intend to have that all rectified soon. I've a mind to even do a budget in writing. So please don't worry about me. I know you must think my wardrobe is pathetic, " I sort of coughed, trying to hide my feeling of abject embarrassment.

He made the tsk tsk sound and said, "*Mais non.* Here is what I want to tell you. You have been twice now a guest in my mother's room. You know her armoires are overflowing with clothing. I believe Marie-France tried to offer you some of *Maman's* things previously, did she not? "

I nodded, realizing that this had not been forgotten, as I'd hoped it would have been.

"It would please me were you to see if any of those things would do for you. Do you agree to that?"

My first instinct was to categorically turn down that offer. All I needed was to invoke sad memories of **Maman** *every time he saw me wearing something of hers. Secondly, her shadow loomed over me every day when I walked into the FCF. Ignoring the rude awakening Robineau tried to evoke that fateful day he told me I would never be accepted because I hadn't known her, I didn't need reasons to be reminded of it by wearing her clothes. Third, I had no idea if any of it would fit me, although the peignoir I had been loaned over there obviously had. But then, night clothes don't have to fit exactly, so I couldn't really use that as a measure.*

I looked at him waiting for a response from me with a sweet, if pained look on his face, afraid he had insulted me.

"I thank you for that kind and generous offer. I'm not sure I can accept. But I will say this: I will go shopping right away for some different stuff to wear to Foundation events and evenings out with you, how's that?"

I reached for my water, and he, instead, stopped me and took my hand and held it in his. "That is not what I meant to convey at all. You look lovely whenever we are together and at work, too. I only wonder…like many women, you seem to like clothes…and perhaps you could use some additions to your wardrobe? I did not mean to imply that I expect you to go shopping just to satisfy me. I would just like to, well, help you. And I know you like Chanel, do you not?"

"Well, yes , but …

"My mother had many Chanel ensembles. I think they would look lovely on you."

"Forgive my curiosity, *Monsieur*, but I'm a little surprised your mother wore the clothes of a known *collabo.*"

"And you also wear them?" he chided me with a little smirk.

"Well, yes, but I didn't buy that **one** Chanel thing you've been seeing me in so much. My college roomie Cass Hyde gave it to me. It was hers. Long story. "

"And you like so much this dress. It looks very pretty on you."

"I can't pretend I don't love Chanel clothes, perfumes, and everything. I guess I should feel guilty about it. When I was in Paris, we learned all about Coco Chanel's nefarious activity during the War."

"Did you?" he asked, rather rhetorically, with that same sly smile.

"Well, yeah---she was a known anti-Semite and a collaborator. From what I heard, she would have been arrested, taken away and dealt with by the Resistance but supposedly Winston Churchill or someone intervened on her behalf."

"Yes, Sarah, you are right. She was called in by the Free French Purge Committee, the *épuration*. She had had a long affair with a German diplomat stationed in Paris during the Occupation. His name was Baron Hans Günther von Dincklage. My father knew him and so did *Oncle* Charles. In fact, after the war Gabrielle lived with the Baron in Switzerland."

"Geez, and she still stayed in business?"

"Not exactly. Not throughout the war at all. But she reopened afterwards in the 1950's. I shall tell you how my mother came to have Chanel suits, which she liked very much by the way, even as she could not stomach Gabrielle — *euh* — Coco."

We sat there at the table and he recounted how, when his mother came to New York and joined forces with many other French ex-pats, as he had already explained to me, she was reunited with a very dear friend of hers named

Pierre Wertheimer, a Jew who had had to flee Paris along with his brother, and later his son. She had known the Wertheimers since her student days, even before she knew her future husband, who, himself, was also a friend of theirs.

"Like my family, the Wertheimers had a branch of their family and businesses in Geneva. They were enormously wealthy and very private."

"Wow, that is like yours. Were they also in shipping and banking?"

"No. Cosmetics, at least at first. Their father had left Alsace before the Franco-Prussian war, and invested in a French theatrical make-up company called Bourjois.

"NO! I love Bourjois!!"

He laughed. "Yes, as do all other women, I would imagine."

He continued his story: "By the 1920's his two sons had grown it into the largest and most successful cosmetics and fragrance business in France. It remains their family business today, even as they have many other holdings. *Alors*, one day when my parents had begun seeing each other but were not yet married — it was 1922 — they and Pierre Wertheimer were at the races at Longchamps. You know the great families of Europe would often frequent the same social venues, and Pierre's horse was racing. A friend of Pierre's named Théophile Bader came into their box with a young woman and introduced her to them. She was Gabrielle Chanel, and my mother took an instant disliking to her."

"Why?" I asked, interrupting.

"Oh, I believe *Maman* said she was rather vulgar. She had already been linked to a social set in England which included some of the royals, who were quite anti-Semitic, as the English upper classes tended to be, and Gabrielle must have been told that Pierre was Jewish, because she already treated him aloofly that day."

"What?! " I asked in disbelief, naïve as ever. "You mean even the royal family were like that?"

"Yes," he answered, "giving off a little chuckle, "but they keep it pretty tamped down these days."

"Gosh, " I said, "and here I had Prince Charles' pictures plastered all over my bedroom walls as a kid. Anyway, sorry…I interrupted you."

Prince Charles on my bulletin board; what a baby I must have seemed to him!

" No, no, it is fine," he smiled, "Pierre's friend, Théophile Bader was the founder of Galleries Lafayette — you know it, of course?"

"Of course! Who doesn't? This just keeps getting better and better!"

"Théophile knew that Gabrielle had created a scent with a perfumer in Grasse. She was selling it in her little millinery shops, and it was very successful with her clientele. You know what she called it, I am guessing."

"Number Five, of course! It's all my Nana ever wore."

"Yes, Chanel No. 5. Théophile wanted the Galleries Lafayette to be the store — *le grand magasin--* that launched the fragrance, but he needed it mass-produced, so he immediately thought of Bourjois to do it, and that is what did happen. They created the business called *Parfums Chanel,* and even as Gabrielle agreed she would license her name and receive ten percent of the stock, she did not participate at all in the business operations. The Wertheimer's put up all the financing, did the production, the marketing and the distribution of Chanel No. 5, and for that they received seventy percent of the profits. Théophile Bader was given twenty percent as a sort of finder's fee."

"And it was a great success, right? Did it make them all even richer than they already were?"

"Oh, *oui, évidemment*. Much wealthier."

"And Coco, too, I'm guessing?"

"Yes, but almost before the ink was dry on the contracts, Gabrielle decided she'd been robbed by the others, especially the Wertheimer brothers, whom she excoriated. She called Pierre, 'the bandit who screwed me.' Her anti-Semitic tendencies were coming to the fore and she would spend decades suing them to regain control over her perfume."

"So did she win the lawsuits?"

"*Non, justement*! And when the war broke out and Paris was occupied, Nazis were seizing all Jewish-owned property and businesses, as well as many other French enterprises such as my family's…except that as I already explained to you, my uncle had warned my father early enough to close ours and move the entire operations to Geneva. The Wertheimers also got wind of horrible things about to happen to French Jews, and they very cleverly bought shares in an airplane propeller manufacturer run by a French Catholic engineer named Félix Amiot. This man was a known collaborator who sold arms to the Nazis, so before the Nazis could take over *Parfums Chanel,* Pierre and Paul signed the company over to Amiot, and fled France for New York. Since Amiot was selling his *matériel* to the Nazis, they didn't take his businesses, and after the war, Amiot gave the companies back to the Wertheimers. By doing that, he was spared retribution from the Allies. My parents also knew this Amiot fellow –he was one of France's greatest industrialists, after all,--and, I am sure, they knew he was a *collabo.* But they understood the gambit of Pierre and Paul, and they probably kept their misgivings to themselves."

"What happened to Coco Chanel?"

"Well, she had closed up her couture shop during the war, and instead lived in the Hôtel Ritz with the Baron, and since she had such inroads to Nazi high command, she tried with all her might to betray the Wertheimers by petitioning the Nazis to give her back her company that she maintained had been snatched from her by Jews. But her efforts proved to be in vain, of course. The brothers no longer had the company and she did not know it."

"Boy, that must have been some battle she waged against them."

"Yes, it was no wonder my mother could not abide her."

"But she bought a lot of those clothes anyway? After the war?"

"Ah, yes, I am coming to that part. *Maman* was great friends with both the Werthheimers, especially Pierre. She saw first-hand how difficult it was for him and Paul trying to deal with all of this in New York. My mother told me later than they had an entire legal team working only on the Chanel lawsuits. And Pierre was worried that even if they won, which they were certainly going to, the spotlight the legal fight would surely shine on Gabrielle's war-time activities, would not only ruin her public image, but also **his** business!"

"Oh, my goodness, that's right. Not good! So what did they do?"

"*Alors,* in the end, the Wertheimers and Gabrielle Chanel settled out of court, and renegotiated the entire original 1924 agreement. They agreed to provide her with back royalties on her brand to the tune of millions and millions of dollars, and give her future earnings of two percent of world-wide sales. That made her one of the wealthiest women in the world."

"Right along with your mother?"

"*Euh…oui, effectivement.* She was not actually as wealthy as my mother, *voyons.* One thing she was, however, she was far more conniving. She made them agree to pay her Rue Cambron rent, her taxes, and all her living expenses---big and small---everything until the day she died. Paul was incensed, but Pierre acquiesced to this; and he did her one other favor, which also served to seal his fate as owner of Chanel."

"Oh, so he never relinquished ownership? He owned **Chanel**?"

And JPA explained to me how that happened. After the war and after Chanel had returned from Switzerland, she had wanted to reopen and launch a revival of her couture business. Pierre fully financed her dream. However, her attempt to stage a comeback with her first post-war collection in 1954 was a massive failure. Her wished-for success didn't arrive until Bettina Ballard, the highly influential editor of American Vogue, *gave the clothes a huge spread in her magazine, and she herself ordered a suit and wore it. After that, the reputation of Coco Chanel was reestablished. And by that time, Pierre Wertheimer had taken outright ownership of the entire House of Chanel.*

"*Voilà.* Chanel is ostensibly Jewish-owned. My mother's great friend obtained for her quite an advantageous position in buying Chanel suits and other things."

"My God, what a saga! So, are you still in contact with the Wertheimers?"

"*Oncle* Charles is, yes. *Maman* stayed in touch with Pierre after the war; they were both amassing great private art collections. Sadly, he preceded her in death -- in 1965. His son Jacques was never very interested in the couture business, but keeps it, of course…his people run it. He breeds horses in Chantilly instead. He leads a sad life, really, living alone in a huge mansion in the 8th *arrondissement.* I understand he is not doing so well mentally. But Jacques has two sons who, I hope, are going to take over and be more serious about it now. I do not know them very well—they are very young, in their twenties. Their names are Alain and Gérard. I have only met them from time to time at functions, mostly in New York. The family has homes in various cities, including Geneva where they live in the same Vandoeuvres section where the d'Arivèque home is, and they, like my family, lead a life of relative seclusion."

"And is Coco still alive?"

"As a matter of fact, she just died this past January. Did you not see it on the television news? "

"No, I must have missed it. I know she was still in Paris when I was there as a student; one of my friends saw her one day sitting in the park of the Palais Royale."

He nodded, and fixed his gaze on me again, with a deliberate demeanor.

"So, Sarah, are you now prepared to come and look over my mother's armoires?"

I thought I would sound like a broken record if I told him even one more time how grateful I was for every little thing he'd done for me since the day I came into his employ.

I gave his hand a little squeeze and thanked him, and promised to come over one day and, yes, look at those armoires.

"It probably can't be for a little while," I cautioned, "because I am moving next week. I'm excited about it, but even though it's just down the hall, and even though I have hardly any material possessions with me, it's still going to take some work."

He was surprised. I hadn't told him about my new apartment arrangements, but when I explained it, he seemed pleased that I could stay in the same house, and genuinely happy for me that Mr. Hyde had given me a break on the rent.

"I'm going to have a real kitchen!" I chirped. "Would you come to dinner some time?"

He nodded and then, catching myself, I quickly added, "I'm sure Jean-Luc would help you climb those stupid steps."

"I should be delighted to come. Do you really do it...the cooking?"

"I really do. Not like your chefs, of course. Don't get too excited."

He laughed. "It is wonderful to contemplate having a dinner prepared by you."

The Chicago Symphony season finale concert could not have been more wonderful with Maestro conducting what was to become one of his signature works: Mahler's *Fifth Symphony*. On the program along with that was Smetana's *The Moldau* and Brahms' *Academic Festival Overture*. I was in no way ready for classical "Name That Tune" by any stretch, but I was getting familiar with works, and more discerning in my tastes. In general, baroque was becoming my most-loved era, and French music the staple of my collective favorites. I knew and liked Mahler's *First* even better than the *Fifth*; but Solti's interpretation of the one he conducted that night impressed me so much with its intensity. It always seemed to me that the maestro had only to flick his hand or nod at them, and the unity of the musicians and the conductor was spell-binding.

As for the Moldau, I swore it had the same tune as the Israeli national anthem *Hatikva*; and the Brahms they played that night was familiar to me, and I loved it.

Afterwards, there was a reception for the subscription series "big donors, " so we were having drinks in the lobby, which was all decorated that particular evening with tall round tables draped in white cloths and tied with big yellow bows. Baskets of wildflowers were placed on each, and they had even hung up little white lights , and strewn them all over, creating a scene as if one were at a fairy tale garden party.

Solti was greatly sought out by all, but he managed to get away and come over to our table, happy to see us. I asked the conductor about *Die Moldau*, and if I were imagining that I knew the tune from singing it in Hebrew School.

"She's very clever, Polo!" he exclaimed. "No, Sarah, you are not imagining it. The Israeli anthem is based on a Romanian folk song called *Carul cu boi*, which translates as *Cart with Oxen*. But this melody itself was a modification of a 17th century Italian composition by a man named Casparo Zanetti, which he called *La Mantovana* and **that** tune was borrowed by Smetana; and that's why the central theme of the *Moldau* bears a striking resemblance to *Hatikva. Voilà.*"

"Well done, Sarah, " commented Jean-Paul.

"Gosh, I swear I never think about Romania, " I said. "I know nothing about that place, what art it has, what is its music. I can't name a famous Romanian. I'm actually appalled at my ignorance."

"They have a tennis player who is poised on the world stage at this very moment, " Jean-Paul laughed. "Soon you will know a Romanian."

"Who is it?" asked the maestro.

"His name is Nastase. Ilie Nastase. You will see—he is destined for great things. Do you like tennis?" he asked me.

"I like to watch it very much! I can't play worth a tinker's damn."

"And how did you find we played the Brahms tonight?" Solti asked us, deferring to Jean-Paul.

"Truly lovely, " he answered.

"You know, " said Solti, "Brahms was a fifty-year-old confirmed bachelor who declared himself to be, and I quote him now, *'Frei aber froh'*, which translates to 'free but happy.' So Polo, do you see yourself the same at –what are you-- forty-five?"

"Not yet, *merci beaucoup*. Let us not rush things."

Were gay men considered confirmed bachelors? I was rather astounded that he'd ask that question to someone who wasn't going to be marrying any woman anyway, and who didn't seem to have a life partner. But then, what did I know?

Jean-Paul seemed mightily uncomfortable at being expected to come up with an answer.

"I cannot say that I am unhappy, Georg."

Solti then turned to me. "Are you *frei aber froh*, Sarah?"

"You bet. And lucky. Sorry I don't know any German to tell you that."

"Ah, you consider yourself lucky? Me, too! I have had an enormously lucky life, and I count Polo's uncle Charles-- whom I heard you just met recently!—as one of the contributors to that. But I have also said many times, and am more and more convinced every day, that I have a guardian angel who guides and protects me. Do you believe in them, Sarah?"

Was he expecting a real answer from me? How about "Where were they in Auschwitz?" On the other hand, if he meant that they were a metaphor for friends or something, then hell, yeah; and standing right there at the high-top in the spiffed-up lobby of Orchestra Hall, Jean-Paul d'Arivèque came close to being mine.

"I...don't know, Maestro. I would like to believe they are somewhere watching over us. I'll have to ponder that a little bit."

A more pressing issue that I had to ponder was that I had just invited my boss to dinner with no pre-thought as to how that was going to even be possible.

Chapter Ninety-One

*Quintet in C Major Adagio + Allegretto, Opus 163...*The Divine Franz

The last week in May, keys to my new place were delivered to me by messenger, and I let myself in to have a look at it and contemplate my future there. A rush of happiness washed over me as I stood in front of the fireplace. "Cute, cute, cute," I said out loud to the empty rooms. But having the new place wasn't the end of the story for me. It was really bare. I had never lived anywhere that I had to completely furnish. I couldn't afford to shop for big-ticket items in normal furniture stores where one could have purchases delivered; and I couldn't go to thrift stores or junk shops because I hadn't the wherewithal to get things back to the apartment. Having to rely on friends all the time was getting old, too. Of course I could go to JPA, and he'd put his entire staff at my disposal. Of course I could ask Jean-Luc to drive me places and help me carry things upstairs, and he would do it. I just didn't want to do that. What must they think of me...taking help all the time with nothing to offer in return?

Luckily the workers Peggy Bergman had told me would move the larger items she was letting me use, did just that. When they were done, I had a day bed in the bedroom with a small bedside table just big enough for a little lamp and my transistor radio, and I had the chest of drawers. So the bedroom was about the most furnished room in the house. The living room got the two mismatched chairs from the studio, and, at least it made for a place to sit and read. I asked the guys to screw two hooks on the ceiling above the wall socket so I could hang the Chinese lamp on its chain in between the chairs. I had them put my kitchen table with its two chairs in the dining "el," and that was it. There were no end tables, no lamps, no sofa, nothing decorative, no art on the walls, and no window coverings. Even though my largest windows did not face any other buildings or the street, I still couldn't just leave them bare, and same for the bedroom one.

"For the time being I'm using sheets," I told Cass on the phone, "but it's too tacky for words."

"And are there curtain rods installed?" she asked.

"At least!"

"Well, you know what you can buy?"

"What?"

"Curtains with the valance sewn right on top...they're of a piece. You wouldn't even need double rods. And they're pretty! I saw some white lace ones at Penney's in Cedar Rapids one time."

And she was right. I found them and they weren't even that expensive. Buying a length that covered the window but didn't go down to the floor was even more economical.

One good thing about moving out of an apartment about to be demolished was that I didn't have to leave it sparkling clean, and the other handy bit about my situation was that I could just transfer the contents of my fridge and kitchen cupboards from the studio to my new ones. At least I wasn't going to have to restock everything from scratch and haul it all up the front stairs.

The room I made my first priority was the bathroom. I had a few cast-off towels and washcloths from my Iowa home, but this time I went out and actually bought a matching set in a pretty green jacquard pattern, along with a green and white striped shower curtain that I could hang on a pressure rod, and a deep green bath mat. I even splurged on glass accessories for the sink—soap dish and toothbrush holder. And this time I didn't shop at Woolworth's either, but sprang for the "good stuff" at Marshall Field's. I liked the idea of having something nice to display, and still have the old ones to use.

Peggy Bergman kept her word, and one day movers showed up with a navy-blue couch. They came in and planted it across from the fireplace. That was actually perfect, as it became a divider between the dining alcove and the living room. I was also pleased that it also wasn't the ugliest couch in the world. It needed some throw pillows and then it would do fine.

The end of summer of 1971 saw me happily ensconced in new digs that I loved. I relished coming home every single night to my comfy living room, my sweet little kitchen and cozy bedroom. I found that what I liked best was being there alone and doing exactly as I pleased. It reminded me of that other summer I'd lived happily in my own place with Cass. I had been carefree then, too, working at a job I liked and coming home with no other responsibilities. I was more alone in Chicago than I had been in Iowa City, of course. There was no Cass, no Soren, no more Pax, and thankfully, no Jerry Cohen either. Plus the symphony season was over, so my weekends nights were also more or less free. Solti was leading the Ravinia Summer Series, which JPA did not attend.

I still had a date every Sunday night, though…with Alistair Cooke! He had begun hosting *Masterpiece Theater* on PBS in January of that year, with *The First Churchills*, but by summer was narrating *Père Goriot*. It was great for me to be steeped in Balzac on the small screen, because I'd just done a synopsis at work of the 1943 film *Le Colonel Chabert* by René Le Henaff, whose theme, like that of *Le Père Goriot* was the profound impact on French society brought about by regime change. I'd written a nice *Moment Culturel* about the Restoration and the July Monarchy.

At the office I was actually busier than I could have ever imagined I'd be. I was screening movies, writing conversation prompts and the mini-lessons to go with them, developing more Culture Boxes, and filling dozens of orders per week for our library's materials. It seemed teachers did even more work in the summer prepping for their classes than they did at any other time of the year. However, the majority of my time in my newly defined occupation as Director of Education was taken up with meetings. All throughout July and August, I was often invited along with JPA to appointments at the French Consulate. The Foundation was specifically working with various cultural attachés there to coordinate our efforts with theirs in the areas of scholarship programs, student and teacher exchange opportunities, and cultural offerings for schools. One thing they did was invite in visiting performers for school assemblies: singers, troupes of actors, poets. JPA was most anxious to help when it entailed housing the various French entertainers and guests who were slated to appear in the Chicagoland schools and colleges. Sometimes it even happened that I went to these meetings on my own and represented *La Fondation.*.

All throughout the summer on Saturdays, I made good on my vow to continue an autodidactic approach to mastering the contents of the Impressionist collections at the Art Institute. Dom, Peter and I faithfully met up for our coffee dates and gallery explorations. They had also shown a lot of interest in my new place and had even offered to help me set things up. Once there, they noticed something I had not: there was a tiny space in the kitchen under a tall window at the far end of the room that they thought would hold a small, round wrought-iron bistro table and maybe two chairs, like people used on decks or little balconies in Chicago. And they had one. They also had a bean-bag chair they could let me use in the living room.

"It's kind of groovy, " said Dom, "and pretty comfortable."

"Yes, comfortable once you're in it, " Peter laughed. "Getting up from it is another story."

"You guys are the best, " I said, thanking them profusely.

And that is when the idea occurred to me how I could begin to repay them for all their generous help: invite them to Thanksgiving dinner with my boss. I had already gone out on a limb with that impromptu invitation to dine at my place I'd given JPA. Why not have a nice dinner and include all the people I owed!?

. "And do you know how I can repay your generosity?" I announced. They looked at each other and then back at me and shrugged.

"I want you to come for Thanksgiving dinner. Last year I sat in my place and ate a t.v. dinner!"

"Ewww, " said Peter, summing up the experience perfectly.

"I swore I would never do that again. Do you have plans yet? Can you come?"

"We'll be here, " said Dom.

"And I also want to invite my boss, is that okay?"

"Sure. I met him that night at the club, " said Dom.

"I'm guessing you don't intend to have Robineau come with him?" Peter teased me. He knew the whole story.

"Please. Let's not sully this conversation by bringing that turd's name into it."

"So you'll do a regular traditional thing then? Turkey, stuffing, the whole nine yards?" said Dom.

"Yep, that's a meal you cook the same whether it's for three or thirty."

"We'll bring something, too. What would you like that to be?"

"Well, it's still early to be thinking about that, but frankly, if you could bring pies, that would be so great. I can bake them, but if I don't have to...even better. We must have pumpkin. Can you bring that and maybe an apple or cherry?"

"You got it."

"I don't know what I'll serve this meal on, " I laughed, "but I have three months to figure it out, don't I ?"

"You know, " said Peter, "you can rent tables, even with linens and fancy china."

"Or, "said Dom, "you could buy paper plates with a cute Thanksgiving theme and even napkins to match!"

"Guys. I don't see me serving Jean-Paul d'Arivèque Thanksgiving dinner on paper plates, but thanks just the same for the idea." I laughed.

By September things in my apartment were still piece-meal and I had to really decide on a budget and also what I truly needed to make life there work. I wrote lists for each room. I needed the least for the bedroom, so that was a highlight, but by the time I had enumerated what was lacking in the kitchen just to cook the holiday dinner, expenditures were beginning to add up.

I discussed all this with Cass.

"I decided the right thing to do would be to invite Annie-Laure and Jean-Luc, too," I explained to her, "partly because they have been so wonderful to me, helping me with all sorts of things since I came to Chicago, but mostly because they are truly my best friends at work." I added, "It's also a great idea because Jean-Paul is totally comfortable being aided by either of them walking places...like up my front stairs."

"I think that will make for a lovely group for your dinner, kid. You are such a good cook! They're going to love it!"

"Well, maybe. The ugly Melmac plates won't do, though, and I don't even have silverware decent enough to set a table for four, let alone six. I also have no coffee table for the living room and if we're going to sit in there to eat, that won't work, especially for someone without the use of an arm."

"Look," she said, "I have the solution and you'd better take me up on this idea."

"What's that?" I asked, honestly not knowing what she'd say.

"Use some of that money of mine my father gave you, and buy what you need to get started out in your new life."

"Oh, no."

"Oh, hell yes. I know you won't go nuts, and I also realize, knowing you, that you'd insist on paying it back. My God, there must still be thousands in there."

"Yes, still more than three thousand. I wish I could just give it to you."

"Let's not stray into that territory again. You can't send it to me. Alan just barely bought the idea that you sent the twins all those birthday presents because you got a big raise."

"Well that was not a lie on your part, really, " I tried to assure her.

I had sent them quite a collection of size two clothes, plus more darling playthings. I tried to curb my penchant for buying toys since Cass had complained of becoming loaded down with material "things", and I knew I was part of the problem there, rather than the solution.

In the end, I decided I would take her up on her offer. I took a deep breath and borrowed two hundred dollars from the fund. With that and what I budgeted from my own stockpiled savings, I bought the requisite amount of dishes, silverware, water goblets, some little juice glasses, and pots and pans— only what I needed, not an entire array of kitchenware. I also bought six over-sized wine glasses, paying little attention to the type of wine for which they were intended. They would just have to do for any color. As the daughter of the proprietor of a bar, I was still embarrassed not to be able to offer anyone a proper cocktail, but that would have meant buying high ball glasses or cordials. I just couldn't do it.

I didn't find any gingham curtains for the kitchen like I had imagined I'd hang in there, but I found some cute print ones that looked almost like *toile de Jouy*, so that was even better. I put the white lace kind on all the other windows, including the little bathroom one that no one could see into anyway.

One of the things I loved and appreciated about Chicago was the conglomeration of diverse neighborhoods and funky streets that harbored treasure, whether that was boutiques, antique shops, little restaurants tucked into alleys, or famous jazz clubs.

Once I started walking home on different routes for a change, I found myself on a street with second-hand stores lining it, and all of a sudden I saw the *pièce de résistance* for my living room. I considered it a true miracle: a coffee table right in the window of a little antique-cum-junk shop in a neighborhood, not far from my own. The table was low and had curvy legs. It was stained dark oak, but had a grey-blue marble top that would go really well with my couch!

"It was fate!" I told Dom when I called him once again to elicit his and Peter's help to carry it the three blocks and ten steps into my place.

It turned out that I could return this favor by doing one for Dom.

He had a very good student who needed a part-time job and loved French. He asked me if the Foundation had any openings for non-skilled but enthusiastic labor, and luckily we did, in the form of my library assistant. I went to Marie-France de Piaget for the green light to have this high school student, Joelle Barton, come five days a week after school got out, which for her would have been at about 2:30.

"She could start at 3:00 and work until close, doing the mailings for films and boxes," I suggested. It was a perfect fit for all concerned.

By mid-September, Cass had big news, too. Alan had graduated in August with an MFA from the Iowa Writer's Workshop, a prestigious degree no matter what the circumstances. His CO work was also coming to an end, and he was heading off to the MLA convention in Boston the week before Thanksgiving to seek a position.

"The U of Iowa said they would keep him on as a part-time instructor in the rhetoric program, but that is low-paying, and he wants to advance in his career, " she explained.

"So you and the kids jump on the train and come to my house for Thanksgiving!" I fairly shouted. "Alan can change his ticket and meet you here in time for the holiday."

"I can't, Sari, " she'd responded, softly with a little sorrow in her voice. "They're too much to handle by myself on a train."

"Then fly."

"No."

"Come on, Cass! They're not infants anymore! They'd have fun!"

"Ha! You don't know toddlers, so I'd reserve judgment if I were you. They're a real handful now. Anyway, I don't really eat…you know… that meal…uh… anymore, and, so, I think we'll just stay here and muddle through."

"Cass, you are *bourrique-bourrique et demi*. I give up."

"I hope that translates into 'best mommy on the planet?'" she chortled.

"As a matter of fact it means stubborn as two mules and then some."

"But promise me you'll come here at Christmas?" she said changing the subject.

"I promise. And Cass, you'll be pleased to hear that I took you up on your offer and borrowed two-hundred dollars from your money."

"Great! I'm happy to help you out, kid."

November arrived that year as crisp and as beautiful as any autumn I'd ever seen. Emily Brontë's words echoed in my memory, "Every leaf speaks bliss to me." There was no turning back now. I'd made up my mind to have the Thanksgiving party, and at that point I went ahead and made arrangements to rent a small table and six chairs, as well as the linens. I'd indeed invite Annie-Laure and Jean-Luc along with Jean-Paul d'Arivèque, Dom and Peter to dinner. Marie-France was not included because I knew she had a standing invitation from friends in New York for that holiday and to take in the Macy's Thanksgiving Day Parade.

I approached Annie-Laure first, and she affirmed that they had made no plans and would be delighted to accept my offer. I then went to Jean-Paul's office one afternoon near closing hour, to seek him out and invite him.

"I am here to make good on my offer to have you to dinner, " I told him, cheerily, "and would like to invite you for Thanksgiving. I've already asked Annie-Laure, Jean-Luc and my French teacher friend from Lincoln Park High school and his — uh *(what did I call Peter? Not husband. Life Partner? Companion?)*-- boyfriend."

I assumed he was doing the math I intended: one straight couple, one gay couple and one mixed couple. What could be more tailor-made?

"I thank you for this very nice invitation, Sarah. I would be delighted to come, and I accept with pleasure."

"Have you ever gone to an American Thanksgiving dinner?"

"Yes," he answered, "during high school in New York, *Maman* and I were invited to many of my friends' homes. But it was Thanksgiving *à la française*, I am sure. What will yours be?"

"Mine will be very traditional with the addition of my Nana's –my grandmother's--recipe for rice pudding. I'm betting you've never had that. It's very different from the Swedish kind-- that's what your kitchen prepared for me last Spring."

"No, I cannot recall ever having any other kind."

"Well, my Nana's recipe is great. So, there will be turkey and all the trimmings. Dom and Peter are bringing pies for dessert. Must have pumpkin pie, you know. Wouldn't be Thanksgiving without that."

"And so what shall I bring to this extraordinary dinner?" he asked, grinning at me.

I wanted to say **nothing**, but then, I knew he'd bring something anyway, so I asked for what we really needed: a bottle of *Rosé d'Anjou*.

"*Parfait. Je l'amène avec grand plaisir.*"

And then, instead of bidding me good night, he asked me to take the seat in front of his desk because he wanted to speak to me about something. I fought off the familiar dread that always came with this action, because I knew in my heart that my job had never been more successful. Joelle was working out well; we were, as predicted, getting many more requests for our services than ever before, and she was keeping abreast of the mailings. The culture boxes were a big hit; our latest one was a great new *Le Petit Prince* puppet theater.

"You realize, I am sure, how pleased we all are with your initiatives for the Foundation's educational offerings."

He didn't give me a chance to respond, so I nodded, and he continued, "Someone requested the film of *Madame Bovary*, did they not?"

"Yes. We have both the 1932 Albert Ray version and the 1949 adaption of the book for film by Vincente Minnelli with Jennifer Jones, James Mason, Van Heflin, Louis Jourdan and Gene Lockhart. That one is in English, of course."

"Yes, I know them well. *Alors*, you included your discussion sheet, I believe, and a cultural article on Rouen and *La Normandie*?"

"That's right."

"Well, whoever you sent it to had contact with a text-book publisher, Dowling Press, and they called me from Des Moines, Iowa, asking to use the *Moment Culturel*, as you call them, in their forthcoming new French textbook. They are adapting an extract of the novel. "

"Wow, that's pretty cool."

"Cool," he chuckled, "yes. But do you give your permission?"

"Well, of course, but anything I write for the Foundation is technically yours, *Monsieur*. It would come under your purview and aegis, wouldn't it?"

"Perhaps, but I explained to them that you wrote them. We would like you to be given the credit for authorship. And to that end, they are also requesting to include similar articles in every chapter of their new series of French textbooks. They would like you to write one for each chapter of three levels of books with twenty-five chapters."

"Wow. Seventy-five '*Moments Culturels*?"

"Do you think you could do it? "

"Oh, gads, there are certainly more than enough interesting things to write about France and the French-speaking world, so that's not a problem. But do they want them in French? English? Easy? Hard? Would the topics need to match the chapter contents? I'd have to consult with them about that."

"Precisely. We would be flying you to Des Moines to do just that."

"Okay. When would this be?"

"They asked for the second week in December."

"I can do that."

"There is one other thing. They have offered to pay in the range of six thousand dollars for this. I should like our legal department to be apprised of any contracts you would undertake. For your protection."

What did he say? Six THOUSAND dollars? And he didn't bat an eye?

"Wait a minute. That would be a donation to the Foundation, wouldn't it?"

"No, Sarah, that money would be your consulting fee."

"But...I'm ... in your employ."

"Yes," he laughed, "you are in my employ! And you also do free-lance consulting. There is nothing untoward about that. Your income tax burden may be affected, of course, but our accounting department will help you file the returns."

"My goodness! That is too generous!"

Too generous my ass! It was like winning Punto Banco at Monte-Carlo!

"You are worth it. Why do you not see that immediately?"

I went back to my office and called Cass, fairly shaking.

"Sari! That's fantastic!" she sang.

"And they want to fly me to Des Moines, but I just had a brainstorm! I'm going to ask him if I can drive the Cit and then I can stop and see you coming and going!"

"Oh, yes! Perfect!! Will they let you?"

"I think so. I have my Illinois drivers' license, now. If they say no, I'll rent a car. God knows I'll be able to afford it! I can pay your father's fund back right away, too. Hot damn!"

"You are really taking off, friend of friends! I always knew you would be a star around there."

"No you didn't. Anyway, you're next in line for karma to smile upon. Your State Fair win has put you on the radar!" Cass' Switzerland scene had indeed taken first prize in the Iowa State Fair art contest. The write-up in the Iowa City Press Citizen had turned out to be prophetic.

"Well, I'll show you the blue ribbon when you come. It's just like something out of the movies! Ha!"

"And I can bring the kids' Christmas stuff with me in the car, so I don't have to schlep it all on the train! This is really going to be outtasight!"

I hung up the phone still in a state of euphoria and so pleased with my decision to drive to Des Moines in December, that I almost forgot all the work I had to do to prepare for Thanksgiving. Coming back down to earth, I sat at my desk and made lists of chores, food and readiness. And on the way home, I did something I had never done in my entire life: I stopped at Clovington's Gourmet Market on State Street and placed an advanced order for a turkey at their meat counter. Then I shopped for all the other supplies I'd need to make all the other dishes: the dressing, the casseroles — sweet potato and green bean; the rice pudding, salads, condiments, and rolls. And I arranged for all that to be delivered--what a concept!-- to my house on the Wednesday before the holiday. The office was slated to close at noon that day, but I would be taking the entire day off.

Chapter Ninety-Two

"Now Be Thankful"...Fairport Convention (Thompson & Swarbrick)

I had an on-going battle with self-doubt over what I had done by inviting these guests, including my boss, to my humble little abode for a big holiday meal.

"Have I gone temporarily insane?" I asked Cass on the phone from my kitchen as I awaited the deliveries.

"You've got this in the bag, " she said.

"What makes you think so?"

"You said yourself, the Thanksgiving dinner is always the same and always good. You've made it dozens of times...well, maybe not dozens. You made it at my house, and you did great."

"Yeah, so like once! But in all honesty, I did help my mother and grandmother with it for my whole life."

"You can do this, " Cass said, and then she added, "I'm glad you called, though, Sari." She sounded worried.

"Why? What's wrong?"

"Well, Sunday when I took Alan to the airport, I saw one of his fellow Workshop grad students there, too--- a girl. I've met her once or twice at department gatherings... her name is Donna something."

"And? So what? Obviously she's in the market for a job, too, like he is. I'm sure a whole bunch of Iowa U people were on that plane to the MLA, don't you think?"

"I guess so, but get this: she waved to him all smiley, but then when she saw me with the kids, she averted eye contact with me and hurried away."

"No marriage survives the Workshop" came into my head.

"Oh, Cass, I'm sure it's nothing. Alan wouldn't be that stupid."

"I hope you're right. We haven't exactly been getting along too well."

I had a sinking feeling that was the case, but didn't elaborate with her on that phone call-- I was too caught up in my own angst at that point-- but I reminded her that my trip to Des Moines would soon be upon us.

"I'll see you in a matter of ...well...just a couple of weeks really!" That buoyed us both up.

The Wednesday before Thanksgiving, I had been right to ask for the entire day off, because the deliveries started coming swiftly around mid-morning. The market drop-off came first, and the new concierge let the man in the front door and brought him-- with a large box and two bags-- to my apartment.

Next the rental company came with the table and chairs, and the guys handed me a plastic bag of linens. I set it all up in the middle of my living room, which was the only free space.

When I laid the table with my new dishes, it still looked drab and bleak. So I rushed out to the little market in my neighborhood and got a bouquet of autumnal flowers. I took it apart, cut the stems down to about four inches, and placed them in small groupings in my new juice glasses. Then I set those in a line down the middle of the table. It did the trick. I had a focal point of Fall colors on the white table scape.

I had also picked up some Thanksgiving-themed paper products—a tablecloth and matching napkins with hay bales, cornucopia, and other harvest images on them. I took the paper tablecloth and put it on my old former kitchen table which was now occupying the corner of the room. That would be the dessert table. I set the matching napkins on it and some small plates. Peter's pies would be displayed there. After dinner we could all just lift the rented table off to one side, and have dessert on the sofa and the few chairs I had. It wasn't perfect, but it would do.

I was happy as a clam in my new kitchen, tiny as it was, so I got busy all the rest of that day, and made the side dishes which would need to be baked, freeing up the oven for the turkey on Thursday. In reality that was indeed a snap. I had it done in four hours: rice pudding, dressing, sweet potato bake, and green bean casserole. In the evening I made cranberry orange relish, another one of Nana's recipes, and put it safely in the fridge. I then cleaned house until it was spotless, which, while I was being a little paranoid about it, was important to me, knowing I'd have these guests who were my colleagues. However, due to the size of the place, cleaning it, too, was fairly quick work. I fell into bed a little after midnight.

Finally, Thanksgiving Day was upon me, and already I was thankful for no ice on the steps or snow on the streets. I prepared the turkey and hoisted it into its rack in the aluminum roasting pan I'd bought. I made another recipe of dressing, and stuffed the turkey with that. I made the requisite foil tent, and put the bird in the oven. A few hours later, the house was awash in the scent of Thanksgiving. Towards the end of the roasting period, I set the other side dishes all around the turkey, cramming them all in the low oven to warm back up.

Dom and Peter were the first to arrive, by plan, and the pies looked glorious on display. Dom had also thought of something else that came to my rescue for that meal.

"I brought our Chemex, " he said holding up an hourglass-shaped vessel with a conical funnel-like neck and a piece of wood acting as a "collar" on it, tied with a buckskin string.

"What's a Chemex?" I asked.

"Coffee! Can't have pie without coffee, now can you?" he laughed.

"Whoa, I hadn't even thought of that." *True, enough. I had never owned a coffee pot and hadn't even stocked in any instant coffee!!* "What an idiot I am! I'm about to serve dinner to French people! *Quelle catastrophe* that would have been! You really saved the day, Dom!"

"Well, you lucked out double then, because I also brought the filters and coffee."

"You are outstanding! I owe you--big time."

"It smells delish in here, " said Peter.

"I can only hope, " I said. "I mean, I shouldn't be nervous, right? I can do this. Everything is ready, but timing it all to come out hot at the same time is another thing."

"We'll help you, " Peter assured me.

So I ran into my bedroom and changed into wheat jeans and the fisherman knit sweater, brown penny loafers and thick beige woolen socks. I put on the pearls and pearl earrings for the hell of it, and pulled my hair into a low ponytail tied with a cream-colored velvet ribbon. When I reemerged, it was time to go to the front door and keep an eye out for the rest of my guests, whose car was just pulling up.

Jean-Luc got out first, as usual, but instead of helping Jean-Paul d'Arivèque from the car, he went around to the back and took out a crate of some kind---I couldn't exactly tell what---with straw seeming to burst out of it. Annie-Laure came around to the curb side and aided Jean-Paul. Then to come up the stairs, she held his cane and took hold of his left arm, while Jean-Luc positioned himself on the right side of him. As Luc carried the crate up, Jean-Paul grasped Luc's arm, and they came up together one step at a time. I was at the top of the stairs to open the door and guide them down the hall to my place.

"*Bienvenue!*" I greeted them. "Come right this way."

We entered my apartment, cooking aromas enveloping us, and I made introductions. It was all "*Enchanté*" with Dom, but poor Peter was the only one there who didn't speak French, so I paid special attention to him, explaining as I presented them, that Dom Lambert was a French teacher, and Peter Weir worked for a theatrical agency, that he was also a production designer for clubs and theater.

"He was in charge of the sound and lighting over at the Ferronnerie for the Edith Piaf impersonator show! " I elaborated, "And he baked our fabulous Thanksgiving pies! A man of many talents."

Annie-Laure reached into the top of that crate of Luc's and presented me with a beautiful candle nestled in some autumnal greenery, and when she saw I had flowers on the dining table, she quickly suggested it would look great on the dessert table.

"It's just gorgeous, " I said, thanking her warmly with a huge American-style hug. "What a great decoration!"

I gathered up all the coats, scarves, and hats and took them in to lay on my day bed. When I reappeared, Jean-Luc was unpacking the rest of the crate, and before I could inquire about it, Jean-Paul announced that "*on va prendre un peu la crémaillère*"-- that he had taken the liberty to bring me a "small housewarming gift." He began to lift out something I found only too familiar: a Baccarat flute like we'd been served in so often at his home and in the office. There were ten of them (!), so Annie-Laure began to take them away over to the dessert table, too.

"Oh, my goodness, " I said as soon as I saw what was happening. "You… shouldn't have… done that."

"I did not forget the *rosé*, " he said smiling at me, "but I thought perhaps afterwards we would like to toast with a bit of champagne, so here are two bottles of each." Jean-Luc took them out, brushing off the straw as he did. Two bottles were Remy Pannier *Rosé d'Anjou* and two were Krug *Grande Cuvée*. They were both cool to the touch.

I just stood there for a moment, acutely aware, yet again, of what a litany, a goddam broken record, I was going to sound like when I launched into how generous and kind this gesture of his was-- just like all the rest.

"*Je vous en remercie, Monsieur, vraiement…c'est trop généreux… I..*I don't know what to say."

I was just babbling, so I took both the wine and the champagne into the kitchen to keep in the fridge, and busied myself looking for the corkscrew that, thank the Lord, I'd remembered to buy when I first moved to Chicago! When I looked up from fishing around in the drawer, Jean-Paul was standing there.

"Sarah, you are upset?"

"Upset? Oh, no! Of course not! It's just, well…**Baccarat**. Really, that's just too much, *Monsieur*."

I was trying –and not succeeding—to convey my predicament of not knowing how I'd ever repay anything he'd done for me. Here we were at the dinner I'd intended would be a start, and there I was, faced with more offerings for which I, again, couldn't even hope to reciprocate. He waved that off.

"Can you please call me Polo?"

"I…I…can't. But I will use Jean-Paul. How's that? At least here."

He smiled at me and said, "Your kitchen is filled with wonderful scents."

"Thanks! Hope hope. Keep your fingers crossed."

Having planned a very traditional family style American dinner, and not a French one, something else I didn't have were any real hors d'oeuvres. Dom appeared in my kitchen and wondered if he might open some wine to get started. That caused my first panic of the evening. What was I going to serve with this make-shift *apéro*? I had celery on hand from making stuffing, and I had carrots in the fridge. But what else could I come up with? I was frantic as I perused my kitchen. There were some club crackers, a jar of olives, and three or four left-over radishes from a salad I'd made that week. I cut everything up as quickly as I could and decided it would do. Then I threw together a dip made from sour cream and dry onion soup mix, used a small cereal bowl in the middle of one of my plates, arranged the veggies all around, and took it in as though I'd always meant to serve that.

I sat for a minute, savoring a few sips of the *rosé*, which was heavenly, and then left again to work on the final preparations for the meal. Dom and Peter excused themselves to come help me get everything on the table, and then I announced dinner was imminent.

Annie-Laure had volunteered her fiancé to carve the bird with my makeshift carving set that was just a kitchen knife and the three-tined long-handle fork. He did a great job, and I dished out the individual plates in the kitchen, not only to save Jean-Paul the embarrassment of not easily being able to pass serving dishes and take his own helpings, but also because the rented table wasn't really big enough to place everything on it anyway. I didn't ask people what parts of turkey they preferred, but just gave everyone some of dark and more of white. I cut Jean-Paul's and covered the meat in gravy so no one would even notice the small pieces. I said nothing when I placed it before him, but I did see him glance at me as he realized what I'd done; he wasn't embarrassed, as I didn't want or expect him to be. He understood that I'd done it expressly to help him out.

Everyone had turkey, stuffing, all the sides, and Nana's rice pudding. I circled the table to provide each person with gravy from a bowl with a large serving spoon because I didn't have a gravy boat or a ladle, and I sent around dinner rolls in a "nest" I'd improvised using two of the paper Thanksgiving napkins in a basket. I put myself at the seat closest to the kitchen door, in case I had to jump up and get anyone anything, and when I finally sat down, my food wasn't any too hot; but I hoped theirs was.

Everyone was very pleased with dinner and addressed their "*compliments au chef*," with Annie-Laure singing the praises of the rice pudding, which she—and everyone else-- affirmed they'd never tasted before. Jean-Paul gazed at me approvingly, (perhaps in some shock that I'd pulled it all off?), calling the dinner *"un vrai triomphe!"*

Dom got the table conversation started by expressing his gratitude for the films and lesson plans coming from the Foundation, to which he had availed himself "often" and which, he said, really delighted his students. I reminded the others that among those students was Joelle, my new assistant. Jean-Paul and Annie-Laure both seemed pleased to hear that, and each looked over at me.

I, in the meantime, decided to broach the subject of driving, rather than flying to Des Moines, since I had the boss, as well as the car expert, captive at my table.

"But Sarah, you do not have to feel that you cannot fly. We are sending you there on Foundation business, after all."

"I just still hate to think of a plane using all that fuel to ferry only one person, " I said, as a final argument, "and the Citroën is such a wonderful car to ride in as well as drive." I paused for a moment to gauge Jean-Paul's reaction, and then added, "And if I drive, I can stop in Iowa City and visit my college roommate, Cass. I…really…miss her…and her kids!"

There! I felt confident that I'd landed the *coup de grâce* argument. That should do it! I looked at Jean-Paul with anticipation of an agreement, but he, instead, turned to Jean-Luc.

"Luc, what are your thoughts of her driving the car of *Maman*?"

"Désolé," he started, disappointing me right off the bat, *"mais il va y avoir trop de risque."*

"Wait," I started, trying to think of more arguments… but he cut me off.

"Sari," he said, addressing me as Annie-Laure did, "it is almost winter. What if something happened to you out on the road, eh? For one thing, *La Citroën* cannot be towed as other cars. She must be put on a flatbed. Besides, no garage would have parts for her on your route into Iowa. I think it would be better for you to drive the small limo, the Mercedes town car."

What small Mercedes limo? I'd never noticed any such car in their parking garage.

"Yes," Jean-Paul agreed, " that is the perfect solution."

"Hold on a minute, " I laughed. "The Citroën was just an idea. I didn't mean for you to hand me over the keys to the castle. I can easily rent a car if it comes to that."

"Mais non, " said Jean-Paul forcefully. "You must take the Mercedes. *C'est fait."*

Wow. How did that just happen?

Annie-Laure changed the subject for me by bringing up the topic of my new place and how much better it was than the studio. All who had seen my previous living arrangements agreed with her. I was happy they liked it, and happy I had decided to have this dinner.

"This apartment is heaven for just me, " I laughed, "but as you can see, it's rather cramped for six. The décor leaves a lot to be desired, too…I know!"

I invited everyone to take a seat on the sofa or chairs while Dom and I retreated to the kitchen to make coffee. Per his directions, I put the kettle on to boil some water for him, and he took out the filters and coffee he'd brought.

"Watch and learn, " he laughed. "I'm going to take that boiling water and pour some over the grounds to 'bloom' them — make them moist. Then I'll pour enough for, let's say, eight cups and we'll wait for it to percolate down through the coffee and filter and into the bottom of the pot. *Voilà.* The best coffee. Well, maybe not the best, " he corrected himself, "to French people."

"It'll be better than anything I could have come up with!"

And it was great. I had brought out milk and sugar, but there was also whipped cream for the pumpkin pie, and I dumped a dollop of that on my own coffee. *"Met slagroom"* I said, remembering Holland, fondly.

I handed around cups of coffee and servings of pie. Jean-Luc took out a pack of Gauloises and began to pass it to the others. Annie-Laure accepted two, lit one and handed it to Jean-Paul! I must have seemed shocked to see this, so she asked me, "Oh! *Tu ne fumes pas?"* I shook my head.

I had smoked in my college days, but not much; and yes, I had tried Gauloises once or twice in France, since all my friends, including Nonnie, smoked them. Just smelling the smoke wafting through my apartment from those cigarettes transported me right back to Boulevard Raspail.

531

I returned to the kitchen to try and figure out what in the world I could use for an ashtray, of which I had none, and no earthly reason before now to purchase one. My smallest Pyrex mixing bowl would have to do.

Everyone raved about Peter's pies, and we all had some of both with Dom's coffee. We sat around pretty stuffed, as people are wont to be after Thanksgiving dinner, but it was still early, so I brought out a bottle of the Champagne and the flutes, and took down some records from my bookshelf.

"Who loves Fairport Convention?" I asked eagerly, and then anticipating their silence, answered my own question, "Just me, I guess? Allow me to indoctrinate you!"

Annie-Laure and Jean-Luc didn't know the band at all; Peter had heard of them, but didn't own any of their albums. Jean-Paul d'Arivèque, it went without saying, was completely in the dark. That left it for me to enlighten this group. I put on *Fairport Convention*, (as *What We Did on Our Holidays* was called in the States), and sat back, basking in the opportunity to turn people on to the music I loved.

"'Meet on the Ledge' has to be one of the greatest songs ever written," I murmured.

Jean-Paul looked at me with an expression of bemused wonderment, as though he were meeting me again for the first time. In all our discussions during my musical "education" we'd rarely spoken of my music. He knew I loved the Beatles, but when I had mentioned other fave raves like Simon and Garfunkel, Buffalo Springfield, Joni Mitchell or Laura Nyro, he hadn't reacted with any real sense of recognition. So I'd just let it pass, and hadn't even bothered to go into the myriad of other music I lived inside of at all times.

We listened to *Liege and Lief,* after that, and after having offered more pie and refilled their coffee cups, I brought out *New York Tendaberry*, regaling them with the story about how when that record had come out, one of Laura Nyro's friends had sent her a telegram congratulating her on her birth. And as I told that story, I wished like anything, that Cass were there to back me up. I was not objective when it came to expounding on Laura Nyro recordings.

"Isn't this just fab?" I gushed, when "Time and Love" finished playing. "She's such a brilliant writer—her lyrics are so evocative, aren't they? And the music! Her soprano voice is more mezzo than, say, Joni Mitchell, but still hauntingly soulful!"

Jean-Luc spoke up in agreement with me and also commented on how many jazz elements he heard in her music.

"Do you like jazz?" he asked me.

"It took me a while to appreciate it, " I admitted, "but I do like it now. Chicago is a great place to live if you like jazz, isn't it? Like Paris."

"*Exacte*," Luc affirmed.

Luc wondered if they could borrow some of my albums and Annie -Laure nodded enthusiastically. I was only too happy to create more Laura acolytes and I heartily obliged. Dom also professed his love for Nyro, and Peter had the best news of the night for me: he thought she was slated to appear in Chicago in the coming year.

"Be still my heart!" I cried. "If you work on that show, may I please please tag along to be your--- I don't know---roadie?!"

"Deal, " he answered, to my thrill. "I'll find plenty for you to do."

Finally, when the evening was over, it was *la bise* all around. I invited people to find their coats in my bedroom, and I accompanied Jean-Paul to get his and help him on with it. Jean-Luc went down to start the car and warm it up, before he returned to help his boss tackle the stairs.

Jean-Paul took my arm and we walked back out to the front room, as he expounded on what "a wonderful time he'd had celebrating Thanksgiving *à l'Américaine."*

"I'm glad," I said, as we gave each other *la bise* for the second time, and I thanked him yet again for his over-the-top gifts.

"I want you to stay home from the office tomorrow, " he said to me. "I see now now why many American businesses are closed on the Friday after Thanksgiving. I shall have to take that under advisement."

"Oh, that's okay... I can come in, " I said.

"*Non.* I am neither *naïf* nor untutored, " he said firmly, looking me squarely in the eyes. "I know you worked very hard on this dinner. You need a day to recuperate."

There was that word again.

"But, *Monsi…er…*Jean-Paul, I already took Wednesday off from work to do all the preparations."

"Then you shall also have Friday… to recover." He put his finger on my lips. "*D'accord?*"

I nodded.

Dom and Peter took back their coffee pot and the left-over pie. "That is just too much temptation to leave with me," I had assured them. They again told me dinner had been great and thanked me for inviting them. I was just as grateful to those two as far as helping me move and all, as I was to Jean-Paul, and for that matter, Annie-Laure and Jean-Luc. All of them had given me loads of support and done favors for me above and beyond. One dinner was a mere drop in the bucket of pay back.

And now I had three days to get my life back together. The rental place was scheduled to pick up on Saturday morning, and I had to admit that extra day at home would give me added precious moments to wash, dry and put everything else away; straighten the place up again, and just decompress. After all, starting Monday I'd be needing to gear up for writing seventy-five articles on French culture as well as Christmas shopping for a pair of two-year-olds.

Chapter Ninety-Three

"America"...Simon & Garfunkel

My office phone was ringing almost as I walked in on the Monday after Thanksgiving. I knew it had to be Cass, so I was worried, and I was right to be.

"Alan got offered a job at the MLA!"

"So that's good news, isn't it?"

"In El Paso, Texas at UTEP."

"Holy hell, you're joking."

"And not only that...we have to move right away. Right now!"

"What?! What's right now?"

"When do you come?" she asked fervently.

"In about ten days. My meeting in Des Moines is on the fourteenth. I thought I'd come the weekend before."

"Oh, phew, then that's okay. We'll still be here until the fifteenth. I was scared we'd be gone already!"

"How did this happen so fast?"

"That's just the way it works...they need someone to start second semester, as it turns out. Alan got the position. It leads to tenure track and everything. And the salary will be good--really good for once!"

"But, Cass...it's Texas. I mean, that's the shits."

"Tell me something I don't know."

We hung up with the promise that I'd call her back as soon as I could process this new and, yes, revolting development. The trouble was, I had many balls in the air at the same time just then at work. Besides preparing for the Des Moines meeting with the textbook people, I had to formalize the dates for the teachers' institute, start lining up a venue and invite speakers. I had to have all the information finalized before I could turn it over to marketing to do promotions. Jean-Paul d'Arivèque had already called me in for a consultation on the institute idea, and as I approached his office, Annie-Laure gave me a funny look, like she already knew something I didn't but was about to find out. She waved me to go right in.

"I am afraid you are under deadline pressures, " he began, "and I want to alleviate some of it."

"Well, not really. I mean, I won't know the *Moments Culturels* deadlines until I meet with them on the fourteenth."

"No, I mean with the teachers' institute. I should like to put that off until September."

"Really? That long? Won't that interfere with the start of the new school year?"

"What then, do you suggest? August?"

"Maybe. *En revanche*, if you want to know the truth, I guess I did realize January was too soon, but I was thinking Spring."

"Well, there is something of which you are not yet aware that will be happening in the early summer, that could interfere with Spring plans. The transition of my office will take place in May with Marie-France retiring to my family home in France, and Annie-Laure stepping into her place here."

"Oh, yes, we heard that news at the reception. That will be a big change all right!"

"*Oui, évidemment.* What was not announced then is that their wedding will take place in June. You know it will be at my home, yes?"

I nodded. "That was quite the present to them! Getting married in your ancestral home. "

"I intend to offer to fly the entire office there for it. We shall close down here for a week, but Annie-Laure and Jean-Luc will be gone one month---two weeks prior to the wedding and two weeks after for the *voyage de noces, la lune de miel.*"

"The entire office, eh? I mean, wowie zowie! Who would imagine that!"

"Yes, and you shall attend?" He didn't give me a chance to answer. "Everyone will be invited. This way, in France, Annie-Laure and Luc can marry in the presence of all their French family members. It will be very nice. There is a chapel on the grounds, and the house is very large. Marie-France will go months ahead of time to open it up, staff it and make the arrangements...with Annie-Laure and her family. After that, Marie-France will stay on, as I announced at the *vin d'honneur*. She will soon be seventy years old! She deserves to live out the rest of her life in peace."

I may have been naïve on some things, but I wasn't a halfwit. Marie-France was obviously his mother figure and, for all I knew, Annie-Laure was like a sister he never had. But still...he had to be the most generous man on the planet.

"So I guess the Autumn is the best time to plan this institute after all," I realized, sort of thinking out loud. "I tell you what, why don't we really put it off until October in that case? Many schools have Fall Break—shorter than colleges do, but still a few days off. Let me do some research on the Chicago schools calendar and we could plan it for then. That will give us plenty of time to really organize it and make it a great début."

"*Parfait!*" He seemed gratified that I was onboard with his initial suggestion. "To that end, I have arranged a meeting with the head of the *Alliance Française* school here in town---to just talk to them about their space. I would very much like you to come with me."

"Yes, sure. Do you have it calendared already?"

"I do. It is Friday of this week, December third. Could you be prepared to explain the idea to them— what we might need in the way of space?"

"Of course. But they understand that this event might not really work for their teachers, right? They just teach language, and this is really meant for the classroom teachers who do culture lessons or even teamwork, you know... with their colleagues in other departments, like history."

"Yes, I understand, and I shall make it clear to them." He looked at me with an amused expression.

"No, no... I didn't mean to infer that you didn't get...er...understand it!"

"*Ne t'en fais pas,* Sarah. I know what you meant." And then, redirecting the conversation, he added, " Also, you did not forget we have a concert on the eleventh of December, did you?"

"Oh, gosh...I ...no, I didn't forget. It's just that..."

"Yes?"

"Well, I've got a bit of a complication now that weekend. I was going to ask you if I could take the day off before the Des Moines appointment and go earlier. I wanted to stop and see Cass and the kids on my way. Now it turns out they're moving away—leaving town that exact week!"

"Moving?" he said with genuine surprise.

"Yes, and far. So it will be the last time I see them for...who knows how long. I was hoping to go for the entire weekend. I didn't think about the concert. I'm sorry."

I could tell that he was very concerned both about me losing proximity with my friend and about our planned concert attendance.

"Naturally you may have the Monday off prior to your meeting in Des Moines. But it would be a shame if you had to miss the concert. It is Tchaikovsky's *Fourth Symphony* that night. A glorious work. Our maestro will be quite disappointed if you are not there."

I realized I was being fussy about this when here he had the plans and the tickets and everything. I was only thinking of myself...and not getting to spend as much time with Cass.

"No, it's fine. I'll leave for Iowa City on the Sunday morning. That will work. I'll have the better part of three days with her before she goes."

He seemed relieved, but I felt like I owed him a further explanation.

"Her husband got a job teaching in...in Texas." But as I said those words I started to choke up. Tears welled up and slid down my cheek. I tried to brush them off my face. I even stunned myself with this emotional display in front of JPA.

"Oh, *là làaaa,* " he said, sounding helpless. "What can I do? You are so upset!"

"No, I'm fine. Sorry." I gestured my embarrassment, shaking my hand in front of my face; but I continued to sob anyway.

"*La pauvre,* " he whispered, offering me a handkerchief.

"I'm...I'm so sorry, " I said trying to catch my breath and find a way to take my leave. "Can we talk about the concert details later? I promise I'll be prepared for the *Alliance* meeting." And I turned and left before he could do anything about it.

I ran from his office in front of a horrified Annie-Laure who, I'm sure, went directly to him to see what was the matter with me. I felt like an idiot back at my desk crying, and realized that Cass' moving was affecting me in ways I hadn't even considered.

Thankfully, no one came down to my office, and I regained composure and got back to work. I prepared a few writing samples to take to Des Moines, and I got together a proposal for rooms we'd need to run the institute in the *Alliance* building.

The main thing I had to do before I left, however, was to shop for presents for the kids, which left me with a real dilemma. I surmised-- and rightly so-- that they would now be cramped for space on the trip. I wondered how they'd manage such a move-- if they'd tow a U-Haul behind the Rambler? Could that old car even make such long voyage, let alone tow anything? If they didn't pull a carrier, though, how would they ever take furniture? I doubted they'd hire a moving van. I made a mental note to ask Cass first thing about this, but even before I did that, I decided that too many gifts would not be welcomed this time.

"It's so sad!" I told Cass on the phone. "I have a huge car and could bring tons of stuff for the kiddos."

"Well," she said timidly, " I better tell you---we had to sell your car. Alan bought a panel truck."

"Sell my car? Was it worth anything?"

"Ha! Almost nothing, as it turned out. But every little bit helped. We have a big enough vehicle now to move quite a load, but not much furniture. We'll take our bed, of course. I do love that bed."

Cass had painted an old iron bed and it was very splendid when she got done.

"What about the cribs? Will you take them?"

"No. Paul and Laura are about ready to be in kid-size real beds anyway. We'll find some once we're there. We are putting down a little crib mattress in the van for the trip out, though. They'll be able to play and sleep on it. We'll use boxes as a boundary and pack the rest of our worldly possessions behind that. There aren't any windows back there at all!"

"Won't that be dark for the kids?"

"Sort of. They'll get some light from the front. "

"Well, " I said, "a long car trip like that will be quite the adventure for the kiddies. Devising a play area for them is pure genius."

"Alan is being a real bear about what we can and cannot take. He's insisting we get rid of everything we possibly can."

"Well, don't go too spartan on me there! You have to take your books, art supplies, and records, for God's sake, don't you? How could you live without Joni, Crosby, Stills and Nash, Laura and Dylan?"

"I know! And Richie Havens and Jimi and Janis? Yeah, we're taking all that. But the worst part is we can't take any of our animals with us...not the cats, our ducks or Gillie, the baby goat. I'm literally sick about it."

"Gosh, of course you couldn't travel with those animals, but you can't just leave them there, can you? Your landlord won't take care of them."

"Oh, hell no. Alan's already talked to some farmers on the other side of the Iowa City airport who said they would take them from us...for free, of course."

Hearing all this, I knew better now than to load up the Mercedes with a lot of fancy clothes for the children. Cass and Alan had "tolerated" what I had bought them every other time, but I knew what with their "back to the land" and simple living attitudes, they were not anxious to accumulate more vestiges of the middle class. So I did my bit and refrained from picking out dresses for Laura or any little twin outfits. I bought them OshKosh B'Gosh unisex bib overalls and cute shirts and sweaters to wear underneath; plus light winter jackets, thinking Texas climate in general would be warmer than Iowa, at any rate.

It wouldn't be Christmas, however, without at least some toys to open that morning. I really scoped out the toy department at Marshall Field's this time searching for great things that would be small enough to make the long haul. The first thing I bought was something they could share: a Fischer-Price

536

farm whose barn doors closed with magnets and had little animals that were just the right size for toddler hands, not so small that they could be accidentally swallowed. I also bought them some wooden puzzles whose pieces could be picked up with little pegs and replaced in the correct spaces.

For Paul, I found a sweet toddler-oriented train set that folded up into the "train depot" itself, and when opened, the tracks fit around the station. For Laura I bought a baby doll, whose plaid suitcase box opened up and made into a bed. It came with a blanket, a doll bottle, a little dish and a bib for the doll, along with an extra dress. The doll itself was soft plastic with hair and features painted on, so nothing like eyes could come off and be choked on by a two-year-old.

I wrapped the toys in holiday paper but left the clothes in their own sacks and hoped Cass would be able to fit them in whatever luggage she was packing. I also intended to give her a wad of her father's cash, but had to decide on what lies I would tell Alan to account for it.

"I'm going to tell him a partially true story, " I announced to Cass on the phone a few days later. "I got a promotion with a doubled salary, which is true. I got a book deal for an insane amount of money, which is also true. And so I'll say I'm giving you guys part of it, which, of course isn't true. How's that?" I was impressed with my own ingenuity.

"You can't do that, " she said. "For one thing, he won't believe you."

"Watch me, " I said.

"He won't accept it."

"I'm not giving it to him. I'm giving it to you, and telling him, not asking. So there. You won't have to hide it, and he won't be able to take it from you, and most important, he won't be able to refuse me the privilege of doing with it what I damn well please."

"He'll be mad at me."

"Cass, for Christ's sake. I'll phrase it so as to make it clear it is for the KIDS. Okay? Can he deny THEM?"

"I guess not."

In the meantime, the meeting with the *Alliance Française de Chicago* had gone well, and they were on board for letting us use their space for a weekend in October of 1972. We presented the idea as a public-school teachers' opportunity so as not to mislead them into thinking we were in any way slighting their teachers. What they were interested in, they said, was a statistical report afterwards on the merits of the institute. They hoped to capitalize on the free publicity for their own organization. Jean-Paul agreed that we would come up with the instrument of evaluation that Dom had also suggested. I had months to think about getting this done.

Jean-Paul and I did not discuss my melt-down in his office when I saw him the next week for the concert date, but he was curious as to why El Paso, Texas was the choice of new residence.

"I guess college teaching jobs are few and far between, " I reckoned. "The Iowa Writer's Workshop is about as prestigious as it comes, though. Jobs must be tight."

"That would seem to explain it, " he agreed. "Still, I am sad for you to now have your friend so far away. Will they live on the campus?"

"I have no idea, "I said, realizing that, indeed, I knew nothing about the lay of the land for them.

The Tchaikovsky *Fourth Symphony* was truly unforgettable under the baton of Georg Solti. Everyone out at the lobby bar for intermission was animated and in perfect accord saying things like "the trumpet fanfare and strings playing the melody were each utterly superb," and "oboe solo in the opening of the second movement was heaven itself."

"It is the oboe which gives the piece such a rarified, soulful sound," Jean-Paul commented to me. I took his word for that, impressed as I always was, at his knowledge and understanding of such things. He then told me something that, while just a random fact, he thought would elicit a deep feeling in me. He told me that the dedication by Tchaikovsky on this symphony had been "To My Best Friend."

"So, " he said to me with a flourish, " you are hearing music dedicated to his best friend, and you leave tomorrow to see yours. I think that is quite emotional, is it not?"

"Oh, it is. You're right."

Our concert-going routine was changed around that night. Instead of taking me home, Jean-Luc drove to the mansion, into the underground garage and dropped us at the lower level door. Then he parked the limo and went to bring the Mercedes over to us. Before I got in to drive it off, Jean-Luc handed me a Shell gas card to use, something I never expected. I shook my head and gestured to him that I was rejecting the offer.

"Yes, yes, take it. You will be on Foundation business. We want to pay for the fuel, " Jean-Paul explained.

"Well, I guess, all right then. " I gave in, and accepted the card from Luc, who told me to have a safe trip and a good meeting in Des Moines, and then went inside, leaving Jean-Paul and me standing in the garage alone.

"Thank you so much for this—for the gas card, but also... again... for letting me drive your wonderful car. I promise to be a very safe driver."

"But if you should get in any trouble, please do telephone me, no matter the time of day or night. You say you are leaving very early in the morning, no?"

"That's right." And then, overcome by a feeling of real gratitude, I leaned up toward him to kiss his cheek. But it wasn't *la bise*. I really kissed him, and only on one cheek, *à l'américaine*. I was pretty sure it surprised him and I didn't care.

I turned to get into the car but he took my arm. He lifted my hand to his lips and kissed it, holding on to it, and said to me, "I wish I were accompanying you on this both sad and happy trip."

"Well, you... you could certainly come along if you want," I found myself saying.

"No, that would not be possible for me."

Yeah, okay, well, that was an understatement.

"Anyway, I sleep on their couch. Ha! And that's if they still have one, " I laughed. "We could get you a hotel room, though. One time I had a summer job as a desk clerk in the Iowa Memorial Union. It's a hotel."

"You are very kind to invite me. *Malheureusement*, I am afraid I have a very full agenda for this week."

"Yes, I understand."

"*Alors*, will you just please promise me you will not drive if your eyes are filled with tears? You must be able to see the road, *n'est-ce pas?*"

Chapter Ninety-Four

"Tristeza"...Lobo & Niltinho

I had to admit it wasn't half bad—well, what I really mean is, it was phenomenal-- driving from Chicago to Iowa in the black 1968 Mercedes 280 SL that I had got to borrow for the trip. The interior was supple leather, of course, and had that fancy burl wood-paneled dashboard. The gear box was "on the floor" but automatic. All the dials and gauges were big and round, and the radio and tape deck were top of the line; no doubt German engineering went into them, too. I had brought all my tapes with me. The Francis Lai soundtrack from *Vivre pour Vivre* might have been the best car trip music ever written.

Having left my house before seven in the morning, the roads were almost empty, and I made excellent time getting to Interstate 80. It was a clear shot from there. I pulled into Cass and Alan's driveway before mid-morning. Cass had evidently heard my car; she came out onto the porch in the robe I'd given her the last Christmas I was there.

I was very happy to see her, naturally, but shocked at the same time, and when we hugged, my fears did not abate. I was five feet two inches tall, and weighed around one hundred pounds-- give or take the few I'd put on since college--but I felt Gargantuan next to Cass this time. Cass, who had always been bigger boned and taller than me seemed to disappear in my arms. I was spooked enough to sit her down once inside and confront her directly.

"Cass, is something wrong with your health? Are you anemic? Something worse? Tell me."

"No, nothing! Why are you so freaked?"

"Well, for one thing, what the hell do you weigh now?"

"Oh, gee I don't know. About the same as usual. Why?"

"Bullshit, that's why. You're iron-deficient, aren't you, Miss Vegetarian?"

"I'm not iron deficient at all. I eat all kinds of leafy greens, " she laughed.

But I wasn't laughing. I was afraid to see the twins, now, for fear they weren't thriving, but when they both came running to us, they seemed fine.

"Your hair is all dry and matted. What has happened to your hair?"

"I just don't have time to get it done, that's all."

"Oh, come on. I'm obviously not buying that."

"Well, look, so I've sort of let myself go, I'll admit. But my priorities are a little changed now, huh, kid? Taking care of two rambunctious toddlers! It's a full-time occupation. You've been here enough to know that."

"So don't you have the church day care anymore?"

"Yeah, I have it. But I feel guilty, you know, taking advantage of that without paying for it."

"So pay for it."

She bristled. "It's about to be a moot point anyway."

"But maybe we can take them in there tomorrow, okay? Let's go into Iowa City and visit the hairdresser, shall we?"

"Yes, okay. I bow to your every command. You can drive me in your fancy mini-limo over there."

Alan heard me arrive and emerged from whatever he was doing in the back bedroom to greet me. "Miss Shrier!"

"Hi, Alan." I gave him a little peck on the cheek. "Congrats on your position at UTEP, " I said trying to disguise my only half-hearted enthusiasm.

"Thanks! It's going to be quite a trek."

"Can you take Route 66?" I suddenly remembered having told Cass all about the t.v. show and that the highway's starting point was Chicago.

"We can take it as far as the Missouri-Oklahoma border, but then it continues north, and we have to go far south. El Paso is right near Mexico, did you know that?"

"Fuck me." I was indeed stunned.

"Shall I help you bring in your stuff?" he suddenly asked. "We sort of cleared off the couch, here, for you. How long are you going to be here? Two nights?"

"Three, actually. I'll go to Des Moines Tuesday morning, but I'll be back that night and be here until you guys leave Wednesday."

"Yeah, all right!"

He and I went back out to bring in my bag and the presents, and when we returned, we headed straight for the babies' room where I could at least put my suitcase down and show Cass the clothing I bought for the kids.

"Oh, I like those bibs!" she exclaimed.

"Do I detect a note of relief in your voice, that I stayed out of the kids' department at Saks?" I chided her.

"No...but where we're going...you know."

"Yeah, I can imagine."

Suddenly there was a thump out in the living room and Laura let out a little squeal.

"Oh, jeepers! God knows what they're into now," Cass said, rushing out of the bedroom.

The interior of the little farmhouse was a chaotic mess with a jumble of boxes in various states of readiness strewn about. The twins were a little too eager to play with the opened contents, too, and had just knocked over a stack of books.

"I have to keep them out of the packing process, " Cass groaned.

"I'll play with them, " I offered. "Let me take out and open one of the puzzles I brought with me."

"I'll make some tea, " she offered. "We're not packing the kitchen up until last."

"That would be nice, " I said, skeptical that she could even find the tea kettle in the morass, even if the kitchen wasn't boxed up yet.

"Some buddies of Alan's are coming over later today to help us figure out how to load the panel truck, van, whatever you want to call it. What they are really are, though, are scavengers. They descended on us yesterday like vultures waiting to grab up everything they think we don't have room for. I mean, it's okay because we need 'homes 'for lots of miscellaneous items, but when a crew comes over to help, and then spends the whole time telling us we'd better leave this and leave that, it just made me feel used."

"Oh put a sock in it, " Alan barked, suddenly chiming into the conversation, and startling me with his tone. He turned to me, "It wasn't as bad as all that. They were right...we do need to jettison most of this shit."

"Well, I'm sorry, then," I announced with an air of mock superiority, "that I brought extraneous Christmas presents, but I did. And you'd better not jettison them. Is that an Iowa Writers' Workshop verb, by the way?"

He pushed by me with a little cuff on the shoulder but didn't act mad anymore. By the time I had done the puzzle with Paul and Laura about fifteen times, I heard cars and motorcycles arriving in the circular gravel drive. I wondered about moving Jean-Paul's car way up towards the empty animal pen to keep it out of harm's way in case beer was involved in this packing effort.

"The guys are helping Alan build a top carrier for the van, " Cass explained. "Our bed and a lot of the boxes will fit up there."

"Well, that's ingenious, I have to admit."

"So, do tell all about this meeting you're off to in Des Moines."

I felt she was trying to evade the issue of her health, but I obliged with the whole story again about writing my *Moments Culturels* for the newest editions of the French textbooks called *Notre France et le Monde Francophone*.

"They said, in essence, that I would be writing one for each chapter of the beginning and intermediate two levels of the text series. At first they'll be in English and then I'll transition to French. I have to see the contents of the chapters before I can know what to write, so I haven't brought any with me except a sample."

"You'll wow 'em, I'm sure!" She hugged me again and then drawing back she said, "Just look at you! So petite and beautiful! What are you wearing to the interview?"

"You might not believe this, " I laughed, "but I went out and bought clothes. So now I can wear some that weren't yours, how about that!" And I pulled out a new black knit skirt and black boiled wool bouclé jacket trimmed in red at the collar, cuffs and pockets. And I showed off my new riding boots. "Look! I'm finally not wearing my seven-year-old college boots anymore."

"Gorgeous!" she proclaimed.

"Okay," I said, getting back to the matter at hand, "what gives with your weight?"

She sighed and looked straight at me. "I'm sort of like afraid to eat, so I don't eat much."

"Why are you afraid to eat?"

"Because when I was pregnant with the twins I was so fucking huge, that's why! Alan didn't like it one bit. It took me forever to lose that weight."

"Cass, that's not true. Alan knew you were carrying his babies---plural---for godsake. I can't believe he would have put pressure on you. I was around for a lot of that, and I don't remember him making a big deal out of how you looked. You were always the most beautiful girl on the Iowa campus. You know that."

"I don't know anything of the sort, " she snorted. "I am terrified of becoming that hippo again. I am where I want to be now, and I can't even fathom putting on more pounds. Being a vegetarian has been the godsend I was hoping it would be. And it's so much healthier! Can you say my children don't look healthy?"

"Well, no, but…"

"But nothing. I cook for them and for my husband. I'm a lot better at it now and I shop with a conscious effort to create fine meals!"

"That's all just dandy, but do you eat these fine meals along with them?"

"Sometimes. Since you asked, you're going to be happy to hear that a lot of the time while they eat dinner, I go off and spend that time with my art projects. I take my own meals alone."

"Well, I'm here for a couple of days. If I cook for you, will you eat it?"

"No, Sari. Thanks for the offer. I'm sure Alan would take you right up on that---he always loves your cooking. But we've started emptying out the freezer and fridge, so there's not much left in there to cook. And we don't want to waste our precious few hours together in the grocery store, now do we?"

"So what will we do then?"

"We'll wing it. How about Pagliai's tonight? The kids love cheese pizza, and I know you are dying to not have Chicago-style thick crust, am I right?"

"Right on, as a matter of fact."

"I love their salads, " she added.

We went out to check on the progress of the truck's outfitting, and one of the guys asked whose "tricked out ride" the Mercedes was.

"Well, that would be me, " I answered, and suggested to Cass that we take the twins and go somewhere to get out of the guys' hair. It was too cold take them to any parks or on stroller meanderings around downtown Iowa City. So I suggested we drive to Cedar Rapids and go to a mall where we could get them some little treat.

Cass and I pushed the twins around the fairly bustling small-town mall done up in a semblance of jolly holiday décor. We wheeled them up close so they could see an animated snowman and some dancing candy canes. They squealed with delight.

"It must not take much to impress a wee one, " I laughed. "This place seems pretty bleak to me."

We parked them at an ice-cream kiosk inside the food court, and got them each a cup of soft serve, which I helped them eat. Once on the go again, whenever we passed by a store display with clothes, Cass would stop and tell me how cute I'd look in this one, or how sweet my figure would fit in that one. All about me; she never said a thing about what she might be secretly longing to wear.

On the way back three hours later, we stopped and picked up the pizza and salad to take home. Alan had given away the coffee table that we had always used for eating near the sofa, but he purposefully had not packed up the kitchen table, so we set that. Cass even had left over Christmas paper plates from the previous year, and our little meal turned somewhat festive. The twins could still use their high chairs with the detachable trays removed, and push right up to the grownups' table. Cass did not take off to the

541

back room this time, but sat with us and ate the salad, picking out the olives and any other ingredients she deemed fattening. But at least she ate the lettuce, chopped up celery and carrots, and cherry tomatoes that came with it. She did not put any dressing on it. I had to refrain from asking her how her plate of nothing tasted.

When Cass took the kids in to get bathed and ready for bed, Alan and I sat down on the couch and he opened up to me.

"She's sick, you know," he stated. "Anorexia. And she also shows signs of bulimia, but not as much."

"What are you talking about?"

"So…what?…you've never heard of anorexia nervosa or bulimia then?"

"No. I mean, maybe I've heard the words but I don't have any frame of reference for them. What is it?"

"Eating disorder. Go to the library and look them up when you get home. Eating illness behaviors are a bitch, believe me."

"Okaaay, so what are they? What does she do?"

"Well, first of all, she doesn't eat. They're afraid to eat. They have an actual fear of it. And when she does put food on a plate, like at dinner with the kids and me, well, you didn't see it tonight, but usually she cuts everything up into tiny little bits and pushes them around the plate all night. That is if she even sits with us, mind you. Most of the time she takes these stupid dry curd cottage cheese containers into our bedroom and hides them all over the place. It ends up stinking to high heaven in there. She mostly eats sauerkraut, the dry curd crap, and lettuce. Period."

"What?!"

"Oh yeah, you heard me. This started out as being a vegetarian, you know, and that was fine. At least she fixed some meals she would eat once in a while. But it got out of control after a time. Now she's afraid to put any calories in her body."

"So what's the bulimia part?"

"Oh, that…yeah, like the other day she ate a package of Oreos. All of it. Then she cried all afternoon, and then… just purged it all after that."

"You mean she threw up?"

"Made herself throw up, to be precise. Put her fingers down her throat."

"Oh, Christ, Alan. She needs to get help in that case."

"She's batzoid you mean."

The twins came bounding down the hall and out into the main room, so I jumped up to help Cass put them to bed. In the nursery, I took a better look at her. She really was skin and bones to the point of looking unrecognizable to her old frame. She lifted Laura up into the crib, and I could see ribs through her blouse. Not only that, her pelvic bones were protruding up over her waistband. Her formerly astonishingly beautiful, huge round eyes, which were still covered in thick lashes, were now sunken back above her cheeks. Her mouth seemed smaller, as if the jawbone had diminished, and her neck was thin and scraggly. She looked three times older than her twenty-four years.

I didn't know what to do. I wanted to leap into emergency mode and become Fix It Sari, but there wasn't any time. I had my meeting to think about and get to; I couldn't put that off any more than they could put off their move. I really wanted to lure her into my car under false pretenses, and whisk her to the ER at U Hospitals. But I knew she'd throw a shit fit if I tried it, so I just repressed all those urges – and did nothing.

The next day when we dropped off the kids at church and got back in the car, I just sat there without starting it up, and opened up a dialogue with her.

"I know you've got anorexia nervosa, " I announced, which obviously gave away that Alan had spoken about it to me.

"I'm in maintenance now, though, " she was quick to respond.

"So you've seen a doctor about this?"

"Not exactly. But I went to the U of Iowa med library and looked it up. I know I'm okay now."

"Oh, that's rich. How can you be so sure of that?" I huffed at her.

"Because I'm telling you. I'm assuring you. Rest easy. "

"Cass, you don't fool me for a minute. I'm not happy about the way you look."

"So let's get to the salon and I'll look a whole hell of a lot better when we're done." She reached around for the seat belt.

"Before we do," I told her, "open the glove compartment and take out that envelope with the Bank of Chicago logo on it."

"No, Sari. I'm not taking it."

"You are. Hey! I'm not arguing about this. If you don't take it, I'll give it to Alan. He'll think it's my money, so he'll accept it. Do you want him to have control over it? It's yours."

"No."

"So, put it in your purse. I'm going to tell him the little white lie I discussed with you over the phone and be done with it. This money will pay for rent for months, plus all the day care you'll ever need in El Paso. By the way, there's fifteen hundred in there, and still tons more left in the account."

She took the money and turned to me with tears running down her face. "Sari, let's please not fight on the last day we may have together for a hell of a long time, okay?"

I reached around, undid her seatbelt, and hugged her.

"Just tell me what's wrong, " I said trying to soothe her.

"Our marriage is off and on shitty, for one thing."

"Then why are you moving to Texas with him? You could come back to Chicago with me!"

"No, no...I didn't mean to imply that I'm not willing to stay with him. I just get hurt feelings, you know? He's non-communicative and, you know, like with my birthday, he doesn't give a damn about being nice about stuff like that. I don't play the hurt martyr. I explain how it makes me feel; but even then, he doesn't care."

"That doesn't sound like any marriage I'd want to be in. But maybe it's that your existence here has gotten saturated with so many hassles. He's been under all the stress of the degree, the CO stuff and getting a real job. Now you can make a fresh start. After all, you're moving to a college town, and you guys will have a new chance to integrate into the community. You'll be a professor's wife. That will come with some status, won't it?"

"Oh, Sari, how can you say that? I hate the idea of cocktail parties and making small talk with Deans and all that rot."

"Well, intellectual stimulation isn't all bad. Besides, I still believe you'll make a name for yourself with art! Don't ever give up that idea, Cass. It's your destiny. And, hell, El Paso will be a whole new market for you."

"You keep thinkin' that, " she chuckled, lighting up a bit. "It's true that having a real salary will have to make some difference. Sometimes here we didn't know where the bread for rent and food was coming from. Our meager savings dwindled to literally nothing."

"Yeah, well, that was your doing...it needn't have if you'd have let me send you money."

But heeding her admonition not to fight, I let it drop and instead asked her, "Will Iowa City still hold fond memories when you leave?"

"The Iowa City we shared will, " she replied. "But Alan's and my particular set up here was oppressive. So yeah, under other circumstances I could dig it here, but I'm anxious to see new places and want my kids to experience the whole world of different, far out things, too. Happy memories are best kept happy—at a distance—in both time and space. For me, at any rate."

"And at least when you get there, you can settle in town, maybe close to the campus, and take advantage of all it has to offer, right?"

"Oh God, no. I don't want to live in El Paso. I'm hoping we can get some little farmstead like here...outside the city."

"Oh, and be isolated and lonely again? Are you nuts?"

She just laughed and I shook my head. *Bourrique, bourrique et demi.*

Cass and I managed to get into the beauty shop she liked in Iowa City. Students were in class, thus not out and about in town much. I treated both of us to the works, and thought it was good timing to get

543

a manicure before my meeting the next day. The girl who did my hair got a little carried away teasing it, however, and I had to tell her to take it down a notch.

"I don't want to walk in there tomorrow looking like Tricia Nixon."

We tried to hit a few of our old haunts and relive our mad, gay and exciting student lives, but in a nod to Thomas Wolfe, it wasn't really working. Our mood was not light. In a last-ditch effort, I insisted we go to the bookstore so I could get some Iowa folders, and then to lunch at Hamburg Inn #2. Cass had vegetable soup, and, knowing I was paying close attention to how-- or if-- she ate it, she did eat it all. But she went to the bathroom twice before we left. I admit I was suspicious... and I sure didn't like that...feeling that I couldn't trust her.

We picked up the kids around four-thirty, and back at the house, the crew was gone. I proposed dinner at a Chinese restaurant.

"That is a winning idea, " Alan enthused. "We can go to the one in Coralville we all like. Family oriented and all that."

Cass ordered bean curd with bamboo shoots, and just as Alan had described to me, she cut it all up into little dice-sized bites and pushed them all over the plate. I had fabulous egg foo young, and the portion was so huge, I shared it with the twins, who really seemed to like it. The kids weren't quite two and half yet, and it still took all three of us to wrangle them in a restaurant setting. Still, all in all, they were pretty well-behaved and ate like little troopers. They ate more than their mother did.

We returned home and turned in early so I could get some sleep before my drive the next day. I arose at the crack of dawn, and had the bathroom to myself in which to dress. I tiptoed around, gathering up my purse, writing samples, keys and sunglasses, and headed out without seeing either of them.

The drive to Des Moines was easy and the roads were clear, which was lucky. Mid-December could have easily been an ice storm, and I was as grateful as hell that it wasn't. The Mercedes handled like a dream on the road and I knew I was completely spoiled, and that I'd be sad to turn it back in when I got home to Chicago.

I found the company's building just fine; it even had parking. I thought to myself, "Toto, we ARE back in Kansas." My meeting was scheduled for ten o'clock and I was there a half an hour early, so I sought out a coffee shop, and had a small orange juice to fortify myself with a modicum of energy.

Once I arrived and presented myself to the receptionist of Dowling Press Educational Publishing, a woman who turned out to be an editor, came to get me in the lobby. She was super friendly, and led me into a small conference room where two other people — both men-- were waiting. They explained that they had heard about me from someone in their organization who had had a vendor's booth at the Mid-States Conference.

"He heard your talk, and ordered one of the Foundation's films just to see how all that worked, " one of the guys told me.

"The lesson plan you provided and your little culture capsule article gave us the impetus to pursue the idea further, " the female editor said.

They proceeded to present me with a prototype of the new text, first level, and that way I could see what the chapters would be containing. Their plan was for me to submit whatever I deemed pertinent to each chapter.

"There will be three levels of this text series, and we will only start with the first one. But even with that, you don't have to do them all at once. Why don't we say, five-chapter increments, " the editor suggested. "You send them in, we will okay them, or maybe make some changes, of course..."

"Sure, " I hastened to agree.

"And then we'll give you the green light to do five more, and so on, until all twenty-five are finished. The roll-out for this new edition is slated for 1974."

"Wow, it takes a long time, then, doesn't it?

"Does that surprise you? "

I responded yes, and added, "And you'll indicate when I should switch to French?"

"Yes, and we will trust you'll be able to tell the level of advancing difficulty, too, within each lesson, and adapt accordingly?"

544

"Right, " I said, trying to sound confident but hoping to hell I could actually do that when the time came.

"Are we correct in assuming, too, that six thousand dollars is an agreed-upon fee?"

"You are," I said, nodding, but almost bursting out laughing. I tried to remain cool and professional, but it was hard when I wanted to skip around the table.

"Mr. d'Arivèque indicated that he would like his legal team to look over the contract, so we're sending it here with you---sign four copies and keep one. Just mail them back to us, by, shall we say, one week from now?"

"That sounds fine, " I said.

A secretary was sent for to bring in the manuscript of the textbook and the contracts. They bundled all that up into a large manila envelope, we shook hands all around, and I was on my way.

I fairly leapt into the car and drove out to Merle Hay Road to get some lunch, since I was starving. My emotions were bouncing off the car roof—elated and really astonished that everything had gone even more smoothly than I imagined it would. And all that money! It was not a mirage! Still, I remained awfully worried about Cass. It depressed me no end that in a few hours we'd be saying our tragic goodbyes with a lot of issues left unresolved. God, what a rollercoaster my life seemed at that moment.

By the time I got back, their place was being emptied out, and the van was loaded down with all their worldly belongings.

"I see I still have a couch to sleep on tonight," I noticed, looking around in amazement at their progress, "but where are you going to sleep?" Their bed was, as described, taken apart and strapped to the top of the truck.

Cass wanted to hear more about my day than tell me about theirs, but she assured me they had sleeping bags in the back bedroom. The twins would sleep in their cribs one more night, and then Alan had arranged for the Episcopal Church to come the next day and cart them off for the day care, along with the couch.

"So that's a perfect solution, " Cass said, and I couldn't disagree. "Okay, now we want to hear how it went Mad-dam-mwah-zelle Shreee-aaair! Are you a textbook writer now?"

"I guess I am!"

"And your salary?"

"Consulting fee, really, but hell yeah, just like they said on the phone: six grand! Hoolllleeey buckets, no?"

"Wow," said Alan, "you struck gold."

"And to that end, Alan, I need to tell you something else. I also got a huge promotion at work...I'm Director of Education for the Foundation now, in case Cass didn't tell you. They doubled my salary. Can you imagine? Doubled! And I am giving you guys a chunk of money. You can't argue...I already gave it to Cass. Fifteen hundred dollars. For your trip or your new place or the kids---whatever."

"Sari, " Alan said in a soft voice, "that's so fucking incredible and generous of you."

"Not really," I said, exchanging a knowing glance with Cass, who looked uncomfortable, but agreed that it certainly was.

"And we love you! And the babies are loving their Auntie right along!" she added.

"This must call for a celebration," Alan said. "Dinner out! There's certainly nothing to cook here."

"Or anything to cook it in!" chimed in Cass.

"I will drive us to wherever you want to go, " I offered.

"Well, then, how about The Mill? Talk about for old times' sake!"

Alan climbed in the back seat with his children and Cass sat next to me, as we took off to spend our last fun night together, as fate would have it-- but of course we didn't know that then--for the rest of our lives.

Chapter Ninety-Five

"Time Is Like a Dream"...George Delerue & Hal Shaper

Back at my desk after the ecstasy of Des Moines and the agony of Iowa City, I had a pile of work to keep me busy for months, and yet enough time on my hands to ponder all the flotsam and jetsam of my strange single life. It brought to mind the memory of a customer who was in our bar one night during the holidays, and I was the hostess. In making conversation, I wondered if she were done with her Christmas shopping. She looked up at me and heaved a great sigh, saying "Oh, I just do that in the pet aisle of the Safeway." She only shopped for her dogs.

I thought about our office closing soon for Christmas break, and how it would be easy to use that time to go back to The Bluffs, if I wanted to. I pictured myself buying a load of stuff and heading home to bestow the bounty of my new-found status on the family. But then I came to my senses.

"Oh, hell no!" I said out loud. Adding more tumult to my unhappiness over Cass would be idiotic at best and insane at worst.

And I was very unhappy about Cass. This was the first time she actually seemed distant to me. Me! As for my attitude towards her, I found I was actually mad! I didn't believe her at all when she said she was well, and I was actually finally feeling anger—real anger-- that she hadn't shared this food repulsion stuff with me when it first started. I could understand her masking troubles and fears with the church people or Prof. Klampert-- if she even saw him anymore--but not with me!

I was perturbed, too, about their move to El Paso, Texas, the last place on earth I ever pictured either of them. Okay, so I was also feeling a little sorry for myself that Cass would be so far away from me when I had always taken comfort in the idea that we were just a few hours from each other in a straight line down a highway or train tracks. How I'd ever manage to get to that farthest outpost of Texas to see her was beyond me.

I also loathed the idea of them living out in the country again, and found myself mulling over and over in my mind all the reasons for how stupid it was. This whole "back to the land" crap struck me as the height of hypocrisy and nothing but hippie nonsense that Cass Hyde—my Cass Hyde—was massively unsuited for. I had noticed, for one thing, how her enthusiasm for seed catalogues seemed so forced. Why was her image of herself that of "farmer" instead of "artist?"

Another thing I ruminated over was how I hadn't liked Alan's attitude towards her at all during my last brief stay, and wondered just how long **that** had been going on. I shuddered to think what would happen to the kiddos if Cass and Alan really did go off the deep end.

I'd also been reading up on anorexia nervosa. People could die from it.

No matter what my mood was, however, Chicago's mood was holiday. One day while heading to lunch at Woolworth's counter, I glanced at a display of Christmas cookie cutter sets and little stacked spiral-bound cookbooks on holiday baking. It gave me the idea to bake up some really fancy Christmas cookies for the office. That would keep my mind off my troubles. I bought the set and a book, and made a list back at my desk of what essentials I'd need to have on hand in order to accomplish this. On the way home, I stocked up; and that night by the time I'd gone to bed around one a.m., I'd baked eight dozen cookies from scratch, decorated with my own renditions of holiday colors made from experimenting with different formulas of food coloring! I made wreaths, bells, Santas, stars and reindeer, who had to remain plain because I couldn't come up with any brown hue for their frosting. Making those holiday cookies improved my mood. It struck me as a nice gesture, too, for people in the office who were so nice to me.

Before leaving in the morning, I made pouches out of tinfoil lined with wax paper, and decorated it all with ribbon. I got there early so I could deliver them to each department of the Foundation. Upon opening the one in the legal office, Hennie wondered if I really did bake them or "Did you possibly stop at the famous Koenig German Bakery on Dearborn and pick some up on your way to work?" But her boss overheard this conversation, peeked inside the packet, and teased me, saying "I doubt any bakery would use those-uh—shades." She picked one up and ate it while I was still there, pronouncing it "*exquise.*"

Later in the day, Jean-Paul d'Arivèque appeared in my office to thank me and extend an invitation. "Last year when you saw my *arbre de Noël*, you expressed your childhood desire to decorate, yes?"

"Did I?" I laughed.

Okay, I did remember telling him that, in my opinion, little Jewish kids all hankered to join in the tree trimming, but I also recalled that he had those priceless works of art as ornaments, which was definitely not what I'd had in mind.

"Yes. Therefore, I should like to most whole-heartedly extend you the invitation to come over and join me this year."

"That…would be very nice, *Monsieur*, er-- Jean-Paul, thank you, but your tree is not the…uh…average Christmas tree. You have Lalique and Boucheron and all those fancy baubles. If there were even normal glass balls or tinsel or something, I could trust myself to help, but really, I'm a klutz. *Je ne veux pas faire des bêtises.* If I broke one of those, I'd never forgive myself."

"*Mais non*, that is absurd. My tree is small. It sits on a table. Even if you dropped something, it does not have far to fall. So yes, you shall come?"

"Okay, if you're sure. I'd love to come over. Thanks! When do you want me?"

I knew French people decorated their trees a lot later than Americans, often not until Christmas Eve. This was already Tuesday, the twenty-first, so he had really put it off, too.

"Come for *apéro* Thursday after work. We can decorate the tree and then have a small dinner in the library. Does that sound nice?"

"Very!"

That day I showed up at work wearing black velour slacks, my white sweater and the black bouclé jacket with red trim that I had worn to Des Moines. I tied my hair up in a red velvet ribbon. Chicago was having unusually warm weather that particular week, so I wore my London shoes instead of boots. I was always amused by ads for clothing that touted "work into evening" wear, and now I had some of it.

I rode home with JPA and we were greeted by Robineau, to my disgust, and when I say we were greeted, I mean Jean-Paul was greeted. I was hardly given a glance, which was fine by me. He didn't dare scowl at me or do anything else rude, however, in front of his boss when I was an invited guest. Luckily he wasn't "on duty" in the library and the other staff treated me with friendliness that more than made up for that rotten little worm's vile attitude towards me.

The tree was set up in its same spot near the French doors, and his staff had already strung delicate white lights on it. We got right to work and I had to laugh. Instead of the usual flimsy boxes with little cardboard dividers that most Christmas ornaments were stored in, his maid had placed an array of beautiful silken boxes with tufted or quilted interiors where the fancy ornaments nestled. At least there were some plain crystal ones that I made a point to hang first. I was thankful that I could do it without my hands shaking. JPA handed them to me for a while, but it was only logical that he, being taller, would put the ones up higher. I took them out and gingerly gave them to him by the hanger. There was some white pearlescent garland that we draped around the tree, weaving in and out through the branches, so that the ornaments looked as though they were perched on it. Our *sapin de Noël* turned out beautifully and even looked different from last year's when we were done.

"It looks splendid, does it not?" he asked me, backing up to take it all in.

"Well, that's just such a magnificent collection of ornaments, " I said, sounding redundant.

"It is your creative placement of the ones that reflect the light, " he said admiringly.

I pooh poohed that idea.

Dinner was brought in on trays and we sat on the Chesterfield sofa to eat it. There was delicious smoked salmon and crab salad, another delectable dish of pasta shells in a light seafood sauce, and lots of bread. We drank Perrier along with chilled Sauvignon Blanc from the Sancerre region, which I also loved. The whole thing was heaven.

When we were through, JPA beckoned, I arose, and he led me to the center of the room where we could view the tree again, shimmering before us. After a moment or so, he turned and looked at me quite intently.

"Did you enjoy the tree decorating?"

"You know I did."

He reached over and took my hand in his, then tilted his head up, inviting me to do likewise. I now noticed that we were directly beneath the chandelier, from which hung a sprig of mistletoe.

Smiling, he said "You perhaps know of this tradition... Would you mind very much if I kissed you?"

I was completely taken aback. "Do you...think, I mean, do you want...to? You don't have to, you know... I accept you exactly as you are. And you do not have to worry that I would ever let on... er...what I'm trying to say is... I fully understand why someone in your position...your status in this city...would need to maintain...a pretense. But I understand. So...you don't have to kiss me."

He reacted as though he didn't comprehend why I would go into such a speech.

"No. I want to."

I was confused, so in the end I just spat it out.

"But, see, I thought that...well... you don't... prefer women. Right?"

"*Comment*? You thought I did not prefer women."

"Well, yes. I just thought you... you know... batted for the other team?"

"*Excusez-moi? Je ne comprends pas.*"

I took another breath and blurted out, "I thought you were gay." There it was.

"Gay? *Homosexuel*? What would make you think that? I am not...gay...as you say."

"What would make me think that? Oh, God."

Something had gone terribly wrong here. I was digging myself into a hole that could ruin my entire life.

"*Alors*, Sarah?" He wasn't angry but seemed very confused and considerably hurt.

"Welllll, you...you aren't married and you're in your forties. You lived with your mother — until she died! You went to a gay nightclub with your gay valet..."

"And saw you at the same one with your gay teacher friend!"

I acknowledged with a little nod of my head that he had me there.

"Yes, but...well, okay, that is true."

His tone became more explicit. "My mother lifted me...quite literally...out of a war... and she stayed with me in hospitals for years. Of course I should have lived with her. This house is enormous! *Effectivement*, there was certainly enough space for us both, as you can see."

His attitude was becoming more animated so I took that cue and ramped up my own rhetoric.

What did I have to lose by then? I'd already for all intents and purposes destroyed the best job anyone could ever dream of.

"Well, yes," I continued with not a little indignation in my own voice, "but I still imagine it might be hard to actually carry on a love life with one's mother peeking from down the hall, might it not!"

"Come with me." And with that, he stood up with the use of his cane, but then tossed it to the side and took my arm. He limped determinedly, holding on to me, out to the corridor and over to the elevator, whereupon we entered and he pushed the button marked 3. It opened onto a large paneled hall with fifteen-foot high ceilings down from which hung huge portraits, like at a palace or a castle. *Fucking Fontainebleau.*

The parquet floors were covered in thick Aubusson carpets down the middle and each room he led me through opened up onto something more wonderful than the last.

"These are my personal apartments, " he said solemnly. *Maman* did not come up here unless invited...or except when I was ill. There is a small bedroom and bath for her off the kitchen, but she did not use it very often. You **know** where she stayed."

He continued, almost pulling me along, "We are in the gallery here. All the ancestors are on these walls. Here we have my father. And this one is both my parents."

His father was very handsome, painted in normal, beautiful clothing, not a military uniform like many of the others, or robes indicating nobility of any sort. And there, finally, I saw *Maman*. The portrait was formal; her hair was swept in an up-do of the 1930's, and she was wearing a tiara in it. She was dressed in a long blue silk-satin gown that perfectly captured the blue of her eyes. Marie-Aveline looked like she'd been painted by Sargent or Nattier and lived in Cunegonde's world of sugar cake instead of one on the brink of war.

548

"I have here seven-thousand-three-hundred square feet of space and half that amount again of terrace. If we were to turn back towards the entry, we would see a library, and on the other side of the gallery wall is the kitchen. Come, I shall show you."

As we passed its open doorway, I could see into the massive kitchen. There was a large marble-covered island in the middle of the room, and all the cabinetry was white.

Continuing down the hall we came to a dining room with an enormous nineteenth-century French crystal chandelier hanging from the coffered ceiling, and a table with places for fourteen chairs! Adjacent to that was the long living room with two seating areas---one rounded with a baby grand piano next to it, and across the room, a canapé with three chairs flanking it, a tufted leather bench opposite from the sofa, and in the center of the whole arrangement, four square glass-topped tables making one large table, but which could be taken apart and used separately.

Behind that room was a wing of bedrooms all with en suite bathrooms, and at an angle from the living room another hall turned right and led to an enormous master suite with an immense sitting area, the same kind of Napoleon Empire sleigh bed his mother's room had, and-- what else?—its own elegant bathroom, larger, even than the one downstairs where I had stayed. From his bedroom there was a door leading out to that terrace he was talking about. It actually did wrap all the way back and around to the library.

"Your place is...so... very beautiful, " I managed to stammer.

"May we go sit down now, please?" he said, leading me, more gently this time, back to the living room. "So you see, I have my own private home here. Does that answer your question about my mother?"

It may have answered the question about his mother, but it didn't answer my real question. I feared I had already destroyed any good will I'd built up with him over the past two years, and I felt so stupid it didn't even warrant trying to apologize. So once again, I just came out with what was on my mind.

"So why aren't you married, then? Please enlighten me, because I don't get it. Any one of a hundred thousand women would want to marry you. You are the sweetest, kindest, most generous man I've ever encountered. You are cultured. Your erudition is known on two continents. You have more money than God. Your taste is impeccable. You have a myriad of friends who adore you...really everyone...all your employees.... revere you. You do good works and spread your largesse all over the city."

I took a breath and looked up at him. I had an inkling that my little rant about all his wonderful qualities would amuse him to some extent, but instead, he had a serious, almost woeful look on his face.

"Sarah, you do not understand. And if I explain it to you, you will perhaps think I am feeling sorry for myself, which I do not. I never do, *je t'assure*. But yes, of course, there have been women. Many women want what I have, what I own...what they think they might inherit when I die . But few of them want...this." He gestured to his withered side.

I vehemently shook my head. "I don't believe that."

"Well, it is true."

"Okay, so what about Marie-France? She loves you the way you are, I'm sure. Why didn't you marry her?"

He laughed a laugh of incredulity. "Marie-France **was** married, Sarah, for more than half of my life! And she was a great friend of *Maman*. I would never see her as anything resembling a lover or a wife. She is mostly like a dear aunt to me. Her prowess—her business acumen in the office-- was very highly regarded by my mother as it is by me. I do love her, but not in that way. "

" All right, so I'll bet maestro Solti knows a hundred women who would marry you tomorrow."

"You need to understand something. The women I have met up to now in Chicago... they only seem to wish to bide their time with me...they pity me, or they would be willing to play nurse until I died. Yes, that is one type. Or some have been honest; they did want to marry me but live separate lives. And then there were the ones who had fetishes for people with orthopedic appliances. Have you heard of that bit of craziness?"

"Fetishes? For ortho.... like for braces and crutches and such?"

"Yes."

"You mean, they ...got off on it?"

"Yes."

"Christ."

"So you are beginning to understand?"

I didn't say anything because what he was explaining had the ring of truth to it. He became somber.

"There was one woman, with whom I was quite in love. We had known one another since childhood. She still lived in France. So we made plans to reunite when I came to Paris for university. I believed we would one day be married. But when we reconnected after the intervening years, she could not get past her shock of seeing me. She made it clear that we could not be together in the way I had hoped."

I was mortified on hearing that story. It must have been a longer one than he had revealed, but, again, I didn't feel as though I had anything salient to add. It wasn't my place to pry.

He was visibly upset. I desperately wanted to flee. But I also wanted to stay in his employ, even as I was quite sure I'd already blown that. I owed him a vast apology.

"Look, I'm so sorry. I shouldn't have misjudged you. I truly regret taking something for granted that I had no right doing. I regret what I said. And I hope you can forgive my jumping to conclusions like that. My father always did tell me, 'Sarah, your mouth will get you into trouble.' And so he was right, damn it." I looked up at him and pleaded, "Just please, please don't fire me, okay?"

"Sarah! Again you are worried about your position at the Foundation? I am not about to sack you! What I want to tell you is… I have fallen in love with you. Surely you suspected."

" WHAT?! Well, no…I thought we were… you know, great friends."

"We are! That is what is so remarkable! You have no ulterior motives! You are the sweetest, smartest, most fearless girl I've ever met. You are energetic, hard-working—tireless, *au vrai dire*-- and spirited. And so attractive…your beautiful eyes are expressive, and in them, I see your depth… that you are a much deeper person than you let on. I loved you almost from the first time you came into my office."

I just sat there dazed, speechless. No man had ever spoken words of such admiration to me before in my entire life.

"You… you love **me**?"

"Could you…do you think you could also love me?" he asked almost plaintively.

I could only nod at him, my eyes welling up with tears. And then we both sort of simultaneously reached for each other. He pulled me towards him with his good arm, and I flung both of mine around his shoulders. We kissed for what seemed to me like a very long time—and over and over again.

"Oh, God, "I murmured, "hold me."

"Yes, *chérie*," he said, kissing away my tears, "and you me."

I pressed myself into his chest and nestled my face in his neck. He was running his hand through my hair and kissing my forehead. I found I was alternately sobbing and saying over and over, "I'm so happy." Finally we both sort of let go and sat up breathless. And laughed.

I dried my eyes with my pretty red-trimmed cuff. "Who'd a thunk this, eh?" I chuckled, sniffling. "Pardon?"

"Who would have imagined this outcome, I meant."

He smiled, took out a beautiful linen handkerchief and handed it to me. "When can we see each other again?"

I shrugged, wiping my eyes. It was a sticky wicket in my estimation. I could hardly stay over at his house, even in his private apartment, and he couldn't get to my house by himself.

"My bedroom—you saw it-- is right down that hall, " he said, caressing my face.

"I can't stay here overnight. You know that. What would your staff say if they saw me leaving here in the morning?"

"They would say, '*Ah, now Monsieur is a very happy man.*'"

"Ha ha. Come on. Be serious. First all your staff would know, and then the whole office. I think too highly of my job at the Foundation to let anyone come to the conclusion--erroneous as it may be--that I intended to sleep my way to the top."

"Sarah, you are so very naïve. You are already at the top, and you got there by your own best efforts and brilliance. And if you paid more attention, you would have realized that most of my close associates at the office have known for a long time how I feel about you. "

"So do they think I'm already your mistress?" I asked panicky.

"Of course not."

"Well, speaking of not paying attention, there's something you don't know, either."

"Oh? What is that?"

"Robineau hates me. And I have to say, I feel the same way."

"To what are you referring?"

"Well, I'll tell you. He was really mean to me the time that first July 14th when I got sick and ended up in your mother's bathroom."

"What did he do?"

"He barked at me in French that I was 'up to something.' He was a real dick...*un vrai cul!*"

I went on to report that every time I was there for some soirée or other, the valet glared at me, was unfriendly to me, sneered at me, and acted like I had to be watched.

"It's as though he was just plain jealous that I took up your time. But the worst came when I was here recovering from the surgery."

Jean-Paul's brow furrowed and his eyes became narrow, as I launched into the part about how Robineau had come into my sick room, and had scoffed at me, accusing me of trying, in his estimation, to wheedle my way into the inner circle. I explained how he had vilified me to the other staff, and how they had felt compelled to come in behind his back and tell me to beware of him!

"And here's the *coup de grâce*, " I said, tensing up, "he came right into my---your mom's ---room and laid it on the line. He said I would never be accepted here because I hadn't known your mother! Like that was your litmus test or something."

I felt good that this was all out in the open now. Listening to me, Jean-Paul's expression turned to an even more fierce show of anger, something I had never seen in him before.

"I am extremely unhappy to learn of this. I shall talk to him at once."

"Well, good luck with that! A leopard can't change his spots, now, can he? You can talk to him 'til hell freezes over, but you should know that I'll never stay here with him in proximity; I want nothing to do with him, and I don't ever intend to be victimized by him again."

"Sarah, believe me, I had no idea! I am so very sorry. You will never have another bad thing like that happen to you in my home. I swear it."

"It's not your fault...don't apologize. He's your valet and you need him. I dig that. He's just so vile."

"Do not think about him now, *chérie*. It will all be taken care of."

We went back downstairs and he called Jean-Luc to drive me home.

"Shall I come also?" he asked me.

"Yes, please."

When the limo pulled up to my gate, Jean-Paul got out, too, and held me on the sidewalk.

"Tomorrow is Christmas Eve. What will you be doing?"

"Maybe with any luck watching some sappy movie on t.v., like *Meet Me in Saint Louis*. That's my fave. What about you?"

"I shall be thinking of you...and longing to be with you. May I come over and partake of the sappy film?"

"Sure... but how?"

"Oh, I think Luc would be happy to assist."

"But I thought you always give the staff Christmas off."

"I do, it is true. So I will bring my bag with a change of clothes, and he can come back and pick me up the twenty-sixth. Would that be all right with you?"

"Of course... if you...want to. But Jesus, Jean-Paul, you'll really be slumming it over here."

"And there is something else I need," he said with mock seriousness while planting kisses all over my face, ignoring my concerns.

551

"What might that be?" I asked, grinning at him.

"That you must call me Polo. Will you do this for me?"

"Yes, all right -- Polo. I will. "

Chapter Ninety-Six

"I Think It's Gonna Rain Today"...Randy Newman

I was in big trouble and the learning curve was not going to be gentle. I had said yes to my boss, now my love, staying over at my place two nights on a holiday with most places closed, and no way to get ourselves to a restaurant for Christmas dinner even if there were any open somewhere in the city. He could only get up to my place with help from his chauffeur and down again the same way. He would be sleeping in a small and no doubt, very uncomfortable day bed, and as for every other facility at my apartment which, it should be noted, would fit inside his library, this was going to seem to him a lot like camping out.

I only had a few hours on Christmas Eve day to run around and try to get some provisions. Yes, I was a decent cook---of drab, quotidian fare. I had not "mastered the art of French Cooking" yet, and even though I'd cooked through several of the famous book's chapters, I certainly wasn't going to try any of those complicated recipes on such short notice.

The French *Réveillon* meal was always oysters and turkey. *Not going to happen either, I thought to myself.* What I eventually decided to prepare for Christmas Eve which was sophisticated enough and very French, would be *oeufs brouillés, salade vinaigrette* and *crêpes*. Elegant French scrambled eggs would have had truffles, but I held out no hope whatsoever that I would find those. I would, however, scavenge for some *baguettes* in my neighborhood and its environs, go to the fanciest markets I could locate, and then pray that the miracle that I'd think of or find something else to make for us on Christmas Day.

Starting at the same place where I'd ordered all the Thanksgiving food, I went in and found myself amidst a myriad of people evidently doing what I was: last minute Christmas. It reminded me of Europe, actually, where all the shops were bustling on that day.

And there it was right on the shelf: MAILLE mustard, and not just the kind one would usually see in America for sale at five times what it cost at Inno. This was *"Moutard au Chablis et Brisures de Truffe Noire!"*

"Oh my God!" I said out loud and the person nearest to me turned around. "Oh, sorry," I said to her. " I'm just floored to find this mustard with bits of truffle in it."

"What can you do with that?" she asked.

"Put it in scrambled eggs!" I replied cheerily. "If only they also had *crème fraiche!*"

"Oh, I think they do have it." She gestured at me. "Go look in the back dairy section." She had to be joking. How could I get that lucky! But bingo...there it was. *Thank you for being Chicago and not Omaha.*

And then it came to me what I would serve the next night: pasta. You can't go wrong with a simple pesto dish, and the French ate a lot more pasta than people realize, I tried to reassure myself. I knew there was some ready-made pesto in their deli counter because I'd seen it there. And going up one aisle and down the other, I just sort of grabbed things: cherry pie filling for the dessert *crêpes*, Christmassy paper napkins, a red plastic salad bowl and tongs, and just for the hell of it, a little sachet of European chocolate snowmen individually wrapped in colorful foil.

I still needed bread and rushed out of the market headed for the Koenig bakery. Even though it was German, maybe, just maybe, they'd have some French bread. Or Italian, even — anything I could grill under my broiler and put the scrambled eggs over.

Walking home from my expedition, thankful that, even though a white Christmas was always the recurring hope, there was no snow to have to plod through. I felt better...better except for the fact that I wouldn't have one thing that could be a gift for Polo. What in God's name could I ever have come up with to offer him? **Nothing**. That was the answer to that. Not in a million years. It seemed to be my fate that all these people I would love to shower with presents already possessed every possible thing one could imagine. I found myself in the same coals-to-Newcastle boat I'd been in years before, trying to come up with a hostess gift for Cass' parents, or for that matter, birthday presents and Paris souvenirs for Cass. Now I saw myself on the horns of that same dilemma once again! Only this time there could be no possible solution.

553

I would obviously resort to testing out the theory that "things are not what's important…people are." My gift to him would be a holiday not spent alone. I would play music for him he'd possibly never have heard and certainly didn't own. I would snuggle up on the couch with him, and make him tell me stories of Christmases at *La Pérégrine*. And finally, I'd let him have his way with me in bed. Merry Fucking Christmas. Literally.

Shit, I thought. I should have bought some of those shearling condoms like Pax had. Oh well, no time now.

He had told me they would call before they came, so I was ready at five o'clock at the front door of the building, which was about half full of tenants by then. There was even a concierge — in the French, not the hotel sense-- living in the newly refurbished space that had housed my old studio. She watched all the comings and goings, took in packages if we were gone, and supervised any movers or repairmen. I couldn't tell for sure, but assumed she saw Jean-Luc helping Polo up to the entry, this time carrying a very beautiful tan leather Swaine Adeney Brigg duffle bag along with what looked to be a picnic basket. Polo was holding his arm and swinging his brace leg up the steps one at a time.

I greeted them with a jovial, "*Bonjour et Joyeux Noël vous deux! Entrez!*"

I motioned for Jean-Luc to hand me the picnic basket as we made our way to my interior door.

"Be careful. It is rather heavy. It was Annie-Laure's idea, " he whispered.

He was right…I could barely carry it, and set it down immediately once inside, where I took Polo's coat from him and asked Luc to put it with the bag in my bedroom. Then Polo wished his chauffeur a nice holiday weekend, and the sweet guy winked at me and made his exit, with the understanding that he would return late Sunday afternoon.

"So what's in the basket? " I wondered.

"Well, since you asked, Annie-Laure evidently mentioned to Jean-Luc, who told my kitchen staff, that perhaps we would have a bit of trouble finding things to eat this weekend."

"You mean, because we're stranded in this apartment. Yes, I thought of that, too."

"There is no other spot I would rather be stranded, " he said, smiling at me. "Look inside. You should find enough to keep us happy."

Well, that was not a lie. There, wrapped in kitchen towels, were dishes of cold lemon chicken, *pâté de fois gras*, *quiche Lorraine*, *terrine de canard et de porc* with cranberries, two small plum tarts and finally, a box containing a beautiful *bûche de Noël*. Topping it all off were three baguettes and another bottle of wine… white, this time, a chardonnay from Domaine Montrachet.

"My GOD! 'Tara is saved!'" I cried, seeing all that bounty.

"What is saved?" he laughed.

"Never mind…just a joke…a bad one… *Gone with the Wind* reference. Ever seen that movie?"

"*Euh, oui, je pense. La guerre civile américaine?*"

"Yep."

I put the food in the fridge and when I came back out, he was sitting on the couch just watching me.

"I am so happy to be with you in your apartment again. I had such a wonderful time here at Thanksgiving."

I sat down next to him and he put his arm around me. He kissed the top of my head and said, almost to himself, "This would be enough."

We kissed and cuddled and didn't do much talking. I drew my knees up under me and just sort of settled into the crook of his good arm, as he kept caressing my hair.

"You have no Christmas tree and you have no *chanukiah?*"

"How do you know that term for the menorah?" I asked him.

"Oh, I have had many Chanukah evenings at friends' homes. Remember, I was raised for a time in New York."

"Of course. Well, Chanukah is over now. My menorah is back on the bookshelf…there." I pointed to the niche off to the side of the couch.

"But it is so very small!" he exclaimed, maybe expecting to see a large silver one.

"I know. It takes birthday candles, no less! Ha!"

He laughed softly and asked me, "When is your birthday?"

"It's in June—the thirtieth. 1948. And yours?"

"The fifth of May. 1930. We are eighteen years apart in age."

"Hmm. So you're forty-one?"

"And you are twenty-three...so young."

We sat there for a while longer as the room began to get dark, and then I turned to him and explained that I did have plans to make *oeufs brouillés* before I knew he was bringing food.

"Please," he said, "do not feel as though you must change your menu. I will be happy with whatever you decide. I know already that you are a fine cook."

"I can make some things well, " I said, "I'm not a chef by any stretch. But I'd like to prepare dinner for you, since I found all the ingredients."

"Then, yes, by all means. May I watch?"

"*Je t'en prie,* " I answered, using the familiar form of address with him for the first time ever, and motioning him to follow me.

It seemed to amuse him that I knew my way around a kitchen. He studied me cracking the eggs individually into a glass first before pouring them into the bowl.

"Why do you do it that way?" he wondered.

"Because that's what my Nana did. She always warned of unknowingly adding in a rotten egg and ruining the entire recipe. I just do it her way."

"Very smart, " he murmured, thoughtfully.

The egg dish turned out fine. In fact, he pronounced it "*sublime.*" He had helped set the table, and I wondered if it were the first time he'd ever done that. Turns out, no, his mother made sure he knew his way around the kitchen in the New York apartment, too. I surmised that New York must have been his only experience with normal life.

"What about Paris when you were in college? Did you live on your own?"

"Oh, no. I stayed in the apartment on the Parc Monceau and there was plenty of staff. An American writer and his family lived on the same *étage* as us. Perhaps you know of him...Art Buchwald?"

"I love him!" I stated, in amazement. " I have all his books at home! Ha! '*Kilometres Deboutish'* cracks me up every time. Is he still there? In your apartment building, that is? Do any of your relatives still live there? Your uncle, I mean?"

"I still have our apartment---*Oncle* Charles uses it, yes, when he comes to town. But the Buchwalds moved back to the States in the early 60's and they live in Washington, D.C. *Maman,* I believe, had seen him once or twice after he came back. "

"That's such a kill that you knew them! Did you enjoy your time in Paris? Was it hard after New York---getting around, I mean?"

"When I was a student in Paris, the house staff included the parents of Robineau...that is how I met him. He is about five years younger than me, and when I was a student at HEC, he became my companion...to help me, you know. He was then nineteen." He looked at me with renewed concern. "I do so sincerely apologize again for the way he treated you in my home.""

"Well, I was loath to bring up his name this weekend, but I guess I am curious as to how you'll get on being without him here. Is it the first time you've been away without a valet?"

"In a long while, yes... without someone...it is not always him."

"Okay. But are you worried about being here alone?"

"But...I am not alone. You are here with me. *On se débrouillera, n'est-ce pas?*"

"Yes... if you teach me ... what you need help with, I'll try to do it."

"Yes, *chérie*, I need you to kiss me, for example."

I kissed him and laughed, "You know what I meant."

I had already made the crêpe batter, so I fried them up for us and again he watched me with an expression of admiration that made me a little self-conscious. I rolled the crêpes with cherry pie filling, topped them with whipping cream and a cherry, and handed him the plate.

"So, let me guess...not that many of your other girlfriends cook for you?"

"There are no other—uh—girlfriends. Just you! And your *crêpes* are *vraiment délicieuses.*"

"Well, I can't take credit for it...Julia Child's recipe."

"Ah, *bien sûr.*"

Then we had the task before us to see what, if any, movies were going to entertain us that Christmas Eve. It wasn't long before we determined that cinematic choices were slim that year. WGN had on *The Bishop's Wife* and WLS had *Holiday Inn*. We chose the first one, and snuggled up on the couch under one of my extra blankets to watch it.

"I'll bet you don't watch as much television as I do, " I told him, slightly embarrassed, but unable to pretend otherwise. "I sort of grew up on it like most American kids."

"You are probably right. What was your favorite program as a child?" he asked. "I know there was Walt Disney."

"Yes, I watched that. My favorite shows when I was in elementary school and junior high were called *Steve Canyon* and *Hennesey*. Oh, and *Seventy-Seven Sunset Strip*. I never missed that one. *Hennesey* was about a doctor and his dentist friend and their nurse pals on a U.S. Naval base in California."

"Really?! Why did you love that program?"

"I liked the stories. I even wrote a letter to the writer when I was eleven years old, and he wrote me back. Can you imagine my thrill? Then he was nominated for an Emmy Award...you know what that is? Like the Oscars except for t.v."

"Yes, I do know it."

"Well, he lost, but my parents let me send him a telegram. He lost to a show with a group of writers, and I said to him, 'Don't feel bad. It took ten of them to beat you.' Something to that effect."

"Very sweet."

"So then he named a character after me."

"*Mon Dieu!*"

"I'll say. The show was slated to air on a night that I happened to be in the hospital. And all these nurses were in my room to watch with me. And the character was a nurse...Nurse Sari Shrier. It was the coolest."

"And why were you in the hospital?"

"Well, I was thirteen and having dizzy spells. They thought I might have had a brain tumor. So I was in for tests."

"A brain tumor? *Mince, alors.*"

"But I didn't. Guess I've dodged two bullets now come to think of it. I had kind of forgotten about that, if you want to know the truth."

I didn't want to talk about illnesses, so I suggested getting out the champagne I still had from Thanksgiving. Polo told me to bring the bottle to him with a dish towel, and he actually took it, and put it into his left hand which he lodged up against his braced knee to hold it steady. He then manipulated the cork off expertly-- with only a small pop of air-- as though he opened champagne for a living. I was duly impressed. I poured it out into the lovely Baccarat flutes he'd given me.

"I sure do adore these," I reiterated, "and thank you again for the fab gift."

At that moment I noticed him take a pack of Gauloises from his pocket, shake a cigarette up from the box and remove it with his mouth. He then put the pack back, took out a lighter from the same pocket, and lit his own cigarette as though there were nothing to it.

"Oh dear," I said, which elicited a worried look from him, as though I didn't want him to smoke.

"Ah, *tu préfères que je ne fume pas?*"

"Oh, no! Go ahead. It's just that I never did get an ashtray. That was dumb of me! I'll go get my trusty bowl."

When I came back, he beckoned me to sit so he could put his arm around me again, and I just nestled in there as he smoked around me and every once in a while, lifted his arm over my head to flick the ash in the bowl on the coffee table in front of him.

"It is true, I do not watch a lot of television. Nor in France, either."

"The nightly news?" I asked. "Do you watch NBC or CBS here? "

"*Non.* It is so much war. America is repeating France's errors in *Indochine.* I already know the outcome."

" How about the election stuff?"

"*Non plus.* And you?"

"Some. I'm very hopeful for George McGovern. When he wins over that sonofabitch Nixon, I'm going to dance in the streets!"

"I should love to be there to see that!" he laughed and drew me closer to kiss the top of my head.

The Bishop's Wife came on and we settled in on the couch to watch it.

"*Évidemment* you have seen this film before?" he asked me.

"Many times. You know, de rigueur Christmas fare and all. It's good, though."

"And you still enjoy it?"

"Sure. David Niven's character is a little obtuse, but who wouldn't love Cary Grant coming down from heaven and mixing it up in their lives?" I laughed.

"Yes, Christmastime typically brings about a preponderance of angelic interventions in one's life, does it not?"

As we watched, however, and the familiar—at least to me—plot unfolded, I began to feel a little squeamish about the portrayal of people who are pursued for their wealth in the story. They also willingly let their money be used to glorify themselves. I got an uncomfortable feeling that Polo might take my movie choice the wrong way.

"I must say, these rich people in the movie are the antithesis of you!" I offered, awkwardly.

He looked at me quizzically. "I see you are sensitive, Sarah. Do not worry---I take no offense at this film. Its message is universal, *de toute façon.*"

"Yes." I said, and gratefully dropped the subject.

Suddenly the television channel we'd been watching the movie on was signing off. Midnight had struck and it was Christmas. I turned to Polo, hugged him and wished him *Joyeux Noël.*

"Do you also celebrate this holiday?" he asked.

"Meh...sort of."

"*Alors, Joyeux Noël à toi aussi.*"

"Say, " I announced, realizing I was getting sleepy and the preparations for bed hadn't even been discussed, "would you like to unpack? Your bag is in my bedroom. I'm going to brush my teeth and change into night clothes."

His coat was in there, too, and I hurried to hang it in the closet since it had been left draped over the day bed. He followed me back to the bedroom where I grabbed my ancient flannel Lanz of Salzburg nightgown to put on in the bathroom.

"Shall I take your toiletries with me and set them on the counter by the sink for you?"

He smiled at me and nodded, hoisting his duffle bag onto the bed. "They are just here." And he handed me a worn leather dopp bag. "This bag was my father's. I always use it to travel."

"Very nice, " I said, "and you've got some swanky luggage there, I must say. Beautiful."

"It was also a gift from my mother."

When I came back in the room, he had taken out a sweater, a different pair of pants, some underwear, his pajamas and that same gorgeous robe I'd seen him in at the hospital that time.

"How about if I put all that on the chair?"

"Yes, fine, thank you. " He looked up and noticed my nightgown, the antithesis of lingerie, if that was what he was expecting. "Very pretty."

"You mean very frumpy... *mal habilée.* I know."

"Sarah, why do you criticize yourself? You are hard on you."

I shrugged, and tried to make light of it. "Oh, I'm just a little embarrassed. I'm thinking maybe flannel isn't what you might be expecting, is it?"

"But it is winter! Of course you would put on something warm."

I felt uncomfortable, but there was no use pretending I had any sexy peignoirs to slip into.

"Now", he explained, "in order for me to undress, first the leg brace comes off. This would be easier, you will see, if I had the full use of both my arms. I am going to show you that the pants leg on that side has a hidden zipper, and if you would just unzip it for me, you shall see how this—*euh*—process--goes."

I bent down to his ankle and found the hidden zipper. The way the pants were made, you could never tell it was there unless you knew it was fitted into a seam. "Boy, that's ingenious, " I marveled, unzipping it as far as it went which was up to his thigh. "Are all your clothes custom-made for you?"

"Yes, but these things can be found for any people who wear leg braces. "

"I had no idea."

"So now the brace is revealed, and I shall sit down. I unlock at the knee and then it will bend, as you already know." He was seated on the edge of my little bed and the first thing he did was draw his leg up with his right hand and reach down to untie his thick braced shoe. While he was in that position, he undid the other shoe as well. He was adept at untying with just one hand. (Lacing them back up again was another story.)

The brace was really heavy and kept in place with a series of leather straps that had to be unbuckled. He did that himself, too.

"I can take it off, but it will go faster if you ..."

"Sure. I just lift your leg **out** of it you mean?"

"Yes, *chérie.*"

That worked. His leg came out of the shoe just fine, and I saw up close this time how contorted his left foot was. I propped the brace, locked upright, against the same chair where his clothes were.

"My heavens, that's heavy!"

He nodded. "It is steel."

With the brace successfully off, he unbuckled his belt, undid the button at the waist, unzipped the fly and then he stood up on his good leg so that he could pull the pants off part way. He looked up at me and nodded, then sat back down so I could gently take them off the rest of the way and place them with the other clothes.

He had on a shirt with cufflinks, which he managed to get undone adeptly from the left wrist first, after which he sort of laid his left arm in his lap, and placed his right wrist close enough to where he could maneuver its cufflink to a position where he could undo it with his left hand! I marveled at the whole thing, confirming that his left hand worked, even if the arm did not. He handed them to me to put aside, and then he began unbuttoning the shirt itself. He was again adroit at getting the job done with one hand. Then he put the cuff of his good arm between his teeth and pulled his arm out of the sleeve. He lifted the shirt over his shoulder and onto the other side and eased it off his weak arm. Slick.

"Now things get a little tricky, " he laughed.

"**Now** they get tricky?"

"My left leg is quite short. The limp will be more noticeable. I shall need you to help me walk to your bathroom. If you hand me the cane and then take my weak arm, please?"

"Polo, " I said, "what about pain? Do you have any?"

"Off and on, yes, " he answered, knowing I remembered that's why he ended up in the hospital. "*Mais ne t'en fais pas.* I shall let you know. I realize my leg looks quite the *bazar.*"

His left leg did indeed look a mess; I'd seen it that one time before but only for a moment. Now here it was, completely unveiled, showing signs of bones having been broken and operated on, scars, visible gashes, and not a lot of musculature left.

"Is it weight-bearing?" I thought it important to ask.

"It can be, *chérie,* but it is a matter of equilibrium. I do not have much chance of balance with the difference in height."

We made the short trip to the bathroom and he was right. It was difficult without the brace to garner any sort of stability. He led with his right leg, and I helped play catch up grasping him on the left. Had he been able to use his left arm, he could have just held on to me, but without that, I had to support him instead. We managed to get to the sink where he could prop up using his good hip. I was glad at least that it was a tiny bathroom with the toilet wedged right between the wall and the side of the vanity. I realized then and there that bathrooms should all have railings and handles and all sorts of aids. I made a mental note to pay attention if I was ever at his place again, to see how his was outfitted.

"Just call out when you're ready, " I said, closing the door.

Back in the bedroom, I had tried to convince myself that it wouldn't be the first time two people slept in a little single bed; Soren and I had done it. But the logistics of this situation led me to offer to sleep on the couch.

"This is a teeny-tiny little bed, " I despaired, " and I'm sure you've never EVER slept in one so small. So I'm happy to let you have it to yourself."

But he wouldn't hear of that.

"*Mais non, voyons.* I am sure we can make this bed work."

Polo had opted to not put on the pajamas he'd brought, and he lay down in his underclothes on the bed and moved in as far as he could to the iron frame. He then beckoned me to come in, too. I scrunched up and we found ourselves in the perfect position to spoon. But soon he turned my head toward his lips, and I wrapped my arms around his torso, positioning myself on top. He was a gentle and nurturing lover; I was immediately aroused and I suspected the same to be true for him. Very soon my nightgown was off and we were slowly rocking together.

"*Je suis là,*" he whispered in my ear, and at that point I gasped and held him tight.

Afterwards I just lay there, with my head on his shoulder and we cuddled. I drifted to sleep in a state of euphoria. When I woke up there was only the faintest hint of morning light coming through the window. Jean-Paul was nestled against me. All at once I was startled to feel his tears wet on my face. Propping bolt upright on one elbow, I became overwrought at the thought that he might be hurting.

"Oh! Oh no! Polo! Is it the pain? Are you all right? It's too uncomfortable, isn't it?"

"*Mais non,* Sarah, *chérie*...no no...everything is fine!"

I breathed a sigh of relief.

"I am in tears because...because this is so beautiful and I never imagined it would happen for me. I did not think it was possible that I would find... someone... you...and here we are together."

I slumped back down with my head on his chest, my heart beating so hard I was sure he could feel it.

"*Calme-toi,* " he intoned in a sweet soothing voice as he stroked my cheek. "I did not mean to frighten you. Let me just hold you."

"Please do."

The bed was big enough after all, I mused. Where there's a will there's a way, indeed.

We both fell asleep again in each other's arms. When we awoke and took one look at each other, we fell into love making again.

After that it was almost ten in the morning. Lover or no, I felt obliged to tend to my houseguest, so I got up and threw on a robe from my closet. Polo sat up and I offered him his from the chair.

"Robe?"

"Yes," he said. "And shall I have you help me into it?"

"*Mais oui, volontiers.*" I knew how to do this—just like his coat. Weak arm in first, bring it around the back, hold it for him to put in his right arm. *Voilà.*

"Can you please tie it -- like you did in the hospital? Do you remember? "

"Of course." I smiled at him, and helped him stand to get the robe all around him and I tied it. Then he sat back down. I had, it seemed, joined the small minion of people he allowed to assist him, and, as if to seal the deal, after having made love to me, he must have disabused himself of any notion that I would ever be doing things for him out of pity. I think—hoped-- he knew full well that this would never be the case.

"Go to my bag, Sarah. I have something for you."

I did as he told me to, reaching into his fancy butter-leather duffle and thinking it was just as I feared: that he'd brought me a Christmas present and I would have nothing with which to reciprocate. I felt a box with ribbon on it. Yep, a present. And then there was something else—a sack that was light but nevertheless bulky. I took them both out and handed them to him.

"Do you know what this is? " he asked me with a twinkle in his eye, lifting the object from the sack.

"Oh, a French press coffee pot? It's a little one...four cups or so?"

"*Exacte.* I knew that your friend brought the coffee to Thanksgiving. Now you have your own."

"Oh, no, another housewarming present? You have to stop."

"And there is a brick of coffee in the bag, too. *Carte Bleue*. It is still quite new in France, but my kitchen has had it shipped over. American coffee is *l'eau des chaussettes*, as we French say."

"Hmm, yes, 'sock water' –I've heard it called that by my French friends. Did you put this kind in our break room, too, then?"

"Of course. Everyone is most pleased. But you do not drink coffee at the office?"

"No, actually. Maybe I'll have to start."

"And this box is your Christmas present."

"But I don't have one for you, so…"

"*Chut.*" He put his finger to his lips. "Come sit here beside me and open it."

It was a small square box that I unwrapped from beautiful silver and burgundy colored Christmas paper festooned with sparkly bells. The silver ribbon was tied in a curly bow and anchored with a seal that I didn't recognize. I opened it gingerly because it was too pretty to rip.

"Oh, it's a little camera!" I exclaimed, seeing the brand Canon. I turned to kiss him. "Thank you!"

"Well, open it further."

It was a "Canon Canonet 28 Walnut"…like the walnut paneling on a car's dashboard. It had a thick, tan leather shoulder strap and also a matching wrist band attachment.

"It takes 35mm film—there is a *pelicule* in the box, " he said, "and it is what they call 'point and shoot'. Do you like it?"

"Like it? What do you think?! I love it! I only have a Polaroid camera---very old that I got for my Bas Mitzvah, and a cheap Instamatic that I took to Europe. This is just such…a …real camera! Thank you so much!" And with that I flung my arms around his neck almost toppling him over.

"I am glad. We may take some photographs later, no?"

I nodded. What a sweet gift it was.

"Now, coffee. This *cafetière* was in my kitchen so it is already washed. And the coffee I have brought with me is of a coarse grind…that is important for the future when you must replenish it, *d'accord?*"

"Right."

"*Alors*, may we go into the kitchen and I shall show you how to make the coffee?"

"Yes, please."

I took the coffee pot and the package of *Carte Bleue*, and he took my arm. The trip to the kitchen was farther than to the bathroom, so we got there slowly, and he sat down at the little café table Dom and Peter had given me. From there he could call out the step-by-step instructions.

First I had to boil some water. I did not have an electric tea kettle, so we had to do it the old-fashioned way, which I knew would take a while. I put the kettle on the burner, and sat down across from him.

He looked at me and smiled and then, out of the blue, said, "I would imagine that you are lonely. Tell me, when is your loneliness the most unbearable---when you are sad or when you are happy?"

"Are **you** lonely?" I asked him purely as a rhetorical question; I couldn't believe he would be. What with the social whirl around him that I had observed first hand, I was taken aback that the word was even in his lexicon.

"It is I who asked you."

"Well, you actually didn't ask me," I chided him playfully. "You told me you thought I was. That's a little different. My friend Cass told me that too, awhile back, because she pictured me living by myself in this apartment, and expressed the idea that, ergo, I would be lonely." I paused, and then answered the question. "I don't really see myself as lonely. But, in all honesty, I suppose maybe I am sometimes." I fumbled around with the empty coffee cup on the table, and reposed my own question, "And are you?"

"Yes, Sarah. Most acutely since the death of my mother."

*Oh, boy, I didn't want to go **there** and invoke any more feelings of defensiveness on his part about Marie-Aveline d'Arivèque.*

I nodded, and didn't say anything.

The tea kettle whistled as if "calling time" and then, as though that entire conversation had never taken place, he got back to his coffee-making instructions. He said we had to wait a few minutes for the water to cool down a little bit, so he had me put the grounds in and shake the glass jar to settle them. Then, when he gave the word, I was to pour half of the hot water over the grounds.

"This is the bloom, " he said, and I had already heard that term from Dom when we made coffee by Chemex. For someone who didn't drink coffee at home, I sure was becoming "steeped," as it were, in the art of making it.

"You see, the hot water is allowing the aroma of the coffee to escape as a gas. Now we wait half a minute. Do you have a kitchen timer, *chérie*?"

"No," I started to say and remembered, "well, yes, my microwave oven does." I set it for thirty seconds. When time was up, he had me stir the coffee gently to break up a crust of coffee grounds that had formed, and mix them with the water before adding the remaining hot water.

"Now put the lid on it with the plunger pulled all the way up. It must steep for four minutes. Set the *micro* timer again, yes?"

When the timer went off for the second time, Polo told me to slowly lower the press all the way down to filter the grounds from the coffee.

"*Voilà*! You did it. Now we drink."

"It's good!" I exclaimed with some surprise as I tasted mine. "Needs sugar, though, don't you think?"

"No, no, I take mine just black. And you know, *cafetière à piston* coffee cannot be kept for long, " he added as we drank it. "It will become bitter."

As we sat there, he looked up from his cup and smiled at me. I felt it was safe enough to venture back into the conversation on loneliness.

"I'm sorry you're lonely, Polo."

"It is ameliorated since you, " he said, "since you came to *La Fondation*."

"So tell me about this woman you loved who called off your engagement at the last minute. The French one, you mentioned."

"Oh, no, she did not call it off ---I had not yet proposed marriage to her. Her name was Marie-Bénédicte, and as I told you, we had grown up together at *La Pérégrine*. Our parents were close friends. She was some years younger than me—I forget these details now. We spent many summers and other holidays together, and we were good for each other—both *enfant unique*—only child. We liked to ride horses, and enjoyed life in the country many weekends together with our families.

"When the war broke out, and I was obliged to leave France, as I explained to you, I did not see her at all for more than ten years. However, *Maman* remained in contact from New York with her family, so we did write letters, too, as teenagers hoping one day to reunite."

He took out a cigarette from the pocket of his robe, and lit it with that beautiful gold lighter. He sat there smoking and drinking coffee as he continued the narrative.

"When I arrived in Paris to further my studies, she was still in *Lycée* in the Loire region. But when I began *HEC*, she was by then eighteen years old and at *La Sorbonne*. So we made a *rendez-vous* at a café Place de la Sorbonne. When I arrived I saw that she was so taken aback at the sight of how I looked, that she could not hide her shock. She even expressed something akin to surprise at my being out in public. The French, as you may realize, tend to hide away their *handicappés*, especially in those days."

I shook my dead dejectedly, "Yeah, I know."

"Well, Marie-Bénédicte, she… could scarcely bring herself to look at me. *La pauvre*. She tried to be kind, but she admitted to me that my physical condition horrified her."

"But, that must have horrified **you**."

"You know, many people look away when I am on the street, even here. But in France, *effectivement*--I believe-- it is much worse. Marie-Bénédicte did stay and talk with me that afternoon. She was pleasant enough, but she made it quite clear that she could not be with me as I was…so different than before. She was honest."

" Well, I guess…in a way, then…her honesty was kind. I'm still sad that that happened to you." I looked at him and put the question out there. "So, was she the great love of your life?"

He didn't answer my question, but instead posed a different one.

561

"What about you? That man…your doctor *nouvelorleanais* whom I met in the hospital. He called you darling."

"That's just an expression where he comes from. He's the one who found the lump in my breast."

"Oh? He was examining you — as your doctor then?"

"No. He found it in the shower."

He stared at me trying to disguise his obvious amazement. "*Ah bon? Alors, you…vous deux* — were taking a shower together?"

"Yes."

"So he was your love?"

"Lover, more like," I said, smirking a little sheepishly at the word. "We weren't together long enough for me to find out if it would be a great love. But I'll tell you this: he and I never could have married."

"Because?"

I didn't want to "bore him with my life's story" and I didn't want the conversation to be redirected towards me.

"Oh, for a lot of reasons. But I asked you first. What was up with Marie-Bénédicte to make her react that way? She already knew you and you two had been very close! For heaven's sake, she must have realized you'd spent all that time in a hospital and all."

It really made me wonder if her response to his physical appearance was at the heart of his being unable to trust the motives of women he might meet.

"Yes, Sarah. I thought that I loved her. Perhaps I only loved the idea of her. And in the past at that. The way she treated me at the café astonished me, I must admit. I had never even considered that would happen."

"Yeah, I really do not understand that, and I don't get why some people can't handle seeing handicapped persons. But I suppose the other extreme is that you get stared at by strangers, right?"

"That is true, yes. The thing is, Sarah, I understand how people are nervous about their emotional responses. They do not know how to act, and they would never simply just engage in conversation, and ask what happened to me. "

"No, I don't suppose so. I mean, the truth is that that would seem too invasive of your privacy."

We finished the coffee with baguette that he'd brought, and sat in the kitchen awhile before he touched my hand.

"*Alors*, would you invade my privacy by taking a shower with me?" he teased.

"Oh, I think that could be arranged." I wondered, though, because I suspected he had a walk-in shower at his place, and I sure didn't. "I only have a tub and shower combo, though."

" Yes, I noticed, " he laughed. "That will perhaps take a bit of doing, I am afraid."

I was nude under my robe, but he still had on his tee shirt and shorts from the night, so those had to come off. I put a chair from my dinette table in the bathroom, and even though it was a tight squeeze, that was eminently helpful. I could easily take off his boxers, but the tee posed other problems. In the end, with both of us doing it, the clothing issues were resolved insofar as removal went.

We then studied the tub situation together.

"If I act as the railing and you take a hold of me, can you step into the tub with your good leg and then bring the other one in?" I asked, pondering the direction of the water and depth of the side of the tub.

"I cannot, I do not believe, put my own leg over the side."

"Hmmm. Do you think if I lifted your weak leg into the tub first, and held onto to you, you could put weight on it just long enough to be able to put the right one in?"

"Perhaps — if you held onto me. But Sarah, as I told you in Delevan that day, I am heavy." He surveyed the tub height again, and contemplated the situation for a moment, and then decided that it shouldn't be attempted after all. "I feel that if my leg gave out, you would not be able to keep me from falling."

"Yes, I worry about that, too. Okay, what about this: I put the chair in the tub and you turn your back to it, and then I help you sit down on it. Once seated, you turn your torso a little bit, and I'll lift your legs into the tub. Then with your cane, and my help, you can stand up, and I'll take away the chair."

"I believe that will work. We shall manage, *non*? Shall we try it?"

I was happy that I'd come up with a potential solution, but something else flashed in my mind I was suddenly hit with the realization that we had another problem.

"The other trouble with all this is," I said, " bathtubs are slick, and if either of us should slip…and go down, it would be *la cata complète*!" I looked up at him and I suddenly bursting into giggles at the thought of us flailing around like that. "It's not funny, " I said, still convulsed in laughter, which made him start to laugh also, "but my God, that would be worse than the Keystone Kops." Regaining composure, I announced, "I'm going to put a towel down on the bottom of the tub. Fuck it."

So that's how we managed to both get in. It was too delicious to be naked next to each other again and not start to caress and kiss. He had a hold of my arm and pulled me gently closer to him and said, "You are so lovely."

If I were blushing, the hot water would have perhaps hidden my red face, and if I were crying, the running water would disguise that, too. I didn't know how to respond to what he said, so I just looked up at him and smiled. But I didn't believe it for a second. If I was so "lovely" why had I gone through three years of high school without a single date?

He was balancing okay on the cane so I stepped farther into the water and shampooed my hair. I took soap and lathered up, dividing the foamy bubbles between us. He laughed and blew some back in my face, and then letting the cane fall away, he held me again. We just stood there, wasting water and time.

Finally, I turned off the taps and picked up his cane from the wet towel on the tub floor. Getting out loomed harder than getting in. For one thing, being wet, he might slide off the chair! I got out and threw one towel around me, and put my hair in another. Feeling happy that I had actually bought new towels, I took one of my nicest ones, put it around his torso, folding in the ends. I brought the chair back into the tub behind him.

"What I want you to do, " I explained, " is to very slowly sit down."

He did it. "Yes? And now?"

"Here, hold your cane for equilibrium and swivel to the side, so that I can lift your legs up ."

"Like so?" he said, doing it.

"Yes. Now scoot using your good arm and leg as close to the edge as you can."

He was then sitting near the rim of the tub, facing the room. Once I gave him the cane, he could use it to stand down. He was out. He then handed it back off to me, and grabbed ahold of the vanity in order to get his bearings in front of the mirror. I replaced the chair on the floor so he could be seated again to dry off.

"Piece of cake, " I said sarcastically, making a flourish with my hand.

"*Tu es génial!*" he laughed.

"Yeah, well maybe, but I have a feeling we might just skip this tomorrow, you think?" I giggled.

But I had to wonder if he weren't pretty damned relieved something awful hadn't happened. This bathtub situation had required a lot more logistics and worry than it should have. Mine had no handrails of any kind! Able-bodied though I was, I realized then and there that if I should ever slip, there wouldn't be one thing to grab hold of, except maybe the shower curtain, which would no doubt come crashing down. I'd be buying a proper tub mat the day after Christmas!

In the end, I had a feeling he couldn't wait to get back to civilization.

Chapter Ninety-Seven

"A Song for You"...Leon Russell

Jean-Paul d'Arivèque's and my two and a half-day, self-imposed Christmas confinement was filled with *le pique-nique* in my living room, *la cour amoureuse* in my bedroom, and music everywhere. And this time the tables were turned. No longer Galatea to his Pygmalion, I brought out record after record of my own choices with which to school him. I had the requisite Fairport Convention, Simon and Garfunkel, Joan Baez, Laura Nyro and Joni Mitchell, plus the Beach Boys, The Beatles (!—well, he knew them, at least), Carol King's short-lived group The City, Leon Russell, Antonio Carlos Jobim, my signed Phil Woods album, Jefferson Airplane, soundtracks from *The Fantasticks, The King and I, Fiddler on the Roof, A Man and A Woman*, and a few other random recordings like *Pentangle* and the one Rolling Stones record I'd bought by that time, *Between the Buttons*.

"But how is it that you love all these different genres?" he asked rather stupefied as he spread out all my albums on the couch. "You have these rock and roll — *euh* — folk rock? — *un mélange, quoi?*-- Bossa Nova, jazz, Broadway show tunes and film music! And I know you like baroque and medieval. Choirs and madrigal, too...and much classical music, yes? And what is more, you love cars!" he laughed.

I laughed, too. "So how come you find it strange? You love a ton of music, and you're so knowledgeable about it. I can't quote even one composer's dates; you know them all. You're the one who rubs shoulders with every classical 'star' who comes to Chicago, let's not forget."

"Yes, yes, perhaps. But I do not follow the range of music that you do. I am stuck in past centuries, I fear."

"Then you might want to get acquainted with our times, *Monsieur*, because believe this or not, we've just gone through-- and are still in-- another true Renaissance. That's not just my opinion, of course. My college boyfriend who was passing through here — you remember? — is writing on this topic now in New York. He's got a big spread in *Rock Scene* –that's a magazine — about the rock and roll explosion. I think it's going to make him famous!"

"Were you also in love with him?"

"What?"

Where had that come from?

"I...uh...well, we ...um, yes I suppose so. But it never would have worked out. Both sets of parents were against us. I didn't care so much about mine, but he did about his."

"So they managed to come between you? *Les parents?*"

"Yeah, sort of. He showed courage, though, in quitting law school and moving away from Iowa and his parents' expectations of him."

"And you? Did you also rebuff yours?"

" Oh, I do that just by breathing."

I wanted to make light of it, but I saw he was serious.

"Polo, it's a little hard to explain, you know? I don't have a good relationship with my parents. I never have. Things with them didn't really hinge on me and Soren."

I didn't expect someone like Jean-Paul d'Arivèque who, from everything I could discern had had an idyllic rapport with his parents, to be able to relate to what my home life had been like, and I really didn't feel like dwelling on it.

"One of my professors at college said something to the effect that very few people have the great fortune to grow up in a home with good parenting. I think maybe you did. I didn't."

"But look at you! You are wonderful."

"No, I'm not. You just think that because we're in this first...call it... 'honeymoon' phase... of our friendship...or love... even. We put our best self out there and keep our worst tendencies hidden. But deep down we know, don't we? That we are less admirable than we would wish to be. We keep all our flaws a secret, " I said, "but we go around weighted down with the guilty knowledge of what imperfect little humans we are."

Before he could answer, I hastily added, "Not that I'm saying you do."

"Yes, Sarah... I agree with you. I am, however, rather startled by your insight into this!"

"So **you**, you are probably that rare person who was parented well. You lost your father at a young age, and that was tragic, of course, but you obviously got healthy feedback from your mother and your uncle, and that provided you with an inner structure...sort of a scaffolding, which allowed you to deal with your — uh---imperfections."

"I cannot disagree with what you are saying; it is true."

"Well, see, it didn't seem to matter what I did. I only got criticized and belittled and marginalized by my parents, especially Sol, my dad. My mother's role was passive. She never would confront him or stand up for me. I always felt he and I didn't get along, and that he was an authoritarian ogre, but, looking back on it, her refusal to ever defend me to him made her even the more abusive parent."

"I cannot believe what I am hearing. You are –how do they call it in psychological terms?-- high functioning! You are bright, happy, and your innocent enthusiasm for all things fires up the room every time you walk in! I have seen this time and again with you. It must be genuine; you could not *faire semblance*...pretend... all the time."

"Yes, well, I guess I got pretty good at compensating. When I was young, I came to terms with my — uh-- feelings of unworthiness at home by throwing myself into school. School was always a refuge for me, and I liked to please teachers enough to get their praise, which I did...sometimes — ha! Not always! And as for work, well, it's not the same thing, of course. I'm not doing it for your praise, although...that's always nice, don't get me wrong, " I laughed. "I just love what I'm doing now. I do believe...I'm sure... I am happy here in Chicago."

"But, if you say you have feelings of unworthiness. That does not manifest at the office, I must tell you. But, do you doubt your ability to be loved? Are you inhibited from accepting love when it is offered?"

"Maybe. I try to fight against that, though, and accept love when it comes along. But just when is that? We don't always know. I mean, there're a lot of different kinds of love. I have had friends whom I truly love, but it isn't romantic. I think I could have loved Clément de Seignard, if you must know ---that family you and your mother knew in Paris, remember? And yet, one night his friends took me aside and told me-- right up front-- essentially, that because I was American and a Jew to boot, it had to be understood that I'd have to forget any ideas of a long-term relationship with him. I mean, they were nice enough about it, they liked me, but even so it was the same thing rearing its ugly head. So, see, it's mostly always about non-acceptance."

"That seems cruel."

"But Polo, it was also cruelty with Marie-Bénédicte... from what you told me, *n'est-ce pas?*"

He shook his head. "I believe it was shock more than anything else."

"Anyway, the fact of the matter is that I couldn't have married my college boyfriend, Soren, for the same reasons I couldn't have married Clément. And certainly not Dr. Pax Hubley, either. None of those families would have accepted me as a wife for their sons."

"I cannot believe that."

"Believe it. It's true. But in the end, that's all a moot point. I never was in the market for a husband when I was dating any of them!"

"But Sarah, you do not present this carefree, happy 'personality' to the world simply as a defense against rejection, do you? I cannot fathom that you would be able to carry off such a thing! Therefore, perhaps I think, rather, you might fear commitment?"

"Oh, I don't think that's it. Hell, I might even have gone ahead and married either Clément or Soren, but, in the end, it was rejection that was on the horizon, not fear of commitment."

I shoved some albums to the side and sat down next to him on the sofa. I wasn't sure he believed me, but I just put it out there and was being honest. He drew me closer again and stroked my hair, lost in thought.

Finally, he looked at me and said, "And you are wrong about me, too, *chérie*. I am also damaged...but my damage shows. If you are flawed, as you say, you hide it well."

"Oh, come on, now. You're the one in this room who knew St. Exupéry! Personally! '*L'essentiel est invisible pour les yeux.*' No more discussion on that score."

565

He laughed, but then got quiet again, put his arm back around me, and said, "I can tell that you do not fear intimacy, but Sarah, I do---or I did, before you. You made it safe for me to act on my feelings for you. You did that for me! You met me, and instead of dreading being seen with me, you showed that you enjoyed my company... in public, too...for who I am and not what I own."

"Okay, let me be completely up front here. It is-- you have to admit-- a little **hard** to ignore what you own, and anyone would be an idiot if they weren't impressed by it. But I could tell right away you were not someone who hid behind your wealth or flaunted it either...you were lucky that your family was able to use that wealth to help shield you from the hardships of the world and the viciousness of other people. Like Sartre said..."

"*Oui,--'l'enfer c'est les autres'.*"

"Exactly."

"Yes, I had an insular upbringing by a very protective and loving mother, but, I am sorry to admit, that rather than protecting me from the world, it only reinforced in me the belief that my physical limitations were *unique au monde...* and that loneliness was my *véritable* destiny because of this. I do not blame *Maman*. She did not intend for me to be alone, I am sure. In fact, *au contraire.*"

I pulled out from under his arm, and repositioned myself to hug him tight.

Vulnerability was about the last thing I expected to see in this man who, his braced leg and weak arm notwithstanding, was embodiment of perfection! The most intelligent, warm, caring, kind, cultured, erudite, sweet, and yes, wealthiest!-- person I'd ever met in my entire life. Any woman would have – should have---been considered the luckiest one on the face of the earth to have him in her arms, and here she was: me! Here he was---right there on my couch, loving and wanting to be loved by: me! Someone will surely wake me up from this dream!

"Oh, Polo. I do love you... so much. Gosh, this happened so fast!"

"Not fast at all, *mon chou*. I have loved you for such a very long time."

It wasn't as though I didn't have grave reservations about becoming the boss' lover. It smacked of stereotype and stupidity. In novels, movies and soap-operas, it never turned out well. Even if my heart didn't know—or give a damn—my head knew this was opening a potential Pandora's box of anguish and woe. Every fiber of my being was sending up an alarm to end this before I got in waaaay over my head. And yet, there I was, giving in to my deepening feelings of bliss and joy. How weak we humans are, I thought. How fragile.

By the time Jean-Luc was set to return, and put an end to our little love-in, my apartment looked the worse for wear. I put on *Revolver*, and sang along to it as I busied myself picking the place up, doing dishes and even laundry, all the while watched by Polo who, I gathered, was amused at this domestic energy.

"I really love these songs. "Here, There and Everywhere" is one of my all-time faves. And I used to iron in in my basement to "Eleanor Rigby.""

"Íron?"

"*Le repassage.'*

"*Mais...comment ça?* You did it for yourself?"

"For the whole family."

"*Mon Dieu.*"

Yep, another French person stupefied by the idea that I did the ironing. It was déjà vue *all over again, as Yogi would have put it.*

"*Non, non...c'est normal.*"

He had a hard time fathoming that, I suppose, given he'd never seen his own mother do anything of the sort, and probably had never even watched a maid do it either.

"Sarah, you work too much. You really must come to my home this week. The office will still be closed, and for *Le Saint Sylvestre*, the maestro and his wife will be in Chicago and want to celebrate with us."

"Us?"

"Yes, he specifically mentioned hoping to see you. Please say you will be there."

"Well, it's not like I have any other dates for New Year's Eve!" I kidded him, leaning over to kiss him on the cheek.

"I have an idea which I would like you to implement. You come with me and Jean-Luc this afternoon and drive *la Pallas* back here. That way you shall have a car and can go where you like. You can drive it to work and to do shopping. You will no longer have to carry provisions, etc. I shall have Luc put a house key with the car key, and then you may come to my home any time you like ."

"But..."

"I know. You do not wish to see Robineau. *Ne t'en fais pas.* I shall take care of him."

I gave a little smirk. It occurred to me that now he was the one being naïve.

"I can't just show up at your place unannounced! Your staff will think that very odd!"

"Hear me out. As far as I am concerned you may come in by the front door any time you like. But since you will be parking underground, you come into the garage and you may enter the house by the door we use *d'habitude* when we get the cars. Once inside, you take the elevator directly to my apartment. *Voilà!* Unless you happen to run into my staff downstairs, no one will even know you are in the house. And, as you realize full well, the people who work for me--in spite of anything Robineau has said to them-- they love you. *Je m'en occuperai....de cette situation avec Robineau.* I shall sort it out."

And with that, I had a car...in Chicago! I had actually forgotten---or repressed-- the wonderful feeling of freedom a car could afford someone. I took it for a drive up to Evanston and to a good old suburban supermarket with an acre of parking! (The stares I got in that parking lot! Whoa! Citroëns were not the norm!)

Mid-week after our Christmas tryst, I tried out Polo's plan. It worked like a charm, and when I thus found myself snuggled into his bed, which was huge, it goes without saying, I brought up another subject that had been weighing heavily on me.

"Polo, I'm not on the pill. And I'm worried about becoming pregnant. So...I brought these." I had picked up condoms in Evanston and, even though I couldn't find the lambskin kind Pax had used, I hoped the regular ones would be okay with my new--- boyfriend? Lover? *Oy vey.*

He smiled at me. "Yes, Sarah, I , too have thought of that. You do not, of course, wish to have a baby when you are not married."

"Oh, God, no! A baby would absolutely ruin my life whether it was out of wedlock or under any circumstances. I just pray I wasn't ovulating this weekend, ha ha!"

He looked at me and smiled again, but this time the smile was half sad, which I noticed, but let pass without discussion.

"So you won't mind wearing one of these? " I asked tentatively.

"No, no. I also have some. I keep them here, " he said, pointing to the side table.

"Oh, good! Whew."

One of these days, I'd have to get a diaphragm or else, I didn't know, some IUD... or something.

"But, Sarah...will you be able to help me put it on?"

"Oh,... sure thing. Hard to do with one hand, eh?" *I wondered how the hell he had done it ...or if he had... with other women?*

"Well, I can do it, but it is, well, perhaps a bit...shall we say taxing," he laughed nervously.

"Hey, it's not going to be a problem," I tried to reassure him.

But then he looked at me point blank and said, "And were you shocked to discover that I am circumcised?"

HUH?! Jeeesus.

"Noooo. I...don't know anyone who isn't." I looked away hoping to hide my acute embarrassment at being asked that question!

"It is not common in France for baby boys to be circumcised as newborns unless they are Jewish or Arab, you know."

"I did not know that."

As a student in Paris I hadn't slept with anyone yet, let alone Clément or any other Frenchman, for that matter. But if I had, I admit that it might have come as a rather rude shock.

"So when *Maman* found out that here in the States doctors do this as a matter of routine for baby boys... regardless of religion...she asked them to do mine."

"What?! When you were a teenager?"

567

"Yes, but I was put under general anesthesia, you know, more than a dozen times."

"Oh, right. So during one of those operations on your leg?"

"*C'est ça. Maman* was concerned about the hygiene."

"Hmmm," I nodded. Nothing for **me** to comment on.

It was almost easier in my tiny bed finding the optimal positions than in his big one, because in mine, there were few choices. We would start out facing each other very close together and there was nowhere else to go... I would just turn and he would lift me a bit to be on top. But in his bed, we had all the room in the world, so he could maneuver on top of me without having to worry that he couldn't use his left arm to aid in this process.

"My arm is not very mobile, as you know, " he explained to me, "but also, the shoulder-- it has pain."

"Oh, shit, Polo. I don't want to be the cause of you being in pain."

"No, no, you shall not. *On va se débrouiller.*"

He could **say** we'd figure it out, but I was still worried. I was worried all the time about him and pain... that pain had landed him in the hospital. It must have been unbearable. Thinking I might hurt him when we made love scared me and made me tense up.

I needn't have been so concerned, though, because he smiled and kissed me tenderly as he drew me near. We slid together as smoothly as we had in the daybed. Our rhythm was in perfect tune to one another, and we reveled in the breathless, and very hot, joy of being together. He was such a gentleman and a gentle man. He made me realize that in the arms of Soren, neither of us had known exactly what we were doing; and that even though Pax was an experienced lover, it now became abundantly clear that we had both been partaking in the act of pleasuring mainly him. Jean-Paul d'Arivèque seemed to know exactly what he was doing, and in such a way as to thrill me. I knew then and there that I would learn wonderful things from him and that I could relax and let go.

"So, " he said, after we'd made love, and he was sitting up in bed, smoking a Gauloise, "we are agreed for the thirty-first, yes?"

"Sure. I'll be here."

"*Très bien.* Now, we have three whole days in which to do things this week. What would you like to do?"

"Oh, gosh...wow...I don't know. Go to the movies? See a play? What do **you** want to do?" I couldn't believe he saw the work hiatus as a time to frolic with me.

"I should like very much to see your home...your hometown. Perhaps meet your family?"

"Excuse me?!"

Oh, crap.

"Are you serious? That's an eight-hour car trip---longer with stops along the way. You wouldn't want to ride in a car that long, would you?"

Please say no.

"I have an airplane."

"Yeah, well...um... huh-uh...no. I can't see us doing that. I'm sorry."

Godalmighty, where had he come up with this idea? That would have been about the last thing I needed to do...show up at home unannounced with some goyishe *man almost old enough to be my father. Not a good idea at all. He had no clue.*

"Very well, it is all right. Let us in that case drive to Iowa City. Just we two. You would, of course, have to do the driving."

"Why do you want to go there!?" I asked, again, completely taken off guard.

"Because, Sarah, it is important in your life, and I should like to see where you spent some of your past. I should like to connect with your life—your formative years-- in some way. "

"Well, okaaaay. It's three hours from here, too, by the way."

"Yes, and I believe we could make the trip in one day...without staying overnight, no? Do you think it possible?"

"Sure."

568

"Very well then! The day after tomorrow? Come for me at around eight in the morning. We could be there in time for lunch. We can go to all your student-days places, and then have dinner and drive back. It would be very nice, I think, to spend all that time with you together… just the two of us alone."

Chapter Ninety-Eight

"A 200 à l'Heure"...Francis Lai

I was rather surprised that no one insisted we use the limo on our day trip. Jean-Luc had put up no roadblocks to taking the Cit out on the highway this time, even though it was still winter and it was the same car that no mechanic would know how to fix if it broke down. I guess they thought if Polo were with me, we could face whatever might happen together, as opposed to my being alone with the car.

The day of our adventure dawned with fair skies, but still freezing cold temperatures out. However, the forecast was for clear and dry weather, which meant the same for the roads. Lucky.

I loaded the tape deck with as many of my faves as I could, and got to Polo's house at the appointed early hour. We didn't take any food with us, thinking that it would be too cold out to eat it even in the car. But he had brought a very beautiful and modern-designed thermos container of *Carte Bleue* and some Styrofoam cups. He handed me an Hermès tote bag with the provisions, and I placed it behind me on the floor.

Polo was not used to riding in the front seat of any car. For one thing, when he sat on the passenger side, it meant his brace leg had to go in first. So he unlocked it, but that caused it to collapse immediately and gave him precious little time to get in. He had to position himself far enough in before he did that, so he would sort of fall onto the seat. I stayed outside the car on his side to see that he made it okay, and to take the cane.

I had to fight a little bit of in-city rush hour traffic, but by the time I was heading towards Interstate 80, we were going against the congestion coming into Chicago, and it was smooth sailing in that magnificent automobile that gave you the feeling of riding on a water bed.

"This is the world's greatest car, " I reiterated to Polo, as I dialed up *Vivre pour Vivre* on the stereo system. He smiled and patted my knee.

"You are a splendid driver. Jean-Luc has already told me this, but I see for myself. He gave you the highest compliment, you know. "

"Really? What was that?"

"He said, 'She drives like a man.'"

We drank the first cups of his wonderful coffee at a rest-stop just west of Naperville. It was a pretty locale, as was that little town, the parts of it, that is, that I could see from the train on my various trips back and forth. The rest stop had parking on one level, but the actual building with the bathrooms was on a higher one. There were no steps but the incline was rather steep up there, so I walked with Polo and when we got to the little brick enclosure, he kissed me as we went our separate ways inside. I waited for him; the downward return trip could be trickier than the climb, just as going downstairs was often scarier for him than going up them.

The ride into Iowa City was smooth and uneventful. I asked Polo about some of the topics I'd had in mind to bring up when he was at my apartment, but hadn't gotten the chance: namely his childhood and holidays in Paris and at *La Pérégrine*.

"In all honesty, *chérie*, I do not have many memories of Christmas. I do recall at some point we were with all my grandparents there...in the country... I must have been very young."

"Were you completely spoiled?" I laughed, thinking I could assume the answer...only child of nobility and all. "Did you always get everything you wanted?"

"I cannot fathom that, but I think you may be right, " he conceded.

Then we talked about Annie-Laure's wedding which was going to be held there, the orchestration it would take to transport something like forty-five guests from America on the private jet to Paris, then on to the Loire Valley.

"So, how will we all get to the town nearest to where the château is?" I wondered.

"That would be Vierzon, " he told me. "I shall arrange for a coach to meet you at Orly, and perhaps it will drive all the way; or else, you shall take the train. Marie-France is looking into all that."

"Ha ha! When I hear the word coach, I think of something gold, shaped like a pumpkin and drawn by white horses. I know you're rich, but that would be hard even for you, " I feigned wonder.

"But, it is a bus to you Americans, *non*? "

"Yeah, I know. I was just teasing you. I took a coach tour of the entire country of France one time."

We had made even better time than I'd envisioned, arriving in Iowa City well before noon. The town was pretty deserted with Christmas break still in full swing. I parked in the downtown area right outside of the bookstore.

"We used to call this place Iowa Book and Crook, " I cheekily told him, gesturing over to it.

We walked across Clinton Street to the Pentacrest. Old Capital was open.

"Do you want to go in?" I felt my inner tour guide coming alive. "This was, as the name tells you, the State capital. It has a cool rotunda, doesn't it? 'Course, it's no *Invalides!*"

"Very beautiful, " he remarked.

"Upstairs it's like a museum almost---they have the Supreme Court room designed to show how the lawmakers must have seen it. Let's go up there and have a look. There's no charge."

He shot me a funny look, perplexed, perhaps, that my concern for cost should be a factor. "Happily."

"Old habits die hard? " I laughed, as I directed him towards the elevator.

"When did this place cease to be the capital?" he asked.

"Oh, in the 1850's or so, I'm sure. Oh wait, there's a plaque. It says it was built in 1842 and the capital moved to Des Moines in 1856. How 'bout that! I wasn't far off. It also says it was the first building on the U of Iowa campus."

The upstairs wowed me, but to a Frenchman, this was neither a very old building, nor a very elegant one, even though the room had a colonial splendor about it. But even if JPA was not impressed, he acted as if he were.

Afterwards, we headed over to Schaefer Hall.

"Home of the French and Italian department, " I announced. "Want to see a classroom? I think they're probably unlocked."

"Oh, yes...I am interested."

"'Course, there's nothing much to see in these classrooms. Most college ones resemble each other. Not like in the Sorbonne, of course."

"It pleases me to see anywhere you were here." He reached over and hugged me.

We next drove over to the residence halls, where there were always some students staying through the vacation, so they, too, were open. I showed him those infamous purple and pink kidney-shaped love seats in the Burge lobby, and then we went outside to have a look at Kate Daum.

"No use going in, " I said. "Nothing to see, and we can't get into our old room. I guess you'll just have to **imagine** Sari and Cass and our mad, gay, exciting dorm life."

As Cass would, no doubt, have described it.

I drove down to the Iowa Memorial Union, whose main entry presented no steps to get in the building, but a lot of stupid ones to get up to the main floor. Luckily there was a good railing and I only had to pay attention to his left side and hold the cane so he could use the metal banister. We took the elevator to the River Room and had our –late, by now-- lunch up there.

"This is where Alan Jones and the grad students from the famous writing program, the Iowa Writers' Workshop, hung out, " I explained. "I came here sometimes with my poetry classmates, too, but mostly Cass' and my haunts were in the basement where the Goldfeather and Wheel Rooms are."

"Then may we see those also?"

"Naturally! We'll go down there and then out to the bridge leading to the art building and the museum. I'll bet you didn't know this, but our—or rather the University's—ha ha—art collection includes some of the most famous paintings in the world."

"I did not know it," Polo responded with mock seriousness.

"I'm not lying! We have this Jackson Pollock that he gave to Peggy Guggenheim and she later duly gave it to Iowa. You'll see it, it's called *Mural*. And then we have a Max Beckmann triptych called *Karneval* that's really famous, too. I used to go over to the museum all the time when I was a student, just to hang out and look at those two. Plus there's a Miró, a Rothko one, and a pretty well-known collage by Lois Nevelson. And then there's Grant Wood. You recognize that name, right?"

"Yes, vaguely."

"He was born in Cedar Rapids, which is right near here, and he went to the Art Institute of Chicago, and also to Paris, and then taught painting here! He's Iowa's most famous artist and his stuff is iconic. Can you picture it?"

"I believe so, " Polo answered.

"You'll know it the minute you see it."

I also explained that we would be seeing the Lasansky pencil drawings and intaglio prints, and I expounded a long time on exactly who he was. "Cass's whole reason for coming to Iowa was to work with Mauricio Lasansky, " I said. "Even after all the years-- and all her disclaimers to the contrary--I'm still unconvinced that someone of her means and family ties to Eastern schools should have ever chosen Iowa. But I'm so glad she did."

We made our way out to the bridge as I had described to him, and across the Iowa River over to the art school and thence to the museum, where my French art collector friend was genuinely impressed by what he saw. As we turned to leave two hours later, who should I see on the brick walkway between the two buildings, but Professor Klampert!

"I can't believe this, " I said to Polo. "There's Cass' professor and mentor! I had a couple of classes from him, too."

He caught sight of me and stopped in his tracks.

"Sarah Shrier! How are you?"

"Professor Klampert!" We shook hands. "I'd like you to meet Mr. Jean-Paul d'Arivèque from Chicago."

"How do you do?" he said, offering his hand.

"Very nice to meet you, " said Polo.

"Please come into my office for a few minutes. Warm up."

I looked at Polo who nodded. "Thanks!" I said. I knew he wanted to find out about Cass, and I, unfortunately, had precious little information yet.

"Your office is very nice!" I exclaimed, as though seeing it for the first time.

"Yes, it's been, shall we say, upgraded since you were a student here," he laughed. His boyish good looks had not at all diminished over the years. His blond hair still fell onto his face, where it still parted like curtains and revealed those incredible azure blue eyes. Unlike when he was teaching, this day he was wearing a plaid flannel shirt with the sleeves pushed up, and a turtleneck underneath it, and jeans. He must have been working in the studio.

"Mr. d'Arivèque is my boss at the *Fondation Culturel Française* in Chicago. I'm the film librarian."

"She is now the Director of Education, more precisely, " Polo corrected me.

"That's outstanding, Sari, " he said. "Good for you!"

"Thanks, " I said, a little embarrassed over the whole thing. "Mr. d'Arivèque has an important collection of French art in his home and in our office. If you are ever in Chicago, you must come by and see it."

"I will! Thank you." And then he got down to the matter at hand. "Sooo, what news of Cass Hyde do you have?"

"Well, they moved, as you know, to El Paso, and I just haven't heard from her yet. I don't know if they even have a phone."

"Well, let me put it this way: will you write and let me know her news when you hear from her? I sure hope she continues her work out there."

"Me, too. And I'll certainly keep you informed." I turned to Polo and added, "You know, he let me park my car on the driveway at his house near here for a whole year!"

"Very fortunate for you, was it not?"

"I'll say."

Polo told him a little bit about the Foundation and his mother's art collection until we decided we'd better let Klampert get back to what he was doing before he invited us in. As we were leaving, my former professor and I hugged each other and he and Polo shook hands again.

"Well," I said when we were back outside, "you wanted to see what was important to me here …he was probably the most influential person in Cass' life her whole time at the U. She never did have master classes with Lasansky. "

We drove out to Alan and Cass' dilapidated farmhouse next, and the place looked a complete wreck. Some remains of their old stuff had been removed from the house and were just set out on the gravel drive and hadn't even been picked up yet.

"I suppose the landlord is redoing some of this and getting it ready for new tenants, " I said, almost as if to convince myself. "It sure looks like a dump."

"And they lived with their babies here?" he asked, as though that were some sort of abomination. His reaction was not unlike Betty's when she saw my studio that one time.

"Yes, this was their home."

We couldn't get off that property fast enough, and I next drove over to the summer apartment Cass and I had shared. "My absolute happiest time was spent here," I told him.

And finally, I took him down Brown Street and my senior-year digs.

"There is it, " I announced as we stood in front of my former house. "You've now seen my entire life at the University of Iowa. I hope you've enjoyed your tour," I joshed.

"I do like it here, " he said. "I wish I had been here with you."

"I wish you'd been in Paris with me," I said wistfully, and meant it. "That whole year I would see couples…nothing but couples…on the *quais*, at the *bouquinistes*, on the bridges, in the parks, and all I could think of was what heaven it must be to be in love in Paris!"

"Come here." He drew me close and kissed me. "Could it not be just as heavenly to be in love in Iowa City?"

We stood there for a few minutes, just embracing in public as though we **were** in Paris, not caring who saw us.

"I guess love is great in any locale, isn't it?" I finally said. And with that, I led him carefully across the uneven brick street and back to the car. I wanted to give him a look around Iowa City's downtown… Things, Whetstone's drugstore, the music shop and the stores. After that, we went over to have an early dinner at The Mill.

"Did you used to eat here quite a lot?" he asked, sampling a piece of stromboli. "It tastes very good!"

"You bet." I pointed towards an interior door. "We came often to hear live music in there."

We lingered over dinner as I talked about college…Cass' and my dorm life, her studio art, and my nearly scandalous brush with a lunatic professor who falsely accused me of a serious offense which I had not committed.

"If you think you can even imagine the *sturm und drang* I would have been subjected to from my parents had he prevailed, or had I not been able to prove my innocence, you can't! It would have been a complete plunge into hell for me."

"*Dieu merci, alors*--- that he did not destroy your university career. But the friend of Marie-France, she helped you, *non*? She would not have allowed a false accusation against you to stand, *voyons*."

"She did help---she believed me over him. Luckily it never came to a hearing, but he still ruined my grade point average and kept me out of Phi Beta Kappa."

"*Alors, là…c'est injuste.*"

"Well, in the end…you know…*tout est bien qui finit bien* and all that. I landed the best job imaginable!"

Darkness had descended, and the Mill shimmered with the Christmas lights that were still up. We realized we had better hit the road. I got back behind the wheel and headed out onto an inky landscape, lit only by passing semi-trailer trucks. We didn't talk much on the return trip; for one thing I was concentrating hard on night driving. The Citroën headlamps were superb, and the way it handled and hugged the road made driving it pure joy. Still, it was a good distance before we'd be reach Chicago.

We pulled right into the city at one in the morning, and got to Polo's home pretty exhausted but happy.

"It was fun, wasn't it?" I said.

"You know I had a marvelous time there with you. Thank you for doing all that driving. I saw for myself that you are a technically superb driver. It must be because you love it."

"I suppose that's why anyone does anything well, " I laughed. "Tennis on the other hand…don't ask!"

I didn't stay over that night, but drove right back to my little apartment and, instead of collapsing right then and there, I sat down with a notebook and wrote a five-page letter to Cass. I had an earth-shattering amount of pent-up news and raw emotion to unload on her. Polo was not gay. We were lovers. I ratted out Robineau. I took Polo to Iowa City and saw Klampert. I had the Cit at my disposal to drive any time I wanted. *Holy Mother of God.* If this letter didn't knock her for a loop I didn't know what would. And then I realized I didn't even have an address to send it to! I decided that if I addressed it to Alan, c/o the English Dept. at UTEP, they would for sure have a mailbox set up for him by the time it arrived, and I was confident he would get it and take it home to her.

When New Year's Eve day rolled around two days later, Polo insisted I had to come over early and go right on to the third floor. I got off the elevator, but much to my abrupt shock and consternation, there stood Robineau and no Polo in sight. I froze.

"May I please speak to you, *Mademoiselle* Sarah?" he said very seriously.

"Go ahead."

"Shall we go into the salon? May I take your wrap?"

I let out an inadvertent huff and, handing my coat to him, I sighed, "Why not? "

He hung my coat up in a closet near the elevator that I hadn't even noticed was there, and then led me all the way down the gallery of portraits and into the living room over to the seating area by the baby grand piano.

I was trying to keep my cool, but my pulse was racing…and not in a good way.

"I wish to offer you my heartfelt apology for…for all the ways I treated you these past two years."

*It **had** been years already, hadn't it, I thought.*

I looked down at folded hands in my lap, and then back up at him. Truth be told, he repulsed me so much I could barely stand to see his face, let alone look him in the eyes. He reminded me of a weasel physically as well as personality-wise. Nevertheless, I was obliged to engage in this conversation.

"And you expect me to believe that? I realize *Monsieur* is unhappy with what I told him, " I said, "and I'm sure he made some points clear to you about it. But I don't see how any of this can come from your own…uh…devices. You're just doing what he asked you to so as to stay in his good graces."

"No, *Mademoiselle*, I want to assure you that I am most contrite… and ….I realize I made…mistakes… a mistake about… you," he said. I thought I detected a bit of panic in his voice.

"Bullshit. Again, am I actually supposed to believe a word you say now?" I sneered.

"Please, *Mademoiselle* Sarah. I could not be more grievously sorry and remorseful. I would feel horrible if I were responsible for your not coming to this home. *Monsieur* told me he has fallen in love with you. That is good enough for me."

Now he was being downright obsequious.

"You were also snotty to my friends Dom and Peter, and you know each other!"

"I regret that, also."

"Look," I said, "I have no intention of staying away from my…uh…job responsibilities in this house for Foundation business or anything. Just keep away from me. Give me the widest possible berth."

"I intend to be very deferential, from this point on, to you, *Mademoiselle* Sarah. But I also need to know that you will not be revolted by me attending to any duties I have with *Monsieur*. "

"What?! No. That's fine. I didn't ask or tell him to fire you on my account."

"But he said he would…fire me…if the situation did not ameliorate, and I promise you, it will. I…I…implore you to believe me."

"Okay. That's enough, then. We're done here. Where is he, by the way?"

"Waiting for you in the library…by the elevator."

I rushed out and back down the hallway. He was sitting there on a modern leather couch like the one the Hyde's had in their Chicago penthouse, looking rather stoic. He smiled a pursed smile at me as I entered.

"Everything all right now? " he asked hopefully.

"I guess so." I didn't want to disappoint him by making this more of a big *mishagoss* than it had to be. *Sol's words echoed in my ears, "Everything's a federal case with you."*

"Sure?"

I nodded. His mood immediately brightened, and he rose from where he sat, and came over to kiss me.

"I have a surprise for you and I hope you like it. Come."

He took my arm and led me back through the gallery to that huge guest bedroom suite that was on the opposite end of the wing from the corner where the master was. He opened the closet door and there hanging on a white satin padded hanger was an exquisite cocktail dress with a heart-shaped white velvet bodice and a full red silk-satin skirt. Underneath it, perched on top of an enormous Saks Fifth Avenue box that the dress must have come in, was a pair of black ballet flats like girls wore in the 50's, except that these had little squash heels, so there would be a modicum of height for the wearer of them.

"For you. I should love to see you wear it tonight."

"It…takes my breath away! " I gasped. "How do you know it will fit me? I—I've never told you my size?"

"Annie-Laure and I shopped for it. She seemed to know."

"Uh, well, wait a second. It's strapless! I don't own a strapless bra to wear with this."

"You will not need one. It has a built-in foundation, like a swimsuit."

I looked inside the bodice. He was right.

"I shall send in Sophie to help you into it, will that be all right?"

"Sophie? Your maid? Yes, that would be very nice. Thank you. That is, thank you for all of it ! I've never owned a dress even close to this!"

"I am pleased you like it because it gives me much pleasure to offer it to you. I shall await with great anticipation seeing you in it in a bit." He smiled at me and left.

It was New Year's Eve but the dress looked and seemed like a Valentine. I called it "My Valentine Dress" from that night on.

The maid came in and zipped me into the dress which accentuated my small waist and softly cupped my breasts into the luxurious feel of the velvet part. The skirt billowed out to just below my knees, and that tea length was flattering, too.

I tried on the shoes, and they fit perfectly. It occurred to me that Annie-Laure may have had a chance to ascertain my sizes when she had gone to fetch the clothing when I was convalescing from the breast lumpectomy.

I stood in front of the mirror with Sophie behind me, and she pronounced me *"vachement belle!"*

"Shall I do your hair, *Mademoiselle*?" Sophie asked, breaking my train of thought.

"You do that?"

"Yes, I like to… very much. "

My hair was in its tried and true half-up-and- half-down "do" I always wore out on special occasions . I had tied the red velvet ribbon in it, as usual. She took all that down, took three long clips out of her apron pocket, and piled my hair into three parts.

Removing one of the clips, my hair fell to my shoulders and she divided that part into three sections which she braided and let hang. She then picked up one of the side portions, divided it again, and braided that. Repeating the same pattern on the other side, I then had three braids. She took the red ribbon and wove it in and out of the three sections and then gathered the braids sort of in the middle of the nape, so it looked like a low braided chignon with ribbons streaming through it.

I was in absolute awe of how I looked.

I presented myself out in the gallery to Polo, who was also very dressed up by then in a beautiful charcoal grey cashmere blazer, soft blue shirt with a blue and green silk ascot tucked into the neck, and grey slacks. His face lit up when he saw me and he held out his arm and beckoned me to turn around. I

575

twirled in a fancy puff of red, and then I ran up and threw my arms around him, taking care not to disturb the braided masterpiece on my head.

"I'm so fucking spoiled, now, " I said, at once embarrassed that I hadn't just said "Thank you!" about a hundred times. "You know, I never went to prom or military ball or any fancy dance in my whole life. I've never owned a formal or a cocktail dress!" I told him again.

"Those boys in your high school must have been *imbéciles* not to take you to those — euh--balls. But tonight you are the most beautiful girl in Chicago."

The *St. Sylvestre* was, like all his parties, fabulous, over the top, *le non plus ultra*. The food was magnificent...mostly huge tiered seafood extravaganzas, and all the other French things one does at the second *Réveillon* of the season: heavy hors d'oeuvres, pastries and more champagne than one could imagine.

He had hired a string quartet to entertain us with an array of music's greatest hits for that genre: Haydn and Mozart, of course, plus some transcriptions of Schubert and Mendelssohn along with my absolute favorite, Fauré's *Pavane, Opus 50*.

Georg Solti sought me out to introduce me to his lovely wife Valerie, who was Valerie Pitts, previously of the BBC. She was wearing a black taffeta dress with a huge stiff white nylon collar that swept past her neckline where her hair, teased up in a perfect flip, just barely grazed her shoulders.

The maestro was interested in corralling Polo for a few hands of bridge, games of which were being organized over at the far end of the great room, where little tables had been set up.

"Polo is a wonderful bridge player, Sarah. Did you know?"

"No I didn't ! There's just nothing that man can't do, " I said admiringly.

"Do you play?" he asked expectantly, his bushy eyebrows raised high.

I had tried to learn bridge in college, but, unsuccessful in my endeavors, convinced myself it was for the best, since I saw kids literally flunk out of Iowa, skipping class to play in the Wheel room from morning 'til night. When I did play, I could never keep track of points or what the face cards were worth. I couldn't grasp the idea of conventions.

"I cheat, " I laughed. "Always need a crib sheet for the point values."

"Oh, but Polo would help you, " he chided me.

"No, sorry. I can't bid either."

The only thing I'd have been able to lead with that night would have been a heart...my own.

576

Chapter Ninety-Nine

"All My Time"... The City (Carole King)

I actually dreaded going back to work after New Year's, 1972. Without putting too fine a point on it, I was about to turn back into a pumpkin. Not that I didn't want to see and be with Jean-Paul d'Arivèque...he was all I could think about day and night. But no matter how I rationalized it, no matter how I excused myself on the grounds of temporary insanity, the fact was that I was now "sleeping with the boss" and it made me feel strange. I wasn't his mistress, at least, I kept telling myself. If a man is having an affair but neither he nor the woman is married, then that term didn't apply. I was his inamorata, though, for sure, and I did not want that to define me at *La Fondation*.

I worried about this from the first time we made love until I knew I would be getting up and going into the office, because his and my work relationship would never be the same, and that was not necessarily a good thing. But each day during the holiday break that I spent with Polo, I stuffed my fears into a remote corner of my being, and gave in to my newly bubbled-up feelings of ecstasy.

When we were together during the vacation, we just fell into each other's arms and had the most fun and revelry I'd ever experienced. Sometimes I would drive over to the mansion and we would go to some gallery he knew the owner of. Or he would take me to lunch or dinner. One time we decided to go to a movie.

Going out to a real movie theater was something he was unaccustomed to, since he usually just ordered films to watch in his library like he'd done with me. But I liked the big screen, not to mention popcorn, and it turned out that he was delighted to be out and about "on a cinema date," as he called it. I had been dying to see *McCabe and Mrs. Miller*. After all, Julie Christie was already in my pantheon and Warren Beatty wasn't too shabby either. It did not disappoint. We both loved it, and afterwards, having coffee in a little hole-in-the-wall diner near Lincoln Park, I got to expound all over the place about the soundtrack and my love for Leonard Cohen.

"That music! I mean, didn't you adore it? And wasn't it revelatory?" I enthused. "They used 'Sisters of Mercy' in the scene when he meets the prostitutes, for God's sake. Brilliant."

"Yes, the music was wonderful. But how did you find the film?"

Every so often, even as Polo spoke flawless fluent English, he would slip into some expression that let on his being a native French speaker. I understood that what he meant to ask was what did I think about the film.

"Well," I said, "loved it ! The cinematography was pure reverie. I was completely blown away. What about you?"

"The film was very sad, I thought, " he said, " but I admired it very much."

"I agree. And it also struck me how a movie so depressing can still be so beautiful at the same time! It's beyond me."

"I was not expecting it to be so — like a western."

"Well, it's really not a western, though, is it? More like the end of the American West...the conquered West."

"It was very emotional, *non?*"

"Yes, very, " I replied. "But I was taken with the idea that the emotions were evoked and made large by all that Leonard Cohen poetry in music. It really brought home the idea that McCabe had poetry in him, didn't it? Flawed though he was. Mrs. Miller knew it, and every one of those Leonard Cohen songs illustrated that idea."

"It was quite a statement about women, also, do you not agree?"

"I do! It's a very feminist film."

He looked across the table at me, and smiled. "I so admire the way we discuss art, you and I, " he finally said. "You are most insightful and intelligent."

"Well, not compared to you, " I protested.

"No, no, Sarah. I consider you my intellectual equal."

"Well, that's not possible, but thank you. I do believe we worship the same gods, so to speak."

"Do not underestimate or diminish yourself. Your creativity, for example, far exceeds mine."

"Oh, Polo, come on. Cupid is making you talk like this to me, " I laughed. But he just shook his head and continued to smile at me.

Often during the holiday interlude, I went to the Lake Shore mansion, followed his instructions and repaired directly to the third floor and into his waiting arms. If my apartment had been like camping in a yurt to him, his place was like being holed up in the Paris Ritz to me.

The reception rooms and his mother's bedroom on the floor below had never struck me as places real people inhabited, even though I had seen that they did. The décor and dimensions suggested, as I had concluded when I first stood and gaped at place, that one had taken up residence in a museum or a palace, and as time went on, I found all that unimaginable opulence everywhere really started to weigh on a "normal" person like me. I could never get completely comfortable on those settees and brocade-upholstered chairs. How could you honestly come to terms with the idea that people actually lived like that?

But Polo's personal apartment, though far bigger in sheer square footage than most people's houses, was more intimate and inviting than the downstairs was. Stately though his living room, dining room and library were, they were at least less grand in size, and not furnished in Louis XV anything, but rather in gorgeous leathers and beautiful comfortable fabrics, even if they did come from Brunschwig & Fils. His personal library had a lot of the same amenities as the big one a floor down, but it was brighter and more of an intimate refuge for reading or listening to music. It had the most modern furniture of any of the rooms. The other rooms were more traditional — but without being Versailles.

The apartment's master bedroom suite was as immense as his mother's on the second floor, and configured with the same layout of sitting areas, a desk, and the Empire-style sleigh bed. But instead of armoires lining the wall, his had a walk-in room for a closet --literally the size of my former studio, with every piece of clothing organized by type or color, and a big center island with old-fashioned haberdashery drawers of all different depths for folded clothing items and accessories. His ties made up a display that could have easily been in some up-scale boutique.

The bedroom walls were not paint or wallpaper, but ivory colored raw silk fabric over foam, making the room all but soundproof. His enormous bed had a tufted leather backing on the headboard end, filled up with pillows. The duvet on top was a magnificent brown, cream and blue Chinoiserie print of more Brunschwig & Fils material, and the linens on it were by Frette. The minute I laid my head on them, the scent of lemon verbena rose into my nostrils. Heaven could only hope to smell like that.

His bathroom was stocked with Porthault towels and robe. And, of course, I did verify that he had a walk-in shower — no tub, and the shower was big enough to hold a small dinner party in it. It was a real steam shower like in some gym or spa, and the shower heads hit at all different levels. I'd never seen that before, and as I had wondered, there were indeed railings on three sides. In contrast to the brown tones in the bedroom, the bath was done up in creamy pale blue wall tiles and grey-veined marble on the floors and counters. Thick Porthault mats covered the flooring so that one didn't slip on it, and the heating was also in the floor, so you didn't step onto a cold surface in the winter either.

"Blue is my favorite color, " I told him the first time we took a shower together in there, and "this is the prettiest blue I'd have ever imagined," I swooned, fingering the tiles in the shower. He lathered my back using a long loofa brush soaped up with Roget & Gallet's signature scent. Just a whiff of that reminded me of Paris, too. It was an aroma that was ever present in pharmacies and in Galleries Lafayette or Le Drugstore's perfume department.

I turned to face him and just stared up at his face. He looked at me quizzically as I gave out a little laugh, because he looked so typically French all of a sudden. It was beyond ironic that his thin aquiline nose was the very one I'd seen a hundred times in portraits by Hyacinthe Rigaud or Charles Le Brun. His round brown eyes were set back into the curvatures of his high cheek bones, and his lips were thin but inviting, because when closed together, they seemed to turn up at the ends into a perpetual smile.

I had come to adore that face. It made me happy just to see it.

On January third, however, the jig was up. That first day back, Polo appeared in my office almost as soon as I arrived, having slept at my own apartment the Sunday night and walked to work as usual in the morning. I had already decided on purpose to not go and see him in his office. I intended to hold fast on this. Our private lives were to be kept private. I was steadfastly determined to ignore any knowing glances or winks or any other signs that would give away that "they knew."

"If you do not kiss me right here and now, " Polo stated, drawing me into his arm, "I do not know how I shall be able to get through my morning, let alone the entire day."

"Polo! People will see us." I kissed him but he could feel my tension.

"Sarah...anyone on my staff who is a sentient being with a *soupçon* of intelligence already knows I love you."

Back at my desk I had to get busy on researching lecturers for the Institute, which, having been my idea, fell to me to organize. Even though it wasn't happening for months, I'd have to use all that time to work out the details. I needed to write up some of the pertinent information so that our monthly Foundation newsletter editors could cover the story at least four times before the actual event, and I had agreed to be interviewed by them. I also needed to do p.r. for it myself, and would be enlisting the aid of our marketing department, which would mean meetings. I foresaw that I was going to be very busy.

In the meantime, I was carefully studying the chapters of the Dowling Company's textbook sample to determine which *Moments Culturels* would go where; then I began writing them. My first deadline was in two weeks. Plus I was handling the film library as usual, and even with the help of my enthusiastic assistant Joelle, the brunt of the responsibility still fell on me.

Also on the first day back, stuffed in our mailboxes were large ecru-colored envelopes tied in coral ribbons and engraved with our names on the front. These turned out to be the formal invitations to Annie-Laure and Jean-Luc's wedding. These invitations were an amalgam of French and American custom: the presentation was like a fancy American wedding would have, but the actual invitations were very different looking. The layout was in the French style with a tri-folded card. Theirs had a cover with a René Char poem in script printed on it:

Et moi, semblable à toi/ Avec la paille en fleur au bord du ciel criant ton nom
J'abats les vestiges,/ Atteint, sain de clarté.

When opened, Annie-Laure's name was in beautiful large type on one side and Jean Luc's on the other. In the middle, going right over the fold, each of them invited us to *"partager leur joie"* and then invitation wording stated that that the marriage would be celebrated at *La Pérégrine, Cher et Loire, samedi, le 10 juin, 1972 à 16 heures en Chapelle*. At the bottom of Annie-Laure's side was printed in much smaller type, *Monsieur et Madame Claude LeBeau, 15, Boulevard Fraissinette- 42 Saint-Etienne*, and on the other side, *Monsieur et Madame Rémy Moreau, 6 Rue Valentin Haüy- 75 Paris 15e*.

There was no response card, but I determined from having spoken to Annie-Laure, that the reason we got these so early was because of all the arrangements that would need be made by her and Jean-Paul d'Arivèque to fly us all to France, get us to the venue and back again, put us up at *La Pérégrine* and entertain us. We were all instructed to let her know if we were coming, and she would take care of the rest. About a month out, everyone would get further instructions. What the invitation did not say was dress code, but the time of day was supposed to be the clue. Tuxedos-- *"le smoking"*-- were not appropriate before six p.m., so that let us know it was not as formal as it could have been. I was relieved about that and would certainly not even think about what I was wearing until way later.

Our previous routine picked up again, also, and I found myself busy at the office and busy with symphony concerts as usual. There was the de rigueur round of social engagements for the Foundation at the d'Arivèque home as well. True to his word, Robineau treated me with almost disarming courtesy, much as I still avoided having to be in any room with him if I could manage it. But I have to admit, butter wouldn't melt in his mouth when he was around me. I guess Polo had put the fear of God in him after all.

To my delight, one of the Foundation's Chicago guests that January was a returning Yves Brunsvick. He was giving a speech on UNESCO to the University Club at U Chicago and had invited Jean-Paul to hear it, at the same time asking if he could stay with him. Polo had been more than happy to oblige him, and knew I would be *"ravie"* to see him again. He organized a small *soirée* for him the evening after his speech.

"I know you don't remember me from that one class, " I chided *Monsieur* Brunsvick, as he kissed my hand again.

"No, " he admitted, "but I certainly do remember you from the last time I was here, *Mademoiselle. Je suis enchanté de vous revoir.*"

He was in great demand that night at the mansion. Almost the entire Foundation staff plus the university officials clamored after him, taking photos for the newsletter, and asking his opinion on various topics. It did not escape me that, before he was a professor in the *Cours de Civilisation Française* at *La Sorbonne*, he had been in the French Ministry of Education, so if I had a chance, I definitely wanted to broach the subject of our Teachers' Institute idea with him.

I hovered around the circle of admirers surrounding him, waiting my turn. "Yes," he was saying, " as a young teacher, I did join *La Résistance* against the Nazi occupation. Against this brutal onslaught were already brewing the ideals which would be enshrined in UNESCO's constitution, namely to contribute to the advancement of human rights and peace. If we got out from under Germany, we already knew we would advocate for international cooperation through education, culture and communication, among other areas."

He could have been Socrates holding court there. Polo would glance at me from time to time, seeing I was mesmerized and still in awe of him.

Brunsvick had first joined the French delegation to UNESCO in 1948, and in ten years he was heading it. "I had the unique opportunity, " he was explaining to the gathered throng, "to work with several *présidents de la République* and many other important leaders, to thereby guarantee that eminent French and European personalities participated in UNESCO's work."

"But even more importantly, " our legal chief Daniel Rosier de Molet lauded him, "you were the architect of the projects with which these personalities, as you call them, were involved!"

Brunsvick smiled. "As you wish, " he admitted, visibly uneasy about taking all the credit.

Household staff were circulating around the group passing out hors d'oeuvres and flutes of champagne, when Polo gathered us all together for a toast to our distinguished guest, after which, a sort of dispersion happened, and I found myself alone with Yves.

He took my hand and held onto it. "You have taken quite the initiative here, " he said smiling at me. "Polo has told me of your idea for the public-school teachers. Wonderful."

"Do you think the first one on *Le Marquis de Lafayette* might be a good jumping off point, *Monsieur*?" I asked, eager to hear his response.

"You could not have chosen a better first topic, I think," he said, looking down at me admiringly. "Did you know, for example, that when the *Marquis* arrived in the Colonies and went to Philadelphia, he could hardly speak any English, but he was a Mason, and they welcomed him in various quarters because of that."

"I didn't realize that. I don't really know very much about him, except what we learn in school, which is precious little. I need to attend my own seminars and glean as much from the them as the teachers," I laughed.

"Well, he dearly wanted a cause and, fortuitously for both parties, the American one was it. He offered to serve without a salary, which helped his commanders."

"And he was made a general at a very young age, I do know that," I said.

"Yes, your Continental Congress granted him a commission at the rank of Major General... at the behest of his advocate, Benjamin Franklin, it must be noted. Your *conférenciers* will have many topics upon which to base their sessions."

I nodded. It was true. I had already read enough abstracts of articles on Lafayette to know that this Institute topic could easily fill a week rather than a weekend. We would have to adjust accordingly.

When the party was finally breaking up and I was preparing to drive the Pallas back to my place, Polo stopped me and took me aside.

"I should like to invite you for *Le Jour de la Saint Valentin*, " he said. "What would you like to do?"

"Oh! Well, gosh, I don't know. But if we could go someplace where I could wear the dress again, that would be fab! It's practically a Valentine in its own right, isn't it? Please don't get me anything else."

"All right. Shall we start here with *apéro* then? I will make reservations for dinner at …perhaps the Palm Court?"

"Groovy."

February 14 fell on a Monday that year, so he wanted us to go out on the Saturday night before, first of all because he was giving Jean-Luc the actual holiday off so those two love birds could celebrate it together, and also because he was no doubt thinking I'd stay at his place the entire weekend, which was fine by me.

Jean-Luc was to pick me up late in the afternoon, and when I stuck my head outdoors to test the temperature, I saw a sky low and overcast with thick clouds, and the misty sort of atmosphere that would indicate snow was imminent, in the same way you could smell rain that wasn't quite there yet. I decided not to wear boots, though, because that would ruin the "look" and besides, we were being chauffeured all over town. If the snow turned out to be deep by the time I was coming home, I'd just have to tough it out in my new little ballet shoes.

Jean-Paul met me as I got off the elevator on the second floor, because, he said, we were having drinks in the main library.

"You are beautiful, " he cooed, kissing me.

"You're not half bad yourself, mister, " I said, noticing he was wearing a dinner jacket and bow tie.

I took his left hand. It had become my habit ever since we'd evolved from friends to lovers, to hold hands with him. It was fortuitous that he had total use of that hand, I had decided. The arm didn't work too well, but the hand had been saved. When I remarked on this he had said, "Just for you."

We got to the library and I expected to see someone---a maid or one of Robineau's lower ranking assistants, for instance, but no one else was in there. We sat down on the Chesterfield couch and Jean-Paul seemed to be preparing me for something. He became quiet. He took my hand-- with his other one this time-- and kissed it. Then he looked intently at me and said, "I want to tell you something."

"Shoot, " I answered.

"I… I have thought about nothing but this for quite some time now. I have here, something I would like to give you."

As he reached into his pocket, I protested, "But I told you not to get me a Valentine's gift, didn't I?"

"Yes, but this is not that." He took out a small square of tissue paper and laid it on his lap so he could undo it. It wasn't taped or wrapped with any ribbon or anything that had to be untied. "This is the ring of *Madame* Schwartz. I thought to use it to … to offer you… to ask you… if you will do me the great honor to become my wife, Sarah. I have, of course, my mother's very large diamond ring, but I felt this would perhaps be more meaningful to you, and not carry the shadow of *Maman* to haunt you any more than you say it already does."

It was true: I had said something to that effect once--that time I "tattled" on Robineau and quoted what he'd so disgustingly told me about not being accepted there because I hadn't known Maman. *I had pointed out that since her spirit permeated the entire Foundation, how could I not know her!*

He held up the ring for my approval. It was a magnificent three-carat sapphire and diamond set *"a l'ancienne"* and so ornate it looked almost Rococo.

However, this offer of marriage caught me completely off guard. I was not expecting any such thing, and knew immediately I could never accept it. I was sitting there in a shock-induced trance at first, and recoiled when he tried to hand me the ring.

"Polo, "I said laughing a little nervously at how insane the idea was, "YOU can't marry **me**. It's out of the question. Every person in the known universe would assume I was the biggest gold-digger who ever lived. So, no. I'm sorry, but I can't accept *Madame* Schwartze's exquisite ring."

"Why do you say this?" he asked, very surprised.

"**Because**, that's why." I stood up and looked at him in a way there could be no crossed signals, no miscommunication. "I'm nobody. From Nowhere. Real nowhere. The nowherest nowhere. You're a fucking French aristocrat and I'm far far out of your league. This is the same old story. Your family would never approve your marrying me."

"What family? There is hardly any family left!"

"You know what I mean. Any French people. I'm a JEW. You're a French Catholic count—duke--whatever! Marry an American Jew? I don't think so. I lived in France, too, you know. I know all about the French ways. I would never be accepted in France as your wife. Not that that bothers **me**, but it would bother you. I know how you were raised...at least until the age of twelve."

"Sarah," he pleaded, "please sit back down. I need to remind you that I do not live in France. Nor do I have any plans to do so."

"That doesn't matter, " I said, **not** sitting back down. Instead I paced around the coffee table. "You're French, and much as I love it, there are things in the French culture that go against me. You know I'm right. You know this Catholic thing? I've already told you I had two close encounters with serious Catholic relationships where I was informed in no uncertain terms ---pretty much point blank-- that I wasn't marriage material for them. Period! Full stop! If your mother WERE still alive, she would politely take me aside and tell me that yes, even though her son is in love with me, we both know such a union would be impossible, blah blah blah. She would be very nice about it but...heh, **we** know."

As he could see I was getting pretty worked up at this point, he beckoned me again to sit by him. I ignored it.

"Sarah, my mother, were she here, would wish more than anything in the world for me to be happy. She would have already fallen in love with you, as I have. I love you. I could not bear to lose you now."

"Well, why can't things just go on as they are then?" I was jittery by now. He, too, was becoming agitated.

"Because I want to be your husband! I want to give you children and I want them, too. I dearly want children. You told me having a baby out of wedlock would ruin your life. I agree!"

"Polo, " I said, stopping in my tracks and just staring at him for a moment. "I don't want children. Why did you get the idea I did?"

He lowered his voice. "But...you love the children of Cass. You would make such a wonderful mother, *chérie*."

"No! I fucking would not! What in the world would make you say that?! I'm pretty damn sure I wouldn't even make a decent wife for anyone. For one thing...and this is a good one!...I've never seen a happy marriage! Ever! I haven't seen ONE happy marriage, Polo. Maybe my nana's was...she always spoke highly of my grandfather, but I was too young when he died to have known them together. Cass' marriage is shit. HER parents have a business pact more than a marriage, it seems to me. They didn't parent her at all. My parents' marriage is shit. They were lousy parents to me. (*Et cetera et cetera ad nauseum!*) You get the idea. Oh, and speaking of my parents, they would never approve a marriage to you either. Not that I really give a damn about it, but they would absolutely crap if I married outside the religion. That's all my father harps about from morning 'til night." I paused and thought about that for a second. "That's probably why I never see myself getting married...to you or anyone else, if you want to know the truth."

Polo was upset, and I could see it in his eyes, deeply hurt. I finally sat down next to him and put my arm around his shoulder. Then I broke down in tears at having done that to him. I sat there and cried, sobbing, "The r-r-ing is beaut-t-tiful. Tha-a-nk you anyway." I reached for my purse to try to find some Kleenex, where upon he took a monogrammed handkerchief from his interior jacket pocket and handed it to me. That made me sob more.

"Sarah, " he said solemnly, "you have laid out many reasons to tell me **no** tonight. But if another one is that you cannot abide my physical appearance and all the complications that go with it, and you simply do not want to tell me that, would you at least be honest with me and say it?"

"What? Oh my God! How can you even ask me that...now?"

Was this what that woman did to him? Made him insecure and fearful?

" NO. There's my answer to **that** nonsense. I think I'd better just leave."

I made a move to get up off the couch when he took my arm. "Please do not go. I need you to listen to what I have to say now. Look at me. "

So I turned to him and sat silently.

"Life...our lives... they are very short and very finite. They can be snuffed out without so much as a fair warning or even a premonition. And we only have one chance to live this one life we are given. We are born into this world alone and we leave it the same way. It is what we do in between those two moments that gives our existence any meaning. And what we hope to do with our lives is to love another person. People say there is someone out there for everyone, but I did not believe that was true for me... until I met you. Everything changed in my life after forty-one years, because of... **you**. And I feel you also love me. How could I feel so loved by you if you did not love me? You do...love me, *non*?"

"You know I do."

"Well, then, that is all that matters! What other people think does not matter. Religion does not matter. That can all be overcome. Yes, I was born a Catholic and christened in the Church. But have you ever seen me attend church since you have known me? Not even once. *Maman* was very *déçue* with the church during and after the war. She lost faith and she did not impose the church on me. Had I wanted to attend Mass, she would have been fine with my wishes, but I agreed with her. When she died, her body was cremated and her ashes flown to *La Pérégrine*. I was very very sad, but not because she did not have the last rites of the church. I do not fear for her immortal soul or for mine. *Oncle* Charles, I believe, is still a Catholic now. His wishes are to be buried next to his wife in Geneva and she is in a church cemetery, but..."

"Well, there you go, then." I saw my opening and interrupted him. "You just said it! He won't approve of your marrying me. He'll be very unhappy about it."

"Not at all! He will not say a word against me...or against you. And Sarah, I would never impose any religion on you...you would be...you are... free to believe what you want, practice as you wish...attend synagogue. I would not change you."

"And if I had a baby, you'd be fine with it being raised Jewish, I suppose? Get real."

"If you did have our baby it would complete my happiness so definitively, I would do anything you wanted."

"Well, you say that now, but I'm not so sure. Anyhow, Judaism is a little different, you know. Even if I don't go to services too often, it doesn't change the fact that I'm Jewish, and can't just get rid of it by saying I don't practice or anything. It's always with me — part of me. In some circles it defines me. If I did have a child, she or he would also be Jewish because — get this-- Judaism is passed through the mother."

I began sobbing again uncontrollably, which even surprised myself. " S—s--so the next time there's a-a- Holocaust, your kid gets it whether you're Catholic or not!"

" Sarah, please."

"And can you imagine — just theoretically, of course-- a boy of ours inheriting your title? A Jewish *Duc de Beuvron*? Yeah, right. That will never happen any more than my becoming the *Duchesse de Beuvron* could."

"I am sorry to correct you, my darling, " he stated, "but it is precisely what would happen....if I used the title, which, as you know, I do not."

"Yes, well, being a duke for you is kind of like being Jewish for me, " I whimpered. "W—w-- whether or not w—w--we say we are, we are. "

I didn't have anything else; I was spent. I felt horrible. My head hurt and I was exhausted from crying. I sat there still weepy, taking intermittent short gasps of breath, trying to regain composure and not doing a very good job of it. For one thing, I now found myself shivering in my skimpy little frock.

Robineau appeared at the door to announce that the car was ready to take us to dinner. We had never even rung for the *apéritif* to be brought in.

Shall we?" Polo said, offering his arm for me to help him up off the couch, which I did. But as he locked his brace and reached for the cane, I said I thought maybe Jean-Luc could just drop me off at my place. "I can't see me walking into the Palm Court with mascara running down my face."

Polo took the handkerchief I was still clasping and dabbed it at my cheeks. "There, " he said, "you look lovely."

"Oh, I bet, " I managed to laugh and he was relieved to see me do so.

"Please come to dinner with me. Please."

His forlorn pleading with me was heartbreaking. I thought better of it, but in the end consented. We walked down the hallway towards the elevator, where suddenly Robineau was standing there holding up a strange wrap that most certainly was not my camel hair one. It was a magnificent full-length black sable coat with an enormous shawl collar that lifted into a hood.

"It is too cold out tonight for you to wear your coat, " Polo said. "I asked Robin to bring this one out of storage for you to have."

Wear, maybe. Keep, no.

I looked at him thinking maybe this was a joke, but he nodded and I slipped into it. "It's the most luxurious thing I've ever had on, " I said, feeling stupid for stating the obvious.

"You look resplendent in it, " he said. "It suits you."

"That is as may be, but we'll take my coat with us in the car so I can give this back after dinner."

He knew that meant I'd be having Luc drop me at home afterwards. I would not be spending the weekend. The dinner date would be strained now, at best, and horribly uncomfortable at worst.

"Sarah, " Polo said, taking my furry arm, "you may not be my *fiancée* tonight, but you are still my Valentine."

Chapter One Hundred

"Yesterday"...Lennon & McCartney

Why, God, couldn't I have just awoken to the calendar reading Friday, February 11 again? In one short hour before an innocent dinner date, my life completely flipped. Now I had to worry about my job, my future, if I would stay in Chicago (well, there was no chance I'd go crawling home to The Bluffs, let's face that) and whether or not Polo would ever treat me as an employee as he had before.

I was desperate to talk to Cass, but I still hadn't gotten her phone number. *They'd been there two months already and I had only received one letter. I didn't even know if they had had a home phone installed where they'd settled, outside of El Paso in a place called St. Anthony, New Mexico.*

Cass had written that she didn't want to be in the city and that this town was a straight shot down a highway twenty-five minutes to the university for Alan. She said she was very happy that UTEP even had an Early Childhood Lab Preschool/Day Care program the twins could enroll in.

"Alan can drop them off when he goes to work, but that means I'm stuck without any transportation all day. Or he can ride the bike there, and I take them in and keep the panel truck."

Neither "solution" was optimal for her, as she could barely drive that van and hated doing so. But at least, it seemed to me, with the twins gone all day, she would have time to devote to her art. Blocks of time were the precious commodity.

So on a whim, I went into my kitchen, pulled the little café chair up to my wall phone, and dialed information for New Mexico, specifically asking for any new listing in St. Anthony for "Alan Jones."

"There is a listing on Calabasas St., " the operator said. "Is that it?"

I looked at Cass' envelope, which simply had a UTEP box number on it, but I told the operator, "Yes" and she gave me the number.

When Cass answered, I breathed a sigh of relief and launched right into a narrative of my last few weeks without so much as a by-your-leave. I came up for air, and apologized to her for not even asking first about her situation and how the kids were.

"Oh, Sari, I've been meaning to call you, too. I just thought you were kind of mad at me when we last saw each other in Iowa City."

"I'm not mad at you! I was, however, damned worried when I left you in Iowa. I have to admit, your letter sounded pretty good, though! Do you like it there?"

"Oh fuck no, " she laughed. "How could anyone like it here?"

"That's what I figured. How's Alan's faculty position? Is he happy he took it?"

"I guess it's fine. He doesn't talk much about it."

"How come? See? That must mean he has second thoughts about moving you guys all the way out there, right?"

"I don't know. He's so noncommunicative these days...about anything. "

"Well, I bet some little people in the house are more than making up for that! Ha! How are they? I miss them so much!"

"And they miss their Auntie ...and so do I. They're fine! They're not really talking yet, but they seem mostly to babble at each other and somehow, they understand! They'll say a lot of single words but not put together any sentences. And they know colors! Oh, you should have seen them the other day: I gave them finger paints! It was too cute. Laura kept asking me for RED."

"Oooh! I need artwork on my walls, so send me some of theirs, okay?"

"Sure. I can walk to the post office from our house."

"Well, far out! At least you're not out in the boonies again."

"Yes I am too, this whole place is the boonies. But you're right...we're in town. We do have some extra land on the side of our house, so I still have a pen for animals — don't have any yet-- and a plot for gardening. And the rents here are so cheap!"

"So Cass, " I asked, feeling the need to address the elephant on the phone line, "how's your health? How's the eating thing going?"

She hesitated and sighed. "Last week Alan did the grocery shopping and he came in, dumped the sacks on the table, and ordered me to cook dinner. I did it. I made fried chicken, mashed potatoes, gravy, green beans and salad."

"But did you eat it?"

"Well, you know, on my maintenance plan I'm still not eating meat, but yes, I ate salad."

SHIT. I knew it. Maintenance plan my ass. But I decided it was something at least that she would admit that to me.

"Well, all right, I'll take your word for it. I'm not going to lecture you or try to run your life long distance. I've got my own lap full o' woe, as Pax might say. But I want to know you're okay."

"I'll tell you if anything happens, I promise."

"Okay, good."

"But what about YOU?! My God, he proposed! If you married him, you'd be one of the richest women in the world!"

"Yeah, well I made it clear that I wasn't about to marry him, so we don't need to fantasize about me shopping at Givenchy. What I'm most worried about is how screwed at work I am. I could lose this job, you realize. I can't even face him tomorrow. What if we can never have another collaboration? What's going to happen if the office turns against me? They all revere him... it's like...he's a god to them."

"I can't believe this will affect your job, Sari. You already have it way under control and all your ideas are simply *brill, dahling.* Just keep working on them and be upbeat around Polo. Act like nothing's changed. You're the fucking Director of Education! He can't just replace you. He created the position **for** you!"

"Well, you keep me in the know about your battle with anorexia nervosa, and I'll keep you up to date on my life falling apart here."

"Sari, I wish you could just hop on a plane and come see us. Could you?"

"I don't have any more vacation time for a long while, honey, but as soon as I do, I'll come down there. Maybe at ... end of summer?"

" Phew, that's a long ways off."

"I'll see what I can do, Cass. Maybe I **could** splurge and come for a weekend sooner rather than later."

But even as I heard myself telling her that, I knew it wasn't too damn likely. I probably shouldn't have given her a reason to think my flying down there on a whim was really possible. However, when we hung up that Sunday afternoon, I was happy just knowing she had a phone and I could reach her any time. I made a mental note to hide away in my office from then on, and call her whenever the mood struck.

Ironically, even before Cass advised me to remain enthused and act like nothing had changed, I had already determined to do just that. Suck it up and be positive. Do my work as usual. Try to avoid the Presidential suite—although that wasn't going to be too possible. Keep it professional and pleasant.

So that's what did happen. Polo and I still had CSO concerts to attend, and we went. It was not as though things were not strained between us, in a social setting especially. He just seemed sad. He tried to be cheery to me but it was as though deep down he thought he'd done something to hurt me by proposing marriage. I, on the other hand, found myself on the verge of tears at these concerts. Whenever the music was poignant my mind would wander back to that night in February. I did overflow with tears during the adagio movement of Barber's *String Quartet*, but since it was among the saddest, most touching music ever written, I hoped Polo just thought I was overcome by that and didn't suspect that I was crying over him.

I didn't see Georg Solti very often, however. If he were conducting those nights, he almost always begged off having a drink with us due to the dreaded necessity of having to schmooze with the mucky-mucks. But the one time he did meet us in the lobby, he took my hand to kiss it and when his eyes met mine, I distinctly saw disappointment in them. Was I imagining that?

As delicate spring rains heralded the humidity that would pervade my third Chicago summer, Cass wrote me some actually rather jolly letters from St. Anthony, which, I can't lie, came as a pleasant surprise, with emphasis on the "surprise" part. She decided she was happy with their new digs, and assured me their life wasn't the "Spartan" one I'd conjured up in my mind when she described them using electricity and other "modern conveniences" sparingly -- what most of us considered necessities. She wrote:

"Life here is just simple, and that makes me pretty happy. We do use kerosene lamps in the living room at night because the soft ambience here in the quiet St. Anthony outskirts is so nice after a long day of work for Alan and child-wrangling for me. When I read at night in bed, though, I use electric lights, don't worry. I made us two wind-chimes and a tinkling mobile that I hung above the front porch. I think it is so sweet and pleasant to hear the symphonies of clacking and jangling the New Mexico winds cause in them. We started a compost pile out of all our garbage and will put it on the garden. I hope to have a big healthy garden this year. I'm planning to buy a hand cultivator---kind of like a plow thingy. We won't be able to grow and produce all we consume by any stretch of the imagination, but it'll provide something."

In another letter, that she insisted she had to write rather than tell me on the phone, she gave me an earful on how I should curate my time... and really my life.

"I know you are unhappy. I imagine you brooding there alone in your little pad. Don't forget, I know you, kid. You think relief from your troubles-- or anyone's (truly I know of what I speak)—can be found in books and music—and shopping haha! I'm sure you find solace and inspiration from them. But what will really make things better for you is feeling and growing and loving...and being loved. What enables the entire train of happiness (and sometimes unhappiness) to keep chugging along, cannot, ultimately, rely on any amount of things. Only people and compassion and love and forgiveness do that. Those are the "objects" that you need. Work can be beneficial and hobbies are fine. I can't deny that doing many projects myself—like painting or sewing—makes me feel fulfilled. But even those things do not define me like being Paul and Laura's mother and Alan's wife does.
Even creating art is the easy part. The hard and complicated part is giving over your life and heart and soul to another person. It's as though we have to learn to do what should surely be what OM hopes we learn to do---be good one to the other. I know you were good to Polo as he was to you. But if that wasn't meant to be, I hope you don't give up faith that you will find 'the one' who is good to you and kind and loving. Like, that is why we are on this earth, you know? And I wish for it to be soon! I want you to be with someone you love. There is nothing finer or more glorious I could hope for you, my sister."

I believed her but the question was, had I given up that person already? I was afraid I had, and that I had "left the cake out in the rain and I would never have the recipe again."

Until it hit me like a ton of bricks: I must skip the wedding in France! Those were the days I could use to go to El Paso. I would fly myself down there first class, for God's sake, and to hell with having to feign enthusiasm for being at the d'Arivèque ducal seat. I would forego a weekend of obligatory *politesse* and instead indulge in a weekend of being Auntie Sari again.

Of course, I was genuinely happy for my dear friends Annie-Laure and Jean-Luc, but they could do without *ungebluzen* me moping around, gumming up their days of joy. The more I thought about the idea, the more I felt relieved to have come up with it! No worries about what to pack for a French garden wedding. No angst over meeting the people who may have known and loved Jean-Paul, maybe all the way back to when he was a kid.

I made an appointment to see Marie-France and tell her I would not be on the plane to Paris. I felt that it would be proper to go first to her before Annie-Laure, because, in essence, the wedding trip was an office event from which I would be absent. Yes, she was the one I must tell.

I expressly did not look his way as I entered the large wing of the Foundation office that housed the top brass, but I knew Jean-Paul saw me approach Marie-France's door from his glass-enclosed "fortress." Annie-Laure was, thankfully, away from her desk. I broke the news to MFP in as matter-of-fact way as I could, and she was at first alarmed.

"Oh, *Mon Dieu*, you're not ill again, are you? Is it your breast after all?"

"Oh, heavens no!!" *My God, I'd never even given a second thought about that benign lump, and gave short shrift to the idea that I would ever have to think about it again.* "No no. This is just about going to see my best friend in New Mexico. It's the optimal time to go visit her…you know, when the office is closed anyway. I don't have any other vacation time accrued."

I was sure she noticed that I hadn't asked her permission to be absent, but had told her I would be. There was an awkward pause in the conversation. It seemed like she was waiting for me to broach the other subject with her, but neither of us mentioned anything about my having turned down the marriage proposal, even though I was pretty sure she was up to snuff on all that…they told each other everything. I assured her I knew how splendid the wedding would be, especially with her in charge of the details, and how happy I was for the couple. I said I would, of course, see her before she left, since she was not returning to the Foundation; that I was very sad about it, and we would all miss her terribly around there, but I was also thrilled that her retirement should take place in her homeland.

And that's when she breached her silence, saying, "I owe it all to Jean-Paul, and so, it should be said, does Annie-Laure. He's the most wonderful man alive."

I couldn't disagree with that.

Chapter One Hundred One

"Time and Love"...Laura Nyro

I was hard at work on the Teachers' Institute. We had the dates set for October, and we had the lecture hall and classrooms procured from the Chicago *Alliance Française*. The teachers for the first Institute would be limited to ten in number, and they would be housed and fed at the d'Arivèque mansion.

I still had to find some experts on the Marquis de Lafayette to give our lectures or else there wouldn't be an Institute at all. With U Chicago, Northwestern, Loyola of Chicago and U Illinois Chicago Circle all within shouting distance, so to speak, I told myself it shouldn't be that hard. But I had a chicken-egg situation on my hands, what with never having put on any event of this type and not knowing if we should present a contract to draw potential speakers, or line them up first and then offer them the perks. At least, I reasoned, the *Fondation Culturelle Française* had enough *cachet* in that city to attract top people who would know we were legit.

I decided I would have to consult with JPA and the legal department before I did anything else, so I set off to do the necessary research in order to present them with a list of French or history profs whom we could possibly invite. I went to the imposing red brick and green glass Harold Washington Chicago Public Library on State Street to find books on Lafayette, and determine if any of the authors were living in Chicago. The first book that caught my attention was one containing the actual memoirs and letters of the Marquis, which I checked out to read myself.

And then I found what I thought might be the perfect book! It was called *Washington and Lafayette*, written by a Pierre Montcalm who was on the faculty of Notre Dame, which wasn't too far away, either. But on the same shelf, I discovered another one about the two generals and "the friendship that turned the American Revolution, " which was written by a U Chicago professor-- a man named Marvin Roizen. If he were contacted, I decided, and didn't want to do it for some reason, perhaps he would know others who would. That was a start. I felt better.

I also sought out Dom, who, besides being a source of information for me, would of course be in the first group to participate. He gave me names of noted French profs he knew of at the various colleges who might be willing to be a part of this endeavor, and I added them to my file.

Armed with all that, I set up the meeting with d'Arivèque and Rosier de Molet and took with me the list of names plus a draft letter of invitation. We met in a small conference room which was adjacent to the Presidential suite. One of MFP's secretaries brought us coffee in a cobalt blue and gold Sèvres Napoleon porcelain service on a Ravinet sterling silver tray, replete with sugar and creamer in the matching sterling pattern.

"Would you please pour for us, Sarah?" Jean-Paul bade me.

I nodded, but in truth I was almost afraid to touch the fancy stuff and hoped I wouldn't fumble the whole thing and expose myself as the klutz I had already many times proclaimed I was.

Our chief legal officer, Daniel Rosier de Molet had been at the board meeting where I had pitched the Institute idea, and he had been favorably inclined towards it, but he wanted more details.

"Tell me again about your goals for this project," he asked me in a kind voice that did not intimidate me or put me on the defensive.

"Well, it seems to me that our overriding goal of everything we do in the education department is to spotlight *La Fondation* and what it has to offer teachers and students in Chicagoland, and possibly nationwide. So to that end I have proposed, as you know, a weekend---call it mini-institute—for teachers. I would like them to be inspired...discover ways to... to beef up their lesson plans with new ideas on how to present this Franco-American content. I'd like the first one to highlight France and America."

"Yes, the role France played in America's emergence from English rule is probably not one taught in too many schools. What age students do you foresee benefiting from their teachers' participation in this?" DRM asked.

"I envision it being on all different levels of study, because I want us to have teachers from elementary, middle school and high school... French language but also American history. I picture us

589

providing enough diversity of lessons to enhance any class. I also see this as cross-curricular, so collaboration would take place, say, between the French teacher and the history one, or in lower grades, the language arts and social studies."

"I see, " he said. "And you've brought us something written out to illustrate by what means you hope to accomplish this?"

"Yes, here is what I propose for the weekend, " I said, handing them a one-page outline that summarized my ideas. I launched into a brief description of what I had planned for the two days, directing most of my attention to Rosier de Molet, since JPA already knew the gist of my proposal. They both listened raptly as I explained.

"I thought an optimal number for our inaugural event would be ten teachers. They would arrive on Thursday evening at the d'Arivèque home to be housed for two nights. I hope we can have a sort of reception that first night—you know, like a get-acquainted *vin d'honneur* where we'd explain the weekend and distribute a packet with the schedule."

"Yes, " said Jean-Paul. " I very much like that idea. They would have time to see their rooms and acclimate a little bit."

"Exactly," I said. "The main event would be a two-day affair. We would provide two breakfasts, two lunches and one dinner. The dinner would be Friday night, and while we won't do anything too formal, I thought French food and maybe a film afterwards? " I glanced up at JPA and he nodded, smiling.

"The breakfasts would be continental, nothing elaborate, but authentically French. After that everyone would board a jitney for the ride to the *Alliance Française* building. Lunches will be box ones, brought over by our staff. For the one dinner, again -- not formal --on Friday night, I thought we could also invite our speaker. Everyone will leave by late Saturday afternoon." I set my pages of notes down.

The two men were very attentive and seemed enthralled by my presentation. JPA would look over at Daniel Rosier de Molet from time to time to ascertain his reactions to it.

"One thing that has changed from my initial idea that you were already consulted on, Jean-Paul," I said, "is that now I believe we should only have one guest lecturer. That would give more time for him or her to maybe go a little deeper into the topic."

JPA nodded and said, "Yes, I see your point."

"Anyway," I continued, "everyone attends the lecture and then before lunch, they actually break out into the first small-group sessions such as we..." I paused to nod in his direction,... " *Monsieur* and I saw at the Mid-States Conference."

"Can you give me an example of what the break-out session would entail?" Daniel asked.

"Sure. There could be, for instance, a lesson-planning session on how to introduce the topic of the Marquis de Lafayette into one's own classes. I envision our library playing a major role in this with our films, our history boxes geared towards younger kids, and a wide range of multi-media materials at the teachers' disposal. We want to introduce them to the really high-quality materials that they can access from us later. And in fact, we have the greatest movie on Lafayette—we could show that after dinner on the Friday! Its title is just *La Fayette* – it's not a new one -- it starred Michel Le Royer."

"Ah, *oui*, of course, I saw that in the *cinéma* in Paris, " Daniel said. "Orson Welles played Benjamin Franklin. *Mon Dieu*, I have not thought of that film in years!"

"When it came out some ten years ago or so, " I remarked, "it was the most lavish and expensive film France had ever produced."

"I saw it, too, " said Jean-Paul. "Orson Welles had played the same role of Franklin in Sacha Guitry's film on Versailles. Do you know if we also have that one, Sarah? *Si Versailles m'était conté.*"

"I've never even heard of that, " I answered.

"In English it was called something like *Royal Affair in Versailles*, I believe."

"Sorry! Doesn't ring a bell. But I'll check our catalogue again. Maybe we have it. I do know Sacha Guitry --at least! We have a bundle of his."

Daniel smiled. "I know when you and Jean-Paul got back from that conference, our film lending really took off. This will elicit the same reaction no doubt."

"I think it will, too, " I said. "Also, we want the teachers of the differing content areas to brainstorm some interdisciplinary activities they could combine forces on. I think kids love a *'changement d'air'* from time to time and our whole overreaching goal is to turn kids on!"

"Wonderful!" said de Molet.

"Continue with the schedule, Sarah, " Jean-Paul spurred me on.

"Well, like I said, we will provide lunches both Friday and Saturday and I feel like we could prevail upon the AFC to use their dining room to eat in. Then, I see us conducting some sort of creative session for them to make bulletin board materials or plan some skits--I don't know yet—but something concrete to take away from their weekend experience."

"I think that is one of the best parts of the whole concept, " Jean-Paul said, obviously pleased with my efforts, "but I am curious as to who you have in mind to lead the afternoon break-out session."

"Yes...well... I haven't exactly figured that out yet either. I mean, I'll certainly do my part, and I'm hoping I can hit up Dom Lambert to have some really good ideas for me. The thing is, with teachers, they're usually pretty creative, and if given the time and materials, I imagine they would be able to brainstorm and come up with some great things in the group setting."

Rosier de Molet laughed, "I never had any teacher as creative as you, Sarah!"

Jean-Paul smiled at me, and said, "We still have time to iron out the details. As I was the day you brought this idea to our attention, I am very impressed with the work you've done so far, and I am convinced that this program could be very successful---for us and for the teachers."

"I heartily concur with you, *mon vieux,*" echoed Daniel.

I added, "The real take-away from this whole weekend, I believe, is that it would serve to elevate teacher awareness of the Foundation, that is, tackling this particular topic, at least. I'm hopeful that if this one is successful, teachers will ask for more. This one on Lafayette might be just the spark that ignites an entire explosion of other programs for us to develop."

"Yes! I am sure you are right, "said Jean-Paul, adding, "if the teachers are enthusiastic about their weekend, they would spread the word. They would, at the very least, return to their classrooms buoyed up about French, history, Franco-American ties and, as a result of all that...about our Foundation."

"And," I added, reassuringly, "don't forget, I still intend to come up with some evaluation tool, so we can gauge if we were successful with our objectives for the Institute. "

"So, what do we want to offer our speaker in the way of an honorarium?" the legal counsel asked d'Arivèque.

"I was thinking in the neighborhood of a thousand dollars, " he answered.

"Wow! " I blurted out, not meaning to do that.

"What? Do you not believe that is the right amount?" Jean-Paul asked me worriedly.

"Oh...no! That's great! I...it just...took me by surprise is all. That's very generous, of course. I don't see how anyone could turn **that** down for a few hours of work!"

It was decided before we adjourned, that we should send out a letter of invitation, under JPA's signature, to any potential speaker, with the added explanation of the offer for an honorarium.

"We will follow up with a contract, " said Daniel.

I was jubilant as I returned to my office. My job had blossomed seemingly from a few flowers into a full garden. I was on target for the Institute, time-wise; I'd written lesson plans and conversation prompts for over fifty of our films; and the culture boxes were coming in and going out smoothly. Most importantly, the *Moments Culturels* for Dowling Press-- numbers one through five-- had been approved already. My topics for those initial ones were 1) French school pupils' greetings to peers versus adults; 2) French official time in the telling time scheme; 3) the custom of having a "chocolat sandwich" for "*le gouter*" after school in France; 4) shaking hands and *la bise*; and 5) a simplified version of the role a café plays in French life. These were written and explained in English; and the writing of them had been fun. I was pleased with the results and hoping the editors of both the Foundation and the company would be, also. I was gearing up to write the next five, and eager to switch to French-- of course, a version of French using a lot of cognates.

I wasn't taking any more work home at night, since I concentrated hard on sequestering myself at my desk, like I vowed I would. I rarely went to the break room, and few people sought me out in my office,

591

no doubt having all heard I'd been responsible for breaking our beloved boss' heart. Even Hennie left me alone, and I quit socializing with her. I figured she'd be on that plane going to the wedding and there might be a chance that she would open her big mouth to me there. Thank God I'd decided not to attend.

I still got heart palpitations and stomach flips every time I thought of Polo or remembered our lovely time together; but I tried to repress it, wanting at all cost to avoid even the *soupçon* of a confrontation of any sort--- neither love nor enmity. The truth was, I felt hollow inside. I was sad, but also angry at myself all over again, especially any time I conjured up the cringe-making humiliation of my having assumed for two years that he was gay.

I was back to lazing around my living room in sweat pants after work, eating soup in front of the t.v., and wallowing in melancholy as I listened to Joni Mitchell sing "now I've gone and lost the best baby that I ever had." So it floored me when, one night, the new buzzer system that had been installed rang in my apartment, indicating that someone was at the outer front door for me. Annie-Laure was at my front steps.

"Annie-Laure! Gosh, is Jean-Luc here, too?"

"He'll wait for me in the car, " she said, gesturing towards the street. "May I come in for a minute, Sari?"

"Yeah---sure. What's cookin'?" *As if I didn't know.*

We went down the hall into my open door. I invited her to be seated on my couch and I sat down facing her. She looked straight at me and pouted.

"It will make me very unhappy if you do not come to my wedding."

"It might make you more so if I do. I haven't been in the best mood lately, you may have noticed. I don't want to mope around at your wedding."

"Then don't **mope** around it, as you say. Be happy and come on that plane! I just couldn't believe it when Marie-France told me you were not coming! So I said I would convince you. Thus I am here. To convince you. It would not be the same without you."

Her demeanor was firm and business-like. I felt I could resist it.

"Sure it would. I'm just one person, and you'll be surrounded with your family and French friends."

"You are my family here, Sari. I very much want you to be at our special day, Luc's and mine. He feels exactly as I do."

"I would also like to be there for you, however, as you know, it's very awkward for me now around the workplace. But at least no one has to see me after hours. At your wedding, I'd just stick out like a sore thumb when all I'd really want to do is go off and hide."

She looked at me again almost calculating what she could come up with that would change the dynamic in the room.

"He loves you, you know. He's also having a hard time of it right now."

"That's another reason I should avoid him. I'm the cause of his misery."

"**Losing you** is the cause of his misery. You could put him out of it by just changing your mind and marrying him. We could have a double wedding!"

"Now you're just being ridiculous."

"*Remarque*, I understand that what happened has made you very unhappy — both of you — but your not coming to my wedding only punishes me. Please don't do it! I absolutely want you there. I've made my life in Chicago, now, and so has Luc, and you are a part of our lives here. A grand celebration of ours would not be the same without your presence."

At that, I was rather taken aback: Annie-Laure sounded like me trying to convince Cass to come stay with me. I sympathized with her. She kept talking.

"Consider that JPA has offered his plane to the entire office so that no one would have to worry if they could not afford to make the trip to be there with us. It is a magnificent gesture on his part...just to make us the most wonderful wedding weekend. How could you live with yourself if you missed it?"

I tried to think of something to refute that, but it was not forthcoming. I was indeed on the receiving end of my own arguments to Cass. I felt my defenses breaking down.

"I'll...I'll think about it."

"I am leaving in another week to start the preparations with Marie-France. I must deliver all the visa documents to the Consulate in a few days. I want to know you will be on that plane. You must tell me tonight that you will."

I had yet not announced to Cass that I had found the days free to come to El Paso, so it wasn't like she would be counting on me or anything. But not going down there also made me sad. I was looking so forward to seeing the twins. What I wasn't too anxious to have to contend with, however, was that Cass had been lying to me about conquering her eating disorder. In fact, I was pretty sure she had tried to pull the wool over my eyes and that we'd have an altercation of some sort. Maybe this wasn't the best time to go down there.

"Okay, I'll come to your wedding. And I also promise not to ruin
it," I chuckled, hugging her.

"*Chouette!*" she yelled. "I am happy again!"

Yeah, well, that made one of us. On top of all my doubts and misgivings about being alone at the festivities, now I found myself in the predicament of also having only a few weeks to find some goddamned fancy summer outfits to wear to this thing.

Chapter One Hundred Two

"Wedding Day at Troldhaugen"...Edvard Grieg

Almost in the blink of an eye, I was packing for the wedding of Annie-Laure and Jean-Luc. The ceremony and subsequent celebrations would take place over an extended weekend, with the office closing on noon on the Wednesday, and the d'Arivèque plane taking off Thursday late afternoon from O'Hare.

We were a group of forty-two employees of the FCF, many with spouses. Hennie was attending with her French boyfriend, Jacques, "Mop" , and they planned to stay on in France and go to his hometown of Nantes. It indicated to me that their relationship was also getting serious.

"I've got vacation days accrued, " she crowed to me, "and we plan on making the most of them. It's going to be a **gas**."

"I presume you will find time to spend in Paris, " I told her, "because being there with your true love is the **best**."

On the day of the flight, we were all to congregate at the office entrance to be bused to the private aircraft section of that huge airport. At least I already knew that drill, having flown on the Hyde's plane. The trip would be overnight, and we would arrive at Orly Airport at around eight o'clock the next morning. JPA had decided that we would travel not by coach to the Loire Valley, but go on a scenic train ride from Paris' Gare d'Austerlitz station to the town of Vierzon, where we would be collected with our luggage, and then go by other transportation to *La Pérégrine*.

We'd been provided with a detailed schedule of events, and I had been forced to come up with multiple outfits suitable for everything from hanging around the *château*, as I imagined this place would be, to attending the prenuptial rehearsal dinner Friday night, and then the wedding itself on Saturday, followed by the resplendent wedding dinner that night. On the Sunday, after the newlyweds departed for their honeymoon to Corsica, the rest of us were invited to tour the city of Orléans, about an hour away. I'd been to Orléans during my year abroad and had absolutely loved it. This time I reckoned I'd get to see a lot more of the gorgeous jewel town than I had the summer of 1968. On Monday the "*trajet*" would reverse and we would head back to the airport in Paris for the return trip to Chicago. The office would reopen on Wednesday with a skeleton staff-- since there would be no Marie-France de Piaget or Annie-Laure LeBeau Moreau! Starting again mid-week would give us a chance to recuperate from any jet lag.

My outfit choices for the trip were discussed on the phone at great length with Cass.

"You need something comfortable for the plane but that doesn't look like you were homeless, sleeping on a park bench when you get off in Paris."

"Well, wish me luck with that. "

"Yeah, don't wear linen pants! They look so chic when you put them on, but you can resemble a shriveled-up raisin when you get up after sitting in them."

"So maybe a maxi skirt? Would that give off too much hippie or pioneer woman?"

"Hmm, yeah. So what about a cute flowered maxi dress of some sort? Look through some magazines. You'll find them. See what you think."

"Okay, so then what shall I take for the wedding? I've seen sketches of Annie-Laure's dress. Oh, Cass, it's really fab---all Alençon lace over silk shantung taffeta with a two-tiered cathedral train. Too gorgeous!"

"Then why don't you buy something simple, like a cocktail dress with a kind of full skirt. That would be garden-party-ish."

"Yes, that's an idea. I'll see what I can find. What about just messing around the manor house? I don't see myself in wheat jeans."

"No, probably not. I can picture you in one of those sleeveless cotton Lily Pulitzer sheaths like The Shrimp used to wear. You remember? Get a pink one. I think you should wear light pink and black together. That's so chic!"

"Yeah! That would be cute to go on a bus tour of Orléans, too. I could wear a sweater with it...doubt France is any too warm even in late Spring."

"Be sure to take pictures with that cool new camera of yours, and send me some when you get back."

"Of course! Good idea. Can't forget to take that."

She was right. I had my new camera to take on this trip---its own maiden voyage.

So I outfitted myself from Saks Fifth Avenue's equivalent of Brandeis' French Room, first in a cotton-candy pink shantung cocktail dress for the pre-nup. It had a black satin ribbon at the waist that tied into a big bow, and billowy sleeves that came to cuffs. It was a gorgeous romantic look, reminiscent of Carnaby Street, and I could wear my London shoes with it. For the actual wedding, I decided to splurge on a full-skirted tea-length dress made of organza the color of pale pink champagne and covered in pink cabbage roses with delicate green stems and leaves. It had a stiff crinoline sewn into it. I felt like a floating garden when I walked out of the dressing room in it to view myself in a full-length mirror. I was convinced that the shoes Polo had given me to wear with the "Valentine dress" *(as I still called it---ugh)* would go fine with this one, too. So I purchased both of those beautiful dresses for the shocking-to-my-system price of three hundred eighty-five dollars (double what the first-class airfare to El Paso was.)

Next I bravely took the escalator down two floors to the "Life Style" department, and found what I would wear on the plane: a knit pants suit in sort of a dusty rose, a little more subdued than the wedding attire. If I took the jacket off, it would remain relatively unwrinkled for the duration of the flight, and I could look half-way put together when we landed. For the country I took a light-weight white sweater I already owned, to wear with the same pants and...this time... loafers. I could wear that outfit with its jacket on the day trip to Orléans, too, and even be reasonably coordinated. And since I didn't care what I looked like upon arrival back in Chicago, I did indeed pack the wheat jeans and a plaid cotton shirt to wear on the plane home.

"So in the end, I just threw money at the problem, " I told Cass, after hearing her oohs and ahhhs at my descriptions on the phone.

"Well, sometimes you gotta go for it, " she said reassuring me that I wouldn't end up penniless for having done this. "Besides, you're a high falutin consultant now. You make a fortune!"

"I guess so, " I laughed. "Yay for little me, eh? Too bad I don't have any decent underwear to do this fashion justice. Good thing no one will be undressing me at this thing."

"Well, you're going to France, for God's sake. Buy some there!"

"No time for shopping! Plus it's **France**. The stores won't be open in Orléans on a Sunday. The only free time I'll have will be at the *château*. So no chance for elegant lingerie on this trip. But thanks for the suggestion—ha ha-- since you remember, I'm sure, how shocked we both were to see those prices for ONE BRA on the Champs-Elysées that time. I thought I'd faint."

"I remember. Let me put it to you this way: whatever under garments you have, you'll look like the Queen of Sheba next to me. Mine are so far gone they'd make rags seem chic."

"Well, Cass, I'll bring you some when I come, but you must be able to find something down there. Don't they have Kresge's or Woolworth's? You can get anything in those stores."

"Probably in El Paso, you're right. At least the kiddos are still doing just great in all those clothes you brought to Iowa City for them," she said, hastily changing the subject. "Thanks again for all that."

"I'll be back one of these days---soon. I will splurge and fly down. It may be end of summer now but I'll come, I promise."

"You have to. I'm desperate to see you again."

It was a balmy and warm afternoon in Chicago when, as instructed, we all met at the office with our luggage in tow and our passports with the requisite visa procured by the Foundation. Naturally, I was the only person there with a plaid cloth suitcase purchased with Green Stamps.

We were whisked out to O'Hare and assembled to board without even any time to lounge around in the lah- dee-dah VIP private flight waiting area. I walked out the door and onto the tarmac, expecting to see the private plane, but what I saw stopped me in my tracks. Everyone else, however, just mingled and kept walking...towards a stairway leading up to...WHAT?!...a Boeing 707! A normal Boeing 707! This was the actual d'Arivèque plane?! I was speechless. It was so much bigger than the Hyde's private jet!

"They must be joking! " I whispered to our assistant copy editor Charlotte, as we stood ready to climb the stairs into the plane. "This plane is huge. I just can't believe it."

"Oh, you didn't know that?" she laughed. "I've seen pictures of it before. Never flown in it, though."

"That was going to be my next question." None of these people seemed as shocked as I was to be boarding a private plane that size.

I saw everyone there but Jean-Paul d'Arivèque himself, but knew he wouldn't have come on the bus with us. We were given the signal to start boarding and up we went…into a fucking magic carpet!

Who knew the interior of airplanes could be reconfigured into flying hotel lobbies! Even though the front of the plane where we entered looked like a regular first-class seating area behind the cockpit-- with pairs of wide leather seats, the usual bathrooms on one side, and the same type of curtain dividing it off-- the next part, which would have been coach, I guess, was nothing like an airplane. It was more like a yacht, replete with a long, completely stocked bar, seating areas around tables for eight, conversation pits with comfortable leather couches and lounge chairs, and more restrooms. Then there were a few more rows of the same first-class-sized seats exactly as in the front. When you got to the very back, there were two closed cabins…I presumed Jean-Paul's bedroom and maybe an office…or a big full bath? I had no clue.

The whole plane was paneled burnished teak, polished to a sheen, and the furnishings were teal blue and seafoam green. Each porthole had white shades with curtains over them. Tables were set with white linens, china and silverware, and each one had a floral display in the cabin colors.

Stewardesses in that same teal colored suits with white piping around the collar and cuffs, wearing white gloves and pill-box hats welcomed us in French as we came in. It was as though I had climbed the stairs into an airplane and immediately fallen down a heavenly rabbit hole.

I was standing just by the cockpit, trying to decide where to go sit down, and out of the still open door, I saw Jean-Paul being helped up the narrow stairs by Robineau. He wasn't having an easy time of it. The space was too steep and small for him to be able to swing his brace leg out and up, so he had to keep the knee locked, and just sort of drag that leg behind him. While he could propel himself up holding the railing on the right, Robineau practically had to lift him up on the left. That must have been the drawback to flying private, I surmised…no jetway at your disposal. I wondered how "normal" people with mobility problems-- but without servants--- managed to get on airplanes that didn't have jetways. Nothing about it seemed easy.

I decided to go sit in the back-- in one of the "regular" but so comfortable broad leather seats near a window, and put my tote bag on the seat next to me, signaling that no one need sit with me.

There was a built-in pillow top on the seat back and a blanket and eyeshade wrapped in plastic left on the seat for us like on a commercial flight. I bet myself I'd be asleep as soon as the wheels started to roll down the runway.

Jean-Paul sat way up in front and not in one of the private cabins, which made me feel relieved that he wouldn't be coming to the back and passing me. He did, however, get on the intercom and welcome us all on board before his Flight Purser took over and gave us take off instructions.

Our newsletter editor, Quentin Masson, and his wife took seats a few rows behind Jean-Paul with Daniel Rosier de Molet and his wife and teen-age daughter, Emilie. Hennie and Jacques sat near the bar with Bernadette, the receptionist, and a slew of others. The sixty or so of us didn't even seem to fill the plane by half. I was amazed.

The stews passed out menus and hot towels while we were still on the ground, and then they took their places up near Polo for take-off. All went smoothly, and we were soon at thirty-five thousand feet cruising altitude, set to cross first the continental United States up to Newfoundland, and then the Atlantic.

I settled in, unwrapped the blanket, curled up on the seat under it, and took out my dog-eared copy of *Setting Free the Bears*, a book John Irving had written at Iowa. I'd brought it along to read on the plane hoping to actually finish it this time on an eight-hour trip. I had not found it to be the proverbial page-turner, but felt obliged to give it another-- more thoughtful --version of that old college try.

John Irving, like Kurt Vonnegut, was a house-hold name by 1972, and I was determined to offer his book a fair shake, even though the truth was I didn't much care for it. One of my professors at Iowa had once said that reading was an endeavor, unlike looking at paintings or listening to music, that one had to work at in order to mine the *treasure it guarded. I came to the conclusion that I must not have been particularly in synch with John Irving, because Setting Free the Bears was not giving up many nuggets from my efforts to read it. So I put it down after about fifteen minutes, and started to daydream about the fact that I was streaking across a continent and an ocean on a private jet… for the **weekend**… to attend a wedding! Was this really my life?*

I looked around at the plane and my colleagues. We were doing a pretty good imitation of the Beautiful People. Actually, I'd been rubbing shoulders with the jet set for the past six years, really. Between the Hyde's' two or three homes, limousines, their plane, stays in exorbitantly expensive hotels in New York and Amsterdam on their dime, my Paris year abroad, my job, the countless soirées and receptions, public concerts, private recitals by world-renowned musicians, dinners out in the most glamorous Chicago restaurants, new clothes. Shit! Who was I? Or rather who did I think I was?! It was not lost on me that this bubble could burst at any given moment, plunging me back to a 1959 crumbling Nash Rambler station wagon before I could say "No.. no more fois-gras for me, thanks."

My reverie was abruptly and rudely interrupted when I looked up and saw coming right down the aisle towards me, none other than Robineau. I became instantly very much more interested in Mr. Irving's Vienna zoo animals.

"*Excusez-moi, Mademoiselle,* " he said leaning in dangerously close to my personal space, "*Monsieur* has asked me to invite you to come to his *place…* for a moment."

Go up to his seat? Oh, Christ.

"Why?" I asked without looking at him.

"I cannot say, *Mademoiselle* Sarah."

"Yes, okay, " I said, hoping not to show any rancor or exasperation in my voice, "tell him I'll come up there."

He nodded and said, "Thank you," and left.

I put my shoes back on, climbed out of the soft blanket and headed up to the front of the plane.

"Hi! " I said, trying to sound nonchalant and cheery at the same time. "You wanted to see me?"

"Sarah, please…sit down here next to me, would you?"

I took the seat and turned in it to face him but not quite look him in the eyes.

"I am delighted that you changed your mind and came on the trip with us. It means a great deal to Annie-Laure and Luc."

"Good, then I'm glad I came, too." I smiled up at him, but he was not looking as "delighted" as he said he was. His demeanor was forlorn, and that was exactly what I feared it would be.

"I have missed you, Sarah."

"But I've been at work every day, " I said not acknowledging what I knew full well were his feelings.

"Yes, you have. But have you? Really been there, I mean."

"Yes."

"No. You are as distant as the stars."

"But still there."

"You see, I feel I offended you…deeply…in some way with my proposal of marriage. You did not take it seriously."

"Yes, I did. You didn't offend me at all. I just told you the truth why it was a preposterous idea for **you** to marry **me**." And then I did look him in the face, and asked, " Do you really want to talk about this here? In front of the entire office?"

For one thing, I was now very afraid I was going to cry again.

"They are not paying attention to us way up here. But we could go into my cabin and talk about it if you would prefer."

"No."

"*Alors*, the main *hésitation* for you…the stumbling…what is this expression?"

"Stumbling block?

"Yes, stumbling block… for you… is your religion, *n'est-ce pas*?"

"Not for me, for **you**. I keep telling you that. I don't care, but you would."

"Why do you insist on proclaiming to me what I would or would not do? What I asked you up here to tell you is I am willing to become a Jew to marry you. Would you agree to that?"

"What?! NO!"

"Why not?"

I lowered my voice to barely a hiss, "Because you're the fucking future *duc de Beuvron*, that's why. You can't be Jewish, and I can't be the cause of all the strife that would come down on you if you did convert. Which you cannot."

"But if as you say, I am *the fucking duc*! I can do what I want!"

"Now you're just messing with me."

"I am sorry. Forgive me?" He raised his hand to my forehead and swept some wisps of hair from my eyebrows. Then he looked into my eyes deeply and said, "I just want you to know that it is true. I am willing to change religions if it would mean that you would consent to marry me."

I just sat there for a minute — seemed like an hour — before saying anything to that. And then I took his hand in mine and felt him squeeze it.

"Look, Polo, I would never ask you to do that. Just so you understand where I'm coming from, people take marriage vows to love, honor and maybe even obey-- although that one is questionable these days, I have to say — but the ceremony doesn't demand that they promise to change who they are, to abandon their identity, their heritage or their souls. I couldn't ask that of you, ever." I let go of his hand and continued,

"You're you and I'm me. We come from different universes. There's a chasm between us wider than this ocean we're about to cross. So let's just face the fact that we can't marry. We can be colleagues — boss-employee, I mean. I'm still filled with gratitude that I was ever even hired by your Foundation. I would do anything for you, and I daresay, so would everyone on this plane! You and I are now dear friends. I even thought…was perfectly willing…to be…to have… you as my lover." I paused, but added hastily, " Even if I now fear that was a mistake."

"It truly saddens me to hear you say that, Sarah. I am more and more convinced that I love you. I had great hope that you felt the same way."

"I did!" I confirmed emphatically. "I still do. But, it doesn't matter. What I'm trying to say is that even though all that may be true, we still just can't be man and wife. Not us."

"I must reject that. I sincerely believe that you are wrong, Sarah. I know in my heart that you are my one love… for all my life…that you are my *beshert*. If I did believe in some God, I would swear that meeting you bore the fingerprints of divine intervention in my life, something I have longed for all these years."

Fuck. Me. I gave up at that point. I could not see the use of more arguing at thirty-five thousand feet with no exit. He used the word beshert *with me. He obviously knew its meaning. He was making this so hard for me I couldn't stand it.*

"Well, I thank you, "I said. " Truly if the situation and the circumstances were different, I'd be very… honored… to be your true love. I really would."

I kissed him discretely on the cheek and went back to my seat. Now I had to hope I wouldn't be nauseous on the plane from anxiety. Now I had to look forward to a weekend of discomfort and just plain sorrow. Now I was right back to wishing I'd never agreed to go on this trip.

Flight attendants came around to serve us wonderful food and anything at all we wanted to drink. They brought out pastry carts and cappuccinos after dinner and gave us headphones so we could watch the movie which was going to be shown, *Elvira Madigan*. I took every diversion offered me to try to block out my feelings of inadequacy and gloom.

It was fitful, but I still managed to sleep curled up across both the seats in my little row because those leather cushions were so incredibly comfortable. That, together with the hum of the engines and the sometimes rocking of light turbulence, put me right out.

I awoke to sunlight streaming in the cabin and to the dreaded cotton mouth. Gathering up the toiletries kit I'd brought on board, I went into the back bathroom to make myself presentable. And there he was: just as I was coming out of the tiny metal door, Jean-Paul's beautiful wooden cabin door opened revealing his figure right beside me. I stepped out of his way giving an awkward little wave. He waved back and smiled at me with a wistful look. I scurried to retake my place.

Upon landing and going through passport control we emerged from the private baggage claim area and into the regular arrivals hall, where I caught a glimpse of Jean-Luc! He was there to take Polo, along with Robineau, by car to *La Pérégrine*. Once outside on the curb, I saw the magnificent car Luc was driving this time: a Rolls Royce! It had to be a pre-war car. It was black and had some sort of coat of arms on the side passenger door.

Holy shit… what next!?

The rest of us were shepherded into a waiting coach to take us to the Gare d'Austerlitz. I wondered who would get to *La Pérégrine* first, and I rightly surmised Polo would. But traveling by train through France was always one of my favorite things, and I reveled in the opportunity to do so again aboard the pretty red and white *"Le Capitole,"* a 1960's version of a *"train à grande vitesse"* or fast train that linked Paris-Austerlitz with Toulouse. All our reservation numbers were in the same car, so we rode as a jolly group anticipating the wonderful reunion with the wedding principals and MFP, and the myriad of events that would keep us celebrating for the next forty-eight hours and more.

The *Gare Vierzon* was, as expected, very small and the train was slated to be stopped in it for less than five minutes, so we had to hustle off with our luggage and then mill about for nearly half an hour while it was determined which of many different cars would be delivering us in groups of five, to *La Pérégrine*. Finally, Daniel Molet stepped up and organized this convoy, and I rode in the last car with him and a lot of the luggage. He'd been there before, so as we were approaching the drive, he motioned for me to take a look out his side of the car so I could see the house as it came into view like a birthday cake frosted in yellow. We drove up a long gravel drive that opened out in front of the house into a wide circle, flanked by boxwood hedges and white wooden crates holding flowering bushes. There was parking for a multitude of cars right there, which astounded me, too.

I was pleasantly surprised by the realization that, though very grand and probably classified as a château, it actually was more of a home than a castle. A manor house was what Polo considered it to be, but it did have one château feature--a real honest-to-God "Rapunzel-worthy" turret on the left-hand side. Beautiful vines of blooming bougainvillea covered one wall, and the upper-story windows in this part all had those little diamond-shaped frames people associate with the classic leaded and beveled glass of the Tudor era.

The main entrance had no stairs in front of it, thus you could walk right in through a double door surrounded, as all the windows were, with long white shutters, the real *"volets"* that could be opened and closed both for security and to keep light out. That main door led into a long-cloistered gallery which connected two symmetrical wings of the house, each three stories high. Attached to those parts—I thought they were attached, but it looked like an afterthought--were two stone houses that might have been granges or stables in the olden days, but were renovated into homes, for whom I did not know. What I came to find out was that the side buildings had housed offices and staff quarters in the days when the place bustled with activity. Marie-France de Piaget had taken the one on the turret side as her retirement residence. It was still enormous for only one occupant. For the wedding weekend at least, the other side would house a myriad staff who would work as maids, butlers, waiters, chefs, other kitchen help, car parking valets and florists.

Once inside that long gallery foyer-- the part of the house that really was a cloister in that it had large arched openings on both sides--there was a table set up to check us in and assign us a bedroom. The wings on each end seemed to me to be accessed only by identical grand, very winding, circular marble staircases, which, even though they had sturdy, thick rope railings, made me wonder if there weren't also bedrooms on the ground floor, since JPA wouldn't have been able to get up those stairs unaided to save his life.

The windows in the gallery let in the bright mid-day light, and gave a superb view to the back garden where I glimpsed an Olympic-sized swimming pool right in the center, surrounded by a pool deck studded with striped cushion deck chairs—what the French call *transats*, just like on Blue Beach at Nice-- and a patio with little conversation clusters of tables and chairs. Marking each *chaise* at poolside were huge urns filled with a riot of colored flowers. In front of all that, there was even a grand manicured *"pelouse"* or lawn that one didn't see every day in French homes.

"Wow, " I thought, "gorgeous!" Too bad no one had told us to bring swimsuits.

On one side of the pool area, formal "*jardins à la française*" stretched out as far as the eye could see, and then at the end, gave way to forest. Off in the other direction I saw the former riding stables, and thought instantly of Corneille the Palomino.

I was not the only singleton guest on the list, but others had already doubled up for rooms, so I was given one to myself. It was so pretty, I almost burst out crying. It was a spacious room done up in cream and yellow. It had a big limestone and brick fireplace, a bed the size of Jean-Paul's sleigh bed in Chicago, and a beautiful hand-carved inlaid writing desk. There was a massive armoire against one wall in the corner for my clothes, and in the middle of the room in front of the bed, was a section delineated by a thick, vintage Surya carpet, upon which were a square antique table and four chairs that had a music motif for the backs. Two comfortable wing chairs had been placed at either end of the mantel.

Another table with a blue gingham cloth and a tall vase of sunflowers stood beside the door leading into my own en suite, which was also enormous. Its floors were made of large, rustic porcelain tiles, and the room had all the facilities scattered about in a haphazard fashion that gave away the attempts that may have been made over the decades-- maybe even centuries-- to modernize it. Nevertheless, it had lovely fixtures and another huge leaded-glass French window that opened outwards and gave off onto the pool.

I was delighted enough with that room to want to just spend the entire weekend holed up in it, but we only had enough time to unpack and freshen up before being beckoned by the schedule to appear back in the foyer for a *vin d'honneur*. There we would be welcomed, and we would meet the French families of the happy couple before heading in to a late luncheon at around two o'clock.

Jean-Paul d'Arivèque took center stage and started right off saying how he and all of us owed Marie-France de Piaget a sincere debt of gratitude. He commended her on the extraordinary job she'd done re-opening and staffing the house. She blushed, but I could tell she was in her element, and also verified with her later, how thrilled she was to be living there for the rest of her life.

"It was a true mission of love, " she assured us, motioning for Annie-Laure and Jean-Luc to come forward. Annie-Laure radiated like the light beams streaming into the room when she stepped up to embrace her former boss.

We were all led to the dining room in the "turret wing" as I started calling the one on the left, to distinguish it from the other one, where an enormous long table was set for twenty-six people and the rest were accommodated on three more round tables for ten. The walls, which had Rococo "*boiserie*" panels painted in a light chartreuse, matched the chair seats. Three huge mirrors hung down from the crown molding near the ceiling: one with a beautiful stone fireplace under it, another with a mahogany and marble buffet under it, and the third one with the main serving table beneath it. Each mirror reflected light given off from four voluminous crystal chandeliers hanging on heavy velvet cords from various points in the ceiling, including one that marked the center of the long table.

During luncheon later, Marie-France mentioned to me that all the furnishing in that room were "fairly recent," as they dated from the late 1890's, which made me chuckle.

I asked her "Is this where the wedding dinner will be held? It's so beautiful."

"Oh, no," she laughed. "The wedding dinner will be set up in tents in the garden. There are three hundred guests expected!"

Jesus.

I noticed that Annie-Laure and Jean-Luc had not come into the dining room yet, and that there were three empty seats up at the head of the table where Jean-Paul was seated. All at once, in they came with...*Oncle* Charles! "Wow," I thought ...again...(Yes, I was wowed quite a bit that weekend), "he must feel very close to her." Just then her parents also rose from their places and went over to greet the patriarch who was walking hesitantly on two canes. They showed him to his place, where Jean-Paul embraced his uncle from his chair, as Charles sat down next to him.

I was watching this little ballet from where I sat, half-way down the enormous table from them, when Uncle Charles caught sight of me and his face lit up in a smile and he mouthed a silent "*Bonjour, Mademoiselle*" to me. I responded the same way, and gave him a little wave. It was wonderful to see him looking so well for his eighty-some years, despite having a few mobility issues, and I found myself hoping we'd get a chance to talk sometime during the festivities.

600

After the sumptuous "light" lunch of *vichyssoise* followed by *bouchée à la reine*, with cheese boards after that, and a dessert of raspberry *profiteroles*, and coffee, we had free time until dinner. MFP stood and announced that they would make available to us bikes and *Solex vélomoteurs* or mopeds for trips around the grounds-- most of which had not yet been restored to their former glory, she warned us. (*Could have fooled me!*) Or we could take them for a short trip into the nearest village called Lury-sur-Arnon or the town after that, Reuilly.

This would be the perfect diversion for me, I realized: to take a moped out and explore the French countryside. Alone! And I almost made it outside to the parked bikes when Jean-Paul called out to me and I turned to see him struggling on the gravel to make his way after me. So I pivoted around and met him half-way.

"Did you bring any French money with you?" he asked with an amused look on his face.

As a matter of fact, I had scooped up the remaining French coins I had kept from 1969, thinking I might buy something in Orléans on Sunday, but it only added up to enough for a few postcards.

"I did bring a few *centimes* with me, " I admitted, laughing, "but... I don't need any, do I?"

"Take this…just in case, " he admonished, handing me a one-hundred *franc* note.

"*Cent francs*?!" That was about twenty dollars. "Oh, *mais, Monsieur*---er—Polo, *non. Ça c'est du trop.*"

"Nonsense. Take it. Please. And you will not get lost, *n'est-ce pas*?" He laughed, and added, "but if you do, here is my card with the telephone number on it. We shall send out a search party for you if you are not back by late afternoon."

I took his card-- and the money-- and thanked him, shaking my head with the realization that this was, as usual, just one more thing for me to not to be able to reciprocate.

The trip into the towns was just the tonic. Surely Roman soldiers had at one time marched the same route I took, and the tree-lined two-lane road had probably seen the kings of France, too. Lury itself wasn't all that quaint, and although it did have an ancient portal that was interesting, it would not have made the list of France's most beautiful spots. But Reuilly, on the other hand, was more of a picturesque iconic French village, famous, it turned out, for the wineries like *Clos Fussay* near-by that offered the wines of the Loire. I parked the *mop'* and took a seat on the *terrasse* of a café to drink a *citron pressé* for a little while, the ideal spot for people-watching on the square in front of Reuilly's church. The weekly outdoor market was set up and bustling.

I saw that a *quincaillerie* was open just across from where I was, so after I'd sat there for about forty-five minutes, I walked over to the open doorway of the shop with its displays of pans, brooms and baskets of dried flowers hanging outside, and decided to buy a filet like the one I'd had in Paris. If I wasn't driving the Pallas to supermarkets any longer, at least I could carry my stuff home in the new *filet* and be reminded of France. It was a cute "souvenir of the wedding weekend."

I draped the net bag over the handlebars and set back off on the return trip. I was able to flawlessly retrace my "steps" on the D918 road and find my way back to *La Pérégrine*, not because there was a sign, but because peeking up in the distance I could see its yellow tower and reddish-brown tiled roof.

"Piece of cake," I laughed "Not birthday cake…wedding cake."

I had plenty of time, it turned out, to bathe and dress for the prenuptial dinner. I wasn't needed at the rehearsal at all, but I did want to sneak into the chapel to see where the wedding would take place. I knew it was out in the garden somewhere, but not near the pool, so I had to do a little sleuthing to find it. Once near, you couldn't miss it. They'd decorated the trees with streamers and the doors with garlands and bows. The chapel itself was bigger than I thought it would be and in a state of major disrepair, which only added to the rustic romance of the whole place.

Inside, the ancient walls were peeling, but I could tell there'd been some sort of fresco paintings on them at one time. There was a center aisle on each side of which were placed those little gilt rental chairs set up in rows. That space could not have held seating for three hundred; obviously not everyone coming to the dinner would be at the service. Up front and to the side, someone had set up one of those newfangled keyboards on metal legs, so there would be music accompaniment. At the very end of the nave, if you could call it that, under a lovely stained-glass pastoral scene-- completely secular with no hint of the usual biblical tales portrayed in churches-- was a high table covered with a white cloth upon which were two tall candlesticks with white candles. There was no crucifix and no other crosses, either embroidered on the cloth or hanging on any parts of the wall.

I was Jewish, but I'd been in my fair share of Catholic churches and chapels in my day, and I didn't see anything in that space which could be used as accoutrements of the Nuptial Mass. That really puzzled me. I wondered what kind of wedding we would witness the next day.

On the far back wall of the chapel I noticed a niche with a large urn on it, and underneath that the wall held little cubbyholes for other interred ashes.

"My God," I thought, "people are buried in here." I looked back outside for any signs of a graveyard, and didn't see any, but it turns out there was one…just farther away…which housed the remains of many a *Duc de Beuvron*.

Polo had told me about the love-temple shrine his mother had erected to house the things she'd put in it to honor her husband; and I knew that was where he had buried her ashes, too. But I couldn't see that from the pool area or the chapel. That folly she'd had built must have been deep in the garden.

The prenup dinner took place in the same dining room where we'd been already; this time the table was laden with large vases of pink and white roses and festooned with ribbons. For this dinner I was seated with the Foundation's legal department, the Rosier de Molets, Hennie and Jacques, Hennie's immediate boss Madeline Guerin and her husband, and De Molet's secretary, Suzanne Lefevre and her husband. I had met all these spouses at various Foundation events, but had never had the chance to really talk to them, so it was very pleasant. No one brought up anything to do with my erstwhile relationship with our *Président*, but they all spoke enthusiastically of the film library, the textbook contributions, and the up-coming event for teachers. I was happy to field their questions, but a little self-conscious to be the center of attention at that end of the table. Hennie was quite subdued, for her, and her knowing glances and the expression on her face from time to time, led me to believe she was taking note of how I was being treated by her superiors. This might have been the only time she'd ever shown deference to me since I'd arrived at the Foundation, and it felt weird.

We had many toasts to Annie-Laure and Jean-Luc and even, as in America, speeches by the "*témoin and témoine*." I could tell this was going to be a sort of amalgam of American and French customs. Annie-Laure's father expressed his heart-felt gratitude to Jean-Paul d'Arivèque for providing the splendid venue for his daughter's wedding, and thanked all of us for coming to share in it. I had no idea what he did for a living, but I imagined this was more than he could have ever afforded to give her, and probably more than any of them had bargained for. But he didn't act embarrassed or rueful at all, and seemed genuinely thrilled for his girl.

The wedding day arrived as bright and fair as the day before. Most of the guests, including me, did not attend the secular legal wedding at the *Mairie* of Vierzon. The deputy mayor, who performed it, was a close friend on Jean-Luc's side, whom, it turned out we would all meet later that night. Breakfast-brunch-lunch was offered any time we felt like eating something. This time the big dining room was transformed into an elaborate buffet with seating wherever one liked. I took mine out to the pool and sat on a comfortable *chaise-longue*, eating finger sandwiches and drinking Orangina under the cloudless azure sky.

We had the entire afternoon in which to prepare for the wedding ceremony. I bathed leisurely and changed into my cabbage-rose dress, and tried to do something with my hair. Too bad that nice maid who braided it before didn't make the trip. My own attempts to braid it even a bit on top were hopeless. I parted it on the side and drew the hair that was most plentiful up above and behind my ear, and secured it with an elastic band. Then I tied a pink ribbon around it into a bow. The rest of my hair hung down straight on both sides. I may have looked like a three-year-old, but I liked the idea that it was fancier than I normally wore it.

I took a seat on one of the wobbly little chapel chairs about three rows back from the altar. Jean-Paul came in with his uncle, glanced at my hair and smiled at me, and they chose seats right across the aisle from me. Polo looked at me from time to time, as though he had something to say, but we didn't chat.

Soon the musician hired to play the electronic keyboard sat down to it and serenaded us with Vivaldi. Notes that sounded like a harpsichord came out of speakers in the back. It was another wow moment for me, as I was not at all familiar with synthesizers. When Bach's *Prelude in C* was struck up, the little machine put out the sound of a pipe organ. We all stood to watch the bride enter.

Annie-Laure was nothing short of a vision. Her taffeta gown was an Empire style covered in the floral motif Alençon lace I had described to Cass. It had a sweetheart neckline and a sweep train. She wore the two-tiered cathedral length veil, covered in beaded lace embroidery, which I'd seen in the sketch, and when Jean-Luc lifted it so they could face each other, his expression was one of sheer awe at her beauty. We all felt the same.

The officiant seemed to be a priest-- he wore a clerical collar and vestment-- but certainly did not perform any semblance of a mass. There was no psalm, no Gospel, nothing like a homily or sermon. Instead he just gave the usual welcome to all the congregants, and then went right into having them repeat normal sounding vows: to each one in turn he asked, "*Prenez-vous Jean-Luc et Annie-Laure comme époux? Et promettez-vous de lui rester fidèle? Dans le bonheur ou dans les épreuves? Dans la santé et dans la maladie? Pour l'aimer tous les jours de votre vie?*" And to all of these questions the couple each in turn answered, "*Oui.*" There was an exchange of rings, and that was about it. The venue may have been over the top elegance, but the actual ceremony was simplicity itself.

The huge dinner tent and smaller drinks stations, also tented, were indeed set up on the lawn, featuring long banquet tables which were illuminated by white lights strewn all over in the trees, and magnificent silver five-globe table-top candelabra adorning every ten or so places down the middle of the tables. Bowls of pink roses were positioned amidst the candles, and the chairs were covered in white cloths with white bows at the back, except for the bride and groom chairs which were decorated in garlands of flowers and marked "*Monsieur*" and "*Madame.*" The overall aspect created was one of nothing less than fairyland.

Sunset there was later than in Chicago, since France is way farther north in latitude, so for a good three hours we could see what was being served. The *château's* great floodlights came on as the gardens darkened, and by the time the pastry chef appeared with the elaborate *croquembouche pièce montée*, the traditional French version of a wedding cake, the gardens were dazzling under twinkling lights and a starry sky. A string quartet set up on the pool deck had played during dinner, but another combo-type group arrived later, and changed to rock music that lasted into the wee hours. Everyone drank champagne and danced.

Still leery of drinking champagne-- even on a full stomach -- I wandered around the grounds stopping at various bars set up, hoping to unearth Coca-Cola or even a Schweppes. But for some reason no non-alcoholic drinks were available, so I went into the house looking for the kitchen to get a glass of water, when I ran right into *Oncle* Charles.

"Oh, Sarah!" he said, startling me, "I was hoping to find you. Would you have breakfast with me tomorrow and take a stroll perhaps in the garden?"

"I would love to, *Monsieur le Duc*, " I answered, remembering to call him that, to which he shook his finger at me and corrected me with "*Oncle Charles*, please."

"I would love to, *Oncle Charles*, but I am scheduled to be on the coach to Orléans in the morning. What time were you thinking?"

"Would it be possible for you to forego the little day trip to that lovely town? I fear I will not have the chance to see you again, as I must take my leave in the early afternoon."

I didn't want to stay back, but I could hardly deny him anything. "Of course I can skip it, " I said.

"*Ah, merci*, Sarah, *c'est gentil*. Shall we meet in the gallery at ten o'clock?"

"That would be fine, " I said, and bade him goodnight as I turned towards where I thought the kitchen was.

Unbeknownst to me, I was wrong, and I ended up in a maze of little rooms and antechambers behind the stairs on the non-turret side. Hopelessly lost, I was trying to retrace my steps out of that rabbit warren when I saw Robineau heading towards what must have been Jean-Paul d'Arivèque's bedroom.

"*Excusez-moi, Monsieur* Robineau?" I called out to him, bracing myself for one of his exasperated barrages of "*Mais qu'est-ce que vous fabriquez ici!*" or "*Je n'en reviens pas!*" or "*Mais vous faites n'importe quoi!*" I expected to hear him bark "*Putain*" at me or "*Punaise!*" or any number of other nasty rebukes. But he said nothing of the sort and instead told me, "*Un moment, Mademoiselle* Sarah, " and motioned out of my range of sight, whereupon Jean-Paul emerged from the shadows in his dressing gown with the pronounced limp that let me know his leg brace had already been removed for bed.

"Oh, God, I'm so sorry, " I said, "I didn't realize…but of course, it's very late… I got a little turned around. I was looking for the kitchen…just to get a glass of water to take up with me."

"I shall have the maid bring it to your room, *ne t'en fais pas*, " he answered …far more sweetly than I deserved at that point. "Will water do or would you prefer a *tisane*?"

"No, no water is fine. I'm sure I could get it myself…I'm just a bit lost."

"Could you…would you mind helping me to my bedroom? And I shall call down to the kitchen…they will send someone with the water and show you how to get back to your room."

"Sure, " I said, taking his arm.

He led me through a series of tiny little corridors that fanned out and ultimately opened up into a palatial bedchamber the likes of which I hadn't seen since class trips to châteaux like Chantilly or Cheverny. I stopped dead in my tracks, astonished at its grandeur and beauty. His room was even bigger than ones I'd seen in the famous castles, and *far* more inviting, with a four-poster bed whose ten-foot high canopy of green silk curtains gathered into a veritable tent over his head — over the head of the noble *Beuvrons*, that is.

Standing with him just inside the door I said that I had been very remiss in not telling him before then that his house was simply splendid, and that I could easily see how he could have been so happy here as a kid. I told him I adored my room upstairs, and thanked him again for making it all possible for us to come.

He was teetering a little since I'd stopped and he had to balance on his good leg, so I realized at once that I need to help him over to the edge of the bed where he could sit down. But as I turned to leave, he took my hand and pulled me back in closer. He put his arm around my waist and I sat down beside him.

"Please stay, " he whispered to me.

"Well, no…I …I…just can't!" I tried to laugh the idea off. "Could you imagine! What if someone saw me leave your bedroom? My God, *ce sera scandaleux*! *La cata complète!*"

But I hugged him and he drew me into a long embrace, after which we sat there in silence for a few minutes, kissing and nuzzling each other. Every time I gave in to these feelings of love that had never abated, the embers were fanned anew, and, in turn, renewed all the misgivings I had about my upbringing compared to his.

I thought about his summers spent in glorious revelry in this house and my summers spent in a puny wooden ranch house with paltry furnishings, a swing set in the backyard and nothing remotely resembling a pool. We'd been asked to "excuse" his garden as "not yet fully restored" and yet it was still divine. Our "garden" consisted of a row of peony bushes delineating our property line and a measly bed of petunias against the house. I had myself more and more assured that he would have been as staggered seeing where I grew up as I was awestruck seeing where he did.

Finally, gently extricating myself, I moved off the bed. He looked up at me and gave a sigh, before ringing for the maid who would accompany me upstairs with the water.

Once back in my room, I set the glass on my table, sat down, and sobbed, trying all the time to fight off those familiar pangs of angst-induced stomach upset. Nothing could reconcile my world to his; and he was kidding himself if he thought otherwise.

.

"That's the Way I've Always Heard It Should Be"…Carly Simon

It's not like I didn't have an inkling of what Uncle Charles wanted to talk to me about. I figured either I would be accused of having broken his nephew's heart by turning down his proposal, or more likely, he was going to have that *tête-à-tête* with me about how he liked me and all, but I surely wasn't suitable to be marrying a future duke. He would no doubt tell me how relieved he'd been to hear that I "did the honorable thing" by turning down Polo's proposal. That actually seemed the most probable to me.

We met up at the designated time and place, went to the dining room where a butler promptly appeared at his side, and offered to bring him anything he wanted from the sumptuous buffet. I, on the other hand, joined the queue, and choosing an assortment of fresh fruit, a croissant, a brioche, some butter and jam, I carried my plate plus a glass of orange juice—a nod to the Americans at the celebration-- back to where he was seated. I had asked for *chocolat* as my hot drink, and was delighted when a server brought it to the table—made *à l'ancienne* in a real *chocolatière*.

He didn't bring up the subject of Polo and me at all, but instead as we sat together and ate breakfast, he wanted to hear about all "*les idées formidables*" for the educational department of the Foundation he said he'd learned I'd been working on. So I went into some detail about the Institute, but all the while feared boring him to death.

After our meal, he asked me to take a turn in the garden with him, as he wanted to have a more private conversation. We found a bench near a bed of rose bushes trained to grow like little trees, the enchanting fragrance of which permeated the entire space around us.

"I shall get directly to the substance of my meeting with you, " he said ominously. "Polo tells me you believe he cannot marry you, that the family would not approve of you, your religion, your background, and so forth. Is this true?"

"That is exactly true."

"He also said you mentioned something I find a bit bizarre, that you do not think you have ever known anyone who had a happy marriage?"

"That…is… what I said, yes."

"I am sorry you did not know me with my wife, Madeleine. We were besotted with each other!" He laughed at his own use of that arcane language. "It is true!" Then he became somber. "Our marriage could not have been more wonderful…until the death of our son. Thierry died---perhaps Polo told you--- in a tragic automobile accident in the mountains. It destroyed Madeleine and, without a doubt, precipitated her own death one year later. Those last months saw her change from a woman who loved her life to a …a shade…a ghost. She became convulsed in an unending spiral of grief and could not regain her bearings. She was so angry at God, you know. So much so that she could no longer bear to attend mass. Our priest tried his best to console her but to no avail. She rebuffed his every effort."

"It is the worst thing I can think of…for a parent to have to bury their child."

"You are absolutely right about that." He paused to collect his thoughts. "What I want to tell you is this: I speak for the family. There are only a few other cousins—distant ones…none of them are in the d'Arivèque Industries with me because they have their own lands…their properties…very nice ones, and they are content with that. Polo's mother's side…*la famille éloignée*, also lived not very far from here…nearer to Bourges. Polo's maternal *arrière grand-mère*---his great-grandmother was also the daughter of a duke. So you see, his mother was already aristocratic when she married Georges-Henri, my brother. There are few of those people still alive. At one time, perhaps, they felt close to Polo, but they never saw him growing up when his *maman* took him to the States, and, of course, he no longer lives in France."

I sat there listening and got the impression that I'd been right about this aristo-peasant pairing up of Polo and me, and I felt sure I was about to hear that it could never work out. I was prepared for it; and I was glad to have my prediction about to be validated.

But that is exactly what didn't happen.

Charles took my hand and kissed it. He looked at me as though he were talking to his own granddaughter, full of love and optimism. "We, the family, for which I am the spokesperson, only want one thing, Sarah, and that is for Polo to be happy. His life has been so lonely. I believe you know the problems he had before he met you. And yes, there is a large difference in your ages, but not insurmountable in my opinion. The fact that you are young only makes it easier for you to infuse the relationship with exuberance and joy. Think of how happy he would be if you two married and had a baby!"

Whoa.

"But *Oncle* Charles, what about the religious differences? I know you're still Catholic, even if your wife …did she renounce it?"

"Not exactly, no. She was still buried with the sacraments of the Church. But Sarah, we do not care what religion you are! Polo said…you stay what you are---Jewish. He told me he even offered to change his religion—if he even has one now--- and I have nothing whatsoever to say about that."

"But you know, no Jew can inherit the title of *Duc de Beuvron.* I think that would be impossible to overcome."

"Do you know in England there are several Jewish members of the House of Lords?"

"Well, yes, but I'm sure that's different. The kings and queens of England have bestowed knighthoods and peerages on commoners from day one. From what I understand, no monarch of France ever formally ennobled a Jewish family."

"You don't think Napoléon did so, however? "

"Well, I don't know. Did he? In any case, your title dates from the *Ancien Régime,* doesn't it? I thought I saw years on the wall in the chapel going back to the 1400's."

"That is correct, " he laughed, adding, "but you do realize, of course, that all the *Ancien Régime* nobility came to an end in 1790! All the titles were lost, and any deference made in using them today is merely window dressing. It is only reminiscent of a bygone era, as the saying goes. But who is to say? If by blood the extinct title reverts to Polo's son, he shall be duke! No one can say a word against him! And that goes for you, also, my dear. If you marry Polo, you **will** become *Comtesse* and one day be the titular *Duchesse de Beuvron.* It is as simple as that. Of course, **no** title means anything in America, and Polo chooses not to live in his native land. The acceptance or non-acceptance of it is moot."

"If I were to marry him, no one in France would ever really accept me! It doesn't matter that I love the country and speak its language. I would never be considered French and possibly neither would my children."

"But Sarah, if you are *Madame* d'Arivèque, the wife of Jean-Paul d'Arivèque, it is not up to anyone else to accept you or not accept you. You are the wife! *C'est tout!* Polo loves you most assuredly and very deeply. For me, that is the essential element! I admire and respect you. We two are the ones who matter!"

I saw his point on that, and it helped a little, but I still had the same nagging doubts.

"*Oncle* Charles, in France I'd just be 'that Jew' who married Jean-Paul d'Arivèque, and in America I'd be 'that little gold digger'---do you know this term?—who got her claws into him. To the French and, I might add, the Brits, I'd be considered classless, *nouveau riche.* And in America I'd be accused of having married a sugar daddy. Any reputation I could hope to have would be painted with the same negative brush."

"Sarah, how ridiculous you sound, *voyons.* You are the bright star at *La Fondation Culturelle Française.* You **earned** your title of *Directrice d'Education ;* you work hard, your ideas are fresh and they are yours alone. No one can say you achieved what you did by virtue of becoming Polo's *paramour.* You never once did 'dig for the gold' as you say. In fact, you are the opposite of any Jewish stereotype. Believe me, I am in banking…I know the black mark society has put on Jews, saying they are *lié à l'argent,* and so on. You are anything but *lié à l'argent!*"

"Well, that's probably because I've never had any!" I had to laugh. "Don't worry—it's not that I don't like money." I paused this time, to gather my thoughts, and he didn't say anything, so I continued, "But seriously, that's one of the things I admire most about your family: you are so generous with your fortune. I know the Foundation employees are highly compensated and I see that they are happy! They feel appreciated. And Polo would do anything for anyone. I've observed him at it time and again. Look at this lavish wedding he put on for Annie-Laure!"

Charles burst out laughing. "Sarah! It could not be more obvious. You have no idea of the net worth of *les d'Arivèque* do you?"

"Well...no, not really. I know it's a lot." I didn't want to belabor the point but he was absolutely right. I couldn't fathom what the family might be worth, and had little to compare it to, other than the Hydes.

"More than you could even **imagine**, I'll wager. Should you marry Polo, you would want for nothing... ever, nor would your children or their children. You know, I am sure, that we French are highly reticent to speak of money. I am going to ignore that convention of etiquette this one time and tell you-- just to give you an idea-- that we are worth more in land acquisitions alone-- world-wide-- than Aristotle Onassis or the Aga Kahn. Our assets are in manufacturing sectors and shipping, art, banking, property, as I said, and we have more cash reserves in our private banks than you could spend in ten lifetimes. There have been no hostile take-over threats to any of our industries. We sold off our shipbuilding division to a Korean enterprise called Daewoo, and I have been consolidating many of our other holdings of late, so that when I am gone and Polo heads the family business, it will be less complicated for him. My nephew inherits everything. Of course, Polo does not intend to live in Geneva and run the enterprise. He will have in place a minion of trusted officers of each division, plus our legal teams and various boards of directors, eager to help him, just as he has at *La Fondation*. I have seen to all of it."

"I'm sure he's grateful to you beyond measure, " I said, feeling very uncomfortable having been made privy to this kind of information. But he continued on.

"I am not telling you this to boast or to gloat. Do not forget the adage, *'Noblesse oblige.'* We have the great responsibility to act as stewards of this vast fortune, to do good in the world with it, and to set an example. It is really you Americans who are the great philanthropists, Sarah. I so admired Marie-Aveline for realizing that and following the example. That is why she created the *Fondation*. Yes, she had several houses and apartments, fine jewels, and all the other accoutrements-- trappings of affluence. But neither she nor her son, nor I, for that matter, go about flaunting our wealth." He laughed, adding, "Well, perhaps except for that 1938 Rolls Royce parked outside. It belonged to my late brother. He loved that car."

*Yeah, that and a fleet of airplanes which included a Boeing 707 and a parking garage in Chicago filled with another car collection. Other than **that**...*

He went on, " I am eighty-five years old. I still go in to my office every day. Not out of avarice...I have all I could ever need. No, because my work is all I have, and overseeing our domain gives my life its true meaning. We are an immense organization...a multi-faceted conglomerate, if you will, and, I must add, a well-oiled machine. And there is one other thing I should like to tell you, Sarah. My family's banks in Geneva---yes there are more than one---are private and were never ever associated in any way with the nefarious actions that took place in Switzerland with the Nazi regime during the war. It is important for you to know that, as a Jewish person in love with Polo."

"It goes without saying, *Oncle* Charles, that I've been overwhelmed with everything I've seen so far of your family. It's all a testament to you... and Polo and his mother."

"Ah, yes, his mother. I also learned you feel haunted by her. It is indeed very difficult to compete with a spirit, is it not?"

"It is."

"But you are wrong. Polo assured me he does not hold her over you. And I repeat, she, as I, would only wish for Polo's happiness. She did protect him and she did create a haven for him, it is true. But she did not want to make it a prison. She gave him much personal freedom and did so very intentionally. She was a good mother, and pushed through her own heartbreak after the death of my brother, in order that Polo would live and find happiness. Were she here with us today, she would tell you exactly what I am saying: we want Polo to achieve a life devoid of loneliness and isolation. He has always felt alone, you know, and quite frankly, unlovable. It has been quite devastating to his ego to learn of ulterior motives of people--women--and others---who befriended him for his money or out of pity. Many people see physical limitations as defining. No one wants that. And then you came into his life with no agenda whatsoever, hidden or otherwise, except to do a good job at your work and help build the mission, as it were, of *La Fondation*. You were…you are… his breath of fresh air. You did not pursue him at all, to hear him tell it."

"Don't forget, and I'm sure he's mentioned to you, that I didn't think he preferred… women… actually, and of course, everything else notwithstanding, it wasn't my place to assume the head of the entire organization would want to go out with **me**. And for that matter, sleeping with the boss wasn't even in my lexicon…until it was."

"Sarah! Your *naïveté* is a constant source of wonder to Polo and me. You make us smile."

"*Oncle* Charles, it seems to me that there is one other insurmountable problem with my marrying your nephew."

"Oh? What is that?"

"Well, it's part of marriage, the way I see it, to be equal partners. Do you agree?"

"Yes, and your point?"

"I could never be one to him. I would have nothing to bring to the union. I can never repay what he's already done for me NOT married to him. I have a background completely dissimilar to his. I don't have the education he does, and…"

He interrupted me. "I beg to differ! You went to *La Sorbonne*! You are extremely intelligent. Even Solti and I could see that from the moment we met you."

"I think you know deep down I'm right. And besides all that, there's not even a gift I can offer Polo—for his birthday, Christmas, or any occasion. A marriage must be give and take, not merely take."

He looked at me with a look that had more softness than admonition in it. "You do not see that giving a man his confidence that he **is** a man, a lovable one, someone who has won the heart of a wonderful, **young**, sensitive, resolute woman is not a GIFT to him? Sarah, we all know you are not obtuse. Please change your line of reasoning on this. It is beneath you to think you would bring nothing to the union."

"Okay, look, I know I do a good job at the Foundation, and I have loads of faith in myself there. But what could I offer him in the way of wifely existence? He has staff that cooks for him, cleans for him, does his laundry."

"Yes, and he has a heavy social calendar that would be made far more enjoyable with you at his side. But I will tell you something else. Are you willing to hear it?"

I laughed – in spite of myself – I wasn't making much headway in my logic. "Of course – tell me – I'll listen."

"Give him children, Sarah. He longs for them and *voilà*—he would be forever in **your** debt. It is something he obviously cannot do for himself, and no amount of money could ever repay the happiness you would bestow upon him."

I began to shake my head, but suddenly Robineau appeared where we had been sitting for what turned out to be more than an hour!

"Please excuse the interruption, " he said awkwardly, "but we have packed your luggage, *Monsieur le Duc*, and the car will soon be here for you."

"*Merci, Robin. J'arrive.*"

"*Très bien, Monsieur le Duc.*" And he left as abruptly as he'd come.

"Sarah, I am an old man…my time is certainly limited. That is why I spoke to you here today as I did. Yes, to put in a good word for my nephew. But I hope I have convinced you that we, the d'Arivèque family, love and accept whomever our dear Polo chooses to be his wife. If that is you…and I fervently hope it is…you have nothing to worry about from us. Polo did not send me on this errand. I told him, of course, but it was more in the way of an offer to speak to you, that is all. I am very fond of you."

"As I am of you, *Monsieur le*…uh…*Oncle* Charles. Thank you for taking me into your confidence. I'm very touched…really."

"So I will bid you *au revoir*, then, my dear, and hope to see you again very soon…*dans un avenir pas trop lointain*, as we say. Perhaps in Geneva? I should like to show you my beautiful city. A little larger than Orléans!"

"I would love that." He reached for my hand again, to kiss it, but I put my arms around him and hugged him as though French people did that, which, as we know, they do not! And certainly not with an octogenarian duke.

I was just giving myself permission to be me.

Chapter One Hundred-Four

"Happy Together"...The Turtles (Gordon & Bonner)

I stayed in the garden after Uncle Charles left and, wandering around in there found another, more secluded spot, this time on a hard cement bench amidst perfectly trimmed square boxwood hedges. I lingered, listening to warblers in the trees above me, not being able see or identify the birds, but taking solace that they were keeping me company and giving me something else to listen to besides the nagging doubts in my head.

I tried to cut myself some slack and chalk it up to youth and inexperience in the ways of the world when it came to all the worry about reputation and what others would think of me. Why should I even care about "them" anyway? People go about their daily lives all the time without giving a second thought to how the neighbors see them or how society might judge them.

As to what I did have to also consider would be the horrific row that would ensue with Sol and Betty Shrier if I married Jean-Paul. That was real. They would disapprove of the age difference as much as the religion difference. They would reject us categorically as family. But hadn't they pretty much done that to me already? Even if I had quit my job and moved back home, gotten a teaching degree at Omaha U and complied in every way to their wishes, who's to say they wouldn't have found other flaws in my character, more ways to criticize me, more opportunities to diminish my accomplishments and undermine my self-worth. More rejection of my soul.

"You can't win with them" I told myself, "so you might just as well forge a new life now."

If I were proud of my work and happy with the services I rendered at my job, and content to live in a big city and partake of its cultural riches, what right did they have to rain all over my parade anyway? I thanked my God and theirs that I hadn't caved into to their demands and gone back.

I wasn't paying attention to my surroundings or the time, caught up as I was, wallowing in my "situation," when Polo appeared at my side. I scooted over on the bench so he could sit down, which he did balancing on his good arm and unlocking the brace.

"I see *mon oncle* had a long talk with you this morning?" he said. "He has now gone."

"Did he tell you I hugged him! Sorry! Emotions of the moment just took over. I'm sure he was shocked, " I laughed, nervously, then added, "I hope we see him again soon."

"If you hugged him, I am sure he appreciated it," he said, smiling reassuringly. "Do you realize it is past two? Did you intend to have lunch?"

"Oh, did I miss it? What time will the coach be returning from Orléans?" I asked, not really caring but trying to make conversation.

"Ah, are you upset that you did not go? I can arrange a car to drive you there. You might still have a few hours to see it."

"Heavens no! I was just curious. I've got plenty to do---need to pack, for one thing. I've got stuff strewn all over that room. Embarrassing for the maid to see," I laughed.

All of a sudden, as though a hand swept down from the heavens and cuffed me upside the head, it dawned on me that I needed to tell him something else. I turned towards him on the bench and opened my mouth to talk. The words were stuck at first but then I just sort of blurted it out.

"Polo...I...I've decided that I **will** marry you. That is, if you'll still have me. I've been silly. I truly love you and only you."

He reached for me in utter amazement and then joy. He took my arm and began to kiss it from the hand to my wrist, to my forearm...and then we locked in an embrace, both of us getting teary-eyed and kissing each other with tender fervor.

"How does this wonderful thing happen that you changed your mind, Sarah?! Was it my uncle?"

"I don't think it's only because of what your uncle told me today, " I said coming up for air. "I— uh-- came to my own conclusions. It's mostly a question of all this analysis. Why analyze anything more? We're in love! I love you so much. This must have been meant to be, otherwise why would it have happened?! I just suddenly realized it, Polo. This isn't logical! It's all about...sort of... you know...fate! It's kismet!"

610

"*C'est le mot juste,* my darling girl, " he agreed. " You have made me the happiest man alive right at this moment. *Merci de tout coeur, chérie. Je t'aime à la follie, tu sais. Pour moi c'était le coup de foudre.* I think I told you before…I fell in love with you the first moment you entered my office that day."

I laughed. "Come on."

He smiled at me. "Well, it seemed that way to me." He held me again to his chest and nuzzled my neck. "I feel like I am in a trance, " he finally said. "I was so very sad, and now, with one word from you, it is all lifted… just like fog rises out of a deep valley. You have turned my despondency back into joy. I was afraid…I had lost you…Sarah. I did not know how I could go on without you."

"But you didn't think I stopped loving you, did you?"

"In my heart I did not, but it was such hell knowing you were in the office, but only as my colleague, not my love."

"I…I just had so many doubts, Polo. I was also tormented, you know. But frankly---in the end, it's love, isn't it? If we don't have someone to love, our life really is empty. I see that, now. I guess I always did know it, but thought I couldn't have it. Just like you."

"Sarah…my God." And he held me in a tight embrace. I kissed his face over and over.

"I've never known anyone like you in my entire life, " I said, stating the obvious again. "I promise to do everything I can to make you happy forever. I love you so much."

Afraid I was going to start crying again, I stood up and he reached for my arm to stand. I took his cane and we walked arm in arm back to the house. If anyone saw us, they were probably pretty damned shocked at the sight of it, but there weren't very many people around, except for staff busily cleaning up from the wedding. We went in, and he directed me to his library off the gallery on the turret side.

"I have photos to show you, " he said, "and I was so hoping to get a chance to be able to do so."

This library was far older than the ones in his Chicago home. The books were all behind tiny diamond-shaped leaded glass doors. There was no overt modernity about the room. Every piece of furniture was antique and all the printed material looked like it would crumble if touched. Just like that night in Chicago, Polo asked me to approach one of the doors and reach in for some photo albums, which I took down. We retreated to a silk-upholstered sofa and sat side by side. He opened the album and pointed out all the family members shown. Some of the figures had World War I uniforms on. Other photos showed him as a little kid…one of them of him at about eight years old wearing lederhosen and knee socks, balancing on a mountain path.

"Oh, look how cute you were!" I said…not teasing. He really was darling.

He tuned to a section displaying his paternal great-grandparents, the Duke and Duchess of Beuvron in splendid fancy dress standing with dignitaries. It could have been a ball or something official. His great-grandmother was wearing a gown with a tiered bustle!

"She and my grandmother, too, got their dresses from Worth, of course, " he told me, "as all the noble English ladies and wealthy Americans did in those days, also. During that era, my grandmother had a salon in the Parc Monceau home. All the literary giants of her time came to it. Even Anatole France and, one time, as I understand it, Marcel Proust."

"Wow. Did royalty ever stay with them…or here?"

"No king or queen that I am aware of, but one time the *Prince de Condé* was a guest in **this** house. To him it must have seemed rather like a weekend in a small hunting lodge, " he laughed.

Polo, can we take these albums back with us to Chicago? I'd like to have more time to look through them."

"That is a very good idea, *chérie.* I should like to explain about everyone in the pictures – at our leisure."

"Well, cool."

"I am anxious now for the others to return so I can share our news with them. "

"I hope we don't see too many rolled eyes."

"Do you really think that could possibly happen?" he chided me. "As you would say, 'come on.'"

"You know, I don't think Marie-France went to Orléans. We could tell her first."

"You are very clever. I shall telephone for her to come over. I believe you were with my uncle when the newlyweds left this morning on their trip, but Marie-France was there to see them off, so I know she did not go with the group."

Marie-France hid her shock well, if indeed, she was surprised at all by our announcement, and she showered us with her good wishes.

"I hope to be at your wedding!" she said. "When do you think you will have it? And would you want it here as well?"

"We haven't even talked about that, " I said, "but we will for sure let you know."

"I think Chicago, " Jean-Paul said, smiling.

The group may have had an inkling that something was up when I wasn't on the next coach, which was chartered this time to take us back to Paris for the flight home. I rode with Polo and the Rosier de Molets in whom Polo confided our news first. We took a limo---not the Rolls-- driven by a different chauffeur, one from Paris who had come down on the tour bus. Robineau traveled with us, too, up front next to the driver. I daresay that was the first time the trunk of such a car had seen a plaid S&H Green Stamps suitcase stacked in it among the Hermès, Louis Vuitton, Asprey and that posh duffle bag Polo had brought to my house at Christmas.

Once on the plane, Polo took to the public address system and announced our engagement to the entire group, so that speculation and rumor wouldn't follow us home. The plane erupted in cheering, and many of them came up to the front with good wishes for us. No one seemed unduly surprised. Hennie, of course, was not on board and missed the announcement. I thought to myself how floored she'd be when she returned and heard the news, but then, knowing how people seem to know everything that concerns Jean-Paul around that office, maybe she did have a hunch about us. She never heard it from me, though.

Upon return to Chicago, Polo asked me to come back with him to the house because he wanted to propose to me again with the ring, which he did. There I sat, in my wheat jeans and plaid shirt while he was as elegant as ever, as though he hadn't driven three hours to a plane and then spent eight more flying back.

"Sarah," he said, slipping it on my finger, "you are the love of my life."

"I'm so honored to wear this ring as a symbol of our love, Polo. I will love you 'til the day I die."

"Will you also promise me something?" he asked a bit plaintively.

"Sure. Anything."

"Please promise you will never leave me. Can you do that?"

I almost laughed, but then I saw how serious he was and said, "Yes, Polo. I promise I will never ever leave you. I can't stay here tonight though!"

We both laughed. I knew what he meant.

"I want you to take the Citroën home, " he said, when I was getting ready to go back to my apartment. "It is your car now."

Once we were again at work, nothing was too noticeably different in our interaction in the office, with the one big exception that an incredible weight had been lifted from my shoulders, and I reveled in the realization that I no longer had the pent-up anxiety I'd been carrying around since Valentine's Day. That didn't mean I was home free, however. A newer angst had taken its place: how and when to break the news to Sol and Betty.

Before I told my parents, however, I felt we ought to have a date set so Polo and I met in his office to discuss that. He and I got out the calendar and he wondered if a summer wedding would "suit me." I said I didn't want a big wedding at all, that no rabbi would marry a mixed couple I didn't think (and I was right), and maybe we should just elope somewhere. Illinois didn't have justices of the peace, but some nearby state might.

"I would rather we marry in court, " Polo said.

I was astonished because I knew then he must have been thinking about this already.

"Fine by me, " I said. "What about if we do it in early September? That way I could have some time to gird my loins to tell the parents, and if they wanted to come, they would have ample time to plan their trip here."

"Yes, darling, " he said, turning in his large desk agenda to the September pages. "What about Friday, the first? *Comme ça* we could go right to the airport after and take my plane to Paris. Would you like that? The city is especially beautiful in early autumn."

"Oh, yes! Gosh, for sure!"

"Then I have a surprise for you," he said, his eyes twinkling as bright as Madame Schwartz's ring on my finger.

"What could be more of a surprise than telling me you're taking me on a honeymoon to Paris for God's sake?" I laughed.

"If I tell you, what kind of surprise would it then be? But, I shall take you to lunch today and reveal all to you."

I returned to my office completely curious about what it could possibly be, and glad that for some reason I'd dressed up a little for work that day. Going out to lunch with Polo was always a more formal affair than my usual ham sandwich at the Woolworth's counter.

When the noon hour rolled around, we went out the front doors of the lobby to a waiting car. Since Jean-Luc was still not back, Robineau was the chauffeur now. I was relieved that for once, I didn't bristle at the sight of him, and he was, as he had been since the "apology," ingratiating towards me. *Could a leopard change its spots? I still had to wonder.*

"First we shall have the surprise, " he said mischievously, "and then go to lunch, is that all right?"

"Whatever you like."

We were driven to the Cook County Courthouse and we got out in front of an entryway -- with no steps! Once inside he seemed to know exactly where he was going. We got in the elevator and went up to the tenth floor…the District Court Judges' chambers. He held hands with me on his left side and guided me to the door of "Judge Harry Lowenstein."

"Do you recognize that name?" he asked me, pointing to the embossed letters.

"No. Should I?"

"Perhaps not. You remember I told you the story of flying out of Lisbon on that Pan Am clipper with a doctor and his family?"

"Oh! Yes. Weren't they Jews and your father paid their way to New York? Oh, no! Wasn't their name Lowenstein? Oh, my God, it was, wasn't it?"

"*Exacte.* Harry was their little boy. Not much younger than I at the time. We would see each other quite regularly in New York, of course, but he went to a different high school than I did. He went to the very prestigious Horace Mann school where he was a top scholar. He came to University of Chicago for law school and stayed here."

"But…I have never met him at any of your soirées, have I? Didn't you stay close?"

"We have stayed very close, *chérie*, " he said, "but he is extremely busy and does not socialize too much at events like those which *La Fondation* hosts. But you are right, I should have invited him to more of our gatherings. I am remiss in not introducing you until now."

Any tie-in of his to his childhood or youth was precious to me, as there were so few of them. I was suddenly very excited to meet this judge.

"Polo! My dear friend! " Judge Lowenstein said, as we were ushered into his nice mahogany-paneled office suite. They embraced to one another with *la bise*, and then he turned to me. "And this must be Sarah!" He extended his hand to me. "It's a pleasure to meet you."

"I'm so happy to meet you!" I said.

He wasn't very tall, slightly shorter than Polo, but very distinguished-looking in a way that gave him stature. His hair was dark and he had a five- o'clock shadow. His eyes were bright behind horn-rimmed glasses. His features were soft and his demeanor intellectual… learned but amiable.

He turned to take hold of Polo's arm. "She's really lovely, Polo. Come, both of you…sit." We took seats on beautiful tufted leather chairs trimmed in brass brads, lined up in front of his desk. "So, you would like to be married here in my chambers? I would be so delighted to oblige you."

"Yes, thank you, *mon vieux*, " Polo answered, "and we are hoping your calendar would be free on September the first."

"I'll make sure of it!" he said. "I can rearrange things if need be, to accommodate you. Will you be writing something you want specifically said at the ceremony? And will there be guests? You will need a witness."

"Oh, gosh, we hadn't gotten that far, " I blurted out. "Can we let you know?"

"Of course. It's only June. We have time."

"Do we need other documentation? " Polo inquired.

"Yes, " answered Judge Lowenstein. You must procure and fill out for me a signed marriage license application, which you can get downstairs in this building. You must present to me valid identification with proof of age, " he laughed, "as if I didn't already know yours, Polo. They will charge you a small fee for all that."

"Do we need blood tests, too?" I asked.

"Not in Illinois, " he answered. "Do you need them where you come from?"

"I've no idea. I just remember hearing about that, is all."

"Well, we in Illinois are no longer concerned with the diseases the tests used to disclose, like rubella…and others."

"What used to happen if one of the couple turned up to have it? Could they not get married then?" I wondered.

"In some instances, no. But that was a long time ago. Even then most often, the disclosure was all that was required. The couples could decide between themselves if it made a difference to their decision to marry. For Jews, it was, as you may know, Tay-Sachs disease that was the primary concern."

"Why, I've never even heard of that, " I gasped with my now-famous naïveté.

"It is a very sad business for families with children who have it, " Polo offered. "It is a genetic condition resulting in loss of neuro-motor ability. It…it leads to an early death."

"Polo has told me you are Jewish. Are you Ashkenazi?" the judge asked me.

"Yes, I guess so. Aren't most of us?"

"I can say with authority on that, yes, most immigrants to the U.S. around the turn of the century and throughout the Holocaust were Ashkenazi from Europe. I'll wager you did not know that the rights of Ashkenazi Jews developed in such French cities as Troyes. The eminent French Rabbi Shlomo Itzhaki--- called Rashi--- had a significant impact on Judaism."

"Wow, France, huh? How about that!" I said laughing. Then I became serious again and all of a sudden worried. "So should I be tested for…that Tay- whatever disease? "

"Your doctor can do it when you are thinking of becoming pregnant."

"Oh, well, forget that, then, phew."

Judge Harry looked at Polo but didn't comment on my remark.

"Polo, " he said, "who will be your *témoin*? Robin perhaps?"

Seeing my face wrinkle into a frown at that thought, Polo quickly said, "No, Harry. Perhaps Daniel Rosier de Molet. I shall ask him first."

"And will you have a bridesmaid or witness, Sarah?"

" Yes! I'll have my college roommate!"

"Splendid!" Judge Harry said enthusiastically. "So write down your preferences for the ceremony and send them over to me. I'll take care of the rest. Will you be having a reception? You may do so here in my chambers if you wish. Not much décor suited for the *Comte de Beuvron*, though, I should add," he remarked with a little tease. "Perhaps you could hire some people to gussy it up a bit?"

"Oh, I don't think we'll be having anything…will we Polo?"

"We shall see. Thank you for the offer, however, *mon cher* Harry. *C'est trop gentil de ta part.*"

We got back into the limo and Robineau drove next to the Palm Court where Polo had asked Bernadette to make reservations for lunch.

"It is so beautiful in here," I said, struck to see it in broad daylight for a change. "Thank you for today. I **love** the idea that your dear friend from childhood will marry us. Can you even believe it! What are the chances of **that**?!"

"I am so glad you are pleased. So… what about a small party…here…let us say… in the Palm Court… after the ceremony?"

"Hah! Here? No party here would be small," I laughed.

"I have already spoken to Marie-France about organizing something. She did such a superb job with the wedding at *La Pérégrine*. She would be only too happy to return and do ours. She could then fly back with us right afterwards. What do you say?"

"I say...whatever you want. I can't say no to anything you ask for, just like I couldn't deny anything to your uncle. Will he come, too?"

"Without a doubt...if he is able."

"God, I hope so. It wouldn't be the same without him. And if he does come, then he must be your *témoin*. *Oncle* Charles and Cass. That would be so perfect. Maybe he'd be able to stay with us in Paris for a while, too? Wouldn't that be too, too cool?"

"**Cool**, yes...as you say," he laughed.

So my next order of business after that lunch was to phone Cass. I knew she'd freak completely the hell out when I announced, "Cass! I'm getting MARRIED!!! To Jean-Paul!!!"

"Oh, kid! You came around??!!"

"I did. Who knows how this stuff works! I just suddenly realized that I loved him to bits, that it wasn't going to change, and, so let the chips fall where they may! He's my beloved and I am his."

"Sari, I am so happy for you. Do you even realize what this means? You are set for life, my little friend."

"You don't think that's why I'm doing it, though, do you?" I was brought up short by that remark. It really wasn't a question, and it irked me that that was the first thing she said to me. If SHE thought that, the whole rest of the world would be sure of it.

"Oh, Sari---NOOOO. Sorry! Of course not. I knew you were crushing on this guy long, long ago."

"Good, because you know, everyone will think I am marrying him for his money due to our ages. But I don't give a shit about his age. I absolutely love him utterly for himself."

"Of course you do. But kid, just think! You won't have to work at all! And you could even go back to school and do something else!"

"Why would I want to do that, Cass? I've told you how much I love my job. I'm not quitting! I've got a ton of projects going around there."

"Well, sure, I mean... I dig where you're coming from. But just imagine...you'll have the means to do all sorts of other stuff, too! You could, for example, go back and get a master's in art history. If for nothing else than to curate the fabulous art collection you told me they have. You're going to be his wife! There's no one else to do it... unless they have a private curator, of course."

"You know what, I think you are absolutely onto something with **that** idea, you little genius. But for the moment, I've just got too much on my plate at the Foundation."

I let that drop and directed the conversation to the real reason I called. "So anyway, Cass, it's going to be September first—a Friday. I will send you first class tickets...for all of you to come. You must be my matron of honor, okay? We're getting married in COURT!"

"Hold on there, now. Not so fast. I don't think that's going to be possible, Sar. Alan's courses will have started up again. He won't be able to leave."

"Well, okay, I hadn't thought of that. Why would they be starting so early? Iowa U never started until mid-September."

"Who knows why Texas does anything."

"But **you** can still come! And if you don't want Laura and Paul at the ceremony, one of our maids will look after them. I'm on great terms with most of them already, and by then I'll be living there. Oh, that reminds me, I'm going to give notice to your dad's company on my place. I plan to write him a nice note and tell him how grateful I have been to live there."

"I'm sure he'll like that," she said, with no enthusiasm whatsoever in her voice. "Sari, I can't make that trip."

"Don't be ridiculous. I'll pick you up, you'll stay with us---the place is practically a four-star hotel-- and I'll arrange for you to be taken back to the airport with us! We're flying to PARIS straight after the---very small—luncheon reception at the Palm Court."

"HA! Well, that really seals the deal, then. I haven't got one thing suitable to wear to the Palm Court anymore."

"Cass. Get real. You can buy anything you want here. Let's say I send you tickets to come into town a couple of days early and we'll shop! In fact, I NEED your help to buy some decent lingerie and negligées for my…ahem…honeymoon in Paris. **Paris**!!"

"I just can't come. I'd like to…really I would. But it will not be possible. I'm so sorry."

"**Cass**! Cut it out! What makes you think I'm taking no for an answer on this? And aren't you just dying to meet my Polo?! Bottom line is: I can't get married without **you** there."

"I managed to do it without you at mine. You'll be fine."

My God, where did that come from?

"That's unfair! And hey, don't think for one minute that I wasn't hurt that I didn't get a chance to be at your wedding either. But I understood the circumstances you were in, and I was in another country. **You're** right here. I…I…just… don't see how you could let me go through this alone."

She didn't say anything so I just kept at her.

"Please, Cass. Just please reconsider. Talk to Alan."

"I don't think Alan would notice if the kids and I were gone, to tell you the truth."

"Why do you say that? What's going on out there anyway? The last time we talked you said he was non-communicative, but that's nothing new."

"You know, I've got to go get my little ones from El Paso, now, Sari…I'll talk to you in a couple of days, okay?"

"Huh? Oh, all right, sure. When you call me to tell me you've changed your mind and are coming to my wedding!"

"Bye, Sari."

Chapter One Hundred Five

"My Old School"...Steely Dan

I gave the Hyde company notice that I would vacate my apartment on August first, which gave me a month to get things sorted out. I had no furniture of my own to move out with me, except Dom and Peter's café table set and bean bag chair, and I wanted them to have those back.

Dom and Peter sat around my living room one last evening, drinking French wine and listening to *Blue*, and I assured them they would be welcome at the d'Arivèque home any time.

"And of course, you'll be staying there the weekend of the Institute, " I reminded Dom. "Too bad Peter's not a French teacher, eh?"

"And you'll be *Madame la Comtesse* by then."

"Yeah, yeah, knock it off."

"Hey, he's still the Count de Beuvron, so that makes you…"

"I know. But it's such a non-starter. Because he doesn't use the title. Like I told you."

"About a million times, " Peter laughed.

"So what did your parents say when you told them you were engaged to a real honest-to-Christ French aristocrat?" Dom wanted to know.

"Not much. But they're coming next week so they'll meet him."

"Oh I wish I could be a fly on the wall for that visit, " Peter chuckled. "They'll think their daughter is another Grace Kelly."

Dom tried to reassure me, too, saying, "Just wait 'til they meet him. He'll wow them, just like he did us. Can you dig it? You have nothing to worry about."

I did worry, though. I dreaded it. But I felt I had to make an overture to them since I was about to be married, and Jean-Paul was insistent on the idea.

"They can stay here with us, " he had offered, "and avoid the cost of hotels."

"No, that won't do. Even though I told them my moving in here with you was only logical since I had to get out of my place, they still consider it living in sin. I pointed out to them that you had done the most honorable thing in asking me to marry you and NOT wanting to merely live with me, but it didn't sway them."

"Yes, well, I understand then, " he said.

"It will be better for them to stay at the Allerton. It's a nice place and they're familiar with it. They stayed there when my father attended some B'Nai Brith convention a few years ago."

I had not been looking forward to the phone call to invite them, but since, as they put it-- "*Oy!* You're calling long distance! "-- they made short order of the call. They and Rozzy would be arriving at O'Hare and I would pick them up in the Citroën.

"I'll be at the gate to meet you, don't worry."

When the day arrived and they disembarked, I was waiting right there. Our initial meeting was more cordial than I thought it would be, except for my father's complaint that my fiancé wasn't also there to greet them.

"He sent you all the way out here by yourself, I see."

My mother hugged me and my sister gave me a peck on the cheek. I hugged them both. Sol was not the hugging type but expected me to kiss him on the cheek, too.

"His name is Jean-Paul, " I reminded them, "and he's waiting for us at the house. We'll go there directly, and then I'll drop you back at the hotel after you meet him. We'll have drinks and hors d'oeuvres, and if you like, maybe we can all go out to dinner later."

"I think we plan to just eat in the hotel, " Betty said.

Do what you want, I said to myself. I have no intention of picking any fights with you this trip.

We exited to the baggage claim and I told them I would go fetch the car and pick them up at the curb.

"You can't miss my car, " I laughed. "It will be the weirdest-looking one out there."

But when I did drive up, they just stood there, dumbfounded.

"Climb in, Rozzy " I said, "and get ready for the best ride of your life. You'll think you're on a waterbed! It's so neat."

I opened the trunk and Sol loaded their three suitcases. Betty got in back with Roslyn, and Sol got in the passenger's seat next to me. I put the car in gear and it rose up slightly higher on the hydraulic suspension, and we took off.

"How in hell did you learn to drive this thing?" Sol said, watching me shift the gears on the column, and wincing a bit as I maneuvered into Chicago traffic on the Dan Ryan Expressway.

"The chauffeur taught me."

"Why?"

"Why not? This was Jean-Paul's mother's car and it was sitting idle in the garage. Cars need to be driven. I sometimes needed a car here---not all the time, of course. It is just good for me and for the car that I drive it. And can you blame me for loving to drive it? Isn't it a dream?!"

We rode the remaining nineteen minutes in fairly pronounced silence, them not asking me much and me not offering much. I drove up to the white limestone mansion and rounded the corner past the topiary garden. But when I took the garage door opener from the visor-- after which the door opened to reveal a parking garage filled with many cars inside-- my mother let out a little squeal.

"Good Christ, " Sol muttered.

"Holy shit!" said Roslyn.

"Roslyn! Language!" Betty hissed.

I parked the car and led them to the door, into the elevator and up to the second floor, where Polo was waiting right there for us. I had used the words "slightly handicapped" to describe Polo, so they wouldn't do something like blurt out any ultra-embarrassing epithets upon seeing him for the first time, but I guess I should have been more specific because my teeny-bopper sister couldn't suppress her shock and my parents were once again speechless.

"Mom, Daddy, Roz, I'd like you to meet my fiancé Jean-Paul d'Arivèque." And turning to Polo, I said, "These are my parents Sol and Betty Shrier and my sister Roslyn."

Jean-Paul offered his hand to each one and they took it with trepidation, like they were being exposed to whatever was wrong with him and would "catch" it.

"I am so happy to meet you all at last, " he told them, to which they had only awkward perfunctory replies. "Welcome to our home. Won't you come in?"

We repaired to the library where they all took seats on the sofa and I sat on one of the armchairs which were to the side, leaving the other one for Polo. The bar was already set up with four Baccarat white wine glasses and a chilled bottle of *Pouilly-Fumé Saint-Bris*, one of Polo's favorite white wines and the only Sauvignon Blanc appellation in Burgundy. But Polo offered my sister the first choice. "Would you like a soda Roslyn?" he asked brightly.

"You have sodas here? Sure! I'll have chocolate!"

"He means pop, " I told her, out of the side of my mouth.

"Oh, well, why did he say soda then?"

"Do you want Coke?" I asked her pointedly.

"Yes."

"Please, " Betty corrected her.

"Yes, please, " she repeated, exasperated.

"I'll get it," I offered, jumping up to go behind the bar to the fridge and take out the bottle, which I opened. "Still bar tending, aren't I?" I laughed, but they didn't think it was funny.

"You never did tend bar at our place, now did you?"

"Just joking, " I said…like any explanation would ever work anyway.

"*Chérie*, would you like to do the honors?" Polo asked me. He had told me ahead of time that he felt it would put them more at ease not to be surrounded right off the bat with his staff. I poured everyone some wine and then I distributed the glasses. Polo had already sat down by then under their still-disbelieving gaze.

618

"So," I said, "how about a toast?" I held up my glass and gestured for them to do likewise. "To *L'Amérique et la France!*"

Jean-Paul gave me a mock scolding look as he tried not to laugh. My parents reacted like that was a stupid thing to toast, but did it anyway. Roslyn said, "What?!"

"Just clink the Coca Cola bottle and don't worry about it, " I told her.

I tried hard for there to be no pregnant pauses or uncomfortable silences. Keep 'em talking, I had decided.

"I related to Jean-Paul how you fought in France during the war, Daddy, and that you saw the Liberation of Paris firsthand."

"I certainly did, " he said, which put me at ease thinking he'd like to have that conversation.

Sol hadn't been involved in anything especially heroic during the Second World War, but everything the U.S. Armies did for Europe was appreciated, and especially by the French. Polo already knew that my father had enlisted and fought from Oran, Algeria, through Italy, France, Germany and Austria. It wasn't nothing.

"Too bad we had to let that son-of-a-bitch De Gaulle pretend like his army did the deal...liberating Paris I mean," Sol chided.

"Daddy...come on now. Actually, General De Gaulle was a friend of one of Jean-Paul's uncles during the First World War."

"Is that so? " said Sol sarcastically, turning to Polo. "I pity you in that case."

"*Non, non,*" Polo interjected, "It is all right. We French knew that we could not have prevailed in either World War without the Americans and the other allies."

"Damn right you couldn't. You'd all be speaking German now if we hadn't gotten over there."

"Okay, let's change the subject, shall we? " I said.

"Not yet, " said Sol. "I'm interested in Jean-Paul (he called him "John Poll") here's war experiences. How old were you when the war was on?"

"I am forty-two now, " he said. "I left France when I was twelve. The war still had a few years to go."

I butted into the story. "His father was in the Resistance and worked clandestinely behind enemy lines in Vichy France for De Gaulle. Unfortunately and sadly, he was killed in a plane crash. It was shot down, actually. Jean-Paul never saw him again. He was in a hospital in New York by then. His mom was with him."

" Why were you in the hospital in New York?" my sister asked.

"I was hurt, you see, " Polo pointed to his brace leg, "and Paris was occupied by then. My mother got me out...of France, that is, and over to the doctors in New York who were the specialists."

"My goodness, " said Betty. "That must have been harrowing."

"It was," I answered.

"This is good wine, " Sol said, as though he hadn't heard a word of the conversation. "You gotta hand it to the French with wine."

"Yes, I am interested in your opinion, of course, as a barman, " said Polo.

But Sol didn't show any further desire to talk shop, except to pointedly correct Polo.

"Barman? Do you mean bartender? I own our business."

"Yes, of course, I know it, " Polo corrected himself at once, afraid he'd offended my father.

"Hey, do you guys want to see some more of the house?" I asked, eager to defuse this situation.

We got up to leave the library, and I caught a glimpse of my father watching intently as Polo lifted himself out of the chair, locked the brace, and took up his cane. We all followed him to the grand reception hall with the Louis XV furniture and the *boiserie* paneling.

"You live in a palace!" declared Roslyn, looking around wide-eyed.

"We don't really live in this part, " I said. "There's another apartment on the third floor that's actually our home. There are many other rooms on this floor, though -- a magnificent, grand dining room, plus a more intimate one—it can still seat twenty though," I laughed. "There's the main huge reception area—like a massive living room—want to see it?"

"Yes, dear, " said Betty, "whatever you and Jean-Paul want to show us. I'd love to see the kitchen."

"It is off to one side on this floor, " Polo explained to her, "down a corridor and then in back. It abuts the largest dining room. I shall be happy to show it to you."

We went to the kitchen through the wing with many bedrooms, so I said, "See, guys, Jean-Paul's cultural Foundation often hosts important out-of-town visitors to Chicago, so there are a lot of guest bedrooms on this floor, all with their own en suite."

"What's a 'on-sweet'? " Roz wanted to know.

"Their own bathroom. You know, so nobody has to go out in the hall and try to find one."

We rounded the corner and Polo led them into the vast kitchen. Betty couldn't stifle a little squeal when she caught sight of the range.

"Oh my goodness! Is that a La Cornue?"

"Why yes, it is, " Polo responded, surprised that she had a reaction. "Do you know these?"

"Well. You can hardly miss those metal strips and brass knobs, can you? Do you cook on that, Sari? What's it like?"

"Mom, I don't do any cooking here. Polo has a chef and an entire kitchen brigade."

"Oh, right. Silly me." She was embarrassed, but added, "It's just magnificent, though."

"And my chef, he appreciates the oven. She's a very fine one, is she not?"

"I—I've just never seen one in person, " Betty admitted. "My mother first told me about La Cornue. She would have loved to have had one like that at the restaurant. I can tell you that."

Hearing that Nana knew about French kitchen equipment intrigued me. "She did? I sure wish she was here."

"Hmm," Betty said, still in a reverie about the stove.

We continued the tour, with me pointing out to them that there was a lot more to see.

"We also have a game room, a music room and several other smaller gathering places on this floor."

"Say, speaking of other rooms," Sol interjected, "would it be possible for Betty and I to take Sarah off and talk to her alone for a few minutes? Maybe you could show Rozzy here some other of your — uh — interesting stuff back in the library?"

"Of course, but there are also hors d'oeuvres coming to us in there."

"Oh… that'd be swell. We won't be long."

So we headed back to the library, and I went with them into a small ante-chamber next door, where a meeting or a group for cards might take place. It had a beautiful Moroccan inlay hexagonal gaming table and six small chairs in there. Roz went back with Polo to the big library and I overheard him ask her what she wanted to do when she got out of school. She said go to college "and become a nurse," which shocked me to hear.

"Roz wants to go into nursing?" I asked, turning to my mother.

"Not like you do, " Sol answered glaring at me.

"What do you mean by that? I'm not interested in going back to school to change careers."

"No, you'll just be nursing your husband. Why didn't you tell us he was a cripple?"

"Because we don't use that term nowadays and besides, as you can see, he has a few physical… uh…issues…but they're not insurmountable by any stretch."

"Sarah, I didn't come here today to start a big *megillah* with you, and I'm not gonna yell at you. But what *tsuris* are you getting yourself into here? That man is almost my age. I went to war at 20 years old. He was only about eight years younger than me at the same time!"

"I was afraid you'd find the age difference between us problematic, but I just want to assure you that I'm fine with it. We're very compatible. We're really in love. He's the most generous, sweet, tenderhearted man you'd ever want to meet."

"You say that now. Wait 'til you have your first big fight and he calls you a kike."

"A what?"

Oh, shit, that was a term I only learned when I read Salinger. I'd completely forgotten it.

"No! That won't happen. He's far too genteel to call me names."

"Gentile, you mean, not genteel. "

"Ha ha. Very funny. You're a regular riot."

"Look Sari, " Betty said, " Daddy and I discussed this already back home even before we met him. We feel you are in way over your head in this situation. You don't belong here. You know in Chicago, the country clubs restrict Jews, there are quota systems in the colleges. Organizations for wealthy people like the Junior League won't accept you. I can see this man has a lot of money, and I can tell you this: all the people in the circles he runs in will look down their noses at you."

"I get what you're saying, but you're wrong. Or if you're right…about other people, I…and by that I mean, we… don't care. Because we know who our friends are and they're all really happy for us."

"Is Cass happy for you? Is he as rich as her parents?" asked Sol.

"More so. He has a net worth we can't even fathom, trust me."

"Well, you won't get any of it when he dies, which, by the looks of it, might be soon. And then what are you? A young widow with no future, nothing to show for however many years you put up with nursing him."

"Okay, I'm not going to listen to this." Sol might have restrained his decibels, but I found mine going up. "No one nurses anyone around here! There's a huge staff that runs this place and yes, he has help. He needs a bit of assistance. But we manage. And yeah, sometimes I help him, …with everyday routine tasks. Most of the time his valet does it. But that's nothing. The man runs a huge foundation and heads up the board of directors. He's the sole heir to an empire! Really! Take my word for it, he's not incapacitated at all!"

"Sarah!" Sol yelled at me, his voice rising in increments at every phrase. "That man can't walk! He can't move his arm! He's in worse shape than Roosevelt was!"

The volume in the small space was ramping up too fast, now.

"Shhhhh, for God's sake. He'll hear you."

"I don't care! I want you out of here!! You pack up and come right home with us. This *fuhcockta* marriage is out of the question! I won't have it!"

"I'm not coming home! What is the matter with you? He even offered to convert to Judaism to marry me! What do you say to that?"

"I say he doesn't know what the hell he's talking about."

"Yes, Sari, that's ridiculous," Betty added, " He doesn't need to because Judaism passes through the mother, so no matter who you married, any children of yours would automatically be Jewish. And mark my words, his family would *geschrei* about it if he did that!"

"I'm not having any children!"

"Well! Finally! A good decision. Not with him anyway. That's the first thing you've said that makes sense since we got here! You find some nice Jewish boy to settle down with, then you can talk about having Jewish children."

Betty added, "Look, honey, be reasonable. It's not too late to start the college of education at Omaha U. You could really be a great French teacher."

"Yeah, why did I send you to Paris to school? To be a glorified secretary?"

"My God, "I snapped at them, "**you two don't even have a clue of who I am**!! I am only twenty-four and I have a good job---that I love! I'm the fucking Director of Education! It pays well. I'm also a consultant to a textbook publisher…that pays GREAT. And I am creating a teacher institute in a couple of months. That's not the job description of a secretary, now is it? And didn't you notice something else? I'm not on drugs or in the gutter. I have no children out of wedlock. What more do you want?"

"We want you back home and not living with some crippled *goyische* man old enough to be your father!"

At that and the recalcitrance on their part, that couldn't seem to be overcome no matter what I said, I began to cry.

"How can you be so fucking narrow minded? How can you judge people you don't even know? Everyone absolutely LOVES him. I love him! More than anything!" I sobbed into my hands.

"Stop that blubbering, Sarah! It's not gonna work on us! You always think you know everything there is to know. You always think you can get your way! Well not this time! Not for something that will determine the rest of your damn life."

Suddenly Polo and Roslyn with her bottle of Coke were standing in the doorway.

621

"I have heard just about enough yelling in this room, " Polo said firmly but still calmly. "Will you kindly lower the tone and come back to the library where we can have a civil conversation?"

"That won't be possible, " said Sol. "We're leaving. We won't be back for more conversation with you and we won't be back for the wedding. Go get our bags out of that car, Sarah. We'll take a cab to the hotel."

"Oh don't be so stupid. I'll drive you, " I said, wiping away the tears with my wrist.

"Look, I'm through with you, " my father said. "Don't think you can come crawling back to us now. It's over. You made your bed. Lie in it."

My fiancé stood there frozen, not believing what he was seeing or hearing. He kept an eye on me as though he thought I would faint at the thought that my own parents had more or less disowned me, and he kept up the effort to engage my father in dialogue which he thought would "fix it." I didn't want to. I didn't even give a shit at that point.

"Mr. Shrier, I love your daughter…so very much… and I have the means to provide very well for her for the rest of her life. She will never want for anything. She is a wonderful and highly intelligent young woman. She's beautiful and creative. I simply cannot believe that you, of all people, do not recognize her great …the person she is…her essence."

"Save it. You say you've heard enough from us…well, I'm not listening to anything you have to say either." He turned to me. "Come on, let's go. Let's get out of here. This…" he said, gesturing to Polo, " this museum you live in. You sure ain't our kind."

I had never heard my father say "ain't" in my entire life unless he was quoting some bizarre colloquialism that wasn't his, like "ain't that a shame." He was beyond embarrassing now. It was pure mortification.

"Come on, " I said, "we need to go back to the elevator. This way."

"Would you like me to accompany you, *Chérie*?" Polo addressed me.

I shook my head no, and we left him standing forlornly in the hall. No one spoke in the elevator, and we all piled silently into the car.

I drove them the five minutes it took to get to the Allerton, and popped the trunk so they could take their bags out. My father pulled them haughtily to the curb and turned to me one last time as I was closing the lid.

"Good luck, " he said, almost spitting at me. "You're gonna need it."

I looked at my mother and she just turned away from me and followed Sol up the steps. Roslyn lingered back for a minute with me.

"Sari," she said, "you must be nuts wanting to marry an old guy like that who's handicapped. Plus that house…geez Louise, you can't even sit on the furniture in there. Don't you miss our house?"

"Bye, Roz. Have fun in high school."

"Yeah, thanks for nothin', Sari. Daddy'll be mad all the way home now and I won't even get to see Chicago."

Chapter One Hundred Six

"I'm Happy Just to Dance with You"...Lennon & McCartney

Jean-Paul d'Arivèque was distraught when I got back from taking my family to their hotel. I wasn't in a great mood about the way things had gone either, but I wasn't as surprised as he was.

"You know what Tolstoy said about all happy families being alike and every unhappy one unhappy in its own way," I said to Polo. He nodded. "Well, you saw our unique one right up close. People like you who didn't have dramarama in their lives—well, you had real drama, I admit—can't fathom it."

"No, what I cannot fathom, as you say, is his animosity towards his own daughter. *Mais qu'est-ce qu'il fabrique?*"

"I don't know. I guess he wanted a boy or some cliché like that. I've always been a disappointment to them. "

"To your mother also? *Alors, là, je n'y comprends rien.*"

"Truth is, I don't think my mother liked being a mother very well. From what I gather, I sort of drove her crazy as a toddler, and he'd come home from work and see her upset and blame me."

"What did he do to you? " He paused and looked at me with something akin to pity. "Did he... hit you?" Polo asked with a strain in his voice.

"I don't remember what went on when I was very little, " I answered, truthfully, "but when I was older, he just screamed at me a lot. He did spank me, but I tended to laugh at that...which just made him madder."

"But why did this antagonism towards you persist, Sarah?" he wondered, his curiosity laced with sadness.

"I'm not sure. I mean, I probably tried their patience; I could be mouthy. But I was also deferential to adults and dutiful, really. Sometimes I think-- with Betty—she held onto deep resentment that she never got to 'self-actualize,' as they say in psych class. She was smart but she didn't have an opportunity to go to college, even though she was accepted. It was the Depression and Nana's family just couldn't afford to send her. She probably hates the fact that she got stuck living in a backwater when I got to go abroad. Stuff like that."

"Usually parents wish for their children to do better than they themselves did. It strikes me as pathetic your mother would resent your capabilities. But perhaps that explains a little bit. What I cannot bring myself to understand is a mother's reluctance to intercede on behalf of her child who is most blatantly being victimized, as I saw here today. You have told me how she never protected you."

"No, she didn't ever take my side against him. I think if some time when I was much younger, she'd made a scene or told him to lay off of me or else she'd leave him or something, he might have toned it down a little. But she never did and she never would. They tried and tried to have another baby, but it wasn't until years later that Roz was born, and by then they considered her a miracle and she became the favorite ever after. I was only eight, but I got the boot."

"*Chérie*, it astounds me that you came through all that and turned out to be *la personne remarquable* that you are."

"Well, I was certainly always looking for their approval-- and rarely got it. But I did from my grandmother. Thank God for saving graces, no?" I laughed.

"Yes, "he concurred. "I am in her debt."

"I guess I just overcompensated by fending for myself, you know? We all have to, at some point, take our lives into our own hands, don't we? You had a perfectly sublime upbringing, but you still had to become your own person."

"It is not the same, Sarah. The aftermath of a happy childhood cannot be compared to the trauma of an unhappy one, and the residue that leaves."

"Yes, I know. Another one of my college profs called it 'family of origin baggage.' He said it can ruin your life. But there must be some conscious effort to just leave it behind and... decide to... live!

Otherwise , how would most of us get through our lives? I would imagine hardly anyone had wonderful parenting like you did."

He came over and put his arm around me. "I am still angry at the treatment by your parents towards you, my sweetheart."

I shrugged, pondering the ramifications of what had gone down there today. In the end, it was all pretty laughable, so I decided to make more light of it than anything else.

"Let's not dwell on them. The whole afternoon was perfectly ridiculous, wasn't it? It was even worse than I'd imagined it, and that's saying something. Ha! I'm glad they're not coming to the wedding now. They'd probably just ruin it."

Jean-Paul felt so bad for me and so affectionate towards me, protective as always, that he pulled me closer and held me to him around the waist. He bent down to kiss the top of my head.

"They said some really horrible things to you, Sarah. I heard most of it."

"I'm sorry you did. They're just ignorant. Don't take it personally."

He snorted. "Oh, *oui!*"

We went back into the library to decompress from what had gone down with my parents, and then I realized I hadn't even told him of my conversation with Cass… about not coming to the wedding.

"You know, the other thing is, Cass also says she can't come to the wedding either. I'm really bummed about that."

"Why ever not? We would of course fly her here. I could send a plane to get them."

"Yes, I already offered her first-class tickets on commercial. She categorically refused. I'm going to call Alan and see what's up. Maybe he can change her mind."

"Yes, *ma chère,* that is a good idea."

In the meantime, he thought it would also be a good idea if we talked about the vows we wanted to exchange at our wedding.

"Did you like the lines Jean-Luc and Annie-Laure repeated to one another?" he asked me.

"Yes, they were fine. I haven't been to many weddings, believe it or not. You know, I **do** like some vows that are Church of England. I saw it in a British movie one time. It went like this: the man held up the ring and said these cool vows. He said 'with this ring, I thee wed. With my body I thee worship. And with all my worldly goods, I thee endow.' Then he took the ring in his hand and she held out her hand. He put the ring partway down each of her digits, stopping on each saying 'In the name of the father — for the thumb, the son for the index finger, the holy spirit for the middle one and then he slid the ring all the way on the ring finger with Amen.' I thought that was so neat. Of course, it wouldn't be right for ours."

"No," he laughed, "not that last part. I shall ask Harry what he would recommend, perhaps? He may know some of the Jewish wedding customs, after all. "

"Yeah? Okay. Secular is fine, too. I like things that are old fashioned like 'plighting thee my troth' and stuff like that. But I'm guessing that might be Christian, also. Believe it or not I've never heard Jewish vows. I've only been to one Jewish wedding — my cousin's-- and since it was all in Hebrew, I didn't understand a word. Can you even imagine promising all sorts of stuff and you don't know what they're saying?"

"I shall do some research. I did like the French version we heard at *La Pérégrine.* Shall we incorporate French into our ceremony?"

"By all means."

So Polo planned our wedding. He sent for the licenses. He read up on various ceremonies — traditional and modern. Troth was not religious, he told me. It was merely derived from the old English word for truth and meant faith. He arranged to have Marie-France come back for the month of August to do the invitations, make all the arrangements with florists and the photographer, and plan the party at the Palm Court with the caterers. And since she didn't want it to seem like she was taking over, she included me in everything.

She even offered to shop with me to find a wedding dress.

"Oh, you mean a white gown and veil and all that?" I asked, laughing at the absurdity.

"*Alors,* it can be any dress you like, not necessarily a gown."

"I just want something simple... and not white."

I was lucky in those days that I was thin. I was short and that didn't help matters, but I never weighed over one hundred pounds and had no "pupik" or bulge in the abdomen, due probably to walking everywhere in that city. Most clothes looked good on me: straight skits were smooth and full skirts accentuated my small waist. My legs were thin but had the proper curves, and my arms were firm, no doubt from carrying groceries upstairs for two years. I hated my smile, my nose, and my hair, but I liked my eyes. As with all great love stories, Polo overlooked my flaws as I did his. I saw only the object of my deep affection when I looked at him, and I hoped the same was true when he looked at me.

I spent August pretty much not working in the office, to my surprise, since I was so busy, not only with wedding details, but also packing up my apartment.

But I did make time to at least look for some sort of wedding outfit, and one day, milling around the Clark Street area, I saw it...right in a boutique window. The shop was called "Rêve" and I'd never even been inside, much as I'd walked past it dozens of times. What caught my eye in the window was not a dress, but a skirt and top, in pale grey knit, with short sleeves on the jacket and a little black leather belt with a bow at the waist. It was simple and beautiful. I could Jackie-Kennedy-it-up with my pearls. It was displayed with three-quarter length black leather gloves and a black straw hat trimmed in grosgrain ribbon. In honor of getting married, I decided to buy the whole ensemble, gloves, hat and all.

The boutique had boutique prices, and the outfit cost three hundred forty dollars, which struck me as too expensive by half, but at that point it was the only outfit I'd even considered. Of course I knew whom I was marrying. Of course I knew he'd pay for that or anything else I wanted. But I was determined that, in lieu of my parents offering me a wedding, I would outfit myself for it, and pay for it out of my own resources.

I didn't know it then, but this was all about to be irrelevant anyway. Soon after we were married, Jean-Paul d'Arivèque insisted on giving me a Carte Blanche credit card, in both the literal and figurative sense of the phrase.

I made a last-ditch effort to cajole Cass to come, and when she rebuffed all my ardent pleas, I phoned Alan at his office.

"Miss Shrier! You're calling me?"

"I need you to help me, Alan. I'm getting married, as you know, and Cass has just refused all my entreaties to be my matron of honor. She's just got to stand up with me. I'm hoping you'll be able to help me convince her. I'll pay for the whole thing—air tickets and all, as I'm sure she's told you."

"She can't make the trip, Sari, " he said without even considering what I was saying.

"Sure she can. But why won't she?"

"You don't have any idea what it's like now. What she's like to **live** with now. For one thing, you would hardly recognize her... she's a real mess. I can't stand to be home, if you must know. I take the kids in with me in the morning and we don't go back there until dinner time. Dinner time, " he sneered, "I use that word lightly because that's a laugh."

"Why? She told me she's on maintenance or something. Doesn't she cook?"

"She doesn't cook. If she does manage to make dinner, she won't EAT, especially not in front of us. She still acts all weird about food. The only thing she does consume is that same revolting crap I told you about. And she continues to hide it like, 'for later' she says—but she won't eat it after all. That is still going on. Just like in Iowa City, the place stinks! Same as ever. Do you hear what I'm telling you? **Nothing** has improved. "

"Oh, my lord, you must be joking." I was truly dejected at this news and the fact that Cass had been—if not outright lying to me—keeping it all from me. Distancing me from her struggle and unhappiness.

"I wish I were joking, " he said. " She weighs next to nothing and says at least once a week how fat she thinks she is. She works out in the garden like it's the Boston marathon or something. Constantly tilling, digging, weeding. But very little to show for all that."

"What about her art? Is she working on that?"

"It's strewn all over the house, if that's what you mean, but no...there's not much output on that front either. 'Course, I don't know...I don't pay much attention to it."

"Well, how are the kiddos? Are they ...thriving?"

"They're fine. Talking up a storm…with a Texas drawl."

"Oh, great, " I laughed, "I hope you can nip **that** in the bud, at least. What about your job? Are you glad you took it?"

"I like it here. It's good. Good students. I –uh – like my colleagues."

"And what about Cass? Is she at least finding some friends among the faculty wives or anyone?"

"Oh hell, no, Sari. Get real. She was in the office one time and we went over to the cafeteria for lunch---she just had coffee, and the guy behind the line told me later, 'I see your wife's one o' them skinnies.' That's what he called her. I told you she looks like shit, Sari. Anorexia is a bitch."

"You know what, Alan? Cass Hyde couldn't look like shit if she tried."

"What she really looks like is some Holocaust victim in Life magazine pictures---you know the ones. She looks just like that. It disgusts me. You need to come down here and see for yourself, I guess."

"Yes, well, I want to. We are, however, taking off for Paris on our honeymoon, and after that I am hosting a teacher's weekend workshop here. I can't get away for a while. But Alan, you need to get her to some doctor down there, don't you? I mean, it's an illness, right?"

"She won't go. Anyway, we'll talk about it if you come. Maybe you can convince her to see one. I hope you do come, Sari. And, you know – about the wedding and all--- I'm real happy for you. I knew you were sweet on your boss when you came to Iowa City, now didn't I?" He laughed. "He sounds real good for you."

"Well, you were right, even if I wouldn't admit it then. And yeah, I wish you could meet him."

We hung up with me sending love to Paul and Laura and telling him to hang in there with Cass and try to help her, a suggestion he spurned with an audible grunt.

In mid-August I moved. Polo sent a retinue of people over to help pack my things and take them out of there. I dropped off the keys with a nice note to John-Wilfred over at the Hyde Industries offices, and that was that. My days as a single girl in the big city came to an end, and I settled into one of the huge guest bedrooms on the third-floor digs at the mansion. I put my clothes in the closet in there and used its bookshelves for my music and little thises- and- thatses. I didn't sleep in there, of course, but it was my private space where I could retreat if Robineau was there dressing Jean-Paul. It was mutually understood, also, that Robineau would spend as little time as possible on that floor, but rather come up in the morning only. He would also pretty much abandon his habit of sleeping in the staff quarters behind the kitchen.

I awoke the day of our wedding to blue skies and temps warm enough for me to wear my outfit without a coat of any kind. I got dressed in "my bedroom," and told Polo to wait for me on the second floor. I had no aisle to walk down, so coming out of the elevator in my dreamy, chic attire to present as his bride would have to do.

He had asked the maids to help me in any way they could, but I told him it was easy enough to get into the clothes without them, and I didn't need anyone to do my hair either, as I was wearing it just parted in the middle with bangs… and my hat.

The elevator doors opened and he was standing there in breathless anticipation. He had on a charcoal grey vicuña wool suit with a white rose in the lapel, and he was holding a magnificent bouquet for me to carry. It was exceptionally elegant, and ever so slightly cascaded with pink and cream roses, white calla lilies, and green and pink hydrangea---my favorite flower, which he knew and had informed Marie-France …all wrapped with a gorgeous ivory satin ribbon secured with pearl pins. He offered it to me as I approached him.

"Oh, that's breathtaking, " I said seeing the flowers.

"You are. *C'est toi qui me coupes le souffle*, Sarah, " he said to me, offering his arm.

Daniel Rosier de Molet and his wife were waiting for us out in front by the limo, and this time Robineau was driving, as Jean-Luc and Annie-Laure rode with us. Annie-Laure was standing up for me in place of Cass. Marie-France had been staying with us, and so of course, she rode, too. We all drove to the courthouse without talking too much but glancing at each other and grinning the whole way there.

Judge Harry Lowenstein greeted our group in his office, and then led us to chambers. Polo and I stood across from one another in the traditional way flanked by our "*témoins*." We signed the papers before the judge and Daniel signed as the main witness. And then the judge began the ceremony with a few words about…Judaism!

He told us that marriage in the Jewish tradition was called *kiddushin*, which translated to "holy."

"*Kiddushin* is the act of two people setting themselves apart from the rest of the world and keeping themselves for each other...for a holy purpose, " he pronounced with an air of Rabbinic authority. "In our Torah, the origin of marriage is the verse **'It is not good for a person to be alone.'** The way I interpret this is that God decided a fundamental part of human existence is connection to other people. We are whole, we are *tov*, in Hebrew, when we are in a relationship with an 'other.' And the deepest realization of this wholeness...of how we grow our soul into a fuller human being...is found through the intimacy of romantic love and commitment to nurturing **another** soul: that is the meaning of marriage."

Polo smiled at me, happy that his dear friend had found a way to weave my religion into our secular, interfaith mishmash-of-cultures ceremony. As for me, I was in awe of Harry Lowenstein.

"We are born into this world alone, " the judge continued, "and we leave it alone, " words I'm sure Polo asked him to re-convey to me since he had given me essentially this same argument when proposing to me the first time. "The moment of marriage reminds us that we have the chance, while yet we live, to surmount that."

At this point Harry directed his remarks to me, saying, "Sarah, Jean-Paul has asked me to conduct the vows in French."

I nodded and handed my bouquet to Annie-Laure who, I could see as I glanced sideways, was tearing up a little. She smiled, embarrassed at her emotion, took the flowers, and stepped back a bit.

"Sarah Elaine, *voulez-vous prendre Jean-Paul Benoit comme époux?*"

"*Oui,*" I answered.

And then, as Annie-Laure had done, I also promised *de lui rester fidèle, dans les beaux ou dans les mauvais jours, dans la santé et dans la maladie, pour l'aimer tous les jours de ma vie.*

The same was repeated by Polo, after which the judge said that marriage required a loving nature and a forgiving heart if it were to succeed, and that the exchange of rings would seal the vows. He asked for the rings, which Daniel took out, and put the first one, a diamond-encrusted platinum band, in Polo's hand, whereupon Polo asked me to hold my hand out and he said, to my surprise,

"With this ring, I thee wed." And he touched the ring to my thumb. "With my body I thee worship." And he touched the ring to my index finger. "And with all my worldly goods, I thee endow." And he touched the ring to my middle finger. "Amen, " he said, sliding the band down my ring finger to rest upon Madame Schwartze's. He had managed to incorporate that pretty ceremonial thing I said I liked from the English movie, but without the Christian part! I was stunned.

I had no such vow ready to make to him and also no worldly goods with which to endow anyone.

Judge Lowenstein took the other ring, a plain one, from Daniel and handed it to me. I took Polo's hand and the judge, prepared for my lack of vows of my own, said, "Please repeat after me: "With this ring I thee wed." I said that. "And, forsaking all others, to thee I will be true so long as we both shall live." Overjoyed, I repeated that, and then he added, "And thereto I plight thee my love." It was perfect! Every element I had dreamed of in my ideal wedding ceremony, I had gotten. It was like a miraculous omen.

And then, in one last astonishing act, Judge Lowenstein reached behind him to his "bench" and took down a cloth napkin wrapped around a bulky object. He set it on the floor near Polo's right leg and Polo stomped on it. It was the glass broken at Jewish weddings to symbolize the destruction of the Temple in Jerusalem.

I thought to myself, "I hope that wasn't Baccarat."

"*Mazel tov!*" cried Harry Lowenstein, joined by the rest of our little party. He then turned to address Polo: "You may kiss...your wife." His voice revealed the poignancy in that phrase for Polo, and Harry did it expressly, showing us he knew of his friend's longing to find someone with whom to share his life.

Polo and I held one another in a long embrace and my eyes were damp with tears of pure joy. Even without Cass there. Even without the blessing of my parents. Their absences had only served to amplify how much I, too, was alone... except not anymore. As of now and up until the day he died, I would never be alone again.

Marie-France had arranged for a photographer to chronicle these moments as well as the party to follow, so we all posed in front of the paneled bench and electric candelabra in Harry's courtroom, and

627

then again out on the grand staircase in the hallway, although we didn't take the stairs anywhere. We all left by elevator to the awaiting limousine and made for the Palm Court in the Drake Hotel.

What with the iconic giant urn rising from the fountain in the center of the magnificent room, the Palm Court didn't need any further decoration, especially for the "simple" wedding reception I was expecting; but Marie-France de Piaget had thought differently. She had ordered the white rounded "club" chairs switched out for those dainty gilt ones and she had them decorated with ivory satin bows on the back. There were crystal bowls with floating pink and blue hydrangeas on each table, and a huge centerpiece of white gladiolas in a beautiful Sèvres trumpet vase on a long table displaying the traditional American wedding cake. Our cake was four tiers high decorated in cream-colored frosting with swags of braided icing looping all around each tier, and flowers at each arch. It was the loveliest cake I could have ever hoped for.

A string quartet played in front of the fountain, and by the time we arrived, the guests were already mingling and being served hors d'oeuvres consisting of an array of delights, that, even though I'd been to many d'Arivèque receptions, parties and dinners prior to this, amazed me with their artistry and *luxe*. There were lobster *mousse*-filled pastry shells, *paté de fois gras* and caviar on toast points; prawns, Swedish meatballs, miniature seafood *soufflés*, Nova Scotia smoked salmon, stuffed mushrooms, Blue Point oysters rolled in bacon and something the waiter told me was called crab legs Chantilly! Dom Perignon flowed like the proverbial river, and at the end of the cake table, huge brass samovars with tea and coffee stood amid an ocean of bone china cups and saucers.

We were greeted by applause and I saw many familiar faces in the crowd. But the first person to approach us was Georg Solti.

"Oh, for heaven's sake! " I cried. "You're back? But you didn't want to come to the ceremony?"

"No, I wanted to surprise you right here...and greet some of my musicians over there."

"Oh my goodness, we have the CSO playing for us? That's pretty lah-dee-dah!."

He took my hand, "Congratulations, *Madame*. Valerie and I wish for you only joy and many years of happiness together."

There were more surprises for me and they really blew my socks off. First of all, Jean-Paul had told MFP to invite C.C. and have Nonnie and Patrick fly in from San Francisco on his dime, afraid that I would feel very at sea with none of my girlfriends there. But C.C. was in Santiago, Chile working for the French consulate, of all things...and so she couldn't get away; and neither could Nonnie and Patrick, what with Patrick just starting his residency and her in grad school. So Polo had also asked his friend and doctor—and my doctor—Fabrizio Garabanti, and had instructed MFP to invite Paxton Hubley. Pax, in turn, surprised me by conveying the O'Haras' "great good wishes." I was thrilled to see him there and thanked my sweet husband for having thought to include him.

"Was your mind sort of blown by this news? " I asked Pax, laughing.

"No, Sari. It makes perfect sense to me. Hell, you're gonna rule the world some day. I really believe that. Your husband is a great guy. I could tell that the time he hovered over your hospital bed like a mama lion protecting her cub. He's crazy about you. Probably was then, too, eh?"

"I guess you are right about that. Remember, at that time I thought he was gay. What did I know?"

" Well, this is one heck of a party. Thanks for inviting me." Before I could demur, he added, "By the way; I have some other news. "

"Oh? Tell me! What is it?" I was expecting him to announce his engagement to some—I pictured--Junior League bombshell future doctors' wives auxiliary member.

"My residency is over now. I'm moving out to The Bay Area... Berkeley, to be exact. I'll be in close proximity to Pat and Nonnie."

"Gee, Pax, that's really far out. I hope we can come out and visit them some time and see you, too. That is so cool you'll be together. But what did your parents say when you told them you were not coming back to Louisiana?"

"They weren't happy about it, as you can guess. But they want me to follow my bliss, don't ya know, darlin'."

"Hmmm." I nodded, but really I was shaking my head. *Their wanting me to "follow my bliss" was something I'd never hear from my parents in a thousand years.*

I had to excuse myself from Pax for a moment because I spotted another unexpected guest in the throng: Yves Brunsvick standing with his sister-in-law Marie-France! He was back in Chicago for another guest lecture at the university, and the timing had worked out perfectly for him to be at our wedding, too. I was so enormously happy to see him that I forgot my French etiquette altogether and wrapped my arms around him before we could even offer one another *la bise*.

"Thank you so much for coming. *Ça me fait un grand plaisir de vous voir ici*, " I gushed at him.

He didn't seem put out at my less-than-dignified greeting, and even laughed. "I'm so delighted to be here and also for you both. Polo is a lucky man today."

"Not as lucky as I am. Will you be back in Paris soon? Polo and I will be there for two or three weeks! I'm so excited."

"You will?! That is a long *lune de miel*! You must come to lunch with me at UNESCO. I shall arrange it with Polo's office."

"Fab!" I said. "I'm anxious to see those Joan Mirós on the walls in there again."

I sought out Dom Lambert and Peter Weir in the crowd, and I took the opportunity to have a taste of the food as I sat for a little while with them.

"You know, Sari, " Dom said, "we really like him. Have since we first met him."

"I'm glad, " I said. "I can't tell you what it means for you both to be here today. I know you had to get a sub, eh Dom?"

"We wouldn't miss this for anything. You know that, " Peter said.

"Well, we'll see each other often…maybe even more than before I was married!"

Of course the entire office was there, and they were all delighted to welcome Marie-France back again, too. Many of the other guests were Polo's acquaintances from the boards of directors of dozens of Chicago arts organizations, the French Consulate, the *Alliance Française*, Marshall Fields and the Art Institute---all invited by Marie-France.

A notable absence was *Oncle* Charles, and when I had asked Polo why he hadn't wanted to be with us on the auspicious occasion, Polo took me aside and explained that he hadn't intended to bring up any bad news that day, but that his uncle had been under the weather and was advised by his doctors not to make the long trip.

"Oh no!" I had cried out, fearfully, "I couldn't bear it if anything happened to him before we can be together again!"

"I was afraid this would worry you, *chérie*, and I do not want you to be upset today—of all days. I am assured that he will recover. He plans on meeting and staying with us in Paris, provided he feels better."

I was relieved and calmed down. We rejoined our guests.

About an hour after we arrived, and before the cake was cut, Polo took the microphone and gave a little speech. He thanked everyone for sharing in "the most special milestone day of my life" and expressed his deep appreciation to each and every person there for their kind wishes and support. He then chastised them, albeit tongue in cheek, for their lack of ability to read, since the invitation had specified "no gifts, please," and there was a table in the back of the room simply laden with beautifully wrapped boxes.

I'm not sure he knew it, but that wasn't even really comme il faut *either. In those days people of any decent upbringing did not bring wedding gifts to the reception, but sent them ahead to the bride's parents' home. Given that ours was organized very quickly and no one had an inkling of where I lived, and didn't want to have stores deliver to the groom's home, which wasn't done either, they just broke the rules of etiquette and brought them. We wouldn't even open them for a month, but that gave me the chance to have Annie-Laure order me some personalized engraved thank you notes that read "Monsieur et Madame Jean-Paul d'Arivèque" on the front. I intended to write each and every one by hand.*

The music at our reception was beautiful and meaningful, starting with my favorite baroque "greatest hits" of Telemann and Purcell. The musicians played some of Handel and a version for strings of the andante movement from Mozart's *Piano Concerto No. 21*, the theme from the movie *Elvira Madigan* reminding me of the plane trip to France for the other wedding. At one point Maestro Solti led me out on the dance floor and his musicians played Pachelbel's *Canon in D Major*, and we improvised dance steps to it. I remember thinking that I must have looked like a dork, but what the hell—it was my own wedding.

When he returned me to Polo, the maestro went back over and said something to his orchestra members, and then took up the mic again.

"Ladies and gentlemen, I give you *Monsieur et Madame* Jean-Paul d'Arivèque." I looked at Polo, startled, as he rose and took my hand without his cane, and limped with me out to the middle of the floor. The music began. It was the Beatles' "I Will". I gasped, and saw that Polo was grinning at me. I lifted his left arm to my waist where his hand was able to grip me. I put my left hand on his weak shoulder and clasped my right hand in his. We stood facing each other and just sort of swaying to the music, imagining Paul McCartney singing "Who knows how long I've loved you?..."and then the refrain came along I drew close enough to put both my arms around his neck and sing along in his ear, "Love you forever and forever...love you with all my heart. Love you whenever we're together...love you when we're apart."

When the song was over, we just stood there, locked together, and Polo told me, "This is the first time in my entire adult life that I have ever danced. You made it possible...and lovely."

"Well, in that case, I'm honored to have been your first partner."

We went back and sat down, but no sooner had I reached for my flute of champagne, then Dom came up and said to Polo, "*Vous permettez?*" and swept me back to the dance floor. The quartet struck up another Beatles tune, "The Word" and Dom and I rocked out to it and sang at the top of our lungs, "Say the word I'm thinking of...have you heard the word is love!"

When that song ended, there was still another Beatles hit, this time "In My Life!" Pax came over to me to request a dance.

"Looks like it's a Beatles trilogy, " he grinned. "I wonder if our esteemed maestro arranged this?"

Polo winked at me and I guessed they both had. Pax and I went over by the fountain and he led me around the floor to the slow pace of "There are places I remember all my life...though some have changed..."

Three of my very favorite songs with three of the dearest men in my life. If I wasn't the most fortunate bride on God's green earth, then no one was.

My lingering twinges of sadness that Cass hadn't been there for any of this also faded away as the afternoon lengthened, and finally we took our leave, pronouncing our heartfelt thank-yous to the guests. We made our way back to Lake Shore before heading to his plane.

"You've made me the happiest girl on the planet today, **Mister** d'Arivèque," I told him as I snuggled up to him in the back of our limo.

"Sarah," he said, cupping my face in his hand and kissing me, "I have no words...except *je t'adore*."

Chapter One Hundred Seven

[Reprise] "I Love Paris"...Cole Porter

After our wedding reception, it had taken three waiters to carry all the presents out to the car. There were several boxes in the iconic robin's egg blue of Tiffany's, which caused delight, but also made me think that these poor wedding guests were in the same boat I was: there was nothing one could offer Jean-Paul d'Arivèque as a gift. So just go to Tiffany's and hope for the best. That was, of course, fine with me.

When we got back to his place---our place---I was greeted at the elevator by Robineau, who addressed me as "*Madame* Sarah" now. *Madame*. I liked that. I still didn't like him, though.

"This letter arrived special delivery for you, " he said to me in a perfunctory tone, which caused Polo to shoot him a look of questioning disdain. So he hastily added, "I ...thought...perhaps you would want to see it before you left for Paris."

It was from Cass!

"Yes! I would. Thank you."

Cass had made an oversized square envelope addressed in big scrolled blue letters to *Monsieur et Madame* Jean-Paul d'Arivèque. Inside was something I recognized immediately upon lifting it out of the envelope: one of her original Switzerland scenes, an especially beautiful woodcut print of a delightful Alpine village. She had matted it and made it suitable for framing of any sort I—or, rather, we -- wished.

I found myself stunned that she had taken the time and energy to get this work of art done, and decided it must have been started just as soon as she'd heard he'd proposed to me. Things in her life were not quite so dire then, I reckoned.

She had printed it out on pale ecru paper and matted it on light tan. The printing itself was done in soft tones of beige, tan, brown and green, and she put in exceptional details of a mountain valley road lined with chalets and cottages winding up through forests towards snow-capped peaks. The roofs of the buildings had exaggerated gingerbread designs, and the houses' small windows were flanked by shutters with hearts carved into them. I marveled at the perspective she had managed to achieve of the small village spread out from the valley up to the tree lines on the sides of the hills. If she had done this from memory of some little place she'd once visited, she was truly gifted; and even if she'd done it by looking at a photo taken decades earlier, she was still a genius.

I called Polo over to see what I'd taken out of the envelope. "Look what Cass has sent us!" I announced.

"Oh, my, Sarah. That is beautiful!" He was genuinely impressed with her work.

"And look, here's a card, too---it's of US!" I lifted out a large pink hand-made paper card with an ink-drawn cartoon on the cover in a style copying Joan Walsh Anglund's figures with only eyes...me in a long wedding dress with a cape over my shoulders, the veil and train secured by a wreath of flowers in my hair and roses in my hand; and Polo in a top hat and tails, holding a long stylized cane. Inside it read:

September 1, 1972 (New Moon)
Happy be this day & Your LIFE together
Sari and Polo
JOY is the most
    Infallible sign of the presence of God* (*OM)
Bless one another and be loved and LOVING.
    Love, Cass

"She is very sweet, " Polo said softly when I showed it to him.

As I was putting it all back in the envelope with the intention of taking it to Paris and displaying it there, I saw there was a tiny note in the bottom addressed only to me. I took it aside and read it.

"Dearest Sari,

It is so golden and warm here that I feel certain it is but a reflection of my two beloved people joining hearts and hands in Chicago. Please write all the happenings and share. I feel so bad that I couldn't make it in with my wedding wish for you in person. The 'reason' is that my life seems to be silently unravelling at the seams. A parade of tears and tearing apart. But that is for another day's telling. Be patient with me. Today is YOUR day of JOY and with all my heart and soul I wish you two all that is glorious and lasting and loving.

PEACE and LOVE, Cass"

"Oh, God, " I blurted out as I read it, which alarmed Polo.

"What is the matter, darling?"

"Nothing... I mean... not that we can do anything about now, " I said folding the little note with the card back into the envelope. "She's having problems, though. I hope when we return I can talk to her about it."

"Perhaps you should go to her next month when we are back?"

"Well, but... I can't because of the Institute. I'll call her, though...maybe from Paris? May I?"

" But...of course."

I didn't want anything to get in the way of our honeymoon, no damper put on it and no worries that would make my new husband fear I wasn't happy...the happiest and luckiest girl in the entire world. That's how he made me feel and that's what I was determined to show him.

"I love you, " I told him, kissing his cheek.

"And I you. *En plus*, I have something for you. Let us go up to the third floor, shall we?"

"A gift? Oh, come on, Polo, as usual I have nothing for you!" It was my same old mantra — only official now.

He put his finger on my lips and said, "*Chut.*" Then he led me into the elevator and up to the bedroom where my clothes hung in the closet. Displayed right there on the floor was a matched set of Louis Vuitton luggage in the brown monogramed-design that was already ubiquitous in France, but not yet the shock-wave popular trend it would become in the States.

I gulped seeing them all placed around the bed and bent down to finger them and open them up to the iconic lining. There was a garment bag, a round hat box, two large oblong "Pullman" cases, a smaller identical one, and the duffle bag carry-on.

"Oh! Polo! A whole set of it!? Holy shit! "

"So you like it then?"

"Like it? Yes, I like it. I love it! Thank you!"

"It is my pleasure to provide you things. And this, you need, " he laughed.

I looked at the array of luggage stacked up on my floor and my eyes glazed over.

"But...but...I don't even have enough clothes to go in half of these!" I said, looking up and seeing him grinning at me.

"That is the point, *ma chérie*. You shall take them empty and fill them up in Paris. *Voilà.*"

"Yeah, like that's going to happen! Ha! I don't think so." I jumped up and flung my arms around him. "And what pray tell, could I ever gift you with for our wedding?"

"You have already given me...everything."

Our plane ride over to Paris had several extra passengers. There was Marie-France de Piaget, of course, planning to stay awhile with us in Paris before returning to *La Pérégrine*. And there was also Robineau and his boyfriend, Maxime whom I did like.

It was becoming clear to me that I had to suck it up and accept the fact that Robineau was going to be in our lives, and to just get used to it; but I didn't want to. Not that he wasn't absolutely polite to me now, as he had been since their "talk." But there was no love lost between us. Even though I dreaded having to see him around, I vowed to stuff it. My husband needed his valet to maintain his routine. He was dependent upon him in ways in which, much as I thought I could step in and substitute, Polo didn't want to ask me to do that, and I understood.

The plane ride over was a little bumpier than I had experienced prior to that flight, and the stewardesses didn't want us out of our seat belts, so going back into the cabin to sleep in the bed was out of the question. Polo and I sat in front again, with Marie-France across from us. I tried to take my mind off of the airplane's instability, and to pass the time trying out for them a new idea I'd had for the Institute.

"I want to provide the teachers with some take-away thing they can all use in class right away, " I explained, telling them that from what I knew about Dom's classes, he had to buy a lot of his own materials, and by extrapolation, I assumed all teachers did that.

"Anything they can get for free and really use is a great boon. So I've thought of a game that could be very generic, yet interdisciplinary and useable in all levels. It's a 'Concentration' game—based on a t.v. show. The game already exists, and the teacher would have to procure the board---places sell these---or make one themselves. But the cards relevant to French could come from us. My idea is art."

"That sounds wonderful, " said Polo. " How would it work?"

"Well, if you ever watched the show on t.v., which I assume you have not, " I laughed, "you'd know it's a solve-the-puzzle game where players had to remember what was behind certain numbers. They chose two cards to be revealed, and if they matched, they got the prize ... on t.v. In the classroom, kids would also choose two cards to be revealed, and if they match, they would earn a point. If they don't match, it's another player's turn. We wouldn't supply the prizes. The teacher could do that—or just give them points on something else, like extra credit."

"I think I remember 'Concentration', " said Marie-France. "Would they solve a puzzle?"

"Not exactly. My idea is for the cards to be the name of an artist, and the match would be a picture of some iconic work of art for him...or her... and the title. In the game I've thought up, on the board facing the players the cards are numbered. So the kid calls out a number—this is in a French class, so they would do this in French, since even beginners learn numbers. The artist would be revealed. The cards with the works of art could be lettered. Students would call out the letter, and if they matched, the kid or team gets the point. And it would just proceed like that. The kid calls out 'numéro cinq'...it's Monet. He calls out 'lettre D' and if it's "Impression: Soleil Levant' he wins the point. If it's "Bal au Moulin de la Galette' or something else –he doesn't get the point, since that would have been Renoir. Get it?" I asked, wondering if I'd bored them to death.

"Yes, I see, " said Polo. "And so we would provide what?"

"Well, cards. A set of cards—well, two sets of them. I'd say in dimensions of five-by-seven or so---I'd have to ask Dom what size the boards take--- one with artists' names on one side and a number on the other, and the second set with art works on one side and a letter on the other. Let's say fifteen of each. I'm thinking those boards hold thirty cards, if I'm remembering right. We would want them to be laminated. If our marketing department couldn't make them up for us, we could probably find a manufacturing source of some kind. I'm guessing this wouldn't be too expensive to do. We only have ten teachers coming to the first institute, so ten sets wouldn't break the bank, I don't suppose. What do you think?"

"I think you are an idea machine," said Marie-France. "Legal might have to be involved, though...the images are no doubt copyrighted."

"Yes, but you know, I think I could find postcards of all of them in the museums in Paris, and maybe they have the copyright place on them and we could contact them."

"Yes, that is probably the case. I would have our people look into the copyright situation before we did anything in the way of reproduction, " said Polo.

At that point the turbulence was becoming more noticeable and all of a sudden the plane lurched down to one side and back up. I gasped, and my arm flew out towards the aisle as if to balance myself. Polo saw how scared I was and put his arm around me.

"The plane can take it, " he said reassuringly, "do not be afraid."

"Easy for you to say!" Marie-France laughed nervously. "Do you forget we are the ones heavier than air up here?"

"And to think I used to love flying, " I said.

As if to take my mind off being scared, Polo started a conversation with me about how he had felt sad for me that I didn't have a "hen party".

"Hen party? That's British, " I said poking fun at him, "but yeah, you're right. Think of all that skimpy lingerie I missed out on not having a wedding shower. Tsk. More of a loss for you, *mon ange*, " I teased.

"I shall make it up to you…and myself…in Paris, " he laughed, hugging me. "You can buy everything you see. In fact, I need to reiterate that I was entirely serious when I said I want you to shop for an entirely new wardrobe there."

"Oh, you do, do you? Well, I won't be turning down that offer any time soon, but will you come with me?"

"I should be delighted."

At Orly we were picked up in a grey Mercedes limo that was to be our car in Paris. Our driver was called Marcel, a rotund guy for a Frenchman, about Polo's age, I estimated, or maybe a little older even. He had a photo of his pretty wife and three children on the dashboard, but it looked to have been taken in the 1950's. He did not wear a uniformed coat and hat like Jean-Luc did in Chicago; instead, he was dressed in a suede jacket and a beret. But he seemed to know all the people in the car except me, and was visibly happy to see them again.

We drove into Paris on the A6 to the *Periphérique* that led us to the Boulevard des Courcelles and into those famous gilded gates of the luxurious Parisian landmark park. I had always wondered, when I went to the Parc Monceau as a student, just who had access to that drive and parking, and figured it had to be the residents. There were actually two such entrances with parking, and each apartment building that abutted the park was more beautiful than the next. The d'Arivèque former *hôtel particulier*, now divided up into posh apartments, was imposing, with those *oeil de boeuf* windows under the mansard roofs that were so iconic.

Our car turned into the private off-street drive right in front of the door to Jean-Paul's apartment building. His residence was on the *premier étage*, or first floor, (but of course, that meant the second floor as we would count them. Only the *concièrge, Madame* Ferand, lived on the *rez de chaussée*.) Polo, Marie-France and I squeezed into the tiny black iron-gated elevator to go up one floor, while the others walked and brought the luggage. Trying to be reasonable, I had only brought the garment bag, one Pullman -- practically empty -- and the carry-on. Robineau took Polo's bags; the rest were brought up by various other house staff members.

The interior hallway was as splendid as the exterior predicted it would be. This place was a palatial 18th century mansion with black and white Carrara floors, and variegated marble walls, the likes of which I'd only seen on visits to places like Fontainebleau and Vaux-le-Vicomte. The place wasn't as grand as those palaces, of course, but the decorations were certainly as opulent. There was a sweeping oriental-carpeted staircase leading up to higher interior levels, and in the stairwell was an enormous brass hanging lantern in the center of the ceiling to light the way.

Inside Polo's apartment, I found myself walking across ancient floors of the usual French parquetry. I got the feeling Marie-France had been there many times; she seemed to know where she was. But Polo led me around to different rooms, so I could see that we had gorgeous views over the park.

The walls of the *grand salon* were covered in priceless art. Right away I glimpsed a Delacroix, one signed Ingrès, and one that looked like a study for Pissarro's famous market scene at Gisors. This room had an elaborate balcony outside of floor to ceiling French doors, with perhaps the most bucolic park perspective of any room. I was expecting to see the ubiquitous silk-covered settees and other Louis XV furniture, but was pleasantly surprised to find a lot of it was much softer, and that even the formal chairs had fluffy cushions on them for comfort. The colors were Versailles-like again, in foamy greens and pinks, all right, but the furnishings were "livable" as opposed to strictly museum pieces.

There was next a magnificent dining room with a lovely coffered ceiling. The room had a view over the courtyard rather than the Parc Monceau, but the beautiful windows were still covered in thick damask draperies, even as light came more from the three enormous Saint Louis crystal and brass chandeliers than from the outside.

Polo wanted to show me the bedroom we would be using. It was his.

"We have a total of six bedrooms not counting three more for staff," he told me, "and **ours**, (*his emphasis*) also has a twenty-four square meter balcony off it. It looks down into the children's playground area of the park. It is very sweet to watch them."

"Cute," I agreed. "I can just imagine you playing down there when you were little." There was enough tree cover to blot out noise from kids enjoying themselves on the various swings and rides, and of course, at night, it was empty anyway, but I knew I was going to love being able to watch all the action from there.

This house, like every other d'Arivèque one I'd been to, had yet another library that dwarfed even Polo's largest one in Chicago, and in the middle of it were two huge tables pushed together to make seating and reading room for twenty people or more. The walls were lined floor to ceiling with completely filled bookcases.

"You have so many books! " I exclaimed not believing what I was again seeing. "Whatever are you going to do with all of them...someday, I mean?"

Polo laughed. "I am not entirely sure. The family, perhaps, will ... "

"What family?" I wondered aloud. "It's only you and *Oncle* Charles."

"No, rather, I meant... the Foundation will have to archive them all, I suppose. I imagine the *Bibliothèque Nationale* may want a few of ours."

He knew and I knew we weren't going to get into it that day, at least, --my unwillingness to give him children.

After I'd unpacked a few things in the bedroom we were to use, I resumed wandering around the apartment a bit. All the bedrooms in the hall where ours was also had their own bathrooms, which I found astounding. When I remarked to Polo that I couldn't believe people in the 1700's had bathrooms like that— in their sleeping quarters—he laughed and enlightened me.

"*Maman* had this home modernized in the 1950's, " he explained. "She came often while I was studying in Paris and she knew I would possibly live here several years. She had spaces reconfigured, and that's when the bathrooms were added to these bedrooms."

"That was more convenient for you, of course, " I said. "But I guess I'm confused. This wasn't your family home in Paris when you were growing up, right? I thought you told me you grew up in the sixth *arrondissement*."

"Yes, darling. Remember, this was my paternal family home. My d'Arivèque ancestors originally bought the building in 1760 to become the seat of the *Ducs de Beuvron* in Paris. It was not the ornate building you see today, and the Parc Monceau was quite a bit smaller—it was not even made truly public until 1793. Even before my mother came to live here-- when I started university in Paris-- my great-grandparents had already remodeled the home in the Baron Haussmann era. And then again later, the electricity and heating were redone...after the First World War."

"So until what your mom added, it hadn't been redone since then?"

"Well, no, although other modernizations had taken place. We have a very nice kitchen now. You shall see it."

"But did you spend any real time here or were you always in the *sixième* when you were growing up?"

"Oh, yes, I spent great amounts of time here."

"And is this the house where your great-grandmother had her salon with famous people?"

"It is."

"What about *Oncle* Charles? Was it he who actually inherited this house when your grandparents died?"

"He and my father inherited it together, Sarah. But as it happened, my grandfather died in 1939, just a few years before his son was also to die. So, yes, my father grew up in this house, but he never lived here afterwards. *Oncle* Charles gave it to me outright, with the understanding that he could use it any time he liked, and of course, since I am only nominally a citizen of France-- and frankly, so is he-- neither of us stays here too often."

He turned to me and placed his hand on my shoulder. "I now want you to think of this apartment as also your Paris home, *mon ange*...yours and mine. I know you love this city. Now you have a place to call your own here any time you like."

"I don't know what to say. Thank you! For starters! I'm just overwhelmed to be in the *Duc de Beuvron* family seat in Paris, and to think your grandparents and great-grandparents inhabited these same rooms and hosted the *literati* of Paris! And that the current duke would allow us to live here, too. It's too much!"

"Speaking of Charles, he arrives tomorrow!"

"Fantastic!" I exclaimed. "I can't wait to see him."

"I believe he feels it was he who convinced you to marry, " Polo laughed.

"Well, I can't say his little pep talk didn't help, " I said, "but I assure you I came to the conclusion all by myself. "

We did indeed welcome *Oncle* Charles back to his own home the next morning and we, along with Marie-France, had a wonderful reunion with him. It turned out he had invited MFP to return to Geneva with him for a few days before she took up residence back at *La Pérégrine*. Polo and I were also invited but we demurred this time. The honeymoon would be just Paris.

That didn't mean we were alone, though, as invitations came in by the dozens for us to meet his old friends. We were invited to the Opéra Garnier music library by one of his closest school chums who was an archivist there. We were given an invitation to dine at *Le Grand Véfour* with other friends who wanted to *fête* our marriage. And yet another invitation came, as promised, from Yves Brunsvick who invited us all to lunch at the UNESCO headquarters over on the Place de Fontenoy. It was a great running joke then that I had already been in that building and Polo never had!

The first thing Polo and I did together in Paris, however, was not go to lunch or to dinner parties or the theater. We went shopping for that wardrobe he'd spoken about in Chicago. I had warned him that I couldn't picture myself sitting in a *couture* salon having clothes modeled in front of me like in some movie. I said I knew he was very wealthy and very generous, but enough was enough. I would go to Galleries Lafayette and buy some things, and even there, we shouldn't "go nuts."

"Nonsense, " he said. "I have an appointment with an old friend of *Maman* in her shop, and she will help us with your clothes. She is not a *couturière*; she's a business owner. Her daughter and son-in-law run the boutique now, and she assures me they have excellent taste and will help you make many choices. Then, if you like, you may also shop at the *Grands Magasins* or anyplace else you like while we are here...*chez* Chanel, Dior or Yves Saint Laurent if you wish. They all have *prêt-à-porter* now. You needn't have clothing made for you by those houses."

"Well, I know, but even still...I'm not going to shop at those places, Polo...it's just too expensive."

I couldn't make any arguments that would dissuade him, however. I just hoped he understood that things like this put me right back in that same position of feeling undeserving of his largesse and unworthy to be his wife. He sort of headed me off at the pass, however, telling me he wasn't trying to shower me with riches because he thought I had nothing, but rather it was because it made him so happy to do it.

"I know you do not feel you could ever afford this lifestyle, Sarah, but that is the point. You can now. I want to do this for you. It pleases me to give you beautiful things. Will you allow me to do it? I would not dream of imposing my taste on you...I trust yours implicitly. What I would like to do is make everything available to you. You choose what you like."

"It's not that I'm ungrateful...not at all! I love clothes and I know I need some. I just don't want you to think you have to provide everything. It isn't fair, especially when I can't reciprocate. You do get that, don't you?"

"I understand," he assured me. "Just come with me to *Madame* Grenville and see what she has, will you?"

"Yes...sure... of course I will. *Volontiers*! And thank you my sweet sweetheart! I love you...and not just because you spoil me rotten."

So we went to the boutique in the seventh *arrondissement* and I was shown beautiful things...cashmere sweaters and wool pencil skirts; tea-length dresses, one in black and white dotted Swiss

636

with a jacket to match; a plaid wool suit lined in silk with a blouse made out of the same material as the lining; and another outfit with a full skirt in buttery tan hues and a muted brown bouclé jacket to go with it.

Madame Grenville also thought I might need evening clothes, so she had curated a few gowns that would flatter my height—or lack thereof---and not make me look like I was playing dress-up. I especially liked a black satin shantung dress with a scoop neck and off the shoulder sleeves. The long skirt was elegant without being "costumey."

She had also chosen a —yes-- little black dress for me with a crisp white collar, perfect for work or going out afterwards. She paired that with a short, belted wool carcoat in powder pink, which would also go fabulously with jeans, I thought. Jeans with cigarette legs, worn with high heels. How much more French could I get?!

When we were finished there, Marcel loaded up the car with all the boxes and bags, and I felt I was set for life. But, as *Madame* had remarked when I tried a few things on, my underclothing was "unacceptable." She chided me that bad undergarments change the way the other clothes fit, and she took my exact measurements, making me promise to come back later that week, and she would have a whole new lineup of lingerie to show me.

"I promised her I'd come back and let her show me all kinds of things my husband would love, " I teased Polo.

Oncle Charles was very pleased when we arrived back at the house after the shopping spree.

"Ah, I see you acquiesced and allowed Polo to outfit you, " he purred approvingly at me. And turning to Polo, he asked if he could spirit me away to the library for a few minutes and have another little private talk while he was still in Paris. Polo gestured, "*Je vous en prie, mon Oncle,*" and winked at me.

We sat down together, whereupon he took my hand in his and said, "It is my duty and my pleasure to welcome you into the family." He was very sweet and genuinely pleased that I had agreed to the marriage. "You have made my nephew the happiest man alive, and for that I am sincerely grateful. I hope you believe me. I love him dearly, and—you know this by now... I've only ever wanted his happiness."

"I do know that, *Oncle* Charles, " I answered, "and I want to thank you for being so kind to me. But I'll go to my grave wondering why in the world he was never married before I came along."

"I believe that old adage, Sarah, that you just know when a person is the one, " he answered. "In any case, do not doubt yourself. You **are** the one. And he's desperately in love with you, as I hope you are with him."

"I am."

"So, my next question, as you may guess, is to be...is there the chance that you two will have children? The d'Arivèque name will die out if you do not, you know."

"Did he tell you I didn't want to have children?" I asked, knowing the answer already.

"He may have mentioned it, yes, " he answered a bit sheepishly. "Do you think you might change your mind? Again?"

"Are you on a mission here to see that I do?" I laughed.

"Not at all!"

"Well, then you've probably heard my arguments against it, right?"

"But not from you."

"I just don't think I'd make a very good mother. And while I do feel that Polo would make a wonderful father, it takes both parents to seal the deal for kids."

"Polo did not have both parents. He turned out fine."

"Well, yes, but he had two extraordinary ones for a while, and then his mother... seemed to be able...well... to be a fabulous single parent. I think he was pretty darn fortunate."

"I am sure you are right, my dear, but that does not preclude your being a good mother, also. You do not strike me as a selfish person at all. I am sure you have much love to give, and when you really consider the circumstances, you know you will have many people to help you at a moment's notice, should you decide to have a baby."

"Yeah, it's not that. I wouldn't especially want to give my kid over to governesses and servants to raise. I'd want to be more hands-on, as they say. But I have little confidence in my ability to do it."

"Well, I am not here to persuade you one way or the other. I just want you to know that you have the chance to shape the history of the family."

"Oh, okay, so no pressure, huh?" We both laughed and he hugged me *à l'américaine*.

"Sarah, you amuse me. I want to show you something. See this ring on my finger? "

I looked at it and saw that it was a jade signet ring with some sort of bird and some intertwined initials.

"It is the ring of the *Ducs de Beuvron*. When I die, Polo shall have it, of course, and if he should predecease you, which I feel is bound to happen, much as I hope you two have a long and happy life together, you will become the heir to this ring. I want you to have it. But I also want your assurance that if you were to have a son someday, he would be given this, as the next *Duc de Beuvron*, and pass it to his children. Will you do that for me?"

"Of course, *Oncle*. If I should ever have children, I will make sure they know who they are. I promise you. I know about the Salic law and that the title can't pass through the mother, though, so if I did have a baby and it was a girl, even if she subsequently had a baby boy, he wouldn't be duke, right?"

"That is correct. But give her the ring anyway. It should stay in the family."

"Well, this is all conjecture at this point, " I said, "but I will do my best to carry out your wishes."

"I knew you would say so. And I have *un petit cadeau de mariage* for you. Come with me."

I followed him back to the grand salon where Polo and Marie-France were chatting, and waiting for us. There was the unmistakable orange box tied with brown ribbon stamped *Hermès Paris* sitting on the table in front of Polo.

"This is a wedding gift from *Oncle* Charles, " Polo said.

"My goodness...it's big. It's not a saddle is it?" I laughed.

"Open it, " Uncle Charles said. "It is for you."

I untied the bow and opened the lid. There it was, under a mountain of tissue paper: the ubiquitous *Hermès Courchevel Sellier "Kelly"* bag in a light tan color. I knew for a fact even then that this purse cost upwards of 12,500 FF in 1972, and I just didn't think I could accept that. I still had my replica one that would do just fine.

"Oh, no," I said, almost in tears, "I can't possibly accept this. It...it has to be a...what?...three thousand dollar bag?!"

"But of course you can!" Charles said. "You would hurt my feelings if you refused it."

I looked at Polo for succor, but he was just sitting there smiling at me. He nodded, gesturing that I should take it out. I lifted it out of the box and held it up to me.

"It...this ...doesn't suit Sari Shrier of The Bluffs, Iowa, though, does it?"

"It suits *Madame Jean-Paul d'Arivèque, Comtesse de Beuvron* quite well, however," said Marie-France.

If my uncle had not offered it to you, I would have, " said Polo, "so you are obliged to accept it, *en tout cas*."

"It's the most beautiful thing I have ever laid eyes on," I said finally, wanting to be gracious about the wedding gift. I knew they could both easily afford it, but it still floored me. I didn't want to be continually reminded that I was a country bumpkin marrying into this family, but I sure felt like I was one anyway; that they were Colonel Pickering and Henry Higgins dressing me for the ball and placing their bets as to whether or not I'd pass the test...or be found out.

Chapter One Hundred Eight

"Nights in White Satin"...The Moody Blues

Almost as soon as I could, I called Cass from Paris. She immediately began to cry on the phone, which wasn't really like her.

"You just won't believe what I'm about to tell you, " she sobbed.

"WHAT? Are you sick...again?"

"No, it's not that. It's Alan."

"Oh, shit, what now?"

"Well, I found out..." she hesitated, as though afraid to repeat it to me, but then almost sobbed into the phone, "that that woman from the Writers' Workshop...that Donna person I saw at the Iowa City airport...is down here! She's at UTEP, too! They're teaching together and they...p- p-planned it all along!!"

"What?! Are you sure?"

"I confronted him. He admitted they worked together, but told me it's just a coincidence...that UTEP had two openings and they **didn't** plan it."

" So...you don't believe him, do you?"

"Not for a minute. He's gone a lot. Says he has to grade papers and attend meetings. I think he's staying with **her**."

"Shit, Cass, I just don't see how he could he do that to you...to his kids!?"

"What if he doesn't love us, Sari? What if he never did?"

"Well, he pursued you all over the country and he rescued you from the dire straits of the home for unwed-mothers. I think he loved you."

I put it in past tense, remembering the last time I was with them, and also how Alan had complained bitterly about dealing with her anorexia when I spoke to him on the phone.

"I might have chosen a different kind of life for myself if none of that had happened," she lamented. "Childless, perhaps. Certainly one with more interesting events in it and... better clothed! Oh Sari, you should see my wardrobe...it's in tatters." She tried to give out a little laugh. "I miss having nice things sometimes...in my wallowing self-pity. "

"Cass, don't worry about that. I will send you a bunch of clothes. Name what you need. It's yours by next month."

"Oh, Sari, there you go again...fixing stuff. You're so good to me, but that's not what I need. I need **Alan** to be good to me. I'm so angry at him! I mean, he never takes me anywhere I can half-way dress up if I even **had** anything to wear. He never gives any signs of love. Gifts are a thing of the past. What it boils down to is that I want Alan to be a different person, which really is a crazy vision from a crazed mind. It will never happen."

"So...what are you going to do? What are your options? Do you feel trapped down there?"

Not letting her answer, I went on with what I thought was a brilliant idea.

"Listen, why don't you tell him you're taking the kids and going back to Chicago for a while? We'll be home in two weeks. I have to run the Teacher's Institute but after that, I'm totally free. We have a huge place, as you know. You can stay with us indefinitely."

"No, no. I'll be okay. This will not destroy us."

"It will if your husband is sleeping with another woman!"

"It's strange, but I feel conflicting thoughts simultaneously about my life and Alan. Sometimes he is really good to us---he does the grocery shopping and once in a blue moon he'll clean up around here."

"Well, that's something...gives you more time to work on art."

"Well, that's another sore point. He thinks any time I spend on art that is salable-- and might make us some extra bread—well, that's a waste. He thinks it's selling out. But I like making cards and prints. I think I can sell more down here than I did in Iowa City."

639

"Then you should do it! Fuck what he thinks."

"Yes, but I get too depressed to work on it. He makes me feel like I don't have any real talent. He always has."

"That is simply bullshit, Cass and you know it. Everyone else in your life has gone bonkers over your talent, including your high school teachers, your parents, Klampert and me. If Alan doesn't think you are an artist, how **can** you love him?"

"Yeah, that's a valid question. But he's the father of my children, so for that alone, I love him. But it's not like I'm a happy person to be around either. I have a hard time being kind to people who are unkind or thoughtless to me, and he is. Sometimes in my most melancholy days I feel like I have left so much of myself behind that maybe my problem is that I don't recognize my own reflection when I encounter it in the mirror." She paused, and then added, as though trying to convince herself, "Surely there is a grace and a strength to be had in getting through shitty days, though, huh?"

I was suddenly overcome with guilt. I felt disloyal to her that I was so happy in Paris with the most wonderful man for a husband. How ironic that she despaired of not having clothes when I had just been showered with them, or that she longed for a gift or any token of his affection, and I felt I had to constantly put the brakes on getting so many. It was actually the first time since Cass had run off with Alan Jones that she ever even hinted at regret at having left material wealth behind. I felt I couldn't share my joy with her, that it would be rubbing her nose in it somehow. I felt stricken by my own happiness. When she wanted to hear all about our wedding and honeymoon, I begged off on the grounds that the call was transatlantic and way too expensive to go into it.

"I promise to write you all the details, " I said, trying not to show overexuberance or in any way lord it over her how wonderful my life was at that moment. So I added, "You remember how Polo's uncle met me in the garden of their château and tried to convince me to marry him? Well, now he's advocating for me to consent to having a baby."

"And how does he propose to meddle into that?" she asked, without sympathy in her voice.

"Oh, no…he's not really doing that. He means well. He's really a sweet man…just like Polo."

"So, Sari, " Cass said somberly, "why **don't** you want to give Polo a child? Isn't that what he longs for more than anything---besides marrying you, of course? Didn't you already know that when you married him, if I recall."

"You know why."

"Well, I think you're wrong. He's right about you. You do love my kids, and you are so good with them! I've observed you…up close and personal. And you can't fake that."

"Maybe we can talk about this more when I get back. In the meantime, I'm going to have to get off the phone now, but I promise to write."

I didn't want to argue with Cass on the phone, especially since we were so far from each other. And I didn't want to let on that she'd struck a sore point with me.

Part of my fantasy of Paris when I was a student there, --due in no small way to the constant public displays of affection that were the norm on the boulevards and quays-- was walking around on the arms of my "true love." But Polo rarely walked anywhere, and during our honeymoon we were driven to all the events we attended, whether in the day or at night. He had wanted to see my dorm and where I "hung out" as a student, and all my favorite places in his city. But again, it was Marcel who escorted us to do it.

"I'm anxious to get out and walk around Paris, " I told Polo, one day after lunch at Vagenende on Boulevard St. Germain, "and we're right here in the midst of my old haunts. You wouldn't mind if I left and just ran around for a few hours, would you? I can take the *métro* home later."

"Of course, *chérie*. I have some papers I must go over that Charles left me, anyway. You go… and have a nice time."

So that's what I did. I went to find the St. Germain des Prés boutiques that Cass and I had frequented together and saw that most of them were still there. I had brought along my own money to spend in Paris, so I didn't have to feel so dependent on my husband, even though I was fully aware of the fact that he would have gladly provided me with any amount of cash I desired. I had obviously only dipped my toes in the ocean of wealth now about to inundate me; maybe a part of me still couldn't believe it.

At the shop where Cass had bought our knit dresses in 1968, I picked up a green and navy plaid cotton skirt and a blue Lacoste polo shirt, and at La Bagagerie, I bought myself a soft brown leather satchel reminiscent of the *cartable* French school children carried, only redesigned to be used as a shoulder bag. I figured I could carry my *Moments Culturels* in it to and from meetings. Across the boulevard at Salamander, I bought a pair of navy sandals in braided leather with chunky block heels. They were soft to the bare foot and as chic as my London shoes.

Cutting through Luxembourg Gardens just like in the old days, I headed up to Inno and bought some chocolate in the basement, and a few other necessities upstairs, like Vergé de France airmail stationery and Roget & Gallet soap. I picked up another *filet* to consolidate the bags into, and then I headed back to the Rue Delambre and straight to Boulevard Raspail. I rounded the corner to *La Maison*, and peeked back into the dorm, to see if the Concièrge was still there. She was! It had been three years, but she recognized me right off. I didn't bother to tell her who I had just become; she addressed me as she always had: "*Mademoiselle* Shree-air." She indicated that she was very busy and didn't have time to stand around and chat. Nothing had changed.

I did ask after my former roommate, though.

"It is a very sad story of Agathe Picard." She spoke in French explaining that Agathe was ill with an insidious disease called Guillain-Barré syndrome "*...déjà très développé paraît-il.*" It could in some cases be fatal! "*Agathe est une invalide dans un état de faiblesse extreme.*"

"*J'en suis bouleversée* " I said, truly saddened, horrified, really, at this news. "*Je pense bien à elle.*"

I thanked her for updating me on this turn of events, but I left the *Maison des Étudiantes* still reeling from the shock about my former *camarade de chambre*. Of course I had kept her parents' address, and would write to her forthwith. It just made me terribly, deeply sad. What were the chances of something so devastating, I wondered? We were still young, after all! Why her?

I headed into the Vavin *métro*, constantly thinking about Agathe, and rode cross town up to l'Opéra to while away a few hours in Galleries Lafayette and Au Printemps. I wanted to face my lingerie dilemma myself this time, and buy some things with my own money that I thought would please Polo. His friend had supplied me with some lovely basics, but it was my intention to provide my husband with some "wow factor," as we would say today, even though that was not me, it's fair to say. My own taste ran more towards preppy "BCBG" Daniel Hechter boy pants and matching bras with flower motifs. Instead I by-passed all that and went to the fancy intimate apparel section, and ogled aisles and aisles of *chemises de nuit, peignoirs*, and *robes de chambre*. I stood at table displays and fingered luxurious *soutien-gorges, nuisettes, bustiers, guépières* and *jarretelles*. There were nightgowns, silky teddies and more sexy items with attached garters than I'd ever seen. If I thought I owed it to Polo to wear stuff like that, I still couldn't figure out what to buy.

I finally decided on a pink Chantilly lace set of bustier with garters hanging down from the skimpy matching panties, and a pink silk robe that covered it all up. I then chose a black lace corset that hooked up the front, and a "body," which was what the sign above the display called a leotard-looking thing. It was the most *agent provocateur* stuff I would surely ever put on my body, I mused. I wasn't on the Champs-Elysées in those shops Cass and I had seen, but even at Galleries Lafayette, it all cost a fucking fortune.

I could have jumped back into the *métro* at Chaussée d'Antin, but I dragged all my bags with me and retraced my steps to Opéra, in order to take the direct Line Three direction Pont de Levallois Bécon to Villiers, so I'd only have to change once with one more stop to get to Monceau.

The Monceau *métro* was on the opposite side of the park from our apartment, so it gave me a chance to walk through the playground area and over to the kiosk that sold toys, snacks and ice cream to all the privileged young patrons. That kiosk, as I remembered from my student days, sold the flavor of Berthillon ice cream called "Cappuccino" — a combination of coffee and dark chocolate pieces in it, which was my downfall. I couldn't get enough of it, and even when I was so strapped as a student, I would shell out the scandalous twenty francs for a two-scoop cone. The price was still the same, and as I ordered it with gleeful anticipation, I recalled my reaction from the past: four dollars! My God, that was enough for an entire dinner with wine (!) at Mille Colonnes.

I decided not to appear at our door licking the cone, so I plopped down in the *parc* and watched the parade of nannies---and sometimes moms-- with their well-heeled little charges...swinging on multi-

641

colored seats, going on baby amusement-park-like rides, or being led around on the backs of patient ponies.

I sat there. How could I watch all those toddlers and children and not think about what *Oncle* Charles had said, and of what was-- by now-- my almost automatic response?

Maybe I was being selfish after all, but, in all honesty, I didn't think of myself as a particularly egotistical person. Yes, I'd had some awfully great luck thus far in my short life, I mused, not the least of which was how good the Hydes had been to me. Still, I didn't consider myself ungrateful to them nor, for that matter, to the source of my incredibly fortunate career and new life, Jean-Paul d'Arivèque. Hadn't I made him happy? Yes, but wouldn't having his child really assure that? And who's to say I'd end up a lousy mother like Betty had been to me? Couldn't I learn from her and Sol's mistakes, and vow to not repeat them? Didn't I have enough self-awareness to be the architect of my own destiny?

And what about this age difference between Polo and me? Wasn't the ring on my finger a signal of sorts to me that I had to now abandon the naïve ways of my youth and actually become an adult? As Director of Education of La Fondation Culturelle Française, *I had a new level of leadership to undertake, and as* Madame Jean-Paul d'Arivèque, *I had a new multi-dimensional role to play, also... wife, helpmate, partner, philanthropist, hostess... lover.*

I licked the treat as I watched someone stroll past pushing a Silver Cross baby carriage like the ones we only saw in pictures of the British royals. Privileged babies. If I got pregnant, mine would be among the most privileged in the world. I wouldn't have to go it alone, much as I was serious when I told Charles that if I did ever have a kid, I would prefer not to hand it over to someone else to raise. But I could have help, and I could still work, keep my job, do my own thing. I could afford a lot of freedom.

The sun was beginning to set and give off that glow the late afternoon spread over the already yellowish and orange leaves of the squared off, manicured Horse Chestnut trees. Paris in autumn was almost unspeakably beautiful. How could anyone be there and not feel optimism and joy?

I speculated that what I had just experienced, sitting there in the Parc Monceau, was an epiphany.

The decision was almost made for me by my surroundings. I would do something just for Polo and proclaim once again that I had changed my mind, that I was amenable now to having a baby. But I wouldn't announce it---or act upon it--- until after the Teachers Institute was behind me when we got back to Chicago. Maybe I could even hold off longer than that and give him the news at Christmas...as his gift.

"Sunshine of Your Love"...Cream

We had been married on Friday the first of September and had flown back from Paris on the sixteenth, cutting our honeymoon short because so much work on the teacher's institute loomed on my horizon.

Not to say that we didn't have a dreamy time together alone and with friends. No one treated me like I didn't belong, and a lot of that was due to Polo. He wanted his friends to accept me, and he always set the stage for that, putting me forward, so to speak, so they would. He always accentuated my accomplishments so as to leave no doubt to his crowd that he valued me for my intellect. For my part, the joy I exuded in being his wife was transparent. I did everything I could in front of his friends to let them know I hadn't married him for his money. It was most serendipitous, we both acknowledged, that we'd forged a deep friendship early on, and projected it in public as well as privately; it was at the core of our marriage.

When we flew back to Chicago, no one else was on board except Robineau and his boyfriend Maxime Aubert. It amused me that I actually liked Max, even as I couldn't figure out what he saw in Robineau. But who was I to judge? They were obviously very compatible, having been together more than twenty years! Max was as friendly to me as Robineau had been haughty, and I was happy to realize that he had seemingly not been poisoned against me.

"So did you guys check out the clubs in 'gay Paree' — little joke — or anything?" I teased Max as we sat in the VIP lounge waiting to board the aircraft. "See what the competition is doing?"

"We sure did!" he answered. "There are some hep cats in that town."

"I'll bet. Where **are** the gay bars in Paris? I know the jazz clubs in the Latin Quarter, but can't say as I've been to any gay ones."

"In the Bastille area, " he answered.

"Isn't it kind of yucky over there?" I said, remembering it from my student days.

"It's up and coming now. Maybe the last affordable central location."

"Hmmm, interesting."

"And guess what else?" he said, his eyes twinkling with intrigue.

"What?"

"They're talking about needing a new Paris Opera and they're thinking of putting it on the eastern side. So that area may one day see a big arts revival."

"Wow. That would be cool."

"Yes," he agreed, "but then there goes the affordability part."

I asked Jean-Paul if he'd heard anything about a new Opera house and he nodded and said, "Vaguely," but that Maxime traveled in more musical and artistic circles in Paris than he did, so maybe what Max said was true. I couldn't imagine their ever leaving the Opéra Garnier.

"*On ne sait jamais*, " Polo told me.

"Right. You never know," I echoed, and I couldn't help musing how right Polo was, though he didn't know it. I was like the cat who had swallowed the canary.

Back in Chicago nine hours later, we headed up to the third floor and our home inside the home. Sophie was up there waiting to unpack for me and put everything away, but I dissuaded her, anxious to take inventory of my literal treasure trove. I arranged all my new clothes into the bedroom closet and then went to find my husband who was in the master bedroom lying down.

"Jet lag?" I asked, hoping it was only that.

"A little bit, " he answered. "What about you?" He patted the bed for me to join him.

"Yes, I tend to get it on the trip back, too. I guess on the way over the old adrenaline kicks in so hard you feel only excitement and anticipation. But coming back the body rebels."

I lay down beside him and he stroked my hair.

"Sarah, " he said with a more serious tone than I was expecting, "do you think you are going to like living here? I feel my rooms up here may be a bit, shall we say, too masculine for you?"

"It's fine, " I said, and then felt I needed to reassure him, adding, "It's not like I'm going to come in here and start redecorating your home, Polo."

"I would be happy for you to do so, *chérie*, " he said, smiling.

"Oh you would, eh?" I laughed. "What if my taste is completely pedestrian compared to yours?"

"Now you are teasing me, " he said. "I know you have excellent taste."

"Well, let's just say that's a work in progress. My apartments so far have been all hand-me-downs and not a reflection of my real taste. I'm working on it, though," I mused.

Little did he know. If I'd had my druthers I'd be living in a Laura Ashley wet dream of cottage prints, chintz and gingham. Needless to say, that wasn't going to happened on Lake Shore Drive.

"*Chérie*, anything you want to change here or redo, you have *carte blanche* from me—freedom to do anything you like. You know that, yes?"

"Oh my, you can deny me nothing, *n'est-ce pas?*" I joked.

"*Exacte.*"

"No, darling Polo. I'm happy with your home just the way it is."

"Our home."

"Well, I'll tell you what. I think I need a little corner of the upstairs---our---library for a desk. I think I foresee me having to work at home some nights on the Teacher Institute and writing my culture articles. Would that be possible?"

"Consider it done. Would you also like some space in there for your own books and the bibelots you had on display at your place?"

"Oh, thanks! That would be great. I can get them out of the boxes in my closet."

"Since you mention the Institute, *chérie*, I have been thinking about it, also."

"Oh?"

"Yes, one thing worries me."

"What's that?" Now I was worried.

"Well, we call it an institute, but that to me implies something like a course. At least more than a short weekend. What do you think?"

"Well," I said mulling that over, "I see your point."

"Yes, to me ours will be more of a *colloque, non?*"

"Yeah. Damn. You're absolutely right. We could call it that. '*Colloque des Profs*' might work."

"Why not call it a Teacher's Symposium then? That way if we get publicity in the wider media, the English title will be more understandable to the public.

"Okay! That's good, Polo! I like it!" I was enthused…at first. "There's only one thing, though--- we've already called it an Institute on some of the initial information and publications we've put out."

"That is as may be, but we can change it going forward. I'll put Marketing to work on it this next week. We still have time."

"All right! The first 'Teachers' Symposium of the *Fondation Culturelle Française*' is born."

What I hadn't planned on back in the spring when I started to organize the Teachers' **Symposium,** as we now called it, was that my work time would be interrupted by a wedding and a honeymoon in Europe! So I felt I had to really step on it to finalize everything in six weeks. Luckily I had written to the speaker candidate, and I hoped that when I got back to the office his acceptance had come in, along with teacher applications.

Things did, as it turned out, come together as planned once I was back at my desk. I had the venue secured well in advance, so that was a load off. I knew I had at least one teacher signed up for real, and that was Dom Lambert. He was willing to help me recruit other teachers in a wider range of areas than just French, but if we only had French teachers, it would still be okay.

A task that I was not looking forward to, however, loomed on the horizon. Once I knew who the teachers would be, I would have to meet with Robineau to assign their rooms. Buoyed by my Parc Monceau epiphany, and in the newly conjured up "role" and philosophy I had vowed to live, it was no more timid Sari, cowed by his former rude behavior towards me. I would not be asking him if I could do this or that, but telling him I would be doing it.

The "Concentration"- type game was a go. I had indeed found artwork postcards in Paris, enough to start pairing up for my card set idea. I had Monet, Renoir, Cezanne, Van Gogh (I decided he could count since he did most of his work in France and the French museums had plenty of them), Mary Cassatt (same thing, and a great tie-in to the Art Institute of Chicago), Manet, Delacroix, Ingres, Fragonard, Degas, Millet, Rousseau, Matisse, Gauguin and Toulouse-Lautrec. For iconic works and, really because these were the images I found, I chose *Impression: Soleil Levant; Bal au Moulin de la Galette, Le Mont St. Victoire; La Nuit Étoilée; Portrait of the artist's mother reading Le Figaro; Bar aux Follies Bergère, La Liberté Guidant le Peuple; La Grande Odalisque; Jeune Fille Lisant; La Classe de Danse; Les Glaneuses; Paysage Exotique; La Chambre Rouge; Femmes de Tahiti;* and *Jane Avril Dansant.*

Polo had taken it upon himself to meet with the legal team to procure the copyright permission, and since we weren't selling the game and since it was for educational purposes, permission was forthcoming, and our marketing department took on the task. Soon I had a dozen sets of the cards. Dom and I tried it out on his game board and he pronounced it a booming success. I would present every teacher participant with a laminated game set at the get-acquainted reception the first night.

Annie-Laure had heard back from Prof. Marvin Roizen, PhD, U Chicago, whose credentials, she felt, were impressive and believed I'd agree that he was perfect for our inaugural event. We issued the official invitation to him for the dinner Friday night and then for the morning lecture. I was also convinced we'd made the right choice to only have one lecturer, given our short time frame for the first symposium. That made it more special for him as an honored guest, and it gave me more wiggle room on break-out sessions.

I met with Polo and Annie-Laure when I had the program itinerary worked out and a tentative schedule of events.

"I have made copies for each of you, " I said, as I handed them a sheet with the detailed schedule and launched right into it. "We have, as you see, a sort of check-in and the welcoming *vin d'honneur* at 7:00 p.m. on Thursday, the 26th. We will have heavy hors-d'oeuvres with the drinks -- but no dinner -- and afterwards I'll give them their Concentration card game. Would that be okay?"

"Of course. That is a good idea for an ice-breaker, " Annie-Laure remarked. "Maybe they could all try it out right then."

"I love that idea!" I enthused. "I'll make a note to ask Dom to bring his game board to show them what they'd have to have to play it in their classrooms."

"Yes, " Jean-Paul remarked, "I think that would be a very nice way for them to get to know one another right away."

"So, then in the morning, we'd give them breakfast--- also a French one, Continental...you know, no bacon and eggs...ha ha. And then the jitney picks them up for the trip to the *Alliance* building. Of course, Jean-Luc could drive you," I added, so Polo wouldn't think he had to ride in a van, "but I'll take the jitney with the teachers."

"Yes, that would probably be best."

I continued, "Once there, you can welcome them again to the Symposium and introduce the guest lecturer. Maybe say a few words about Lafayette..."

Polo interrupted me. "Oh, now you are having me make another speech?" he laughed.

"Well, the *Fondation* is your baby," I chided him. "I just thought you'd want to play a leading role in this."

"*Eh bien*, I shall be happy to speak...and sing your praises."

I went on to detail the remaining events of the first day—Friday. Dr. Roizen would give his lecture starting at 10:00 with a Q and A period afterwards that could last until noon. Then lunch would come, delivered by staff from the mansion and served in the AFC dining hall.

"And remind me again of this lunch, " Annie-Laure interjected.

"Oh, you know, a box lunch—something light but nice. Nothing that we'd have to cook or heat up even."

"Very good, " she said, jotting notes down in her Filofax.

I went on to explain to them how the afternoon would be in three sessions. "I could lead one, and I think Dom could be persuaded to do another one. For the third one, I think we'll have a brainstorming session and let **them** come up with ideas on how to put what they've learned into practice."

"What will your session's topic be?" Annie-Laure asked me.

"Well, I thought I could present them with an overview of what we offer in the way of films and lesson plans that would go with the theme of France's role in the American Revolution. I'd bring along a Culture Box of costumes related to that time period, too, to show them and explain how they can check those out from us for their own use. Teachers love a hands-on approach, I think. It's all in the cause of learning how to get kids excited about French and history. I hope to inspire them to go back to the classroom and get kids fired up about how 18th Century events shaped our lives."

"And what about Dom's? What would you have him do with the teachers?" Polo asked.

"Well, I'll consult with him, of course, and not just assign him something, but my ideas are in the realm of conversation prompts. Dom teaches all levels of French. I think he could come up with varying degrees of difficulty speaking about the topic. And frankly, if there are non-French-speaking teachers in the group, these discussion topics would work in English, too! But like I say, I'll talk to Dom first."

"She is so clever, is she not? " Jean-Paul commended me to Annie-Laure.

"*En effet.*"

I must have blushed a little at that, but not wanting to encourage it, I got right back to giving more details of what I had planned for that last session on Friday.

"Like I said --brainstorming. I'd like this to be a lesson-plan time, dealing with Lafayette. That is, after all, the *raison d'être* of our weekend. I'd like them to create something concrete, like I've mentioned before—something for them to take away, like maybe a bulletin board. We could provide some basic materials-- images of the Marquis, for instance, some lettering stencils, poster board, markers and the like. I realize this would be another expense for the Foundation, Jean-Paul."

"Perfectly fine. That is why we are doing it!"

I looked up from my paper at him and smiled. "Thank you!" *Marie-France's words echoed in my head: "He's the most generous man alive."*

"So I see that each teacher will come away with a meaningful tool for use with this—*euh*—lesson," said Annie-Laure, realizing that she didn't quite have a grasp on how it would play out in the classroom.

"The Lafayette lessons would make up a unit, Annie-Laure. Teachers could integrate it into their textbook lessons, teach it on its own, or team teach it with another subject area completely different from French."

"I think that sounds splendid, Sarah!" Jean-Paul said.

"As usual, your ideas are very carefully thought-out," Annie-Laure added.

"Well, thank you. I obviously have a great partner in Dom. He's really wonderful, and I know he'll help me. So that would be about it for the first day. I envision a nice—bit more formal—French dinner for Friday night—perhaps Dr. Roizen could attend...maybe with his wife? I'm not sure he's even married."

"I shall be happy to check on that and issue the invitation, " Annie-Laure offered.

"Thanks so much! And then, what about a French film in the library? Would that be okay?"

"Of course! What film do you propose? Our Lafayette one?"

"Oh, I'm not sure yet...maybe they'd like a break from the Marquis!" I laughed. "What about something fairly new...like Truffaut? *Baisers Volés*? That's called *Stolen Kisses* in English, and much as it did play here in Chicago, maybe some of the teachers haven't seen it. Anyway, they can see it again, if they have. The sound track alone is heavenly. Charles Trenet is always a winner."

"Yes, that would be a good one," Annie-Laure agreed. "It is one with a nice ending."

"So then, let's look at Saturday. Another breakfast at the mansion and then back to the AFC. This whole day would be sessions, of course, as we have no other speakers. Naturally, we will give them breaks often and the same type of lunch as the first day. "

"And what about the Saturday sessions?" Polo wondered.

"Well, I see us needing time for them to develop lesson plans. The more I'm reading about Lafayette, the more I'm becoming interested in his writing. I think I'd want to develop a lesson on his major contributions to the Declaration of the Rights of Man. Did you realize he played a key role in that document's becoming an instrument of the French Revolution?"

"Yes, *tout à fait.* But what about the American Revolution, darling? That is, after all, your primary emphasis, is it not?"

"Yes, you're right. I think the more actual lesson development that goes to topics related to Lafayette with emphasis on the American Revolution, the better. One other thing I would like to incorporate into these would be art. They could examine French culture of the same period as Colonial American culture. They would, for instance, be able to plan French vocab lessons around the topic and also weave in language arts with poetry or readings. I can lead that part, and thus again promote what the *Fondation* can do for them in all this. "

They both looked at me, somewhat overwhelmed, so I reassured them that it was going to be so great for teachers to come away from the weekend laden not only with ideas, but with actual things to use immediately in class.

"At the end of the second day, the teachers will reconvene to finish the bulletin boards, try out the game again, review how to use the Culture Boxes, and everything... and just tie a bow around all the tangible teaching tools and ideas they've gleaned from coming to our symposium."

"It is simply a wonderful thing you've got in store for them, Sarah. I am so filled with amazement at its scope. And you referred to the cost...we have the means and we are so eager to make this come to fruition for you. It will be my pleasure—and I'm sure the Board will concur—to finance this symposium entirely. *Ne t'en fais pas, chérie.* Do not ask the participants to pay for anything."

"You don't realize how grateful they will be. I don't think you're really aware of this," I told them both, "but teachers don't have a lot of budget in big inner-city schools, for materials. Anything they can get for free, they've got to love. They will be astonished that we're providing all the materials for the weekend, but I'll also emphasize to them the free access to our film library and our resources. That has to be a boon to teachers. Word of mouth will enlarge our sphere of influence immensely. It already has."

I stopped talking in order to gauge their reactions, and saw mounting satisfaction in both their faces.

"It will be a momentous occasion, Sari! " exclaimed Annie-Laure. "I am most anxious to help in any way I can, all right?"

"You got it, " I said gratefully.

"And may I also congratulate you once again, " said my husband, "for all your work and creativity with this project."

"Polo, " I said, still feeling awkward to address him in front of Annie-Laure like that, "your generosity in sponsoring all this and paying the honorarium for Dr. Roizen and for all the supplies, is far beyond anything I've done. If this is a success, and I so hope it will be, it will be because of you."

"*Au contraire,* " he insisted.

I felt better knowing the plans were coming together, and I huddled with Dom to go over it all with him like I did with my Foundation colleagues. We also had the list of teachers who had applied. Dom and I went through the candidates, and chose eight women who would represent French teachers of junior high and high school levels, social studies teachers of elementary and middle schools, and an art teacher with a K-12 endorsement. They were all from different schools so we assumed they probably didn't necessarily know one another, and we just randomly assigned them roommates.

"Oh shit! I've got an idea!" I exclaimed realizing all of a sudden that the rooming situation would not have to be scuttled due to his being the only guy. "Have Peter come!...to the reception, the dinner and breakfasts, at least. If he doesn't want to go to the sessions, that's fine, but at least he can be your roomie."

"Wow, Sari...thanks, " said Dom. "I think he'd really like to hear the talk by Roizen, and," he added, "at least Jean-Paul already knows Peter."

"Yes, my husband will be happy we came up with this solution, I'm sure. I mean, you would have had a room of your own in any event."

I had the office send out the requisite acceptance papers and a schedule of events to each participant. I also put in a note about how the name was changed to a symposium rather than an institute, for just the reason Polo had explained to me.

And then I finally had to face Robineau for the room assignments. He was perfunctory with me but not rude, and I was the same with him.

"If I recall, all the rooms come with their own bathrooms, is that right?" I asked. I still hadn't even seen the entire panoply of guest rooms in "my " house.

"*Oui, Madame* Sarah, " he said.

"Okay, so closer to the date, I will present you with the list of which people should get which room and you can have them ready for the arrivals, yes?"

"Of course."

"Good. And we're set for the reception, dinner , breakfast and the box lunches to be delivered, correct?"

"Everything will be as you wish , *Madame*."

"And then, all that will be left at the end is for the jitney to bring them back here to collect their things. It will all be over by four, Saturday afternoon."

"Very good, *Madame*."

"And Robineau...thank you a lot, for all your help... and thank the staff for me. I want you to know that I really I appreciate all this."

"*Je vous en prie, Madame*, " he answered without the former stink in his voice.

Well, that was refreshing.

Meanwhile, it wasn't as though the Symposium was my only workload item. The library was coming into its own, and films were flying out of there at a much ramped-up pace. I was grateful that I still had Joelle for another school year as my assistant. She was as happy with the job and the opportunity to use her French around the office as she'd been the first year, and so I spoke only French with her, too.

I was also writing batches of *Moments Culturels* for the publishing company's next level textbooks, and they, too, had switched to all French. In a stroke of luck the chapters in the mid-level book each dealt with a different region of France, so my regions lessons for the documentaries in the library dove-tailed with that project. The last, most advanced level would be literature, art, theater and science in the French speaking world. I could see my way clear to having those written within the year. I hated to think my consulting job would be coming to an end, but if there was one, maybe there would be more.

Jean-Paul d'Arivèque had also heard again from the Mid-States Conference on the Teaching of Foreign Language, which wanted his presence repeated at their spring 1973 conference, which was taking place this time in Minneapolis. Their idea was for him to do a session rather than give a speech, and they thought the Foundation should also have a booth at which to disseminate its publicity like had been suggested last year. He tentatively accepted and then came to tell me.

"My darling, I do not mind sitting behind the table handing out information or talking about *La Fondation*...of course I shall do that. But I do not feel capable of presenting in a session. Would you do it?"

"Sure... I'll do it. We have six months...I'll come up with something. Maybe I'll present on the outcome of the first Symposium, except what will we do if we got so much positive feedback that eighty teachers wanted to come! Ha! That would be a problem!"

"We must give them an abstract next month! We do not have six months to prepare."

"Don't worry, Polo. I'm sure I can come up with something. It will be fine."

He looked at me skeptically. I thought for a minute.

"Well, how about that idea I had before of incorporating cuisine into teaching about the *anciennes* regions of France...or something? Do you remember me talking about it?"

"Vaguely, darling...you have so many good ideas!"

"Each region has a cuisine specialty, so I could devise a way for the teacher to assign the class into teams or partnerships and each could research a different region, make a cuisine sample and bring it in. Or, they could cook something in the classroom...maybe borrow the home-ec room for the day. I'll work it all out. I'll make them sample lesson plans and instructions, and throw in some of my own *Moments Culturels* on the French regions. Will that work? Do you think they'd like it? Maybe I'll try it out with Dom's class first and photograph the results---present a slide show or something."

He stood there staring at me somewhat in disbelief. "Sarah, I just mentioned this and already you've thought up a collection of ideas to make it a reality. You truly astound me."

"Happy to help!" I reached over and hugged him.

"Star Trooper"...Yes

Each night after work, Polo and I would come home and be offered dinner in the downstairs part of the mansion, where he'd always taken meals. It seemed so formal to me, so I broached the subject of my maybe cooking dinner in our apartment's kitchen. Polo was surprised at the offer.

"But my *chérie*, that would mean you would have to plan the menus and do the shopping for food! You would return here tired after a day in the office, and have to start more work?"

"Well, honey, what do you think the average American working wife does every day of the year? Just that."

"Yes, I see. I am sure you are right. But Sarah, I feel you would be exhausted. Perhaps we must simply go out for dinner more often."

"Yes...but still, restaurant meals are very exp...too...elegant."

It wasn't that I didn't love going out to dinner with Polo, but the nagging sensation I had wasn't really about doing things together in public, but rather not being with each other in private. What couple doesn't sit around the dining room or even kitchen table and rehash the events of the day or the nightly news and kibitz and share their opinions about whatever comes up?

Well, I had sat in that park vowing to grow up. Maybe the "new" Sari would have to give up old habits, "dress for dinner" and make the best of it. Even if I wanted to offer to cook some simple things for him, what if he considered the meals I knew how to make mere slop?

"I have the solution, " he said all of a sudden, as if reading my mind. "I shall have the cooks make us dinner upstairs, and serve, perhaps, lighter fare? We can eat in our own dining room. How is that?"

"Or maybe the kitchen?"

"Do people eat dinner in their kitchens?" he asked, genuinely non-believing.

"Are you really asking me that?" I laughed.

"I see that I should not, " he recovered, also laughing.

So we settled into this "compromise" routine. Sometimes I did change for dinner...into jeans, but Polo didn't change. His clothes were really never very "*décontracté*" --casual, but he didn't say anything when I got out of work clothes-- especially if I'd dressed up for a meeting or something-- and lounged around in the evening in my old duds. Sometimes he would ask me to help him out of his suitcoat or blazer, and into that sort of "smoking jacket" I'd seen him in before, the one that tied in the front. He had several, but unfailingly, all of them were silk or satiny, one more elegant than the next. The man just didn't know from laid back.

I was young but had also already developed habits, like watching t.v., even when I ate dinner. We did watch more t.v. than he ever had, and we even bonded over some shows like *Bewitched*, *Hogan's Heroes*, *Masterpiece Theatre*, *Laugh-In*, and a new show, *Wall $treet Week with Louis Rukeyser*. But none of that would have been his idea. He had spent upwards of two years introducing me to the cultural offerings of Chicago, and a month after moving in together, I got him into American (and British, it should be noted) television!

I also listened to radio more than he did. He would put music on the stereo, the speakers of which were wired to carry all throughout the apartment, which I loved; but he rarely listened to radio. I, on the other hand, was addicted to WLS and WFMT. I was even used to leaving it on all night, which felt so strange to not do anymore, that I dug out my faithful little transistor radio –the one Cass had given me all those years ago—and took it into our bedroom to play ever so softly next to my ear at night. When Polo eventually found out about this, he was touched at my stealthy desire not to disturb him; he had a radio placed on the nightstand on my side.

"Listen to whatever you like all night, " he told me, " it won't bother me."

"It might."

"No, darling. With you in my bed, nothing would bother me."

He always put my wishes before his own. His same philosophy permeated the little stuff as well as the big stuff: we only have a short time together to be happy in this life. We mustn't waste it worrying about minutiae. He considered all "life-style" things like radio listening to be in that category. I could learn a thing or two from this man.

As for me, I knew I had to step up my game, too, and do whatever I could to make him happy…or at least not cause him any pain.

To that end, I acquiesced completely to his need for Robineau to be in our lives; and I reiterated that to Polo. I assured him that I was "over it" — that Robineau was a part of our domestic scene, and the Major Domo of our home.

"You simply can't do it without him, Polo, " I said, "and I fully realize that and am on board with it."

"I appreciate you telling me this, Sarah. I feared for so long that you would be unhappy with the situation and that there was little I could do about it, save give him the sack."

"No, no. I understand now."

What I said was absolutely the case. They had a routine. At least during the work week. I realized I could not be a part of it. Robineau had many duties besides helping Polo dress. Twice a week he would appear after dinner to escort him to the basement "gym" and swimming pool for therapy and exercise. Sometimes I went with them, changed into my swimsuit, and got in the pool, too. Swimming was about the only sport I could even do with some expertise, and I had a cute bathing suit: white top and black pleated skirt with a patent-leather belt across the hips. I had had it since high school and still liked it. Polo thought it was *"très mignon"* and that I was *"très mignonne"* in it. While the therapists exercised his legs, I would swim laps, and when they were done, we would play around and swim together. Again because of his arm more than his leg, he wouldn't be able to get out of the pool by himself without a lot of struggle, and I wasn't much help due to how heavy he was, so staff would do it, and Robineau would help him dry off, put a robe on over his wet swim trunks, and take him up to the apartment in a wheelchair so he didn't have to put the brace back on only to take it off again for bed.

If it were not a therapy night, Robineau would appear around ten o'clock to help Polo get undressed and into pajamas. And in the morning promptly at seven-thirty, he would reappear for the reverse.

"I know this must seem like the *'lever et coucher'* to you, " he said to me only half kidding with the reference to Louis XIV's routine at Versailles.

"Ha ha! " I laughed, "that's good! But, no, I get it." I sure wished I could be of some help though.

Instead, I would go into the other bedroom, the one that held my clothes, and use it for my own preparations for the day. We would meet up again for breakfast in our dining room upstairs and embrace like we hadn't seen each other in two weeks. Robineau would be long gone.

However, on the weekends, things subtly changed. Polo had evidently made other arrangements with his valet shortly after we got back from the honeymoon. Gradually I began to notice that on the Saturday and Sunday we slept in later, and no one bothered us. I could help Polo into the bathroom, put on the brace, and even to get dressed, especially if we were just staying in for the day.

On Sundays the maids would bring up both the *Chicago Trib* and the *Chicago Sun Times*. They would arrive with one of those gorgeous wooden trays like I'd only seen in the movies, containing a coffee service and baskets piled with croissants and brioche. We would happily stay in bed, cuddling, reading the thick newspapers, and nibbling at the continental breakfast. That was my favorite day; it invariably led to late-morning love-making before we actually got up and showed our faces anywhere in the house. We joked about the conjecture probably going on out of our hearing, but we reveled in our private tryst routine.

We cherished our time together alone, and although his physical needs precluded things like romantic little trips away just the two of us, we turned his apartment into our true love nest and settled into it and into each other's arms as easily as if we'd always been there.

My marriage and married life were as sweet and wonderful as Cass's were sour and miserable. In fact, worry about Cass and her dead-end situation in New Mexico consumed me even as I finalized plans for the Symposium. I spoke to her often on the phone from my office.

"My marriage was a holy thing in my heart, " she told me near tears one day.

She seemed to be crying a lot.

"But that didn't mean that I didn't have moments of imagining another existence. It's just that now that's all I do. I thought we were bound by the ribbons of our souls, " she said, " but he's acting more and more like he wants to be single again."

"Well, what is he doing? Is he threatening you with divorce or what?"

"That's the thing…he's acting like we're divorced already, but he doesn't leave. When he's home, which isn't always, he won't speak to me. If I speak to him, he walks away."

"Cass, that is called abuse. Get out of there!"

"I realize it is… I put up with it because I'm not strong enough… within me… to fight."

"Yes, you are. Fight for your kids' sake!"

"Oh, yeah, that's another thing, he believes the way to handle three-year-olds is by force."

"He doesn't… **hit** them, does he?" I snapped, already hot under the collar.

"No, but he yells at them."

"That's abuse!" I repeated.

"I know. It makes me feel so awful that I have actually let go of any love that I had for him. I don't believe in **us** anymore. I don't feel loved or productive. I'm a mom twenty-four hours a day and, the fact of the matter is, Sari, I don't always feel like being a parent either."

"Well, don't tell **him** that. He'll take the twins away from you and they'll descend into the ninth ring of hell for sure."

"Oh, ha! I'm sure he wouldn't want to be the single parent of them."

I paused and then said, very pointedly, "Cass, I'm sending you some plane tickets. I want you to pack up what you can and get out of that goddamned desert and come home to Chicago. We have a fucking mansion and you can stay here until you figure this all out. In my house, you'll get whatever help you need with Laura and Paul."

"Oh, Sari, "she sobbed, "you are my all-time constant sustaining person and I love you. But I can't come back to Chicago, admitting defeat to my parents. They'll just yell at me and tell me they told me so ad nauseum."

"Okay, so yeah, that might be what happens. But you can stay with me and not even contact them until you know what's what. They don't have to know you're back in town even!"

"No. Anyhow, I just can't leave here yet. Besides, you're a newlywed for God's sake. You can't have people invading your conjugal abode so soon."

"My conjugal abode, as you call it, is a bazillion square feet! We could all be in here for days and never run into each other if we didn't want to."

"Couldn't you come down here and visit?"

"Not for a while, Cass. For one thing, I've got a teachers' symposium to run in a few weeks. "

"You have truly come into your own and blossomed in brave and beautiful new ways, haven't you?! I'm so proud of you, damn it!"

"Thanks, sweetie, " I said, "that means a lot to me. Now I just wish you would leave El Paso, St. Anthony…whatever… and come here!"

"And I wish **you** were coming here."

"Well, Polo did offer me the chance to fly down and see you. I'll really try to do it. I promise. Even if it's just a longish weekend."

"Oh, thank God, yes! You must come!"

"What if we both come? Then you could meet him!"

"Uh, what? Gee, Sari…I don't have any place for him to stay in this crummy house. Anyway, I thought you said you guys travel with some kind of entourage."

"I'm not sure I would have called it an entourage. But maybe we can come just the two of us. I can handle it, and anyway, he'd love to meet you and my two little godchildren!"

"No, Sari… really, it won't work. My home is a wreck, no pun intended."

"Well, we could stay in a hotel."

"There isn't even a decent one in this whole town!"

"Okay, so maybe we'd have to stay in El Paso?"

"I guess, " she said, sounding so downhearted on the one hand and panicky on the other, that I let it drop.

"Okay, then, we'll cross that bridge later. I have to stay here for the next few weeks and then I'll look at the calendar and work something out, okay?"

"Yeah, that would be better."

But I wondered if I really could make sense out of anything with Cass and Alan. What could have gone so wrong with their seemingly impassioned union, one that had produced two beautiful children, to cause it to just break? It wasn't as though he were some *schlepper* with no education. While he wasn't necessarily ambitious, he seemed to have a decent work ethic, and being a college professor wasn't nothing, after all. He had convictions and held to them, so much so that he'd become a Conscientious Objector and had fulfilled all the requirements for it. Even if his poetry hadn't gotten into many reviews or magazines yet, it was undeniable, I'd always thought--especially when I'd first met him-- that he had the soul of a poet. His love for and knowledge of music had also been revered by Cass, and his boyish good looks had captured her heart.

And as for Cass, it wasn't as though I was hallucinating when it came to her looks and talent. She really had been one of, if not, **the** most beautiful, intelligent, cultured, and talented artists at the University. Alan knew from the start that he was damn lucky to be the one she chose. They might not have been on the same socio-economic strata when they got married, but who was I to even comment on that!?

No, to me, this was the same old thing I had always believed: there actually **was** no such thing as a good marriage. As simplistic as I may have been making it, and aside from the arguments put forth by Jean-Paul and Charles d'Arivèque to allay all my fears, I silently stood by my belief.

It made me wonder when the other shoe would drop in my own marriage.

"Rêverie"…Claude Debussy

The Symposium Weekend was soon upon me. Things were going according to my schedule; our ducks seemed to be lining up in nice rows. The teachers all began arriving at the Mansion at the appointed hour, and Polo and I were there to greet them. We had decided to also invite Professor Roizen to the pre-symposium reception. He had admitted that he did not know much about the Foundation, but was eager to educate himself. He was fairly floored by the interior of the house and mentioned to us how even the French Consulate in Chicago didn't have as fine a décor, not to mention anywhere near the space. I explained to him that we hosted many of their visiting dignitaries because of that specific fact.

"I can see why!" he laughed.

When Dominique Lambert and Peter Weir arrived, Polo was quick to welcome Peter and put him at ease that his "guest status" was no less important than the teachers'. Dom was grateful and impressed with Polo's hospitality to his boyfriend. No gay unions were sanctioned in the 1970's, and, while Dom didn't go around living in fear for his job, the truth of the matter was that if he'd ever "come out" in those days, he could easily find himself **out** in more ways than one-- namely, on his ear.

Robineau had his staff at the ready; everyone was shown to their rooms and invited back to the main reception area for the *vin d'honneur* and the welcome from my husband, who announced how pleased he was, in the name of the *Fondation Culturelle Française* to accord them *"un chaleureux acceuil"* and that *"La Fondation est à votre disposition avec beaucoup d'offres dont vous pouvez en profiter."* I do believe I noticed some not so subtle surprise at my husband's physical anomalies. There was a little twittering from the back of the room that I could overhear, but to be fair, most of them were more shocked at their surroundings than at their host's withered limbs.

I handed out a page to each of them with the next two days' schedule, and gave a brief summary of why we had chosen the Marquis de Lafayette as the symposium topic, which led me to a more formal introduction of the guest speaker, Dr. Roizen. I then presented them with their "Concentration" game cards and briefly explained what they'd need in the classrooms to make it work. Dom had come prepared with his Concentration board to show.

"We are not providing you with the game boards, " I laughed, nodding to Dom, "but my friend *Monsieur* Lambert here will be able to tell you where you can get yours if you don't already have one."

The teachers seemed genuinely impressed with how they were being treated so far, and like Dr. Roizen were duly amazed at the opulence of the mansion's interior, and the hospitality afforded them.

We served the hors d'oeuvres and mingled in the reception rooms. I gave a little impromptu tour of the art hanging on the walls, which took us to the bigger of the dining rooms and the library.

"Tomorrow night we're going to watch a movie in here after dinner," I explained to the group.

"Wow" was the chorus heard most. By the time my jaunt through the house was over, the teachers were fired up for the weekend and champing at the bit. But their beds beckoned and Polo and I saw them to their quarters. Then we, too, went upstairs.

"I am so deeply grateful for your willingness to host this, " I told my husband, feeling obliged to remind him yet again that if it weren't for him, none of this would be taking place.

"It is you, darling, who must be complimented."

"Well, let's wait for the evals to see if this had any of the desired impact , shall we?" I laughed.

"But of course it shall have an impact! And a great one."

"Hope so."

The following morning was bright and chilly. Remembering that we were only a few days away from *La Veille de la Toussaint*, I dressed in a black wool pencil maxi-skirt and a black cashmere sweater. I threw on my black boots, tied my hair up in a black ribbon, and added a silk *carrée* in hues of orange and dark yellow to accentuate some dangly Halloween jack-o-lantern earrings I'd picked up the previous year at Woolworth's. Whimsy. If teachers weren't into whimsy, I decided, their lives weren't worth living.

Polo's chef went all out with a very nice French breakfast the teachers loved. Chicago had several decent, authentic French *boulangeries*, which, since none were anywhere near my old apartment, I hadn't even known about when I was single. But obviously if something were French in Chicago, Polo's staff were on top of it.

We piled into the jitney, as planned, with JPA being driven over by Jean-Luc, and Dr. Roizen meeting us there. The *Alliance Française* also had some Halloween décor going on in the interior and looked inviting. Their president welcomed us, and then he took me aside.

"I'm afraid there's a little glitch, " he told me, and seeing my alarm, added, "but I'm sure we can straighten it out."

"What?" I asked, afraid to hear the answer.

"It's the dining room...for your lunch. I'm sorry to tell you it's not available like I had said it would be. Our people are not here and we can't get in there to use it at all."

"Oh...well, we weren't preparing any food in your facility, " I explained, "just going to use the tables for our own lunches. We can eat in the classrooms---not a big deal."

"Ah, good! In that case, the problem is solved. Thank you for understanding."

"No...that's fine." I was relieved it wasn't something far worse.

I hurried in to where Jean-Paul was introducing Marvin Roizen, hoping he wasn't wondering what had become of me and why I wasn't there for the start of his speech. He did look up at me puzzled and I mouthed *"Ça va"* at him, and sat down.

Professor Roizen gave an inspiring lecture about the Marquis, taking care to mention that if one were to do serious research on him, she or he would start at Lafayette College in Easton, PA., where hundreds of the Marquis' personal papers could be found, along with other belongings dating from his stays and visits in the United States.

"He had far-reaching impact, " Roizen said, "on the American Revolution, the French Revolution and on Franco-American relations that last to this day. France rendered us a great service in our Revolution, " he said, "and we reciprocated in the two World Wars."

His talk was every bit as wonderful as I had imagined it would be, and he showed pictures of artifacts, such as letters from Lafayette to Washington, on the overhead projector. He spoke of the veneration "Americans and the French also have for this consummate soldier and champion of the rights of man." Lafayette, it turned out, also had amazingly modern views on the abolition of slavery far ahead of his time. "He even wrote to George Washington after the war and encouraged him to free the slaves of Mount Vernon and turn them into tenant farmers." Everyone gasped.

"We didn't learn that one in school!" one of the teachers said pointedly.

I watched as the small audience took copious notes and nodded in agreement and appreciation during the talk and I felt certain they were being inspired to come up with many ways to convey the excitement to their classes. The Q and A period after the lecture was spirited, with every single teacher participating. Roizen was adept at fielding questions and engaging discussion, so apart from having their curiosity piqued and their queries addressed, they were also getting an impromptu master class on teaching! They applauded vigorously at the end.

JPA and Dr. Roizen left after the lecture since Polo had invited him to lunch at the Drake Hotel's Cape Cod room. It amused me to hear he'd planned this because it was about the most Colonial American ambience you could come up with in downtown Chicago. Polo charmed me. Meanwhile, when my own staff arrived with the lunch boxes, I had them delivered into the classroom where the break-out session would be happening, and the teachers were none the wiser that we couldn't use the dining room.

After our lunch, the first session was Dom's. He planted the seeds of lessons that they would work on in depth the next day by putting them into small groups and instructing them to sketch out thematic units together. There would need to be vocabulary lists, conversation prompts, reading and writing activities. The emphasis was kept on the Marquis de Lafayette, with interdisciplinary ideas at the fore. I noted that Dom had put forth the suggestion that the art teacher and the social studies teacher collaborate during that session. I thought that was sensitive on his part; neither of them spoke or taught French. So I sat in with them for a few minutes to provide some ideas of how the Foundation could be of special help to them, and assure them that my session, to come next, would illustrate that even further and bear me out.

Dom was also a master teacher, and served during his session as more of a recorder than "sage on the stage." As groups voiced their ideas, he put them all up on the board so nothing would get lost in the cyclone of wonderful brainstorming.

About halfway through that session, I had to absent myself and go into an adjoining room to prepare the next one, my own. Luckily for me by then I could speak off the top of my head without any notes about The Foundation, the d'Arivèque family, and my domain, the library: its offerings and our amazing resources for schools, teachers, and students on every level. I set out all the handouts and our film catalogues for them, specific information on media about Lafayette, the American Revolution, the Regions of France and food...for starters. I had procured lots of posters on the French regions and especially from the Haute-Loire, whose *syndicat d'initiative* was only too happy to provide me with a dozen posters of the Château de Chavaniac, where the Marquis was born. I also had samples of our Culture Boxes and provided some of my *Moments Culturels*.

By the time we started the bulletin board creation activity at about 4:30, I was afraid that fatigue would set in, and, even though people were enthused and brimming with so many ideas---too many, really, to be able to execute in the short time that remained---I decided to table it until Saturday. Dom agreed with this impromptu change, and encouraged me not to worry that I'd rearranged the timetable at the last minute.

"Now you'll know, " he said, "for next time, how long activities can take. Don't sweat it. Everyone will be happy to be back at the Lake Shore mansion to relax a bit before the evening's festivities. Trust me."

The dinner was magnificent, and probably more elegant than I, and certainly the teachers, had really anticipated. The chef and his staff had come up with hors d'oeuvres of tiny smoked salmon tartes with *crème fraiche* and dill, which were passed around with champagne in the reception area; after which we went to the smaller dining room for dinner. The first course was a butternut squash and caramelized onion *galette,* followed by *poulet à l'estragon* with *asperges blanches*. We finished with *salade verte,* a cheese board and, of course, coffee, which came with the desserts: meringues with lemon *crème anglaise* and apple *tarte tatin.*

This time we had Mrs. Roizen with us as well as our distinguished lecturer. She was slight, with blondish-grey hair in a page boy, blue eyes sparkling under her bangs. She wore bright orange-rimmed glasses, and had a vivacious demeanor. She begged me for a quick tour around the house after dinner, because, as she explained, her husband's enthusiastic descriptions of the place had captured her imagination. She and I finished up in the library, and I invited the Roizens to stay for the film, even though it would be getting over rather late.

"We would be delighted, " they assured me, and we all settled in to watch it together in the beautiful surroundings of a darkened ambience still lit dimly by the hundreds of twinkling lights on our terrace.

On Saturday morning everyone was anticipating their wonderful French *petit déjeuner* and reveled in it just as I had done in Paris as a student. I again loaded the group into the van for the return ride to the AFC where the first activity of the day was taken up with game making.

Besides the artist "concentration game," Dom and I taught a game of classroom "baseball, " and how to play it with two teams and the room set up with desks as mock "bases" and a podium for "home plate." It consisted in rolling a die to see what base they would land on if they answered a question correctly (one was a single, two a double, and so forth. A five was an out, and a six was a walk). I had made up a set of sample questions using facts about the Marquis de Lafayette and other American Revolutionary War trivia to get them started. Dom pointed out that this game could also be used to review an entire chapter of a text before an exam, and, depending on the students' level, the questions could be in English or the target language. I also demonstrated how to keep score on the board and pointed out that students would be tapped to do that.

Dom and I played this and the Concentration game with the teachers to give them an idea of how it would work, and by that time the morning was spent and lunch was again brought in.

The afternoon was divided into a session I gave also, on skits with puppet theaters, and songs that tied in to 18th century American and French life, geared more towards elementary classes; and then the teachers were gathered into a larger room with the array of materials at their disposition with which to finish creating bulletin boards that would illustrate the themes we had presented to them over the course of the two days. The Foundation once again provided all the art supplies: paper, stencils, scissors as well as a guillotine cutting board, and ready-made photos of the Marquis, George Washington and several of various Continental Army soldiers.

The teachers had become quite animated when they realized that they would be going home with a bundle of goodies, and by the afternoon, they were indeed believers, since everyone came away with useful, hands-on, educationally sound materials for use in their classrooms.

Interdisciplinary activities would become a major trend in American education in the future, and our symposium had shown how these lessons meant to enhance the areas of French language and culture, could also tie in neatly with American history, language arts, and social studies.

The sessions were enthusiastically received. I was happy as I passed out evaluation forms, anticipating good news and feeling like our first symposium had gone far better than in my wildest imagination.

Jean-Paul d'Arivèque had turned up near the end of the afternoon in time to see the exciting bulletin boards that had been created. Everyone thanked him profusely and gushed that we should "please have another *colloque* just like this one!" What they mostly conveyed to him was that before they came, they had really no idea of what the *Fondation Culturelle Française* offered, and they let it be known to a person how grateful they were to him and his unbelievable generosity. He grinned at me, slightly surprised, I think, at the adulation.

When it was over and the teachers had dispersed from the mansion, Polo and I retreated back to the third floor where I flounced down fairly exhausted on the couch in our bedroom and he looked at me, exclaiming, "*Quel triomphe!*"

I teased him, "Didn't think I could do it, huh?"

"Of course I did! *Tu parles.* But I must confess, it exceeded anything I expected! "

"Well, that's because Dr. Roizen was so fantastic. He really turned them on! We were lucky to find him for this. And Dom. Dom helped me beyond measure, too."

"I think it is much more than that, Sarah. Why do you hold back giving yourself the credit you deserve?"

"I don't hold back. I did a good job. I admit it. And I was thrilled to do it. But you know how I feel about the whole thing: I could not have even come close to doing anything of this sort without your financial backing --**you** and your Foundation. Does it ever occur to you that no school or school district or educational association puts on workshops or institutes for teachers like this where everything is **free** for the participants? Not one! Dom emphasized this to me again and again. They have no resources to do it! That convention we went to and will go to again...well, educators have to pay a lot to participate in those. If they're super lucky, the school will pick up part of the tab, but that's rare."

"Yes, all right. I understand. But do not underestimate the role you play in everything educational we do. If it were not for you, the *Fondation* would be a mere *soupçon* of what it currently is in the educational wing. I was absolutely correct in naming you *Directrice d' Education.*

"And I'm delighted you did, *Monsieur!*" I said, kissing his cheek.

"So we shall celebrate your magnificent achievement of today by going to dinner. You must wear your red and white "Valentine" dress, and the sable coat, *d'accord*? I shall take you somewhere wonderful."

"Oh, so I'm dressing up as a princess, eh?"

Well, after all, it was almost Halloween.

Chapter One Hundred Twelve

"Aujourd'hui C'est Toi"...Francis Lai

Word of the Symposium and of its great success had spread. The office went nuts. Many of the departments had worked with me to promote it, acquire the necessary legal clearance, make up the materials and pay for it all, so those colleagues had a vested interest in its success. When the evals came in, everyone felt their efforts had been rewarded.

Hennie came down to my office having taken a circuitous route from the break room.

"People are over the moon about your teachers' weekend, " she announced, with the new deference she'd shown me ever since I'd become Madame d'Arivèque.

"Well, I do think it was pretty far out."

"So, do you plan on doing more of them?"

"I hope so. Maybe annually or something. Not right away!"

"It was a lot of work, wasn't it?" she commented, astutely...for her.

"Yeah, of course, but this organization has teamwork down cold. We should bottle it or something."

"You're funny."

"Heck no---I'm serious. The way this place hums along and everybody supports everyone else...just incredible to me."

"Due in no small part to JPA, I'm sure, " she added.

"Absolutely, " I agreed.

Dr. Roizen had also sung our praises to his university's college of education, and they contacted me to make a presentation about organizing something like that to one of their faculty committees. When I consulted Polo about it, I had made the suggestion that I invite them to our offices rather than my going over to Hyde Park.

"Yes, darling, " he'd answered. "I should be very pleased to have them get acquainted with the Foundation as they hear your admirable presentation."

"My 'admirable presentation' notwithstanding, " I laughed, making air quotes, "it's always great for a group that is entirely education-oriented to find out first-hand what we do here. I'm very proud to be a part of it...as you know."

Right on the heels of that, the publishing company in Des Moines for whom I was consulting called me to present my *Moments Culturels* ideas at several other conferences around the country, especially with their reps at the MLA. That national convention was always held the week before Thanksgiving, as I was so acutely aware, and that year it was to take place in Philadelphia. The editor who phoned me said that they would make all the travel arrangements, and especially the housing, because hotel rooms had long since been booked.

"We have a block of rooms," the person on the phone told me, "and you can have one of them. You may have to have a roommate, if that's okay."

I said that that was fine.

Jean-Paul d'Arivèque was delighted.

"You are becoming sought after, " he said to me.

"Oh, I doubt that."

"No! I am surely right."

"Well, I'm happy to go but don't forget I'd been hoping to go to St. Anthony for Thanksgiving and see Cass---**both** of us. Even if the holiday is a sore point with Cass in a way. She won't eat that meal, and all the festivity revolves around food. I would gladly cook it, but she wouldn't want me to, and also I get the impression her house down there isn't conducive to gourmet anything."

"We shall take them out for Thanksgiving dinner...perhaps in El Paso, and she can order what she wants."

658

"Yes, that's an idea. From what she told me, you and I would probably have to stay in El Paso anyway. I'm sure there would be someplace open on Thanksgiving, " I said, not at all sure that that was true. "I can't lie, though. Even though I'm dying to see them, it might be kind of depressing down there. Besides that, I like holidays at home."

"Would she consent to come here if you...or perhaps I...spoke to her about it again?"

"Nope. Not even going to try."

I did call Cass, however, and tell her of our tentative plans.

"Will his valet come with you... I hope to hell not?" she asked.

"I guess he could, since we'll be staying in some hotel. But he may be needed here instead because right after that, the Foundation is welcoming a contingent of French art gallery owners who were invited by the consulate, and Robineau is the manager of this whole place, you know."

"Oh good! Maybe he won't be able to make the trip, then. But can you do everything for Polo on your own?"

"I've done it before, I can do it again. I don't mind at all. The only sticky situation is his weight and if he falls, I'll have a hell of a time trying to help him up."

"Yikes."

"I can't wait to see the twins!!" I exclaimed, changing the subject. "Shall I bring goodies for Christmas with me? Or will you change your stubborn mind and spend the next holiday at my house?"

"Yes, go ahead, 'Auntie Santie' and spoil them like you always do."

"They're probably little people by now and no longer toddlers?"

"Exactly. They seem to be thriving at the day care on campus, I will admit that."

"So does Alan still take them in the mornings?"

"Well, hardly ever. He lets me keep the panel truck here so I can drive them."

I wondered if that were true, given what Alan had told me on the phone some months back.

"Do you guys get snow down there? That truck doesn't seem very road-worthy to me."

"Luckily it doesn't snow very much here, but the van is not road-worthy at all! It's a junker. Still, though... what can I do?"

"You could leave!"

"You're a broken record. Let's not get into it again, okay?" she said, sounding like she could become really exasperated if I pressed it.

"All right, you win. Look, I'll call you closer to our arrival date, but I'm guessing we'll be there the Wednesday before Thanksgiving, and leave on Sunday, how does that sound?"

"You know, kid, I'm still not sure this is a great idea. I'm kind of...well, you know... in over my head."

"Cass, for heaven's sake. We're not going to come down there and judge you...on housekeeping or anything else. Can you please be glad to have us and to meet Polo and for us to see your kids?"

"Sari, what I also hope is that you'll see my kids again and finally change your mind and decide to have one of your own. From what you told me before, Polo would so love that. Wouldn't you want to do it...for him? Look how good he is to you."

"Well, smarty, believe this or not, during my honeymoon in Paris, I did have a sort of epiphany, and I have decided to get pregnant."

"You have?! Wow! Fantastic!"

"But I haven't told him yet, so please don't say anything, okay?"

"Why!?"

"Because I want to make the news a sort of gift to him at Christmas. I mean, look at the bind I'm in...forever more, by the way, not just now. There is nothing I can ever give this man! Nothing! I mean, your parents were bad, too...I really struggled to come up with things to bring to them when I visited. But this is worse. He's my husband, my love, my life partner, and what will I ever possibly be able to bring to the equation? His clothes are all custom-made. He has more jewelry than King Midas---he doesn't really wear any of it, but you know what I mean...I can just imagine their bank vaults. Hell, there's a vault in our house! He owns a world-class art collection and more books than three public libraries. His music isn't my music, although, yes, I could maybe give him some I like...but that's stupid."

"That's not stupid, and the point is, you can give him anything you like...if it's from you, it's not what he already has."

"Yeah, well, I'm not the creative genius you are. It's not as though I could make him any sort of artistic thing."

"He smokes, right? Get him a monogrammed cigarette case---go to Tiffany's or Cartier or someplace. Put yours and his initials on the back or something unique. Have it engraved with a quote from *Le Petit Prince* if you can't think of anything else."

"Cass! That's a great idea! My God! You truly ARE a genius!!!"

"Happy to be of service, " she laughed.

I hadn't heard her laugh in a while. It sounded like the old her.

"Cass, I love you! I can't wait to see you."

So I went to the Modern Language Association and partnered up with Dowling Press. I did indeed have a roommate at the hotel, which was very old, but very unique: the rooms had two bathrooms--one on each side, and so we never had to share anything! I'd never seen that before. They wined and dined me along with reps from any university or school that might be interested in their line of books. My contributions to their texts were on the high school level, but they assured me I would represent their company very well, and they pointed out the great side-effect of my being there was the public relations work I could do for the Foundation in the realm of post-secondary education. It was a point on which I could not disagree.

However, around the end of the second day, when I went off to do a little shopping in Philly, an exciting city I did not know at all, I began to feel a cold coming on. My throat was scratchy at first, and I blew it off as strain from all the talking and *schmoozing* I'd been doing. But when I got back to my room, I felt feverish. I went down to the hotel lobby's shop and paid some exorbitant price for over-the-counter cold medicine and plodded back to my room, feeling like hell.

In the evening, all the French teachers...and invited guests like me... were to meet at one of Philadelphia's oldest establishments for drinks, an ale house called McGillan's, before going on to dinner at a place called Le Club Colonial, one of the few French restaurants in the city.

"You'd have thought that with all the help the Marquis de Lafayette gave us during the American Revolutionary period, the greatest city of its time could have established a few more French eateries, " I said hoarsely to my roomie Marion, a rotund, very blond Minnesotan, who was a Spanish professor from McAllister College, and thus, not going to the same place as I was.

"You sound like you're coming down with laryngitis, " she told me, concerned. "It's a by-product of conventions like this." She gave out a little laugh but I wondered if she were afraid she'd catch it from me. Truth is, I was Typhoid Mary at that stage and didn't realize it.

At the dinner I could hardly swallow. My throat was in agony by then; I couldn't breathe at all, and I was so hot I kept shedding garments to try to find some relief. By the time we got back to the hotel in a cab, it was all I could do to stagger up to bed.

In the morning, I managed to get up and out to the airport where I arrived at the gate armed with some Neosynephrine I'd bought in one of the airport shops, and taken into the bathroom to put in my nose so I'd have a fighting chance of not flying in abject sinus pain. I still felt hot, and thought of nothing but falling into my Chicago bed. It occurred to me that I'd better sleep in "my room" that night, in case what I had really was contagious.

Polo met me at Midway and I fended off his embraces on the grounds that I felt ill and he might catch it. He was worried.

"Yes," he said, taking a look at me, "you are pale, darling."

"I think I have a fever. And I'm tired, plus I kind of hurt all over."

When we got home I took off my coat and careened over to the first couch after our "hall of ancestors" entry. I really was exhausted. Polo immediately summoned Robineau and he, in turn, called a maid to help me get undressed and into bed. And she brought a thermometer in, too.

"Oh, *Madame*!" she exclaimed, removing it from my mouth. "You have a very high fever!"

"What is it?" Polo wanted to know, very worried.

"One hundred two point three."

"I shall phone the doctor."

"What doctor?" I didn't have one except the French Ob/Gyn and the illustrious surgeon, neither of whom would be interested in treating someone for a cold.

"My doctor, " he said, and left the room.

I fell asleep fitfully and was awakened by the touch of a man's hand on my shoulder who wasn't my husband. It was Polo's doctor, Philippe Tromblay. Polo introduced us to each other, and thanked him for coming over. Even in 1972, it struck me as odd that doctors still made house calls, but I soon learned that any d'Arivèque summons of a physician was met by a complete willingness to oblige.

"How do you feel, Mrs. d'Arivèque?" he asked me.

"Like hell, " I answered, poetically.

"I would like to see inside your mouth, please. Can you open wide and say 'ah'.
I did it.

"Your throat is very red, " he said, "and your eyes are watery. Do you also ache anywhere?"

"Yes, everywhere, " I admitted.

"You have a high fever." He turned to Polo standing in the doorway to my room. "I think we should move her to the hospital."

"The hospital!?" I said incredulously.

"I believe you have flu, " he answered. "The Hong Kong flu is still lurking about, you know, and the other strain is called London flu. Chicago has seen that, too."

"Oh *mon Dieu!*" exclaimed Polo. Hearing the word flu no doubt conjured up latent fears of the same outcome his uncle had succumbed to during World War I. Polo turned to the doctor very anxious, "We must get her treatment as soon as possible!"

"Now, now...I'm suggesting the hospital as a precaution, mostly. She is young and not apt to become critically ill from this, but it's better to be safe than sorry, don't you think?"

"It's okay, Polo, " I moaned. "But you mustn't get near me if I have flu, okay?"

"Nonsense."

"No, she's right, my friend. You steer clear of her for the few days or at least until a day after the fever breaks. I'll let you know."

Polo was distraught as he watched me get up wobbly, and gather some things to take with me to the hospital. Jean-Luc would drive me, but that worried me, too...he could catch it as easily as Polo could. The doctor went ahead to admit me.

I was put in a private room and checked on almost hourly. I had no idea if this were routine or if my husband had paid for extra nursing, which did turn out to be the case, but I slept through most of it anyway. I couldn't eat much and only took clear liquids at first. I had a breathing treatment and was given acetaminophen instead of aspirin to bring the fever down. Polo sent me a huge bouquet consisting of pink and white oriental lilies with pink roses and greens, in a beautiful, tall glass vase with pink ribbons festooned throughout the top of the bouquet. Various nurses and aides came in to admire it.

"Lucky girl, " they all invariably pronounced me.

After two days, the fever broke and I was considered out of the woods enough for visitors, so I found Polo sitting at my hospital bedside. I was feeling better but afraid I still looked like shit. He kissed my hand and held it in his, telling me how uneasy it made him feel to see me ill.

"But how do **you** feel?" I asked, just as concerned that he was about to come down with it, too.

"I am fine, " he assured me. "However, you and I do have a problem, my darling. The doctor says you must stay in here for another few days."

" Oh, Polo! " I suddenly called out, coming to my senses, and panicking, "We can't go to Texas now, can we?"

"Doctor Tromblay believes it would be unwise to do so, and I agree," he admitted.

"Will you call Cass and explain it to her then?" I asked.

"Yes, *chérie*, do not worry."

I had him write her number down and told him to phone her as soon as he could. But he reached for the phone in my room and placed the call from there.

"Oh, geez, " I muttered, "that's going to cost another fortune."

661

He waved off my remark, shooting me a look of amused disregard, and when she answered the phone, I was entertained imagining her shock at who was on the other end of the line.

"Cass, "he said tentatively, "this is Jean-Paul d'Arivèque *à l'appareille.*"

"She doesn't really speak French," I called out from bed.

"I am so sorry to have to ring you with some bad news. We are not going to be able to come for Thanksgiving next week after all. Sarah has been taken ill and I am phoning from her hospital room."

There was a pause on our end and I surmised she was worried.

"No, no, not that. She has the flu. She returned very ill from Philadelphia, and we had to admit her to hospital. Yes, I am sad to not be able to meet you also. Yes, my dear, we shall look forward to a trip down there as soon as we can arrange one."

I waved my hand at him and signaled that I wanted to talk to her, too.

"Here is Sarah, Cass. She wants to say a few words to you. *Au revoir, et à très bientôt, j'espère.*" He handed me the receiver.

"Hi Cass. I'm so sad we won't be coming. Yeah…I know. Tell them soon, though…Christmas! Yes, I agree; he is indeed. Yeah, I'll be fine. Bye…kiss them for me."

I hung up just as an orderly came in with broth for me. "Could you get a cloth and some disinfectant and wipe down the phone receiver?" I asked him. "Thank you so much."

"She says you sound really nice, " I told Polo.

"And she also. I am very very distressed…mostly for you… to miss the trip. But like you said, perhaps nearer to Christmas."

"For sure. I'll start planning it as soon as I'm out of here."

I still don't know what strain of flu I had that year, but I was stunned by how weak it made me for days and days, and how much weight had just fallen off me, even though I hadn't had the stomach variety, for which I thanked God.

When I did get discharged from the hospital, it was the actual day before Thanksgiving, and I was in no shape to prepare the meal. Polo wouldn't even hear of me expending what little energy I had to do any such cooking, and had already arranged for his chef to create a version of it. The dinner he came up with, minus Nana's rice pudding and some of the other American standard side dishes, consisted of a turkey stuffed with chestnut dressing like the French do at Noël, and *pommes de terre gratin dauphinois*, with *tarte tatin Chantilly* for dessert, both of which were also "wrong." I didn't care, though, and just thanked Polo for what I took to calling my Thanksgiving *à la Lafayette.*

I did begin to feel like my old self by the weekend after Thanksgiving, and I was happy to get back to the office when it reopened on the Monday. I couldn't wait to go on lunch break and put Cass' idea of a gift for Polo into motion. I went out onto Michigan Avenue up to the seven hundred block to Tiffany's to look for a cigarette case.

I approached the clerk standing at a long, elegantly curved glass display case. The young man, nattily dressed behind the counter, was not very tall, but very blond and wearing tortoise-shell horn rimmed glasses that almost hid his brown eyes awash in long eyelashes. His thin fingers conjured up piano playing in my mind. He smiled at me as I walked up, but didn't exactly act eager to be of service to me.

"I'm wondering if Tiffany's has any cigarette cases…you know, like people used to use …at least more than they do now."

"Naturally, we have them, Miss," he said, with measured nonchalance. *Miss? I guess I still looked pretty young, but he must not have noticed I was wearing a wedding ring.* "Do you have a particular style in mind?"

"Style? Square? What other styles are there?"

"I just meant, did you want, say, an art deco type or a modern one? Perhaps one harkening back to the Roaring Twenties?"

"I'd like to see art deco, I guess. In gold."

"I have an art deco case here, " he said, turning to lift one out of a drawer behind him. "However, it is in sterling silver."

He placed it on a cloth-covered stand before me on the glass.

"This is a Dunhill signed authentic Art Deco case. As you can see, the lid, sides and base are all matched perfectly and it is fitted with a rose gold double catch. It has a vermeil interior and it is hallmarked and signed, 'Dunhill London.'

"It's gorgeous, "I said, a bit stunned. "I'll be... wanting... to get it engraved, also, if I buy it. How much is it?"

"Before engraving it would be four hundred eighty dollars."

"Fine, I'll take it."

"Would you please print exactly how you would wish it engraved?" he said, taking out a pad of paper and handing me a silver pen with which to write.

I liked the idea of both our initials on the back, JPA & SES so I had them do that in a blocky style, and then on the inside of the lid, *"L'essentiel est invisible pour les yeux. On ne voit bien qu' avec le coeur,"* which was to be done in cursive lettering.

I had to fill out papers with my information on it, and so when I gave him my name as Sarah Shrier and the office phone number, I instructed him that I did not want it delivered to our home or to my workplace, but said that I would come and fetch it later myself. However, when I wrote out the check for five hundred fifty dollars, covering the cost plus engraving, and it had Sarah S. d'Arivèque imprinted on it, the clerk looked down at my wedding ring and back up at me, and then, taking the check, he said he would return with my receipt. When he came back out, he had another, older and more distinguished looking person with him.

"Mrs. d'Arivèque!" he greeted me, extending his hand. "I am David Blume, head of this department here at Tiffany's. I am so happy to make your acquaintance."

"Thank you. I'm happy to meet you, too." I said, almost laughing at the sudden overly-friendly demeanor.

"We are completely at your service, and I hope you will call on me personally for any future help in purchasing from Tiffany."

"Well...uh, thank you. That's very nice of you. Do you...know...my husband? The cigarette case is for him...it's a surprise."

"Everyone knows your husband, Madam!" he said matter-of-factly. "And of course we will treat this with the utmost discretion."

And there it was...my first outing as "little gold-digger who'd married the richest man in the world and who had his bank account at her disposal." Boy, would I ever be welcomed at this establishment from now on!

I got back to the office and called Cass to thank her again for the suggestion and tell her my Tiffany's exploits.

"Sari, why are you so damned paranoid about being his wife?" she said sourly. "Maybe they were treating you with the deference all Tiffany's customers should be shown."

"Oh right. Where did that come from? Were you treated just like any old customer as Cassandra Hyde? Or your mom, do you think?"

"Well, I admit, our name was also known, though Hyde probably wouldn't send up the red flag d'Arivèque would. But you could try cutting the world some slack. No one thinks you married for money."

"Oh, I wouldn't be so awfully sure about that."

"Anyway, I wanted to talk to you about coming down here. I'm back to thinking it's not such a good idea... at Christmas anyhow."

"Oh? Why not?"

"Well, for one thing, wouldn't you really rather be home with him announcing the idea of having a baby?"

"I can still do that. What's really going on?"

"See, um, we're not in a very cool place around here just now."

"Because?"

"Alan is involved with that Donna woman and I'm just so angry about it all the time."

"Well, Cass...aren't those grounds for divorce for chrissake?!"

"**I do not want a divorce!**" she screamed.

663

"Why the fuck not?" I yelled right back.

She began to sob. "Because of the kids! What do you think? If I filed for divorce, I'd have NO WAY to provide them with anything. As for Alan, he'd probably demand custody just out of spite, as a way to keep me from them, and then where would I be?!"

"Cass, that cannot be true. I'll help you. Your parents will help you for that matter. The Hyde attorneys would make mince-meat out of Alan! You have GOT to get out of there and let us HELP you."

"I…I…can't. You have to let me do this my way, Sari. I know you're all prepared to whirlwind in here, as you always do, and take over for me…"

"I do not!"

"…but this time, I have to handle it myself."

"Bullshit. And furthermore, adultery is grounds for divorce. Period."

"Listen, kid, you don't know the half of it. I don't think there's any legal way to force him out of our house…unless he was an alcoholic or if there was consistent brutal treatment of me or the kids."

"There is brutal treatment of you! What do you think carrying on with another woman while he's still married is?"

"Ethically he's an abomination, Sari, but the cruelty aside, it's legal. He can also withdraw all our money from the joint account and I can't do anything about it."

"So," I said, hearing that little bombshell, "your father was right about him all along, huh?"

She just began to cry again. She was exhausted from sorrow and I was furious and disgusted with Alan.

"He told me the other day that the marriage was a mistake from the beginning! "

"Oh, fuck him."

"And I can't afford the luxury of self-pity, Sari, because goddamnit, I've got to be a good mommy to these two kids! And I don't want you to come down here and have to witness the thoughtlessness of another Christmas without the slightest kindness from him, no compromise, no reconciliation. Just the uncaring things that account for his attitude… the dull, plodding indifference that he is, by now, famous for. I'm repelled by him."

"Well, yes, I am, too. That doesn't mean I still wouldn't like to give him a good piece of my mind."

"Not what we need, Sari…you surely hear me."

"Yeah, okay. Listen, after the holidays then, I'm coming down, with Polo and maybe a lawyer or two! How about that?"

"We can talk about it later. I'm not divorcing him. He'll have to file on me if he wants out of this union."

"Well…Christ, Cass, he probably will! You've got to not roll over and give him everything."

"I won't."

"You say that."

"I promise."

"And what about…you know…your weight? Are you eating?"

"Sari! You've just got to stop!"

"Look, five minutes ago you yourself told me you were afraid of losing Paul and Laura! If he thinks you're not eating, that could be misconstrued easily as unfit to be a mother! Why don't you **think**?!"

"**Okay**! I'm sorry. You're right. You **are** right. I'm going to make sure that doesn't happen."

"Jesus, Cass."

"I'm sorry, Sari. I know it's 'cause you love me. Everything will be okay. I'll talk to you soon."

And with that, she hung up, leaving me to stew in my own juices of despair. With an unhealthy dose of rage.

I was still stinging a little bit from that rebuke of Cass' to the effect that I swooped in and ran her life; so I decided that backing off plans to go down there at Christmas was the right thing to do. Work was popping anyway, and it was everything I could do all of a sudden to keep afloat. I found myself in demand to speak, and was asked to several Language Association dinners to address audiences on running *mini-colloques* for educators. I was also invited at two different small Midwest film festivals to speak on the Foundation's film library.

Because of all that, I was out of the office several days a week in Chicagoland and once or twice in other states. Our public relations arm had a hard time keeping up with requests for me to be in the local media, and I was also sought out for interviews by some national press as well. Anything that brought attention to the Foundation pleased our head of PR, Gabrielle Pasquier, but it didn't make her job any easier since she felt she had to keep track of it all so that she could write it up for our own newsletter.

After the Symposium, Polo, too, was in great demand. He was guest of honor at the Annual Conference of the Federation of *Alliance Française* chapters, which, conveniently, was held in Chicago that year, and I attended with him. They'd asked him to expound on the idea of partnering with the local *Alliance* to house the classroom portions of our program, and about half way through his remarks, he had me join him on the stage and go into more detail about the results of evaluations we'd done on it, and to speak to its future.

Then in mid-December 1972, Jean-Paul d'Arivèque got word that France was going to recognize *La Fondation Culturelle* of Chicago for a special medal from *l'Ordre des Palmes Académiques*. I had heard of all the honors of the French government, but it wasn't until I went to the various meetings that I actually met people wearing the little bar or rose insignias in their lapels which indicated they were members. Polo was pleased but surprised at this notice and said he honestly didn't know how it had come about, since normally one is nominated and must send their CV to the Embassy or Consulate.

It turned out that the *Consul Général*, Monsieur Pierre-Yves Boasson, who'd been to the mansion many times for official and unofficial events, had skipped some steps and gone right to the *Ministère d'Education* in Paris with his nomination of Jean-Paul and his Foundation. As it happened, Polo and I were invited to the Consulate one evening and Monsieur Boasson explained it.

"My term as *Consul Général* is coming to a close, " he said, "but I want to still be here to award you the honor. So this will happen the first of the year. The official list comes out on December 15, and we will have a ceremony in late January."

"I would like it to go especially to my wife," Polo announced, completely out of the blue as I sat there.

"Oh, no!" I spoke up, astonished. "No. This is for the Foundation, not me. It must be **you** representing."

"Sarah, *Palmes Académiques* is an education honor, " Polo stated deliberately and slowly. "You are the guiding force behind everything we have done in that field." He looked back at Boasson, "This honor should go to her."

"*Mon cher* Polo," said the *Consul Général*, "that is perfectly fine with me. The honor is really for *La Fondation*---which is unusual in itself because it is usually reserved for a specific person---and whichever of you accepts it is doing so in the name of the organization, *non*?

"Yes," I quickly added, "so it should be our *Président*."

"You see what I am confronted with here?" Polo implored Boasson, not exactly kidding, "With this one, she never wants to take the credit for the splendid work she has done."

"That's not...really...true," I tried to argue, to little avail.

On the way back in the car I did try to make my point a little more seriously with Polo.

"What I keep telling you is that my job wouldn't have existed without you. You are the *raison d'être* for the Foundation, and it is you who should be in the limelight. The way I see it is that I am implementing your vision at all times."

He looked over at me and didn't say anything at first. I couldn't tell if he were about to blow up at me for embarrassing him in front of *Monsieur le Consul Général*, or if he were going to hug me.

"I do not bring this up to put you ill at ease, *ma chérie*, because of comparisons to you with my mother, but what you have done in the short amount of time you've been here surpasses her wildest dreams for our organization. You have brought her vision to fruition. I could not do that. And I am so very grateful to you." He lifted my hand to his lips.

"Polo, I'm not freaked out by comparisons to your mother. You need to believe me on that."

"But the unkind words of Robineau to you?"

"Yeah, I was upset by what he told me that day...you know...long ago. But I told you -- I've put his scorn behind me now. All that is over. Marie-Aveline doesn't threaten me. If you want to know the truth, I calmed down after *Oncle* Charles spoke to me about her. I'm sure if I'd known her, I would have loved her. I mean, you do…obviously…and the office reveres her, as they do you." I put my arms around his neck, and whispered in his ear, "And, for what it's worth, and this goes without saying, I love you to the end of days."

He drew me closer and we embraced and kissed and nuzzled one another until the car pulled into the garage at home, where I sort of straightened my mussed-up coat and hair to be a little more presentable on exiting the car. I could see Jean-Luc's bemused expression in the rear-view mirror already.

The office closed for the holidays and things settled down as we prepared to spend quiet times together, interrupted only by invitations to Christmas cocktail parties and New Year's Eve events. Chanukah had come and gone by then that year. It had started on November 30th, when Polo had presented me with a beautiful silver menorah to replace my little Woolworth's one, and we set it up on a table in our part of the house in a window near the piano. He seemed to enjoy watching me light the candles each night, and I wondered if he thought some alien had moved in with him. We didn't exchange gifts for that holiday and it occurred to me that Chanukah wasn't any fun with just grown-ups anyhow.

The d'Arivèque Christmas tree was always ordered from some florist and set up as usual in the grand library on the second floor. Ever since I'd made the flip remark that Jewish kids must surely wish to be able to decorate Christmas trees, Polo had invited me to decorate his. Now we were married and it was, he told me, my chance to "go wild" and do whatever I wanted to with it.

"Hell no, " I'd told him. "I wouldn't change your decorations for the world. I still feel that if I broke one of them, I'd have to commit suicide is all."

He teased me that he couldn't tell if I were really serious.

,   "What if I offered to go with you and buy all new ones?"

"Oh now, come on. I'm not going to even entertain **that** idea. Part of this whole *megillah* is taking out the ornaments and remembering them…where you got them; which was your fave and why, who gave them to you. That's why people pack them away and bring them back out year after year, and all that. I would never deprive you of it."

"Sarah," he mused, "until you came over that fateful night, and were so enamored with the tree, I had never even touched those ornaments. The staff put them up every year. I want you to decorate it. I want to decorate it with you. But I never did want to do it myself, and frankly, I cannot recall where most of them came from at all. Just the one I chose with *Papa*, as I explained to you."

"Okay, I hear you. We'll do it together and I'll be happy to do it. But not with new ornaments. Let's just use yours and I'll have to be very careful. You can hang the most expensive ones…if we can even discern that at all."

And **that** gave me the most wonderful idea I'd had yet in our marriage. When the cigarette box was ready and I went back to Tiffany's to get it, I came up with the perfect way to announce to Polo that I was ready to have a baby. The obsequious Mr. David Blume was only too happy to oblige me. I picked out a sterling silver baby rattle from the store's very chic collection of non plus ultra ornaments "for the tree that had everything," and I had them engrave it "Baby's First Christmas, 1973." It was for sure a gamble. Could I even get pregnant right away and have a baby by next Christmas? Well, I deduced, it was worth a try anyway. I would present it to Polo by way of announcement. So, indeed, that was tempting fate somewhat, but, I figured, if it didn't work out, I'd simply put the thing away and get something else for our tree the year we really did have a child. No big deal.

I was so pleased with myself that I just had to call Cass and divulge the plan.

"Can you imagine his shock when he opens it?!!" I squealed to her.

"Hah! I hope he doesn't have a heart attack, " she joked.

"I hadn't thought of that, " I said, worried all of a sudden. "But I don't think that will happen. I hope to hell not!"

"This will truly make him happy, " she said, softly. "I'm glad you changed your mind, Sari."

Her words were happy but she sounded sad anyway.

"You still sound kind of down, Cass, " I said. "What's going on out there now?"

I think she was afraid I'd start in on her again about coming to Chicago, but for some reason, she opened up to me.

"Oh, Sari, " she said, beginning to sob, "you were right about Alan. He's threatening me now about the anorexia."

The timbre of her voice showed a fear I had never before heard from her. I hesitated to even ask for clarification, afraid it might set her off, but I took the plunge anyway.

"Soooo," I ventured slowly. "I thought you said... you were on maintenance. Not really on it? "

"I was! I am! But...he...says that he's sick and tired of the way I don't eat normally — whatever that means---and never gain any weight. He says it's detrimental to the kids to see me like this, and that he has a mind to start proceedings against me for sole custody of the twins." She paused and then sobbed into the phone, "He says I'm an unfit mother – just like you told me he would!"

"Jesus. I knew it."

"Don't you dare tell me you told me so! I just couldn't take it!" she sniffled, still almost yelling at me.

"I'm not. I didn't mean it that way. Calm down, Cass. I'm on your side. I'm always on your side."

She regained her composure and then confessed more to me.

"So, the bad news is that I ate a package of chocolate marshmallow cookies yesterday. How could I have done that?!" She burst out crying again.

It should have occurred to me what she would say next, but it didn't.

"I threw it all up afterwards."

"You purged you mean?"

"Yeah."

"Cass, in terms of your illness, I don't know what to say."

"You don't have to say anything. I'll work on it."

"But...from what you've done so far, I'm...beginning...to think...maybe you need some professional help." I tried to be gingerly in my approach to this. "What if...and this is just a thought...your parents could help?"

"NO, Sari. DO NOT tell them!! You've got to SWEAR to me you'll not tell them. That would be a betrayal on your part. I...I'd never forgive you."

"All right! Christ! It was just a suggestion. But you'd better do something! You say you don't want to lose your children!" *And I didn't want to lose patience!*

"I will get ahead of it. I refuse to lose them. And Sari?"

"What?"

"Thanks for all the loot you sent them. I'm not wrapping it — just like you. Leaving it out as though Santa brought it."

"You're welcome. You know I love doing it. Do you have a tree up?"

"Nope. West Texas isn't exactly conducive to Christmas décor. I'm sure you can imagine...they put lights on cactus plants down here."

"Yuck. Please. That sounds ghastly. But...give those two little sugarplums loads of kisses from me, and try to have a merry Christmas, okay?"

"Well, that's not going to happen, but thanks."

So I spent the holidays sick with angst over Cass' predicament, followed by butterflies in my stomach with anticipation of Polo's joy.

Polo had only celebrated eleven Christmases in France, and when I asked him about his traditions...opening presents on *La Veille* or on *Le Jour*, for instance, he told me that as a little child he'd had the most presents on St. Nicholas Day, so neither Christmas Eve, which was *Le Réveillon* meal, nor the next day, which was quiet. He didn't grow up enough there to attend Midnight Mass with the adults, and once the war started and Paris was occupied, the family moved down to an emptied out *La Pérégrine* and most festivities came to a halt. In New York, he spent the first two and a half years in the hospital, where he said he found the feeble attempts people made to bring a little holiday cheer for the children stuck in there at Christmas or Chanukah depressing.

"*Maman* did not set up a tree at the apartment, nor did she bring one to my room. It wasn't until the 1950's when she went back one summer to the Paris house that she even had the old family decorations shipped to New York, " he explained. "By that time, I had no nostalgia for them and really very few memories of Christmas at home."

"But a few?" I asked.

"Maybe a few, " he admitted, with a smile.

So we decided to start our own tradition doing our own thing opening up gifts on Christmas Eve. He had already presented me with the gorgeous menorah that first year of our marriage, but I made him promise there would be no Chanukah presents for me from then on. If the holidays happened to coincide, then fine. What I did not want was yet another occasion to raise more conundrums of what I could possibly give my husband as a gift, let alone eight days of them!

So on December 24, 1972, we sat down in the big library where I had requested the chefs fix us that same wonderous seafood buffet and champagne, and as we nibbled at all the goodies, Polo handed me a small, square box wrapped in gold foil and tied with thin red satin ribbon.

I gave it a little shake and...nothing moved. He watched me with raised eyebrows and a smile curling up to one side of his mouth.

"Oh, my God. Good grief! What did you do?!" I exclaimed, amazed to unwrap a coral colored box lined in aged beige velvet containing a circular pendant locket on a chain of platinum gold. The locket had a raised heart on it with a *fleur de lys* in the center. It was green pearlescent enamel surrounded by diamonds, seed pearls and emeralds and marked on the back "August Hollming-St. Petersburg 1899." It was the most exquisite necklace I'd ever held. I turned it over and over in my hand, not saying anything.

"Do you like it?" Polo asked.

"I...yes, of course, I like it. I love it. Thank you so much for this...incredible...thing...gift!" I reached over to kiss him and he held me.

"I love you so much, Sarah."

"I know you do. Right back at you."

"Do you recognize this name...August Hollming? It's actually August Fredrik Hollming."

"I don't, to tell the truth."

"No... well, he was not as well-known as his place of employment...the House of Peter Carl Fabergé."

"Fabergé?! Okay then, so this is priceless and I can never wear it in public?!" I burst out laughing.

"Of course, you can wear it! I want you to! We shall not keep this in the vault, *voyons*." He chuckled. "Do try it on." He couldn't help me on with it, but it was long enough that I could slip it over my head without undoing the beautiful round barrel clasp.

"There," Polo said, admiring me " it is lovely on you. You know, Hollming was never as famous as Fabergé but he made some beautiful things for them. He was Finnish, and not Russian, but he settled in Saint Petersburg---I assume because at that time in the late 1800's Russia was a great market for jewels and *objets d'art*."

"So did Carl Fabergé know about him and hire him? "

"Not at first. He had to take the qualifying exams to become a master goldsmith, and after he passed them, he set up his own workshop. That is when Fabergé offered to have his *atelier* moved into the same building as the Fabergé one, and for all intents and purposes, it was Hollming who ran the entire operation. He is the one who produced some of the very famous miniature Easter eggs and such. Cigarette cases...you know, the *bibelots* that Fabergé was known for."

"Oh? Cigarette cases, huh? Fancy that, " I said, getting up to go over to the table where our Christmas tree was set up. I reached under it for my first robin's egg blue Tiffany's box, which I hadn't bothered to rewrap since I had asked them to substitute a lovely red bow for the usual white one.

"This is for you," I said, handing it down to him and then sitting back down. "After what you just gave me, I doubt it will measure up, though."

He struggled a little bit with the tie, but he opened the box easily with one hand. He saw my cigarette case and exclaimed that " c'est un très très beau étui à cigarettes."

"Do you like the engraving on the back?" I asked.

He took it out and turned it over to see our initials. "Oh, yes, very much! I shall treasure this, *chérie*."

"Open it up."

He did so himself and was moved seeing the inscription. He looked back up at me and I half expected him to start to cry, but thankfully, he didn't.

"It is *magnifique*," he told me, and he took my hand in his, kissed it, and held onto it until I gently extracted it and put my arms around him. "But guess what? That's not all," I said.

"You are being mischievous, now?"

"You could say that." Back at the tree I took out the other, longer, Tiffany blue box.

He slipped the bow off this one and the ribbon fell loose. He opened the box and separated the tissue paper to reveal the baby rattle. He didn't have to turn it over: the engraving was visible right there. He read it out loud, "Baby's First Christmas, 1973."

"*Mais… alors…qu'est- ce que c'est que ça …?*" he looked up at me with his mouth agape.

"I've changed my mind—yet again!-- about having a baby, Polo. I've had…what you'd call…a change of heart now. So I hope next year when we're decorating the tree, this can hang on it."

I looked at him and he was staring at me.

"Sarah! Oh Sarah! You…**do** want to have a baby?"

I nodded. "Let's go for it. What the hell. If I turn out to be a lousy mother, you'll more than make up for it because you'll be the best *papa* ever!"

"*Mais non*, my darling! You shall be a perfectly wonderful mother! You have made me *l'homme le plus heureux de la Terre* tonight! Complete happiness. Happiness I never even dared hope to have . Even so…you have done this."

I knew my abrupt about-face would have an impact, but once again, I felt embarrassed enough to deflect his exaggeration of my powers over him.

"Well, my love, we're a regular mutual admiration society, aren't we?"

He looked at me quizzically and I just smiled up at him. We both knew that we were about to spend the rest of our nights that holiday season trying to make his fervent wish come true.

By the date of the *Palmes Académiques* ceremony on January 29th, I had missed my period and suspected I might be pregnant. I didn't say anything to Polo, until I had set up an appointment with Dr. Bertram, and she confirmed three days later that I was probably about twenty-eight or nine days pregnant.

"Well, how about that?" I crowed. "He was a pretty damned straight shooter!"

Chapter One Hundred Thirteen

"Things we Said Today"...Lennon & McCartney

Winter in Chicago at a house isolated by a highway in front and Lake Michigan in the back, could be either quietly beautiful with that filigree ice on the branches that turned nature, or in our case, the veranda, into a misty wonderland; or it could engulf us with the howling north wind that blew blizzards across prairie and lake. Either way, the temperatures made going out in it prohibitive, and driving a mess. On a blustery night in early February, we were slated to appear again at the French Consulate-- at the last official duty of Consul General Boasson-- a cocktail party honoring the newly appointed French Ambassador to the US, Jacques Kosciusco-Morizet's first visit to our city. Even though it was only a short drive that I certainly could have done in the Pallas, I was happy for Jean-Luc to be taking us. The wind was constantly whipping up snow on the streets, and a steady freezing rain laid down a sheet of ice the minute it touched the pavement...or windshield.

Polo was so sought after in that city, that if we didn't put a cap on it, we could have been gone every night of the week. I was the one without very many close friends in town, so I left our social calendar up to him. He was always so pleased to have me by his side in public, and made a point to treat me, in any social situation we found ourselves in, like he valued me as his equal ---a nice compliment, especially given our age difference.

His friends accepted me mainly because they saw the change in him and they, being true friends, recognized and relished his newfound contentment. Even his acquaintances from the worlds of philanthropy and the arts treated me with deference because he treated me that way.

I was young, still pretty naïve and insecure in my new role as Madame Jean-Paul d'Arivèque. I found I was continually plagued by fear that I wasn't really the person he thought I was, that the whole thing could, without any warning, come crashing down around me. These doubts and presentiments had no bearing in reality. Polo never gave me a reason to believe he didn't love me with all his heart. So why did this anguish hang over me like overripe fruit about to fall from some laden tree limb?

Was our marriage too good to be true or too true to be good?

I was in "my" bedroom getting ready for the evening at the Consulate, caught up in a funk that I had to dress up and look more sophisticated than I felt. If I wore my gorgeous new locket, like he said he hoped I would that night ("the perfect venue for it"), would the other guests see me as "Nellie Nouveau, " or worse, merely avaricious? Then again, shouldn't my delight at being with him outweigh all the insecurities which invariably welled up?

My pensiveness was abruptly disrupted, however, when Polo appeared in the hallway outside my door whimpering in pain. He called out to me, and turning to see what he wanted, I heard his cane drop and saw him collapse, as he tried to reach around and grab his spasming right calf. His brace leg was flung out straight, since he couldn't unlock it in time.

I gasped to see him writhing in agony on the floor.

"POLO!" I screamed.

" It...ouff...is...a...cramp!" he cried out, "aîeeee."

"Oh, God! What can I do!? Are you all right!?"

"Ouille, uuuugh!" He was trying to rub it out.

I approached him to take his arm and try to lift him.

"No! Sarah....*Aieee*!...No, no... I am too heavy for you...the baby."

"I know...but...you can't get up."

"Please call Robin. Ring him by dialing seven."

I did what he told me to do, and Robineau was up there in a nanosecond. He lifted Polo to a standing position, leaning him on the brace leg while holding him on the left side.

"The pain..it is so bad!" Polo blurted out, still wincing.

Robineau switched sides and put Polo's right arm around his shoulders and I took hold of his left one, and together we got him down the corridor into the bedroom and onto to the bed. Robineau undid the hidden zipper in the left pant leg, unbuckled the straps and took off the brace. He then removed the pants altogether to reveal Polo's right leg. He ran to the master bathroom and brought back rubbing alcohol to massage the leg, which he seemed to know how to do quite expertly. At the same time he dialed the doctor on the bedside phone. Not wanting to just stand there helpless, I went to the other side of the bed and climbed up beside my husband, taking his left hand in mine and stroking it.

Robineau left and went down to await the doctor and escort him up, so I was alone with Polo, and very concerned.

"Is it better now? Are you okay?" I implored him.

"It hurts, " he said still cringing. "Thank you darling. I shall be fine."

"Well, if you are, that will be Robineau's doing not mine. Jesus! He seemed to just go into emergency mode right there. I didn't know what to do."

"He has had more practice with this than you have, *chérie*, " Polo sighed, in continued distress.

A doctor I did not recognize at all arrived with Robineau, who absented himself from the bedroom, but stayed up on the third floor in case he was needed. I got off the bed and stared like a deer in the headlights, still petrified.

"What was the pain on a scale of ten?" the doctor was trying to discern from Jean-Paul.

"A twelve!" he answered, trying to laugh about it, and then he introduced me to him. "Please meet my wife Sarah. Sarah, this is *le docteur* Lemoine. He is my pain specialist."

"Pierre, " he said to me, offering his hand. "*Enchanté, Madame.*"

"*Enchantée, Docteur,* " I answered, and, relieved he was there, I added, "*Merci d'être venu.*" As usual, the house call was a given, but Polo, too acknowledged his gratitude.

"*Alors, mon vieux,* " said Lemoine, "*l'hôpital?*"

"*Ah, non, quand-même, Pierre.* I think I shall be better soon. We have a dinner to attend tonight."

"I would advise against that, " said the doctor, firmly.

He turned to me and asked whether I knew about Polo's history of this recurrence he suffered from cramping and spasming in his legs.

"She knows I was in the hospital awhile back for it, " Polo offered.

"Yes, I knew he had, at various times, bouts of severe pain."

"But you never saw it up close until this one?" he asked me.

"No, not an attack like this. I saw him in the aftermath of it that one time, like he said."

"Ah, well then, now you know. This one came on in the right leg, the good one. Most of the time the attacks happen in the injured leg. This one was more of…perhaps…a tremor with an outside secondary cause such as… stress-induced? When it occurs in his left leg, it is a permanent aftermath of the trauma he sustained all those years ago."

"So…you're in pain…terrible pain… a… whole lot of the time and you just don't let on?" I was incredulous at this thought.

"It is all right." He tied to assure me, and then turned back to the doctor. "Please do not give her reasons to worry about me. She's pregnant."

"Oh, congratulations!" Dr. Lemoine exclaimed, beaming at me.

"Thank you, Doctor, " I said, smiling, but not wanting to talk about that. "Do you think he should go to the hospital now?"

"If he doesn't wish to, that's fine. I can give him some muscle relaxants today and see how he is in the next couple of days. If the pain continues…"

"Yes, then, hospitalization for sure, " I said.

"They cannot do much differently there than here, " Polo said to me.

"Yeah, well they can tend to you around the clock a lot better than I can." I turned to the doctor and added, "I'm afraid I'm a rotten nurse."

Dr. Lemoine said he'd call around the next day, Sunday, and would assess the situation again then. Robineau showed him out and I stayed up there with my true love.

"I'm going to change back into 'civilian' clothes, " I told him, "and then I'll return and smother you with kisses. You know when I was little, if I ever hurt myself, Nana would tell me she'd 'kiss it and make it all better.' And you know what? For some strange reason it always did."

"I should be in favor of this…*euh*…medicine…" he laughed. "Please administer it to me as soon as you can."

Robineau reappeared to help Polo into pajamas and to give him the first dose of the medication… some sort of benzodiazepine… that the doc had left. Robineau actually was a good nurse, or at least a good orderly, for which I was grateful, since my fright hadn't really abated much by then. I snuggled with Polo for a while, but he was getting drowsy, probably from the pill, and I left to go work in the library on my latest batch of *Moments Culturels*.

I sat down at my desk, hardly able to concentrate, and just stared up at the lovely Alpine scene Cass had gifted us. I loved it with a passion and had hung it right above where I worked.

I decided to call her then and there to help assuage my worry about my husband.

"This was new, " I sighed, retelling the horror I felt at seeing him in excruciating pain. "I was *nulle*, too," I added, pronouncing the word in French.

"Did you panic?" she asked.

"Well, yeah, sort of. I would have panicked more had we been out together when it happened. Now I'm afraid it will happen again out of the blue…and keep happening. He can't take falling down like that. What if he'd broken some more bones?"

"Not good, " she said. "But kid, at least you didn't flinch when he told you to call ol' what's-his-name."

"No… and the guy was righteous this time. I've got to hand it to him."

"Well, then it's good that you two get along now."

"Yeah…I'm not sure we get along. We go along, though."

"So, listen, "she said, her voice trailing off, "I've got to put the kids to bed. Call me later this week and let me know how he's doing, okay? And you, too! How do you feel? " It was as if she caught herself and remembered I was "with child."

"I figure I'm almost home free," I told her, "without even a hint of morning sickness thus far. And isn't it true that if I make it through the first few months without it, I probably won't have any?"

"I hope that turns out to be the case, " she replied.

Except for Cass…and now Dr. Lemoine, no one knew our big news, as we'd agreed to not announce to the office or other friends until I'd made it through the first trimester. But I was anxious to share what I was going through with Cass, even though there wasn't a lot to tell yet since I wasn't going through much of anything.

Polo did get better, and Dr. Lemoine backed off from putting him in the hospital. He stayed home for a few days, even as I returned to work as usual, and by the middle of that next week, we were both back to our routine of commuting to the office together.

Polo had asked me to take a pregnancy hiatus from work but the reality was, I just couldn't do that, even if I had wanted to, which I did not. I had too many irons in the fire and too many commitments lined up to be gone from my desk. He had, however, insisted I move into the presidential suite of offices, so that did happen. But I missed my little projection room office with its isolation. As my belly "grew, " I was completely visible in the glass house that was Polo's office area. People were too polite at first to confront me; I guess they just thought I was getting fat.

At the beginning of the pregnancy, Polo had insisted I get a whole new wardrobe lined up. He even offered to take me back to Paris to procure it, but I demurred. Even though, in those days, I didn't have to dress in maternity clothes that made me look like, say, Lucille Ball on her t.v. show the year she was pregnant, I had no intension of "showing." No expectant woman, with the possible exception of some hippies, walked around in 1973 with the bump protruding.

I went to Saks and completely outfitted myself in sensible loose-fitting work clothes, pretty empire-style dresses that would look fine once it was obvious. I basically bought the clothes in various sizes, and put them away until needed.

Saks' maternity department was stocked that year with a lot of what I called pinafores---little mini-jumpers to wear over pants with long-sleeve shirts under them. I chose some cute flower-print tent dresses, too, and a couple of "maxi" length jumpers, one in plain black wool and one for spring in a nautical theme with a "middy" tie at the collar. I splurged on one elegant, silk shantung outfit of skirt, top and jacket all in the same color: salmon. It would be perfect to wear out to our more dressy events like the symphony or ballet. I also bought a maternity swimsuit, far uglier than my real one, so that I could continue to swim with Polo and get exercise myself.

Valentine's Day was on the horizon, and, instead of looking forward to it as one of my favorite days, I was dreading having to once again come up with some idea to show the very real affection I had for my beloved.

"Thinking up something unique for the man who has absolutely everything, or could buy anything in the world he didn't have, is going to be the death of me!" I said to Cass, back on the phone in my office.

"You're giving him what he wants most, " she said, "so don't angst over it. Stress isn't good for the baby."

She was right.

And then it hit me: something I could give him uniquely from me each and every year...a photo of us together...in some lovely frame. But I didn't want to go to a photographer and have portraits taken, I wanted more candid shots. I approached Annie-Laure with my plan.

"I will make some pretense of going in to talk to him, " I told her, "which won't be hard, I do it all the time. And you will have my camera—you know, the one that he gave me -- and you can snap a few photos of us through the glass. I'll try to stage it a little bit so we're either looking at one another or one of us---probably me---is looking towards you. Do you think you can do it?"

"I'll try," she said. "I can't promise anything. Why does it have to be like that though? Could I not just come into the office and take your picture together?"

"Well, maybe we will eventually have to do it that way, but let's try some completely candid ones first."

She and I chose a day I knew his schedule would keep him in the office; I gave her the camera, and the plan proceeded as envisioned. I took him in a rough draft of the abstract for my presentation on the cuisine regions of France, and leaned over his shoulder, pointing out some wording. I looked up and she took the photo from her desk using the zoom feature on the Canon.

When I got the film developed, it turned out that several of them were actually okay and would certainly work for their intended purpose. I thanked Annie-Laure profusely and we commiserated on how hard it was going to be for me to gift this man.

"But of course, you have the perfect present...in there, " she said smiling at my stomach.

I nodded. That's what I kept hearing.

I found a frame that would look nice on his desk and matted the photo, which I had printed out in five-by-seven size. I wanted to make him a frilly valentine of my own---maybe paint it. But I was forced to acknowledge that I had no talent for such things, so I just went to Chicago's most wonderful card shop, Verso, on Delaware Place and bought him a cute one. On the outside was a stylized red candy apple, the kind with the big stick like you'd see at the Christmas market in Strasbourg. Out of the top of the stick, pink and white flowers were blooming, and in front of the stick, a red ribbon banner curled around with Happy Valentine's Day written in white to stand out. Inside, the message was pretty stupid. It said, "Let's bite into our life together."

So I added my own message in red, borrowing a verse from a poem by Rosemonde Gérard to her husband Edmond Rostand. Hers was made famous by Alphonse Augis, a jeweler in Lyon who, in 1907, created a medal with her lines engraved on it that read "*Chaque jour je t'aime d'avantage, aujourd'hui plus qu'hier et bien moins que demain.*" I changed it up a bit to read what I would write on all subsequent Valentine cards of our entire marriage: "*Je t'aime… plus qu'hier mais pas autant que demain.*" Under the verse I gave credit where it was due: "*d'après R. Gérard.*" I signed it "Sarah". Polo didn't call me Sari and even though I'd tried to address this issue with him (since being called Sarah reminded me that Sol only called me that), Polo couldn't seem to use my nickname. But since he pronounced my name "Sah-RAH," I decided that was different enough, and I could live with it.

"Ah, " he said, grinning, when he took the photo out of its box. "A family portrait...of the three of us, *non? Que c'est sublime!*

That year Polo offered me a silk Hermès *carrée* in hues of brown, tan and cream on a background of red. The design was called "Carnavale" and had a large palomino horse in the center, wearing a black saddle, and plumes on its head, surrounded by other, smaller horses, some in pairs, with their riders adorned in plumage, also.

"I chose the colors to complement your Kelly bag and also to wear with the fur coat I want you to have... the sable one...of my mother."

"The sable one?"

"*Exacte.*"

"You know I think that is an extremely beautiful coat, Polo. But don't you think sable is a little bit extravagant at this point?"

"Do you wish to have a different type of fur then?"

"No! I'm not saying I want some other fur coat. Not at all. Your coat is terrific. Look, never mind... I'll try to...you know... force myself to ...live up to it." I laughed to ease any tension he might have been feeling.

He seemed relieved, and said again that he felt I looked simply beautiful in it, and how happy he had been the first time he saw that it fit me.

The day after Valentine's, the phone rang in my office and I guessed—partially correctly -- that Cass was calling me to see how the holiday had gone and what gift I had managed to come up with for Polo. I heard her voice on the other end of the line and immediately launched into my doubts about having a sable coat.

"He really wanted me to have it, but also be happy with having it."

"Hummm, " she said, without much conviction in her voice.

"I know!" I cried, "You think I'm too young to wear sable, don't you? I was afraid I'd be laughed right out of the room when we got to the restaurant."

She didn't say anything, and I decided she must have been put off by my crabbing about so crass and materialistic a thing as a fur coat, which, given her current philosophy of living, she wouldn't be caught dead in.

Ignoring her silence, I continued, "Well, of course, I shouldn't worry what other people think, should I? I mean, I'll end up in the loony bin if I let it get to me, huh?"

Suddenly I heard her muffled crying on the other end of the line, and realized my harping on Polo's coat wasn't even registering with her. Something was terribly wrong, and it brought me up short.

"Cass! I can't understand you too well. What's the matter?"

"Oh Sari! I'm so unhappy! Everything here is going wrong. I...I'm going to ask Alan if I can bring the kids to Chicago and visit you. Is...is that okay?"

"Of course it's okay. Don't ask him...tell him! I've invited you a million times already. But...what happened?!"

"See, he really threatened me this time...because I'm sick! I'm ill, Sari! I can't lose my children just because I'm not well!"

"You're not going to lose the children!"

She calmed down a bit. "So, anyway, here's the deal. I can't let him suspect anything. It can't look like I'm running off with the twins. So that's why I'm going to ask...I'm going to tell... Alan that you invited me, which, as you say...you did, right?"

"**Yes!**"

"And he'll think it's just a visit and it won't raise any suspicion that I'm 'stealing' the kids away, but Sari, that's what...I...am doing! Oh, God! I don't know what I'm going to **do**! Can we stay with you?"

"Of course! You don't even have to ask that. And listen, I think you need a lawyer."

"Yeah, I know. We can talk about that. Can you send me those tickets you were going to before?"

"Cass, I actually think it would be a better idea for you to fly with us in our plane. I want us to come down there and get you. I want you to pack up a whole bunch of stuff so you can stay a long time. Your art supplies, and everything."

"Well, I...I can't...because he'll **realize** what's up if he sees stuff gone."

"Oh, all right, but put in plenty of clothes for the kids. It's cold here."

"Sari—knowing you, you'll just go out and buy them anything they don't have anyway!"

674

"Well, you're right about that. Never mind what I said---pack what you want. We can replace everything."

It was not lost on me on me that she hadn't put up a fight about flying in our plane rather than have me send her the tickets.

"So, listen, try to stay calm and act normal. Pretend like you're going on just a little break at my house. I'm going to talk to Polo and we'll look at the calendar and decide when to travel. In the meantime, if Alan wonders why we're coming down there, tell him I'm coming for a textbook conference in Texas. It's almost true...the publishing company I deal with in Des Moines is actually a subsidiary of one in Houston. I could easily be attending confabs with the parent company. Tell him since we were going to be there anyway with our plane, we invited you back to visit. *Voilà*. I mean, you don't need to lie outright to him, but just if he questions you."

"Believe it or not, I doubt if he'll ask me anything. He rarely talks to me unless he's ranting. And he makes no bones about not being here now. He told me he lives in El Paso with Donna and that's just the way it's going to be. He wants me to leave...just not with the kids. I actually think he wants to use them to leverage money out of my parents! Augh!"

"What an asshole. Don't you worry. Any lawyers we get...us or your parents...will eat him for lunch. You know that, so just play it cool. I know it sounds hard, but you can do it. Am I right?"

"I guess so. Talk to you soon, okay? Try to come soon."

"I'm on it."

I saw her willingness to leave him as a good first step towards getting better, too. She needed to turn her anger on him and not back on herself-- in the form of starving herself.

Chapter One Hundred Fourteen

"Beware of Darkness"…George Harrison

*In the 1960's I didn't know from anorexia nervosa, bulimia, or any other eating disorder. Had I been paying more attention, I probably would have recognized these syndromes on the campus of Iowa U, but I was categorically **not** paying attention. I was a thin girl, and I ate everything under the sun without gaining weight. As a matter of fact, most girls in my dorm were "on the thin side" or "normal," except of course for the few who were obviously fat, but just like in high school, not much was ever made of that. If those girls were being told things we would now find offensive, such as "but you have such a pretty face," they weren't freaking out about it, at least not in my presence. If they were being bullied or demeaned behind closed doors, I didn't hear about it. There was one seriously unpleasant heavy girl on my dorm floor, Bevy Anne, who did nothing but waddle around the halls slurping big take-out cups of pop, and telling everyone else to "pipe down." But no one disliked her for being fat; we all hated her because her personality was odious and she was mean. It had occurred to me more than once to thank my lucky stars I hadn't gotten her as a roommate.*

*Cass was taller than me but we weighed about the same-- one hundred pounds or so --the whole time we roomed together. I wore all her clothes and she could have worn mine. Everyone hated dorm food, so there were meals we didn't especially relish eating, but I never noticed that she didn't eat certain foods or was picky out of the ordinary. I did put on a few pounds in Paris but how could you not? The food was so amazingly good and on every other block was a boulangerie or patisserie offering up windows brimming with your heart's desire. Because I walked so much over there, I could eat **almost** with abandon and not gain an inordinate amount of weight.*

Since, personally, I would rather die than vomit under any circumstances, purging could not have appealed to me less, although from time to time, especially during bouts of stomach flu, I did realize that being sick could cause a person to lose five pounds without even thinking about it. Even so, that struck me as a disgusting and, indeed, an unacceptable way to get a desired side effect. Had I been more aware, I might have realized that girls were sneaking off to purge at parties or after dinners or during study hours, and I undoubtedly must have seen some binging going on and not recognized it as such.

None of my psychology lectures had pertained to eating disorders, and the topic hadn't come up in any sociology courses I took either. No one seemed to care about over-achieving perfectionists and their poor self-esteem. In all our late-night talk-a-thons, girl coffee dates, or dining hall get togethers, no one spoke of their struggles with body image or chronic, potentially fatal, bouts of anxiety over food. I never heard anyone self-diagnose their eating habits as having anything to do with anger, anxiety or fear.

I never assigned meaning to food. It never would have dawned on me to try to get back at my parents for favoring my little sister and treating me like a non-person by not eating; or for feeling the only control I had over my own life was epitomized by what I put in my mouth. I surely felt bad sometimes, unsure of myself, put upon to study so hard and achieve, unhappy at not having a steady beau, but it had never even occurred to me to use food – either too much of it or too little-- as a way to compensate for bad feelings or things anyone had done to me, including Betty and Sol. Food deprivation was never, for me, a means of punishing my parents or myself, just as over-eating was never a substitute for love or a consolation for not having the love I craved. No. If eating for reasons other than because you felt hungry, or starving for reasons rooted in your emotional state were common then, I was absolutely unaware of it. I did have enough self-awareness to realize, at a fairly young age, that being raised by Sol and Betty Shrier was no picnic, but by some miracle – and it must have been a miracle! – I'd come out of childhood, luckily, with adequate coping mechanisms.

Cass seemed to have some conscious knowledge of what was happening to her, but it had been Alan who had introduced me to the vernacular of anorexia; she had obviously educated him and herself about it. It wasn't unknown, after all, having been referenced in literature since the Nineteenth Century, and in some Western Civ class we briefly talked about religious fasting that turned ugly. And, yes, it afflicted women, especially.

I asked Polo one night if he'd heard of it.

"It was said that Mary Queen of Scots had the problem, " Polo told me. "The French called it *l'anorexie hystérique*." Polo also mentioned how shocked he had been as a student in Paris in the fifties to see women who had **not** been in concentration camps walking around looking as though they had been. One of his close friends had a sister studying dance seriously at the Opéra de Paris, and he knew that, like ballet dancers from time immemorial, she practically had to starve herself to stay as thin as the masters demanded. Polo had also asked me one time if I had noticed Cass exercising to some ridiculous extent, and I said I had not.

"We both hated gym classes, " I assured him, even after regaling him with our exploits concerning fencing in the halls of Kate Daum. "I did know, however, that there were girls...like the guys...who were jocks, but it never dawned on me that some of them were exercising at a mad pace to burn up every calorie they'd taken in that day. "

But if I'd been truthful...to myself as much as to him, I would have recalled how Alan Jones had described Cass doing just that when he told me about her disease. That should have sent up a red flag, but instead I had just ignored the ramifications of it all.

Nor did I bring any glory upon myself being a sympathetic ear for Cass after I first realized she was ill. "I'll cook for you!" was my answer to everything. She couldn't be honest about her feelings towards her parents or husband, but I couldn't be honest about my reluctance to accept this malady, and thus I wasn't of any meaningful help to her either.

I approached Polo with a bit of trepidation when I realized I had offered up his airplane to go get Cass and the kids and bring them back to Chicago. In my heart I knew that was impulsive and that I should have checked with him first.

"I apologize for not asking you this rather than telling you. I feel ashamed, and I'm truly sorry."

"Sarah, " he said, shaking his head, looking sad. "You must consider that plane-- and anything else I own-- yours, as well as mine. I know how much you worry about Cass. I am glad you have offered to fly down to bring her back here. I will make the arrangements for any date you wish."

I just stood there for a second, wondering anew what I ever did to deserve this guy!

"Polo, thank you so much! You are too good to me, you really are."

"Ne dis pas de bêtises. It gives me pleasure to do things for you."

I hugged him and we just stayed there in each other's arms, until drawing back a little, he added, "I would like Robineau to accompany us, if that is fine with you."

"Rien n'est parfait, comme dit le Rénard, " I thought to myself, and then said out loud, "Sure, that's okay."

"It is because I do not want you lifting anything heavy, of course, " he explained.

Because I was pregnant and thus a semi-invalid in the eyes of my sweet husband, Polo didn't want me loading luggage, nor could he do it, and neither, he surmised, could Cass. After the bout with pain Polo had undergone, I wasn't exactly unhappy to have Robineau along, just in case, but Cass knew the whole saga of his and my rocky start, and I wasn't too sure how she'd take having him there.

"But, will he want to go on a trip where he has to be valet to everyone and not just you?"

"Oh, I do not think he will say anything, if I ask him to do it. Perhaps, however, it would also be a good idea for Jean-Luc to arrange a rental car for us and for him to drive it? That way there will be the two of them to do what we need."

"Whatever you think best, Polo. I'm all for it."

So we planned to go at the end of February, and I gave Cass the heads up on who all would be there. She was fairly flabbergasted, but did not put up a fight.

"Plan your arrival time to be shortly after noon on a Friday, " she counseled me, "so that Alan will be in class. He isn't prone to cancelling or skipping out on his teaching schedule."

"Good idea," I agreed, giving her credit where due. He wouldn't realize until he got home, if indeed he did go home, that his wife and kids were gone.

"He will just assume I'd come for you and that we'd all left, I hope," I told her.

"Yeah. That's the plan anyhow. "

I also told Cass not to come greet us at the airport. She knew the drill with private aircraft: we would be landing in a separate part, quite a ways away from the terminal, and since Jean-Luc would see to picking up the rental car, we would then just drive straight to St. Anthony.

"I just feel so embarrassed by my house, " she sighed. "I hope you all don't plan on staying too long. "

"No, of course not. And if you have your luggage all stacked at the door, the guys will just load it up and we'll be off."

"I just want you to know how grateful I am, " she said, "and I am excited to meet Jean-Paul after all these years!"

"He, too. He can't wait to meet your kids." And then it occurred to me to tell her also: "Sort of prepare them, will you? Explain to them that he was riding his 'horsey' and it got scared by a loud noise and he fell off and got hurt. I mean, they're only three and a half, but they might understand that, right?"

"I'll try, " she said and then paused and added, " How…how… you know… how bad is he? "

"Well, not that bad to you and me, but they won't get it. And don't worry, he won't be offended if they stare at him or are afraid at first. I'm sure once they see us together, and they get to know him, they'll love him."

I thought the bigger shock anyone was in for on that trip was what she would look like. Based on what I had seen in Iowa City months earlier, I felt I had to prepare the others, too, for meeting my anorexic friend, so as soon as we all boarded the plane, I asked Jean-Luc and Robineau to join us at the front for a few minutes.

"I feel compelled to explain to you that my friend is ill. Even when I last saw her, it shocked me that she doesn't look like she used to. She looks, really, like a mere caricature of her former self. She was so beautiful in our days at school that every guy in the room would turn to stare at her when she walked in. I can't predict what you'll see when we get there this time, though."

"What was different?" Jean-Luc asked.

"Well, do you know what anorexia nervosa is?" I asked.

"Not exactly."

"It's a disease---a disorder—where the person is afraid to eat. She herself explained it to me but I wasn't prepared for what I saw when I visited them. It was on that trip where you said I couldn't drive the Cit to Iowa, remember?"

"Oh, yes, indeed. You took the small limo."

"That's right. Well, I drove to the house and expected my usual welcome. Instead, this emaciated shadow of a woman greeted me. It was awful! Cass had these gorgeous violet eyes before, and now they were sunken into dark sockets which made her cheek bones stick out. Her mouth had also lost bone structure somehow, you know, like what happens when the elderly lose teeth and bone, and their mouths seem to shrink in. And her chic hairdo was gone. Instead her hair was dull and unkempt. All this---what I would call-- star quality she had when we were students, was over, " I concluded, giving a shrug.

I guess they didn't know exactly how to react to my spiel, but Polo put his arm around me and shook his head sadly in a show of empathy. I knew that he felt bad for me having to deal with all this emotion.

"Let us just hope she will get better soon in Chicago, " he said, trying to reassure me.

"Oh, she will, " I answered resolutely, and I believed it.

"I know you love her, " my husband told me, drawing me nearer to him in the two seats, nestling my head into his chest, "but this may not be as simple as you think."

"Yeah," I reluctantly admitted, "I hear that."

*Even as we flew down to El Paso on a mission, so to speak, my intentions were not on seeing to it that Cass got help for an eating disorder as much as on getting her out of a crappy marriage, protecting her rights to have her children with her, and seeing her happy again with me in Chicago! I was naïvely buoyed up by a steadfast belief that if those problems worked out, she would go back to eating "normally." If I'd been heeding the signs from the start, I'd have known that she hadn't been "eating normally" since we were in Paris together, and what I was doing---well-meaning or not, and it **was** well-meaning--- was stepping in to take control of the situation and "fix everything" for her. Control was the issue, and what I didn't realize at the time was that I wasn't part of any solution.*

As we got closer, I was fidgety and nervous about how we'd manage to "get her out of Dodge."

"I just hope we can pull this off, " I finally admitted.

"What about her parents' involvement?" Polo wanted to know.

678

"Oh, I don't think she'd be too happy if I contacted them just yet. I mean, I'd sure like them to have a relationship with their grandchildren, but that's going to have to come from Cass, don't you think?"

"I am not *au courant*, *chérie*, to give an opinion. I believe the Hydes would want to see their daughter, but I do not know them as you do."

"Look, I agree with you, but I didn't want to bring them up with her right now. She's too fragile. I think she's very wary of being in the same city as they are. But I promise to broach the subject as soon as I can. Okay?"

"Yes, darling. You do what you think is best."

The plane landed in Texas and it was show time. We waited for what seemed like an eternity for Jean-Luc and Robineau to return with a nine-passenger Ford Country Squire station wagon.

"That's the perfect get-away car, " I laughed when I saw it.

"We are not committing a crime, *voyons*!" Polo said, not laughing.

We took the route Cass had given me and it was a quick trip straight up Highway Ten to the sign that announced we were entering St. Anthony, New Mexico-- city limits and state line both. She had told me that if we took the main business street heading west, at the end where it looks like the countryside is coming up, that would be her house: red and white with a wind-chime hanging over the front porch.

"There it is, " I called out. "Just as she said."

Jean-Luc pulled into her short driveway and turned to look at me.

"If you two would wait here, " Polo said, "we will signal you to come in and get the luggage, is that all right?"

"*Oui, Monsieur*, " answered Robineau, getting out and coming to open the car door for his boss, and help him out. The Ford sat lower than other cars, and it was harder for Polo to maneuver.

When the car doors opened and shut, two little faces peered out from behind the front door to see us.

"HI!!!" I shouted, and ran up to get them.

"Auntie SARI!" Laura squealed, and then Paul joined in, "Auntie Sari!!"

I leaned down to grab them both and swept them into my arms. Then I turned to see how Polo was making it up the one step onto the porch.

"Look!" I said, "here's Uncle Polo! Can you say hi to him?"

"Hello!" Polo offered.

Both kids were shy and cowered back behind me rather than greet Polo. Then Cass appeared at the door and we hugged each other. She felt skeletal in my arms.

"Cass, finally!—I'd like you to meet my husband, Jean-Paul d'Arivèque!"

Cass extended her bony arm and hand to him, and he took it but gave her *la bise* instead of shaking her hand.

"So happy to meet you at last, " she said. "I'm so sorry it's under these circumstances."

"Cass, it is indeed my great pleasure to meet you. Sarah has told me so much about you. I feel I do already know you." But he shot me a very concerned look behind her back as he reached around for her shoulder and kissed her cheek.

"Yes, me, too, " she said, motioning us in and glancing out onto the driveway to catch a glimpse of my former arch enemy. "Excuse this place, please, " she pleaded.

"No, no, it's fine, " I said, actually horrified. The house was a disaster. Dust was literally covering every surface as though it had snowed in there. The carpet was not clean enough to have children playing on it. Her kitchen sink, visible from the front door as we entered, was piled with dirty dishes and pans, and the countertop had dried-on food sticking to it. I shuddered.

"Have a seat. I mean, I know we're not staying long, but it's just so good to finally be together, isn't it?" she said.

"Yep," I answered, searching furtively for signs that she had prepared what I'd asked her to for the trip.

We sat down on dilapidated furniture. Only a few works of her art hung on the walls, which made me hope she'd packed up the rest at least.

"You're taking your art, right?" I asked.

679

"Some, yes, " she said.

"Where is it?"

"Just in the bedroom."

I got up to go find it and see what else we should be ferrying out of there. She excused herself from Polo and followed me to the hall where I found a few stretched canvases and her paint box on the floor.

"We're taking these, " I said.

"No, Sari...they're just nothing."

"Well, what about the paints?"

"Yeah, okay, " she sighed.

"Cass, it's a Boeing 707! There's a shit load of cargo space."

"Jesus, " she laughed, "a Boeing 707? You're richer than my parents now."

"Did you pack some of the kiddos' favorite toys, too?" I wondered, not seeing as many suitcases as I thought I would.

"Yes, Sari...stop your stewing. They'll have plenty to do. I even left out a few things for them to play with on the plane."

"Very good ! It pays to have a stewardess for a mommy."

We went back out to where Polo all of a sudden had two curious little curly blond heads bobbing around him.

"Did your horsey hurt you?" Laura was asking, patting at his leg.

"Yes, "said Polo. " He didn't mean to. But I'm better now, see?"

"Is your arm still ow-y?" asked Paul.

"It does not hurt me, " Polo said, "but... it does not work too well. "

Suddenly Laura leaned up to his arm and kissed it. "All better, " she said.

Polo smiled up at me. "The same remedy as your Nana had?" he laughed.

"Works every time, " I said.

I sat back down on the couch and scooped Laura and Paul into my lap.

"Oh boy! Guess what we're going to do!" I said to them with mystery in my voice. "We're going to go for a ride on a BIIIIIG airplane! Won't that be fun?"

"Yeah!" they both cried.

"And you guys can play on the plane and we can have yummy snacks, too!"

"And candy?" Laura asked, with a little gleam in her eye.

I burst out laughing, not prepared for how astute she was. "Oh, I don't know about candy. We'll see!"

Cass was sitting on a wooden chair across the room from me when suddenly with a hint of panic in her voice, she called out to me.

"Oh!" she said in pain, "Sari!"

I slid the kids off my knees back onto the couch, and went over to her.

"Can you come with me into the bathroom? " she whispered.

"What's wrong?" I asked...and then saw blood on her skirt. "Oh, Cass!"

"Yes, I'm spotting. Let's go."

I shot Polo a look that said I didn't know what was wrong, and then took Cass by the arm. She was doubled up. Once we were in the hall and out of sight of the others, she shoved her fist between her legs and clutched at her skirt.

"I'm bleeding but I don't have my period, " she said, panting. "I haven't had it for a year."

"You're not pregnant, are you?" I asked alarmed, even as I firmly believed she couldn't be.

"Christ, no! Kid, I don't know what this is!"

"Well, what can I do for you?"

"I need to change." She slipped out of her straight navy skirt and then I saw it. She was literally a cadaver in front of my eyes. Tears welled up and I couldn't help but gasp.

"Oh, Cass. What in hell... do...you...weigh?!"

"No, Sari, "she said, starting to sob, "please don't let's get into that. We're just about to leave."

I sat her shaking body down on the toilet and took off the panties that were coated in blood. "Is this urine? Is there blood in your urine?"

"I don't think so. It seems to be coming from my vagina but it's not menstrual."

"Yeah, but we'll have to treat it like it is and have you wear a tampon or something on the plane, won't we?"

"I have some maxi pads. Can you get me one? In the bottom cabinet there."

I did as she requested and then I went out to find her some clean clothes in the bedroom. Luckily, as was her plan when she talked to me on the phone, she had had no intention of packing all her belongings so as not to raise suspicion with Alan, so I found clean underwear and another skirt, which, I remarked, was strangely similar to the one she'd just taken off.

"I guess I'd better take a few of these pads, " she said.

"I'm taking the whole box, " I replied. "Have you seen a doctor about this bleeding?"

"Huh-uh. But I will. It feels like I'm going to wet my pants all the time!"

"Well, that can't be right. Maybe it's a yeast infection or some other UTI?"

"I...don't know." She began to cry again. "I can't...seem...to be able to make it stop."

"Hey, it's okay. We're going to get you some help. Everything will be all right." I leaned over and put my arms around her. She was so frail and so small, I was afraid she would disintegrate onto the floor in a heap of powdery feathers at my feet and be blown away by the slightest breeze.

I left her to clean up and when I rejoined Polo and the kids, he was visibly upset.

"Sarah, *chérie*, she is so very ill, " he whispered solemnly to me out of the range of hearing by Laura and Paul. "I think I should have an ambulance meet the plane. I shall alert the pilot."

I looked at him and nodded. "That might be a good idea."

I went out to the porch and asked Jean-Luc and Robineau to come in.

"I think we're about ready to load up, " I said.

Cass had three suitcases in varying states of dilapidation ready in the bedroom, plus a couple of boxes, a knapsack with the kids' toys, a garment bag and her old art caddy that she'd brought to Iowa all those years ago. I gathered up more of her art works and took them out myself. She'd done a large woodblock print of what looked like the New Mexican landscape in back of her house, and she still had some of the Swiss series printed out in varying stages of completion. I pictured her in my house recuperating and working on her projects, just like in the past. I also took down three paintings she had on their walls.

"Alan might miss those and become suspicious, " she said when she came out of the bathroom and saw me.

"Fuck Alan," was all I could reply.

I saw Cass start to take her house key off the key fob to leave on the kitchen counter.

"Don't do that, " I said. "Take your keys. Leaving the house key **would** tip him off."

"Yes, that was stupid of me."

What I was really thinking, however, was that we'd have to send someone back to get all her belongings and those of the kids. I didn't give the slightest damn that Alan would be forewarned of any pending break-up.

Once we had everything, Cass climbed in the far back seat with the twins, Polo and I sat in the middle seat, and Robineau sat up front with Luc.

I turned back to Laura and Paul. "Isn't this car fun?" I sang out, and they nodded. "Pretty soon we'll all be in that big airplane I told you about!"

Cass had her frail arms around each child. I reached over to take Polo's left hand and held it all the way there. Only the driver and his passenger in the front wore the lap seat belts; no one in the two back seats bothered to use them, as we sped down the highway to the El Paso airport. The station wagon pulled up to a small building off in the private plane section of the airfield and we all got out. The luggage was set aside until Jean-Luc could return the rental car, and we went in to wait for flight plans to be filed and the d'Arivèque plane to be refueled and readied.

There was a little coffee bar in that lounge, so I went up and got Cass and Polo each one, and then I noticed a single vending machine against the far wall. It happened to have apple juice in those small drinking cups with the peel-back lids like you'd see on a hospital tray, so I got each of the kids one, and sat them down to drink it. Cass slumped into a leather chair, looking awful but at least not bleeding that I could tell. I could see that Polo was keeping an eye on her, too, and was nervous about it. When we boarded and Robineau helped him up the stairs to the plane, Polo stopped at the cockpit to talk to the pilots. I suspected it was about having the ambulance waiting at Midway. Our flight crew members, Amelia and Maggie, were delighted to see children board, and one of them went off to get those little wing pins the commercial airlines hands out to kids.

"I always kept a few of these from my days at BOA, " she said smiling.

"Oooh," I cooed at the twins, "look at those! Now you're real pilots."

We settled them into seats by a table and I offered Cass the cabin in the back, but she wanted to sit with her children.

"This plane is three times bigger than my dad's, " she laughed softly, somewhat dazed by the fact that we were to have the entire aircraft to ourselves. She looked around at all the amenities it had. "It's very beautiful in here, I will say."

"Yeah, not too bad, is it?" I joked back, still feeling pretty much dissociated from the fact that it was mine. I sat down next to her to break the news that she was going straight from the plane to the Chicago Med Center.

"Cass, this is a three-hour flight, and then when we land, we've arranged for you to be transported directly to the hospital. I hope you're fine with that." I braced myself for arguments.

"Yes. Okay," she sighed. "What about the kids?"

"I'll take them back to my house and believe me, they'll be well cared-for by our maids. I'll ask especially for Alicia…she's wonderful and loves children. She was a 'summer girl' in Evanston before Robineau hired her." I knew Cass would recognize that nomenclature Chicagoland called nannies in those days. Even though she hadn't spent much time in Kenilworth, she was, after all, from there.

"Oh, good, that's all right, then, " she said, and laid her head to the side against the soft leather seat back, too exhausted to argue.

When Paul and Laura finished their juice and had a few other snacks, they both lay down on the couches and fell asleep. It would be night when we landed in Chicago. I'd brought along new ski jackets for them to wear off the plane, too, as the drop in temperature from El Paso to Chicago in February would be striking.

I settled in with Polo in the front of the aircraft where he always sat if he wasn't in the private cabin.

"I think you had better ride in the ambulance with her, " he told me.

"Oh, okay…I just told her I'd be taking the kiddos home."

"I can do that, *chérie*," he said, "but someone has to be with her to get her checked in, no? And you can sign for her and take responsibility for the eventual bills."

"That's so nice of you, you sweet man, " I told him, hugging him. "And once we get home, I'd like Alicia to be the one in charge of them, is that okay?"

"Of course." And he called over across the aisle to Robineau who came up to our seats. "Robin, when we arrive back at the house, please ask that the children be put *aux bons soins d'Alicia*."

"*Très bien, Monsieur*," he replied, nodding and showing none of his old exasperation.

The flight was smooth, thankfully, and uneventful. When we landed at Midway, the emergency unit pulled up to our plane. Medics boarded with one of those collapsible gurneys and Cass got up on it of her own accord.

Cass motioned for her children to stand next to her. "Momma isn't feeling very well, so I'm going to go see a doctor, okay? Uncle Polo will go with you to his house and you'll see how pretty it is there. He'll read you a story before bed, too!" She looked up at me and said there were books of the twins' in the knapsack and I relayed the message to Polo.

I got the kids into their new jackets while Robineau helped Jean-Paul descend the stairway. Then I took the kids down and handed them off to Jean-Luc. I kissed Polo and climbed into the back of the ambulance after they loaded Cass in.

"I'm going along to check you in, " I told her, taking her hand to hold on the way. "It was Polo's idea. Isn't he sweet?"

"The sweetest, " she said with a noticeably weakened voice. "He's everything you described and more. I love him already."

"I knew you would. So don't worry about anything, okay?"

Chapter One Hundred Fifteen

***Pavane pour une Infante Défunte*...Maurice Ravel**

I'd never been in an Emergency Room before, and had especially not ever arrived at a hospital in a rescue squad. I expected a flurry of activity, orderlies and nurses running hither and yon; doctors meeting the gurney in anticipatory readiness. But none of that greeted us, as we pulled into the Chicago Medical Center around ten p.m. The waiting room inside was almost empty and, while the EMT's were directed to wheel Cass into a little curtain-enclosed cubicle, there was no urgency about it. They pointed me towards a desk where I was to sign her in and I watched them take her away.

"Are you her next of kin?" the woman behind the counter asked me.

"Um, no, I'm her friend. But I brought her in---we flew up from Texas just now. And I will be responsible for the bill."

She seemed surprised to hear that, but handed me a clip board with papers to fill out anyway.

These were the days long before sweeping privacy acts prohibited anyone who wasn't a relation or the person with the health power of attorney to make decisions for a patient. HIPAA laws were not yet on the horizon, and it would even be the better part of the year before HMOA73-- the law that made it legal to profit from health care-- was signed by Nixon. Though I was not a blood relation to Cass, I could act like one. Since she was conscious, however, I didn't have to make decisions on her behalf.

Not really knowing Cass' whole health history, what childhood diseases she might have had, or if she'd ever had any surgeries, I finished up with what I could of the paperwork. I put down what I knew, including what was happening now, namely that she was suffering from anorexia nervosa and that she was experiencing bleeding from the vaginal area, but hadn't menstruated for over a year.

I set the papers back on the counter and went down the hall to find where they'd taken her. Parting the curtain a bit, I walked right in, and no one told me to leave. The doctor on call was young, and I assumed he must have been a resident. There was a nurse in there, too.

"How is she?" I asked, making my presence known.

"She's stable. Not bleeding, that we can tell, " the doctor said, adding, "Her blood pressure is pretty low, though."

I walked closer to Cass and asked how she felt. She just shook her head "no." She was certainly not feeling great.

"We did a quick pelvic exam and have a hunch she may have uterine prolapse, " said the doctor.

I must have looked like I had no idea what he was talking about, because he motioned for me to follow him out to the hallway.

"Are you related to her? " he asked.

"I'm not…but a very close friend. What is that condition you just said?"

"Uterine prolapse. Her uterus is slipping down the birth canal or vagina rather than staying in its place."

"Oh, God. What in the world causes that?"

"Well, believe it or not, it is usually the obese women who are prone to this, or women who have had many children. However, we see it present in anorexia nervosa patients, also. They often lose weight very quickly, and so **much** weight that it causes amenorrhea, which is the cessation of menstruation. That in turn causes a major drop in estrogen hormone production, coupled with sudden electrolyte imbalance. All that can lead to uterine prolapse. "

Christ. I'd never heard of any of that.

"What can you do for her?"

"Typically what would happen now, I'd say, is a hysterectomy, but we'll have to call in an Ob/Gyn on a consultation. The problem is, she's not in any condition to undergo surgery just now. Her weight is only eighty-one pounds and there is a risk of putting her under general anesthesia, because another result of anorexia can be weakening of the heart. I believe she also has a condition called bradycardia, which is slow heart rhythm."

"And? What does that do?"

"Well, it can be a factor in sudden acute ventricular arrhythmia, which is serious."

"So are you saying that she might not even be strong enough to withstand surgery to correct the uterine...thingy?"

"Prolapse. Yes. She may not be able to tolerate anesthesia."

"But you... don't...you can't... mean she could die on the table or something, do you?"

"She could go into cardiac arrest during the surgery. Or afterwards."

I was reeling at this completely unexpected horrible news, but felt I had to buck up and be brave for Cass's sake. I thanked him for talking to me, and asked if Dr. Pauline Bertram could be called in on the case, since we needed an Ob/Gyn.

"I'll check into that, " he answered. "Does she know the patient?"

"No, she knows me. My name was Sarah Shrier when I was her patient."

"Okay, I'll get in touch with her."

"That'd be great, " I said, feeling some relief.

"Also, "he added, "does the patient have actual relatives in town?"

"She does."

"You might want to let them know her situation."

"Can I talk that over with her first?" I asked.

"Sure."

I nodded and went back into the ER and Cass's little space. Cass was lying on her side whimpering.

"Are you in pain?" I asked right away.

Her voice was very small but she told me no. "I'm just so fucked."

"Hang in there."

Another nurse came in, interrupting our conversation, and said that they would like to admit her, and that if I waited back in the reception area, she would come get me as soon as they had Cass in a room upstairs.

"It will be on the fifth floor. I'll come down and get you."

So I went out to the waiting room area and leafed through a copy of *Mademoiselle* Magazine's Christmas issue from three months prior. I started to read an article about "Cheery clothes and things to make even if you're all thumbs, " but I couldn't concentrate on anything besides trying to digest what had been explained to me about Cass' medical situation.

It had taken over an hour for them to examine her and get her into a room, and, by the time I was summoned to go up to the fifth floor and could see her, visiting hours had long since ceased. They let me go in anyway. She was in a private corner room, much nicer than the one I'd been in years ago. I was glad they put her in a private one, but felt remiss in not having been the one to request it.

I went over to the head of the bed which was half blocked by a nightstand. "Cass, " I said gingerly, "they think it'd be best if your parents were told about this."

"Yeah, that's okay. You can call them. They'd find out sooner or later anyway."

"Okay, good, I will. " I paused but then continued on. "So, they explained to you about uterine prolapse and everything?"

"Yes. I have to have a hysterectomy, don't I? Isn't that the irony of ironies, though? I got pregnant when I wasn't prepared for it, and now won't be able to have any more children if I decide I want them."

I wasn't showing yet, but it didn't escape my mind that I was standing there pregnant all the while she was reeling under the news that she never would be again.

"Well, I know, but you have two of the most terrific ones now."

"How are they, by the way? I miss my babies."

"You know, sweetie, I haven't been home yet. But I'm sure they're fine, and I'll bring them to see you right away tomorrow morning."

685

A nurse's aide came in and tinkered with the bed to make it go up so Cass would be in a sitting position. She had brought in some broth for Cass to drink. Without asking if Cass wanted it, she opened the lid and set it down on the bed tray, pushing it over in front of her patient.

"We'd like you to drink this, " she said in a nice but authoritative voice. She stood there for a minute waiting for Cass to start drinking, and when she wouldn't, the tone became more forceful. "Come on now, let's give this a try, okay?"

I shot her a look that said, "Lay off" and scooted over to put my arm around Cass's shoulders and prop her up a little closer to the tray table.

Cass acted like she was being made to drink cyanide. She closed her eyes and crinkled up her nose to take a tiny sip, after which she pronounced it abominable.

"You can do better than that, " the nurse's aide called out as she was leaving the room.

"Oh brother, " I said, "is this what you're going to have to put up with in here? What a jerk."

Cass was agitated. "They'll put me on a feeding tube, won't they?" she whimpered.

I hadn't even considered that. I thought feeding tubes were only for people who were unconscious!

"Oh, hell no! But… just give it another go… you know, so you won't make them mad, " I cajoled her.

She took the cup in her bony fingers and looked at me out of the corner of her eye. It was the old habit of not eating in the presence of anyone that was flaring up again, I thought. So I went to the other side of her bed to reach the phone.

"I've got to get home, you know? It's almost midnight! I'm going to call Polo from your phone, if that's okay." It didn't matter if it was or not; he was paying for the hospital room after all.

Polo answered on his end, and I let him know I'd take a cab and be there soon.

"Oh no, darling. Jean-Luc is right here waiting with me for your call. He'll come get you."

"Oh, gosh, that's so nice of him. Tell him I'll be at the regular entrance on Erie Street."

I kissed Cass on the cheek, told her I'd be back first thing in the morning, and left her room. Out at the nurses' station, I asked which bank of elevators would take me to the main hospital entrance and then waited down there for Jean-Luc. He came in the Citroën and I climbed into the front seat with him.

"How is she?" he asked kindly.

"Not too damn good!" I replied, feeling overwhelmed and helpless at the same time.

"The children are fine, " he said, reading my mind. "You were right about Alicia…she's wonderful with them. She put them in the bedroom off the kitchen on the third floor, rather than so far from you in one of the big ones on the second."

"That's a good idea, " I said. "That way they won't be too scared if they wake up and their mom isn't there."

"She stayed with them until they fell asleep, " he said, and laughed, "she may still be there, for all I know."

"That is above and beyond. And so is this, by the way. And thank you for coming on the trip and all. I really appreciate it."

"Je vous en prie. Ne vous en faites pas!"

I walked into our house pretty exhausted, and went up to the third floor where Polo was waiting for me in the room closest to the elevator, which was the library. My forlorn and weary demeanor must have been a give-away to him, and he gestured for me to come over to his embrace. I just started sobbing and sobbing, and in between heaves and floods of tears, I told him that her condition was serious and that she could, in fact, die from it.

"Anorexia nervosa has destroyed her, " I wept. "Her uterus has detached from its normal place and is coming out through the birth canal! Can you even imagine?!"

"No, darling, I cannot," he answered sadly.

"And her heart's weak also, " I whimpered. "Anorexia, it turns out, is just slow suicide. I'm actually getting angry at her now! How could she do this to me!"

"But Sarah, *calme-toi*! You mustn't think this has anything to do with you."

"**Yes it does!**" I sobbed again. "How could she leave me?"

Polo looked at me with the most unhappy demeanor I'd ever seen on him, at least not since that night I exposed Robineau. I'm sure he was concerned about Cass, and wrought with anxiety over how I was taking it, but, as I wallowed in self-pity, I also wondered if Polo had thoughts that I valued Cass' love above his. I was afraid my unthinking comment may have hurt his feelings, and it struck me that I probably owed him an apology, but I found myself unable to acknowledge my self-absorbed thoughts. Instead, I plunged ahead with the business at hand as though it hadn't happened.

"I need to call her parents, but it's too late now, isn't it?"

He looked at his watch and nodded. "The morning will be soon enough."

"What a fucking goddamn mess this whole thing is!" I cried out, really to myself. "If she doesn't get better, Alan will take the children away from her. He really will be able to prove in court that she's an unfit mother."

"Sarah, you cannot let these thoughts and events overtake you. You are doing everything in your power to help her, and so am I... doing everything I can to help you."

"Yes, I know you are, and I love you for it. And I'm grateful, I really am."

"Darling, you are carrying our child now. You have to stay calm."

"Yeah, I will. I'm fine. Please try not to worry about me so much."

Unlike my best friend, who was now fighting for her life, I was in the peak of health, getting excellent pre-natal care. And even though there were lots of things I did worry about in the first trimester of my pregnancy, stress wasn't one of them. I was told that stress may, yes, exert an effect on the baby's development, that long-term stress releases hormones that could actually cause a premature birth, but I didn't have long-term stress, and I was sure there wouldn't be any negative effects on my child. I knew Polo was reading up on pregnancy issues and medical stuff, and I wished he weren't. It was making him more anxiety-prone and causing him to be even more over-protective of me than he usually was.

Polo and I went to bed. It was very late. I wasn't too keen on having intercourse while preggers, but I did snuggle up and cuddle with him every night. I realized I had to reassure him that everything was great with us and our baby. I just couldn't manage to do a decent job of suppressing all my own heightened emotions over Cass. I resolved, lying on his shoulder, to do better.

The next morning, quite early so as to catch them at home, if they were indeed in town, I phoned the Hydes. I recognized the voice of their housekeeper Lottie Brandon on the line. I told her who I was vis-à-vis Cass and she said she remembered me. I was in luck that the Hydes were there and that John-Wilfred had not yet left for work. Lottie told him who was on the phone and he picked up with a rather chipper greeting to me.

"Sarah...er... Sari! Good morning! What can I do for you?" He must have been surprised that I would be calling him.

"Good morning, Mr. Hyde, " I said hoping my voice didn't crack. "I'm sorry to call you at home. I need to tell you that Cass is here in Chicago, and she's in the hospital—at the Med Center."

"She's here? In Chicago? In the hospital? What happened?"

"Well, I – uh- my husband and I—I'm recently married -- Cass is very sick...she....we just flew to El Paso Texas and brought her and her children back with us. Alan didn't come....he's still in El Paso."

"Texas? And you say she's ill?"

"Yes, extremely. I think you and Mrs. Hyde should go over to the hospital right away – this morning. I'm leaving in a few minutes to take the kids to see her."

"What's wrong with her, exactly?"

"Um, do you remember that time you were visiting her in Iowa City and she was so thin and you thought she was anemic? Well, turns out she was actually starting to suffer from a disease...it's called anorexia nervosa. They don't eat and after a while everything just goes downhill from there. She weighs eighty-one pounds."

"My god. "

"She's in the hospital now with complications, including a condition called uterine prolapse plus she has a weakened heart. The doctors really think you should be with her."

"I see...Julia and I will come right away...see you there, then?"

"Okay, good. I'm sure you will be happy to see your grandchildren, too! They're wonderful."

687

"Are they? Thank you for calling us, Sari. We'll see you at the hospital. And Sari, I did see something in the paper that you were married -- to Mr. d'Arivèque -- so congratulations!"

"Yes, Jean-Paul d'Arivèque. We met through my work at the Foundation."

"That's terrific."

"I can't wait to introduce him to you, " I said, and we both said good-bye.

I jumped into the shower and afterwards, put on what I wanted to be a "cheery" outfit, as much for myself as for the kids. I picked out a violet purple and blue flowered Laura Ashley "sack" dress with a flowing skirt and a little white laced collar. I paired it with a light purple cardigan and even threw on pearls.

I ordered breakfast for the twins to be brought up to our kitchen on the third floor, and then I went in to wake them. I dressed them alike this time in one of the many outfits I'd bought for them that Cass had packed.

"We're going to see Momma this morning, okay?" I told Paul and Laura, who were sitting at the table eating oatmeal and toast with marmalade. They nodded, and kept on eating. "You both are good little eaters, aren't you?!" I exclaimed.

"It tastes good Auntie Sari."

"Did you have fun with Uncle Polo last night?"

"Yes, "said Laura. "He read us a story."

"Oh, good. He's a great reader, isn't he?"

"Why is Mommy sick?" Paul asked in an uncharacteristically sad voice.

"Well, she's just awfully…uh…tired, and doesn't feel well." I really stumbled at that one. How could I explain what was the matter with their mother to three-and-a-half year-olds? "When she sees you, though, she'll feel better!"

"Where's our daddy?" asked Laura.

Good question! The sonofabitch would also have to be told where Cass was, I reckoned.

"He's still back home teaching, " I told them.

I cut the conversation short so I could get them into their jackets and down to the car. I had a kid's hand in each of mine, and Polo took hold of my arm as we all went together in the elevator.

"Why do you have an elevator in your house, Auntie Sari?" Laura wanted to know.

"Oh, I guess because it's so big, " I answered, hoping that would suffice and I wouldn't have to go into how Uncle Polo can't walk up stairs.

"Yah, it's pretty big," echoed Paul.

When we got to her room, Julia and John-Wilfred Hyde were already there! Cass' bed was raised up at the head and she was propped up on more pillows. Her gaunt face lit up when she saw her children. Her parents stepped away from the bed and the kids ran up to it. She could reach down to hug them with her bony arms around one each.

Polo and I approached the Hydes for formal introductions. John-Wilfred shook Polo's hand warmly and kissed me on the cheek. Julia and I also sort of air-kissed each other, and she surprised me by saying how happy she was for us, adding that when she read about it, she realized who Polo was and that she had known his mother.

"Of course, I knew Marie-Aveline from the Symphony Board!" And then turning to the kids, she just stared at them a moment. , "My God, they look just like their father, " she whispered. "Those ringlets of blond hair and those blue eyes."

"I know!" I said, but I was still quite sad that they didn't get the beauty that was their mother's when I first met her. Not that they weren't darling; they were. Both of them had grown into round-faced little sprites with rosy cheeks and happy dispositions.

Cass wasn't paying any attention to us since she was engrossed with her children, so the parents asked us to accompany them out to the hall for a minute.

"Did you speak to the doctors yet?" I asked.

"Yes, and one of them told me you asked for her to be on the case. I appreciate that, Sari, " said Julia.

"Yes, well, she's great." I turned to Polo and informed him I had asked for Dr. Bertram to consult.

"Ah, yes," he said to the Hydes, "she is Sarah's doctor…and a dear friend."

"So…we've decided, "said John-Wilfred, "to contact Alan Jones and tell him what is going on."

I nodded, thinking it was a crappy idea, but inevitable, given the prognosis we were all facing.

"Of course, you know, they want to operate on her, but consider it a huge risk. But they have to do it."

"Can't they wait just a few more days to give her a chance to stabilize more?"

"Not really, " said her father. "Her condition is critical with this uterine prolapse business."

I saw that the Hydes were genuinely concerned about their daughter, and Julia confirmed it with me. Out in the hall, she took me aside and confided to me that she now felt bad that she hadn't flown with her husband to Iowa City that time, and that this very morning she had told Cass she was sorry for having cut short her university years. She said she'd asked Cass to forgive her.

"I love her and I hope made that clear to her, " Julia proclaimed to me. "I told her that I would love to have the children stay with us while she recuperated."

I just stood there pretty startled for a minute. There wasn't much I could say except that it made me happy to hear that a reconciliation of some sort had taken place between them. Julia added that she was thankful I'd called them, and that she'd had time to have a real heart-to-heart with Cass. I nodded and then it hit me that Julia was talking as though she thought Cass might really die! I opened my mouth to refute that, but all at once John-Wilfred came over to suggest we go back in the room lest we would arouse concern in Cass.

She, in turn, was anxious to have her children meet their grandparents.

"What shall they call you?" Cass asked her mother, but Polo intervened into the conversation.

"You know, in France, we call our grandparents *Mamie* and *Papi*, "he said to the twins.

"Mee-mee and Pop-pop?" asked Laura, not having understood.

"Close enough, " Cass laughed.

Julia and John-Wilfred were not as cold as I expected them to be towards their new offspring either. In fact, when the nurse came in to check Cass' vitals, Julia wondered if we all wouldn't like to go with Mee-mee and Pop-pop to have some hot chocolate in the cafeteria and let Momma get some rest.

"Let Sari stay here, " Cass said, "I need to talk to her."

"Okay, " said Julia. "What about you Mr. d'Arivèque?"

"I should love to accompany you, " he said, adding, " and please, you must call me Jean-Paul."

They all traipsed out with John-Wilfred bringing up the rear, holding his arm up as if to sweep them all out. I heard Julia mention the name Georg Solti as they left the room.

"Sari, I want to talk to you about the kids."

"Shoot, " I said, pulling a chair right up to the bed.

"Will you agree to take them if something happens to me?"

"But, Cass, I'm expecting—you know-- my first child right now. That would mean we'd become a family of five right away!"

"Yes, so?"

"Well, yeah, I guess I see your point. We can certainly afford it and I already love them. But what about your parents?"

"They wouldn't do it!"

"Oh, gee, you don't know. I can't see them letting Alan have them!"

"No but with you having them, they won't have to ever see Alan."

"I can dig that."

"But, for now, you know, he is their father, so he has all the rights. If I left a document saying you were to get custody, he would probably fight you."

"Cass, this is all conjecture. You're not going anywhere! You might be in the hospital for quite a while, but Alan can't just come and grab them away from you. Your parents and my husband all have batteries of lawyers who would make things very hard on Alan if he tried anything."

"I may not make it, you know that."

"Cass, you simply have to get well. You must decide to and then do it. You…you just can't leave me! You can't let me go through pregnancy and childbirth alone now, can you?!"

689

I was being half-way facetious, but she wasn't having any of that.

"Sari!" she snapped, "I can't be there for you!! I can't even be here for ME!"

She flopped back onto the bed and turned on her side to cry. I got up and leaned over the mattress to stroke her hair.

"Come on, Cass, I didn't mean it that way. I'm sorry, okay? You just have to get well, that's all that matters. Of course, I'll take your children if the powers that be will let me. Don't worry about anything. Just rest. Try to be calm."

She continued to sob into the pillow when I noticed bright red blood oozing onto the sheets.

"OH SHIT!" I hissed, and ran out of her room to get help.

Nurses rushed in and very quickly undid the various monitors she was hooked up to, and rolled the bed right out of there in a big hurry.

I didn't know where they were taking Cass but I suspected into emergency surgery. I ran to the elevators to go find the others.

I found Polo, and the Hydes, and trying not to show too much alarm in front of the kids, I said we'd all better get back up there and told them what had happened.

We sat in Cass' room and a different nurse came in to inform us that she had indeed been taking into surgery and that Dr. Bertram had come right over. Polo wondered if Dr. Fabrizio Garabanti could do the surgery.

"I don't think he's on call, " said the nurse, but she agreed to check on it.

"Oh, do you know Fabrizio, too? " Julia asked him.

"Yes, *Madame*. He is also a great friend of mine. I am sure that if he is indeed here, he will help us."

Julia realized that she was talking to someone who might have been his patient as well as his friend, as she looked over at his braced leg.

John-Wilfred asked me if I had Alan Jones' phone number by any chance, and I did! I kept a small leather address book with all my friends' and relatives' addresses and phone numbers in my purse at all times. I took it out and gave it to him, and he, in turn, picked up the hospital phone in Cass' room and directed his office to get ahold of Alan and tell him that his wife was in the hospital in Chicago and perhaps he would like to come be with his children.

"Tell him that I will pay for him to stay in a hotel here, " Cass' father added.

I sneered as I overhead this conversation, thinking it'd be about the last thing Alan would want to do.

A nurse came back in and told us we could wait at the surgical floor waiting rooms if we wanted to. The doctors would come out and talk to us after it was over, she said. There was even a playroom that the kids could go to on that floor.

"That's a great idea!" said Julia. "Do you want to come with –uh—Mee-mee to play?"

"Yaaayyy!" they said, first one and then the other.

At least they have each other, I rationalized, because I couldn't bear to think of them as orphans.

The rest of us went to wait it out together. My palms were sweaty and I felt like my heart would give out from beating so hard. She could die in there or she could survive it and still die. She could survive and live, of course, but given her condition, I was beginning to see that the twins could easily be at our place up to or past my own due date of mid-September, because Cass was going to need so much rehab and treatment for the anorexia, not to mention the heart problems. Well, that would just have to be, then, I said to myself. I was sure Polo wouldn't object, and we had enough staff to keep everything going. I was, after all, only nominally the lady of the house.

Julia reappeared with the kids before we had any news.

"Sari, " she said, "I think I'm just going to call for my car and take the children home with me to Kenilworth. Do you think that would be all right with Cass? We have some toys still around someplace, and my housekeeper and staff will take very good care of them. It's no fun waiting at a hospital for a mommy who might not even be awake for hours. What do you say? That way I can come back here and wait with John-Wilfrid."

Her request took me completely by surprise.

"I—um—well—sure, I think that would be fine, Julia, " I said, smiling. Cass wouldn't find out about it until much later and she and her mother could duke it out if necessary as to where the kids should stay while she was recuperating.

"All their stuff is at our house, though, including their toys."

"Oh, we'll bring them back later this afternoon. Hopefully they can see their mom then and go home with you."

"Okay. That will work." I thought they should get to know their grandparents and if she was willing to let that happen, who was I to thwart her good intentions?

In the meantime, John-Wilfred Hyde's personal secretary showed up at the hospital and was sent to find us in the surgery wing. She said she had spoken to Alan Jones, and that he would drive up to Chicago and be there in the next two days if possible. Cass had told me it had been a twenty-hour trip from Iowa City, which they broke up into two full days of driving. Chicago was another three, almost four hours from there. We shouldn't expect to see him before Cass had been out of surgery for two full days, really, so I put that out of my mind.

Finally Dr. Garabanti came out of the OR pulling off his mask, his blue scrubs splattered with blood. He came over to where we were gathered on the couch. "She made it through the operation, " he said breathlessly.

"Oh thank GOD!" I cried out, realizing that my hands were shaking as I put my head in them.

"She's not out of the woods by any means, however, " he said. "We have her lightly sedated and will keep her that way. Her blood pressure is low and her breathing is shallow."

"Thank you, doctor. We are so grateful, " said John-Wilfred, offering his hand.

"You're welcome," replied Fabrizio. "I didn't realize at first that this was your daughter—er—and Julia's. And my dear chap, Polo! What are you doing here?"

"The young woman you just operated on is a close friend of my wife's."

"My God. What a small world we do inhabit, " he said, laughing. "How is my former patient? I had a wonderful time at your wedding party, my dear. *Mazel Tov* again!"

John-Wilfred knew nothing about my having had surgery from this same doctor, but given Garabanti's world-wide reputation, he couldn't have been very surprised.

What was astonishing to me was the way that the upper echelons of Chicago society were woven in and out of the same organizations, causes, charities and cultural worlds. They didn't always know one another, but they knew the names. The Hydes had obviously crossed paths with Maman d'Arivèque *many times, but they didn't necessarily put two and two together about her son, let alone her son and me. It occurred to me that after this we might be seeing a lot more of each other. I had great hopes for a grand reconciliation between Cass and her parents and I envisaged a life in Chicago that finally included my best friend and-- the frosting on the cake-- seeing the twins grow up. They would be four years older than our child, but that wasn't insurmountable. I started day-dreaming about how they would all be great friends.*

"When can we see Cass?" I asked the doctor eagerly.

"Not for some while, I'm afraid. We're keeping her in the ICU for the time being."

"Intensive care? Wow. Okay, this is still really bad, then, isn't it?"

"I'm afraid it's not good," he replied, not mocking me at all. "So the family can visit her once on the hour for about ten minutes."

"Just…the family?" I asked, incredulous that I had come all that way with her in the years between 1966 and now, and wouldn't be able to be with her during this crisis.

"Well, we can bend the rules for you, Sarah."

"Oh thank you!" I wanted to hug him.

It turned out that Julia didn't have plans to camp out at any hospitals waiting to see her estranged daughter for ten minutes of every hour. Her father couldn't be there too much longer either, since he had an empire to run, and my sweet Polo, who didn't want to leave me alone for a second, also had to go into his office. So, between the bending of the rules and people going off to do other things, it really was just me up there most of the time. I always carried a notebook in my purse, so I took it out and wrote *Moments Culturels* during the time I wasn't in with Cass. And when I was in with her, she was pretty much non-responsive. But I talked and talked to her.

691

"Oh Cassssss?" I cooed. "Guess who's here to seeeee you? I can bring Laura and Paul, too, " I assured her. Whether the twins were in Kenilworth or back at my mansion in the good care of Alicia, I could summon them to be with their mother with one phone call.

I gave Cass pep talks, telling her she had to get well, or that there was a movie I was dying to see with her, or that it would be so great for her to convalesce at our place because we'd have so much fun! I told her what the Chicago weather was and what books I'd been reading.

"I just finished *Jonathan Livingston Seagull*, and wanted to throw it across the room when I got done, not because I didn't like it, but because I was mad I hadn't written it! Isn't that a kill? It's just like that time Soren and I were in the bookstore, and he felt the same way about *Love Story*!"

There wasn't any response from Cass to any of my soliloquies. I began to wonder if they had indeed "lightly" sedated her or if they'd put her in a medically induced coma. The ten minutes I was allotted always flew by and then I would work for the rest of the hour until I could see her again.

When, after two days, her vital signs stabilized once again, they moved her out of the ICU and into a different room, this time on the same surgical floor I'd been on. It had a solarium at the end of the hall which was quite lovely, where we could gather if we didn't want to all be in her room at the same time.

By the third day after surgery, Cass had not awakened, but she was breathing on her own, which I took to be a good sign. The Hydes, Polo and I, and even sometimes with the twins, took turns with her in the room. The kids couldn't understand why their mommy didn't answer them when they spoke to her, so we kept their visits to a minimum. It just confused them. I didn't have a lot to speak about to the Hydes, but they weren't cold to me at all.

And then Alan arrived. He asked to talk to her doctors, and, identifying himself as the husband, was allowed access to all medical staff, who discussed with him the prognosis. He then went straight to the third floor and found me first.

"Miss Shrier! How is she?" He seemed chipper and smiled at me.

I wasn't smiling back. We went into the hall by the solarium door to talk.

"You know what, I'm not Miss Shrier anymore!" *Asshole.* "She's not good, as I'm sure you can imagine."

"Well, I've come to take the kids back with me."

"Oh you have, have you? Well, we'll just see about that. When she wakes up, she'll be wanting to see them first thing."

"From what I've been told that could be a long time from now."

"Who said that? She's just sedated now because the surgery was so traumatic. She's got a bad heart, in case you're interested."

"Look Sari," he said pulling my arm towards a bench right outside the solarium a few steps from her room. "Anorexia nervosa changed her into another person, and you know that. She hasn't been the girl I married for over a year now."

Just then, a woman with long blond hair wearing a bomber jacket and boots came up to him.

"Sari, this is Donna. We were in the Workshop together and she also works at UTEP with me. Donna, this is Sari Shrier, Cass' best friend."

"You brought **her** up here with you!!?" I was flabbergasted. It would have plunged a dagger into Cass' already weak heart if she knew, and if I'd had one, I'd have made a pre-emptive strike and done it to him in her name.

"Nice to meet you, too, " Donna said sarcastically.

Alan's tone also turned impudent. "We're not staying in Chicago and the Hydes can save their money. We're just picking up Laura and Paul and then we're out of here."

It panicked me to think that he could walk out of there with the kids and we'd never see them again. I toned down my rhetoric and tried to stall him a little. "Are you at least going to speak to the Hydes? I think they might want to see you or something. Shall I go get them?"

"Yeah, go ahead."

I went in to get them. Julia refused to see him, but John-Wilfred took each twin by the hand and led them out. I followed them, and Polo followed me. Alan and Donna had moved into the solarium which was empty, and when he saw his kids, he waved to them. When they realized their father was there, they

692

were happy and squealed "Daddy!" at him. He held out his arms and they ran into them. He looked up and saw us all coming, so he motioned for Donna to take the kids off via the stairwell.

"Go down to the main lobby to wait for me, " I heard him tell her.

As John-Wilfred approached, Alan stood up, but it wasn't necessarily a sign of respect, more like a stance for a show-down.

"I'll be taking my kids back to Texas, Mr. Hyde," he said.

"I wish you wouldn't, " said John-Wilfred. "My daughter will be bereft when she wakes up and finds out what happened to her children."

"That could be weeks. They need a parent."

"Oh, now you're a **parent**?!" I screamed. "After you abandoned them all in that isolated slum!"

Polo had caught up to us all from down the hall, and came up to me, taken aback at my behavior. "Sarah! Please!"

Alan ignored me, and told John-Wilfred that he would be living full time in El Paso now and gave him his card. John-Wilfred said that he intended to send his staff to New Mexico to clean out Cass' things.

"Be my guest, " replied Alan with a sneer.

John-Wilfred pivoted and went back down the hall to Cass' room, and when he was out of hearing, I turned back to Alan and went off on him again.

"Alan! You ASSHOLE! This is all your fault!!!"

Polo was extremely uncomfortable at my public display of animosity, and at the same time very worried about what an emotional outburst could do to his unborn child.

"*Chérie s'il te plaît! Calme-toi!! Calme-toi!*" And he went up to Alan to introduce himself. "I am Jean-Paul d'Arivèque, Sarah's husband. How do you do?"

"Nice to meet you. She's a little wigged out; I dig it. "

"You just wait, " I snarled. "The Hydes have a legal team that will annihilate you! If they file for custody of the twins, they'll crush you, and I'll testify on their behalf!"

"*Oh, là, là, là, là, là, là,* " Polo droned.

"I mean it!!" I was right up in Alan's face. "Abandonment! A mistress!! You bring your fucking mistress to your wife's sickbed? Are you fucking insane?!! You arrogant prick!"

This time Polo let his cane fall and he grabbed my arm and pulled me towards him. He couldn't really lead me away, however, so I just stood there seething. Alan got up and just shook his head as he sort of laughed off my rant.

"Nice to meet you, Mr...." he let his voice trail off and made a gesture in the air as though to say, "whatever your name is."

"Sari, the Hydes know where I am. And by the way, the court doesn't usually take kids away from the biological parent."

And with that he turned and headed for the stairwell.

"Yeah, well biological parent is ALL you are. YOU FUCKER!"

Polo was not happy with me at all. In fact, it was the first time he'd ever shown disappointment or anger with me that wasn't tempered by hurt. This time, I hadn't done anything to him, but he still took mighty offense at his wife's crude outbursts. He took hold of my arm, probably afraid I'd run after Alan on the stairs. I couldn't look at him, but I jerked my arm out of his grasp.

"Let go of me! I need to get back in there. " I picked up his cane and handed it to him, huffing away before he could say anything more to me.

When I got to the room, though, residents and nurses were swarming around Cass' bed, and her parents were off to the side of the room frozen with fear. I recoiled as I came in and saw the scene. Cass lay lifeless on the bed.

"OH GOD!" I wailed. "NO!!! Oh no!! No... oh please... no...no... no!"

"Sari, come over here with us, " Julia said. I burst into tears.

The young resident doctor moved out of the group and looked at us, shaking his head.

"I'm so sorry, " he said, and left the room.

I became engulfed in hysterics and even Julia and John-Wilfred showed more emotion than they had the entire time Cass was ill. They both wept a bit, all the while trying to comfort me. Polo had come back in time to see this horror story unfolding. His anger with me melted away, and he just hastened to my side to hold me.

Every time I glanced at Cass motionless in the bed a few feet away, I became convulsed all over again with grief. I was gasping for air, crying, and clinging to Polo.

"Oh my God," I sobbed, " she's **dead**!" It was as if I needed to say it out loud to believe it.

Self-pity overwhelmed me as much as sadness for Cass. I wasn't proud of that, and was especially aware that my feelings were a monumental set-back to my sworn "adult Sari" persona.

All I could think of was how alone I felt, and whatever was I going to do now… without her?

FIRST EPILOGUE

"Fire and Rain"..,James Taylor

Cass was gone. Just like that. She had simply vanished from my life... like a dream at dawn.

For some time I found myself floating despondently in a fog of abject denial. For weeks I still had lingering feelings of anger mixed with a hearty dose of guilt over her death. Everywhere I turned, I expected to see her. If the phone rang in my office, I assumed it was her. Or I'd think of something I had to tell her, and then go into shock all over again that she wasn't there for me to call. If some memory of us together would drift into my consciousness, I would dissolve into floods of tears. Often the crying jags would just overtake me without warning. I couldn't seem to shake off the wretchedness I felt; the sorrow stabbed me in the gut each time it reared up. It threatened to turn into self-loathing, and even though I tried to talk myself out of **that**, at least, and give myself a break, I couldn't. I wasn't stiff upper lip at all.

"It probably does not help that hormones are raging inside your pregnant body," Annie-Laure said one day when she saw me crying through the glass walls, and came into my office. She put her arm around my shoulders. "I know your husband is worried."

Jean-Paul d'Arivèque could see that I was inconsolable, and he didn't push me to "get over it" or anything of that sort; but I didn't want him to see the depths to which I had plunged. I tried to hide it from him because he already worried too much about my emotional state. In fact, Polo was doing everything in his power to help and support me. Mourn her, yes, but also cope with the loss. He actually tried often to draw me into conversation about Cass, feeling that it would help the healing process.

"I shouldn't have nagged her so much, " I would sob to him when remorse overtook me. "She told me that I just swept in and took charge. I was only ever trying to help her! I was always, always on her side."

He tried to offer his interpretation of events. "Please, darling, do not make all this worse by blaming yourself. Part of the anguish you are experiencing is that you were not prepared for her to be as ill as she had become in El Paso, no? Her last phone call to you was a cry for help, do you not think so?"

"I guess you're right."

"When we saw her there, it was a shock. She so was painfully thin, Sarah. I could feel her unhappiness merely by looking at her, and I suspect you knew in your heart that the situation was desperate."

"The fact is, Polo, I don't really understand anorexia nervosa. Cass had what would seem to me to be the most wonderful childhood. I mean, not with her parents, I'll grant you that. But her houses were veritable dream palaces...her room in Kenilworth would have been my heart's desire. She was sent to terrific schools and camps and world travels. She had every material possession she ever wanted. Her clothes were beyond beautiful. SHE was beautiful...inside, too. And yet, even at Iowa, she always doubted who she was. It became apparent to me that she felt she couldn't live up to the expectations she set for herself, even as an artist. She was never confident in herself, especially with such indifferent parents, particularly her domineering mother. And then her marriage with a dismissive husband is where things really fell apart. But I still don't really get it."

"But, chérie, her life must have been quite lonely, do you not see it? Except for the parts of it shared with you, I mean to say. And do you not realize that she expressed this loneliness by eating—or rather not eating? Her food deprivation—and also the binging—they are a direct assertion of her feelings."

"That would mean she knew what she was doing, though! No. I can't accept that!"

"But my sweetheart, perhaps you must."

"No!" I started to sob again, and between gulps for air stated, "I firmly believe...know...that her eating disorder just got out of control. I can't make myself accept that she was trying to...you know...kill herself."

He took me in his embrace. "Now, there, I believe you, darling. Shhhh. Even on the plane back, I know you talked about her getting well and recuperating at our house, and then how happy you would be to have her in the same town again."

695

He was right about all that. I did envision her at our house, regaining strength…and weight…all the while bringing up her children in our midst.

"I had a jolly little fantasy about her being back in Chicago with me, I'll admit it," I conceded to him, managing to laugh a little. "Sort of the textbook definition of *naïveté*, huh?"

"Perhaps," said Polo, looking at me with reverence in his face, "but also love. You are lucky, Sarah. Do you know why? Because love never dies. Yes, your heart is broken, but Cass is in there, among the pieces."

"I'm lucky to have you, is what I'm really lucky for."

Polo caressed my cheek and cupped my face in his hand. "Sarah, nothing that happened to Cass was your fault or your doing. Please forgive yourself, darling. Promise me. You must. You know I cannot bear to see you suffering."

So I tried harder after that not to agonize so palpably, at least not in the office, because I did realize it upset him to see me so lost in grief. Now that we were working right next door to each other in a big glass bowl, I made a concerted effort to stay very busy and in control of my emotions.

Polo often invited me to lunch at fine Chicago restaurants, but he was also booked up with myriad noon meetings, and so from time to time I reprised my former rendezvous routine with Woolworth's lunch counter.

One time in late March I was on my way back to work and suddenly, once again, overtaken by sorrow, I decided to just walk it off, and went out window shopping, hoping, in vain, to see in the new displays on Michigan Avenue any hints of a budding Spring. At one juncture, I caught sight in a store window, not of any metaphorical crocuses or buds, but of myself. I let out an audible gasp. I had been scolded by Dr. Bertram to gain weight, and even though I as yet had only a slight beginning of a thickening under my winter coat, my face had taken on the distinctly recognizable aspect of a full moon.

All at once, I made the decision to change my appearance. This was a sort of corollary to the epiphany I'd had in the *Parc Monceau*: If I were to put on the mantle of adult Sarah-- *Madame* d'Arivèque, mother-to-be-- getting rid of student Sari Shrier would further that goal. What was really going on, however, was that I just never wanted to glimpse myself again in any mirror and see the Sari I was when Cass was still alive. When we were Sari and Cass.

I went straight into Saks to the hair salon, where I barged right up to reception without an appointment, and begged to see any hairdresser who happened to be free. A Mr. Demitri took me in, and I asked him to cut three inches off my hair, and shape it into an inverted bob, making the back short and the sides noticeably longer in front. I kept the bangs. Since this was such an impulse move, naturally, I hadn't consulted Polo, and only presented it to him as a *fait accompli*. He was surprised but asked for no explanation, and I offered none.

"You are very beautiful, " he said, motioning for me to turn around so he could see the whole effect. "I like it very much."

"And what if I had shaved it all off or dyed it pink?" I laughed.

"Then I would love you just the same, " he asserted. And I believed him.

The next thing I did was clear out my closets. Luckily I had saved the huge box from Polo's amazing gift dress all those months earlier, a fortunate foreshadowing of the possibility it would come in handy someday. I took it down from the shelf, and used it to pack away all the clothes that Cass had ever given me: the blue dress with the pink sash from college, the Scottish kilt from England, the fisherman knit sweater; and the Chanel jumper with its blouse. I also put in the red purse from *La Bagagerie,* and the faithful little transistor radio. They were precious keepsakes to me, but I just couldn't bear to have them around reminding me not only of her but of us. I kept out the fur hood and the Hermès gloves that had been Christmas presents to me from the Hydes. I couldn't do without the hood, and the gloves went so well with my camel coat, that even though seeing them made me feel sad, I reasoned that maybe by next winter--by the time it got cold enough again to wear them—then perhaps I'd be able to appreciate something that would make me think of her.

I stored away the box with Cass' outfits, and kept the wardrobe Polo had bought me in Paris, which of course I would need again later, as well as the frilly lingerie and other items I'd purchased there on my own; but I made the decision to get rid of all the rest of my old clothes. Every single thing was put in bags to be hauled away and donated to a women's shelter in Chicago. I would soon be wearing only maternity clothes anyway, and once baby was born, I rationalized, I could replenish my entire wardrobe at my leisure.

It was beginning to sink in, too, that I would be able to go anywhere I pleased and buy anything I wanted.

As for the rest of my efforts to keep the sadness from taking over my life, I had projects up to my eyeballs to distract me. I worked almost the entire nine months of my pregnancy, with the blessings of Dr. Bertam, but under the concerned eye of Polo.

"I figure I'll be out of commission for up to a year after the baby is born, " I explained to him, "So I really need to get as much accomplished as humanly possible."

But, of course, the real reason was that work took my mind off desperately missing Cass.

*   *   *   *

As much as anything else, the mitigating circumstance that helped me get through my grief was planning the Mid-States presentation and the second teachers' *colloque* to be offered by the Foundation. With that next convention looming, we were committed to the idea I'd come up with about a class project on the Regions and Cuisine of France. It had been submitted and accepted, so there was no turning back.

Dom Lambert had readily agreed to let his two sophomore French III classes be my guinea pigs.

"Remember, they're the 'middle children' of high school," he reiterated. "Anything to spice up their class would be welcomed,"

Dom and I huddled together several afternoons at his school, scoping out his classroom and developing the plans, which were ambitious.

His students would be divided into teams--partnerships, or in some cases, threesomes. We made up a packet to be given to each one containing a calendar of the three-week period that would comprise the project, delineating what was due when and what classroom activities and media would take place on what specific dates. We devised the academic plan, consisting of a research paper on their region's history, geography, tourist attractions and cuisine specialty. There would be, in conjunction with the paper, an oral presentation to the entire class about their region, on which the other students would be expected to take notes. The partners would also bring in a tasting sample of their cuisine specialty, with the caveat that if the recipe they found needed alcohol in any form, it was to be left out!

"Can you imagine the scandal if even a hint of alcohol was present in the classroom?" I laughed.

"Can you imagine me getting fired?!" he retorted. "Not so funny."

"You're right...sorry I made light of it. Do you trust them?"

"I have to! But I'll tell them I reserve the right to taste everything ahead of time, and that if someone defies this rule, there will be heavy consequences."

Obviously, the 1970's was a more innocent time!

One big element of the project would be an **in-class** cooking activity, where, under careful teacher supervision, the students would make a typical French dish. This would take place over a two-day period in the project: one to cook it and one to eat it and watch a film.

"Well, they're going to like that!" Dom mused.

"I envision your classroom arranged in 'stations' and the students in the same sort of 'brigades' one would find in a restaurant kitchen. They'll cook in your room, that is, barring the idea that you can just take them down to the home ec room, which I doubt, am I right?"

"I would guess you are, yeah, but how would a kitchen be set up in my room?" Dom asked incredulously.

"Okay, see, I'm thinking that you rearrange the desks into groupings, and make signs that say Station One, Station Two, etc., and place them around the room. The kids would draw numbers to know which station to report to. At the stations would be chopping, frying, assembling, and so forth. We would use tables you already have in the classroom to set up fry pans, cutting boards, and other stuff. Of course, you don't have a sink in your room, but you're close enough to the bathrooms. It should be okay."

"Don't you think the principal should get involved in this at all?" he wondered. "I mean, it probably wouldn't hurt to have permission."

"Well, sure. Whatever you think is required."

I told him that in doing research, the two dishes I thought we could cook, riffing off real recipes from Julia Child, were *coq au vin* and *boeuf bourguignonne.*

"Dom, I think we could do either of those... with non-alcoholic wine, of course! "

"Well, they're classics all right. I like the idea of *boeuf bourguignonne.* Do you think we could pull that off? How would it actually cook?"

"That's the thing! I saw something really cool in a magazine. It was an ad for Rival's new cooker called a Crock Pot, and that's what gave me this idea. I will buy two of them, and two Sunbeam electric frying pans."

I told him that I would also purchase **everything** he needed to try this in class, and afterwards, he could keep all the supplies for future use.

"You figure out a way to make cooking stations and I'll supply the rest. You can fashion the work space out of the desks or tables pushed together near enough to electrical outlets. The end station would be called 'assembly', where you would have the Crock Pots on those electrified carts you use for audio-visual showings. Granted the students at that last one won't have as much to do," I added, "so put kids there accordingly---maybe some you don't trust with knives, haha!"

"I have some discretionary budget, Sari, and I can provide the food part of this."

"Not this time, okay? I don't want you to spend your precious supply budget on my idea. We will require a lot more than food-- all the utensils, too — like slotted spoons and spatulas, knives, measuring cups --all that stuff like the home-ec people have. We want to replicate their kitchen. Just clear out some storage space in your book cupboards because you're going to need it!"

I also explained that I would give him all the media, films, filmstrips, as well as posters and print materials that had poured in from the French *syndicats d'Initiative.* He and I would also write a game of 'baseball' to review the material, and finally, the exam over the entire unit.

"And we can team teach this, if you like, " I offered, "especially on cooking day. You, of course, would be in charge of all the discipline and classroom control issues. I'd just get to be the fun teacher, " I laughed.

"Thanks a lot!"

"Also I would like your permission to photograph the entire three weeks, and use those slides in my Mid-States presentation."

"Sounds great! You have my permission to do anything you want! " he said, and admitted he would be relieved to have help.

I then had the idea to ask Polo if Dom might accompany us to Minneapolis so that he could be at the presentation to answer any questions the teachers might have that only another teacher could provide. Polo was enthusiastic about that idea, and Dom was delighted to accept.

I was absent from my desk at the Foundation much of the three weeks our experiment in Dom's classroom took place. The students had protested a bit at first about all the work components they saw on their calendars, but the research and execution of the project was so enjoyable, that the griping faded away to nothing, and everyone seemed on board. Dom was a super sport about rearranging his lesson plans to accommodate this project, and still accomplish course objectives he had for his sophomores. I felt bad about his added work.

"The silver lining," he assured me, "is that the project comes just prior to student registration for the next year's classes, and maybe they'll have had so much fun, they'll want to stay in French."

"And they'll have learned a ton, don't forget that part!"

Cooking day came off like clockwork in both sections. The students were indeed assigned to their brigades and did their jobs of cutting up onions and mushrooms, frying meat, assembling the sauce at the Crock Pots, where Dom did the pouring of the non-alcoholic wine. We evened out the work per station by adding salad-making, where they used a French lettuce dryer from Polo's kitchen to spin-dry butter lettuce; and we gave them the recipe and ingredients for vinaigrette dressing to accompany the next-day's tasting.

Dom took the salad makings home to his fridge overnight, but the slow-cookers were left simmering away, with notes to the janitors not to turn them off! The scents wafting from his classroom intrigued all passers-by the next day, and we were greeted with a chorus of "Where's that coming from?!" and "Does that ever smell good!"

During the whole project I had taken slide photos in the classroom, documenting the room preparations, the ambience, how the Foundation materials were used to decorate the space, and how it was set up. More importantly, I photographed the students in action giving their presentations, cooking, watching films, and reviewing for the test at the end. All the slides would serve to illustrate my talk.

"Wait 'til you see this!" I announced, breathless, to Polo and Annie-Laure as I burst into the Presidential suite after the last of the team-teaching sessions with Dom. "We really pulled it off! When you view the slides, you'll be impressed at all we could accomplish in a normal high school classroom! The kids were fantastic! It turns out I like teaching!"

"That does not surprise me, " Polo stated, and they both laughed.

The day of our departure for the Mid-States came, and once again, we were loaded down with materials to disseminate, so it was decided Jean-Luc would accompany us on the trip to help Dom carry the boxes and to be of service to his boss. This was to be merely a one-day jaunt, and Robineau would not have to be there.

Dom met Polo and me at our home for the ride out to the airport. At the plane, Polo motioned for us go up first, and once on board, out of Polo's hearing, Dom exclaimed,

"Jesus Christ! You weren't kidding about this plane, were you?"

"Yeah, well... no!"

"I mean, you said it looked like a yacht inside and, geez, it does!"

When we landed in Minneapolis and took a cab to the McIntosh Convention Center, we checked in (and made sure we all had the requisite credentials this time!), and then Dom and I took the presentation materials and went to scope out the assigned room; while Jean-Luc carried-- and Polo arranged--the other materials in our *Fondation Culturelle Française* booth. They would man the table together until the designated hour for my presentation, at which point Polo would just leave the packets for Luc to hand out, and he would join me.

I started my talk by introducing the *Président* of the FCF, and giving the teachers a little teaser about the bounty of information available that awaited them if they availed themselves of our services, both in execution of the project I was about to describe, and also in their classes in general.

I then introduced Dom as the teacher they would see in the slide presentation.

"Please meet my great and good friend, the master teacher who piloted this project."

Polo sat rapt in the back of the room, and Dom passed out various handouts as I proceeded through the salient points, starting with what the Foundation had provided in the way of media on the regions of France, and how the whole thing was organized on the calendar. It took about forty minutes for me to get through the entire slide show and my speech, after which I got a rousing round of applause and Dom and I both took questions.

"My main trepidation, " said one participant, "is that my administration might not allow cooking in the classroom."

Before I could answer, another chimed in, "Yes, and my home-ec department chair would never in a million years let me borrow her equipment." People laughed but there was more than one nod in agreement.

"Did you have to buy all that stuff? You must have **some** budget!"

"Most schools have strict prohibitions against **any** food from the outside!" another one declared.

Polo gave me an uneasy, worried look. This was the very first time in my Foundation career that I had faced antagonistic backlash about **anything** I had proposed!

I tried to ease their concerns. "I understand what you are saying, " I told the group, trying not to acknowledge that they had presented any real roadblocks. "Even though my slides keyed in on the in-class cooking part, you can leave it out! Look at the hand-out. There are plenty of other components to the unit without actual cooking. And if your school prohibits outside food, just change that part of the students' instructions and have them bring in a **picture** of the cuisine specialty. The cooking day on the calendar could be replaced with the baseball game — or any other game-- just as easily."

"What about the time frame? " another one added. "I don't think I could spare three weeks of my curriculum to devote to one unit!"

Others mumbled sympathetically.

I felt myself flush a bit, and nervousness welled up. I could see this whole thing going off the rails.

"Well, obviously you can pick and choose, " Dom spoke up, coming to my defense. "You could always just do a few of the activities in class, especially the first time you try this, and then maybe map it out for a future Intersession project, if your district has that."

"Or do the cooking as a French Club activity, " I suggested, trying to exude calmness. "Maybe outside of the school day, you could cook someplace else…and of course, eliminate the grading component."

Dom added, "This just takes some brain-storming about your proposed syllabus. You can always get together with your department, your colleagues, and plan some extra time in the next year's curriculum if you wanted to build in some project days. It doesn't have to be three weeks. You change the calendar of activities as you see fit."

"Did you do that when you took three weeks out to do this activity?" someone chided him.

"I'm the French department head, " he retorted, smiling. And they all laughed.

"The whole point, " I said, trying to regain their attention and redirect the focus, "is the students! You saw in the slides. That was a real classroom with tenth graders. We didn't stage anything! They were engaged, enthusiastic and willing. The kids loved this even though it was hard work for them! Culture is the wow factor for you. We don't learn a foreign language to merely show our proficiency in grammar. We do it to live in the culture. If you just showed the media alone and did nothing else, it would whet the students' appetites to want to visit France…and keep taking French!"

Everyone seemed to calm down about their previous trepidations. I ended by reminding them that anything they could possibly need to get started was available to them at no charge from the Foundation's library.

"I really hope you'll take advantage of what *La Fondation Culturelle Française* has to offer you, " I said, concluding my talk. "Please pick up an evaluation from our convention rep by the door on your way out, and put them in the box in the hall. Thanks for coming!"

When the room was emptied, I turned and slumped down on one of the chairs, spent.

"Nothin' but net, " Dom said, putting his hand on my shoulder.

We exited into the hall, and Polo put his arm around me, warmly, probably as much with relief as pride.

"You were *magnifique!*" he whispered in my ear.

"Oh, *tu parles*, " I scoffed. I didn't feel magnificent.

"Your wonderful pictures told the whole story! You are a good photographer, *chérie!*"

"So you're glad you gave me that cool camera, huh?" I laughed.

I was gratified that my part was over, and in the end, I was convinced that we'd given a successful presentation, even if it did have some mild rebuke at the end.

In the corridor Polo tried to hold me close, but all at once we were surrounded by a mob of teachers who had stayed after, wanting to meet him. When he could get free, we left to find Jean-Luc back at The Foundation's display in the arena center. Approaching the booth, we saw that we were practically out of the materials we'd brought, so we abandoned it, and went to the Conference Luncheon. I ate the meal this time.

"I feel certain your evals will be excellent, " Dom assured me.

"Not every teacher is so obviously creative as you both are, " Polo said. "Had they just thought a moment before being so swift to criticize, they would have seen the solutions by themselves. *De toute façon*, let us not dwell on any unfavorable aspects. Over and above everything else, this was once again a triumph of public relations for our Foundation, and another great achievement for my *Directrice d'Education!*"

"Hear, hear!" Dom echoed.

"Without you, Dom, I couldn't have done it, and without you, my sweet and generous husband, neither of us could have!"

"Well, that is as may be. This time, I agree that you did need a budget to get this accomplished, as that teacher noted. I am happy we could provide it."

"Yes," Dom quickly added, "I thank you again for all that, *Monsieur*."

Polo waved him off and changed the subject, informing us, with a hint of conspiracy in his voice, "I have a surprise for the both of you. Do you mind flying back to Chicago terribly late?"

We shook our heads no. "But why?"

"I have procured tickets for a performance tonight at the Guthrie. Do you know this theater, Sarah? Dom, you do, no doubt."

"I've heard of it, " I said, "but I've never been here before."

"I've never been to it either, " said Dom.

"They are presenting *Candide* tonight!"

Given my checkered history with the work, you'd have thought I'd have at least **heard** *of the musical.* "My old friend Voltaire? How cool!" I cooed.

"Bernstein, actually!" Dom corrected me.

"*Oui*, it is a musical; *effectivement*, it is more of an opera, " Polo chuckled.

Even as I was a big West Side Story *fan, at that point I had never heard a recording of* Candide, *never seen an excerpt from the show, didn't know the music, and had no knowledge of the Broadway play. And though it had, essentially, flopped when it opened in 1956, it would be revived and restaged many other times — for London's West End, by the Scottish Opera and many others, and be hailed as brilliant, and Bernstein's homage to European music. I knew Leonard Bernstein was conductor of the New York Philharmonic, of course, and that he did "Young Peoples' Concerts" on CBS television. But I didn't know his own music until* Westside Story.

Dom was familiar with it.

"Can you imagine what it must have been like in those sessions?!" he exclaimed, "Lillian Hellman, for God's sake! She wrote the play's book. *The New Yorker* panned the show in their review as 'too serious' — think about that! And then a bunch of other collaborators were brought in to fix it...Dorothy Parker! Stephen Sondheim!"

"An unknown Sondheim, " Polo reminded him gently. "But in the music, Sarah, you will definitely hear foreshadowing of *West Side Story*. And you will see that Bernstein has a deep understanding of choral music, the division of vocal parts, melodic shape, phrase lengths, harmonic complexity, and so forth. I believe you are going to love this."

Before heading to the theater, Polo had also undertaken to make dinner reservations at St. Paul's oldest French restaurant, *La Petite Maisonnette*, a tiny but fabulous eating establishment in a Victorian cottage on one of St. Paul's celebrated old streets. There were barriers, as usual — narrow steps up to the door — but luckily Jean-Luc was there, and it wasn't half as daunting as, say, climbing to my former apartment had been.

Our meal was perfection, with an especially intriguing salad after the main course.

"That is literally the best vinaigrette I have ever tasted!" I said a bit startled at the delight to my taste buds as I took the first bite.

"It is the house secret dressing, " Polo informed me. "Very famous."

"How do you know this stuff?" I wondered, very impressed yet again with my husband's cultural prowess.

"For one thing, this restaurant was given a fine write-up in *Gourmet Magazine!*" Polo told us.

"I can see why, " Dom remarked. "It's terrific! Thanks so much for inviting me."

We had wonderful seats in the venerated Guthrie theater that was almost theater in the round. The stage had a circular platform with trap doors, and the production values, lighting, sound and costumes were all fabulous. I sat entranced and enthralled from the opening bars of the overture, which I immediately recognized as the theme music to The Dick Cavett Show (!!), to the final curtain. I loved every minute of it!

"Oh my God, how could I have not known about this?" I fairly screeched at my husband as we walked to the cab Luc had managed to flag down for us after the show.

"It is sublime, is it not?" Polo remarked.

I basked in the glow of *Candide* all the way home, and the touchy moments after my presentation faded into oblivion. It wasn't lost on me that, once again, the arts had the power to cleanse the palate of one's troubled soul.

Back in Chicago, at nearly two in the morning, Jean-Luc dropped Dominique first at his place before heading on to Lake Shore Drive.

"Success, right?" he asked me as I accompanied him to his apartment door.

"Success. And thank you so much again for all the work you did." We gave each other *la bise*.

A few weeks later, the evaluations came in. Polo called me next door to his office.

"Mostly rave reviews for you, *chérie*!" he called out, waving the paper around.

"Mostly?"

"Nearly perfect. *Ne t'en fais pas!* Once again you accomplished something very important for our Foundation. I mean it. Dom was excellent, of course, and very magnanimous in letting you into his classes. But you came up with this idea—you alone -- and almost *à l'instant* if you remember! And then you executed it with—*je ne sais quoi dire...la grâce!* And not only in the classroom with Dom. The way you gave that lecture demonstration to the conference participants! I feel, Sarah, you are a born teacher. I do not believe people can learn to do it."

"Well, my darling Polo, many teachers' colleges would beg to differ with you. And if it were true, then were my parents right to insist I leave Chicago and get my teaching degree?"

"*Ah, non! Tu plaisantes!* I did not mean that. You must never leave me."

"You needn't worry on that account."

"But it is just that I am more and more convinced that I chose my most deserving and capable *Directrice d'Education* for the Foundation. I am so enormously proud of you."

*   *   *   *

I was becoming increasingly huge with child and beginning to look very much like a beached whale. As pleased as Jean-Paul d'Arivèque was with the seriousness and skill with which I pursued my duties as Director of Education, he still fretted a lot about any stress I was under, and whether I had the stamina to do everything I was doing. So once the conference and symposium were "put to bed," I turned all my attention to having a baby.

Polo doted on me every minute we were together. In the evenings I would heave myself onto the leather sofa in our library and spread out with my swollen feet in his lap where he would rub them and massage my legs with such a gentle caring touch, that, I admit it sent me rather into a trance.

I would lift his hand and place it on my stomach to feel the kicking of "Lumpkin," as I called "it." He would in turn take my hand, kiss it, and work his way up my arm, which would pull me up into a sitting position and over closer to him as he kissed my neck and then we would find ourselves in an embrace.

"I am more excited about our having this baby than any man has a right to be, " he told me.

"You have a right to feel any way you like," I assured him, *so thankful that, as Oncle Charles had predicted, I had found a way to make him so happy.*

Polo sweetly announced that he wanted to give me something special as a baby gift.

"You must tell me exactly what you would like to have, darling," he admonished me. "I want it to be splendid."

So even though I tried to protest, reminding him that he'd already given me so many things, he insisted I come up with something suitable for this milestone occasion. We didn't have the saying "push present" in our lexicon in 1973, but that's what he had in mind. Since I already had received the gift most wealthy French women were offered for the occasion-- the *Hermès* Kelly bag-- I asked for a really nice baby buggy or stroller. It wouldn't do to be cooped up in an apartment all day. I had to have a way to get the baby out into more fresh air than even our enormous terrace offered.

He sent Annie-Laure, who was by now my closest friend, to shop for it in New York, where lavish European baby accoutrements were more readily found than in the Midwest. She came back with none other than the navy and white Silver Cross "Kensington" pram that would basically come apart and reinvent itself into a stroller as the baby grew. It came with a lovely white piqué cotton bedding set consisting of an elegant coverlet and a pillow whose case had *broderie anglaise* trim and silver crewelwork detail. I'd only seen those actual prams in the Parc Monceau or in pictures of Prince Charles being wheeled in Windsor Great Park or somewhere. It had to be one of the most magnificent baby carriages anyone ever pushed down Michigan Avenue.

Another big discussion, of course, was where to put our baby's nursery on the third floor. Even though it was farther from us, we decided to turn the room nearer the kitchen into the baby's room.

"It would be more convenient for preparing bottles, " I reasoned.

"And you shall be doing that yourself?" Polo asked me, surprised.

"Uh... yeah! And laundry, too. And to that end, I wish to have new machines up there, " I told him, " and I want them to be like in all French homes-- in or near the kitchen. We've got plenty of space in the pantry."

"You have thought of everything, " Polo said admiringly.

Polo had also insisted on giving me free rein to decorate the baby's room any way I wanted to, and I decided on white. We didn't know the sex of our child, and I wasn't slated to go through amniocentesis to find out; so a white nursery was easy to decorate, and also chic.

Polo did suggest, however, that an interior decorator friend of his named Trudie Harris should help me.

"She can take you to the design center at the Chicago Merchandise Mart," he proclaimed. "You've heard of it, yes?'

"Yes. That would be super! Thanks!"

We needed Trudie's credentials as *entrée* to the Mart, but I already knew what I wanted, so she helped me find the best vendors for a white baby bassinette, white Valencia crib, two dressers, a changing station, and a Roche Bobois puffy leather glider armchair.

"I'd like the chair to add some color...what do you say to red? And do you suppose we can get wallpaper that is *toile de Jouy*?" I asked her, as we walked up and down the cavernous showrooms. "I'm envisioning shades of gray and white, with light crimson and blue highlights. What do you think?"

"That—uh-- sounds great!" she said, rather taken aback at my having already done her work.

"I figure if I have a girl, I could accent the room in pink—pink bedding and wall hangings—since gray and pink are always pretty together. If it's a boy, the gray would lend itself to looking more boyish, with blue accents."

"You're the boss, " she said.

"I also would like accent fabric to match the wall coverings. Can that be had?"

"Sure. Are you thinking pillows?"

" No. I want gingham for pillows. I was thinking of window coverings. I picture festoon shades."

"I like that!"

Trudie knew many people in the trades, and when I found everything I wanted, she arranged the shipping to be on her timetable. She and her team would need to get in and redo the basic room features before any furniture arrived.

I met her again one afternoon in the tea room at Saks where she had brought with her sample rolls of the *toile* wallpaper and matching fabric she'd found. It had a recurring motif of children in Seventeenth Century garb playing with hoops. The design included hot air balloons, and foliage, along with rabbits, deer and even elephants! I loved it. Afterwards, I went straight up to the store's baby department, and chose a gingham bumper set to put in the crib, and a few matching pillows for the red chair. Naturally I had them wait to see if I'd need blue or pink before shipping them to me.

Trudie and her crew came like a swarm of worker bees, and transformed the old bedroom in a matter of days. Polo had been confident that I'd know what furniture to look for, but he was blown away by the wallpaper and color scheme. He stood in the nursery with me and marveled at the ambience for our baby.

"Trudie!" he exclaimed when he saw her coming down the hallway from making a phone call. "It is a magnificent transformation! You have done something superb in here."

"Oh, heck no, Jean-Paul. Your wife here designed the whole space. I just got her into the Mart. She knew exactly what she wanted and how the color scheme would look. I'm going to feel a little guilty charging you. But, I will, of course!" she laughed.

Polo just looked at me and nodded. "I should have known it, " he said. "It is you who are the wonder."

It gave Polo a real thrill to go with me to shop for the baby. He loved heading up there and adding little things to the room: a Teddy bear and a few baby toys on the shelves; some cute receiving blankets in the dresser. We laid out baby towels and positioned a new-fangled bouncy infant seat I had picked up so there would be somewhere I could put "Lumpkin" before he/she could really sit up.

More than once I came home and found Polo just sitting in the nursery, taking it all in.

Annie-Laure had also concocted the idea with her boss to give me a surprise baby shower in the office one afternoon in early September. She had planned it to take place at the close of business hours, and had told our receptionist to ring my phone about five minutes before quitting time, and invent some reason to bring me out there. Bernadette came up with the scenario that an unhappy teacher had shown up with complaints about a film she'd ordered.

"Oh, gosh, Bernadette, I'm bushed. Could you please handle it? Just take her name and tell her I'll get back to her tomorrow."

"Ah, *non*! She insists upon seeing you now, *Madame*."

"*Nom de Dieu*," I muttered, hissing. "Shit!"

So I got up and waddled on down the hall. Turning the corner towards the main lobby, I was met by a room full of balloons, serving carts set up with every sort of pastry, champagne cooling in buckets (Coke for me), a stack of gaily-wrapped boxes sitting off to one side, and forty or so people all clapping and laughing, with Polo in the center of the room looking pretty contrite for having perpetrated this hoax.

"Whoa!"

Bernadette came forward to give me *la bise*. "*Je m'excuse*," she laughed.

Polo and I were overwhelmed by the generosity of his employees, which only served to illustrate in my mind once again, their devotion and great admiration for him. We got a vast array of lovely-- mostly yellow or white--unisex infant gowns, kimonos, booties, and bonnets from *Jacadi*, *Petit Bateau*, *Tartine et Chocolat* and other famous French shops; plus bath toys, stuffed animals, and books.

I admit to being stupefied at all the French layette.

"What did you do?!" I squealed to Polo, "Send them on a shopping spree to Paris for God's sake?"

"No, " he answered, looking almost sheepish, "but we had some meetings there to which I sent Daniel and his team."

Well, obviously not Hennie or I would have heard about it.

Annie-Laure and Luc approached me with another large gift box which they beckoned me to open. What I lifted out was perplexing.

"It's a...well, not a kimono but... sort of like that...a bigger one?"

"It is a sleep *sac*, " she announced proudly. "I got it in New York at *Le Berceau des Étoiles*. French women swear by these, " she explained, "for helping baby to sleep calmly."

Polo was so intent on seeing to my every need and desire during the pregnancy, that he had, without my knowledge or prompting, arranged several lunches with his dear friend and our wedding officiant, Harry Lowenstein, to educate himself on Jewish customs, and to familiarize himself with any religious or cultural events and ceremonies I might want for our child. He even inquired about rabbis Harry might know in the city to call on for performing ceremonial rites. Polo told him that I had already decided we were not going to have a *bris* if the baby were a boy, since the doctor could do the deed right there in the hospital; but I did sort of want a naming ceremony...for either sex.

Polo couldn't disguise his relief and joy, when reporting back, that his friend had been so helpful.

"Harry assured me he is delighted to have been able to provide a list of rabbis he knows in town who would love to have us at some Shabbos service to name our baby, " Polo announced to me, hoping I would be pleased.

"That is so sweet of him. What a guy, eh?"

"Yes, " he said, and then became solemn. "Sarah, he tells me often that his family all felt they may have never gotten out of Europe if it hadn't been for my father. Even though I make a serious case for just the other way around as well---that my mother could not have handled bringing me to America without them and their medical aid. But he will not hear of that."

"I'm guessing deep down he knows, though, that his parents, being doctors, gave your father the precious gift of at least a modicum of relief that his wife and child would be looked after on the trip over. I'm sure he was wracked with worry about it before that, since he knew he couldn't go. But yes, Georges-Henri may have saved their lives in the end."

Polo and I knew we needed to have discussions on names for our child, but he wanted it to be my choice, and he was anxious to discuss with me what Harry had told him about how Jewish babies were often named after close relatives who had recently died or after someone who had held a special place in the hearts of the parents.

"I should like you to have the final say, " he told me. "Any name you like will be fine with me."

"No, *mon ange*! I couldn't exclude you from a decision that important."

"Harry explained to me that there are hardly any circumstances where Ashkenazi Jews name babies after living people, " Polo said.

"Yeah, that's why it's very rare to see the suffix 'Junior' or 'II' after the name of a Jewish person, " I acknowledged.

Without really announcing anything to Polo at first, I'd been doing quite a lot of thinking and soul-searching about the name, and even before the discussion about Georges-Henri and the Lowensteins, I had it in mind that the clear choice if we had a boy would be to name our baby after Polo's father. And since I said I'd want a baby-naming in a synagogue, I also had to come up with a Jewish name. So I went to the Chicago Public library and did some research. Finding an equivalent for George wasn't that easy. That name derived from the Greek for "tiller of the soil" or some such, and one translation I found for it was Yaniv. I liked that name. It turned out Henry was a little bit easier. The consensus was that name was Chayim. So Yaniv Chayim it was. But usually the ceremonial name included, I discovered, " son of " or Ben, so I needed a Hebrew equivalent for Polo. However, in the case of the parent, any Hebrew name could be used – it didn't need to be a transliteration. So I decided – unilaterally – that Polo should take the name of the Israeli Ambassador to the US at that time, Yitzak Rabin. I loved the guy, and every time I saw him on the news, it just reinforced what a great leader he was. He had overseen Israel's victory in the 1967 Six-Day War and obviously Golda Meir had enough faith in him to make him her Ambassador to our country. That was good enough for me. Yaniv Chayim ben Yitzak it would be!

As to a girl's name, I felt the only person for whom my baby should be named was my grandmother. It wasn't as though I didn't like the name Marie-Aveline; I did – at least the Aveline part. But I still recoiled a little bit at the ghost of Maman haunting us. The thing was, I no longer felt in any way threatened by her memory, nor did I harbor a whit of animosity towards her; but I still didn't want my daughter to carry the burden of that name with its myriad of connotations into the future. Not all people in Chicago and Paris knew the name Jean-Paul d'Arivèque, but everyone *knew Marie-Aveline.*

I did feel guilty about it, however. Polo had adored his mother, and was completely devoted to her memory; and there I came, not wanting to brand our girl with her name. It was selfish of me because my *fervent desire, and an idea with which I had yet to bring up with Polo, was to name her after my own Nana, who had been Clara Louise Dalkin Hershorn. A name I loved in France and elsewhere, had always been Claire. Wouldn't that be so perfect? As far as a name that began with A,* ostensibly *for Aveline, I loved the Dutch name Anja...like my friend at the Sorbonne.*

Finding a Hebrew name for Claire would prove to be harder. From the Latin for light, I couldn't find a nice equivalent in Hebrew! Elior meant God's Light, so I took that as a possibility. My other choice was to just find names in Hebrew that began with the letters C and A. It could be Chanah, Chava or Chaya. Any of those were okay, but in the end, I preferred Elior. As for A names, I liked Avigail or Aliza. So I picked Elior Aliza Bat (daughter of) ...ME! My name was already Hebrew...for Princess. Ha! Good one.

Finally I broached the subject. "As far as names go, I think if it's a boy, we must name him after your father. Georges-Henri is a beautiful name and it also works for my own maternal grandfather whom I didn't know very well, but who was the love of my Nana's life. His name was also Harry—isn't that ironic?--but everyone called him Hal. The Henri part could stand for him also, at least in my mind."

Polo was overwhelmed at my offer to give our baby his father's name. He was on the verge of tears when he took me in his arms, "Thank you my darling. I am very touched that you would think to do that. If he were here, he would be very pleased."

"No, silly! If he were here, we wouldn't be using the name," I laughed. Then I got serious and looked at him, adding, "And if your mother were still alive, it would have pleased her, right?"

"More than you know," he answered softly. "And if the name might also invoke the memory of your dear Nana's husband, then I think that's splendid!"

"But, Polo, if we do name our kid Georges-Henri, I'd like to call him just plain Henri, or even Henry when he starts school, at least while he's little. Later on he can add the hyphenated name back in if he wants to."

"Considering he will be an American, and the French name could be hard for his little school chums, I think this is a fine idea."

"So, if it's a girl, what are your thoughts?" I asked, afraid he now expected a girl to be named after his mother, Marie-Aveline Chantal de Maurignac d'Arivèque.

But instead he asked, "Do you have a preferred one?" as if he expected that I must.

"What do you think of Claire-Anja?" I asked him rather timidly.

"I like that, " he said, although I had a hunch he would agree to anything. "But, *chérie*, I am wondering if you would want to name her Cassandra?"

I had wanted to name her after my grandmother Clara and shockingly enough, I hadn't even considered Cassandra!

"You know, " I mused, realizing the perfection of it, "both Nana and Cass had names that begin with the letter C, so that does work. And your mother's name, Aveline, is why I picked an A name. I thought..."

"Wonderful!" he grinned at me and then beckoned me to come closer. He whispered into my ear, "I love you so deeply, I can hardly find a way to... "

I put my finger over his lips. "Shh. I know. And I love you, Polo. So much."

"So! It is to be Georges-Henri or Claire-Anja d'Arivèque then? How marvelous!" He was delighted.

Dr. Bertram had arranged for us to begin taking pre-natal classes at the hospital one night per week. At first Polo assumed I'd be going by myself. He said he would feel too awkward showing up in the class with his physical limitations on full view, and also given his age. I tried to laugh all that off and assured him he'd be welcomed by one and all, but he said he just couldn't do it. However, the doctor convinced him that he should be there to get in on the all the information with which I was about to become bombarded.

"Having this baby is your great desire, " she chided him. "You should go with your wife."

"I see that I must admit you are right, " he said, acquiescing in spite of his misgivings.

This was not a class on labor and delivery, although those things were mentioned. Rather, our class had a practical curriculum of baby care: how to bathe baby, tips on sleep patterns (we were instructed to place baby on the tummy in those days!); how to soothe the baby, how to hold the baby, trouble signs, when to call the doctor, and so on.

They did show us a film of the delivery of a normal, healthy, natural childbirth. Many of the couples were already enrolled in Lamaze, which we were not. I had opted to have an epidural and the least pain possible. Even though the debate raged, I didn't think epidurals were risky, and even as the proponents of natural childbirth warned of babies who would be born drugged, I blithely ignored them.

However, the big debate between breast feeding and bottle feeding did come up, with members of La Leche League invited to (read: butted into) the class on more than one occasion. I wasn't intending to breast feed, which came under scrutiny by those advocates of it.

They could make you feel like child abusers if you decided to NOT breast-feed.

"I understand the part about the baby getting some good immunity from the get-go, " I said to Dr. Bertram. "But, considering that I've already had one breast surgery, and I'm not sure I even **can** breast feed, I just don't want to start with it. Formulas are high quality now and I just prefer the bottle method."

I couldn't help but remember the nightmare Cass went through trying to breast feed the twins.

"I won't pressure you to breast-feed, " Dr. Bertam assured me, "but I think you should consider it carefully."

"Actually, I've already made up my mind," I told her deferentially, but also resolutely.

Polo didn't seem to care one way or the other. But then, he wasn't the one upon whom the propaganda was being foisted from the other side.

When I actually did go into labor, I didn't even realize it was labor; I thought all I was having was some cramping. But the date — it was one day before my due date-- should have set off some warning bells! We were watching the *Johnny Carson Show* and it suddenly dawned on me that these "cramps" were coming in measurable intervals.

I was laying on the couch as usual, eating my tenth or so popsicle of the evening, my head resting on Polo's lap. I put down the stick and looked up at him. He looked down at me and smiled.

"I think I'm in labor, " I said nonchalantly.

"What!" He tried to sit me upright. " Are you having contractions?! Shall we time them?!"

"Yeah, I think they're about ten minutes apart."

"*Mon Dieu!*" He reached for the phone and dialed Jean-Luc. "*Il est l'heure!!*" he panted into the phone. He struggled to get off the sofa in haste, and this time he helped **me** up. We had the little overnight case packed and ready to go, and out of nowhere, Robineau appeared with it to take me down the elevator. It was a balmy night, so no need for a coat. I hoisted my rotund self into the car and off we went on what was only a five-minute ride.

Everything else is a little blurry for me now; my water had not broken, and they took me into a room –decidedly not the pretty birthing room-- to give me an enema and start a drip prior to the epidural. They said I was dilated to six centimeters when I got there, so I'd evidently gone through the first stage of labor not realizing that was what it was. We moved into the birthing room about an hour later.

I was awake but, of course, soon after that, feeling no real pain.

We had arrived at the hospital around eleven p.m. and at four in the morning I gave birth to a healthy six-pound- two-ounce baby boy: Georges-Henri Benoit d'Arivèque, the *de-facto* future *Duc de Beuvron.*

Because I didn't do Lamaze, Polo wasn't by my side coaching me through contractions or helping me do breathing exercises, but they didn't make him sit out in a waiting room either, like fathers-to-be in 1950's were relegated to do. When we were getting close, they brought him into the room, helped him put on disposable scrubs to wear over his real clothes and had him wear an operating room cap. He tried to act calm---for me---but I could tell that he was anything but. When they showed him the baby crowning, he became even more animated. Beads of sweat appeared on his brow and he kept glancing around nervously at me to make sure I was okay. By the time the baby was born, the new father was an emotional wreck, deliriously happy, but concerned for his wife.

"Is she all right?" he kept asking the nurses.

"I'm fine, " I would groggily answer.

I was more interested in the baby's Apgar score. One minute after birth they measured it and again at five minutes. Our baby was doing great, with eight's on all the factors measured. They put him on my stomach for me to hold first, and I remarked how HUGE he was, which struck them as terribly funny since, given his birth weight, he was considered small.

Then Polo was offered a chair pulled up right next to my birthing bed, and they placed the baby in his right arm and sort of stood over him since his left arm would be of no use if anything happened, which, fortunately, it didn't. My husband was overcome with gratitude that they had let him hold his son before the baby was even thirty minutes old. After they'd taken our baby boy from him, and placed him back in the little plexiglass bassinette, Polo leaned over my bed with tears in his eyes. "*J'en suis éperdument amoureux.*"

The first six months, we didn't even use our gorgeous *toile* nursery, but instead installed this very beautiful, fancy wicker baby basket on wheels that Daniel Rosier de Molet and his wife had gifted us, for Georges-Henri to sleep in at the foot of our bed. The nursery over on the other side of the kitchen was actually too far away for me to hear the baby and react quickly enough; it would be another decade before baby monitors were the norm. Polo said he felt bad that I had to get up and do all the changes and night feedings by myself, but I was young and healthy, and made it clear to him that performing any baby task was not only **not** a problem for me, but was my special joy. Sure, I was tired, but it wasn't as though I were the typical new mother who also had to keep house, cook, do laundry, and maybe even go back to work after six weeks. And even though we did not have a nanny or even a designated maid there in our third-floor digs, I was a pampered, very spoiled, new mommy with dozens of staff at my beck and call and no chores whatsoever except to care for our infant son.

We were both thoroughly enthralled with him! He was pretty, with light brown hair and except for my color of brown eyes, his face and features took after the d'Arivèque side. He was twenty inches long at birth, which seemed tall to me, and he gained up to around sixteen pounds by six months old. He was fed on a schedule—not a rigid one, but not demand feeding---and was sleeping through the night in no time.

"That French sleep sack you found for me was a wonderful invention, " I praised Annie-Laure.

I created quite a scene strolling him around in the English baby carriage. People stared at me as I walked by them, or they stopped me to see the baby inside, which I'm sure wouldn't have happened if I'd been wheeling something less grand. But my instincts told me that bad things were on the horizon for a baby to be out on the city streets with all that exhaust and other toxic elements in the air, so my routine changed and I would fold the pram into my *Cit*, drive him to Lincoln park, and push the buggy there. I had the be-all, end-all baby car seat of the day, too: a GM "Love Seat" that cost thirty dollars and strapped in on the back seat. They still made the kind of car seat I'd gotten Cass for the twins five years earlier, but a very young baby couldn't sit in one of those, and since safety concerns were beginning to be touted, experts rejected-- with good reason---that old fashioned hook-over-the-seatback-type carrier.

*   *   *   *

It wasn't too long after I had my baby that I got a phone call from Julia Hyde. I was a bit startled by it, but I just thought she'd done the math or something, and was calling to inquire after our new child. That wasn't the case, however! Instead, she had quite an announcement for me: she and John-Wilfred had indeed filed against Alan Jones for custody of Cass' children! And they had won! It actually didn't come as a shock to me that their lawyers must have been superior, but the kicker was that Alan hadn't put up much of a fight at all. Alan was still a vociferous opponent of capitalism in all its forms, with a special contempt for the Hyde Industry's money, and was an easy target for the battery of attorneys to paint as incapable of providing for the twins. And, according to Julia, whatsherface -- Donna -- who was far more avaricious, hadn't relished, in the end, the idea of becoming the default mother of toddler twins unless a boatload of cash came with them.

Even as kindergarteners, Laura and Paul were old enough to understand that they had been shuttled twice back and forth from El Paso to Chicago, but that they were now going to be staying permanently with their grand-parents, who would be known as *Grand-mère* and *Grand-père*, rather than Mee-mee and Pop-pop. And I didn't judge Julia negatively this time, when it became apparent that those children would be raised by governesses and servants, and sent to private schools in limousines. Being back with Cass' family in her former surroundings struck me as much more desirable than their staying with Alan. Julia also told me that I would be welcomed to see the twins as often as I liked, and I immediately answered that I would really love that!

Julia Hyde would come back into my life in another way not long after that, much to my surprise.

We ended up living one town away from the Hydes because by the time my son was a year old, I got a bee in my bonnet that we had to bring him up in a smaller place than the mansion on Lake Shore Drive, and in a greener place than Chicago. I don't know if my small-town ways were flaring up, but at some point in the first year after our baby's birth, I decided it would be better to raise him in the suburbs.

The only towns I considered were the three just north of Chicago: Evanston, Wilmette and Kenilworth; however, I soon ruled out Kenilworth. I didn't want him to live on any sort of estate, isolated from neighbors, behind walls. I wanted him to be able to ride a bike on the sidewalk in front of his house, or walk to a park, and, even more important, to the neighborhood school. I wanted for us to be able to take him Trick-or-Treating on our block. I also wanted us to raise him ourselves, without a retinue of nannies, maids and valets.

Jean-Paul d'Arivèque was not too keen on the idea of leaving his family home.

"But your house would be tantamount to raising our baby in the *Chateau de Versailles*, " I blurted out without bothering to use all the calm, logical reasons I had prepared for the conversation.

"And so *evidemment*, you see yourself as Marie-Antoinette in need of her *Petit Hameau*, *n'est-ce pas?*" he teased me.

"Of course not!"

"*Chérie*, you must realize that not living here would be very difficult for me. You know I use the pool, have therapy, host guests, put on receptions. None of that is *facultatif*, darling. It is the routine. Plus I count on you to be at my side for social occasions, do I not?"

"I know, but I'm sure we could work something out. Maybe I could see my way to employing **one** nanny for the times I had to work or be at the Foundation. But that social whirl will not be all the time. Maybe some nights you would still sleep at the mansion, but most other nights don't you think you could be driven home to us?"

He sighed heavily. I just sat there, hoping the bloom wasn't off the rose of our marriage just yet in his eyes. Neither of us said anything until I broke the silence.

"I want our child to be educated at the neighborhood school, " I said deliberately, staying unruffled, "where I can drive him and pick him up at first. Then later when he's a bit older he could walk with neighborhood kids. That is never going to happen in Chicago."

"Sarah, we can afford to send our little boy to the finest private school in the city. In the world, for that matter."

"I realize that, but I want him to have a more **'normal'** upbringing is all. Look, when I was a kid, especially a teenager, I had all kinds of glorified ideas of boarding school and desperately wanted to go to one. But I had a crappy home life. I think our kid will have a happy one, and since you became a father rather—uh-- later in life, wouldn't you want to be with him as much as possible? Think about it."

In the end, Polo caved to my wishes but allowed as to how he still thought the logistics would be very hard to manage.

"However, if you want to start looking for a house in the closest possible suburbs-- Evanston or Wilmette—I have a friend who owns a real-estate agency in Chicago, and I could have them start a search for you with one of their agents, and see what is available."

"Oh thank you, Polo! You won't regret this."

He gave a wry little laugh. "I hope I do not!"

I went with Martha Trefton, a bubbly but not undignified career real-estate agent, who cut to the chase right away as we drove off in her car.

"With no budget restraints," she fairly sang, "obviously you are not going be the typical suburban client!"

"No," I laughed, "this house hunt could be easier than most, but I do need to warn you, I'm pretty fussy."

As I laid out my must-have list, I had a few things that were non-negotiable, written in stone: no grand stair entries; the door to get inside must be as flush to the ground as possible. I had to have a home that was mainly on one level, but if that wasn't to be, then at least the master bedroom and one other one had to be on the ground floor as well as laundry. The master bedroom had to have a nice, big bathroom. I wanted a minimum of four bedrooms and just as many other bathrooms, along with a decent-sized kitchen.

"There should, ideally, also be a fireplace—either in the living room or in a big family room or den." Lake Shore had many fireplaces, one more ornate than the next. But we didn't use them, except for the one in the library, because there was no comfortable furniture on which to laze about in front of any fires.

I also set down my wishes to her that there be a pleasant back yard for play, and that I wanted a pretty tree-lined street. I had not stipulated a certain style of architecture, but told her, "I don't want modern or cookie-cutter, you know… architectural ersatz." I also didn't want anything that resembled what they called "baronial, " and no copies either of castles; nothing Spanish, no Italianate villas. That left Colonial, Tudor, Cape Cod or country cottage.

"So I just have to find you the moon and the stars?" she joked.

I explained that I wasn't on a time bind and if we found something that **almost** met my criteria, we would be able to renovate or redo parts of it to comply more exactly to what I wanted.

We drove around and I looked at a few homes, mostly Colonials that didn't suit me for one reason or another. She seemed to think a stair chair lift would solve the problem of two story, but I didn't like the way those things looked. Putting in elevators wasn't practical either; most suburban American houses were not set up to accommodate the shaft that would be necessary in order to install a real elevator.

And then one day I got a call.

"I've found it!" Martha exclaimed in glee over the phone.

The place she had found was in Wilmette on Linden Drive, only a short hop to the beach of Lake Michigan. It was designed specifically to resemble a Norman French country house. She described it as white brick with a round driveway circling in front and an entry flush with the walk. The property was on a normal street and not an estate, but the lot was full of old-growth trees that afforded a lot of privacy, and even though we had side neighbors, they weren't terribly close.

We met the agent representing the sellers as soon as we could, and he elaborated on the architectural style for us.

"The original owners built it just after the war in the style of a French farmhouse near the town of Dives-sur-Mer, where the man, as a young soldier in World War II, had mistakenly landed when he parachuted behind enemy lines. He'd gotten blown off course and had ended up in a field near that town instead of Saint Lo. A family of farmers took him in. In homage to them, he tried to replicate their house."

"My husband will love that story."

The house had different wings, and it was all on one level with the living space in front, which included a large formal dining room and a den, as well as the very spacious front room. There were six bedrooms in a separate wing, with another two for a nanny or domestic help on the other side. There were five bathrooms or half baths; not all the bedrooms had an *en suite* but the master did, which was what mattered to me.

The front door opened into a vestibule and the living and dining rooms were on either side of a central hall. This was a rambling, expansive house, but nothing about it screamed mansion. It lent itself more to the word cozy and that suited me just fine. The living room was only small compared to our Chicago digs; for a family home, it was immense. In it was a gorgeous Clinker brick fireplace with intricate carved masonry designs and high windows on either side of it. Another, larger bay window gave out to the front sweeping lawn, and even had a window seat, something I'd longed for since visiting Cass' house and seeing the one in her bedroom.

My agent remarked as to how there would be plenty of room for two comfortable sectional sofas and probably three other separate seating areas, forming a U-shape on each side of the fireplace.

"You could easily set up a bridge table and chairs in the back there, " she added.

And the kitchen! It was my dream. French doors led from an eating nook to the brick patio out back and that park-like back yard I was hoping for.

"That would be lovely for barbeques or other outdoor activities," I noted, and Martha could only agree.

The room itself was huge, not the chef's kitchen we had on Lake Shore, but perfectly suited for family needs. It was done in shades of yellow and white with a Viking stove and Sub-Zero fridge that looked like a cabinet instead of an appliance. There was a spacious island in the center with a marble top and much storage below on one side; stools lining the other. There was a small "extra" sink built into the island, also, but the main sink under the widows was a huge double farmhouse one set in a marble surround, with a wonderful high faucet/sprayer. Cabinetry was opulent; the cupboards were tall and expansive.

I could see myself cooking in there even if Polo could only envision us having staff.

"But I want to cook for us," I told him, laughing. "I want to put the baby in a grocery cart and do the shopping, too."

"Sarah, " he said, giving me that perplexed look of his, " *ma chérie*, please be realistic. You have a career in Chicago, do not forget. You are still *Directrice d'Education de La Fondation*."

"Well, I know that. Don't worry, I can do my job at the Foundation and also go grocery shopping!"

*In 1954, the price of the house that my parents built and where I was raised, was seventeen thousand dollars with the lot in one of The Bluffs' most desirable neighborhoods costing them another five grand. The Wilmette house, in 1973, was on the market for two hundred five thousand dollars! I thought that price was a **fortune**, simply outrageous, but that was typical for houses in the suburbs on the North Shore. When Polo saw it, and realized that*

I'd want to change most of the décor, paint or paper the walls, and renovate any bathroom or kitchen plumbing fixtures that were outdated or not to my taste, he consulted with both the owner of the real estate company and his trusted legal team at the Foundation, and then authorized me to offer them one hundred eighty thousand – all cash, quick close. They didn't even counter, but accepted that price outright.

By the time Georges-Henri was twenty-three months old, we would be moved into 776 Linden Drive. Linden was just the kind of quiet street I had visualized, with stately homes, but not walled or gated. At one point the street lanes divided and a little park was installed at the top of the block with cross-walks leading to it. Mature oak trees lined it, which was just what suited me—I could walk my baby up and down shaded sidewalks and be completely *chez moi.*

But Polo had certain caveats to this arrangement-- things I'd never even thought of.

"Sarah, I do not wish to put too fine a point on this, but we shall need more security than this house affords us as it is."

"Why?"

"Why? *Quelle question!* Did you not realize there is a complete security detail at our home on Lake Shore?"

"Not ...really. Is there?" I laughed a bit but he was serious.

"Yes, darling, and do you know who has been trained as the security chief?"

"No."

"Robin."

Ugh, I should have known.

"Who trained him?"

"A professional security company. It was the same for me when I lived in Paris. It is the same for *Oncle Charles* in *Génève.* And I should like them to also consult on the new house."

"But, again...why do we need that? What will it entail?"

"*Chérie,* I am a modest man, and I do not flaunt our *richesse,* as you know. But we are extremely vulnerable to crimes that every wealthy family must face. Kidnapping, assault, theft, *et cetera.* Our entire residence on Lakeshore is wired with alarms. All the art pieces are individually protected. You are always telling me that our furniture looks as though it should have ropes in front of it. Well, it is true, the pieces in our public reception rooms and the dining rooms, the bedroom of *Maman*...most of the entire floor... are museum-quality, and are thus catalogued, insured and protected."

"Okay, I understand that. But what I have in the Wilmette house isn't like that. You have curated furniture and accessories in our Lake Shore home. I wanted comfortable, livable stuff---nice!---I'm not saying junk, but nothing worth—uh-- cataloguing! Things are more...you know...normal in there." *There was that word again.*

I had not exactly skimped on furnishing the new house, and I loved the way my home was decorated when I got done with it. But I can't take all the credit for that. Julia Hyde had shown an interest in helping me when I mentioned to her that we'd purchased a place in her neck of the woods. She informed me that she also had an entrée into the Merchandise Mart, thanks to Hyde Industries, and that she would be happy to take me there again and introduce me to a myriad of vendors, decorators and tradespeople. Even though her degrees weren't in interior design, she was knowledgeable about all aspects of it, and offered to guide me towards procuring everything I –and my husband – wanted. I was happy to accept her offer, if a bit perplexed by this sudden interest in me. I mean, I guess the Hydes had always liked me – in fact I knew it. But it occurred to me that she might have taken pity on me knowing whom I married, and that I might not be up to the task of taking on decorating a place that would rise to his level of "style." She didn't come right out and say that, but even if she had, I wouldn't have been able to argue with her. I had spent enough time in up-scale American and European homes and museums to begin to cultivate my own taste, but I appreciated her guidance.

When completed, our Wilmette home was retrofitted with Porcher bathrooms that had marble walk-in showers and cabinets full of Porthault linens; there were Waverley, Brunschwig & Fils and Laura Ashley wall coverings and fabrics used on comfortable decor; a large Henredon dining set, and bespoke furniture from several North Carolina manufacturers. My color scheme was very light washed-out blue and white (no surprise there) with scattered accents in cherry red on ancillary pieces. The living room was the grandest and most formal room in the house. I figured we would be entertaining in there, so I went with large-scale elegant furnishings; there was nothing

711

demure about it. I chose to keep the walls that light blue with cream crown moldings and baseboards. One entire wall was windows, which we changed out to beveled glass French doors. The drapes were silk damask, the palest slate blue and white stripes. I had three tufted linen sofas flanking the fireplace, all different, but variations on the theme of comfortable yet timeless "French country house." There was, as the realtors had both expounded upon, plenty of space for a large octagonal white lacquered game table with matching chairs upholstered in the same fabric as my drapes, and a gorgeous mahogany bar towards the back of the room, surrounded by several other conversation nooks. The carpets on top of the beautiful, high gloss oak floor of the living room, were thick slate blue hand-knotted Persian rugs that Julia helped me find. There was a huge French crystal chandelier hanging over the coffee table like a piece of jewelry, and two enormous curio cabinets to house glass and sculpture pieces that Polo loved.

However, it was the family room in this house where I achieved my own interior design dream. The room had beautiful cherry paneling on two walls, with another entire wall of Palladium windows. However, the fourth wall, housing the fireplace, I considered my masterpiece of decorating. I had it painted a soft red, with a cream mantel flanked by hurricane lamp sconces and topped with a huge antique mirror. The furnishings in there were far less formal, featuring my preferences for cozy ginghams, stripes, or even a pop of plaid on armchairs surrounding a huge leather sofa, and hassock. I had custom bookcases with glass doors installed in the family room where I displayed many of my own favorite things and small objets d'art like Herend figurines of animals and Staffordshire dogs. As planned, we chose not to display any of Polo's priceless objets d'art.

In the dining room I had an enormous china cabinet full of Royal Copenhagen table services in both the traditional pattern and their Flora Danica for entertaining; my everyday dishes were Limoges and Quimper. I asked Polo if I could "borrow" some of Marie-Aveline's antique plates to line an archway into our pantry, and he was pleasantly surprised and pleased to let me take them to use in the new house.

But I did not consult Polo on bringing art works from Lake Shore to display on our walls because I didn't want museum pieces in there. However, bare walls wouldn't do either, so I chose reproduction prints from artists like Boudin and Turner with a bent for scenes of the sea to enhance our surroundings.

Julia Hyde played a pivotal role in all of this, went with me several times back and forth on shopping expeditions, and pronounced at the end of it that she was pleased with the results. It occurred to me over and over to wonder why she cared so much about my new beginnings as a wife and mother, and our move to the smaller home. I speculated that maybe it was due to her having watched her own daughter die, and maybe it had made her rethink the way she had parented Cass. Perhaps taking me under her wing was her way of atoning in some part for that.

So while our home was certainly nice, upscale, tasteful and full of beautiful things, I still felt it was just a private house, not a showcase, not a manor house and not in need of enhanced security. But Polo was adamant.

"Sarah, Georges-Henri d'Arivèque will be in there."

"Ah. You think he could be at risk for…kidnapping?"

"Yes."

"Seriously?"

"Yes, darling. Robineau has already approached me with the idea of having a trained caretaker who would act as a bodyguard live on the premises with us, as well as several other servants."

"No." Tears welled up in my eyes. " I… have… no intention… of even entertaining that thought."

"Please hear me out. Will you, *chérie*?"

I nodded. I certainly didn't want to make him mad at me when he was, until this, giving in to everything I wanted. "Okay. What?"

"There needs to be a wrought-iron fence around the entire periphery of the property and a gate that opens electronically. That is the minimum of protection needed."

"Oh great, so when Georges-Henri wants to ride his trike on his own sidewalk, he has to be buzzed in and out?! What about trick or treaters? We won't even get any!"

"Sarah! You are being ridiculous now! That is one night on the entire calendar!"

"Well, yeah, but an electronic gate ruins my vision of normal family life!"

Polo became firm. "We cannot have a **normal**…as you see it… American life, darling!"

"You can take the girl out of The Bluffs, but you can't take The Bluffs out of the girl" raised its ugly head. *Where had Adult Sari disappeared to? She evidently still had a ways to go.*

"You're obviously right about that, " I conceded, calming down. But he could tell I still wasn't happy about this.

"Now do not get *ungebluzen*, Sarah!"

He didn't deserve my moodiness, so I snapped out of my pout. I was being selfish and stupid. One of these days we would get the word we were dreading that *Oncle Charles* had died, and the papers would no doubt print the news that Jean-Paul d'Arivèque had become, whether or not he used the title, Duke of Beuvron, one of, if not **the** richest man on the planet. Living right there in Chicago and Wilmette. Of course there would be a heightened danger to us all. He would be as renowned as the black wolf, as the French say. Hell, he already was.

"I agree to all your security demands...er... I mean...wishes, Polo. I'm sorry I acted like a naïve fool. You're right. You always are."

And so it came to pass. Polo had given in to me about raising our child in the suburbs and I, in turn, gave in to having a trained security "caretaker, " a live-in nanny, and a housekeeper who also cooked. We had enough bedrooms in the home's back wing for the domestic help, and the caretaker would live in a very nice apartment we had built over the garage.

I assured Polo that I was on board with all this. "It does make sense, in the end," I told him, " because some of the time I surely will have to be gone, and we'll need for full-time babysitter in the home."

Polo was relieved I'd come around. "I also admit to feeling safer knowing that Bernard ("Bernie") Mason, will be on site, " he added. "He was hand-picked by Robineau. I am confident it is the right decision."

Annie-Laure had offered to help me hire the other staff, and she made all the initial overtures to the agency involved. It was decided we would interview for nannies at Foundation headquarters. So I bought a portable playpen, and took Henri into work. This gave Polo a chance to *kvell* over his little one as people from all departments filed in to see our baby and his father's obvious adoration.

For the position of nanny, I chose a young woman named Genevieve Basset, who had gone through junior college hoping to major in early childhood ed., but who had been obliged to interrupt her studies when her father died suddenly and left the family hard up to make ends meet. She'd gone to work in a Loop coffee shop, but all the while longed to work with children. The idea of living in our home was the answer to her prayers, she'd told me, as her mother still had two teenagers at home.

The housekeeper-cook we hired turned out to be a friend of Annie-Laure's mother named Jeanne-Marie Dufour, who, with her husband, had moved from Annie-Laure's home town of Amiens, France to Highland Park in the mid 1960's to be near her daughter, married to an American she had met while he was working in France for NATO. When American bases were, in essence, kicked out of France, and her children moved to America, Jeanne-Marie and her husband found themselves an ocean apart from her daughter and grandchildren, so they decided to emigrate. Annie-Laure's mother had kept in touch with them through the years, and Annie-Laure tried to visit when she could, too. Jeanne-Marie had become recently widowed, still fairly young at sixty-two. Our situation was perfect for her.

"She won't have to live alone anymore and can still see her grandchildren and the rest of the family when she likes, since they live really not far from you," Annie-Laure told me. "She's not a chef, but she's a wonderful French cook."

"Sounds great, " I said. Jeanne-Marie could take care of the meals and supervise housekeeping. She wouldn't have to do any heavy domestic chores, since Polo offered members of his staff as cleaning help several times per month, (and he provided them with a hefty salary bonus that came along with that.)

Both nanny and housekeeper started working for us almost immediately after we moved in, and a routine was established. Our household was, at least, more laid-back, more "*décontracté,*" I remarked to Polo, than his on Lakeshore was. Polo's great dream of fatherhood was fulfilled, so it was no surprise that he wanted to be a very involved *Papa*. It didn't take long for him to see the benefit of being a family unit in the more conventional environment the Wilmette home afforded us.

Robineau did not come out to spend the night when Polo was in Wilmette. They worked it out that Jean-Luc would bring Robin along any mornings he was coming to drive Polo back to Chicago. That way he could still help Polo get showered and dressed for work, and be back to run the household on Lake Shore Drive as usual. This was about a seventy-minute round-trip process, if the traffic wasn't too heavy. When I was needed at the office or wanted to work there, I drove the *Citroën* in myself; and on those occasions I might also drive Polo home with me in the evening.

I consulted Jean-Luc on the best car to provide for Nanny Genevieve, suggesting to him that I'd noticed out in the suburbs that the Volvo was a very popular one. Luc agreed and suggested a Volvo station wagon. He accompanied me to the Evanston dealership and we test drove a few cars before I picked out a brand new, 1975, yellow 1800 ES sport wagon, for which I wrote out a check for five thousand dollars and change. This was a stylish auto with a wide rectangular rear tail-gate window, which caused it to be named "Snow White's coffin" in Europe. It was not the boxy icon the Volvo station wagon would become later. I loved driving it, myself, too.

Nanny took charge of all things having to do with George-Henri—meals, laundry, naps, etc., and it was agreed that I would take over whenever I wanted to; when I was home, it would be up to me to make the decisions about schedule, playtime, and discipline. But it became apparent to me from the start that Genevieve and I would get on famously, and we pretty much dovetailed our activities with the baby. Our schedule was a little different than most, though, because I wanted our little one awake past seven when he could have playtime with his father.

As new parents, Polo and I had had a serious conversation about what the child would call each of us. It was obvious that any kid of ours would have a leg up on becoming bilingual, and that even though Polo did not consider himself a French count, but an American citizen, he was, for all intents and purposes still French, and as such, should speak French with our child.

"So he should use the French term for you, and you should be *Papa* –pronounced in French of course-- like your father was to you."

"But you do not wish to be *Maman*, I am imagining," he laughed. "Am I right?"

"Well, as a matter of fact, you are. I think, as you know, that there can only be one *Maman*, and that's not me. So I think I'll emulate Cass on this one and be what she called her mother, which was **Mummy**."

Cass's children had called her Mama, and that seemed too old lady to me. I had always liked being at Cass's house when we were in college, and hearing her call Julia "Mummy," as though she were hoping the moniker would produce the closeness the word conjured up. Plus it was British, and I still had a nostalgic longing for England.

Because we did live close to Kenilworth, it turned out that I was able to see the Jones-Hyde twins fairly often-- at least until they were about eight. They were, of course, quite a bit older than my son, but happy to be invited over anyway, and they liked to play with him. Their governess would bring them to our house to play, and they came to his birthday parties and other celebrations. We treated all the children as though they were cousins, and we even socialized a bit with Julia and John-Wilfred.

The Hydes announced to me that, starting with third grade they were taking the twins out of North Shore Country Day School and relocating to Switzerland with them, in order to place them in *Le Rosey*, that posh school Cass had attended for one year. Julia and John-Wilfred had decided to initiate a sort of pre-retirement phase, and elongate their annual stay in Gstaad, where the school had their winter trimester, and the twins would have family there part of the time.

"*Le Rosey* is one of the most exclusive schools in the world, " Julia explained to me, and I already knew it, "but not the most rigorously academic." She gave a little laugh. "They'll have a chance to develop their creativity as well as the regular subjects."

"Let's face it, " said their grandfather, "these children will have no trouble getting into any college. And they'll be turned into great skiers as **Roseans!**"

I was not surprised at their decision. *Le Rosey* had a reputation that preceded it, and a clientele of the wealthiest families in the world. But the idea of the twins being there, so far away, also gave me pause and sent twinges of sadness through me. I reckoned, however-- possibly to make myself feel better-- that at least they had each other, and their special twin kinship would be their saving grace. Plus any time we went to Geneva, we could also see them.

When our Georges-Henri was three, I started him in nursery school in Wilmette and finally began to meet other mothers. It was interesting that few of them had any inkling of who my husband really was. What they did notice was that I drove a really funky car. (When Henri started primary school, it was usually I who drove him and picked him up; my blue *Citroën* or Nanny's yellow Volvo were both cars that were easy for him to spot.)

Most of the moms I met at Henri's school had left their own careers when they married and settled in the Chicago suburbs. They were young, wealthy, Junior-League types, willing to take on many volunteer duties, especially at the school. They were well-groomed and exquisitely dressed --to appear casual. Their jeans were Ralph Lauren and their sweaters cashmere. These women's days were peppered with hair and nail appointments, spa treatments, facials and exercise classes. Their calendars were brimming with board meetings, garden club gatherings, golf and tennis dates, and bridge luncheon parties. They took part in things that were completely anathema to me like riding in the North Shore Hunt Club or sailing. They traveled with their husbands, and they owned secondary vacation residences, many in Door County but also Colorado, Arizona, and Southern California. They all had cleaning help, some had summer girls, and others had full-time nannies, but even they didn't employ the kind of staff I had in Chicago.

I was something of an anomaly to these women. I worked outside the home. I had not given up my career after marriage...quite the opposite. Sometimes they indicated to me how floored they'd been to see me on the t.v. morning shows. They were friendly to me at the school, but they couldn't quite figure me out. I only occasionally orbited through their galaxy.

They may have had their suspicions, but the jig was up, when, at one point during Chicago's autumn arts gala season, the Foundation hosted some cocktail parties for various boards Polo served on, and a group of the nursery school mommies showed up at our Lake Shore home, and were duly astounded to see that the "lady of the house" was...me. You could almost see the wheels in their heads turning as the bombshell realization hit them that we were **those** d'Arivèques.

"Oh, here we go, " I whispered out of the corner of my mouth to Polo, even as he smiled at our guests gasping in disbelief. Polo knew right away that my unspoken presumptions were that once they got over their initial shock, they'd be judging me. He pre-empted my whining by taking me aside and reminding me that he didn't give a damn about what anyone else thought of his marriage.

"*Je m'en fous*! Anyone with a *soupçon* of intelligence, they will not think ill of you or have any malice towards you for having married me."

"You are impervious to slander and scandal, Polo. I'm not."

"Darling, please. Let us not dwell on this. I chose you to be my wife. If other people cannot accept that, you must agree it is their problem, not ours. Am I right, Sarah? I will always protect you as best I can from any spiteful acts towards you, the sort perpetrated by Robineau in the beginning, for instance. But we must let go of troubling thoughts that keep us from enjoying our life together. Yes?"

I nodded. What he was implying was that I needed to keep to my vow to **grow up**! Insecure Sari Shrier had not been fully tamped down yet. Sarah d'Arivèque needed to step in and finish the job.

After that, anytime I showed up at Henri's school, everyone greeted me in a friendly way that I perceived to hold a slight deference I hadn't seen before.

"*Ça c'est possible*, " Polo laughed, when I related the change to him. "As long as they are *amicale* towards you. "

"Yes, they are...to my face," I chortled.

"That is what matters! What anyone says about us behind our backs, we cannot control, *de toute façon*."

And as usual, he was right.

*   *   *   *

It was great to have a fenced backyard for Henri to play in. And that led me to my next project with which to confront Polo: getting a dog. I felt strongly that little kids should grow up with a dog. For one thing, in theory it taught them some responsibility at a young age, and for another, if the temperaments were well-matched, a kid and his dog could become the greatest "best" companions. Polo was leery of this, but as usual, he could not refuse me, and I went by myself to the Evanston pet rescue center and found a very young male Beagle.

"Might be a mix," the animal control officer told me. "We think he may also have been the runt of the litter. We took a whole slew of 'em from a puppy mill up the highway towards the Wisconsin line. We're *guesstimating* his age at about five or six months old. There were three more of these and about six cocker spaniels. People should be in jail, " he added, shaking his head. "Already adopted out most of these."

"I think he looks pretty much like a beagle, " I said. "Do you really think he's a mix?"

"Hard to tell, " he answered. "Seemed to me like the pure-bred ones were the cockers. We aren't sure of the rest. He may turn out to be bigger than a beagle…might have some other hound mixed in. Can't really say."

The officer brought the dog out of a cage, and I got down on my knees. The puppy came right over to me as I extended my hand for him to smell, and then I petted him and rubbed him behind the ears. His tail wagged in appreciation of all the attention. His face was a beautiful tan and the ears were a bit darker. He had white around the nose and throat, tan with a black "saddle" on his back. The rest of him was white.

I adopted him and brought him home.

"What should we call him?" asked Polo, smiling down at me on the floor with the dog, giving me that look that said *I'm not so sure about this, but I can deny you nothing.*

"How about *Guillaume le Conquérant*, since we live in a Norman French house?"

"Do you think our son will be able to pronounce that any time in the near future?" Polo asked me with a twinkle in his eye.

"Okay, we'll name him *Guillaume*, but **call** him Willy. How's that?"

"Parfait… comme toujours, mon chou."

I took the dog's muzzle in my hands and cooed in his face, " You're Willy now!" I stood up and moved away from him calling, " Here Willy! Come!" The dog just stood there, looking bewildered-- but so cute!

I thought it was going to be curtains for Willy, however, the first few nights we had him. He didn't like being put to bed in his kennel and he howled. Unceasingly. Afraid the neighbors would hear him and complain about the noise, I stayed with him, sang made-up doggie lullabies to him, and soothed him into the wee hours of a few harrowing nights until finally he got the message that he LIKED the kennel---it was his safe place in the end. Eventually, he happily went to sleep in it.

I took Willy to obedience training back at the Humane Society in Evanston and he passed the Level One class with flying colors. He could therefore, "sit," "stay," and "come" on command. I also taught Henri to be very gentle with the puppy, and Henri soon learned to treat his dog as "Nice, Willy."

Nevertheless, a month or two into this pet experience, I hired a dog trainer to come out and teach him to signal when he needed to go outside. He'd been paper trained when we got him, but I wanted to sort of nip that and start him on going outside by "telling" us. After a few lessons with the trainer, he would sit at the French doors off the kitchen and bark once to be let out. He also barked to be let back in if somehow we weren't paying attention.

We made quite the Norman Rockwellian scene at night in our sweet Wilmette abode, the four of us: Polo took to sitting in my newly acquired red and cream-striped arm chair to the side of the fireplace in the family room, with me usually on the floor at his feet with our baby boy and his Beagle puppy. Willy reminded Polo of how much he missed having a dog after leaving France at twelve years old, and he told me over and over again what a good decision it ended up being to get the pup.

Henri could toddle around pretty well, starting at about fourteen months old, pulling himself up by holding on to something, like his Papa's knee. By the time we moved to Wilmette, he was walking unaided. He was a fast crawler, too, and could give the dog a chase on all fours. He liked all toys he could push or ride on. The dog was really in for it when Henri figured out he could chase him around on a Big Wheel.

Henri loved toys such as soft plastic boats that he would play with in the bath, and he loved going to the beach near our house with big boats and sand toys. He was all for rides in the carriage, converted now into a large navy blue and white stroller. Often I took him and the dog, too, which required me to maneuver the leash carefully so as not to monopolize the entire sidewalk. On days not suitable for a foray to the beach, Polo and I sat out on our patio in the glider while Henri and Willy ran around the grassy lawn. It did not escape either of us that I had achieved the home life I craved.

*   *   *   *

Jean-Paul d'Arivèque and I got pregnant two more times in the next five years of our marriage, but neither of the pregnancies made it past the first trimester.

716

The first time I didn't even know what was happening really. My pregnancy with Georges-Henri had gone almost flawlessly, with hardly a minute of morning sickness or discomfort. So I wasn't prepared at all for things to go wrong.

I was in about the eighth week of my second pregnancy. It happened so fast. One day everything seemed fine, but the next day, I woke up with some cramps and a little spotting. I didn't think much of it. Then by evening, my breasts had no more of that tenderness they had had, and I began to think something was amiss. It had happened too early for me to notice things like no movement, but for whatever reason, I just didn't feel pregnant anymore. The following morning I called Dr. Bertram, who saw me right away. Stethoscope in hand, she became quiet and looked up at me with sorrow in her eyes and a frog in her throat. I was right.

"I...I am not sure what went wrong, " she said, softly, shaking her head. "There's no heartbeat."

Polo and I were shocked more than anything else, but we determined to put the anomaly behind us and keep trying.

It took us longer to get pregnant the third time.

The next miscarriage occurred with more drama. It was 1977 and I had taken Henri to pre-school and driven on into Chicago. I was at the office doing some work on a presentation I was to give in a few weeks for Northwestern's film school-- just the usual--- telling of the offerings available to them from the Foundation, a speech I could truthfully deliver without preparation. But I'd decided to update our catalogue to hand out. All at once, at my desk, I felt a bad cramp, and then the ooze of blood between my legs. This wasn't spotting; it gushed. And I screamed. Polo came in panicked to see me. I ran into the bathroom adjacent to our offices and left a smear of blood on my chair which made him nearly hysterical as he called out for Annie-Laure to get Dr. Bertram on the phone. There wasn't time to get immediate help; the doctor couldn't just walk out of her office and come to me. But she sent over one of her nurses, who confirmed that the slough of blood and mucus was a miscarriage.

We bypassed going to Betram's office. I was promptly admitted into the hospital, inconsolable and nearly hysterical.

"But WHY?! What the hell is up with this when it was so easy the first time?!" I sobbed out loud to the doctor, while Polo leaned over the bed to hold me and kiss the top of my head.

"You know, " she answered quietly, "it is often nature's way of saying there would have been something wrong with the pregnancy or with the baby. It is a case of chromosomal abnormalities."

"It is because of my age, is it not?" Polo asked her with deep resignation.

"Oh, not necessarily. Lots of men older than you become fathers. But on both sides, your mothers had difficulty becoming pregnant after the first child. It could be something genetic, really...from either of you."

She tried hard to reassure him, but I could tell he didn't buy it. I certainly hadn't assumed or given him any reason to believe that I felt his age was the reason. However, he could not hide his despondency from me and the temporary depression that set in with both of us scared me. It seemed to vindicate my old adage that no marriage was ever really happy. Now I was afraid mine would join those ranks.

In the ensuing months, those real fears that I could never again make him happy resurfaced within me, but Polo, ever so perceptive, caught wind of what I might be thinking, and sought to reassure me that his and my love had grown even deeper and more beautiful because of the sorrow.

"*Je t'adore, tu sais,* " he would coo at me.

"And I adore you."

But we did not ever conceive another child. I went on birth control pills and we made the conscious joint decision to have no other children. We would cherish Georges-Henri for the rest of our lives and not think of what could have been.

In light of the decision, Polo and I discussed at length the dangers of even unwittingly smothering our now only child with our affections, because he was such a precious part of both of us. We saw the results of other parents' overprotection. The terms "helicopter parent" and "Tiger Mother" had not yet come into use, but "Jewish mother" certainly had, and the behaviors existed. We saw it in evidence with many of Henri's little friends, and we tried even harder to avoid any such situation with ours. We made a concerted effort to treat him as a kid and not as a *Petit Prince* or a little *Mashiach*.

I had read up on studies of "poor little rich kids" and their sometime tendency to never be satisfied or satiated with their lot in life, always demanding more of everything, even playing one parent against the other. I did not see this in my son. To be sure, he didn't lack for anything: toys, clothes or outings; but he seemed to be content with whatever came his way. He loved us and he loved his dog, not making much of a differentiation. He was curious, and he could amuse himself as happily alone as when being stimulated by outside sources.

Henri was a good student in the Wilmette public schools, polite to his teachers, whom he professed to like each year, and eager to get up every day and go to school. Liking school was big in my book. I had liked it because it was a refuge for me; he liked it because he was being creatively and intellectually guided and challenged, and because he had some nice friends. Dom had told me that by the time students arrived in his high school class, if they hated school, it was almost too late to be of any real help to them. You had to like school in the elementary years to be a success later.

For his part, Georges-Henri, albeit with some lapses, was remarkably even-tempered and non-demanding. However, he certainly wasn't perfect. Like every kid, he could be cross, sulky and irritable at times, and it was only logical that, since I was the one around him most, doing the most discipline, like many other mothers, he turned his irritation on me.

One night when he was about eight years old, Polo heard him giving me attitude and talking back. "Georges-Henri, " Polo addressed him sternly, "I do not want to ever
hear you speak to your mummy in that tone again, do you understand me?"

The boy was so surprised at having been called out in such a way by his normally soft-spoken father, whom he adored above all other human beings, that he stood up from his toys, came over and hugged me, and said, "Yes, *Papa*. I'm sorry, Mummy."

And that, surprisingly enough, just about did the trick. It wasn't our only behavior issue, but Polo's nipping that attitude stuff in the bud paved the way for Georges-Henri to interact with me in a more respectful way from then on. He wasn't only told to do so, either; he had his father as a role model on how to treat his mother. In the end, what I concluded was that all his life, our son treated me so well because he observed his father doing so. And it worked the other way around, too. He saw me as a most loving wife to his dad, taking the physical limitations completely in stride, with no embarrassment or self-consciousness about giving Polo the help he needed. From the time he was old enough to observe us, our kid saw a mother who deeply cherished her son and adored his father, a father whose wide-open heart overflowed with gratitude as much as love, who delighted in heaping affection on both his wife and son.

If our life with Henri was idyllic, it was not lost on me that one of, if not the main reason why, was the lack of stress in it. I may have had some work decisions to make and some time constraints associated with being a working mom, but I was never faced with the choice between buying groceries at the end of the month or paying the rent. I didn't have mounting bills, an unfaithful or inebriated husband coming home at night to control or abuse me, or a kid who had to go to school with shoes falling apart.

There was a pithy saying making the rounds in those days, mostly in pious conservative circles, which I would normally have eschewed, but which, for some reason touched a chord in me: **"The best thing a father can do for his children is to love their mother."** *If only Alan Jones had espoused that, I pondered, how different Cass' life might have been.*

Georges-Henri grew securely in the loving cocoon of both his parents, but he was obviously **not** being raised by us "as normally as possible." It wasn't normal to have a full-time nanny, a working mom and domestic help, two large homes in Chicago, a summer house in France, ancestral homes in Switzerland, a *pied-à-terre* in New York, and parents who took him along to many a reception and cultural activity. We tried to live with a routine for him, however, and simulate suburban family life as much as we could. He adapted, and for all we knew, he thought all little kids had the same life as he did. I believe that later on, when Henri understood why he didn't have any brothers or sisters, he even became rather protective of me. He had a sweet sensitivity—not that rare in boys—but he seemed to feel more deeply than your average child and pre-teen.

As for that "summer house in France," something else I really wanted was for our kid to have as close as possible some of the upbringing Polo had had. One way of replicating that was to spend summers at *La Pérégrine*. Polo was quite surprised when I suggested this, having not used the house in decades except for the special wedding. Since Marie-France de Piaget was living there, however, the house had come alive again, and I argued that if we took our boy over to see her (and also Uncle Charles in Geneva), she would become his son's *de facto* honorary grandmother. The idea pleased Polo immensely.

To that end in France every summer, we tried to give Georges-Henri a country experience as comparable as possible to his dad's when he was a boy at the same house, complete with his dog and even, later, a pony to ride. He was free to roam about and swim and play. The one thing that was different, however, was that there were no cousins in the vicinity as there had been in the 1930's, so we made a concerted effort to invite village children over as playmates. A few times we even spent Christmas there, too, and Marie-France made a big production of taking Georges-Henri to Orléans to look at all the beautiful shops.

*   *   *   *

Of course, I had written to my own parents that they had a grandson. I got no direct reply. I say no direct one because it happened that one of my Omaha cousins, Karen Shrier, came through Chicago on business and contacted me. I met her for drinks at her hotel. She acknowledged that the information on Georges-Henri had reached Sol, Betty and Roslyn, but that my letter had not arrived in a timely manner. They had moved, and the post office had taken its sweet time getting mail forwarded to them.

"They live in Omaha now, in a high-rise near the Med Center. Here's their new address, " she said, taking out a piece of folded up paper. "I decided you may as well have it. You never know."

I took the slip of paper and put it in my billfold. "So is Roslyn at Omaha U?"

"Roz is in nursing school at Clarkson."

"So she really did that, huh? I don't get it. She doesn't seem the nurturing type or the science brain either. They probably forced her into it so she'd meet a nice Jewish **doctor**."

"Well, if they did, that's down the road a tad. She's a pretty serious student."

"How can she have any sort of college life living in an apartment with her parents? Jesus!"

"You know, they sold the bar."

That came as a shock to me. "**Really**?"

Karen didn't want to talk about The Spot, however. "Uncle Sol is still incensed by your marriage, Sari. He feels any children of that union would be 'illegitimate.' He's a pretty stubborn guy."

"Why illegitimate when we're married, for God's sake?" I asked indignantly. But she just shook her head.

"Your father is a piece of work" she added, as if that were news to me.

"Well, not knowing my wonderful husband and their terrific little grandson is their ultimate loss. They're pathetic."

"I will tell Aunt Betty that I saw you. She plays *mahj* now with my mother and her friends. Can you believe it? **Your** mother playing with them!"

I knew what she meant. Anti-social didn't begin to describe Betty. My mother could be all smiley with the patrons of her drinking establishment or in the restaurant, but with her family, and especially with me, she had ice water running in her veins.

"How's..her...uh, their health and all? Everyone fine?"

"Oh, yeah, you know; hell, they're still pretty young. I don't think they would have closed The Spot, except that the city's tearing down that block for a new road into the downtown. They got a heck of a buyout for the building."

"They're lucky Nana left that to them, then. Or did they have to pay my other aunts for their shares?"

"Oh, I believe, if I'm not mistaken, that your grandmother left the other two gals their part of the value of The Spot in cash in her will. I guess they didn't ever know what they could get for that real estate. I think everyone made out."

"Well, bully for them then."

"Not like you did, though, eh?" she squinted a knowing look at me. Word must have got out that I married someone wealthy. *She had no idea.*

"Well, it's my husband's uncle, if you must know, who is one of the two or three wealthiest men in the world. Think Ari Onassis or the Aga Kahn."

"Shithouse mouse!" It was a saying we cousins had often used at home.

"Yeah, " I said, " too bad my parents weren't nicer to me. They wouldn't be living in an apartment near the Omaha Med Center. They'd be living on easy street."

"Meet on the Ledge".....Fairport Convention

We lost Polo in July of 1989. My nearly sixteen-year old son had a father, it turned out, only two years longer than **his** father had had one. Nevertheless he, sadly, likewise found himself, at a young and formative age, in that same strange land of grief, clinging to a mother who, herself, was reeling.

By the time Polo really began to be very ill, Georges-Henri was, thankfully, in school in New York City, and did not have to be home to witness the loss of his father by agonizing degrees. Up to that moment, our boy had lived a privileged and happy life.

    *   *   *

Our little one had gone through public grade school in Wilmette, as I had envisioned. Polo and I derived much pleasure in all the things we did that added up to the typical American elementary school experience: we attended every music concert, every holiday program, and parent-teacher conferences. No one's buttons burst as regularly as my French husband's did, seeing his young son's science fair projects or hearing him narrate the third-grade's *Frosty the Snowman* program.

Because of the need for clandestine security around Georges-Henri at school, the principal knew who we were. But we certainly did not advertise either our wealth or our position in Chicago's philanthropic world, although many of the parents, like the ones at Henri's preschool, did eventually figure it out. Suffice it to say, however, if any class project, field trip or equipment need arose, Polo was the first to donate all the funding needed...anonymously.

Henri was an enthusiastic pupil. He took part in each and every new experience offered him: anything music-oriented, science club, junior quiz-bowl and space exploration group. At our country club, he had perfected swimming and had become quite good at tennis.

The only sport he didn't do as a child, but that we intended for him to, was skiing. The Hyde-Jones children were experts at it, and Henri wanted to be one, too. But that would have to come later, once he was in school in France.

In Wilmette, elementary school ended at fifth grade, and as I contemplated his further education, I began to reject the various middle school options available to us. Everyone in our part of Chicagoland was intent on getting their kids into New Trier High School, which had, for decades already, been named one of America's ten best schools. New Trier was a fallback for us, too.

And to that end, the choice of Middle Schools loomed large. At that point, since Henri was just finishing fifth grade and about to enter the next phase, a dilemma was presented to us the same as for other North Shore parents: we didn't especially like the choices his elementary school fed into. Lots of parents we knew from among his friends were at odds about where to send their children for the years from sixth grade through eighth. Most of Polo's colleagues in the various organizations he was associated with couldn't understand why our kid was in the public school in the first place. I had begun to come around to thinking that they and Polo might be right: we could afford the best schools in the world, so why didn't we avail ourselves of them for Henri? I began to research private schools available to us, and chose the Chicago Latin School which was located fairly near our mansion. We could even all commute in together.

The three of us went to visit the school and were impressed with it. Henri wasn't eager to leave behind his neighborhood friends, but the new school offered much that was to his liking, including private music lessons—he was already getting quite good on the piano—and chess club, as well as many sports besides the typical soccer and basketball. The headmaster assured us that new students were welcomed even by "lifers" who had started there together in kindergarten.

Middle School age was a risky time to initiate change. Kids would rather put up with the hell they knew than the heaven they didn't. I just had to hope that his life to that point had not been hell and that he'd get used to the next school and like it, too. True, Middle School was an unfortunate age to have to start over making friends, but we reasoned that Henri's self-esteem was securely intact; we felt sure he would adjust.

Attending Latin meant that our schedule was stretched to the limit with his after-school activities, just like every other American household. I had achieved "normal" after all. The problem was Hebrew School. I had started Henri at Evanston's Temple Emanuel's Sunday School, and he attended sporadically all through his childhood. But the years leading up to age thirteen and the Bar Mitzvah signaled a change-over to Hebrew School, and the reality was that I did not see a way to fit it in.

"We shall have him prepare privately, then, " Polo had suggested.

"Yes, that's a possibility. The trouble is, having a Bar Mitzvah all alone, like in the Rabbi's study or something, strikes me as sad. He'll feel left out."

"He will feel that way anyway, *chérie*, if he does not go to the other children's celebrations."

He was right. From everything we knew, the Bar Mitzvah of that time period among the wealthy congregants was far different from my small-town days where we had a simple party on our patio, and I got to invite my school friends (none of whom, it should be noted, had ever stepped inside a synagogue). Even in Omaha in my day, families grouped together for bigger dances and parties sharing in the expense and, in most cases, not leaving anyone out. In Chicago, the Bar and Bat Mitzvah parties turned into productions that would shock Cecil B. DeMille. It was beginning to be popular to hold them in Israel, too, at venues like Masada; or even worse, to have them at "destinations" like French *châteaux*, Tuscan villas or the Costa del Sol.

We had a château in France and we could afford to fly Henri and all his classmates anywhere in the world, but we never would do that. The idea that these people were all trying to one-up each other and outdo themselves made me physically ill. In the end, we decided it would probably be better to keep him out of that competitive crowd.

So we sat Henri down the summer before he started Latin and explained to him that it didn't really matter if he had a Bar Mitzvah or not, and it was his prerogative to have one even as an adult if he so desired, but we had decided to take him out of Hebrew school.

"Are you terribly disappointed?"

"No...but what about the other kids? "

"You mean the parties?"

"Kind of."

"Well, sweetie, they might still invite you. But remember, you'll be in a different school by then and have different friends."

Our boy was eleven years old, and he knew that he had a Jewish identity, which was ever my only goal in the first place, and to which Polo had agreed eagerly from the beginning. But during that summer before he started Chicago Latin, some of his friends were over and they did bring up Henri's impending absence from the Hebrew School prep class and the Bar Mitzvah.

"Are you not going to have a Bar Mitzvah because your father is too handicapped to hold the Torah up on the *bima* with you?" one of them had wondered.

Henri asked me point blank, admitting that he couldn't understand why his pal had said that. He told me that it had made him wonder if this had anything to do with his quitting the class.

"Absolutely not!" I had retorted. "Good grief. Isn't it awful that people still can't handle seeing or being around anyone who's different? Don't you have any handicapped kids in your school?" I had asked him. He had shaken his head no.

I confronted Polo with this conversation later, and remarked again that it was a different world in 1984 than it had been growing up in America during the aftermath of the polio epidemic.

"Children do not understand the ramifications of what they say, *chérie*, " he had consoled me.

"Yeah, but they get that crap from their parents." It infuriated me that this must have come up in some dinner conversation or other at the kid's home.

Georges-Henri had settled into Chicago Latin well, kept busy with academics and a lot of music. He played piano and started violin lessons, too, as well as singing in the choir. He was fortunate enough to be in a school where he could be boosted into high school French classes since he spoke it so differently than other middle-schoolers. We still wanted him to take French, especially for the grammar and literature.

I still had a bee in my bonnet about him experiencing a life that paralleled his father's, and to that end, we spent at least a month every year at *La Pérégrine*. This pleased Polo, especially since we could see that Henri loved it there. So I began to think up other ways for him to emulate Jean-Paul d'Arivèque's upbringing, and one loomed on the horizon: for him to attend the same high school as his father had, the *Lycée Français de New York*.

"I know we've only just put our kid at Latin, but what do you think of the idea of transferring him for high school in New York… to your old school?" I asked Polo, having bounced into his office one day brimming with enthusiasm.

"I like it!" he had answered, but then just as quickly had become pensive. "But, darling, I cannot move to New York for four years. It simply would not be possible. Could you live there with him…without me? Perhaps I could fly in every other weekend or something?"

"NO!" *I couldn't face the idea of leaving Polo for even a week at a time. That would not work at all for me to move to New York without him.* "And, just to be clear, I also don't want him living in your…our… apartment by himself with just servants either, even though the staff are, of course, more like his friends. We don't even know which of them would be willing to accompany him."

"Yes, I see that this presents a great stumbling block for us, does it not?"

"A big one." I had shrugged and left his office, saying, " Let me get back to you on this."

Polo and I were faced with this dilemma the whole time Henri was in middle school: how to figure out the logistics needed to get him to his father's alma mater. It wasn't a boarding school.

"Perhaps he would be just as happy finishing high school in Chicago, *après tout*, " Polo had remarked when it seemed like whatever solution we pondered wouldn't really work.

"I suppose, " I had sighed. "But I want him to have a bilingual education and graduate with the real French Bac, so he can go to college in France if he wants to."

"Well, we could always send him to Le Rosey where the twins are. They seem to love it."

Cass' children had been at that fancy locale since third grade, and indeed liked their schooling in Switzerland. Their grandparents' arrangements to live over there for long periods of time had worked out better than they could have dreamed, according to Julia. Laura had plans to come back to the States and enroll in college at Vassar. I was hoping to be able to see her if and when I could get Henri settled in New York. Paul had taken the Oxbridge exams and was to embark on a seven-year medical program at Oxford. It was to be the first time ever that the twins had to face living in different cities.

"Oh, gosh, Polo…I thought New York was far away. I don't think we want to be across an ocean from him just yet."

We had invited the Lowensteins over one night and brought it up at dinner. Harry Lowenstein's lovely, but rather shy, wife, Rachel, had become quite good friends with me. Rachel, it turned out, had a degree in early-childhood counseling, and she became my touchstone once in a while, for advice on all things K-6…both at home and in developing materials at The Foundation.

It was Rachel, who, in the end, proposed a solution that I felt could answer all our prayers.

"Harry," she said at dinner, "you still have family in New York who should be able to tell us which of their friends might have kids at that school. We could ask their advice, couldn't we? Maybe one of them would even take, like, an 'exchange student' into their home for the school year!" Rachel had suggested.

"Do you think so?" I had asked incredulously.

"It couldn't hurt to consult with my nephew," offered Harry. "I'll get in touch with him right away."

Harry did contact his nephew, Richard Lowenstein, whose own children attended Horace Mann school, but who, it turned out, did know people with ties to the *Lycée*. He discovered that one of his best friends from childhood whom he hadn't seen for years, had a child—a boy—who went there. And they were Jewish.

"You have to be kidding me, " I had laughed when Polo announced the news to me.

"Does that make a difference?"

"No, but you have to admit that's kind of serendipitous, don't you think?"

We then had more than one long talk with Georges-Henri about going to the same high school as *Papa*. Naturally we broached the subject delicately with him.

"Are you still on board with the whole idea of *Papa*'s high school?" I asked him, "because we won't insist you go there if you want to stay in Chicago with us."

We made it a point to say that he wouldn't be forced into doing anything he didn't want to.

"I think I want to go to *Papa's* school!" he answered with more enthusiasm than I'd imagined.

"Well, darling, you understand that *Papa* and I can't move into our New York place with you, don't you?" He nodded, apprehensively. "And you see, I also don't really want you living in New York all alone in our apartment with only the servants. That wouldn't be any fun would it?"

"No, I guess not."

"Mummy and I could come visit very often, " said his dad, "but we still feel it would be too lonely for you, Henri. Do you agree?"

"I --don't know — I suppose you're right, *Papa.*"

So we explained to our son that we had come up with this idea, and had spoken to "Uncle" Harry---(as Henri called him)—about his staying with a family there, the Reniers, who had a boy in the school, too.

"That way you'd go to school every day with a friend and come home to his family at night. Wouldn't that be just about perfect? If they're nice, of course. We would only do this if you liked them, too. And we would still come very often to see you!"

"I like that plan, " said Henri. "If they're nice."

"We must all go to meet them, " Polo said.

I knew Polo was all for the idea, but he and I were nevertheless a little bit apprehensive even as we set it in motion: it was still a rather bizarre situation, to board Georges-Henri with strangers. It had been more than a decade since the Getty heir was abducted in Rome, but Robineau brought that up often in any talk of sending Henri away, too.

Arrangements were made with the Foundation's New York staff to have the d'Arivèque apartment readied for us, with a car and driver at our disposal, too. The three of us—and Robineau—landed in New York and were thus duly met on the tarmac of JFK and driven to Beekman Place. Polo's *maman* had continued to use that residence all her life, as she spent a lot of time in New York; Polo and I had only been there at very sporadic times in our marriage. He was emotionally attached to the place, however, and always felt happy returning to it.

The day we'd been invited over to Philip and Cheryl Renier's place, we rode with lingering trepidation to East 80th Street right near FDR Drive. The building was nice but certainly not fancy, and their apartment was a classic pre-war six that had been tastefully redone and made brighter and cheerier, it seemed to me.

We were greeted at the door by someone I took to be their housekeeper, and led down a fairly long corridor into a cozy living room with a white sofa and two overstuffed royal blue chairs around a glass coffee table that rested on a lovely white bouclé rug. Off to each side of a white rock fireplace were two other small gilt armchairs upholstered in blue and white gingham. "Cute!" I thought. I liked that room right away! It was awash with light from two south-facing windows behind the chairs, and except for the rug, all the floors were polished cherrywood.

The Reniers were all waiting for us in there. After introductions were made, we began to feel comfortable with them right away. Philip was affable, with a nice smile and, I thought, debonair good looks. He was tall and slim, and wore brown linen slacks and a cream-colored silk shirt. Cheryl was petite and blond, her hair held in place by a wide headband. She was bubbling with cordiality, anxious to make it clear from the onset that having Henri wouldn't be an imposition of any kind. She presented their son to us, who stepped forward to shake our hands, and acted friendly right away to Henri, offering him a seat near him.

Philip explained that they didn't pronounce their last name in French, even though his family had indeed immigrated from Alsace after the First World War.

"We say it like *Ray-NEAR,*" Philip laughed. "But we do speak French, both of us…and of course, Roger does, too." Funnily enough he pronounced his son's name "Roh-ZHAY."

"He's better at it than I am, " Cheryl said, motioning us to take a seat, and reaching for a coffee service that was on a narrow table behind the sofa.

"Coffee?" she asked in a friendly but polite tone.

"We appreciate so much your willingness to take in another teenager," I said.

724

"You know, " Philip said, "I grew up with the whole Lowenstein family...in their building in the 1950's. I would do just about anything for that crew. They are the epitome of 'good people,' aren't they?"

"Indeed they are," offered Polo.

"Roger, are you just finishing up your freshman year at the school?" I asked.

"Yes, *Madame*, " he answered.

"That's what I understood. Henri here will be an in-coming freshman. Does that bother you at all?"

"No! I think that's actually better, " he said. "I can show him the ropes."

I smiled at Henri, who seemed to like the idea, too.

"We have enough bedrooms for them to not have to share Roger's, " Cheryl said. "And there's also a guest bathroom."

"Well, that does sound perfect, " I had to admit.

Harry Lowenstein had already run a background check on these friends of his nephew's. Philip was a wine *négociant* for Vine Street Import Company, and thus traveled to France six times per year, as well as to Portugal, Spain and Chile among other locales. Cheryl worked as a media salesperson for an advertising company. They made over one hundred thousand dollars per annum, four times the median income for the 1980's, which was a very comfortable living; but in New York, it didn't indicate excessive wealth. The big break had come for them when they inherited their apartment from her parents, and could thus live on the Upper East Side without having to invest their capital in the purchase of a home.

After about an hour of conversation about Polo's teen years in New York at that same school, and how his mother had worked with the first French delegation to the emerging UN, then had left New York to start the Foundation in Chicago, we came to the point in our meeting about actually having our child live with these people.

We liked them right away, and I think they liked us, but it was still a lot to ask of them to take in another kid. We also spoke at some length about the security detail that was a part of our son's existence, and we explained that our staff person Robineau and we would arrange it all, including with the school, and that they would have to do nothing.

"We know you are doing this out of deference to the Lowenstein's," Polo said, "and it is quite a generous offer on your part. But we feel we would like to provide you some remuneration, too."

"Oh, no, we couldn't accept rent or anything of the sort, " Philip said. "Consider this just a favor---like you said on the phone—a sort of exchange student/host family thing."

Polo smiled at them but continued. "What we have in mind is this, " he stated, "we would pay Roger's tuition at the *Lycée Français* for his remaining three years, and then offer him a scholarship from the *Fondation Culturelle Française* to do undergraduate work at the college of his choice...perhaps even in France? *Pourquoi pas?*"

Philip and Cheryl sat dumbfounded across from us and Roger just said, "Wow." Tuition at a school like that, at the high school level was, in those days, upwards of twelve thousand dollars per year, about the same as an Ivy-League college. Polo was offering the Reniers somewhere in the neighborhood of eighty thousand dollars, give or take, over the next seven years.

"That is awfully generous of you, " Philip said, still in disbelief.

"It would be our pleasure to do it. After all, you'd be doing us an enormous service."

We left things up in the air for a few days for them to consider Polo's offer and for us to spend time with Henri really feeling him out on his thoughts about the arrangement. In the meantime, I invited Cheryl Renier to meet me at the Russian Tea Room to go over more details of our son living with them...his food preferences, medical insurance information...his religion. Since this was a private exchange and there were no agencies involved to serve as buffers, we were in a bit of a precarious situation if something went wrong. I wanted to reassure her that we had a support system there in d'Arivèque Industries staff, and that, in any event, for any reason, we could be in New York within hours.

"You know," I told her, laughing a little bit nervously, "all my adult life I've been accused, as it were, of being naïve. This time I'm not. I want to assure you that I'm aware this whole thing might not work out. They're kids. Roger might not really be too keen on having his home invaded by another boy.

Henri may not like the school. And it's okay if it doesn't work out. The world won't come to an end. If for any reason you all — or Henri — can't make a go of this and be happy, we'll come get him. "

This seemed to hit her as a surprise. She stared at me without a response for a good long moment and then said, "I –uh – understand what you're saying, but I'm very optimistic that this will all be fine! The boys seemed to like each other ---at first glance at least. I actually think it's going to be great for both of them. To have a quasi-sibling, I mean. Roger had a younger sister…" her voice trailed off, and she looked down at her hands around the Lomonosov teacup.

I was startled at this revelation; no one had mentioned another child.

"Oh!"

She looked up at me with tears in her eyes. "She died from osteosarcoma when she was three years old."

"I am so very sorry, " I said to her, feeling awkward and ill at ease for being in the dark. "I..I just can't imagine what that must have been like."

She'd been so perky and amiable — they both had — that I had no clue they'd been through such unspeakable sorrow as to have had to bury a toddler.

She unbuttoned her cardigan to reveal a heart-shaped locket engraved with an R, made into a brooch that she wore pinned to her blouse on the left side of her chest. Touching it, she looked at me and said, "I keep her close to me always. I think about her every single day. Her name was Rose."

I smiled and nodded, but couldn't find any more words.

"Don't worry, though, " she added, "that I'd be trying to replace her with your son."

"Well, no… that…"

"I just think Roger will also benefit from having a — you know — special friend around the house. It's been nine years since Rose passed away. I took…and continue to take…solace in Judaism."

Yet another curve ball to me. Judaism had its mourning rites and customs, true, but I never saw them as particularly comforting. The religion didn't do a thing for me when Nana died.

"We're practicing Reform Jews, " she stated to me emphatically, "and we go to Temple every week. But I won't insist that Henri accompany us if he doesn't want to."

"He may want to, " I said…and it was true.

Thus all the arrangements with the Reniers were made. We would be bringing him for the start of term just before his fourteenth birthday in mid-September 1987, and that gave us the chance for one last "*grandes vacances,*" **two** months spent at *La Pérégrine* together in our little family unit before he'd be leaving our home.

La Pérégrine, *however, was a sadder place than at any other time in Henri's life because our dear Marie-France had died there a few months earlier. We all loved her, but especially our boy whose only grandparent relationship was with her. We had all gone back for her service. Unlike Polo, she still had family in the region who came to* La Pérégrine *to express their deep gratitude to Polo that their cousin had lived such a full and happy life in the company of the d'Arivèque family, first with* Maman *in New York and Chicago, and then ultimately back in France not far from them. But they asked that the burial take place in her* "pays natal" *of the* Poitu, *and so at that point no trace remained of her at* La Pérégrine. *Her death had been our young Henri's first encounter with grief.*

We had not asked any of Henri's friends to go on vacation with us and our faithful Willy that time, but Henri had friends now in the village, and he could have them over any time he liked. We had, however, invited Robineau's boyfriend Maxime to accompany us on this sojourn in order for Polo to still have, as always, the services of his primary valet, but also for the two of them to be able to get away from Chicago, "*en couple.*" It had been in the back of Polo's mind for some time to offer the chance for Robineau and Maxime to take a vacation together for any amount of time during those two months that Maxime could get away from his club.

The house was plenty huge for them to be able to stay in a section that would be completely private, and for them to be able to take advantage of the pool and gardens, to have a car and go all over the region--- up to Paris if they wanted to. To that end, I'd even availed myself of the d'Arivèque staff to order tickets to the finals of the French Open for all of us. Georges-Henri loved tennis and was becoming quite a good player. It would be a thrill for him to see the stars of the day, Boris Becker, Mats Wilander and Ivan Lendl play in person.

Contrary to the way Robineau had NOT welcomed me into the fold all those years ago, he was as devoted to Georges-Henri as he was to his father; and as much as I had loathed Robineau for a very long time, I trusted both him and Max implicitly with my son by then.

Things at *La Pérégrine* that summer, did not go as smoothly as I had planned for our idyllic family respite before Henri entered high school. I began to sense little signs that something was wrong with my husband. Polo always tried hard never to complain about pain around our kid, but I could tell that he was straining to keep it under wraps. One day as we sat around the pool at the *château*, Polo was hurting and it had become obviously too acute to ignore. I noticed he was trying to rub his leg but not able to reach the part that was giving him the worst trouble. I saw him struggling and asked if I should take over massaging.

"Let's swim, " he said, smiling weakly. "That might soothe it."

The large swimming pool at *La Pérégrine* had been refitted with shallow steps that made it easier for Polo to maneuver into and out of. With the brace off, Henri and I could get him into the water by Polo putting his right arm around my shoulder and Henri taking hold of his left side. We had some of our best times swimming together, too. Even Willy got into the act.

My semi-successful fencing escapades at Iowa U notwithstanding, swimming was just about the only sport I had excelled at as a kid. Sol and Betty had had the foresight to force me to take swimming lessons, and had got me into classes at one of the neighborhood private pools, since the public one in The Bluffs had been shut down in the polio crisis. I wanted the same and more for my child. He shouldn't be like me...completely nil at athletics. I knew that playing sports – on a team or just socially – would serve to raise his self-esteem and provide lasting skills that he could use in adult life to form ties to his community. It was Julia Hyde, however, who had suggested we join their country club in Kenilworth where Henri could also start swimming and tennis at a very young age. If the Hyde twins were home from Switzerland, we would all meet up there, as they always loved seeing Henri and he relished being with them.

Once he we got Polo back to the chaise longue that day, however, I reached over to feel his leg and noticed edema. I could see that my fingers left marks when I pressed down on his skin.

"Does your leg hurt more with the brace on or off?" I asked, concerned about the swelling.

"Well, both, *chérie, les deux*. But I suppose more with the brace on."

"Then, we have to see a doctor, " I said, matter-of-factly, but with a nonchalance that would hide how scared as I was. "I think since we're going to Paris anyway for the French Open, we can consult up there. We can call Fabrizio and ask him to recommend someone, can't we?"

"Sarah, darling, I think I'd rather return to Chicago."

I was stunned to hear him say that. He and I both knew this was to be our last hurrah at *La Pérégrine*. Once Henri was in high school in New York, we might not be able to ever get a block of time like this again. But I acquiesced without argument because Polo's demeanor led me to believe this was too serious to ignore his wishes.

"Okay...if that's what you want, that's what we'll do. We can all go to Paris, and drop Henri, Robineau and Max at the *Parc Monceau* apartment, and then you and I can fly out---and take the dog. I'll make the arrangements with Robineau to bring them back after Roland Garros finishes."

"We shall send the plane back for the three of them."

"Polo," I laughed, "it's a direct flight from Paris to Chicago. They can fly commercial." And then I added, "First class, of course."

He picked up the brace and I helped him get it on. This was a lighter one he'd been wearing for about a decade, and I hoped the only problem was that it needed some adjustments.

"It's probably just the brace, " I said, closing up the top Velcro. "Maybe it's got out of whack somehow."

"Try not to worry, darling, " he said, reaching out to hug me from the chaise longue. "I merely want to consult my own doctors there."

"I'm not worried."

Well, that was a big white lie.

*   *   *

Ten years earlier, when Georges-Henri was in preschool in Wilmette, I was making my first forays back to work full-time and thus, I was in the office with Polo one Spring morning when he got an urgent call from Marie-France de Piaget... from Geneva. Polo motioned through the glass wall separating our workspaces, for me to come into his office. *Oncle* Charles had died.

"Oh Polo, " I said, draping my arms around his shoulders from behind his desk chair and leaning in to kiss him, my face wet with tears, "I'm so dreadfully sorry, darling."

"Yes, we were expecting this, but I am still surprisingly shocked and very saddened."

Oncle Charles had been in failing health off and on for some months, and we had gone over to see him several times even before that, because he so delighted in seeing our little boy. Already in his mid-eighties the year Henri was born, Charles was still spry and still went to work as "*Président- Directeur Général*" of the entire d'Arivèque dynasty. But even Polo had begged him to slow down, so that he could enjoy having our child around as much as for any other reason. Marie-France had taken to spending time in Geneva with him, too, not only because they were great friends, but also because she knew many sides of the business and was talented at being of help to him. It was she who eventually would oversee his funeral arrangements which were set long before he died and in place when we got there.

It had taken us a few days to wind up the projects we were working on and arrange to take our son out of school so he –and his dog---could accompany us to Europe. We had planned to be in Europe for about three weeks, but to return in time for Georges-Henri to participate in all his end-of-school activities. We flew into Paris that time, and were driven to *La Pérégrine*, where Henri, Nanny Genevieve and Willy could stay while we continued on to the funeral in Geneva.

It was decided that I would then take Marie-France back with me to *La Pérégrine*, so Henri could have some quality time with his honorary *grand-mère*. Polo explained to me that he would be obliged, in any case, to remain for a while in Geneva to consult on the business side of things with the Board of Arivèque Industries and his dear friend, Chief of Operations, Stéphane Hardouin and his entire team. Stéphane would set everything in motion, but this meeting could not even take place until a respectful period of mourning had been observed. I had met Stéphane several times already over the years of our marriage, and knew he was *Oncle* Charles' hand-picked successor. He was very fond of Polo, and in no time I came to rely upon him and trust his judgment, too, exactly as if he were part of the family.

Oncle Charles' funeral was a Mass of Christian Burial in the *Basilique Notre Dame de Génève*, followed by internment next to his beloved wife Madeleine.

"United again, " Polo pronounced, when it was over, "after twenty-nine long years. How he missed her."

Polo looked noticeably tired and pale at the cemetery, and seemed to have more trouble than usual getting around. Many people were coming up to him, naturally, and he felt he had to give each one his undivided attention, but I was anxious to get him back inside for a rest. The funeral had started at eleven o'clock and it was past two by the time we all were to gather in the venerable, ancient *Auberge de Briquessert* in Geneva's Old Town. Marie-France had chosen it because it was a favorite of Charles.

After the meal, when people were still paying their respects to Polo, Marie-France took me aside to also express concern about his demeanor and carriage.

"I gave Polo Charles' signet ring this morning, " Marie- France told me, "and I'm thinking this hit him harder than he thought it would, " she offered. "I'm afraid maybe he's feeling more pressure as the head of Arivèque—everything—and also the *Duc de Beuvron* now."

"Of course, he is in deep mourning for Charles, " I agreed, "but I see this as more physical. Don't you notice it? His gait is off-kilter, even more than usual."

"You are more astute than I, " she said.

"The thing is, he still wears that heavy brace. But goddamit, this is 1977! Surely there are lighter ones made now. I can't believe his doctors haven't switched him to some newer materials. There have to be braces and other orthopedic equipment made with aluminum or some alloy or something...anything lighter than steel. *Nom de Dieu!*"

"Sarah, you are right! I shall make some calls, " she said, in her old office-manager tone. "We're in Switzerland, after all! Braces have been being made here since the sixteenth century!"

"They have?" I asked, knowing nothing about that.

"Yes! In the eighteenth century it was a Swiss doctor, Jean-André Venel, who became famous as the father of orthopedics, namely by inventing various braces and appliance to treat deformities in crippled children. Have you never heard of him?" she asked incredulously.

"No, never."

Later when I finally got Polo alone, we sat back down at an empty table.

"Marie-France and I are worried about you, " I told him, without wanting to sound too alarming. "It seems to me that you're having trouble with your leg again. Are you in worse pain?"

"A bit, yes."

"Well, it occurred to me…to both of us… that your brace is just too ancient! You should wear a more modern one---lighter!"

Polo was a little stunned but then laughed softly, "I do love you, you know. I should have realized you would take it upon yourself to see to me."

"Marie-France and I both notice it, and, I must say now, Polo, I'm mad we didn't think of this before. Why didn't your docs at home make it their priority to provide you with more modern orthotics, as they are calling them now? They read the journals. They should be in the know."

"But darling, I never brought up the subject with them, either, now did I?" He put his arm on my shoulder.

"Yeah, I know…you're about to tell me to '*calme-toi,*' aren't you?"

"I would never tell you to calm down."

"Yes. You would." I laughed. "Now let's get you back to the house."

We were staying in *Oncle* Charles' villa on Lake Geneva where we always used to stay when we visited him, even though he had relocated to his penthouse apartment in the city center after the death of Madeleine. The lake house was much smaller than *La Pérégrine*, but it was a veritable little jewel….that still had nine bedrooms! In deference to my husband, they always made up a bed for us in the sunroom on the first floor because there was no elevator there.

The look of it was more Swiss than French, with intimate living spaces all accented by light woodwork and pale walls. The Swarovski chandeliers and beautiful carved wood furnishings were all gorgeous antiques, but comfortable, too, and many rooms had spectacular views of the lake. The best thing about the house was its entrance: very similar to our home in Wilmette…the circular drive was only one step down from the front door.

We had stayed at this house often enough through the years for Henri and me to become very comfortable there, but for Polo, it was another home away from home, and he loved being there. However, this house did invoke sadness for him, too. He was there in mourning for the third time. Lake Geneva did have a calming effect on the place, however, and we sat together on plush lawn chairs on the back terrace, and rested, watching the pristine blue water swish softly against the shore mere yards from us.

"Do you feel…sort of like an orphan now?" I asked Polo with a small amount of trepidation.

"*Eh, oui,* " he sighed. "But *remarque,* I am so lucky to have had him for such a long time, am I not?"

"Yes. You needed a father, but also, he needed a son. Funny how life takes a tragic turn and then it ends up better than you'd have thought."

Polo looked over at me and then reached for my hand. Tears began to appear from the corners of his eyes. I got up to offer him a Kleenex I had in my pocket from earlier.

"Thank you darling, " he whispered to me. "I am not crying from sadness for the two of them--- my father and uncle, so much as from gratitude for you."

The first person Marie-France had turned to when she took up the gauntlet to find Polo some help, was Stéphane Hardouin's executive assistant.

"Naturally, we have many contacts in the medical field here, " she said. "I shall get in touch with someone who can advise you."

A couple of days after the funeral, we were notified by Hardouin's secretary that we had an appointment with a Doctor Marcel Bellechasse at Geneva's prestigious *Institute Orthopédique*. The doctor was very nice, around the same age as Polo, and of course, he was familiar with our name. It was likely that *Oncle* Charles had contributed funding at some time or other to their institution.

729

He explained that Polo would be measured and fitted with a custom brace made out of aluminum by their orthotics specialists, and they said the process could probably be expedited, but couldn't be done overnight or anything, so it was fortunate we had already planned to be in Switzerland more than a few days. He would need to examine Polo with the new brace, too, to make sure everything was perfect.

Because of the change in our plans, it was decided that Marie-France would go back to *La Pérégrine* alone after all to be with Henri, and I would stay in Geneva with my husband. Polo and I agreed that Henri was in good hands with his nanny and our staff there; he knew it was his home. But having "*grand-mère*" with him before his parents could come back would make him even happier.

MFP was nearly eighty years old the year Charles died. We weren't sure how many more times Henri would be visiting her either before she was no longer able to enjoy him.

Polo had several appointments at the *Institute Orthopédique*, with doctors but also with technicians. The former did all the preliminary workups, and the latter fabricated a brand-new state-of-the-art leg brace. The new, lighter brace made a lot of difference to Polo, and was definitely the right thing to have done, albeit late! It was certainly going to be easier for me to help him maneuver it on and off because these new ones did not have the leather straps that had to be buckled. They had Velcro! The clinicians at the *Institute* were amused and a little curious as to how we didn't know braces could come with this closure, which had been invented by a Swiss engineer in the 1950's for heaven's sake.

"George de Mestral named his invention after the French words '*velour*' and '*crochet*', " Dr. Bellechasse's colleague explained, "because of the way it worked with fabric strips that are 'hooked' together."

"Genius, " I noted.

Since I had stayed in town with Polo, I also accompanied him to his business meetings, and it was conspicuous now that the staff referred to him as *Monsieur le Duc*. Charles' death meant, of course, that Polo was now the *Duc de Beuvron* and I was *Madame la Duchesse*. Sometimes thinking about that made me giggle, but there wasn't much gravitas to the event anyway because we didn't use those titles. We had arranged, however, for Georges-Henri to have dual citizenship like his father, in case he should ever live in France as the next titular *Duc de Beuvron*.

Charles' organization had all the ducks in a row with the battery of legal and industrial experts, bankers and board members that were in place to help Polo manage what he needed to as sole heir to this extremely vast empire. Except for the selling off of division assets, there hadn't been much else that would change the way things had always been before Charles died. Polo was never involved in the day-to-day running of the enterprise and he would not need to be now. It was all carried on by carefully appointed family retainers and business partners. Charles had set up a retinue of professional men and women--- bankers, accountants, stockbrokers, real estate managers and others — all looking after our well-being. Polo assured me that only the most honest people of impeccable integrity were involved on both sides of the Atlantic, and that one day when it would be I who was head of the Foundation, he surmised, (against my admonition for him not to talk of such things), the organization would all run as smoothly for me as it did for him.

After the death of Uncle Charles in 1977, Polo also inherited the office buildings and factories of d'Arivèque Industries world-wide. In Switzerland he now owned outright the headquarters building in Geneva, the villa on the lake, Charles' penthouse apartment, and their family home in the Vandoeuvres district, which I had only ever seen one time.

"Are you going to keep that?" I had asked Polo when we were going through the papers with *Oncle* Charles' personal attorneys.

"For the moment, yes, " he had answered. "It still has some nostalgic hold on me, I confess. My grandparents visited Charles there, as did my father once in a while. Someday perhaps we may spend some time there as well." But we never did.

There was, almost immediately upon the death of Charles, another enormous infusion of money and securities for Polo's own private use. He could pour it back into the Foundation if he so chose, or he could just put it in the bank — in Geneva, New York, Paris or Chicago.

When we had married, Polo immediately put my name on all his accounts and made them joint. I did the same and put his name on my bank account, even if that was a joke. I still had that same bank account from when I first moved to Chicago, and I continued to earn my Education Director's salary, which I considered "my money" and didn't ever think about what was at my disposal in Polo's name. We had signed no pre-nuptial agreements. From time to time, for instance when my taxes were due or when large household expenses came up, such as when I bought the Volvo station wagon, he would instruct his accountant to "infuse" my account with some extra money. I had protested that I really didn't need it; it was always too much. I remained thrilled with the salary I made and happy that I earned it.

However, back in Chicago after *Oncle* Charles' funeral, Polo took me into his office one day, and said we needed to have a little *tête-à-tête*, in light of what he had recently inherited. He announced to me that he had made some changes, and had set up a new trust I would oversee for purposes of philanthropy outside the Foundation. It was to be in my name only.

"There are surely causes you would like to support, no? " he had asked me. "This is your money to do with as you like, just as your personal bank account always has been." The difference was the amount in it. "I'm starting you out with five million dollars, Sarah. Does that please you?"

Please me?! I could buy a Senator with that.

"Polo...I don't know what to say. I...I'll do some research and come up with...the best...organizations I can to... spend it wisely."

" You can give it out to people, too, darling. Perhaps your parents? A little peace offering?"

Oh, HELL, no.

"Um, yeah...maybe."

He smiled. "Well, there are so many deserving causes. There is a new group calling themselves *Médecins sans Frontières* which is, I think, very interesting. Also many libraries, nature centers and so on. You do as you like."

"But darling, you must also set down clear instructions as to the philanthropies **you** support and the funding you do personally, too, with the amounts and everything." I knew what galas we attended, what dinners and balls we had calendared, and the groups we entertained at our own home. But he and I had never decided together upon the recipients of d'Arivèque gifts or money.

"Of course, *chérie*. It is all taken care of. If I did not consult with you before it is only because I did not want you to think I saw our marriage as a philanthropic business partnership. It is a partnership in the most correct sense of the word, do not misunderstand. I see you as my equal completely in our marriage."

"I know you do. I wasn't worried about that."

"Good! Because of course, you always did worry—you said it many times—that you were not able to bring your fair share to our marriage, and, much as I vehemently disagree, I also did not want to burden you with too much of the financial side, lest you feel even more hurt that you haven't been able to contribute. But since one day you will be directing the enterprise, it is probably time for us to start easing you into more of the details of the operation."

We had already begun to implement some changes with an eye to the future of the Foundation. For one thing Polo and the board had directed the hiring of a new staff of arts funding experts, several extra people who would be adjunct to our marketing department, not charged with raising money, like many arts organizations found themselves needing to do, but with dispersing it! There was an even wider range of organizations we wanted to support.

I had also added to my own department, an entire group of scholarship administrators. I initiated the plans to offer three times more scholarships than we had in place when I first arrived at the Foundation. We fanned out to provide funding for French studies at Laval in Québec, to the *Alliance Française* of Chicago for their own study abroad programs, and for students who planned on becoming French teachers; they could use the money at any accredited college or university in the world. I worked closely with the Consulate in order not to duplicate their own scholarship programs directed by the French government, but to augment the funding in places where it was most needed, and to give specialized grants to students, say of drama to attend the Aix-en-Provence festival or to film students to travel to Deauville or Cannes.

To a great extent this also meant enlarging the number of pages in our newsletter once or twice a year to include the forms needed to apply for these opportunities and the pages needed to promote them. Polo decided we needed more copywriters, contributing editors and photographers, so Annie-Laure was charged with the task of filling the positions.

Around the time Henri was safely ensconced in elementary school, I approached my husband with an idea that had been in the back of my mind since Cass had brought it up years before.

"Polo, " I had said, initiating the discussion casually one evening, "I'm not sure I ever told you this, but before Cass died, she told me something interesting. She said I ought to go back to school and get a master's degree in art history…if for no other reason than to be able to curate your family's art collection with a few more bona fides." I hesitated a moment waiting for his reaction, hoping it would be positive. "What do you think of the idea?"

"Darling! I think it is a marvelous one!" he had exclaimed right away. "Would you go to U Chicago or Northwestern? I presume not back to Iowa City?"

"Let's see if I can even get accepted somewhere first! But no, not back to Iowa City. I hope Northwestern. Without your having to endow a library or something," I joshed, but was only half kidding.

I couldn't even apply to graduate schools without taking the Graduate Record Exams, and found them to be surprisingly difficult, especially the math. I knew I'd bombed that part, and sure enough, when my results came back, I'd scored very high in English, barely passable in math. I applied and was accepted to Northwestern. The d'Arivèque name on the application probably didn't hurt.

I had more free time than the average "working mom" who goes back to college, but I still scheduled most of my classes in the late afternoon or evenings so I could continue to take Henri in the mornings and get in some office time, too. I'd opted for the M.A. with thesis, rather than the M.S. with Comps, so I had nine less hours of coursework to do.

"See, they give leeway for the classes one must take in order to write the thesis," I told Polo, showing him the grad school catalogue. "It's a three-hour seminar on writing it and six hours called 'thesis'."

"Yes, I see, " he said, not knowing much about the intricacies of American liberal arts degrees. "It seems, nevertheless, to be quite a bit of work, Sarah."

"Believe it or not, darling, I still think this will be easier than what I had to do that year in Paris!"

So when my schedule was worked out with an advisor, I was obliged to have eighteen hours of art history, among which some classes were obligatory, and some could be electives. My coursework required study of many different periods from classical to modern, and from varying cultures. But for six of the hours and for the thesis part, I could concentrate on what I wanted to write about: French art, and Impressionism in particular.

The coursework I'd done at the *Sorbonne* and the Saturday mornings I'd spent meeting up with Dom and Peter at the Chicago Art Institute stood me in good stead. By the time I was thinking of a thesis topic, nearly two years after I'd begun the process, I chose one that was not only a hot topic because not much had been written about it, but also one dear to my heart: *Les Effets de Neige dans les Peintures Impressionnistes,* Snow Effects in Impressionist Paintings.

I called Dom first to run my idea by him before putting it in writing with my advisor.

"Nearly all the major Impressionists painted *en plein air* in the winter," I proclaimed over the phone. "Of course, Monet was the predominant leader of that movement, as well. But also---imagine this-- Caillebotte! I love him. And Pissarro! Pissarro even used that as a title!"

"You picked a winner, " Dom said. "We've got one right here in Chicago on loan ---I'm sure you've seen it."

"I know!" I knew he was referring to Monet's *The Magpie*, which French art historians credit with starting the entire Impressionism movement five years before it got its dubious title at the *Salon des Refusés* with the publishing of a harsh critique of Monet's work "*Impression: Sunrise.*"

Polo was enthusiastic about my thesis topic, and also lauded Monet's bird perched on a gate in the snow.

"Did you know, *chérie,* when Monet painted that one, it was during one of his darkest periods?"

"When he was almost destitute?" I asked, thinking I was pretty up on Monet.

"Yes, that, of course. But also because it was at that time that his family rejected him completely. They did not like his choice of *métier* because he never brought in enough money, and also, they did not approve at all of his relationship with his companion, Camille."

"*Plus ça change, plus c'est la même chose, alors,*" I sighed, thinking of Sol and Betty who, one hundred fifteen years after Monet's family, also did not approve of their daughter's career choice or of her companion!

I was not your typical grad student in one other way: I had a private plane at my disposal and a house in Paris I could go to anytime to do research or wander around in the *Jeu de Paume* and *L'Orangerie*. I took Henri twice on these trips, with Nanny Genevieve, too, and we roamed Paris, ate *glace cappuccino* in the *Parc Monceau*, and played in the *Jardin d'Acclimation* in the *Bois de Boulogne*. I encouraged Genevieve to check Henri into the playground in the Luxembourg Gardens, too, and to go off by herself and enjoy the Latin Quarter. Henri had a fair French vocabulary by then, but more relevant was the fact that his desire to play overcame any language barriers.

"You'd better not let on to the other members of your study group where you disappear to, " Dom had chided me, "or Polo's plane will be filled."

Once my abstract was accepted, it didn't take too long to write the thesis, which I did in longhand and later had one of the secretaries at the Foundation type for me using the MLA format. At least that hadn't changed since my undergrad days at Iowa.

Before the thesis defense, I told Polo that I had an idea I wanted to run past the President of the Chicago *Alliance Française*. I had become quite close friends with him, given the number of *colloques* I had put on there by then, as well as the guest lecturers we had hosted for them at our home.

"I'm going to ask him if I can be one of their speakers. You know, they have those monthly luncheon meetings where people talk on every different subject?"

"Of course. And you will speak on your thesis topic, I am guessing?"

"Yeah! A little dress rehearsal for the defense. What do you think?"

"I think it is a brilliant idea; *pourquoi pas?*"

I told the AFC that I would show slides and speak in French. Having the world's second largest collection of French Impressionism at their fingertips, Chicago *Alliance* members were sophisticated and knowledgeable. If I could engage them, I would surely do fine with my committee.

When my talk was over, Polo pronounced, "My darling, you have **wowed** them, as you would say!" *Turns out, I had.*

Twenty-one years later, Charles F. Moffett would publish one of, if not the, definitive works of research on this same topic, and his book would be touted as the "first thorough investigation" of the subject matter of Effets de Neige.

I donned the purple hooded robe of Northwestern University to march down the aisle and receive the Master of Arts in June of 1983. The PhD candidates were even more resplendent in their puffier sleeves with satin stripes, their tams and fancier frills, but I was so happy with myself at having hit this milestone, I didn't even pay attention to the different ranks. I could hardly restrain the joy I felt floating up to the stage, as if the Dean were standing on a podium in the clouds.

Afterwards, Polo, the Lowensteins, Annie-Laure, Jean-Luc, Nanny, and Henri met me behind the curtains where those of us who had rented the regalia were obliged to hand them back in. Everyone rushed to congratulate me, give me *la bise*, and tell me how happy they were for me. Henri was bubbling over with "I saw you up there, Mummy!" I leaned over and pulled him close, and told him how glad I was, in turn, that he was there with me to see it.

I'd asked Nanny to bring my faithful little camera and she took pictures of us before I relinquished the hood and gown. Henri had a fun time trying on my mortar board and holding the diploma. Polo radiated with pride, hugging me again and again.

We all repaired to the Club in Kenilworth for a luncheon that made Henri cry out, "It's just like your birthday, Mummy!" when he saw the table decorated with beautiful bowls of orchids floating on water, balloons tied to my chair and a small but lovely stack of presents at my place. I had a hunch Annie-Laure had organized it, and I was right. She also had an orchid corsage for me to wear, and pinned it onto the lilac-print, lavender silk shantung Christian Dior sheath I'd picked up for the occasion on one of my Paris research jaunts.

Georges-Henri was anxious for me to open his present first. Polo had taken him on a special father-son outing to buy me a sweet graduation card, which Henri had picked out, Polo reported to the group proudly.

"And I colored the envelope! Nanny helped me," Henri announced, showing it off.

"Well, talk about a work of art!" I exclaimed. "That is gorgeous!" Henri had drawn --no doubt Nanny Genevieve had had a hand in it —a cartoon picture of the *Citroën* with a dog's face hanging out the window, a boy in the back seat, me behind the wheel and his dad in the passenger's seat. A streamer was drawn on the side of the car with the word "*Félicitations!*" on it and thought-bubble appeared above the car saying "Yay, Mummy!"

"Open it!" Henri bubbled.

I pulled out the card to reveal a picture of a dog not unlike our beagle, holding a rolled diploma with a ribbon around it in his teeth.

"Oh, my goodness, it's Willy!"

"Yes, " Henri stated matter-of-factly.

"*Oui, c'est ça,* " Polo laughed.

The package held something that took my breath away and proved once again how incredibly thoughtful Polo was. I figured he would have wanted to get me something really exceptional for the occasion of my graduation, but I certainly wasn't expecting what I opened. It was a square ostrich-hide Montblanc "Sartorial" portfolio in the same color blue as the Citroën, with my initials stamped in gold on the lovely brass clasp of its outside flap. I had no idea where he might have procured such a valuable thing. It was obvious that it hadn't been his mother's because it still had a tag on it, not with the price, of course, which must have been astronomical. I figured Marie-France might have had something to do with this.

Inside he had put a copy of my thesis, which he'd had leather bound also.

"That will, of course, go into our library," he said as I held it up for all to see.

I hated to show so much emotion in front of the others, so I choked back the tears that were welling up in me and almost spilling out, and I drew a long breath as I stared at this amazing gift.

"Thank you so much!" I sang out to the both of them and got up to hug them each and give my son an extra-special smooch. "I love this *portefeuille de ministre* with all my heart. I'll use it!"

"Yes! "said Annie-Laure in a more animated tone than usual, "you will, because my present will go inside, too. Open it next!"

I took a look at the cards and hers was attached to a letter-paper sized flat package, which had wrapping paper over a manila envelope. I gave her a furtive look of mock inquisitiveness, as though I might be unwrapping one thing and then another. Inside was a catalogue of some sort, and all at once I realized what it was and gasped audibly: a complete inventory of the d'Arivèque art collection replete with a thumbnail photo, the title of each work, the artist, the year produced, the year acquired… in fact the entire provenance of each one.

"*C'est le tout, quoi!*" I marveled at it, leafing through it.

"*Oui!*" she laughed. "Now you have something to curate!"

I thanked her profusely and showed Polo, who obviously knew it was coming, and indeed had probably given her access to all the files from which to compile her list.

"*C'est une merveille,* " I said understating my awe for it. "*Je vous remercie de tout coeur,*" I said thanking them both since the card was signed "Annie-Laure et Jean-Luc."

"This will become invaluable to you, *chérie*, in the future. *J'en suis sûr.*"

I didn't want the Lowensteins to feel left out or that anything they could have offered me would never have lived up to these other presents, so I fussed over the last gift on the table, an iconic Tiffany box, cooing, "Oh, that robin's egg blue box! And I'd know this ribbon anywhere! You guys shouldn't have done this!"

Inside the box was a gorgeous very simple twenty-four carat gold, large-linked bracelet with no ornamentation except a safety chain hanging from its elegant art deco-looking rectangular clasp, which was engraved with my initials, "SESA."

"Oh, this is too beautiful!" I uttered quite overcome. I held it up and the rest of the table oohed and ahhhed over it. I slid it on.

"Lovely, " Polo pronounced.

"Thank you so much! I will treasure this."

As we ate lunch and Polo bragged about "my wife's triumphant lecture on *les effets de neige* at the AFC."

I couldn't help but let my mind drift back to my graduation from Iowa. Yes, Sol and Betty and Roslyn had come, but my parents had hardly said anything about only the third B.A. achievement on either side of the family, so incensed were they at that moment that I hadn't graduated with a teaching certificate, was not coming home to get one and then a teaching job, and worse than all that... my boyfriend was Catholic.

*   *   *

During the years when Georges-Henri was growing up in Wilmette and I was in grad school, I started socializing more with neighbors, other moms and my fellow art history students. The end result of most of these newly formed acquaintances was that I got "drafted" into being on committees for the school, the Wilmette library and parks, the children's museum, and study groups. There were some instances when I couldn't tell if they wanted to know me or just tolerated me for my money, but I heeded Polo's advice to me from long before, and didn't worry about it. Even if some of the participants were suspect, the causes were not, so I joined in and contributed generously of both my time and resources. I also still hung out with Dom and some of his faculty friends, many of whom had ordered films and tried out my lesson plan ideas for them. "We're your little guinea pigs, " Dom teased me.

But Annie-Laure had become my most esteemed colleague. I loved and admired her deeply, and felt so lucky she had come up through the ranks to take on a pivotal role at the Foundation. Polo saw our relationship develop and told me on more than one occasion how pleased he was about it.

Annie-Laure was essentially being groomed to completely take over Marie-France's former role, and as such was offered a place on the Board of Directors, which led Polo to bring her and her husband Jean-Luc into his office for a talk about their future.

Polo knew Luc had obtained his "Bac" in France years before, but it was a "*Bac technique*" and Polo had a different idea for him. He wanted him to take the TOEFL exam and enroll in a Chicagoland college or junior college with the goal of obtaining the bachelor's degree and eventually going to law school, with the intention after that of joining the administration of the Foundation and assuming a seat on the board. It would take quite a few years, but Polo told them he would be pleased to finance the whole endeavor and welcome Luc to the fold as more than chauffeur/head of the motor pool. Part of his immediate task, if he chose to accept the offer, would be to begin finding his own replacement and groom several of his other people to take over as chauffeurs and mechanics, too.

Annie-Laure must not have been expecting this because she was shocked...and overjoyed. They both were. I had to believe Polo was doing that in part for my sake. He was thinking ahead to when he wouldn't be there and I would assume the titular, and actual working title of *Présidente de la Fondation*. He felt I would need people I knew and could rely on, which was true. I had told him many many times that I was not business-oriented; therefore, it was agreed that my most trusted advisor and mentor would have to be Daniel Rosier de Molet. Daniel would be charged with keeping in place a vibrant and committed board of directors at my disposal. More importantly Daniel and his team would be my liaisons to Geneva, as they were Polo's.

As for me, I had become something of a minor celebrity on the lecture circuit. After I did the Mid-States conference twice, I began to be invited to speak on behalf of the Foundation all over the country on the subject of the integration of culture studies in the French classroom.

"National guidelines are beginning to be generated, " I told my various audiences, "by the Council on Foreign Languages. Culture studies are the wave of the future, both 'big C' and 'little c'. Culture is becoming an important component of the teaching of modern languages."

To that end I was asked to give talks and workshops on lesson planning using resources from our Foundation, among other entities. Traveling so much meant that I had to be away from Polo and our little one. I admitted to needing Nanny Genevieve, just like I'd been admonished by my husband. Even so, I tried to be away only for a day or two at the most. It was handy to be married to someone who put a private plane at my disposal. Just turning thirty, I still had a full reservoir of energy, and my work was so stimulating that I loved everything about it. The thing that brought me the most job satisfaction was the fact that I continued to consider it an honor to work for Polo, just like I had from day one.

In Chicago, my reputation had also begun to precede me. After one of our regular CSO concerts, where we were to meet the maestro in his dressing room afterwards, some of the orchestra board members ambushed Polo in the hallway to bring up some funding idea, and I went on into the Green Room. Georg Solti greeted me warmly, then took me to one side of the room to *kvell* over my most recent success: an appearance on the "Windy City Today" show, Chicago's local morning television show.

"They'd asked to interview me about a recent talk I'd given on the region of Bordeaux, France at a travel agents' convention," I explained to the maestro, softening my voice. "Polo and I don't go on the air too often, though. If people knew how supremely generous he is, he'd be flooded. We try to keep that part on the down low," I laughed.

"Polo told me you are doing such a fine job for the Foundation's educational wing, " the maestro said. "I don't know how you manage to juggle all the things you do, go to graduate school, work and keep a second house and raise your child."

"Oh, I admit it's a little frenetic around our place. Nanny Genevieve has proven to be a godsend and I rely upon her more than I ever thought I would."

The maestro looked at me with an expression of real esteem in his eyes. "He is so very proud of you, you know."

"I... do try... my best to represent him."

"Yes, of course, " he smiled, and placed his hand on my shoulder, "but Sarah darling, whenever he speaks of you or your work-- or, for that matter, you as a mother-- his heart overflows with admiration."

I blushed at hearing this from the world-famous orchestra conductor. I didn't know what to say.

"Well," I finally said, "you know I'm so desperately in love with him."

"I know!" he grinned at me.

*   *   *

Polo and I lived mostly in Wilmette, but that didn't mean we'd given up our calendar of social events in the city; we continued to host visiting dignitaries at the Lake Shore Mansion, as a favor to the French Consulate or any other organization who desired our assistance.

When the university of Chicago announced an "International Colloquium of Faith and Religion," Polo was asked to have several speakers stay with us. One of them was Alain Badiou, a world-renowned professor of philosophy at the *École Normale Supérieur*.

For the first-- and only—time, Polo declined to house a guest as requested.

"His father, Raymond, and my *Papa* were in *La Résistance* and worked together at times, " Polo said, which made me even more curious as to why he would not invite the son. "And Alain is a brilliant man with a great body of knowledge at his fingertips. He is, in France, *une grosse tête*. It does not surprise me that Chicago would consider it a feather in their cap to get him for their event."

"So, why, then, do you refuse to have him?" I asked.

"Because, my darling, for the simple reason that I know him, and even as he would no doubt keep his opinions to himself in our home, and even though he has professed all his life to never equate philosophy with politics, among his colleagues-- who all acknowledge his academic prowess and genius, there is a belief—*il y a l'impression très nette*—that he is widely thought to be a garden-variety anti-Semite."

"Oh...well, don't exclude him on my account. I couldn't care less---I've never heard of the guy."

"But darling, he was quite active during *Les Evenéments de Mai*! 1968 in Paris. You were there!"

"Not exactly, Polo. Don't forget-- I got there in June. Anyway, my French was so elementary in those days I wouldn't have been able to follow the slightest debate or news item on the t.v., which I didn't have access to anyhow, by the way."

"*Bon, alors, ça ne fait rien*. No matter. I will not have him in my home."

It was a prophetic stance on Polo's part. Decades later when Badiou published a book called Circonstances 3: Portées du mot 'juif' *—The Uses of the Word Jew', controversial publicity sprang up between* Le Monde *and another newspaper,* Les Temps Modernes, *where Badiou was labeled an anti-Semite by the past president of* Collège International de Philosophie, *Jean-Claude Milner, as well as Frédéric Nef and others.*

Polo and I had had many discussions on religion in our short seventeen years together. I often questioned him on his belief system or, rather, lack thereof, and he confronted me with the same. He professed to have followed his mother's lead of renouncing faith, and I couldn't ever come up with a good explanation of why I had one.

"Do you believe there was some intentional creator who made us for a purpose?" he would ask me. "What do the rabbis say?"

"I don't know," I had answered more than once. I did not tend to talk to rabbis as friends.

"One time in college," I had told Polo, "we had a guest rabbi for the High Holidays at the Iowa City synagogue – a young guy – very avant-garde for the times. He gave the dvar torah – like a sermon-- about how God was not a puppeteer. He had bellowed at us from the bima, 'What would make you think you were so important as to pray directly to some personal God for ...anything?' I thought about that a lot, and afterwards found myself becoming irate. So I confronted him. I said that if my kid is ever laying in a hospital with a chemo drip going into her arm, I'm going to jolly well need to sit on the edge of the bed and pray to **someone** with all my might to intercede and save her!"

"What did the rabbi say to that?" Polo had asked, "Was he surprised that you confronted him?"

"Oh, he just mocked me. He was condescending. He told me, 'God is not a puppeteer, but if it makes you feel better --- go ahead and pray. Send up many prayers for your child.' But I remember thinking he didn't really believe that it would do any good. I think he was just taken by surprise that anyone would argue with him. He didn't retract what he said, and I didn't change my mind either. But that particular sermon did take me farther away from Judaism that day, I think. Not towards Christianity or anything, but it was food for thought, since I know so many Christians who feel a personal affinity towards **their** Lord."

"And so, what do the rabbis say about where HE was in Auschwitz?" Polo had smirked. " For that matter, I wonder what do priests say! It wasn't only Jews who died there."

"Yes...I know." I hadn't been able to come up with a good answer and only thought about what I'd read on the subject. I knew that when Eli Wiesel came out of the Holocaust, he came out of it without God. "I have no idea, " I continued. "I suppose Christians would say that there's an afterlife where consequences will follow for how we conducted ourselves in this life. Evil will be punished."

"And then they go and contradict themselves by professing that it is only by faith alone that one attains heaven," Polo reminded me. "Deeds do not count."

"Well, " I said, "if that's the case, then surely religion really doesn't make any sense at all."

"The fundamental problem, as I see it," Polo had concluded, "is not whether bad people are punished after death, but why innocent ones are punished during life. In what way could the suffering and horrid deaths of good people, which I and all of us have seen in our own lifetimes – some more close-up than others--- in ruthless historical events like wars or in random occurrences we hear about daily, ever make me want to believe that there is a loving or caring God?"

I couldn't argue with him, but again, I couldn't offer up an explanation from my own religion to that conundrum either. I couldn't defend my belief in the God of Judaism except in sophomoric terms of the religion having provided me a guideline to living or some such. And in that I also failed miserably. If there were not ten commandments but six hundred plus, what was the point of trying? I told him I supposed that religion was ultimately a search for the meaning of life. Judaism did teach Tikkun Olam, repair of the world, that one should leave the world a better place for having been in it.

Jean-Paul d'Arivèque would certainly leave the world a better place for having been in it. He had already described himself to me as being an Existentialist more than anything else. In college, both in America and France, I had studied Existentialism in literature and philosophy, of course, and knew its basic tenets. I also realized that Existentialism, per se, wasn't really even French, but I felt the Frenchness of the body of work put forth by Camus and Sartre permeated Polo's soul and that's what he emulated. Polo embraced the idea of conscious involvement, and how each individual could – had to, really – create his or her own meaning in life. As they – and he – saw it, there were reasons to live a moral and 'engaged' life based on human values rather than revealed divinity. We had discussed this very thing many times. Polo remarked to me often that what he always believed was that we have the capability to be the architects of our own lives, no matter how we were raised---well or not – or who our parents were, et cetera. He liked to point out to me, in light of my work as Director of Education, that my creativity, which he assured me I had more than he did...and I didn't believe it...was an act of will. He said it was his belief that if life is to have meaning, then that meaning is ultimately what we are able to give it.

737

Several times I'd asked him if he saw himself as spiritual at all, if not religious in an organized way. He would always affirm that he did.

"But you gave up your faith. Do you still believe in some version of God?"

"Sarah, you and I both believe in beauty and art, do we not? We see the divine in nature. Those are the realms in which I encounter God."

"So you're saying you take it as a manifestation of God – or at least a divine spirit, in nature, of course, but also in the creative aspect of the human mind?"

"Mais oui. Listening to Mahler's First, I become enveloped in the transcendence of those sounds. As do you, n'est-ce pas?"

"I do!"

"Alors, that is my church. Just as the Sologne Forest is, and our terrace overlooking the waves lapping at the shore of Lake Michigan."

Later on if anyone tried to console me that Polo's death was God's will, my immediate rejoinder was always, "Well, that's just bullshit."

* * *

I had had forebodings of the fateful day to come because my husband's health had already begun years earlier to show some subtle and some not so subtle signs of decline. His heart had weakened due in great part to a life of other physical struggles. Getting around became more tortured. He was frequently out of breath, sometimes dizzy and always in pain.

He and his doctor probably knew what was coming far earlier than I even realized. Polo didn't let on much to me, but even by the time he couldn't keep how he was feeling to himself, I know I must have tried to repress the realization of it. I held on tight to my belief…and fervent hope…that modern medicine and expert care, coupled with my deep love for him would ward off the unthinkable for an indeterminate very long time.

Unfortunately, they did not.

Even as Polo still had his same internist, Dr. Pierre Lemoine, who always took the time to explain the situation to me every time something new came up, I was lucky that I could always turn to Dr. Fabrizio Garabanti to re-explain what was going on, and, more importantly, for assurance about what was being done for Polo.

In the spring of 1989, I had moved with Polo back into our Chicago mansion to be nearer to the medical center. Lemoine had eventually needed to call in specialists to consult on the case – cardiologists and an electrophysiologist – and plans were being made to move Polo from the Lake Shore mansion into the hospital. The cardiologists wanted to run a new battery of tests, and it was just easier not to have to drive in every day from the suburbs. Besides that, they weren't one hundred percent sure Polo would tolerate the testing. When Dr. Lemoine decided he needed to transfer Polo, he'd asked Fabrizio to come over to the house to be with me when he explained the necessity for this.

"Our son Georges-Henri is in school in New York!" I told them, my voice beginning to show panic. "I need to go get him and bring him back to Chicago while his dad is still home! I don't want to drive from O'Hare to the hospital with my son terrified that he's being rushed to his father's death bed!"

"No, no that is fine," said Fabrizio, calming me down. "Don't you think so, Pierre? Jean-Paul is not in any immediate grave danger. If the first order of business will be to run more definitive tests, in any event, that can wait – a few days, even a week."

"Oh, good. So then, could we both go to New York and get Henri?"

"Well, no Sarah, " Fabrizio answered before Lemoine said anything. "Let's not go that far. Jean-Paul must stay here. Traveling is never that easy for him, as you know, even under optimal conditions – your own plane and all. But now it would just be impossible."

Polo and I had always had to take into consideration his disability and any potential effect on trips we might take, outside of going home to France. We agreed that more often than not, I would travel alone if I wanted to visit some city, because the accommodations he needed simply were not available, or because it was too hard for him to get around for sightseeing. I felt sad for him; he didn't know the cities I loved like London, Amsterdam, Copenhagen, or even San Francisco. He was never bitter and he took a lot of pleasure in seeing my enthusiasm for travel, and also for showing Henri the places I loved. Most of the time, though, we just stayed as homebodies, which didn't displease us. At least we could be together in France, both in Paris and at the country house.

I tried to remain cool and upbeat when I went in to tell Polo that I was embarking on a trip to New York to bring Henri home early. There was, however, no sugar-coating this. Polo's time to be with us was running out.

In the back of my mind (and not only because of that ridiculously cruel altercation with my father when he came to Chicago and tried to talk me out of marriage, warning me that I'd end up a young widow) I'd always known and feared the moment when our life together would come to an end. Polo did not shrink from the reality either. We each had a heightened and poignant awareness of the need to grasp at any opportunity to say how much we loved each other, because we knew the chances to do so were only becoming slimmer.

"You've made me the happiest woman on the planet, " I assured him, "and I love you more than life itself."

It wasn't too poetic, but it was the heartfelt God's truth.

He had also brought up the subject.

"Sarah," he had confided to me one day that spring, "I want to tell you something."

Dread had shot through me like lightning, the same lightning the French language uses to describe "love at first sight." Why must love be laced with fear?

"Shoot, " I'd said, trying to sound carefree and probably not succeeding.

"You know I have loved you, quite literally from the first time I met you?"

"You've said it many times."

"Well, I want you to know that I am also consumed with pride for you and your accomplishments."

"I know you are, Polo, and I appreciate that."

"But what you do not realize, I believe, is that you are so different from any woman I would have expected to marry, or been expected to marry, I should say. The French women--"BCBG"-you know what that is – they would never have taken on the career you did. They would not have become my partner, my sustainer, my face to the public. My own mother was different from her contemporaries because she was thrust into the role of father and mother; and also, it must be added, because she lived in America. But even as you will be taking my place as president of the Foundation…"

"One day! Not yet!" I interjected, always in denial.

"…much as you will be taking on that role, you already have done a monumental job for the organization! I have spent two decades in awe of you, darling. What you have done as my wife for the organization is just immeasurable."

"Well, I'm…very happy to hear it, but remember, I was already an employee when we married."

"You were, it is true. But time and time again, you exceeded all expectations and proved yourself so capable, so enthusiastic representing our raison d'être. *You grew our educational division in ways I could not have even predicted! And more importantly, you blossomed into an expert, broadening your horizons and talents. You always say what a waste it was for your Cassandra to have died without becoming recognized as the great artist she was. But you do not give yourself credit either! You, too, are so very artistic---all the lesson plans you wrote, the textbook editing, the film projects and culture materials."*

"Polo, you've got to remember something," I always felt I had to remind him at moments like this, "I lead a very privileged life. I don't have to do any of the chores of normal wives. Much as I wanted to sometimes! I am pampered with spa treatments and a hairdresser who comes to me ---and charges you a fortune for doing so. But the bottom line, the most fortunate part of it is that I have a job I love. "

"Which you are exceedingly good at! I cannot imagine any other woman I might have married, especially from the French 'aristocracy' – entre guimets," *he said, making air quotes, "doing what you do or accomplishing a fraction of it. Yes, they would have perhaps made good hostesses on Lake Shore, but nothing more. They would not have been prepared to do real work."*

"Oh, but I'm guessing that's changing, don't you think?"

"I do not. And something else, ma chérie," *he said, taking me in his embrace, "I remember how sure you were that you did not want children, that you thought you would make a terrible mother. Well, one only need look at our wonderful son to see how wrong you were on that."*

"He is wonderful, I grant you that. Mostly because he has your temperament! Ha! "

739

"No, Sarah, I do not believe that. You have been the guiding force in his life. You wanted to have the Wilmette house and you chose the schools. When he was ill, it was you who stayed home and took care of him. You read to him and taught him, and helped him with his schoolwork. You are the one who saw to his religious education, and you arranged for his private lessons, music, sports. You drove him and his and his friends all over Chicago. You traveled with him."

"**You** played with him... with his toys, many of which you bought him! And you attended – attend-- all his school functions, even at great distance! Don't sell yourself short!"

He looked at me and shook his head. "It is not the same. We both love him dearly, but you, as his mother, love him enough to discipline him and by the example of yourself, instill in him the qualities he shows always: he is kind, always deferential to adults, and a serious student...as you were."

"Okay, come on, Polo. Let's just agree that we both got lucky and our kid turned out great! We can both take credit, but most of all, **you** desperately wanted this child. Do you think that gets past him? He knows you adore him, but he also knows what he means to you. You were always there for him...for anything. And let's not forget something else: we didn't have any financial challenges as parents, thanks to you! Do you think that is the reality of most parents? It isn't! And on top of that, we have both been so favored with great employees. Genevieve was the most wonderful nanny I could have ever wished for, and everyone who works for you-- in the households and at the office –hell, they think you walk on water!"

So there it was: the moment I had been dreading for months, and the horrendous task looming before me: to summon Georges-Henri home to cope with what we both feared would happen.

I had alerted the Reniers before I flew out to New York and explained the situation, that I would be there to take Henri home. Final exams were over although the results were not yet in, and Henri would have to miss the end-of-term dance and some other parties. But none of that was important; it would just be better for him to spend as much time as possible with his dad.

The Reniers were heartbroken as well, understanding the magnitude of my having come out there to get my son. Out of the earshot of the boys, they told me they would be anxious to travel to Chicago if they could be of any help at all, and also if the worst should happen, they would attend the funeral. The Reniers had truly become Henri's second family, and they made it a point to assure me that he was welcome to come back for senior year, which was what I intended, too.

On the plane home I knew it would be stupid to try to pretend that this was not that big of a deal or that it wouldn't take anything less than a miracle to change the path we were all on, he and I...and his father.

"You've heard the story about how your grandfather simply disappeared from this earth and your dad never saw him again. Much as that saved *Papa* some pain, in the sense that he didn't have to watch his dad get sick and suffer, like you have, don't you think you are luckier because you get to say good-bye?"

"But Mummy," he had implored me, " why does he have to die from this? He's been sick before and come out of it."

"Yes, but not as sick as he is now. His heart is just giving out, sweetie." When my eyes welled up with tears, it didn't matter if I tried to keep my voice from shaking; the jig was up.

"I just can't imagine him gone from my life, " said my wise son.

"You and me both, kiddo, " I sobbed, hugging him. "But we'll let him know how very much we love him to pieces in the meantime, won't we?"

Polo did brighten up as soon as Henri was home again. The doctors let him stay in our Lake Shore house a bit longer than they had told me before I'd left for New York, simply because they could see that it did the patient good to be with his kid at home.

Henri was anxious to share his school activities with his father, and wanted to discuss the literature part of his *Baccalauréat* preparation with him. He had the summer reading list so every day, he would read parts of works to Polo and they would discuss them. The work most fresh on his mind was Anatole France's *Le Crime de Sylvestre Bonnard*, and Henri spent hours beside Polo's bed, reading passages out loud. The parts about the city of Paris intrigued Henri, who had been to the capital only rarely on all our trips to France.

"He had quite a view from his window," commented Henri, referring to the text. "Listen to this part:

'Tout ce que je découvre de ma fenêtre, cet horizon...qui me laisse apercevoir l'Arc de Triomphe comme un dé de pierre, la Seine, et ses ponts, les tilleuls de la terrasse des Tuileries, Le Louvre de la Renaissance...; à ma droite, du côté du Pont-Neuf, ...le vieux et venerable Paris avec ses tours et ses flèches, tout cela c'est ma vie, c'est moi-même, et je ne serais rien sans ses choses qui se releètent en moi avec les mille nuances de ma pensée et m'insporent et m'animent. C'est pouqoui j'aime Paris d'un immense amour.'---(Anatole France, 1881)

"I wish now we'd spent as much time going around Paris as at the country house," Henri said, wistfully.

"Do not worry, *mon grand*, " his dad assured him. "You will have a whole lifetime to get to know Paris. Perhaps when you study there for college? You would like that, no?"

"Of course, *Papa*. You and Mummy both did. I'm sure I will, too."

"Well, then you will be able explore it to your heart's content, *alors*, will you not?"

"Yes, and you won't have to live on one hundred dollars per month like I did!" I chimed in, delivering the mail to the bedridden patient. "And have your friend bring you food from her stewardess job."

"Oh, Sarah, " Polo said wistfully, looking up at me with longing in his eyes, "how many of us can say we had our dearest friend in Paris with us to share adventures in the best years of our lives? *Tu avais tellement de la veine, chérie.*"

"You're right, but then, I had **you** to share Paris with after that, and it was even better."

The time came too soon when the hospital was the only option left us. The doctors had Polo transferred by ambulance and we followed with Robineau driving because he wanted to stay at the hospital. He and Polo had had a long talk at one point, I found out later, and Polo had insisted that Robineau be there for me...for anything. And, it must be noted, he always tended devotedly to the needs of Georges-Henri.

Polo was in the same oversized private suite he'd been a patient in previous times, and there was enough room in there for several chairs and even a cot, which they brought in for me to be able to stay with him all night. But Robineau preferred to sit outside the door in the hallway on a chair he took out of the room. He looked like a plain-clothes cop guarding a witness.

"You don't have to stay here all day, you know " I had told him, upon returning from the coffee machine and handing him a cup. I even had tried to joke, saying, "No one's going to kidnap him from here."

"No, of course not, "he had answered softly, "I know. But I prefer to be here. If it's all right with you."

"It is, " I had assured him. It had been almost two decades since he and I had exchanged unkind words. He'd been the model of decorum with me since the incident where I told my husband that his valet hated me. It was painfully apparent that Robineau was reeling. He was awfully choked up at the hospital. He was younger than Polo, but had known him a lot longer than I had. I thought about their relationship and how the d'Arivèque family had to mean so much to him. Sometimes Maxime came to the hospital, too, and would sit out there with his boyfriend, consoling him. We all needed consoling, that was for sure.

For quite a while, I was still not facing reality, believing that Polo would be discharged in ten days or so, like he always had been. I would sit there, watching the heart monitor as the meds dripped into his arm, and I was sure that at any moment the beeping, which was an erratic and scary cacophony of random noise, would return to normal, regular intervals, and the doctors would give me the good news that he was going to make it.

Henri rode over on his bicycle every morning or afternoon to be with me and his dad. That meant I had to be the stronger person and not go into too much drama in front of him, lest he feel even more like an orphan than he already did, knowing he was about to lose his beloved father. He couldn't be expected, at nearly sixteen, to have to take on an inconsolable mom, too.

741

Henri and I would slip out for little breaks, sometimes to the cafeteria and once in a while to the chapel. He asked me if we should pray the *Mi'Sheberach* prayer, and it amused me that he was so culturally Jewish.

If we'd prayed Mi'Sheberach in synagogue in the Bluffs during the Torah service, I never recognized it.

"Do you know I never knew that prayer as a kid?" I remarked to him. "I only learned it taking you to Temple in Evanston. I don't even know all the words by heart. It wasn't really until Debbie Friedman put the words to music and mixed in some English, that it became popular and a true part of the services."

"I heard Debbie Friedman herself sing it at Temple Israel in New York, " Henri said, "and I thought of *Papa*."

" Wow! What was that like? Was she cool?"

Cool? It wasn't as though he'd told me he'd seen Paul Simon on the street or anything.

"Heck yeah!" Then he got quiet again and said, "I prayed for *Papa*. Do you pray too?"

"Hey kiddo, you bet I do," I said, trying to comfort him, "I do pray. I pray for a miracle every day. I pray for this not to be the end...not yet. It's too soon. We just can't live without him, can we?" *I prayed for God to be a puppeteer.*

I stayed round the clock, leaving only to go back and shower and change. I pulled a chair close to Polo's bed and talked to him whenever he was awake and they weren't doing things to the various cords and lines attached to his body. Sometimes, after everyone else was gone, I climbed up onto the bed and lay down next to him with my arm over him, my head nestled on his chest.

"I shall always be with you," he told me, over and over.

Dr. Garabanti, who really wasn't even physician of record or consulting formally on the case, came by every day to see me. He wasn't trying to buoy up my spirits as much as comfort me, to explain things that were happening, to give me a medical play by play. This did more than anything to convince me that Polo wouldn't be going home.

Fabrizio was kind but he didn't sugar coat anything.

"His heart is weakening, and pretty soon the other organs will start to fail."

When it did happen, no one was with him except me. Henri had left; Robineau had had to attend to something at the mansion. Inside the room was dark and still, but outside below the sky-scraper hospital window, Chicago's night lights were never so beautiful. And the stars were twinkling their brightest as I stared out the window, too, when suddenly the monitor went off and people rushed into the room.

It was over. I slipped the wedding band and Uncle Charles' signet ring off Polo's fingers.

They let me stay in the room as long as I wanted to, and I rang the house for someone to bring Henri up. I fervently needed our son to be alone with me and Polo one last time.

Neither of us could hold back the tears as we clung to each other next to the bed. I reminded Henri that we were only looking at the shell of our beloved.

"Remember what *Le Petit Prince* told the pilot?" I sobbed, and Henri nodded, silently. " H-h-he -s-s said, '*Je ne peux pas emporter ce corps-là...mais ce sera comme une vieille écorce abandonnée'.*" I recited it from memory, and Henri joined in, " *...ce n'est pas triste les vieilles écorces...*"

I gave Henri the d'Arivèque ring that had been worn by the dukes of Beuvron for centuries, and explained to him that Uncle Charles had been very determined that it be passed down to Polo's children. Henri took it gently from me and put it right on. It fit him, as it had his dad, and he assured me he would wear it, and keep it for his own children-- if he ever had any.

Polo and I had already discussed preferences pertaining to his death, which were for him to be cremated and to have his ashes taken to *La Pérégrine* to be kept next to his mother's in the shrine she'd built to house his father's "remains." He told me he desperately wanted me to do the same when the time came, but that if I didn't want to be cremated, he understood. Harry Lowenstein could help me choose someplace nice to be buried and Georges-Henri would have an actual grave site to visit, if he wanted to.

"No, no, I only want to be with you, that's all."

Georges-Henri and I huddled together in our search for some abatement of the heavy clouds of grief surrounding both of us. We planned Polo's memorial service in Chicago, which, at the suggestion of Maestro Solti, we accepted to hold in Orchestra Hall.

"We should have music, poetry and pictures, " I said to my son. "What do you think?"

"Absolutely," he answered. "I'm glad now that you took so many slides and photos, Mummy."

"Your *papa* once gave me a terrific camera, " I told him wistfully, "and I used it a lot. I'll have our production department make up a montage of them, " I said, "and put music to it. That can be playing in the background on a big screen while people eulogize him. That will be nice. Right afterwards, you and I will fly to France, what do you say?"

And that is exactly what did take place. We put the announcement in both Chicago papers, the *New York Times* and also in *Le Figaro*, which did a long story on his life. I opened the memorial service to all who wanted to come. People from the hospital, the French consulate, the arts and culture organizations, the Art Institute, and the *Alliance Française* joined in with the staff of the Foundation. Many Foundation and d'Arivèque Industries board members and administrative staff flew in from all over: New York, Paris and Geneva.

Special people sat with Henri and me: Daniel Rosier and his wife, the Hardouins, Annie-Laure and Jean-Luc, Robineau and Maxime, the Hydes along with the twins, Maestro Solti, the Lowensteins-- every one of Harry's family still living in the United States came-- as well as the Reniers, Dom and Peter, Fabrizio and all the other doctors.

I had invited the Maestro and Harry to give formal eulogies, but before they were presented, I had instructed the funeral director to announce that anyone else who was desirous of speaking should come up. I had expected one or two of the Foundation staff, including Annie-Laure, who gave a moving speech, but after her, more than a dozen men and women headed to the microphone. Each one to the last person paid tribute to Jean-Paul d'Arivèque's lifetime of courage, perseverance in the face of pain and physical adversity; his kindness, generosity, and his deep understanding of history, literature, philosophy, music and art.

I arose after they were done to thank them all warmly and to introduce the two main speakers. Before I did so, I read some lines from Alfred de Musset:

> **"La Vie est un sommeil/ L'amour en est le rêve.**
> **Et vous avez vecu/ si vous avez aimé."**

"Life is a long sleep and love is its dream. If you have loved, you have lived. Polo taught me to do both."

I then introduced our son.

Georges-Henri had come to me with a poem he wanted to read, by a poet he had just studied in the previous term in school at the Lycée Français de New York: WH Auden's "Stop All the Clocks."

"I adore that poem," I had told him approvingly.

"Did you also study Auden?" he wanted to know.

"Yes. I love him."

"Did you know he was a fa---a fairy?"

"Yes, I knew he was homosexual. Do your friends use that term?"

"No. Worse."

"Well, don't."

But the irony was not lost on me that I had spent nearly two years believing my boss was also gay.

I had asked Henri if he were positive he wanted to get up in front of that crowd and read the poem. He assured me he was.

"I think I want to take part in the service, Mummy, " he had stated, "and I don't want to make a speech. So this will be good, don't you think?"

"Yes, honey, I do if you really want to, " I had answered, my heart, broken though it was, swelling with pride.

I felt I had to delve a bit into his motives. I didn't want Henri to feel that I expected him, at not-quite sixteen years old, to step into his father's shoes. He already realized that everyone who knew Jean-Paul d'Arivèque was in awe of him, and I was afraid that Henri would worry that he could never live up to that if he weren't perfect or super-

*human; and that if he **weren't** those things, he wouldn't be worthy of love — mine or anyone else's. I didn't want being Polo's only child to put a crippling burden on him...one that he would never be able to overcome.*

My son's lips were quivering as he recited, but he got through it. I felt he'd chosen that poem as much to express his mother's anguish as his own. It was very touching for me to watch Georges-Henri stand up in front of a throng of mostly strangers and do that, and I was bursting with pride for him.

Georges-Henri had picked out the poem completely unaware of how prescient and ahead of his time this was. Five years after that, the film Four Weddings and a Funeral *would come out using this same poem as the focal point of the funeral portion.*

Up to that point in the service I had stayed--remarkably, I thought—emotionally together. However, it was Harry Lowenstein's eulogy that broke my composure. It wasn't until he was almost finished, when he looked right at me and quoted the lines from Tome IV, Book 5, 4th chapter of *Les Misérables* that Victor Hugo had penned over a century earlier. Harry explained that he and his wife had recently been to New York and had seen the musical version of it that had opened at the Broadway Theater. He went on to quote from Hugo: "*La reduction de l'univers à un seul être, la dilatation d'un seul être jusqu'à Dieu, voilà l'amour,*" and to tell the mourners that those were the words — if paraphrased-- from which he believed the lyricist of the new musical took inspiration for the last lines of the show. "To love another person is to see the face of God."

Harry held forth, looking up and speaking directly to me. "I believe this is what transformed Jean-Paul d'Arivèque, Sarah. You allowed him to know this, to see the face of some God. I noticed a completely different Polo after he met you, and (nodding to Solti in the front row next to me) I know the Maestro feels the same as I do. The memories of the day I married you two and how joyous he was—and you also, of course--- are indelibly etched on my heart and will stay there forever."

I lost it at that. I burst into tears and tried in vain to muffle them. I was in front so couldn't see the rest of the audience, but I felt their stares on me. Georges-Henri put his arm around me and I clutched at his hand sobbing, all the while trying hard to get a grip.

It was a beautiful and moving tribute to Polo, even as grieving wears one down, and we found ourselves exhausted after the memorial and reception, Henri and I. But the next day, we rallied to fly out, as planned, with Polo's ashes to France.

*   *   *

When my son and I got back from our mission at the beginning of August 1989, we decided to stay in the Chicago house for the month before I took him back to start his junior year at the *Lycée*. Jean-Luc hadn't been doing much of the chauffeuring anymore since he was in school full-time, but he picked us up at the plane and drove us to Lake Shore Drive. No one said much, but the atmosphere felt heavy.

"The entire household is still grieving," he told me, which I believed. "*Monsieur* Robineau asked if he could speak to you upon your arrival."

"Sure, " I sighed. "Call him from here and tell him I'll meet him at the elevator on the second floor."

As I got off and Henri continued up to our apartment on three, Robineau was waiting for me. We went into the library.

"I wanted to see you, " he said. I nodded and he just continued. "*Monsieur* spoke to me before he died about staying on in your employ...he asked me... to see to any of your needs and concerns. But I am freely offering you my resignation if you so desire it."

"I didn't ask for it."

"No...but given the history between us, I would not be in a position to argue with you if you were to."

"I ...would like... you to stay on."

"And I would like to!" he said, more than a little surprised.

"Of course, valets only work for men, but I still need a house steward...a *major domo*-type person. You've been managing this operation since I met you. I couldn't possibly think of anyone better to do the job. Your pension and health insurance are vested with the Foundation. As far as I'm concerned, you always have a job here…as long as you want it."

"I am very relieved to hear it!" he laughed. And then he got serious again, adding, "and I want you to know something else. I am still stinging after all these years, from the rebuke *Monsieur* gave me that fateful day he found out about how I had behaved towards you."

I looked away, not wanting to get into it again with him. I wasn't feeling in the least contrite, but I didn't want it brought up either.

"You see," he continued, "I am truly very, very sorry. I was wrong in many ways. I did not realize until it was almost too late for me how deeply he loved you and how you changed his life. We heard it in the eulogy and I know it to be true. During the weekend of *Madame* Annie-Laure's wedding in France, I can tell you that *Monsieur* was terribly distraught and sad, feeling that he had lost you. I had never seen him in such a depression. But then, when you accepted his proposal after all, well, the difference was nothing less than astonishing."

"I wanted to accept it but circumstances stood in my way, until I spoke to *Oncle* Charles that weekend. It was as much his doing as mine."

"Well, to whomever goes the credit, I am so grateful it did work out. And I also want to tell you one more thing."

"What's that?"

"Well, it is that I also came to see that your work and yours alone fulfilled the aims of *La Madame's* Foundation. I shall do everything in my power to assist you in continuing to carry out your work."

"Goodness. Thank you! I…appreciate that. Very much. And since we're having this little …uh…chat, I do want to also thank you for how you've been so devoted George-Henri. I'm really grateful."

He nodded. There wasn't much more to say. He asked me if I intended to keep living in Wilmette and I said I did, except that until Henri had to go back to New York, we'd be staying on Lake Shore Drive.

What I didn't tell him was that I wanted to sleep in Polo's bed again, to feel his presence, glean any last remnants of his scent there, see his things in the room, listen to his music---our music--- and just let myself ache with missing him.

I took Henri back to New York in our plane, but just two weeks after that, it was his sixteenth birthday and he asked to fly home to celebrate it with me rather than have me come back and do a party with the Reniers and his friends.

"Sweet sixteen doesn't mean anything for guys, " he laughed, "and I've been driving for years!"

It was true. I taught him to drive at *La Pérégrine*, and he drove all over the property. He still had to get his license in Chicago, however, and did so while he was back. Jean-Luc took him, and when he came home victorious, he drove me out to get a malt.

"I know your birthday's sad this year, " I told him, as we dined on cheeseburgers and shakes at the same diner Cass had taken me to years before. "Mine, too. All our holidays and occasions will be now. But I truly believe *Papa* is looking down on us and wants us to have fun…and remember him, of course. "

"It's like what you told me, Mummy. I feel him with me all the time."

"Me, too. I know he's here with me and I think about him constantly."

"But do you think you'll remarry? You're still pretty young."

"Uh, thanks, I think!" I teased. "No, darling. It's not something I'd ever consider. It certainly wouldn't be fair to someone else who, no matter what or how, could never live up to your father. I wouldn't put anyone in the position of having to try, either."

Roger Renier graduated that year with his French *Baccalauréat* and headed off to William and Mary for college, paid for with his promised "scholarship" from us. Henri continued to live with the Reniers even without Roger there, and the two boys saw one another on breaks. Henri even went down to visit in Williamsburg for a weekend, and really liked the campus, but he was determined to go through the French university system and was headed off to the Sorbonne once he had **his** Bac in 1991.

I was happy… and sad… at his graduation. Polo, of course it goes without saying, would have been bursting with pride.

"It is such an ironic tragedy that your father isn't here for this, " I said, almost crying behind the menu at Tavern on the Green, where I'd taken him for post-Commencement lunch, just the two of us. "You were his every heart's desire."

"I know, Mummy. You were, too."

"Well, some other people weren't here today, either, and I've decided I want you to meet them."

"Who?"

"Your grandparents. You only have one set of grandparents, and you've never met them. They only have one grandson and they've never met you. I intend to do something about that."

"You're bringing them to Chicago?"

"No. We're going to Omaha. That's where they live now. It isn't where I grew up, but I'll show you all that, too. Are you up for it?"

"Sure!"

"It risks being rather unpleasant, I'll be honest with you."

"Well, you've told me you didn't get along."

"That's putting it mildly. But hey, maybe they've mellowed."

'They didn't like *Papa*, did they?"

"They didn't give themselves the chance to get to know him, Henri. It was me they didn't like."

He didn't say anything, just made a face of exasperation.

It was not my intention to show up unannounced, of course, so I wrote to them, but I phrased it in a way that would leave no doubt that I wasn't asking for permission to bring them their grandson to meet, and that if they refused to see us, there would be hell to pay. I told them I intended to gather the entire remaining family to meet Henri, and if Sol and Betty didn't see us, I would feel fine condemning them to all the other relatives for being heartless assholes who rejected their only grandchild. I knew it would cause enough Jewish angst to show them I meant business. They agreed to see us.

We flew out in the d'Arivèque plane and were met at Eppley Airfield with the car I had rented. I drove it myself, sort of strangely happy to be behind the wheel of an American car again. The traffic there was nothing in comparison with Chicago, of course. There wasn't even a freeway one had to maneuver onto from the airport into the downtown. Omaha was a sleepy little burg compared to every other city I had to navigate.

It was warm out, so to meet my parents again after all these years, I chose a Christian Lacroix silk chiffon, sleeveless, belted day dress with matching coat in a shade of cornflower blue. I wore three-inch high spike heels in light tan and carried my Hermès Kelly bag and the blue croc Montblanc document folder Polo had given me. My hair was long enough to put in a French twist; I'd let it grow out again a bit after Polo's death. I still had bangs, and I wore square tortoise-shell Chanel sunglasses.

My outfit was elegant in its simplicity, but the message it sent was clear: I was sophisticated and worldly. It put my family far out of my league. I was not exactly out to flaunt my status or rub their noses in the fact that I was the dowager Duchess de Beuvron, but I was also not that little girl they drove to Iowa City all those years ago either. I had achieved-- in spite of their constant disapproval of just about everything I ever did-- a reputation of my own that far exceeded anything they ever could have imagined. If I **were** out to send a message to my parents, it was not to mess with me.

Henri wore khakis and a blue, green, yellow and pink madras plaid short-sleeved shirt. He brought along a navy hopsacking blazer for when we went out to dinner and met up with aunts, uncles and cousins.

"Henri, you cut a real dash, to coin an old phrase one only still hears in England now," I told him admiringly.

He was guaranteed to make quite a first impression on his new extended family. He had longish— not too long—light brown hair, and he had my shape of large rounded brown eyes. His nose was not Semitic like mine, nor as aquiline as Polo's, but still rather long and straight. His cheekbones were more rounded than mine, so that was d'Arivèque, too. His mouth was thin like the portrait of his French grandmother showed. He had beautiful teeth, which I did not, and when he laughed and the little lines appeared around his eyes, I saw my Nana in him, too. Henri was a mix of all his origins, but decidedly more d'Arivèque than Shrier.

I pulled into a parking space on the street below their apartment building near Clarkson College. It was an urban renewal area in 1991, and I was surprised Sol and Betty had picked that part of town to move to. I surmised — correctly — that they must have done it for Roslyn's schooling.

We went up to the eighth floor — a high one in that building — and rang their bell. I heard the high-pitched yappy barking of a little dog! Betty answered the door, taken aback by her daughter and grandson standing there. She stood there expecting me to hug her, I guess, so I did. Henri leaned toward her, and she kissed his cheek.

"Hi Mom, " I called out, offering her a kiss on the cheek also. "Don't tell me you have a DOG!" I reached down to pet a little apricot miniature poodle who was jumping and twirling at my knees. Henri bent down to pet it, too. "This is your grandson, Georges-Henri. You can call him Henry."

"Come in!" she exclaimed, still not really believing what she saw. "Get down Gigi!" she called out, pushing the dog away.

The front door gave onto a long corridor where there was a closet, and off to one side, a powder room. Their apartment was spacious, I had to give it that, with the three "public" rooms, living room, dining "el" and kitchen all visible to each other, and a large picture window at the end of the living room, where sliding doors opened onto a sort of balcony-cum-deck. The tiny terrace was big enough for a small grill, some potted plants, and a café table with two chairs, but not capacious enough to host a gathering.

I saw Sol off in the distance in a Barcalounger-type chair. He made no effort to get up to greet us. So I waved over to him. "Hi, Daddy."

God, that sounded strange. I think it shocked Henri that I called him that, but there wasn't any other moniker to use: Dad didn't fit, Father was too phony, and I couldn't call him Sol. I guess Daddy was a stab at some sort of affection. It had been when I was little and still was; only it didn't achieve the goal.

"Sarah," he nodded, in the way of greeting me. "Bring my grandson over to meet me."

"Is he disabled?" I whispered to my mother. She shook her head "no".

What a jerk he was in that case.

I approached his chair with Henri and before I could do formal introductions, Sol said, "I'm your **Zayde**. That's your **Bubbe**."

"How do you do, " Henri answered perfunctorily, offering his hand to his grandfather and smiling. "I'm Henri." He pronounced his name in French.

"**Henry**, if you want, " I told Sol.

Betty invited us to sit down while she went to the kitchen, which we could see from where we were sitting through an open pass-through. She was bringing out food. Henri jumped up to carry the tray for her.

"I see he's quite the little gentleman, " said Sol with almost a snicker in his voice.

"He's got a lot of the old man in him, " I answered.

"That's so sweet, " Betty said, handing it off. "Rozzy will be home in a little while. She's taking off early to see you."

"So, " said Sol, asserting his authority over the visit, "to what do we owe this visit? I hear you flew in in your own plane? Must be important."

"I wanted you to have a chance to meet your only grandson. What could be more important than that? He just graduated from high school in New York and he's leaving soon for university in Paris."

"Just like you, then, eh?" Betty said.

"Both of us. Jean-Paul also went to the *Sorbonne*...and then the French equivalent of Harvard for his business degree."

"Yes," said Henri, "I hope to follow in his footsteps because, of course, one day I will head up the Foundation...as Mummy is doing now."

"Not the business end of it, though, " I quickly added, laughing.

"You're a widow at a young age, now, aren't you?" Sol said, ignoring talk of the Foundation. "What are you, forty-something?"

"I just turned forty-three. I presume you remember the year I was born."

"Just like I predicted that time you brought us to Chicago."

747

"Yes, and it's very unfortunate. We miss him more than life itself. I have to tell you though, in the French culture, a widow is a revered and honored person. But of course, I was always revered by my husband. And I adored him." I looked up at my son and he nodded.

"We both miss *Papa* so much!" Henri added.

My parents stared at us as if we were recently landed aliens invading their space.

"So you speak French pretty good, huh?" Sol asked his grandson.

"He's bilingual, " I answered in his stead.

"How's yours then?" my father smirked.

"Not bilingual, but I'm fairly fluent."

"Why aren't you bilingual?"

I ignored that, and took the opportunity to launch into another reason for my visit.

"Listen, " I said, "we came to town so you could meet Georges-Henri, but also so that I could tell you… I would like to acknowledge… that my education, especially in Paris, of course, was the catalyst for my having obtained the job I did get right out of college…at the French Cultural Foundation in Chicago. And to that end, I have come here today, prepared to pay you back for that education."

In the middle of my announcement, however, the front door opened and in came Roslyn, dressed all in white: uniform with little pins on the collar, white hose, white squishy shoes. She was taller than I expected, certainly taller than me, and her brown hair was parted in the middle and pulled severely off her face into a low ponytail.

I got up and went to give her a hug, and Henri followed suit.

"Is this my nephew?!" she chirped at him.

"It's nice to meet you, Aunt Roslyn, " Henri dutifully said, offering his hand and also kissing her on the cheek.

She shook his hand and then turned her attention to me, saying, "Wow, aren't you something!"

"And you…in your uniform and all. I kind of thought nurses didn't wear all that white anymore. The ones who took care of my husband wore these cute little pastel outfits. Pants, mostly. Some of them wore pants and matching jackets with cute prints, although that was mostly in pediatrics, I should say."

"It depends on the hospital, but in any case, I'm a nursing supervisor. I wear white. But look at you! You look like a million dollars!" And then she laughed and said, "Well, duh! Maybe I should say **billion**. Aren't you an heiress or something?"

"She's the *Duchess de Beuvron*, " Henri said with pride. I smiled but shook my head at my son. Not only did I not use the title, of course, just as Polo had not, but it wouldn't have registered with them or meant a thing anyway.

"So," I continued, "I was just telling Mom and Daddy that I came to offer them compensation for their having paid for my education." I turned back to address them. "I'm in a position to pay you back…with interest…and I want to do it. "

"We're comfortable enough. We sold the bar, you know, and the building, which was the real reason we have money now, as you can imagine. It's only with real estate that one has any true wealth."

I had mentioned in my letter that I'd had a visit with our cousin who'd brought me up to snuff on the news of them selling the business.

"Yes, I understand. Nevertheless, with this money that I'm prepared to offer you today, your future…and that of Roz, is secured. I have brought you a check for two hundred thousand dollars."

"WHAT!?" shouted my sister. "My God, you **are** loaded."

Betty was the first of the parents to say anything. "My, Sari, that is an awfully lot of money…and …very generous of you."

"But we don't need it, you understand, " Sol was quick to add.

"Sol, it's **very** generous of her, " Betty snapped at him. "Please."

"No, it's fine," I said to her specifically. "I intend for you to have it whether or not he thinks you need it."

Roslyn, sensing a fight she didn't want to be a part of, suddenly said, "I'll bet Gigi needs to go out…she's my dog, really, you know, and I'm dying for some ice cream. How about I take my nephew

748

with me and we go walk over to Goodrich? We can sit outside on their picnic benches. What do you say Henry?"

"*Tu veux y aller avec ta tante*? "I asked Henri.

"*Volontiers*, " he answered, also anxious to avoid witnessing any altercations, much as I'd warned him there could be some.

Roz gathered the dog up in her arms, along with her purse and the leash, and they left.

I got out the large checkbook from my Montblanc portfolio, carefully tore out the check, and laid it on my lap.

"I'd also like to ask a favor, " I said turning to my mother. "I've been trying to remember some stuff from my Sorbonne days...you know...some of my old haunts to tell Henri. I find that I'm just foggy on details, so I'd like to borrow back that file of my letters...you know the one... that Nana put together. I know you kept it in your bedroom desk at the old house. Can I have it? You don't mind, do you? I'm sure you haven't reread them in decades, am I right?" I got up to go to the bedroom.

Betty stopped me. "Sari, " she said, "I ...don't have those anymore."

"What?!" I laughed, "Not possible! Nana and I were always going to maybe make them into a book! I have an entire publishing department at my disposal, so I just may do it...unless the writing is too awful."

"You're not listening to me. I said they're not here. Sit back down." And then she got defensive. " Look, I got angry at you one day, and I threw them out."

"You did what?" I said, backing down into the chair again.

"I have a right to get mad. I got mad. I tossed the file."

"But...for Christ's sake, what could I have done to you that got you **that** mad at me?"

"Who cares what it was!" bellowed Sol. "We had plenty of reasons!"

Seething with rage but trying not to blow up, I carefully replaced the portfolio in my lap.

My tone of voice was cold and angry, but I didn't scream at them. Instead, I answered deliberately, "No. You didn't. I gave you precious little real trouble and you goddamn well know it. I went to school and got good grades. I worked in your fucking bar every vacation, every school break! I graduated college, got a job... no drug charges, no out of wedlock pregnancies...no nothing! I married a **wonderful**, caring and generous man, whom you hated before you ever got to know him! Your biases and your prejudice mortified me! You embarrassed ME, not the other way around."

I didn't want to, but at that point I just broke down and sobbed. I was nearly forty-three years old, yet they could still upset me that much, and it made me furious at myself.

"Oh, now she's blubbering, " Sol snorted from the other end of the room. "Figures."

I regained composure. "So, okay," I said, straightening up in the chair. "since you hate me so much, I rescind my offer."

And I tore up the check right in front of their eyes.

I got up, put my coat on and gathered my things to walk out of their apartment.

"But Sari," called out Betty. "What about dinner tonight with the family?"

"Tell them I'm dead to you, " I sneered, "...and then be sure to explain why, since I can't."

I went down to their lobby, sure I could intercept Henri and my sister as they came back in. I sat in an armchair with one of those paisley patterns in shades of green and magenta that was supposed to invoke "traditional elegance" but was made out of cheap materials, which gave it away as crap. I sat there, took my checkbook out of the portfolio, and wrote out another check for the same amount... in Roslyn's name only. "At least she'll have a retirement account," I sniffed.

When they got back, Henri was surprised to see me sitting there, and Roslyn said, "Oh no, I can just guess. There was a big blowup of some sort, wasn't there?"

"You could say that." I looked at Henri and shook my head. Then I turned back to Roz. "Why do you live with them anyway? So you can be expected to wait on them hand and foot after you get back from a long day at work, and then be doomed to have to nurse them in their old age to boot? That's no life. Here, take this."

I handed her the check and she gazed at me with her mouth agape.

"Move out of here. Get your own place. Jesus Christ!"

749

I motioned to my son. *"Allons-y mon grand."*

We said our good-byes to my sister, all of us acknowledging without words that it was probably for the last time. Henri and I left, got in our rental car and just sat there parked for a little while, as I explained to him what had happened with his grandparents, and that we'd be having dinner by ourselves that night. I told him that I was sorry about his not being introduced to the rest of the family. "And I'm never coming back here, either, so I'm afraid you won't ever meet your cousins and great aunts and uncles. I'm sad about that, sweetie."

I drove him to The Bluffs and showed him my old house, looking exactly the same…ugly. Henri was not a snob; in fact, just the opposite considering the privileged upbringing he'd had. But I could tell he was pretty shocked at the little town he was being driven around in. I think he thought I must have been very poor.

Henri, as a little kid, had one day come home from elementary school and had asked me point blank if we were rich. Some classmate had told him he was "filthy rich," which sounded like an adult-generated term to me. I had brushed off the question then, but later, when the topic came up again, I answered him truthfully. I said that yes, he was a wealthy boy, born into privilege like his papa had been. I had told him that I was certainly not from a wealthy family, and that was okay. What mattered was that we were rich in love, and so lucky that the work we did to help other people enriched their lives and ours.

By the time he got to about sixth grade, he knew what it meant that our family had four residences, staff, fancy cars, a plane, and many other trappings of "entitlement." But Polo and I, at every stage of our son's development, had been very circumspect in explaining to him who he was, who his family were, what we owned, where his family fortune came from, the Beuvron history and the rest of it.

Henri had even been so astute as a child to ask me how it was that his dad's leg and arm couldn't have been "fixed, " since he had so much money.

"It's not as though they didn't try, sweetie," I had answered.

But it's what I left unsaid at the time that I'm sure he understood later: all the money in the known universe couldn't repair Polo's shattered limbs. We loved him with all our hearts no matter what he looked like. I don't think it was lost on Henri even then that we can never lose sight of what's truly important.

Henri had grown up in a ritzy suburb, and he visited the Hyde twins in an even wealthier one. None of the housing he was ever in looked anything like my old house, a completely non-descript, cream-colored ranch with redwood fencing in the front. He had a hard time imagining what it must have been like to live there, since I didn't talk much about it and, for that matter, about my past in general. I had taken a little album with a few pictures of me as a kid with me when I went to college, because I had already started keeping scrapbooks by then, and one of them was a red book with black paper pages where I'd pasted childhood photos on with those sticky corners. Henri and Polo had both seen that book, but it didn't show much of the house, which, even though it was custom built and had an interior that was Betty's mid-century modern dream of blond Heywood-Wakefield furniture--her idea of "having made it in life"-- the architecture gave the idea more of tract house or mobile home.

"Look at this side yard," I said to him, inching the car past the driveway. "I used to go sledding on that little hill. "

"That must have been fun, " he said, trying to sound anything but pitying for me.

"Yeah… hell, we didn't know. We thought it was a mountain."

I drove him downtown to see where the bar had been. This was not looking the same at all, since the entire block had been torn down to make room for…nothing.

"A grassy knoll with some trees planted. Too big to be a median, too small to be a park. Now that's some great urban planning," I sneered. "Typical." *The past had been erased in ways both small and large. My recorded recollections of my time in France destroyed, memories of my Bluffs childhood bulldozed.*

After that, we crossed back over what would have been the Aksarben Bridge, but which had been turned into a nameless Interstate one by the year I'd graduated high school. I laughed, as I explained to Henri how nervous it used to make me to drive over the bridge, and how only leather driving gloves did the trick to give me courage.

"I'm going to take you some place very special for dinner, " I told him, "my family's favorite pizza place. It's called Caniglia's, and it's in South Omaha's Little Italy. Omaha pizza is far different from Chicago's or New York's, for that matter. I hope you'll like it."

"I like pizza from anywhere," he assured me.

The interior of the restaurant was not noticeably different than how I remembered it, at least that's what I told myself. The darkened room with its paneled walls and oil-cloth tablecloths, big globe lights and filigree columns in the back brought the old days back to me, even if my childhood recollection was fading and untrustworthy. The pizza, however, was exactly the same. I ordered my childhood favorite: mushroom with Romano cheese instead of mozzarella.

"I do love it when stuff we remember from the past doesn't change!" I exclaimed to him as the waitress set the oblong tray on our table. "See, this is *pizza Napolitana*! You've never had it before. It's real South Omaha stuff," I remarked to him, picking up a rectangular thin crusted slice, and placing it on one of the small plates before us.

I was glad I got to share some good memories that day after all.

*   *   *

Henri was headed off to university in Paris, and, for the first year at least, I wanted him to live in a structured environment. I felt the Parc Monceau apartment was too big and too isolated to be a good choice, especially since, again, he'd just be living there with servants.

Henri was not part of a program as I had been, because for one thing, he'd already passed his entrance exams to be able to attend French university, and for another, he was already fluent in French. But because he was American, he was eligible to live in the *Pavillon des États-Unis* out at the *Cité Universitaire*, a sort of campus of international dormitories where all my American guy friends had lived in 1968, a few *métro* stops past Raspail where *La Maison* was. Living in the dorm to begin with was what I wanted him to do, and he did not disagree with the plan. I told him after that first year he could get an apartment in any *arrondissement* he liked, and possibly have roommates.

"Or you can find some studio you like," I said. "I won't be dictating where you live later. But when you do go into an apartment, I want you to be responsible for your own upkeep and do the cleaning, your own laundry and… at least some cooking."

"Yes, Mummy," he had laughed, "I will."

There was still one problem, however, and that was Robineau. He was adamant that Henri would need some sort of protection in Paris just like everywhere else he'd gone to school, and expected me to send a bodyguard with him. I had to agree to that, and Robineau made arrangements for the security detail to live in the *Cité Universitaire.*

Henri was aware of his circumstances, but, as always, we tried to keep it as low-key as possible. If he'd been the playboy sort, a big drinker or a casino-loving, horse-race-following young aristocrat , it would have been different; Henri was as normal a college freshman as I could have asked for…slightly nerdy, rather shy, and studious. I trusted that he would make friends easily enough, but I wasn't afraid he'd get to Paris and start throwing his money around and go nuts in any way. In any case, I made five or six trips a year there, to be with him at various intervals. He would leave the dorm, sometimes for a week at a time, and live with me on Parc Monceau.

In Chicago, I was still grieving dreadfully, and the aching in the pit in my stomach never abated. I didn't expect it ever would. I knew I would feel the pain forever, and accepted — intellectually at least — that I had to do everything possible in order to maintain some sort of equilibrium. If I were to become catatonic, if I were, for instance, to walk into Lake Michigan and keep on walking, where would that leave my kid?

I had never contemplated suicide. Even in my worst times growing up in the Shrier household on Moorline Hill, I never gave it a thought. I didn't have those voices in my head telling me I was worthless, even if I had them out loud at the dining room table. Something… and I have no idea what…inside me loved me. I guess I loved myself, in spite of Sol and Betty. So while I plotted my getaway constantly, I never plotted the definitive one. I had this dream life, somewhere deep inside of me, and it kept bubbling up, spurring me along to try to fulfill it. And I had to be alive in order to do that.

I knew in my heart **and** in my head that I wasn't going to be able to get over the grief by hoping it would go away in time. I'd lost the love of my life. I knew I'd never find another love like Polo. But I also couldn't see my life grinding to a halt, either. Yes, I was horribly wounded and hurting more than I ever thought possible. But I couldn't fall apart because I had to live...for Henri. And grief was contagious! I didn't want to spread it to my son or envelope him in mine. He had to grieve in his own way.

I did, however, emphasize to him that each of us had the d'Arivèque legacy to uphold. I said that we would get through our horrible grief by honoring his father's memory. He would continue his schooling at his dad's alma mater, and I, especially, had to rally to keep Polo's vision alive, and continue to uphold my beloved's memory by doing his work. Love compelled me to grieve, but it also propelled me to live.

I threw myself into every project with renewed vigor. I doubled the Foundation bequests to each cause and organization that were dear to Polo's heart. Every time I gave money, I did so in his name. And I started the biggest scholarship to date, **the Jean-Paul d'Arivèque Memorial Grant in Education,** in the sum of fifty-thousand dollars, What differentiated this bequest from others we gave was that it was earmarked for aspiring future French teachers who would agree not only to graduate with a degree in French **and** education, and then teach French; they also had to agree to stay in the profession for at least ten years.

I continued to privately support all of Polo's and his mother's past cultural organizations, and in so doing, I was also invited to take his place on most of their boards of directors, which I declined. I was fine sitting on any board having to do with art, but I didn't feel I could do justice to the other ones, especially those his mother had established and he had stepped in to serve on. They would continue to receive our financial backing, but not my time, which I devoted to *La Fondation*.

By the mid-nineties, I made what I believed to be a monumental decision, and I called a meeting of our own directors to announce it. I would be closing the Michigan Avenue offices and reopening them inside the Lake Shore Drive mansion. It was a logical step. I wasn't living there, and while we did continue to host visiting dignitaries, which we would still do even after the remodel, in essence over fifty thousand square feet of space on five levels was going to waste.

I consulted with John-Wilfred Hyde, still not quite retired at that point, and we drew up plans which would leave the basement level with its parking garage, pool, offices behind the pool where the vaults were, and all staff quarters as they were, only adding in a mail room and distribution center for our newsletter. But the rest of the space would be completely reconfigured on the other four floors, including the top floor ball room which Marie-Aveline had made use of for grand events, but Polo and I never had.

The mansion lent itself perfectly to making a beautiful new headquarters for the entire workings of *La Fondation Culturelle Française*.

The first-- or ground-- floor would continue to be space used for large public receptions, and all the "museum furniture"—as I called it-- would be brought there. We would move the music room down there, and create large conference rooms for board meetings, a huge dining room, catering kitchens and four guest bedroom suites. There would be a reception desk area, also, for two-fold use: to greet and guide people to the other offices, and to take care of overnight visitors.

All the works of art in the d'Arivèque private collection that hung on the walls of the Lake Shore mansion were re-catalogued, taken down, and put in storage in our lower level vaults in order to make way for the remodel; they were to be hung back up in the new spaces, mostly on the first and second floors.

In my role as curator of the art collection, I had begun making inquiries as to where I might loan our art, so that the paintings and sculpture could be seen by a wider public. I didn't believe in the idea that wealthy private collectors and corporations bought art and then secluded it away for no public showings. I would never sell our collection off, but I certainly would share it.

On the second floor, which had previously held the grand reception rooms, the two dining rooms, and the dozen or so guest bedrooms, along with that huge bedroom where *Maman* had lived, we put in the President's office suite, the film library—set up exactly as it had been on Michigan Avenue with a screening room as its office—and the areas for the press secretary, the revenue officers and account managers, the legal department, marketing and advertising. The great library was on that floor, set up only to be a library, and so I gave instructions to leave it exactly intact, and to remodel around it, which was not hard, since it occupied a huge corner of that level. It made me sad to go in there and not have Polo with me, but it also soothed me to be able to keep it exactly as he had.

I turned *Maman's* bedroom on that same floor, which, I always said, was bigger than any apartment I'd ever had as a single person, into my own *pied-à-terre* for when I had to stay in Chicago. I put her huge Napoleonic sleigh bed in one of the guest rooms downstairs, and brought in Polo's bed from our former third floor apartment, and partitioned off an area that was still plenty big to be my bedroom. I kept her bathroom the same, but next to that put in a little galley kitchen. Her sitting room area became my living room and the terrace was accessible from that. I kept her green silk draperies because they already matched the settees and chairs.

The vast majority of my clothes were in Wilmette, but I brought some in to put in Marie-Aveline's armoires. Polo had always wanted me to have whatever of his mother's wardrobe I liked, and, much as I didn't want to wear her clothes, I couldn't bring myself to get rid of Chanel suits, Givenchy and all the other *haute-couture* dresses, etc., so they were all still there. The sable coat and all her other furs were kept in cold storage, also in our vaults. That stayed the same.

I had the workers take down all the family portraits that lined that great hall leading into Polo's and my former living quarters, and had them shipped to *La Pérégrine*. It was only right for the ducal seat of the family to house these, I'd decided. After Polo's death, I had continued to take Henri to the house often in the summers, and as a young man on his own, he also went there frequently. I thought it would be very fitting to have the gallery there lined with the family portraits.

"Henri has always loved the place, " I told Annie-Laure. "For all I know, he'll keep it long after I'm gone."

My belief in the importance of La Pérégrine in Henri's future turned out to be prophetic.

On the fourth floor, which had been nearly ten thousand square feet of ornate ballroom, I installed the entire publications department. Our newsletter had grown by leaps and bounds, and there was still no such thing as the internet on which to publish it, although our operations were beginning to switch over from manual production to computerized. I had glass-enclosed offices for the editor-in-chief, the deputy editor, features editor, various associate directors and editors, copy chief, and the research departments.

It took nine months for this project to be achieved to my-- and the Board's-- satisfaction, and in the fall of 1996, the move was completed. As a bonus, since the d'Arivèque family owned the Lake Shore building outright-- in fact, I owned it outright-- moving the offices saved our organization over three hundred thousand dollars per year on rent alone.

Most of the time I continued to live in Wilmette, much as I was lonely out there without my beloved or my son. I maintained a heavy lecture schedule, speaking at language conferences and university education colleges, mainly in the Midwest but sometimes nationally. I visited Nonnie in San Francisco several times as we established scholarships for her students who wanted to study French. She was thrilled we set one up for study in Paris where she and I had met and become such good friends.

One time while Henri was studying in Paris, just before I was planning to visit him, I was invited by the Chicago Art Institute's curator of French art to a conference of her colleagues from other museums. I found this serendipitous because I would be meeting these people and then shortly thereafter, be able to see some of them in Paris. However, along with French institutions, there were many others represented...from England, Holland and Italy, among others. It was there that I met people from London's Courtauld Collection. They proposed an idea to me: to see their institute on one of my overseas trips, and perhaps eventually loan them some pieces from our collection. Since I was planning to be in Paris right away after that anyway, I took them up on the offer, and detoured first to London. I was so impressed with it, that I decided that this should be the first place I really would loan out paintings from the d'Arivèque collection.

For the opening five months later, Henri joined me in London as they unveiled the rooms whose signage announced, "*Unless otherwise indicated, all works in this gallery are on loan from the collection of Jean-Paul and Sarah d'Arivèque.*"

My son and I stood there and he put his arm around me and gave me a little squeeze because we both knew how emotional it was to be there without his dad.

"All the things we do like this--in his name-- unite him with me, you know " I said to Henri. "He was my whole *raison d'être*, and also, naturally, my dearest, closest friend... my compass."

"I hope I find a life partner with as deep bonds of love as you and *Papa* had, " he told me.

"I hope so, too, " I said, hugging him.

*　　　*　　　*

George-Henri had finished his *License* degree at the *Sorbonne* in three years and, in 1998, was preparing for *HEC*, where his father had done his business degree. He had indeed found a nice three-bedroom apartment in the *6ième arrondissement* , not far, really from where his father had lived as a child, near the Jardin du Luxembourg. Someone had once told me that there were no such things as coincidences, and I wasn't sure I believed that, but I did believe in serendipity, and the irony that Henri had chosen a place so near his father's maternal family home in Paris was not lost on me.

Henri had a cadre of nice friends, guys and girls, and two roommates who shared the rent, unknowing that they were only paying a fraction of it as their "share" and we were picking up the rest. This was "livin' large" for a student, but not for a multi-millionaire.

This time Robineau had installed his "agent" to protect Henri in the building with the *concièrge's* knowledge, and had hired a housekeeper for the three guys who kept an eye open as well. I still didn't see any present danger for my son in Europe, but Robineau, I'm sure, would have considered that naïve as ever.

I was invited to Geneva every so often for d'Arivèque Board meetings, and brought Henri along when he could get away. The two of us were treated with much deference and kindness, even as the directors all knew we were not only ignorant of the scope of our dynasty, but also ill-prepared to understand the workings of such a huge conglomerate. To that end, another one of the leading directors, a close personal friend of *Oncle* Charles, named Bénédict Levesque, whom I had met previously several times, did me a favor and gathered into a binder, the history of the family business and current holdings, mostly to show Georges-Henri so he'd had a better grasp on what he would one day be dealing with, and also to help me keep things straight, too.

The d'Arivèque financial holdings had historically been in private banks, which, as early as the seventeenth century, were already headquartered in Geneva, and thus out of harm's way during the French Revolution. The dynasty had invested heavily in the nascent industries of large-scale copper mining, rail and sea transport, diamond mines and oil exploration. They had been lenders and investors for centuries to countries, kingdoms and consortiums.

D'Arivèque employed over four thousand people, had more than ten thousand private clients world-wide, and managed an annual turnover of over thirty billion Swiss francs, French francs, sterling and dollars.

"We do not hide the money, " added Bénédict Leveque, as if reading my mind. "We pay millions and millions in taxes to any country in which we do business. But our main holdings are here in our private Swiss banks, of course, and thus safe from the ravages of stock markets and fly-by-night despots."

Henri was grateful for the impromptu education one particular trip, but approached me afterwards with some trepidation, to tell me that all those subsidiaries, funds, and businesses made his head swim. About a year into his graduate studies, during one of my impromptu visits to Paris, my son seemed a bit more agitated than normal and asked to have a talk with me at the Parc Monceau apartment.

"I think I've chosen a different path than *HEC*, " he announced to me "I would like to change direction and go into hotel management and hospitality, and I think I want to do it in Geneva at *École Hôtelière*. Oxford has a program in that, too, " he continued, "but I think with our family ties to Geneva, that is where I belong."

"Goodness! You've obviously been giving all this some serious thought for some time, haven't you?!"

"Yes, I should have mentioned it to you earlier. It's just that after our meetings with Levesque, I realized that I'm not cut out for international banking."

"I'm all for whatever it is you want to do, darling, " I said, "just a little surprised."

"Mummy, " he continued, "there's another part of my plan I haven't told you yet."

"What's that?" I laughed. *This kid had it all going on!*

"I want to take over *La Pérégrine* and turn it into a luxury hotel. Would you be very angry at that idea?"

"Angry? Are you kidding?! I think that's a great idea!"

"You do? Whew!" His relief was visible. "But what about *Papa* and *Oncle* Charles? Would they be angry with the repurposing of the family home, do you guess?"

"They…they're gone now, honey. I can't answer for them. But I think they'd be happy to know the home would be saved from going to waste—or to ruin. You don't plan to tear it down, right?"

"Oh no! I want to keep it the same on the exterior---mostly. " He added laughing, "Maybe redo the parking area."

"I would be for that, " I agreed.

"It's really your house now, Mummy. Are you sure you are in agreement with this idea?"

"YES!" I answered, hugging him. And then suddenly I thought of another part of it. "And you know what, Henri? France really doesn't have the kind of places Americans are calling 'destination venues'—like for weddings and other special occasions… you know? The French have all those spas in the Alps and *Massif Central* and such, the thermal ones like *Évian* and *Volvic*…those have been around since the Romans. But not spas like America has…to pamper-- mostly women-- or have weekend getaways or bridal parties or even the entire wedding. We had Annie-Laure's wedding there but your place could really become a wedding destination!"

"Mummy!! You're brilliant!" he swept me up into his arms.

"Well, I don't know about that! After all, **you** were the one with the hotel idea." I grinned at him. Then I got serious again. "It's still really difficult for entrepreneurs to make a go of it in France. In my day, a young guy like you would have had a hard time implementing such a new idea. The French don't take to changes in the traditional ways of doing things. But I hope that's changing. I think you've got a great chance to make this a success, especially if you emphasize that it's sort of a French-**American** place."

Even if entrepreneur was a French word, being one in France was not an easy road. But in all honesty, my kid was in a better position to gamble with a new venture than most. He had all the income he'd ever need from his father's estate, and didn't require outside capital to fund his venture. Henri wasn't really risking anything by trying. La Pérégrine, in whatever permutation, would always remain in the family.

"Yes, Franco-American! I can just see the signage! Maybe we can line the entry drive with both flags. What do you think?"

"I think you'll have a terrific business once you reconfigure the château the way you would like it to be."

He looked at me a little sheepishly. "The other thing is, though, Mummy, since we're on that subject, I'm also wondering if you would undertake to see to the actual renovations. You did such a phenomenal job of remodeling our home into the offices of *La Fondation*. Would you work your magic on *La Pérégrine* also? Make it into a real—destination-- as you call it?"

"Well, I'd…sure…I'll do it. I'll hire Hyde Industries again. Did you know Laura has taken over from her grandfather and is the head of it now? That will be easy enough."

"I was hoping you'd say that! I'm not trying to dump this on you, Mummy. I'll be the one who does the work once it's up and running."

"I understand, darling. I'm so happy you've thought of what you really wanted to do and found a niche. And you want to live there, too? Full time? "

"Yes. I hope that doesn't make you sad."

"Of course not! What are planes for?" I laughed. "All I mean is, we will make sure *La Pérégrine* is still a home, and retain the ducal seat, at least part of it. What do you think?"

"I give you free rein, Mummy. I trust your taste implicitly."

" Ha! We'll see about that!"

So while Henri did his graduate degree in Geneva (living in *Oncle* Charles' penthouse, instead of the Lake Geneva villa we always stayed in, both of which I now also owned, of course), *La Pérégrine* was completely revamped. In order to fulfill this mission, I immediately consulted with John-Wilfred Hyde. I said I knew that he was by then stepping back from the actual day to day operation of his businesses, and that it was Laura who had taken on the mantel of CEO, but I wanted to run the idea by him first, and invited him and Julia to come over for a visit and assess the place. They still traveled often to Europe in the 1990's. Paul was becoming a well-known pediatrician in London, so they liked to be there as much as possible, especially during Wimbledon. Laura had returned to the States for college, graduating from Vassar in 1991.

"She then entered the Wharton School with an eye towards business," John-Wilfred had explained to me. "But she definitely inherited her mother's artistic talent. Even though she considers herself to be more creative than anything else, she did superbly in graduate school. I have complete confidence in her abilities to take over our company."

"Well, her artistic bent will serve her well, in any case, " I had replied, "running a huge industry that designs as well as builds."

Laura Hyde put me in contact with her architects who brought to fruition our plans to overhaul the interior of *La Pérégrine*, all the while keeping the original integrity of the château intact on the outside, exactly as it had always been.

First and foremost, the place would now be set up as a hotel, but as I'd indicated to Henri, it would remain the "Ducal seat" and family residence as well. Hyde Industries drew up plans that would enable a lovely home on the ground floor, but would be enlarged to accommodate up to seventy-five guests in thirty bedrooms or suites on the upper floors. Large kitchens designed to provide catering for as many as five hundred were to be installed in augmented space near where the original kitchen had been, and in the private quarters, another, far smaller, kitchen would need to be added.

The entire "turret" wing, where Marie-France had lived out her retirement days, was converted into a state-of-the-art spa, with space for services that would include salons for facials, exfoliation treatments, spa pedicures and manicures, massage, hair, makeup, yoga studios, meditation spaces, a sauna and aroma therapy rooms. The long gallery separating the two wings was redecorated to highlight what it now became: the hall of ancestors, housing all the portraits from the Chicago mansion.

The front entrance was turned into an official reception area, and on the wall above a beautiful, high antique check-in desk, hung a portrait in oil of Polo and me that he had had commissioned shortly after our wedding. He had it done from one of our formal wedding photos. It had turned out quite well...not too stuffy but still elegant, befitting a future duke and duchess of something...and Georges-Henri had asked me specifically if he could have it.

Behind the front desk was a separate office, and behind that and down the hall were the family's residential quarters, including Polo's original bedroom, where I'd gotten lost all those years ago. Henri insisted that this bedroom was to be my room any time I came to stay with him, and it touched me deeply. We didn't change one iota of the décor in there, which had been more or less the same for centuries. However, instead of the rabbit warren of small rooms and alcoves around it, all that was opened up, creating a new, more modern master suite, and carving out four more, albeit smaller, bedrooms, bathrooms, a living room, a private dining room, a t.v. room or *salle de séjour*, as the French called it, the family kitchen and laundry facilities, and, most importantly, a room that could someday become a playroom for toys if needed (and I fervently hoped it would be!).

La Pérégrine's library to the side of the entry adjacent to the "turret wing" was also preserved and left the way it was, since it, too, had existed in the home for five hundred years. It was not to be a public room, but could be made available for meetings or private guest functions. Inside the spa we added another, smaller "salon" where hotel guests and spa clients could relax, read, peruse magazines and the like. The lobby also had a seating area, but a little less quiet, since it had a television and some storage for games and a few toys for guests with families.

The two sweeping staircases on either end of the gallery were kept intact---they would make gorgeous backdrops for wedding photos, after all. But the house needed to have a completely different elevator installed, not the cage type so often seen in France, but one like hotels had—wide enough for luggage carts...and wheelchairs, for that matter.

The chapel, which was kept more or less non-religious, was enlarged to accommodate bigger crowds, and some exquisite landscaping was done around it to accentuate the wedding venue aspects of it. All the gardens were brought back to their original splendor, just as Marie-France had envisioned when she took up the task two decades earlier.

I flew over several times with the architects and construction engineers to watch the transformations. Henri was still a grad student when most of this was going on, but he was kept in the loop on every aspect of the design and came over from Geneva almost once a month to observe the progress. He seemed very pleased. And he also had ideas of his own for the property.

"I would like us to offer tennis and horseback riding lessons, too, " he told me. "It might attract more families to come for holidays."

"I like the idea of the stables not going to ruin," I had responded, "and you're right: tennis courts are a must. We already have a lovely pool area. Tennis and swimming just complement each other."

Robineau had taken a keen interest in the idea of turning *La Pérégrine* into a hotel, and one time just as I was slated to go over, he approached me to say that he was wondering if I would consider letting him finish out the rest of his career working for Henri there. He was, after all, mostly the equivalent of a hotel manager, ever since the days when the Lake Shore mansion housed many guests per week. He could help Henri staff his place and get it off to a good start.

I was greatly moved by this offer. Robineau was about twelve years older than me, still five years away from retirement age, but his boyfriend Maxime...called "partner" now...was ready to hang it up in the club business, and agreed he'd like to live out his life back in France.

"I think Henri will be delighted at the prospect of having your help and expertise. Of course I agree to your plan, and I'll continue to pay your salary and benefits from here."

The part of *La Pérégrine,* the turret, which Marie-France had inhabited for more than a decade at the château had been designated as the spa, but in the remodel there would still be plenty of room for a handsome two-story apartment to be reinstalled in the front part nearest the circular drive. I was happy to hand those lodgings over to Robineau and Maxime, and let it be their home.

However, once it was agreed upon that Robineau and Maxime would be retiring in France, I had also had another idea.

I called them both into my office one day shortly before they were to leave Chicago.

"You know, I've been giving this move of yours some thought, and I think I've come up with something that will interest you both. I own Uncle Charles' Lake Geneva house now, and of course, I will be bequeathing it to Georges-Henri, with the further intention of his heirs having it one day. However, it is sitting empty. Henri really only uses the city apartment in Geneva. I would like to offer the villa to you both. Use it as a weekend getaway now while you, Robin, are still working; but later on it can be your retirement home if you'd like to live on Lake Geneva. My only stipulation is that you may not, yourselves, bequeath it to anyone. It will still be in my name. If I pre-decease you, you won't have to worry that Henri would sell it out from under you. In any event, I'll discuss all this with him. In the meantime do you like the plan?" I asked breathlessly, realizing I hadn't given them a chance to speak to the idea at all.

"I...I'm overwhelmed!" said Robineau, who'd been to the Lake Geneva house many times as Polo's valet.

Maxime grasped me by both hands. "Such a gesture, *Madame.* What can we say?!"

"Say yes... and you don't need to call me *Madame.*"

*   *   *

Georges-Henri came back to Chicago, after having obtained his Master's equivalent in hospitality management, to surprise me with something else: he had met a fellow EHG student—a French girl.

"I've fallen in love, Mummy, " he told me. "I want you to meet her, but I wanted to tell you first. "

Her name was Delphine de Bettencourt. Her father was a lawyer who could trace his ancestry back to an ancient noble Norman Catholic family, one who also had famous members of the French Resistance in the more recent history. Henri had been struck by their having that in common when he first met her parents.

"When I met them, they immediately knew the name d'Arivèque, " Henri said, "and told me about the links between my grandfather and their family."

"Well, honey, " I said, "almost everyone in France knows the name. But of course, I believe them, and, yes, I too find it interesting."

"They live in Paris, but their *maison secondaire* is near Orléans. That's where Delphine spent most of her summers. Otherwise during the school year on weekends they went to her grandparents' place in Normandy. The paternal family seat is a Norman château."

"Orléans is not far from *La Pérégrine,* " I noted. "That's also ironic, isn't it?"

"More than you know!" he laughed. "She's told me she feels deeply rooted in 'the *Orléanais,*' as she calls that part of the country."

Henri and Delphine had gone through school in Geneva together, only not on the same level. Three years younger than him, Delphine went straight to the Geneva hospitality school from *lycée.* She received the equivalent of a Bachelor's degree from there, not a Master's.

"Still, with that in common, " Henri explained to me, " we feel that we could run *La Pérégrine* as a hotel superbly together."

"Does she want to do that?" I wondered.

"Absolutely, " he answered. "I've already taken her there to see it. I'm sure when you meet her, she'll tell you all about the ideas she has for the spa and turning the place into a real resort. She loves the idea that we offer equestrian lessons and also put in games like croquet…you know, add more family-oriented activities. She also would like **us** to have a large family. Well, I'm getting a little ahead of myself."

"Then, I can't wait to meet her!"

He had not yet officially proposed to Delphine, but flew her to Chicago to meet me first. We hit it off right away. She was very personable and friendly, though in the French way…deferential to me as Henri's mother and very formal with me, using *vous.*

I was captivated by how beautiful she was, and it also struck me funny. She was the antithesis of me when I first met Polo: unlike me, she was rather tall, especially for a French girl, with a massive mane of shoulder-length blond hair, which was so thick that when she reached around and pulled it off her face, it fell right back in front and cascaded down her cheek. She had blue-grey eyes framed with thick lashes, but hidden behind orange tortoise-shell square glasses. Her nose was perfectly formed and turned up just a little bit at the tip, and her lips were full and round, pretty in red gloss. Besides being so physically striking, Delphine was, I could tell right away, very bright. Henri had already mentioned her high marks in the school they both attended, but I could also gauge this by her thoughtful, well-reasoned opinions on subjects from ideas she had about spa cuisine at *La Pérégrine,* to Jacques Chirac's ascendancy to *Président de la République* from mayor of Paris.

I saw right away that Henri had fallen deeply in love with this girl, and I had no objections whatsoever, nor would it have made any difference if I had. But I felt obliged to have a serious discussion with them both, so over a dinner catered up my office's private dining room, I confronted both of them, but mainly Delphine, with the fact that even though my son was the heir to the d'Arivèque name and all that came with it, he was still a Jew; and her family would not be the first bourgeois French people to reject outright the idea of such a marriage. The conversation we were about to have harkened me back to the one I'd had with *Oncle* Charles in the gardens of *La Pérégrine. It was déja vu all over again.*

"Are you two prepared to be confronted with a rejection of your union by your parents, Delphine?" I questioned her bluntly.

"My parents like Georges-Henri very much, " Delphine offered, knowing full-well what topics were about to come up.

"Mummy, we wanted to talk to you first, though, before we ask *Monsieur* and *Madame* de Bettencourt for their blessing."

I think in his heart Henri knew I would never stand in his way of marrying whomever he wanted. He knew of the debacle that ensued when I had announced my pending marriage to my parents, and what their reaction had been when they had met his father for the first time. Owing to that alone, he felt secure in the knowledge that I would never have done such a thing to him. But the Bettencourts could have been a different matter. Delphine assured me that things had gone well when Henri was introduced to them.

"Even so, won't they be expecting you to marry in the church?" I asked, feeling I already knew the answer.

"My parents and grandparents, for that matter, have no problem with the idea that I would be marrying outside the church, " Delphine answered slowly and deliberately. "It is, as you know, the mayor's office ceremony that is the legal one in France."

"Yes, I realize that the clergy in France are not vested, as we say, with the legal authority of the state that they are in the U.S. But are you also telling me you never dreamed of a big church wedding? Henri told me you have strong ties to *Orléans.* And you never wanted to be wed in their lovely cathedral

758

with all those Joan of Arc stained-glass windows lining the nave? Wouldn't your parents want to see you married there?"

"It is very nice, you are right. But no, I do not mind at all. As for my parents, they would have a harder time with their future grandchildren being absent from celebrating *Noël Réveillon en Normandie*, at the country house. We have gathered there every Christmas of my life, " she laughed.

"In any case, " I hastened to add, "Henri might not even be able to **be** married in a cathedral. I don't know about in France, but here, he couldn't be married in any Catholic church, let alone a cathedral, without –I don't know—at least a dispensation if not a conversion. And even then, I'm not sure."

"I don't plan on any conversions, Mummy, " Henri interjected.

I looked at Henri. I could see that he was uncomfortable and guessed what he was feeling: the elephant in the room that still hadn't been addressed was that, regardless of where they got married, the probability was that I wouldn't be having any Jewish grandchildren. He was very concerned that this would bother me.

He needn't have worried.

"You know what? If there are future grandchildren in my life, I promise you I will love them more than life itself. But Delphine, " I pressed her, serious in my tone, "it's not a secret that when push comes to shove, not only could Henri very well **not** be accepted –but myself either for that matter, as potentially the other grandmother—by your family, I mean. You both know the systemic anti-Semitism going back to the Middle Ages in France was pretty much thought to have dissipated before the War. French Jews were highly assimilated. And then look what happened…it resurfaced again, and we found out when neighbor turned on neighbor, didn't we?"

"*Madame* d'Arivèque, " she responded just as seriously, "we French---all my family--have many very recent memories of that horrible period during the war. My parents and grandparents talked to my siblings and me about it all our lives. We studied it in school, and they did not…*comment dit-on dorer la pilule?* " she looked up at Henri.

"Sugarcoat…"he answered.

"*Oui*, they did not sugarcoat it in school either. None of the French…we make no excuses for the Vichy government. My grandparents, especially, they were appalled by the atrocities that happened in their lifetime! And no one is more indignant over it than my father. His firm has handled several famous cases of Holocaust compensation and restitution. We all take on the mantle of shame, believe me. I assure you, *Madame*." She was practically in tears.

"I believe you Delphine." And I did. I reached over to put my hand on hers at the table. "But one can't just get rid of Judaism. It's in you."

"And I've never tried to hide it, have I?" Henri said.

"No, Henri, " I laughed, "you haven't. You practice more than I do."

I think I felt better that night after our little dinner discussion, but of course, the real test lay ahead of me…in Paris.

During her stay in Chicago, Delphine was shown all around the city by my son. We all stayed in the Lake Shore mansion, but Henri took her to see his childhood home in Wilmette, too, and they spent time on the beach near our house.

"She seems to like Chicago very much, " Henri told me one afternoon when Delphine had gone out shopping. "She loves the fact that the stores here are so huge…and cheap!"

"Well, compared to Paris, I'd say she was right."

I took the opportunity while Delphine was out on her own to take Henri aside and tell him the story of the wedding ring I wore. He knew something about it already, but I reminded him that it wasn't his grandmother's ring. Hers, consisting of a five-carat diamond from De Beers that had been made into a beautiful Ascher-cut engagement ring, was still in our vault in Chicago, only ever having been worn by her.

"Your father did not offer it to me because I was averse at the time to wearing things that had belonged to your grandmother. And besides, after I'd heard the story of the Schwartzes, you can see how special *Madame* Schwartze's ring became to us. But I know *Papa* would be thrilled were you to propose to Delphine with his mother's ring. It's extremely valuable, but that's not the main reason you should have it. It's very beautiful, and also has so much sentimental worth. Would you like me to get it out for you? You don't have to use it---if you'd prefer something of your own choosing, I completely understand."

"Oh no, Mummy, I'd love to offer Grandmother's ring to Delphine. I think she'll really see the significance in that. Also, I've been thinking about suggesting the wedding take place at *La Pérégrine*. I think she'll like that."

By the time I met *les de Bettencourt*, I got the impression right away that they, too, saw the significance in their daughter's enormous engagement ring. The thought entered my mind that they might be willing to overlook the fact that their *gendre* was a Jew, when a future grandson of theirs would be the duke of Beuvron, not to mention heir to one of the world's greatest fortunes. All of that was, however, merely conjecture on my part. They would never have brought the topic of money into any conversation with me, nor I with them. But the d'Arivèque family name and reputation were so widely known all over France and Europe—far more than in the States-- that they could hardly disguise their elation that their daughter was going to be the wife of the scion of that family.

"We are so fond of your Georges-Henri, " Véronique de Bettencourt told me, smiling broadly as she welcomed me into the foyer of their classic *pierre de taille* apartment building in the Eighth *arrondissement*, and led me in the little black cage elevator to the fifth floor, while the kids climbed the six flights.

Hubert de Bettencourt was standing on the thick carpet in the hall outside his open double doors of the apartment *à gauche*. We exchanged warm introductions with handshakes, but not *la bise*.

"I travel to London often for business, " Hubert said in perfect English when we were settled inside being served Campari aperitifs by their maid, "and Delphine insisted I must see your art collection at the Courthauld. Just magnificent."

Delphine was one of four children: older sister Béatrice was married and had a baby of her own – their first grandchild.

"She is a beauty already, " said Véronique, "our little Mathilde. *C'était le. coup. de. foudre!*"

Yes, love at first sight…I'd experienced it when laying eyes on Paul and Laura and then my own baby; but one often hears of the unbridled joy one experiences seeing grandchildren for the first time.

Béatrice lived in the suburb of St. Cloud with her husband Lionel, who was a lawyer, having been taken into his father-in-law's firm; brother Jean was a student at the *Fac de Médecine* in Paris' sixth *arrondissement*, and younger brothers Mathieu and Quentin were in high school at Lycée Montaigne, and still living at home.

We had a wonderful dinner that night at their house, and everyone talked amicably about a wedding at *La Pérégrine*.

"The children seem to be determined to be the first ones to be married at the new wedding venue, " said Véronique. I waited for the other shoe to drop about no nuptial mass. "We couldn't be more pleased."

That did surprise me, and I echoed her sentiments. "And I want to assure you that as we get closer to the date and when you have a guest list, we can arrange transportation to and from *Orléans*, in case your guests prefer town hotels rather than being in the not-quite-finished country house. "

I had no idea how many guests she planned to invite, but I assumed it would be a lot.

"That is a very kind gesture, " said Véronique.

By the time the actual wedding date rolled around, however, almost a year later, *La Pérégrine* **was** refurbished into a hotel, and the celebration was a truly splendid affair, just as beautiful as Annie-Laure's and Jean-Luc's wedding, and three times bigger. We took a page from Marie-France de Piaget's planning and put up two tents in the gardens this time, and then lit the place up as splendidly as she had with fairy lights.

Just like Polo had done for the other wedding, I flew my entire staff and special friends over for this one, and it turned out I was the one to put my guests up in the *Orléans* region so the bride's family could have our château.

The pair were legally wed in the village mayor's office, as prescribed, and there were two officiants at *La Pérégrine*--- a de Bettencourt family friend priest and Judge Harry Lowenstein-- to perform the second rites. Not much mention of God and none of Jesus, but like I always believed, you can have the words "The Lord" and take it to mean either.

* * *

Henri and Delphine were pregnant within a year of their wedding, and they decided — or rather their Parisian Ob/Gyn did — that they would have their baby at the American Hospital of Paris, which was really in the western suburb of Neuilly-sur-Seine, just a few miles from the d'Arivèque Parc Monceau apartment. Henri and Delphine had settled in there a couple of weeks prior to her due date, and that made it easy for her mother, especially, to see her often. When Delphine went into labor with my first grandchild, Georges-Henri phoned me to tell me he thought I still had about twelve to twenty-four hours to get there, but for a first baby, the speed was surprising, and I arrived to a hospital room full of the de Bettencourt family already cooing over the beautiful Jeanne-Pauline. They named her, without the shadow of a doubt, for Henri's father, and I had absolutely nothing to do with it; they thought it up all on their own to honor Polo.

I burst into tears when Henri placed her in my arms. She was blond, an absolute towhead with flaxen wisps framing huge gray-blue eyes. Her cheeks were rosy and very plump, and her mouth was a tiny bow. She looked like a baby in a Reubens painting, and I couldn't take my eyes off of her.

Back at home I resurrected some of Henri's nursery items for use when they all would come visit me, and I took it upon myself to stock in a new supply of Petit Bateau layette items and a few sweet toys from Le Nain Bleu before I left Paris.

The baby was born in June and by the end of summer the three of them had come to Chicago to see "*Mamie-Sari*" as I was to be known to my grandchildren. *Mamie* was the French term of endearment for the grandmother, and my granddaughter's French *Mamie* was already the designated *Mamie*. It was only logical---she would be there so much more often than I, and besides, the mother's mother, to me, **is** the grandmother of record. I was certainly always closer to my Nana, Betty's mom, than I was to Sol's mother who was *Bubbe*. My paternal grandmother didn't live long enough for me to adapt to that name, and she was no longer living by the time Roslyn even came along, so there was never really a *bubbe* in my life. I didn't like Granny, as English grandmothers were called, because it sounded like such a crotchety old person. I guess we had *The Beverly Hillbillies* to thank for ruining that. I didn't want to be Grandma, either, and I also rejected Nana. There was only one Nana. So I was left with "*Grand-mère*" which sounded altogether too remote, or Grand-maMA, the other Briticism, which I dismissed on the grounds it would make me sound too haughty.

"I don't want her to call me just Sari, " I moaned to my son and daughter-in-law. "I hate that when kids call their relatives by their first names to their face."

"Then why not *Mamie-Sari*?" said Delphine. "That differentiates you enough from my mother, and she won't mind."

"That works!" I said, relieved.

Little Jeanne-Pauline became known to us as **Pauline**, and she was followed in quite short order by Louise-Aveline (which I thought was a beautiful name and very generous of Delphine to have yet another of her children named for a d'Arivèque family member.) Their third child, a boy, was Charles-François Hubert, so named in order for the future *Duc de Beuvron* to once again be a Charles, and also to honor Delphine's father, ignoring the Jewish taboo of naming after someone still alive. Hubert de Bettencourt's buttons were bursting.

All three of my grandchildren had blond hair and blue or hazel eyes. None of them had any coloring at all which resembled my side of the family. It was just like Cass's children both taking after Alan. Genetics was a crap shoot, and I was bemused by the results in our case. My three beauties were all the spitting image of their gorgeous mother.

From the age of about eight or nine, Pauline, Louise and Charles were sent to Le Rosey for school. Henri explained to me that since the school was relatively close to their home, and since it was a protected environment with the security apparatus in place for many a wealthy family's children -- not just ours -- it was the logical choice. Robineau approved, but as expected, still insisted that his own security team reside nearby.

761

"Delphine and I both run the business here in Vierzon, " Henri had said, "and this way we can be sure the children have a stable academic environment of a higher echelon than anything in the Loire Valley, and not have to commute to Paris for boarding school."

"You know, I think it's a great opportunity, " I said, "Obviously, Le Rosey is world-renowned. The Hyde-Jones twins are the products of that school, so I'm well acquainted with it. Their mother went to it as well for a time. It's a little hard for me to fathom them away from you so young, but obviously the other families do it."

"We miss them, of course, but we go up to Rolle frequently."

Henri and Delphine were interested in *La Fondation Culturel Française,* and acutely aware that one day decisions would have to be made as to whether they would stay in France, or come back to Chicago to run it. More than wealth acquisition, stewardship of the family empire was always at the forefront of any of our future planning. When they wanted my advice, I freely gave it. But I really did not intend to meddle in their lives in that regard.

"I feel certain, " I told them, "that with three children, you will have ample opportunities to decide who will take over what. Your son, for instance, might really want to step into Uncle Charles' shoes and direct d'Arivèque Industries. And maybe the girls would want to carry on in the tradition of their great-grandmother."

"**And** their *Mamie-Sari!*"

Henri and Delphine indicated that they would indeed like to preside over the Foundation one day, and probably move back to Chicago, which pleased me no end. *La Pérégrine* could possibly be run by one of their children. The future of all of it seemed bright to me.

Every summer throughout their entire childhood, my three Norman-French-American, Catholic-Jewish grandchildren came to be with me, and played happily in the back yard, at the beach and at the country club where their father had spent his childhood. At first Henri and Delphine-- or one of them-- would fly over with the kids to spend big chunks of the *grandes vacances* with me, too. But pretty soon, the kids came without their parents.

My grandchildren did not attend synagogue in France and they were, for all intents and purposes, raised a bit more Catholic than anything. However, their father made sure they knew they had Jewish— and American—roots, and if the timing were right, he made it a point to bring them home to Wilmette with me for Jewish holidays and Thanksgiving. If Chanukah fell outside the dates of Christmas vacation, then they came for at least part of it in Chicago. If it happened to coincide with the Christmas frenzy, then I went to them and we did both holidays in France. This pattern repeated itself in the Spring. If they could be there during Passover, we had it at my home. When Easter morning came, we hunted eggs and baskets full of candy and toys in my garden. If they couldn't be in the States for Spring break, no matter what, I always sent them Easter presents.

If I was at *La Pérégrine* for Christmas, I was always invited with them for *Réveillon* up to Normandy and the de Bettencourts' eighteenth-century half-timbered manor house on the estate dominated by their family's decaying château. The little kids had the great advantage of many cousins to play with in Normandy.

Véronique remarked one Christmas when they were still quite young, that the children would soon be old enough to travel alone under the auspices of the airlines, but I reminded her that I would be sending my own plane to get them. She was speechless for a minute, as though she'd forgot who we were.

"Ah, yes, of course, " she smiled. "I should have realized it."

The Boeing 707 was Polo's personal plane, not the Foundation's, and I had sold it 2003, opting instead for a Hawker Horizon by Raytheon. The 707 was past its prime and also, with old habits dying hard, I felt too guilty flying around in such an enormous plane when we'd gone through an oil embargo for one thing, and the carbon footprint left by one passenger only in a huge airplane was too much for me to bear. The Hawker Horizon was really small in comparison to the other plane. The cabin no longer resembled the interior of a yacht. But for the trips I made and the people who normally travelled with me, it made a lot more sense. My plane was called a "super mid-size" and mine was configured to carry fifteen passengers comfortably. It had a forward right-side galley behind the cockpit, two lavatories, and a seating area with table in the back with a double aft-side divan, before you entered a very tiny extra bedroom-type cabin at the tail. All the upholstery was high quality leather, and the cabinetry was mahogany. The price tag, including customization, was in the twenty million dollar-range. I employed two pilots and three flight attendants on rotating schedules.

If I were heading straight to *La Pérégrine*, I would fly into Geneva and be picked up for the short trip to Vierzon. But if I were over for meetings, researching, or otherwise on Foundation business, I lived in our Parc Monceau place; and Henri and Delphine would bring the kiddos up to see me. They loved playing in the park, and I loved watching them there. But these were poignant times when I fervently wished Polo could have been with me, and I always remembered my "epiphany" sitting in that garden decades earlier.

La Pérégrine Spa and Resort became, over time, a huge success, accomplished by the hard work and creative direction of Delphine and Henri, and in no small part also by Robineau, whose managerial skills were invaluable to the young entrepreneurs.

"We couldn't really call it a *'station thermale'*, " Henri said, " because there are no springs, no *sources*. So we thought having the name in English would indicate a certain *cachet* of mixed cultures."

Late one summer after they'd been open for business for not quite five years, Henri telephoned me in a state of nervousness I hadn't really ever heard in his voice before, at least not since Polo's impending death. He was rather beside himself because the entire spa and all the guest rooms had been booked for a weekend party by a member of the vintner branch of the de Rothschild dynasty.

"Mummy, what if we aren't up to clients of that caliber? Do you know them? What if they're impossible?"

"Nonsense, " I told him, "not only are you up to it, but an event like that could seal the deal on your place as **the** destination venue in France! I do not know any Rothschilds but I bet *Oncle* Charles did. I'm sure this is a feather in your caps! *Bravo vous deux!*"

"But Mummy, won't you please come over? I'll feel better if you're there — just to be with our kids and sort of lurk about, keeping tabs on it all. Please say you'll come."

"Sure, honey! Don't worry. Everything will be fine. Have a big confab with Robineau, though, to make sure the best staff are on the job and know what is expected of them."

I did fly over for the Rothschild spa weekend. The honoree was one of Baron Philippe de Rothschild's great granddaughters. The occasion was her pre-bridal "hen party." The wedding itself would take place on their grand estate of *Château Mouton*, but the bride-to-be wanted to have something less formal and more fun for her friends leading up to the nuptials.

Dozens of young women, all in their mid-to-late twenties, arrived unchaperoned by any *grande dame* with the name of Rothschild, so Henri didn't have anything to worry about on that score. They were all very polite, if a little giddy by the Friday evening, after drinking champagne all day, and having a great time partaking of Henri and Delphine's menu of spa services. Each one had a "Bridal Exfoliation Treatment" done with sugar and sea salt; the "Spa Joyous Massage," an "Anti-oxidant Soak" and most of the other "normal" offerings like pedicures and manicures.

Out in the back garden where we had all sat around the pool summer after summer, Henri had added a Jacuzzi and then enclosed the entire patio, pool and all the seating area, under a heated glass dome, so that guests could swim year-round. It was a big hit with the de Rothschild party, and at the end of their stay, they all raved to Delphine about the experience. *La Pérégrine* was cutting edge for France, and one of the girls, who wrote for the style section of *Paris Vogue,* recognized that. She vowed, as she was leaving, to make *La Pérégrine* a household name.

Their tab came to fifty-four thousand euros. The bride-to-be presented Henri with her personal check and in a matter of days the transaction went right through. When they had left, Henri looked over at me and we burst out laughing. He had worried for nothing. In fact, we were both giddy and I was exceedingly proud of my son. It was 2009 and at thirty-six years old he was a happily married father of three, a dutiful and appreciative son, successful in his chosen field, cognizant of his present and future duties...an all-around great guy. I could not have wished for more.

One day, several years after the Rothschild party, which did, I must add, put *La Pérégrine* on the map, I was in my office on Lake Shore Drive when a call came in that was announced to me as Henri by our receptionist. I panicked for a second, since I was always afraid I'd get a call out of the blue from him that one of the children was sick or some terrible disaster had occurred.

"Henri? What's wrong!?"

"Nothing's wrong Mummy. But something strange happened a few minutes ago. I thought you'd want to know about it."

"What?!" I was still distressed.

"Well, we have a family booked into the resort –it's a man with his daughter, son-in-law and four grandchildren. They're here from Paris…you know, just for a relaxing holiday with swimming and such for the kids."

"Okaaay. Nothing strange about that."

"Well, I was working in my office as usual… you know, with the door closed. One of our staff was registering them, when all of a sudden the gentleman—he must be in his seventies at least—turned rather pale and asked my clerk why a portrait of **Sari Shrier** was on our wall!"

"Really!?"

"So my clerk was a little confused because she only knows you as *Madame* d'Arivèque, and didn't really know to whom he was referring. So, she tells him she'll be right back, and comes to get me. I go out to talk to him and he asks me the same question. I tell him, 'That's my mother!' and he is dumbfounded. Finally he gathers his composure and says he knew you when you were a student in Paris! His name is Clément de Seignard and he told me to be sure to say hello from him! What do you think of that? Do you remember him at all?"

Oh, my God.

"Yes, darling, I remember him. I knew him quite well…and his parents. His father knew your grandmother well --- and *Papa* too. He was the director of several art galleries Marie-Avéline frequented in Paris. He became curator of the Musée Marmottan. They were very kind to me when I was at the Sorbonne. It's a long story how I met them… And Clément's father, Renaud, knew I was in Chicago, too, but at the time I wasn't married, and trust me, nothing would have given him the *soupçon* of an idea that I would one day be *Madame* d'Arivèque."

"So Mummy, why don't you fly over here and see him? He didn't check in with a wife—only his daughter and her family."

"I wouldn't want to intrude on their holiday, Henri. But I tell you what, give them every possible service they might want, all the terrific treatments, diversions and activities and goodies for the children, and all their wonderful meals….*le tout, quoi*…everything. Tell him it's compliments of the house since he's an old friend of your mother's. And charge it to my account."

Fin

We used to say
There'd come the day
We'd all be making songs
Or finding better words
These ideas never lasted long
The way is up
Along the road
The air is growing thin
Too many friends who tried
Were blown off this mountain with the wind
Meet on the ledge
We're gonna meet on the ledge
When my time is up I'm gonna see all my friends
Meet on the ledge
We're gonna meet on the ledge
If you really mean it, it all comes round again
Yet now I see
I'm all alone

But that's the only way to be
You'll have your chance again
Then you can do the work for me
Meet on the ledge
We're gonna meet on the ledge
When my time is up I'm gonna see all my friends
Meet on the ledge
We're gonna meet on the ledge
If you really mean it, it all comes round again

      Richard John Thompson

                        Fairport Convention

Made in the USA
Monee, IL
03 September 2023

42103962R00420